Author's Copy
(Ordered January 7th, 2025)

ISBN : 979-8-9917808-0-3

Trigger and content warnings for this work, as well as art, poetry, and fun stuff like that can be found online at: **rarust.com**

I am not on social media, but please do still post fan work with the hashtag **#dto** or **#dtofanart** so I can find it! <3

TABLE OF CONTENTS

PART ONE

PART TWO

PART SIX

DEATH TO OSIRIS

R.A. RUST

Part One

No admittance except on party business.

Chapter 1
B.B.E.G.

"The sky is blacker than the deepest void of nothing, and there is a sense amongst you all that this is the end. In the molten soil ahead there is a creaking and groaning like the unearthly sounds of a ship ready to sink. It only takes a moment of these rumblings, which seem to shake the ground beneath you, for a clawed scaly hand to burst up through the landscape. It clamours at your feet, forcing you backwards toward the endless sea of magma. The stench of brimstone is briefly overshadowed by one of ammonia and rot. Its source: a black billowing smoke crawling out of this ever-widening crack in the ground like the ashen clouds over Pompeii. The smoke battles its way into the featureless sky and blends with it, obscuring your vision of whatever creature it's emanating from. You can, however, hear him."

Partha's hand danced quickly across his keyboard and the next words to leave his lips were modified by his voice-changing software. He put on something of a posh accent and spoke slowly so as to emphasise the deep ethereal nature of the modulator, starting with an evil chuckle: "'Ahahaha. What a perfect mistake you three so-called heroes have made by rousing the likes of Zenryll the World Eater from his eternal slumber in this accursed divine prison. I have had millenia to revel in my hate, and now I must consume!'" He deactivated the voice-changer and continued in his normal Bermudan accent, "The smoke finally settles as Zenryll leans forward. His head hangs over you, the size of a galleon. The individual scales, black and grey in colour, are easily larger than Hector's shield. His breaths are thunderous and push around the smoke as he smiles a mouth of draconic teeth taller than giants. He is eager to play with the three fools who would dare challenge him…. Roll initiative."

One of the 521,239 viewers of this live stream was a sixty-three year old woman living in a cabin in the Tennessee wilderness. She was leaning toward the laptop screen unknowingly, and when her brother came into the room, she was surprised by his voice: "Gracie, stop biting your nails, dear. What are you watching? Party the Kid?"

She pulled her hands away from her mouth and smiled at him. "Johnny! Yeah, it's the last session; come watch." With a pat on the nearby ottoman, he smirked, rolled his eyes, and joined her.

Among the other watchers was a forty year old French woman named May Day. She had the stream on her left monitor, but she wasn't watching as intently as most, instead paying more attention to a chat window on her middle monitor where she was rapidly messaging someone named Lanni. Her room was dark and lit only by LEDs from her computer tower and the three screens enveloping her. Fortunately, because of a cybernetic augmentation in her brain and over her corneas, she was able to counteract the eye-strain that would otherwise be affecting her. To achieve such a thing, she needed only to activate a software she had written and downloaded into the augmentation which would inhibit her ability to see blue light.

When she heard the initiative rolls sounding on the VTT, she finally looked to her left. She giggled at the size difference between the player tokens and the black dragon they were fighting, then returned her attention to her conversation with Lanni.

Partha reduced the volume of the music after the rolls had been made and laughed at the results. "Thyne, how the fuck did you roll higher than him?"

He did not have a webcam active like the other three, but the viewers could hear him as he giggled and took a drag from his cigarette. His voice was deep and pleasant, with a London accent: "You really shouldn't have given me these boots, mate."

Partha laughed in turn and replied, "Well, it's no matter. You're first. What do you do?"

"Hmmm. I… cast…."

The first two rounds of combat were brutal for the party, even with Partha fudging rolls behind the scenes to save the players from being killed in one hit. He unfortunately couldn't stop his father's character from being downed, but he took the opportunity to have Zenryll say something that he knew would change the tides of the battle: "After Roosevelt falls, Zenryll lets out a booming laugh and says," he activated the voice-changer to sound more menacing, "'It is truly pathetic how you struggle. You would die for this? You must not know the consequences were you to actually slay me.'"

"What consequences?" asked the players in tandem.

"'Ahahaha! You amuse me, mortals. You come down to Hell to release and slay me and do not understand your own ends! If I am felled, then the land my domain rests beneath will crumble into this prison with me, taking all who live upon that land with it.'"

"What land?" asked Partha's father.

"'Why, Akeddlon, of course.'"

"Oh, I see," said Thyne, "This is what you were referring to, isn't it, Party?"

Partha nodded and deactivated his voice modulator. "It is. And it's your turn What does Helio do?"

The pause between Partha's question and Thyne's answer was too short to allow an actual ponderance, indicating to the other players that this was at least somewhat planned before the session: "I take the oil lamp from my bag." At this, Partha showed his audience and players an image of a Middle Eastern style oil lamp he had commissioned from the same man who had written the score for this entire campaign. The lamp was black with a deteriorating ornate design in its more natural brass colour all across the surface. "And," continued Thyne, "I call forth my marid patron."

Partha started to speak, but he was interrupted by another player: "Wait, is Helio a warlock?" This was a development others may have expected given the personality of Thyne's character, but it was not known to anyone save for Partha that he had taken levels in a class other than bard.

"Yeah, I took three levels in it before we even reached level ten."

"Is that why you betrayed us back in Elderriver?"

"No," he laughed, "That was just because Helio's a twat. Anyway, Party, what happens when I rub the lamp?"

"As you run your hands across the design, they are blackened. At first, you think you must be wiping away the dark colouring, but in fact, your very soul is being swallowed up by darkness. This is merely an external expression of it. The others don't know this is happening— the soul magic isn't visible externally, but you can feel it. Where most would find it perturbing, though, you know that this darkness around your soul is pleasant. Out of the lamp pours an aromatic smoke, smelling something like cinnamon and petrichor. It takes on the humanoid form of your friend and patron, Seif." Partha feigned an unplaceable accent for this character as he spoke for him: "'Helio. What ails thee now?'"

"I smile at him and hold my bleeding side. 'Seif, please grant me a wish. There are an unfathomable amount of lives on the line.'"

"Seif smiles back at you, but he seems confused. 'Helio, this isn't like you! What do you care of death and rot?'"

"'It is an entire country, Seif! Millions of people! I wish for you to move the entire population of Akeddlon to another continent.'"

"Seif frowns at you and crosses his arms. 'And why should I?'"

Thyne let out a shuddery breath. It was only a game, but there was still a real pressure weighing on him. He lit another cigarette, chained from the remnants of his last, and replied with a quaver in his voice, "'Seif, please. I'll do anything. Zenryll must be defeated.'"

Partha leaned back in his chair and smiled wickedly. "Seif is touched. He briefly cups his hand around your face lovingly and whispers, 'Okay,' before looking up into the void above. He raises his hands and mutters an invocation. His magic is dark and pours across the landscape in almost the exact same manner as Zenryll's black breaths of toxic smoke. While he is casting this spell, you both notice that Zenryll is smiling again. His booming laugh shakes the earth as Seif's arms fall to his sides. Your marid friend looks to you and whispers, 'I'm sorry....'"

"Wait," said Thyne, "He can't do it!?"

"He cannot."

"Party, what the fuck, mate!? We talked about this before the session!"

His wicked smile returned, but he otherwise ignored the outburst, saying instead, "Franky, it's your turn."

He arched his brow. "I was under the impression I acted after Zenryll."

"He's still channelling, so his turn is more or less skipped."

"Okay," he stroked his scruffy chin, "Standby."

Francis took a moment to ponder his options, and it was in this brief moment of dead air that a woman watching from Arizona rushed into her kitchen to retrieve a tray of almost-burnt cookies from the oven. Her name was Dezba Meadows, and she was one of Partha's oldest fans at sixty-seven years old. Table-top games like the ones he often streamed reminded her of her late husband. When he was alive, she never took the time to fully understand the games' complexities, so there was always a pit of guilt in her gut when she watched Partha's streams and found herself so invested and able to comprehend the rules of the games with ease. When she came back into the sitting room to resume watching the stream, Francis was finishing his turn, having hit the dragon with a high-damage spell as well as his sword.

"Good hit, Franky. He's very low," Partha praised before taking a sip from his Piña Colada. "Thyne? You could probably finish him off, and it's your turn."

The Englishman held his head and leaned on his desk. Smoke from his cigarette danced circles around him. His voice was muffled for the audience due to his hunched posture: "If I kill him, all of Akeddlon will die, too. Is that a certainty, Party?"

"As far as you know, yes."

A shuddered breath. "I... don't think Helio would do this. He's evil but...." He leaned back and took two quiet drags as he pondered. "Okay. I turn to Seif, take his hands in mine and say, 'I wish for you to kill him. You have so much more blood on your hands than I do. And if he isn't destroyed, he will slowly devour the entire world until there is nothing left.'"

Partha steepled his fingers as he listened intently to the question. "Okay, Seif will need a moment to process that request, and by that I mean *I* need a moment." His steepled fingers bisected his face as he leaned on his thumbs and scanned his computer screens.

"How many people has Seif killed?" asked Francis.

Partha took a moment to process the question before answering, "Oh, I don't know. At least a couple thousand."

Francis nodded and drank from his flask. While Partha pondered, all three of the players responded to some of the questions from the livestream's chat.

"Okay," he said after eight minutes of wordless deliberation, "Seif is shocked by Helio's request. You feel his grip around your hands tighten. His eyes widen, and after a glance back at Zenryll's towering silhouette through the smoke, he whispers to you, 'Helio, I have killed oh so very many people, but you're asking me to kill millions so as to not have the blood on *your* hands? This is….' He trails off and squeezes tighter onto your hands. His face is featureless, but you can sense him seeming to cry when he finally says, 'Okay… I'll do it.' He releases your hands and takes a step back, turning toward Zenryll and raising his arms. He begins channelling a powerful spell. Zenryll's turn is next, but he has this final round before his channel is finished, so Franky: one last turn. What do you do?"

He fiddled with his flask's lid noisily. His teal-green eyes scanned his laptop's screen. "To clarify: Zenryll will die? I can wait for Seif to kill him or kill him myself?"

"Correct."

"And, if one of us succeeds at killing him now, all of Akeddlon will also immediately be destroyed?"

"Yes."

"But if he finishes his channelled magic…? What happens then?"

Partha's wicked smile returned. "You're not certain, but the prophecy spoke of the entire world being devoured over the course of several decades."

He fidgeted with the flask again. "So, this is truly our last chance to stop this…. Hector will not be responsible for the destruction of an entire country. If it will take several decades for the entire world to be devoured, mayhaps we will still have time to stop it. So…" He took a swig from his flask and wiped the excess rum from his lips. "I approach Seif and place my hand on his shoulder."

Partha tilted his head. "He looks at you."

"'Seif… don't kill him.'"

There was a moment of stunned quiet from everyone. Partha was visibly baffled by the request but, after clearing his throat, he said, "He stops channelling. His arms fall to his sides, and he pulls you and Helio into a loving embrace. He whispers an invocation neither of you recognise, and everything goes black. You can't feel anything anymore, but you hear him whisper, 'I love you,' afterwards." Partha took a deep breath to calm himself. "It comes around to Zenryll's turn, and you hear a rumbling sound as his channel is finished. Out of character, I will tell you that the entire plane is collapsing in on itself, and you are all sinking into the floor as it turns from basalt rock to liquid magma. But, because of Seif's magic, you feel no pain or upset and see nothing but darkness. You feel at peace as your lives fade out into nothing. I suppose the prophecy rings true: Zenryll escapes Hell and begins devouring the world, and… that's the end of the campaign."

A loaded silence followed. Those who had watched the stream over the years and come to love these characters were blindsided by this ending. Many shed tears at the conclusion, some more enraged than others, evident by the onslaught of negative messages reeling into the chat. When Partha caught glimpses of his fans' opinions, he let on a pained smile and said, "I'm going to go buy another drink. Thyne? Did you still want to play something after this?"

Thyne looked up from his phone at his friend's webcam and said with a low voice, "Yeah. There's no hard feelings, mate."

Partha's smile became less pained, and he even let out a tipsy titter. "I'll hold you to it!"

It was interesting to see Partha stumbling to the door for those watching. When he stood, he leaned heavily toward the right of his desk and quit the room with his strides staggered and body slanted the entire way.

While Partha was gone, his father took to answering the chat and keeping the stream interesting. Thyne silently appreciated such a thing: it allowed him to text with Francis:

〘 Bring me something sweet and bad for me. 〙

〖 Have I upset you? 〗

〘 No, Franky. There wasn't anything we could do. I don't know why Party didn't warn me about the dead man's switch. Whatever. Just bring me some food. 〙

〖 What would you like? 〗

〘 I don't care. 〙

Francis looked up at his computer from his phone and briefly read some of the chat messages. His brow furrowed as he felt offended on his friend's behalf. "I'll be back, too," he said before pulling a cover over his webcam.

Richard opened his mouth to reply to Francis, but he was interrupted by Partha coming into his room with a rum slushy for each of them. Still walking with a slanted posture, he brought them to his father's side and said, "The ship is listing. Should we be concerned?"

Richard took one of the drinks and rustled his son's hair. "Thanks, Party. We'll be okay. Hardly a list; I think you're just drunk!" He laughed but stopped when it seemed to offend his son. "You did good with the game." Partha's gaze flicked to the chat, but his father grabbed him gently by the chin and pulled his attention back to him. "Your talent to create narratively compelling stories under all this pressure and in only a few seconds always astounds me, son." His smile was pure and loving enough to infect Partha, and the chat was made less hostile after it became clear how much the negativity was affecting the game's drunken host.

"Thanks, Daddy."

While Partha made his way back to his own computer, Francis appeared at Thyne's side with three takeout containers stacked precariously in his left hand and a strawberry milkshake in his right. He took a sip of the frozen treat, declaring it as "the friend tax," then set it on the white wooden desktop in front of Thyne.

After muting his microphone, Thyne smiled weakly at him and sipped through the striped paper straw. "Smells like Indian," he muttered.

Francis nodded and passed him the top two boxes. "Your favourites."

Thyne opened the containers to find butter chicken over rice in one and Chinese sugar doughnuts in the other. He offered a warm smile to Francis. "I love you, mate. You want to stay here? Me and Party are going to play *Counter Strike.*"

With a drunken blush and grin, Francis nodded and pulled a chair from Thyne's vanity to sit beside him.

"What'd you get?"

He opened the last container to show his friend the vegetable pancit inside.

"Do you need a drink?" He reached for his mini-fridge and passed a can of diet ginger-ale to his friend without waiting for an answer. "Just remember to use a coaster, you wanker."

By then, Partha had returned to his computer. "Where's Franky?"

Thyne unmuted his microphone. "He's here. We're eating. Opening my game now."

"That was an interesting conclusion, Partha," commented Francis, "Were you planning that from the beginning?"

He drank some of his slushy to stall answering the question. "I don't want to talk about it," he said eventually.

"Oh! Apologies, my friend."

Thyne shared his screen with Partha so the streamer could show both gameplay perspectives for the audience as they wound down with some simulated violence. Of the millions of people who played the game the world over, Thyne was among the top fifty in terms of skill, which was much the same story for him across multiple games and genres. He was often approached by esports managers and developers for various games, but he rejected all offers. Gaming was a hobby, and he didn't need the money, no matter how ludicrous some of the sums were. He valued his freedom and privacy more than almost anything, and he was happy to share streams of his footage with Partha's audience to help bolster the younger man's career. There were sometimes viewers who tuned in solely to watch Thyne and Partha gaming together, and the streams wherein the older party was mentoring Partha were especially popular. He was a good teacher and never asked for compensation for his time or advice.

After only ten bites of his pancit, Francis put the mostly-full container in the mini-fridge beside Thyne's desk then scooted his chair closer to lean on his friend's shoulder while he gamed. For the first few rounds, Richard was the most talkative of the group. Thyne was taking bites of his butter chicken during lulls in the game-play and Partha was drunk and overly affected by the negativity after his campaign. Despite that, it was only Francis who had fallen completely silent. He had his hand on Thyne's thigh without either of them noticing, and his eyelids were heavy. Tiredness was not to blame for his relaxed state, but bliss. The room was dark but not uncomfortably so. There were LED strips embedded into the crown moulding all around the ceiling. They were a warm peachy pink colour which bled down into the vibrant pinks, blues, and purples from the computer tower, monitors, and keyboard. It was therefore violet in the chamber, but the white of the moon was cutting through the airy curtains above the bed and bathing the men in smokey moonbeams. Francis had no ability to smell, so he was made especially curious by the idea of what all the smokey scents might have been adding to the ambiance. Some of it was from Thyne's three cigarettes of the night, but he also had a stick of dragon's blood incense on his altar that was only just then burning out.

"Franky?" he heard Thyne coo and snatched his hand from his friend's thigh. "You don't have to move that, mate." He took Francis' hand and put it back where he had absentmindedly rested it, bringing a blush to both of their faces. Thyne smiled through it and gestured to his keyboard. "Do you want to play?"

He shook his head and hesitantly relaxed his trembling hand on Thyne's thigh.

"Okay, just let me know if you change your mind." He kissed his forehead then returned his attention to the game. Considering Partha was drunk and also already not much better than average, Thyne was holding back while he played. There were several moments he stopped moving to take bites of his food or smoke, but he was only punished by the enemy team once out of seven instances. Overall, he was having a great time. He had his best friend drowsily draped on his shoulder, his favourite foods, his favourite cigarettes, and another close friend somewhere out in the Atlantic getting sloshed while they gamed. They won most of the matches they played thanks to Thyne, but he prioritised joking around with Partha and Richard.

In the interim after the campaign's confounding conclusion and the switch to this FPS game, Dezba had found herself gripping tightly onto her knitting needles. The steam from her latte and freshly baked cookies had faded away. The scent of chocolate and coffee lingered in the dry air, and the desert outside was as silent as her empty home. It wasn't until the conversation turned to talks of Thyne's upcoming birthday that she noticed sounds creeping back into her perception. More present, she noticed a rare rain outside making her feel small and protected. She relaxed her posture and finally released her deathgrip on the needles. With a sigh, she set them down and sipped on her latte as she resumed listening to the boys talking on stream:

"And how old are you turning?" asked Richard.

"Old," was Thyne's simple reply.

"Oh, don't bother, Daddy," slurred Partha as he died in the game, "He's jus' gonna say he's turning sixty-nine again!" He laughed drunkenly and struggled to read some of the chat messages on the side of his screen while he waited for the next round.

Richard laughed too. "I suppose it's none of my business."

"So what do you want for your birthday?" asked Partha.

Thyne took a moment to ponder. He stopped moving his character in game to stroke his chin with his left hand and absentmindedly killed an approaching enemy with a flick of his right shortly thereafter. "Well, you know what I like. We can talk about it off stream." There were things he wanted to mention to his friend without the burden of an audience. Thyne was quite a secretive individual, so there was hardly anything known about him to Partha's fans. He was British, that much was evident from his voice, and it was understood that he was at least fifty years old. He smoked like a chimney and enjoyed violence in all the sorts of games they played. But even after four years of being a regular part of Partha's streams, the fans were forced to speculate further than those few facts.

Dezba groaned at Thyne's insistence to speak about his gift off stream. She knew it was his right to keep himself so guarded, but as a long time fan of Partha's work, she felt entitled to at least a scrap more of information. There was a small part of her that saw her husband in him, and she would never admit to the small crush she therefore had. Of course, there were boundaries she would never cross. She didn't even use the chat when she watched the streams, so she was hardly the type to actually try attracting his attention. That she was filling a void of loneliness in her soul with this parasocial bond was something she was only vaguely aware of.

The boys continued playing for hours, even after Richard had to go to bed and while Francis was mentally absent. Partha maintained his drunkenness but never pushed it to a point of incoherence. His skills in the game were hindered, but Thyne was able to make up for it. Usually, the Brit would be harsh on Partha for the inane mistakes he was making, but with Francis leaning on him the entire night and the smoke in the air, it was far too blissful for him to snap at his distant drunken friend.

All of the calm of the night, however, came to a screeching halt when a stranger started blasting a song through his microphone. It peaked and clicked and growled like sandpaper on a chalkboard, but Thyne was still able to recognise the song before he quickly muted the offender. Partha was slower to mute it, but he seemed much more outwardly startled by it than Thyne, and Francis' only reaction was a flinch and a pat on Thyne's thigh in an attempt to comfort him.

For the following three rounds, Thyne was entirely silent. He did not engage in Partha's drunken banter, nor did he acknowledge the comments from both of his friends about how he was being suddenly very harsh on the enemy teams. The fourth round following the outburst, Thyne single-handedly killed the entire enemy team in twenty-six seconds, which was indicative to Partha that it was time to end the stream and talk to his friend more privately. He bid his audience adieu and quadruple checked that his stream was ended before turning his attention to his private call with Thyne and saying, "You can turn your camera on now. What's wrong?"

After checking that Partha wasn't streaming anymore, Thyne plugged in his webcam and opened its cover. Onto Partha's screen therefore came live footage of his two closest friends sitting together in Thyne's London home.

During the day, Thyne's room was a soft pastel pink with lace and flowers and other forms of stagnant beauty. His altar, which he devoted to all manner of gods, was equally gentle in its sightliness: small marble idols sat atop a short antique bookshelf behind him with a stick of incense almost always lit in front of them. At this late hour, however, the area had all but lost its airy regal nature. The moon must have sucked away the colour of the room, leaving it in a state of grey and black that matched Thyne's dark clothes and many piercings. It was lit only by the pink, indigo, and violet LEDs around the ceiling and coming from Thyne's computer tower.

A warmth that was otherwise absent entirely from the room emanated from his lighter as he flipped it open in a flourish and lit himself another cigarette. The flourish brought attention to his missing fingers, which were currently replaced by cybernetic prosthetic ones: his right middle and left ring fingers. Partha had always assumed it was a joke when he claimed to be old, because looking at him, he didn't look a day over thirty. His features were somehow simultaneously soft and angular. His cheekbones were sharp and led into his slightly-cleft chin with the grace of a dancer. His pale skin was smooth, free of pimples, and always clean-shaven but speckled lightly with freckles, especially on his cheeks and nose, which were usually redder than the rest of him either from wrath or flirtatiousness. His hair was naturally brown, evident by his well-groomed eyebrows which were currently (and usually) furrowed with rage, but as long as Partha had known him he kept the soft wavy locks dyed pastel pink and somewhere between short and shoulder-length. His teeth were straight and pearly white despite his constant smoking. His upturned eyes were sharp with irises coloured the same amber of dying embers. One of his most distinctive features was his perky nose, which was in desperate need of poking. Very rarely, Partha would witness it holding up a pair of big round reading glasses, but Thyne tended to not often need them.

Slightly behind the Englishman's white and pink chair, sat in a white antique dining chair and adjusting himself to lean on Thyne's shoulder again, was Francis, a Frenchman. He looked about the same age as Thyne, but his skin was more tan and therefore slightly more worn. His hooded eyes were deep and captivating. They were an odd sort of hazel that fluctuated between navy blue and sea green, usually (and currently) somewhere in the teal between. Small gold hoop earrings dangled from his ears any time Partha saw him to the point that he could only assume he slept in them. His sharp jawline was hidden under a forest of wild brownish beard which matched in colour and unkemptness with his brows, but when it was clear he had recently bathed, he would be clean-shaven or graced with a pleasant shadow of stubble. His hair, usually in a ponytail, was long and blond, sometimes quite literally "dirty" blond. In fact, he seemed allergic to hygiene most days. His teeth were straight but rotten and yellow. Parts of them were even brown. He would occasionally go long enough without showering that his hair would start to mat, and he would absent-mindedly roll it into locks. The nasty bastard had no sense of smell, so he must have reeked. Luckily, Partha had never had the misfortune of meeting him in person, but in private conversations with Thyne, Partha learned that Francis smelled often of the ocean, booze, and woody colognes. "Usually pleasant," was how Thyne described him, but Partha was willing to bet he was noseblind because of his constant proximity to the disgusting oaf and obvious crush on him.

The two friends were usually sitting while talking with Partha, but he knew their heights and how dichotomous they were to their respective builds. Thyne was only 5'8", but he was athletic and would sometimes not wear a shirt on calls, showing off the well-toned body he was clearly quite proud of having. Francis was the taller of the two at six foot, but calling him lanky would be an understatement. He was visibly malnourished. It was a wonder he was even still alive. Partha had only ever seen him consume alcohol and the occasional take-out. His attitude was boisterous and his wardrobe flowy enough, however, that it was hardly noticeable most days how physically weak he truly was.

On the other side of the call, sitting in a standard cruise cabin, was Partha. His single father was a sailor, so as far back as the kid could recall, he was living on ships and travelling the world. When he was only ten, he started taking fencing lessons from some of the sailors who often worked with his father, and when he was twelve he started entering unofficial tournaments in various ports. In one of these unregulated events, he was fencing with a boy a few years older than him, both of them unmasked, and his opponent accidentally took out his left eye. He was rushed to hospital where the injury sustained was deemed too gruesome to save the eye. At first, young Partha was struck with an understandable upset at the situation, but after a heartfelt apology from the teen and a few months of healing, he decided to lean fully into the aesthetic. He became obsessed with pirates and history in general, which led to his interest in designing, sewing, and wearing costumes, which led quite naturally into tabletop gaming and roleplay.

His costume currently was somewhat draconic and overly detailed. He even utilised his missing eye to give himself a glowing prosthetic one. Since the session had ended, however, he had taken out the uncomfortable device, as well as the headpiece, to instead wear his eyepatch, which was how he tended to present himself. His hair was its natural black, but it had been dyed almost every colour under the sun at least once. It usually fell past his shoulders, but at the moment it was freshly buzzed due to a fiery mishap in the galley a few days prior. He often wore hoop earrings not dissimilar to Francis', though they were more noticeable against his darker features than the blond's. His height was only an inch shorter than Thyne, but his build was much more average than the Brit's. He was twenty-three, but he looked slightly older, no doubt from all the sea air and sun he saw. His family had Indian ancestors, but neither he nor his father had any meaningful connection to that culture. By birth, they were Bermudan, but they both considered themselves citizens of the world considering how often they travelled, never setting anchor anywhere for very long.

His face was ovular and pleasant, with a Grecian nose, bent slightly sideways from a different childhood injury wherein it was broken. His lips were thin but pillowy and his cheekbones were soft and hardly noticeable under his smooth brown skin. His smile, which was not an uncommon default for his expression, was pleasant with teeth all straight and clean. Though his jawline was soft, his chin was pointed and angular, drawing a harsh distinction from the rest of him, especially when he would let his facial hair grow into a goatee that suited the pirate aesthetic he loved so much. He was objectively attractive, and perhaps that was why he had such an easy time playing into the sailor stereotype of being a horndog.

Thyne took a drag of his cigarette, inhaling all of the smoke as he closed his eyes to try calming his racing heart. It didn't seem like he was going to answer Partha's question, so he tried to change the subject: "What do you want for your birthday?"

Thyne shook his head, his eyes still closed as he took another drag. It was as he blew out a puff of smoke that he opened his eyes to glare into the camera. "Party, have you heard of Maitland Music Group?"

He shook his head.

After yet another drag, he leaned back in his chair and held his hand out on its armrest to ask for Francis to hold it. Once their fingers were intertwined, he let his cigarette hand hang limply off the other armrest and said, "Maitland Music Group is a company that was established in 1921 by a Welsh man named Joe Thomas Crump, or J.T. Crump as he was usually called. He named it after his wife at the time, who would become the real head of all of its dealings. It was her idea originally, but it was 160 years ago: women didn't exactly have too many opportunities to do that sort of thing.

"They're a huge sound design and music company now. Always have their hands in movies, games, and whatever the fuck else. Have a few record labels, and I think a brand of biscuits for some bloody reason." He rolled his eyes. A drag. "But they started off by selling sheet music for instructors and schools. Their competition never sold anything original (or at least nothing good), but Maitland was different. Over half of the songs in their books were award-winning, original, and, in a lot of cases, free for commercial use. Some of the more precious ones took a longer time to reach the public domain, but now all of the original recordings are free for anyone to use. That song in the comms, or what was audible of it, sampled a piece called *Charcoal Diamonds* composed in 1932 for an entire orchestra. Their methods in producing so much original music were... unethical to say the least."

Partha nodded, though his brow was knitted. Thyne was petty as Hell, but this seemed incredibly random. What did he care about the unethical business practices of some random company a hundred something years ago? How the fuck did he know all of this anyway? And off the top of his head! "Does this have something to do with your birthday?"

Thyne nodded. "I want a gang," he said after his next drag as if it was a sufficient explanation.

Partha tilted his head. "For your birthday?"

He nodded but didn't elaborate.

"Franky, do you know what he's asking for?"

Francis had been so mentally absent that hearing his name made him physically start. He looked around to determine his location then found Partha on Thyne's computer screen. "Apologies."

"He says he wants a gang," said Partha as if Thyne was not present.

"Yes. Like that game you play with us sometimes. Oh, what was it?" He stroked his scruffy chin. "Ah! Gang Theft Auto the Seventh."

Partha snorted at the misnomer and noticed Thyne, still grumpy, smiling as well. "Well, he said as much. I don't know what you mean, though."

Francis opened his mouth to reply, but Thyne held up his hand to stop him and leaned over his desk to look up into the camera, making the bags under his eyes more evident even as the smoke from his cigarette slightly obscured the picture. His voice was low and wrought with bloodlust. "Party, I want a gang. I want to take down Maitland. I know you have underworld contacts, and all my attempts to start one with Franky have fallen flat." He leaned back again. "But if you can't handle it, then just get me a plush from your next port to add to my collection. Or maybe a Grecian idol of Aphrodite or Charon for my altar."

Partha's eyes widened as the request seemed to sober him. He nodded more and more enthusiastically as he started to understand, a smile creeping its way across his lips. "Okay! A gang! I can do that for you. Hopefully I can do it on time, but if I don't get replies quick enough, it might be a few days after your actual birthday." He sipped on his cocktail and started up another queue for them to resume playing their game. "But I have to know: why?"

Thyne shook his head and smiled wickedly. "I knew you'd pull through for me, Party. If it all goes well, I'll tell you all about it, but for now I'm keeping mum."

"Fair enough," said the sailor as they were put into another match.

Chapter 2
The Bardbarian

He could hear them through the door, but he couldn't understand them. The muffling was too strong, and his grasp on Spanish was too weak. Hateful words swarmed his head. His arms and legs were zip-tied to the chair, but what most irritated him was the bag on his head.

The door to his chamber opened. He snapped his gaze up and tried to see the newcomer's face through the bag and the dark surrounding it. Unfortunately, he only managed to make out the vague shadowy figure of the man approaching. He smelled like gunsmoke and blood.

"So, you and I are going to have a little chat," *said the kidnapper as he noisily dragged a chair across the room and sat backwards in it to face his prisoner. He sounded American, but Dale supposed that he could have learned English from an American as a child. It wasn't entirely impossible for a Mexican to know both languages. He continued:* "You got a name?"

"Fuck you, beaner. Ye ain't fed me yet, an' Ah ain't had no water, neither. Ye cain't let me die. It's a war crime."

The kidnapper snort-laughed and said, "That's so cute. Okay, you want some food? I'll go make you something before we talk."

Dale arched his brow. His confusion was evident in the way he muttered, "Okay," *as the kidnapper promptly left the room.* "... Cute?"

When he returned about an hour later, the aroma of a well-seasoned steak or pork-chop and vegetables filled the dark little room. Dale was immediately drooling and looked up to spot the shadows through the burlap over his eyes. He was surprised by a light filling the room, and the subsequent ambient humming of the fluorescent tube above him sent a chill down his spine. He was torn from the present and haunted by a memory, immediately catatonic.

He didn't notice the bag being removed from his head and the plate of food being set on the seat of a chair in front of him. He didn't hear his kidnapper talking to him. He didn't even see him. The smell of gunsmoke and the hum of the fluorescent light were the only things he could perceive.

After some amount of time, what felt like years, the light flickered out, and he was finally able to wrench his gaze from it. The sunspots in his vision blotted out the face of his kidnapper as he tried, to no avail, to make out even a single feature. He did manage to notice that he wasn't in uniform, however. Strange....

"Eat up, dude. It was real expensive. Cost an arm and a leg," said the kidnapper as he pushed the chair with its plate and bottle of water closer. It was only then that Dale noticed his arms had been untied. He held his head, pushing back his mullet-mohawk and sighing. "What's the matter? Not hungry anymore?" asked the man. He sounded genuinely disappointed.

Dale took another moment of quiet before relaxing enough to reach for the offered food. Surprisingly, he had been given both a fork and a steak knife. After the obvious thought of attacking the stranger crossed his mind, he decided to eat first and cut into the pork-chop. He was halfway through the meal when he opened his water and downed almost all of it, only then noticing that the man was still in the room and watching him with a sadistic smile. His stomach dropped. "Fuck," he said as he set down the fork and leaned backwards, "It's poisoned, ain't it?"

He seemed to take offence, pressing a hand to his chest and saying, "Of course not!"

"Then why ye smilin' like that? Ah know that smile. That's a killer's smile."

The grin grew wider. "A smile nonetheless." He gestured vaguely at the meal. "You enjoying it? I made it myself."

With an arched brow, Dale squinted into the darkness to try and perceive the face of this man with more detail. He didn't look like a beaner.... He looked... he looked like a kike. No. A muslim: even worse. His short black hair and thick beard seemed especially dark against his pale skin. Maybe he was some mix of both? He certainly *wasn't white. Maybe Italian. Too swarthy for Dale's liking regardless, and his killer's-grin was made more disturbing when he spoke again, unprompted:*

"It's your captain."

Dale blinked. "What is?"

He gestured to the food. "The meat. It's a cut of your friend's thigh." He leaned down to fully show his face to Dale, his white teeth shining through his dark facial hair. "Wha'd'ya think about that, you nazi fuck?"

Dale smirked to match this man's energy and spoke with the air of a viper: "I think ye're a shit cook." To punctuate his statement, he stabbed into a chunk of the meat with his knife and ate it.

The man's wicked smile became nigh-hysterical, twitching his eye as he stood upright. "Oh, I like you. Maybe in another life, we could have been friends." He lit a cigarette and tipped the chair over to knock the plate of food onto the floor and sit himself where it had been. After a drag, he noticed Dale's hand around the knife handle tightening and said, "Gonna stab me after I fed you such a nice meal?"

"Ah ain't friends with no guidos or kikes or muslims."

He reached across the opening between them and easily took the knife out of Dale's hand before leaning back into his chair casually and tossing the blade up and down as he smoked with his other hand. "So here's how it's gonna go: you're gonna tell me where my husband is right now, or I'm gonna waterboard you until you either yap or die."

"Oh, great, ye're a faggot, too."

A sigh. "You know... I only asked for your name to be courteous. Should I use the one I saw on your records?"

He started.

"Aha, don't like that, do you?" He smiled wickedly. "I like the cut of your jib, man. Just tell me where my husband is, and this'll all go a lot smoother."

"Ah don't know where yer beaner faggot boyfriend is."

"Alright," he stood and opened the door to shout something in Spanish. The only words Dale could pick out were "agua" and "trapo."

"Ah honest to God don't know! Ye cain't waterboard me! That's a war crime, too."

The kidnapper chuckled. "I fed you your own captain, and you still think I'm abiding by laws like that?" Dale was quiet and pondered the question. "You're not a prisoner of war, bud, because I'm not a soldier. Now...," he took a rag and running *hose from someone outside of the room. Dale tried to reach to untie his legs, but he was unable to move, as if he was still tied up. The kidnapper spit his cigarette on the ground as he approached and said, "Where's my fucking husband?"*

Orange County and Los Angeles were in a state of perpetual flooding. The elite who still lived in the hills were relatively unaffected, only treated to the odd visage of the shoreline below seeming to creep closer with each passing month, but most of the denizens were suffering. Those with the means tended to move further inland, so a lot of the celebrity scene was slowly transferring to Vegas. One thing that hadn't changed was the horrible stench: smelled like piss and pretension. But hey! The complaints of the residents from decades prior had all but vanished: no more traffic, no more wildfires, and all the yuppies were quite literally being flushed out.

A lot of the remaining businesses and residents had moved to levels above the ground floor. The "underground" crime scene had also, ironically, moved up the ladder and was often situated physically above the more legal goings-on.

One of the bank towers downtown was so flooded and damaged, engineers had informed its wealthy owners that repairs and reinforcements on the lower levels would cost more than constructing an entirely new and better building in Vegas, even accounting for the cost of real estate in the sin city. Unsurprisingly, the permanently-flooded building was abandoned, and whatever remained of a city authority warned the residents not to enter.

On the streets that crisp January evening was only about a foot of water. Or rather… "water." With a thick layer of trash floating on top of it and the rotten fetor of dead fish wafting up from every inch, it was more like a sludge than the Pacific ocean. Being born in 2049 and spending most of his childhood in the city, the tall man wading through the flood toward the abandoned bank tower had never seen the Pacific ocean in its natural beautiful blue state. His long black hair was pulled up into a hair-claw so as to not accidentally make contact with the scum and seagull shit, but the guitar on his back was given less care. Its case wasn't water-tight, but he wasn't worried about the instrument. In fact, he wasn't worried about most of the filth around him. Other than the stench of rotting carcasses and bird shit, he was of the horrid mind that it was an exquisite visage.

Despite how pleasant he found the views, his heart did ache as he climbed over waterlogged supercars peeking out of the heaps of garbage like islands of hope.

Perhaps if it wasn't seawater and so polluted, he and his brother could take one of the abandoned Ferraris or Lamborghinis to repair and refurbish. Alas, no amount of scavenging around the city for working parts from other cars would make such an endeavour worth the cost of the parts and supplies they would need to purchase outright. Even if they could successfully refurbish and repair one, they would have nowhere to safely store it. Their apartment building was not permanently flooded like the bank tower, but the cars in its parking lot were all long ago destroyed in various high tides, including the few they had modified and parked there. Shortly after losing two cars, they started renting a garage in the hills to store the car they had built together, among three others, but the rent for that, paired with the rent for their apartment, was wringing them too dry to even pay their water bill.

With a sigh, the man climbed onto another rusted luxury car and grabbed the bottom rung of the bank tower's fire escape ladder. It was a skyscraper with a proper indoor fire escape, but since the floods started destroying the lower levels, the people who had moved into the building, whether legally or otherwise, had all added other means of entering the upper floors such as this ridiculously long exterior fire escape.

He pulled himself up onto the staircase and started climbing. There were other ways into the building, but this method would keep him the driest. Most people took a makeshift staircase on the opposite side of the building because this fire escape was at least twelve feet off the ground. It was still eight feet to the bottom rung while standing on the car beneath, but even if it was reachable by people shorter than this dark musician, it required a feat of upper body strength that most did not possess to reach the stairs.

He shook out some of the water from his pants' legs as he climbed to the thirty-second floor. His breaths were loud and laboured when he knocked on the window.

A woman approached when she noticed him and helped him inside. "You must be Mr. Velvet!"

He coughed and held his knees, holding up a finger to her, silently asking for a moment to catch his breath.

"Oh! You poor thing, you probably need some water." She reached into a nearby refrigerator and rushed to him with a bottle.

"Thanks," he said hoarsely as he tore off the lid and downed its entirety in a matter of seconds. When he was finished he squeezed it into a crumpled heap of plastic and tossed it aimlessly over his shoulder.

The woman was upset to see the bottle destroyed, but her grin remained. "Well, Mr. Velvet, you're early. Welcome to Stickerbomb! We're excited to have you perform for us tonight. Follow me!"

The room he had entered was once a corporate break room, but since being claimed by this club, everything floor to ceiling had been covered in vinyl stickers. There were parts painted over with graffiti of various skill levels and a bulletin board on one of the counters propped up against the wall. It had various papers pinned into it, and he was able to catch a glimpse of the schedule for that night as he was led out into the hall. Rather than stickers covering every inch of it, the walls, ceiling, and floor of the hall were cluttered with graffiti, random scraps of wallpaper, fake flowers pasted to the wall, mosaics made with broken CDs, and occasionally a vinyl sticker or two or twelve or fifty.

He was led up a set of stairs to what was once a studio apartment. The walls and ceiling were painted matte black, and the floor was plated with steel. The black leather couch on a cow-print rug must have been reupholstered after being fished out of a soggy dump judging by the vague scent of mildew hanging in the air. There was a bong and lighter on a distressed wooden coffee table which the hostess informed was free for him to use. He seemed interested, so she smiled and said, "If you have a particular preference on what you'd like to smoke, Mr. Velvet, we have—."

"That's just a stage name, you know."

"Hm?"

"Red Velvet isn't my real name."

"Right!" Her smile became more nervous. "Mr. Roach? Was it?"

He nodded and ambled over to the couch. "Just Roach. Get me the cheapest shit you've got. I'm easy to please and broke as hell." He plucked up the bong and gave it a whiff. "Is this used?"

She strained to keep grinning, a panic in her eyes. "It's clean."

He shrugged and leaned back in the chair, kicking his feet up onto the table and pulling out his phone. "Good enough." She took the hint to leave and fetch him some weed, and he opened an e-reader on his phone to pick up where he last left off in *The Phantom of the Opera*.

While Roach was waiting for his set to start, his brother was sitting at a poker table fifteen stories above his. It was their twelfth game of the evening, and the river was approaching. When it came to his bet before the last community card, he pushed all $63,353 that he had won up until then into the pot. The three men to his left folded at the show and grumbled angrily under their breaths.

His name was Karson, but he had come to be called River on account of never having lost a game of Hold'em if he allowed his hand to cross the fifth street. It was often whispered that he was a cheat and a scam artist, but when confronted in the past, he never had anything up his sleeves. He usually only ran in illegal circles, so cheating was often met with violence. Despite the fact that it was only ever speculation that he cheated, he had met his fair share of fists to the face or threats on his life.

Counting cards was frowned upon, as was memorising what cards were in play, but even if he had some amount of integrity, these were too automatic for him to easily stop doing. He would also count shuffles and watch cards sliding across each other and subsequently, as if by magic, know which card lay in what position in the deck with anywhere between seventy-five percent and complete accuracy.

When the last card was revealed, he laughed haughtily, and after it was confirmed that he had won, he started to pull in his money from the pot by the armful. He was stopped halfway through the gloaty display, however, by an angry player to his left grabbing him by his large upper arm and yanking him halfway out of his chair. It clattered to the floor as he stumbled to his side and forced a smile at his attacker.

"What's wrong, Benny? You shouldn't have folded, dude." He giggled as they both side-eyed the man's would-be winning hand.

"You've got a lot of nerve, Roach." He snapped his hand up from River's arm to his throat and squeezed.

"Oh yeah?" he choked out, "Rematch, then. Double or nothing." He was released and punched square in his nose, but he showed very little upset as he held it and added, "We can even use that deck you think no one knows is marked."

It was around this time that the hostess from the club returned to Roach's dressing room with the weed he had requested. He thanked her with an expressionless nod. As he started to pack some of it into the bong, she explained that the fridge and cabinets were stocked with snacks and drinks for him to "help yourself! But please don't take more than two bottles of water. You understand."

"Of course." He took a hit and nodded as he set the bong back on the table. "Thank you."

"I'll come get you fifteen minutes before your set." She looked at the time on her phone then smiled at him. "There are graffiti pens in that basket there if you'd like to add something to the walls in here. It's a new idea, so we've only got a few contributions since the renovations." She gestured to a small doodle on a column behind him of a salt shaker with three signatures around it and another contribution on the opposite wall that was too small and far to interpret as anything more than some colourful lines.

His heart was made lighter by the novel idea of letting artists leave their marks on the walls, but he didn't let it show on his face. After another nod and unemotive stare, the hostess scurried out of the room. Another hit of the bong, he finished the paragraph he was reading and pulled the basket of paint pens to his side to start digging through them.

Being an adept artist, it only took him ten minutes to finish his piece. After drawing a small black and red striped ant over his messy signature, which read *Red*

Velvet, he clicked his marker closed and took a step back to admire the work. A praying mantis with a backwards baseball cap was doing a trick on a bicycle. There were some scribbles on either side labelling the various parts of both the bug and the bike with their proper scientific/mechanical names.

"It needs something else," he muttered as he tapped the pen against his palm. While he was busy trying to think of something to add, his phone buzzed loudly on the coffee table. He brought it to his hand and looked at the new message:

⌈ Hey! Did you catch the stream? Your music was great for it. But anyway... I was wondering if you'd be interested in some more long term work. Work more like what you did with my father way back when. If you remember... Anyway... sorry for bothering you. (ó﹏ò) Call me... Please. ⌋

Roach considered the offer for an agonising three minutes before Partha saw the indicator that he was typing a reply:

⟦ You'll learn I don't tend to forget things. I remember the job with your pops. Shit hit the fan, if you recall. I know you were still just a kid back then. What's the job this time? ⟧

⌈ Hahaha yeah! (´∀ ' ;) Shit did hit the fan, huh? One of you went to prison, right? But anyway, it's kind of hard to explain, and I don't want to do it over text, so... can we just call? ⌋

Roach's heart panged at the unwanted reminder from Partha, but he showed no outward signs of emotion as he called him.

"Hello?" answered the kid.

"What's the job?"

Roach's voice was so cold and deep it brought a chill down Partha's spine, evident in the way he stuttered his reply: "Oh, uh. Hi. So, erm. Well, you remember Thyne from my stream?"

"Yeah."

"It's his birthday on the third."

"Mmhmm."

"Yeah, so he asked me a favour."

"Get on with it, kid."

His panicking breaths were audible through the call as he sputtered, "Right! S-sorry. Well he wants—. Um. He wants to start a gang."

Roach let out a huff. It was somewhere between a scoff and a laugh.

Partha laughed nervously. "Yes, it's a silly thing to ask for as a birthday gift, but he's a good friend, and I quite like the idea of being a real pirate instead of just pretending."

"Why should I not hang up on you right now?"

"He has a job in mind! He wants to take down this company. Some music company. Maryland Music? Martian Music? ..." Roach's air shifted as Partha continued to struggle recalling the name. After the rambling, he let the call hang in silence. "Are you still there?"

With another moment longer of pondering and wordlessly savouring Partha's panicked energy, Roach replied: "Tell your friend to meet me February tenth, at the Waffle House on Ninth and Brittle. Phoenix, Arizona. 10:30 in the morning. Tell him to show up no later than noon, or I'm out." Without waiting for confirmation from Partha, Roach hung up and returned his attention to the art on the wall. He snickered at his own thoughts as he decided what to add and uncapped the pen to finish the piece.

"Mr. Roach," he heard the hostess' mousy voice as she knocked politely on his door.

"It's open."

She cautiously entered the room and looked at his art as he closed the pen and tossed it in the general direction of the basket, missing horribly.

"'Praying for'… what does that say?"

"It says, 'Praying for the downfall of man.'" He stifled a laugh, choking it out in his throat to instead offer her a set of cold hazel eyes.

A nervous ha. "Because it's a praying mantis?"

"Yeah, dude. Mantises are notoriously evil. Have you ever met one? Assholes. Capitalists! And zealots to the nth degree. Probably started the crusades. Even the American one." He stifled another laugh, coughing it away by clearing his throat. "Anyway, is it almost time for my set?"

She offered an odd smile and tilted her head at him. "Yeah…."

"Alright. Let me just finish this bowl." He took another hit from the bong and blew a cloud of smoke above her. "Big crowd?"

She gave his art another look and giggled as her gaze trailed back to him. "You artist types are so weird. Yeah, it's kinda crowded. You'll do great, though. You nervous?"

"Not in the slightest."

She laughed again and, when he was finished smoking, led him to a backstage area to help him hook up his guitar and loop pedal to do a sound check. It was a disgusting looking instrument with crusty duct tape holding the whammy-bar in place and a few exposed wires where there were once volume and tone dials. What was once a white base was yellowed by Gods knew what. There were a few scrapes coloured in with markers of various hues and a plethora of dark scuff marks. It was a miracle the thing wasn't electrocuting him as he played some impressive arpeggios. "Thanks," he said as he started to tweak the tone and distortion, and she was intuitive enough to know he was asking her to leave him be.

When it came time to take the stage, Roach was as expressionless as ever. Perhaps it was awkward for the crowd to see him so unenthusiastic to be on the stickerbombed stage and unimpressed by their polite cheering. He didn't care. He carried around a deadened energy that was somehow equal parts intimidating and relaxing. The crowd was brought to silence as he moved the microphone to the side of the stage wordlessly. He could sing, but his loose plan for the night was to only provide improvised guitar instrumentals.

Stickerbomb was a decades-old club in LA, but it was only after the floods that it became more than just another loud crowded place to get high and flail around. Roach had played for them as a DJ before they embraced the punk scene, and he liked to think he was part of the reason they opened up to the idea after he played a remixed grunge song during his last set. This was only his fourth time playing for this club, but it was the first time since the county was placed under a permanent flood watch. It was also his first chance to play something other than EDM.

The crowd was quiet under a haze of smoke that seemed to vibrate as he slammed his hand across the strings and sent a growling howl through the air from his falling-apart instrument. There were scattered cheers as he let the sound hang over the crowd until it seemed he had their undivided attention. After he started on a melody, it was only after an impressive run that the audience's silence was broken by an uproar of applause. He had hardly even noticed the crowd was there, having lost himself in the music, so when they pulled him back to reality he offered an acted smile and stopped the lead with another loud growl from the strings. As the looping backtrack he had created continued, he pointed to a random member of the audience and told him to come on stage.

"Get the microphone," he said with a gesture toward it. The stranger rushed to the microphone and took a second one offered to him from a stagehand. He brought one of them to Roach and tried to hand it to him, but, "What am I going to hold that with? Telekinesis?"

The audience member blushed and brought both microphones to his mouth where they screeched with feedback until he pulled one of them away to his side and laughed nervously into the other. "Sorry."

Roach gestured with his head to be offered a microphone, and when the nervous man was holding one to him he said, "What's your name, dude?"

"Mathew."

"You play any instruments, Mathew?"

"Nah man."

"That's chill. What's your favourite song?"

"Uhh. *Hot Garbage.*"

"Your favourite song is one of mine? I'm flattered." It certainly didn't show on his face. He started playing the mentioned song absent mindedly. "And what's your favourite… hmmm… rom-com? Make sure it's a cheesy one, Mathew, this is serious."

He chuckled, and the crowd started shouting out answers as he stroked his chin. He heard one woman's response and pointed. "Yes! Yeah that's a good one. *The Princess Bride!*"

"Inconceivable!" Roach ran his hand up the neck of the guitar and started playing the main theme from the ninety-four year old movie. It sounded much less fantastical than the original given the distortion on his guitar, but it excited Mathew to hear. "Not really what I meant by rom-com, but a great choice nonetheless. Thanks, dude. Go ahead back down into the crowd, but set up the mic on the stand right there would you?"

With the microphone ready for him in the centre of the stage and Mathew hopping back down to his place, Roach improvised flourishes to the theme then leaned into the microphone and said, "I like this, you guys. You're chill as Hell. I think my next album will be called *Rodents of Unusual Size*. Yeah?" He took a step back, shredded on the guitar, let out a genuine chuckle to the subsequent applause, then leaned back to the mic. He quoted the scene of Westley and Buttercup in the fire swamp exactly and added a musicality to it. He even sang some of the lines. When he was finished with that scene, he asked for the crowd to suggest other scenes, but before he could get on with the Miracle Max one, he heard a voice from off stage to his left:

"Tony! TONY!"

He stopped playing, letting another note hang in the smoky air, and turned to see the person trying to get his attention was his brother. "I'm kinda busy, dude."

River peered out from behind the curtain at the crowd before quickly hiding back behind it and whisper-shouting something in an unplaceable language.

Roach replied in the same language, making no attempt to not broadcast it to the entire room. To the audience, it sounded something like Arabic, something like Greek, and something like Korean. None of them could possibly understand or place it. After another reply from River, Roach addressed them, "It's been great, guys, but I gotta blast." And with that, he dropped his guitar into one hand and flipped it around so that he was holding it almost like a battleaxe as he kicked the loop pedal off and quit the stage.

The brothers could hear the confused announcements from the host as River led Roach out of the club and to an interior stairwell. By the time they were in the unlit column of concrete steps, River was fully sprinting, leaving the black-lunged Roach leaning on his knees and coughing when the door to the stairs closed behind him. "Sonny," he complained hoarsely, "Slow down, dude."

"Did you not hear me!?" he called up from three flights below, "They have *guns*, Tony!"

"Yeah yeah." He shooed away the concern and coughed again. "Where are they?"

His voice was getting progressively quieter as he replied during his rushed descent: "We were playing on forty-seven, but I lost them around thirty."

Roach rolled his eyes at the panic and started a meandering sort of amble down the stairs. He lit a cigarette and took a drag as he leaned into the centre of the stairwell and looked up as if it would help him find the people trying to kill his brother. The darkness of the stairwell was black as pitch, but neither of the Roaches had trouble navigating or seeing their surroundings.

When Roach reached the landing for floor thirty, he lingered and smoked. His gaze was locked on the door like a Western hero about to have a quick-draw duel. He almost surprised himself with the speed at which he suddenly reached up and knocked on it.

Someone on the other side: "Did you hear that? Where's Benny?"

At this, Roach opened the door. He got a good glance of the hall on the other side wherein there were four angry criminals with pistols in their hands that were quickly aimed in his direction. In only two seconds, he saw this, said "Wanna buy a knife?", flashed the balisong knife in his inner pocket, slammed the door closed again, and slid to its side to avoid being shot. Three rounds pierced the door. One of them grazed his calf, but his adrenaline was pumping too hard to fully feel the pain.

When the criminals bursted into the stairwell, he had already climbed to the floor above theirs. As they were struggling to light the area, he did a little jig and started playing his guitar. Unbeknownst to him, it was still wirelessly connected to the sound system in Stickerbomb, so the crowd was treated to a confusing glitching ghost melody as he played a slow ethereal mish-mash of whatever songs came to his mind, the most prominent of which was *No Surprises*. He could hardly hear his guitar, but his haunting voice echoed like a siren's through the stairwell as he serenaded the unseen men whose flashlights were flickering on and flailing around.

The men came into his view a few measures into the song, and all four—. (Wait. Five now. Must have found Benny). All five of them fumbled with their guns. The clips fell out of a few of them, and the others seemed to fly out of their hands and into the impenetrable darkness as if they were snatched away by apparitions. Flashlights were quick to find Roach and the mad grin he wore while strumming his guitar. "Careful, boys, this place is haunted," he taunted, and, while two of them were looking around for their fallen clips, the other three came rushing up the stairs toward Roach.

When they caught up with him, the audience in Stickerbomb was startled by the loud twang of the guitar's final deathly wail when Roach spun it around into the head of the closest attacker. The sound of his skull cracking was like a snare in Roach's improvised song, and he silently lamented that he had not recorded it for sampling.

With his hands free, Roach produced a butterfly knife in each and opened them with a symmetrical skillful flourish.

Knife to throat. Dead. Knife to throat. Dead. Another two blades produced from different pockets. A gun's clip clicking back into place only to be pulled from this panicking stranger's hands and replaced with a stab to the gut, heart, throat, eye, and gut again. Last knife in poor ol' Benny's back as he tried to flee.

River knew it was over when he heard his brother's hysterical laughter echo down to the bottom floor. He leaned into the centre of the stairs and called up to confirm, "You done?"

It took an entire minute for him to stop his maniacal guffaws, and when he did he said simply, "Yeah."

They brought the bodies and broken guitar down to the flooded parking garage, dumped them unceremoniously in the slimy garbage water, then made their way home together.

Chapter 3
Trolls and Ogres

"We're sorry, this number is not in service at this time," the phone nagged before swiftly hanging up on him. He sighed and hung his head, looking down at the device and trying not to cry. Laughter and the deep voices of people he'd rather not think about were muffled through the walls of his closet-sized room. He had a mattress they must have pulled out of a gutter, a CRT television, and a broken walkman. His boss, Grisha Morozov, was a collector of antiques, and the fondness he had for this man was the only reason he was afforded such "luxuries" as these. The others who worked for the Morozov family were not so fortunate, and, of those with rooms, his windowless eight foot cube was somehow the largest.

The chuckles and boisterous Russian conversation from the living room above him were broken by the sound of glass shattering followed by a reeling rage. Jean-Jacques ran a hand through his long hair at the sound but otherwise ignored the shouting. He was a thirty-six year old Frenchman with the sides of his head shaved, showing off the tattoos on his scalp. Like most of his tattoos, they had a heavy focus on engineering and aeromechanics. On the left side of his head were some aesthetically pleasing messily scribbled equations, and on the other side were schematics for a turbojet engine. They were hardly disconnected from the ink on his neck and shoulders, running down his arms and torso. His tattoos were piece-meal in style, all received at different times, but he had enough pieces to cover most of him, especially from the waist up. He didn't have much money, but (what could generously be called) his colleague was a tattoo artist. That Jean-Jacques was always down for another piece made her giddy, and she never charged him with money, only with favours. His favourite tattoo was the *Albatros L 58* schematic that bisected his throat vertically, with some of its thin outer lines curving up onto his face in a way that suited his strong jawline beautifully. Even as heavily tattooed as he was, however, he had no piercings to speak of.

His eyes were so dark a brown they were often regarded as black, and his pale skin made them seem all the darker in contrast. Naturally, his hair was dark, but he had bleached and dyed it mint green after being told it would suit his facial structure by one of his employer's friends. He had done this for fear that he might upset his superiors were he to disregard the comment, but he had to admit that it *did* suit his boxy facial structure. His high cheekbones seemed sharper because of it and gave emphasis to the kind slant on his eyes. He tended not to grow out his facial hair, but he could sport a dark beard and still look handsome.

His build was lean and slightly taller than average at 5'11" with hands always caked in callouses from his line of work which had him often reeking of kerosene, even freshly showered. If it were up to him, he would dress in a grungey or punkish style, but more often than not, he had the choice between coveralls, coveralls, or coveralls. At least he could choose the colour…? (Sometimes). And when he could, he chose black or dark blue.

After tying his hair into a quick ponytail, he stood to open the suitcase, which acted as his dresser. It was absent of clean clothes (at least any that would be able to handle the forecasted blizzard), so he took the laundry basket of dirty clothes off the foot of his mattress and sauntered sleepily toward the washing machine down the hall. $13.50 from his wallet, he cringed as he paid to start the load. One of the other workers had left a bottle of detergent behind, so, with a quick glance around, he poured a capful into the machine and hurried to replace the bottle where he had found it. His last bottle of detergent had cost him $144, and it was $50 to buy a capful from the vending machine in the corner. Seeing as he was only paid $7.50 an hour, the theft seemed justified. If his line of work didn't leave dangerous chemicals on his clothes and coveralls, perhaps he would go longer without cleaning them, but he was already pushing his luck by wearing each piece at least four times.

"There you are, Martial!" sang a drunken Russian entering the laundry room behind him.

Jean-Jacques' spine tensed. He spun on the balls of his feet and forced a smile. "Monseigneur Grisha. W-what can I do for you?"

He draped his heavy arm over Jean-Jacques' narrow shoulders and squeezed him. It was a friendly sort of half-hug, but because of the context of their relationship, the little Frenchman was perturbed and pouring sweat. "Motya say you cannot fix military plane. I tell him, 'My little Martial can fix anything!'"

He gulped. "M-military plane, sir?"

"Da! So Motya say, 'Little Frenchman is useless. You give too much credit, brother.' And so, I get mad and throw my bottle at him! Talking about my little Martial like that!" He puffed out his cheeks which were red both with rage at the story and from his drunkenness. After a hic and a cough on his cigar smoke, he continued, swaying Jean-Jacques around as he led him out of the laundry room. "So we wrestle!" He laughed. "And of course I won! And afterwards I say, 'I will buy ten antique gun planes and my Martial will make them good as new!' He says, 'Grisha is mad! I bet ten million dollars he cannot fix the planes!' I say, 'He can fix ten million planes! I bet hundred million he will make gun planes good as new!'" The guffaws that followed sent a chill down Jean-Jacques' spine.

"W-what kind of—." Gulp. "What kind of g-gun planes, sir?"

"Haven't decided yet!" A drunken hic. By then, he had led the Frenchman out of the basement and into the kitchen. He finally took his thick oppressive arm off of Jean-Jacques' shoulders then stumbled to the counter to start pouring himself another glass of bourbon. After a swig, he wiped a spillage off his fat chest and gestured toward the fridge. "Make comfort, JJP. Where is little dog?"

"Sh-she's staying overnight at th-the dog doctor, sir."

He frowned. "Is little dog okay!?"

"No." He took an apple from a nearby fruit bowl and fidgeted with it nervously. "She needs surgery. It's very expensive, sir. D-do you think you—," he stopped himself.

"Grisha pay for little dog's doctor bills?"

Jean-Jacques' eyes were watering as he nodded helplessly.

Grisha rushed to him, scooped him up into a hug, and pushed his head into his chest. Jean-Jacques' thin body was awkwardly arched around Grisha's fat stomach, his feet dangling at least a foot from the ground. "Oh! We do not cry, we do not worry! Little dog will be good as when she was little puppy! Grisha will pay for doctor."

He sniffled and cried into Grisha's chest, eventually feeling vulnerable enough to reach his arms up around him to return the hug. His voice was muffled by the fabric and broken by his sorrow, but he managed to choke out a sniffly, "Merci, Monseigneur."

His fat arms squeezed him harder, and he pet Jean-Jacques' head, shushing him lovingly and rocking gently from side to side. "We do not cry, we do not worry, JJP. Grisha loves little dog, too."

When the long embrace came to a close, Jean-Jacques was invited to dinner with the family and quite literally could not refuse. There was, however, some time before the cooks would be finished, so he called the veterinarian to schedule his dog's surgery then spent the rest of the time before supper doing his laundry.

Dinner was a feast of traditional Russian dishes with a sprinkling of other goodies like fresh rolls, Korean barbeque, and an entire four-cheese lasagna. There were sixteen people attending the meal including Jean-Jacques, though he was the only one not a part of the Morozov family.

He was buzzed on a glass of vodka soda when the table started to fill with food. To his right was Grisha, and to his left was Motya. They were brothers with Grisha the older and fatter of the two. Motya was large in his own right, though. He was nearly seven feet tall and a bodybuilder. Jean-Jacques sitting between them with his average build seemed even smaller for it. His shoulders were tense. Even drunk and feeling somewhat welcome at the table, he was making himself small so as to not touch either of the brothers. These two in particular were the most temperamental in the group, and knowing that they both had blood on their hands and had each attacked Jean-Jacques at least thrice meant he was on his best, most docile behaviour so as to not anger them. At least… while he was sober.

Most of the conversations were in Russian. He knew enough to follow along, but when he was dragged into a chat, he responded in English. As the night grew older, the temperature in the desert outside plummeted, and it was not long into dessert before all the Russians started talking about the snow outside. There was a competitive sort of way they spoke of it, and by then, Jean-Jacques was on his fifth vodka soda. He laughed at Grisha's claim that he once raced frost to the bank of a lake by swimming only slightly faster than it. All eyes were on him as he so blatantly disregarded the claim, but only Grisha's were angry.

"Why is Martial laughing?"

He hiccupped and swayed. His tone was mocking and haughty, speaking in third person to mock him further: "Martial is laughing because it's a funny thing to picture: your fat ass doggy-paddling away from a blizzard." He howled, and all the rest of them laughed at the visage he evoked. Grisha's furrowed brow softened at the comment.

"He's right, son," said Papa Gennady in Russian with a chortle, "Jean-Jacques, punch him in his fat face for telling such foolish tales!"

He winced at the command and looked sheepishly up at the behemoth.

Grisha stood without regarding Jean-Jacques and pointed angrily at his father. In Russian: "I'm telling the truth, you bastard! Sister was there! Tell him, Roksi!"

"Go out into the blizzard, then, fatass!" He laughed at his son's rage. "Jean-Jacques, go fight him in the snow while we watch."

They all turned toward Jean-Jacques who shrank in their dark oppressive gazes. There was a moment of quiet before Grisha picked him up by his collar and growled in English, "Outside, pussy! Else Grisha won't pay for little dog's surgery."

Jean-Jacques nodded with worry at first, but as he started to pump himself up mentally for the fight, he managed a drunken smirk. "Let me go, then." After he was dropped, he maintained his balance, downed the rest of the bottle of vodka from the table behind him, then stomped to the front door. The Morozovs followed him with Grisha at the head of them.

The cold was deadly, but they were both too warm from their drunkenness to fully notice. The others huddled around on the covered wrap-around porch while Jean-Jacques and Grisha circled each other on the snowy lawn.

This was not his first time fighting someone twice his size, and the way he held up his fists after removing his shirt was indicative of such a thing. The tattoos all over his torso and up his neck were intimidating, even to Grisha, who knew this man to be rather meek. The fat man removed his shirt and tossed it toward his sister in one swift motion, whereas Jean-Jacques' was off before he had even left the porch.

Once Grisha had his fists up, Jean-Jacques thrust himself forward and skillfully grappled the larger man. He deftly dodged a punch in his approach before rounding to Grisha's back and spinning up onto him. He had one arm locked around his fat neck and the other was pinning one of his hands up against his shoulder by its thumb. Grisha's free hand was trying to make room between Jean-Jacques' arm and his throat to stop choking, but the smaller man's knee slammed into his middle-back and brought him to his knees. He tapped on Jean-Jacques' arm to stop the fight, and the Frenchman released him.

After catching his breath, he turned toward Jean-Jacques, who was being praised by the rest of the family, and tackled him into the snow while his back was turned. The wrestling that ensued was fast and brutal. Jean-Jacques was no match for him in this manner. His only hope was to escape, but when he finally did manage to wriggle free, Motya was an immovable wall between him and the house. "Monseigneur Motya, p-please let me—." He was shoved to the ground by the mass of muscle and spat on. They cursed him in Russian with so much drunken slurring and drooling that he couldn't parse the words of the foreign tongue from each other. Not that he needed to know what was being said. They made abundantly clear what they thought of him when they took turns kicking him in the stomach hard enough to take away all his breath. The snow against his bare skin started to burn, and the wind howled angrily as he was beat to a bloody pulp by the brothers. Even Roksolana, their teenaged sister, joined in after a while.

All he managed to understand as they finally finished with him and started to walk away was one last comment, this time in English, from Motya: "Drink more, little Frenchie. It'll hurt less." They laughed as they left him curled up in the snow and tempestuous blizzard.

Fortunately, he was only about thirty feet from the front door, and they hadn't locked it. When he came inside half frozen to death, he was met only with cold glares from the entire group. There was a worry in the back of his boozy brain that perhaps he had ruined his chances of Grisha paying for his veterinary bills, but he also knew this lot to be fickle and unpredictable. He'd probably wake up to a pile of blueberry pancakes drenched in syrup and a big glass of orange juice to help his hangover. Grisha wouldn't apologise, but he likely wouldn't acknowledge this violence at all.

They were wordless as he moved through the living room to the cellar door. Their gazes stabbed through him, somehow more icy than the snow currently clinging to his skin. When he finally managed to make it to his room, he sank into his bed and shortly thereafter found himself holding his side. He tried to peel his hand away, but his fingertips felt stuck in something. After standing and looking in his floor-length mirror, the extent of the damage done to him was made more clear. He had a bloody (potentially broken) nose, a swollen bloody brow, a black eye, small cuts in his shoulders from the dry cold and acidic snow, bruises larger than his fist all over…. But the most unsettling image and the reason he was holding his side was because he, at some point, had been slashed by some sort of blade.

Memories of the scuffle were hard to distinguish, but he seemed to recall a moment wherein Roksolana flipped open a hidden switchblade in her shoe while he was being kicked from all sides. His adrenaline and drunkenness were finally fading, so it was with shaking bloody hands that he started digging through his belongings. He was out of bandages in his first aid kit, but it had disinfectant. He poured some on the wound without thinking and hissed at the horrible pain. His hands were too shaky to thread a needle, so he fell on the floor and crawled to his suitcase, where he had dumped all his clean clothes. He dug around and found a sock, which he pressed to the wound then secured to his side with the entire roll of gauze in his kit. It had been used for several similar injuries in the past, so it was hardly sterile, but he had little else of a choice.

Once that was done, he was finally able to address how deathly cold he was. He had warmed significantly since coming back inside, but he still found himself piling all of his laundry, still warm from the dryer, and all of his blankets on top of him.

As he warmed himself, he took out his phone and tried to call his sister again.

"We're sorry, this number is not in service at this time."

He hung up and shivered. "Merde."

After forcing away the dark thoughts of what might have happened to her since they last spoke, he checked his email for updates about his dog. They had sent him a picture of her playing with a toy and wearing a bow on her head. It brought a weak smile to his face, but the worries that her surgery might not be covered after the fight soured the otherwise happy moment.

He was about to start a game of chess on the phone when he received a text message from Grisha:

⌈ I just ordered three gunner planes. They'll be here in two months. And another six after that in August. They're all different models, I think. I'm sure you'll have fun with them! ⌋

He sighed and closed his eyes. "Merde."

Chapter 4
Short Rest

For Thyne's birthday, Francis appeared at his doorstep at three in the morning with a flawlessly-wrapped gift in each hand. Still awake at such a late hour, Thyne was quick to pull on some pyjama pants and call down to his friend to come inside. Francis used his key and was in Thyne's bedroom thereafter. He set down the gifts on his well-made bed and pulled the shorter man in for a loving embrace.

"Merry birthday, Thyne."

"I'm surprised you remembered." They retreated from the hug, and Thyne noticed a distinct lack of a boozy smell on his friend. "And you're sober?"

Francis' eyes welled with tears. His voice cracked as he replied, "I can offer only one last apology, but I would never ask for your forgiveness, for I know I am not worthy of such a thing."

Thyne tilted his head. His smile soured into one more concerned and perplexed. "One last apology? Are you going somewhere?"

"Unfortunately for you, no."

He shook his head, his smile entirely gone by then. With a thoroughly furrowed brow, he asked, "Why would that be unfortunate for me?"

Francis opened his mouth but it lay there in silence before he shook away his thoughts and plucked up one of the presents from beside them. "Open your gifts."

Thyne took the offered box and looked at it with a dumbfounded expression. After a while, he set it back on the bed and reached up a hand to cup around his friend's tear-stained cheek. His voice was soft and loving: "Frankenstein. What's going on?"

He took Thyne's hand away by the wrist and averted his eyes. "You need not worry yourself with my burdensome troubles. There's no more time to waste. Open your gifts."

Thyne's concern and confusion compounded, but he leaned down to grab one of the presents and carefully unwrapped it so as to not ruin the work his friend had done to make it look so picturesque. This first gift was a leatherbound journal with a leather strip loosely wrapped around it. He started to unravel it, but Francis stopped him by gently resting his hands on Thyne's and saying, "Now the next one."

The journal was replaced in Thyne's hands with the next gift, and he offered another odd expression to his friend. "Franky, why are you—?"

"Open it."

Thyne tried to open it carefully, but after only a moment, Francis reached out and tore the paper so he would get to the gift inside more quickly. It was so out of character for Francis, Thyne was baffled to blindness. His eyes rapidly blinked and brain tried to process why Francis of all people was being so impatient. When he finally came back into himself, he was able to parse that the gift in this larger box was a World War Two style helmet. He read the name on the inside: *O. York*. "Oliver's helmet?"

"Do you like them?"

His gaze bounced between the presents then flittered up to Francis' ocean blue eyes. He was wreathed in the smoke from the incense Thyne had lit only a minute before the sudden visit. When he lit it, he asked Aphrodite for a sign. Was this—?

He didn't have more time to question it before Francis' lips were on his. He melted into the kiss, dropping the helmet on the carpet as his arms went limp and eyes fluttered closed. After what felt like a million years of bliss, Francis opened his mouth and danced his tongue with his best friend's split one. Thyne's cheeks were hot and heart racing. His stomach was stirring up with butterflies, and when Francis retreated, Thyne tried to pull him lecherously toward the bed.

"No," said Francis with a trembling lip. There was a long pause, after which he whimpered, "Thyne, I love you more than anything."

He beamed. The kiss had him on cloud nine, and his reply fell from his lips like the smoke of a cigarette: "I love you more than that."

"I am so indescribably sorry."

"Why are you—?" There was a visible shift in Francis' air, and Thyne's smile soured.

Francis' dumb grin followed before he swigged from his flask. "Thyne, my dear. What's the good word on the gang situation?"

He sighed and plucked up the gifts to bring them silently to his bedside table. After setting them down and sucking up a slimy ball of sorrow in his sinuses, he turned toward Francis and replied with only a slight quaver in his voice: "Party got us a contact. We'll be flying out to the states a week from now. Or, realistically a little sooner, so we're not late for the meeting."

"Bully! I haven't been to the states since they were colonies!" He laughed drunkenly before taking another swig and noticing the rain picking up outside. "What do you say to a movie or two?"

A sad smile. "Okay, Franky. I'll meet you in the living room."

"I shall obtain all your favourite snacks," he proclaimed. He popped down to the shops to get snacks, and Thyne started carrying blankets, pillows, and plushes downstairs.

On his third trip to the bedroom to put his computer to sleep, he found himself drawn to the gifted journal. His curiosity got the better of him, and while he heard Francis downstairs organising whatever he had bought, Thyne opened the little notebook.

With a quick fan of the pages, he was able to tell that the entire thing was filled with perfectly straight lines of the calligraphy Francis called his handwriting. He peeled back the pages until he was on the first and let out a soft gasp at what he read.

Francis called something up to him, and he was quick to close and hide the book under his pillow. "Coming!"

The first movie they watched all cuddled up in a mountain of pillows and blankets was Thyne's favourite: *The Wizard of Oz*. Francis had remembered (or more likely read a reminder of) Thyne's favourite snacks, so the Brit was treated to apple and fruit juiceboxes, gummy peach rings, pop rocks, and a chocolate orange. Francis, on the other hand, was content with just his bottomless flask of rum and a sleeve of stale crackers from Thyne's pantry. He had his best friend curled up in his arms sipping adorably from a juice box and snuggling a fluffy plush sheep. There were versions of him that would savour such a thing, but he was instead an inebriated shell of himself, only drinking more heavily as the hours elapsed.

While the credits rolled on the first film, Thyne looked up at Francis and asked, "Wanna watch your favourite, now?"

"What e'en is it?" slurred the drunkard.

Thyne frowned. "You don't remember your own favourite movie, Franky?" He reached slowly for the flask and tried to take it from his friend.

"Shtop! Thass mine."

"Franny, I'm worried about you," he whispered.

He averted his eyes. Even this drunk, he was ashamed of himself. "Sorry."

"What about something new? We're going to America soon. Maybe a Western?"

He sighed and glared at his flask before turning toward his friend and sobering up enough to force a smile and nod.

Thyne beamed and took out his phone to stream to his large television. "How's *Shanghai Noon* sound? Have you seen that one yet?" Francis shook his head, and Thyne said, "Good. You need to lighten up, mate. Here." He passed him the last apple juice from the six-pack and kissed his cheek. "Drink this instead of that brown muck you love so much."

Francis smiled hesitantly and briefly set down his flask on the couch beside him to fumble clumsily with the juicebox's straw.

"Oh, you muppet," joked Thyne as he opened it for him. He took a sip, calling it, "the friend tax," then snuggled back up against Francis' bony body with his peach rings in his right hand and his plush lamb nestled under his left arm.

Francis maintained his drunkenness for the rest of the night and into the morning, but he had the wherewithal enough to keep from blacking out or slurring again. By noon, they had watched a few more movies, and Thyne's eyes were aching and bloodshot. The bags beneath them were darker than usual. He rubbed them with a cute yawn as the last movie's credits rolled.

"Have you happened upon some rest?" asked Francis.

"If only," he smiled sadly, "Far too loud up here." He gestured to his head then stood to stretch his legs. From his new position, he noticed a thin layer of snow outside and smiled. "Oh, Franky! Look how pretty! It never snows in London anymore! It's for my birthday from Marena!" He giggled and rushed to his coat closet. "Let's go out! Oh, I should gather some of it too! For spells!"

As Thyne was zooming all around and bundling himself up to go out into the soft winter afternoon, Francis ambled to the foyer and watched him. "Merry birthday," he said as he rubbed the back of his neck, "What would you like?"

Thyne rolled his eyes and dumped an armful of winter clothes in Francis' arms to act as a coat hanger while he struggled with his snow pants.

"I could bring you something from Ancient Egypt if you'd like. Isn't one of your gods Egyptian?"

"Franky, how many times do I have to tell you that Giovanni and Arjun have thoroughly ruined my faith in Osiris as a God? Not to mention the bloody company." He snatched his coat out of Francis' arms and glared at him as he pulled it on. "My Gods are Charon, Thanatos, Aphrodite, Marena, Brigit, and the lwa Kalfu. Write it down!"

"Oh that all sounds familiar. I've written it already." A dumb grin as Thyne attached his false fingers and tested their mobility. "How about something from Ancient Greece, then?"

"Shut up." He snatched away the gloves in Francis' hands. "You already got me something. Stop ruining my mood with your stupidity."

"Oh," he laughed with a drunken blush, "Well good on me, then."

In his private hangar at the Heathrow airport, Thyne had two planes stored. They were both considered classics, though one was only seventy years old, whereas the other was well over a century vintage at that point. The younger of the two planes was a fighter jet he was only legally able to fly for three reasons. One: It was defunct in all major militaries of the world. Two: The custom paint job was made up mostly of pastel pink and mint green. It depicted a variety of adorable animals and candies as well as a happy face on the nose of the plane. It looked both unprofessional for a military and nonthreatening in general. And the third reason he was able to fly it: bribery and blackmail of the bureaucrats blocking his way to registering it. That he could still technically load it with weapons was something no amount of bribery could handwave away, however. For him to arm the plane was strictly forbidden, as was flying it out of EAU airspace. He could illegally fly it into the states for their meeting in Arizona, but there was only room for himself in the *Sukhoi Su-57*. Not to mention it wasn't worth risking his pilot's licence. Besides, he didn't mind all the limitations. For Thyne, it was mostly a leisure vehicle he would bring to air shows to perform highly dangerous and impressive feats of airmanship.

The second plane of his was comically large in comparison to the fighter jet. Most private jets would only be slightly larger, but this old beast was an *MD DC-8*. It had belonged to a variety of commercial airlines until Thyne snatched it up before it would be entirely gutted and, with Francis' help, returned it to its former glory. Its interior had been entirely redone, and the livery on its exterior had been replaced with a sleek colour-shifting and pearlescent lemon yellow/light pink paint. It was by far the oldest plane in the skies, but it flew as if it had just come off the line way back in 1965. Because the controls were so old, there was even some trouble certifying its airworthiness with the authorities when he first tried to claim it as a flying vessel. There were minimal modifications made to the cockpit from its last refurbishment in 2034, so Thyne had to hire a test pilot to come out of retirement in order to certify the machine.

Their flight plan to get to America involved stopping in Iceland to refuel then again in Toronto before finally landing at a private strip and hangar Thyne had bought in the middle of the New Mexican desert. Francis and Thyne were usually joined at the hip. That the scruffy man would be sitting in the cockpit while his friend flew the plane was therefore nothing new to the pair. What *was* new was that they would be flying over the Atlantic. Francis had a crippling fear of the ocean and especially of crossing it on a vessel he wasn't in full control of. He trusted

Thyne entirely: the man was a phenomenal pilot, but his fear was rooted in betrayal and trauma he had yet to heal even after what felt like an eternity. It was possible for him to get to America without having to cross the ocean, but he insisted that he would be at his friend's side on the plane to save his life should the worst case scenario occur.

After loading their luggage into the cabin, Thyne sat in the cockpit to start doing calculations and running over the details of his flight plan. Francis was already buzzed in preparation for the gruelling day of thalassophobia and PTSD ahead of him. He came into the cockpit and sat in the First Officer's seat. He was vaguely familiar with the controls and the jargon on the chatter, so, at least until his inevitable panic attack, he had volunteered to operate the comms with ATC. Thyne, however, refused it when he smelled the rum on Francis' breath: "I'll do it, you mug. Just sit there looking pretty."

The take off and first half hour of flight were much like any other trip across Eurasia or Africa for the pair, and because Iceland was a long-standing member of the Eurasian Union, there was very little paperwork necessary to legally plan a private flight from one to the other. Francis' panic started to rile up when he could no longer see land through any windows. Even when he left the cockpit to look out the windows in the cabin, he could see only ocean. He returned to his friend's side, visibly shaking. Thyne briefly removed his hand from the engine throttles to squeeze one of Francis' hands and smiled sadly at him. "You're safe with me, Franny. Only another hour, and we'll be in Keflavík. Okay?" He removed his hand from Francis' with some difficulty. "I have to keep my hands on the controls, but you can come sit on the floor beside me."

He did as was offered and wrapped one of his vigorously-trembling hands around Thyne's thigh. He squeezed tight and pulled himself as close as possible. The middle console was in a highly inconvenient place for him to feel his face on any part of his friend. Thyne noticed the difficulties and, with little else he could do, he quietly sang for Francis his favourite song: *The White Cliffs of Dover.*

His voice was a gift from the divine, and even though singing brought about a panic in him almost as fervent as the panic in his friend, he was cool enough under pressure and focused on his love for Francis and the safe operation of the plane to manage his way through the entire song with only three pauses to catch his stuttered breath. The gesture did not go unnoticed or unappreciated by Francis, and by the time the song was finished, his shaking had all but subsided.

They landed in Keflavík shortly thereafter, and while they waited for the plane to be refuelled, Thyne suggested they go into the airport for lunch. Francis had calmed significantly by then, so on their way inside he said, "Thank you for singing to me, Thyne."

"Only for you, mate."

While they wandered around the gates to find somewhere to eat that sounded appealing, they passed an American Chinese restaurant chain and Thyne stopped in front of it. He grabbed one of Francis' wrists and pointed wordlessly to the counter.

"Oh bully! It's hardly *real* Chinese food, but some fried rice does sound pleasing to the senses." After a while of standing in line it was their turn to order, and Francis, like a Western asshole trying to show-off, tried ordering in Mandarin. He was fluent in the language, but his verbiage was quite antiquated, stilted, and odd, not dissimilar to when he spoke in French or English. Luckily for him, the worker knew Mandarin, but he glared at the white man speaking it so strangely while he ordered. Thyne spent the entire interaction rubbing the bridge of his nose standing behind his friend and hiding his blush.

The worker replied in English, his Icelandic accent thick: "An orange chicken and shrimp fried rice. Is that all, sir?"

Francis was going to reply to order some drinks, but Thyne started to shove him away and said, "That's all. Cheers, mate." He produced his credit card without removing his wallet from his pocket and passed it to the irritated employee. It was almost immediately given back after a quick wave over a chip-reader. Thyne took it and read the e-receipt displayed on the previously transparent middle section of the card as he shoved Francis to a nearby table.

"170 Euros. Greedy bastards," the Brit muttered angrily.

"You do not desire a beverage?"

He looked up from the credit card, transferring his glare from the total price to his friend's confused grin: "Francis, can't you speak English to them?"

"He *did* know Mandarin, Thyne. I know not the reasons for which you find yourself upset with me."

Thyne rolled his eyes and leaned on his elbow. "It doesn't matter. Go buy us drinks from a vending machine."

Francis went pale. "A vending machine?" He gulped. "I don't know how to operate those, my dear. You are aware."

Thyne let on a wicked grin as he finally slid his credit card back into his wallet. "All the better, mate. Practice makes perfect. I'd like a diet cola." He passed him a different card while he had his wallet out. "And get yourself something. There was an alcove that way with soda machines and between them was one selling canned cocktails, you bloody drunkard."

Hesitantly, Francis dragged himself out of his chair and wandered in the direction Thyne had indicated. When he spotted the aforementioned machines, a pit of dread formed in his stomach, and his steps into the alcove were small and unconfident. He could swear they were sentient the way they seemed to be looking down on him from on high. He whispered in his native tongue of French: "Thyne desires a soft drink. Do it for him." He could see into two of the machines and spotted a bottle of diet cola in the one on the far left. With a shaky hand, he fed it the card. It beeped happily as it took the bank information, but when he took it back out, it seemed evermore impatient with him to get on with the transaction:

Beep.

'*These buttons make no sense.*'

Beep!

'*By God! Hush you damnable machine. I'm trying. 6-F?*'

BEEP!

'*But oh! Where are the buttons I'm meant to press?*'

He was looking for physical buttons on the machine, but it had a standard touch screen which was currently flashing a message that it verbalised after another round of impatient tones:

Beep.

Beep!

BEEP!

"Please proceed with purchase."

He stopped time and held his aching head.

Francis was of a mixed breed; not of different human races but of different species entirely. He was half-human, this much was true, but there was also alien blood in his veins from a long extinct race called Etren. It was this ancient other-worldly genetic material that afforded him supernatural powers, the primary of which was his control over the fourth dimension. (Another of these abilities was his passive tolerance of cold down to the absolute-zero brought about by time being stopped as it was then).

After a long while alone with time unmoving around him, he found the lock to the door of the vending machine and aged it to dust. Sweat beaded his brow at such a use of his power, and it didn't help that the door he then had to pull open was much heavier than he had anticipated.

Still, he managed to open it and took three diet colas for Thyne, shoving them into his mostly-empty rucksack, then closing the door and sliding to the side to observe the cocktails on offer.

After stealing himself five daiquiris and a Manhattan, he returned the machines to their states before he had ever approached them by ageing them both backwards by a few hours. The drinks were therefore refilled in the machine, but his bag still contained the ones he had stolen. He resumed time when he was satisfied with the look of them and sauntered confidently back to Thyne, passing him one of his sodas and cracking open one of the daiquiris for himself.

By that point, because he had taken so long being stressed and confused before abusing his power to steal the refreshments, their food had already arrived.

"Cheers," said Thyne after swallowing a mouthful of orange chicken, "Did you figure them out, or did you cheat?"

Francis pouted like a child and opened his chopsticks. He puffed out his cheek and averted his eyes before shoving a skillful mouthful of rice into his blushing face.

Thyne giggled. "You're cute, Franny." He took another bite and looked into the paper bag for the complimentary cookies as if they would spawn magically in between his last glimpse and now. With a sigh, he pushed it to the side and complained, "It's a shame we don't have any fortune cookies, or we could split one like a Christmas cracker."

Francis took the bag to look for himself. "They did not provide any? How much did this cost you?"

"Oh, Franky, don't make a scene. It's okay. We'll get some next time."

Ignoring his friend, he stood and rejoined the queue. Thyne's reaction was to hide his blushing face from the strangers all around. His vast fortune could get him out of a lot of trouble, but he didn't like the idea of drawing unnecessary attention to their little "vacation" to the states. They were on their way to America to meet up with a criminal for the express purpose of doing more crime. Still, he was angry enough about the lack of sweets to not pull Francis back to their table. He watched the scene play out in quick glances:

"Hello, it has only been thirty-six minutes and five seconds since my last foray with this...," he looked around, "establishment.... I trust you remember me?"

He was still speaking Mandarin, and it only added to the irritation already plain as day on the worker's face. He slow-blinked and sighed. To appease him, he replied in Mandarin: "Yes, sir. What do you want now?"

"It's no trouble, really, friend. We are merely missing our complimentary cookies of good fortune."

His voice was droning and bored: "We're out of fortune cookies, sir."

"Oh my! Well, when does the next shipment come in?"

He rolled his eyes and clicked a few things on a nearby tablet. "We'll have them again when we open on Friday."

"Right. Well, I'll see you then!" He took two steps toward the table before using his control of time to send himself to Friday and walk back to the counter, which was empty of patrons and starting to close. The same worker was sweeping up behind the counter when Francis suddenly appeared. A slew of vulgar Icelandic exclamations followed as he dropped the broom and held his racing heart. After catching his breath and picking up the fallen tool, he droned, "We're closed," in Mandarin, clearly remembering this weirdo.

"Oh, what a shame. When do you open?"

After a moment of irritated silence he approached the counter and leaned on his hands. "For the love of God, what do you want?"

"I was hoping to get two of your cookies of good fortune for my friend and I. We were here——."

He was interrupted by a handful of fortune cookies being thrown into his chest. "There! Now get out of here!"

He fumbled to catch them all, but before picking them up off the floor he beamed his rotten teeth and said, "Thank you, sir!"

With six fortune cookies in hand, he travelled back to Sunday, February eighth. To those nearby when he returned, it seemed the fortune cookies in his hands had appeared there magically, but, though the action was seen by three strangers, none of them questioned him. They merely watched him with mouths agape as he went to the table and set the cookies in front of Thyne with a big dumb grin down at his friend.

"How's that, then?"

Thyne offered a blushy smile and took one of them to start opening it. "Cheers, you bellend."

Satisfied with his gesture, Francis nodded once and sat back down to shovel more rice into his maw.

Thyne offered half of the unbroken cookie to his friend, and they cracked it open like a wishbone. Francis' half was the one with the fortune, so he pulled it out and popped the cookie in his mouth while it was still full of rice and soy sauce.

Don't be afraid to seek out help from loved ones.

"What does it say?"

He passed it to Thyne.

"Do you know why you're getting this message?"

Francis had long ago lost all faith in magic and gods as higher powers, but he knew his friend was a warlock and quite spiritual. To the question, rather than shutting down the idea that it may have held a deeper meaning, which was how he truly felt, Francis merely shrugged.

"Well, you can always lean on me, Franny!" He beamed adorably, his little button nose scrunching up and eyes pushed closed by his freckled peachy cheeks.

Francis matched the smile with one of his own, but it was slightly soured. He was perturbed by dark thoughts the fortune had aroused in him. Still, he sounded cheerful enough when he replied, "Likewise, my friend."

It was lucky Francis had drunken himself blind. He wasn't exactly observant, nor was he a pilot, but Thyne was giving him worried glances all the same. Had he noticed the alert about Engine Two? Surely he wouldn't understand what it meant, but Thyne's response would be telling that something was wrong. And in the middle of the Atlantic? "Fuck," he muttered. This was exactly the sort of situation that had Francis a drunken mess in the first place. He was sitting in the First Officer's seat, but his posture had been slumped with his aching blurry gaze unable to focus on even his own hands.

Thyne was careful in his movements to not be caught in Francis' periphery. Slowly, he pulled his left hand from the yoke and reached into a cubby. His panicked glances toward Francis as he scanned the instruments probably weren't doing him any good at seeming calm.

"Wuh's that?" slurred the drunk when he managed to notice Thyne pulling a small three-ring binder of hand-written notes onto his lap.

"It's nothing," he lied. Sweat was beading down his spine as he turned to a checklist he had written decades prior to prepare for the error he was seeing. He pushed up his big round reading glasses to keep them from falling into his lap as he followed the list's instructions. That was until....

"Franny?" he cooed after swallowing a lump of dread in his throat.

"Huh?" He looked at him and tried not to touch anything when his body swayed.

"There's some switches over there," he pointed to the panel over Francis, "Can you read them?"

Francis tried to read them, but when he retroactively processed what was asked of him, his gaze snapped down to the rest of the controls. He noticed one of the throttles was pulled all the way back and an illegible orange line of words in the centre console that he had only ever seen when there was some sort of trouble with the plane, not to mention the notebook in Thyne's lap. The fear that struck him sobered him like lightning. His eyes were wide and face pale as he looked into his friend's amber eyes.

"Oh Franky! It's okay! Don't you worry your pretty face about it. It's just an air conditioning thing." He forced a laugh. "Why don't you go into the cabin and look for a winter coat in case it gets cold in here?"

Francis took his friend's words with the utmost seriousness and stopped time before rushing into the back of the plane and tearing it to pieces looking for the warmest clothes he could find. He returned an hour of his own time later, more sober now, and resumed time with an armful of layers for his friend. "Is this enough? Oh, Thyne! It gets mighty cold up here! Are you going to be okay?"

Thyne frowned at the sudden apparition of winter gear. "Oh, would you look at that, it's all fixed!" He laughed anxiously. "So go take your time putting those away and put on some music, won't you?"

If Francis were more perceptive, even the expert liar Thyne was faltering enough to be caught out in his deception. With all the compounding issues piling onto his already frazzled mind, he was visibly anxious. He was calm under pressure, but he knew Francis would not share in that steadiness if he figured out the real issue. At least not when they were out here in the middle of nowhere with only a void of various blues outside.

Francis kissed Thyne's forehead and left the cockpit with the clothes to start putting them away. He knew his friend was trying to imply that he shouldn't use his power, but he assumed it was because he needed time alone to fly the plane without distraction. While not untrue, the real reason Francis was temporarily unwelcome in the cockpit was because of Thyne's anxiety that he might discover that an engine was having issues. It did cross his mind that perhaps Francis would look outside and see the engine on fire or smoking or maybe even missing entirely, but with a quick check of his tail camera, those fears were quelled. Whatever was wrong with the engine was internal.

When Francis returned to the cockpit some fifteen minutes later, he took Thyne's phone and streamed a playlist to the bluetooth surround-sound in the cabin behind them. "Loud enough?" He asked as it played clearly through the half-open door.

"Plenty loud," he said with a dismissive wave of his hand. His gaze was still on his instruments, and as he finished a third checklist, the alert on his screen finally disappeared. He sighed a breath of relief and pulled out a cigarette to take a relaxing drag before turning toward his friend and smiling weakly. "Are you okay?"

He pointed out the front windows. "There be Canada." The shoreline of Newfoundland extended past the edges of the windshield. "And we flew over Greenland."

"So... you're feeling okay?"

His smile soured. "I am not crippled by fear."

"Well, come and watch the horizon and let it calm you."

He nodded and sat back down. "How about a travel game?"

Thyne let out a long smoky breath as his racing heart finally started to regulate its speed. "Sure. What game?"

Chapter 5
Party

In a world slowly flooding, expanding the fleet from twenty-eight in 2020 to fifty-six in 2081 was only natural for a company that had the means. *Aquillius' Revenge* was a premier luxury cruise ship and the newest addition to Canopy Cruises and Hotels' fleet, having its maiden voyage in late January. For civilian sailors like Partha, it was impossible to work for long without at least once winding up on a Canopy ship, and *Aquillius' Revenge* had been his home away from home since it first set sail out of Marseilles.

As a worker, his room was below the surface, so when they were near land the layer of garbage, scum, and flotsam on top of the water would hinder his vision of the sky. It was for this reason that, on one of his days off near Panama City, he decided to climb up to the bridge where his father, the captain, was steering with masterful skill through the canal. With a breadth of over seventy metres, the newly-widened canal could still hardly hold her. 386 metres long and tall enough for thirty-two floors excluding service floors at the lowest and highest points: she was a monster, but still not the largest vessel in Canopy's fleet.

She was a state of the art model made mostly of a nigh-indestructible glass (laced with diamonds), cold black steel, and (occasionally) carbon fibre. When the waters were calm, the gargantuan windows on either side of her tall bow revealed what appeared to be a fourteen-storey hotel within that overlooked an indoor pool, lush gardens, and several lounge areas. Those with private balconies in the fore of the ship therefore had a good view of the common area below as well as the sea ahead. Above that was a large bar, lounge, and restaurant that overlooked the flatter top of the bow. Even further up still were more guest rooms, and at the very top of the monstrous vessel was the bridge. The aft was similar to the bow in that it also had towering expanses of glass to reveal the structures within, making the entire ship seem something of a human terrarium floating along the seas. The parts of the ship that weren't towering windows were matte black steel with lights embedded throughout in geometric patterns that almost resembled a circuit board. The colour of these lights could be changed to nearly any hue but would often alternate in a sweeping gradient between red, white, and blue.

It took a while to reach the top of the ship from its bowels, but when he did finally make it there, Partha danced onto the bridge wearing a flowy poet shirt and a rapier on his hip. He was singing a sea shanty between sniffles, and those few who were in good enough spirits to join him stopped sharing in his levity when they noticed the sounds. His father's tone was serious and reprimanding as his son came up to his side: "Party, why are you sniffling?"

"Relax, Daddy. It's just a cold!" He beamed. "Where's the city!? I want to see it!"

Richard squinted sceptically.

"What?" A nervous chuckle.

He grabbed Partha by his shoulder and looked deep into his eye.

"Daddy, I'm fine," he said with a huff as he pushed the hand off of him. He averted his gaze and pouted like a child. "I just wanted to come see the city."

Richard sighed. It broke Partha's heart when he heard the disappointment lacing his father's tone. They left a lot of words unspoken as the captain gestured ahead of them and said, "Shouldn't be too long before we can see it, but I'd bet it's flooded like Hell by the looks of it."

"Well, I hope not. I was hoping to go into town tonight."

He laughed. "You'll have to wear those wellies that make you look like a child." Partha pouted, at which Richard laughed again and pulled his son in for a half-hug. "Why don't you stay in with me, hm? We can go down to the bar and get drunk together. Maybe we can do a one-shot. Don't you want to spend some time with your old man before whatever shenanigans you're going to get up to in California?"

The lightness in his tone and the good points he made brought a grumpy reluctant smile to Partha's face. "Okay, Daddy," he said as he finally relaxed again, "I'll go prepare something. What game do you want to play?"

"Surprise me!"

Entirely bubbly again, he was beaming before quickly kissing his father on the cheek and dancing back out of the room and down into the bowels of the ship where his small cabin was situated.

The flooding in LA was especially bad when they arrived, so the behemoth ship was not allowed to dock or tender. The passengers who were scheduled to have exited the vessel in LA were forced to stay on board, so it was with a lot of upset that rumours started to spread around the ship when it came to a stop and met with a small coast guard boat. Some of the passengers claimed to have seen "that one-eyed waiter from the restaurant just jumped into the water and swam out to the coast guard boat! Why can't we do that?"

It was true. Partha gave his father a series of hugs and cheek kisses in an emotional goodbye before donning a life vest and climbing an emergency rope ladder all the way down to the surface of the water where he jumped from about ten feet up. Once he was on board the coast guard boat, he gave another goodbye to his father over the radio, and the cruise ship's engines rumbled back to life to immediately start chugging it through the sludge toward Hawaii. He thanked them for bringing him to the docks then stumbled around the city for a while looking for his meeting location with Roach.

After an hour of being officially lost, his phone started to ring.

"Hello?"

"Where are you, kid?"

He looked around. "Uhhh…"

"Are you in California?"

"Yeah. I'm somewhere in LA. I can't see the Hollywood sign…. Does that help?"

"Not really. Are you on dry land, at least?"

"It's not flooded here, if that's what you mean." Partha continued to observe his surroundings and started to describe them as he saw them.

Roach interrupted him halfway through his rambling: "Okay, I know where you are. Just stay there, and I'll come get you."

"Are you sure? I can—."

After a quiet curse in Arabic, Roach interrupted him again: "Yes. Stay exactly where you are. I'll be there in ten."

Partha opened his mouth to protest, but by then Roach had already hung up, and subsequent attempts to call him were sent directly to voicemail. He pouted and walked to a nearby bus-stop to sit on its bench and make notes on his phone for homebrew magic items inspired by whatever garbage came into his view.

About ten minutes later, he was pulled from his thoughts by Roach's deep voice: "Hey, kid."

Partha looked up at him and blushed. He had forgotten how handsome and intimidating he was. The mere sight of such an encroaching figure turned Partha into a blubbering mess. He stood and fumbled with his phone for a moment before shoving it in his pocket and offering a mock salute to Roach. "Aye, sir, I'm right behind you."

Roach nodded once and shoved his hands into his jacket pockets. "It's this way," he droned before turning and walking them back toward his apartment in Compton.

It was rare for Partha to be somewhere entirely new to him, especially somewhere seaside, so now that he wasn't worried about trying to find a specific location, his gaze was wandering all around and taking it all in. About a minute into their walk, the click of Roach's lighter as he lit a cigarette returned Partha's attention to him, and he jogged up to his side to ask, "Can you tell me about all this stuff?"

"All what stuff?"

He gestured vaguely. "The city!"

He followed the gesture and stopped walking. After a drag of his cigarette, he had finished scanning the area, and his hazel-greys landed squarely on Partha.

It was like he had been shot through the heart with a spear of ice when Roach's eyes hardened on him. "It's... no big deal if not." He blushed and averted his gaze.

"What's there to say, Party? It's a shit hole." He smoked and continued walking wordlessly.

Partha had met Roach in person twice before, but he had never seen his apartment. He was therefore put into a petrified state when Roach opened the front door and gestured him inside.

It was dimly lit with a plethora of candles that were fighting with the stench of cigarettes and weed to make the apartment smell decent. It was an uncluttered sparsely furnished space but also the very antithesis of clean. Dust danced lightly in the haze. Smoke faintly obscured the entire room to the point that Partha could only see the outlines of guitars hanging on the back wall. There was a faint flickering glow from the flatscreen television, which Partha would later see was playing static. It sat on a half rotted thin leather trunk only about a foot off the ground and lit the sitting area, which was furnished with a soggy scratchy couch and a "coffee table" that consisted of a piece of particle board nailed haphazardly to a stack of three broken industrial pallets.

Above the television, a chill struck Partha's spine to see some thirty knives stabbed into the drywall. Most of them were butterfly knives, but there were bowie and switchblades here and there. Hell, he even saw a butter knife amongst them. At the sight, he grinned nervously at Roach who replied with a flat, "What?"

"N-nothing," he sputtered and allowed Roach to lead him into the apartment and give him a lazy tour. Once inside, it became increasingly evident how many bugs there were.

They. were. *everywhere.*

Roaches, earwigs, woodlouses, ladybugs, moths, spiders, ants—.

"Ah! It touched me!"

Roach withheld a chuckle as he watched Partha squeal and flinch away from a moth only to have another fly onto his shin.

He shrieked and batted at his pant leg to get the moth to fly away, eventually finding himself huddled up as close to Roach as possible.

"It's just bugs, dude. Relax. They can't hurt you. I take care of the venomous ones." He pet Partha's soft head condescendingly. "Anyway, there's the kitchen." He gestured vaguely to a galley which was visible from where they were (what could loveably be called a breakfast nook), over a half-wall that obscured the counters and sink behind it. Partha could see the cabinets in the back of the kitchen and, though it was lit dimly with the dancing lights of candles, he noticed several vermin crawling around the doors and even onto the fridge, which was stained like several other furnishings and walls with splatters of— well... best not to think about it, actually.

Roach brought him down a hall. The first room he was shown was a messy bedroom and perhaps the most cluttered space in the house. It had a lot of laundry strewn about its floor, spilled playing cards and board games shoved haphazardly under a built-in desk on its right wall, books in a discordant mess about the area with a couple on the unmade bed, and an electric lamp on the document-laden bedside table. It was giving its light to Roach's brother, who was laying on the bed and regarded Partha with a quiet, "Hey, kid," before returning his attention to whatever book he was reading. In his lap, he was petting one of the twins' five dogs, the other four of which were also in the room and approached Roach when he entered.

He crouched down and pet each of them lovingly, giving them little kisses on their heads and letting them lick his face as he spoke Arabic in a baby-voice to them. When he stood back up he introduced them each to Partha: "That's Daisy, Diana, Aphid, Hugo, and the one on River's lap is Angel. You saw that little paddling pool on the porch, too? That's for Malfeasance, my mallard. She must have flown off for a bit, though."

Partha had what could generally be described as 'the creepy crawlies,' but he was made considerably less disturbed by the friendly pups and squatted to pet and greet them all. He was treated to a couple puppy kisses before Roach led him to the next room which he explained was, "The dog's room." It was by far the cleanest in the apartment with only a scattering of dog toys on its floor and considerably less grime than the other chambers.

Next, he was shown the bathroom but told not to use it because the twins had no running water. "We'll get you an empty vodka bottle or something." Partha forced a smile and tried to get used to the idea of staying here. He didn't have much else of a choice (unless he wanted to waste money on a shitty hotel). He didn't want to be rude to the twins by refusing their generous invitation to stay there, and he had already been told that River's bed would be his, after all. It would be rude to complain after the sacrifice.... Not to mention: Roach was absolutely terrifying.

The last room he was shown was Roach's, at the end of the hall. Now, the rest of the apartment was disgusting, that much was true, but *this* room was the very definition of filth. There were unidentifiable stains on the terracotta tile, the rug, the walls, the fucking *ceiling* somehow. His bed was an undressed mattress on some milk-crates with a single sheet and pillow. Cigarette butts littered the floor. Instruments were strewn about, leaning against and hanging from the walls, as well as piled in one of the corners. The laundry hamper was tipped over and spilling its mostly-black contents across the rug. There was a rotten wooden desk covered in graffiti and vinyl stickers, the surface of which was littered with crinkled and stained looseleaf papers. The candles in this room weren't lit, so Roach had flicked on the overhead light and gone inside, giving the entire hazy atmosphere an uncomfortable yellow tint and an irritating repetitive squeak from the ceiling fan.

"Look, dude. Isn't it cool?" said Roach as he gestured to some sort of shadow-box on the wall. Partha came inside to look at the display and winced when he saw it was full of pinned insects and spiders. "You find any bugs that look like this one, this one, these three, or these two, you tell me, and I'll take care of them, alright? Don't fuck with them. Especially not these ones."

Partha gulped. "O-okay, sir."

"Alright, so, you've seen the apartment. You got any questions? Plans? You can't bring anyone else here, of course."

'God why would I ever want to?' "Erm. No plans. But. Um... Is it always like this?"

"Yeah, dude. I'll let you know the rules and stuff later. Nothing overbearing, don't worry. For now, I'm going to call Perlie. She'll pick up some dinner for us. What you thinking? You better not be a pineapple on pizza guy."

A strained grin. "Um. Yeah. Heh. Pizza is fine. Whatever you like. But, uh, oh!" He gestured to some of the instruments as Roach turned the light off and led him back toward the living area, "You can't play music around Thyne."

"Huh? Why not?"

"He freaks out. I mean, not always, but—. Just don't play stuff around him. It'll upset him, and I don't really know why."

He almost frowned but refrained from emoting. "Alright, well, I've got my PC hooked up to the TV, so if you want to play a game while we wait for Perlie, I'd be happy to show you. No streaming from here, though. Sound chill?"

He saluted. "No streaming. Sir."

An amused huff. "You're a dork, dude." With that said, he called Perlie, asking her to bring them a couple pizzas and sodas, then sat beside Partha on the couch and lit up a bowl. "Help yourself to the weed and alcohol around."

"Are any of these alcohol bottles filled with piss?" He cringed at the thought.

Roach shrugged. "Probably, but you'd be able to tell just by looking or the good ol' sniff test."

"Right...." He sighed and held out his hand to ask for the bowl, which Roach happily passed to him.

Perlie arrived a few minutes into Partha playing an RPG on Roach's TV. Roach helped her carry the pizzas to the coffee table and invited her to sit with them and smoke. She took him up on the offer and didn't seem bothered at all by the mess. In fact, when she sat beside Partha, she casually flicked a cockroach off of the armrest then leaned on it to look at him and smirk.

She was a Korean woman with straight black hair all the way to her lower back. Her physique was fit, perhaps moreso than Thyne, and her chest was flat. Her face juxtaposed to her body but not in an unflattering way: where the rest of her was muscly and made of jagged edges, her face was soft and lips pillowy. Her eye makeup put an emphasis on her naturally thick eyelashes, which she batted flirtatiously at Roach any chance she got. Her fashion sense seemed expensive and flattered her body type beautifully. Currently, she was wearing a form-fitting double split maxi dress made of faux black velvet that was somehow clean all the way to its ends despite how much garbage she must have had to wade through on the way to the apartment. She was free of tattoos or piercings, and the skin of her face was smooth and seemed to have never even heard of acne. There was a blush on her cheeks which may have been mistaken for rouge if not for its coming and going based on her proximity to Roach. Given the overwhelming smells in the apartment, Partha had trouble determining her scent, but he figured the sweet vanilla smells were coming from whatever lotion or perfume she was using to stave off her cigarette stench. Her nails were manicured and painted with rainbows, and her air was somehow both proud and shy.

One thing that caught Partha's notice as particularly interesting were the scars on her arms. They seemed... purposeful, but he struggled to imagine they were brought about by suicidal or depressed inclinations. They were daresay artistically designed. He only had a mere glance before he averted his eyes, but there was undoubtedly a symmetry to them, each of her upper forearms had an intricate hexagon of slashes with extended lines. It seemed her right arm had a pentagram, and her left had what looked to be a key. Beyond that he couldn't see in the cursory look he got, but he noticed there were more scars on her thighs and chest.

"Cute kid," she spoke of Partha as if he wasn't there, "Where'd you get him?"

Roach ruffled his hair and ignored his offended expression. He laughed once through his lips and answered truthfully about where they had first met: "Comic Con."

Chapter 6
The Knight and the Riddle

To allow time for the mechanics to look over the troublesome engine, Thyne and Francis stayed in the Toronto airport hotel. There were two beds, but when it came time to sleep, they wordlessly cuddled up together in the same one. Neither of them, however, got even a wink.

Thyne was chronically exhausted. It was rare for him to get a full night's sleep, and it may have been an entire week since he had slept more than four hours at once. The voices in his head were incessant and often said things too interesting or important to ignore without the aid of sleeping pills or deathly exhaustion.

Francis, on the other hand, was not an insomniac. He had a friendly relationship with sleep. It was easy to capture and easy to release. But that night, with Thyne curled up against his chest listening to his heartbeat, he was perturbed. A dark sort of madness took him. This was… romantic. And Thyne… Thyne was just a friend. Wires were crossing. Things were happening that simply would not happen were this real life. The butterflies in his gut and lightness of his heart were blackened and turned to stone. He felt himself sinking into the abyss. The unlit room around him became the fathomless deep of an astral void. Were Thyne to look up at his face, he would have seen his teal eyes unfocused and staring into a nameless nothingness akin to Death.

At seven in the morning, Thyne left to answer the door. Francis didn't notice his absence the way he didn't notice any part of his present reality. The morning light through the shutters was similarly unperceived until Thyne opened the window.

Francis' gaze slowly trailed to the source of light. '*My angel Thyne*,' he thought as he saw his friend sitting at the desk and haloed by the morning glow.

He lit himself a cigarette, and the sight of him looking through a pile of paperwork about his plane's engine brought Francis slowly back up from the depths of his own madness. After a swig of his flask, at a quarter 'til eight, he stood and started to dress himself.

Thyne looked up briefly, the big round reading glasses on the tip of his button nose catching the glare of his cigarette embers like little fireflies. "Good morning. You alright? Already drinking I see." He sounded disappointed.

"And you're already smoking!" said the offended party, "Cast your stones, then! We all have vices." A sigh and swig. "Good morning or afternoon or whatever wretched hour it is."

He offered a sleepy smile. "Someone woke up on the wrong side of the bed, hm? Why don't you pop down and get us some breakfast? It's free with the room."

"For what offerings do you yearn?"

"Oh, you know what I like, Franny. Whatever looks good." His smile strengthened when he wiggled his nose playfully at his cranky friend. "Love you, idiot."

"Don't say that! You do not love me."

Thyne started. He could practically feel his own heart breaking, but before he could fathom the strange outburst, Francis had quit the room, slamming the door behind him.

"Hello?"

"Is this Roach? I'm Thyne. Got your number from Party."

"Yeah. What's up, dude?"

"We might be a tad late for the meeting."

"Why?"

"My plane's engine is acting up."

"You have a private jet?"

"Yeah, and? Anyway, the engine is acting up, and the mechanic says——."

"What I said to Partha stands."

"What did you say to Partha?"

"I told him if you're not there by noon day-of, I'm out."

Thyne took the phone briefly away from his face and squeezed it hard enough to almost crack the screen. When he brought it back up to his ear, his tone was one of poorly masked rage: "So you'd have me crash my plane into the middle of the desert?"

"I'd have you fly commercial," he laughed one ha of disdain, "Rich prick."

"Now listen here, you rotting carcass of a man! I am not just—."

Click.

He shouted and threw the phone across the room. "BLOODY TWIT!"

Francis watched his friend barrel out of their suite. To the outrage, he merely rolled his eyes and resumed doodling an eighteenth century galleon on the hotel notepad.

The mechanics on call at the airport for Thyne all started when he slammed open their office door and stomped up to the only one he had ever seen in person. He pointed up into his face and growled, "What's wrong with it?"

The man was unaffected by the threatening posture and gently pushed Thyne's hand out of his face. He looked him up and down and smirked. "I've given you the time estimate to fix it, sir. You could buy a new engine from the manufacturer in Detroit, but that will still take at least a week to get here, let alone install. And it would be inadvisable to buy a new engine without replacing the three older ones."

He threw his paperwork into the man's chest. "Will it make it to New Mexico?" the mechanic arched his brow. "I asked you a question, you Canadian slag! Answer me!"

"Your engines are very old."

"I didn't ask how bloody old my engines are! I asked if I can make it to New Mexico without the second one!"

His glance flickered briefly to the plane behind Thyne. "Should do."

"Good. Look over all the engines to make sure they don't explode or fail further. Got it?"

"It'll cost—."

"Oh, hush, you know I'll pay you more than enough." He opened his wallet and took out his card. "Give me the reader." The mechanic happily handed him a small machine. After a long while of Thyne pressing on its screen and typing things, he handed it back with a huff. "That should be enough."

The mechanic smiled at the amount. Thyne was paying each of the workers €100,000 for the job to be completed by the next day. "We'll get it done sir."

"Good. I'll see you tomorrow."

"Have a good day."

"Yeah yeah."

The next morning, Thyne was awoken from a two-hour doze by a call from the mechanics telling him that his plane's working engines would be able to get him to New Mexico, "but you can't cross the ocean again without getting it properly fixed, alright, bud? It can't make it that far. Especially with nowhere to land if things go sideways."

"Cheers, mate. I'll fly out around noon."

"Safe travels. Hope whatever has you in such a rush is worth the risk."

"I'll be okay. I'll send you a selfie when we're back on land."

"I would actually appreciate it, if you could. I don't want it on my conscience that you flew into a mountain or something."

"I'm a good pilot…. Sorry for shouting at you yesterday."

"No problem, bud."

After the quick exchange, Thyne drowsily dragged his feet to a convenience store and withdrew as much cash from its ATM as was allowed. He also bought himself an armful of energy drinks, a case of cigarettes, and a variety of candies including gummy cola, red licorice, chocolate eggs, and pop rocks.

Once they were airborne again, Francis was his usual helpful self in the First Officer's seat. He was handling the radio for Thyne and lightly monitoring the instruments, which was a huge weight off Thyne's shoulders when the engine started acting up again. He followed the instructions from the mechanics for how to handle the alert and flew safely from Toronto to the private strip outside of Albuquerque. Flying through American airspace (especially with a broken engine) was a little terrifying, so he was glad to be back on solid land after the buttery smooth landing in the desert. He parked it in the hangar at the end of the runway and let out a long relieved breath. After lighting himself a cigarette, and before they left the cockpit, he remembered to send a picture of himself and Francis to the Canadian mechanic.

In response to the picture, he replied: ⌈ Hey now! Glad you're both safe. Now that I'm technically not in your employ anymore, I wanted to ask you out for some coffee next time you're in Toronto. ⌋

Thyne blushed and hid the screen from Francis to reply: ⟦ If you had caught me at any other time, mate, I'd be interested. Unfortunately, I have a boyfriend. ⟧

⌈ A shame. Well, glad you're safe regardless. You two be careful down there. The states are crazy. ⌋

⟦ We will be. ⟧

The first order of business now that they were on the ground was getting a mechanic to start immediately on the engine. Because they were in the states, however, it would be unwise to make their presence known in legal channels. Besides the crime they were planning, they would also be flying back to Europe with American citizens in their plane. Such a thing had been illegal for several years: Americans were not to leave the country for leisure. Most business trips were also forbidden. The rules, as ever, applied less frequently and with less enforcement for the ultra wealthy, and while it was true that Thyne was technically among that crowd, he was not a capitalist. He had no businesses nor regular employees. He peddled no goods nor services. The only property he owned was his home and personal belongings. His money did not accumulate or multiply in any manner outside of interest. It sat in a bank account being slowly drained since

He would therefore not be able to manipulate the law the way
'oat and business-minded than him.

_ ᵤnto the cabin of the plane once he was certain the engines were
_ᵤ and dropped himself into one of the black leather couches with Francis
following him like a loyal dog. He sat beside his friend and annoyingly propped
his dirty boots up on the coffee table, but Thyne only rolled his eyes and took
out his phone.

"Are you going to summon a car?" asked Francis.

"Good idea, mate. Why don't you go pinch us one?"

"Thyne...."

"What?"

After a while of silence he looked at Francis' knowing expression and smiled.
"Right. Well, I suppose I'll get us a taxi or something after I find a mechanic."

Francis chuckled and swigged from his flask. Yes, he was drunk, but such a thing
was easy enough to remove by ageing himself a few hours. The true lapse in
memory from Thyne was briefly forgetting that his tipsy friend didn't know how
to drive in the first place. It was amusing to consider because he was once a
legendary pirate captain who sailed into hurricanes as if they were merely drizzles
of rain. Not only that: since discovering his supernatural abilities, he had travelled
to a time with ships powerful enough for interplanetary travel and had therefore
piloted several sorts of spaceships with prideful confidence.

Without fully realising it, Thyne had an arm around Francis, who was curled up
and cuddling him while they both used their phones. With only one free hand,
Thyne utilised his split tongue to hold his cigarette still when he puffed on it, and
Francis brushed any subsequent fallen embers from his abdomen and lap thoughtlessly. The former pirate was texting with Partha about the journey ahead of them,
and Thyne was searching the dark web for a less-than-legal mechanic who
wouldn't ask questions.

After about an hour, he struck paydirt: a member of the Russian mafia was
looking to buy historical planes. Thyne had him on a call within fifteen minutes:

"Someone with a fondness for older things, are we?"

"Da. You have plane for me?"

"I might. But I have a price."

He laughed. "Funny Englishman. Grisha is not looking for handouts."

"Good. My price isn't money, however."

"Oh?"

"You must have a good team of mechanics to be so nonchalant in your initial
post here: 'Any plane at least fifty years vintage.'"

"I have best mechanic in America!" He coughed on his own haughty laughter.

"Lovely. Where?"

"He lives with me in Yuma, but we are in Albuquerque for week."

"The stars align, then. I'm just outside of Albuquerque. Deliver your mechanic to me to fix my engine, and I'll get you damn near any kind of plane you want."

"For free?"

"No, you dolt. For your mechanic to fix my engine. I'll pay him for you, too." He rolled his eyes and looked for Francis to share his disgust, but he instead blushed when he noticed they were snuggling. He pet Francis' shoulder who leaned backwards to give an upside-down grin to Thyne.

"This sounds too good to be true," said Grisha, "send address."

"Alright." He took a moment to text Grisha's burner with his current address. "And sent. Happy to do business with you. Be drafting a list of planes in case I can't get your first choice."

"Will come armed. No funny business."

"Come in a tank if you want. I don't care. Just get here fast."

After dropping his dog off at the groomers, Jean-Jacques followed Grisha's big black sedan out of Albuquerque and into the desert. When the roads turned to dirt, he was glad to have a helmet that covered his entire head and filtered the air like a gas mask. His motorcycle was an odd sight pulling in behind the luxury sedan, but Thyne was able to determine who Grisha was when he stepped out of the back seat, a hulking mass of Russian pride. He beamed at Thyne. "You must be doorman, hm? Where is Mr. Chamberlain?" He looked around the hangar.

With his nose wrinkled and brow furrowed, a red-faced Brit pointed up into Grisha's fat face. "You better watch your tone, twat."

"Oh!" He chortled and held out his hand to shake with Thyne's. Grisha's grip was strong, and he was shocked to not be met with a limp-wristed unenthusiastic handshake in return. This little pink-haired twink was already impressing and befuddling him. He looked at the nearby plane. "You have nice looking plane. I have two *DC-8*'s."

"Oh?"

"Is shame how you painted it, though. Looks like girl plane." Thyne glared. "You wanted list!" he announced as the memory popped back into his mind. He produced a list written on the back of an unpaid parking ticket of his desired plane models.

Thyne snatched it away and gave it a quick scan. "A *Mosquito*? Like from World War Two?"

"You said any plane!" He swapped to Russian to call him something akin to a, "Faggot bitch," for daring to go back on his promise. The other two Morozovs with him joined in a hearty chortle at the assertion and added to it with slurs of their own.

Once their laughter died down, Thyne offered Grisha an angry smile and spoke in perfect Russian: "I'll get you your damn plane. Now get off my property, and leave your mechanic with me for as long as he needs to fix mine. Capiche?"

Grisha blushed and sweated hearing Thyne speak Russian. What followed was baffling. Jean-Jacques watched with his jaw agape as his boss began daresay grovelling to the smaller man: "Apologies. I work mostly with Americans and other Russians. We are proud people. We would never.... Erm. We would never carry ourselves like you do, but that doesn't mean you're a faggot. Please. For antiques so old, I cannot afford to upset this relationship so immediately. I want more than planes from that era."

He looked at his glittery black manicure as if to further emphasise the label that was so flippantly put on him. "A shame, really. Let this be a lesson to you to show some restraint before opening your fat trap. You'll get a plane, and, perhaps, if I find it in my heart to forgive you, I'll find you a hmmm," he stroked his chin, "*SVT-40?*"

Grisha whimpered, and Jean-Jacques gasped to see him lower himself. It wasn't a full bow, but it was submissive in nature. "Yes, please!" The only people he had seen Grisha act so weak in the presence of were his brother and father. This British man was alone, and Grisha had two well-armed mafiosos behind him. In fact, it seemed more and more like a one-sided deal. What was Grisha getting out of this besides a few promises from a stranger?

Were he not drooling over Thyne's classic plane, Jean-Jacques probably would have warned his boss of the potential deception at play. Thyne had an odd air about him. They kept talking, and the mechanic perked up hearing his name when Thyne asked for it and Grisha answered, "His name is Jean-Jacques Paul Martial, but we call him all sorts of things like JJP, Martial, *zhopa*," he chortled.

Before he knew it, Jean-Jacques was being taken aside by Grisha, and Thyne was leading the others into the jet.

"You fix his plane, no? How long?" asked the Russian of his mechanic.

"I don't know what's wrong with it, sir."

"Keep in touch with me. Tell me if he hurts you. Will kill him. He says he will pay you. Tell me also if he does not."

He looked up at Grisha and arched his brow. "Why are you bowing and begging him if you don't trust?"

"I trust enough. He is no nark." He gestured vaguely. "He gave real name. I sent to Natalya. She says he is billionaire." They both looked at Thyne as he escorted the other Russians into his plane for some drinks. "He is little bit famous, too."

"And that makes him trusty?"

"No, but if he *is* trustworthy, Grisha needs be on his good side, no? To get antiques."

"And if he's not?"

He shrugged. "Is easy enough to kill little faggot men who forgot to bring body-guard, JJP." He laughed and lit a cigar. "Come inside. He mentioned aged whiskey."

They drank together for about an hour before Grisha felt a sudden sting on the back of his neck and brought the entire conversation to a screeching halt. He flailed his arms around and spilled some of his whiskey on the fluffy pink rug, but his panic was stopped by Thyne's calming voice: "It was only a wasp, mate. Are you allergic?"

"Da. I leave now."

"Au revoir."

After Grisha's car was out of sight, Thyne turned toward Jean-Jacques and smiled. "You're French?"

"Oui, Monsieur."

He nodded and spoke in flawless French: "I suppose he'll want half of whatever I pay you. Is that right?"

"He'll want more than that...."

"Then I suppose you'll have to keep most of this hidden, hm?" He led Jean-Jacques toward the rear of the plane and opened a drawer in what looked to be some sort of sleeping quarters. The Frenchman couldn't see what was inside, but when Thyne turned back around he had a wad of cash in each hand. "How does 450 sound?"

"450 Euros, sir?"

He laughed. "No, 450 thousand."

He was stunned to silence and pale-faced.

"Is that enough for your labour? I will tell Grisha I paid you only fifty thousand."

"If he finds out...," he trailed off and swallowed a lump of dread in his throat.

"Mull it over. Anyway, you can start working right away. First thing you'll need to do is make a list of parts and tools you'll need. You can text it to me. Now give me your keys. I'll be taking your motorbike."

"B-but sir, how will I get food?"

"There's food in the plane. You can sleep in it, too. Right here if you like." He gestured to the bed, which admittedly looked quite comfortable.

Jean-Jacques hesitated, but as he watched Thyne put several stacks of cash on the bedside table, he sighed and passed him his keys.

"Thank you. I'll take good care of it. Now, is there anything you need that isn't accounted for? Medicine? Recreational things for whatever hobbies you have? I don't expect you to work 24/7." Jean-Jacques stuttered incoherently. "Just add things to the list as you think of them. I'm in a hurry." He cupped his hands around his mouth as he left the room, shouting into the fore of the plane: "Franky! Let's go!"

The drunk was startled from a staring contest with the wall and stumbled out of the cockpit into his friend's strong arms.

"Oh, Franny, you reek of rum."

French being a flowy language already, when Francis replied in his native tongue, it was utterly incomprehensible.

"Sober up, now. I won't have you falling off the bike."

While Francis used his powers to reduce his blood-alcohol level, Thyne had a visible thought and returned to Jean-Jacques. "Where is your helmet?"

He bit his lip. "I usually use it while I work to listen to music."

Thyne shooed the idea as if it were a pesky fly buzzing around the room. "Nonsense. The sound system in here is phenomenal. You'll have to leave the stairs down to be able to get in and out, so blast it as loud as you like. And if that doesn't work, I have wireless earphones in the settees up front. They fold open like piano benches."

"And safety glasses?"

"Add it to your list, Jean-Jacques." He was growing audibly annoyed by the constant chatter. "Now, I really would like to keep waffling on, but I reiterate: my mate and I are in a hurry." The comment made him consider asking Francis to bring them to Phoenix using his power to avoid being late, but he shook his head to remove the thought. Francis could get them there, but Thyne wanted to make the drive himself. He hadn't driven a motorcycle in decades, and he'd never been to America. This was a perfect opportunity to see the wild western landscape.

"And what of my dog, monsieur?"

"Your dog?"

"Oui. I left her in Albuquerque with the groomers."

"We'll get her for you," he said as he was leaving, "Just text me the information."

It was nearing 10:30, and they still hadn't seen the Waffle House, so Thyne pulled off into an alley. He took out his phone and read the message from Partha again:

⌈ He said 10:30 a.m. Phoenix, Arizona. At the Waffle House on Knight and Riddle streets. And don't be late, or he's not going to help. ⌋

He rubbed the bridge of his nose. "I don't understand, Francis, we've been all around this bloody city, and we still haven't seen either of these streets." He took out a crinkled paper map from his back pocket and gave it another scan. "They're not on the map, either!" He tore it in half and huffed.

"I'll go find the restaurant."

A sigh. "Cheers. You're a blessing."

Francis stopped time and started wandering the streets at a leisurely pace in search of a Waffle House. From Thyne's perspective, he teleported a few inches to his left immediately, but he had truly walked the entire city at least three times. "I believe it is three blocks in that direction at the crossing of Ninth and Brittle."

Thyne's face turned bright red, and he may well have had steam shoot out of his ears with how comically angry the news made him. "I'll kill that fucking idiot!"

Francis smiled softly. "We'll scold him his ineptitude later. Come now. Shan't be late."

As much as Thyne enjoyed motorcycles, he much preferred cars, and this preference was made especially evident when he parked at the Waffle House and had no door to slam. He almost kicked the motorcycle on its side, but he managed to restrain himself and instead lit a cigarette. He was averting his gaze of Francis and only retroactively heard him say, "I'll go secure us a reservation." By the time he had processed the outrageous claim, Francis was already inside making one of the workers roar with laughter. Thyne couldn't help but smile at the sight as he took another drag and felt himself simmering down.

His gaze trailed the parking lot, and as he smoked he noticed a car pulling into a space near the back of the property. Fortunately it was not blocked by other cars, so Thyne could properly ogle it. It was a *Locust*, and from the looks of it, a classic model: a *Patanga* from the 2020's with four seats. The paint was a colour-shifting pigment that was simultaneously blue, black, and deep violet. The windows were tinted too dark to see the man inside, but he felt whoever it was looking his way and averted his eyes. *Locust* was a luxury car company, but this one looked modified. With one last puff on his cigarette, he checked the time, noticed it was 10:30 on the dot, and flicked the half-finished fag across the lot to walk hastily inside.

When he opened the doors, it felt like he was walking back in time. The jukebox started playing Connie Francis' *I Will Wait For You* as soon as he set foot in the establishment. The décor and furnishing must not have been changed since the 1950s, matching the old song. There was a sort of post-war bittersweet levity in the warm air that he had not experienced in over a century. It wrenched his gut in an inexplicable way as he ambled to the booth Francis had found on the side of the building. His hands were in his pockets without him fully realising until his phone buzzed. A message from Partha:

⌈ Did you make it? ⌋

A slight groan. ⟦ **No thanks to you.** ⟧ He was much calmer than he would have expected of himself after the reminder that Partha had nearly ruined everything. He credited the calmness to the music, the sweet smells coming from behind the counter, and the overall ambience that had transported him back to a simpler time. He leaned on his elbow and opened his messages with Roach to update him: ⟦ **We're here. I have pink hair. You can't miss me.** ⟧

⌈ **Got it. Can't miss me, either. I'm 6'6". Be inside in a minute. Finishing this cigarette.** ⌋

Thyne's eyes widened and cheeks flushed at the message. *'He's so tall.'* He turned toward the parking lot to look for him and spotted someone who must have been him smoking near the *Locust*. When he turned back toward Francis, he started fanning himself with one of the laminated menus and forced a nervous grin.

"Are you perturbed?"

"I'm alright."

"You look to be sweating. Shall I ask them to turn up the air conditioning unit?"

"Franky, stop."

He looked around. "This establishment seems as displaced from time as I am."

Thyne nodded, but before he could comment on the odd way the place was making him feel, the entire world was thrust back into the horrid humid present as Roach dropped himself into the booth beside Francis and across from Thyne. The music stopped just as he sat down, and all that could be heard in its wake was the clattering of cutlery in the open kitchen and the murmur of other conversations.

"You must be Thyne," he said to the Brit before turning to Francis, "And you are?" His voice was deep and smooth with a charming American accent that had Thyne short of breath. If he wasn't so enamoured he may have noticed that Roach was playing up his ignorance. He had definitely seen Francis on Partha's streams, evident by the cadence of his words.

"Androme Francis Horatius Alexandre Anaxagoras de Tremblay," replied Francis with his hand held awkwardly to his side for shaking with Roach's. "But you can call me Francis."

"Anaxagoras, huh? Your parents astronomers?"

He smirked and shook his head. "No, but I am."

Roach took his hand, his grip so strong it nearly broke the pirate's frail fingers. "An aptronym, then. I sort of have one, too. Call me Roach."

After the pleasantries, Thyne was finally calm enough to lower his menu and give this man a proper look. The first thing that was immediately evident about him besides his height and impressive muscular build was his sense of style. He had an aesthetic he tried to achieve; one that very much clashed with the desert heat. Thyne couldn't see his legs because of the table hiding them, but from his glance at him in the parking lot he recalled that Roach was wearing black pants that had more holes than a colander, the ends of which were tucked into his black combat boots. Looking at him now, he could see the finer details of his outfit:

His nails were well manicured, filed to points, and painted matte black. His long and slender fingers were covered in various rings. All of them were thick and most had some sort of design that seemed to say something about his personality. He had three on his left ring finger: two plain wedding bands, and a third more intricate one. Where the others were mostly silver and bronze, this one was accented with gold. The design was of an ankh. There were two rings on his right hand that were a gas mask on the ring finger and its canister on the first, connected over the middle finger by a little chain tube from the mask. He had a few jewelled ones, all dark and in cool hues. A rat. A crow skull. One that resembled razor blades....

The veins in his hands were evident even in this resting position which was unsurprising given his obvious strength, and on the back of his right hand was a small tattoo of a honeybee. What Thyne could see of his wrists were absent of jewellery, but they were mostly covered by the tattered sleeves of his falling-apart black denim jacket. It had patches sewn into it, some of which were scrap fabric of various patterns and colours, but a few of them were more political. He had one on his front left pocket that plainly had an anarchy symbol on it and one down his right sleeve of a guillotine. The sight had Thyne's heart fluttering and blush returning.

Under his jacket was a black t-shirt purposefully stained with bleach in the shape of a ribcage. And under his shirt, Thyne spotted the slightest hint of a ball-chain around his neck. 'Dog tags no doubt. He must have served in the war.'

Roach was speaking with Francis, so his posture had shifted. He rested his head on his hands and therefore leaned slightly over the table. It made Thyne have no way to really observe his face, but he noticed the hair-claw holding up a mass of long black hair. From the size of the claw, he would wager the hair must have at least fallen to Roach's lower back if not his arse. He noted how clean and soft it seemed while still somehow matching with the rest of his dishevelled appearance. His scent, as well, was pleasant (at least in Thyne's opinion), being overwhelmingly the stench of cigarettes but with undertones of gasoline, sandalwood, and basil.

Thyne, having not listened to a word of their conversation, was briefly nervous he would be invited into it when Roach turned to face him. However, when they made eye contact, whatever Roach was saying was immediately silenced.

He was a time capsule. His eyes: a portal to the past. Thyne could see it all like he was living through it again. The smell of basil drowned out every other scent like an aromatic tsunami. *Heart and Soul* seemed to be playing, though the jukebox was silent. He could hear the ethereal but distinct laughter of his long-dead lover and saw his face in place of Roach's. Visions of the war soon overwhelmed the more pleasant memories, but even despite all the trauma running down his spine and into what remained of his hands, his dread was indicated only by a slight tremble in his fingers as he brought his left hand up to his chest and grabbed at a pair of rings suspended from a chain around his neck.

Roach was equally shaken by the gaze but for reasons less obvious to him. In all his conscious moments, he had never forgotten anything that had ever happened to him, with the only exceptions being times he was asleep, blacked-out drunk, or too high to function. And yet, here was Thyne, whom he was sure he had never met, feeling as familiar as his brother. He saw straight through to his soul. It was unnerving, as were the butterflies that stirred up his stomach at the sight. Despite how pleasant and comfortable he was making him feel with a mere gaze into his golden honey eyes, he told himself that Thyne was not to be trusted. He wanted to check the clock, wondering if it was time for his next prayer, but Thyne's gaze was too mesmerising to wrench himself free of it.

They looked into each other's eyes for what felt like a century: both of them left utterly speechless.

Francis, sensing something strange was happening, flagged down a waitress who came over and interrupted the odd staring contest:

"What can I get for you all?"

Roach was the first to break eye-contact with Thyne, and the Englishman was finally able to better observe his facial features. His pierced nose was Roman and skin a pale olive colour, slightly sunkissed. His features were sharp and masculine, his face clean-shaven but with a five o'clock shadow forming. When he had seen his eyes he actually hadn't cognised what colour they were, instead seeing only into the past. Retroactively, however, he realised they must have been deep grey or hazel-grey based on the vignette on the visions looking into them had brought about. His ears were adorned with somehow more piercings than Thyne's, and as he spoke, Thyne caught the faintest glimpse of a piercing on his tongue.

Roach turned back toward him, but the Brit was quick to turn away so as to no longer stare slack-jawed at the handsome stranger he seemed to already know. He beamed a nervous grin up at the waitress. "Do you have tea?"

She smiled wide. "Oh my goodness! Are you British?"

His blush returned, sweat beading down the back of his neck. "Yeah."

"Oh, I love your accent! It's so cute! Are you on vacation?" He nodded. "And you came all the way out to Phoenix?" She chuckled. "Are you enjoying it at least?"

Finally coming down from the strange high that had struck him upon seeing Roach, he let out a bit of a giggle and gestured to the other two. "I only came here because these two wankers wanted to."

She turned to Francis and Roach. "Oh, are you two from Eurasia, too?" Francis nodded and Roach shook his head, to which she implored them to divulge where they were from.

"I hail from France," answered Francis, though the claim in conjunction with his antiquated British accent confused the Arizonan.

"Compton," said Roach without giving her the decency of eye-contact. He was staring at Thyne the way Thyne had stared at him, but the Englishman was trying not to notice.

She laughed. "Wanted to come somewhere dry, huh?"

He nodded dismissively and finally pulled his gaze away from Thyne and up to her. "This one was asking about tea."

"Right. Sorry for the tangent. What type of tea did you want, cutie?"

Thyne smiled at her light flirting and wore his blush with more pride than before. "I don't suppose you have any oolong?"

She arched her brow. "Is that a brand?"

He sighed. "Just a black tea with sugar and cream. And as far as my meal," he held up his menu to feign looking at it, but he was truly using it as an excuse to flick his gaze up at Roach between glances at random words. "Just some bangers. I'm not very hungry."

"Bangers?"

"Oh, right." He looked at her. "Sausage links?"

She nodded and wrote it down. "Okay, but since you're from out of town, you have *got* to try the waffles. They're really good. They're basically the only halfway decent thing we serve."

"Okay, then some waffles for all of us. Franky, what did you get?"

He hadn't ordered yet, so the waitress looked at him to listen to his answer. "The waffle alone shall sate me."

She nodded and left them, coming back only a moment later with their drinks. Thyne frowned at the cheap bag of tea but steeped it and gave Roach a few quick glances before clearing his throat. In spite of all his nerves, he found Roach's eyes and managed to keep himself from looking away or blushing again as he asked, "So… how do you know Partha?"

"Did a job with Richard a while back. Party was just a kid."

"What was the job?"

Roach did not dignify him with a response.

"Okay…. Well as far as the gang is concerned, what do you bring to the table?"

"What's this? A job interview? Piss off, dude. I could ask you that very same thing," his tone was irritated, but his mien was blank.

An awkward quiet followed, after which Thyne asked, "Why did you bring us to a diner?"

"Well, I wasn't expecting to eat here. Was just to meet up. I was thinking we'd probably want somewhere more private to talk about our plans."

A beat.

"Why did we not meet in Compton?" asked Francis.

"Because the job's out here."

"What do you mean the job's out here?" said Thyne after a very unsatisfying sip of his tea. "Partha didn't tell you? We're going to take down Maitland. It's in England."

His facial expression was deadpan, but his words were daggers: "You'll excuse me, Thyne. I'm not going to leave America indefinitely to take down a company with two strangers. You have to prove that you're serious about this." He gestured at him with an air of disdain, "I mean look at you with your private fucking jet and no-doubt designer clothes. Playing games with Partha and thinking you can suddenly just play pretend you're poor for a few days for a thrill. Just a couple of spoiled brats looking for a crime sherpa. Worthless, yuppie, liberal piece of shit." He punctuated the disparaging rant with a sip of his seltzer and a glimmer of wickedness in his hazel-greys.

Francis was all smiles until hearing the insults and assumptions, but of course, it was Thyne who was the most taken aback by the bombardment. He squeezed so hard onto his teacup that it started to crack and drip onto his mechanical middle finger. All the good feelings that the initial look at Roach had brought about were replaced with boiling hot rage. His brow was furrowed and teeth grinding into each other, but he was silent. His mind painted a flickering fire around Roach. It played imaginings of what his screams of agonised pain might sound like, and it vignetted his vision with red as he felt his blood pumping all throughout his body, even across the whites of his eyes.

The silent tension was made more awkward when their waitress returned and placed their food in front of them wordlessly.

Once she was gone, Roach continued, "I just don't want to help some rich asshole take down a rival company to line his own pockets, so you have to prove to me your mettle. I need to know you're in this for more than just Maitland."

Thyne's voice was low in both volume and pitch as he spat, "Fuck you."

Roach sighed. He spoke sternly but with much more empathy this time: "You'll do this job with me, and we'll go from there."

"Fine," said Thyne as he slammed himself backwards into the hard booth. He grumbled things to himself in Italian and under his breath about the presumptuous nature of their new friend and how his good looks were the only reason Thyne hadn't threatened his life.

"Is he always like this?" whispered Roach to Francis.

Francis was mid-bite of his waffle, so he covered and spoke through the mouthful: "You spat a lot of venom at him, my friend. He is reacting accordingly. In fact, he is being markedly reserved. I'm surprised he hasn't set you alight."

Roach sort of chuckled and looked back at Thyne. "Listen, I think we got off on a… weird foot. To say the least." He held out his hand. "Clayton Roach. This ain't my first rodeo, as they say. I've been burned before, and you must understand that I can't just blindly trust you."

Thyne rolled his eyes, huffed, and grabbed the offered hand. Roach tried to squeeze as hard as he had with Francis, but Thyne's grip was stronger than his, even with his missing fingers. It took Roach off guard, loosening his own grip. "Clarence Crump," said Thyne firmly, as if he was daring Roach to challenge the name.

Francis dropped his fork and offered Thyne a wide set of eyes. He whispered in French, covering his face from Roach in the process: "Why are you telling him your real name?"

Thyne ignored him. "So, what's the job?"

Roach was intrigued after his earlier research of the company, but he didn't emote and moved on as if he didn't understand the implications of Thyne's apparent surname. "Small bank just outside the city. We'll hit it and quit it, lose the cops, swap cars to my *Locust* out there, and head back to Compton. Masks are a must, and I'm not going in. I'm pretty identifiable even with a mask," he gestured to himself, "so I'll be getaway."

"Are you any good at driving?" asked Thyne with an almost disgusted expression.

"Of course I am. We'll need a car for the first half of the job, though. I can't lose my baby. Rebuilt it with my brother." There was a beat as Thyne looked at the *Locust* again.

Roach continued: "If you rented a car with your real name, we should probably steal one instead. I can hotwire no problem." He took a bite of his waffle to punctuate his sentence, and it was only with that bite that Thyne noticed he had put ketchup and mustard on it. All sense of trying to figure out this job came to a horrified standstill, at least for Thyne. He looked from Roach's plate to his drink and noticed he had poured some of the cream into his seltzer. Francis was enjoying his waffle with syrup and butter like a normal person, but when he noticed Roach putting ketchup on the waffles he tried it, too. He even salted it.

Thyne watched them eat with an ever-horrified face and turning stomach. "Franky, did you trick him into putting ketchup on his waffle?"

Francis, caught with another mouthful, looked up at Thyne and shook his head.

"Oh, hey. You like it?" said Roach when he noticed he had apparently influenced Francis' decision.

Francis nodded and swallowed. "Aye, 'tis pleasing with the syrup, too."

"Good thinking." He poured the syrup over his ketchup and mustard covered waffle and took a huge bite.

Thyne ate some of his waffle in silence as the two lunatics across from him enjoyed what could hardly be called food anymore. After a chuckle from Francis at something or other, Roach looked across the table and spoke calmly: "Heya, Clare. What's wrong?"

He caught the faintest glimpse of Roach's eyes before quickly looking back at the syrup pooling up in his waffle. "Don't call me that."

"Sorry." He pointed with his fork. "So what's with the missing fingers? What happened?"

He glared. "None of your business."

"Guess that's the same answer if I ask about the tattoos on your forearms."

"You guess correctly." An angry smile.

Roach shrugged and continued eating, the sight of which gagged Thyne.

"Oh, come on," he said through his mouthful, "It can't be worse than British food."

Thyne was offended on behalf of his people, but after tasting this cheap diner waffle and noticing that it was objectively better than almost anything he had ever bought from somewhere similar in England, he let out a slight chuckle. "I'll concede the waffle is pretty good, but you've obviously never had a good black pudding or steak and kidney pie."

Francis leaned in to whisper to Roach, though it was clearly just for the gesture and not to actually keep anything secret: "His boyfriend jests with him on the subject, as well. It's cathartic."

"Boyfriend?"

"Yeah," answered Thyne, "He's an Italian chef."

"You Europeans and your *culture*. Let me guess, he makes great spaghetti?"

Thyne arched his brow, catching on to the jealousy Roach was making great efforts to hide or perhaps didn't even recognise in himself. "Obviously."

"Well, I'm about finished with this waffle," said Roach as he took a sip of Thyne's tea. "What do we say to stealing these forks and getting the Hell outta dodge?"

Thyne went pale. When Francis saw his friend's reaction to the suggestion and processed what Roach had said, he was concerned and confused. "Have you just suggested cribbing the cutlery, Roach?"

Deadpan, he turned toward the pirate and said, "Yeah. Your first test. If that's too much for you losers, then how do you expect to start a gang?" An amused and irritated huff. "No-good liberal motherfu—."

Thyne slammed his hand on the table. It rattled all of their plates and cutlery and even briefly silenced the entire diner. After the short lull, he pointed at Roach, his face as red as a cherry. Try as he might, he couldn't formulate a coherent response, blinded by all his confusing emotions, so after four seconds of wordlessness, he slammed his hand back on the table where his fork was laying, took it, and stomped out of the restaurant.

"Well, isn't he just a charmer," joked Roach as he spun his fork down his fingers and stood. He offered a gentlemanly hand out to Francis and paid their bill on their way outside, making absolutely no attempt to hide his thievery.

Chapter 7
Critical Fail

This Valentine's Day would be her thirty-ninth wedding anniversary, but it was her fifteenth anniversary without a husband. After her first Valentine's Day as a widow, she was too afraid to be alone with her thoughts, so, like the past thirteen years, she packed her pickup with goods to drive out to Phoenix. There were three boxes of knitted blankets, shawls, and purses she intended to donate to the local homeless shelter. Her duvet covers also needed to be dry-cleaned, so they were scattered about the bed of the truck in garbage bags.

With the lid closed over the bed, she packed some tupperware with baked goods she had spent all week making. Among them were gingerbread, chocolate chip, and snickerdoodle cookies, lemon and raspberry tarts, and blueberry muffins baked just that morning. She buckled the tupperwares into the passenger seat, giggled at the sight, then started on the three-hour trek into town.

Traffic was light, and as she passed the exit to the reservation she reached over to the radio to turn up the volume. Music was a salve for her aching heart, but even the advertisements were welcome on a day so lonesome and bittersweet as this.

Dezba was an elderly woman ageing like a fine wine. Her wrinkled face held soft brown eyes that seemed to sparkle like the night sky, and her bright white smile was the sweetest in the world. Her skin was dark and warm like a desert sunset. She smelled of lavender and vanilla with hints of cinnamon, and her fashion sense was surprisingly "with the times" for her age. She didn't chase trends, but she didn't dress the same as she had in her youth, usually sporting something to hint at her

Navajo roots while also being comfortable. Being an active woman, she typically also sported pants as opposed to skirts and dresses.

She sometimes wore her long grey hair in a pair of braids or neat bun, but she just as often let it flow naturally all the way to her mid-back. It was soft and slightly wavy but always managed to tangle with her earrings when she was younger. She had since given up on dangling jewellery entirely.

Her first stop in Phoenix was a craft store. She shivered on her way to the door, commenting under her breath about the dusting of snow on the ground from the previous night. The warmth inside was almost as hot as she felt the desert usually was, so her shivering was soon replaced with sweating as she shed her coat and leaned lazily on her shopping cart. Though she came to the store with a purpose, she wandered its aisles aimlessly and came to the checkout counter with a cart full of things she did not need. The two reasons she came to a craft store in the first place, however, were actually necessary: a variety of yarns to knit more goods for the shelter and a bouquet of fake flowers she arranged herself in the flower aisle. This month she chose Lionel's favourites: hydrangeas and poppies.

With her truck even more loaded up with goodies than before, she snuck a cookie, sipped her water, and made her way to the shelter. The young men working there were excited to help her unload the boxes of knits, but she refused a lot of their assistance. She was old, but she wasn't knocking on death's door like they seemed to think. She had a home gym she used regularly, and her doctors were always singing her praises. The boxes weren't that heavy, and she even managed to earn herself a few flirtatious comments from one of the employees as he watched her haul one inside and lift it up to the counter. The last of the comments and the only one she replied to was something like, "Shame to always see you alone on Valentine's Day, Miss Meadows. Would you like to go for some coffee together?"

She smiled sweetly and blushed just-so. "That's very sweet, son, but I'm far too old for you."

"Aw. Come on, Miss. Age is just a number. Besides, it doesn't have to be more than a friendly outing."

Perhaps on another day, his flirtations would have won her over. He was a hand-some young man, after all, but she was too brokenhearted to fully appreciate him and turned him down with a gentle, "I'm sorry, son. I'll be too busy visiting my late husband's grave."

He frowned and dropped the subject. "I'm sorry. Here, let me get that last box for you."

"Thank you."

After the boxes were all inside, she brought her tupperwares of baked goods in and set them on the counter with a fiendish grin. "These are for anyone who wants them. Have a nice breakfast." The few homeless people who were in the lobby watched the food with soft smiles, and one older gentleman thanked her kindly and entreated God to bless her as she left.

With her business at the shelter finished, she made her way to the dry-cleaners and happily took a cherry-flavoured lollipop from the lobby as she dropped off her duvet covers. She beamed at the clerk as he ran her card through his machine.

"Have a good day, ma'am," he said with a smile returned.

"You, too!"

Her only errand left was to cash a social security check, but her bank was an hour out of Phoenix. So, with a crunch of her lollipop, she parked at the edge of the graveyard, took the bouquet she had made from the passenger seat, and ambled through the tombstones until she saw her husband's. After replacing his old sun-faded fake poinsettias with the new flowers, she sat across from the headstone and sighed. A weight pushed down on her shoulders, and her eyes watered. "Hey, sweetie," she whimpered, "Happy anniversary…"

Though livestreams weren't something she liked when he was alive, and Partha hadn't even made a channel yet, she liked to talk about his streams to her husband. She knew he would have enjoyed watching them with her, and perhaps in another reality they did. She had learned so much more about tabletop games since his passing, and it always choked her up with guilt when she used the jargon so readily. She only wished she could have shown the same level of interest in her husband's hobbies when he was alive. She wasn't dismissive of them by any means, but she was far more focused on trying to start a family or the horrors her parents and siblings were suffering than his "silly little games" at the time.

After her talk with the grave, she stood and wiped the tears from her eyes, taking in another desert breeze before getting back in her car and letting the radio's pop music of the day ground her back into the present.

As she left the area and started toward the bank, she passed the post office and vaguely remembered ordering something. Lucky she stopped to check: she had a small package in her post box. She didn't remember what was inside, so it was sort of like a gift from her past-self when she cut it open with a switchblade from her glove compartment. "Oh!" she said and smiled at the set of expensive gemstone dice. "Well isn't that sweet? Thank you, Dezba. Oh, you're welcome, dear." She giggled at herself and hummed a happy little diddy as she shimmied the wooden case holding the dice into her purse.

On the sunset drive through the desert, with lightning storms visible far in the distance, she hit a minor bump in the road, and her radio powered down. A sigh. The pickup was a gift from Lionel on their tenth anniversary, so it had most certainly seen better days. This wasn't exactly a new issue. She tried to slam the dash with her fist a few times, but all it managed to do was turn the lights for the clock back on. The silence didn't bother her at first, but as the sun sank below the horizon, and the only light became the flashes of lightning in the distance or the headlights of other cars, her thoughts darkened in that same way.

It felt increasingly futile to continue existing the way she was. She had lost everything and everyone over the years. Her sister, the last of her relatives, had passed away on New Year's Day. Likewise, the few friends she had had either died or abandoned her. Younger folks didn't seem interested in her as a person, and if they were, it was because they assumed she would support them financially. Her marriage and the trips she took with her husband in this very same truck were the closest to true adventure she had ever reached. But where was she going in it now?

The bank…. On Valentine's Day…. Alone….

When she arrived, she parked on the side of the building and turned off the engine, but rather than go inside, she rested her forehead on the steering wheel and squeezed her eyes shut. 'No,' she scolded herself silently, '*Dezba, don't cry in public. Don't cry.*' Her body responded to her internal dialogue with a loud sniffle and shuddered breath. "No," she said aloud and looked at herself in the rearview. The way she glared into her own eyes seemed to help, but then she caught a glimpse of the dice in her purse. Her lips started to tremble at the sight, and it only took a moment for her façade to crack. She held her face in her wrinkled hands and wept.

Every anniversary and even on their wedding day itself, she gave Lionel a new set of dice. This was the first set she had bought for herself in her entire life, and she hadn't planned to pick them up on such a heartbreaking day.'*Why? Just to break my own heart. I don't have friends. Who would even play with me?*' "Oh, Lionel!"

After an hour of mourning and self-pity in the car, she sucked up the last of her sadness and made her way inside just before closing. Unsurprisingly, the small local bank was empty of patrons. A bell jangling over the door as she opened it broke the silence.

"Oh, hello, Dezba!" said the young clerk, "Are you okay?"

"I'm fine, Wendy. Have a check to cash." She hobbled up to the counter and slid it to the teller.

"Alright, just let me get this put in for you. You wanted it all in cash, or did you want some in your checking account?"

"Cash," she sniffled and looked down into her purse to fiddle with her wallet.

"Having a nice Valentine's Day?"

"No…."

"Oh no! What's wrong? Husband out of town?"

"Something like that," she muttered.

"Well, I don't have a date tonight either. Closing up soon. Maybe we could go see a movie or something. As friends, of course."

She sighed. "Yeah, maybe."

Wendy returned her attention to her computer and clicked around. While she waited, Dezba heard the door open behind her by the chime of the bell. Almost immediately after, Wendy's eyes went wide. She held up her hands and backed away from the counter.

"Get down! On the ground!"

Dezba turned slowly and saw two men with guns outstretched. The one closest to her was wearing a full-face motorcycle helmet, and the other man was wearing a grey headscarf covering all but his eyes, which were hidden behind a pair of sunglasses. One of the guns Dezba recognised as an *Astra A-100*. She briefly admired the paint job: a gradient from deep blue to hot pink with a pearlescent finish. The other man's gun was an old flintlock pistol, and her eyes sparkled at the sight. She had never seen a gun so old in such fine condition, and he seemed quite confident in its ability to fire the way he had it aimed at Wendy.

The one with the motorcycle helmet took an intimidating step toward Dezba. "I said on the ground!" The *Astra* was close enough to her thumping heart she could almost feel its deadly energy reaching out and grabbing her soul to threaten it. With a gulp, she looked down at the scratchy carpet.

But… what did she have to lose?

None of this felt real.

It was happening so fast but so excruciatingly slow.

Her gaze trailed from the forest-green floor to her purse, and before she even fully understood her own motivations, she was reaching into it.

Wendy watched Dezba's movements with watery eyes. It seemed her life would be saved by this kindly old lady. She knew Dezba to always have a gun in her purse, and a hysterical half-laugh choked out of her when she saw the older woman cock the weapon. She would be saved! Oh, thank the Heavens for this lovely old woman and her kind heart! A hopeful smile. Trembling hands clasped in thankful prayer. *'Thank you! Oh! Thank you, God!'*

With such a rapid incline in emotion, it was especially jarring when it all came crashing down around her. The barrel of Dezba's gun was suddenly a third on the panicking teller.

"Why'd you stop? I said cash. Now," demanded Dezba.

Thyne and Francis gave each other a confused glance. "Should I kill her?" asked Thyne in French.

Francis opened his mouth to reply, but he was suddenly wrenched from his place in Phoenix and dropped halfway across the world in the Icelandic airport getting fortune cookies for his friend. From the others' perspectives, he had disappeared outright and in an instant. Thyne closed his eyes and inhaled a deep breath to contain his rage. He was thankful for the moment afforded to him by this strange old lady who was, for whatever reason, robbing the clerk for him.

Tears were waterfalling from Wendy's eyes as she tried her best to calm the broken heart beating up into her throat. She opened her till and started to fill a drawstring bag with the money from inside. She was taking a long time due to her hands' incessant shaking and difficulty seeing through all the tears. Her worst fears came true a moment later when she felt the cold metal of a gun pressed against her forehead and heard the strange man's voice with its thick southern accent: "You best hurry up now, darlin', else I'll pop you right now."

She hurried to fill the bag with the rest of the money then tossed it in their direction. "Th-th-th-that's all," she cried. As the man took it and turned for only a moment, Wendy quickly pressed her panic button.

"What about the vault?" asked Dezba.

"Nah, Em, don't worry 'bout the vault. They don't keep much in 'em, and we gotta scram," said Thyne as he grabbed her by the back of her jacket and started to drag her outside. From the doorway, with his gun still trained on Wendy, he said "You didn't press that button did you, little miss?"

Her eyes went wide, and she shook her head vigorously.

He smiled, but it was only evident to her through the tone in his voice as he cooed: "Good girl. Then I don't gotta kill ya."

The door closed behind them, and it felt as if Wendy had just been pulled out of a burning building of billowing smoke with how relieved her breaths felt as they roared through her lungs.

In the parking lot, the barrel of the gun was shoved into the small of Dezba's back. Thyne's words brought a chill down her spine as he whispered, still in a Southern accent, "You're coming with us. Gimme your gun."

She passed him her gun immediately and let him push her to a burnt-orange SUV across the parking lot. There was a man drumming on the steering wheel, and when they approached, he unlocked the doors. He was wearing a headscarf like the other man had been, but his was black and white gingham, and he wasn't wearing sunglasses. "Where's Toto?"

"Iceland," growled Thyne as he slammed the door where Dezba was then rushed to get into the passenger seat. "Just drive."

"Who's this?" He asked as he pulled the gearshift down to reverse and started to leave.

"I don't know. She helped, but the girl saw her face."

Roach put the car in drive, but before speeding away, despite the sirens in the distance, he turned around to look Dezba up and down and said, "Which car is yours?"

It was finally starting to hit her what she had gotten herself into, so her hand was trembling as she pointed to her pickup.

"Does the teller know your name?"

She swallowed the dread in her throat and nodded timidly.

Roach shoved the gearshift back up to park and opened his door. "Be right back."

Despite Thyne's protestations, during which his false Southern accent was starting to slip, Roach went into the bank flipping open a butterfly knife and re-emerged seconds later closing it, this time much bloodier. Dezba's stomach turned, and she averted her gaze. Thyne was watching him with wild fury in his veiled eyes as he walked casually up to Dezba's truck and tore off her licence plate with his bare hands. He broke into the passenger door by slamming his elbow into the window, after which he tore open the glove box and took everything from inside.

When he came back to the car, his door still open, he slid into his seat and tossed the licence plate and contents of the glove box into the back (save for the switchblade, which he kept for himself). "Dorothy, give her a marker, so she can redact her info. When you're done blacking everything out, lady, put the papers in with the money, so we can burn it all." She was confused by the demand but took the offered pen from Thyne and did as she was told. With that settled, he finally closed his door and sped out onto the road, cops arriving on the scene only a few moments behind them. "I didn't see Toto in there," he said as he turned down the music and drove in a relatively pedestrian manner considering their current situation. "Did he bail?"

"No, he's just a bell—. A bitch. I'll text him." He slid the phone out of his pocket to send a barrage of angry texts to Francis.

While he was busy doing that, Dezba looked behind them at the oncoming police force and asked, "You have a spare mask somewhere?"

The glove compartment popped open a moment later, seemingly before Roach had even reached down to touch it, and he grabbed a bandana from inside to toss into the backseat. "God I need a cigarette," he grumbled.

Dezba took a deep breath and tied the bandana around the bottom half of her face. She took a pair of embroidered driving gloves out of her purse, gingerly pulled them over her wrinkled hands, and tied up her long grey hair. After a few breaths to calm herself, she took another gun out of her purse and rolled down her window to aim back at the cops and shoot out one of their tires.

Roach and Thyne both flinched at the sound, Thyne turning around to immediately scold her. He was stopped before he managed a single syllable, however, by Francis suddenly appearing in the seat beside her and explaining in a faux Russian accent: "Apologies, comrades. Who's the lady?"

"I'm calling her Auntie Em. She's fucking crazy," said Thyne with an impressed intonation, "Emmie, I appreciate the enthusiasm, but please stop shooting at the police, love."

"Fuck you, this is fun." She let off three more rounds, leaving the four cops that were behind them riding on a rim each. It was only when she leaned back into the car, out of ammo, that she noticed Francis beside her and gasped.

Thyne rolled his eyes and cocked his own gun. "If you're going to shoot at them, at least kill them." He leaned out of his window so far that his arse was on the threshold and aimed down his sights at one of the cops driving behind them. When he let off his round, Roach simultaneously swerved around a car in front of them, so Thyne instead shot the windshield of a passer-by. He reeled back into the car and immediately started shouting at Roach, his false accent entirely forgotten by then: "You bloody moron! I thought you said you knew how to fucking drive. Let me drive!"

"I do know how to drive, fuckface. Hey! What the hell are you doing? Get off of me!"

Thyne had climbed up onto Roach's lap and shoved the gearshift to the left, changing it from automatic to manual. Luckily, being so tall, Roach always drove with his seat as far back as it would slide, so there was enough room on his lap for the smaller man to sit. Still, he had to recline it as far as it would go, accidentally knocking Francis' lap quite hard with his headrest. "Sorry, buddy," he said with a mostly-hidden giggle as Francis started.

"You think *you* need a cigarette, now *I* need a cigarette," whined Thyne. His legs were crossed, so he didn't have direct access to the pedals, but he had full control over the gearshift and wheel. "Clutch!" he shouted.

Roach let out a small sound of pained exertion as he struggled to find the clutch, trying to see around Thyne at where his boots were as well as trying to move his legs while restrained by the 160-or-so pounds of weight on them. He managed to push in the clutch at the right time for Thyne to change gears, but it was a close call.

"Oh, you bloody twit! Do better! Do better!" He stretched his legs into an odd and amusing position, his right foot on the ceiling as he shoved his left foot down toward the pedals to press them himself.

Even under these non-ideal circumstances (saying the least), Thyne skillfully drove into the median between either side of the highway and drifted across the desert sand, turning them swiftly around in a cloud of dust. Once they were driving the opposite direction with an impressive acceleration on the other side of the highway, he shouted, "Francis! Would you kill the bloody pigs already?"

"Got it." He shifted to the front passenger seat in the blink of an eye, and behind them, on both sides of the interstate, all of the cruisers turned suddenly into each other, causing a massive pile-up. Their sirens wound down to silence, and Thyne returned to sitting with his legs criss-crossed over each other on Roach's lap. He let out a few laboured breaths he had been holding and said, "Alright, we can slow down."

"You can get off of me," said Roach.

"Right, sorry." He climbed into the back seat with Dezba and sat behind Roach as he put his seat back upright. After sliding a pack of cigarettes out of his pocket and removing his helmet to light one, he offered one to Dezba.

She shook her hand at the offer but couldn't shake the feeling that Thyne sounded familiar. And... did he call that other one Francis?

"Let me have one," said Roach.

"Only if Franky can promise no one will see your face." He looked at Francis.

"Franky," whispered Dezba as she sort of stared at Thyne, her eyes thin and trying to figure out what was going on.

"I'm on top of it, Thyne," he said as he removed his headscarf.

Dezba gasped loudly. Thyne, not paying her any mind, was having trouble getting another cigarette out, so he took off his gloves, revealing the cybernetics beneath. He wrapped his arms around Roach's shoulders to uncover his mouth, shove a cigarette between his lips, and light it for him. When he finally leaned back in his seat, he clicked on his seatbelt and took a relaxing drag. As he opened his eyes, he was greeted with an expression of confused shock from their new elderly friend. "Take a picture. It'll last longer."

"You're Thyne," she pointed, "but you're so young."

His eyes went wide as he recognised what was happening. "It's a British name! You have me mistaken for someone else."

"No no no. You're Thyne, and you're Francis," she pointed at him as he sipped from his flask, "and you are.... Well I don't know who you are, but you two are on Partha's streams!"

Francis turned around and beamed a smile at her. "Always nice to meet a fan. What's your name?"

"F-Franky! What the Hell do you mean it's nice to meet a fan!? She just helped us rob a bank!"

"Yeah! Lucky that, considering I was trapped in Iceland for a spell. I like the cut of her jib." His dumb grin looked especially punchable.

Thyne rubbed his aching temples and tried to actively forget his place in reality, but Dezba wouldn't allow it: "Why did you tell everyone you're old? And, you," she pointed at Francis, "Why are you disappearing and reappearing? Am I losing it?"

"Yes!" said Thyne with too much enthusiasm to believably take the excuse, "Yes, it must be dementia or something."

"Come now, Thyne, we can tell her." He pressed a hand to his chest, but Thyne dove across the car to slap a hand over his mouth before he could say more.

In Italian: "Franky, I will kill you so help me God. You keep your stupid mouth shut. At least until we're back in Europe. Capiche?"

He glared and licked Thyne's palm.

"Ah, gross!" He pulled it away instinctively and wiped it on his trousers, but his gaze was deathly on his friend.

Francis shoved his hand into the backseat and introduced himself as, "Androme Francis Horatius Alexandre Anaxagoras de Tremblay. And you are?"

She was hesitant to take his hand. "Dezba Meadows."

"Listen, lady," said Thyne as he scooped her up by her shirt collar to pull her close. "If you so much as *think* about telling someone what you saw here or who we are, I will find everyone who has ever meant anything to you and burn them alive in front of you, and when I'm done with that, I will pull you apart with a pair of needle-nose pliers, sentencing you to a slow and painful death. Am I clear?"

She was surprisingly resolute despite the fire in his eyes and the heat to his words. "Crystal."

He shoved her away. "Good. Now put your seatbelts on. You're all idiots. Especially with this one driving." He slapped the back of Roach's seat, which prompted his half-smoked fag to be flicked into his chest from the driver's seat.

"I saw how you looked at my *Locust*, Dorothy. And to think, if you weren't such a dick, I was going to let you drive it."

Thyne rolled his eyes and crossed his arms, looking out his window at the passing desert as he grumbled, "What a bloody fucking nightmare."

Chapter 8
Inter-Party Conflict

Partha was curled up on the couch and cowering from a cockroach on the other side while River got dressed in front of him. His gaze was locked on the insect as it moved, but as he noticed River undressing in his periphery his lustful heart won out over his fear of the bug. He ogled the gymnast's shirtless body, the rest of the world fading from his perception. That was until River leaned down and slapped him across the face. "Hey, dumbass! I'm fucking talking to you."

"Oh!" He held his cheek and looked around. "Uhh. Um. S-sorry."

River flicked an earwig off of Partha's shoulder then stood back upright to look around the floor. He picked up a shirt and gave it the ol' sniff check. "As I was saying," he began as he dropped the dirty shirt in an overflowing hamper and looked for another, "I'm going out of town, but I'll be back in time to join your silly little gang." Another sniff test, a quiet gagging sound, another shirt added to the laundry hamper.

"Okay. Where are you going?" He said as he tried and failed to keep his attention on River's face as opposed to his half-naked body.

"Vegas." He finally found a shirt that didn't reek and pulled it over his rippling abs, much to Partha's chagrin. At least he was still only in boxers on his lower half....

It took a moment to retroactively hear River's answer, but when he processed it, no longer distracted by his shirtlessness, Partha clicked his teeth into a flirtatious toothy grin. "Oh? City of sin? Can I come?"

A glare. "I'm not interested."

Partha whined like a dog. The dogs lazing about the room all lifted their heads and looked at him. "Not interested in…?"

"In fucking you?" He laughed and resumed his search for pants. "I'd say try Tony, but I don't think you're really his type."

He tilted his head. "What's his type?"

After adding a second pair of pants to the hamper he sighed and cursed in Arabic about how he would have to do laundry before his trip. With that decision made, he started throwing all the clothes around the room into the basket, even removing his shirt again to add to the heaping pile. He picked up the hamper and leaned it on his hip before turning toward Partha. "Follow me."

He stood and followed River outside, embarrassed for him when he noticed that he didn't seem to be covering himself. He leaned toward him and whispered, "Don't you want to get dressed? You're only wearing boxers."

"Relax. It's just down here under the stairs, and I know everyone who lives here. Have to shower in their apartments." He led them to the laundry room. It only had two sets of machines and one small lattice window at the top of the back wall. There were stains on the floor and walls from past floods, but it was clear from the three steps up into this room that it was usually quite dry. The overwhelming stench of mildew was therefore misleading. "Anyway," continued River as he started filling the washing machine, "Tony's not into dweebs. He's enough of a dork himself."

"Hey!"

"What? Are you not a dweeb, dude? I've seen your streams. You're adorable and all, but it's all kinda trite, and Tony's already told me how little he thinks of you."

His lip trembled. "No he didn't! Why would he think little of me? I helped you two smuggle people out of the states!"

River smiled wickedly. "I asked him why he agreed to do this for you, and he said something like, 'I was bored, and Partha was a cute kid. I figured I might as well hear him out and maybe show him and his friends what real danger looks like.' He said he wanted to take you all down a peg. And he was especially angry yesterday on the phone."

"Angry?" Partha was finding it impossible to recall any outward expression of emotion from Roach but most especially he could not fathom him being angry.

"Yeah, dude. You guys called him up to try and play pretend you're pirates when he and I are living in squalor. But he was mostly mad that Thyne has a private jet. He's pretty anti-capitalist, so you can imagine how much he detests all of your wealth." He dropped a handful of detergent pods into the machine and let the lid fall closed with a loud bang. After turning a few dials on the back of the machine, he leaned on it casually to face Partha as it started to fill with water.

"He doesn't hate us! We're not pretending!" He stamped his foot and shouted one syllable of frustrated angst. "Stop smiling like that! You're laughing at me, and I don't appreciate it."

He chuckled. "I *am* laughing at you. I mean, are you serious?" He pointed, starting at Partha's feet then circling up toward the rest of him. "You're dressed like it's Halloween, and you lost a bet. With the eyepatch and everything." He lifted up the patch and caught a quick glimpse of the scar underneath before Partha pulled his hand away. His smile wavered. He hadn't expected it to be covering a real injury. "Anyway, no. You're not coming to Vegas with me. They'd eat your little twink ass alive."

"Stop."

"Or what? Or you'll hurt me? Go on, then. Try and hurt me." After such an invitation, and with his rage compounding, Partha did not hesitate to punch River square in his all-too-chuffed face. "Oh," said River as he held his nose. It didn't hurt much, but he was impressed nonetheless. "Well, look at that. I didn't think you'd do that."

"So stop mocking me, now."

"Alright alright. I'll let up for a bit."

"And let me come to Vegas with you."

He laughed. "Now don't push your luck, kid. You're staying here, but you won't be alone. Perlie's coming over." He rubbed his nose again as the pain started to worsen. "She's coming to babysit." A mocking grin.

"I don't need babysitting, you fucking dickhead. I'm twenty-three years old!"

"Oh? Well what will we do if you overdose?"

All the colour washed from his face. "W-what? Overdose on what?"

"Oh, that's adorable. You think I haven't noticed." Partha stuttered incoherently, and River watched every moment of it with sadistic hungry eyes. After getting his fill, he chuckled and said, "Relax. She's coming over to dogsit. You think I'd leave you alone with my fluffy babies? I hardly know you. Even if you weren't bumping coke, I'd call her to watch them. And y'know, since you're so horny, you should try laying her. She's probably desperate and lonely enough."

"You said you'd stop mocking me!" He punched him in his gut.

He coughed and bent over to hold his stomach. "Alright! Jeez, kid. Chill out."

"You're a real cunt, River."

He managed a shit-eating grin and replied sarcastically, "Come now, Partha. You'd say such things to your gracious host?"

Francis kept the police off of their immediate trail, but neither Dezba nor Roach were told how. With the more leisurely pace he afforded them, they were able to talk about their journey ahead. It started innocently enough (at least as innocent as conspiring to commit violent crimes could be):

"So, I assume you figured out your plane's engine?"

"No," Thyne huffed, "We flew here with it broken to appease *you*, you rotter."

Roach took a drag of his cigarette and flicked the ashes out into the cupholders in the middle console. "Well, that was stupid. Why didn't you just fly commercial or drive in? You'd willingly bring your pilot to America?"

Were he sober, perhaps Francis would have corrected Roach's assumption that Thyne had a private pilot, but he was instead staring blankly at his flask between swigs and listening to the music playing through the stereo from Roach's phone.

Thyne smirked and decided not to tell Roach he was his own pilot. "And why shouldn't I? He came of his own free will."

"Oh? Or was it because you pay him, and if he didn't fly you here, he'd lose his housing, next meal, or whatever other essentials?"

He giggled. "You really are a muppet."

"Whatever. So, how do you plan to get us out of the country?"

"It won't be a problem."

"Really? Because I've seen the direct consequences of getting caught, and it's what I would call a very very big problem." Another drag. His tone and mien remained deadpan, but he was evermore irritated.

"Well, we won't get caught then, will we, mate?"

He scoffed and looked for Thyne in the rearview. In order for them to make eye contact, it moved without him touching it, seemingly from some sort of remote on the driver's console. "Better not, or I'll kill you."

Thyne's lips curled into a sarcastic grin. "Right."

He turned his attention back toward the road and smoked while the rearview readjusted so he could see the road behind him again. There was a brief lull, during which Thyne took out Dezba's pistol and observed it. She turned toward him and grinned. "You like it?"

"Oh this? Yeah, I've never seen this model. What is it?"

"It's an *Anubis 78*. It only came out two years ago."

He arched his brow and observed it longer. "From... Osiris?"

"Yeah from Anubis." She was beaming as she took out her second gun to show him. "You like guns; you might recognise this one."

They traded firearms, and Thyne briefly pored over the older model. "A *Baretta*?"

"A *Baretta*...?" She rolled her hand around its joint to implore him to guess further.

He opened his mouth to take a guess, but Roach snipped from the front: "You two put the stupid fucking guns away."

"Or what, mate?"

"Or nothing. I just don't like 'em."

He laughed, passing the pistol nonchalantly back to its owner. "What kind of American doesn't like guns?"

"This kind of American." He pointed to himself. "They're for pussies."

Thyne laughed more and nudged Dezba's side with his elbow. She was nervous, but he ignored the upset and leaned over the middle console to look at Roach. "You're having a laugh. They're for soldiers and revolutionaries. I assumed you were both of those things, but I suppose that anarchy patch on your jacket is just for show, hm? And these?" He grabbed the ball-chain around Roach's neck and yanked the dog tags he had hidden underneath his shirt out into the open. He held them in his palm and started to read them, but Roach snatched the tags away and flicked his lit cigarette into Thyne's face before he could make sense of the words.

"Don't fucking touch me, dude. Guns are for pussies, and that's just facts."

After brushing the ashes out of his hair, Thyne grabbed Roach's half-smoked fag from the middle console and took a drag. He blew a cloud of smoke rudely into his face and smiled. "Oh yeah? And what, *oh wise one*, is a weapon not for 'pussies'?"

Thyne immediately had the blade of a balisong knife pressed gently along his right cheekbone, pulling him closer to Roach.

"Knives?" he laughed as if there wasn't a blade on his face, "You can't take down the government with knives, mate."

"Watch me." He closed the knife and dropped it noisily into the cupholders.

"Oh, so *edgy*," taunted Thyne, "Well, while you're getting gunned down before you even get to the palace doors, Dezba and I will be on the roof with snipers taking out the entire monarchy. Right, Em?"

He shooed Thyne away with a flick of his wrist. "Shut up, dude. You've never even used one in combat. Guns are shit. They're loud, cumbersome, ugly, easy to trace back to you, and, worst of all, they make it too easy."

Thyne arched his brow and looked back at Dezba to see her reaction. She was visibly perturbed, so he nudged Francis' shoulder. In French: "Are you hearing this, Frankenstein?"

"Hm?" He looked around as if he had just come up from the bottom of a well. "Something about firearms?"

He swapped back to English, his tone mocking, "Roach thinks guns are for cowards. He says they make things too easy."

Francis blinked. A beat. "I... don't care."

"You don't care that he's mocking us for using guns?"

The way he looked at Thyne was like that of a defeated soldier. In whispered French: "What does it matter, Thyne? What does any of this matter?"

He frowned. "Franky, shh. It's okay." He caressed his cheek with his knuckles then returned his attention to Roach. "You say they make things too easy. How?"

He took a drag and turned up the volume of the music, refusing to elaborate. It was just at the close of an alternative rock song, and when the next song started up, Thyne's entire world went dark, stopping his next sassy remark before it could even form in his head.

All of the songs until then had been of various genres. It was Thyne's guess that Roach had all of his music shuffled, and after so much variety, maybe he should have anticipated something like this happening. From the first note alone, he was transported some century and a half back in time. His eyes went hollow and hands ached. He fell backwards into his seat and grabbed at his face with trembling fingers. He had put his gloves back on, and since they were covering his cybernetics, he was dissociated enough from time to forget his missing digits. His breaths were laboured, and just before he was thrust into the throes of a violent panic attack, the music stopped entirely.

"We do not play opera with Thyne present," Francis asserted, "In fact, it be most provident for us to avoid music of any genre in his presence."

"What the hell, dude? Why?" He reached back toward the dials, but the barrel of Francis' flintlock was immediately on his temple. "Okay, shit!" He snatched his hand back to the steering wheel. "Can't handle knives. Can't handle music. I'm beginning to wonder if there's anything you rich pricks *can* handle."

Francis ignored the comment and lowered his weapon. He stopped time and swapped places with Dezba to sit himself in the back beside Thyne. When he resumed time, his panicking friend was quick to scramble into his arms and ground himself with the sound of Francis' thumping heart.

Dezba gasped and let out a faint scream at the sudden change in location, but Roach observed the show of supernatural power with his regular blank expression. "Anyway," he said as if there was nothing odd to address, "Will we be flying to England with the broken engine?"

"No. Thyne has hired a mechanic to repair it."

"And what do you plan to do while that's being fixed? Maybe buy a hotel just for yourselves then abandon it to let it rot? Buy another plane and fire your old pilot since it was clearly his fault in the first place?"

Thyne's breaths were calm by then, but after the comments, he started to huff angrily.

"Well, I am unaware of Thyne's machinations, but—."

"We're here." Roach blurted as he pulled into a parking garage and drove up three storeys. After parking in an empty area, taking up four spaces, he popped the hood. "Everyone out. Come on. Dezba, don't forget your licence plate, but give me the bag of cash and your registration. You blacked it all out, right?" She nodded and passed him the bag. "Good." With that said, he got out of the car and lifted the bonnet.

Thyne thanked Francis with a kiss on the cheek and asked him to help Dezba to Roach's *Locust*. When they stepped into Roach's view, he clicked a button on his key-fob to unlock the car on the other side of the garage. A satisfying ding echoed to them, so he slid the keys back into his pocket, tossed the bag of cash haphazardly under the hood, and returned his attention to the SUV's engine.

"What's your problem, mate?"

Leaning on the hood as he held it open, Roach scoffed and rolled his eyes. It was the first explicit show of genuine emotion from him that Thyne had witnessed, so it made especially clear how irritated he was. "God dammit, dude. Would you just go wait in the *Locust* and shut the fuck up?"

"Ay! You stop being such a bloody cunt! I did your stupid robbery! Franky got the pigs off our arse. We stole the forks. We've done everything you've said, so why in God's name are you still not taking us seriously?" After a slew of muttered curses he flicked open his lighter with an automatic flourish and lit a cigarette.

Roach leaned on the chassis and watched Thyne smoke. He was admittedly quite adorable with his cheeks all pink and nose scrunched up under his knitted brows. His hair looked soft, but his skin looked softer. His eyes were—. '*Come on, Clayton, get it together.*' "You ever killed anyone, kid?"

"Kid?" He scoffed. "Roach, I assure you I am much older than you."

"Dodging the question," he muttered as he flipped open a butterfly knife and started cutting tubes and cords around the engine.

"What does it matter if I've killed anyone?" He rolled his eyes and crossed his arms, using his tongue to hold the cigarette in his mouth as he puffed angrily on it.

Closing his knife, Roach stood upright and eyed Thyne. His posture was lazy and leaning further back than normal. "Listen, Dorothy…. I'm sorry."

"You what, mate?"

"Said I'm sorry. I'm out, man. You've never killed anyone, and your plane isn't even working. You did the heist, but Francis disappeared in the middle of it, and you dragged in some old lady. You're not exactly the criminal type. I don't want to help some lib take down a company." He plucked Thyne's cigarette out of his mouth as if to punctuate the sentence.

The Brit huffed smoke out of his nose like an enraged dragon. "You call me that one more time, and I'll burn you alive."

He stifled a laugh. "What? A 'lib'? Well then enlighten me how I'm wrong! You've got a private jet, employees, no doubt you have at least one house (though

I'd wager much more). You've been ogling my *Locust*, so I'd guess you like cars. Maybe a *Ferrari* or two back in London? And what else? Other than your probably-designer outfit and expensive cologne? You're a capitalist pig like all the others. Let me take a guess at why you want Maitland gone, *Mr. Crump*. Is it because Daddy wrote you out of the will? Or is it because he fired you from your cushy do-nothing job?" He tisked and started smoking the stolen cigarette as he returned his attention to the mechanics under the hood.

Thyne crossed his arms and leaned on the side of the car, a smug air about him as he talked down to Roach: "Alright, if we're making assumptions how about I give it a go, yeah? If I'm just some hypocritical liberal, then I guess that makes you a washed-up rockstar wannabe, posing as a leftist, but the moment you're presented with the resources and manpower to make an actual change, you want to quit at even the slightest excuse like a coward."

No matter how much he tried to hide it, there was a shift in his air. The comment stripped him bare and struck him to his core. He even briefly stopped working on the car. It was wordless in the beats that followed while Roach finished sabotaging the mechanics and started a small fire with the battery. He stood and flicked the cigarette under the bonnet before dropping it, tossing the keys to Thyne, and saying, "A keepsake for you."

Thyne fumbled them then jogged up to Roach, who had started his way to the *Locust*. "Come on, mate, you can't just quit."

He averted his hazel-greys from the pleading honey eyes of the much shorter man. Still wordless, he got into the *Locust* then gestured with his head for Thyne to get in the passenger's seat. After he connected his phone wirelessly to the stereo, he passed it to Francis and sat in silent thought. He had started the car, but he was looking out his window with his fingertips gently pressed against his lips rather than driving.

"Roach?" said Francis after a while, "Wherefore have you entrusted me with this cellular device?"

"Play what you like from it," he replied. It seemed speaking aloud about something unrelated to his reeling thoughts had freed him from them. He finally looked at Thyne again. "You guys need a place to stay until your plane is fixed?" Thyne's golden eyes were hopeful. "Don't look at me like that, man." He averted his gaze. "My apartment is a mess, and it's all the way in Compton, but if it'll be a long time, I wouldn't want you trapped in some hotel until we leave for Europe."

He squeaked happily and lunged across the front seat to hug Roach. "Thank you!"

"Alright alright," he pushed him away, "Chill out, dude." He turned toward the backseat. "You got any pets, lady? Family living at home?"

She shook her head.

"Good. No need to go back, then. If we get caught it'll be your fault." He spoke matter-of-factly. "Hope you're all ready for a long-ass road trip."

He changed gears to start leaving, but he braked when Francis said, "Speaking of pets. Did Jean-Jacques not have a hound we needed to fetch for him?"

"Yeah, and his motorcycle. It's in an alley nearby."

"Jean-Jacques?"

"He's the man fixing my plane. We'll have to bring him his bike and dog at the airstrip."

"Where's the airstrip?"

"About an hour outside of Albuquerque."

Roach sighed. "Alright. And the dog?"

"The dog's in Albuquerque."

"Well, if we're going to Albuquerque," he turned toward Francis, "play the Albuquerque song, dude." Francis stared blankly. "You don't know that one? Where'd you find this guy, Thyne?"

"I've never heard it, either," muttered the Brit.

"Oh, you two are such weirdos. Dezba? Have you heard it?" She nodded. "She gets it. Give Dezba the phone, and she'll play it. It's exceptionally silly."

It was a quick drive to the alley where Jean-Jacques' motorcycle was parked, so neither Francis nor Thyne actually had the time to listen to the entirety of the lengthy song Roach had requested. Dezba moved to the passenger's seat of the *Locust*, and it wasn't long later that they were on the empty highway through the stormy midnight. It was painfully cold, so only half an hour into the drive, Thyne pulled off onto the shoulder and waited for Roach to pull off behind him.

"What's wrong?" shouted Roach.

Thyne got off the bike and held his arms as he shivered his way over to Roach's open window. He flipped open the visor on his helmet and shouted, "It's bloody freezing!" A gesture to the beginnings of a snowfall around them. "You got a jumper or jacket in there?"

Roach shooed Thyne away from the shoulder to make room for his door to open. Thyne thought he would go look in the boot, but once he was outside, he instead took off his jean jacket and shoved it into Thyne's chest. "Best I got."

It was warm from his body heat, so the Englishman did not hesitate to pull it over his goosebumped arms. "Franky!" He called through his clattering teeth.

"Yes?"

"Get me a jacket."

"Another one?"

"Yes another one, you idiot. It's snowing!"

"From...?"

"From the town we just left!"

91

Francis nodded and struggled with the motorcycle's kickstand for an embarrassingly long thirty seconds before finally disappearing and reappearing at Thyne's side with a fluffy sweater outstretched toward him, tags still dangling from its right sleeve.

"Cheers, both of you," he said as he pulled on the sweater then redonned Roach's jacket overtop of it.

"We're good to go, then?"

Thyne nodded and flipped the helmet's visor back down.

"Won't Francis be cold?" asked Roach.

"You need not worry yourselves," said Francis.

Thyne elaborated: "You've seen him teleporting all around…. He's—. Just—. He doesn't get cold."

Roach shrugged. "Whatever, man."

They continued their seven hour trek to Albuquerque with only bathroom, fuel, and snack breaks. After about five hours, Francis disappeared from the back of Thyne's motorcycle, and when questioned about it at the next gas station, Thyne said simply, "He's at the airstrip waiting for us."

Perhaps the most noteworthy aspects of this trip, however, were Roach and Dezba's scattered conversations. It started after about an hour of quietly enjoying the *Locust's* custom sound system via Roach's shuffled playlist:

Roach turned down the volume. "Dude, I've gotta ask: what happened in the bank?"

"Well… what do you mean?"

"Don't play dumb with me. How'd you wind up putting yourself in this predicament? You regretting it yet?"

She watched the dark desert roll by her window. "I don't regret it."

"Have you done this sort of thing before?"

"No."

"You know I killed the teller, don't you?"

"… I know."

"And that doesn't bother you?"

"It does…."

There was a long beat of quiet.

"It was for your own protection, you understand."

"I don't want to talk about it."

"Fair enough."

He turned up the music, and it wasn't until after their second snack stop, two hours later, that he brought the topic back up:

"It must be strange for you: giving up your life as you know it entirely. And for a bunch of strangers. Criminals. We're not good people, Dezba."

"Oh, hush. You think I don't know that?"

"I just don't know what could have compelled you to join us. Did Thyne force you?"

"It was my choice."

"Was it really?"

She glared at him. "What do you want me to say, son? You want me to say that I'm scared and want to go home? That I didn't expect the people trying to take me hostage to be criminals? I knew what I was getting myself into. I pulled my gun on Wendy. I saw the fear and betrayal in her eyes, and I know that you killed her not but a few minutes later. What's done is done. What's gone is gone. At least now I won't have to go home alone." Roach was quiet. "The biggest surprise," continued Dezba a moment later, "was finding out that the men who had me at gunpoint were Thyne and Francis. Do you know about Partha and his streams?"

"Of course. I do the music for them. Partha's back in Compton as we speak."

A weak grin. "Really? I'll get to meet him?"

"Don't get all star-eyes, Emmie. You know what they say about meeting your heroes."

"Well, it's clear he's involved in some sort of criminal activity if he's friends with you lot. I'm still coming to terms with all this, but I don't regret my choice."

"Just don't say I didn't warn you. He might disappoint."

"Oh, you stop. He's a good kid with a good heart."

"Debatable."

She rolled her eyes, and it was followed by another few hours of wordlessness. At their next stop for refuelling, Roach made everyone wait for him to, "do a *Qada* prayer, since you assholes made me miss *Isha*. And after that I've got to do the *Fajr* salah before I miss that one, too."

They were understanding, but the impatient Brit was loudly complaining after about twenty minutes of waiting. Roach was praying out in the desert quite a distance. They could hardly see him through the snow as it started to pick-up, and when he walked back after about half an hour, he was shivering and holding his bare arms. "Alright," he said, "You guys better have bought me a soda like I asked."

"It's in your cupholder," said Dezba, "But you're cold. Should we get you a coffee?"

He nodded (rather adorably) and got back into the *Locust* to blast the heat.

Dezba and Thyne went inside to get him his coffee and ended up also buying another energy drink for Thyne (the fourth of the night). When he came back outside drinking it, there was genuine concern in Roach's tone when he said, "We can get a hotel for the night, man. Those things'll kill you drinking them so often."

"I'll be fine. We'll sleep in the plane. Come on. I don't want to delay any longer than we have to." He chugged the remainder of the drink, put his helmet back on, and got back on the bike.

It was only another hour before Albuquerque was visible in the distance. The snow had let up, and by the time they were in the city, it was late enough into the morning for businesses to start opening. This included the doggy hotel where Jean-Jacques' miniature schnauzer was staying. They beelined for it, and as soon as Thyne had a confirmation text from Francis of the dog's information, they picked her up and put her in the *Locust* where she immediately took a liking to Roach.

Dezba closed her door, and Thyne leaned down to look through her open window. "About an hour left. Are you still okay to drive?"

"I should be asking you that, dude." He gave the dog a treat from his glove compartment and pet her as she curled up in his lap. "This is an adorable little pup. What's her name?"

"Juliette."

"Oh?" He looked down at her and scratched behind her ear. "I wonder if one of my dogs will be her Romeo."

Thyne rolled his eyes. "Let's just go, unless you have another six hour prayer to do."

"Don't be a dick, dude. Your legs must be jelly by now anyway."

"Yeah, they're absolutely destroying me. Precisely why I'd like not to dawdle."

Roach nodded, and they started back on their way again. The last hour of the trip was made much more lighthearted by the dog in Roach's lap. She was excited by the car moving and propped herself up on his door to look out at the passing landscape. There was a moment at a red light where a dog in another car had Julliette starting to growl and bark, but Roach made a shrill clicking noise and hushed her in Arabic as if she were one of his own dogs. She was submissive and obedient to the sounds despite not understanding them, and Dezba commented, "You're so good with her. You must have a kind soul."

"I assure you I don't."

She was going to argue her point, but she took his word for it when the memory of his knife covered in Wendy's blood flashed through her mind.

In the warmth of the car and feeling more comfortable around Roach, Dezba fell asleep on this last leg of the trip. With his only conversation partner snoring in the seat beside him, it was lucky the dog in his lap was keeping him awake enough to not doze off behind the wheel.

When they pulled into the hangar beside Thyne's *DC-8*, Roach wanted to lay into him for the sheer size of the plane, but he was too exhausted to formulate his feelings into coherent thoughts. He opened the door and let Julliette run across the echoey chamber to her owner, but Thyne, Dezba, and Roach gave Jean-Jacques only cursory greetings before dragging themselves like zombies into the plane and collapsing onto the first vaguely-horizontal surfaces they could find.

Roach awoke to his alarm for his afternoon prayer. He rubbed his tired eyes and sat up, taking in his surroundings. The interior of Thyne's plane was spacious and decorated in blacks and pinks. The leather couch on which he had fallen asleep was adorned with fluffy pink throw pillows that had left chaotic sleep lines on his left cheek. The ceiling had a repeating diamond pattern of white and pink LED strips, and the lighting other than that was a cylindrical floor lamp bolted to the ground beside the couch. On the pink sofa across from his, Francis was drooling onto one of the black throws, his left arm hanging off of the furniture and bent on the floor, spilling whatever was in his flask onto the rug. Between them was a black coffee table with a curved line of stained-pink glass running through its midst. The only thing on it currently was Jean-Jacques' motorcycle helmet.

Roach stood and took his long black hair out of its hairclaw, rubbing at the back of his head where it had pulled painfully on his scalp while he slept. While he massaged away the pain, he wandered about the cabin, hunched to avoid the low ceiling, looking for the others. Dezba was sleeping on a daybed in another chamber behind the living area where he and Francis had been, and Jean-Jacques was cuddling his dog in a proper bed at the aft. Thyne, however, was nowhere to be seen. He wanted his jacket back, but he needed to pray and decided it best to do it outside even in the cold. Luckily, there was a knitted throw blanket on the back of the couch he had hardly disturbed during his sleep, so he wrapped it around his shoulders, awkwardly washed himself in the cramped lavatory, and jaunted down the air stairs. His legs ached from sleeping in his jeans, so he was glad to have to stretch them walking around the perimeter of the hangar looking for a regular-sized door to the outside. He eventually found the door to the desert, but when he opened it, he stumbled directly into Thyne, spilling hot tea and coffee all over both of them.

"Oh you twat, you did that on purpose!" He shoved a handful of wax paper bags and a reusable tote full of snacks into his chest. "Hold this."

"What's all this?" He asked as Thyne was picking up the fallen drinks.

"I couldn't sleep, so I walked down to the petrol station and bought everyone breakfast, but you've just ruined it." After a few angry huffs, he stomped into the hangar to a small table near the door and set down all four of the spilled cups. He managed to save two, "both coffee. Gross," and brought them up into the plane. Roach trailed behind.

After setting the bags of baked goods and gas station snacks on the coffee table, Roach followed Thyne back out into the hangar and said, "Hey, man. If you want me to take you somewhere in the *Locust* just let me know when I'm done praying, okay?"

Thyne rolled his eyes and waved his hand around dismissively at the idea. "I'll be inside reading."

"Oh? What are you reading?"

"A book."

It took all of Roach's self control not to roll his eyes at the answer. Thyne left before Roach could ask for his jacket back, so he pulled the blanket further over his shoulders and went outside. When he was finished praying and returned to the plane about fifteen minutes later, he found Thyne on the pink couch reading a leatherbound journal. He had Francis' head in his lap, petting his dirty blond hair mindlessly.

"Psst. Did you want to go somewhere?"

Thyne patted Francis' shoulder gently. "Let me get up, love." The drunkard sleepily nodded and sat up just long enough for Thyne to stand before collapsing again. Roach noticed his flask was missing and spotted it on Thyne when he stood and stretched his legs.

"Is that a flask in your pocket, or are you just happy to see me?" he joked quietly.

Thyne rolled his eyes and whispered angrily, "Would you prefer I let him keep it?" He closed his book and opened the black sofa's base like a piano bench to put it inside before making his way to the *Locust*.

In the driver's seat, Roach's tone was chipper when he asked, "So, where to?"

"How far is Kansas?"

He exhaled an amused huff through his nose. "Good one. No but for real, where do you want to go?"

"Did I fucking stutter?"

"You're not joking?"

"Obviously not, you idiot."

"… You just want to abandon everyone?" Roach was surprised by how willing he was to go along with the spontaneous idea.

"What? No! I didn't say that at all."

Another amused exhale. "Kansas is really far, dude. Not to mention even further away from Cali."

He blushed with embarrassment, but his brows furrowed with rage. "Then where do *you* suggest we go?"

He shrugged. "Back to the gas station you just came from, if you want. There's not much around here but desert and mountains. Could just be a joyride."

"A joyride for you, sure, but what would I get out of it as a passenger?"

Roach almost laughed but stopped it before it showed on his face. "I'm not letting you drive my *Locust*, man. I'll let you DJ, though. You got music on your phone?"

"Of course I do."

"Well, connect it to the radio. I'll look for places nearby. Maybe we can go get lunch or something."

They were both on their phones in silence for a moment before the music suddenly blared, startling both of them. Only a split-second later it was at a reasonable volume.

"Sorry," muttered Thyne. He was so startled he didn't stop to think as to how the radio had gotten so quiet so quickly without either of them moving. Maybe it was some sort of feature of the custom stereo system.

"No worries, dude." He returned his attention to the map of the area. "There's a Desert Mart not too far. They have those in Eurasia?"

"No."

"Weird. Well they're all over *this* shit hole of a country. It's a retail chain. They sell basically everything. If there's anything you might need or want for your stay in the states we could go there."

"Desert Mart, it's called? Does Osiris own it?"

"Yeah, why?"

"Franky—. Well, he was probably drunk, but he told me when I first brought up this gang idea however many years ago—. He said he wants to take down Osiris."

A scoff something like a laugh. "Yeah, definitely drunk. That's impossible." He kept looking around his map, but before his next suggestion the music caught his attention. He listened to the accordions and Russian lyrics. "What's this?"

"What's what?"

"The song, dude."

"Oh! It's an old Soviet song. I can change it...."

"Nah, man. This is cool as Hell. I wanna sample it. What's it called?"

"Крутится, вертится шар голубой." Roach looked at him blankly and blinked. "I'll just text it to you. It's one of my favourites."

"Oh? And what are your other favourites?" He started to back out of the hangar through its smaller side garage door. It opened automatically as he reversed toward it. Roach didn't have a remote for it, but Thyne was too busy looking through his phone for his favourite songs to notice the oddity.

"It's from my favourite movie. I don't know if you've seen it." He turned up the volume and played *Over the Rainbow*.

97

"*The Wizard of Oz?*"

Thyne beamed. "Yeah! Have you seen it?"

"I actually haven't." He was embarrassed to admit it. Why was he embarrassed?

Thyne clapped adorably. "Oh! I'll get to show it to you!"

"Guess so."

They were on what could generously be called a road when Roach glanced toward Thyne, having noticed movement in his periphery, and saw an unlit cigarette hanging out of his mouth. He leaned over and snatched it quickly out. "No. No smoking in the *Locust.*"

Thyne pouted and snatched the cigarette to slam it back into the box then look out at the desert rolling by. "Cunt."

Roach rolled his eyes. "Not all of us are billionaires who can afford new upholstery annually. You smoke in your cars?"

"I do."

"Disgusting."

"So I won't be allowed to smoke in your apartment, either?"

"What? Of course you can smoke in the apartment. I've already told you it's a mess."

"Wouldn't want to '*ruin the upholstery,*'" he said the quote with a mocking posh voice and holding an invisible glass of wine.

Roach let out a one-syllable chuckle. "Dude, you're gonna laugh when you see it."

"What's the difference, then? If you don't care about your furniture smelling like smoke, why does it matter in the *Locust?*"

"Because my brother and I basically built this car from scratch, and we got our couch at the dump. It doesn't mean shit to me." He shrugged. "And besides, if the upholstery gets ruined in the car, we're the ones who will have to replace it. Not to mention pay for the materials."

"You're both mechanics?"

He nodded and started listing, counting each item with a finger: "Mechanics. Interior Techs. Paint Techs. Drivers. Engineers. All things car, basically. I'm actually excited to get to talk to Jean-Jacques. I've always wondered how similar aero-mechanics are to auto mechanics."

"You've got all those skills, but you choose to be a musician and criminal instead?"

His only response was a sigh and roll of his eyes.

"I didn't mean it as a bad thing. I respect it."

"Oh, shut up. No you don't."

"Why wouldn't I?"

He looked at him between glances through the front windshield: "You're rich as

Hell. If you were me, you'd give up the art for the money. You'd leave Compton to go somewhere more stable and slave away at some body shop ten hours a day waiting for retirement. Desperately trying to 'pull yourself up by your bootstraps'. You don't even like music according to Francis. Who the fuck doesn't like music, dude?"

"You sure do like to make assumptions about me, mate. We're listening to music from my phone *right now*. I even introduced a new song to you, if you recall."

"But you don't like opera, and apparently my library on shuffle is a risk factor for making you pissy. Though, I think I'm beginning to gather that there's probably not a damn thing on this planet that isn't at risk of sending you into a tizzy."

Thyne huffed, but getting too angry at the comment would only prove it correct. He rolled his eyes and pouted for a while, his gaze tracing the rolling horizon again. Three songs later, he disconnected his phone from the radio and, in the newfound silence, said, "Play whatever you want, then."

"It's fine, man. I like all music. Just play whatever. I realise there are some genres that just aren't for everyone. Opera's not exactly popular. Just seemed like an over-reaction when Franky literally pulled a gun on me over it."

"I have a complicated relationship with music."

"Oh? Care to elucidate some?"

"No."

There were about ten minutes of silence before Roach slid his phone out of his pocket and used its voice function to, "Connect to JXF43421." The speakers dinged. "Play 66535478KL113NM.ktp."

"That's quite the name," muttered Thyne.

"It's a project file. I'm still working on it." The song started with a discordant MIDI melody that transferred slowly into an arpeggio on a jazzy sounding electric guitar. The percussion was synthetic and minimalist. There was a reverb on the entire track that made Thyne wonder if it was recorded in a big empty room, but it must have been digitally added considering it was on almost all layers of the track including those that were created on the computer. The reason Roach played this song in particular for Thyne wasn't evident until the bridge:

It sampled the original studio recording of a song once sold by Maitland and used in a ballet what made it famous. Thyne instantly recognised it from the first blare of brass. He had turned off the stereo before he even realised he was moving.

Back to silence....

Five minutes later: "So what's the problem with Maitland?"

Thyne only shook his head and wiped a tear from his eye before it would give away his sorry state to Roach. He couldn't handle being mocked for it, so he elected to stare out the window and listen to the voices.

About fifteen minutes later, Roach parked across two spaces in the back of a large parking lot. The Desert Mart he had mentioned was almost as barren as the land around it, but there were a few cars scattered around the lot. "You wanna go in, dude?"

He had stopped crying by then, but his voice was still whimpery when he nodded and said, "Alright."

The cold from the night before had been entirely replaced with unbearable heat. Thyne shed both of his outer layers when he stepped out into the sun and could swear he felt himself catching fire under its merciless stare. Roach seemed to be struggling, too. He pinched the front of his shirt and fanned himself with it as he watched Thyne. Before they started toward the front, Roach pressed a button on his fob to lock the doors: a satisfying beep, and when that was finished he pressed another button. All of the windows turned instantly to mirrors, reflecting the unrelenting desert sun, and on the roof a small solar panel opened up.

"You like it?"

"I understand the mirrored windows, but what's the solar panel do?"

"I made it myself. It's powering the AC while the car is off. Save the battery, y'know? The reflective tinters were my brother's idea. Couldn't begin to explain how he made them work. He's better at that sorta shit than I am."

Thyne smiled weakly at him. "Impressive, mate."

They started toward the doors. "Thanks, dude. I don't know if I've ever used it in heat this bad, though. It's gotta be getting up to the triple digits, y'know? Maybe already is."

On their way inside, a patron was leaving, and Roach stopped when he spotted her drop half of a submarine sandwich in a trash can outside. Thyne didn't notice he was walking alone until he turned around and, to his horror, saw Roach reaching into the garbage bin.

"Oh Gods, mate. Are you serious?"

He found the sandwich and pulled it out. After brushing off some napkins and a cigarette butt from the top, he looked at Thyne with a dumbfounded sort of air to him. "What? *She* clearly doesn't want it."

Thyne slapped the sandwich out of Roach's hands and dragged him by the wrist into the store. "I will *buy* you something to eat, you nasty wanker."

"Aw, but it's tuna salad."

"Well, she obviously got it from here, so I'll buy you a new one! Now come on. Petulant rat." He rolled his eyes and huffed, but Roach could see the sides of his mouth struggling to keep downturned.

"So you're going to buy me lunch? Like a date?" He fluttered his eyelashes and nudged him playfully.

Thyne laughed. "Shut up." His gaze left Roach and took in the massive interior of this store. "Are you sure this isn't a mall? How many floors is it?"

"They're usually five, but I think this one's only three."

"And this is all one singular store?"

He nodded.

"I am genuinely astounded."

"Well, let's start with that date, hm?"

Thyne blushed and gently bumped into him while they walked. "As long as you promise not to eat out of the bin there, too. I swear, you're worse than Franky."

"Worse than Franky?"

"The man will eat anything."

Roach smiled, but it was short lived. He didn't notice at first, so when Thyne looked up at him and made him more consciously aware of his expression, he wiped his face clean of emotion.

Thyne frowned. "Why do you do that? Let yourself smile. It's okay, mate."

"Well, would you look at that? This Desert Mart has elevators. They don't normally have those, disabled people be damned."

Thyne puffed out his cheek and sighed. "Just take us to the bloody bistro for your sandwich, you tosser."

Chapter 9
Adventuring

Jean-Jacques was awoken by slobbery kisses on his face from his dog. He scolded her in a drawling sleepy sort of French that was hardly intelligible, but she ignored it and jumped on his chest, her tail wagging a million miles an hour. He was only half awake until she barked, and his eyes shot open. His breaths were laboured as he looked around the room in a panic. He was hugging the dog tightly to his chest and shushing her, but when he realised where he was, he released her. While she was playfully biting at his hand as he swayed it around lazily, he was using his other hand to rub the sleep from his eyes. That he had not heard Grisha shouting at him to, "shut up little dog before I kill it," was a boon on his mood, and when he finally left the sleeping chambers in the back of the plane he was happy to find Dezba and Francis sitting in the settees at the fore of the vessel.

"Good morning," said Dezba as she brushed the powdered sugar from her scone off of her hand and held it out to shake his. "I'm Dezba. You must be Jean-Jacques. Sorry we didn't talk much last night."

He shook her hand, but before he could respond to her, he snipped, "Non! Juliette, non! Couche!" He gently tapped the dog's curious snout as it sniffed a chocolate muffin on the coffee table. She almost seemed to glare at him before promptly leaving the plane, the click of her claws on the cement outside getting quieter as she sniffed around for food her owner would not so *heartlessly* deprive her of.

"Sorry for her," he said as he rubbed the back of his neck and tossed an anxious smile around the room.

"Don't be sorry, son. She's precious! Come sit!" Dezba patted the seat beside her, and he did as she asked. "Have some breakfast. Thyne bought it for us. Isn't that sweet?"

He looked around the cabin. "Where is he?"

"Thyne and the tall one are procuring supplies from a retail market some fifteen miles eastward," replied Francis, "Need you anything?"

Jean-Jacques generally understood English, but the antiquated manner in which Francis spoke made him question his grasp on the language. "Need me anything?"

"Francis, don't you know French?"

"Oui. I was born in France."

"Well, why don't you ask him in French, then?"

Francis didn't understand why she was making such a request. Jean-Jacques knew English, and if someone knew English, surely they could understand him when he spoke it. Still, he repeated the sentiment in French, his verbiage just as antiquated in his native tongue.

"Are they at the Desert Mart?" he replied in English so as to not be rude to Dezba. Francis nodded. "I should text Monsieur Thyne?" The other two shrugged.

Shortly after this conversation, Thyne's phone buzzed in his pocket, but he didn't notice from the midst of an argument with Roach:

"Dude, don't you have any faith in people?"

"No, I don't! Exhibit A!" He gestured at Roach.

"Exhibit A? What the Hell, man? Exhibit A is you! You're the one with a billion fucking Euros in the bank!"

"So you wouldn't trust someone like me in this ideal world of yours, then?" He smirked haughtily, having backed Roach into a metaphorical corner.

Roach stuttered for a moment and allowed his brow to furrow and fists to clench. He poked him in his chest as he shouted, "I'd fucking *kill* people like you, and who would fucking stop me!?"

Luckily, the Desert Mart was a ghost town, so their bickering was somewhat private. It just so happened they were in a large section of the store meant for children, so while Roach was voicing his violent thoughts, they were surrounded by a dichotomous visage of hyper-saturated colours and fluffy plushies. Thyne grabbed one and threw it into Roach's chest. "Come off it! You bloody twat, you're absolutely unbearable!"

Being attacked by a (plush) bear, in combination with Thyne's unintentional pun while throwing it, Roach's anger all but evaporated. His expression blanked, but he was stifling a laugh. "You're adorable, dude. I can't take you seriously right now."

He shouted a frustrated holler and stomped away from Roach, disappearing into an adjacent aisle where he sat on the floor and took out his phone. He leaned on the soft wall of plush toys behind him and finally noticed Jean-Jacques' message:

⌈ Your strange friend told me that you're out at the Desert Mart. Could you pick up dog food and a leash? ⌋

Though Jean-Jacques' message was in French, Thyne texted replied, ⟦ yeah. ⟧ in English before opening his messages with Francis: ⟦ This wanker is really getting on my bloody nerves. ⟧

⌈ You write of Roach? ⌋

⟦ Yes, idiot! ⟧

"Asking Francis to come teleport you away from me?"

He looked up at the mocking grin on Roach's punchable face and threw his phone at him. "You leave me alone!"

He watched the phone bounce off his chest and fall on the floor while taking a bite of his sandwich. Through his mouthful: "Nah, man. You're cute when you're angry. I think I'll keep bugging you."

"I will light you on fire!" He scrambled to his feet and opened his lighter in a quick flourish. He held the little flame between them, his shoulders heaving with each angry huff.

Roach finished chewing and calmly blew the flame out before taking another bite. "Do it. It'd be the best cooking you've ever done."

Thyne's reply was a lot of incoherent grumpy noises until he flicked the lighter back on and tried to put it on Roach's shirt to burn it. He dodged the incoming hand and grabbed Thyne by his outstretched wrist before he could fall, plucking him up off the ground like a bemused giant and chuckling as Thyne thrashed around cursing him.

He blew the flame out on the lighter again and dropped Thyne on the floor where he tumbled and nearly broke his arm. "You won't hurt me: you need my help." With that, he finished his sandwich and tossed the trash on the floor behind him.

Having been humiliated so succinctly, Thyne refused to let Roach see him crying. With his gaze on the floor and never going further up Roach's form than his knees, he reached for his nearby phone. After grabbing one of the plush toys and hugging it, he leaned against the aisle again and sent a message: ⟦ Come here, Franny. Take me away from him... ⟧

Roach's stomach stirred up with butterflies at the sight of Thyne so defeated. *'He's even hugging a teddy bear.'* "Come on, let's go to the pets section and look at the fish." He leaned down to offer his hand to Thyne, but he was suddenly in the appliance section with Francis standing in front of him. "Woah! What the fuck, man? Where's Thyne?"

"You have greatly upset and offended him. I am here to defend his honour."

"You challenging me to a duel or something, dude?" He sort of scoff-laughed as he looked around for Thyne. "How'd you teleport me like that?"

"Look me in the eyes, or I *shall* challenge you to a duel!"

He gave Francis his unamused dead-inside hazels, but they filled with intrigue when he noticed Francis' eyes were pale green. He was certain they were deep blue, sometimes teal. This shade of green seemed impossibly light to be natural. It made him realise retroactively that there was once a stream of Partha's where they were brown.

"Thyne is at the hangar and away from you. In addendum, I have procured the necessary and requested materials from all crewmates and brought said supplies to the hangar with him. You need only enter your car and return it to reunite with the rest of the crew."

"How'd you teleport us, Francis?"

"Thyne has asked me not to divulge such information…. Though such be me yen."

"So tell me anyway. He's not the boss of you."

"I shan't betray his trust."

Roach blew a sigh through his lips, puffing out his cheeks in the process. "Really twisting my arm here, man. I can't exactly threaten your life, 'cause you'll just blip away, but I really wanna know. Can I convince you? Could fix a car for you."

"I can't drive."

"Could teach ya."

"If I desired such a thing, I would choose my beloved Thyne as my mentor."

"Beloved?" His posture straightened. "What do you mean?"

"I mean I would rather my beloved Thyne teach me to drive be—."

"No, dude. Why are you calling him that?"

"Calling him what?"

An amused exhale. "Nevermind. How'd you teleport? You can tell me, dude. I'll keep it secret."

Francis groaned. "Alas! I will tell you, but Thyne will be angry."

"Thyne's always angry."

He pursed his lips. "Well, the truth is," he leaned toward Roach and whispered into his ear, "I am only half human."

Roach was leaning down, but Francis was only six inches shorter than him, so it wasn't very far. He replied in an unintentional whisper: "What's the other half, dude? Vampire? Wechuge?"

Francis chuckled and leaned back to speak normally. "No. It is an alien race called Etren, so ancient they existed before Pangea."

"So all Etrens can teleport?"

He shook his head. "No, I am unique in that regard."

He blinked.

"So, now that your curiosity has been sated, shall we depart?"

"You're coming with me?"

"A ride in your vehicle would be leagues more desirable than walking the entire trek back to the hangar."

"You can't just teleport back?"

"Oh, I suppose my answer to your inquiry was insufficient. I do not teleport. I control time."

A genuine grin so wide it bared his pearly white teeth. "That's rad as Hell, dude. Is that why you talk like a douchebag?" With a giggle, he noticed himself smiling, and as quick as it came, the smile was gone again.

Francis nodded. "I was born in 1657."

"So, do Etrens' eyes change colours a lot, then?"

He stroked his chin. "I don't think so. I've never met one."

"Then why are your eyes green right now, dude?"

"Oh, are they?" He pulled up his left sleeve and started to push his arm through time. Tattoos animated across it as if they were being penned and erased by a ghost beside him. Roach watched the display with his jaw agape. "Here it is. These be the notes pertaining to me eyes."

He showed Roach a tattoo of notes with flawless penmanship. He had to round over to his side for the words to be legible to him, but, because they were organised and specialised to Francis' niche needs, it was still hard to understand anything other than numbers and colours and, "does that say microwave?"

"Yes. Those eyes see in the microwave range."

"And that says radio, then, for the same reason?"

"Indeed."

"Do they work? Wouldn't you need receptors in your brain or something to make that work?"

He shrugged. "Of all my academia and pedigree, I have never forayed into the fields of medicine or neuroscience. But yes, I can see in those ranges when I am using those eyes."

"I assume they swapped your eyes entirely for different pairs. Did they do brain surgery on you when you got the ones that can see in infrared or whatever?"

Another shrug. "Mayhaps. I don't recall. I was not conscious for most of the procedures."

"Well, man, this is all wild. Good thing you didn't challenge me to a duel, huh? I'd definitely lose."

Francis pushed his eyes through time until they were replaced with his birth-given ones. With that settled, he pulled the puffy sleeve of his poet shirt back down over his tattooed forearm. "Yes, of course you would lose, but I thank you for reminding me that I came here to defend my beloved Thyne's besmirched honour."

"Okay...."

They stared awkwardly at each other for a moment before Francis finally spoke up: "Thyne is not to be mocked nor ridiculed nor 'man-handled' any longer, lest I slay thee."

Another beat of quiet staring.

"...Is that it, then?"

Francis shrugged. "I suppose."

Roach couldn't help but chuckle. "You're a hoot, dude. Let's blow this popsicle stand."

Jean-Jacques would need a scissor-lift to work on the plane, so while they were at the store, Roach and Francis bought a trailer to tow it behind the *Locust* with any other tools Francis deemed too heavy to fetch for the mechanic on his own. After being sure that the hangar was stocked with everything Jean-Jacques would need to fix the plane, it was time to start packing the *Locust* for the long trip back to LA. Francis' luggage consisted of a half-empty satchel he tossed carelessly into the back of the trunk, it having only a single change of clothes, a decanter of cologne, and two canned cocktails from the Icelandic airport.

Amongst the things they would take, Francis had offered to go to Dezba's house to pack her a bag. She appreciated the offer and gave him her key and a vague list of things she'd want, including her knitting needles and best yarns. When she inspected the suitcase's contents, she was disappointed to see that he hadn't under-stood which yarns in specific she requested, but it showed with only a slight purse of her lips. Ultimately, she thanked him and kept quiet to the miscommunication. She was mostly still having trouble coming to terms with the fact that he had super powers, let alone how they worked.

Roach's luggage was almost as light as Francis'. He hadn't expected to be away from home longer than a couple days. His shirt changed that morning from the bleach-stained t-shirt to a navy blue Nirvana shirt with not only its sleeves removed but the entire sides. It would help keep him cool in the oppressive heat of the desert on their long drive west, but the main benefit for the others was the way it showed off his strong arms and even allowed peeks at his abs when he leaned over. Otherwise, he was wearing all the same clothes he had left home in.

Unlike the others, Thyne had packed a lot before leaving England then packed even more in the grounded plane when he found out from Jean-Jacques how long it would take to fix the jet. It was by the time he had brought his fifth bag out to the car that Roach stopped him before trying to Tetris it into the small trunk. "Come on, dude. What could you possibly have in all these?"

"Jean-Jacques has given me a time-frame, and it will be at least a month, if not three entire months before my engine is fixed. So, put it in the boot, and mind your business."

He closed his eyes to take a calming breath and contain his rage. Thyne really had a knack for pushing his buttons in a way he had never come across. Usually stone-faced and in complete control of his emotions, he would never admit to how vulnerable and out of control the angry little Brit could make him feel.

When he came back with a sixth piece of luggage and a pillow, he claimed, "That's everything."

"It's not all gonna fit man. What's in this one? It's so fucking big, it's not gonna fit with all this other shit." He picked up a hard rolling suitcase that he had noticed was suspiciously light when he first tried to fit it in the trunk.

"None of your business! I need it, so just shove it in there or put something on the trailer you bought, you mangey bellend!"

Roach averted his eyes to hide their aching need to roll into the back of his head and unzipped the suitcase. Thyne tried to throw himself over the lid before Roach could lift it, but he was too slow. When he saw what was inside, he could not stop the smirk that followed. A set of soft hazel-greys on Thyne: "You need it, do you?"

Thyne's face was bright red. "You shut up!"

"Come on, man, this is adorable."

He slapped at his hands to try and close the luggage. "Shut up! Shut up! Just close it and put it in there before someone sees."

They looked toward the plane where Dezba was chatting with Francis and Jean-Jacques over what remained of breakfast.

Roach closed the suitcase but took it out of the trunk. He rolled it toward a door to a side room. Thyne rushed over to it to try and bring it back to the car, but when he turned around, Roach had all of Thyne's other bags hanging off of him. He gestured with his head for Thyne to open the side room door, and once they were both inside with the luggage, he flicked on the light. It was a small mostly empty chamber that was probably once used as a break room for staff of the old airstrip. Now it had only a flickering fluorescent light over a large metal table.

"What are you doing?" asked Thyne as Roach started piling his bags onto the table.

"Dude, you suck at packing. You filled your biggest suitcase with nothing but plushes, you adorable little dumbass. I'm going to repack for you."

His face somehow became redder, and he huffed once. "I was in a rush because *someone* gave me a strict time limit!"

He started unpacking the plushies from the suitcase, holding back smiles and laughter with great effort. His voice was nearly cracking with joy when he replied, "And your best friend controls time, so what's the problem, dude?"

"Right, remind me to flay him for telling you. But his powers don't work like that, and you didn't know he had them at the time."

"He said he wanted to tell me. Why were you making him keep it secret?"

Thyne was stupefied by the question and blubbered nothingness before managing a coherent thought: "Are you high?"

"Not at the moment. Why? You got some weed in one of these?"

Poor Thyne was so apoplectic with rage he couldn't form a single syllable of coherent speech. He held the sides of his head and tried to capture a thought in his reeling mind, but everything went silent when he saw Roach unzip the bag with his boxers in it.

The next thing he knew he was half on the floor and half in Roach's arms. "You okay, man? You need some water?"

"What happened?"

"You fainted. You want me to carry you to the car or plane or something?"

His brow furrowed, and he shoved Roach off of him, sitting himself upright. "Leave me alone, mate. How long was I out?"

"It's only been like a minute. I caught you before you hit your head on the concrete, but I still think you should get some water and maybe be wary of falling asleep. Come on, dude, I'll carry you. There's no shame in it."

"I can move on my own, thank you very much," he snipped and stood, gently slapping away Roach's hand when he offered it for help.

Thyne went to the *Locust* and sat sideways in the passenger's seat, leaning on his knees and holding his head in his hands as it seemed to want to spin right off his neck.

Alone, Roach allowed himself to smile at all of Thyne's stuffed animals. Amongst the other things he felt necessary enough to pack were fourteen novels, all of which Roach had copies of at home, big round reading glasses, a case of juiceboxes, a case of cigarettes, a fluffy pale blue sweater, and a packet of bang snaps. There was a warmth burning his cheeks and butterflies stirring him up inside. "Adorable," he muttered as he packed.

When he was finished, he had managed to turn Thyne's six bags and pillow into just two bags. Not everything was included, however, so he brought out the things he hadn't packed and crouched down with them in front of Thyne. "Hey man, Cali's hot as Hell. I don't think you'll need these blankets or jackets. If you do somehow get cold, we've got jackets and stuff at home. And I've got lots of books including all the ones you wanted to bring." Thyne didn't move or respond at all. "Sooo… if you're okay with that, I'll bring this stuff back up into the plane, and we can get going. Sound chill?"

A vague nod.

"Great. I also left this guy out." He dug into his armful of things and pulled out an antique teddy bear that was hardly keeping together. "Seems important." Thyne still wasn't moving, so Roach gently set the bear on the dash then carried the other unpacked things back into the plane. He dropped them on the coffee table while the others were mid-conversation and announced, "We're leaving in a minute or two. Stretch your legs while you can."

After two hours of watching the vast orange wasteland pass them by, Thyne's grip around Oliver's teddy finally started to relax. The water bottle Roach had given him before the trip was unopened, but he found himself growing thirsty. The others had been talking and listening to music from Francis' phone, but Thyne was focused entirely on the voices and his text messages.

"Oh, hey you. You're finally awake," said Roach when he noticed Thyne stirring in the back. He stifled a laugh at his own reference, but he was glad to see a small smirk from Thyne in the rearview.

His voice was soft and sweet: "I wasn't asleep."

"Yeah," he coughed to cover a chuckle, "You were trying to cross the border? Walked right into that Imperial ambush, like us and that thief over there." He gestured to Francis in the passenger's seat.

Thyne giggled. "Muppet."

Dezba, also in the backseat, leaned toward Thyne to try and glimpse his phone. "Who have you been messaging? Partha?"

"No. My boyfriend. I should message Partha, though. Still haven't laid into him for taking the piss with that address."

While Thyne typed out an angry message to Partha about the mistaken street names, Roach commanded everyone's attention by asking, "Who's hungry?"

They pulled off the interstate for some lunch, but rather than taking them to a restaurant, Roach parked at, "A petrol station? We just filled up. You know I'm absolutely not running low on cash, don't you? We could go to a proper restaurant."

He shooed away the idea. "Nah, man. This place has a restaurant-type-thing inside."

"'Restaurant-type-thing'? What the bloody Hell does that mean?"

"Just come inside, dude. Stop being such a stick in the mud."

Despite Thyne's continued bitching, they went inside. Roach brought the others to a computer monitor where they could get something made-to-order. So, while Thyne, Dezba, and Francis were busy perusing the options, Roach went outside to smoke and investigate a vending machine he had seen on the side of the building. It seemed to be powered-down, but he could see through its door that there were several goodies on offer. With his cigarette between his teeth, he used both hands to remove his industrial piercings. After some fidgeting, they both extended and revealed specialised hooks on the ends: lockpicks. He pushed them carefully into the vending machine's lock, and after only thirty seconds, the door clicked and creaked slightly open. He pulled it open the rest of the way and immediately grabbed a sandwich from the bottom shelf.

"What are you doing, son?"

"Oh, hey Em. I'm getting some lunch."

"Why are you getting it from there? Thyne's paying for us. I'm sure he'll pay for you, too."

"Nah, man. I want this." He held up his sandwich. "I fucking love egg salad."

"Roach honey, I don't think that machine is plugged in. You might get sick if you eat something perishable from it."

He ignored her concern and perused the machine's drink options. "Why'd you come out here anyway, Emmie?"

"Thyne was looking for you."

"Why didn't he come out, then? He's probably dying for a smoke."

"I think he stayed in because he's having trouble paying with Euros. He asked me to come get you to figure out what you want for lunch."

"Well, tell him I'm golden. And, uh…," he took out his wallet and tossed it to Dezba. "Here. My treat. PIN is 3825."

She brought the wallet inside looking for Thyne. He was fuming and rattling something off she didn't catch, then, a moment later, Francis translated to Spanish for the worker they were speaking with. She didn't know the language, but from the way Thyne was waving around his cash, she could only assume he was still having trouble paying for their food with his foreign currency. When he felt Dezba tap his shoulder, he spun around and shouted, "What!?"

"Don't yell at me. Roach said he'll pay."

He snatched the wallet out of her hand and opened it, but his anger was replaced with embarrassment when he saw a condom in the folds of the leather. He cleared his throat awkwardly, muttered, "Lo siento," to the worker, then pulled Francis back to the monitor with Roach's card in hand. "What did you want, Em? I'm sorry for shouting."

"Just a turkey club for me, and it's okay, son. I just feel bad for the workers. It's not their fault they can't accept foreign currency."

His blush deepened. "Euros are worth so much more than the Monopoly money they use over here. I just—. I haven't had any issue using it this entire trip until now."

"Well," began Francis, "it is not dissimilar to having dropped two bars of gold on the counter.... I know from experience."

He sighed. "Yeah I know. I'll tip them a lot. What do you want, Frankenstein?"

"I'm not hungry."

"And what did Roach say he wanted?"

Dezba rubbed the back of her neck. "He found a vending machine outside."

"Well, guess it's just our sandwiches and some sodas, then.... Bollocks. It's asking for a PIN. Franky, go ask—."

"3825," said Dezba.

After leaving €340 in the tip jar, Thyne brought the food outside and stood beside the car to light himself a cigarette. Dezba was stretching her legs against the curb nearby, and Francis was laying across the backseat drinking from his flask. A quick scan of the area later, and Thyne spotted Roach approaching the car with a bottle of chocolate milk in one hand and a half-eaten sandwich in the other.

"I suppose you still won't let us eat in the *Locust*?" complained Thyne.

"You suppose correctly."

He scoffed. "Fine, but I'm going to take my sweet time eating."

A shrug. "No worries, dude. I should do my afternoon prayer while we're stopped anyway."

With an eye roll and another drag of his cigarette, he noticed a spot of pale blue on Roach's sandwich and coughed on his own smokey breath. "Stop!" he managed to say hoarsely.

"Stop what?" He looked around.

"Mould." He coughed. "Mould on your bread."

"Yeah I know." Another bite.

Thyne gagged. "You're gonna be sick, mate."

"Nah, dude. I eat mould all the time."

Talk was small for the next few hours of travel. There were some road trip games tossed around the car, and when those got boring, some surface level "What's your favourite __?" type questions were the new default. It wasn't until Dezba asked about one of Roach's tattoos that the conversation took a turn:

"So, do the hieroglyphics on your arm actually mean anything, son?"

"Mine? Yeah, it's a story."

"What's the story?" asked Dezba.

"Well, it's only half of the story. My brother's tattoo is the other half."

"But what's the story?" whined Thyne.

Roach took a deep breath to calm himself as Thyne, yet again, grated on his nerves. "My half is an account of Set chopping Osiris into fourteen pieces, and my brother's half depicts the story of Set taking out Horus' eye."

Dezba had leaned forward to trace a line of the small hieroglyphs down his arm. She retreated when he was finished with his summary and asked, "Is Set like a God?"

"He's not *like* a God. He *is* a God."

"What's he the God of?"

"If you don't know, I'm not telling you. Why are we talking about my tattoos anyway? Let's talk about Thyne's. Thyne, what's with the spoon on your forearm?"

He glared at Roach through the rearview.

"Is that what it is? A spoon?" She turned around to look into the backseat and held out her hand, asking to see Thyne's arm.

He let her hold his wrists to get a better look at both forearm tattoos and said, "To answer your question, Dezba, Set is the God of sandstorms, chaos, destruction, and violence."

There was the slightest blench in her before she fully retreated from Thyne and looked at Roach with a horrified set of big brown eyes. "Is that true, son?"

His grip around the steering wheel tightened enough that his knuckles went white, but he remained otherwise deadpan. "Yeah."

"Do you worship this God of violence and destruction?" She didn't realise she was rubbing at the cross on her necklace to comfort herself.

"I worship the same God as you. My appreciation and acknowledgement of other Gods doesn't discount my devotion to Allah. Fucking Hell, Thyne, why'd you tell her, dude?"

He feigned a frown and mocked, "Poor little Clayton."

"Francis, tell us why Thyne has a spoon tattooed on his arm," demanded Roach. Despite his best efforts to sound calm, there was a rumbling rage on the lower ends of his already-deep register.

"Don't you dare, Franny."

Francis nodded. "I shan't."

"Thyne, you're a real prick, you know that? Now Dezba thinks I'm some sort of monster."

His sarcastic pout persisted. "Are you not?"

He slammed his palm against the steering wheel. "That's it. I'm stopping for a cigarette." He pulled off at the next exit and parked haphazardly across three spots in a strip mall parking lot. The outward expression of his rage had all but evaporated, so when he slammed his door and rushed away from the car lighting himself a cigarette, the other three were startled by the sound. They watched him smoke from the car, but eventually Francis stepped outside and approached, much to Thyne's bemusement.

"I apologise for Thyne."

"Leave me alone, dude."

"The spoon is a memorial tattoo." Roach stopped smoking mid-drag. "For his late lover, Oliver York."

A slam of the car door caught both of their attentions. "Stop fucking telling him things!"

Thyne rushed up to them and grabbed his big-mouthed friend by his wrist to attempt dragging him back to the car, but Francis wriggled free and said, "No, Thyne. He's helping us. He's part of the crew. He deserves to know more about us."

"Oh yeah!? Well then, why don't you tell him about how you put your bloody wife into the betting pool during a game of dice like she was no better than a few quid!?" He savoured the subtle shock in Roach's eyes before continuing, "Or how you were *enslaved* but still somehow manage to be a greedy selfish bastard on the daily." He turned toward Roach: "If you really want someone to lay into for being everything you hate, it's this cunt right here."

As quickly as he came, he was leaving and lighting himself a cigarette on the other side of the parking lot.

A warm breeze blew the hot ash from Roach's durry into his arm. It snapped him out of some sort of trance. "You bet your wife in a gambling game?"

For the first time since they had met, Francis was blushing. "I… I knew I would win…."

"Dude…. That's fucked up."

His lip quivered, but he sucked up his sadness and drowned it in rum. With a wipe of the excess dribble from his lips, he said, "I know, and you will be delighted to learn that my life has been a maelstrom down into Hell ever since the fateful blunder."

"Guess you were enslaved afterwards, then? By her? When was this?"

"No. I was enslaved as a child. Juan Ya was much more blunt in her anger with me when she made an attempt on my life. She even—." His voice broke into silence, which was quickly filled by the sound of his rum sloshing against the side of its metal prison. He drank more than could possibly still be in the little flask.

Roach took a drag from his cigarette and trailed his gaze from Francis to Thyne off in the distance. "Go keep Em company, will you?"

When Francis had gone back into the car, drinking the entire walk over, Roach flicked away his cigarette and approached Thyne.

"What do you want now, you bellend?"

"I just want to…," he eyed Thyne's tattoo, "Apologise."

Noticing where Roach was looking, Thyne crossed his bare arm over his stomach to hide the tattoo and glared. "Then do. You have a lot to apologise for."

The subtlest of scowls. "Sorry for pushing about the tattoo. I didn't know you've lost someone so important to you. I've uh…. I know the feeling." He held up his left hand and wiggled one of the rings on its third finger.

Thyne's glare softened. Smoke fell from his slightly-parted lips effortlessly, dancing through the arid air around them. "How old are you?" he whispered.

"Thirty-two." A beat. "But anyway," he shoved his hands in his pockets and squinted into the setting sun over the flat horizon, "We're losing daylight." It seemed like he wanted to leave, but he lingered and watched the colourful sky. Now that he had reminded himself of his late husband, he was letting his perfect memory entertain him with recollections of a cross-country trip they had taken together. On the trip, it was during a sunset just as prismatic as this that he had proposed. The only other time he had seen the sky so explosive with colour was during the war: a mortar had shelled some sort of tanker truck with a variety of chemicals that exploded beautifully into prismatic clouds not unlike those on the horizon. It was a memory as welcome in his mad mind as his wedding.

A minute of silent reminiscing later, he muttered, "See you back in the car," and turned to leave. Just as he took his first step, however, he felt a pinching pain on the back of his neck and immediately grabbed the area. "Fuck. What was that?" He turned to Thyne.

"What was what?"

"Did you just do something to my neck?"

He shook his head while Roach rubbed at the sting. "There was a wasp flying around…."

He immediately started to search for it. Thyne could swear there was a light in his eyes that wasn't there before. "Where? I love wasps. What kind? I hope it was a cuckoo."

"A cuckoo?"

His eyes were smiling despite the deadpan expression on the rest of his face. "Yeah, dude. They're this sick kinda turquoise colour. Sorta like Franky's eyes, now that I think about it." His reeling mind seemed to sadden him, and all the light drained from his eyes, "Oh, but it wouldn't be a cuckoo if it stung me." He rubbed the spot again and resumed looking for the bug. "Anyway, I'll see you back at the car, but flag me down if you find the wasp again."

"Why?"

"So I can catch it."

"Why do you want to catch it?"

"To add to my collection, dude. I'm an entomologist." Roach noticed Thyne's cheeks flush at the comment and found it odd, but he decided not to ask about it. "Alright. Let me go make sure Franky's not hurling on the upholstery. Your comments really got him upset and drinking…. Y'know… more than usual."

Chapter 10
The Inn

The room was spinning. His heart was racing. Another round of shots slammed against the bar in unison, but the sound was silence compared to the blaring bass shaking the walls.

"Where are you from?" he shouted to the woman who had been drinking with him for the past thirty minutes.

"The hills," she shouted back, "What about you?"

"Bermuda."

"What?"

"BERMUDA!"

"Like the triangle?"

He laughed at her, but the music drowned it out, making him seem to only be smiling. "Yeah sure, like the triangle. You wanna go somewhere quiet?"

Her brow furrowed. "I do *not* need to go on a diet!"

He shook his hands. "No! Do you want to go somewhere *quieter?*"

"OH!" A giggle he could only see. "Okay! My place or yours?"

"My place is in the middle of the Atlantic."

"Okay!"

He offered his arm for her to link with his and started to lead her outside, but on his way someone else caught his eye. With her still on his arm, he approached the attractive man. "Hey! Wanna drink?"

He didn't hear.

"HEY!"

"Oh, hey! You're Party the Kid!"

"DO YOU WANT A DRINK!?"

"HELL YEAH!"

After another hour of drinking and shouting over the music, Partha and his two catches of the night finally went outside where they could hear each other. "Your name was Caroline. And yours was…?"

"Oscar. I'm a big fan, man."

"Well, let's go!" He turned toward Caroline, who was looking at him just as expectantly.

After a moment of awkward staring, Caroline giggled and said, "Why are you looking at me?"

"We were going to your house in the hills."

"What? I thought we were going to your hotel room."

"I don't have a hotel room. I'm staying with a friend."

"You said you had a room in *The Atlantic*."

He laughed. "No, I said my house is in the middle of the Atlantic. Like the ocean. Because it's in Bermuda."

"Bermuda is a place? I thought it was a triangle, like cute or isosceles." Both of the men howled at her ignorance, but she was too drunk to be offended, instead joining them in their laughter. "Okay, well we can go to my house," she said as she linked her arm back up with Partha's and waited for Oscar to link up on his other side.

In her luxurious mansion, they got up to the expected behaviour. Partha did a line off Caroline's chest and another line off Oscar's penis not too much later. He was the centre of a satisfying sandwich for round one, but round two was a double-team on Caroline. His heart was beating so hard, if he weren't stupid drunk he would have rightfully worried for his health.

In the morning, Caroline's cook made them all a lovely breakfast and her signature "hangover cure" which was an abhorrent mix of sweet tea, pickle juice, orange juice, and pepto bismol.

By two in the afternoon, Partha and Oscar were leaving and shared a cab down as far as cars could travel toward the flooded parts of the city. Partha got Oscar's number and let him take a sober selfie with him under the condition that, "no one finds out about us, okay? That was a one-time thing, and I don't wanna get cancelled again for sleeping with a fan."

"No problem, man. I don't want you getting cancelled again, either. People are so annoying. It's not *your* fault Farah was married."

"Exactly!"

"Did you know she was married?"

"Yeah, but it was *her* choice to cheat."

"Heh... yeah. Well, thanks for the selfie... and the sex." He chuckled nervously.

"Of course."

They parted ways, and Partha made the long trek back to Roach and River's apartment. When he went inside, Perlie was painting the dogs' nails. All of them except for Aphid rushed up to him to greet him, and he happily crouched down to be smothered in puppy kisses. They got nail-polish on his pants, but he didn't notice until after the greetings.

"You look like shit," said Perlie, "Where have you been?"

"What does it look like? I've been wading through the garbage out there all morning. I need to shower."

"Showers here don't work. Roach's gym card is over there on the TV stand, though."

"The gym is flooded."

"Yeah, it's bad today, huh? Well, my house is probably blocked by the flood, then. Guess you could try someone else in the building. They're all friends with the twins, but since neither of them are here... uh... good luck."

He sighed, grabbed a change of clothes, and went outside to try his luck with the neighbours. No one answered the first two doors, and the third was an angry old woman who closed it on his face only halfway through his hurried explanation. Fourth time, it seemed, was the charm. He was given attention by a middle-aged heavyset woman who was crossing her arms and leaning on her door frame to look him up and down judgmentally as he blubbered at her:

"Hello, ma'am. I'm staying with the Roaches for a while, and they don't have running water, and the gym is flooded, and I'm not from around here, so I don't know anyone else around, and as you can probably smell, I really need a shower. Heh. And anyway, long story short, I was wondering if I could maybe use yours?"

She was wordless and attacking him with her eyes for an agonising three minutes. "What's in it for me?"

He let out a breath he had been holding and put on the most charming smile he could muster. "Well, what would you like? I don't have much to offer other than money or my body." He wiggled his eyebrows.

"Deal." She let him inside. Once the door was closed, he tried to lean in and kiss her, but she stopped him with a hand on his chest that hit him like a wall. "What are you doing?"

"Oh... uh... er... I thought...."

"Money." She laid out her hand.

"O-of course!" He took out his wallet, his hands trembling as he opened it and started to count through his cash.

"All of it."

He could have left and tried a different neighbour, but he was feeling far too awkward now that the door was closed. With a nervous gulp, he took all of his cash out and handed it to her. In various currencies, it totalled something like €1,780.

While she counted it: "Down the hall on the left."

After his shower and another awkward exchange with the stranger who had rented it to him, he rushed back to the twins' apartment and spent a good twenty minutes just cuddling the dogs and scrolling through his phone. Thyne's angry message about the address mix-up made his lip quiver and eyes water, but he cuddled Diana closer to keep from crying in front of Perlie.

"The flooding is letting up, so I'm going to go buy some food while the streets are clear. You want anything?"

He looked at her and sucked up his sadness. "Sure."

"What do you want?"

"Dunno."

"Alright, well just give me the money for it, and I'll text you what they have."

"Cash?"

"Gotta be cash in LA, dude. Most places here don't have stable enough electronics or internet connections to take cards. There are some in the hills, but I'm not going all the way up there." He murmured something. "What?"

He sniffled. "She took all my cash."

Perlie snorted. "Thicker woman just downstairs?" He nodded. "That's Helena. She's a bitch, but she loves Roach. I think they dated." She stroked her chin. "Anyway, in that case, I'll see what I can afford for you."

"Thank you."

"No problem. If you decide to go out, make sure to lock the dogs in this room."

After she left, he spent another four minutes feeling sorry for himself before dragging his luggage closer and rummaging through it for his coke. There was only a dusting left clinging to the inside of the bag, and he felt his heart skip a beat. "I can't be out," he said before sitting upright and starting to properly dig with both hands through his belongings. "There's gotta be another bag."

The dogs were stirred up by his frantic energy, and by the time he was dumping his duffel out on the floor, the puppies were both barking. "Hush! Hush!" He said as he slammed his hand around on his things to separate everything. "No! No! I can't be out!" His breaths were laboured. "Stop barking! STOP!" Aphid joined the younger dogs, but his bark was much deeper and quieted the puppies. "SHUT UP, APHID!" He nearly hit the panicking dog, but he managed to keep control of himself. Still, he was shaky and desperate when he grabbed the bag and started rubbing the vaguely-dusted plastic on his gums.

He collapsed on the floor, weeping, and when Aphid saw this, he rushed over to him and started nudging him with his nose. "I'm okay," he whimpered to the whining dog before pulling him in for a hug. Aphid was trembling almost as much as Partha.

Another fifteen minutes elapsed, during most of which Partha was the foundation of a comforting dogpile. With Aphid calmer now but still in his arms, he kicked his phone toward his hands and called his father.

"Heya, kid. How's LA?"

"Daddy," he whimpered, "I... I'm... sad." He couldn't bring himself to admit that he was using again, but there was a depression starting to weigh on him like the depths of the ocean.

"Aw, Party, what's wrong?"

A beat.

Richard knew what the lack of response must have meant. "Well, kid, you said you wanted to do a vlog while you were there, right? Why don't you pop out that selfie stick and go film something for the fans? Maybe the Hollywood sign!"

"I don't know, Daddy. It's really ugly here...."

"Well, it'd be good for you to go out and get some not-so-fresh air." He chuckled. "It doesn't have to be for the fans. It can just be for me. I haven't been to LA since before you were born. It's where I took your mother for our honeymoon."

Partha wept. His mother died when he was too young to remember or miss her. What made him emotional was the idea of ruining whatever magic was left in his father's heart for his late wife by showing him what LA and Orange Counties had become.

"Don't cry, son.... It'll be okay. I won't be able to come get you for a couple weeks, but I'm sure there's another ship you could get some work on to get out of there sooner. Are you having second thoughts about the whole... um... the crime thing?" He sounded hopeful, which only broke Partha more.

"I'm out of blow," he cried, "Oh, Daddy, I'm sorry! I know you spent so much on all that rehab, and I'm sorry! I just need it! I need more...." A long beat of silence followed, broken only by Partha's sniffles and mewls. "Daddy? Are you still there?"

"Yeah, kid. I'm still here. I love you. I worry about you, but... you're a grown man. You can make your own mistakes." He meant to say 'decisions,' but he didn't correct himself. "I just want you to be safe and happy and healthy. That's all I ever want."

"I know," he whimpered, "I'm sorry."

"You don't have to be sorry, Party. Just, go outside and do your vlog, okay? Focus on your work and being creative. It'll help you feel better."

"...Okay."

"Alright? I gotta go, now."

"I love you, Daddy. I'm sorry."

"I love you too, kid. I'm always so proud of you...."
Click.

'*The darkness come again.*'
Thyne in his arms.
'*Mind is playing tricks again.*'
Flask on the floor.
'*I cannot face this veil again.*'
Perhaps if he could smell he would note the scent of cheap fabric softener on his pillowcase. If he could see, he would note the mundane furnishings in the room around them. His mouth smacked of thirst, but when his flask fell from his limp hand an hour prior, it may as well have fallen to the bottom of the sea. The weight of Thyne on his arm and chest—. The deafening silence of the desert outside—. It was all white noise.

Thyne had turned off the light two hours before then. He had fallen asleep an hour and a half after that. But to Francis, time was a series of eternities. There was nothing in his present reality to prove itself to him. '*Who's to say I'm not still in the void?*'

He decided to test reality.

In Mandarin: "I love you."

Thyne stirred.

In an alien tongue from Jupiter: "I love you, Thyne."

A groan and incoherent mumble.

Francis said it again in Ancient Sumarian.

In Swedish.

In Ancient Greek.

Old English.

Welsh.

He said it in every language he did not share with Thyne. If he replied with anything less than confusion—.

"I love you, too, twat," he mumbled sleepily as he turned onto his other side and shoved his back into Francis' embrace. "Go to sleep."

Tears welled in Francis' eyes and poured down his cheeks. He was crying, but he couldn't feel the sensation physically, nor could the sleepy man in his arms. He was unaware, but his test was flawed: he had forgotten that Thyne knew Ancient Greek (not to mention the number of times he had drunkenly slobbered the confession in Mandarin before then). To Francis, it was all the proof he needed that he was, '*still in the void.*' … "It feels so real sometimes."

An eternity of silence followed.

"I miss you, Thyne. I miss you more than anything…. More than anything."

Thyne turned back toward him and said something, but Francis was lost. He heard only a pulsing wail like the sirens at the end of the world. He felt the rocking of a ship and the salt of a breeze. He tasted his own blood. And soon thereafter the darkness opened up and took him. It showed him the imminent end like a haunting spectre of death. He whispered mad nothingness into the cloud of future memories. There was a warmth and familiarity washing over him. The ship kept rocking, but the sirens became the pleasant squeals of friendly gulls. The taste of blood became the taste of salt and lime. The darkness became his greatest love.

"Francis!" The visions all turned out like a light when he felt a strike across his cheek. "Franky, what's going on!?"

His eyes fluttered open. The bedside lamp was on, and bathed in its yellow glow, straddling his increasingly intrigued body was, "My angel Thyne." A soft smile.

Thyne blushed and started. He readjusted to be sitting more upright and only turned redder when he noticed Francis was at attention. "Are y-you okay, Frankenstein?"

His smile saddened but remained. After a peck on the knuckles of Thyne's left hand, he tossed it gently to his side and said, "I am lost again, but you always find me."

"Lost…?"

He smiled sweetly. "Yes, dear. Always a little lost out here."

He looked around. "In… America?"

He floated his hand around in a vague meaningless gesture.

Thyne stopped straddling Francis and curled back up beside him, but to say he was concerned would be an understatement. He wrapped his strong arms around Francis' lanky torso and squeezed. "I'm right here, Franky. It's okay. Just try and get some sleep."

Thirty minutes of silence elapsed, but to Francis it was another thirty forevers.

Thyne's eyelids were leaden, and his grip had loosened significantly, but he was still conscious enough to understand his friend's whispered question after the quiet half hour:

"Will you be there at the end with me?"

His voice was hardly coherent, his face smushed up against the side of Francis' chest as he mumbled, "I'll always be with you, you muppet."

Francis' dark heart sang, and, thanks to the light from the lamp and his mad worries being quelled for the moment, he finally fell asleep.

Dezba was roused from her slumber by incomprehensible mutterings from across the room. When she finally managed to keep her aching eyes open, she spotted Roach, kowtowing near the window, facing the far wall. After a few syllables, she was able to determine with a good amount of confidence that he was speaking Arabic. '*Must be praying,*' she thought as she sat upright and stretched her arms.

It had been Roach's decision for the two of them to share a room. He was the one footing the bill, so Dezba had assumed it was because of the price that they only rented two rooms for the night. It was therefore something of a surprise when Roach revealed his reasoning to her the night before: "You're staying with me, so you don't get any ideas about running off to the feds," he had said.

Running hadn't once crossed her mind since her first moments in that burnt orange SUV. She even shot out the tires of the police chasing them! She hadn't tried to run in the ample opportunities before then. Why was he worried she would run or seek out the authorities? More confusingly, the comment made her question if she had been kidnapped. It had seemed like her choice to join them, but... '*Does Stockholm Syndrome set in that quickly?*'

Roach finished his prayer and stood. "Oh. Good morning. Did I wake you?"

"It's okay, son."

"Damn. I'm sorry. I was going to go outside, but—."

"I said it's okay."

"Just as well, we should get going soon anyway."

"How much longer is it to Compton?"

He looked at his phone for the time. "Based on my last trip this way, I'd say about twelve hours."

"Is that including stops?"

He nodded.

While Roach excused himself to go shower, Dezba watched the sunrise and pondered the new state of her life. She would never see her home again or bring a truckload of goods to the shelter. She would never again greet her neighbour or his dog on his morning walk. The memories made in that home were all she had of it now. Nothing would ever be the same....

She smiled.

Nothing would ever be the same!

She would never again go to sleep in an empty home. She could bake treats for these new friends and their pets. She would! And she'd find a good store on their way back to Compton to get more yarns to knit them all sweaters and hats and gloves and socks, and '*Thyne seems to like teddies!*' She would also get to meet Partha! Maybe, if she was particularly lucky, she'd get invited to one of his games. She tapped her feet around excitedly.

The only thing that even slightly wavered her good mood was the fact that she would never be able to visit Lionel's grave again. '*But, he's with me in my heart. He would love all this! It's like a real life D&D adventure!*'

Roach finished his shower and came into the main room with a towel draped over his sopping-wet hair and another tied around his waist, covering his navel. Dezba's attention was caught by the movement, but it lingered disrespectfully because of his Adonis body.

"Throw me that shirt, would ya?"

She took a moment to wrench her gaze away from him to find the shirt and tossed it over. It started to unfurl so soon after it left her hand that she was already apologising, but she supposed the throw was better than she had thought because it floated all the way into his hands.

"Thanks. You alright? You look a little manic." He tossed the towel from his head onto one of the beds and pulled on the same sleeveless shirt he had been wearing the day before.

"I was just thinking about how much my life is changing."

"Exciting, isn't it?"

"Oh, yes!"

He disappeared behind the bathroom door and pulled his pants down from their place hanging over it. "You leaving anyone behind?"

"No."

"No friends or family to report you missing, then?"

Her smile dissipated. "No...."

He reemerged from behind the door with his pants on and a hair claw holding up his wet mane. "Lucky us, hm?"

"Lucky?"

"Yeah, dude. You joined us, are willing to help our criminal endeavours, and you don't even come with baggage? We made out like bandits. Pun intended."

A sheepish grin. "Oh, don't flatter me, son. To be honest, I don't know why none of you have killed me yet."

He stopped putting on his socks to look at her. His deadpan expression was hard to read, but she felt more vulnerable than ever in his harsh hazel gaze. "You want us to kill you, Em?"

The colour drained from her face. "N-no!"

"Then why would we kill you?"

"I'm no use to y'all. I'm just an old lady with no experience doing... uh... crimes, I guess."

"No use to us, hm?" He pulled on his boots and started tying them. "You seemed to know a lot about the guns in your purse."

"I do know a lot about guns.... But that hardly seems like something worth keeping me around for. Thyne knows about guns, too. Am I not a liability?"

"Dezba, do you want me to kill you?" She shook her head. "Then why are you talking about yourself like that? To be honest, out of the three of you, you're the only one I *don't* want to kill right now. Thyne and Francis are really grating on me. Especially that stupid little Brit." He finished tying his shoes and stood. "Speaking of: I'm going to go wake them. Get ready to go. We'll grab breakfast in the lobby then skedaddle."

She chuckled at the silly word and stood to start getting ready while Roach left the room to go knock on Thyne and Francis' door.

"Yes yes, we'll be ready to go soon," complained Thyne as he finished putting on his third outfit of the morning. He turned toward Francis and posed. "What about this one?"

"I fail to comprehend why you keep changing, my friend. You were pleasing to behold in the first two just as you are beguiling in this one."

He rolled his eyes and smirked. "Okay, but does it look good for the area?"

"If you mean to ask if you will look photogenic in the desert wearing that, I will say yes and no. Yes because you always look photogenic; no because the pastel hues in that shirt will blend into the bright desert background."

"Okay, well, I'm not wearing black in the desert, so I guess I'll just blend in."

Roach knocked again.

Thyne scoffed and stomped to the door to open it. "What do you want?"

"You two stop wasting time. I don't want to have to get another hotel."

"Well, you wouldn't have to worry about it if you'd let me drive while you sleep."

"You're not driving the *Locust*, dude. I barely trust you enough to show you where I live, if I'm being totally honest."

Thyne huffed and turned away. "Franky, bring my bags to the car, will you?"

"Sure."

"Cheers, mate." Once Francis and all their belongings had disappeared from the room, Thyne turned back toward Roach and shoved him out of the way to step out into the hall. "Happy?"

"Doesn't it exhaust him to so needlessly use his powers?"

"If it did, he wouldn't have used them, now would he?" An angry grin.

"I don't know. I think you're abusing him, dude."

Red.

RED.

Thyne had never seen more red in a single moment since the day he was born. He reached for his lighter, but it wasn't where he left it. Without further hesitation, he punched Roach in his gut hard enough to knock the wind out of him. "YOU DON'T FUCKING TALK ABOUT US LIKE THAT, YOU HALFWIT SLAG!"

Roach coughed and held his abdomen. He wheezed through his black lungs and spit a mouthful of bile on the ugly hall carpet. It took all of his self-control not to stab Thyne in the throat, so when he looked up at him from his hunched-over position, he could not stop the rage from showing on his face. "Motherfucker," he coughed, "I will flay you alive."

"I'd like to see you bloody try." And with that, he finally started patting around his pockets to find where he had put his lighter. It wasn't on his person, so he left Roach in the hall and returned to his room to tear it apart.

Two minutes of Thyne's frantic search later, Roach leaned on the arch of his open doorway and cleared his throat to get his attention.

"WHAT NOW!? Don't you see I'm busy, you inbred mongrel!?"

"Whatchya looking for?"

"None of your business."

Roach watched wordlessly for another minute before clearing his throat again. Thyne turned to scream at him, but he was silenced when he noticed Roach holding up the lighter and wiggling it. "Looking for this, I presume?"

"You give that back!" He dashed madly to the door, but Roach held him back with one arm and held the lighter up to the ceiling, far out of Thyne's reach. "How did you get that!?"

"What? You're surprised I managed to pickpocket you?"

He huffed and tried to dig his nails into Roach's arm to make him release his grip, but he remained unfazed.

"I'll give it back, but you've gotta agree to something."

"No, I bloody don't! Give it back, you lunatic! I'll sic Francis on you!"

"Firstly, you will stop referring to your supposed friend like that."

"Like what!?"

"Like he's a weapon you can wield and not a person with a heart."

"I love him more than you could possibly know or understand, you heartless bastard. Mind your own business and give me my fucking lighter!"

"And why should I? If the inscription is to be believed, this was Oliver's lighter, and who's to say you didn't treat him just as poorly as you do Francis?"

"I don't treat Francis poorly." He managed to free himself from Roach's outstretched arm and tried to punch him again, but he was grabbed by the throat and plucked off the ground with ease.

Roach walked them inside and kicked the door closed behind him. His tone was quiet and dark with a hint of pure evil in the backs of his eyes as he half-whispered: "Now you listen here, you rabid leech. Partha asked me to help you with your gang, but what you clearly need are some lessons in anger management. So. Lesson one." He crushed the lighter in his hand as if it were as fragile as an egg. Thyne whimpered at the sight, his eyes immediately welling with tears, but he couldn't respond with Roach's immense grip around his neck. He was pulled closer and felt Roach's breaths hot on his neck as he whispered: "What do you hate more, Clarence? Me or Maitland? You can't do this without me, and you know it."

He had been flailing his legs around since he was picked up, but he finally managed to get some purchase on something and used the leverage to throw himself backwards and out of Roach's grip. He wanted to attack him again. He wanted to scream and shout and light him on fire, but he was weeping and struggling to breathe too much to even muster up a single word.

Roach crouched down in front of him and dropped the broken lighter on the carpet between them. Its fluid was dripping from his hand when he grabbed Thyne by his chin to force eye contact. He was shocked to see a smile on Roach's face. The sadism behind his perfect teeth was palpable, and it was only made more evident when he let out a dark but genuine chuckle and said with a low voice: "I'll see you at the car."

Chapter 11
Somewhere to Long Rest

Thyne was no stranger to flooding cities, especially considering his boyfriend lived in Rome, which was experiencing similar levels of flooding as California. One thing that did differ greatly between the way the two were flooding, however, was the response to the ongoing disaster. He was always under the impression that this part of California was one of the most important places in the states, but it seemed that was far from the case (at least as far as government aid was concerned). When the permanency of the issues were made unmistakably evident, and after a lot of protests and racket from the citizens who hadn't fled, the entire county was sent nothing more than a few days worth of rations and some raincoats. In Italy, on the other hand, the threat was taken much more seriously much sooner. It still left a lot to be desired, but hotels and empty apartments in the Alps were seized by the state to turn into "temporary" housing for all those displaced.

Roach avoided the floodwaters and drove them up into the hills where he parked in the garage of a small house beside two other cars, one of which was hidden under a tarp. When he started to leave the garage shortly after the engine was turned off, Thyne spoke up: "Aren't we going to get the luggage?"

"Nah, I'll get it later."

The garage door was manual, so just as he had left the car to open it for them, he closed it, easily able to reach the top because of his massive height. Thyne started to walk toward the front door, but Roach stopped him by asking, "What are you doing?"

"I thought this was your flat."

"Fat chance I could afford this place. I'm just renting the garage. We've got a long ways to walk." He looked at Dezba. "Is that going to be an issue?"

She rubbed the back of her neck. "I should be okay."

"You're going to carry all of our luggage on this 'long ways to walk' later?"

"Yeah, dude. Come on. Hope you have your rain boots on."

A few minutes into their trek, Thyne and Francis stopped when they noticed an opening between two of the houses that allowed a good view of the city. They watched the sunrise, Roach and Dezba joining in after noticing what had caught their attention. The daylight creeped between the buildings and down the flooded streets. Its golden flakes reflecting off the sea were far and between. Not only was the smell sickening even so far as they were, but the sheer sight was all manner of upsetting. It was like a nightmare the way the sun seemed to reveal more and more rubbish clinging to the roadways. Prismatic pools of oil floated between the opaque layer of garbage and death. It made the hairs on the back of Thyne and Francis' necks stand on end to see the city of angels drowned as it was.

"Nice view, eh?" said Roach. He didn't sound like he was joking, and they all three looked at him with horrified expressions. The light in his eyes died when he looked away from the sunrisen sorrowful visage and saw the disappointment and disgust on their faces. "Anyway. We should keep going. I don't want to miss my morning prayer."

So on they went.

The infrastructure was prepared (poorly) to handle millions, yet it seemed this small group wading through the sludge and garbage was the only terrestrial life in the entire county. That is to say: there were birds enough to blacken the sky were they to all fly at once. There were rats and roaches and maggots. There were stray cats and dogs fighting with vultures over scraps of meat from the many fish carcasses. Most harrowing of all: there was a haunting sort of feeling weighing on their souls, as if actual angels had drowned in the sludge. But they were the only *people* in sight for the majority of their trek.

Because of the lack of light under the opaque layer of litter, the water was much colder than the LA sun would otherwise allow. Francis had felt something swim by his legs only a few steps in, so he was immediately grabbing at Thyne and trying to mask the utter terror tearing through his chest. The Brit reassured his friend and let him piggyback on him, which was an offer Francis did not hesitate to take.

When they got closer to the city, they saw a woman paddle by them in a canoe. The water was to their waists at that point, which Roach insisted was rare even at high tide. The only other people they saw were some highschoolers making their way home from a makeshift school in the upper floors of a skyscraper. According to their local guide, the school was only still operating out of the charity of a few elite philanthropist-types still living in the hills.

Before taking them to his apartment, Roach led them to the same building with the school in it. Francis' anxieties left him with a sizable sigh as they were led to a stairwell, and Roach started climbing. Thyne carried Francis up the first flight before dropping him off of his back and informing him that he wouldn't be carrying him up the rest of the stairs after Roach's comment that they would be going to the fifteenth floor. After three flights it was Dezba who needed help, and before she could bother Thyne for a lift, Roach offered to carry her the rest of the way.

When they finally reached their designated floor, Thyne was miffed to see that it wasn't Roach's apartment but a makeshift supermarket. "We definitely don't have enough to feed you all at my place," was his immediate explanation when he saw the red tint to Thyne's cheeks and his furrowed brow. "Be a doll and buy as much food as we can handle carrying. Your cash will go for miles here. I'll be looking for dog food after my prayer."

"Will there be a need to ascend another fourteen flights of stairs to arrive at your apartment?" asked Francis.

Roach shook his head as he set Dezba on the linoleum and caught his laboured breath. "My building only has two floors."

Francis continued as Thyne stomped away to go picking through the shelves: "Have thee any allergies?"

"No," was Dezba's reply, and Roach's was: "No, but I do *try* to stay halal."

"Alright, I'll go make certain he does not ignite the building or provoke further inexplicable ire in himself." And with that, Francis jogged up to Thyne's side and followed him around the store.

The offerings were limited to say the least. Most everything was canned, and it was clear that a lot of it had been skimmed off the floating garbage piles from the city streets. On the side of the building, what was once a large office had been converted into a greenhouse. The fresh ingredients on offer were directly from the vine. Thyne's rage was soothed to a mere simmer at the sight of something so odd and uniquely pleasant in an otherwise dismal apocalyptic city. He plucked an orange from a tree and a bunch of grapes from a vine, but he feared harvesting anything else would kill the plants. As he shopped, he shoved his finds into Francis' chest where he dropped them without a care for if his friend had a hold of them or not.

With each new item, Francis would stop time to grab the object, and once his arms were full, he "spawned" a reusable bag from behind the counter to fill instead. It went that way for most of the shopping: Thyne grabbed something and dropped it in front of Francis where it would make its way into a bag in an instant. All the while, the Brit was huffing and puffing, not even certain anymore what had set him off in the first place.

His frown was replaced with a bright smile and light air when he spotted a horribly water-damaged box of fruit snacks. It was a wonder he could even read such an illegible bleeding slab of cardboard, but he ran over to it excitedly and spun it off the shelf. "Frankenstein! Look! Gummies! Make them good again." He passed the box to his friend with both hands outstretched, this time waiting for the Frenchman to have a good hold on it before releasing his own. He watched the damage wane, and after about a minute, it looked brand new. He clapped his hands quietly and hopped from one foot to the other as he watched, snatching it back when he felt it was "good enough."

They all met up at the register and moved everything into the cart Roach had half-filled with things like dog food, boxes of gelatin, a gallon of milk, and a plethora of canned goods. All Dezba had felt worthy of bringing to the register was flour, baking powder, and sugar. She complained while the others moved Thyne's choices into Roach's cart: "There aren't any eggs or vanilla. I hope you have some at home, Roach."

"Vanilla, yes, but it's a damn miracle I found this gallon of milk, to be honest, Emmie. Dairy and fresh meats are really rare around here."

"Oh," she frowned and took her things back out of the cart, "Well, I can't bake you all cookies, then."

"Not so fast, there, Em. I have a duck. She lays an egg every day, give or take."

Dezba beamed. "Why didn't you say so, you prankster!"

"You have a duck?" asked Thyne.

"Yeah, dude. Her name is Malfeasance. And——. Well, I already told you about the dogs."

"Your dogs don't try to eat her?" asked Dezba.

"Nah, man. I've trained them so well, I could set an entire roast chicken in front of them— well not so much the puppies, they're still learning —but anyway, I could set an entire feast in front of them, and they wouldn't flinch unless I told them it was okay to eat it."

Thyne was the only one moving things from his bags to Roach's cart and interrupted, "Do you really need twenty-six cans of tuna, Roach?"

"Yeah, dude. Just buy them. Your Euros will be worth so much, I'd say we should buy even more, but then we'd have to carry it all."

Thyne rolled his eyes.

In the end, groceries enough for all six of them, plus the dog food, was $14,457. Thyne cursed under his breath at the obscene number. "Are you certain? There must be a mistake."

Roach leaned down to whisper, "That's dollars, dude. Just give him the Euros."

He huffed and opened his wallet to take out a handful of cash. "Tell me when," he said to the clerk before starting to count it aloud.

Roach knew the conversion rate and did the math in his head in a matter of seconds. $14,457 USD was equivalent to about €2,400. Knowing this, it was amusing to see Thyne count out €5,403 before being stopped by the cashier. '*Rich prick doesn't even know or care that he's getting scammed,*' he thought as he watched Thyne hand over the money and start to pack their reusable bags.

There was no denying that Roach was the strongest among them, so he had the majority of the bags, most of which were full of canned goods. Thyne, the second strongest, had the second most bags, but because he would be carrying Francis, Dezba had the remaining goods.

Going down the stairs was predictably much less exhausting than climbing up, so it was only Dezba who was winded when they reached the bottom floor. The sloshing sound of the sludgey Pacific that had creeped its way into the building sent chills up Francis' spine. Before they had even touched the "water", he was grabbing at Thyne's shoulders and muttering in a low French ramble, "Don't make me go in again. Don't make me go in again, please, Thyne."

With the lanky pirate on his back, Thyne was the first to wade back into the water, making his way quickly to the exit and onto the street. Noticing Dezba's exhaustion, Roach offered to carry her despite the immense weight he already had from his seven bags of groceries. She politely refused and followed Thyne outside, to which Roach only shrugged and said, "Suit yourself."

On their way to his apartment, they passed what used to be the library. Roach lamented the books lost due to the flood waters, "but the ones on the second floor fared okay. Now it's mostly just a good spot to get drugs or a blowie from a stranger."

"What kind of drugs?" asked Dezba.

Roach hesitated to respond, and something caught his eye: a passing can of diet cola on the heaps of trash all around them. He slid the handles in his hand up his arm and plucked it from the surface of the thigh-high water. To his pleasant surprise, he found that it wasn't empty. The pull-tab was still sealed, so he cracked it open and took a sip. Even more surprising was to taste that the liquid inside was actual cola and still fizzy. He drank half of the can in one shot and offered the rest to his travelling companions.

Thyne was disgusted at the sight, but he wasn't shocked to see Francis' arm reaching over his shoulder to take the half-empty can and finish it. "I thought you liked cola, Thyne," was his comment when he was a few sips in. He was not dignified with a response.

The water was only ankle-deep around Roach's apartment building, so Thyne put Francis and his grocery bags down in the parking lot and rested his hands on his knees to catch his breath before he would have to climb the stairs.

The building was in the Spanish Colonial style. It had twelve apartments, all of which were different shapes and sizes. They were built in a square with their doors leading out into a closed courtyard around which the entire building was constructed. The only way into the courtyard (and therefore the only way into the apartments) was through a black iron gate at the front, above which was a bell-tower. There were stains from the flood waters all along the foundation that mostly stopped where the water currently rested: ankle-deep. Because of a step up into the tiled courtyard, it was perfectly pleasant and lush within. There were four garden areas evenly spaced from each other and each had a towering palm tree surrounded by other tropical plants and flowers in the brush. The terracotta tile elsewhere in the courtyard was beautiful in its various shades of orange and tan.

When Roach unlocked the gate and led them into the verdant square, he turned to his left and spotted four women on one of the second-storey balconies. Two of them were in their forties, and the other two were pushing sixty. The younger two were drinking what looked to be iced lemonade from mason jars, one of the older two was sewing patches into some children's clothing, and the only one not in a chair was ironing. There were some children playing outside, and Roach recognised three of the kids as belonging to the younger women on the balcony.

All four women noticed Roach, but the one ironing was the first to speak to him: "Hola, Jefe! ¿Cómo estás? Who are your friends?"

He waved and shouted up to them with a more charismatic tone than he had ever offered his partners in crime: "Hola, ladies. My friends and I are going to go kill some CEOs."

The women laughed and cheered at the notion. They spoke amongst themselves in Spanglish, too distant to understand, save for a comment something like, "I like the little pink-haired one." It was said entirely in Spanish, so Thyne didn't know they were referring to him.

Francis leaned in to whisper, "They like your hair," as Roach replied to the women, also in Spanglish, though his was much heavier on the English side of the line.

Thyne and Dezba exchanged a look that communicated silently their inability to understand the Spanish, but they were able to piece together that Roach was fairly good friends with these ladies and that they were warning him of "that girl" in his apartment. Francis interjected once with a wordy Spanish sentence, which brought about laughs from all of the ladies on the balcony and a huffed one-syllable chuckle from Roach.

After their conversation, Roach continued to lead the others through the court-yard, walking through the group of children as they were playing and rustling the hair of one as she passed them. He commented something entirely in Spanish to the child, who replied in-turn then ran off to continue playing with her friends.

They carried their groceries up to the second floor, and Roach led them to his balcony. There was a paddling pool turned makeshift-vivarium in the corner and a set of wicker chairs in front of a grimy window. The duck quacked happily when she saw her master and splashed the clean-looking water out of the paddling pool with a flap of her wings.

"Hey, now, no splashing," he said with a playful tone as he set down his many grocery bags to go give her a hug and kiss the top of her head.

"Who's adorable now?" muttered Thyne.

"I heard that," said Roach as he patted Malfeasance on the head and stood, jingling his keys on his way to the door.

Thyne was beet-red and averting his eyes with a cute little pout. "Let's just go inside and get these groceries put away."

Right on cue, Roach unlocked the door and pushed it open, gesturing dramatically inside. "'Mi casa es tu casa,' as they say."

The smell that wafted into their faces was much more crisp and aromatic than the rotten stench outside. It was complex and interesting. Most assuredly, amongst the smells were the unpleasant odours of cigarettes and, to a lesser extent, weed, but it was clear that some effort was made to mask those scents with woody candles and spiced incense. It wasn't an overly great smell, but compared to how the interior appeared it was a damn miracle.

Thyne had never seen a more disgusting flat in all his years. In the few milliseconds he had to process the sight, he had already spotted three bugs, one on the wall, one on the ceiling, and one on what could hardly be called a rug. He noticed the five dogs coming calmly to the door to greet their master, but made immediate eye-contact with Partha, who was sitting on the stained couch looking despondent. He jumped to his feet and rushed to Thyne's side as the group funnelled into the sty. "Thyne! I've missed you," he whispered as he pulled him in for a strong embrace.

Dezba had immediately spotted the drywall over the television with the thirty-odd knives stabbed into it. For the first time since the bank robbery, a palpable fear struck down her spine like lightning, and her hands began to tremble. She looked around to see the others' reaction to such a thing, but they didn't seem to care. Her stomach was a maelstrom pulling all the colour from her face. There was something in the pits of Francis' eyes that seemed to catch a glimpse of her fear, and she was soothed quite a lot when he grabbed her hand wordlessly and let her squeeze hard enough that she may have broken his brittle bones.

"This is Perlie," said Roach as he gestured to a woman who had, until then, remained quiet. "And, well, Partha, she already knows who you are, so I suppose I should say: this is Dezba."

Glances and polite nods were exchanged, but they weren't given time for handshakes before Roach clicked his teeth and lined up the dogs in front of him. He pointed to one of them, a black and tan doberman: "This is Diana." And the next, a brown pit-bull with her tongue hanging out of the side of her mouth: "Angel." The next was a hairless dog with something of a mohawk and a chunk missing out of his left ear. His skin was dapple, and his name was, "Aphid. Got him in Mexico. He's got PTSD, so don't fuck with him." And the last two dogs were puppies who were growing bored of sitting around and had started play-fighting with each other. He spoke another Arabic command to break them up, but it took three tries for them to finally stop and look up at him. "The cocker spaniel is Daisy, and the mutt is Hugo." They perked up after hearing their names, their heads on tilt as they wondered what he was doing. With another command and a gesture of his arm, they all hopped up from their positions and dispersed, most of them back to whatever room they had left, but Daisy had found a chew-toy on her way and decided to lay on the living-room rug to gnaw on it.

While Partha and Perlie were mingling with the newcomers, Roach was carrying groceries into the kitchen. On his last trip, he took the bags Thyne had been carrying and, when he reached the galley, promptly dropped them on the floor.

Thyne heard the clamouring of the cans and rudely left his conversation with the others to rush to Roach and glare at him. "Be careful, you bellend." He crouched down and dug through the bags to check on his fruit snacks. The corner of the box had been crushed but it was otherwise intact. After shoving it under his arm with a huff, he stood to tear it open and grab three of the packs. He wanted to set it on one of the mostly-barren counters, but he saw a cockroach crawl across one of the cabinet doors above them and gagged at the thought. "How do you live like this?"

"Oh, quit bitching, dude. Go to a hotel, then."

"You know I can't get a room without using my card or ID."

"Then suck it up, buttercup. My brother's room and the dogs' room are clean, and since Sonny is in Vegas, that's where you'll all be staying. Dogs with me."

"I can clean up for you," Thyne offered helplessly, "Fucksake, I can hire cleaners and carpenters to come disinfect the place and replace drywall and," he trailed off as he saw another bug, "Good heavens, Roach, it doesn't have to be this bad." He pulled out his wallet and started thumbing through his cash. "How much will you need?"

Roach was silent, and though he did not emote, there was a clear anger in his air. "I like it how it is," was all he said in response before grabbing one of the bags of fruit-snacks from Thyne's hands and leaving the kitchen to regroup with the others.

Dezba's eyes kept trailing to the wall of knives and their harrowing shadows being thrown all about the room by both the light from the television and the candles surrounding it. Partha followed her gaze to see what had her so enthralled then slowly led her to the couch to sit down together while the other four talked amongst themselves.

If she had met him in almost any other circumstance, she would have been over-joyed and rattling off all sorts of questions and anecdotes. She had been a fan of his for almost five years, and he had only been streaming for six. But she hadn't even given him eye-contact for longer than a few seconds before her gaze would fall back on the knives. She swore she saw bloodstains on … almost all of them.

"Roach is good people," whispered Partha as she continued to stare at the intim-idating display. It finally wrenched her gaze away from it, and she paid some of her unsettled attention to the one-eyed man beside her. "I worked with him a few years back. Him, his brother, and his husband were using our ship to smuggle non-Christians and Catholics out of America after the bans. We ran twelve trips before my father and coworkers started getting really worried that the authorities would catch on. Roach insisted we continue. All three of them did, actually. His husband promised to take the fall for all of us. So we went another three trips, but they figured us out after that. Just like he promised, Roach's husband took the fall and was the only one to go to prison, though I think Roach and his brother were arrested briefly. In total we managed to save…," he stopped and struggled to recall the number.

"4,222 Catholics. 1,598 Jews. 652 Muslims. 1,852 agnostics and atheists. And the rest were other religions like Hindu and Wiccan. In total: 8,413 people," Roach finished Partha's story for him, bringing about a harrowing quiet in the dimly-lit room. All eyes were on him as he sauntered over to the coffee table and took a bottle of gin from the ground beside it. "Do me a favour, Party, and let's not talk anymore about it."

A terrified nod from Partha. "Yes, sir."

Roach looked down at Dezba, who shrank in his oppressive gaze. "But Partha lied to you," he said before taking a swig from the top of the bottle, "I'm not good people."

"Son, helping that many people is more than—." He silenced her by noisily pushing everything off of the coffee table and sitting on it to stare at her with lifeless eyes. She straightened her posture and met his gaze with one just as confi-dent despite her thumping heart. The witnesses of this sudden staring contest held their breaths. The spiced air was still and silent. Minutes elapsed, and as it seemed someone was about to break the silence, Roach flipped open a butterfly knife from his pocket. The others all took a step toward him to stop whatever they thought he was going to do, but he held up his hand and ordered, "Wait."

With them stopped, he set down the gin on the table beside him, turned his attention back to Dezba, and held the knife gently in both hands. His gaze fell to it, and Dezba's followed. She noticed his fingers were trembling just-so. Thoughts tumbled over each other in her mind, but she wasn't certain what to say or do. Luckily, Roach broke the silence again, but she gasped when she heard him speaking Navajo. His accent was thick and borderline incomprehensible at times, not to mention his grammar was all over the place, but she understood enough of what he was saying about the knife, himself, and his husband.

She placed a hand on his knee and shushed him before replying in the same language but without all the mistakes: "I'm going to hope that your strenuous grasp on the language means you misspoke. I cannot believe that number otherwise." He averted his gaze. "But even if you said it right, well… I'm not going anywhere. I can feel your soul. I swear I can almost see it. It is dichotomous…. It does scare me. But, all beautiful things are dichotomous and scary. The sun. The sea. The desert. Life itself…. You are a complete and complex person, and I am excited to learn more about you. About all of you. Your husband loved you, and he's with you now, and he'd be proud of you for…." She trailed off and blushed. "He'd be proud."

Roach scoffed at the notion, and she spotted a tear trailing his cheek. "Anyway," he said in English, wiped his face with the back of his hand, and pushed down all his feelings, "House rules time. Everyone on the couch."

Confused but glad that some of the tension in the room had been extinguished by whatever was said in Navajo, the others did as they were told. There wasn't enough room for everyone on the sofa, so Francis sat on Thyne's lap, and Perlie sat on the coffee table, all of them looking up at the towering man like a group of school children.

"Firstly, I want to make it abundantly clear that I am not going to Europe without my dogs and duck. Is that going to be a problem for your pilot, Thyne?"

A sarcastic grin. "He likes dogs."

"Good. Now, for the three of you who don't know this all already: all of our power is solar. Don't waste it, or we won't have enough at night to do anything." He gestured to the many candles and lanterns around them. "We light the place with candles. I already know that Perlie and Party have lighters, so who else needs one?" Dezba raised her hand, and Roach slipped an extra lighter out of his pocket to toss to her. He eyed Thyne, knowing he had destroyed his lighter, but the Englishman met his gaze with an irritated smile. "You don't need one, Thyne?"

He wiggled his nose.

"Found another?"

He took Oliver's lighter out of his pocket to show him. It wasn't pristine, but it wasn't destroyed anymore. After a beat, Roach silently deduced that Francis must have fixed it magically and moved on: "Next house rule: we don't have running water. We shower in the neighbours' apartments, but it would be rude to ask that for you all. Perlie has a shower at her house, but if that's too far for comfort or blocked by too much water, there's a gym down the street a bit. We piss in bottles. Perlie uses the neighbours' bathrooms." He eyed Dezba but didn't have a good solution for her. "Anyway, those are the only 'rules'."

He took another swig from the top of the gin bottle, and Thyne couldn't help himself: "Aren't you Muslim?"

He froze. His movements were slow as he lowered the bottle from his lips and reached out to his side to drop it on the ground where it somehow didn't shatter on the rug. "Too right."

The Englishman shrank and hid slightly behind Francis. He was expecting something like, 'Mind your business,' or, 'Shut up.' That he immediately dropped the alcohol was spine-chilling for a reason Thyne couldn't quite grasp.

His dead grey eyes finally relinquished their grip on Thyne's soul and trailed lightly to Partha. "Hey kid, do you know that Francis is a time-traveller?" His gaze flicked briefly back to the Brit, a hint of pleasure and malice in it.

Partha beamed. "Oh? Are you DMing a game? What system are you using?"

"No, kid. In real life."

Partha laughed nervously. "Good one, mate."

"It's true! He can control time."

Before Partha could reply, Thyne peeked out from behind Francis and said with an irritated grin, "If you're finished telling us your rules, why are we still here?"

Roach ignored him. "I'm surprised how quickly he told me after meeting me, too. Partha, you should be offended as his close friend."

Thyne pushed Francis off of him and stood to step up into Roach's space. "Why are you trying to tiff, mate?"

Roach looked down at his scrunched up nose and red cheeks. The conversation with Dezba had rebroken his heart, and the comment about his drinking made him feel even worse, but… looking into Thyne's eyes now was somehow soothing. He felt lighter as he observed his face, noticing how beautiful it was. His skin was pale but with red freckled cheeks like a dusty porcelain doll. His eyes were the perfect yellow of rotten apples, and his aroma of cigarettes and cologne was as intoxicating as the gin on the floor. The darkness under his eyes was evidence of insomnia but made him look like an exquisite apparition. His soul was a wildfire, and Roach wanted nothing more than to see him let loose, destroying everything in his path.

Thyne pretended not to notice the admiration in Roach's eyes and repeated, "Why are you trying to start a tiff?"

"I'm just having fun," he muttered.

Only about twenty seconds had elapsed since Roach's confirmation that Francis controls time when Partha's gaze snapped to the former pirate. His jaw was agape, mouth smiling, and eye glittering. "Wait! Franky! NO WAY! What's your full name?"

He let on a smug smile and pressed a hand to his chest: "Androme Francis Horatius—," he was stopped as Partha finished his own name for him, growing evermore excited with each syllable. He jumped up to his feet then looked at Roach with the boyish glee of a child meeting Superman. "Do you know who he is!?" No one answered, mostly because Partha didn't give them time before turning to Francis and exclaiming: "You're the famous pirate Captain Androme de Tremblay!"

Francis chuckled, his air still smug. He stood and bowed politely to Partha. "The one and only."

Perlie crossed her arms and scoffed. "If you can actually control time— which is a new level of insane even for you Roach —then why don't you go back and fix things y'know? Kill Hitler. Stop America from outlawing Catholicism and non-Christian religions. The war with Mexico. Any of it."

His smug smile faded. "Alas, I am not so powerful. I cannot change a past I have experienced, despite all my attempts, even if I have only *learned* of an event's unfortunate unfolding."

She rolled her eyes. "How convenient."

"Don't bother with Perlie," said Roach, "She's sceptical of this kind of thing."

"Oh, I'm so sorry for not being a raving lunatic like you, Clay. What good is he outside of his 'time control', hm?" She turned toward Francis and continued, "Because I'm not so easily fooled as my dumbass ex-boyfriend over there."

Francis looked defeated by the question for only a moment, and it was all Thyne needed to be thrown into another fury. He pointed at Perlie and shouted, "OI! What good are *you*, slag!?"

She feigned ignorance in a sardonic and catty manner, poking her puffed-out cheek to mime pondering. "Oh, did I need to fill out an application? I didn't realise the group of criminals would need my résumé. Do you want the scented ones? Or are you allergic to fun, too?"

Thyne lunged for her, but Roach grabbed him by the back of his shirt and pulled him away before he had even made two steps. "Perlie, stop antagonising him. Thyne…." He grabbed him by his shoulders and looked at the raging fire in his eyes. "I know what you need, dude. Here." He looked for something on the rug, and, when he found it, he bent down to pluck it up. "Promise not to burn anything or any*one* while I go down to the laundry room and wash it for you?"

Thyne eyed the little porcelain whatchyamacallit and pouted. "What is it?"

"What is—?" He stifled a laugh, letting out a slight snort in the process. "Dude, you've never seen a bong before?"

"You bellend!" He groaned loudly and turned his attention toward his friends to rant in French: "I have had it up to HERE with these American cunts! The flat is disgusting. Roach keeps antagonising me. Perlie's being a bitch, and we've only just met her. I don't need weed, God dammit! I'm perfectly calm!" He screamed. "Party. Franky. We are leaving! LEAVING! We're better than this, and we can take down Maitland on our own!" He stomped toward the door. In English: "Come on, let's go."

Francis sighed and offered an apologetic smile to the others. "He's stressed," was his excuse, "Thyne, my darling, calm thyself in the courtyard with a cigarette."

The hot-headed man rolled his eyes and slammed the door behind him. Roach watched the outburst and quit the apartment to keep Thyne from running off.

"So?" said Perlie, "What good *are* you, Mr. Time-Traveller?"

Francis hesitated to respond, so Partha jumped to his defence: "Do you hear yourself!? What good is the legendary pirate Captain Androme de Tremblay!? He sailed through hurricanes regularly and with ease! He was—. Uh… *is* perhaps the best fencer to have ever lived, never once losing a duel of blades in his entire life. His red flag was an omen for slavers and rapists and—."

"Party, I didn't ask about this dead pirate. I asked what this guy cosplaying as him is bringing to the table for the gang. I'm not even sure I'm going to join you guys yet, so I'm literally just trying to help you not get scammed on account of Roach's insanity. I guess like attracts like, though, because you're just as mental for believing him." She turned toward Dezba. "Do *you* believe him?"

"The truth is, Perlie," said Francis before Dezba could answer, "I don't have a sufficient answer for you. I'm not good for much of anything. Like I said, when I go to the future and learn of a certain past, it means that past is set in stone. I can't change it. If I go back to it, it is exactly how I learned it would be…. But I'm trying…. Always trying to fix it…."

There was a long quiet, after which Dezba whispered, "What did you learn that you're trying to fix now?"

He looked her way but averted his eyes almost immediately. "I dare not speak it further into existence. I must hold out hope that there remains a chance to stop it."

Thyne was lighting a cigarette and rushing through the courtyard when Roach called out to him from the balcony: "Hey, where are you going?"

He stopped, but he didn't turn to face Roach. His eyes were welling with tears. Yet another attempt at taking down his mother's company would be stopped before it even started. He knew he was unlikeable— unlovable, even —but it didn't make it hurt any less when he continued to ruin things for himself with his unkempt fury. Maybe a bowl *would* calm him down. Maybe something stronger….

"Thyne?" shouted Roach, "Come back up, dude. I'm sorry for being a dick."

He spun on the ball of his foot and glared. "Why?"

"Why what?"

"Why do you want me to come back up?"

141

He lit himself a cigarette and shrugged. "You do what you want, man. Just seems kinda crazy to run off now that things are finally gonna be calm for a bit."

Thyne moved closer, but he stayed on the lower floor. "Roach, why did you agree to this job in the first place?"

He shrugged. "Seemed fun."

Thyne glared sceptically, and Roach felt like his soul was being violated. "You're lying."

With shifty eyes he said, "Nah, man. Sounded fun. Hand on heart."

"What heart?"

"Fair enough." He leaned on the railing and hung his head. "It *did* sound fun," he said without looking up, "but if you must know…." He looked at him. "A subsidiary— record label— of Maitland… fucked me." Thyne smiled wickedly. "Yes yes, gloat all you want. I'm a dumbass. I got played. They said, 'Sign here for seven-figures' and I signed away my entire backlog for a couple grand and a dunce cap." He took a drag. "But, when you called me a poser leftist… I don't know why it hadn't occurred to me before then." He seemed to want to say more but smoked instead.

"Why what hadn't occurred to you?"

"Taking down Osiris would be great, don't get me wrong, but we're in agreement that it's impossible, right? Even with Franky's power."

"Obviously."

"But I was thinking… I have two companies in particular I'd like to see destroyed for much more substantial reasons than Maitland. They're both smaller than Osiris, of course."

"Everything's smaller than Osiris."

"Right." A drag.

"What companies?"

"Eir Lilac. Baumbach. Heard of 'em?"

"Eir Lilac: yes. Baumbach: no."

"Baumbach Corrections. It's a prison company." Thyne nodded and smoked in silence. "You think the others will be down?" asked Roach, "To take down more than one company, I mean."

"Well… theoretically this is a gang, not just a one-off, so I would hope as much." He stroked his chin. "Party complains a lot about Canopy…."

Roach hung his head again to hide a smile, and Thyne took the opportunity to climb up to the balcony and lean backwards on the railing beside him. They smoked together wordlessly for a minute before Roach broke the quiet: "I'm sorry, by the way."

"For?"

He flicked away his cigarette butt and stood upright. "I dunno for strangling you?" He almost laughed. "Or did you like it?" A cheeky grin.

Thyne averted his gaze to avoid answering the question.

"Come on, dude. I'm just messing with you." He nudged him with his elbow. "Lighten up. I still think a bowl'd do you good."

"Maybe." His voice was nearly inaudible.

"Well, let's go back in. Gotta give you all the 'grand tour.'" Thyne followed him inside, and they interrupted the tail-end of the conversation about Francis. "Toto. Em. Follow me." He gestured with his head, and once they were trailing him, he started down the hall. The first door on the left was, "Sonny's room. He's out of town. Dezba and Perlie will stay in here." He briefly flicked on the overhead light to give them a better view. The room was small, but it was much cleaner than the rest of the apartment. The full-size bed was made-up haphazardly with a hound-stooth duvet and some plush toys thrown about on top. A wall of shelves full of playing cards, dice, and a few board games was freshly dusted. The floor had been swept, and an air-freshener was plugged into the wall giving the entire room a pleasant aroma of lavender and pine. It wasn't pristine, but it was a lived-in sort of room that had been cleaned with the expectation of guests.

Across the hall was, "The dogs' room. For the lads." He flicked on the light to give them a look. It, too, was relatively clean, and the dogs were currently lounging about and playing with toys. There was noticeably no actual bed in the room but instead two large dog-beds almost as thick as mattresses. They looked... more comfortable than the floor at least. The smell was another lavender and pine air freshener but with a hint of the unmistakable scent of dogs. There were leashes and harnesses hanging from a coat-rack beside the door which Roach gestured to and joked, "Now boys, those are for the dogs.... The ones for people are in my room." Dezba snorted at the joke, but Thyne only blushed and Francis... well let's just say none of his many PhDs were in sex education. The only other things of note in the room were a pile of loosely-folded blankets on a low table against one of the walls and a box of pet toys in the corner. The bottom half of the window was blacked-out with duct tape which Roach explained was because the glass was missing from it. "It can get quite cold in here, so if anyone is cold," he stopped to lead them to a linen closet. It was just as clean as the other rooms they had been shown, which was beginning to be odd enough for comment.

"Why are the sitting room and kitchen so disgusting if this is how the rest of the flat looks?" asked Thyne.

Roach sighed and pointed to the remaining two doors in the hall. "Bathroom—but again, we don't have water, so just piss in bottles —and that's my room." He turned back toward Thyne with a gesture that loosely dismissed the little touring party. "Sonny keeps it cleaner than I do, and he's been gone for a few days, so he hasn't been cleaning up."

"That's rude that you make your brother clean up after you like a child," remarked Thyne, and the others dispersed, having no interest in hearing yet another pointless tiff between the two.

Once they were gone, Roach rested a hand on Thyne's shoulder and looked down at him with a slight disappointment in his air. After a beat: "Dude... why are you so hostile with me?"

Thyne was expecting another debate, so the question threw him off. "What?"

"I'm asking what your problem is with me. It seems you want to pick a fight at any chance you can. You want me to kick your ass again?"

He sputtered incoherently before managing to reply, "If you do, then Francis will defend me, and I don't want you getting hurt." A satisfied nod. *'That oughta teach 'em.'*

"Sure. So why are you so hostile, then, if you don't want to hurt me?"

He tried to shake his way out of Roach's grip, but it was clear he wasn't going to be allowed to leave without an answer. "Stop," he whimpered, "Please, I don't know. *I don't know.* I have anger issues. I don't know."

"Okay, so then why are you always angry with me? Have I done something wrong?"

He was rubbing his eyes but looked up and furrowed his brow to assert, "Yes!"

"What have I done wrong? Other than the obvious."

"You've accused me of being in leagues with the worst sorts of scum in the world because of my plane and my wealth. You don't even know why I want to take down Maitland, you just assume it's for profit."

"Oh no, Thyne. When you claimed to be a leftist, I did some research. I'm confident I know your motives, now."

"Oh yeah?"

A smug, closed-lips smile creeped across his mouth as he nodded and hummed a simple, "Mmhmm."

"So then why do you think I'm doing this?"

"Clarence Elna Biggs Crump," this immediately sobered Thyne which subsequently tripled the smug air in Roach, "Son of Maitland and Joseph Crump. Born February 3rd, 1920. 'Dead' at sixteen. Brought to the present via Francis' power, no doubt to avoid the impending war." He pulled up Thyne's chin with one of his fingers to be sure his rare smile was not going unnoticed. With a playful teasing tone and a knowing smirk he said simply, "Mommy issues?"

Thyne's breaths were laboured and hands trembling. Why had he given his real name to this wanker? "Fuck," he breathed and reached for his cigarettes. They spilled out of the box, however, when his wrist was grabbed and turned over in an intimidating display from Roach.

He leaned in. His whispers into Thyne's flushed face reeked of smoke and gin: "Doesn't explain the plane, *mate*."

He glared. "It's a plane, not a plane factory."

"Oh yeah? Let's assume you're perfectly innocent, then. For funsies. You 'don't exploit people,' so you must pay your pilot a lot. How much?"

There was a beat wherein Thyne donned a shit-eating grin and whispered, "I don't pay him at all."

The answer visibly baffled Roach, who watched with a jaw slightly agape as Thyne pushed him out of his way and walked to the sitting room to cuddle up on the couch beside Francis. He leaned on his friend and whispered things in French, giggling as he retreated. Francis chuckled with him then "saved" him from a bug about to crawl on his leg. Thyne, who was usually quite squeamish around bugs, stopped him from flicking it away and let it crawl onto his hand. He held it up for Francis to see and squealed through a huge closed-eyes smile. "Look, Franky! A woody wig! Look how cute!" He poked at it to see it roll into a ball then waited patiently for it to start crawling around again.

While Thyne was playing with the little woodlouse, Partha, who had been interrupted by his coming into the room, resumed pestering Francis with endless questions about his life as a pirate. Francis was mostly honest, but when Partha asked, "Which of the stories about how you died is actually true? Or I mean… which one was the one where you came to the future?" Francis winced and asked to be left alone.

With Partha's attention off of Francis, it was finally Dezba's time to be proper excited to meet him. She tapped his shoulder gently and explained that she had been a fan of his for a long time and pestered him with questions the same way he had just done to Francis. Partha was much more dramatic in his answers and happy to divulge absolutely anything. Clearly he liked talking, especially about himself.

Between all of that, Roach called Perlie into the kitchen, and the two were relatively alone for the first time since they had dated. Immediately, Perlie was stepping into Roach's space and rubbing her hands up his chest, but he pushed her away gently. "No, Perlie. We need to talk."

She pouted. "About what?"

"If you only agreed to do this job because you thought we'd get back together, I have to warn you to go back home now. We're not getting back together. Ever. We didn't work once, twice, thrice: we won't work a fourth time."

"Well," her tone was lecherous, "we don't have to get back together to *enjoy* each other's company." She walked her fingers up his chest, her eyes all over his body and rarely on his face.

He grabbed her hand and tossed it aside. "Don't touch me. Are you here to do a job or not?" She puffed out her cheeks and pondered the question. "Well, while you're thinking about it——. Thyne! Come in here."

He emerged in the doorway a moment later. "Yes?"

"It's time to talk shop. Perlie here is an expert in international law. She was a spook before she met me."

His face soured at her. "For the yanks? CIA?"

She nodded, a slight blush on her cheeks. "It was the only way I could think to leave the country. You understand."

Thyne and Roach made eye contact. It was clear to Roach that the Englishman was immediately distrustful even before he asked, "You sure she's no nark?"

"Swear on my life, my brother's life, and my pets'. I wouldn't have her around me if there was even the slightest chance she wasn't good for it."

For the rest of this conversation, Thyne's gaze on her was scrutinous, but he allowed it to continue with such a passionate vote of confidence from Roach.

"So where exactly are we going?" asked Perlie.

Thyne answered, "Franky has a place in mind in France."

She nodded and took out her phone to start taking notes. "Paris? Marseilles? Be more specific."

Thyne called Francis into the room and caught him up to speed. "...so she's asking where precisely."

He donned a rotten smile and said with the gravelly sort of seadog accent only a true pirate could achieve: "Aye! Where else but The Palace of Versailles?"

 # Chapter 12
Bardic Inspiration

Perlie went back home after that night, and a week elapsed. Bickering between Thyne and Roach was a constant. Some days it was political debates, others it was petty squabbles over nothing of any real consequence like video games or matters of personal taste. Unrelated to them always butting heads, Francis was increasingly drunk, and Partha's mood was in a constant downturn.

Dezba was caught up in the middle of it all. She tried to tend to them each individually and as a group, but to no effect. At the end of the week however, she approached Partha while the others were off in the city and finally figured out what had him so upset. She was heartbroken to learn it was because of his cocaine withdrawals and commented, "I thought you went to rehab."

"I did, but I'm a worthless fuck, so it didn't stick."

She hugged him, but he didn't move at all, simply letting her arms wrap around him as if he were a corpse. "No, sweetie, no! Don't say that. You're not worthless. Your streams were the only thing that was keeping me sane before I wound up here."

His tone was monotone and defeated: "It doesn't matter."

"Oh, son, it does! Look around you. You have Francis and Thyne and Roach. They're good friends of yours, right? Doesn't that matter?"

He looked through her. "I'm just a waste of space, Dezba. Leave me alone."

Her heart hurt, but she left him to try her hand at baking in Roach's kitchen. Before she would dare attempt using the oven she would need to clean, so she went downstairs with a bucket, an unopened bottle of dish soap, and a hand towel.

Using the sink in the laundry room, she cleaned the bucket and filled it with soapy water. It was heavy, so when she brought it back upstairs she was sweating and had to take a break at the landing.

Malfeasance quacked curiously at her, and she gently patted the duck's head before opening the front door and asking Partha to, "carry it inside for me, please?"

He dragged his feet to the door and did as she asked wordlessly. Once it was in the kitchen where she wanted it, he trudged back to the couch and collapsed into it, not even flinching when a cockroach thereafter crawled across his bare back.

After washing him a cup and getting him some water from the sink downstairs, she gave him the controller for one of the video game consoles across from him and the television remote. "Play something to escape reality for a bit, okay?"

He lazily grabbed the controller and droned, "I guess."

Back in the kitchen, she rolled up her sleeves, tied up her long grey hair, and got to work. Two hours later, Roach returned, dropping a bag on the floor beside the door on his way inside. "Hey, Party. You alright, dude?"

"No," he muttered.

He walked over to look at the TV. "*Minecraft,* hm? You playing online?"

"No."

"Wow, really? You're good at building!"

"Thanks."

"Chin up, man. You want something to take the edge off?"

He blinked and looked vaguely at Roach. He was still laying on his stomach across the entire couch, so his face was mushed into the cushion.

"I've got weed, liquor, cigs." He stroked his chin. "Unless Perlie took it, there's some codeine cough syrup in the fridge. You want some lean?"

He let out a groaning incoherent sound, but Roach understood it to mean yes.

"No problem, dude. You want ice in it?"

Another affirmative non-word sound.

He rustled Partha's short hair to attempt comforting him then made his way to the kitchen. "Em, what the fuck are you doing?"

She beamed and whispered, "I was going to make cookies for Party since he seems so down."

"Why the fuck are you cleaning my kitchen?" She couldn't be certain, because Roach's emotions were always so well veiled, but she felt like he almost sounded... scared.

"I... er. I'm sorry. I just figured it'd be a nice gesture, and uh... I didn't want to bake anything that might make people sick."

His eyes were shifty, but as she went on, they darted all around the room with more and more fervour. "It's too clean," he muttered then spotted the pail of

148

soapy water on the floor. Without thinking, he put the shank of his boot on the lip of the bucket and pushed it forward. Dezba tried to stop him with a series of sounds and gestures, but he didn't pay her any mind. It tipped toward her and splashed all over the area, briefly flooding the kitchen and pouring out into the living room. While Dezba was trying not to slip on the soapy tile, Roach opened a cabinet and started pouring entire tubes of dried spices onto the wet ground. "Too clean," he muttered on repeat. His movements were manic and hands trembling. Each time he emptied a container, he would drop it and its lid on the floor just as haphazardly before finding another thing to dump.

After four containers of dried herbs, he reached for the unopened bag of sugar, and Dezba grabbed it out of his hands before he had even processed she was near him. "Now, son. Don't go pouring sugar everywhere. Why don't you go play *Minecraft* with Partha? I'll leave this mess on the floor and make cookies."

"Too clean," he muttered and tried to find another thing to spill. "Too clean."

She cupped a hand around his face lovingly, trying to catch his frantic gaze. "Clayton...."

Her tone was soft, and her warm hand around his face soothed his racing heart. After almost two minutes, his hazel-greys finally landed on her and stayed there.

"There we go. It's all okay, son." She pet his cheek with her thumb and made soothing shushing sounds.

"Don't clean again," he said in an almost-whisper.

"I won't. Just go sit down. I'm sorry for upsetting you."

He nodded... and nodded... and nodded.

"Shh, honey. Stop. Stop." His head finally stilled again. "Now, what kind of cookies do you want?"

He shook his head. "Fridge. Need the fridge."

"What do you need from the fridge, honey?"

"Cough syrup. Ice. Soda. Cup."

She grinned with fiendish playfulness. "Making lean, hm?"

He nodded again, but before he could lose control, she pinched his face with her free hand by his cheeks, and said sternly, "Go sit down. I'll bring you both a glass."

"Not for me," he said through his smushed lips.

"Okay, just the one for Party, then."

It wasn't his plan to join Partha in inebriation, and it was haram to drink alcohol, but the debacle of his kitchen being suddenly clean had him reaching for a bottle of vodka on his way to the couch. He pushed Partha's legs out of his way, dropped down into the cushions, and flicked the lid off with his thumb. After a swig from the top, Partha droned, "What's wrong?" His tone was uninterested, but he did genuinely care.

"Too clean," muttered Roach, "Hand me that joint."

Dezba came in with Partha's lean after Roach's first puff on the doobie. She noticed him white-knuckling a bottle of vodka and frowned. There was no way of knowing that cleaning the kitchen would have done this to him, but that didn't make her feel any less guilty for it. Her tone was soft and motherly as she addressed them, "Well, boys. What kind of cookies do you want?"

"Cookies?" said Partha between sips through his straw.

She smiled. "Yes! I can make gingerbread, snickerdoodle, sugar, or oatmeal."

Partha nearly smiled when he answered timidly, "Snickerdoodle."

"Snickerdoodle? Does that sound good to you, Roach?"

His tone was monotone and gaze locked firmly on nothing: "Yeah."

She pet them both on their heads then sauntered back to the kitchen to start making a dough.

"You want some lean?" droned Partha when he noticed Roach's dead stare into the abyss.

"Lean?" He looked at the glass and took a moment to process the question. After a moment, he replied with his tone entirely back to normal: "All yours, kid. I don't fuck with opioids."

Another few minutes passed, and Partha had sat up to nurse the beverage, no longer playing his game. He dropped the controller on the cushions between them and looked over at Roach. "Where's the joint?" Roach puffed on it and passed it to him. Partha noticed the bottle of vodka still in his hands. "You're drinking?"

"Shut up, dude."

Partha smoked then leaned his head on the back of the couch, staring up at the yellowed ceiling. "What's in the bag?"

Roach was leaning forward on his knees and briefly looked over at the bag he had brought in with him. "That one?"

"Yeah," he said without moving.

"I went out scavenging. It's just random crap."

"What were you scavenging for?"

"Anything useful. Scored some glass for Perlie's glasswork and some interesting trash for myself."

There was a beat, during which Roach took another two swigs of vodka. It would have continued to be silent, but Partha had a sudden thought and lifted his head. "Hey, Roach?"

"What?"

"Since Thyne isn't here, could you play some guitar?"

He was pleasantly surprised by the request. "Well, sure!" He took a guitar from the wall behind them and checked its tuning. After a few arpeggios to warm his fingers up, he asked, "Any requests?"

"No, I like when you just jam."

"Alright. Just a second." He hurried in and out of the kitchen so as to not upset himself with its newfound cleanliness and returned to the couch with a shot glass on his left ring finger. Using the glass as a slide, he leaned far back into the cushions and improvised some calming blues.

Partha listened with his eyes closed for the first five minutes. He let the music and drugs take him where they pleased. It eventually awakened his soul enough that ideas for his campaigns started to tumble through his mind, and after those initial five minutes he opened his eyes to write the ideas in a note on his phone as they came to him.

Dezba swayed gently and hummed to herself when she heard the music filling the apartment. It reminded her of when her father would spend hours delighting the entire family on quiet evenings with his guitar. The smell of her cookies in the oven worked in tandem with the sound to bring her back to her youth, putting a lightness in her heart and a smile on her face. She would usually clean up her workspace while things were in the oven, but to keep to her word, she instead went to the entrance of the kitchen and watched Roach.

The boys were so lost in the music that when Dezba came in fifteen minutes later with their cookies all stacked up on a plate, neither of them noticed her until she said something.

Roach didn't stop playing and said, "Thanks, Em. Just set them on the coffee table and pop a squat."

She pursed her lips at the suggestion. She knew if she set them down they would have at least a couple bugs on them within the following ten minutes. With a sigh, she relinquished the plate to the middle of the table, took a cookie for herself, and sat down in a rocking chair Roach had found that very same week to continue knitting a sweater she had started a few days prior.

Despite the mess, the candlelight and setting sun mixed with the smokey air and music in such a way that they were all three comfortable and relaxed when Francis and Thyne came in about an hour and a half later. Partha called out to them with a weak grin, "Hey guys. Dezba made cookies."

When he heard the guitar, Francis looked at Thyne with a worried expression. "I'll tell him to stop. You go outside." To Francis' surprise, Thyne shook his head at the prospect. He approached the sitting room cautiously and watched Roach play like a dog watches a newcomer. His head was on tilt and curiosity burned in his heart.

Roach hadn't noticed them despite Partha's greeting, and when he opened his eyes a moment later and saw Thyne, he immediately stopped playing. "Shit, dude. I'm sorry. I didn't hear you come in."

His amber gaze traced the neck of the instrument down to its body then up to

Roach's face. His hands were trembling and heart racing, but there was something odd within him that had him whisper, "Keep playing."

"You sure?" Thyne nodded. "Alright, but just say when, and I'll stop." He started back up again.

Thyne's stomach sank. His throat clogged up with either vomit or tears, perhaps both. His hands shook and neck sweated, but he didn't stop Roach. He watched him play with a curious expression, and when he noticed Francis beside him, he said in French, "Why am I not...?" He didn't wait for a response and turned back toward Roach to take three cautious steps closer.

Roach didn't stop playing as he looked up to Thyne and asked, "You want me to teach you, dude?"

"I know how to play," he muttered as he bent over and gently pressed his fingertips to the base of the instrument to feel it vibrating.

"You do? Well, do you want to join me, then?" He gestured to a guitar on the wall behind him.

Thyne's gaze trailed slowly up to a pristine parlour guitar that their host must have taken special care to keep so clean and polished in such a sty. It looked suddenly like a monster, and Thyne physically leapt away from it.

Roach stopped playing. "You alright?"

He was already hyperventilating and holding his chest.

"Woah, hey. It's okay, man. It's okay." Roach stood to help Thyne, but he disappeared. Francis had brought him far out into the city in the upper bedroom of an abandoned mansion. He laid him on the bed and held him for ten minutes.

When he had calmed down, he whimpered, "Franky?"

"Yes, dear?"

"Go ask him to hide all the guitars from me somewhere, except for the one he was playing. Then.... Then take me back."

"Aye. I will." He kissed the top of Thyne's head and stopped time. After dragging his unmoving body back through the city and setting him in one of the wicker chairs on Roach's balcony, he went inside and resumed time in the sitting room.

Partha and Dezba started at his sudden return.

"Thyne is on the balcony."

"Is he alright?" asked Partha.

"Per his wishes, you are to ensconce all instruments with the exception of that one."

Roach grabbed the indicated guitar by its neck and looked it over before looking up at Francis and asking, "Why?"

Francis did not dignify him with a response, instead grabbing an electric off of the floor and asking where to put it. Once all but the slide guitar were in

Roach's closet, Francis summoned Thyne inside, and they all sat around the living area again.

"I'm sorry," began Thyne as he lowered himself onto the settee, "Play it again. Please."

"You sure you'll be alright, man?" He took the guitar back off the wall and eyed him.

"Please," he whispered.

Partha and Dezba were leaning forward and watching the scene as Roach hesitantly started to play again. Francis swigged his flask when the song started and crossed the room to sit beside Thyne and hold him, were he to panic again.

Shivers shot up and down Thyne's spine, but he was much less perturbed by the music than he would have expected. He could go for a cigarette, but he didn't need one. He had always wanted to play a slide guitar, but they were, *"for the poor and uneducated,"* as his mother had said. It also helped, he wagered, that, "Your B string is out of tune."

Roach stopped and looked at the guitar as if he could see it being out of tune. He played down each of the strings to hear them. "No it isn't."

"It's flat."

Roach pulled out his phone to prove that Thyne wasn't hearing things right. He opened his tuning app and handed it to Thyne, whom he asked to look at the screen. He played each of the strings in order again, slowly to be sure the tuner could hear them. According to the app, each of them was exactly in tune up until the penultimate string. Thyne held up the phone and pointed to it. "See?"

Roach's eyes widened when he saw how *minutely* flat the note was. The animated needle on the app was hardly even askew, enough that the app still dubbed it a B. It might have only been off by half a degree. He played it a few more times, each time more and more baffled that a human being could have possibly heard the difference. "I guess you're right...," he reached for the tuning knobs to fix the issue, but Thyne stopped him: "No no! It's good like that. It makes it wrong enough that it's not upsetting me. At least not as much as usual."

Roach arched his brow and reached for them anyway. Rather than fix the B string, he turned it even further in the wrong direction then plucked it again. The app, which Thyne was still holding up to show Roach, dubbed it a B flat. Roach nodded once before resuming his music, now with an out-of-tune note that gave it a discordant sound despite the music being improvised.

Thyne smiled, his eyes welling at what he considered a very sweet gesture. Roach didn't even know why the instrument was so upsetting to him, yet he was still somehow making him... making him miss it.

Francis' arms around him became less and less necessary. Roach played just as calmly as he had been before, but now Thyne was scooting closer every few measures until he was out of Francis' grasp entirely. He felt free. He felt bold. He—. He—. "Can I play?" he blurted out.

Francis gasped and smiled wide at Roach as he passed over the guitar. He also tried to offer the shot glass, but Thyne refused.

Francis moved closer to Thyne to be beside him and ready to take him away and comfort him at a literal moment's notice, but he was beaming. "Good show, Roach! I haven't had the pleasure of hearing Thyne's guitar in aeons of my own time."

"I've never heard it," said Partha, his eye sparkly as he moved from the couch to the coffee table to get a better look at Thyne. Dezba, as well, was watching intently from her rocking chair, her knitting needles limp in her hands.

When the weight of the instrument seemed to press down on his lap like an anvil, Thyne blushed and let out a breath with as much force as if he had been punched. He looked down at his trembling hands and let out a few quick huffs to try mustering up his strength. After removing his prosthetic fingers and handing them to Francis, he finally took up the instrument ready to play. Panic tried to paralyse him, but it was only a wave of trembling that shot down his spine like lightning.

His trembling fingers made quiet little dings as he set them gently on the strings, ready to play an A minor chord. He took three quick breaths, after which it seemed he was ready to hand the guitar back to Roach without having played anything. He started to push it off of his lap, but it was stopped by Roach's hand suddenly resting on his knee. "It's okay," was all he offered. He would have said something more poignant, but he didn't know what was so triggering about this to Thyne.

He looked into Roach's deep grey eyes and could swear he was Oliver. The aura around him was calming, and when it was paired with the warmth of Francis' body rubbing up against his, he pushed out one long breath and closed his eyes. Letting their energy be the only existence he knew, he played the chord.

The B string being out of tune made him shoulders tense, but he relaxed them when he recalled that it was out of tune on purpose. Another calming breath, another chord, this time a D. He briefly pulled his hand away from the neck and shook away the ache in his fingertips, his eyes opening and a nervous smile on his lips. "Don't have my callouses anymore," he muttered.

He returned his hand to the neck and closed his eyes again. Rather than playing another chord, his hands started shaking evermore, and his facial expression winced at his own reeling thoughts. After almost an entire minute of this, he opened his eyes and sputtered out, "What do I play?"

Roach had leaned closer, his brow furrowed with concern and intrigue. When Thyne's eyes opened, he sat back upright and lost the emotion from his face. "Well, what do you like to play?"

An anxious laugh. "I don't."

"If you don't like to play, why'd you ask for the guitar?"

His gaze darted all around, landing on Dezba for some reason. She wasn't helping to calm him, but she also wasn't upsetting him. Still, he wondered if it was some sort of stage-fright because of her presence. She surprised him in the midst of this panicked gaze by speaking, her voice maternal and loving: "You don't have to prove anything to any of us, dear."

"Yeah," concurred Roach with a newfound jubilance as he patted on Thyne's knee, "Just jam out, man! Improvise something!"

"Improvise?" His brow furrowed, and he looked back down at the instrument as if it was an entirely foreign object. "Improvise…," he repeated in a whisper. It was like he had never heard the word the way it seemed to befuddle him.

"Yes," said Roach as he leaned down to try and catch Thyne's gaze. When their eyes met, he clarified: "Just play whatever comes to mind. Let the music take you where it wants to go."

"I—," his face was getting redder and hotter, "I never learned how to improvise."

Roach was surprised and endlessly intrigued, but he didn't let it show on his face. All he said was, "Just play something. It doesn't have to be good or musically coherent."

Partha piped up, "Or you could play a song you really like. Maybe one of Roach's."

Francis added to the thought: "And, to ease into improvisation, you could change something about it. The key, perhaps? I am not so musically literate."

"Do you want sheet music?" asked Roach.

Thyne shook his head. After a long while of quiet, his eyes closed. With the calming air around him soothing his nerves, he started plucking on the strings. The B string being out of tune surprised him yet again, and he opened his eyes to look down at his hands as they played. Even with his two missing fingers, he was managing the melody. In fact, when he recalled the half-step decrease in the B string, he was able to make the correct chords and notes on the fly by always pushing that string a fret further up than was typical.

Roach's eyes widened as he watched, physically taken aback by the talent on display. He had been playing guitar since he was eight years old, but he couldn't even *fathom* how Thyne, who had apparently not played for long enough to lose his calluses, was playing it so flawlessly. He watched him form the correct chords in spite of his missing fingers and the mistuned string with his jaw agape.

He started with a skillful rendition of Leonid Utyosov's *Curly Haired Man* which Roach recognised as one of the songs Thyne had played from his phone in the car. A few bars in, Partha noticed it was a waltz and hopped to his feet. He approached Dezba, bowing politely and with overacted dramatics as he offered her a hand and asked for a dance. The old woman was flustered by the request and tried to explain that she didn't know how to dance, but Partha insisted that he would teach her.

While Partha was waltzing Dezba around the barren little apartment, Thyne started playing another song in tandem with the Soviet one. Francis and Roach recognised it as The Four Seasons' *Beggin'*, which was being folded into the melody flawlessly and in three-four time. This medley was something that would have taken Roach at least a month to finalise, and here was Thyne playing it entirely on the fly. It had him at a loss for words.

A moment after introducing the second song, Thyne beamed at Francis and Roach. His smile struck down into Roach's soul and fluttered up his stomach with all sorts of nervousness, but he showed only subtle surprise on his face, carried over from when Thyne had first started playing. He had the sudden idea to test Thyne's sight-reading abilities and took a pile of crinkled messy papers from one of the openings in the palettes that made up the coffee table's base. After thumbing through the pages to the fourth, he set it on Thyne's lap.

He looked down and saw the torn-out page of a sketchbook with several skillful drawings on it. The part he was obviously meant to read was a hastily scribbled page of sheet music. The song was titled *Dumpster Fire* and Thyne immediately started to add it to the medley of other songs. It was like a tapestry of music the way he weaved the pieces together so beautifully and without fault, changing keys where necessary to make it cohesive.

When he came to the end of the handwritten composition, he resolved the melody with a few quick chords then shoved the guitar off his lap to curl up in Francis' arms and attempt quelling the panic that had overcome him again.

Roach's jaw was still agape as he took back his instrument, his eyes never leaving Thyne as he dropped it carelessly onto the ground. Dezba and Partha returned to their seats and watched the exchange as it unfolded:

Roach was trying to catch Thyne's attention again. Francis was able to shake him a bit to turn him toward the baffled man, and Thyne faced him slightly, hiding most of himself under a throw blanket from the back of the couch. "Did I do something wrong?" he whimpered.

Roach shook his head. "Teach me."

"What?"

"That was the most impressive thing I've ever seen. Will you teach me?"

He sputtered a lot of nothingness, eventually managing to say, "I don't know how I could."

"Leave him be. He is unsettled," said Francis when Thyne buried his face back into his bony chest.

Roach's expression hadn't been overly emotive, but whatever emotion there had been was immediately lost. "Sorry," he muttered and leaned back in his seat to swig from his vodka bottle. He kicked his boots up on the coffee table and bit down on a cigarette. While he was lighting it, he gestured vaguely to the television and said, "Party, show them what you built."

While the energy in the room mellowed, with Dezba knitting again and Partha showing his *Minecraft* house to his friends like a child, Roach's phone rang.

"Hello?"

"Tony… I don't know what happened.…"

Roach replied in a language he knew with utmost certainty that no one but his brother could possibly place: "What's wrong? Do you need me to come out there?" He set down his vodka on the coffee table and made his way toward his bedroom to find a suitcase.

River laughed weakly. "I don't remember how it happened. I don't remember."

"What happened!?" He slammed a suitcase onto his bed and flicked it open to start tossing things haphazardly inside.

"I just woke up—." He hissed, in pain. "I just woke up in an alley about two minutes ago with a knife in my gut."

In the sitting room, though there was a tension caused by Roach's sudden alertness, the others were relatively calm. Francis was still holding Thyne, and Partha was listening to some of Francis' tips on building in the game as well as savouring his compliments. Dezba was rocking gently in her chair and starting on the left sleeve of the sweater.

Roach rushed back into the room, silencing their conversation and catching all of their attention. He kicked a guitar case toward the television and walked up to it to start pulling knives out of the wall, dropping them into the case without a care for whether they were closed or open or even for the random garbage already inside it. He was still on the phone and speaking in the same language he had chosen to use when he first sensed River's upset.

The language he was using, to Partha's ears, sounded like Arabic for the most part, but it also was distinctly *not* Arabic. It was as if the language had been put in a blender with Latin, Italian, German, and Russian. No matter how it sounded, it was utterly unrecognisable to Partha, who could only surmise that Roach was upset. Thyne, on the other hand, was more intrigued by the language than Partha. He had a much closer understanding of it and could even pick out some of the words. His boyfriend and metamours all three spoke something similar. They had been teaching it to him since he joined the polycule.

Francis understood it entirely, but he was drunk and polite and minding his own business.

Thyne sat up and squinted at Roach as if he would be able to understand it better with a more scrutinous eye. "Is that Old Egyptian?" he muttered.

Roach turned around to face Thyne with eyes all wild set in the midst of an

157

otherwise unemotive mien. "It's Demotic. My brother is in trouble. I'm going to Vegas." He tossed the last of the knives he had taken from the wall into the case then disappeared back down the hall.

Thyne stood and followed. He was looking into River's room, where he thought he heard Roach, when he suddenly ran into him in the middle of the hall.

He was holding a suitcase that popped open when they bumped into each other and cursed in Arabic accordingly.

"What's wrong?" asked Partha, who was starting to stand up to match the frazzled energy of their scrambling host.

Roach crouched down and started piling the spilled contents of his luggage back inside. Thyne had assumed the call was over considering Roach wasn't holding the phone to his ear anymore, but he heard the person on the other line shouting. Roach pulled it up to his head and spat more of the ancient tongue to River, but in the middle of his reply Thyne took the phone and held it up to his ear. "Hello? Is this Sonny?" He paced down the hall with a finger curling around his hair.

"Who are you? Give the phone back to Tony."

"Tony?" He smirked at Roach, who was obviously enraged with his breaths heaving but his face showing none of it.

"Roach? My brother? You sound British. Are you Thyne?"

"Yes. What's wrong? Roach says you're in trouble, and—," he held up his finger at Roach when he tried to take the phone back, as if he had any right to have hijacked the conversation in the first place, "—he said you're in trouble, and I think we could help."

River chuckled. "Yeah, maybe you can talk some sense into him. I probably shouldn't have called at all. I was just a little shocked, but I'll be fine. I don't want him coming out here. I'll be able to drive back. Just need a few hours. Isn't the first time I've been stabbed."

"Stabbed!? Are you okay?"

He laughed, but the laughs became a pained cough. "Yeah."

"When will you be here?"

"Late tonight if I can help it."

"If you're sure you'll be okay."

"Yeah, tell Tony to meet me at the garage."

Thyne relayed the message, covering the receiver to say it, then back to River: "Has he told you about our plans to take down Maitland?"

"Yeah, he mentioned a couple other companies, too." He paused to groan as he readjusted his posture. "I think I've got another for the list."

"Oh? Which one?"

"Canopy." He coughed.

Thyne covered the receiver again and looked toward Partha, who had joined their little powwow in the hall. "Don't you work for Canopy Cruises a lot, Party? They treat you poorly?"

"God, don't remind me. I have another trip with them next month. Not looking forward to it."

Thyne smiled and replied to River, "Alright, consider them targeted. Would you like to talk to Roach again?"

"Yeah, just to say goodbye."

"Alright, here he is. I'm excited to meet you. My boyfriend is a doctor. I'll give his number to Roach to give to you. Not sure how much help he'll be from Italy, but better than nothing."

"Thanks."

He passed the phone back to Roach then took out his own to text his boyfriend.

Roach finished his conversation in Demotic and sighed when the call ended. "You're such a fucking prick. Didn't you ever learn any manners? That was rude as fuck."

"You yanks are too polite," he joked, his eyes still on his text messages. He had finished his quick back-and-forth with his boyfriend, sent Roach his number, and moved on to his thread with Jean-Jacques to expedite the repairs on the jet for the sake of their injured friend.

Despite the population, culture, and businesses of Los Angeles slowly invading Las Vegas and spreading its borders, it was still the country's capital for sin and debauchery. Despite the lawmakers outlawing things left and right for being sinful and unchristian, they dared not make the mistakes of their forefathers by outlawing alcohol, and likewise dared not outlaw gambling in the few places it was legal like Vegas. It was good for business after all, and the American government was truly nothing more than a Christian-themed façade plastered over the three companies who were actually running the country. One of said companies was none other than Canopy Cruises and Hotels, of which River had a very suddenly bad opinion.

He wasn't exactly a great fan of his country or the businesses that ran it, but he was the kind of neutral-minded man whose convictions and morals were not his own. That is not to say he could be easily persuaded or manipulated— quite the opposite in fact —but he found little in life that excited him enough to stand behind a cause that his brother was not also standing behind with the boldness River had come to admire of him. It was only once that he had been truly burdened with a moral dilemma on his own. The dilemma in question was over ten years prior, when he and his twin were only twenty:

Roach and his fiancé, Silvino Alvarez, had fled to Mexico after Roach got into some trouble with the law. Shortly after moving, they established the date they would get married. Unfortunately, it was the very same week that River was scheduled to fly down for the wedding when the laws came into place putting strict guidelines on who could leave the states. American citizens, especially citizens with as many missed days of mandatory mass as River, could not easily leave. Likewise, Roach could not re-enter the states, not only because of the warrant out on him, but also for fear of being accused of breaking the lockdown laws, the punishment for which was sometimes death.

The brothers missed each other dearly from across the border, but Roach was able to live in Mexico with some of his new in-laws. He worked a body shop to help pay for himself and his new spouse, all the while with a great hope that one day the laws would be lifted or at least old enough to be more easily dodged. River had never been to Mexico, so all the stories of how colourful and nice it was from his brother and brother-in-law were a nice contrast to the ever-darker days in New York City, where he was living for the time. He heard stories through their sister of the flooding getting so bad that their father had to leave Compton. She even said he used his Egyptian passport to flee the states entirely.

But the dilemma in question wasn't for seven months after this forced separation of the twins. May fifteenth and sixteenth, 2070: an invasion of and, the day after, war declared on Mexico.

At first, he was as unfeeling as ever. War wouldn't faze his brother. He trusted Roach to protect himself and Silvino's family. He trusted Silvino would be strong. Perhaps, even, with the madness of war, the brothers would be able to reunite. Such was his thinking until four days after the war was declared. He checked his mail. He could swear the paper was a ton of bricks with how heavy it felt in his trembling hands as he read it.

Conscription.

Mandatory.

Evasion would be met with execution.

What followed was some of the most emotion he had felt in all his life. He found himself in a brief training program a week later, but it was like he had sleep-walked to it, suddenly rousing from his trance when he first fired a gun and felt its stock push into his thumping chest. "Fuck."

Some of the men who would train the new soldiers were adamant in calling the Mexican people all manner of horrible thing and even depicted them visually as the "savages" who once presided over their land in times too ancient to fathom. On the *flight down to the border, he was dead-eyed and deaf as the other soldiers tried to make some semblance of sense of the situation. There were a handful who were excited to "rid the world of those vermin," but they were few and far between. Over-whelmingly, the drafted soldiers were confused, angry, and desolate. River was the latter. He tried to think of a plan to escape, and, for the first time in his life, consid-ered sacrificing himself with the risk of execution for the sake of doing what he knew was right: running as soon as his feet touched the ground. But... he never had to fully commit. His two weeks of emotional turmoil were closed with his unaddressed dilemma being solved for him:*

When he got to the war camp, he was trapped. It was guarded and fenced like a prison. He wondered briefly if he had been tricked into a concentration camp. There was a path out he could have climbed, if only not for the barbed wire on the stucco walls. He couldn't run. As his hair was buzzed off and he was handed more guns than he could hold, there was a knowing way his commanding officer looked at him. River was quite good at reading others' emotions despite not feeling many of his own and deduced that no one truly wanted to be there. Even the men who had been reeling their racist spiels on the plane had had their glee extinguished by the Texas air. "Aim high. Waste ammo," were the officer's instructions, spoken with a shaky voice.

Other than this one instance, wherein his officer solved his crisis for him, he had never been presented with something so divisive without a default position given to him by the love he held for his brother. If Roach didn't feel strongly about something, it wasn't worth feeling anything about at all, as far as he was concerned. He paid little mind to politics, even after serving in such a political war against his will. Neither of the twins were allowed to vote due to their many absences from church (not that voting even mattered), and now that they were living in a nearly-lawless city, it seemed silly to pay attention to much of anything outside of his interests when Roach was there to protect him like he had their whole lives.

The trip to Vegas had been something that Roach had asked him not to do, citing the inability to protect him as his reasoning. Were he a more emotional man, perhaps he would have taken offence that his brother still thought so little of him that he worried he would need to be guarded at all times, but, with a look to the wound in his gut, there was no doubting that he most certainly *did* need said protection. Still, the deed had been done, and not only had Roach talked him through the first-aid, but now he had the number of some doctor willing to work with what was becoming a criminal organisation (and for free no less).

With some pictures of the wound and knife sent to this new number at his request, River was instructed how to redress it for the long drive back home and given no more than three weeks before he would have to be treated in person. It took about an hour and a handful of pain-killers, but he was eventually able to pack his bag (including the knife), and rode the elevator down to the parking garage.

He replayed the night on repeat the entire drive back to LA. He tried to decipher exactly when he was drugged but, despite his best attempts, couldn't put it together entirely. There was one thing for certain, however, and that was where his drinks were coming from and his physical distance from the other players. The casino had drugged him, there was no doubt in his mind, but he wasn't entirely sure if they were also responsible for the attempted murder.

He drove into their four-car garage at about three in the morning and smiled when he saw Roach inside fiddling with something under the hood of the *Locust*. River hadn't even fully stopped the car by the time Roach was opening his door and lifting his shirt to inspect the wound. He made quiet prayers to Allah for mercy when he saw its severity and hugged River, holding back tears.

His brother was the only person in the world whom Roach allowed to see his unfettered emotions, and it was something River greatly appreciated. He pet Roach's hair as he cried into his shoulder, hissed a bit in pain, and said, "Come on, Tony. Let me get out of the car, at least."

Roach retreated, wiping his eyes and nodding. He sniffled and whimpered, "Okay. I'm sorry," as he backed up to make room for the other 6'6" giant. He offered a hand to keep River steady, and once they were both standing and the door closed, he pulled him in for a more proper and much tighter embrace. It surprisingly didn't hurt, acting more like a pleasing pressure on the wound.

"Alright," said Roach after a good ten minutes of holding him. He retreated slowly, holding River by his shoulders, and looked into his identical grey eyes like a mirror. "Did you bring anything overly important that needs to come to Europe with us?"

"Just the knife you said you wanted and some cash."

Roach looked into the backseat and spotted a backpack. "In there?" River nodded, so Roach took the bag and dug through it for the knife. He let out a short ha laced with hysterics and eyed River wildly. "Who did this? I'll kill him with his own shitty knife."

"Shitty?" He sort of laughed.

"Oh, Sonny, don't get me started." There was a part of him that wanted to point out every flaw with the cheap blade, but he shook away the desire and slid it back into the backpack. After zipping it, he surprised River by scooping him into his arms to carry him.

He called in pain as the wound was jostled around but settled and wrapped his arms around Roach's neck when the ache somewhat subsided. "You're going to carry me the whole way back?"

"I am," he said as River moved the backpack to place on his stomach.

"I can walk, Tony. It really looks worse than it is."

Roach left the garage, waiting for River to close it before continuing down the driveway and toward the sinking city. He shook his head in response to River's claim and replied, "It doesn't matter. I don't want it getting infected. We might have to post up for a while here because Thyne's damn jet is broken. *God*, he's getting on my fucking nerves. You know he took my phone right out of my hands when I was talking to you! And he complained about the apartment and tried to give me a big wad of money— and Jesus Christ, the *money* thing. Don't get me started on him. That stupid little cockney lib with his private jet and cocky little grin and—," he groaned in frustration.

River arched his brow and opened his mouth to try and calm him, but when he saw Roach's face, he immediately read every emotion in it. Rather than speak, he thinned his lips into a wide smug smile with a knowing set of eyes on his twin.

"What are you looking at me like that for, dude?"

His voice was sing-songy and teasing: "You *like* him."

He blushed and started. "No I fucking don't!"

River giggled. "Oh, so you weren't upset at all when you found out he had a boyfriend?"

Roach pouted and rolled his eyes. "No," he lied, "He's no good for anything. He just wants to play pretend with Partha that they're pirates, then he'll drop us like everyone else."

"Perlie and Poppie didn't drop us."

"And the *pirate* thing. You know one of them, Francis, he controls time. He's from 1657. Party says he's some legendary pirate, but he's just been stinking up the house with all the rum he's constantly drinking. I've never *seen* someone drink so much, Sonny. He even uses his power to refill his flask, so he never runs out."

Roach showed no signs of stopping his mad rambling, so River commented under his breath, "I guess we're just brushing past the time-travel thing then."

"And after learning about his powers, it was simple enough to deduce that Thyne was plucked right out of 1936 when he was sixteen and brought to the future, presumably to get revenge on his mother by taking down her company. Just avoided World War Two entirely! The coward. And another thing: on that stupid private jet of his, he apparently doesn't pay his pilot at all, and I just don't even know what to make of that because like…"

He continued to ramble about it, but River stopped listening. It was almost immediately obvious to him that Thyne wasn't paying his pilot because he was his own pilot, but he snickered at the realisation and withheld it from his reeling brother. *'This will be hilarious later, and I'll have to commend Thyne for tricking the big dope,'* he thought.

"…and made fun of *my* taste in food when he's literally *British*. God, you've got me going, Sonny, you bastard. I just want to punch his smug little face the fucking—."

"You mean kiss."

"What?"

"You want to kiss his smug little face."

He rolled his eyes and scoffed, but there was a slight smile on his lips that told River he was entirely right in his assumptions. "I could drop you, you know." He glared, but it was mostly playful. "Anyway, let's talk shop. Canopy will be tough to take down, but Partha has connections, no doubt, and he'll do literally anything I say because he's terrified of me."

"So Baumbach, Eir Lilac, Canopy, and Maitland. We'll be in Europe for a lot longer than I thought."

"Just as well. Fuck this place." He spat on the ground with disdain. "It hadn't occurred to me that we could go after more than just what Thyne wanted until he called me a poser leftist. God!" His grip around River tightened as another frustrated growl vibrated his chest. "Can you believe him!?"

River's eyes were half-lidded and grin even more amused. "I thought you wanted to talk shop, Tony. If you hate him so much, why'd you bring him up again?"

He huffed a few more times, another blush on his cheeks as he saw the look on River's face and felt butterflies stir him all up. "Anyway," he managed, "Francis wants to go after Osiris with nothing but a flintlock and a prayer, I guess. He's absolutely bat-shit. These people are just so—."

"They sound fun."

He was disarmed by the comment enough to smile at his brother and sigh. "I guess you're right. They're making things more interesting, if nothing else. Now, shut up for a second." And with that, he lifted River over his head to wade through a particularly deep part of the floodwaters.

 # Chapter 13
Deception Check

Along with all five of the dogs, Thyne perked up at the sound of a key turning in the apartment door's lock. He heard the muffled voices of Dezba and Perlie on the other side, and smiled weakly at them when they entered. He hesitated to return to his bored posture leaning on his arm watching Partha struggle with a boss in a classic souls-like game. Perlie was holding three appetising beverages, and Dezba had a drink carrier with another four. He swallowed some saliva that the sight of the drinks was drawing from his sweet-tooth.

Just as Thyne had hoped, Perlie declared, "I brought everyone milkshakes!" Her voice was cheery and smile wide for the first time since he had met her, and the jubilance was easily contagious and passed all around the room. "We've got strawberry and vanilla," she set two of her cups on the coffee table and took Dezba's carrier with her head on a swivel. "Where's Roach?"

"He went out with River for something this morning," replied Partha after dying in the game. He gave them all a quick glance but was otherwise uninterested and lethargic.

"Oh," Perlie's smile deflated, "River's back?"

Thyne decided on a strawberry milkshake for himself but handed Francis a vanilla one in case he wanted to steal tastes of the other flavour. "River? Is that Sonny?" he asked between sips.

She nodded and rolled her eyes. "Yeah. Don't call him Sonny, though. Only Roach can call him that."

Dezba shuffled through the living room to her rocking chair and nursed her milkshake while watching Partha play and listening to the conversation.

"Do you not like him or something?" asked Thyne.

She scoffed and pulled a chair from the dining table to where she had been standing. She slammed herself down into it like a pouting child. "I was just hoping not to have to deal with him just yet. He's a cunt, plain and simple."

Partha started at the curse, taken by his game to a more professional mindset where such words were cause for alarm. He wasn't streaming, though, so when he remembered that with one good look around the room, he beamed a nervous smile to Perlie then returned to his game.

"This game looks much worse than I remember," commented Dezba.

"You used to play?" He paused it to look at her.

She blushed and smiled nervously. "Yes, I was quite good."

"Oh? Well, here. Beat this boss for me, then. Thyne won't." He sort of chuckled and passed her the controller.

"Oh, son… I don't know. It's been so long."

"We're all friends here," he said with a slight smile.

When Dezba took the controller, Thyne wanted to comment, but he was too intrigued by Perlie's upset to let the conversation be derailed further. "What's so wrong about River?" he asked her.

She laughed, but it was derisive and straining in her throat. "He's a coward and a cheat. You know why they call him River? Because ever since he started playing poker in underground circles, he's never lost a *Hold 'Em* game where he let his hand get all the way to the river. And his reputation just feeds into it, because people will notice him bluffing his way to that round and fold simply because they assume he would not be so reckless as to get that far without a winning hand. Of course, he doesn't do that every time. I've seen him fold in a game of *Standard Poker* with a royal flush just to throw people off his trail. He's such a lifeless husk of a man that he can lie his way through the entire game and—," she stopped and rolled her eyes with another scoff. After a sip of her milkshake and a deep breath: "He took my mother for all she's worth, and when I begged him to give her back her money, he laughed in my face. It took me 'convincing' Roach to get it back for her, but even Roach didn't want to cross his brother."

"Oi! He shall be confounded indeed," said Francis with that gravelly undertone of a salty sea-dog. "Whatever sort of cheat he is, Thyne's a better one."

Thyne smiled.

She seemed intrigued, but ultimately glared and turned her attention away from them to watch Dezba and stew. *'Can't fight fire with fire,'* was her thinking, but she was wondering if maybe Thyne would be able to knock River down a few pegs. Her mother had thought the same thing, being a former Las Vegas magician, and her father was a professional criminal who was no stranger to underground gambling. Perlie, herself, was quite good with cards considering some of her work in the field as a spy would involve joining games with criminal types. Therefore, when River cleaned Mrs. Moon out, it came as a huge blow to the entire family's egos.

But there were more reasons Perlie was in a huff at the idea of seeing River sooner than she was mentally prepared to handle. She kept mum to their odd past, wherein she had found herself madly in love, and he had callously rejected her: *She had let him win his last hand of the night despite orders from her bosses and invited him to her hotel room for an illegal weapons deal. When he came into the luxury suite, she confusingly brought him to the kitchen. She took his phone and destroyed it in the garbage disposal, to very little upset from River. Once it was sufficiently destroyed, she opened the refrigerator and started taking out all of its shelves.*

He watched her do this with an odd expression but enough curiosity to stay. He peered into the fridge looking for the gun he was trying to buy, but it was evermore empty until suddenly he was being pulled by the wrist into it and the door closed, the two of them with their chests touching and his tall toned body struggling to fit into the small space. He was a good sport about it and joked, "If you wanted to chill with me you could have just asked."

It was part of the reason she had fallen for him in the first place, and it was in the pitch-black chill of the cramped little box that she confessed: "I know you, Karson Roach. You need to get out of New York, and you need to do it tonight. In March of last year, you won a hand in a game much like the one we just played. One of the other players was a heavyset man with short blond hair and a disgusting wart on his forehead. You cleaned him out entirely of the money he was willing to bet. Do you recall?"

His heart was beating hard enough into his chest that she could feel it as he swallowed and let out a strangled, "I remember."

"That was the CFO of Osiris International. He wants you killed. My job is to kill you, but River, oh River, I could never! I want you to know me as intimately as I know you. The things you did in the war: defecting to Mexico's side as soon as you could, having no casualties to your name until then. You're a hero, Roach. I can get us two tickets to anywhere in the world, and we could be together, and if you don't love me as madly as I love you after a month in that new place, I'll help you get back home or change your identity or anything you need. Just please give me a chance."

She cringed at the memory of what he had said next, after what felt like an eternity of silence: *"If your job is to kill me, then I welcome you to try."* It was pitch-dark, but she could both hear and feel the cocky grin through which he said such a thing. Having rejected her so callously, he pushed open the fridge door and simply walked out of the suite without ever saying another word to her. That was until she chanced upon a meeting with his brother several years later. She first mistook him for River, but after some flirtations he confessed to being his twin. Her thinking at the time was 'close enough,' and that became something akin to love over the next few years of their on-again off-again relationship.

It was shortly after this confusion with Roach that her father was found out as a professional criminal, and she left the agency when they tried to have her kill him in a wildly ill-advised test of her loyalty. What had her interested in the group now was the possibility of Francis being the suspected time-traveller her closest friend in the agency was always trying to pin down and capture. She had major doubts that Thyne could beat River in any sort of gambling game, but if Francis was one and the same as the fabled *Jumpman* as the CIA had dubbed him, then surely he could use his time-travelling technology to outwit River.

But if one thing was drilled into her head while working in the CIA, it was that space aliens and 'impossible' technology such as that were always to be treated as foreign and hostile reconnaissance, usually pinned on China but in more recent years accredited to Italy or Brazil. She had read the secret files on what happened at Area 51 over a century before; there was no doubt that aliens were real and had visited Earth on countless occasions, the file detailing just the most famous case of such a thing going wrong for the would-be invaders. Even with this knowledge and the pictures and the files and her old friend's yammering about time-travel, she was a sceptic. She had never seen anyone anywhere do anything, no matter how impressive, that a human could not have done. Eye-witness accounts meant nothing to her, especially when it seemed no one could agree on what *Jumpman* looked like. Sometimes he was a blond with blue eyes like Francis, but just as often he was something else. Black hair, black voids for eyes. Shaved-head and hete-rochromia. A broken-nosed ginger with wrinkled hands. Usually described with tattoos, sometimes described as having none. What were the tattoos of? Notes, usually, but sometimes described as various other things like playing cards, sailing ships, skulls, flowers, etc.

It was her thinking that *Jumpman* was a centuries-old cult or criminal organisation who only accepted male members and had them stationed all over the world. Maybe Francis was a part of it, but it hardly mattered to her anymore now that she was out of the agency, and with her obsessive friend dead in the war with Mexico some four years ago.

After all these reeling thoughts, she heard the door behind her open and turned to see Roach carry River inside and set him down. Thyne hadn't seen him when

Roach brought him back the night before, so this was the moment he learned that they were twins. The room was made a little hotter at the sight. He crossed his legs and turned his attention to the television to desperately hide and hinder his blush.

River let out a quiet curse when he noticed he was bleeding through his shirt. It brought a sadistic smile to Perlie's lips, which she wiped quickly away when it caught Roach's gaze. "I brought you a milkshake," she informed and gestured to the only remaining drink.

While River went to the bathroom to tend his wound, Roach grabbed the milkshake and plopped down on the couch looking at memes on his phone. Everything was relatively calm, so it was strange how quickly Partha shuffled out of the sitting area to go looking for River.

The bathroom door was open, so Partha slipped inside and closed it silently behind him. In a whisper: "Did you get it?" River glared. "Oh! Uh… I'm sorry. Do you need anything?"

He gestured to a cabinet standing in the tub. "Get me a clean rag and some antiseptic."

Partha opened the tall cabinet and grabbed a rag. It smelled clean, so he passed it to River then started digging around the disorganised mess for a bottle of antiseptic. In his rummaging, he spotted some medical needles still in their wrappers. They were all different sizes, and he eventually found a single syringe in the back. It had visible residue inside of it, and he felt a chill climb up his arm. "Why are there so many needles in here?"

"Mind your business, dude. I need something to clean this out. It probably got some flood water in it."

"Right. Sorry." A moment later he found the mostly-empty bottle of rubbing alcohol and passed it over. He watched River tend to the wound, and the very instant it seemed he was finished, he blurted, "So! How much did you get?"

"Jesus, dude. You're like a drooling mutt. Give me a minute, would ya?" He held his wound and took a few laboured breaths.

Partha twiddled his thumbs and rocked back and forth on his feet.

"Here," snipped River. He pulled a plastic bag of white powder out of his front pocket and tossed it into Partha's chest. "Keep it up high. If my dogs get into it, I'll feed you to them."

"Y-yes sir. Thank you!" He opened the bag and desperately gummed some of it.

"Yo! Dude, chill out! That's a lot, man. Do I need to take it from you?"

He guarded it like a precious artefact. "No! It's mine! I'll pay you back when we get to Europe. I'll pay you triple whatever you paid." He looked at the bag. "How much *did* you pay, anyway?"

"He said it's three grams," said River with an inquisitive tone, and Partha nodded. He took a moment to massage his wound and ponder whether or not to tell him the truth. "Three grand."

Partha snorted. "Wow. You got big-time scammed."

He shrugged. "Either way. Guess you owe me nine."

His laughter died down. "Oh. Right." He looked at the bag again. "Well, anyway. Thanks. You didn't tell your brother about it, did you?"

"No," he lied.

"Good. Don't tell the others, either."

"You got it, man. Now help me out there. I want one of those milkshakes before they're all gone."

Three days elapsed. Francis, on Thyne's behalf, had challenged River to a game of cards, and the gambling addict would have sooner keeled over than refuse the opportunity after such braggadocious claims made by Francis of his cardist friend. The most cluttered area in the apartment was the dining room table, but after the challenge was issued and accepted, it was cleared and prepared for a night of games and merriment. Roach and Perlie went out into the city to gather snacks and sodas. Dezba baked banana-nut muffins. Francis only drank half as much as usual. And Thyne and Partha were biding the time playing a fighting game wherein Thyne won every round even when he tried to go easier on the kid.

Once the table was set with a plethora of treats, and they were all sat around it, Francis suggested *Liar's Dice* as the first game of the night. They had to use coffee mugs to hide their dice, and it was lucky Roach had stolen some extra ones from one of the stores he and Perlie had visited. Francis had to teach all but Partha, Thyne, and River how to play, but with everyone finally able to understand it, the night kicked off with a variety of winners. Francis won the first round, Partha the next two, and Perlie the last. Then it was time for a different game, and Thyne suggested *Standard Poker*. After winning both games, he was feeling confident that all the horror stories Perlie had spun about River were entirely fabricated. He hadn't won a single game yet!

Still young, the night continued with some less intense games. Thyne suggested *Gin Rummy*, which was apparently a favourite of Roach's, and after getting smoked three hands in a row by him, Perlie suggested *Hand and Foot*. She immediately claimed Roach as her partner, and Thyne predictably claimed Francis as his. Partha and River were the other team, and Dezba, left out of the teams, took the opportunity to bake a sub-par green bean casserole for dinner. She was a good cook, but their ingredients were limited, as was her time and attention while trying to keep up with the conversations in the other room.

After Roach and Perlie's victory in *Hand and Foot*, River finally suggested *Texas Hold 'Em*, "and with actual betting this time."

Perlie frowned at the idea and tried to dissuade Thyne from accepting the challenge: "Don't listen to him. That's *his* game. He'll clean us all out."

"Oh?" Thyne smiled wickedly at River, "Ante up, then."

Perlie rubbed the bridge of her nose and sighed as River happily dropped five thousand of the dollars he had won in Vegas into the centre of the table.

Thyne took what remained of his cash from his wallet and gave a handful each to Dezba and Partha for betting, then matched River's ante and started shuffling. The light was dim and the air smokey. Everyone, including Roach, had been drinking, so there was a healthy buzz about them all. The first game was a dud for both of the cardists: Partha giggled as he collected his winnings.

The three smokers (Roach, Thyne, and Perlie), clicked their lighters almost in tandem as they lit up their third and fourth cigarettes of the night. Another hand was dealt, this time by Perlie, and another hand was folded by both River and Thyne.

River eyed the Englishman as Francis organised his winnings. His gaze was harsh: making Thyne feel like a field mouse and River the hungry hawk overhead. A light breeze brushed over them from the open living room window, snuffing out three candles and sending a chill down Thyne's spine. River's smile was wry and mocking Thyne's very soul with only its presence. Words seemed to slither out from between his teeth like a snake's tongue when he said, "Ante up, Thyne. We don't have all night."

He laughed anxiously and tried to ignore the sweat beading on the back of his neck. *'It's time to start cheating.'* "Okay, but we should use my deck this round."

River's smile became more evidently entertained. "Naturally," he said and changed the deck he was holding for the one Thyne had provided. They had only played one of the prior games using it when it was shuffled into the stack during *Hand and Foot.* "So," said River as he started to shuffle it, "Ante up."

"Right," he said as he matched the ante in the pot and looked at the cards he was subsequently dealt. Two fours. He eyed the backs of the other hands in play, reading the subtle markings and determining that he currently had the best hand. River, in particular, only had a good hand in that both of his cards were diamonds.

During the first round of betting, Francis and Dezba folded.

Three cards were added to the board: the four of spades, the six of clubs, the king of diamonds.

'Another diamond for him, but if the next two aren't, he's got nothing.' He eyed the top card in the deck and read its marking as the king of hearts. Feeling confident, he

upped the ante, forcing Perlie and Roach to fold. Despite his horrible odds, River matched the bet and dealt the turn to the board. Just as Thyne had expected, it was the king of hearts. If the last two games were any indication, this would be when River folded. Thyne could read that the next card was his last four, and when he upped the ante again, Partha folded.

His amber eyes hardened on River's hazel-greys. If he didn't fold now, he would lose his claim to fame of always winning after the river card was dealt. So, when he said simply, "Call," Thyne was stupefied. He watched the money fly out of his hand and into the pot. Then came the river: the four of hearts, just as Thyne had read. He eyed it like it was an unrecognisable foreign entity. He couldn't help but be sceptical of his impending victory. After all of Perlie's talk and River's poor luck all night, was it really so easy to trick him? Why… why had he let his nothing hand get this far? Thyne felt sweat bead on his brow and his heart wrenching. '*Surely, he would not risk his entire identity on a nothing hand,*' he thought as his gaze darted all around the room. It landed on the backs of River's cards again: '*Two and eight of diamonds…. That symbol means two. That means eight. That means diamonds…. Am I reading it wrong? Why would he risk his title over this? … But oh, this is exactly what Perlie said he does. I can't fall for it. The cards are marked for Gods' sakes. I know what he has, and he has nothing.*'

River's mocking smile was fiendish. He watched the wrinkles in Thyne's forehead and the stupefied look in his eyes, which were locked on the back of his cards. With a dramatic slowness and grace, he looked blatantly at the back of his own cards then held them closer to Thyne to make it easier for him to read the markings. The action brought quiet gasps from Partha and Perlie, but Thyne's mind was too reeling to notice.

In Arabic, Roach said in a low voice: "Sonny, are they marked?"

He laughed darkly and pulled the cards back toward himself to eye his brother with a balletic air and sadistic smile. Also in Arabic: "Of course they are, Tony. And would you look at him *squirm*. I could watch it all day."

'*Two. Eight. Diamonds. Two. Eight. Diamonds.*' Without thinking, Thyne reached down and looked at the back of the king of diamonds from the board to confirm, '*Yes, that DOES mean diamonds. What the bloody Hell is happening?*' He was visibly sweating and hands trembling. Because he was entirely absent from reality, when River said sternly, "It's your bet," he physically started.

"Y-you can bet first, mate," he said with a nervous grin.

River's tone was calm and almost regal as he said simply, "Okay," and tossed in the remainder of his winnings from Vegas. He turned to Roach immediately after and asked in English, "Where are the keys to the *Locust*?"

All the colour drained from Thyne's face. River side-eyed him and donned another sadistic grin when he noticed the mental anguish he was causing.

Roach's expression was deadpan, but River could read him like a book. "Don't look at me like that. Put the key in the pool. Chop chop."

With hesitation, Roach scoffed and took the key out of his pocket to toss into the pot. Thyne watched in horror as it tumbled across the table and into a nest of cash.

"Now," said River as he turned back to face Thyne and gestured at the pot, "Your call."

'He would never—. Roach would never—, and I would hope his brother would never—. Why would he bet the car if he has nothing? I must be reading them wrong. I must be. Two. Eight. Diamonds. Maybe it means—.' He looked down at the community cards. 'It must mean four… and that would give him two pair, and that would give him at least something to hold over me.' It completely slipped his mind that all four of the fours were accounted for and that they were, in fact, his win condition. 'Two. Eight. Diamonds. Or—. Or—. Four. And the kings. And the kings….'

"It's your call, Thyne," sang River.

Francis' pocketwatch was the loudest thing Thyne had ever fucking heard. Ticking the time away like a hammer into his skull. He wasn't buzzed anymore, but maybe he had misread. He must have, because, 'Why risk his title? And why would he bet the Locust—? And why would Roach agree if—. If—.' He slammed his cards face-down and stood. "I FOLD!"

All he heard as he rushed out of the apartment was a deep and villainous chuckle from River. Thyne's ego was shattered by the display, and a deep crimson was all over him. He sat in one of the wicker chairs on the balcony and looked down at the tile, his hands in his hair and wrapped around his wildly spinning head as he tried to make sense of what had just happened to him.

Francis stood to go comfort his friend, but he was too curious to leave without learning what had happened. He leaned down and turned over Thyne's cards, showing the entire table his pair of fours, then looked expectantly at River.

With the shittiest smuggest grin the pirate had ever seen, River laid out his two and eight of diamonds with a poorly-stifled giggle.

Francis glared at him. "You will pay for this transgression."

"On the contrary, Francis: I have just *been* paid." He laughed again and started to gather his winnings.

Chapter 14
The Hells

Per doctor's orders and with a lot of pestering their lone aeromechanic, it was only two weeks later that the group was finally, mercifully, leaving Compton and heading to the airstrip in New Mexico. Roach had brought all the luggage up to the garage that night rather than sleeping and returned in the morning while everyone was eating the waffles Perlie had made for breakfast. After blowing out all the candles, Roach asked Francis to "teleport" everyone and all his pets to the garage to avoid another eight-hour hike. After a swig of rum and a nod from the pirate, they were all on the driveway leading to the twins' locked garage.

All seven of them, plus the animals, could not comfortably fit in just one car even if Francis used his power to meet them at the airstrip. River was too injured to be expected to drive the long-haul to New Mexico, and upon setting him down, Roach stared at the keys to his *Locust* for nearly an entire minute. He sighed and brought them over to Thyne, holding them up and prepared to pass them over. Thyne beamed and held out his hands to catch the keys, but Roach held up his finger and gave him a spiel: "Remember: no smoking or eating in it."

He nodded. "Yes yes. I remember."

"It's a hybrid, but don't charge it at charging stations. They usually install spyware on the software as soon as you plug them in. It has solar panels and regenerative braking."

"Okay. May I have the keys now?"

"Don't go over ninety miles per hour, and don't off-road it."

He made grabbing motions with his hands. "I get it, mate!"

Roach sighed and looked at the keys again. "Just… take good care of it, dude."

"I will!" He huffed but tried his best to hide his impatience behind a forced smile. "I'm a great driver, mate. You can ask Franky."

He ignored the comment and hesitated for another thirty seconds before finally relinquishing the keys. He averted his gaze as he dropped them into Thyne's then started commanding the dogs into the *Fiat* he would be driving. It physically pained him to leave the *Locust* entirely out of his or his brother's control, but Thyne had been begging to drive it for so long, at least it would be a good test of his trustworthiness and ability.

The twins had four cars in total in their garage, all of which were fitted with (or being fitted with) a plethora of modifications and aftershop improvements. Of course, there was the *Locust*, which was brought initially to Arizona for its many illegal modifications that could help it evade the authorities: a radar tracker, a police radio monitor, bulletproof windows with an almost opaque tint, and a mechanism which could remotely cover the licence plate from inside the vehicle. It was a 2027 model with a sleak and sporty body despite its four doors called a *Pantanga*. The two front doors were switchblade-style but the back two were coach, which was a divisive design choice in its heyday but made it a uniquely sought-after classic vehicle in 2081. The brothers had bought theirs for dirt-cheap from a junk-yard because it wouldn't run, missing almost all of its internals save for the engine block and coolant reservoir. It was a joint project to build it back up, but because River was often the only one making them any money, it eventually became Roach's baby more than his brother's. If they wanted to escape poverty, it was perfectly possible they could sell the car to some yuppie for at least seven figures, but such a thing was unthinkable.

Beside the *Locust* was a car they had covered with a tarp even though it was shel-tered by the garage. When questioned by Partha on the precaution, they explained that it was too big a risk, when they came and went from the garage, for someone to chance a glimpse and want to steal it. Thyne, almost as in love with cars as the oversized grease-monkeys, plainly demanded he be allowed a peek, so River lifted the tarp to show him. It was a beautiful matte black 1969 *Mustang*. He briefly turned the key just enough for the lights to turn on in order for Thyne to see all the electric-blue neon lighting around its chassis. He nearly fainted at the sight. "Forget the *Locust*! I want to drive that one!"

His hopes were dashed as the tarp flew back over the vehicle and he was informed by River, "Can't. It's not finished. The *Ankh*, too." He pointed to a 2067 *Osiris Ankh*: an SUV with a record safety rating and wayback seats. This car in particular was still painted with its primer grey and missing its right side passenger door, so it was patronising to hear River continue with, "They're both missing a lot of parts."

Thyne looked at the last car with a twisted face, his nose all scrunched up as if it reeked. "Okay, then I'll drive the *Locust*." He most certainly did not want to drive the *Fiat Multipla* which, despite all the modifications and the lovely purr of its non-factory engine, was, Thyne wagered, the ugliest model of car to have ever been invented. The twins had added a skirt, neon, a new coat of sporty black and white paint, illegal mods like on the *Locust*, etcetera. But as far as Thyne was concerned, there was no polishing that turd that would make it worth being caught driving. When he learned of the roll cage inside and saw how thick the tint on the bullet-proof windows was, he was slightly more intrigued, but ultimately he would drive the *Locust* with Dezba, Francis, and Partha as his passengers. Roach would drive the *Fiat* with River and Perlie and all the animals.

With Thyne following Roach, they drove five hours before breaking at a gas station, then another two and a half before ultimately stopping in Flagstaff, Arizona for the night. Roach rented them a large luxury suite with the last of his savings, and they rode up to the top floor to fan out and find themselves a place to sleep. The suite had three bedrooms, so the natural divide was the twins in one room, the ladies in another, and Partha, Francis, and Thyne in the last. Partha, however, would not end up in the suite that night. After doing a line in the bath-room, he got dressed in his sluttiest crop-top and leather pants to go down to the hotel bar and find a stranger or two to share a bed with. River was feeling weak because of his injury, so he was the first to conk out, and the ladies were shortly to follow, both of them being morning people moreso than night owls.

It left Francis, Roach, and Thyne in the living area of the suite where Roach was connecting his gaming console (an Osiris branded machine called *The Sarcoph*) to the TV. Francis was unsurprisingly drinking while he watched Roach play, and Thyne was sprawled out across the couch with his back against Francis' side, scrolling his phone through depressing news article after depressing news article. An hour into the quietude, he complained under his breath that Francis needed to bathe or at least brush his teeth, but he didn't think he had said it loud enough for anyone to hear.

It was cold in the suite, so after a few minutes of shivering, Thyne went to his room to retrieve Oliver's teddy and a blanket. On his way back to the living room Francis passed him by and went into their private bathroom. Thyne didn't think anything of it until he heard the shower start and felt his stomach knot up with guilt. Still, he didn't stop him and rejoined Roach in the living area. The calm air was made awkward as he curled up under his blanket snuggling his antique teddy on the complete opposite side of the couch as Roach. He watched him struggle with the same boss six times before commenting, "You are absolutely rubbish at this game, mate."

Roach shrugged and relaxed his already-relaxed posture even more. "Whatever, dude. Not all of us are no-lifes like you."

Thyne pouted and huffed. "Wanker."

He paused his game and looked over at him curled up in the corner of the couch. "You cold, man? Come over here. Sonny's always complaining that I'm like a radiator."

They both blushed, though Roach's was far more subdued than Thyne's. "I—. Uh—. Yeah, I'm cold."

He held out his arm for Thyne to come curl up in it, and after an awkward moment, the offer was taken. When he was cuddled up in the admittedly-warm arms of the irritating anarchist he said, "Okay, but you have to let me beat the boss for you." He reached out from under his blanket and made little grabby motions with his fingers.

Roach passed him the controller and lit himself a cigarette. He held the mostly empty box up to Thyne, but the offer was declined, so he slipped it back into his pocket and watched Thyne easily breeze through the boss battle. It might have actually been a record-breaking amount of time, but when he commented as much, Thyne shooed away the idea. "Y'know," said Roach as Thyne continued through the level, "Why don't you go for esports? I've seen you play on Partha's streams. You're like God-tier. It'd probably make you more money, and more ethically."

Thyne glared up at him, his little nose all scrunched up and cheeks red. "You don't know what the Hell you're talking about."

He was outwardly unaffected by the furious expression, but as he took a drag of his durry he was pushing down all sorts of admiration and adoration. Thyne was criminally cute, and pushing his buttons was just too fun. "What?" he said with smoke on his breath, "Are you not actually that good?"

Thyne scoffed and returned his attention to the game, not dignifying Roach with a response. He knew that's what he wanted: another bickering match, but it was far too warm and familiar in his arms to entertain him with one. It was actually starting to become embarrassing for Roach how consistently wrong his assumptions about Thyne were.

Francis returned to the sitting area a few minutes later wearing sweatpants and one of Thyne's hoodies. The black sweater was oversized for Thyne, so it swallowed the lanky pirate up like a poncho. His long blond hair was down for the first time since Roach had met him and dripping all over the hardwood on his way to the sofa. He plopped down beside Thyne and leaned against him with his bare feet propped up on the coffee table as he drank and watched the gameplay.

Two hours later, Thyne beat the game and passed the controller back to Roach. He sat up and stretched before bidding Roach goodnight and dragging Francis by the wrist into their room. In spite of his deathly exhaustion, his first order of business was bathing. He didn't realise how much he had needed a proper shower with hot fresh water not full of salt and garbage until he was treated to the pure unscented water from the tap in this suite. He stood in the shower as it massaged his back for almost half an hour after he had finished cleaning himself, only roused from the relaxing trance by Francis' careful knocking on the door and asking to come in. Shaken from his mindlessness, he turned off the water and wrapped a towel around his waist before unlocking the door for his friend and going to the mirror. He had more pimples than usual thanks to the horrid mess and humidity in Compton, so he took out an acne cream and gave his face a good scrub with it.

Francis took a piss and rinsed his hands thoughtlessly, to which Thyne stopped him and scolded him to scrub them more, "and with soap, and don't forget to scrape out from under your nails, and dear Lord, Francis, your beard is mad. Take a razor to it before I go mental. Can't hardly see your beautiful face."

It wasn't out of the ordinary for Thyne to be so openly demanding or flirtatious with Francis, but this time in particular seemed to strike him differently than all the others. The shameless ageless man, upon being reprimanded, actually blushed. His heart fluttered and stomach twisted. Maybe it was the rum, which he never seemed to stop drinking, but if it was the rum, something must have gotten into his flask to make him not himself. In the mirror, he noticed himself blushing then noticed himself noticing. It sent his thoughts as reeling and wild as his heart, and as the colour creeped across his cheeks and nose, Thyne's brow arched.

"Frankenstein?" he cooed, "I'm sorry. Are you okay? You don't have to shave. I like the beard." He tried to swallow the self-reproach overcoming him.

Francis nodded mindlessly and started to wash his rough hands again. At a certain point they were clean, but he kept scrubbing. He wore down the provided bar of soap to nearly half its size. It took so long that by the time Thyne had finished with his skincare and brushing his teeth, he was still scrubbing down his hands to the bone. Concerned for his friend, Thyne grabbed him gently by his shoulders and propped up onto his tip-toes to sensually whisper into his ear. His hot breath sent chills all up and down Francis' spine: "Franky, come to bed. I'm sorry. I didn't mean it. You know how I am."

He nodded but continued scrubbing, only stopping when Thyne reached down and turned off the faucet. He was brought like a sleepwalker to the bed where he sat while Thyne dressed himself in a pair of pyjama pants, showing his bare ass to Francis as he bent down to take them out of the suitcase.

"It's quite hot," mumbled Francis while he watched.

Thyne looked at him and fumbled ungracefully into the pants, "Hm?"

His blush returned. "Nothing."

"Should I turn on the air-con?"

Lucky the room was as dimly lit as it was, or Thyne would have easily seen Francis sweating and blushing as he sputtered, "I will simply remove my blouse."

"Oh *no*," he said sarcastically before rushing over to the bed and hopping into it beside his friend. He gathered an armful of plushes and shoved himself into Francis' arms before reaching up and turning out the light. "Goodnight, Frankenstein."

"May your dreams be as lovely as your soul, my dear."

With Francis' frail arms wrapped around him Thyne couldn't help but feel immensely safe. This, he knew, was where he belonged. He loved Giovanni, and he had the capacity to love others. Even Arjun, his metamour, in all his faults, was charming. But no one on Heaven or Earth could make him feel as safe as he felt when he was in Francis' arms.

This was good enough, he wagered. They had kissed several times. They had had sex the once. If all they would be forever was this, then that would be enough for him. He just wanted to be close to him. His favourite smell was Francis' oceanic aroma and the woody colognes he wore. His favourite feeling was Francis' rough hand intertwined with his. His favourite sound was the quiet thumping of Francis' heart when he laid his weary head down on his chest. If not his heart, then his soft singing in those moments where no one could hear them or when Francis thought Thyne was sleeping or too drunk to recall.

As luck would have it, after about half an hour of quiet, he blessed Thyne with just such a performance. His whispery singing sent pleasurable chills all up and down Thyne's half-naked body. His stomach twisted all around and heart soared. It was Francis' favourite song, sleepily sung for his greatest love with the vague assumption that Thyne was sleeping. But, oh! How lucky to be awake to hear the warm tones of the song as they sent low rumbles through Francis' chest and therefore all along Thyne's bare back. When the song was over, Thyne turned around, to Francis' sleepy shock. It was hard to see in the dark of the room, but if he couldn't see it, he could definitely hear the smile when Thyne whispered, "You're so good to me, Frankenstein."

Francis kissed his forehead and finally opened his tired eyes for more than a few microseconds. "Hello," he whispered with a playful tone, as if he had only just awoken.

After all of the excitement of robbing a bank and laying low in LA, being surrounded by such interesting people, and even made able to play guitar properly for a few minutes——. After all that, Thyne was feeling bold, and with that boldness, he leaned closer to Francis, letting his mouth hang open and longing just a few millimetres from his. It took what felt like a millenia, but he eventually felt him lean in and press his scruff-covered lips to his.

It was meant to just be a peck to satisfy Thyne's wanton lust, but Francis found he couldn't pull himself away.

The room was getting hotter, and Francis was becoming alert in more ways than one. After a moment of their lips simply sitting against each other, he melted Thyne by opening his mouth and making the kiss much more passionate.

Francis loved Thyne. He wanted to be with him in every way imaginable. There were parts of him that wanted things he couldn't explain or understand. He wanted to dominate him in a loving and consensual way, but he would dare never say it, let alone admit it to himself. He wanted to see Thyne riding him, but he would dare never say as much either. Everything he had, from his soul to his body to his earthly possessions, he wanted to share with him.... But he would dare never say it.

Thyne did not want him in that same way: he had convinced himself as much.

With their tongues intertwined, Francis felt Thyne's soul pouring into his. He was slowly pushed onto his back as Thyne straddled him, the kiss hardly ever stopping. He felt hands run up his chest and quiet moans of pleasure into his mouth. Thyne's breaths were getting faster and hotter and harder, and Francis shuddered at the sound of it.

"I love you," said Francis so quietly it was hardly audible.

"Oh, Francis. I love you so much. I've loved you since the moment I met you."

He moaned at the declaration and reached his hands down the back of Thyne's pants to take two large handfuls of his bottom. It made Thyne's breaths shudder, and his words were shaky with pleasure, anticipation, and dread all at once: "Oh, Francis, you want me?"

"You're all I've ever wanted," he said truthfully.

They kept kissing, Thyne starting to unconsciously make grinding motions into Francis to stimulate himself.

It was heaven.

It was bliss.

It was perfect a kiss....

But... Francis' mind was clouding.

This room—.

This life—.

It was dark...

...So dark... and and and aNDdand&&&&&&&&&&&&&

desolate.

He squeezed harder onto Thyne in desperation, so much so that the little Brit moaned in pained pleasure, but the darkness did not waver. "No," he pleaded quietly with his fading sanity, "Don't take him from me again."

Francis started to weep, and Thyne stopped everything to caress his face and make soothing shushing sounds. "What's wrong, Franky? I'm here. I'm right here."

"You're not," he bawled, his voice still a whisper but only just. His eyes were blurred with tears too much to see anything but darkness. "Oh, have mercy. Not again. I love him. I love him."

"Francis? Who? I'm right here."

He shook his head. He shook it and shook it. Faster and faster until suddenly slamming it backwards into the pillow. His trembling hands had moved up to Thyne's waist and were clawing desperately at his back. "I'm sorry. Oh, please! God, have mercy." The faithless man instinctively fell back onto old habits and muttered desperately: "O mi Iesu, dimitte nobis debita nostra, salva nos ab igne inferni, perduc in caelum omnes animas, praesertim eas, quae misericordiae tuae maxime indigent. Salva nos ab igne inferni. Salva nos ab igne inferni. Salva nos ab igne inferni. Salvō me ab igne inferni. Salvō me ab igne inferni. O mi Iesu…"

Thyne was befuddled and concerned and downright scared. He put both of his quivering hands around Francis' cheeks and tried to shake his head a bit to snap him out of his stupor. After that didn't work, he kissed, or rather *tried* to kiss him, but it was nothing more than pressing his lips against Francis' while he continued to pray. With tears trailing his cheeks, he leaned over to the side table and turned on the light.

Francis hissed at the suddenness and stopped his mad prayers. After the start, his eyes fluttered open. He saw Thyne, the angel, haloed with a glowing yellow light and vignetted by the blear of tears in his eyes. "'Tis fantasy. He loves me not." He wept. "Say your piece, angel, but torment me no longer."

"Francis, I'm so scared for you." He was weeping and trembling, but his voice was low and steady, "What's happening? I love you so much. I'm so scared. Do you know who I am?"

He nodded.

"Who am I?"

"My angel Thyne."

He blushed, but he was far too concerned to take it lightly. "I'm not an angel, Francis. I'm just a man. Do you know where you are?"

He nodded.

"Where are you?"

"Hell."

He shuddered, stunned out of his weeping. Stunned to silence. It may have been days before he swallowed the terror coursing through him and made his voice as gentle as he could to say, "No, Francis. We're in Arizona. Do you remember? We drove here. From California."

He shook his head, his eyes still too bleary to see anything but vague shapes.

"We did. Here. Stand up." He got off the bed, but it was an ill-advised decision, for Francis immediately fell deathly still and quiet to the point that Thyne worried he had actually died. He climbed back onto the bed in a frenzy and pressed his ear to Francis' chest. When he thankfully heard the wild thumping of Francis' heart, he moved his attention up to his face. Scooping his head up into his hands, he made more quiet shushing sounds. "Francis, please come back." His words were hardly comprehensible through all his tears.

"Angel Thyne?" He spoke clearly and calmly as if he was trying to start a casual conversation.

"I'm just Thyne. Clarence. No angel."

"How long have I been dead?"

He took a deep breath to try and calm himself enough to answer. "You're not dead."

"If I'm not dead, then what's the angel Thyne doing kissing me?"

Thyne sputtered incoherently, wept, and eventually managed to ask, "You don't want me to kiss you?"

He shook his head, and Thyne's heart shattered. "I'd like the real Thyne to kiss me, but he would never."

"Yes he would, Franky. *I'm* the real Thyne. I'm *right. here.*"

"No," he said with a very final sort of tone, "You're not."

Thyne had no idea what to make of this, but he decided that Francis couldn't be reasoned with. He must have been drunk and hallucinating, and it'd all be better in the morning. He laid down beside Francis' body, it feeling very lifeless, and hugged his own knees. Everything was a blur, and he was shuddering and quaking with his silent sobs until the light of morning roused him from an exhausting horrid sort of sleep.

Chapter 15
Murder Hobo

As they were crossing the border from Arizona into New Mexico, Dezba's phone rang loudly over the music Francis was casting to the stereo. Thyne's immediate reaction was to snap at her: "You still have that thing activated!? You've been tracked this entire time! And you shot those cops with traceable rounds! Fuck fuck fuck! You bloody imbecile! It's a fucking miracle we haven't been found yet. Gods! They're probably already raiding my plane! Franky, get ready to—."

"Thyne, honey, I took out the SIM card and destroyed it when you asked me to. Quiet down: Party's sleeping. It's just a calendar reminder. And lucky, too! How far are we from Crownpoint?"

"Why?" he snipped, still coming down from the frenzy he had whipped himself into.

"There's a gun show today. If we're quick we could catch it and get the sorta shit you definitely can't get in Eurasia." Her tone was that of an excited child asking to buy fast food on the way home from school and not that of a woman asking to buy firearms that would be illegal in almost any other country.

"I have guns at home," was his reply.

"But Thyne, you don't have American guns."

"I have a couple." He sounded defensive. Dezba chuckled and asked for his phone. "What!? Why?" His thinking after the question was that she had lied about the SIM card and wanted his phone to return the call of whoever had called her.

Her tone was maternal in that it was both loving and stern: "To call the twins and tell them to divert to Crownpoint."

He huffed and puffed, but after a moment he tossed his phone into the back. "Hyello?" answered Roach.

"There's a gun show in Crownpoint. It ends at midnight. We should go and stock up on the sorts of weapons we can't get in Europe." He didn't respond. "They have knives, too," she lilted.

A beat. "Are you sure?"

"Mmhmm."

"Alright…. Text Sonny the address. Also, while I have you on the horn: we're pulling off at the next exit. I need to pray."

"Sounds good." She relayed the information to Thyne then back to Roach: "I'm hungry, anyway. See you in a minute, son."

"Yup. Later, Emmie."

They stopped for lunch at a drive-in restaurant, per Thyne's insistence. Luckily, there was an inside portion open for customers, so Roach was able to go into its restroom for his ablution. Thyne, having had two energy drinks by then, needed to piss, so he was only about a minute behind Roach into the men's room. When he went inside he stopped and stared. "Uh, mate?"

Roach looked at him. "What?"

"What are you doing?"

"What does it look like I'm doing, dude?"

"… It looks like you're washing your feet in the sink."

He finished with his left foot and swapped to his right, his now-clean left foot pressing on the top of his boot. "Wow, I almost didn't recognise you without your stupid hat and smoking pipe. Where's Watson?"

"Why are you washing your feet? Did you piss on them?"

Roach finished cleaning his right foot then sat on the counter beside the sink to put his socks and shoes back on. "You never washed your feet before, man? I'd heard about how unhygienic you Europeans are, but I didn't think it was *that* bad."

Thyne rolled his eyes and went to a urinal. "You're one to talk about hygiene. You'd probably drink toilet water."

"I've actually had a cocktail called toilet water. It was good." He dropped back down onto the ground. "Anyway, I'm gonna go pray now, so just order for me from the counter."

Though Thyne still didn't know why Roach had washed his feet in the public bathroom's sink, he did remember to order him something halal. Roach appreciated the gesture when he found out that Thyne was actually the one who had ordered for him rather than Perlie or River. Despite appreciating it, he didn't express his gratitude with more than a simple, "Thanks, man," before continuing outside to sit at a picnic table. "Don't know why you wanted to come to a drive-in so bad, Thyne. And why didn't you order for yourself and Francis yet? I'm *not* letting you eat in the *Locust*."

"Well, you say that, but I was thinking maybe it would be okay because— I don't know if you've put it together yet —but we can't fly your cars over to Europe. They'll just be in my hangar until you… come back home." The last few words sort of struggled to escape him. No matter how irritating Roach was, for some reason he didn't want to imagine having to say goodbye.

It hadn't crossed Roach's mind that his cars wouldn't fit into the plane. It looked big enough for at least one, but in hindsight, he supposed there were probably wiring and mechanics in the space he assumed his car would have fit. After finishing a bite of his food, he sighed and eyed Thyne for nearly a minute. "Fine," he said eventually, and Thyne lit up like a puppy. It brought a slight blush to Roach's cheeks that he couldn't thwart, so he averted his eyes and grumbled, "If there's a single stain on a single thing, I'll—."

Thyne hugged him and kissed the top of his head, noticing in that split-second that he smelled divine. "You're the best, mate! I've always wanted to go to a genuine American drive-in!" He rushed back to the *Locust*, dragging Francis along by his wrist, and excitedly ordered from the carside menu.

Partha was roused from a long nap when Thyne and Francis returned to the car. "Are we there?" he yawned as his sleepy gaze trailed all around.

Thyne finished ordering then beamed at his sleepy friend. "No, we're getting lunch. What do you want?"

"Roach is letting you eat in the *Locust*?" It was clear he was asking as a way to remind Thyne of the rule, but after he nodded excitedly, Partha arched his brow and joked, "What'd you do? Blow him?"

Thyne rolled his eyes. "Shut up, mate. Now, what do you want? This is the last stop before the gun show Dezba wants us to go to."

"Gun show?" He vaguely recalled murmurings of the earlier conversation, but he had mostly been asleep during it. "I hope they have flintlocks! I want a gun like Franky's." His eye sparkled adorably. "But, oh, uh—. Lunch." He leaned on his window and muttered, "Let's see the menu…."

Crownpoint was once a small unassuming town in the Navajo Nation, but when war was declared, it was seized by the United States government and turned into an important military hub. Over the course of the war, it saw an influx of new residents, businesses, and general city development, turning what was a humble village just a decade prior into one of the biggest cities west of the Mississippi. A lot of its Navajo roots were ruined by this sudden uptick in population, but most of the residents who had lived in Crownpoint before the war were still living there after it. The mayor, in fact, was a Navajo woman named Nokomis Nakai. The war was still raging in the south of Mexico, but the army had officially withdrawn in the summer of 2076 which was not ironically the first year of the annual Crownpoint gun show. Dezba had made the drive out for the show in 2078, but after her truck broke down on the way back home, she accepted she would likely never go again. It was because of this earlier resignation that she was especially giddy as they approached the convention centre.

Other than her, the only other members of the group who were even half as excited were Perlie and Thyne.

River wasn't a bad shot, but he was a relatively passive man. If he was taking up arms it was because his brother was taking up arms. He could kill and feel nothing afterwards, so, like most things, it wasn't something for which he held any strong feelings or opinions.

Partha was intrigued despite having never shot a gun in his life. He had a passing interest in firearms, but he knew so little about modern models, it seemed wiser to just trust the others to guide him. The idea of going to the gun show had aroused in him an all-too-brief internal dialogue about what he would do when this gang inevitably had to take a life.

And Roach…. Roach was actively irritated by the oversaturation of right-wingers, liberals, and guns in general. He was annoyed to have checked his dogs and duck into a pet hotel for the day and regretted not just spending the time with them in a park somewhere, but he was making the most of the situation, evident as early as the check-in:

They were searched and scanned briefly for weapons. To avoid drawing attention to himself, not only did Thyne dye his hair back to its natural brown in the men's room of a drug store before coming to the show, he also put on a fake Southern accent all throughout it.

They made their way through the lax security line and River paid for all of their tickets except Dezba's with his cash from Vegas. Dezba had a membership card in her purse that let her in for free.

Before Roach was given his badge to enter, the guard with a metal-detecting wand who had already found all ten of his balisong knives asked, "That's a lot of butterflies, chap, but do you have any guns?"

To this, Roach flexed his massive biceps. "Just these," he joked.

"Ha. *Ha.* Never heard *that* one before."

"Lighten up, man. No. I don't have any guns. I don't like them. I got dragged here by the old lady." This got a nervous sort of chuckle and judgemental look, followed by a proper laugh when the guard saw him point to Dezba in the distance and realised that Roach wasn't referring to his wife.

"Quite the GILF, huh?" the guard commented.

Roach pointed to a gun near Dezba with his thumb and asked, "'Gun I'd like to fuck'? Yeah. She's a beaut." He put his hands on his hips and eyed the rifle as if he actually did have lewd thoughts about it.

The guard laughed quite heartily, but it dwindled to an awkward quiet when he saw Roach's unemotive mien. Back in his cold grey gaze, he cleared his throat and said, "Well, anyway, you can have your knives back, chap."

"Thanks, dude."

When Francis was asked about his gun, he answered, "Yes, of course it fires. What good would it be if it didn't?"

"It's mighty pretty," replied the guard who had found it, "I'm not really into the vintage ones like that, but my wife would love it."

The thinly veiled insult went entirely unnoticed by Francis, and he beamed his rotten teeth. "My wife quite fancied them, too!"

"Alright, Captain Jack. Just hand me the gun and any other weapons you have on you. You can get them back on your way out."

"Is this not a gun show? I was under the impression I could show others my gun."

Thyne kicked his shin and stepped between them. "Sorry 'bout him. Here's his gun."

Once they were through to the show, Francis grumbled to Thyne, "There best be a smith selling his finest rapiers, backswords, and cutlasses."

"Don't get your hopes up, Francy Pants."

The showroom floor was vast, and once they were all inside, Roach stopped Dezba by her wrist before she wandered off. He brought the entire group to a quiet corner and huddled them up to say in as low a voice as was still audible for them, "Sonny, divvy up the cash. Em, don't buy anything that can be traced back to you, and only use cash. Okay?" River started passing out equal stacks of money, but Roach stopped him when he tried to give some to Partha. "Are you crazy? None for the kid."

Partha scoffed and whispered back angrily, "Hey! What the Hell? I can handle a gun!"

"Shut it, kid. You're coming with me. Everyone else can split up however."

Thyne, for once, split himself away from Francis. He didn't tell anyone his reasoning, but he was actually hoping to find a gift for his best friend. Luckily, Francis was an oblivious and unassuming sort of man and didn't even think to question him. When he and Perlie were the last two left, he offered her his arm to link up and escorted her wherever she asked to go. The other groups were the twins with Partha and Thyne with Dezba.

The main showroom floor was split in half: independent vendors and collectors on the right and the entire left half of the floor was dedicated to Anubis Incendiaries, a subsidiary of Osiris International. It was an elaborate series of booths, stages, and aisles of firearms for sale. This half of the showroom only ever had a handful of patrons exploring it, and more often than not, they were mocking the stock. Gun-nuts like Dezba were generally of the opinion that Anubis firearms were made too cheaply to be worth their inflated prices, but with the right amount of modifications and care, they could be flipped for a profit and made viable. There were many lawsuits buried or settled out of court regarding how frequently their least expensive shotgun model, the *Geb 17*, exploded in people's hands. It was never recalled or outlawed, but after the death toll for their faulty weaponry reached the triple digits, the company released a public apology and promised to remodel it.

Other than the *Geb 17*, there was the *Nut*, which was the standard-issue pistol for the military during the invasion into Mexico. Like a lot of Osiris products, it was named after an Egyptian deity. Unfortunately for said Goddess, the *Nut* was "affectionately" nicknamed by the soldiers the *Busted Nut* for having sub-par effective range, being infamously inaccurate, and firing unreasonably loudly. The only Anubis gun that was universally accepted as being …decent was the *Anubis 78*, which was naturally also their most expensive pistol model.

When Francis tried to take Perlie into this less-crowded half of the floor, she protested, "No. Anubis is trash. I want to find a vintage collector for a *Tommy* gun," so they went searching for an antiques collector.

Thyne and Dezba were the most knowledgeable in the group on the subject of firearms, so the left half of the floor may as well have not existed to them. They found a lot of strange sorts amongst the independent vendors, one of which had Thyne's vested interest. He was a hillbilly type with hardly any teeth that combined with his accent to make him difficult to understand, but his wares were unique and intriguing. Thyne inquired about their odd appearance and was answered, "They's made 'a mah 'cycled beer and sody-pop cans."

"You made 'em yerself?" asked Thyne.

"Yessir Ah did. Lotsa time t' mahself since the missus died."

"You don't happen ta have any snipers do ya?"

He eyed his pieces then grabbed a bolt-action rifle. "Ah done know how t' make a scope, but reckon ye could buy one from summon here an' 'tach it on thissun."

"Can I see?" Thyne took the gun to look it over then eyed Dezba for approval.

"What's the range on it?" she asked.

"Lemme see." He looked at the tag hanging off the side of the stock. "'Bout half a mile, ma'am. 'Course was jus' me testin' without a scope, so might be longer withun."

Thyne had to take a moment to roughly convert the number to metres in his head then looked at Dezba again.

She gave him a maternal smile and rubbed the small of his back. "If that's the one you want, sweetums."

"This yer ma?"

He blushed. "Er. Yeah."

"Well, ain't that juss preshus? Me an' the missus always wanted kids a'r own, but times, they was tough, and mah nephya hates 'Murica, so natcherly he ain't a fan ah guns er Mr. Park er nothin' else what like Ah like."

"Well, what a shame," said Dezba awkwardly, "Jody, honey, are you going to buy that gun?"

It took a moment for Thyne to realise that his false name was apparently Jody. "Oh," he said as he looked up at her, "You think I should, Mama?" The blush on his face was bright and impossible to hide, but luckily the room was sweltering. It could be chalked up to the heat. After paying $23,000 for the handmade weapon and leaving the booth, he passed it to Dezba to look it over for him with more scrutiny.

"Did I get scammed?" he asked after a few minutes of her examination.

"Son, I think you may have scammed *him*. This is beautifully crafted. It must have taken him so long."

He beamed. "Really? Will it take a scope from one of my snipers back home?"

"Probably." She gave it another once-over and passed it back to him. "Good find! Although, the paint job is a little…. You should probably get it repainted and coated with the last of your cash."

"I was planning on it, actually. Do you think they'll paint it in a pastel colour without getting all homophobic on me?"

She shrugged. "Most people don't really care, but if they ask, just say it's for your daughter."

His stomach sank. "Heh…. Yeah."

She noticed his upset and incorrectly identified it: "Oh, I'm sorry for going along with the whole 'I'm your mother' thing." She blushed. "Hope that wasn't too weird."

A beat. "It was a little weird, but it wasn't because of you."

"Yeah," she said with a nervous chuckle that trailed down awkwardly. They both had complicated feelings about the subject, but it all remained unsaid. "Let's go find someone to repaint it before we run out of time."

While they looked for a booth offering custom repaints on the floor, Partha was bothering the twins to go to the second storey because, "that's where the black-smiths are, and I want a new rapier, since *someone* won't let me get a gun."

After a sweep of all the independent vendors on the main floor, Roach agreed: "Yeah, if that's where the knives are, we should go up there. Sonny? You coming?"

River shrugged and followed them up the escalators into a much smaller but still substantial showroom floor. The majority of vendors on the second floor were food stalls, but just as Partha had deduced, it was also the location of all the arti-sans and blacksmiths. As well, there were a handful of activities like a carnival-style shooting game, archery, and axe-throwing. On their way to a semi-famous black-smith on the far end of the hall, Roach stopped them at the shooting game. He shoved Partha toward it and said, "Here ya go, kid. You can shoot the BB guns and maybe they'll give you a coupon or something."

Partha glared at Roach. "I am *not* a child."

"Oh, I know. Wouldn't want to see an actual child with as much nose candy as you, man." He shoved his hands in the pockets of his sleeveless hoodie. "Sonny, buy him a game. Let's see if he can even hit the target."

River bought him a game which consisted of "ten shots. Every hit on the target is a dollar off anything at the shop. A bullseye is five."

Partha snatched the offered BB rifle out of the woman's hands and hunkered down to aim at a paper target hanging about twenty feet away. It was only slightly larger than a standard A4: he missed the first shot by a mile. With a look back at Roach and River, who were thoroughly unimpressed, he wiped his brow and tried again. It took six shots before he figured out how to best aim the rifle, and his last four hit the paper near each of its corners. The woman running the booth pulled it up to him by pressing a button that would guide it forward. Once it was within reach, she tore it down, circled the four shots with a marker, and passed it to him. "Happy to do business with you, sir. You can redeem it at either of those booths with any purchase over $50."

He thanked her anxiously then slipped out of the way of the next patron. After giving the paper to Roach as they walked away, he looked up to him with a hopeful expression.

"You didn't hit the target," said Roach bluntly.

"I hit the paper, though!" He pointed to the circled parts.

"Yeah yeah." He crumpled it, tossed it on the floor behind him, and shoved his hands back into his pockets. Partha was glaring at him, but he ignored the upset. "Let's just go look at the knives already."

There was a long queue for the blacksmith, so it was ten minutes later before they were close enough to inspect the goods on offer. River was disinterested and looking at something on his phone, so it was only Partha and Roach looking over the wares. Roach was ultimately unimpressed with the selection. Not only were there no butterfly knives, but he didn't see any good switchblades either. There were a few swords that caught Partha's eye, however, so they waited in another shorter line to inquire about them.

"Oh, hey!" said the craftsman when they reached the front of the queue, "You're Party the Kid! I love your stream! I actually have a sword you'll want to see. Just a second." He disappeared behind one of his dividers and emerged a moment later holding a long thin case made of black faux-leather. He brought it to the table and laid it across the glass cover over an assortment of daggers and bowie knives. Opening it to show Partha, he explained, "This is Helio's rapier! From your game! That last session was crazy, huh?"

Partha's jaw dropped as he reached out to touch the blade. "It looks just like the art!"

"Yeah, I did my best guess at the hilt base." He picked it up and showed the bottom of the handle where a large polished gemstone was mantled. It was an opaque pastel green colour with white and gold formations inside. "It's variscite. I believe Thyne said it was his favourite gemstone? I know Helio was only his character, but I figured—."

"It's beautiful!" He looked up at Roach and beamed. "Do you like it?"

He shrugged. "It's cool. Yeah. Not really a sword guy."

"But you designed it. Does it look how you imagined?"

He eyed the sword, but before he could answer, the smith was starstruck for a second time. "Wait, you drew the art for the game? You're—. Yeah! You're Red Velvet! You did the music, too, right?" Roach nodded. "Wow! I'm flabbergasted! I listened to your stuff after Party mentioned you, and I just gotta say, man: big fan of your second album."

"Oh yeah? What's your favourite song?"

He stroked his chin. "Probably *Electric Chair.*"

Roach very nearly smiled. He had never been recognised outside of a show. The ego stroke was nice, but before he could reply, River grabbed his sleeve and said in Arabic: "Don't you need to pray?"

He looked at the time then through the windows. "I should." He turned to Partha and the smith. "Pleasure meeting you, man. I gotta go, though."

"Oh, can I have a picture first?"

"No."

He was gone before the blacksmith had fully processed the answer, so his smile was a little broken and baffled when he looked back at Partha. "Anyway, what can I do for you?"

He pointed to the rapier and said, "How much?"

"Uh…." He laughed nervously. "I wasn't planning on selling it." Partha frowned.

"B-but! I mean! Uh... For you?" He looked at it again, and when he started back up he sounded like he may have cried, "$3600?"

"Deal!" He ignored the upset (though he did notice it) and took out his credit card.

Partha hugged the rapier's faux-leather case like a plush as they walked off. He beamed up to River, who took him aside and leaned down to whisper: "Nevermind the sword, dude. Do you still want a gun?"

He blinked. A confused grin. "I do, but didn't Roach say—?"

"Screw what Tony said, man. You did great with the BB gun. He's just being a dick."

"I—. I did?"

He nodded. "It was rigged. That gun's effective range is only about fifteen feet. I looked it up while you were talking to the blacksmith guy. I also looked up the dimensions of the spot they rented for that booth: it was easily twenty-five feet from the shooting line. You hit it four times. That's great! Besides... I was going to get you a gun either way."

"You were? Why?"

He shrugged. "Important to keep morale high, and you clearly want one. No harm no foul, I say."

"Wow! Thanks, River! Let's go back down to the main floor, then! I saw some pistols that looked really fucking cool."

He giggled and agreed.

After his ablution, Roach was stopped before he left the restroom by a tall husky man with a square face and bushy eyebrows. He was bald and heavily tattooed, and his breath reeked of whiskey. "Hey you," he slurred and attempted to shove Roach backwards, "Don't think I can't see that symbol on your shirt."

He looked down at his sleeveless black hoodie which was bleach-stained across its entire front with an unmissable anarchy symbol. "You mean the one I'm not even sort of trying to hide?"

"Ye—." Hic. "Yeah! You're Antifa, ain'tchya!?"

Roach looked around the bathroom. There were only two stalls and three urinals, none of which were currently occupied, nor were the sinks. When he looked back at the drunk he nodded. "Yeah, I'm their leader."

"'Course y'are," he slurred and proceeded to mumble something under his breath that Roach didn't understand nor care to decrypt.

After a beat, Roach whispered, "Are you going to fight me over it?" There was a sick longing in the back of his eyes and the beginnings of a mad grin twitching his lips.

He stumbled and caught himself on Roach, who helped him back to his feet. "I might! I heard you speaking Arab to your brother upstairs."

"Oh yeah? And I came in here to clean myself before I pray to Allah. Does that scare you?"

"I ain't scared 'a no Muslim terrorist!"

"Right. If you were scared you wouldn't have followed me into the bathroom to try and pick a fight." The way Roach spoke was like magic. It convinced the drunkard that he had wanted to engage in a physical fight when he had only approached to bother Roach verbally.

"'Xactly! So put 'em up!" He held up his fists.

Roach's hands remained firmly in his pockets. "Is this you defending your country then? You know I fought in the war. I'm a veteran."

His posture became less hostile. "Oh, you did? How many beaners did you kill?"

Roach's teeth briefly ground into each other, but he unhinged them to be able to speak coherently: "I fought *for* Mexico."

When his boozy brain had finished processing the claim, he swung at Roach and missed horribly without even a move to dodge. "You're a traitor! A traitor and a murderer!"

"Yeah," agreed Roach as he dodged a sloppy second swing. "You should leave before I prove you right." There was a flash of evil and rage in his eyes to match the sinister nature of his voice, but it went unnoticed.

Another swing, another miss. By that point, the man started to panic. He rushed to the door and threw himself across it to block Roach from leaving. "I can't let you buy no guns! No guns!"

"Oh, don't worry about that. I don't like guns."

"Then what're you doin' here at—." His eyes went wide. "You're gonna bomb the convention!" He tried to rush out of the room, but the door wouldn't budge. It wasn't locked: rather, it was as if someone was holding it closed.

"I might," continued Roach as he paced slowly behind the panicking drunk, "but bombs aren't very good, either. They make a nice mess of things, but they have that same problem that guns have." He waited for the man to inquire, but when he didn't, he continued anyway: "They're too quick. Too easy." By then he was close enough to touch. He turned him around to flip open one of his knives and held it up to his throat with one hand, covering his mouth with the other. "I like knives," he whispered with a glimmer of unholy wickedness in his eyes, "There's so much more time to savour all the blood—. The screams—. The begging—." He took a deep breath through his nose and smiled wide, his teeth perfectly pristine and straight with particularly sharp (though not vampiric) canines.

"You're crazy!" shouted the man through Roach's hand.

He nodded wildly. "Oh yeah. So tell me—. Tell me why I shouldn't kill you right now."

He was sobered evermore by the encounter. His breaths were laboured as he tried to lean away from the knife only to be stopped by the door behind him. Roach only had a few inches on him, and they were likely in the same weight class, but this man felt smaller than he had as a child. His mind kept telling him to kick Roach in the nads and flee, but his body wasn't his own. He was paralysed. He felt the knife start to dig into his skin and blurted out, "No! I have a son!"

Roach's smile was slightly agape as he looked longingly into his next victim's panicking blue eyes, savouring the fear. His voice was low and almost lecherous when he breathed, "And?"

"And I'm all he has!"

"Oh?" He laughed darkly. "Then I should get rid of you, so he'll be raised by someone better."

He sputtered incoherently, trying not to cry, and Roach gave silent kudos to him for holding it back. "Leave me be! I haven't done anything to you!"

"Keep your voice down, or I'll stop considering letting you live." Roach had already decided to kill this man: the conversation was just an excuse to hear him beg for his life. "It's true you haven't done anything to me…."

"Then let me go," he said with a significantly lower voice.

Roach rolled his eyes. His emotions were plain on his face: another indication that the man in his grasp would not survive the encounter. "This isn't fun anymore. What's your name?"

"Peter."

"Heh. Peter." He giggled. "Don't make me laugh, dude. It'll be too loud."

He was too baffled and terrified to form a coherent reply.

"Alright, well, Peter." He sighed and frowned. "You've been an impressive disappointment. I just hope you bleed better than you beg." And with that, the man was stabbed quickly to death, first in his gut, then his chest, then his throat. He screamed briefly into Roach's hand, but his lungs filled with blood too quickly to be heard from the other side of the thick oak door. Roach was careful not to get blood on his clothes, but he let it drench his hand and painted some of it down his face when he was finished killing him, letting out a breathy moan at the feel of it.

He turned out the lights at the same time that the body hit the linoleum, then locked the door. Without any issue in the now-unlit windowless room, he cleaned the crime scene and only heard two attempts at opening the door in the duration, both of which were immediately abandoned when it became clear that the bathroom was locked with its lights out.

Only ten minutes later, Peter's body was hidden in the drop-ceiling, the blood had been cleaned from the doorway, and Roach was washing himself in the sink with the lights on and door unlocked. Besides the inhuman ecstasy in his eyes, there was no evidence of the murder to be found when the next stranger entered and beelined for a urinal.

Roach was on his phone texting his brother in code to inform him of the crime when he stumbled into Perlie and Francis on the main showroom floor. Perlie had found a *Tommy* gun, so he was quick to comment, "You've gotta do the voice when you use that, Perls."

"What voice?" she asked.

He finished texting River and slid his phone into his back pocket to give her his undivided attention. "What voice? Oh—." He took the gun and held it close to his waist as he put on an accent something like a 1920s gangster and mimed he was smoking a cigar: "Ah, see, put the money in the bag, see."

She and Francis both giggled. "I'll have to work on it, then," she said as she took the gun back. "Did you find any good knives?"

"No, and I still need to pray, so I'll have to catch you two later."

"There was a cosy little lounge on the top floor we just came from. Could probably pray there without having to deal with too many assholes," informed Perlie, and Francis held up the martini he had purchased in said lounge to emphasise her claim.

"Hey, thanks." He nearly smiled, but when he moved to leave them, Perlie stopped him with a hand flat on his chest.

She pushed him back in front of her and looked at him knowingly. There was a glint in his eyes that she recognised. He was happy. *Too* happy considering how grumbly he had been about coming to the gun show in the first place. He hadn't even found any knives yet. There was only one thing that would put that glint in his eyes. After crossing her arms and making a point to look him up and down, she said, "Making our own fun, are we?"

He allowed himself a slight grin and said, "You're worse than Sonny."

"Worse? Or better?"

"Yes."

She giggled again and shooed him away playfully.

As Roach departed, Francis felt his phone vibrate. A message from Thyne in Old Egyptian: ⟦ **Partha got recognised. Go into a bathroom stall and change your appearance. We're trying to lay low.** ⟧ He looked up from his phone at Perlie. "Would you be willing to hold my drink while I go to the lavatory?"

"Of course, dude." She took the drink. While she waited patiently for him to return, her eyes scanned the convention, eventually landing on the logo over Anubis' side of the showroom. It was at least fifteen feet tall and hoisted to the wall another ten feet over a stage. This was an expanded and more artistic rendition of the vector logo they etched into their products, depicting a balancing scale with a feather on its right disk and three bullets on the other, their weights evidently equal. In the simplified version, the only hint of Anubis was his hand at the top of the scale, but in this more detailed version, it also included the god of death himself, holding up the scale and gesturing to it with a cartoonish smile. It made her sick to see such a blatant bastardisation of what was once a holy figure. She rolled her eyes at the lunacy of it, especially when she was reminded of their slogan written underneath: *Light as a feather*. She was an atheist herself, but she knew that there were people (like Thyne) who worshipped old gods like the ones Osiris seemingly had an obsession with disrespecting.

Her thinking did amuse her when she reminded herself of the company's many attempts to incorporate Set into its products, though. In all three instances, they were met with a great misfortune. Their first attempt was an artillery company which they created to help arm the war efforts with tanks, mortars, and missiles. It lasted a year before it came to light that the alloys they were using for all of their products were laced with a deadly amount of lead. The tanks were especially dangerous, and, when paired with the heat in the Mexican sun, they also doubled as human broilers. In just one year, the company had killed over a thousand of their own mercenaries and American soldiers with the shoddy products. After enough backlash, they shut down the subsidiary and shelved the idea until after the war.

The second attempt at incorporating Set into their branding was for their table-ware line. Some executive somewhere was really proud of himself for thinking to call it the *Table Set*. The product itself was cheap garbage but nothing dangerous. The misfortune for the *Table Set* line was rather that the main factory was destroyed in an EF5 tornado that tore across North Texas and down into South Texas (one of the newly-acquired states) in 2077. They gave up on the line shortly thereafter and shelved it for another year.

Their last and most recent attempt to bastardise the god of destruction and chaos was in a pet-supplies line. They called it something like *The Set Animals*, but it went belly-up before it ever went to market because of insider-trading. Though it was rumoured to actually be shut down because the CEO's six dogs all mysteriously died in the span of a year.

Francis returned to Perlie's side with his appearance altered. His hair was dark brown and cut into an Ivy League style. His eyes were so dark a brown they were effectively black, he was clean-shaven, and his teeth were significantly less rotten. She didn't recognise him until he took his drink back and thanked her as if there was nothing strange about him.

"What did you do?"

He was surprised by the question (somehow) and stopped mid-sip to say, "Oh, apologies. Have I startled you?"

"You just had like a whole disguise kit on you?"

He tilted his head. "I used my control over the fourth dimension to alter my outward appearance." It was almost like she didn't understand or believe that he could control time. Weird.

She rolled her eyes. "Okay, sure. Why, though?"

"Because Thyne thought it prudent."

With a slight smile she surrendered. "Whatever. Do you want to go see if the line died down for that blacksmith upstairs?"

"A capital idea!"

They went upstairs, River bought Partha a flintlock pistol from a vintage collector, and Thyne dropped off his rifle with a painter to be picked up a couple hours later. While that was all happening, Roach had made his way back downstairs and found himself in the Anubis half of the showroom. He was just as irritated by the logo and slogan as Perlie, but he wasn't aware that Osiris guns were generally considered overpriced trash. There were a few other people browsing the wares, but it was significantly quieter than elsewhere at the show. He stopped to inspect a table of butterfly knives, but after reading *Made in Mexico* etched into each of the latches, he left them alone. They were high-quality blades and not overly expensive, but he couldn't morally justify adding any of them to his collection.

Inevitably, he wandered deep enough into the labyrinth to be surrounded by rifles, and one model actually caught his eye. He plucked it off of its rack and observed it as if he had any idea what a good gun was like. It had two stocks that folded out and downward and was typically fed drum magazines hidden behind each of them, flush against the stocks. The odd design made it easier to dual wield the semi-automatic assault rifles by allowing the gunman to rest the weapon on his or her forearm without fear of it sliding off. At least, that's what the Anubis marketing team said, but in actuality, it got far too hot after extended use for that to be viable. This gun in particular was white carbon fibre with black accents made of an ultra-light aluminium alloy.

"Ah, you like the *KR-44* do you?" asked a worker.

A cursory uninterested glance his way. "Yeah," he muttered, "had one in the war."

"Oh you have good taste! Were you an officer?" He shook his head, still not dignifying this worker with eye contact. "They were a favourite among officers, but I didn't think you could order them if you were a lower rank." He stroked his scruffy chin. "Is there a rank above officer?"

"It's not really a rank," he said and finally looked at the young man, "This gun also looks like a dick, which is just hilarious." He folded up the stocks to prove his point, but it didn't look very phallic and made the worker laugh awkwardly. "At least... it does with the drum mags in it. It's such a stupid design. Horribly impractical to hold. Had to modify mine to remove one of the stocks. Anyway, mine also had an under-barrel grenade launcher and a silencer. Where are those parts?"

"Oh, right this way, sir!" His strides were bouncy as he rounded to the other side of that same aisle and gestured to an assortment of modifications. "We call it the kicker, but it's real name is some number I don't remember," he said as he passed Roach the grenade-launcher, "Do you know how to attach it?"

"No. You attach it." He passed him the rifle and crossed his arms behind his back to walk down the line of mods, observing them.

After adding the grenade-launcher to the bottom of the gun, he rushed up to Roach's place and gestured to the silencers. "These three will all fit. This one is the quietest, but it does hamper the range the most. This one is the best for—."

"I want the quietest one. Attach it."

He was a little panicked because of Roach's intimidating air and rushed to screw in the silencer. "And would you like to also add a scope? Maybe a flashlight or laser—."

"No. How much is it like that?"

"If you sign up for our—."

"Shut up and tell me how much it costs exactly how it is right now." He took out his wallet and opened it, waiting for a price.

The worker stuttered and brought him swiftly to a nearby cash register. After pressing on the screen a few times he said, "Your total would be $21,186, sir. But with our warranty—."

"Lucky I've got just a little more than that." He began counting out the money, starting with $500 bills, but when he set it on the counter he saw the worker nervously holding a clipboard out to him. "What's this? A survey?"

He chuckled. "Uh. No, sir. You can't buy a gun without filling this out. You know how it is with liberals. They want to make it difficult for us to—."

"Yeah yeah. Don't gotta tell me twice how shitty liberals are." He snatched the clipboard and read silently:

THANK YOU FOR SHOPPING WITH US! YOU ARE A VALUED CUSTOMER OF ANUBIS INCENDIARIES. PLEASE FILL OUT THIS FORM TO PROVE THAT YOU ARE MENTALLY FIT TO BE ABLE TO PURCHASE FROM US! AND REMEMBER, WITH A WEAPON FROM ANUBIS, YOU'LL FEEL LIGHT AS A FEATHER!

There was more, but he stopped and eyed the worker. "What is this corporate bullshit, dude? There aren't any forms like this at the independent vendor tables."

"Right, well, that means that the independent vendors are liable in court if the weapons they sell are used for crimes."

"Uh huh…." He passed the clipboard back.

He was too perturbed by his tall bulky frame and lack of emotion to ask him to fill it out himself, so he took up the pen and started to ask him the questions from it with a nervous sweat soaking through his shirt collar:

"Right, uh. What's your first name?"

"John."

He wrote it down. "And last?"

"Jameson."

"Let me guess: you want pictures of Spiderman?" he joked and smiled at Roach, but was met with a petrifying deadpan gaze that immediately erased the lightness. "Right. I'll just write that down... And your occupation?"

"Accountant."

"Race?"

"What do you think?"

He swallowed a lump of dread and muttered, "I'll just put white.... And uh... birthdate?"

"Today, 2050."

"Oh? Happy birthday!" He wrote it down. "Gender?"

Roach's air became ten times harsher.

"Right...." He gulped and ticked off the 'male' checkbox.

"Are we done yet?"

"Almost." He cleared his throat. "Forgive me, but I have to ask these things, and they get more personal."

"More personal than my personal details?"

He laughed nervously. "Maybe. Heh. So uh... Firstly: have you ever bought a gun before?"

"No."

"And are you buying this gun for someone other than yourself?"

"No."

"Alrighty. Have you ever had... suicidal thoughts?"

"No."

"Good! Any thoughts of harming others?"

"No."

"And have you ever killed anyone? If so, how many and under what circumstances?"

"I've never killed anyone."

"Have you ever been diagnosed by a mental health professional with any of the following:

"Depression?"

"No."

"Bipolar Disorder?"

"No."

"Antisocial or Narcissistic Personality Disorders?"

"No."

"Gender Dysphoria or Dissociative Identity Disorder?"

"No."

"Schizophrenia of any kind?"

"No."

"Wonderful. Do you have any vision impairments? For example: do you need glasses or contacts when you drive?"

"No."

"Do you partake in recreational drug use such as alcohol or marijuana? If so, how often?"

"No."

"Okay. And… do you have more than twenty missed days of mandatory mass?"

"No."

"Perfect! You're doing great, sir. There are only a few more left." He cleared his throat nervously. "Have you ever been associated with an anti-government revolutionary or terrorist group such as Antifa, Isis, or the KKK?"

He scoffed. "No."

"Oh, and just because a lot of people get confused with that one: yes, neo-Nazis do count for that question, even though they're not actually a terrorist group."

"I'm not a nazi."

"Good. Good. Are you currently in or have you ever been in a gang and/or mafia?"

"No."

"You're acing this, sir. Have you ever attended a protest, peaceful or otherwise?"

"No."

"Have you ever served in a formal military, American or otherwise?" He was under the impression that he had, so when Roach said, "No," he smiled nervously at him. "I… may have ticked the 'yes' box already…. You said you had this gun in the war, so I thought…." He trailed off, hoping for Roach to respond. When he didn't, the nervous worker quickly grabbed another form and started to copy the answers over.

Roach was a patient person, but he was greatly enjoying watching this man squirm thinking he wasn't. He leaned over menacingly and said in a low voice, "Is this really the best use of our time?"

The man laughed nervously and shrank away from the encroaching giant. "Just a second, please. I'm sorry, sir." Standing back upright, Roach crossed his arms and watched him catch back up on the new form, ticking the 'no' box instead of the 'yes' on the penultimate question. "And, lastly," he said with a quivering voice, "have you ever been arrested and/or imprisoned?"

"No."

After writing a few more things and signing on a dotted line, he passed the clipboard back to Roach. Pointing with the pen to a different dotted line at the bottom, he said, "You just sign there to assume responsibility for the firearm and to confirm that all of the above is true."

Roach scribbled something vaguely legible as *John Jameson*, but his handwriting would be God-awful even if he actually gave a shit about this form.

"Great. I'll take the cash now." Once he had the money sorted in the till he asked, "Would you like the receipt, sir?"

"Yeah."

"There you go. And would you like a complimentary case of ammo for your brand new best friend?"

He stared blankly.

"Heh. I'll take that as a 'no.' Have a good day, sir, and happy birthday again!"

"Yeah. Later, man."

As "John" walked away, the worker, a middle-aged man named Linus, let out a relieved sigh. While he was walking it to a filing cabinet, he found himself absent-mindedly rereading the form. It was his immediate assumption (and a fair one at that) when Mr. Jameson said he was in the war but not the military, that he was a mercenary. Mercenaries were relatively common at shows like this, but if one thing was well-known about them, it was their wanton bloodlust. They were often hired to do things deemed too gruesome for the military. Linus' gaze lingered on the tick next to 'No' beside the *Have you ever killed anyone?* question. He gulped and trailed his green-eyed gaze down to his own name and signature. Sweat beaded his brow. '*I need to get the gun back. I cannot lose this fucking job.*'

After being sure that his colleague would be able to handle the booths he was running (and promising to buy her a snack for the trouble), he rushed out of the area and into the crowded half of the main showroom. Luckily "John" was very tall, so it would be easy to spot him amongst the crowd. At least, that was Linus' thinking for the first half hour of searching. After scouring all four storeys of the convention centre and bringing his coworker a bagel, he was back down to the first floor when he finally saw the tall man. He was wearing a lighter coloured shirt than Linus recalled, but he supposed his memory must have failed him. His voice was mousey when he rushed up behind him and said, "Mr. Jameson? Mr. Jameson, sir?" Despite his anxiety around the tall menacing man, he reached up and tapped his shoulder.

"Hm? What do you want?" said River as he turned around.

"S-sir. Uh." He averted his eyes and poked his fingers together. "So, I figured out that you lied on that form, and so, I have to unfortunately ask for the gun back."

River immediately understood this man was someone who had met Roach and apparently sold him a gun. He made his expression as deadpan as possible and replied, "Remind me who you are."

"R-right. Um. I'm Linus Terk. I sold you that *KR-44*? About an hour ago." He looked up at him with a nervous grin. "You'll be fully refunded, of course."

"I don't have the gun."

Linus was made even more flustered. "Y-y-you don't? Did you put it in your car or something? Did you also l-lie about— er— buying it for someone else?"

"I didn't buy a gun for anyone else."

"Heya, River!" said Partha as he approached, "Thanks again for buying me that gun! I just put in the car!"

Linus glared at him. "AND you lied about your name!"

River pressed a hand to his chest and allowed himself to emote again. "Sir, I think you have me mistaken for someone else."

"I suppose you have a twin brother named John, then?"

It would be easy to say yes, find Roach, and get all of this sorted out that way, but… River was *bored*. He hadn't had *any* fun at this gun show, so he decided to play. "I don't know anyone named John," he said flatly.

"Sir, I need you to get the gun from this young man's car and give it back, or I'm going to have to call security."

Partha arched his brow at River and stood on his tip-toes to whisper into his ear, "What's going on?"

He replied so Linus could hear, "This man has me confused for someone else."

"Either you're lying or… or… he looked *just* like you!"

"He's upset because you bought me a gun?" asked Partha.

River giggled. "He's certainly grumpy about *something*."

"I'm getting security, sir, and you will know no fury like mine."

"Okay," he said and wiggled his fingers at him, "Tootles."

Just as he was leaving, Roach approached with a cup of lemon Italian ice. His newly acquired gun had a checkered strap now and was hanging off his back by it. "Hey, bro. I bought a gun."

River ignored him and looked back at Linus. Without so much as a twitch of the brow to indicate his lie, he said, "I have never met this man in my life."

"Oh, hey!" said Roach when he noticed the worker. "You're the guy who sold it to me. What're you doing out of your cage?" He was referring to the Anubis section of the showroom to make a quick joke, but his tone and mien were so unexpressive that it was harrowing more than it was funny.

"Mr. Jameson. You have to give the gun back."

"What?" he said with the little plastic spoon still in his mouth. "Why, dude?"

"You lied on your form!"

"No I didn't."

"What did he lie about?" asked Partha.

"He said he's never killed anyone, but I have a very difficult time believing that a mercenary who was in the war hasn't killed someone."

Roach took another bite of his Italian ice while Partha answered, "Mr. Uh. Jameson hasn't killed anyone, sir."

"And I'm just supposed to believe you? How do you even know him? And you," he gestured to River, "Come on, man. Why are you pretending not to know him? I can't lose this job. Just give the gun back, and I'll give you your money back, and it'll be like it never happened."

"I don't know him, but," he turned toward Roach, "You're right. He *does* look just like me." He smirked at his brother. "Do you live with your birth mother in England making the ugliest wedding dresses ever?"

Roach swallowed his mouthful and nodded. "I used to, but we moved to the states when I was eight. Do you live with your birth father in a Californian vineyard?"

River giggled. "Yes, I did until the floods. He lost the estate, so we came here to New Mexico. Maybe we were separated at birth! Was there a boat involved in your parents' love life and half of a picture in your dresser of them eating dinner on said boat?"

Roach opened his mouth to continue the stupid bit, but Linus held up his hands and shouted, "Enough! Stop fucking around and give me the gun back." He tried to take it by the strap but was easily dodged.

Roach wiped the condensation from his icy treat off his hand onto his pants leg. "Listen, dude. Hand on heart," he laid his hand flat on his chest, "I've never killed anyone."

Linus huffed. "Fine! Guess there's nothing I can do, then."

"Guess not." He ate another bite of his dessert, looking Linus dead in the eyes.

"I—. I'm leaving!"

They all three waved sarcastically as he stomped away, but Roach stopped when he overheard a stranger behind him say, "...in the men's room, yeah."

And another stranger's response: "The *ceiling* is bleeding?"

"That's what I heard."

"Well!" said Roach rather suddenly, "We should probably get going. Don't want to have to get another hotel."

Part Two

No one can love who has not a heart.

Chapter 16
A Bad Witch

The way the headlights shattered was cathartic. The air hissing out of the tires was like applause. She could hardly see through her tears. She could hardly breathe between hysterical sobs. After smashing the windshield with a few slams from the bottom of her bat, she knocked off the driver's side mirror and left the garage to resume crying in her *Camaro*.

Aspyn Temm was an attractive woman with wavy auburn hair, brown eyes, and smooth pale skin. Her 5'4" frame was perfectly curvaceous by conventional standards: wide hips, large breasts, and a slim but not unhealthily thin waist. The natural curves were also accentuated by a cosmetic surgery she had received which increased the size of her already plump bottom. She underwent the procedure at her father's insistence when she was only sixteen. Luckily for her, he never got to see the results having died in a mass shooting before her flight back to England from Taiwan where she had undergone the operation. She was therefore able to attend the funeral without fully realising what he was probably planning to do to her when she got home.

Now, as a thirty-six year old woman, her mother had just retired the year prior and left Aspyn the owner and CEO of an independent bakery in Piccadilly Circus. Her mother was an exceptional baker and had a shrewd mind for business, but Aspyn was rather lost upon inheriting the establishment. Even with several years worth of lessons from her mother before being passed the mantle, she still wasn't even entirely sure how to go about hiring bakers.

It was unfair. All Aspyn wanted was to explore the world. She was a mountain climber in her free time, but now that she was responsible for a business in one of the busiest parts of London, she was forced to stay in England working. Even her car was breaking down, making it impossible to explore the nearby areas. Only two months into operations, the bakery was failing, and when she found out that her boyfriend was cheating on her that morning, she fired all of the workers and closed it indefinitely.

After destroying his *Jeep* and having a good cry in her beater on the streetside, she drove to her cramped little flat and collapsed in bed to rot away to nothing. Her cat jumped up onto her and started kneading at her back fat, but she ignored the discomfort it brought. '*At least someone cares about me,*' she thought as she turned around to pet the tabby. He meowed at her with a concerned air, and she quelled his worries with a whispered, "Don't worry about me, Meatloaf. I'm done dating." He curled up on her stomach to help calm her.

That night, she squeezed into a short halter-topped dress and thigh-high boots. The dress stopped just low enough on her thigh to not reveal too much while still leaving about two inches of bare skin before the start of her matte black boots. It was wine-red and silky with a deep V-neck that she was glad to see showed a tasteful amount of her cleavage. The outfit wasn't warm enough for late February, but with a duster she would be comfortable enough to make the walk out to the underground and catch a tram to central London. Before leaving, she followed an online video tutorial for her make-up look and ordered a few of the promoted items with a card she most definitely couldn't afford to pay off. Once her makeup was done, she quickly curled her hair into large ringlets, filled her cat's food bowl, and kissed him goodbye.

When she entered the pub, things were already in full-swing for the night. The music was loud but not uncomfortably so, and the bar was crowded. She waited around for a chance to order something, and once she had a Manhattan in hand, she migrated to the least-crowded corner of the building. She found a high table with a couple stools around it and sat on one, careful to cross her legs to not accidentally flash anyone, then took out a notebook from her purse. With her duster draped over the table underneath it, she started writing.

It was hardly a conducive environment for productive writing or financing, but she didn't expect to get any work done. She only brought the journal and pen to look more aloof and approachable by prospects. Her plan wasn't working as well as she had hoped for the first hour of her being there. She had managed to get some planning done for a mystery novel she wanted to write, but no one had approached her. In fact, the only people who had come near her were piss-drunk and stumbled into her table, spilling vodka on her duster. They apologised and left almost as soon as they came, so she couldn't even use it as an excuse to talk with them. '*Just as well,*' she thought, '*They look like uni kids anyway.*'

Her luck changed about a half hour after this incident when a handsome young man, likely in his late twenties, leaned casually on the table and said, "Owamya, miss. I can't help but notice you're all alone over here. Someone stand you up?"

She was flustered by how attractive he was. He was dressed in a dark brown business suit with a plaid vest and a crisp white dress-shirt. His swarthy hair was slicked back and curled out into cute cowlicks at the base of his neck. There was a shadow of mahogany-tinted facial hair that accentuated his sharp bone structure and matched his thick eyebrows in colour. His voice was as deep as his dark eyes, and he had a cute Brummie accent.

Aspyn smiled and pushed some of her curled hair behind her ear to seem more sheepish. "No. I came alone."

"Oh? And were you hoping to stay that way?"

She let out a shuddery breath, taken aback by his forwardness in a very pleased way. "I don't know. Did you happen to know someone who might want to accompany me?" She batted her eyelashes at him and let the blush on her cheeks shine.

He rubbed his jaw and tilted his head, seemingly only to look sexier, before leaning in to say in a low voice, "You wanna go somewhere quieter?"

She lowered her voice to match the volume of his. "Where'd you have in mind?"

He retreated and offered a charming smirk. "There's a lounge down the road a bit. Much more dignified crowd than here."

She was playfully offended. "Oh? Are you insinuating I'm not dignified?"

"Quite the opposite, miss. You look far *too* dignified to be out here with the swine."

A flirtatious giggle. "Okay," she said with a blush as she slid her journal and pen back into her purse, "What's your name?"

He helped her down from her stool and wrapped her duster back over her shoulders, using the motion to smoothly drape his arm around her as he led her toward the exit. "Rory Couch. And you are?"

"Aspyn Temm," she said before he opened the door for her and led her out into the crisp winter air. "I hope it's not too long a walk."

"It's not too far," he assured her and held out his arm to offer to keep holding her. She tried not to seem too eager to accept the offer but was adorably quick to lean into his side and let his body-heat warm her as they walked.

Perhaps it was ill-advised to have so readily gone outside with a stranger, but she had pepper-spray in her purse and knew the area like the back of her hand. His air was also innocent and gentlemanly. If he didn't accept 'no' as an answer, she would be genuinely shocked. Besides… there were very few things someone so handsome could ask of her that she would refuse. As they walked, she decided to get to know him a little more. She had sworn off dating, but, '*Well, if he wants to, I could be convinced.*' "So, what do you do?"

He smirked. "I own about half of this town, Miss Temm."

"You what, mate?"

"It's true. I own eighty-three properties in London alone, including that dreadful club we've just left."

She sputtered incoherently.

A light chuckle. "I was checking in with the owner. He's three weeks behind on his rent, so I hope you don't like the drinks too much. I'll have to shut it down if he doesn't pay me by next week."

'Okay... maybe I swore off dating too quickly... He could pay for the bakery. No. He could RUN the bakery for me. And all I'd have to do is put out for him: the most beautiful man in London?' She smiled anxiously at him. "You must make a lot of money."

His smile soured. "Well, sure, but...," he trailed off.

She recognised the offence she had caused and hurriedly course-corrected: "Any interesting hobbies, Mr. Couch?"

He seemed to relax. "Yeah, of course. I like to read, birdwatch, golf. I keep up with American football even more than I keep up with real footy. And—. Promise you won't laugh?" She nodded. "I quite like to bake, and I'm good at it, if I do say so myself."

'By God he's actually perfect.' "Really? Well, I have a bakery here in town."

His grin was cute and innocent. "That's great! We should bake together sometime."

Before she could respond, he opened the door to a towering building and gestured her inside. It was opulent to a degree she had only experienced on her post-graduation celebration in Dubai. The floor was black marble with prismatic veins flowing across it, giving it the look of an alien ocean of oil. The walls were adorned with priceless artwork, and where there weren't Renaissance paintings bigger than the square-footage of her flat, there was intricate moulding in stark blacks and crisp whites. The crystal chandelier looked to be at least three metres tall and hung from a ceiling just as ornate as the walls. His dress shoes clicked against the marble almost as loudly as her kitten heels as she followed him past an empty reception desk to an elevator.

Once inside, he hesitated to press anything and smirked at her. "No trouble with heights, I hope?"

She shook her head, her eyes still sparkling like the chandelier.

"Good," he said, finding her utterly adorable. After pressing the highest number on the panel he explained, "It's a rooftop lounge. Have you ever seen London from so high? And on such a beautiful night?"

"No, I haven't," she said after stopping herself from swooning.

The elevator opened to reveal a smokey chamber with low ceilings. The walls, floor, and ceiling were all dark oak, and the haze of cigar and marijuana smoke made it difficult to see the other side of the room. There was a pianist serenading the inhabitants from a dimly-lit platform, and to the immediate right of the entrance was a semicircle shaped bar where a well-dressed bartender was currently mixing a martini. Rory's first order of business was to take Aspyn out onto a balcony which, thanks to the cold, was empty. With the glass door closed behind him, he rushed up to her beside the railing and gestured out at the glittering city. "What do you think, Miss Temm?"

"It's beautiful!" She beamed at him but quickly returned her attention to the view.

He leaned backwards on the railing beside her. She was busy looking at the city, but he was rather enjoying the sight of *her* quite a lot more. He patiently waited for her to have her fill, and when she noticed he had been looking at her with hearts in his eyes, they both blushed but didn't break eye-contact. His voice was low: "I'd love to get to know you better, Miss Temm."

She swayed gently from side to side and stepped into his space. She was short, so his 5'9" frame was comfortably tall comparatively. She ran her hand up his chest then cupped it tenderly around his cheek. "Oh yeah, Mr. Couch? And how do you mean?"

He gently coiled a hand around the small of her back to pull her closer and leaned down to kiss her. "We'll take it slow."

She nearly pouted but managed to suppress it to instead pull him in for another kiss. "You're not married are you?"

"No, ma'am. I'm eligible."

"Good, I'm bloody sick of cheaters," she said curtly then resumed kissing him.

Having only broken up with her boyfriend that morning, she was eager to lay Mr. Perfect here to shove it in her ex's stupid cheating face. And, being as perfect as he was, he was able to read her intentions and led her back inside to the coat closet. With someone's scarf tied around the doorknob, he let his hands explore her body, followed shortly after by his lips and tongue. The small room was increasingly hot and humid, and she felt especially beautiful and worthy of love when he easily lifted her to wrap her legs around his back. None of her past lovers had been strong enough to do so, and the most recent scumbag had blamed it on her weight. 'Love' felt like a strong word for this man she had just met, especially while he was railing her against the wall, but in the moment it was all she could think. She tore someone's no-doubt designer scarf in her many moments of ecstasy and managed to whisper all of her moans save for the last one.

When they were finished having fun in the coatroom, they checked each other's appearances. He was wiping off her lipstick with a makeup wipe from her bag while she slicked his hair back as neatly as possible without more gel. "I hope—," he began as he cleaned her cheeks of some smeared mascara, "I hope this isn't just a one-time thing, Miss Temm."

"Call me Aspyn," she whispered.

"It's not a one-time thing, is it?"

She shook her head. "I hope not!"

He smiled and passed her the dirty makeup wipe. "Good. We've done this rather backwards; will you let me buy you a drink?"

She poked his chest. "I'll *make* you buy me a drink."

"Wouldn't have it any other way, Miss Temm." A cheeky wink.

The drinks were almost as expensive as her rent, but she basked in this sudden fantasy of being swept off her feet by a handsome rich gentleman. He was a good lay, too, and the hints at a submissiveness in him had her short of breath. Everything was falling into place perfectly, and she had to stop herself from imagining a life with the young man she had only just met.

After two drinks each and an hour of chatting, Rory had to momentarily excuse himself to go talk with someone because he was, "trying to secure this deal for weeks, and he looks *just* drunk enough to sign. Terribly sorry, ma'am. Just a moment, okay?"

"Take your time," she said with a sweet smile and watched him scamper off to a group of drunken businessmen. After about fifteen minutes of her sitting alone at the bar and nursing her cocktail, the bartender passed her another. "Oh, I don't want to spend his money without—."

"It's not from Mr. Couch, miss. It's from Mr. Abraham." He pointed across the room, and through the haze she saw a man raise his glass to her. She winced at the sight. He looked to be roughly as old as the sun. The few patches of pure-white hair he had were unkempt, and the cigar in his shaky grip made his hands seem smaller than a child's. His suit was ill-fitting and a gaudy green satin that made him look like a cartoon character. His eyes were sunken so deeply into his skull he looked to be the living dead. None of the men sitting at his table were attractive by her standards— by *any* standards, but they were all perfect tens— no— *elevens*— when compared to the dinosaur that had apparently refilled her cocktail.

"God," she scoffed and looked at the bartender, "I've been chatted up by some ugly blokes, but I think he takes the cake."

He sort of grinned. "Do you not know who that is?" She looked at him again then back at the bartender to shake her head. "That's Tatum Abraham." She still didn't recognise him, so, while Rory was on his way back to her, the bartender lowered his voice and leaned in to inform her: "He's the CEO of Osiris International."

Chapter 17
And Your Little Dog, Too

When the cars pulled into the hangar, Thyne noticed Perlie was driving the *Fiat* with Roach sprawled out across the backseat reading. He couldn't see what book it was before he had closed it and opened his door. The dogs that had been piled all over him rushed out into the large empty space and zoomed around the plane, eventually meeting up with Juliette and making fast friends of her. After watching them play for a moment, Roach stood and folded the book in half vertically to fit it into his back pocket, making the British bookworm cringe. He would have berated him if not for the need to speak with Jean-Jacques about the repairs.

The aeromechanic was working on something on the underside of the faulty engine when Thyne approached. "When do you think it'll be fixed?" he asked with a mousy voice in French.

Jean-Jacques smiled nervously at him. "Good evening, Monsieur. I've been working as quickly as possible. It's difficult to do this sort of thing alone in the short amount of time you said you needed it. I know your friend is hurt, though. Check back in... twenty-four hours should suffice."

"Thank you for hurrying. I'll pay you even more for the trouble, of course."

Jean-Jacques nodded and returned his attention to the engine, so Thyne wandered back to the cars to help move the luggage and new weapons onto the plane. Once everything was in the cabin, he gathered everyone save for Jean-Jacques and sat them down to address them collectively:

"If we try to leave the country without landing at an international airport for a search of the plane, they'll shoot us down, so I have agreed to land in Detroit.

When we land, Francis will stop time and bring all of you, all of the animals, and all of the weapons to a house we bought in the city. It shouldn't take longer than an hour, but I opted for a house to be certain you aren't found hiding somewhere in the airport itself. Is everyone on board? ... Pun unintended."

They all nodded vaguely, except for Perlie. She stood and crossed her arms. "You really expect me to believe this insanity?"

Thyne rubbed the bridge of his nose. "Franky, bring her into the other room or something just to shut her up about this."

It hadn't occurred to Francis to use his powers to prove they existed to her. It hadn't really occurred to him that she didn't believe he had them.... He took a swill from his flask and stood, stopping time as he found his footing then dragging her outside of the plane back to the cars. He adjusted her to be mostly upright but near enough the cars to catch herself on the *Locust's* hood if she fell forward. Confident she would be okay, he readied his flask for more drinking and resumed time.

Just as planned, she fell forward but caught herself on the car. After calming her racing heart, her gaze snapped up to Francis. "What the fuck did you just do to me!?"

"I used my control over the fourth dimension to—."

"Oh, come off it! What the Hell is going on!?" She stomped back to the plane and approached Thyne. Scooping him up with both hands by his collar, she shouted into his face, "How did he do that!?"

He puffed out his cheeks and pushed her gently off of him. "I didn't believe him at first either. He had to take me back to Ancient Greece to convince me. I trust you won't waste his time like that, though." A sarcastic grin.

"Waste his time!? If he controls time, then how the fuck—?" She stopped herself and looked at the four others who were still sitting on the couch. After scanning all of their faces, she hardened her gaze on River and muttered, "What's going on?"

He put his hands behind his head. "It's exactly like they say, Perls. He controls time. Maybe he's that *Jumpman* character Lydia was always rambling about."

"Dezba? You believe this, too?"

She smiled sweetly. "Why don't you sit down, honey? I think Thyne wanted to say more, and this is a lot to take in. I'm *still* coming to terms with it, to be honest."

When Francis came back into the room, Perlie turned to him and snipped, "Prove it to me! Stop time right now and show me."

"If I were to stop time and leave you unaffected, you would immediately perish. Time unmoving is air unmoving is absolute zero, and were you to somehow not freeze to death in an instant, you would not make it to your second breath on account of the air you inhale becoming nothingness until your exhale replaces it with carbon dioxide."

She scoffed. "Well, how convenient then, that you can't prove it to me!"

He rolled his eyes and pushed up his sleeves to hold his forearms out to her and push them both forward and backward in time. Tattoos scrawled across them each then un-wrote themselves. Her jaw dropped as she watched, and when he was fairly confident she was stupefied to silence, he pulled his puffy blouse sleeves back down and plopped into the settee between the twins. To Thyne: "Carry on, my dear."

"Thank you, Franny. The next thing I wanted to say was an update from Jean-Jacques: his current ETA is about twenty-four hours from now. Everyone make yourselves comfortable in the meantime. Unfortunately, the food offerings are limited on the jet, so I figured I'd go out and buy some more for both the trip and the wait. Not to mention, Giovanni has texted me a list of medicines and chemicals he wants that are illegal in Eurasia."

"You're going out now?" asked Roach.

"I was going to. Yes."

He looked at his phone. "It's almost four in the morning."

"And your point?"

"Someone should go with you."

"Why?"

Partha butted in: "You can't split the party, Thyne!"

"Is someone offering to come with me, then?" He sounded irritated, and his gaze on Roach matched the tone, but the other twin could see longing in his eyes.

River's thin fingers were over his mouth a moment later, stifling a chuckle as he could practically see three seconds into the future when Roach would say, "I'll go with you." His quiet tittering made Thyne's harsh gaze snap over to him like lightning. If he were anyone else, he may have been perturbed by the wild look in those golden honey eyes, but he only stifled another laugh.

"Oi! You got something to say, mate?"

River's movements were like that of a Victorian lady trying not to divulge a piece of gossip the way he crossed his arms and lowered his hand from his face with an elegant slowness. "I think you're adorable, Thyne. Go on, you two."

Thyne wasn't sure what his reaction to the comment may have been, because his train of thought was stopped abruptly when he saw a ring on River's left ring finger that was remarkably similar to the one on Roach's. River's was the same size and colours, but the golden symbol on its face was of a was-sceptre rather than an ankh. Only a fraction of a second later, River buried his hand in the pit of his elbow, fully crossing his arms and hiding the ring, so Thyne started his way to the car with a lingering eye on him.

Roach patted Perlie's head a couple times on his way to the door then hopped down the stairs to follow Thyne to the cars. "Now, Thyne, you didn't think I'd let you drive the *Locust* again, did you?"

His tone was playful, but Thyne was angered as if it wasn't: "Fucking twat. You let me drive it all the way here!"

Thyne didn't notice himself walking toward him while he snipped. It therefore caught him by surprise when Roach took just one step and was mere millimetres from him. He pinched Thyne's chin to hold it up and looked down at his reddened cheeks and scrunched up nose. His voice was soft and tone still playful: "I'm fucking with you."

"Oh," said Thyne as he averted his eyes.

Roach retreated and bit down on a cigarette. With it between his teeth he said, "But shtill can't schmoke in it, sho," he lit the fag and took a drag before finishing the sentence, "relax, dude. Have a smoke with me."

Thyne rolled his eyes and took out his cigarettes. He opened his lighter with a flourish, but before he brought it up to his unlit durry, Roach leaned in and pressed the tip of his cigarette to Thyne's. The brit was beet-red as he inhaled to steal the light, and after Roach retreated, he immediately averted his eyes. "Cheers," he muttered.

"Where'd you learn those lighter tricks, man? They're cool."

It took him a moment to stop reeling internally, and when he noticed Roach leaning on the side of the car, he leaned on it, too. He let the smoke calm him and finally looked back at Roach to answer his question: "I taught them to myself."

"With a real lighter?"

"Yeah. I didn't try it with fluid in it until I was confident, though."

"Reminds me of practising with my dummy knife." He slipped out a butterfly knife from his back pocket and opened it by doing a trick, tossing it into the air, bouncing it off his forearm, and catching it by its handle perfectly.

Thyne giggled. "I'm sure that's less impressive with a dummy knife."

"Yeah," he let himself chuckle slightly, "we should swap tips. I'll teach you the knife tricks, and you teach me the lighter thing."

"Maybe…."

A beat.

Roach leaned further into the side of the car, closed the knife to return to his pocket, and broke the silence with an attempt at small talk: "So, I saw you reading my books back in Compton."

"Yeah…."

"Anything you liked?"

"I'd read most of them already, but I had only ever read Dumas in its original French, so I read your copies."

"Of?"

"*The Count of Monte Cristo*, and the *D'artagnan Romances*."

Thyne wasn't looking at Roach to see him beaming innocently, but he heard it in the tone of his voice when he replied, "Did you like the English translations or the originals better?"

He tried to catch a glimpse of Roach's grin with a flick of his amber eyes in his direction. By then he had already hidden the display of emotion, so Thyne sounded disappointed and uninterested when he said, "The French is better."

"Oh," said Roach to lead into another awkward beat of silence.

Halfway through his cigarette, Thyne turned toward Roach and tried to look at the book in his back pocket. "Speaking of reading: what's that you had in the car?"

He tried to grab it to see the title, but Roach turned swiftly away and held it still behind his back. "Nothing."

Thyne giggled. "Why *that* reaction? Is it smut or something?"

"No."

"Then what is it, mate?"

There was a brief quiet, after which he cleared his throat and quoted the novel with a voice low and tender: "You people with hearts have something to guide you, and need never do wrong," a pause, "but I have no heart, and so I must be very careful."

Thyne blinked, but after a moment he recognised the quote and smiled from ear to ear. "You're reading *The Wizard of Oz*?"

There was a blush he couldn't stop as he passed him the book and rubbed the back of his neck. "Don't read too much into it...."

He was giddy, but the way it seemed to make Roach uncomfortable had him immediately overthinking to the point that he upset himself and returned to smoking in silence. When he was finished, he flicked the cigarette butt on the floor, stamped it out, and droned, "Come on, let's go."

The first half of the drive was silent. The stereo and air conditioner were off, and the soundproofing on the car was top-notch, making the sounds from the outside nothing more than an almost-inaudible ambient hum. It was visually quiet too. The desert was dry and lifeless: an endless horizon of shadow. It wasn't uncomfortable, but it wasn't a relaxing sort of quiet, either.

Roach's gaze was fixed on Thyne's cybernetics for quite some time as he had his hands resting lazily on the bottom of the steering wheel. Thyne was too busy driving, and the car was too dark, to notice Roach staring. '*Ask about it,*' thought Roach to himself.

'*But then he'll ask me something, and I'll have to refuse. I'm not ready to tell him things.*'

'*Clayton, you fucking moron. If you're too distrusting to tell him something personal, then he sure as fuck won't want to tell you either.*'

'But… maybe if he tells me and flips it on me… maybe I can give him crap since I'm reading his favourite book.'

'Favourite movie, actually. He never said it was his—.' "Hey, what's your favourite book?"

Thyne started at the sudden break in silence. "Oh. Uh. Does *Othello* count?"

'Shit. And here I thought I was being romantic.'

'Romantic, Clayton? Why are you trying to romance him? He's a rich prick, and he has a boyfriend. Who's a doctor, and a chef… and Italian. You can't compete with that.'

"Why do you ask?" said Thyne when Roach didn't reply.

"Uhhh. Just curious."

"Well, what's *your* favourite?"

He blushed and was immediately thankful for the darkness in the car to hide it. "I—. Er. Don't have one."

A brief knowing glance. "Come on, mate."

"I don't have one," he said more forcefully.

"Fine. Keep your secrets."

And… back to silence…. Roach's gaze returned to Thyne's cybernetics, and after a good four minutes of staring he heard himself blurting out, "What happened to your fingers?"

Thyne scoffed. "Wouldn't *you* like to know?"

"Yes," he muttered.

There was a while of quiet, at least five minutes, after which he sighed and said, "Alright. I'll tell you, but you have to promise something."

'Oh, here it comes,' thought Roach. "What do you want me to promise?"

"When I'm done telling you, you have to answer a question too."

He sighed. "What question?"

"Ah ah ah, Roach. Promise first."

"Alright. I… promise." The word was strangled in his throat.

There was another beat. Roach was going to ask for the promised question upfront, but Thyne finally spoke up. His voice was nearly a whimper: "I cut them off myself."

Roach was stunned to silence. When he spotted a tear on Thyne's cheek he averted his gaze to avoid seeing him cry. "Why?" he whispered.

"My mother…," he trailed off and blushed as he recalled Roach's teasing him for having 'mommy issues.'

To Thyne, the genuine tenor of Roach's voice was like the warmth of the autumn sun back in 1939 when he said, "You don't have to tell me."

A moment later their eyes were locked, despite the darkness and the tears blurring Thyne's. "It's not just guitar." Roach seemed to understand. He seemed to maybe even… remember…. "Singing and piano, too. I was going to have to start learning the violin. That's when I...." He sniffled and returned his eyes to the road. "That's when I cut off this one." He held up his left hand.

"And... the other?"

He shook his head and pulled onto the shoulder. After putting the car in park, he held his face to weep more openly. Roach put a hand on his back. It was warm and comforting. After a sorrowful few minutes, Roach reiterated that Thyne didn't have to talk about it, but he sucked up most of his sorrow and answered: "The other one I cut off during a mental breakdown triggered by hearing a particularly brutal Chopin piece."

His voice was a breath. "What song?"

"*Ballade Number One.*" He sniffled and wiped his eyes. "Have you heard it?"

"I've heard it."

He let out a shaky breath and whimpered, "I could never get the coda."

Roach's hand trailed down Thyne's arm and grabbed his right hand gently. There was a not-insignificant part of him that wanted to kiss the wounds and quote something romantic from *Othello*, but he stopped himself. Instead, he simply rubbed the soft skin of Thyne's hand with his thumb before retreating and saying, "Thank you for telling me. You can ask your question, now."

Thyne nodded and took a deep breath to flip a switch in his mind and make a few silent prayers for strength and protection from his Gods. After only about a minute, he was calm again and said, "I know you killed that man in Crownpoint."

Roach went pale. All the tenderness that had softened his air dissipated. A cold shell immediately hardened over his heart and soul, but he was still too scared to reply verbally.

"My question isn't why. I know why." A beat. "My question is... Should I be worried I might find Dezba, Francis... myself... any of us—. Should I be worried we might wind up in a ceiling, too?"

Roach's breaths were faster than normal and heart racing, but he tried to hide it. "Of course not," he managed.

"Because if you hurt me... again... and I told him, Francis would kill you. Roach, he could kill you in ways no one else could. He could age you to dust. He could shoot you while time is stopped, and you wouldn't have any way to stop him. You wouldn't even know until you met your maker. He could bring you to Antarctica back when it was colder. Hell, he could bring you to the bloody moon!"

"I get it...."

Thyne's hands traced up the steering wheel to ten and two, and after a long exhale, he put the car back in drive and returned to the road. After two more minutes of awkward quiet, he spoke again. His voice was hushed and harsh: "Roach, if you somehow hurt Francis, in any capacity, there is nothing on Heaven or Earth that would stop me from making you suf—."

"I won't hurt Francis. I won't hurt any of you. You called me a poser leftist, and I intend to prove you wrong. I'm here to kill corporate elites and squash as many companies as we can. I want to cause chaos, and I want blood, but if I wanted any of you dead, you would be."

The assertion shut him up for the rest of the drive. When he pulled into a space in the parking lot of the same Desert Mart they had visited almost a month prior, he turned off the engine and rested his forehead on the steering wheel.

"What's wrong?" whispered Roach.

He glared. "What do you *think* is wrong, you maniac?"

"I hope you weren't under the impression that we were going to take down Maitland without killing your family."

A sigh. "Roach, you really don't know what you're talking about."

"If you intend to try taking down these companies without killing people I—."

He sat up. "Oh, stuff it! Of course we'll be killing people. We just bought a load of guns, didn't we?" He rolled his eyes and leaned on the steering wheel again. Under his breath: "Idiot."

Roach let out a relieved sigh. "Well, it's good we're on the same page, then. Come on, dude. Let's get you some juiceboxes and sweets." He left the car and rounded to Thyne's door to open it for him. Taking Roach's helping hand, Thyne finally peeled himself off of the wheel and dragged himself out of the car. "Alright dude," said Roach as they started walking toward the entrance, "I've got another question for you." Thyne groaned. "I really don't buy your claims that your wealth was made even somewhat ethically, but I'm willing to be proven wrong. How'd you wind up a billionaire without exploiting anyone?"

"If you must know: Francis stole it."

"He stole a billion Euros? Come on, man. How would he—?"

Thyne stopped halfway to the doors and eyed Roach, who also stopped. "In 1874 Francis went into a hidden diamond vault, stole everything inside, and left it. He was never caught or even suspected because he did it all while time was stopped. He sold the diamonds at various times *before* 1874 then put the money into two accounts in Italy way back in 1475 where it accumulated interest over time. He hid a good amount of treasure, as well. I'm not telling you where."

"Well... colour me impressed." He stared for a moment then spun on the ball of his foot to stride toward the store.

They took a shopping cart from the parking lot and started filling it with produce when they entered. They were drowned in more awkward quiet, exchanging only vague glances and gestures as they grabbed fresh ingredients and snacks. As Thyne put a container of fresh rosemary in the cart, Roach made note that it looked exactly like a sprig tattooed on the forearm that didn't also have a spoon inked on it. It was odd, but considering the spoon tattoo also had a sprig of herbs around it, he could only assume that this Oliver person was a cook, and both of the tattoos were memorials to him. It sent his mind wandering as aimlessly as his feet. They were leaving the produce section when he said suddenly, "You lied."

Thyne's dreary eyes were slow to find Roach. "About what?"

"You said you didn't exploit anyone to get your riches, but you exploited Francis."

The calm in his air became rage. His knuckles were white and teeth grinding into each other. "He *gave* me that money, you fucking twat. I didn't fucking ask for it."

Unfazed by the expected outrage, Roach shrugged. "You're lucky to have him, huh?"

"Exceedingly," he growled.

Roach smiled outright. "You're cute when you're mad."

He scrunched up his nose and pointed into Roach's face. He didn't have a good comeback, so he stood there in silence before deflating and storming off with the cart.

"Hey, wait up, dude." He jogged up to him. "I'm just pushing your buttons, man. You two are cute."

Thyne blushed and averted his eyes. He was still grumpy, but he calmed himself down and replied with less venom on his tongue, "Yeah…. He's an idiot, but he's my favourite person in the world. We've been through everything together."

"That's like me and Sonny. I've saved that asshole's life too many times to even count."

Thyne let out one amused exhale and was quiet. When he finally turned back he eyed Roach's hands and said, "I saw he has a ring like yours. What's that about?"

If he had been looking at Roach's face, he would have seen it lose a lot of its colour. He rubbed the back of his neck and averted his eyes. "Well, you also see the tattoos on his arms are pretty similar to mine? I always wear this ring, so he has one to match because we like to always be able to pretend to be each other. It's gotten us out of a lot of troubles."

Thyne nodded to regard the answer and looked into Roach's hazel-greys where he saw just the slightest glimmer of panic. "What sorts of troubles?"

"Ah, well it's gotten us *into* troubles, too. When I met Perlie she thought I was Sonny, and I played along. She hinted at her feelings for him, and I knew he wasn't interested in anyone except—." He stopped and cleared his throat. "Anyway, I thought she was beautiful, and we got back to my place, and long story short, I found out she was CIA and…," he trailed off.

"And?"

He grinned fiendishly, but he hid it behind his hand to cough away the emotion. When he lowered his hand back to the shopping cart's handle, his face was as deadpan as usual. "I almost killed her. Told her to stay away from Sonny. And—.

Well, it's not really my story to share anymore. We slept together (after I was certain she knew I wasn't Sonny, to be clear), and things went from there. She's a real handful. We dated on and off for a couple years."

"And you're still together?"

He was perhaps too hasty when he replied, "Oh no no no!"

Thyne smirked. "So, how do you know she's not a nark?"

He was quiet for a while and averted his gaze. "I just do."

"I hope you don't think just because she's shagging you that she won't go right back to the feds the moment she—."

"I'm not sleeping with her anymore. You don't know what you're talking about, dude, so why don't you shut the fuck up?"

Thyne arched his brow. '*Interesting*,' he thought, '*Does he still love her?*' A beat. "Why'd you break up?"

He sighed. "I'll tell you, but you've got to tell me something first."

"Tell you what?"

"Tell me about Oliver."

Thyne huffed. "That's hardly fair, Roach. I've told you plenty about me, and I still know next to nothing about you."

"Fine. Fine. Fair enough. I'll... tell you later. Remind me."

He glared. "You think I'll forget."

"I do."

"I won't."

"We'll see."

They continued shopping with only meaningless banter until it became another political debate that carried all the way to the parking lot. After they finished packing the car with the groceries and supplies, Roach got into the driver's seat, Thyne stomped to the passenger's side, and they slammed their doors in tandem.

"You're a real piece of work, dude. You know that?"

"At least I'm not a delusional anarchist. We could never start with anarchy. It'd just turn into even more of a libertarian Hell than it already is!"

"At least *I'm* not gullible enough to trust a bunch of suits in power to evenly distribute fucking anything. Socialism isn't good enough, and state communism is only good if someone altruistic is in power, which is a fucking oxymoron."

"*You're* a fucking oxymoron!"

"That doesn't make any sense, you—." He groaned and grasped desperately at the air, straining his fingers as he willed them not to close into fists. It was another unwanted display of his true feelings: Thyne could break through his unemotive façade quicker and more reliably than anyone he had ever met. He took three deep breaths to calm himself when he felt his facial muscles straining and returned to his default nothing-expression. "Forget it. We should hurry so I don't miss *Fajr*." Another calming inhale. "Does your pilot need a lift?"

Watching him calm himself down helped Thyne come back down from his own frenzy, so when Roach asked about his pilot, he was able to smirk. "No."

"Are you sure? He can't live that nearby. The airstrip really is in bum fuck Egypt."

"He's not far."

"Where's he staying?"

"In the hangar."

Roach started. "He is? Why haven't I met him?"

He giggled. "You have."

"Oh! Jean-Jacques is a pilot *and* aeromechanic? That's sick."

Thyne only grinned wider and let Roach believe his own assumption.

———————— ✦ ————————

Jean-Jacques worked through the night. He tried to be quiet, but there were some things he simply couldn't help from being loud. River easily slept through the noise, and Francis had drunken himself deaf, but other than the two of them, there was hardly any sleep to be had. Those who couldn't sleep kept to themselves and quiet, however. Roach finished reading *The Wizard of Oz* then perused the books Thyne had in the plane, settling on *A Connecticut Yankee in King Arthur's Court*. Dezba resumed knitting the sweaters she was making for the group, and Perlie gave herself a manicure with some nail polish Thyne had in the jet.

The Brit himself hadn't even lied down to attempt sleeping. Instead he cracked open an energy drink, had a cigarette outside, and ordered two tankers of jet fuel to come to the airstrip to fill the plane. He asked Jean-Jacques for a recommendation on who to call, so the tankers and their operators were affiliated with the Russian mafia the same as the Frenchman. After finishing his cigarette and making the order, he approached Jean-Jacques. "Good morning, Martial. I've just ordered the fuel. It'll be here in a few hours. Will you be finished by then?"

"Should be," he said as he wiped some sweat from his forehead. "Can you hand me that?"

Thyne gave him whatever the tube-thing he had asked for was and sipped his drink. "Thank you for working through the night. You're very hard-working. I can see why Grisha spoke so highly of you."

He grimaced. "Please, Monsieur. Do not talk about Grisha."

"I'm sorry. I suppose you don't want to know that he's coming to pick you up with the tankers...."

Jean-Jacques stopped working and looked at him with panic in his black eyes. "Monsieur! Oh no! I—," he trailed off to a whimper.

"He insisted. I'm sorry, Martial."

A sigh. "It is okay. I was only hoping to ask you…."

"You want to come with us?"

He lowered the platform he was standing on to be at eye-level with Thyne and looked into his amber eyes. "I couldn't help but overhear— I'm terribly sorry — but is it true you're flying to France?"

"We'll be going to London first, but we will eventually make it out to Versailles, yes."

He stepped down and grabbed Thyne's forearm as he was trying to take a sip of his drink. His voice was a whisper. "Monsieur, please take me with you. I have been trapped in this country for so long. I'll do anything to get back home. I'll even join your gang."

"Hm… The issue, Martial, is that your boss is already on his way to the hangar."

"Tell him… tell him I ran off! I will take Julliette and my motorcycle and go hide somewhere while you upload the fuel and pay him. And when he is gone I will come back. Oh, please, Monsieur! I am a slave to the Morozovs! I'll do anything to get back home and see my sister."

Thyne peeled his hand off of his wrist to take a sip of his drink and, after a moment, nodded solemnly. "Finish the repairs, then, and I'll find somewhere for you to hide."

"Oh! Merci merci merci, Monsieur! You're saving my life!"

"Yeah yeah, quit your grovelling. It's not that big of a deal, and we could always use more hands."

He nodded excitedly. "Oh, yes! I'll do whatever you need!" And with that, he hurried back to work.

When he finished with the engine an hour and a half later, Jean-Jacques rushed to find Thyne and ask him where to hide. He was instructed to stash his motorcycle in a side room, the key to which only Thyne had, but hiding in the building with his yappy dog seemed dangerous. He was going to ask Francis to take Jean-Jacques and his dog somewhere far away, but Roach came in from a campfire he had made outside where he was preparing to make elote for everyone. "Hey, what's going on?" he asked as he sensed their nervousness. "You need help with something?"

"Yes, actually," said Thyne as he passed Juliette to him, "Take Martial and his dog out to the Desert Mart while the plane is being refuelled, and don't come back until I say it's safe."

"Uh… okay, but why? I was going to make brunch."

"Would you, for once, simply do something useful and not complain about it?"

He closed his eyes to keep control of his facial muscles and the tenor of his voice. "I'm not complaining. I'm confused. I would think that fueling the jet would be something the pilot would need to be present for."

Thyne slapped his own face and dragged his hand down it slowly, pulling at the bags under his eyes as he groaned. "*I'm* the pilot, you moron."

"Oh."

"So, take Jean-Jacques and his dog and keep them hidden from the *Russian mafia* after him. Can you handle that, or do I need to 'exploit' Francis like you keep telling me not to do?"

Roach looked at Jean-Jacques with an odd air about him. He was impressed, but it wasn't evident to the others. His voice was monotone and eyes unemotive as he trailed them back to Thyne and said, "I can handle it."

"Perfect! So go!"

Roach had a quick chat with his brother and Dezba before leaving with the Frenchman. After being in the *Fiat* for about ten minutes, Roach broke the silence by asking, "Why do you keep scratching your neck, dude?"

"There was a… guêpe in the plane garage. I don't know the English word." He took out his phone to use its text translator. "Wasp?"

"Interesting… Did you see it? What colour was it?"

He shook his head. "No, Monsieur Thyne told me, but I didn't see it."

He leaned on his door to ponder. "You can play some music," he muttered and gestured subtly toward the radio.

Jean-Jacques connected his phone to the stereo remotely and looked at Roach nervously. "I don't have a lot of English songs."

"Yeah," said Roach thoughtlessly, "It's fine, man."

When they reached the Desert Mart, Jean-Jacques opened his door to go inside, but Roach stopped him. "Dezba gave me her card in case we wanted anything, but I was just gonna hotbox while we wait for the call from Thyne to go back."

"Hot box?"

He took a bong out of the glove compartment. "You want some?"

"You can drive after this… 'hot box' smoking?"

"Yeah, man."

He forced a smile. "Okay…."

"You can just say no, dude."

A relieved sigh. "I don't think it is good thinking."

"Fair enough." Roach returned the bong to the glove compartment. When he leaned back, Juliette had stuck her head between their seats, so he patted on his thighs. She curled up in his lap, and his large calloused hands enveloped her in loving pets and headpats thereafter.

"She likes you," said Jean-Jacques with a genuine grin.

He scooped up her head and spoke in the sort of baby-talk reserved for dogs: "Yes she does! Yes she does! Who's a good girl?"

They spent about an hour in the car listening to Jean-Jacques' music and talking with each other. Roach learned that Grisha had trapped Jean-Jacques in America by destroying his visa and passport almost ten years prior. He said he hadn't spoken to his sister in almost six years, and the last he heard, she was in trouble. Roach was foolishly optimistic and hopeful for their reunion. It led into a talk about Roach's siblings:

"I get it, man. I don't know what I'd do if my sister dropped off the face of the planet like that."

"You have a sister?"

"I have one sister I know very well and a baby sister my mother took with three of my brothers when I was just six years old. So… I only have a few memories of her."

"Your mother kidnapped your brothers and sister?"

"No… I don't think so. I think it was a sort of agreement my folks made since they wanted to divorce but had eight kids. And of course, divorce is expensive and arduous and just outright illegal half the time, so… I mean, I was only four at the time, but my understanding is that it was amicable. It's just a shame we've never seen any of them since."

"I'm sorry to hear it."

He gently rubbed Roach's shoulder, but Roach was feeling too vulnerable and only allowed it for a moment before pushing his hand away. "Well, I should go in for my ablution. You want to come?"

"Ablution?"

"Yeah. Gotta clean myself and pray. I'll be back."

Jean-Jacques was perfectly content to wait for Roach in the car, but after a few minutes, Juliette started whining. She was watching the doors waiting for him to return, and after some futile attempts at calming her, Jean-Jacques took the keys out of the ignition and opened his door. In French: "Come on, you whiny little brat. We'll go see if they have any free goodies for *good* dogs. Be a good dog, okay?" She tippy-tapped her paws on the hot pavement when she jumped out, so he picked her up to carry her before she got hurt.

Once inside, he set her down and led her to the pets section. She was picking up toys from the lowest shelves and bringing them to him, and it broke his heart to not be able to buy them for her. "No, sweetie. Put that back. I'm looking for the free treats for you. They usually have a little jar somewhere." His head was on a swivel looking for them, so he lost sight of her but heard her squeaking on a toy in the aisle he had left her in.

While she played, she spotted Roach passing by and caught his attention with a little bark before picking up one of the toys she wanted and rushing over to him.

"Oh my, you are just precious, aren't you?" He crouched down and played with her, but he was looking around as she tried, to no avail, to beat him at tug-of-war. "Where's Martial?" Usually after praying, he felt rejuvenated and light, but there was something heavy in the air. He stood and scooped up the dog, still playing with her toy. She dropped it, but he brought it back up to her mouth before it hit the ground, then his attention was firmly at eye-level. "Martial?" he called out as he looked around, "Jean-Jacques?"

Only a few steps into his search, he spotted him at the end of an aisle being held up by his throat. The man strangling him was even more muscled and at least three inches taller than Roach. His whispered Russian was threatening as it slithered from his lips: "You think you can just run away from the Morozovs? You know there's only one way out. I'll kill you, then I'll bring Grisha your little dog to kill her, too."

Just as Jean-Jacques' vision started to darken, he saw a horror he would never forget: Motya Morozov's head being split open by a butterfly knife flying cleanly through his temples. It disfigured grotesquely. It bled profusely. And the sound it made was unholy.

How the Frenchman got back to the car sprawled across the back seat with Juliette trying to give him her new toy to help him feel better was entirely a blur. He wasn't sure what happened to the body, but he vaguely remembered the box for a 180 gallon aquarium with a bloody handprint on the side. The smell of iron was seeping into the *Fiat* as they drove....

When they stopped, Jean-Jacques sat up and saw Roach with a spade, stepping into the desert sand. He looked around for the road and saw no sign of it. Everything went black again, and by the time he came to, he was back in his bed in the plane being awoken by puppy kisses from Juliette. They were flying, and when he stumbled out into the living area, he saw everyone else sitting around and chatting idly.

"Hey, man," said Roach when all eyes turned to Jean-Jacques, "We'll be in Detroit in about an hour for the search, then you'll be free of this country forever. Come sit down. We were just going to play a game."

Chapter 18
No Place Like Home

Thyne landed at the Heathrow airport and parked in his private hangar where there were five people waiting patiently inside for him. They were sitting around a fold-out table playing a board game called *Senet*, and three of them smiled wide when they saw the doors open and the plane start to pull inside. Once the engines had powered down and the hangar was closed again, Thyne lowered the air-stairs and rushed out of the plane to the group.

Firstly, he threw his strong arms around one Dr. Giovanni Loomis XVIII. He looked to be no older than thirty, but his full head of hair was white and spindly. He had it pulled back into a tight braid with its base quite high. The hair itself was thin, so the braid tapered out at his shoulders. His skin was pale and smooth, and his eyes were paler. He had no irises, so it was often assumed he was blind. His vision was perfect however and was, in fact, better than average. His heart-shaped face was thin and came to a pointed chin, on which Thyne had never seen so much as a shadow of facial hair. Though his features were narrow, his nose was broad and chiselled and Roman, almost as if it didn't belong to him. His eyebrows and eyelashes were as pale as the hair on his head, but even with all this paleness, he still somehow managed to be pleasing on the eyes. At least to Thyne. His build was a little more lean than average, and his height was the same 5'11" as Jean-Jacques, though the heel on his dress shoes gave him another half-inch.

His style was almost as antiquated as Francis', but Thyne had seen him wear more modern clothes from time to time. He smelled currently of vanilla, cinnamon, and sage, but it was common for him to smell of all manners of pleasant things. His hands were gangly and almost creepy, especially compared to the rest of him which was attractive if not a little odd, and in his left hand was a small duffel bag nearly overflowing with medical equipment. After kissing Thyne, he bared his pearly perfect teeth into a quick smile, showing his sharp canines. With a thick Italian accent: "I like your hair. Why isn't it pink anymore?"

"Had to dye it and haven't had Franky fix it yet. I don't want to waste his time, you know?"

He shrugged. "Where is the wounded one?"

"He's inside. The thinner twin."

Giovanni nodded and rushed into the plane to immediately start treating River's injuries. Thyne moved on to hug the woman who had been waiting for them. She wrapped her arms around him calling him, "Pop," and held him tightly, trying not to cry.

She was a woman of mixed race with her curly black hair in tight braids that flowed neatly to her bottom. Her teeth, though not bared at the moment, had sharp fangs just the same as Giovanni's, and her scent was just as pleasant but with more flowery notes. Being the same height as Thyne and of average build, she was able to bury her face into his shoulder to hold back her tears. She looked to be in her mid-twenties with smooth dark skin and a spritely spirit, but her clothing said otherwise. She was wearing an antique of an outfit, it being a widow's mourning gown and veil from the mid-nineteenth century. The veil was all covered in tears and dark make-up as she retreated from Thyne's embrace and wiped her cloudy blue eyes underneath it. This was Neodesha Loomis, the daughter of a freed slave from a post-civil war America and Giovanni. If her outfit didn't speak of this origin, her Texan accent hinted at it. "Oh, Pa, I told myself I wouldn't cry. I'm sorry."

Thyne's eyes were welling up after seeing Neodesha become so emotional, but he sucked up his sadness and forced a smile. "It's okay, Shay."

On January fourth of that year, Thyne's daughter and Neodesha's wife, Rosemary Chamberlain, had passed away. Thyne wept lightly at the funeral, but it was only two days later that he had to show up for Partha's livestream for the penultimate session of his campaign. He promised himself he would not let on how heartbroken he was to Partha or Richard (and especially not the audience) during said stream. He was too secretive a person to even tell Partha that he had a daughter, let alone that she had died, so, after getting a memorial tattoo for her to match Oliver's, he was quick to bottle up the mourning. When he saw an opportunity to ask for help forming a crime syndicate to take down his mother's company and received a meeting date from Roach, he spent the interim crying alone every night in his room and drinking much more heavily than was characteristic of him. Francis had helped raise her, but Thyne hadn't seen him cry at all, so he felt alone in his upset to say the least. Grief had haunted him in America, but he had all but forgotten its name before seeing his daughter-in-law bawling her eyes out like she was now.

Still, he managed to swallow the emotions, helped by one of the three remaining men coming over and slipping his arm around Neodesha's shuddering shoulders to bring her away and comfort her privately. While they were busy, Thyne gave a hug to one of the men who had yet to say anything to him or smile whatsoever. He held his hands up to try and shoo away Thyne's hug before he could touch him, but the Englishman ignored the gesture and wrapped his strong arms around him. He was a six-foot tall gangly half-Chinese fellow with sunken dead eyes that seemed to always be looking into a void rather than the world around him. Down both of his cheeks were deep vertical scars, three on each side. They were parallel with each other and seemed to imply that he had once been mauled by some sort of animal. His left eye sagged below the right, indicative of a stroke, but he looked no older than forty. He was plainly irritated by the hug, evident by the way his dark eyebrows flattened, and his black eyes seemed to pierce through Thyne like a dagger.

When he suffered his stroke, this man forgot his own name, so he was therefore called Melchiresa by those who knew him. It was the name the public had given him back in the early 1700s when he was a menacing threat to all human life on the Atlantic. Unlike the others, his teeth were not pointed and were instead all false save for three or four, which were as rotten and yellow as Francis'. His shoulder-length black hair was slicked back and curled at its ends, and there was the vaguest hint of stubble showing on his strong jawline. His features were chiselled and pleasant, if not for all the suffering he had clearly experienced, the marks of which he wore without a care. His style was simple and dark but, like the others, anti-quated. He wore a black poet shirt, black leather pants, and black boots, and his scent was a woody cologne not unlike the kind that best suited Francis' natural musk.

After being shoved away, Thyne kissed Melchiresa's scarred cheeks and approached the man who had taken Neodesha away. He stopped holding her, set his cane down on the table, and held out his arms to Thyne with a wide inviting smile, the white of his fanged teeth peeking out from underneath his large black moustache. He was the tallest of the waiting party at 6'1", and his embrace was physically cold but emotionally warm. His build was more muscular than Melchiresa's and Giovanni's but not as much as Thyne's, and he walked with a limp and cane due to an injury in his left knee. His face was boxy, and his skin a pleasant Mediterranean tan which made his wavy black hair seem all the darker. His age appeared to be fifty, and his eyes were a piercing icy-blue. They were actually quite unsettling and seemed out of place considering his otherwise swarthy features. His style was the most polished and modern of the group: a three piece suit. He had taken off his coat however, revealing a crisp burgundy collared shirt with a sharp black vest overtop. He usually wore gloves, but Thyne saw a pair on the table and was made a little sick at the thought that he might see the eldritch-esque horror that lay in the centre of this man's right palm. Luckily, he didn't catch sight of it before he pulled the gloves back over his hands and spoke to Thyne with his grizzled tone and thick Italian accent: "How are you feeling? Have you been okay?"

This was Arjun Catatone XIX, Giovanni's husband and Melchiresa's partner. He also considered himself Neodesha's father despite having no blood relation to her and was hugely protective of her to an almost offensive degree.

"Please, let's not talk about her, Arjun," said Thyne, "Have you brought some cars like I asked?"

He pouted to show his concern for Thyne's well-being and patted his shoulder. The attempts at comforting him were met with a death glare, so he smiled and moved on: "Yes, we parked them in the garage just over there."

"Good, we picked up a few stragglers, so we'll need the extra room. There are also some dogs and a duck."

Arjun's blue eyes lit up. "Oh! Where!? I *must* see them."

Thyne glared again. "In the plane. *Don't* take them."

"Oh, faugh. I won't."

He left to go greet the others (especially the animals), and Melchiresa followed.

The last of the group of five was a man about Thyne's height with an average build. He had pale freckled skin, bright green eyes, and wild ginger hair. His fiery goatee was especially unkempt, and he reeked of cigarettes and alcohol. Viktor East was his name, and he was only around out of necessity. None of the five people in the welcoming party were entirely human, but Viktor's otherworldly ability was particularly powerful. Thyne had long ago manipulated and more or less enslaved him to use it to his own advantage. He had the ability to both sense and control microorganisms. Any living cell (or sometimes even smaller) was something he could manipulate. Unsurprisingly, he was also a medical doctor, but the level of trust between him and the others was strained to say the least. Since he had left the plane, Thyne and Viktor had made brief eye-contact to regard each other, but neither of them so much as uttered a greeting. Thyne continued ignoring him and approached Neodesha, who had sat back down at the table to hold her weeping face.

"Shay, please," whimpered Thyne, "Your crying is going to make me cry."

"Oh, I'm sorry, Thyne, I just loved her so much."

He bit his lip to hold back his tears. "So did I." His gaze became a glare on Viktor who swigged from a flask and quit the area to go into the plane with the others. Thyne turned his attention back to Neodesha and tried not to cry. He felt himself choking up, so he tried to change the subject: "We're going to take down Maitland. Do you want in?"

"We?" She sniffled and dabbed at her eyes with a handkerchief. "Who else?"

"Francis, Partha, and some Americans."

"Are they in the plane?"

He nodded. "It won't be just Maitland. Some other companies, too."

She seemed a bit befuddled, but as she pondered the offer the thoughts of her late wife were being washed away by imaginings of violence and vengeance, just as Thyne had intended. After a moment of pondering, she managed a small smile and nodded. "Okay. Maybe it'll help me feel better."

"It will." He offered his arm for her to link up with, "Come on, I'll introduce you. They have puppies, too."

She let out a strangled laugh and whispered, "Okay, Pa." They heard gaiety from inside as if someone had told a joke, so she linked up with Thyne's arm to join the others.

Thyne's home in London was a four storey townhouse with a fifth level in the form of a basement and a sixth as a loft in the mansard roof. The building had two exposed sides, for it lay on the corner of Primrose Street and Properfield Lane. He therefore sometimes referred to the house as "The Prim and Proper." From egress to cornice, it was painted entirely in a minty pastel green colour. Even the fire escape had been painted, and the monochromatic nature of the building gave especial attention to its architectural intricacies. The three floors above the first had a column of bay windows which jutted out from the façade over the sidewalk. The ornamentation adorning them was intricate and beautiful, much the same as the decorative elements around the entire exterior. There were two entrances into the building: a door to the basement in a window-well where a garbage bin and two recycling bins were, and the front door, which was tall and surrounded by windows, the designs on which were single diamonds in the centre of quadrisected stained-green glass.

To the right of the building, under a tower of apartments, Thyne owned a six-car garage where they parked the three cars Giovanni, Neodesha, and Arjun had brought from Italy. Thyne was annoyed that he had to move one of his supercars onto the streetside to make room for them, but it seemed important to hide the cars full of illegal weaponry more than the *Lamborghini*.

Thyne led the group inside and filed them through a white wooden door immediately to the right of the entrance into a sitting room. Before entering the living area, Roach caught a glimpse of the rest of the hall. There was a narrow staircase tucked away to the right, the base of which was only a few feet from the sitting room door. The moulding was an ornamented white that seemed to creep its way across the ceiling like some plague of beauty and excess, but it met with the white tiled floor with much more humility. The walls between the moulding were a muted pink colour with a peek-a-boo floral pattern only visible when the light from the crystal chandelier caught it at just the right angle. And there, at the end of the hall, was a smaller door to the back courtyard, through which Roach could spot a still-dormant garden in the beginnings of awakening for the springtime.

The sitting room was much the same as the hall with its chandelier, complex crown moulding and much more simple floor moulding, white floors, and pink walls. The furniture inside was intriguing. It caught Roach's interest that the pieces seemed to be from different eras. Under the large window looking out onto Primrose Street was a daybed built into the wall such that it made a flat bay with the window and two large bookshelves on either side and underneath. Atop the bed were three plush toys, all pastel pink and nestled on a white throw blanket of long alpaca fur. The colour of these stuffed animals (a teddy bear, a lamb that could act as a throw pillow, and a small pig plush) matched with the lightly-patterned upholstery of the bed beneath them. The curtains were sheer and silky and pinned up on one side of the window. Roach couldn't help but picture Thyne in the nook reading, for it seemed to be expressly built with such a purpose in mind. As he was imagining this, however, Thyne rushed up to the daybed, stepped on it with one foot to give himself some quick height, and pulled down a thick black shudder from a roll hanging over the area. It covered the entire window and most of the bookshelves, throwing the room into immediate darkness, which Thyne alleviated by turning on the chandelier.

The other seating in the room looked antique. The pink pattern of the bench matched with all of the sitting chairs and settees, but the white wooden moulding that made up the base of these pieces was carved in a bygone era. They had similarly coloured throw blankets and plushes to decorate them, but even with those added touches they hardly looked inviting compared to the thick foam cushion of the daybed. The rug, which spanned nearly the entire small room, was thick and warm to counteract the cold unfeeling marble underneath. It was patterned and pastel, but its style looked to be something more like from the 1960s which contrasted the antique furniture that must have been at least sixty years older. There were paintings, photographs, and other decorations arranged as gallery walls on either side of the room with a settee beneath each of them, and at the end of the square room opposite the window, over the fireplace mantle, was a large wall-mounted television, the stark black of which was somehow both ominous and comfortable.

The group was invited to sit, and Thyne automatically grabbed a plush to snuggle it absentmindedly as he sat on the settee on the outer wall. They all filed into the room and followed suit, though no one else save for River grabbed one of the toys. Roach, however, lingered in the doorway. He noticed that Thyne had taken off his muddy shoes and left them on the porch, his feet now only covered by socks with llamas or sheep or some other adorable fluffy animal on them. In fact, everyone had taken their shoes off. Roach did not like to remove his boots unless he was cleaning his feet, and usually he would trample all over the rug without a care… but it was fluffy and so light in colour. His boots were no-doubt caked in mud from the rainy outside….

"What's wrong, Tony?" asked River as whatever the others had been talking about seemed to die down with a tapered laugh.

All eyes were on him, and he eyed his brother. His expression was blank, but River knew his comment was unappreciated, as if Roach was glaring daggers through him.

"Nothing," he said before trudging into the room and, as expected, tracking mud onto the crisp white and pink rug. He sat across from River, who was shoulder-to-shoulder between Thyne and Partha on the opposite sofa.

Now was a good time to talk about their plans, so Thyne cleared his throat. "Right. Well, I have enough spare rooms for everyone to stay here for the night, provided Giovanni, Arjun, and Melchiresa don't mind sleeping in their usual room. Then, in the morning, we can all drive out to France. Franky has some mad idea to go to the palace of Versailles, so we'll follow his lead. He's assured me it will keep us hidden." A beat. "Jean-Jacques. Did you manage to contact your sister?"

He fidgeted with the zipper of his hoodie and averted his eyes. "I am trying, Monsieur. She still has not answered her phone, but I am always trying."

"Arjun is very good at finding people, and I would assume so is Perlie? Maybe they can help." The two named parties nodded to regard the assessment. "Anyway, if we want to stay here a bit longer, that's okay, too. You know… before we start committing crimes together." He smiled, though it seemed sort of anxious as his eyes were bouncing from Giovanni to Francis to Roach and back again. Finally, they rested on Giovanni, and he said something in Italian, to which Giovanni nodded and quit the room.

"I've never been to England," said Dezba with an air of excitement, "If it's okay to stay, I'd like to explore."

"I haven't been since I had a job out here, and I never got to see very much of it, so I'd love to join you!" said Perlie.

Thyne nodded and fidgeted with the ear of the teddy he was holding. "Well, Giovanni is making dinner, so as long as you two don't get overexcited and eat out. I promise you nothing here is as good as what he can make."

River snorted. "Well, yeah, because it's British food."

Thyne smiled weakly. "You two can go ahead," he said, though he continued, and it stopped the ladies from leaving too soon, "Partha. You've been to London, right?"

He nodded proudly. "Have a boyfriend out here, actually."

Thyne rolled his eyes and furrowed his brow. "Well, keep it in your pants for the night, and show these two around, will you?" His tone was snippy and irritated, and Partha was quick to do as he was told, shuffling out of the room like a dog with its tail between its legs. Perlie and Dezba followed shortly after him with deflated attitudes but not as defeated as his had been.

"Oh," said River once they were gone, "Where will the dogs sleep? Or Malfeasance. Is it okay to have them in our rooms?"

"Dogs, yes. Duck?" He looked at the duck as she hopped up onto the couch where Dezba had been and quacked at Roach for headpats. He put her in his lap and pet her as Thyne continued. "Does the duck need a lot of space?"

"She'll be okay," answered Roach, and she quacked playfully up at him when she heard his rumbling voice. He smiled at her with his eyes. "Sonny and I can stay in a room together, and if it has a bathroom, I'll fill the tub for her to splash around. If she makes a mess I—," he sighed, "I'll clean it."

"*You'll* clean it?" He chuckled. "Do you even know how to clean?"

Thyne was beginning to understand the subtleties in the minute changes of Roach's expression, and the secret laid deep in the back of his eyes. It was unemotive, but there was an unmistakable agonising glare that seemed to want to behead the Brit for even daring to ask such a question.

Arjun, mercifully and quite suddenly stood and therefore brought everyone's attention to him. He clicked his cane once against the ground as he announced, "I'm going to go to the kitchen to talk with my husband. I suspect he'll want me to go out to the market. Androme, old boy," he eyed Francis. Once he had the drunk's attention, he said something in Old Egyptian. Francis replied in the same language with a sarcastic tone, and with that settled, Arjun turned and offered a hand to help Melchiresa from his seat, who took the gloved hand and followed dutifully out of the living room. Viktor followed them on their way, glad for an excuse to no longer be sharing air with Thyne.

Thus it was only Thyne, the twins, Jean-Jacques, Francis, and Neodesha in the sitting room. There was evidently still something on Thyne's mind, and now his gaze was almost always locked on Neodesha.

With a curiosity too burning to retain his deadpan expression for much longer, Roach decided to get himself alone with him. He cleared his throat and demanded, "Thyne, show me to my room."

His eyes widened and the light freckling on his cheeks was hidden by a pink blush. "Oh! I should have shown everyone…." He stood and turned to set down the plush, but it was comforting his frayed nerves, so he pulled it back into his arms and said, "Alright, everyone follow me."

Neodesha's room was one she had evidently used in the past because Thyne said to her, "You know where your room is, love, but if you want a different one just—."

"Oh, Pa, don't make me sleep in there without her!"

Her eyes were welling with tears, and there was a clear quaver in Thyne's voice as he swallowed his own before replying, "Alright, is it okay if Jean-Jacques stays in it?"

She nodded and wailed into her hands. "Go on and do your tour, Pa," she managed to be coherent despite the sobbing.

Thyne nodded and continued without her as she filed off into the kitchen, still crying.

Jean-Jacques' room (what was apparently meant to be Neodesha's) was directly across the hall from the sitting room. Thyne opened the door to show him and averted his own gaze from looking inside. Where the colour scheme of the rest of the house thusfar had been airy and light, this room was not allergic to darker values. Against the short left wall was a well-made bed with an ornate quilt that seemed old like a lot of the oddities in the house. The blanket was mostly a burnt orange colour that contrasted with the white metal bed frame and white wooden floor pleasantly. There was a large window behind it draped nicely with orange, white, and green curtains, the latter of which were blackout curtains but currently pinned up to the sides with the other drapes. The walls were white, but there was a clear effort in the rest of the furniture to bring about more natural colours. The dresser, bookshelf, chest at the end of the bed, rug, etc. It was all shades of brown, orange, and green. There was a fireplace on the right wall with an ornate white frame and a mantel spotted with family pictures which were too far to make out much detail. Lastly, in the back right corner of the room was a door that Thyne informed Jean-Jacques led to a private half-bath.

The Frenchman peeled off from the group and ambled to the garage to grab his bag, bringing his dog with him for a walk.

"Franky, you'll room with me unless you'll be off somewhere else." Roach noticed himself feeling jealous by this prospect, but he predictably didn't say or express as much.

Francis grinned, a drunken flush on his cheeks and slight slur to his words: "Your bed is comfortable."

Thyne blushed and fidgeted with his hair. "Alright, well go on up. I want to get a few matches in before tea."

Francis nodded and politely pushed his way past the others to climb the stairs, his footsteps waning as he seemed to start on another set of steps. "Follow me," said Thyne to the twins.

Their room was on the second storey and had a sizable private bathroom, which Thyne made a point to show them to be sure it was good enough for the duck. The tub was large, and Roach was excited to spoil his pet with it. He rushed over and started to fill it with lukewarm water while she quacked happily at the sound.

River watched this with a small smile before quitting the bathroom to explore the bedroom where he and his brother would be staying for an undetermined amount of time. He called the dogs into the room from the doorway where they had been loyally waiting for permission to enter. They zoomed inside and around the area while River started arranging some of the pillows on the floor for them.

Thyne lingered awkwardly in the bathroom watching the tub fill with water. He wasn't sure whether to leave them to their room or stay and give them a more proper tour. His nervousness was evident in the way he brought the teddy closer to his mouth and breathed in its lightly perfumed scent. "H-how did you end up getting a duck?"

It was hard to hear his mumbling over the sound of the water, so Roach turned it off when the tub was about halfway full and gently set Malfeasance inside where she immediately started swimming around and quacking with delight.

"What was that?" asked Roach as he wiped his hands off on a small towel that had been folded neatly on the counter.

"How did you get her?"

"Saved her from an alligator in Florida a while back. It got one of her legs, but I killed it and, let me tell you, we ate good that week."

"That's a sweet story," said Thyne before the muttered addendum: "...I think."

Roach nodded and smiled. He gently lifted Thyne's head by his chin so their eyes would meet. The simper was soft and rare and beautiful beneath his sharp grey eyes, but Thyne felt sick with guilt. He noticed himself eyeing Roach's lips and leaning toward them before pulling himself away and averting his gaze as best as he could while his face was being held by the chin.

Roach spoke in a low almost-whisper that would sound sensual if not for what was said: "It wasn't a wasp that stung me, Thyne. What was it really?"

His eyes widened and locked with Roach's. The smile that a moment ago seemed sweet and kissable was sinister and harrowing now. He wriggled free of Roach's grasp and took a step backwards, every sort of upset on his blushing face. Looking to his side through the bathroom door, he saw how close River was. "Bloody Hell!" He flinched away. "You two are... creepy. There's a linens cupboard right there. I'm going upstairs to be with Franky. Just... leave me alone."

Roach's smile faded back to nothingness, but he didn't seem angry. He gestured with his head to dismiss Thyne who thereafter rushed to his bedroom.

"Thyne, my darling, what ails you?" asked Francis when Thyne slammed and locked his bedroom door behind him. He stood from where he had been lounging across the bed and met Thyne halfway through the room, pulling him lovingly into his arms. Thyne pressed his face into his friend's jabot and breathed in his scent as he was pet and shushed lovingly by the taller man. After seeing Neodesha still in her mourning gown—. After all the bickering with Roach and all the mad mess in Compton—. Now that the gang was underway, and he was home and safe and sober in Francis' arms—. With no further ways to distract himself, he plainly broke down. He had been pushing away the feelings for so long they hit him like a freight train.

Francis led Thyne to the bed and laid him down. After kissing his knuckles softly, he stopped time to climb into the bed beside him and resumed it with his arms wrapped firmly around the weepy man. "What's wrong, love?" he whispered.

It was with great difficulty that Thyne managed to speak through all his bawling. The words came to him quickly but left his mouth with great spouts of mewling between them. "You… you… remember her… don't you?"

There was a long solemn silence, at the end of which Francis said in a low voice, "Of course I remember her." His tone was so cold it sent a shiver down Thyne's spine.

He looked up at him with sopping golden eyes. "Why… aren't you… aren't you… crying? Why… why haven't you… why haven't you cried?"

Francis looked at him and somehow smiled, though it was detached and forlorn. "It doesn't matter why I'm not crying, Thyne…."

Thyne shook his head and squeezed his eyes shut. What did he mean? He must not have wanted to say the reason because it would upset him even more. Or, 'Oh, Gods!' he thought, 'He's not saying that he never loved her, is he?'

Francis kissed Thyne's forehead as his eyes were darting all around, and it soothed his reeling mind. That he was so calm and collected and staying strong for his friend was both appreciated and stirring up a worry in Thyne. He wept for half an hour, and when his weepiness started to wane, Francis' gaze trailed listlessly down to his quivering lips. The grieving seemed to stagnate, and Francis, without fully realising it, was kissing him. It was slow and tender and only paused for brief moments as the stuffy-nosed Thyne had to stop to take breaths.

For Thyne, this was another way to stave off the hurt. He had wanted Francis for his own since the moment he met him, and even if the drunkard had kissed him in the middle of his daughter's funeral, he still would have kissed back with the same overwhelming amount of excitement and ardour as he was then. Francis' beard was softer than it looked, and his lips were like liquid gold with how rich and lucious they felt on Thyne's. He tasted like salt and rum, which were, in any other context, some of Thyne's least favourite flavours. But in this context? Kissing the one man he had always loved but never called anything but friend? There was no better taste.

For Francis, however, the kiss wasn't so simple. He wasn't mourning Rosemary because, as far as he was concerned, she had died aeons ago. It wasn't that he had learned of her death that long ago in his own time. He learned of it and attended the funeral only two months prior, just the same as everyone else, but even then, it felt to him like burying a stranger. In the time he had spent with her shortly before her death, her presence was hardly registered. She was an idea, and a pleasant one at that, but she wasn't any more real to him than Thyne was right then hanging on his lips. He felt his body reacting to the kiss, but his mind was a bottomless pit from which there was no escape.

Thyne retreated, and Francis smiled at the sight of him.

"Francis, I don't know what to do."

"My angel Thyne," he cooed, and the words put visible panic in Thyne's eyes.

"No! No no, not again! Francis, please don't say it. Don't say it. We're not in Hell. We're in London, and I love you, and I know you love me, and...," he said more, but by then his bawling state had returned and rendered him incomprehensible.

"*You're* not in Hell," he said calmly, "But I am."

He shook his head, unable to bring the words to his trembling lips that he so desperately wanted to shout out: '*No you aren't! Please! I need you so much.*'

Francis could see how he was affecting Thyne and decided to offer something of an explanation. He kissed his knuckles tenderly then cupped Thyne's quivering hand around his cheek, letting the warmth of his body ground him as much as he could possibly be grounded. Apathetically, he said, "It was a void of nothing."

"What was? Oh, Francis!" He dropped his head onto his chest and wailed.

He pet Thyne then lifted him up by the chin. His voice and demeanour up until then had been callous and blunt, but now he spoke tenderly with an air of warmth and love and heartbreak: "If you don't love me anymore... I can leave."

Thyne was so hurt and confused and worried that he could only cry harder at the comment. He wanted to beg him not to leave, but words were impossible and drowned by all his tears.

"It's all so fleeting, my darling." He pushed some of Thyne's wavy brown hair behind his ear. "Don't you see?"

He shook his head, not to answer the question but in a wordless attempt to beg Francis not to finish his thought. "Frankenstein, what's happened to you?"

The light in his eyes went out like a candle in a hurricane. "I'm sorry."

Thyne clawed at Francis' face with desperate trembling hands. "Please. No. No, Franky. No." That was the same cold look he had when he said they were in Hell back in Arizona.

The light came back with a bit of a jostle of his head. He smiled again at Thyne and said coldly, "I'm sorry, Clarence. She's in a better place now."

Thyne surprised himself by slapping Francis across the face in a sudden bout of rage. He was immediately apologetic and weepy again as the red shape of his hand started to form under the beard. Francis was unfazed by the hurt, which only made Thyne feel all the worse for it. "Oh, Francis! I'm sorry! Oh, please don't talk about Rosie right now. I'm so confused and upset, and I don't know which way is up. You've lost your mind, and I can't bear to hear you say it again."

He was somehow still smiling a genuine and pure smile. "Don't worry, Thyne, I'm here."

"*Are you?*"

Mad tears streamed Francis' cheeks down to his still smiling lips. "Well, where are we?" He looked around. "Ah, yes. London."

He cupped his hands around Francis' face and kissed him, but he didn't seem to notice until Thyne had retreated and was looking at him with panic and desperation. "Franky, what's going on? Why do you not know where you are or who I am anymore?"

This befuddled Francis. "Are you not my angel Thyne?"

"I'm Thyne, but I'm not an angel."

"So says you," he chuckled haughtily, "You're my angel Thyne." He nodded to concur with his own assessment.

Thyne dropped his head onto Francis' chest again, but he was too exhausted to continue crying. His entire body ached. His teeth were tingling the way they did after a panic attack. His breaths were laboured and strangled in his phlegmy throat. He felt Francis petting him and welcomed the half-perceived touch.

There was some rustling, and when Thyne wiped the blear from his eyes, he saw Francis had lifted his arm, the both of them looking down at his inner forearm. Tattoos flashed across it as he used his power to age it through the years. When it started to visibly grow older, however, he slowed how quickly he was pushing it through time. Another wall of notes then Thyne watched the wrinkled arm, covered in liver spots and fading scars, as the next note started to show itself. The handwriting, which until then had been penned with Francis' usual calligraphic script, was now the scrawl of a madman with no efforts made to beautify it.

It revealed itself letter by letter, and with each new stroke, Thyne's gut wrenched more and more. Some of the other "pages" of notes had been titled things like *Blackout* for the times when he was blackout drunk or *Rosie's Childhood* for things like her first words and steps and the like. Others were only labelled on a date-by-date basis and put into an order that always seemed haphazard to Thyne when he would catch glimpses of these tattoos.

Francis had a particular way of measuring dates and rarely used the Gregorian calendar. He had explained years ago, after Thyne inquired, that it made more sense to him to use his own birth year as "year zero" and every year after to be written with a positive number and every year before with a negative. He used the standard 24 hour clock and made his own months, just one for each season. With some guidance, it was simple enough for Thyne to understand. He knew Francis was born on December 13th, 1657 in the Palace of Versailles, so the notes were not incomprehensible to him the way they were to everyone else.

Seeing his friend's arm wrinkled and haggard was upsetting, for he had never, in the hundreds of years they had spent together, seen any part of Francis show any trace of an age beyond forty. But, truly, it was the contents of the notes that affected him most as they showed themselves:

It started with the title for this set of dates, which was not tattooed but rather scarred into his flesh. He watched as the skin opened up, started to bleed, then scarred over in a matter of seconds. It read, *HELL.*

A chill swept through him, and he pulled himself closer to Francis at the sight.

The first date started with its year, the way he always wrote his notes. Thyne saw the negative symbol and the first few digits and assumed it would be the month and day next, but it kept going. More and more digits until it finally stopped, the numbers nearly wrapping around Francis' wrist:

-15,998,233,254.

It did not name a day or month or time, and underneath this unfathomable year it said simply, *The Void.*

Thyne wanted to ask what it meant, but there was more, so he kept his mouth shut to see the next note: *363 ; autumn 54 ; 12:02:45 to 14:23:02* and under that: *Raped Thyne.*

The chill that had swept over him before was now body-wide trembling as he pulled himself even closer to Francis' bony body. It took him a moment to figure out what year it had been, and when he did, he recalled the day in perfect clarity. He held that moment in the highest regard. It was over eighty years of waiting, saving himself for Francis, and it culminated in a blissful loss of his virginity to his best friend and one of his truest loves. After reading Francis' misinterpretation of that day, likely because of the horrible afterwards, Thyne sat up and looked Francis in his ocean-blue eyes. "Franky, no! No you didn't! I love you. Oh, Gods!"

Francis' gaze was numb and cold and lifeless. He shook his head at the idea, and when Thyne laid his head back on his chest he could see that the notes were still going. It was four names into a list of exact dates and times, but he wasn't sure what they meant until he saw the one beside Rosemary's and recognised it as the day she died.

Thyne's name was on it, along with Roach's, River's, Dezba's, Partha's, Perlie's, Neodesha's, Viktor's… in between them were some names he didn't recognise like

May and Dale. He was able to surmise that they were not in order, for his own name was the first on the list. Thankfully, this lengthy list eventually came to an end, but then there were four more date-ranges, unlabelled. After the first two Thyne instantly understood what the following two were: the world wars....

Then came the last date, set only ten days after the close of the fourth war. It was labelled, unnervingly, in Francis' regular handwriting:

The end of the world.

He let all of the information sink in and shuddered with fear. His teeth began to clatter, and after a moment of such a reaction, he felt Francis' rough hand on his shivering jaw, pulling him up for a tender kiss.

It took thirty minutes of silence and shaking for Thyne to finally be able to bring words to his lips. His voice was just as shaky as the rest of him, and he looked into Francis' eyes as if he was looking back and not through him. "Francis... What did the first one mean?"

His gaze was still absent, and it made his unfazed voice all the more chilling. "I travelled to that year and found myself in a void of nothingness. There are no words in any language for what it truly was... I've come to call it Hell, but 'void' works just as well. I was trapped and accompanied only by my own madness until my birth in 1657. It didn't matter that I had been to times between the dates. I was not shown the mercy of being sent into different versions of myself to watch helplessly like I usually am. I was not shown a mercy for so long... I fear often... In fact I am quite certain that I'm still there." He finally looked at Thyne and somehow managed a happy smile, though there were sorrowful tears in his eyes. "Before I unintentionally cast myself into Hell, I was certain time was real and logical and measurable. Before then, I was certain that things mattered." He paused but dared to add with a whimper, "that *I* mattered." A tear trailed his cheek, but a genuine smile remained on his weathered face. "But there be only one thing that matters to me, and it was the only thing that kept me soul from withering out and dying in that endless merciless nothingness."

A beat.

Thyne's voice was but a breath: "What was it?"

"You."

Chapter 19
The Emerald Palace

The men who had met with the others in the hangar only slept through the following day in Thyne's house in a private room on the fourth floor. A pleasant evening shower roused them, and after dinner they were all four on their way back to Rome in Giovanni's *Khnum Series X*, a luxury electric car from Osiris with five seats, a hatchback, and the longest charge mileage of any car on the market. They left Neodesha behind in London to join the others for their more nefarious activities, but she was given a stern talking-to by Arjun in Italian before he departed: "Don't get yourself into any trouble, and remember to call me every night, and don't forget to wash up, and here's your inhaler, and don't go out when it's too hot, and eat healthy we know how much junk Thyne keeps around the house, and take time to grieve if you need it, and use Androme's powers to keep you safe, and come back home any time *any time*, and…" so on and so on.

The next morning, Dezba, who was quite excited by the sizable kitchen, volunteered to make brunch. She used the remaining fresh ingredients Arjun had bought to throw together vegetarian taco salads for everyone. Thyne took the opportunity of the meal to address them all at once. He asked for an update on Jean-Jacques' sister and was happy to hear, "Yes! Monsieur Catatone found her new number. She answered, and we spoke all night! She's alive!" His smile was contagious. "She is in Marseilles. I told her we were going to Versailles, and she said she would meet us there."

"That's great, Martial. Will she want to join us, too?"

"I did ask, and she agreed. She will be of good use for your cause, I think."

"Oh?"

He nodded excitedly. "She is… um… She is like a computer magician."

They sort of tittered, and Thyne replied with a big beaming grin, "She sounds like a good asset for the team, but I'm absolutely buzzing that we get to reunite you two. You said it's been ten years since you were home last?"

He nodded, but as Thyne redirected the conversation, Roach perked up and eyed him. It made Jean-Jacques realise that he didn't remember telling Thyne how long it had been, but he supposed he *had* told Roach.

"Well, has everyone had their fill of London, then?" said Thyne, "I'm itching to get this gang started."

"What's the plan once we have a more secure base of operations, anyway?" asked River.

"We'll take down Maitland and Canopy and whatever else."

River blinked. "Right, so you have a magic wand to just evaporate companies at will, do you?"

He was quiet for a moment then furrowed his brow.

Before River could chastise him further, Dezba spoke up: "I actually had another company in mind, and it's kind of small. Maybe we could start with it?"

"What company?" asked Thyne.

"It's an energy company in America… I know we just left there, but—. Well, we could figure something out. It's called New Clear."

Roach let out an amused huff. "That's a stupid name. Why haven't I heard of it?"

She shrugged. "Maybe it was only local to my area."

He pulled out his phone and looked it up, scrolling through the results as he munched on his salad. While he was reading about it, Partha said, "I've heard of it. They provide a lot of the power in the new states. They're a public company. What if we killed shareholders until they're too scared to keep trading?"

Roach stopped reading and looked at him. Through a mouthful: "That's a damn good idea, kid." He looked around, particularly at Dezba and Neodesha, to see if anyone was perturbed by the violent plan. No one was outwardly upset, so he took another bite and nodded once with approval at the kid.

Partha beamed. "Thanks!"

"Well, there you have it, River," said Thyne, "The plan when we get to Versailles is to establish our base then start looking for New Clear shareholders to assassinate them." He looked at Dezba. "Things are getting real now, love. This is your last chance out, so speak up if you can't handle it."

"Last chance out?" Roach huffed. "We can't let her go, now. She knows too much."

Thyne glared at him then softened his gaze on Dezba. "Ignore him, love. You'll be safe either way."

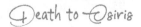

Dezba's gaze was nervous on Roach, but when it trailed to Thyne, she felt pacified and free to express a desire to leave. Feeling comfortable, still she asserted, "I'm here for the long haul. I want New Clear taken down for personal reasons. I'll help make it happen." As she said this, she mentally prepared herself for the inevitability that she would have to watch someone be murdered sooner or later. It was a hard reality to swallow, but when she thought back on the mining New Clear had done on Navajo land and the side effects of its recklessness, she was having a much easier time burying the upset under a decades-old longing for vengeance.

<hr />

Dezba was riding with the twins and Perlie in one of Giovanni's cars. There was an unwarranted feeling that she was bothering Partha in the back of her mind, but the main reason she was in this car instead of the one Partha was in was the same reason the twins had been adamant on driving it: it was a *Lamborghini* from the 1960s. She didn't know much about cars, but the twins' excitement was enough for her to want to give it a try. Not only was she riding in an antique luxury car for the first time in her life, the location was even more exciting! She hadn't been to Europe since her honeymoon in Lisbon almost fifty years ago, and before that a school trip to Rome when she was just a girl.

River had been healed entirely by Giovanni and Viktor, so he was driving, Roach riding shotgun, and Perlie was in the backseat behind him. The two ladies had grown quite close in the short time they had known each other. It helped the older of the two feel less lonely, and she was constantly beaming, happier and happier by the day. Not just because of Perlie; everyone in their little rag-tag gang was so kind to her! Except maybe Roach, but she still liked him quite a lot. She knew he was only threatening around her because he didn't fully trust her yet, and that was fair enough. She wasn't expecting Neodesha to join, but she was happy to add another sweater to her roster. She could only hope it wouldn't be offensive to Roach to give them out on Christmas.

She hummed along to the quiet music and, once she had had her fill through the windows, her attention turned to the others in the car. Her smile flashed all around as she quietly admired her new friends.

Perlie was a beautiful young lady with a dark cloud over her head that seemed to dissipate when she was giving gifts to her friends or spending quality time with them. Dezba had even come to see her lighten up when it was just the two of them, but it was clear that her guard was only let down with an abundance of caution. It was sad to think that such a young woman had hardened her heart to the world. She reminded Dezba of herself at the same age, and upon coming to such a realisation she had warned privately: "Perlie, one day you will look back on these years and wish you had not let so many people and experiences pass you by. It's okay to be scared to open up. You don't have to bare your soul to everyone you meet, but at the end of the road, you'll wish you had been more brave and let someone else carry the load with you."

Unlike most youngsters she was lecturing, Perlie had actually absorbed the advice, and it was clear in her actions afterwards that she was trying to be more personable with her friends. One such example was just then: the simple act of offering Roach a candy from Dezba's purse and asking how his stay in London had been.

He was a hulking brutish figure with a heart seemingly just as iced-over as Perlie's, but Dezba had caught him secretly smiling at his brother on several occasions and once at Thyne. An artist and an anarchist, he was much more of a bleeding heart than he let on, and Dezba found it endearing. She liked to think that he kept himself closed off from the world because it did not deserve the exquisite soul behind those deep grey eyes. While in Compton, she had taken it upon herself to listen to every song he had ever released in an attempt to better understand him.

As he sat in the front seat of the *Lamborghini* doing flourishes with a butterfly knife and sucking on the spicy candy Perlie had offered him, Dezba couldn't help but see him through all his walls. His music had opened just enough holes in them that she was able to see straight through to what he truly was: a man so in love that it drove him to madness. He was so overwrought with emotions, he was always on the brink of hysterics. The subject of his love songs, though? She couldn't say who it was. Perlie had mentioned dating him, but Roach's air toward her was too cold to be the subject of any of his more recent songs.

While Roach and Perlie were chatting, she turned her attention to River, looking at him through the rearview mirror. He noticed her staring after only a moment and commented on it: "What? Am I driving too fast?" He laughed, for they were hardly even at a crawl due to the traffic.

The way his eyes creased when he laughed— the way it came and went in flashes— the way his gaze seemed so much colder than his twin's despite their identical faces—. He was dead inside, and she could see it as plainly as he could see her. He seemed to read her mind as she pondered the state of his being and what he was really thinking. His eyes thinned into a glare through the mirror.

'Yes,' she thought, '*Roach must have inherited all the personality and soul.*'

"You don't know me," he muttered, almost as if to be replying to her thoughts. It seemed neither Perlie nor Roach heard him.

She averted her eyes. His gaze was so hard it felt like she was being stabbed. Clearly River had a soul. He loved his dogs and brother and swept the floor with everyone at cards with a huge smile on his face afterwards. He was a dancer and a gymnast and must have had *some* good reason for agreeing to put his life on the line for their cause. Yes, he definitely had a soul… *'but only just.'*

She looked at him again, and he immediately met her gaze in the mirror. "Hey, everyone," he announced to the entire car to shut up the other two. He was trying to intimidate her, but she didn't let it faze her. "Let's play a road trip game, yeah?"

Perlie clapped excitedly. "What a good idea. What's the game?"

His gaze was so constantly locked with Dezba's that she began to worry for their safety, but with a glance down to the road every second or so, he was driving perfectly passably. It helped that the traffic was pretty stop-and-go to get into The Channel Tunnel.

"Twenty questions. Tony, you go first."

Roach blenched. He hadn't been paying attention to the conversation and was instead more focused on the knife he was dancing around in his hand. He had his knees up on the dash (though that was less of a choice and more because of his height), and his posture was hunched and lazy in the bucket seat. He closed the knife and, a moment later, said, "Okay, ask away."

Perlie was the first to ask a question: "Is it an animal?"

He started playing with his knife again, like a bored fidget. "No."

"Is it a person?" asked Dezba.

"No."

"Is it the *V12* in this car?"

He paused his fidgeting to let out an amused exhale and mutter, "Sonny, you're really no fun."

"Wait, was that it?" asked Perlie.

"Yeah."

"Alright, Perlie, your turn."

She took a moment to think of something.

Dezba asked her question first: "Is it an animal?"

"Yes."

"Is it a tiger?"

"River! It's no fun if you guess it so quick!"

He shrugged. "Alright Dezba. Your go."

She understood what he was trying to do now, so she was determined to pick something completely unexpected. He didn't know her as well as he knew the other two, so she had a good advantage. *'There's no way any of them know what Anaye are, but I'll be extra specific and choose Ye'iitsoh just in case.'* "Okay, I'm ready."

River spent a moment glaring at her in the rearview. There was a good long while of traffic being stopped, so it was completely unbroken eye-contact. After what felt like three minutes straight, he asked, "Is it something Navajo?"

"Okay," she laughed nervously, "What's the deal? Can you read minds or some-thing?" After seeing Francis teleporting all around, she wouldn't be surprised.

"Don't need to read your mind when I can read your face like a book."

"And I suppose my face said, 'I'm thinking of something Navajo' somehow?"

"No, it said, 'I don't want River to guess mine immediately like he did for the others, so I'll think of something he definitely won't know about.' And I'll admit that you're correct to assume I'm ignorant of that culture. I'll defer to Tony, who has read up on it."

He, again, seemed surprised to be invited into the conversation. "Oh. Uh. Is it from mythology?"

"Yes, but I don't want to play anymore. I want to figure out what's going on with River."

"What do you mean what's 'going on' with me?"

"Can you read minds? We've already met a time-traveller, so don't try to tell me that sort of thing is impossible."

He laughed. "Nah, man. I can't read minds."

She glared, unsatisfied and unconvinced. "I can't quite figure you out."

"Ah, just how I like it!"

She couldn't help but smile at him. He was off-putting, but at the end of the day, she would consider him a friend just the same as she would Perlie or Roach or anyone else that had stayed in Compton with them. There was no denying that his skills, whether supernatural or not, would be useful in their criminal endeavours, and she was happy to put her elderly life on the line for any of these fine people she had the privilege to call her friends.

The trip through France was downright lovely. The vistas were breathtaking, the stops for snacks and Roach's evening prayer were in historical towns that could have been explored for weeks. The conversations were pleasant, and Roach even opened up slightly, telling the others a series of stand-up style jokes that had their sides splitting. The control he had over his face remained strong, and he didn't laugh with them, save for a few amused snorts here and there. At a certain point, River asked him to drive because his eyes were watering and abs aching, making it hard to see the road and control the vehicle.

They made their way to the planned destination, following Thyne's car to a manor in Orléans. It had been built for Neodesha and her late wife as a wedding gift from Thyne and Giovanni. It wasn't subtle that the fathers had the secondary motivation of trying to lure the ladies to Europe to be closer, but that didn't make the manor any less beautiful or luxurious. Neodesha hadn't set foot on the prop-erty since Rosemary's passing, and she was quite put-off by the idea that it was the intended destination of this first European road trip.

Still, with Thyne at the wheel, he led the other two cars to Orléans. He didn't need any guidance from maps or GPS, for it was a trip he had taken at least four times a year, usually more. When Rosemary was in Europe for a birthday or holiday, even if she was alone, she had always told her doting father, and he would always drop everything to come see her. This was the first time he had made the drive since her death, and he was only able to keep his heartbreak at bay with a pack of cigarettes and the company in his car.

There were trains from London to Versailles that were much more convenient than driving, not to mention Thyne had a plane, but the cars belonged to Giovanni and were expected to be returned so as to not be caught up in the gang's illegal activities. So the plan was to park them in Neodesha's garage where Giovanni and the others were already waiting for them, take a train to Versailles to see what Francis had in store for them, then drive the rest of the way to Rome and fly back to Versailles to start things proper.

After parking in the six-car garage, Thyne chained his cigarettes to the last of his pack, lighting the next with his last as he had been doing for the past four hours of the trip, and started to silently bring suitcases and bags from the boot into the house. Giovanni and Arjun had come out into the garage to greet them and help bring things inside, but Neodesha was immediately crying into Arjun's shoulder. Being at the house was rousing all manner of painful memories for her, and Francis, nearly blind drunk, had managed to gather that Thyne was also upset. He used his power to stop time, retched into one of the nearby recycling bins, then stumbled his way up to Thyne's place suspended in time in the middle of the den. He took the bags from his hands and brought them to the base of the stairs, too drunk to trust himself carrying them up, then went back to where Thyne was and wrapped his arms around him, hugging him from the side and bracing himself to catch him from falling. When time resumed, Thyne's cigarette fell out of his mouth as he nearly fell forward, but Francis caught him and pulled him violently into his arms for a hug.

His throat was immediately clogging up, and he pushed Francis off of him with an enraged shout. His face was red and lips trembling as he took the cigarette off the rug and took a huge drag from it. "Francis! I had gotten here the entire way without crying and—," his voice broke, and it enraged him enough to turn away and start stomping back to the garage for more bags.

"Thyne," said Francis with a gentle grip around Thyne's wrist.

He stopped and snipped, "What!?"

"I'll unpack the cars. Please."

"Please what, Francis!?"

He pulled him in for another hug, gently this time, and Thyne reluctantly allowed it. He bit through the filter of his cigarette as his face curled up on Francis' shoulder. He spat it out and wrapped his arms around Francis' back, breathing in his scent and closing his eyes so tightly he could see stars. "There's no time to cry," he whimpered.

Francis shushed him tenderly and pet his hair before stopping time and moving them both backwards through it. The building around them, in fact the entire town, disappeared into a thick wood then a field. It was briefly ocean then back again, then, somewhere in the mesolithic, Francis resumed time, still holding Thyne. His voice was soft and smile sweet when Thyne retreated to look at the field of poppies around them. "There's always time to cry, Thyne. So very little time for anything else, in fact."

"Oh, Francis!" He wailed and threw himself back into his best friend's frail arms. The gesture to bring him somewhere so private and disconnected from the present did not go unappreciated, but he said not a word of thanks, instead letting himself break down entirely.

They stayed in this time for three entire years as Thyne grieved, and there were moments, he thought, where it seemed Francis was grieving, too.

While in this mesolithic version of France, Francis would use his power to refill Thyne's cigarette box and lighter fluid the same way he used it to refill his own flask. He used it, too, to keep their stomachs full when they could not find something to hunt or somewhere safe to sleep. It was a lot of aimless wandering and crying and talking about the daughter they had raised and lost. Rare were Francis' tears, but when he was drunk enough to lose himself, Thyne was there to hold him, be strong for him, and sometimes break down with him.

The years passed like molasses, but by the end, Thyne felt he had finally finished grieving his daughter. He thanked Francis for the gifted time and privacy to be able to fully lose himself, and after a kiss and a smoke, Francis brought them back to the manor in Orléans at the same second they had left.

With his energy renewed (especially because there had been no voices keeping him awake in mesolithic France), Thyne was antsy and hurrying everyone to go inside and sleep. Their train would leave the next morning.

Even after the three years of mourning, sleeping in the house would be nigh-impossible for Thyne. The voices were much quieter in Europe, but the grief was still gnawing at him. It was only because of Francis' arms around him and his whispering singing of an old Chinese lullaby and sea shanties that Thyne was able to relax and rest at all. He didn't sleep more than an hour, but he was able to at least rest his eyes for a full six.

As the morning sun crept into their room, Thyne stirred and turned to look at Francis, who was surprisingly still awake. "Are you excited?" There was a clear sleepiness to Francis with how weakly he nodded and smiled. The sun was dappled over him by the tree through the window. It was a river of honey and gold pouring over him, and his deep eyes, like the depths of the Atlantic, sparkled in the dancing light. No matter how rotten his teeth, Thyne was always of the mind that his smile was the most beautiful in the world. "We're finally going to take down mother's company, then I'll never have to hear any of those bloody songs she made me write ever again."

"More than just Maitland," he breathed.

"Yeah, but you're mental if you actually think we can take down Osiris." He giggled quietly and batted his eyelashes.

Francis' smile soured, and the sparkling light of the sun was suddenly avoiding his eyes. "I know," he whispered, but it was strangled.

Thyne cupped his hand around Francis' face and shushed him lightly. "Oh, Franny, I didn't mean it. We… we can do it." A forced smile.

"It's the only way to fix what I've done."

He arched his brow and pursed his lips into an expression of concerned confusion. "Hey, it's okay, Frankenstein. You didn't do anything wrong."

He nodded and sighed. "I have, but there's no use dwelling. We must act while we are still able." He got out of the bed and took a swig from his rum to return his drunkenness from the less-desirable mere buzz he had had all night, which was beginning to wane and hurt.

There was rustling in the rest of the house, too, so Thyne stood. They had slept in the master bedroom because Neodesha was pained too much to set foot in it but did not want a stranger inside, nor did she want it to be left empty, "Case she's in there as a spirit."

He wiped the sleep from his eyes, yawned, and slipped on a pair of Rosemary's slippers to shuffle downstairs, Oliver's teddy in his arms. A clattering of pans in the kitchen brought him there, Francis following like a loyal hound. Giovanni, Arjun, and Melchiresa would be driving back to Rome that night while the others were busy in Versailles, but they were nocturnal beings, so Thyne was surprised to see his boyfriend in the kitchen looking for ingredients in the empty cupboards. "Good morning, love," said Thyne with a sleepy smile.

He smiled briefly at Thyne but focused his attention on Francis: "Buongiorno, ragazzo. Go to market and fetch us the ingredients for zabaione and croissants for breakfast, some sort of frittata affogato for lunch, and whatever you like for dinner, but you know what I will and won't cook." He took out his wallet and tossed it to Francis as if he wasn't just as rich as the chef. "Oh, and don't forget drinks like coffee and tea and wine and some fresh herbs." He flailed around his hands as if getting tired of his own voice before adding on, "And something to make sweets for Thyne."

Francis rolled his eyes and dropped the wallet onto the marble countertop. In a flash, the rest of the counter-space was filled with foods. Among them were the ingredients Giovanni had asked him to find, but there were also things Francis knew Thyne always wanted such as juiceboxes, candy, and tea. The fridge and freezer were also full, and after the other two in the room had taken a moment to look around, Francis said, "No time to waste. Make us breakfast, master. And quickly."

Thyne came over and kissed the chef's pale cheek, mostly to be sweet but partly because he was standing in the way of the juiceboxes. He sipped on the juice as he wandered out of the kitchen to find Francis, who had suddenly disappeared. He heard footsteps on the stairs and went to investigate. "Good morning, Dezba. Keeva's making breakfast." He sipped again as he watched her walk downstairs only to realise he had called Giovanni by his real name. "I mean Giovanni."

"Oh, how lovely. I'll go see if I can't help."

"You didn't happen to see Franky up there did you?"

She shook her head, and the two went their separate ways, Thyne wandering upstairs and Dezba to the kitchen.

"Good morning," she said as she came into the room. She looked around at all of the ingredients with a huge smile. '*Oh, yes! I'm definitely going to make all of these fine youngsters some cookies tonight.*' She started to pick through the ingredients to inspire her future endeavours, but she stopped after a moment and apologised. "I should have offered to help you already."

"You cook?"

She beamed. "I'm no European pastry chef, but I've won a lot of baking contests over the years."

"Oh? How exciting. Well, if you want to help with breakfast, how about you show your chops with some croissants? I've already measured out the flour." He gestured to the measuring cup to his right.

"Okay, you scoot over, son, and I'll make the best croissants I can." She would have given herself more credit and claimed that they would be the best in the country or better, but considering they were in France, and this man was a chef, she decided not to oversell herself.

"'Son?'" He laughed. "Signora, I have watched entire civilisations from birth to death. I have been a king and a god and have fathered enough children to perhaps constitute an entire nation worth of people. I assure you, that I am no one's 'son'."

She pinched his cheek. "That's nice, son. Now chop chop! Need this ready before the train leaves." Missing the train they planned to take would only delay them by about an hour, but it helped to put a fire under everyone's asses to have something of a deadline.

"Sí, but first you must go fetch my doting husband. He'll play us some music on his harmonica while we work." He beamed a smile, which gave her a good view of his vampiric fangs, and she easily returned the grin before going off to find Arjun.

Breakfast was lovely. Dezba's croissants were on par with what Giovanni could have made, and it surprised everyone to learn that they were not his own. The praise she therefore received was met with big blushing smiles from the older woman, and she promised more goodies in the future, which predictably excited Thyne most of all. Giovanni, Arjun, and Melchiresa were left to clean up the mess from breakfast after the others shovelled down the food and almost immediately rushed off to the train-station together. They walked speedily for most of the trip, but when the station was visible they saw their train and bolted for it. Luckily, the conductor had seen them and delayed leaving until they were on board.

Roach, despite being very fit, was heaving the hardest after the short run. He held his knees and coughed a few times. After seeing this and a few minutes into the ride, Thyne stood and approached Viktor. He had joined them per Francis' insistence. His power would apparently be needed when they reached whatever place they were being brought. The ginger watched Thyne approach with a scowl and scoffed quietly when he sat in the empty seat beside him. Thyne looked at his hands before sighing and saying in Viktor's native tongue of German, "Fix Roach's lungs. And Perlie's too while you're at it."

He did not do as he was told but asked, "Want me to help the kid, too?"

Thyne's head perked up. He found Partha then looked back at Viktor. "What's wrong with him?"

"You're kidding. A slight scare would send him into cardiac arrest. He's nearly blind in that one eye he has. Eats worse than you. I can hardly even see him with my eyes because my extra senses are just screaming constantly of his blood pressure." He chuckled. "He might do more blow than I do."

Thyne eyed Partha and frowned then back to his hands. "Yes, please. Help all of them."

"Oh okay, so the scar on the little French one, too, then? Seems he got stabbed about the same place as River."

Thyne looked immediately at Jean-Jacques, who was laughing at something Roach had said. '*Stabbed?*' "Did he say who hurt him?"

Viktor shook his head. "He didn't *tell* me about the wound."

"Yes, help him, too, but take him aside to tend to him like a doctor. He's skittish."

"Alright. Also, the heavier twin swallowed a coin or a rock or something. I'd guess a week ago." Viktor chuckled and Thyne rolled his eyes amusedly at Roach. "Anyway," continued Viktor, "I hope you'll have fun in the palace. Francis once took me where he's taking you."

"He did?"

"Yeah, when we dated. We fucked on the couch. And the beds. And the kitchen floor. Really everywhere. Careful where you step." He laughed heartily in Thyne's face, making enough of a mockery of him that the Englishman stood and returned to his seat beside River, leaving Viktor alone once more.

The Brit puffed out his cheeks and crossed his arms to pout. After a brief glare at Francis, he looked outside at the passing buildings and tried to focus on the gang and the catharsis he would feel after destroying his mother's company.

When they arrived at the palace, they purchased tickets to tour it and stood around in the crowded line as they were slowly slogged through its grandiose halls. Thyne had never been to the palace, so his jaw was agape as he looked all around at the splendour. It kindled an already-burning fire in him that seemed to send his spirit to a time he had never seen. He felt a kindred understanding with the commoners who had taken it upon themselves to behead the bourgeoisie during the French Revolution. He was disgusted by the gaudy opulence of the palace, but the rage it fueled was pleasant. This was a good place to remind them why they were organising. His wandering gaze fell to Francis at his side, and he had a visible thought. He leaned in and whispered, "Franky, this is how you grew up?"

"For the formative years at least," was his reply.

He looked around again with this in mind. "How awful it must have felt to be ripped away from this and shown the real world. Shown the real world through slavery, no less."

"Could have done without the slavery, of course, but I would have rotted here. If I had never left, I may have never met you, and there is no greater tragedy I can fathom than that."

Thyne looked at him and blushed at his innocent smile and romantic comment. "Yeah."

"So," said Roach as he rudely leaned his head down between theirs, resting an elbow on each of their inner shoulders, "Why are we here?"

Thyne glared, but Francis' smile remained. "There be a sequestered haunt not too deep in the palace's bowels. We must secure an opportunity to slink away, so I may show the lot of thee the manner in which to locate and enter it."

"Sounds rad." He turned to face Thyne. "Wish you lived here in its heyday, huh?"

His glare hardened. "Of course not."

"Oh? And why not? Rubbing elbows with other elites. Dressing up in gaudy outfits. Never having to face the poor but pretending to care about them. It's the liberal dream." Thyne didn't react, so Roach sighed, rustled Thyne's hair, and stood upright. "Guess I need new material to get you all riled up."

A sarcastic grin. "Yeah. Guess you do."

As quickly as he had come, he returned to a conversation with Neodesha and Perlie, leaving Francis and Thyne alone at the front of their little group. "His erratic nature is quite becoming of him, don't you think, my dear?" asked Francis.

Thyne rolled his eyes. "You say 'erratic,' I say downright 'mad.' And no. It isn't."

"Oh? Well, I'm growing quite fond of him. He'd make a wonderful first mate."

Thyne's amber eyes snapped to Francis and burned wildly. "Hey! What the fuck, Franny? I thought you and me were best mates!"

"We are! I meant he'd be a good pirate. That's all, Thyne. Please don't be angry."

Thyne scoffed and rolled his eyes. As he crossed his arms and ambled along with the tour group, Francis gently rubbed his shoulder until he relaxed his arms. To his surprise, Francis then intertwined their fingers together until he found an opportunity to peel the group away from the crowd. The few minutes they were holding hands calmed Thyne entirely and even lightened his mood to one brighter than any he had felt the rest of that day— the rest of that week, even. It was perhaps actually the best he had felt all year.

Once they were separated from the tour group, Francis led them through an employee hallway to an empty part of the palace. This new wing was entirely empty of people, giving it a much more luxurious feel than the roar of the crowd they had just abandoned could ever offer. Francis pointed to cameras as they moved and used his power to stop them in time for just long enough that the group could sneak through their sightlines undetected.

It took only five minutes of dashing across halls and waiting for employees to pass, after which they were brought to a fireplace at the end of a massive ballroom. He placed his hand on the marble tiles around the hearth and said, "We're here. We haven't much time, so the lot of you pay careful attention." He counted the tiles vertically then horizontally, aloud so as to give makeshift coordinates for this specific tile. There was a noise near the other end of the room, and holding the ballroom's cameras in time was beginning to drain him of all his energy, so he pressed the tile— or at least he *tried* to press it. It wouldn't budge, so after a few seconds of his frail hands both pressing into it, Roach stepped up and pushed it in with ease.

A mechanism clanked behind the wall, and after some very rusty-sounding gears turned, the back of the hearth slid to one side, revealing a small wooden door. It was painted green, which was a stark contrast to the golds and whites all around. Francis held his aching head and gestured weakly to the door, through which the group filed inside as quickly as they could. On the other side was a long corridor, painted the same ugly green as the door had been. It started narrow and necessitated crawling until, about three metres in, the ceiling slowly slanted upwards, or perhaps the floor was slanting down. Either way, none of them had gotten to the end of the corridor before Francis entered behind them and closed the door. He got their attention with a weak holler, and they all struggled to see him as he pointed to a lever hidden in the stone behind the door. He pulled it, and they heard the same mechanism that had opened the hearth for them as it creaked the marble tiles back over the hidden door. When he heard the last of the movements in the wall, Francis was finally able to release his hold on the cameras in the ballroom and, once he was where he could stand, he took a moment to himself leaning on the wall and gaining some semblance of his strength back.

This secret channel led them to a multi-chamber suite of sorts. Its furnishings were from the mid-nineteenth century and looked as if merely touching them would turn them to dust. The main room was lit with sconces, which seemed to light automatically as they entered but was clearly Francis' doing when he appeared in the middle of the sitting area leaning on his knees and spitting onto the rug. He had stopped time to give the suite a quick once-over, changing his eyes to a pair that could see perfectly in the darkness to do so. He wanted to be sure there weren't any other people already inside and destroy cameras were he to find any. Everything was considerably dustier and more decrepit than his last visit with Viktor. He took out a handkerchief and flicked it over some of the furniture, kicking up clouds of dust that thereafter hung in the air unmoving. After a good dusting of the living area's pieces, he brought time to a crawl and lit each of the sconces. His lighter would no more than spark if time was not moving, so it moved at a snail's pace until he had lit the room, after which he stopped it again and looked through the other chambers.

The bedrooms were dusty like the living room had been, so he flicked at them with his handkerchief until deciding to finish his walk-around and afterwards restore the furniture pieces with his power. The reason he had returned to the living area so exhausted and without having done this, however, came when he entered what would later become his and Thyne's room. Inside, he saw a rotted cadaver under the satin covers on the bed. He was not as perturbed by the death as his companions may have been were they to see it and approached to observe her. He found a note in her hands. After a quick read, he learned that she was a young woman named Natalya who had found the secret chamber while working for the palace and came down into it in 2020 to commit suicide. After another look over her, he noticed she was holding a rosary.

If there was one thing Giovanni had drilled into him as a young man it was that the stench of death was so indescribably unpleasant that he should thank every sort of god that he had no ability to smell it. He worried that the others may have already suffered the fetor, but no one had said anything. The door to this room had remained closed until he himself had opened it, and since time was stopped when he did, it had technically not been opened since she came inside to kill herself. He was already quite exhausted from holding the cameras in time like he had, but this was a situation he *had* to resolve. He rubbed the bridge of his nose and crinkled the suicide note slightly as his hand tried to ball into a fist. After this brief upset, he closed his eyes and said a traditional Catholic funeral prayer for her. He stumbled on a few of the lines, not having a perfect memory of the prayer, but he managed the entire thing with a good enough accuracy before opening his eyes, looking at her skull, and whispering, "Forgive me."

It took a great deal of his power to age her to the point that she crumbled to dust at the slightest touch. With his handkerchief, he brushed the dusted corpse off of the bed and under the rug, followed immediately by the note. He pocketed her rosary to bury more properly had he the time, after which he tried his best to age the air in the room backwards. This was even more difficult to do than turning the cadaver to dust, and he had no idea if it was working to hide the stench. At an arbitrary point, he stopped and hobbled his way back into the living area, closing the door to this room that may have still had the foul odour of death, and resumed time in the middle of the room when he simply could not hold it still any longer.

"Frankenstein, are you okay?" Thyne rushed over to him and pressed his hand under his elbows to give him support. "What is this place?"

After spitting a few more times, he stood and wiped the would-be vomit from his mouth. "Viktor. The walls. Please." He gestured to the muted green walls which were peppered with dust. There was walnut moulding along the floor and crown of the room, and the ceiling was plastered in an artistic swirling pattern and painted with the same toxic emerald green as the walls. There were four doors visible from this main sitting area, each of which led to a bedroom, and on either side of what must have been a hearth at some point were two short hallways that led to two more doors each. In the sitting room, tucked away in a corner near the entrance, was an upright piano, and in a similar alcove on the opposite side of the entrance was an old bookcase with half-rotted texts likely several centuries old.

"The walls, yes," said Viktor, "I'll counteract it."

Francis nodded and groaned as he used his power to restore one of the settees to a more sound state before plopping himself down into it. "This be a secret room my friend Oriane and I used to play in. She, unfortunately, fell ill and passed away when she were only eleven. The paint is laced with arsenic, and the walls are reinforced with lead. Lucky we have Viktor, or this would be nonviable. With him, it will act as its own defence."

There were concerned murmurs and shocked expressions at the mention of the hazardous materials. "What do you mean we're lucky to have Viktor?" asked Perlie.

"You know that Francis can control time, ja?" replied Viktor in his thick German accent, "I am of a similar ilk. In short: I control microscopic life. Blood cells. Skin cells. Plant cells. (Even smaller still in some cases). I can alchemise cells into different types, heal them, give them cancer, so on and so on. It is how I know that you," he pointed at Partha, "are on an unreasonable amount of cocaine." He howled with laughter.

Partha blushed and hid himself behind his hand as he sank down into the seat beside Francis. On the time-traveller's other side was Thyne, who was holding him lovingly, petting his hair, and whispering gracious and comforting words in French.

Roach hid his perturbation about Viktor and approached one of the settees. He seemed to be coming to sit across from them, so Francis waved his hand to reverse the sofa's age just enough that it would support his weight, which was perfectly timed with the large man dropping down into the cushions. "This is good shit, dude. They don't call you Mr. Frantastic for nothing, huh?" Francis nodded dismissively. "Once you're feeling better, we can start planning on how to use this place effectively. Until then—. Jean-Jacques?"

Jean-Jacques smiled anxiously at him. "Yes?"

"Where do we need to go to meet up with your sister?"

"Oui. There is a cafe we have decided. It is not very far away. She texted me ten minutes ago saying she will be there in an hour. But, since we're busy here," he rubbed the back of his neck, "I can go alone…."

Roach seemed to glare. It was imperceptible with the eyes, but Jean-Jacques felt it strike straight through to his soul. "Nonsense," purred Roach, "We'll all come with you."

Chapter 20
A Good Witch

Because he had to stop the cameras again to hide the group as they left, Francis was exhausted to a point he collapsed onto a bench in one of the palace's many gardens. The others stopped and waited patiently for him to regain his strength, the three smokers all taking the opportunity to have a cigarette. After Roach's offer to carry Francis was declined, the tall man chatted in Demotic whispers to his brother: "I've found it's much easier to breathe since we came to France, particularly here in Versailles. What do you make of it? Is the smog so bad in America?"

River shrugged. "Must be."

"Have you noticed a difference?"

"No, but I don't smoke."

He pursed his lips. "I'll ask Perlie, then." He floated over to her and asked in English, "Have you had an easier time breathing in France, too?"

She tilted her head and pondered. After a deep inhale of the flowery springtime air, she smiled. "You know what? Now that you mention it: I think so. Yeah."

"I didn't think the smog was so bad in America."

She nodded and stroked her chin. Roach was floating away to go chat with Francis, but she grabbed his wrist and pulled him closer. "Wait," she said and leaned in to whisper, "I don't think it's the smog."

"Hm? What else would it be?"

She hid her hand behind her torso and pointed slyly to Viktor.

Roach's eyes widened, but he quickly removed the expression from his face and nodded once at his friend. "Not sure how I feel about that if you're right…." They both eyed Viktor, but Roach's gaze trailed to Thyne and hardened into a glare. He left Perlie to take Thyne away and leaned down to whisper angrily at him: "Is your German friend fucking with my lungs, dude?"

He tilted his head adorably.

"Don't look at me like that, you cute little fuck. Is he using his alien powers or whatever to make it easier to breathe?"

Thyne smiled softly. "I told him to. You could hardly run three metres without hacking up a lung, mate."

He pursed his lips and stood upright, still unsure how to feel about it. On the one hand, he didn't like the idea of a stranger somehow having access to his vital organs, but on the other: he felt amazing. The best he'd felt in years.

"You're not feeling even worse are you?" He glared at Viktor with the venom of a thousand cobras.

"No." He sighed. "No, I feel better."

He beamed. "Good!"

Roach looked at Viktor then trailed a nervous set of hazel-greys back down to Thyne. "Are you sure it'll be okay?"

"Mmhmm. Don't worry, mate. He's been protecting me and Frankenstein from stuff like cancer, overdoses, dehydration— that sort of rubbish —for decades."

It was around this time that the smokers were finished with their durries, and Francis was feeling strong enough to walk with them to the cafe where they would be meeting Jean-Jacques' sister. It was a short distance, so they arrived fifteen minutes before her. Thyne offered to place an order for them while they waited. In the end, he bought a croissant and coffee for Dezba, a lemon tart and iced water for River, a hot cider for himself, and a box of macaroons to share with the rest. Neodesha was sneezing a lot the entire time they were outside, but the fits calmed when she was sitting at one of the little cafe tables with its lacy white parasol.

They waited in the courtyard, taking up three of the small tables, but Jean-Jacques sat alone across from them. He was messaging his sister and looking for her between glances at his phone.

When they finally spotted each other, May standing across the street and waiting for a car to pass, it seemed the entire world stopped turning. Before his vision blurred with tears, he managed a good look at her. She had gained weight since he last saw her, quite plump now, but it helped to fill her out where she seemed almost malnourished a decade prior. Her heart-shaped face was kind and framed aesthetically by her stark white hair. It was straight and cut in a neat line just below her chin. The slight slant to her dark hazel eyes was distracted by the bags beneath them. Her skin was pale, paler than he remembered, and she wore a grey gingham sundress with a pair of ankle-high kitten-heeled boots above which was the lace from a pair of white ruffle socks. Off her shoulder there hung a simple black purse, out of which a wire was connected to her phone, which was presumably because (she had mentioned) it was dying. When she spotted him, a wide white grin split her face and pushed her eyes closed. She waved madly at him, and as soon as the street was clear, she rushed across it and scooped him up into her arms.

She had slight difficulty picking him up to spin him around considering she was four inches shorter and not in the best shape, but she managed the feat and set him back down to hold him tightly. They embraced for two wordless minutes before she retreated and wiped the tears from her cheeks and snot from her perky nose. Her French was slightly accented with a hint of Scottish from her birth mother, whom she had mentioned she was staying with for most of the past decade. "Jean-Jacques, I can't believe this is real!"

He nodded and wept, unable to formulate any coherent verbiage.

She hugged him again, and after they had come to terms with this dreamlike reality, she wiped her eyes again and asked, "Where are your friends?"

He gestured to the boisterous three tables across the courtyard. They had quieted to watch the sweet reunion, so when she looked over, most of them waved lightly at her.

"Oh! They're precious! Introduce me!"

He nodded and brought her to the gang, introducing them each up until she saw Partha and squealed happily. "It really is him! I watch your streams!"

A chuffed smugness overtook him. He replied with his overinflated ego on full display, but Thyne had stopped listening by then. He was looking at May with a sceptical glare. Over her left eyebrow there were three silver balls, evenly spaced. They could have been mistaken for piercings, but he noticed a dull grey square no larger than a millimetre on the white of her eye near the tear duct.

When she noticed his staring and had finished being introduced to everyone, she smiled anxiously at him and pushed some of her hair behind her ear, revealing that her ears were modded with half-inch gauges. "Are you looking at my cybernetics, Thyne?" she asked nervously.

"Yes," he droned and finally paid her a less scrutinous gaze, "You must have them removed to join us."

Jean-Jacques smiled and feigned upset: "Oh no! I guess she can't join."

May glared lightly at him. "Nonsense, JJP." Her glare softened but remained faintly when she returned her attention to Thyne: "I've jailbroken it. Osiris doesn't have any access to it anymore."

"You can't be certain of that," he huffed.

"I can be. You probably don't know a lot about computers. JJP said I'd be the best with them of the group. Is that true?" He only glared, so she continued as if he had agreed, "It is only technically an *Eye of Osiris*. I had it installed for convenience and almost immediately hacked it. The hardware is good and, obviously, not something I could have installed myself."

"Prove it to me."

She stroked her chin. "I'll have to think of a way to do just that. Until then, I need to thank you all so much for saving my brother. Anything I can do for you I'll do, including joining your cause."

They finished up at the cafe only fifteen minutes later, the general consensus being that they should all return to Neodesha's manor in Orléans. The train ride back was pleasant, with May getting to know everyone a little bit better and made excited by the idea that she would get to meet six dogs when they arrived at the manor. She was told plainly that she would also be meeting two vampires and a legendary demon-pirate, but even if she believed the claims… she was still more excited to see the pups.

All of the animals, including Roach's duck, which she was delightfully surprised to meet, swarmed her when she laid down on the living room rug and let them smother her in kisses and snuggles. It was an endearing sight, and after she was done giggling and playing with them and told all their names, she was introduced to Giovanni, Arjun, and Melchiresa.

Giovanni, Dezba, and Viktor cooked a bountiful meal for the entire group that night, and they all agreed to reconvene in the morning to speak more seriously about the gang and their plans moving forward.

May and Jean-Jacques shared a room, if for no other reason than to have more time to catch-up, but after a lot of pleasant chatter, Jean-Jacques looked at the time and lowered his voice to a whisper. It was just past two in the morning, and he could see May was growing tired. "May," he began with the air of a conspiracist, "I think we should run."

She arched her brow. "What? Why? These people saved you, didn't they?"

"I have merely traded one cage for another. This criminal business is wicked and will only end in bloodshed: I fear it will be ours."

She pursed her lips. "JJP, this isn't like you. Why aren't you more grateful? They reunited us! Without Arjun finding my new number and Thyne smuggling you out of the states, you'd still be trapped there with the Russians!"

"I know. I know." He sighed. "I just… don't want either of us getting hurt. Can't we go to your mother's house in Scotland? I… don't technically have my engineering degree anymore… but I can still manage to get work somewhere. I'll be a line-cook or dog walker or——."

She crossed her arms and pouted. "Jean-Jacques, these people saved your life and reunited us. Now, unless you want me to go back to Scotland and pretend you're still trapped in America, you will go along with whatever they ask of you for at least a month. Then we'll talk about it again. Fair?"

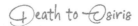

He sighed. "You would really leave? Act like we never reunited?" She nodded pointedly. "Fine. One month."

A smirk. "Good. Now come here!" She pulled him over and gave him a noogie. "I missed you like Hell! Let's get some sleep, but I want to hear all about your tattoos and the good things in America when we wake up."

———◦◦———

After a hearty pancake breakfast courtesy of Dezba, all fourteen of them sat leisurely in the luxurious furnishings of the manor's largest living area.

Francis addressed the group: "There be numerous intricacies and details we must excogitate, but Thyne hath cavilled at my desires to dive headlong into those depths without first— what was it, dearest? Something to do with the aesthetics?"

Thyne nodded. "I couldn't sleep, so I took some notes." He pulled out a pocket-sized notebook and flipped through about four pages before settling. "Firstly, I think we should split into two separate but intertwined entities, at least as far as outside observers might notice. I realised that a few of us are undoubtedly better at stealthy quiet sorts of missions, and the rest are best going guns-blazing." He smiled lightly at Francis. "I had an idea to give each of these sects a name and—."

"You're naming the gang?" Roach chuckled. "What are you twelve, dude?"

He scrunched up his nose. "Shut your mush, you bellend. We're naming ourselves because otherwise the media will, and they will only propagandise and call us something horrific." He flicked his notebook then returned his attention to Francis. "Anyway, I think we should also have calling cards to be certain our actions are all connected by the media and make clear that we are organised." A beat. "I have an idea for the names." He stood and slipped his notebook into his back pocket as he approached Francis. He took up one of his hands in his own and knelt down, almost as if he were about to propose. "'*Allow me to kneel before you, sire, most respectfully. We will embrace each other on the day we shall have upon our temples, you the crown, I the tiara.*'"

Roach crossed his arms and spoke with a playfully indignant tone: "I thought you said the French was better."

Thyne smiled at him. "Yes, but that quote in particular stuck with me." He stood. "I figured Franky could be the unofficial leader of what we'd call *The Crown*, aka: the guns-blazing sect, and I'd be the unofficial leader of *The Tiara*, for less bombastic missions."

Roach's tone was playful, but his posture was still unamused: "How very British of you."

Thyne's face went red and nose scrunched up again under a furrowed brow, but before he could start up his fit, Dezba cooed, "I think it's sweet, Thyne. Did you have an idea for the calling cards?"

He took a few breaths to calm himself and smiled as kindly as he could at her. "Yes, actually, thank you, Em. I think *The Crown* should leave crowns, obviously. Franky could get them from the middle-ages, I'm sure. And along with them: playing cards, specifically the king of hearts." He blushed and grinned at Francis. "And for *The Tiara*, tiaras and queen of hearts cards."

"I like it," announced Partha with a beaming grin. "I want to be in *The Crown!*"

"Don't get carried away, kid," said Roach, "You're going to be at the base making masks and costumes, and that's about it."

"What the Hell, Roach!? Who died and made you pope? I'm gonna be—."

"We can unriddle what you shall do for us at another time. Thyne has more to say."

"Thank you, Franky. Yes, I also figured we could do with some code names. Me, Franky, Roach, and Dezba already have ours, but I spent some time thinking of the rest. Except for you three," he gestured to Giovanni, Arjun, and Melchiresa, "You three aren't joining us, right?"

"That is correct," replied the doctor.

"Viktor isn't really a part of it, either, but I thought of one for him anyway." He cleared his throat and looked at his notebook to read from it: "I'm Dorothy, Franky's Toto, Dezba is Auntie Em, and Roach is the Tin Man. Here are the ones I thought of for everyone else: Party, you'll be The Lion."

"Not sure if I should be offended, but it does sound cool."

"I thought you'd like it, mate." They smiled at each other. "Anyway, then there's May and Jean-Jacques. I figured you two could be East and West." They nodded, Jean-Jacques with considerably less enthusiasm than his half-sister. "Perlie is Glinda. River is the Scarecrow, and, since Neodesha is already a city in Kansas: we might as well just call her Kansas." He lowered his notebook and threw his cute smile all around the room. "How's that?"

River sort of chuckled. "Doesn't the Scarecrow have no brain?"

His smile became forced, almost sarcastic, and he wiggled his nose at River.

"Well," interjected Roach, "I think it all sounds great, dude. You said you had a name for Viktor, though."

"Oh, right. I don't know. I think I was just tired." A nervous glance at the ginger.

"Tell us!" whined Partha.

"Well, I was going to call him Oz."

"Why does *he* get to be Oz?" complained River, "Isn't that the main character?"

"No." Thyne glared at Viktor. "No, I chose Oz for him because he's a fraud and the most mercenary scumbag I know." The ginger's reaction to the claim was a lazy shrug and slight frown but nothing more.

"Well, now, hold on," said River with a little chuckle, "*I'm* not the most merce-nary scumbag you know?"

Thyne's face was turning red again, so before he blew a gasket, Roach stood and ushered him to a seat to address the group. "The names are good. Now, let's talk about our first target."

Chapter 21
The Beetle

Dezba couldn't sleep, so she lounged in one of the antique settees and resumed knitting Perlie's sweater. She had finished Thyne and Partha's already and had Roach and River's both halfway finished. The haunt was quiet, with Francis and Thyne in one room, the twins in another, Neodesha and Viktor in one, and May and Jean-Jacques together as well. She assumed they were all asleep, but the truth was only May and Neodesha were asleep of the lot. Partha was also entirely absent: out on a job somewhere in the Bahamas for at least another week.

She was humming quietly to herself as she knitted, but she didn't notice it until Jean-Jacques sat on the settee across from her and commented, "You have a good voice."

A blush. "Thank you, son. What are you doing out here? The gang's first job is tomorrow. You should sleep. You'll need your strength."

"I can say the same thing to you."

She giggled. "Right, but I'm old: I've done plenty of sleeping in my day." He tried to laugh, but something was upsetting him. After setting down her knitting needles on the seat beside her, she leaned toward him and whispered, "What's wrong, son?"

He sighed and ran his hands through his hair. "Madame... How did you become with this gang?"

"You're asking how I joined?" He blushed and nodded. She chuckled and told him about the robbery and how she had pulled a gun on the teller instead of the robbers.

His eyes widened at the story. "Why did you do this?"

Her smile weakened but remained. "I was lonely and had nothing to lose."

There was a beat, during which he let his gaze trail around despondently. Just as she started to pick her needles back up, he spoke up again: "Are you regretting?"

"Not in the slightest, son." This seemed to perturb him, so she moved to the seat beside his and grabbed his knee gently in an attempt to comfort him. "Are you having second thoughts?"

"I am having many thoughts," he replied, "Third. Fourth. Fifteenth maybe. I see my sister in her bed here in the arsenic château and must be worried. I feel…. I worry…." He was having trouble capturing the thoughts and translating them to English as they formed a dark cloud over his head. Dezba's grip on his leg tightened soothingly, and he let out a long exhale. "I should have stayed with Grisha. May will be hurting."

Dezba wrapped her arms around him and pushed his head down into her bosom. "You shush. You did the right thing. You're finally reunited! And she was excited to join. The others will protect her from harm."

He breathed in her scent and let it soothe him. She smelled of fresh linen, chilli peppers, sage, and, after spending most of the day with Roach and Perlie, cigarette smoke. It was a pleasant smell, especially in contrast with the musty old air in the toxic chamber, but he was still perturbed when she released him. He sat back up and leaned on his knees, looking down at his hands as they were clasped lazily together.

"Son?" He looked at her soft smile and offered a weak grin in reply to it. "Everything will be okay. Whatever is meant to happen will happen." A beat. "Are you religious?"

"There is no god for me, Madame."

She cupped a hand around his cheek. "Then I'll have to ask mine to protect you."

The serious tenor in her voice and the warmth of her hand was a salve to his anxiety, at least for the night. He managed a weak smile and whispered, "Merci, Madame."

"Now. Go get some rest, son. There's a big day ahead of us."

"Oui. But, you must sleep, too."

"I will. Goodnight, dear."

"Bonne nuit."

Francis awoke with Thyne in his arms and no recollection of the night prior.

They were both shirtless, but such a thing was not out of the ordinary. What *did* confuse and disorient him was how dark it was. There were no windows in the haunt, so he was at a dissonance with time that was unsettling to one claiming to be in control of such a thing. Thyne was on his phone, however, and Francis managed to spot the time at the top of the screen while his friend messaged a group chat May had made for the gang. 7:32 in the morning.

When Thyne felt Francis shifting behind him, he finished typing out a joke to Roach and Partha, lit a lantern on the bedside table, and turned around to look into Francis' waking eyes. "Good morning." His voice was honey: sweet and smooth and soft. "Did you sleep well?"

"I slept.... What happened last night?" Thyne frowned, and it became clear after fifteen seconds of silence that he wasn't going to answer. "Did I hurt you?"

"Not... physically...."

Francis' lip trembled. He sat up and averted his gaze from Thyne's perfect form. "Damnable wretch that I am," he muttered.

Thyne's hands were soft as they ran up his back in tandem with a slew of shushing sounds. "Franky, it's okay. I can't imagine.... I mean.... I don't blame you."

"Blame me for what?" he whimpered.

"For losing your mind...."

He squeezed his eyes shut so tightly he saw stars: a desperate attempt to stop the tears. His head was pounding. His heart ached. His limbs tingled and tongue smacked of a thirst for rum. After swallowing all of his upset, he managed a quiet, "What did I say?"

"Franky, it doesn't matter. We don't have to—."

"It does matter!" he snipped, turning around to flash a wild broken set of sea-green eyes at his friend. "It does.... Tell me. Tell me, that I might know the difference between the Hell I've made and the Hell I truly deserve. I wasn't even drunk last night...."

A beat. Thyne sighed and dropped his hands off of Francis' shoulders to look down at them in his lap. "The truth is, Francis: everything you said was beautiful.... Up until I realised you were lost again." He looked at him, a tear trailing his cheek. "But I promised I'd find you when you're lost, and I intend to keep that promise no matter how much it hurts."

"You don't deserve such a burden. Leave me lost when I'm lost. I be not worthy your time nor your affection."

He glared, his button nose all scrunched up. "Androme Francis de Tremblay, you take that back right this very instant."

"Perish the thought, Clarence. I shan't burden you."

"You aren't b—."

"I am! You have just stated the pain it brings you! What is that if not a burden? What am I if not a putrid blight on your otherwise pleasant existence?"

His glare hardened. "Francis, you're my best mate in the entire world. I love you. Now you stop all this self-loathing and apologise."

He averted his gaze and scoffed. "Faugh. I 'apologise.'"

"Like you mean it, de Tremblay."

He glared. "I apologise for burdening you."

Thyne huffed. "You're a bellend. I could strike you."

"Then strike me. It is no better than I deserve." Thyne grabbed at the air angrily to stop himself from taking the invitation, and Francis chuckled sadly at the sight. "If you only knew what I'd done, Clarence. You'd kill me...."

"What could you have possibly done that has you so self-loathing? When we met, you were so obnoxiously full of yourself I *could* have actually killed you with how fuming mad it made me. So what happened, hm? What did you—?"

"I've killed us all, don't you see? It is with that very same arrogance of which you speak that I stripped bare the world of its last shred of hope. Oh, so careless! So reckless! And I shan't elaborate, because I shan't drag you further down into this Hell of my creation. Carry on— I beg thee— carry on thinking there is hope, because if there remains that divine fire in your soul there remains something worth saving."

Thyne may have responded when he finished processing the words, but his thoughts were interrupted by a gentle rapping on the door. "Come in," he said with a slight quaver.

May pushed open the door and quickly covered her eyes when she noticed they were both shirtless and assumed they were naked. "I'm sorry. Um. Dezba made breakfast, and Roach is asking where you two are."

———— ◆ ————

After breakfast, which Francis did not eat, he and Dezba found themselves in a quiet debate away from the others: "Dezba, I advise strongly against it."

"I don't care, Francis. I'm coming with you, and that's final."

"We will be killing someone. Blatantly. You are not mentally prepared to be in witness of such a thing."

She scoffed. "Son, I have seen plenty worse done to my friends and family by New Clear than what any of you could possibly do to one man in a few hours. You're underestimating me. In fact, I want to be the one to pull the trigger. You didn't even eat the breakfast I made. You've never eaten anything I've made. If you don't trust my cooking, why should I trust your judgement?"

He took pause. She was not ready, and he knew it. He had had extensive electronic communications with their target during his preparations pretending to be a broker. Cillian Atterberry was not a plainly evil tycoon bent on irradiating the Navajo people: he was a liberal-minded man-child who had fought to protect the land. Perhaps Francis should have told her as much, but, as a captain, this was the sort of behaviour he would reward with compliance. She would learn to trust his judgement after the inevitable upset watching Atterberry die would cause her. And, if she did manage to kill him, he would show humility and grace in the after. "It is my own business why I prefer not to eat most meals, no matter the cook. But… regarding the matter of your insistence to join us on this first very vital mission, I suppose I should hook you a disguise. A shame Partha is absent, but Perlie or May may pass muster as temporary hair and makeup artists."

She took her leave and found the aforementioned women, asking them to help disguise her, and Francis travelled to the not-so-distant past to secure her a designer dress and handbag, both of which would be vintage enough to be impressive rather than outdated in 2081. Once he had given them to the ladies, he found Roach. The brute cleaned up nicely, Francis had to admit: wearing a crisp grey business suit with a navy blue plaid vest underneath. His long black hair had been slicked into as small a bun as was possible and secured with several hair ties and bobby pins, and his piercings had all been removed. He was clean-shaven and smelled of cherry, oak, and spiced cider.

"You look beguiling, my friend."

"Not so bad yourself, hot stuff," replied Roach with a purr. Francis was wearing a forest green suit with subtle golden pinstripes that gave him an ethereal sort of look when the light caught them just right. His hair was short and dark brown, slicked back neatly, and his face was free of its usual mad beard. Even his brows were neater than usual, and his teeth were pearly white. Roach wondered why he let them be as gross as they typically were if he had the ability to fix them so easily, but as the strange sort of man who enjoyed filth, he almost preferred them yellowed and rotten. His aroma was more pleasant than usual, though: a woody cologne he typically wore but with no undertones of rum and salt.

Francis held out his hands, entirely ignoring the compliment and flirty nature in which Roach had said it. "Now, show me your arms and hold still that I may remove thy tattoos and piercings."

Roach hesitated. "Will it hurt?"

Francis nodded dismissively. "It will. Hie. We have but an hour before our flight departs, and thy false identity is bound to score us a profiled delay."

He still hesitated. "If it'll hurt, I don't want to do it."

Francis scoffed and rolled his eyes. "It will hurt no more than it hurt to initially receive the tattoos, and in much less time. Are you afraid of pain like a petulant child, or are you an adult prepared to assassinate someone?"

Roach pursed his lips. The fact of the matter was that he *was* afraid of pain, but he didn't say as much. Francis' words flayed him, so he could only stand idly as he let the pirate take his arms and push them backwards through time until his tattoos disappeared. It itched at first, then stung like the needles initially stung, then nothing, all in a matter of three seconds. Likewise, the holes in his ears, tongue, nose, and brow all stung, then a sharp pain the way they stabbed into him when he first received them, then nothing.

"There," said Francis when he was finished, "Now, why does your hair remain unshaven? I expressly informed you to—."

"No, Francis. That's where I draw the line. I haven't cut my hair in four years. I like it this long."

"And it shall be returned to that length or longer when we're finished!"

"I'm not shaving my head. You can't make me."

Francis scoffed. "Faugh. Suit yourself. The obstreperousness among the haunt— by god! Dezba has also wormed her way into the boarding party, so I must take leave to briefly send electronic letters and make calls in order to secure her an audience alongside us. Do you remember your character?"

"I remember everything, Francis. Dezba shouldn't come with us, though. She won't be able to handle it."

"You dare believe such a thing has failed my notice? Faugh! She insisted, and I am inclined to let her see what a grave error disobeying my orders can be."

He sighed. "I'll go talk to her."

"Nay! Let her anguish her unfounded misjudgement and rue the day she defied me."

"Francis… I didn't know you were so… cruel." The realisation stirred up his stomach with butterflies, but he remained outwardly unchanged. '*I suppose I shouldn't be surprised. He was a pirate, after all,*' he thought, '*But what beauty to see him giving into that darker side…*'

Francis waved his hand with an air of disdain. "We make the beds we lie in. It be her own yen, the remorse she yet suffers."

"Well, I suppose I'll go give her a run-down on the script, then."

"Yes, yes. I will join you both to inform her of her false identity in a matter of minutes."

They finished their preparations and, with Francis helping them not miss their flight by teleporting them into one of the airport's bathrooms, they boarded their flight to the United Arab Emirates. They were quiet during the trip, only exchanging cursory glances and sometimes a word or two. Chatting casually would hinder their ability to keep in character, not to mention Francis was still quietly irritated with Dezba.

In a line and with a confidence that matched the business-types they were trying to take down, they filed into a towering skyscraper in Dubai. They walked through metal detectors and let security search them for weapons with the sort of irritation of "honest" business people who knew for a fact they were unarmed. And it was true that they were not armed. Francis would be sneaking their weapons inside with his power. When asked for IDs they passed the false ones Perlie had made for them to security and waited with feet tapping impatiently. Dezba had no experience acting, but thusfar she hadn't done anything poorly enough to be called out for it. They were visibly wealthy and, as was usually the case, eccentricities were not only accepted; they were the norm for the types of people the three of them were pretending to be.

The elevator ride was long, but they exchanged no words with each other nor even the slightest of glances. When the doors slid open, they walked with just as much determination as they had downstairs, making their way through more security, and were finally escorted to the penthouse by two of Atterberry's personal guards who were large enough in one way or another to daresay dwarf Roach.

After a moment of waiting, they were brought to a living area that overlooked the opulent sinking city, bringing a pit of disgust to Roach and Francis' stomachs. Their host, Mr. Cillian Atterberry, was an American man whose wealthy father would bring him to Dubai as a teen for business dealings, and he, "fell in love with the view. But where are my manners? You must be Mr. Mathews," he said as he shook Francis' hand, "And Miss Williams." He shook her hand. "And...," he seemed taken aback by Roach's intimidating air and shook his hand slowly and for a longer time than he had with the other two, "I'm terribly sorry, sir. Your name was?"

"Al Su'ud."

"Right!" He swapped to Arabic: "And you don't know much English, correct?" Roach nodded. "Well, I'll do my best to say everything twice for you, but since the others both don't know Arabic, it's probably best that I conduct most of the meeting in their native tongue. Is that fair?"

"Incredibly fair. My business with you is more private, anyway."

He smiled and swapped back to English: "Well, come in! Come in! All of you! Take a seat anywhere you like." He made a big gesture for Roach to understand that he was being invited to sit. "Have some wine!" He poured glasses of chardonnay for each of them including himself. Once they each had a glass and were seated on the uncomfortable couches and sofa chairs, Cillian sat across from them and took a sip of his. He was a handsome young man, no older than forty. His build was evidently average, if not thinner than average, but his suit fit it nicely.

The creases in his forehead and cheeks that only showed themselves when he smiled were deep and dark against his pale skin, and his hair was medium brown and styled in a neat quiff. His eyes were dark and deep-set in his face, and his pointed chin was clean-shaven. An expensive cologne could be smelled in wafts as he moved about the area, and Dezba was of the mind that it was far too rugged a smell for him with its notes of pine and ginger.

He started the meeting with a genuine laugh, delighted to have guests, and spoke with a lilting tone like a songbird: "It's so wonderful to have you! I've been looking forward to this deal all month. I trust your flights here were pleasant?" He barrelled through the question without leaving room for their answers. "And what a beautiful day for it, too! You know my son— he's going to a private school in Sweden —he says when he comes to Dubai he never wants to go back because of the weather." He laughed at his own anecdote. "Can you believe it!? He's just like his old man! I said the same thing to his grandfather when he would take me here.

"And, I can tell you're curious about my boy," they were not, "Well, he's interested in trading just like me, and he's turning fifteen next month! I'm excited. I think I'm going to buy him a property here, even though he's been begging me for more stocks. He's lost far too much on the ones he does have! Like I would ever— but, oh my, how I do run on. I'm sorry." He sipped his wine and set it down on the large amethyst geode that was acting as a coffee table. "Let's get down to business, no? So, Mr. Mathews, let's start with your proposal."

Francis cleared his throat and put on a flawless posh English accent, which had taken him a year disconnected from the present with Thyne to perfect. "Yes, I was interested in your stocks in New Clear. Do you have a lot of say in how it runs?"

"Oh, yes, sir, I do. Like I told your broker last month, I've been trying to get them off that Native land in the states for years now, and I've gotten a few of the mines cleared since I've become the majority holder!" He beamed, especially at Dezba. "We're losing money for it, but I have other investments, and I just couldn't stand it if I was a part of a company that has been hurting so many marginalised people."

Her gut wrenched. She wasn't exactly thrilled to learn Cillian had a teenaged son they would be depriving of a father, but learning that he had been fighting back against the mining sent her head spinning. She looked around for the exit and bit her lip. Was it too late to back out? Why were they killing him if he was on their side? *'But, oh… Francis probably didn't know, and now that he does, we'll apologise and leave him alive, and it'll all be okay.'*

Francis looked at Dezba briefly then back to Cillian. "Is that all?" He made a good effort to sound unimpressed and haughty.

Cillian read the acted emotion just as Francis had intended and shook his hands at the idea worriedly. "No no no! I practically own the company, they're just not doing anything else that needs stopping. But you wanted to talk about the sale, so let's talk about the sale!"

Now that Dezba may have been having a change of heart, Roach looked around the room.

"What's wrong?" asked Cillian in Arabic.

"I'm looking for the guards and servants."

"Oh!" He blushed. "I'm sorry. Did you want something to eat? My wife told me to get a charcuterie board, but I had heard that could be considered rude to Arabs. Oh! I'm so stupid. I'm sorry."

Roach ignored his blubbering apologies and the odd rumour. "Do you have servants and guards in the house or don't you?"

"No sir, not during the weekdays. I only have guards posted at the elevator to the penthouse, but I've never had servants. It makes me uncomfortable to have someone else do things for me if I'm not a guest in their home."

"Is that so?" asked Roach, but he did so in English. Cillian didn't notice at first and simply beamed and nodded. "So the workers at New Clear, the company that you 'practically own,' don't do things for you?"

He went pale when he noticed Roach was speaking English. His heart dropped into his gut and weighed him down into the stiff cushions of his couch. "N-no."

"They don't? Is that why you've blocked their attempts to form a union for sixteen years in a row? Because they don't do anything for you?" His expression and tenor were blank and calm, but he was enraged, and his anger was helping Dezba reconnect with her own.

Cillian looked around in a panic, sensing the sudden danger upon him. What he was looking for, he wasn't certain. "U-unions—. They— er— they're bad for business. Y-you know that, Mr. Al Su'ud. They st-stifle progress."

He stood, and Cillian's breaths were immediately hastened and laboured. "Em, if you don't do it now, I will," said Roach, his voice chilling them all to the bone.

The panicking man noticed suddenly that "Miss William's" hand was fidgeting with something in her bag. She was biting her lip and looked up at "Mr. Al Su'ud." After a faint shake of her head, there was a knife in Atterberry's throat, and he was struggling to scream out for help, gurgling on his own blood instead. With his last few moments on this mortal coil, he watched in horror as the woman was physically held back from helping him, and her mouth covered.

Roach whispered into her ear with a forceful tone, as forceful as his strong arms around her and calloused hand over her mouth: "For your husband, Dezba."

She was bawling and shaking her head as best as she could from within his strong grasp. She tried to shout, "No!" but managed only a muffled sound before her face was squeezed even harder by Roach. *'Dear God what have I done!?'* She was watching this man die!

Roach's breaths were hot in her ear and voice low and deep and spine-tingling: "If you don't calm down, I'm going to have to kill you. Are you going to make me do that, Emmie?"

Her breaths were sniffly and laboured and her muffled bawling was heartbreaking, even to Roach, but the threat made her gather enough of herself that she stopped fighting against him.

He released her, but seeing as he could easily grab her again, she stood in stunned silence and watched in horror as Cillian bled out at her feet.

Francis eyed Roach with a slight nod before reaching into his briefcase and pulling out two of the items from inside: a mediaeval lord's crown and a single playing card: the king of hearts. He waited for Cillian to finish flailing around and leaned over him, putting the card and crown on his chest. He took Roach's knife out of his throat to clean via chronomancy and tossed it back to the murderer. Francis' tone was apologetic but determined as he looked to Dezba and assured her, "It has to be done. It *has* to."

They gave her ten minutes to get a hold of herself, after which Francis fixed her makeup with his power, and they all three left the building with the same confidence they had entered. The body wouldn't be discovered until the next morning.

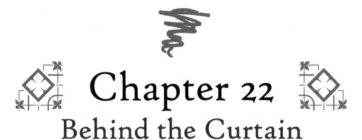

Chapter 22
Behind the Curtain

When they returned to Versailles, Francis and Roach were quick to notice that Thyne and River were missing respectively. In an unintentional chorus, they asked, "Where's Thyne?" and "Where's Sonny?"

May perked up as Perlie helped Dezba into their shared bedroom to calm her. "I was researching and managed to track the location of the next shareholder. He's at a casino in Paris, so Thyne and River rushed out to try and intercept."

Roach took out his phone and started to type on it as he ambled to the sofa, but Francis seemed more concerned: "Have they boarded a train for such an excursion?"

"I think so."

With that, Francis outright disappeared.

River and Thyne started when the chronomancer suddenly appeared in the seat across from theirs on the train. "Bloody Hell, Francis." He had a hand over his startled heart and his breaths were coming down from the brief scare. "What are you doing here?"

"It is unappreciated and unwise of you two to try killing this man before—."

"Don't worry about it, Frankincense," said River, "We're not going to kill him."

"We wouldn't be so reckless. Don't you trust me, Franky?"

"What are you going to do if not kill him?"

They both smirked, Thyne's more subtle than River's. "Well," began the American, "reconnaissance, what else?"

Thyne nodded and reached across the small area between them to gently rub Francis' knee. "Go get some rest, love."

It took Francis a moment of quiet to process the request, but after a slow nod and a swig from his flask, he stood and disappeared from the train.

It had been quiet between Thyne and River before Francis showed up, and for a while after he left it returned to such silence. Thyne was reading, and River was watching through the window as France rolled along beside it. For about ten minutes, Thyne had been reading but not processing any of the words. His thoughts were instead reeling and the voices very talkative. Everything was so loud in his head, it was sudden to River when Thyne grabbed his arm and said, "Oi!"

"Hm?"

"Why did you do it?"

"Why did I do what?"

"When we were playing cards back in Compton, why did you keep betting?"

River smirked. It was a mocking smile with a glint of amusement in his hazel-grey eyes. He was so much colder than Roach even despite his willingness to express his emotions outwardly. The only difference in their appearance, other than River's less bulky build, was that his face was ever-so-slightly thinner than Roach's, but in moments like this he looked so dissimilar he may as well have had the head of a viper. His only response was a haughty chuckle in the back of his throat.

Thyne's fists clenched. No one had ever made him feel so inadequate as River could, at least not in regards to something outside of his musical capabilities. His stomach was stirring up with every possible emotion and three particularly loud sins: envy, wrath, and lust. He had always thought himself the best cardist and manipulator in the world, but here was River, able to play him like the devil played his fiddle. "Why did you keep betting when you had nothing? I know you saw the cards were marked. Could you read the markings?"

"Of course."

"Then you knew I had a better hand."

"Yes."

"So why did you bet your brother's car? Don't you care about him?"

He chortled. It was proud and deep, warbling around like a cartoonish fat-cat villain. "Thyne, you're adorable."

His little nose scrunched up and brow furrowed. "Answer the question!"

"Which one? You asked two questions." The jeering smile was looking more and more punchable by the second. He was eyeing Thyne the way a hyena eyes its prey: with sadistic pleasure and relentless mockery.

"Both!"

He feigned thought and stroked his chin, which was beginning to shadow with stubble. "Hm, I suppose I do care about my brother." The sardonicism stung like a wasp. He was going to continue teasing, but Thyne surprised him with a knowing smile of his own. "What's got you so entertained, then?" asked River.

"Me? Oh, nothing," he lied and leaned away to return to his book. "I just wonder what you would do if you weren't holding all the cards anymore. If I hadn't folded."

"But you did fold." His tone had lost its jeering nature to instead become monotone and tinted with the slightest bit of worry. "What are you talking about, 'holding all the cards'?"

Thyne hummed a taunting giggle that echoed the one River had offered only moments prior. He ignored the question to look back at his book and resume reading, though he did have to turn a few pages back to pick up what he hadn't read while his thoughts were reeling.

River, though confused and vaguely concerned with Thyne's sudden emotional flip, leaned on his hand and looked back through the window. Everything would come to light in time. If Thyne thought he had the upper hand, it would be all the more satisfying to let him revel in it for a while so the fall would be that much greater when River inevitably regained the high-ground in this battle of wits.

When they reached the casino, they were quick to spot their next target and slid into some of the empty seats at his blackjack table. Using cash Thyne had withdrawn on the train, they bought into the game and observed their competition.

Thyne and River both turned on their charm and chatted up this next target, as well as all the swine he wallowed with. After seven hands, they had become "friends" enough that River's invitation to go buy dinner somewhere expensive in Paris was accepted by three of the other players.

Amongst the drunken fiends that accompanied them to dinner was the next majority shareholder of New Clear (the man they had come to intercept): a portly old Irish-French fellow with kinky orange hair who seemingly had more freckles than dollars. His name was Pól Barre, and he was by far the most sober of the lot, save for River and Thyne. They were also accompanied by a middle aged Belarusian woman named Aliaksandra who, as far as they could tell, was the daughter of an oil baron and had a lust for old men, money, or (most likely) both. The only person she hadn't been flirting with all night was their last guest, on account of his clear interest in Thyne and River.

Said guest was Tatum Abraham, whom Thyne and River immediately recognised as the CEO of Osiris International. He was a racially ambiguous dinosaur of a man with wiry hairs that held onto his leathery scalp with the desperation of a climber hanging from a cliffside. He was thin and frail, and his deep Canadian accent seemed to be dubbed over his "real" voice with how unfitting it was in contrast to his sickly appearance. He smelled mostly like cigars and cologne, and the horrid rank of his breath was drowned by the grace of the Gods under all the rum he had been drinking. It was a very real possibility that if either of the men he was flirting with were to actually bed him, he might die from the increase in heartrate alone.

Thyne and River were independently observant enough to deduce that he wanted them to "fight for him," so when they were brought to their table at the restaurant, they feigned a small argument over the seat closer to him. It was lucky he was so drunk, because, even accounting for all of their prowess in deception, it was quite clear to anyone sober that neither of them were actually excited with the development. He was making creepy comments about them all throughout the meal and afterwards invited the both of them to his penthouse.

No matter how uncomfortable it made them to even think of what might happen when they got there, they agreed and bid adieu to Mr. Barre, who would be chaperoning Aliaksandra back to her home in his limousine. As they parted ways, the boys reminded him of the meeting later that week that had been scheduled. After the dinner, they were faced with the long trek to Tatum's penthouse. He wanted an arm around each of them, but he couldn't reach River's shoulders, his hunching posture putting him at a *towering* 4'10", so it was Thyne who was helping hold him up as they ambled downtown.

They brought him to his bedroom and, when he tried to kiss Thyne, he was pushed away and reassured, "We're going to go get ready," in as sensual a tone as the disgusted Englishman could muster.

Tatum was too drunk to notice the upset and smiled. "Okay, the bathroom's down the hall on the left." He pointed, his hand trembling under the weight of all his years, and they were quick to slink away into the restroom.

Their voices were whispers: "We should just kill him," suggested Thyne.

"We can't just kill him. We were the last ones seen with him, and *you* were stupid enough to use your real ID to get your drinks." He poked into the soft of his shoulder to emphasise his upset with the misstep.

Thyne rubbed the area, dreading the bruise that would form, and scrunched up his nose. "Oi! You used your ID, too!"

"No, I was only drinking water. I just asked the waitress to serve it like gin and charge me accordingly."

"Oh." He looked down in shame. "Well, he looks about on death's door as is. We could probably just wait for him to die." He giggled. "But jokes aside: I still think we should just kill him."

"I'm sure you do think that. You think a lot of stupid things."

His freckled cheeks went pink. "Stop it! If we won't kill him, that's fine, but I am *not* going to shag him."

"We should at least consider it. Think of all the things he might tell us if we gained his trust by…," he trailed off and gagged at the thought.

"I don't care if he has the bloody nuclear launch codes, River. I'm not sleeping with him."

"Pussy. I'll do it, then."

Thyne winced away from him. "You'd really do that? He's drunk enough you can probably just ask him whatever you want to know. Either way, we should call the others to give them an update and get ideas for what intel we might need. This might be our only chance to go after Osiris."

River put his hand over Thyne's phone when he pulled it out. "I'll go learn what I can and skip before he wakes up in the morning. Get Franky to come get you." He was pale at the thought of what he might have to do with Tatum once Thyne was gone.

"River, you don't have to do this…."

His brow furrowed and whispers grew louder: "You've just said it might be our only chance. I, personally, couldn't give any less of a shit, but let it be known that I'm a fucking team player. So do you want to take down this company or not, fuck-head?"

Thyne gagged again at the thought and held his mouth to keep the vomit in. "I'll text Francis."

A moment after his message was sent, Francis appeared at Thyne's side and looked at River. "Karson, you are truly offering to bed that monster for the sake of the cause?"

He nodded but just barely.

Francis scooped up his hand and kissed its knuckles tenderly. "Your commitment will not go unappreciated. On my honour, I shall repay it to you tenfold." A beat. His tone went dark: "But River… I need you to kill him."

"Fine. Now go. He'll be wondering what's taking so long."

Thyne stopped Francis before he would blip them back to Versailles and took a pen from his inner pocket. He looked at it for a moment before passing it carefully to River. Francis watched with intrigue and concern plain on his face. "River," began Thyne with a very serious tone, "If you can't kill him, press this to the back of his neck and click it once." He demonstrated and mimed clicking it into Francis' neck. "Can you do that?"

River took the pen with an arched brow. "What is it?"

"I'll tell you eventually, but for now: just do it. Please."

"Okay."

They disappeared, and River was left alone in the penthouse restroom. He went to the mirror and leaned on the counter to look into his own hazel-grey eyes, pretending they were his brother's. He knew damn well that this was something

Roach would never do nor something he would ask River to do, but taking down Osiris was important to Roach, ergo, it was important to River. His own convictions on the matter were muted and malleable, but Roach had audibly fantasised about the fall of Osiris International on countless occasions. If he were lucky, he'd be able to kill Tatum without having to even see him shirtless, but he would go however far was necessary to prove his dedication to the political movement Roach was a part of.

After a few deep breaths, he left the restroom and found Tatum in the bedroom already undressed. "Oh, you're back. Where's Landyn?"

"Family emergency. He had to go."

He looked toward the front door and muttered, "I didn't see him leave…."

River sucked up all his upset with one big inhale, removed his shirt to distract the old man, and stepped closer.

He returned to the haunt in the wee hours with a backpack full of papers and ledgers. There was no one in the living area to greet him, so he threw the bag onto one of the settees and rushed into his room. Roach sat up and met him at the door. "Sonny! Are you okay? Did you sleep with him? Did you kill him?"

"No, yes, and no." He wrapped his arms tightly around his brother and shuddered. Their dogs all crowded around him with concern.

Roach pet his long hair and made soft shushing sounds before scooping him up and carrying him to the bed. "What happened? Was it worth it, at least?" He helped the dogs onto the bed to snuggle up with River, who lazily pet them as he replied:

"Remains to be seen. I hope so."

"Why didn't you kill him?"

"I… I tried. I don't know…." He looked at his hands. "I tried to strangle him— played it off as a kink thing— but something odd came over me. I couldn't do it…."

Roach was visibly baffled by the assertion. "You're not saying you actually cared about him, are you?"

"God no. I don't know what it was. It seemed supernatural… I've never had trouble killing before, and I— well I was going to do it for you, so I was determined, to say the least." He sighed and rubbed the bridge of his nose. "Can you just run me a bath? Scalding hot, please. I want to burn away my skin. That was disgusting."

"I'll get right on it. You did a good thing, Sonny. It won't be in vain." He kissed River's forehead and gave him a grateful couple pats on the shoulder before rushing out of the room to the bathroom to draw a hot bubble bath with milk and honey.

After his bath, River knocked on Francis and Thyne's door. Thyne was still awake, so he dragged himself to it.

"Here's your pen back."

"Ta. Did you use it?"

"I did what you said. He said it hurt. I had to think of a lie really quickly. Why didn't you tell me it would hurt him? What did I do to him?"

"I should have told you, yes. I'm sorry." He pocketed the pen. "Anyway, I take it that you didn't kill him, then?"

River glared at him. Thyne was an expert liar, but River was even better at detecting deception. Something was off about the questions. "What do you think, Thyne?"

"I think you probably couldn't kill him. Francis worried as much."

His glare hardened. "Elaborate."

"No."

After a moment of a quiet angry stare-down between the two, Francis appeared beside Thyne and said, "Thank you, Karson. The files you found will be of great import and assistance. I apologise for giving you an impossible task. My hopes that you could succeed where I failed were unfounded."

"Impossible task? What are you fucking talking about?"

"You couldn't kill him. It's no matter. You did as Thyne asked of you and retrieved those documents. That will be enough."

Francis was lying or at least not telling the entire truth just the same as Thyne seemed to be. "You're both scumbags. Tell me what you're hiding. I just did something unspeakably horrid for your sakes. The least you owe me is honesty."

"In due time," answered Francis with a sigh.

River scoffed and left them to go back to his room and attempt to sleep.

———— ◆ ————

There was a week's lull. Their murder of Cillian Atterberry was newsworthy, but it was not world-shattering. There were even a few news outlets that only covered it in passing comments, if they covered it at all. It was the day of the meeting River and Thyne had set up with Pól Barre, and Roach was taking his brother's place for it. There was much protestation at the idea, especially from Francis: "You risk our security to what end!? You were not present when the meeting was scheduled. Even if he believes you are your brother, you still cannot know exactly what was said: suppose he references a conversation River forgot to recount for you or misremembered. There be no justification for such recklessness!"

"No reason, Francis? I would assume you, of all people, would see the reason. I'm going to protect Thyne in case things get bloody."

To this, Francis' tan face went scarlet. "Dog! He needs no protection from the likes of you! You offend us both. Not only can I save him from anything at a moment's notice, he is a venerable man of his own ilk, a war veteran, and of immutable character!"

"Relax, dude. I want to help. Besides, I pretend to be Sonny all the time."

"Faugh!"

Despite the protest, Roach and Thyne left that afternoon with a promise from Thyne to his worried friend that he would make sure everything went smoothly. The meeting would be much more casual than the one in Dubai, so Roach had his hair in a messy ponytail and his tattoos visible. They were similar to River's for moments just like this. He was wearing his typical combat boots and torn black jeans, but his collared dress shirt was more apt for their destination.

He had been staring at Thyne for a while on the train. They were sat across from each other in a private chamber, and Thyne was evidently enthralled in his copy of *Beowulf*, unknowingly biting his lip and pulling his wavy brown hair behind his ear as it fell into his vision and dared to interrupt the story. It was a tranquil sight. Roach thought, in fact, that it was outright precious. The Brit's outfit was endearing and adorable, despite its business-casual style. The colours were light and played well together. His shirt was a silky patterned piece in light pinks and yellows but with shining gold buttons which were only buttoned up to his chest, revealing a lot of his bare skin. His suit jacket was muted green tweed and matched his pants in colour and texture. His hair was loose, but it seemed curlier than usual on account of his shower a half-hour before the trip. It was even still wet on its ends and had dripped unpleasantly a couple of times onto the pages ensorcelling him.

He felt Roach's eyes on him and looked up to meet them.

They both started.

Roach had been staring dreamily with his eyes half-lidded and a small smile, but neither of them had noticed until then. He averted his gaze and rubbed the back of his neck, immediately trying to divert the conversation: "So, war veteran, huh?"

Thyne closed his book and nodded. "You are too, right?"

"Yeah. What war were you in?"

"World War Two."

Roach scoffed. "Don't lie to me, Thyne. You're no good at it."

He glared, but it was a much softer glare than was typical for him. Pained, perhaps. Offended. Sad. He didn't reply verbally at first, instead pulling up his left sleeve. He reached across the space between them and grabbed Roach's rough hand in a white-knuckled grip, slamming it down onto his forearm and running one of Roach's fingers along something raised beneath the tattoo of a spoon and spices. "You feel that? You see it?" He asked, his tone one of muted rage.

Yes, Roach felt it. There was a line of what felt almost like braille down his arm. It ran the length of the spoon's handle. When he leaned closer to see what he was meant to be looking for, however, he didn't see anything save for the tattoo.

"That's from Auschwitz." He threw Roach's hand away and slammed himself back into his seat.

Roach went pale. He was silent for a while as he recontextualised everything he had ever thought about Thyne, who was a few more pages into his book when Roach's quavering voice broke the quiet: "Why were you there?"

He didn't look up from his book and spoke curtly: "Prisoner of war."

"I didn't know they sent prisoners of war to…," he didn't want to say the name.

"Well, they did," spat Thyne, "We were enslaved just like everyone else. Especially so when they found out I was a communist and in love with a man."

"In love with what man? With Francis?"

He finally looked up. His expression was surprisingly calm if not a little irritated. "What about the American Crusade, hm?" A sarcastic grin. "How was that? Was it fun?"

'*Well, yes a little,*' was his first thought, but he restrained himself and said, "No, of course not."

"Didn't get sent to any concentration camps for being married to a man, hm?"

'*Now, how the fuck does he know I was married to a man?*' He rubbed at his wedding ring anxiously. He hadn't said anything about having a husband… had he? Thyne had such a knack for making Roach doubt his perfect memory it made him sick. He didn't respond and held his aching stomach.

"That's what I thought. Why don't we trade war stories some other time?" It was clear with the enraged smile he used to punctuate the sentence that by 'some other time' he meant 'never'.

The train pulled into the station about ten minutes later, and Roach's air was still that of a scolded dog. He was averting his gaze and making himself small… or rather "small". He picked at his nails, chipping some of the clear polish from them and wishing he could have them black like he usually did. Just trying his best not to think about the war. He was so rapt in thought that he didn't notice the train had stopped until Thyne stood and grabbed his bag.

"Come on. We've got a maggot to kill." He slung his backpack over his shoulders and left the train, Roach trailing behind with his head low and his hands in his pockets.

"I'm sorry," he muttered as Thyne led them through the city in a bit of a hurry.

"Oh, shut up," he said, dismissive of Roach as a whole. His head was on a swivel, and his hand was on Roach's wrist to lead him through the crowd.

Once they were at the docks and waiting in the evening sun for their new "friend," Thyne finally gave Roach more of his attention and noticed his dejected air even through his deadpan expression. "What's wrong with you, then?"

"I had assumed that when you were presumed dead at sixteen, that it was because Francis took you to a different time. I didn't think you'd actually served in…," he trailed off. Thyne pulled up his sleeve to show his tattoo again, but before he could say anything Roach averted his eyes and put out his hands, as if it was blinding him. "No no, I believe you. Don't make me touch it again."

Thyne sighed and looked at the time on his phone. "We're early, and I think it's just about the perfect time to pry." A wicked grin. "You thought I'd forget, but you said you'd tell me why you and Perlie broke up. So out with it."

After a beat, Roach's tense shoulders relaxed, and he lit himself a cigarette. He muttered in Arabic, "Might as well," before leaning down to light the fag Thyne had put between his teeth with his own. The Brit blushed and stole the light from Roach's durry, his attention entirely on the taller man as he prepared to tell his story:

"Used to be my dad had an auto shop out in Compton where me and all my siblings worked with him. It's one of the only occupations that hasn't been entirely replaced by some huge corporation, so that's why he was adamant that we all learn the trade. I worked with him the same as everyone else, save for Sonny, who was living in New York City and going to university. Dad didn't really approve of him leaving the shop, but he also couldn't, in good faith, try to stop him, especially considering he was paying for school himself. Anyway, the shop did well, and he even got to teaching the basics to my best friend back in high school, whom I later married.

"When Sonny and I were just four years old, Dad had some extra income coming in, and he offered us, and the rest of our siblings, to each choose an extracurricular activity to get lessons in or whatever. Sonny chose gymnastics, and I asked for piano lessons. I was basically obsessed with music from then on. I knew seven different instruments by the time I was just fifteen, and I know my dad knew because he'd come bursting in my room to… 'complain' about the volume.

"Even still, I had always thought he'd be happy for me when I told him about my first gig, but he wasn't thrilled by the news. He more or less implied that if I left the shop he'd kill me. A few years later, Perlie and Sonny met, and she warned him to stop fucking around in the crime rings he was frequenting. The CIA had a hit out on him." Roach sounded proud of his brother for the 'accomplishment'. "So while that was going on in New York, Compton and LA were starting to get really bad with all the flooding, but I had that seven-figure offer I told you about. The scam, to be blunt." He took a drag and sighed.

"When I told Dad I was leaving the shop to take the offer, his reaction was actually really disturbing. It was only one other time that I had seen him get so angry that, rather than going around throwing shit and being violent, he was outwardly calm. He said coolly to me, 'Get your faggot ass out of my house.' It really sideswiped me because he had never been anything but polite to the boys I had dated and the man I would end up marrying. But," he shrugged, "I chalked it up to him just being angry that I was leaving the shop, so I moved to that same apartment you saw in Compton and let him be for about six months. Just giving him loads of time to cool down and getting things in line to finally sign with my label.

"Well, LA was getting really bad by then, and after the pier collapsed, folks started getting really scared. The label bailed on me and moved to Vegas within a week after my last contact with them, but they had already taken my entire backlog legally, so I lost a lot of revenue and had no legal recourse because, well I mean, what was I going to do? Sue them? Anyway, Dad must have heard, because every other time I tried to call him he sent me to voicemail, but when I called about that he actually answered.

"I said, 'Things are getting bad here. I have an online friend out in Detroit with an empty shop. She wants to offer it to you for a good price. But Dad, I need money, and my offer fell through. Can I come back home?'

"His response was, 'Welcome to the real world, Clayton. You've made your bed, now lie in it. Don't you ever fucking call me again. I never want to see you, hear you, or even smell you for the rest of your miserable life. I won't even tolerate seeing Karson because he looks too much like you. You're dead to me, and so is he, and it's your fault. You're a worthless sack of shit, and I wish you'd never been born.' And, well," he somehow let out a small chuckle, "that was the last thing he ever said to me." He finished his cigarette and flicked the butt off the dock and into the sea. His next words hit like a punch with how plainly he said them: "So I started shooting up. Heroin. Got high every night if I could help it. When Perlie first broke up with me, it was because she found all my used needles. She gave me a few more chances because, frankly, she's obsessed with both me and Sonny, but I'm the one that broke things off most recently."

Thyne was pale and cold. After processing the information for a while, he asked, "Do you still...?"

"Nah. I'm eight years sober."

"That's good."

"Mr. Harley! Mr. Burakgazi!" The portly Mr. Barre shouted with his arms out as he approached with a woman by his side. He shook their hands vigorously, almost getting the better of Roach's strong grip with the sudden vitality of his own. "Come! Come! She's just been cleaned!" He gestured behind him and started to lead them all, including the woman they hadn't greeted yet, to a large yacht. The ship was called *Saoirse* which Mr. Barre explained was the Gaelic word for

'Freedom.' He helped his lady friend onto the boat before anyone else, then Thyne, Roach, and lastly himself.

His first order of business was the "Grand Tour" of the six bedroom houseboat which ended in the cockpit. He would be their captain for the evening, and he tried to send them out to the sitting area for drinks while he pulled her out to sea for a good view, but Roach implored, "Oh, Mr. Barre, I'm actually interested in captaining my own vessel one day. Could you show me how?"

His fat cheeks went red with delight and the stress put on them by his toothy grin. "Of course, son!" He wrapped an arm around Roach's shoulders and showed him to the controls, explaining quickly but in a good amount of detail what each of the components did, using some of them as examples like the one to unlock the steering wheel or turn on the engines. Were he anyone else, Roach might have heard nothing but a load of hot air and passionate rambling, but he was paying him the utmost attention, his brow furrowed with concentration.

While Roach was listening to Mr. Barre's mouth run as fast as an auctioneer's, Thyne was sitting across from the unknown woman in the living area. She wasn't the woman he had met the week before, and he was fidgeting anxiously as he worried she might be a prostitute and thus not deserving of the fate ahead of her. After a moment, he could only assume she was French and thus did not understand their English conversations until then. He held out his hand and introduced himself under the same fake name he had used at the casino and in French: "I'm Landyn Harley. And you are?"

She glared at his prosthetics with disgust and refused to shake the offered hand. Her French had a thick Russian accent: "What has happened to your finger?"

He blushed and retreated the outstretched hand to rub the back of his neck. "I had to have it amputated after a car accident," he lied flawlessly.

A sceptical glare. "And your other hand? Was that a car, too?"

"Diabetes," he lied again, "So what was your name? I know Russian if you'd rather use it."

She took the offer and spoke in Russian thenceforth. "Klava Melnik. I work for the fat one."

"Oh? What do you do, if you don't mind my asking."

"I do mind your asking, actually."

He cleared his throat awkwardly and twiddled his thumbs, his gaze slowly trailing around in search of something to fixate on while his mind was reeling for ways to suss out if this woman was a business person or not.

It took two agonising minutes, but mercifully, Roach and Mr. Barre entered the room. The sound of the engines spooled down shortly thereafter, replaced with the gentle lapping of water against the hull.

"Oh, Mr. Harley! I see you're getting acquainted with my broker, Miss Klava

Melnik. I'm terribly sorry to have not introduced you to her. I like to have her around as my arm candy." He chortled and hobbled over to the seat beside Thyne to squat down into it, a grunt of effort as his lap pushed up into his belly.

Once they were all sitting, it was time for some reconnaissance. The sun had only just set, so they had plenty of time before Barre would want to go back. It turned out that Miss Melnik did know English, so they conducted the meeting in it to be sure Roach understood, since he knew neither French nor Russian.

There was a lot of wine being poured, and a lot of chatter from their red-faced host. He was boisterous and boastful. "Yes! I'm the second majority holder of New Clear, although, did you hear? That bastard Atterberry died!" He choked on his own laughter. "Surprised someone didn't off him sooner! He split up his shares across a bunch of charities and whoever else when he died, so, I guess I'm the majority holder now!" Another chortle. "He was willingly losing money for all of us. I would have hired an assassin if I knew how to do that sort of thing." At this, Klava covered her mouth politely to hide a ladylike giggle. "But besides New Clear I've got a foothold in basically any company you can name."

"Osiris?" asked Thyne.

He laughed and nearly choked on his wine. "Oh, of course, my boy!" He slapped his back with his fat old hand. "What was it you did again? I imagine all this talk of stocks is rough on you as a…," he waited for Thyne to fill in the blank.

What had he said he did? It was over a week ago, and he was as drunk as he had been the entire night when the question came up. There was an awkward silence as he forced a smile. If he said the wrong thing, Barre would surely know.

"He's the CFO of my company," said Roach when it was clear Thyne had forgotten.

"Right! The pharmaceutical one," said Barre.

Roach nodded. "Yes, and you were interested in acquiring some of our stocks. I presume that's why you brought your broker to the meeting."

The Irishman had a visible realisation. He looked at his wine then at Roach with a drunken grin. He had completely forgotten the point of the meeting. "You lot had me talking a whole lot of nonsense, didn't you!?" He laughed. "Very well, Klava, work your magic. I'll go find something to eat to stave off the hangover for you thin folk." He grunted as he stood, nearly falling backwards under his own weight, but once he was on his feet his jaunty steps to the galley were spry.

Roach watched him leave while he sipped on his wine, a glint in his eyes that Thyne had never seen in anyone and could not identify. When Mr. Barre had disappeared entirely into the bowels of the ship, Roach's voice rang out in an almost musical way, "Two for the price of one, no?" He eyed Thyne, and the glint became recognisable. He had never seen it in anyone else, but he knew it. He'd *felt* it. This was the sadistic gaze of a killer excited to see blood, and it had Thyne short of breath. The room was suddenly very hot, and he tried to drink away the onset of lust by downing what remained of his second glass of wine.

"You're offering?" asked Klava who was confused by the comment.

Roach looked at her and let on a dark grin. "Oh, how darling! How should we do it, Dorothy?" His eyes flared up with murderous passion again, and Klava noticed.

She shrank away from him. "I am no prostitute, if that is your thinking," she said with as much confidence as her compounding fear would allow.

He stood and grabbed her wrist to pull her to her feet, draping her arm across his chest as if about to lead her in a dance. "Of course you aren't!" His voice was low, but it was even lower when he spoke directly into her ear: "If you were, I wouldn't kill you."

"Kill?" She took a moment to let the word sink in. Roach was watching her with an open-mouthed grin, seeming to wait for her to understand what was happening. It was sadism to a degree Thyne had never known, and he almost said something… almost. When Klava finally opened her mouth to scream for Barre, all of the air in her lungs was suddenly sucked out as if she had suffered a rib-shattering gut punch. She was, however, untouched. In fact, Roach had released her arm immediately after revealing his intentions to kill her. With both hands on her throat, she made the universal signal for choking and eyed Thyne with pleading panicked eyes.

He averted his gaze. She wasn't in the cards, so he hadn't mentally prepared to kill her, but he wasn't going to save her, either. He wasn't even sure how she had started choking. "I'll go take care of Barre," he muttered as he started to pull on a pair of gloves before grabbing his backpack. Giving her one last look, he quit the room to find the galley.

Thyne was unfeeling as he sped through the halls, clicking a clip into his handgun and cocking it. He checked the safety, and by then he was in the galley.

"Oh, hello there, Mr. Harley! I—." He dropped the plate of cheeses and crackers he had prepared and held up his hands. "Don't shoot! Don't shoot! How much do you want? Whatever they're paying you, I'll triple it!"

"I don't want your fucking money."

Barre was going to offer more. He was going to offer everything he had, but there was a muzzle-flash, a pain in his chest, then a long horrifying silence that ushered him out into the abyss.

It was lucky Thyne was strong, else he wouldn't have been able to roll over Mr. Barre's corpse to its back to access the bulletwound that had directly pierced his heart. He cleaned the wound with a dish towel then placed the tiara and queen of hearts card from his bag over it. With that settled, he made his way to the nearby deck. He took the gun apart, tossing it in pieces into the water, but when he went back inside to get the bloody dishrag and wine glasses, he heard Roach in utter hysterics. Concerned, he rushed back to the sitting area, greeted with a horrifying visage:

Roach was covered in blood from head to toe. A butterfly knife in each of his twitching hands, he was hunched over and laughing uncontrollably. His breaths were the hoarse wheezing kind before a coughing fit, but his laughter was crisp and deep and harrowing a sound. His fingers were spasming all around as he did flourishes with his knives, the tensing and relaxing of his hands not helping to make said flourishes look anything close to graceful. The tops of all of his fingers, in fact, were bleeding, and just as Thyne entered the room, he witnessed Roach send both of the blades directly into Klava's throat.

He didn't notice Thyne at first, but when he did, pure terror crossed his face. He tried to mask it, but the hysterics were too strong, and rather than snapping back to normal, he was now in a terrified fit. '*FUCK FUCK FUCK, CLAYTON YOU DUMB FUCK! You let yourself get carried awayyy~~~. Fuck! He didn't fucking sign up for this shit. He didn't know I'm a goddamn maniac, and now—.*' He looked down at the corpse and tried worthlessly not to admire it. '*What will he do? What will he say? I can't kill him, but he can't have seen me this way. I—. I—. God dammit, do I love him? Best just—. Just—.*' He looked around in a panic for an escape. The only thing his mad mind could think to do in the moment was dive into the sea and '*swim to shore and disappear. Sonny will find me somehow.*'

Almost as immediately as they had made eye-contact, Thyne watched Roach back away from him, stumbling over the coffee table and falling backwards with a loud crash as its wood splintered and cracked under his weight. He scrambled to his feet and started to rush away, seemingly to the back deck, so Thyne gave chase and grabbed his wrist firmly just as he was trying to dive into the sea.

"I'm sorry!" wailed Roach, and now the hysterics were overwrought sorrow. "Oh GOD! Please drink more. Drink until you forget what you saw. I can't kill you! I can't!" He kept speaking, but the rest was in Arabic and would have been hard to decipher even to a native speaker through all of the tears and sniffling and choking on his own emotions.

Thyne somehow smiled. "What's the matter, mate? We've got plenty of time to clean up. There's a shower on the boat. And I'm not going to nark on you, if that's your worry." His tone was so soothing and sweet, it made Roach cry even harder.

Thyne shushed him lovingly and tried not to notice the splatters of blood on his face as he wiped away his tears tenderly. His breaths betrayed him, however. They were shuddering and scared, but Roach couldn't have known it was because he was concerned for him and not because of what he had just witnessed. At least not until he clarified, "I've seen so much worse than that, Roach. You'd have to—," he stopped and giggled at his next thought, "You'd have to be a CEO or something for me to be upset about this. Now, come inside, mate. It's cold, and I want you to get cleaned up before morning. When we're finished cleaning up, I'll have Francis take us back to Versailles."

His hysterics were stifled and soothed slightly. He was still twitchy and letting out the occasional bout of crying or laughing, but Thyne helped him up the stairs to one of the bathrooms. It was almost as big as Roach's apartment, which added rage to his cycling emotions.

Thyne blushed as Roach took off his shirt to reveal a blood-soaked chest beneath. His eyes were wide and taking it all in with big black pupils, but he managed to catch himself staring before Roach did. "Do you need help?" he whimpered, his voice stifled by his lust.

Roach was calmer than before, but his reaction to the comment was different to what he usually would have done. Under normal circumstances, "No," would have sufficed, but he was overcome with the waves of emotions he usually suppressed. Thyne was so fucking beautiful, he just couldn't help himself from grabbing him by his cute freckled cheeks and pulling him in for a violent and passionate kiss.

Thyne melted. Roach tasted of blood and champagne. His tongue was sweet. His trembling lips were soft. The Englishman could smell nothing in that moment but the crisp aroma of basil. He was surprised to be kissing someone he so constantly wanted to set ablaze, but he was almost as taken by a maelstrom of overwrought emotions as the man on his lips. Roach would have kept going, but Thyne was more present than him. He pushed himself away and spoke softly, "We can't. I want to… I think… but you're not okay, and we have a lot to clean. I— I'm sorry." His voice was mousy and gaze averted, but he looked up once during the comment.

Roach whipped himself internally: '*You fucking no good son of a fucking bitch. Why the God damn Hell did you kiss him? Moron! He has a boyfriend! And even if he didn't, he's clearly in love with Francis. Fuck! Idiot!*' His voice was quiet and ireful, though it was clear from his facial expression that the anger was directed inward and not at Thyne. "God fucking dammit. I'm sorry."

"Don't beat yourself up over it. We'll… talk about it later." He stood on his tip toes and hesitated before kissing Roach's cheek, looking around awkwardly, and saying, "I'll clean up while you shower."

 Chapter 23
The Lion

There would be a week's lull. Thyne and Roach had not taken time to address the matter of their kiss, and the tension between them was especially amplified when Giovanni, Arjun, and Melchiresa came to the haunt from Rome per Francis' request.

Partha had found out about Roach's secret hobby of junk-bashing when he walked in on him making a sculpture of Charon on the Styx out of trash he had been collecting. Rather than continue to steal crowns and tiaras from mediaeval lords, Partha was elated by the development and suggested that they create the rest of the crowns and tiaras by junk-bashing, "as a team!" Roach was embarrassed to have been caught cutting, melting, and glueing trash together. It was an art form he put a lot of heart into, as much as his sketches or music, but he was ashamed of his passion for it. He never did anything with the sculptures when they were finished. He tended to keep the ones he liked best and take the others apart later to make something nicer. His ideas of beauty were usually vile to others, and that he was making something so recognisable as a Greek God was rare. He usually made kinetic sculptures, things from his favourite works of fiction, or depicted the sort of filth and sin and violence he loved so much. He worried it would get out that he was making a sculpture of Charon, but after a good few threats on Partha's life he was confident it would stay between them. Still, he agreed to the idea to craft crowns and would allow the kid to take all the credit for the ones he made.

With the half-secret plan underway, it was a leisurely time for everyone except Partha and Roach. Not only were they making crowns and tiaras for the next ten targets, which they would kill simultaneously, they were also making masks. Roach would lock himself in his room chain-smoking and working even more tirelessly than Partha, day in and day out. It was a nice escape and excuse to not have to face Thyne after crossing a line and kissing him…. Not to mention he had kissed him while he was covered in blood and out of his mind. He spent most of the week scolding himself internally for the debacle. Certainly there would be questions later how Partha managed to make all of the crowns and masks by himself, but Roach would refuse to admit to the hobby no matter the scrutiny.

Partha, unlike Roach, was not content to work alone and posted himself up in the living area daily to chat with anyone who would join him while he worked. He'd ask others to help by doing smaller tasks or passing him supplies as he needed them, but he was working just as slowly as the lonesome twin in the other room if for no other reason than he wouldn't stop blabbering.

Thyne's only "mission" during this lull was to supply the haunt with medical supplies, per Giovanni's request. He bought everything on the list diligently, with Francis trailing along beside him as he wandered the city and stores. The old pirate seemed to be "back to normal" with his jovial chatting, but Thyne dared not to inquire if time travel was to blame. If this was a version of Francis who had yet to see the void and the end of the world, it would be plainly evil to imply he would see such horrors and be changed for it, but if this was the same Francis who thought he was in Hell, Thyne kept quiet if for no other reason than avoiding hearing him say it again. The list his boyfriend had provided was boring him, so by the time he was finished he sighed and said, "He didn't put plasters on here. We're getting plasters if he wants them or not."

Francis smiled and nodded, following his friend to the bandages where he picked out every sort of childish colourful package he could find. He giggled evilly at a particular box, and Francis approved with his own evil giggle. The designs on the bandages in that box were all unicorns. "He bloody hates unicorns."

Francis agreed with a playfully wicked grin.

May's only "official" responsibility during this leisure time was to hide people from the cameras as they came and went, if Francis wasn't teleporting them around, but she took upon herself a secondary mission. Years ago, she had created an artificial intelligence. She was a lonesome woman, especially after she lost contact with her brother when he was trapped in the states, so it quickly became her best friend. She named it the Learning Algorithm Neural Network Intelligence or LANNI and personified it as a woman. She asked Lanni nicely to help her keep track of the gang in the media, and though she could have taken some time to relax thereafter, she spent the week almost exclusively sleeping and keeping note of what was known about them. To her relief, their base remained hidden, as did their identities. Lanni found a CCTV video of Francis, Roach, and Dezba when they first entered the tower in Dubai, but their faces were unrecognisable in the few frames they had been caught. Roach looked directly at the camera in the last few frames, but then it went offline, and no other camera footage of them existed anywhere online. To be safe, Lanni scrubbed these few seconds of footage, leaving no other trace of her tampering.

Dezba, feeling bad that Partha was allegedly the only one making them masks, decided to help by knitting some balaclavas for each of them, but she had only finished one by the end of the week when Roach entered the sitting area and called for a meeting. Once everyone was gathered, he spoke clearly and calmly:

"We have enough to make the final blow to New Clear, but it will take everyone. At least everyone except the Italians. We have ten more targets, and I still think it's best to take them all out simultaneously. May?"

She perked up. "Yes?"

"Will that work?"

She was like a deer in headlights. "Well, I don't know much about business, but I've hacked a few email accounts and have seen that a lot of shareholders are worried. They've all been supportive to each other. In denial, I think." She sweated and beamed a nervous grin. "Is that good?"

"Perfect. Thyne, your target is Mina Paulauskas. She's——."

"I have to kill her alone?"

"Is that a problem?"

He shook his head in a bit of a panic. "No, sir."

"That's what I thought. Francis, how many can you take out at once with your power?"

"Hm? Oh, all of them, but I think it's important to make a scene."

"I agree. That's why Partha has been making masks for everyone."

"I made some, too," said Dezba with an adorable grin.

"Good going, Em. So anyway, Thyne has Mina. Jean-Jacques, you and May will go after Elodie Harrison. Can you handle that?"

They both went pale. Jean-Jacques stuttered, "Oh, Monsieur Roach, I d-d-don't know if I could actually kill——."

"So you can't?"

"Monsieur does not have trouble with it somehow, but——."

"We can handle it," said May, startling her brother. They whispered angrily in French back and forth, but Roach ignored them and moved on:

"Good. Sonny, you and Perlie will have two targets each. They'll be at a banquet. I sent you the names and details just a moment ago." River nodded and pulled out his phone to look at the message. "That leaves Garey Howard for Dezba, but I don't trust her alone, so Francis, can you babysit?"

Francis was nodding when Dezba's brow furrowed. "I'm older than all of you! I don't need babysitting."

Roach rolled his eyes, but his expression was blank again in an instant. "Older than a few of us, sure, but half these people are vampires or some shit. Francis doesn't even seem to have an age at all. Regardless, are you asking to do the mission alone? You think you can kill a man? You were getting cold feet with Atterberry. Why should I trust that you'll kill Howard?"

She stuttered, but his intimidating air was weak against her unwavering will. "Fuck you, I can do it. He killed my husband."

Roach let himself smile for her. "That's the spirit, doll. So you'll kill Howard, but Francis, you'll take care of him if she bails, right?" He nodded. "Nice, and Francis, your target is Pandeli Duff. He's the most heavily guarded, but I trust you can handle it."

"Of course I can."

"Neodesha, you're with me. Giovanni says you're the guns blazing type, which will rhyme nicely with my knives."

"Oh, yessir, I won plenty'a duels in my day, I tell you what. And not in the way what Papa Arjun 'wins'."

Arjun laughed one loud ha.

"Great," continued Roach, "so, everyone get masks, get information on your targets, and reconvene tomorrow at noon to plan the kills properly."

Everyone started to reach for the masks in front of Partha who scrambled after Roach. "Wait, sir, who's my target?"

He stopped and turned to look Partha up and down. This little fucker. What did he want now? He was only here to look pretty and probably fuck things up later. Roach was almost annoyed enough by the sheer gall of him asking such a thing to emote, but he remained deadpan and droned, "What do you mean?"

"Well, you only named nine targets, and I guess you forgot to tell me which one was mine." He poked his pointer fingers together and averted his gaze from Roach's sharp grey eyes.

"Neodesha and I have two targets."

He looked up, hope in his big brown eyes. "Sir, I can take care of one of them for you! Or I can come along to help."

"You?" He half-scoffed, half-laughed. "No thank you. We don't need a liability. You'll stay here with the Italian creeps and their kraut flunkey."

Thyne, from across the room, glared at Roach at the insult to his lover and metamours. How he heard him from such a distance and over the conversations that had roared up was unknown, but Roach did notice the glare.

Partha's shoulders deflated. "But, sir. I'm not a liability. I'm—."

"I assure you, no one will be challenging you to an honourable duel of blades or an arts and crafts contest."

Partha huffed. He wanted to point out that Roach also liked "arts and crafts," but they were close enough to others that he feared for his life if he let it slip.

"You'll stay here, and you'll keep making masks and crowns and the like. I've seen how you've snuck out of the palace every night. I followed you one night. How am I supposed to trust you if you're doing what you're doing?"

Panic tore through Partha like a tsunami. He froze, his eye wide. "What?"

"If I catch you sneaking out again, kid, I'll kill you."

"W-w-what do you think I'm doing when I—?"

"Dude, come on. You're not exactly passing your stealth checks, if you catch my meaning. Stop going out, or I'll fucking kill you, plain as that. You're putting us all in danger for no good reason. You'll have plenty of time to get your dick wet after New Clear is done for."

Partha's face was red hot, his shoulders shrinking. He was suddenly very envious of tortles for their ability to hide in their shells. The only way out of the haunt was through Roach, so he made himself small and slinked off to his room to sulk in shame.

The next day, the group met back in the common area at noon, some more late than others (*coughcough*Francis*cough*. The man could control time but didn't seem to ever show up on time for anything). They discussed the upcoming missions and exchanged information. Dezba cleaned and prepared all the guns that were requested and suggested mods to make the jobs run more smoothly. Those who were together had matching masks, and those who were alone had unique ones. Partha spent the entire time pouting in the corner like a child, and Roach was quietly amused at the sight. Once everything was in order, they broke from the haunt leaving Melchiresa, Giovanni, Arjun, Viktor, and Partha to guard it. For extra security leaving without being caught by the cameras, Francis first teleported everyone to Neodesha's manor in Orléans, then they split ways, some of them taking the cars from her garage, some of them leaving on foot.

Partha sighed as everyone disappeared. He had never spent much time alone with these "creeps" as Roach had called them. They didn't seem interested in conversing with him, but three of them were sitting on the sofa across from his making him feel awkward and obligated to talk to them. He was extroverted enough that it wasn't awkward to talk with strangers, it was just... *these* strangers he wasn't so fond of. "So," he cleared his throat, "You're dating Thyne? He's a good guy."

They all laughed at the assertion, and Arjun joked, "Sure, and I'm the pope."

Partha blushed and averted his eyes. "Well," he conceded, "He's a good friend, at least."

Their laughing died down, and Giovanni said, "You met him through that game he likes to play, no? Something about dragons?" Partha's face lit up like a child's. He nodded fervently. "What's it called?"

"Dungeons and Dragons, but there are a lot of different TTRPGs, and his favourite is actually this sci-fi dystopia one called Paranoia, and it's really silly, but most people only play the fantasy ones like DnD. He's really good at it, at least at the entertainment and roleplaying aspect of it. He's not like a power-gamer or anything, but but *but* he's also not horrible at strategy and stuff. He was Dezba's favourite on my stream, and based on the fan art I've seen of the characters I'd guess she was in the majority. His characters are usually evil, but—."

"Okay okay, I don't care *that* much," he laughed.

Partha scrunched up his nose, offended on his friend's behalf. "Aren't you dating him? You should be more interested in his hobbies."

He waved his hand around as if the idea was a bothersome fly. "Yes yes. He's wonderful, and his interests are very trite and adorable."

"Trite?" He grabbed his chest with a gasp. "Sir, you are being incredibly rude. I have half a mind to tell Thyne what you're saying about him!" What was Giovanni on about? Trite and adorable!?

"Tell him, if you like. He'll find out anyway."

Giovanni returned his attention to the newspaper he had been reading, but Arjun was still interested in the conversation. He arched his brow at Partha. "How does the game work?"

The offence Partha had felt for his friend was washed away by the question and replaced with a huge smile. "I could set up a one-shot for the lot of you! The best way to learn is playing."

Giovanni seemed irritated with the idea, but after some talking with Arjun in what Partha assumed was Old Egyptian, he reluctantly agreed. Partha immediately sat them on the floor around the coffee table and started bringing dice and books and binders from his bedroom. "We'll start with 7E! Viktor? Do you want to play?"

"I am not a child."

Partha pouted. "It's not for children."

His only reply was a roll of the eyes and a swill from a bottle of absinthe, so Partha scoffed at the idea of inviting him again and returned his attention to the three who seemed actually interested (at least Arjun and Melchiresa seemed interested. Giovanni was going along with it to appease them).

After helping them understand the game mechanics at the most basic of levels, they made their characters, and Partha waited impatiently as Arjun drew all three of them (quite skillfully, he had to admit). Finally, he played some music on a portable bluetooth speaker and started to set the scene.

It took a while for them to understand how roleplaying worked, but Arjun and Melchiresa picked up on it quicker than he expected. Or at least… Partha *assumed* Melchiresa understood. He still hadn't said a word since they landed in London. Thyne had told him in the past that Melchiresa wasn't a mute but only spoke around people he trusted entirely. After recalling this fact, Partha passed him a small notepad for writing his dialogue, which he… never used. Oh well! It was more important to try and help Giovanni understand the concept of roleplaying. He seemed almost offended by it.

"You mean I have to pretend? Like a child?"

A roll of the eye. "Yes, you have to pretend like a child. Just give your character some traits and play them up. Even if you don't have them yourself."

Arjun giggled and teased. "Giovanni, my love, you have no imagination. This is why you're no good at all at pranks."

Still, they managed to have some fun, and Giovanni eventually— well no, he didn't get the hang of it, but Partha eventually learned to just *deal* with him not understanding how to roleplay. He tried to compare it to acting, but the old Italian seemed just as put-off by that idea, so Partha submitted to Giovanni just playing as a half-orc version of himself.

Melchiresa played an elven rogue, and Arjun played a goblin bard. They were mid-level, so Partha put them up against some interesting monsters. It was during one of these encounters that something unprecedented happened. The music was tense, the board (though makeshift and with random items representing the tokens) was thick with enemies. Partha heard a voice. It was soft and angelic with a great depth and varied layers, its accent vaguely Italian, vaguely that of a pirate: "I'd like to search for traps."

Partha looked around for infiltrators, but he realised shortly after that it was Melchiresa who had spoken. "Oh!" He beamed his bright white teeth. What a beautiful voice! Why did he hide it away? "Okay, well, roll for perception with advantage."

It was the only thing he said the entire night, but Partha felt honoured to have heard him speak. The gesture did not go unappreciated nor unnoticed. They played well, and, as most one-shots were wont to do, the session ended before the story was concluded, so they scheduled another session to continue a couple days later. Partha was getting grand ideas about finally being able to stream again with these three, which morphed into ideas for a West Marches style campaign with the entire gang.

Chapter 24
Dorothy

It was the first time Thyne had been alone since Rosemary's passing, and the world felt more empty than it ever had. He hadn't really processed how vital Francis' presence was for his sanity until he was on the train to Leipzig to kill Mina Paulauskas. He finished *Beowulf* only two hours into the trip, and afterwards he was trapped with his own thoughts and the voices. They. were. incessant.

He tried not to remember Rosemary. He squeezed shut his eyes and tried not to see the fresh memorial tattoo for her on his right forearm. No matter all his trying to shut out the thoughts, she was all that was on his mind. It wasn't for her that he was doing this, it was for him. In fact— tears welled in his eyes at the thought that— well, he hadn't ever fucking done *anything* for her, had he? He'd raised her, sure, but that was his job.

And...

Fuck.

She wasn't even his daughter. She never even knew... Not even adopted but—. He shuddered at the thought.

It was his fault she had been killed so mercilessly as she had.

It was all his fault.

"Fuck," he muttered and grabbed his eyes. He squeezed them to try and force the tears back into his stupid fucking skull. "Idiot." During his three years in the mesolithic with Francis, he had been consistently reassured that it wasn't his fault, but Francis wasn't there to calm him now. It was just him and the voices and the horrible state of this hollow meaningless world without her. '*Oh, Clarence, you bloody git. Not good enough. Not good enough. Never good enough. It's all my fucking fault.*'

He pulled out his phone. Initially, he wanted to look through his messages with Francis to try and find something stupid and silly to keep his mind off of things, but only two seconds into his mindless scrolling did he see the old message he had sent to Francis: ⟦ He killed her. I heard it all. He told her about what I did to her. To him. She denied it. And when he proved it to her, she wailed. Francis, I've never wanted to die more than I do right now. Lucky the loft hatch door is stuck shut... I was trying to get to the roof. ⟧

And Francis' response, so wrought with tenderness and love that it made Thyne sick to read it back: ⟦ It's not your fault. You were a perfect father to her. Where are you? I shall be there post-haste. Please don't leave me, too. ⟧

He exhaled, but it was shuddery like the breaths just before and just after a great fit of wailing grief.

Something else, then.

He went onto a social media site and scrolled through random memes. Some of them gave him a chuckle and a reprieve. He sent a couple to Francis and Partha. He considered sending some to Roach but refrained. But after an hour of this time-wasting, he was still on the train... alone... and trapped in this reality where he had been the cause of his own daughter's death.

He needed Francis now more than ever: he needed a way to keep himself together. He opened their messages and typed a long one: ⟦ Oh, Franky, I don't know what to do now that she's gone. It's all my fault. I wasn't even her father. She probably hated me in those last moments. She would have hated me all along if she knew. She would have hated you, too... I need you. I need you so much. I don't want to do this anymore. I just want to go home to London with you. I want you to hold me and let me cry until I don't have any more tears then let me cry some more. then when I'm done, you can cry while I hold you, and we can be alone together. That's all we ever are anyway. ⟧ By the time he was finished typing, tears had fallen down onto his thumbs and the screen. After reading the message back, he deleted it all, leaving it unsent, and closed the phone to look out at the blurry sunset.

He tried to focus on the voices, but as he did, he could only truly process the absence of hers. Tears trailed his cheeks, and he sniffled a few times, but by the time the train pulled into the station some eight hours later, he had hardened his heart enough to get his job done. He weaved through crowds to the general location he knew Mina Paulauskas would be. Lighting himself a cigarette, he walked and tried to smoke away his lingering grief. It worked well enough, and eventually he was standing shoulder-to-shoulder with the shareholder.

He "accidentally" bumped into her, spilling some of the contents of her purse onto the sidewalk. With a good excuse to start talking, he picked up the fallen tampons and makeup and snacks and passed them back to her. "Terribly sorry, Miss," he said in German with a French accent.

"Oh, no, *I'm* sorry, sir. I shouldn't have left it unzipped." Her cheeks were blushing bright as she shovelled the tampons back into the bag, followed by the rest of the items.

Thyne had shaved his head the night before, but his dark brown locks were longer now, almost to his shoulders, thanks to Francis' chronomancy. His freckles were covered by concealer and foundation, lucky it was waterproof from all the crying and now the rain over Leipzig. His face had been aged to roughly fifty, which was still not even a third of his actual age, and he was sporting a well-trimmed goatee. He wore a crisp brown suit with gold cuff-links, dark brown leather gloves to match the suit and cover his prosthetics, and his umbrella was stark black. He held it over her as she struggled to both zip her purse and keep her own umbrella from flying away.

"Here, let me hold that for you." He took the handle of her umbrella and held it away from them. By then, the crossing sign was blinking for them to hurry over the street, and she was flustered even more by the sudden rush. Thyne was cool and calm and wrapped a hand around her back to gently guide her while she was focused on her purse, and, once they were on the other side, she sighed and looked up to see him, finally finished zipping her bag. She was short, standing at only 4'8", so his 5'8" frame was large against hers.

Taken aback by how handsome he was, she smiled nervously, now with the blush even darker. She hadn't noticed that he was holding his own umbrella over her, and the way his dark hair was sticking to his forehead as it was battered down with rain made her feel guilty, more so than she already did for being such a nuisance. She liked to think of herself as a shrewd and ruthless businesswoman, and by most accounts she was, but her guard was all the way down. She was only in Germany to visit her dying mother in hospital, so her thoughts were far removed from business. The rain seemed to be God's way of reminding her of the horrible state of things in her life, but this man was beautiful, and he looked quite wealthy. Even if he wasn't, she didn't care as much about potential partners' wealth as she used to. Two financially-crippling divorces from heartless businessmen had made her actually sort of *want* to find someone poor and kindly.

But she was getting ahead of herself. She had only just met him, after all. "Oh, you didn't have to get all wet on my account," she stuttered, her English accent shining through.

"Nonsense, Miss. I'm the one who caused the entire scene, anyway." He passed her back her umbrella. "You look upset. Is it because of the tampons?" He sort of laughed. "It's nothing to be embarrassed about! I grew up with six sisters and two moms," he lied handily, "It's a wonder I ever learned to shave!"

She smiled at the anecdote, but she was still blushing. After averting her eyes, she decided to be bold and said, "Do you want to go somewhere to get out of the rain?

I can buy you a coffee." It almost hurt her English soul to offer such a thing. *Coffee.* Disgusting. But that was the sort of thing people offered in movies, and life was suddenly feeling very much like a movie. She, unfortunately, was misreading the genre.

"Oh, how kind of you! Do you know a place? I'm not from around here, but you sound foreign, too."

"Yes! I'm from England, but my mother lives here, so I've been visiting all my life. There's a local place just up the street here." She pointed vaguely in the direction and started to walk that way, waiting to be sure he was following.

They shook off their umbrellas under the awning and slid them into a cubby meant for them before going inside. The air conditioning cut through Thyne's sopping wet suit like an icepick. He was therefore excited to be getting a hot cup of literally anything. He held himself and shivered, and when Mina noticed, she hastened the transaction with some bribery she tried to hide from him. She was peculiar, wasn't she? Thyne had expected to have to flirt and turn on the charm to get her somewhere private, but it was seeming like she was into him without any effort at all on his part. It wrenched his gut to know what he was planning. Part of him wanted to tell her to run. Not to trust people so readily. He had to close his eyes and listen to the other voices for a while to remind himself that her death would be necessary to cripple New Clear. It didn't help her case when he started to think about how nice a roaring fire sounded to his freezing-cold soul at the moment.

"I'll take you to one of my houses here," she said as they grabbed their drinks from the counter. "I've got some of my brother's clothes you can borrow. And blankets." It was hardly appropriate to be inviting a stranger to her house, but he looked so painfully cold, and it was her fault he was so soaked in the first place. It was the least she could do! But, she realised as they went back outside, she didn't even know his name, so she inquired.

"Oh, how terribly rude of me. I knock your bag from your hands, take your generous gift, and don't even introduce myself." He held out his shivering hand to shake. "Émilien Porcher. And you?"

She shook his hand and offered another blushy smile. "Mina Paulauskas." She was well known in elite circles, but she was confident that this man, who she was beginning to think was a commoner, would have no reason to recognise her name. Even if he would recognise her, she wasn't the kind of person to lie about that sort of thing. If this really was some sort of meet-cute, it would hardly do her any good to start off the relationship with such a bold faced lie as giving a false name. And what name would she even give? If he only wanted her for her money, she wanted to know as soon as possible. She wouldn't be played the fool again!

Mr. Porcher took her up on her offer of going to one of her houses, tossing his half-finished coffee in a bin on the way. He even politely held his umbrella over her again as she accidentally dropped hers digging through her purse for her keys. This was one of her newer properties. She had bought it to rent out to tourists, but seeing as it still had a broken sink in the kitchen, she refused to let it be seen by the public. Besides, she had been visiting Leipzig so much with her mother's illness, as did her brother and his wife, that the place had become like a home away from home anyway.

She shuffled Mr. Porcher inside, playfully scolding him for letting himself get even wetter by covering her with his umbrella again. "Okay, you rascal, you stay here. I'm going to go get some of my brother's clothes, and we'll put yours in the dryer so they get warm before you have to leave."

She rushed upstairs before he could protest, so he looked around her house. It was blandly decorated, and he could only assume it was because this was a property she intended to rent out. Then again, she had her brother's clothes upstairs, so maybe she just had boring taste.

He wandered around the first floor and got to thinking about how he might do it. Some of of his fellow gang members were finishing their jobs, so his time was running out. His brain kept coming back to thoughts of fire, but he had to push them out each time. He usually only reserved such measures for people who had personally crossed him. Miss Paulauskas had been nothing but kind to him, so he would have trouble emotionally pulling off such a thing as burning her alive. It seemed needlessly cruel. Though, if he were being honest, it seemed needlessly cruel to be killing her at all. She was naive and nervous and charmed by him. Not to mention… her appearance was making him pity her more than he would have ever expected from himself, and he couldn't quite place why. That he was there to kill her and had apparently charmed his way into her house made him feel like the sorts of monsters that would kill and rape vulnerable women for no reason.

He had this foolish idea coming into his head on repeat that she could be convinced to give up her shares and fake her death. That he might not have to go through with it.

But why did he want to spare her anyway? Because she was nice? So what she was nice!? She wasn't nice to the natives when she pushed for more mining on their lands— further into their lands. She wasn't nice to the workers when she blocked attempts at unionising and cruelly demanded to cut their health benefits because so many of them were getting cancer. Her bottom line was more important to her than all those lives.

He looked around at the boring décor in the kitchen and noticed one piece on the wall that said *your text here*. "What the Hell?"

"Okay, I didn't know what you liked, so I brought down more than I should have. Here are some shirts and pants. Here's a pair of his wife's pants in case his are too small, but I made sure they look as masculine as possible. Then some socks, of course. I figure you can probably just keep wearing your own shoes."

"Oh, thank you." He took the clothes as she sort of threw them into his arms. "And some gloves?"

She started. "Gloves! Right!" She said it as if he had asked for them, and she had merely forgotten. "I'll go get some. Do you want thick winter ones?"

"Something thin will do fine. I'm just cold." He smiled.

She rushed back upstairs and came back down with three pairs of gloves. "Alright, you can get dressed in the dining room if you like. It has these beautiful French doors I had to pay a pretty penny to install, but they don't have windows, so you can be perfectly hidden away in there."

He took the offer and dressed himself in her brother's clothes, finishing by pulling the gloves over his hands and, for the first time, touching something in the house: the door handles. He pulled the doors open and struck a pose when she saw him. "Ta-da!"

She giggled and patted on the seat of the sofa beside her. "Come sit and chat, if you like."

He went back and grabbed his wet clothes. "Where's the dryer?"

"Oh, don't worry. I called my maid to come take care of that for me. I don't really know how to use the machines, and I don't want to ruin your clothes. They're so nice. Where did you get them?"

"When will your maid be here?"

"Oh, she's probably not going to be here for a few hours. Is that okay? Oh no! Am I being inappropriate!?" She covered her red-hot face to hide her shame.

Now he was really on a time crunch. He simply would *not* be killing an innocent maid. The foolish hope that Mina might be "fixable" flashed into his mind again, but that would take too long. He needed to act now. While she was busy worrying herself sick, Thyne went back into the dining room and lit himself a cigarette. She was ready to cry when she heard him leave. This would hurt his soul.

With a few cautious glances over his shoulder as he quietly clicked the pieces of his pistol together, his hands started to tremble more and more with every shuddering breath behind him. After twisting on the silencer, the gun was ready. He looked at it for a moment but set it down gently on his wet jacket. He turned toward her, hiding what was behind him with his body, and leaned on the table. After a drag from his cigarette he said, "So, what's with the weird decorations in here?"

She blushed and chuckled sadly. "Oh, this was meant to be a rental, but since my mother's been so sick, we've been using it for temporary housing."

He nodded and took another drag, thoughts furrowing his brow. After exhaling, he spoke again but much more coldly: "How many people do you think you've killed, Ms. Paulauskas?" It was in English, accent and all.

Her spine tingled and posture stiffened. She looked up at him like a frightened cat. "What?"

"From the natives being irradiated to the starving workers who can't afford food or healthcare or proper shelter in the winter— how many people?"

She stuttered a lot of nothingness.

The foolish hope returned. He took a drag to quiet it. "You do understand that all of your wealth is stolen, right?"

"What do you mean? No it isn't. Who are you, really?"

He sighed out some smoke and pondered. "Alright, I'll level with you, love. I'm going to show you something, and if I hear the slightest of peeps or see the slightest of movements, my generosity will immediately run out. Are we clear?"

She didn't understand until she saw him pick up a silenced pistol from behind him. She inhaled a quiet gasp, but she closed her lips tightly so as not to scream.

"Good girl. Now, I'll ask you again. How many innocent people do you think you've killed?" She shook her head. "You may speak, just don't scream."

She let out the breath she had been holding and pressed a hand to her heaving chest. It felt like her heart was being stampeded by a million horses. "I haven't killed anyone," she managed.

He cocked the gun and aimed it at her. "Wrong answer, love. One last chance."

She felt light-headed and couldn't catch her breath anymore. Before she knew it, she had fallen unconscious on the plain blue rug.

'Well, that didn't help me feel any better about this.' He pulled out his phone and used his nose to navigate it. Once it was ringing, he held it up to his ear between his shoulder and head and started to take the tiara and card out of his bag.

"Dorothy, I'm a little busy," answered Roach.

"I don't know if I can do it."

He scoffed. "What's wrong with you, dude? You killed Barre just fine. Kill her, too! You have to!"

He sighed and pulled the phone away to hang up. After a moment of staring at the unconscious lady, he took another drag and took off one of his gloves to call Francis.

"Yes?" he answered immediately.

"I need you to come here."

"Address?"

"Right, I'll text it to you."

"Okay."

He looked out the windows to try and figure out the street name, but he had to resort to snooping. Luckily she had something in her mailbox, so he texted Francis the address, and a moment later his friend appeared in the sitting room.

Thyne rushed over and wrapped his arms around Francis, bawling into his shoulder. "Oh, Francis, I can't."

"She's not dead?"

He shook his head and sniffled.

Francis looked at her unconscious on the floor. She was short and had light brown hair with photogenic freckles and a symmetrical face. He didn't notice any makeup on her except the mascara running down her cheeks, and her lips were full and pink. She had pearl earrings and soft features, but with big round eyes and a sharp brow, able to easily set into an expression of rage. It was no mystery to Francis why Thyne was having trouble with her. She looked a lot like Rosemary.

He stopped time and took the silenced pistol from Thyne's hands. Nothing could stop Francis from taking down as many companies as possible if that was the only way to get to Osiris. He *had* to take down Osiris. It hardly mattered if it was Rosemary herself on the floor of this bland little townhouse. He walked over to her, resumed time just long enough to shoot her in the head, then stopped it again to walk back over to Thyne and hold him.

Thyne jumped at the sound, but Francis had only left his grasp for a nanosecond before he was crying into his shoulder again.

"Thank you," he mewled. "We should go. Her maid is coming."

"Grab all the evidence. I'll put the tiara and card on her."

They split ways, and when they reconvened in the front hall, Francis stopped time to bring Thyne and everything he was holding back to the haunt, specifically in their shared bedroom. Thyne immediately dropped all of the evidence on the floor, including the cigarette from his mouth, and collapsed into the bed. Francis gave him his flask, kissed his forehead, and said, "I'll be back. You did well." And with that, he was gone.

Chapter 25
East/West

Among the vehicles in Neodesha's possession, there was a motorcycle. It was without tyres, however, so after some quick instructions from the twins to Francis, he appeared with two tyres. With some failed attempts at finding the correct type, the twins installed them in a matter of minutes. "There ya go, West," said River as he tossed Jean-Jacques the keys.

"It seems unwise for the two least battle-ready crewmates to be riding in a vehicle so vulnerable," Francis had commented.

"Don't worry about us, Franny," replied May.

"I will continue to worry about you, but you are aware and capable of contacting me should the need arise. I will be monitoring my cellular device closely."

May and Jean-Jacques' masks were made of fabric, May's being a black knitted balaclava courtesy of Dezba, which Partha had decorated (for some reason) with thin chains and zippers and safety pins. It wasn't her first choice, but she had conceded that to her little brother. He was therefore wearing a balaclava that had been stitched together out of various scraps of fabric. It was mostly black, but the patterns on it were colourful, and there were a few scraps that weren't black. Fabric was chosen over the bulkier plastic masks with more character because they would be worn under their motorcycle helmets.

They wore leather jackets and pants, though May made an effort to wear clothes a few sizes too large to attempt hiding her womanly curves and thus anonymize herself further. It was difficult given that she was by far the most shapely of the women in the gang, and the humid spring air would be broiling her. She had wide hips, a comparatively slim waist, and slightly larger than average breasts, whereas Neodesha and Dezba's builds were much more average, and Perlie was flat-chested enough that she could pass as a man if she refrained from speaking and hid her feminine face. The twins had a similar problem to May in that their builds were very distinct. 6'6" wasn't exactly a common height, and while May was only 5'8", she sympathised with their plight. She could hide her curves with enough layers, but, really, the twins' only defence was that there were two of them.

May hardly looked related to her brother, to the point that it could be assumed one or both of them was adopted. They were half-siblings, and it was evident that whoever their shared parent had been wasn't carrying the heftiest of genetic information. Her skin was the same pale peachy colour, and her irises the same dark brown, but otherwise, her soft heart-shaped face with thin eyes and pillowy lips bore hardly any resemblance to him. Her hair was straight, where Jean-Jacques' was wavy, and hers had slightly less volume therefore. She slicked it back with a headband and pulled the balaclava over her head. It made evident a slight slant in her eyes, pushed up at their ends by her sharp cheekbones, and they were made more striking for it.

Once her brother had his balaclava on, she pushed some of his mint-green hair under it and out of his face, then they pulled on their helmets. Their weapons were in a backpack that May was wearing on her front, hidden beneath her jacket, making it look as though she had the gut of a man who drank exclusively beer. It helped anonymize her, but it made sitting on the back of the motorcycle difficult. Jean-Jacques tried not to complain as he was poked in the back by the uncomfortable metal in the bag, but he was whiny by nature, at least around his sister. After a few irritated sighs and grunts, she turned to sit backwards on the seat.

"No no, you can't sit backwards. You'll fall off." He spoke in French, as did she:

"It's okay, JJP, I'll be okay. If you're so worried, we'll take some of that rope to tie me to you, but that sounds like a hassle when we get to Bordeaux."

"I won't let you. Put the backpack on your back. We'll have to stop somewhere to take the things out of it, anyway."

She sighed, ready to protest, but his eyes cut through her. They, too, had the same sort of harsh angle as hers that was emphasised by the balaclava and open helmet visor. He felt guilty and was putting on a front of anger to try and make her do what he wanted without having to admit such a thing, but Jean-Jacques was a simple man, especially around May. She had no trouble understanding why he did and said what he did. She stood and swapped the backpack to her back, over the jacket.

"There, now come sit and connect our helmets. I don't know how this brand works, and it's a long drive. I want to be able to talk and listen to music."

She did as he asked, taking only a few seconds to link the helmets together wire-

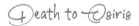

lessly. He started to take his off, but she stopped him, only using the buttons on the bottom of hers to accomplish what, to her, was an incredibly mundane task. "Alright, can you hear me in your headphones?"

He nodded and flipped down his visor. "Thank you. Let's go."

Neither of them were overly thrilled about returning to Bordeaux. They had grown up on a vineyard there and had less-than-stellar memories associated with it. *When Jean-Jacques was ten years old, he was caught in the guest house's garage building some sort of machine. He had snuck in after he learned that their grandfather had a workshop inside, and the young engineer was all too ecstatic at the prospect of power tools and scrap materials and whatever else he might find in such a paradise. When their father found out about his forays into the worskship, he scolded him harshly. He would be a winemaker like the rest of the family, and he would stop putting himself in danger to make "worthless machines."*

May was only two years older than him, but her own dreams had been dashed in the same manner when she was just eight and told explicitly that girls were, "No good for STEM. Get off that computer, and if I catch you on it again, I'll throw it in the river!" The dejected look on little Jean-Jacques' face as the workshop door slowly closed and their father dragged him back to the main house was the same horrible heartbreak she had felt when she watched her hand-built computer sinking to the bottom of the river. He wailed and reached out for the tools and wood and the dreams he felt slipping away, and that's when May stepped in:

"Papa, let him go. I dared him to go in there to help me with a robot I wanted to build," she said, "It wasn't for him." She took the emotional abuse her brother would have therefore suffered and, later that night, snuck into his room to explain that she had started hiding money for him to go to school for engineering. She would cover for him when he wanted to go build in the shop, and she was always willing to lie and take the brunt of the scolding and horrible words for him.

When it came time for Jean-Jacques to start taking over the vineyard, May sold a computer she had built in secret as well as the rights to an AI program she had created. She gave all of the money to Jean-Jacques and told him to go to America to study at MIT like he had always dreamed. He applied with some of the money they had been saving, but his acceptance letter came in the mail. Unfortunately, May couldn't cover for him anymore when their father found the letter and opened it before Jean-Jacques got the chance. He shredded it and demanded that Jean-Jacques stay to be a winemaker, but May put him on a plane to Massachusetts that night.

It was after he graduated and "Got my first job! I'm so excited, May, and I'll always be in debt to you!" that they lost all contact. She had assumed the worst, so when he managed to reconnect and said he was coming back to France thanks to the gang, her elation could not be overstated.

They hadn't had much time to talk alone since their reunion, seeing as they were both thrown into the midst of this gang, so what Jean-Jacques didn't know was why May was so confident in her ability to get their job to kill Elodie Harrison done. In fact, no one but Lanni knew what May had done only two years after losing contact with her brother.

"I'm not looking forward to seeing father again," said Jean-Jacques, as if it was a given that they would stumble across him.

"Father's dead."

"Oh!" He took a moment to ponder the news. "Well, good."

"Yeah."

Other than that, on their five hour drive, they talked mostly about old friends, family, and what had happened to Jean-Jacques in America. They made a couple of stops on the road to stretch their legs, which felt as if they were turning to goo after a few hours on the bike. When they got to Bordeaux, May was surprised to see Jean-Jacques driving them home. "Where are you going?" She hoped he wouldn't say it.

"Where do you think?"

"We can't go back to the vineyard!" There was panic in her voice, so he turned around and headed back toward the town centre, but his curiosity was burning him up. "If father's dead, then isn't it your vineyard, now?"

"Just go somewhere else. We don't have time to go there. We have to find Elodie."

He didn't press the issue further, despite how much he wanted to, and drove them to a below-ground parking garage where Elodie was likely to be parked. They found her brand new 2081 *Ferrari Ghiandaia.*

"Park over there. She'll be out any minute now. Lucky we caught her with your stupid detour." She slapped him in the back of his helmet.

"Okay okay! Don't hit me!" He did as she said, and when he turned off the engine, though it was an electric vehicle, evidently it was making a pleasant ambient noise because without it, the garage was made eerily quiet.

They took off their helmets and started to dig through the backpack. "Here, you're the engineer. Do you remember how Dezba said to put this back together?" She held out some of the pieces of a pistol to him.

He picked up two of the pieces with trembling hands and swallowed his nervousness. He put them together as Dezba had instructed, but he afterwards let out a shuddery breath and looked up at his sister with teary eyes. "May, I don't know if we should do this."

"These people saved your life! We owe them everything. If they want to take down this company, and they say this is how to do it, we have to do it."

He was regretting not having gone back to the vineyard after all. It was wrought with horrible memories, but anything was better than this. "We could just run away," he sniffled.

He was so soft and sweet, she couldn't help but be endeared. Her tone was gentler, as was her gaze. "Put the gun together, give it to me, and go outside while I take care of it. Okay? Big sister's got this." She patted his head gently.

He shook his head, tears falling out of his eyes. "May, my job is to keep people safe, not... this."

"Okay, shush shush, you big baby. Go outside. I'll figure it out on my own."

"But you might get hurt! Oh, May! I should have just stayed in America fixing planes."

They heard a sound from the other end of the parking garage, and May was quick to reach into the bag in search of one of the knives they had borrowed from Roach. She awkwardly opened it, sliding the clasp onto its end to lock the two halves of the balisong handle together, then whispered to Jean-Jacques, "Stay quiet and cover your eyes."

Without waiting for a confirmation from him, she crouched and dashed across the garage to hide behind some of the other luxury cars around Mrs. Harrison's. She peeked down at where the sound had started and heard high-heeled footsteps getting closer. Her stomach dropped when she saw Mrs. Harrison had two beefy bodyguards walking on either side of her. They were talking about the deal she had just made, but May only heard pieces. Something about buying a wine company.

She looked to Jean-Jacques, who was fidgeting with something in his hands that she couldn't see. *'I guess it's all up to me. Hope they don't have guns.'* She snuck her way through the cars to try and meet them at the *Ferrari*, but she was spotted by one of the guards before she got there. "Hey! Who's there? What are you doing?"

"Merde merde merde!" she whispered as she slipped between two of the cars to try and intercept them. She managed to get rather close before she heard them start to panic, so she jumped over the two cars between her and Elodie, who was shrieking like a banshee, and stabbed the shareholder in the chest. One of the bodyguards pulled her up by her shoulders, and she flailed around in his strong arms, throwing her weight around as best as she could. Then, the entire world seemed to fall away as she saw the other guard, who had checked Mrs. Harrison's pulse, stand and pull a pistol from inside his jacket. He cocked it and aimed it at her.

A gunshot echoed like a thousand years of thunder. Surely she was dead, right?

But, no, she wasn't. In fact, it was the man who had been aiming his gun at her who had been shot. She managed to kick away his gun as he fell, and now she was wrestling the last remaining guard off of her back. She managed to wriggle free, took the knife from Elodie's unbeating heart, and stabbed it through the second guard's eye. The sights, the sounds, the adrenaline: it all wrenched her gut, and she wasn't even certain what exactly had happened. It was all so fast. Who had shot the guard that was about to kill her? Who had seemingly helped her wriggle free from the other one?

"May," his voice was a whimper, "We have to go."

Reality came back to her like a trainwreck. What had she just done!? She dropped the knife and stepped back to see the three corpses. Her hands... her body... she was entirely covered in blood. Her breaths started heaving, but when she realised that Jean-Jacques was crying, she sucked up all of her panic and rushed to him. With a kiss on his forehead and warm hug, she said, "Yes, yes. Get the crown and card from the bag."

She only noticed he was wearing their backpack when he swung it around to his front and pulled out the king of hearts card and crown made of trash. He set them with trembling hands on the pile of bodies then averted his bleary eyes. "We have to go," he repeated, his voice somehow sounding calm.

It was the first time he had ever killed someone, and he was doing everything in his power not to vomit.

For May, however, it was her... second ... foray with murder.

They drove back to Orléans under the cover of night, not a word spoken between them on the entire trip, and not a single stop to rest or try and make sense of what had just happened.

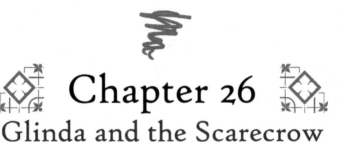

Chapter 26
Glinda and the Scarecrow

"Denise Louis. She's from Georgia (the state, not the country). She has the most shares in New Clear, now that Atterberry and the other one are dead. She's only in Paris for the weekend for this banquet, but her son lives here. He owns a lot of restaurants in the area, particularly ghost kitchens, but he has a couple proper establishments, too."

"I don't care about her son, Perlie, just get on with the actual targets."

"Right. Well, I'll show you their pictures when you're not driving, so that's all the easily verbalised info for Denise. Next is Séverine Renard. French. Owns the venue of the banquet. She has the least amount of stocks in New Clear of all our targets, but she's still in the top ten, so y'know… not an insignificant amount. She's been sued a few times for false advertising for some sort of—," she paused to read quietly, "Ah, I see. It's a pyramid scheme. That's all the info we found on her. Next is a married couple. Elouan and Claudie Monette. Their portfolios are separate, so each of them has their own stocks. Claudie has a few more than her husband but they seem about middle-of-the-pack in the top ten. Doesn't look like they've ever caused any trouble in the company or… otherwise." She read quietly again, for about ten minutes. "Either they're very good at covering their tracks, or they're just a couple old-money do-nothings that invest in whatever seems smart and let their money print itself. They're not even landlords or anything. Hm." She flipped through the papers a few more times then pulled out her phone to do some more research.

The drive from Orléans to Paris was short. It would have been shorter if they had left from Versailles, but their cars were in Orléans, so they had to go there first.

Well, truth be told, they didn't *have* to go there first. If River had gotten his way, they wouldn't have taken a car at all. They could have taken a bus or a train to Paris then run away on foot. Both of them were adept at blending into crowds, Perlie moreso than River considering his size and her training as a spy, but River was a free-runner and a gymnast. He longed for the thrill of the chase. They didn't have a solid plan yet, so he decided to try and talk one out with her for the rest of the drive.

They parked in a multi-level garage near the venue and walked around the building's exterior to scope it out. "What's the banquet for, anyway?" asked River as Perlie slowed to take a smoke.

She squinted into the mid-afternoon sky, looking up at the façade of the towering skyscraper. "It's to celebrate a merger, I think."

"Well, no time like the present. You ready?"

She nodded. "You remember the radio channel?"

He looked at her with a flat brow: irritated she would even ask.

"Looks like you'll have a good vantage point from that building." She pointed to another building on the corner of the same block that was almost as tall as the one with the banquet being held inside.

He nodded, and they split ways. Perlie flicked her cigarette butt into the gutter, which was already teeming with garbage anyway, and walked into the venue. She rode the elevator to the twentieth floor and followed signs to the security check and official entrance to the banquet. After flashing her false ID, she claimed to work for the wait staff. While the security guards were explaining that she needed proof, and she pretended ad nauseum not to understand, a random waiter who had been let through said, "Oh! Hey! Let her through, she's one of the caterers."

"You know her?"

He nodded and beamed at her. She was certain she had never met this man before, but the guards let her through on his good word, and she was quick to thank him once they were inside.

"No problem," said the man when she thanked him, "I've seen you around. What's your name, again?"

"Barbara," she gave her false name and shook his hand.

"Osmand. Nice to finally meet you. Anyway, good luck with the event!"

Thinking about it more, she still had no idea who he was. She'd never met anyone by that name, had she? But then it suddenly hit her: he was CIA. He had given a false name, too. She couldn't recall his real name, but she had done one job with him in the past that went utterly horribly. '*What the Hell is the CIA doing infiltrating this event?*' She snuck into a custodian's closet and activated her radio. She would have felt much better if River was with her now, but he didn't know French, so he had to be her eyes in the sky. "River, we have a potential issue in here," she whispered into her earpiece.

"What is it?" he said through heaving breaths. He had just scaled the decorative top of the building to stand in a faux bell tower. His bag was on the ground and his tall body leaning on one of the jade-green pillars.

"The CIA is here."

"Just find the targets and try to get them to my side of the building if they aren't already."

His lack of concern was somewhat comforting. He must have had a lot of confidence in their ability to get the job done, so she started wandering. Firstly she went to the kitchen to change into a uniform and grabbed a tray of champagne flutes. While she was doing that, River was looking through a pair of binoculars into the building. He counted the floors by their windows and stopped at the twentieth and twenty-first.

"I don't see them," he said after a while of looking, "I don't see you either."

She "scratched her ear" to turn on the earpiece without having to toggle it, so he suddenly heard a quiet murmur from the party as she walked around. She didn't respond yet, but he heard her speaking to someone in French and therefore didn't understand her saying, "Excuse me, sir, but this table is actually reserved for someone else. If you'd like a view through a window, though, I can show you and your friend to one across the hall."

"Oh, thank you, Miss," he said as he stood and took his coat from the back of his chair. He wasn't one of the guests of honour, so he felt a bit bad for having accidentally taken one of their tables (apparently). He helped his wife out of her seat, and the two shuffled slowly after Perlie as they were led to a window on the side of the building where River was looking. She could see the top of the building, so when River started complaining that he still couldn't see her, she had to force a smile for the shareholders. "Thank you so much, and I'll go get you a free dessert for the trouble."

She headed back toward the kitchen, and in a hall she whispered into her earpiece, "Look again, dumbass. They're right there."

After another few seconds of complaining, he snorted a quick laugh and said, "Oh, there they are. And the other two are just above them. Lovely."

She didn't respond, the calamity and clattering from the kitchen indicating for River as to why. After grabbing two plates of cake, she brought them to Mr. and Mrs. Monette, as she had promised, then continued to work the event like a regular caterer. She passed by "Osmand" a few more times during the night, and at one point she was able to get him alone and pulled him into a laundry room. In English she whispered, "What are you doing here?"

"You know I can't tell you that. What are *you* doing here? Didn't you resign?"

"Yes, I resigned. I'm a PI, now. Just investigating some paranoid businessman's wife for signs of adultery. Now, I've told you why I'm here, so tell me why you're here. Please."

"You know, I always had a thing for you." He smirked, and she had to stop herself from cringing.

It wasn't that he was ugly. By all accounts, this fellow— whose name continued to escape her —was drop-dead gorgeous. He was in his mid-forties and had the beginnings of grey in his dark hair, giving him a nice salt and pepper look. His face was perfectly symmetrical, save for a photogenic scar on his forehead and one of his eyes being brown where the other was blue. His build was the kind a super-model might have, and his face was just rugged and handsome enough to match. His skin was on the darker end because of his Latin heritage, and he sported a perfect handlebar moustache that, on anyone else, would look ridiculous.

No, she certainly didn't have a problem with his appearance. But... He continued speaking and made evident his true nature: "I'll tell you... for a kiss."

She only ever had eyes for River, and when he continuously denied her, she settled for his twin. Even if that weren't true, however— even if she had never met the twins —she still would have never found this man attractive. She actively avoided missions he took, and it was clear with the way other women would jump to work beside him, that his creepy behaviour was encouraged far too often. It seemed evident, as well, that he only wanted Perlie because she *didn't* want him.

"You don't have to kiss him, Perlie," whispered River, but she was already nodding, and Osmand was already leaning in. She needed to know what the CIA was doing at the banquet. It wasn't the first time she had jeopardised her safety and comfort for a mission, and it likely wouldn't be the last.

The kiss was... fine. His moustache tickled her lips, and his breath reeked of wine and some sort of sugary vape flavour, but it was... fine. Inoffensive if she didn't think about it beyond the physical sensation. He retreated, and she forced a smile. "Okay, now tell me, please."

He looked around to be sure they were still alone and checked her ears for earpieces. He leaned in toward the ear River wasn't in and explained in an almost inaudible whisper: "We're here to protect the shareholders of New Clear Energy. There's been a terrorist group after them, and their CEO sent us here as security detail to investigate."

It took every single ounce of her acting ability to wipe the paleness from her face as he retreated. Evidently, she wasn't doing well at hiding her anxiety, and he started to arch his brow. Her heart raced and beat up into her throat. He was figuring it out! Fuck! He was figuring her out!

There was nothing for her to do except pull him in for a passionate kiss, which he gladly returned. Her panicking eyes were darting all around as he closed his to enjoy her soft lips. Before she knew it, she was reaching up for his throat. She started to strangle him, but she played it off as a kink, and he nodded as best as he could. With his last bits of consciousness, he started to unbutton his shirt, but he tapped her arm to try and stop the choking. She didn't stop, and he finally realised what was happening moments before passing out.

"Fuck," she whispered as she watched him tumble to the ground, "River I wish you were here. Fuck."

"What happened?"

She didn't respond. She had to kill him, and she had to do it fast. Luckily, the laundry room hadn't been disturbed since they entered, but it was only a matter of time before someone needed a clean tablecloth or napkin. She looked around and, with no sharp objects in sight, made the wise decision to search the unconscious man's body.

"Oh, thank God," she whispered when she found a hidden blade in his wristwatch. She quickly unlatched the watch and used the blade to slit his throat in one fell swoop, pocketing the murder weapon shortly thereafter and rushing out of the room. She went to the changing rooms, grabbed her things, and carried them through the crowds with her head down. Once she was alone in the halls again, she informed River: "I'm leaving. You can do the rest without me."

"Okay. Go wait in the car. I'll wait until they've served the dinner like we agreed."

It was an excruciating three hours in the car before River finally showed up. He tossed his bag in the back and started the engine with the slow ambling pace of a man just off of work and not one who had just killed four people.

"Did you do it?"

He nodded and smiled, but his smile turned when he noticed she was on what was probably her sixth cigarette of the evening. "What's wrong? He didn't rape you, did he?"

Bless River for being so blunt. "No. Just an unwanted kiss, but he's dead now, so—."

"You killed him?"

"Yes. We have to leave, and we have to do it three hours ago."

He drove them out of the city, passing wailing sirens of police cars on the way. "We didn't leave any tiaras or cards," he lamented as he got onto the highway.

"River, they know about us."

"What do you mean?"

"The CIA was there to protect the shareholders from us."

"Oh." He took a moment to ponder but ultimately just shrugged. "Fat load of good they did, hm?"

"How can you be so calm about it?"

"Forgive me, but I'm not exactly afraid of the CIA."

She may have taken offence if she hadn't resigned from the organisation because she felt they were inefficient and kissing the asses of major corporations far too much, among other reasons. Instead of offence, the comment made her think back on her first encounter with River and the fated meeting of his brother however long later. It almost immediately wiped away her worries, replaced with bittersweet memories and silent rumination on what might have been. About fifteen minutes of thinking later, she couldn't hold it in any longer and spurted out: "River, why did nothing ever happen between us?"

"Perlie, you know I love you," he patted her on the knee, "but I love you like a sister."

She sighed and leaned on the window.

"You know, I think Partha might like you," he suggested.

A scoff.

"Or Jean-Jacques."

There was less derision in the scoff replying to that thought, but it was a scoff nonetheless.

"You and Dezba have been getting along better than anyone."

She glared. "Dezba's just a friend."

He smiled knowingly. Perlie had a crush on their elderly friend, and River could see it from a mile away. "Of course."

"She's over twice my age, River." He shrugged, his knowing smile still present. She leaned on the window again and muttered, "She wouldn't want to be with me, anyway."

"You know what I think you need, Perlie?"

"Stop talking."

"What you need is to be okay with being alone."

She rolled her eyes. "You're one to talk."

"Am I? In all the time you've known me and of all the stories from before we met, have you ever heard of me being overly obsessive or clingy with anyone?"

"Yes," was her gut reaction.

"Oh?" He was intrigued. "Pray tell who."

"Your brother."

He smiled again, a slight laugh leaving his nose. "I'm not obsessed with my brother, Perlie."

"You'd be dead without him. You ought to be."

"I'd be dead without him, yes, but I don't see how him saving my life would at all translate to an obsession on my end. And besides, we're brothers. We stick together."

319

"So how can you tell me to be okay being alone if you have him around all the time?"

"Perlie, you started this conversation asking why you and I never fucked. I'm not fucking my brother, so this is a non sequitur."

"Fine, then how do I be okay with being alone?"

"Well, you are alone. So deal with it."

She rolled her eyes. "Very insightful. Good talk."

"You want the truth, Perlie?"

"Obviously."

A beat. "Most of the time, I'm only okay because I *do* have someone."

She sat up and looked at him. "Who?"

He told her, and five minutes of stunned silence later, they were parking in the manor's garage in Orléans.

Chapter 27
Auntie Em

Dezba's target was an elderly man living in Bern, so she was given some Euros and a pocket-sized notebook from Thyne with handwritten notes on how to buy herself a train ticket and navigate in both Orléans and Bern. He was forward thinking enough to have put translations for almost every word and direction she would need, but she worried about how she would sneak her weapons onto the train. When she voiced this concern, Francis held out his hand and said, "Give me the gun." She hesitantly did as he asked, and, in an instant, the case was gone, and his arm was lowered. "It's buried beneath the rose bush beside his mailbox. Make no hesitation to text or call if I am needed." So with that, she took her purse and went off to the train station.

While she sat alone on the train, she looked down at the instructions (her only reading material) and tried to memorise the few French and German translations on it. Her attention, however, slid away from the impromptu lesson without her noticing. She was instead admiring Thyne's handwriting. It was slanted and cursive and elegant, but he dotted his i's with hearts, which endeared her and sent her thoughts on a different path.

The small crush she used to have on Thyne was all but gone now that she had met him. Not that she thought less of him, and he was technically older than her by a great amount… she just didn't see him the same way now that he felt more real. Besides, she was uninterested in romance. These people were her friends. In fact, they were the greatest friends she'd ever had, save for her husband, God rest his soul.

In her youth, Dezba was a horrible person: a neo-nazi. Being that she wasn't "pure," they treated her like she was less than human, and she would have expected nothing better. When she fell out of that crowd after having met her liberal husband in her mid-twenties, her edges were softened, but she still voted for the party that would eventually outlaw non-Christian religions, invade Mexico, and remove even a charade of democracy in America. She was of the mind that it was a good thing to force everyone to be a good Christian like her, but her husband was Catholic. When the last presidential vote in the country was held, she elected into power the man who would later father the current dictator. One of his first acts was to outlaw Catholicism.

Even still, she wasn't changed yet. She hid her husband's religion from outsiders and disagreed with the law, but she was still a blue-blooded American patriot who worshipped the three most important things in the world: God, freedom, and guns. It wasn't until she tested positive for her first pregnancy when she was just thirty-two that she was faced with the horrible reality she had helped create:

"I'm sorry, miss. Its heart isn't beating, and by now it should be."

"Can't you revive her?"

"We can't. If it were ten years ago, we could abort it, but you're going to have to carry it until you miscarry or have a still-birth."

They had been trying to have children for almost two years. It was thought that her husband was infertile. The day she found out she was pregnant was the happiest of her life, and the day she found out it was already dead was the worst. She felt robbed by God and, for the first time in her life, missed church out of spite for Him. She eventually miscarried, mourned, and got back to praying, even apologising to God for having forsaken Him in her fit of rage.

Then was her second pregnancy. She had already disillusioned herself slightly from the far-right after being forced to miscarry, but the second pregnancy was what made her walk away from it entirely. The first few weeks it was looking healthy and happy, and she thanked God ad nauseum for the miracle.

Too hasty was her gratitude, however. When she was only two months along, she was warned that her uterus was volatile. She was monitored closely, and a lot of doctors lamented that the pregnancy was going to be Hell and suggested that she fly to Canada for an abortion. At that point, she was pro-choice, but her choice was to see it through. She was confident in her God and in her body and the doctors' careful monitoring. A miracle baby would be born, by the grace of God! She didn't care if he would come out mentally handicapped or physically deformed or paralysed, she would have a son of her very own.

And it all seemed to be true. It seemed she would have a son who would, more than likely, have some form of mental incapacity, but she was elated all the same. She threw a baby shower and decorated the nursery. She read children's books to her unborn son and held a poll with her friends to decide on a name. She hoarded parenting books, and her husband even went so far as to buy a puppy for the baby to have a play-mate to grow up with.

There was no sound more earth-shattering...

No pain more palpable...

Than the silence that followed her final contractions...

"Why isn't he crying!?" she heard her husband wailing and coming over to look at what had come out of her. She was hardly conscious from the twenty-hour labour, but that silence was something even a dead man would have understood.

She was examined for a while after the ordeal, though she was hardly ever paying any attention to what was happening. She felt like she had died and gone to Hell. Her entire body ached, most of all her heart. Little Jody Meadows would never come home to sleep in his crib, which she and her husband had spent six hours assembling. They had spent all six of those hours talking with pride and playfulness of their great future as parents.

It wasn't until she heard the word "cancer" that she started to fully cognise what the doctors had been doing and saying to her. "You have uterine cancer, miss, and due to a complication during the birth, we need to extract your uterus, or you'll die."

Maybe they would have adopted if Lionel hadn't been diagnosed with leukaemia a few months after her operation.

It was at his funeral that she forsook God entirely, the last remnants of her far-right beliefs following suit.

Now, on the train to Bern, she was unrecognisable as that same woman. She was kind and rebellious and a little on the silly side. Her faith in God had slowly returned, but she didn't take much seriously. Still, she knew when to make herself strong and stoic for the sake of others. The few friends that remained after Lionel's death were all either also diagnosed with some form of cancer, which she later learned was because of the uranium mining on the reservation, or they retained their far-right beliefs. Her loneliness was slowly revealed to her over the years, and it wasn't until that very same year that it had fully hit her just how unfathomably alone and desperate for companionship she was.

And now, not only was she adopted into a group of people who treated her as an equal and a friend and never disregarded her jokes or opinions or anything she said at all—. Not only was she finally getting to live out a maternal role by nurturing the gang members when they were upset or confused or just needed to be held and protected from the harshness of the world—. Not only did she consider these people her best friends and new family, but she also agreed to carry out their far-left political acts, even of violence, so that she might be able to redeem and finally forgive herself for the vile acts in her youth that helped bring about so much suffering, some of which was her own.

The train stopped quicker than she expected. She must have been lost in thought and not aware of time passing or the sun setting. The walk from the station to Mr. Howard's house was short, and when she was nearing the old mansion, she pulled on her mask and gloves and used the cover of night to hide behind the rose bush beside the mailbox. Francis had left a trowel on the ground, so she used it to dig up enough of the dirt that she could slip her hand into the case and wriggle out the gun.

Howard made it much easier for her than Atterberry had. He was living in his home city of Loveland, Ohio when New Clear was mining on Navajo land. He was openly pushing for it and lobbying politicians to try and take all native lands from their pseudo-sovereign states to become official United States territory "like God intended!" Publicly, he denied the Holocaust, but privately he acknowledged and celebrated it. He fell for all the same propaganda Dezba had once let rot her brain, but Howard went further still. In his old age, he had mellowed, but he had still publicly disowned his daughter for marrying a Jewish man, and his money still flowed into the evilest of hands.

She snuck around the property trying any doors she could find, but none of them were unlocked. She could have broken a window, but she was reasonably confident that the property had some sort of security alarm system. On her treks around the perimeter, she had spotted a balcony on the second floor. There was a water drainage pipe beside it, and if she could manage to climb up onto the balcony, the door would surely be unlocked. If it wasn't, at least she could break the windows with potentially less risk of an alarm sounding.

She hooked her purse around her shoulder and took a moment at the base of the pipe to stretch. She shook it gently to be sure it would hold her, then suddenly started to climb. The pipe bent and creaked under her weight, but she made it to the balcony in one piece and immediately rushed for the door.

Unlocked. Hell yes.

She snuck inside, cocked her shotgun, and started to slowly sneak through the dark room in which she had found herself. A leisure room, evidently. She spotted a foosball table near the balcony doors as her eyes adjusted to the dark.

It seemed she hadn't been noticed yet, despite the racket she had made climbing to the balcony, so she pressed further into the house. Her heart nearly burst out of her chest, and she sucked in a shrill gasp when she heard something in the hall ahead of her, but all the tenseness in her shoulders eased when she saw a small orange tabby. It mewed at her again.

She crouched down and swung the gun to her back to reach her hand out and make a soft, "Psspsspss," sound to lure it closer. It rushed over at the invitation and purred as she pet it. "You're just the cutest little thing, aren't you?" she whispered playfully.

When the cat was finished with her, it started to trot away, and she followed it briskly but with cautious glances around the halls and many chambers. Her gun was in her hands again, and after enough twists and turns and one trip down a spiral staircase, she heard a television and stopped following the cat to instead investigate the sound.

It was a large vacant cavity of a living room and seemed hardly comfortable at all with its harsh architecture, lack of colour, and cold marble flooring. She was standing behind a chair where she could see someone sitting with his old wrinkled legs sticking out of his bathrobe. His feet were disgusting a sight and nearly gagged her, but she kept it together and silently slipped a pair of earplugs out of her pocket. As she was putting them in, careful to make as little noise as possible even in her breathing, she heard a loud roaring snore from the man. Confident, therefore, that he was asleep, she finished putting in the earplugs and walked around to his front. Her strides were strong and determined as she aimed the gun for his wrinkled white face. He awoke, presumably because of her footsteps on the hard marble. His breaths were laboured and hands raised, but his heart was beating so hard and so suddenly that he reached one hand down to grasp at it.

She watched as he was potentially having a heart attack. He looked at her with pleading eyes that caught her off guard. She hadn't expected him to look so pitiful and helpless. She hadn't expected getting to him to be so easy. There was a slight quiver in her hands which was evident to him in a rattling of the gunmetal as she looked down the sights.

"You killed my husband," she muttered.

He tried to speak, but his heart was still hurting and had seemingly stopped his breathing.

"And my son." Her finger tightened around the trigger slightly.

"Please," he said after a huge inhale, "I've never killed anyone, you must have the wrong house!"

She couldn't hear him, but she was able to read his lips to some extent and shook her head at the idea. This was Garey Howard, she was sure of it. Even if she hadn't been given a picture and information from *The Crown*, she had seen his slimy little face in years far past. When he was younger but still far from youthful. Even back then, the permanent bags around his eyes were like dark sacks of leeches, and now they made him look even more dead than he had in the past.

"Fuck you, Howard," she said loud enough that she knew he'd hear, then, with one quick inhale, she pulled the trigger back.

Immediately, she set down the gun on the coffee table and pulled the crown and card from her bag. She threw them haphazardly onto his chest and left through the back door, running as fast as she could through his garden and took off one of her gloves to use her phone. She texted Francis: ⌜ **Help!** ⌟

He appeared a few feet in front of her, and she had to scramble to stop running, even still tumbling into him. He stopped her from falling and asked, "What's wrong?"

"Take me back home!" she wailed. "I'm so scared!"

She suddenly felt a chill, and through her blurred vision she was able to notice that the wind was slow around them. His embrace was soothing as he pressed her head into his chest and pet her wispy grey hair. "I am here. All is well. Have you done it?"

She nodded and sniffled into his chest.

"'Tis me yen to return thee to Orléans for now, is that okay?"

She nodded again and hugged him tighter. "Don't let go!"

"I cannot tarry. Others need me." He kissed the top of her head and pulled away. "I've slowed time as much as possible for us, but we cannot linger for long. You shot him, did you not?"

"Yes!" She cried.

"He was vile. Not all of these people deserve what we're doing, but he did. He always did." He hugged her again, able to see how much she clearly needed it. "Shh, Dezba, my dear, you did well. You are invaluable to us, I hope you know, and what more, you are an exceptional friend and woman." A second later, they were in the manor in Orléans, and all of Roach, River's, and Jean-Jacques' dogs were swarming them. Francis gently helped Dezba onto the settee and clicked for the dogs to jump up onto it and smother her with kisses. "They'll have to pass muster for now. We'll be able to regroup within the hour. Merely stay here and try to stay sane." He kissed her knuckles politely then disappeared, her hand still hanging in the air where he had brought it to his lips.

Chapter 28

Toto

It came and went in waves. His sanity was an ever-flooded island in an endless sea of pitch. Whether or not he was still in the void hallucinating was never something he could know for certain. The most disorienting of observations he could make were those of Thyne's affection for him. Before the void, Thyne never thought of him as anything more than a friend. They had never kissed, as far as he knew, and physical affection was rare. It took being thrust into a void of nothing with only his own consciousness— it took probably three hundred years of the some sixteen billion to begin hallucinating his angel Thyne as this god of beauty and romance— it took another century of being accompanied by this illusion— for Francis to finally realise his own affection for Thyne. It was deeper than the ocean and vaster than the sky. Unrelenting like a tempest and as unwavering as the North Star. His love for Thyne was all he ever knew for certain anymore.

But, in those moments of sapience, when he was more certain than not that the world around him was real and crumbling, it was not for Thyne that he pursued his heroic endeavours to save it. It was not for humanity, for his children, for his friends, or even for no reason at all.

It was for himself.

He was reckless and stupid in his past. He travelled time foolishly and without regard for the consequences, and in his reckless stupidity he travelled too far too fast and found himself in a world upended and dying. Ice was a fantasy. Rivers were black. The ocean: a rotten sludge of death. Those who caused it fled to the stars, and those who mattered were left behind to wither like the wind. Inhabiting only three seconds of this time, he travelled further back to see what had caused it.

Idiot.

Now he knew the cause. He stupidly even studied at a university, as he was wont to do, and received his umpteenth degree in history. And after that, what did he do? Well, he ruined things even more, of course! Served for Eurasia in World War Three for two of its excruciating twenty years. Already knew "the good guys" would win. Just fought for pride, really. He was starting to realise his mistakes by then, however, which was why he dipped before the war was over. Still, he was too proud to admit it even to himself, and that pride was what led him to the distant future again. With the sea all rotten and the sky blood red, World War Four broke out, and he saw it through to its finish— to the end of the world.

Just a vast lot of nothing lay after.

And no matter his panicked jumping forward, humanity never seemed to return. Life in general, never seemed to return.

Not after fifty years. Not after a hundred. Five hundred. A thousand. Ten thousand. A million.

And with one more reckless mistake, he travelled backwards as far as he could. Perhaps if he went far back enough, he might find the cyclical nature of the fourth dimension folding back on itself. Maybe he'd get another chance. He hadn't ruined everything. That was impossible. Surely.

15,998,233,254 years before his birth: that was as far back as he could go before he collapsed into what had become a dense jungle around him. He laid there for an unknown amount of time. Perhaps hours. Perhaps days. When he stood and took his first six steps into the jungle to try and determine something about his current location, he was suddenly transported off of Earth entirely, and his consciousness was thrown into a version of himself he didn't recognise. He could feel his own heart was irrevocably shattered, but he tried not to notice.

This version of himself was also in a jungle, but it was alien. The trees were white and red, and there were two suns in the sky. The gravity was not as strong as Earth's, and his steps were lighter for it. He found a clearing in this jungle that had a ritual circle made of painted stones and metal rods in the middle. He sat in the centre of the circle, around him the metal outline of a pyramid, and as he sat, a slow wind danced through the trees.

"You don't remember this, Francis, because it hasn't happened yet," he said, seemingly to this version of himself that was watching it all unfold. His voice broke in the next: "Hold this in your haughty heart long enough that it breaks you: there is no one and nothing less deserving of life than you." Tears blurred his vision, but he closed his eyes without regard for it, and sat upright.

Exactly ten thousand years passed, and though the version of Francis observing it was unseeing while the years elapsed, he could still feel the wind and the warmth of the sun. He could still hear the trees rustle and sense the shifts in weather. Things were still real. His eyes opened, and the bright white that followed quite literally blinded him, bringing on a different sort of darkness: a visual nothingness. But, he could still hear, and he heard someone walking toward him. This other version of him seemed unconcerned and refused to move.

When he was only a few feet from Francis' body, likely on the outskirts of the ritual circle, the newcomer spoke: "I am beyond impressed with you. Your name?"

"Rome," said this future version of Francis. Why?

"You are welcome here forevermore, Rome. How would you like it to happen?"

"Back of the head, but keep my skull."

"Very well."

The unseen person walked around to the back of him, and he felt the very distinct nip of metal from a gun barrel on the nape of his neck followed swiftly by...

Nothingness.

Void.

Hell.

Only his soul remained, cursed with perception and sentience.
For a year.
A century.
A millennium.
A megaannum.
Gigaannia.

And in such an abyss, it took only three "days" (whatever those were) to begin hallucinating. He lived entire imagined lifetimes. He was god to entire imagined galaxies. His soul spasmed and thrashed against its binds, but it only ever ended shrivelled like a worm on hot pavement, having never found a way out. So... he made his own escape, and that escape was his angel Thyne: the many imagined forms of his greatest love in existence and nonexistence alike. Rudely— inappropriately— selfishly— Francis did whatever he wanted with this dream-Thyne. He imagined trifles and dangers to protect him from. He razed entire galaxies just to sate his insatiable lust for blood and fire. He held him and sang with him and loved him dearly. His biggest mistake, however, by allowing his soul free rein to do as it pleased in this void of nothing, was how inexcusably libidinous it was. He had millennia worth of sexual fantasies with his angel Thyne: used what he could hardly remember of his likeness to satisfy himself.

Things felt distinctly real again when he witnessed his own birth and re-lived the first thirty-five years of his life, up until the moment he was thrown into the sea in a mutiny and attacked by a shark as he tried desperately not to die. His consciousness was thrown all over the world for a few decades following, usually witnessing things he remembered living through but sometimes seeing himself and Thyne being romantic together. Surely, that meant it wasn't real.

It was in his sty of an apartment in Marseilles when he finally found himself in control of his body again. That he remembered how to move when the weight of the atmosphere felt so crushing and his body felt so foreign— well surely that also meant it wasn't real.

Thyne knocked on his door, and he opened it.

He was crying. "Can I sleep here tonight?"

He gestured to the bed. A few hours from then would be when he raped Thyne. Whether or not Thyne agreed that it was unwanted, Francis would always consider himself as nothing more than a rapist. He was testing reality. He was using him. And what's worse was it was their first and only time having sex.

If it was real, then what that future version of him had said was true: he was more deserving of death than anyone to have ever lived.

If it wasn't real, which was only slightly less likely, he was still deserving of such a thing for raping Thyne with his mad mad mind.

With no concrete evidence on the state of reality, Francis recalled a robotic friend from his past. In the chest of said robot was an hourglass with a plant inside of it.

This plant was what some might call god. It was sentient but unable to fully control itself while being used as a power source for this other sentient sapient being. Francis knew that, were this plant to be destroyed, so, too, would everything be destroyed. It was only because it existed that anything else did, though it most-assuredly hadn't created anything. The correlation between the two was unknown to the mad time-traveller. All he knew was that destroying everything would include his own consciousness, and either everything would end, or it would remain, and he would know, at least for a while, that he was still in the void.

Through a sheer force of will, when he went back in time, where he already existed in a ship between Andromeda and the Milky Way, he managed to break the laws of his own power— the laws of the universe. Surely, it was more evidence that he was still in the void that he existed in two places simultaneously.

But when he reached his hand into the chest of his robotic friend and former lover to grab his hourglass heart— when he started to squeeze it to destroy the plant within and thus the entire multiverse, he looked behind him to see Viktor standing there. "We shouldn't," he said with a hand on Francis' shoulder.

Francis looked back at the hourglass and suddenly realised how very real it was that he had his hand around the heart of existence, ready to destroy it. As his will to destroy everything tapered out, he flickered in and out of this secondary place until he reappeared fully on the spaceship between galaxies, no longer breaking the laws of reality.

It was this harrowing memory that actually gave Francis hope:

If he had managed to change his own past once by being in two places at once, surely he could prevent the future he saw, or at least use the gaps in his knowledge to prevent the end of the world. And since Osiris International was responsible for the start of World War Three and thus the beginning of the true end, he was determined to see it destroyed before the war's start.

No

matter

what.

His time left to fix it was running out, and now that he was such a shell of himself, his arrogance all but gone, he was finally able to understand the very concept of being in a rush. He was finally able to grasp that, yes, even he, the "mighty" Captain Androme de Tremblay, chronomancer of unbridled and unmatched power, could *run out of time.*

He countered it as best he could. Where everyone else was living in real-time, he had slowed his own perception of it by twenty-five percent if for no other reason than to give himself the illusion of having more time. He rarely moved through the third dimension without stopping the fourth, teleporting even just three feet sometimes. Those few nanoseconds were precious. At least… when he cared— when he was able to understand that he wasn't still in the void. The moments he was mostly certain he was real were the moments he spared no expense and wasted no time whatsoever.

But more often than not, it felt like he was dreaming. His ability to parse things as real came and went like waves to the shore of his ever-shrinking sanity. The sea of madness inside him was as vast and endless as the void that had held him for so long. It was as deep as his love for Thyne and as dangerous as his own reckless hand on the fourth dimension.

Before leaving Orléans, he pushed his phone forward through time until it had messages and call-logs from the future. He noted the exact times Thyne and Dezba would need him then pushed through the tattoos on his right arm to make note of it. He pushed his arm a bit further, to see if he had left himself any messages from the future, and sure enough he had… er… would. He had notes on the rough times the others would finish their jobs, and one part in particular mentioned that Dezba and the dogs would need to be taken back to Versailles. That was good to know, because the dogs currently were in Versailles, so now he knew that, at some point, they would change location.

Though he had said he preferred for the others in the group to make big scenes out of their kills, he kept time deadly still for the entirety of his own mission. Firstly, he had to find his sword, so he went to a museum in Spain from which he had once stolen it and reversed the age on the part of the wall where it once sat until it appeared again. He pulled it down and aged it backwards further, until it was gleaming and sharp. With his sword sheathed and time still unmoving, he walked some 5,400 miles from Barcelona to Chengdu.

His target was a Polish man, but he was on business in China, and seeing as Francis was the only person in the group who knew the language, and it was by far the furthest, it only made sense to assign him this job. That Roach gave it to him because Duff was "the most heavily guarded" made absolutely no difference. Francis walked into the building where Duff was currently in a business meeting, sitting at a conference table with several other elites. He weaved around the many guards and citizens on his way to the conference room with the same amount of disregard as he did with anyone else when time was stopped.

At the head of the table was Duff, and though time was unmoving, Francis rushed to him. In the same motion that he unsheathed his backsword, he beheaded him. Time was still stopped, so it stayed mostly in the same place, and no blood had splattered or started to pool.

He opened his bag and took the card and crown out to set on the table, but he noticed that to Duff's left was Tatum Abraham. Francis' knuckles went white around the hilt of his sword. It would be so easy to kill him, too.

But… he recalled from his history lessons that the death of Tatum Abraham was the first domino in what would eventually lead to World War Three. His rage hurt him physically, and he had to drink himself six entire flask-fulls of rum, downing most of it in one go then refilling it with chronomancy to the point that it didn't once leave his lips. He dropped the flask, but it hung in the air because of time's still state. After wiping the excess from his lips he held up his swordarm, ready to behead Tatum, too.

Abraham died of old age, not of a mysterious beheading. This could be the first domino in a *new* chain. His arm shook as he held the sword up, and no matter how many times he tried to swing it down and behead the CEO… he couldn't. Whether it was a physical, magical, or mental block, he wasn't sure, but it was heartbreaking all the same. With three more flask-fulls of rum in him, he left the conference room having not killed anyone except Duff.

He walked the long way to Berlin, his mind ever foggier from the alcohol, and by the time he got there all his boozy brain wanted was Thyne. He found him walking beside Mina on the street, and came up to them. Time was still unmoving when he wrapped his arms around Thyne's muscular torso and craned his neck down to cry. "Oh, Thyne, I'm so sorry," he wept, "Damnable wretch that I am. If I had ne'er plagued thee with my deplorable presence, perhaps thou might know bliss and blitheness for aye."

Thyne had absolutely no awareness of these lamentations: to anyone but Francis, they did not exist. It must have been three hours before he released his friend and stood behind him as he resumed time. He watched him walk off with Mina, the rain pouring down over him. The street was empty save for the three of them.

Shortly after helping Thyne, Dezba would need him. When it was time to help her, he was similarly already in Bern and ready for her text. The innocence and fear in her heart wrenched his gut as she held him tightly and asked him not to leave.

"Others need me," was his excuse. A lie on the face of it. Just the same as he couldn't stand to see Thyne broken, he couldn't stand to see Dezba broken either. Things were feeling far too real by then, and even on the several walks from Orléans to Versailles and back again, carrying a dog or two each time to comfort Dezba in the manor, the harsh cold of unmoving time was cutting through him to his bones and reminding him of just how alive and horrible he was.

He left the dogs with Dezba and disappeared from her to find himself back in Thyne's home in London. Alone. He drank himself blind and tried to forget. He had three hours until someone would need him again, so he laid in Thyne's bed and stared at the moulding on the ceiling as it swirled and bobbed around like the surface of the ocean.

More rum.

More.

More.

Until he took up his phone and saw a new message from Thyne.

⟦ Please come back, Franky. I need you. I love you. ⟧

He went to him and held him and kissed him and, with enough romantic inter-actions of the sort, he had achieved his goal of slipping back into the dreamlike reality of Hellish void where nothing was real, and only Thyne mattered.

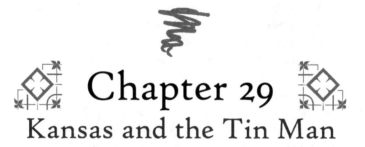

Chapter 29
Kansas and the Tin Man

Roach and Neodesha had to drive to the train station, so they took the last of the three cars and made their way there. Cigarette smoke and music filled the cabin for the entire trip, so they didn't talk much. Neodesha was watching the country roll by and thinking about how different it looked to American road trips. She made a brief comment on the matter, and Roach agreed, pointing out the difference in scenery, the road signs being in French, and the speed limits and distance markers being measured in kilometres.

It wasn't until they parked and the engine had stopped that the silence between them was made painfully obvious. Roach filled it immediately with the click of his lighter as he lit himself a third cigarette of the day, but Neodesha wasn't made uncomfortable by the quiet. She beamed him a smile when he looked toward her. "This is just like in the good ol' days out West! Why, I ain't felt so alive since—," she was saddened by her own next thought, "—well since my wife and I would do this."

Roach patted her shoulder, but it wasn't the time to be having a deep sorrowful conversation. She appreciated that he pushed past the upset and changed the subject by asking, "So, what's with all the vampire stuff, hm? You and Arjun and the doctor.... And the other one." Melchiresa was perhaps the only man Roach had ever met that unsettled him, and a chill ran down his spine as he thought back on his dead-eyed stare, scarred face, and unnerving quietude.

"Oh, we ain't no vampires, Mr. Roach, that's just what the folks got to callin' us."

"Well, you're older than sin, no offence, and the doctor is your father? So he's even older, still. I presume they're part alien, then, same as Francis?"

"Oh yeah, that's my Pop. He and Arjun are about the same age. When ya ask 'em they say they're billions." While she replied, Roach reached into the backseat and started to unpack their bags and divvy out the supplies. "But yeah. They were made in some lab er somethin'. I don't know the whole story."

"Naturally," an amused huff, "Was he a good father, at least? If you don't mind me asking."

"Don't mind at all, honey. He's a sweetheart, and I love him to death. He and Arjun helped my Ma. She'd just been freed, so she didn't have any money and folks was left and right always fixin' to kill her and call her unchristian things. She was just a regular human, so she died when she got real old, but she wouldn't'a got to be so old if not for Pop and Papa Arjun."

"Arjun's not your father, though, so why do you call him that?"

She laughed. He passed her a mask, and she started to poke at its details with her long French-tipped nails. "Well, him and Pop been together forever. Pop has lotsa kids, but Papa Arjun, for some reason, took a likin' to me. He usually hates kids, so I don't know why. But he done protected me and saved me and— well if I'm being honest he's overbearing and still treats me like a little girl, but I can tell he's just...." She pursed her lips in thought then looked up at Roach to meet his hazel-grey eyes with her milky blue ones. "You know Papa Arjun ain't never loved no one but me and Pop and Melchiresa. Maybe Uncle Franky. Maybe Thyne. And he's billions, like I say." She dropped her voice to a whisper as if Arjun might hear her and leaned in to cup her hand around Roach's ear. "He ain't never lost no one he loved, if you get my meaning, Mr. Roach." He shook his head. "Mr. Roach, if I don't come back home after this heist, I don't know what he'd do to you. What he'd do to *everyone*. What he'd do to himself, even."

When she retreated Roach nodded once then pulled his mask on. "Good thing you'll come back." And with that, he opened his car door, flicked away his cigarette, and grabbed his bag from the backseat. While he was leaning into the car, he addressed her again, now with her mask on: "Excited?"

She beamed, but the mask hid it. "'Course I am, honeybuns. Let's go!"

Roach's mask was complex and seemed to cover his eyes, though there were obscured openings for them. It was almost entirely black with a gunmetal dry-brush overtop to bring out the details. It was made mostly of things like plastic forks and bottle caps and soda can pull-tabs, but amongst the things that were left in their normal form were more sculpted parts. Those parts were in the shapes of letters across his entire face and were painted bright red to stick out amidst the grey. The words said *STAY CALM* in a simple sans-serif sort of font. Neodesha's mask was practically the same as his. The words on hers were much the same as

Roach's in size, colour, and sentiment, but they were written in French: *RESTE CALME*.

They stood on either side of the car in the parking garage and both wrapped their long black hair up as tightly as they could. With some help from each other and a lot of bobby pins, they were confident that the hair would stay and pulled up the hoods of their jackets. Both hoodies were black but had red spray-painted words on them. On the fronts, in English, they said, *don't be a hero,* and on the backs was the same sentiment in French.

While Neodesha was finishing up her preparations, like putting on her gloves, Roach took the keys and opened the trunk. There was a cardboard sign inside which he propped up against the open lid. It read, *Free car. The tags are fake. Courtesy of The Crown and The Tiara,* in almost every modern language the gang knew: English, French, Spanish, Italian, Mandarin Chinese, Korean, Arabic, Russian, Papiamentu, and German. The handwriting for most were different, with Francis' Chinese perhaps the most beautiful and Roach's Arabic the ugliest. He dropped the keys in the trunk and took one last look at the signatures each of the members had left. They had all signed with their codenames, and Roach had spent a sleepless night doodling depictions of the gang members as the characters Thyne had named them after (or simply a tornado in Neodesha's case) under their signatures.

Neodesha grabbed her shotgun and bag from the roof of the car, and with the thumping of both of their car doors, they walked confidently to the stairwell. After some calming deep breaths from both parties once they got to the bottom floor, they both rushed out onto the attached platform and slid through one of the open doors into the train. They were in the thick of it now, evident by all the screaming. Neodesha aimed her gun at the doorman and demanded in French, "Get inside!"

The screaming passengers on the train panicked, and some of them tried to leave, but Roach put one of his arms in front of them on the south end of the train as Neodesha aimed down the north end of the car.

This was a train to London, not to mention English was a popular second language in France, so most people backed down when they heard Roach's deep and commanding voice shouting, "Back in your seats!"

Neodesha had her gun on the back of the head of her kidnapped operator and was forcing him to the front of the train, closing and locking the exit doors as well as the ones between the cars on their way.

Roach took the other direction, doing flourishes with his butterfly knives as he walked to be sure the passengers knew that he was also a deadly threat (if his imposing air wasn't doing that enough already).

This was a standard passenger train, but, in true elitist fashion, Roach's target had rented out the last three cars for himself. When he arrived at the first of said cars, he had to punch through the glass of the door and did so in three strikes, during which he definitely broke at least one knuckle. His adrenaline was pumping far too hard to notice the pain, however, and he made his way into the empty car with the slightest of cackles escaping his lips.

On Neodesha's end of the train, she had finally reached the front and forced the conductor to start moving. Her target was less of the "ew peasants" type than Roach's, so he was sitting in the standard seats. She, therefore, had to start walking back down the train to find him. When she got to the third car she thought she saw him, but her attention was swiftly brought to one of the passengers standing and rushing at her. She aimed her gun at him and shouted for him to stop in both English and French. He slowed, but he was still approaching, so she took two steps back and shot the ceiling to show that the gun was loaded. The scattered holes and loud boom it created brought screams from almost every car in the train.

She laughed at their fear but sounded threatening again when she barked, "Back to your seat! Go on, get!" He did as he was told, and she continued her search.

Roach looked around the cars for cameras, and when that proved fruitless, he continued to the last car where he saw his target heading. A maniacal "ahahaha!" escaped his lips again as they started to quiver into a twitchy smile. He loved so very much when they tried to run. A wave of pleasure coursed through him like a high. He looked down the last two cars, through the windows, and saw his target leaning his head out the door of the last car, debating whether or not to jump onto the fast-moving tracks below.

Roach closed the knife in his left hand and threw it up into the air. It hung there at his eye-level as if suspended in time, and he lifted his now-empty left hand toward the door across this empty car. After pulling the shade over the broken window behind him, he looked back at his target. They made eye contact, and just as the man had started to jump off the train, Roach twisted his outstretched hand and the two doors standing in his way were blasted open telekinetically.

"I wouldn't do that if I were you!" There were clear hysterics on the end of his tone and another, "ahaha!" as he grabbed his knife from where he had suspended it in mid-air and started doing flourishes with it again. He approached his target at the end of the train menacingly.

This man, a Scottish bloke named David Lithgow, was only twenty-five and had been gifted his stocks from Daddy's will, but it didn't matter to Roach one fucking bit. He'd die just as nicely as anyone else. Maybe one of the other gang members would get all mopey about killing some spoiled brat who could theoretically be "fixed" or at least robbed blind, but of course, it wasn't anything personal. As Mr. Lithgow was known to say, and as Roach quoted when he was close enough to be heard without shouting: "It's nothing personal, mate. It's strictly business."

David would have jumped from the train. He had tried, but something was hindering his ability to move, and it was clear that whatever was happening was something supernatural when he felt himself floating over the ground back into the car ahead. The door closed behind him as if by magic, and his attacker put a hand on his shoulder. He pinched it hard with his large hands. Hard enough that David called out in pain and bit his lip to keep from crying more than he already was.

At the other end of the train, Neodesha found her target: an American man, coincidentally also named David. She aimed her gun at him when she spotted him, which brought screams and raised hands from everyone in the general vicinity. "David Cruz. Get in the aisle. Now."

He nodded and swallowed a dry fear in his throat. His heart was beating hard, but he was presenting as quite calm. He put his hands on his head when he was out in the aisle and looked at the armed woman to wait for more instructions. "Back of the train. No funny business or I shoot, got it? I'm only moving you outta the kindness of my heart to these poor folk who got all caught up in this and ain't got nothing to do with it."

When Neodesha and Mr. Cruz came into the empty penultimate car, they saw Roach had taken his mask off and was sitting on a kitchenette counter with one leg propped up on the other. He was looking down at Mr. Lithgow, who, for some reason, was sitting real still-like in a passenger seat across from him. Neodesha was confused, but she brought Cruz to the seat beside Lithgow's and told him to sit.

"What are you doing?" she asked Roach.

He smiled and took a drag of the joint in his hand. "Want some?"

"I don't smoke no Devil's lettuce, Tin Man. Now I'll ask ya again: what are you doing? Why's Mr. Lithgow just sittin' there like a stump on a log? Ain't you gonna kill 'em? And why's your mask off?"

"Well, I can't smoke with my mask on, Kansas." He laughed like a lunatic for three syllables, but managed to cough away the display of emotion and return to a deadpan expression afterwards. He didn't want Neodesha to see that much of him, but it was hard to hide how God damn excited he was.

She aimed the gun at Roach. "Answer my questions!"

Another hysterical laugh gagged in his throat at the sight of the barrel on him, this time brought about by fear, but he managed to stay stone-faced and took another puff of weed. "I'm celebrating."

"You ain't killed 'em yet! What're you celebrating?"

"Oh, I'll kill him. I'll kill them both if you let me." A murderous gleam flickered in his eye, and Neodesha had seen it enough to lower her gun. She had worried he was in leagues with Lithgow, but that glint of madness was all she needed to see to trust him again. Lithgow must have been staying still for fear of death if he tried running.

"No, I ain't gon' letchyou kill 'em both, Mr. Tin Man. I wanna have some fun, too."

He gestured to Cruz as if to invite her to kill him and smoked as he watched.

She aimed her gun at Cruz, but before killing him she looked back at Roach and lowered it again. "Well, now. What're we celebrating? Should I wait? We've got 'bout five hours 'til we're in London."

"Oh, it's just a cheeky little joke. Weed. 420. You know?"

She was still wearing her mask, but the way she shifted her weight and the monotone nature of her voice made evident her irritated confusion: "No. I ain't got no dang clue what you're on about, Mr. Tin Man."

"You know 420 and its relation to 'the Devil's lettuce'?"

"I reckon I heard it here and there."

He nodded and took another drag, blowing a few smoke rings and stopping another laugh as it tried to climb out his throat. After coughing away the madness, though it remained in his eyes, he gestured to Lithgow and said, "He'll be my 420th."

She smiled beneath the mask, and it was audible in her reply, "Well look atchyou, Mr. Tin Man! Why, you're a regular monster, ain'tchya?" She laughed. "I reckon that's cause for celebration, but ain'tchyou wanna celebrate with the whole gang after you done it?"

"Oh, come on, Kansas. Why would any of them want to celebrate this level of depravity?" The difficulties he was having with remaining deadpan were evident in how heartbroken he sounded.

She shook her head slightly when a befuddlement struck her. She was going to reply, but one of the Davids was starting to whine about not having been killed yet, so she shot Cruz in the head then leaned on her smoking gun as if it hadn't happened at all, her attention still entirely on Roach. "You don't know 'em very well if you're thinkin' they won't wanna celebrate with ya, Mr. Tin Man. Least the ones I know well ain't so far off." She giggled. "I mean Pop and Papa Arjun have sent more people to Heaven (or Hell) than anyone could count."

"They aren't in the gang," he said matter-of-factly.

"Well, sure, if you ain't gon' include 'em on 'count of them only guarding the base, but what about Thyne? Or Uncle Franky?" She panicked that she had not used their codenames, but Lithgow would be dead before the train stopped, and no one else was around. She searched for cameras, but Roach's lack of mask was comforting enough that she didn't fret more than a few seconds.

"What do you mean?" He arched his brow.

More befuddlement could be surmised in the way she seemed a little taken aback. With a slight chuckle, she explained, "Mr. Tin Man, honey, you're all mixed up 'bout them if you're thinkin' they're saints or something."

"Certainly not saints, but 420 is a lot, isn't it?" He was almost embarrassed by what he was beginning to fear was a low number.

She shrugged. "I reckon not far off from them, like I said."

He pursed his lips. A moment of thought later, he put the joint out with his gloved fingers and pocketed it. "Well, if you don't mind, I like to be alone when I do it."

She raised her hands in an understanding and embarrassed manner, as if he had asked to be alone to do something inherently private. "I get it. I'll go back to the front to get the train to pass London so we ain't gotta deal with a whole city. Don't forget to put your mask back on 'fore you come outta here."

"Thanks. Let me have your bag for the crown and stuff."

She passed him the backpack then left him be.

As soon as he heard the door close behind her, he smiled wickedly down at Lithgow. He stopped holding the shareholder's head telekinetically and leaned down to whisper into his face with a playful tone, "What do you think of all that, hm? You scared?"

He spat in his face and refused to speak.

Roach's eyes fluttered in pleasure. He bit his lip then stood and stretched his arms. After wiping the spit from his face, he tasted some of it off of his finger then smiled again at David. Without warning, he punched him hard in the face, breaking his nose. "Now," he hopped back on the counter, "I want to hear *all* about how evil you think I am."

"I think you're pathetic."

He nodded, still beaming. "Mmhmm. And?"

"I think it's fitting your name in this disgusting terrorist cell is Tin Man, you heartless bastard."

A twitchy smile and one single twitching eye let way for the longest cackle of the night. It was raw madness in its most unadulterated form, sending shivers down David's spine. "Okay okay, enough about me." He caught his breath and wiped a tear from his eye. "What about you, hm? Why don't you deserve to share your buddy's fate over there?" He pointed to the bloody corpse beside them.

"Doesn't matter if I deserve it."

This visibly intrigued Roach. "Oh?" He clapped quietly. "Oh, do go on!"

"Why do you think I deserve this, Tin Man?"

"Oh plenty of reasons, David," he replied with the tone of a chatty coworker, as if they were sharing gossip and not this man's last words, "Do *you* think you deserve it?"

He averted his gaze. A sombre cloud formed over his head, and when he glanced back at Roach, he said simply, "Yes."

It seemed genuine, at least to Roach, and he was made thoroughly elated by the admission. "You do deserve it, don't you?" He laughed, but it wasn't hysterical and instead a simple chuckle to fill the space and further emphasise his smile. "Why?"

"Cheated on my wife. Traded in ivory. Stole my father's company and stocks then watched him die penniless." He looked up at Roach with an expression as if to be asking if that was a sufficient answer.

Roach's response was the loud imitation of a buzzer. "Wrong!" He giggled. "Try again."

"What do you mean 'wrong'? Just kill me already, you fucking psycho."

Roach stepped down from the counter again, punched him in the face, (still smiling), then hopped back up and swung his legs back and forth. "Don't tell me what to do." He started doing flourishes absent-mindedly with one of his knives. "Anyway, no. The reason you're going to die is because of all the innocent people you've killed. Or, I suppose it was your father, but—," he shrugged, "Whatever."

"Then you've got the wrong guy because neither of us have ever killed anyone, you delusional, deranged—."

"You think 420 is a lot. Wait until you hear about all the thousands your father knowingly drowned in Washington or the slaves he owned in Vietnam. I'm sure he passed the surviving ones down in his will to you. You'd know all about it, wouldn't you? Since you killed him for his capital?"

He rolled his eyes. "So you think you have some sort of moral high ground. Some sort of vigilante shit, then. Just kill me. I don't want to hear your manifesto."

"No no, you misunderstand. I'm deplorable. Or, as you said, 'a heartless bastard.' Kansas said, 'monster,' it's really all the same. It's all true. I'm not any better than you or your father or anyone else. I'm only picking your brain because you're entertaining me. If you didn't want to talk you shouldn't have been so interesting!"

He groaned, growing impatient with Roach's mad chatter.

"Alright alright, I'll stop bothering you. I'm not *that* heartless." He giggled. It was mostly sane and genuine until the very end where it seemed to crack like a whip into what was briefly pure madness. After catching his heaving black breath again, he stood back up, still doing flourishes with the knife. "Okay, just one more thing."

"As if I have a choice."

"Exactly! That's the spirit! Well, so just between you and me," he leaned over him, one hand on the seat behind David's head and the other with the knife closed and gesturing between their chests as he spoke, "I'm writing this album. It's kind of for me, kind of for no one, and kind of for this guy I like. And well, one of the songs' lyrics is going to be nothing but last words from the people I kill while I'm in this terrorist group with him. So, I'm just hoping you can give me something poetic, since you seem like a really cooperative guy. Definitely the best for conversation since 312."

"Eat my shit."

He frowned, but his tone was almost friendly: "David, you know that won't do."

He spat in his face again, refusing to speak.

"Well, you're absolutely no fun at all!" He pouted and stood back upright. "If you don't say something better I *will* give you a manifesto."

Lithgow remained silent.

When it was clear he wasn't going to say more, Roach hopped back up on the counter and got comfortable. After clearing his throat he made true on his promise: "The history of all hitherto existing society is the history of class struggles. Freeman and slave, patrician and plebeian, lord and serf, guild-master and journeyman, in a word, oppressor and oppressed, stood in—."

"Dear Lord, just shut up and kill me, you fucking psycho!"

A mad grin. "That'll do." He hopped down and reached into his bag, which he had set on the ground beside him. Confusingly for David, he pulled out a stapler, which he opened and clicked a few times with a wiggle of his eyebrows at his victim.

"Why do you have a stapler?"

Roach frowned, but it was short lived and replaced with a beaming smile. He much preferred that as David's last words. What a funny line it would be in a song without context! Even with context, he was tittering at the prospect. He didn't answer verbally, instead pulling out his king of hearts card to wiggle between his thumb and first finger. He used his telekinesis to hold David still again so he couldn't ruin his very good last words with some random rubbish then stapled the card to his forehead. He pulled out the crown and placed it on his head, adjusted it as if he was a sculpture and not a human being about to be murdered, and opened his knife.

420 and counting….

Chapter 30
I'm Melting

The day following the slaughter, Roach and Neodesha were the last of the group to return to Versailles. When they walked into the haunt, everyone's attention turned from their phones and laptops to the two of them. Roach dropped a heavy backpack on the coffee table where it made a loud clattering sound as it seemed to deflate. "For you," he said to May with a gesture toward it before lighting himself a cigarette and sitting beside Thyne on the settee.

May looked inside the bag and squealed like a schoolgirl. "Oh! Roach! I could kiss you!" She pulled out a handful of cell phones from inside and held them up for the group to see with a beaming grin.

"Where'd you get all those?" asked Partha.

"Passengers on the train. I saw some of them recording us. Had to take their phones." He smoked and looked down at his own phone to power it on. Its screen was cracked, and the speaker didn't work, but it would pass muster for what he needed at the moment. It was why they all had their phones or laptops out: checking the news. When he sat down, Daisy crawled from Thyne's lap into Roach's, so he pet her as he scrolled.

"Idiot! Don't you know cell phones are one of the easiest things to track?" said Thyne.

Roach shrugged. "Relax, man. I turned them all off, took out the SIM cards, and we're in a lead box down here."

Thyne opened his mouth to scold him more, but May reassured him that, "It's okay, Thyne. Even if these are getting tracked somehow, it'll only help me establish a route to hack into all the systems tapping into the spyware and send it all haywire."

He scoffed and returned his attention to his computer, trying helplessly not to worry.

Save for the sounds May was making as she sorted through the phones, the room was quiet. Neodesha was standing behind Roach and Thyne's place on the settee and leaning on her elbows to watch their scrolling, Roach on his phone and Thyne on a laptop.

The only one not checking the newsfeed was the only one not present: Francis. Roach was curious, so when it seemed Neodesha wasn't going to ask, he said, "Where's Captain Dumbass?" He didn't even look up from his phone as he spoke.

Thyne looked at Roach then shook his head and turned back toward the laptop. "Don't be such a bellend. He's in the other room resting."

Roach nodded and looked toward Francis and Thyne's bedroom door. He considered going to it and talking with Francis in private, but his thoughts were stopped by Dezba piping up from across the room: "I got it! I got something!" She pointed down to her laptop then added, "I'll send it in that group chat May made."

A moment later they all had the link in their private chat, so they took a look.

Terrorist Cell Out for New Clear Energy!

It detailed the aftermath of all ten shareholders' deaths and explained that New Clear stocks were practically being given away by anyone with any sort of substantial amount of them. There was also mention of the car found in the train station parking garage. It was seized by the authorities, and fingerprints were found on its interior. The article stated that the owner of the fingerprints remained unknown, but it was their best lead other than the eye-witness testimonies from the passengers on the train. Roach's height was mentioned and guessed at something between 6'2" and 6'8", and their genders were guessed correctly, but they otherwise had nothing. Not even skin or hair colours.

Thyne finished reading before anyone else and immediately turned to glare at Roach. "Fingerprints!? You bloody git!"

Roach stifled a laugh. He held out his hand, and after a moment more of irritated squawking he noticed what Roach was trying to show him. "Oh," he shrank and blushed, "I guess it was Neodesha's." River and Roach had both burnt off their fingerprints long ago in preparation for their job with Partha smuggling American refugees out of the country.

"Don't you worry, Pa," said Neodesha, "I ain't registered them anywhere nohow."

He forced a smile at her then let his gaze fall again. Diana was on the cushion beside him, so he clicked quietly for her and pat his lap. She perked up at the sound but didn't understand, evident when she tilted her head and looked at Thyne.

Roach said a command for her in Arabic, his deep voice rattling through Thyne's spine and sending chills down it therefore. The dog did as she was told and crawled up into Thyne's lap, looking up at him expectantly for pets.

"Cheers," muttered Thyne to Roach as he pet the dog and continued trying not to worry about... well... everything.

"I got something, too!" shouted Partha. Everyone looked at him. "I'll send it in the chat." After the notification crossed onto their screens, a room full of irritated glares were set on Partha. "What?" He smiled anxiously but with a good amount of genuine amusement in it.

"We're not going to a renaissance faire, kid," said Roach as he looked back at his phone and watched a live feed of New Clear's crumbling stocks.

"Well, hear me out! It's one of the biggest, but I've never been able to go. It only lasts three days, so it won't take too long, and I'll make costumes for everyone, and it'll be a good way to relax after you all just...," he sort of laughed, sort of choked up with fear, "Well you all just killed ten people, so I can only imagine you need something fun and light for your mental health."

Most everyone rolled their eyes, scoffed, or sighed and returned their attention to the screens. Dezba, however, reached over Perlie's lap to pat Partha's knee and said, "I think it's a good idea, kid, but we shouldn't celebrate until we know for sure this worked."

"Not to mention," added Perlie with a bitter tone and harsh glare on Partha like a viper, "we have to make sure none of us are going to *prison*, you fucking moron."

"Speaking of prison," said Roach, still not looking up from his phone, "When are we going after Baumbach?"

Thyne opened a tab to research the company. "They don't have shares. How would we take them down?"

"We don't even know if this worked yet," said River.

Roach shrugged and took a drag, ignoring the concerns and keeping his attention firmly locked on the phone.

After a few hours of quiet, Giovanni set down his computer (it confused him anyway) and went into the kitchen to prepare everyone a meal. After dinner, for which Francis did not join them, they started to peel away from the main room and disappear into their bedrooms.

By three in the morning, the only two remaining in the common area were Thyne and Roach. Even the dogs had all left to follow River to bed.

"The stocks are tanking, dude. It's working." Thyne's hands were trembling. He didn't seem to notice Roach was speaking. "Hey," he pressed a hand gently on Thyne's shoulder, successfully spooking him.

"Bloody Hell. When did you get there?"

"I've been here all night, dude. You okay?"

"Yes," he lied and slammed his laptop shut. "I'm going to bed."

Roach watched him leave with an arched brow. Rather than go into his and Francis' room, Thyne went past it to the bathroom, the reasons for which were made evident by the sound of him brushing his teeth a moment later. Roach stood and slipped his phone into his pocket and, with these few minutes, decided to finally go into Thyne and Francis' room with the hopes of speaking to the pirate in private.

"Thyne?" whimpered Francis as he looked toward the opening door. He frowned when he saw Roach's tall shadowy frame instead and let his head fall back into his pillow. The room was black as pitch with no windows and all its lights extinguished, so the light pouring in from the living area was like sunlight into an ancient tomb. It reeked of booze, and Roach could hear the sloshing of more alcohol as Francis tipped back his flask.

"Can I come in?"

"Whatever."

He closed the door gently behind him and crossed the room, avoiding obstacles and things on the floor as if it was brightly lit. He sat on the edge of the bed, careful not to lay on Francis' sprawled legs over the covers, and looked at him. With a sigh: "Francis, I know you've expended a lot of yourself for us, and I just want to first say that we all appreciate it." He didn't respond. Just drank more. "And anyway, it's good that you're resting. I don't mean to be rude, but I did want to talk to you. Alone. Before Thyne comes back from brushing his teeth." A moment later he heard the shower turn on. "Or… I suppose we have a bit more time than that."

'*We never have more time,*' thought Francis, but he drowned out the woe with rum and slammed his arm down to the bed. He couldn't see Roach, but he glared in his general direction and slurred, "Wherefore do'y stir me?"

Thanks to the lack of light, Roach wasn't keeping his expression blank. If Francis could see him, he would have noticed him looking anxious and running a hand through his long hair, seemingly in an attempt to stall his own words. In fact, because he was taking so long to reply, Francis used his power to push his eyes through time until he had a pair with perfect night-vision. They made eye contact, both able to see each other now despite the complete darkness.

"Well," began Roach, his voice a bit wobbly as he tried to not find Francis' eyes going entirely black disturbing, "It's about Thyne."

Though Francis could see him now, he didn't recognise Roach. He vaguely recognised that he was in the Palace of Versailles, but it was in the same way that a dementia patient recalls places from his past. He felt simultaneously like he was still a child, like he was in the void, and faintly understood reality as it was. Hearing Roach say such a name as "Thyne" was like hearing a demon speak of Heaven.

What did this tall stranger know of angels such as Thyne? Why did he dare utter such beauty with his lips so foreign and wrong. "You know not me angel Thyne," he heard himself say and chased the assertion with more rum.

Roach arched his brow. It didn't seem Francis was questioning his closeness to Thyne; it seemed more like he was saying that, for a fact, Roach had never met the little rage-machine. "What do you mean?"

He gestured at him with his flask, splashing some of the spiced muck from inside onto the both of them as he flailed it around: "You know nothin' of me angel Thyne, you *heathen!*"

"Francis, how much of that rum have you had?"

He slurred a lot of angry French.

"I don't know French. But anyway, we can talk when you aren't foaming at the mouth and mad with rum." He said this, and Francis seemed ready to dismiss him, but he didn't move for the door.

"WELL!?" shouted the drunkard.

Roach looked at him with a soft frown and brow furrowed with concern. This was not the same man as he had seen on Partha's streams. This was not the man Thyne had spent hours talking about like a schoolboy with a crush nor the venerable pirate captain Partha had gushed about. As he looked at Francis with this piteous expression, his concern became muted rage, and his brow furrowed inward rather than outward. "I can't believe you do this to him," he spat, "I thought you loved him."

Francis scrambled from the bed and reached for his hip. He grabbed several times at the air beside him and stumbled around. It was clear he was looking for the sword on the floor behind him, so Roach pulled it up into his own hands telekinetically and flipped it around, holding the blade to offer the hilt to the drunk. Francis took it and nodded appreciatively before flailing it around drunkenly until it was aimed at Roach's throat... mostly.

"What are you going to do, Francis? Are you going to kill me?"

He swung the sword, attempting to behead Roach, but it slipped out of his hand in mid-air and hung there. He looked at his empty hand, then at the floating backsword, his confusion impossible to overstate.

When Roach subsequently stood, his six-inches on Francis seemed like a mile as he looked down at him and grabbed him by his throat. Having no lungs, Francis did not need to breathe and therefore didn't choke, but he flailed around in the grip as he was lifted from the ground.

Roach's expression was one of utter disappointment. Rage was still pumping through him, but Francis was far too pitiful in his drunken madness for such anger to remain. He sighed and dropped him. "You need to pull yourself together, dude. This is pathetic. Thyne loves you. I came in here to ask you how far your own feelings went, but I see now that they can't be very deep. I wanted your blessing to pursue him romantically, but I've clearly always had every right, since you evidently don't love him like I could. Like I may already." Unknowingly, a lot of things in the room had started to float upwards by a few centimetres in his overly-emotional state, so when he finished berating him and turned to leave, everything fell back into place with a loud thud. He slammed the door behind him and flicked on his lighter for a smoke as he crossed the common area to his and River's room.

Francis was left alone and struggling to stand in the midst of his and Thyne's room. He grabbed his aching head with both hands and tried to parse reality. What was real? What wasn't? Who was that tall stranger who somehow knew his angel? He shook his head, his long blond hair brushing against his arms and scaring him. He jumped and reached for his sword again after the touch. There was no one there, however, and after a while of this madness, he heard the door open and saw his beloved angel Thyne come into the room wreathed with the dancing glow of fire from the lanterns in the room behind him.

"Oh, angel Thyne," he cried and wrapped his arms around him, "A demon visited me! He said I didn't love you, but I do!" He lamented further, but his drunken slurring and bawling made it entirely incomprehensible.

"I know," said Thyne as he pet Francis' hair, "Come to bed, my precious Frankenstein."

He awoke with no recollection of the prior night. In fact, he awoke with no recollection of the entire yesterday. He changed his eyes back to a human pair, now brown, and reached immediately for his flask. When he stood, it was clear he was still buzzed, so the rum would help to stave off the killer hangover on his horizon. He held his head and regained his balance before leaving the room, bumping his hip on one of the bed posts on his way.

"Rise and shine," said Roach with a sarcastic tone, "Welcome to the land of the living. Can only presume by the flask in your hand that you don't intend to take anything I said to heart, hm?"

Besides Roach, there was no one else in the room. Francis, who usually had a good handle on time, flicked open his pocketwatch and asked, "9:43? Post meridian?" How long had he slept?

Roach nodded and rested his boots on the coffee table, leaning back in the sofa. "Quite the long one. Partha and Sonny were taking bets on if you were still alive."

"Where's Thyne?"

"Everyone left."

"They have forsaken us?"

"They're flying down to Rome to stay in the doctor's manor until everything with New Clear blows over." He smoked on the cigarette Francis only just noticed in his hand. "That and prepare for the stupid renaissance faire Party wants to drag everyone to in July."

He rubbed his aching head and sipped from his flask. "Wherefore hath they left thee in their wake?" Roach gestured to the seat across from his, and Francis reluctantly rounded to its front to lower himself into it. Once he was seated, Roach pulled his feet off of the coffee table to lean forward, his elbows on his knees, and fingers steepled in front of his face. After a while of no verbal response, just Roach's dead eyes on him, Francis looked around nervously. "Your staring is perturbing me. Speak."

"Thyne asked me to stay behind."

"Wherefore?"

"Because you're hurting him."

All manner of upset crossed Francis' face. Anger. Heartbreak. Guilt. But it all ultimately culminated in a pair of sagging shoulders and averted eyes. "I know."

"You do, don't you. So why don't you do anything about it?"

He sighed. "What would you have me do, Clayton?"

"Well, a little AA wouldn't do you any harm."

"AA?"

"Alcoholics Anonymous?"

He deflated and looked at the flask in his hand. "You want me to stop drinking, but I have always been this way. It be not the rum that hurts him. It be me rotten soul. If anything… the rum makes me less burdensome. It keeps me grounded… mostly. Though, I concede, I shouldn't drink so much as to become a bessoted fool with blacked-out memories as I have yesternight…."

"You sound like an addict, but it's not like Thyne asked me to get you off the alcohol, so I'll not overstep. What I *will* do, is insist that you tell me what the fuck has you so depressed, dude. You're not the guy he and Partha ramble about, and I want to help you be that guy again."

Francis scoffed at the idea. "The one who bet his wife in a game of dice? The man who never saw his children again after being cast into the sea in a mutiny? The one who—?" He stopped and held his aching head before revealing to Roach that he had doomed the entire planet. "No. I shan't be him again. I am infinitely— desperately— so very much trying to *not* be that man."

"Okay, fair enough." He raised his hands to concede the point. "I won't ask you to regress, but you've gotta tell me what's wrong."

He opened his mouth to answer but held his tongue. "I shan't burden you, too. It is bad enough that I am burdening Thyne… You don't understand."

"Then elucidate further, why don't you?" He rolled his wrist around its joint and leaned back in the settee, his boots dropping onto the coffee table and smoke filling his lungs again.

It seemed increasingly pertinent to know whatever had happened the night before, so Francis pushed himself back through time enough that he would relive the entire day and thus be able to recall it when he came back into himself across from Roach. "You're angry with me," was all he offered after experiencing the forgotten talk.

He sighed out a big cloud of smoke. "I mean, yeah, I am, man. But I'm willing to hear you out, so come on, dude. Tell me what's got you so fucked up."

"Roach," a beat, "I know you believe I love him not, but reality is quite to the contrary. I love him far too much, and he could never love or deserve such lowly scum as I. You have my blessing to pursue him. A million blessings. I merely want him happy, and I cannot gift him the blitheness he deserves from purgatory. The purgatory in which our romance rests, as well as the one burdening my blackest soul of sin. You... remind me of Oliver." He wiped a tear from his eye, though he did try to disguise it as an itch on his nose, and because he had no lungs, his voice did not quaver. "Oliver always made him so happy. Never brought him down into the depths with him while he was sinking. He was too strong for that." He eyed him again with the implication that Roach was just the same. After a while of staring, Roach let on a small smile, and Francis broke eye contact to drink more from his flask.

"But Francis?"

"Hm." He stood and offered his hand to help Francis to his feet. The ageless man took it, though his movements were slow and confused. Once Roach had a good grip on it, he pulled him to his feet swiftly, causing him to stumble. Their hands were still together, despite Francis trying to pull away. He looked up at him. "Are you mad!? Unhand me."

His eyes went dark and dangerous but in a somehow soothing way. His voice was low and crisp: "Francis, if I'm as strong as you say, then I'm plenty sturdy enough to help you from sinking into whatever it is you feel is taking your 'blackest soul of sin'." He was playfully mocking of the term. *'What peculiarity in him to treat me thusly. I attempted to decapitate him not but fifteen hours ago.'* Francis sighed and averted his gaze, but Roach grabbed his face by the chin to turn it up again and maintain eye contact. "You don't have to tell me, but I think you should."

"It be not thy burden to bear."

"So you're going to let it crush you into dust right before my eyes, then? In front of Thyne? I want to help you. Not just for him but for you. You're a good man, Francis. Better than you think. Better than me to be certain. You don't have to bear whatever it is alone. That's what your friends are here for, and I *do* consider you a friend."

Tears were trailing his flushed cheeks, down to Roach's thumb where it rested uncomfortably on his chin. After a moment of silent consideration, he replied in Demotic, his voice mismatched with the crying in its clarity and softness: "You may have learned that the universe is only some fourteen billion years old. It is not. It is as ageless as I am." He took a step back and wiped his cheeks. "I've ruined everything, Clayton. I've doomed all life on Earth. And perhaps that does not matter in the grand scheme, because nothing truly does except for him, but it is still something I strive to undo. Osiris will start World War Three, which will mark the beginning of the end. If we can somehow stop Osiris… we can mayhaps postpone— perchance even save humanity from my blunder.

"What more: not only have I personally wasted the world, I have also destroyed myself. It was the same sort of reckless disrespect for forces outside of my control that I—," he looked up at him, his stolen brown eyes sopping wet with tears, "I was trapped in a void of nothingness for sixteen billion years." The unimaginable number hung in the air. "'Twere only me and mine own madness to keep me company, and I can never be certain if I've escaped. When Thyne is romantic to me (something he never was before the void), I am sent back directly into that nothingness where I hallucinated him ad nauseum. The rum is the only thing—." A beat. His voice lowered to a whisper: "My mind is not so fractured as to constantly wallow in the nothingness when I am besotted.

"But… it matters not." He looked at the flask in his hand and tried to drop it, but he couldn't bring himself to do such a thing, instead finding himself drinking from it again almost as if his hand had a mind of its own.

Roach brushed Francis' cheek softly and wiped away some of the copious tears on it. He replied in the same language Francis had confessed in: "Do you feel better?"

He stopped drinking and looked at the flask again. From his flask to Roach's kind face and back again. His features seemed so much softer than before. His hulking frame seemed less like an imposing wall of muscle and instead a warm place to rest his weary head. Without thinking, he dropped the flask and wrapped his arms around Roach's warm body, pulling his face into his chest.

Roach returned the embrace tenfold, craning his neck and squeezing Francis tightly but tenderly. He held him for an entire ten minutes before Francis finally retreated.

"Thank you," he whimpered.

"You're not the reason for the end of the world, Francis, and even if you were, I'd still want to be your friend." He used his telekinesis openly to bring the flask up from the ground and continued, "Now, I'll hold this for you. Okay?"

He nodded. "I'm sorry."

"I'm sorry for saying you don't love Thyne."

He wiped his eyes and nodded again.

"Now!" his tone changed to one much more airy, as if he hadn't just been told something as harrowing as he had. He pressed his hands to his hips and spoke in English with a tone as if reciting a speech for some soldiers: "To Rome! Party will make everyone costumes for his silly little faire. Dezba is no-doubt knitting us other goodies as we speak. The doctor will cook us grand meals. And all while we watch New Clear crumble." A flash of sadistic evil in his eyes. "And with your blessing, I can woo Thyne." His tone swapped immediately to one of concern and slight fear: "Do I still have your blessing?"

He smiled sadly. "Aye."

"Oh, come now, Franky. Why so down!? Do you want me to woo *you*, too?" He laughed. "I've never written two albums at once, but I could certainly try."

Francis blushed, but it came and went in the same way as a warm wave of happiness came and went over him. He would have loved to be able to delight in something so light as flirting with this handsome brute, but his slight smile became a frown as the weight of the world fell back on his shoulders.

Roach laughed again and grabbed Francis by his collarbone. They made eye contact, and as soon as they had, Roach leaned down and kissed Francis on the cheek. He lingered beside his ear afterwards to whisper, "How's that, hm?"

Francis' stomach fluttered and heart soared, but it, again, was pulled immediately back into the dark. "You shouldn't waste your time with me, Clayton," he managed.

"Ah, but you control time, don't you?" He was beaming as he leaned back and looked down at him. "You probably don't know how beautiful it is to waste it."

Francis allowed his mind to reel, trying to claw his way out of the dark. It was helped immensely by Roach's wide unwavering grin and the hand on his shoulder. After a while, his cheeks were faintly pink, and there was a slight smile on his lips. "You have telekinesis," he stated rather suddenly.

"Have a couple other 'gifts,' too. So does Sonny. Don't tell anyone, though."

"Well, haven't you wondered about it?"

"How do you mean?"

"Giovanni could run some tests. You may chance have Etren blood like myself."

"Ha!" He pulled him into his arms and gave him a noogie. "More reason to get to Italy, then! Let's drive! Can you teleport us to the garage in Orléans?"

"Okay."

———— ◆ ————

The first leg of the drive to Rome was beautiful. Roach played some rough recordings of the songs he had been writing for Thyne to hear Francis' opinions, all of which were brimming with kind words. They stopped for dinner at a fancy restaurant, which was Roach's idea, but rather than go inside, he brought Francis to the garbage in the alley beside it and explained, "Rich people throw away the craziest food you'll ever see." Francis didn't eat much or often, but when he did, he was content to consume almost anything. Nothing could ever be worse than a sea biscuit wrought with maggots. He was endeared by Roach's idea of a good time and happily participated in the dumpster-diving, allowing himself, at least for the night, to "waste some time." After the lovely little dinner date eating out of the dumpster, they found a cheap motel and booked a room.

Roach showered, prayed, and fell asleep rather quickly in one of the two beds. Before he was entirely asleep, however, he mumbled to Francis that he should wake him if he needed anything and emphasised that it wouldn't be a burden on him at all.

Francis laid himself in the other bed and tried not to notice the hangover creeping across him. For hours, he stared through the window at the overcast night sky, polluted by the light and haze of the city. It was four in the morning, and the room was deathly quiet. By then, there was only Francis and his thoughts, and his thoughts at the moment were obsessing over how neutral and nothing a shade of grey the sky was. After long enough of staring, the entire horizon started to shift and sway and shrink and grow. The room started rocking, and he sat up swiftly, a hand to his racing heart. Back and forth and back and forth. He could hear the sea outside lapping against the hull. A thunder in the distance. It would be another long night sailing through a storm.

He threw the blankets off and moved to stand, but when his feet touched the carpet he let out a curt gasp and reeled away. Some sort of fungus on the floor? He looked around for his boots, and it wasn't until then that he recalled where and when he was. Just a motel for the night. He felt eyes on him, but after a quick scan around the room, he was confident he was alone. That Roach even existed had completely escaped his notice.

He laid back down and reached for his flask. It wasn't on his bedside table, so he patted around on his person to no avail. Why was he here? He couldn't remember. And with no rum… Rum… What was rum again? His brow furrowed as he tried to recall something so basic about his everyday existence. '*A drink*,' he recalled, but the taste and purpose escaped him. The act of drinking in general… It had been so long… Since he had lips… Since he had a body at all…

He had been fully returned to the void. The darkness and silence in the room were enough to plunge him back into it like the crew who cast him into the abyss to die.

Roach was awoken by Francis' sudden start and was watching him with a curious expression. He had asked him aloud what was wrong, but Francis didn't even register his presence. Now he was sitting upright and watching. It seemed Francis was going back to sleep, but Roach knew now that he had trouble parsing reality from the nothingness. "Francis are you okay?" He whispered.

Another voice in the void. He replied internally, '*Aye. I be sorting the lines again.*' There were parallel shadows on the ceiling from the shutters, but to Francis they were something to occupy his mind: a vague hallucination his soul conjured for him to sort.

Suddenly he felt sick and heavy and like the world was falling to pieces. He grasped around for something and clutched onto the first solid thing he touched. "What becomes of me? Where are the lines? Which god do I kill for this!? Oh! The world is gone and destroyed!" But just as he lamented such a thing, the world was back again and much warmer than he recalled it being.

Wait....

He looked around again.

The lines had shifted. *Everything* had shifted. There was someone else in here with him. Someone right beside him.... His face was incomprehensible. His lips were moving, but it was like he was speaking ... Arabic? Soft Arabic whispers and the sudden feeling of bugs all over. But... it didn't frighten Francis. He looked down at his arms, which he suddenly recalled he had, and watched the imagined vermin crawl around.

Roach finished the whispered prayer for his friend before pulling him in closer and petting his long blond hair gently. "Francis, what time is it?"

"Time." He blinked. Time was a very important thing, he knew, but... "What is time?"

"Where are we?"

"You don't know?"

"Francis, tell me where we are, please."

He looked up at him and smiled wide. Whoever this man was, he was beguiling. "'Tis similar to Hell, but thy pulchritude is in excess. Oh, but mayhaps you are Lucifer, himself." He seemed sobered by his own comment and looked scared. Terrified, even.

Roach frowned and kissed his forehead. "Would that bother you?" Francis started to nod, but he stopped and shook his head instead. "What can you see right now?"

He was looking through Roach, which was what prompted the question. When he processed the words, however, his gaze trailed around. "Well, the lines are gone. There is a grey rectangle there, though." He pointed to the window. "And all this fog. Or—," he smiled wide at Roach, "Are we on a cloud!?" He confused himself with his own question and giggled. "What business hath a demon atop a cloud?"

It hadn't crossed Roach's mind that Francis didn't have his nightvision anymore without those big black voids for eyes. (It hadn't crossed his mind in conjunction with the idea that Francis felt trapped in the void, at any rate). After the nonsensical answer to yet another attempt to ground him, Roach finally reached over to the lamp and flicked it on.

Francis started and tried to scramble away, but Roach held him still and made calming sounds. The light, despite being instant, seemed to pour across the floor and up the side of the bed. It vanquished all of Francis' little bug friends from the blankets and his arms as it consumed him, and when it reached the ceiling he looked at Roach and accidentally spoke his thoughts aloud: "A handsome gentleman in my sheets. I hope I am not scandalised."

Roach cupped his hand around Francis' cheek and whispered, "Francis, where do you think we are?" His voice quavered just-so, but he remained otherwise stone-faced and strong.

"I...," he looked around, "I know not."

"Do you know who I am?"

He frowned. "I want to."

There was a long beat wherein Roach tried to think of another way to help. *'Don't encourage the hallucination. He needs to be grounded, but, oh, I don't know what else to do! Allah, lend him strength.'* With a sigh, he hesitantly said, "I know your angel."

His beaming grin was pure and innocent. "My angel Thyne? Where is he?"

"Oh Francis," he lamented on a weepy breath. He managed to suck it all up, however, and stood with the madman still in his arms.

The world was falling away again, but this tall stranger was so strong and sturdy, Francis felt that nothing could stop him. He was taken to a chair on the other side of the room.

"Get that guitar."

"Guitar...," He looked down into the chair. Guitars were for music, he recalled. He wasn't sure what they looked like anymore, but he grabbed the only thing he could reach, and when it let out a whimper like an animal, he dropped it. It didn't fall, however. Instead, it floated over to one of the— beds! That's what they were —where it fell with a quiet thump into the blankets.

Roach set Francis down, sitting him up on the bed and stopping him from trying to grab at things. He held a hand over his mouth when he started to ramble again.

He wasn't sure what was happening, but after a moment of being moved around and quieted, Francis finally understood what the stranger wanted of him.

Except… he wasn't a stranger, was he? No! Francis had met him! He was happy to see him again after such a heartbreaking death. When he stopped rambling madly and rested his hands in his lap with a beaming smile at who he now assumed was a ghost, Roach sat on the bed across from him and picked up the instrument.

"I was not aware you played guitar."

This intrigued Roach enough to postpone his song. "What do you mean?"

"If you be learning for Thyne, I would warn that such a gesture is unwise."

"Francis, who do you think I am?"

He tilted his head like a confused pup. "Oliver York?"

He went pale, but he pushed out all the thoughts that came of such an oddity to instead start strumming on the guitar. "What's your favourite song?"

The absentminded strumming was helping him to understand reality quite a lot. Besides singing casually, Francis wasn't musical at all, so the idea that something so complex could come from his own madness in the void was a far-fetched notion. He even managed to recall his favourite song: *The White Cliffs of Dover.*

As soon as he'd said the name, the tune being played slowed and changed key. He played a simple plucking pattern and sang for him, his voice sounding how Francis imagined a vulture would sing were it a passerine. *"There'll be blue birds over the white cliffs of Dover. Tomorrow, just you wait and see…"*

Francis pressed a hand to his chest and joined in, the two of them singing in chorus: *"There'll be love and laughter. And peace, ever after.…"*

They sang it in its entirety, and afterwards, Francis was lucid again. He stood and crossed the small distance between them to hug Roach as hard as his weak little arms could muster.

"Come on. I'll hold you. Let me put the guitar down."

He stepped back to let Roach prepare then practically dove into his arms. "I'm so sorry."

"You don't have anything to be sorry for, Francis."

"How did you know what to do?"

"I didn't. But music is magic."

He pulled himself closer to Roach. As close as physically possible. "My gratitude cannot be overstated. I apologise so sincerely and deeply. I—."

He lifted Francis' head up and looked into his eyes. "Shut up, dude."

Francis managed a soft smile.

"You don't have to keep going it alone. I'm here. I'll help keep you grounded."

"Thank you," he whispered.

"Nothing to thank me for. I should be thanking *you*."

"Why?"

"For trusting me…. For letting me waste your time, even if only a little."

There was a beat, during which he was unconsciously eyeing Roach's lips. '*No,*' he scolded himself, 'He hath taken enough of my torturous presence. Villain as I am, I do not deserve—.'

"You keep looking at my lips like that, dude, I'm gonna think you wanna kiss me." His tone was playful and smile flirtatiously jeering.

He averted his eyes. "You don't want to kiss me," he managed eventually, even sounding dejected despite the blush on his cheeks a moment prior.

"Oh? Are you a mind reader, too?" His tone was still playful. Francis arched his brow at him. "Can you read my mind, Francis?"

"No."

He smiled again in a mocking way. "So what do you know about whether or not I want to kiss you?"

"You *shouldn't* want to kiss me, then."

"And why not? Pray tell."

"I'm insane. Do you not recall what has only just occurred?"

"If you're saying it would be an inappropriate time, then fair enough, but that's not what you're saying, is it?" Francis shook his head just-so. "You're trying to insinuate that I, for some reason, would not want to be with someone who would *dare* to need my help sometimes."

"It is more than needing assistance from time to time. It is madness. It is constant. It is abuse to you. To Thyne. To everyone around."

"Oh, Francis, stop it. If that was abuse, then you can abuse me all day. No, it would have been abuse to let you be. I couldn't stand to watch your soul rot and rip apart. I prayed for you. I held you. I sang with you. And, before you can go accusing me again, I most certainly *do* want to kiss you. Quite suddenly, I'll admit, but the desire is real and present. Madness is alluring and beautiful to me, and I'm not so sane myself. If anyone here is some sort of monster not deserving of kisses and love it's m—."

Francis pressed his lips to Roach's so quickly he didn't notice until he was already tasting him. Their tongues were intertwined for a long passionate moment, their hands moving all over. Francis got a good feel for Roach's strong chest, and Roach's large hands explored the bony pirate. It was sudden and unexpected, but they were both undressing each other, Roach was panting, and the room was getting hotter.

Before things went too far, Roach wriggled his wallet from his pocket and fished out a condom. For the first time since they started kissing, there was a considerable pause as he leaned back to show it to Francis, his brow furrowed inquisitively.

Francis blushed and shuddered, but he nodded after a moment. "I've never bottomed before."

Roach smiled wide. What an unexpected thing to hear from an allegedly ageless being. "No time like the present, ay, bed bug?"

He nodded and, growing impatient, wrapped his hand around the back of Roach's neck to pull him back to his lips so the night could continue.

Part Three

When all the world was drinking blood.

Chapter 31

Lust and Play

Whoever had done this to her was certainly someone he didn't want to cross. His eyes traced her naked form with increasing horror at every new sight.

"What's wrong?" she asked in Italian, her American accent subtle but present.

"What... *happened* to you?" he whispered.

Her heart sank, and she pulled a blanket over her chest. With her gaze averted, she muttered, "Cross them out, if you like."

He held up his hands and stood. While pulling his pants back on: "I'm sorry. You're very pretty, but this is... this is too much."

"It was from my ex. We're not together anymore. He won't care. It's my body, not his."

He shook his head and pulled his shirt back on. "I'm sorry. I—. I'm not comfortable continuing, even if your— uh— ex is somehow not the possessive type."

Tears blurred her vision as she watched him rush out of the hotel room. After a shuddery breath, she pulled the blanket off of her chest and looked down at her body. There was a tinge of regret for what she had let him do to her, but more than anything, she was... proud. Even though they weren't together anymore, and he was adamant that they wouldn't get back together, she wore the scars with contentment if not outright grace.

After getting dressed in her dark satin dress and clipping up her long black hair, she went back to the bar to try her luck again. She had lost count of the number of people who had rejected her after seeing the extent of her scars. After ordering a glass of gin, she tapped on the bar repetitively to try and stop herself from reaching for the phone. '*He's probably with—*,' her stomach turned at the thought, '*Yeah…. Best not to call him.*'

But her ex wasn't the only person in her contacts. She nursed her iced liquor and wrenched her phone from its place in her bra to start scrolling through the names. One stuck out in particular, but before she could make the ill-advised decision to call him: "Is anyone sitting here?"

Perlie looked up to see a beautiful auburn-haired woman beaming at her. She had asked in English with a posh accent. "Uh… no. No one's sitting there," she managed.

"Great!" She hopped up onto the seat and ordered herself an Old Fashioned. "Good thing you know English. I've been really struggling with Italian."

Perlie turned off her phone's screen and slid it back into her bra. Her tone was cautiously optimistic: "Yes… I know a lot of languages."

"Oh do you? That's always so impressive to me. I only know English." She giggled, already a little buzzed. "You sound American, though. Italy's a long way from home for you, innit?"

"A long way indeed…." She watched the woman take her cocktail and couldn't help but wonder if her luck for the night had changed. After some mental adjustment to get out of her own way, she smiled flirtatiously. "I'm here on work. You?"

"Oh? What do you do?"

"I'm a broker," she lied easily.

"Oh! Maybe I should hire you." A chuckle. "I recently started dating this guy, and he's really business-minded. He lives here in Rome, at least sometimes. I've only been here for a couple weeks, but it's like an alien planet. Everyone's so nice, and the language is really difficult."

Perlie frowned. '*Of course she has a boyfriend*,' she thought with a sigh. After leaning on her elbow and taking a lazy sip of her gin, she retorted with much less interest: "Yeah it's a tough one."

"At least the alphabet is easy, though. I tried learning Nepali because of my semi-annual trips out to Everest, but I just couldn't do it." Perlie rolled her eyes at this bimbo who probably just looked into the language because she wanted an easier way to berate the underpaid overworked sherpas who carried her to the top of the mountain. "Everest is beautiful," she continued without noticing Perlie's upset, "Have you ever been?"

"To the top of the tallest mountain in the world?" She scoffed at the notion, and Aspyn finally noticed her upset.

"What's wrong, miss?"

Another roll of her big brown eyes.

After a moment of observing her, the auburn-haired woman noticed the scars on Perlie's forearms and asked with a courage and bluntness only brought about by alcohol, "What happened to your arms?"

She sort of glared. "What does it look like?"

"It looks like you cut yourself. You know there's always people out there who care about you…."

She drank the rest of her gin only to slam the glass on the bar and ask with poorly-veiled anger, "And your name was?"

"Oh, terribly sorry, miss. I'm Aspyn Temm." She held out her hand.

"Perlie Moon," she droned as she limply shook the offered hand. "You should learn to mind your own business, Miss Temm. I didn't do this to myself."

She blushed and rubbed the back of her neck when her hand was released. "I suppose I should, but… well if it wasn't you, then who was it? It's clearly not accidental."

She groaned and flicked her eyes to the bartender. When she had him, she tapped the bar, and he nodded to acknowledge it. With Perlie's brown eyes back on Aspyn, she snipped, "My ex, if you must know."

"Oh my! That's awful! I'm sorry to hear it. I've never been in an abusive relationship like that, so——."

"It wasn't abusive. I let him do it. I love him." She sucked in her lips after the last declaration and glared at her next glass of gin as it was set in front of her. Maybe she was drunk enough…. She didn't love Roach…. Right?

Aspyn tilted her head. "You *let* him?" After another glance at the scars she pursed her lips and held one of her hands over Perlie's tenderly. "You don't deserve that, mate. He clearly didn't treat you right."

Perlie snatched her hand away and drank more despite the buzz already affecting her. "What's *your* boyfriend like, then?" she spat.

She blushed and retreated. "Oh, he's uh——." She rubbed the back of her neck and looked at the tiled floor. "He's nice."

Perlie glared. "And?"

"He's… he's nice. I don't know. I'm not——." She stopped when she realised how the next part would sound after chastising Perlie's ex. Still, she was too drunk to think of another way to word it, so she said it anyway: "I'm not allowed to tell people we're dating, so I can't say much about him."

"Right…."

"He has a pet rabbit, though. I can talk about her." She giggled. "She's all brown like——."

"Forgive me, Miss Temm, but I couldn't really give less of a shit about your boyfriend's pet rabbit." A bitchy grin.

Aspyn frowned and took her cocktail away from the bar to find a conversation partner less mean, and thus Perlie returned her attention to the name in her contacts list that seemed to be pestering her. Halfway through her gin, she was drunk enough to dial it.

"Ayo Perls!" he shouted, "Whuzzuhp!?" An adorable laugh.

"Party… I want you."

He started and blushed. "Uh… Just a sec." He stood upright from the couch in the sitting area of Loomis Manor and shuffled out of the room up to his suite, rudely abandoning the group mid-conversation. Once he was alone, he locked his door and started going through his suitcase for something slutty to wear. Holding the phone to his head with his shoulder: "Alright, where do you want to go? We doing a date first or what?"

'*That was easy*,' she thought before stuttering out, "I'm at a bar nearby. Come buy me a drink."

"Yes, ma'am!" he said with a grin so big she could hear it. "I'll just get dressed and—. Is it black-tie or can I come in a crop top?"

"Wear whatever you want, kid."

"Hell yeah. Text me the address. I'll be there in ten."

They hung up, and Perlie looked down at the phone with a lump of regret already stirring up her stomach. She hadn't expected it to be that easy….

Once he was dressed, Partha formed a line of cocaine on his suite's kitchen counter, snorted it in one swift motion, and snapped an eyepatch over his missing eye. He kicked open the fridge, took out a bottle of seltzer, and chugged it as he left the manor without telling anyone inside where he was going.

He was usually not the kind to litter, but he had seen Roach littering. Being the sort of easily-influenced man he was, halfway through his walk, he tossed his empty seltzer bottle on the pavement. It shattered on the streetside and mixed with a plethora of garbage already settled there from various high tides bringing trashy flood-water there. '*Hell yeah, that felt awesome. I should tell Roach.*' He snapped a picture of the mess and texted it to Roach with its only caption: ⟦ (¬‿¬). ⟧

Perlie was taking the first sip of her third gin when Partha leaned on the bar beside her and wiggled his eyebrows. "Hey there, pretty lady. Did it hurt?"

"No," she snipped.

He giggled. "Relaaaax. I'm just messing around. See you've already got a drink, so would you wanna go to an actual restaurant? My treat."

She sighed and looked at her full glass of gin. "I don't know, Party. Whatever you want, I guess."

"Hey. What's wrong?" He wrapped his arm around her hunched shoulders and pet her gently. "Did someone fuck with you? I'm not the toughest guy around, but I'll kick his ass if I have to."

She smiled weakly at him before returning her attention to her drink. "Thanks, kid. No need, though. It's not anyone else that's the problem."

"Well what's wrong, then?" He sat beside her where Aspyn had sat and spun from side to side in the swivelling chair.

"Let's just go." She downed half of her gin in one turn and stood.

Partha hopped up, drank the rest of her gin, then escorted her outside. She was a little chilly, but he hadn't worn a jacket, so he looked down at his cropped-off hoodie and asked, "You want this?"

"And what good would that do me, kid?"

"I'm just trying to be a gentleman." Rather than remove his only top, he wrapped his arm around her shoulders and led her to a nearby restaurant. "Oh," he said when he noticed it was closed, "What time is it?" They both looked at his phone as he pulled it out and saw that it was midnight. "Shit. I'm sorry, Perls. We could go back to the manor and make s'mores or something if you want. My suite has a fireplace."

She managed a genuine grin, the first of the entire day. "That sounds really sweet, Party."

"Then onward, fair maiden!" he shouted with an invisible sword held out ahead of them, "To the corner store to procure the crackers of Sir Graham!"

She giggled and let him lead her ever-drunker body to the corner store. While he was getting the ingredients for s'mores, she grabbed a soda for each of them from the back.

When they entered the manor, everyone else was still awake and chatting in the sitting area. Arjun was playing a jazzy tune on the piano but stopped to shout toward the door when he heard it open: "Use protection!" He howled with laughter that was echoed more quietly in the others before returning to his music, improvising lyrics about the two of them and the importance of using protection like an afterschool special.

Perlie and Partha both blushed when they heard this, but neither of them paid anyone the decency to even show their faces, immediately climbing the stairs to Partha's suite instead. Once the door was locked behind them, Partha kissed Perlie all the way to the couch where she let him shove her down and run his hands up under her skirt. The knot of regret was stirring her up again, so after a few minutes of heated passion, she pushed him away and averted her eyes. "Uh… maybe s'mores first?"

He blushed. "Right! Sorry. Okay, sure. S'mores first." He had already taken off his hoodie, so he looked at it for a moment, trying to decide if it would be more awkward to put it on or leave it off. After some thought, he tossed it aside and brought their shopping bags over to the coffee table. With a sip of his soda, he crouched down by the fireplace and futzed with it, trying to figure out how to get the gas started.

Perlie nursed her drink and watched him with a light smile and lilting heart but a burdensome leaden feeling in her stomach. *'What will he say when he sees? Should I ask for the lights to be off? Would that offend him?... Although... seems pretty resilient. Would anything offend him?'*

Once the fire was started, Partha sat on the coffee table across from Perlie and beamed at her. "You're pretty."

Unimpressed, she droned, "Is that your usual material?"

A slight frown. "No."

"Then hit me with the classics."

He looked down at the box of graham crackers and fidgeted with it. "Well, the 'classics' aren't genuine. They're the 'I'll say anything if you fuck me' type things. But you've already said you want me, so why would I play games with you? You're pretty. Simple as that."

She rolled her eyes and leaned on her elbow. "Well, whatever. Thanks, I guess."

"You don't think you're ugly, do you?"

She shrugged. "Roach always said I was pretty."

"Well, he's got good taste." They both immediately recalled his horrible taste in food and how much he genuinely enjoyed filth, so Partha added, "...in people." She huffed an amused chuckle and looked down at the bags on the coffee table. "Alright, let's make s'mores and maybe play a one-shot or something, then I'll show you the best night of your life!"

She was going to mock him for the mighty claim, but she didn't have the energy to be playful nor mean and instead simply agreed. They listened to music from Partha's playlist, all of which was annoyingly EDM until Perlie asked to play something from her phone and filled the room with gentle classical music. Partha found it incredibly boring, but he was nothing if not compliant. The music paired with the crackling fire to give the entire suite a warm and cosy sort of feeling. They had moved to the rug in front of the fireplace to play rummy, and after losing horribly for the third time, Partha leaned over the mess of cards and kissed her.

This one wasn't stirring her up with dread at first. She let him unzip her dress and push her down gently to the ground, but she was nervous. Her breaths quickened. Mostly sober by then, all of her thoughts were wrought with worries of what he'd say when he pulled down the front of her dress. The lights were already off, but the fire would illuminate her. Her breaths stifled, and she grabbed his wrists as he sat up and tried to pull down the dress. "No," she whispered.

He released the fabric and retreated his hands. "I'm sorry."

"I—. I—. Just... put the fire out first."

He pursed his lips. "Perlie, I've already told you you're beautiful. I'd like to see you, if you'll let me. Plus... I mean I'll be better if I can see what I'm doing. I've only got one eye, so it's harder in the dark." A nervous ha.

She bit her lip and let out a shuddery breath. "Okay. Okay fine. Whatever. Fuck it." She pulled down the dress for him. "Take me, Partha."

His gaze devoured her. She was more scar than skin. It was admittedly pretty. The scars were purposeful and beautifully designed. They framed her small breasts and danced like briar vines down her ribcage and impressive abs. Some of them were designs of roses, and he couldn't help but notice a scar in the shape of a roach just below the belt. It pulled some of the colour from his face, and looking at the rest of her scars in this new context made him... a bit jealous. He couldn't help but want a photogenic scar from Roach somewhere, but—.

"Cross them out," she whispered, "Make your own."

His breath stifled. He had played more dominant roles in the bedroom on several occasions, but he had never gone so far as knife-play. The idea scared him at first, but he almost immediately flipped a switch in his brain to a more sadistic mindset. He stood and walked to the kitchen to get a knife. When he noticed his hand trembling around its handle, however, he set it down and eyed the door to his room. Perlie sat up and started to stand, but he pointed at her when he noticed and said forcefully, "Down."

Her heart fluttered, and she nodded. Once she was laying back down waiting for him to get whatever he was getting from his bedroom, a wide grin had crawled across her red lips.

He returned to her smoking a joint with one hand and wielding the rapier he had bought in Crownpoint with the other. After swapping the music back to his own favourites and turning it up so loud that the bass shook the floor, he took a moment to hype himself up internally. The way she laid herself out vulnerable and longing made it easier for him to make the first mark.

Against all odds and every expectation she had of him, it was just as he had promised: the best night of her life.

Chapter 32
Sorrow and Love, Glory and Love

Roach and Francis arrived in Rome in the late afternoon, and once they were closer to the manor, Francis helped with the directions. Or rather... he "helped."

"Go west, I say! West!"

"Sorry, Captain Dumbass, I forgot to bring my compass."

"It's down that street right there and oh dear god you've passed it again."

Rather than turn around for the umpteenth time, Roach parallel parked in the next available space and reached over the middle console to pat Francis' thigh. He looked him in the eyes and smiled in a fiendish but playful manner. "You're not so good at this wasting time business, but you'll get better."

It disarmed Francis enough to have him smile and sigh. "I am merely... in a hurry."

"No hurry no worry, man. We'll get there when we get there, and it will be exactly when it was meant to happen." He took up one of Francis' hands and kissed its knuckles tenderly.

After blushing briefly, he rattled off with panicked eyes, "There are only fifty-seven months until the wretched beginnings of World War Three, followed by two annums of my own mindless valour-seeking. Further still! The world will suffer another—." He was shut up by Roach's finger over his lips.

"Shhh, little bed bug. It's time to waste some time. You can't save the world without resting. Fair?" Francis nodded. "Now, get out. We'll just walk from here."

He sighed and said, "Okay," through his squished lips.

They had to wade through some flood waters on their way up to the manor; it brought to mind their time in California. The Mediterranean was not nearly as much awash with litter, but Roach still managed to find an unopened tin can floating by them. It had lost its label, but it had a pull-tab, so he cracked it open and showed the contents to Francis, who was piggy-backing on him to avoid the sea. "Fruit cake in a can! You Europeans are wild." His gaze trailed around the water's surface, which was up to his waist at that point. He was looking for a fork, as if the sea of garbage might provide one, but he eventually gave up the idea and used his fingers to pinch out some of the snack. He shared it with Francis on their walk, but the pirate refused more than two bites. It wasn't that he didn't enjoy it (he did), he was merely hyper aware of his eating habits and did not like to eat more than once a week if he could help it. Because of his Etren blood, even if he did not use his control of time, he could go an entire two years without food, so it truly was an unnecessary activity to him. He explained as much to Roach when asked, but it prompted the question, "Why don't you eat more, though? It'd help you bulk up a bit. A fresh breeze could knock you over, dude."

"Alas, such is my hope. I spent my youth in shape not unlike yours. If I never have to live in such a body again, it will be too soon."

"Huh? You?" He tried to imagine him as anything other than the glorified corpse he was now. "You didn't like being strong?"

"I much abhorred it, yes. It made me far too useful a slave." He flailed his hand around to try and free himself of the conversation and redirected it by saying, "Release me. We will arrive soon."

Loomis manor sat at the front of a vast property. It was a verdant plot with rolling hills of what was once a vineyard but was too flooded and salted to be useful by then. There were footpaths every which-way in a labyrinthian manner that would necessitate a map for those unfamiliar with them. The walkways wound through gardens, around fountains, between buildings, up and down the hills. It was an objectively beautiful Italian vista, but Roach found it exquisite to the point of exhaustion. He was far more interested in its darkest most unkempt corners, in the graveyard tucked away behind one of the nearby knolls, and in the secrets that the old manor must have held.

Francis seemed to know the area with just as much familiarity as he knew the palace while he led Roach through its southern side. It was a curious enough phenomenon and long enough of a walk that Roach inquired: "Do you visit the doctor often? You seem to know your way around his property." He tossed his empty can of fruitcake on the ground around this time and shoved his hands in his pockets.

"This was once my place of residence," answered Francis as he watched the littering.

"Back in your pirating days?"

"Nay. Priorly."

"When did you start pirating?"

"When I eloped with my wife. We both lived here for a time, working the vineyard and helping Master Drusus keep everything clean."

"Master Drusus?"

"Oh! Drusus is Arjun's real name. And Giovanni's is Keeva. They respond to both just as easily."

"Interesting. So they were your parents?"

He chuckled softly. "Master Keeva was respectable enough, I suppose."

He arched his brow, but realisation struck his face a moment later. It hadn't crossed his mind, but now that it had, he was visibly enraged. He stopped and looked at Francis with a stern set of cold grey eyes. His voice was a growling whisper: "Is Thyne *dating* your former enslaver!?"

He blushed and gestured at an opening between the vine-wrapped outer wall of the manor's main building and a small guest-house beside it. "Lo! We may take this path. I suspect the flowers will be abloom in the gardens." He started down the narrow pathway, but Roach grabbed him by his bony little wrist and pulled him into an embrace. He tried to push himself away, but Roach was immovable. His strong arms were woven tightly around him like a cocoon. "Roach, please," he whimpered as he wriggled around.

Roach's whispering voice was breathed into his ears so delicately it was almost as if he was having a thought of his own: "I'll kill them. All of them."

He finally managed to push himself out of Roach's arms. "This conversation is finished, Clayton. I will not speak on it further, and if you attempt to bring harm on any of them or otherwise disrespect my wishes, my trust in you will be forever fractured."

He pursed his lips. "Fine."

"Now let's go." He passed Roach to go back toward the front of the manor, no longer interested in the path between it and the guest house.

"What about the gardens?"

He flailed his arm around to shoo away the idea. "Forget it."

Roach watched Francis leave. "I guess I'll have to have a romantic walk through the flowers alone, then." He started down the path, his boots crunching on the gravel and the click of his lighter sounding as he moved.

Francis groaned and stopped time to catch up with Roach, resuming it to walk beside him. "You really are just like Oliver, you know." This was a sort of playful jab at both Thyne's late lover and Roach simultaneously.

He smoked and smirked. "Tell me more about him."

Francis noticed that Roach's pace had slowed to a meandering sort of amble, so he reluctantly slowed to match it. "Do you know why Thyne's memorial tattoo to him primarily depicts a spoon?"

He shook his head and interweaved the fingers of his free hand with Francis', his eyes hardly ever leaving the gangly blushing pirate.

"When we first forayed in that American eatery, you proposed we nick the cutlery, aye? Well, just before the war (that is: the second world war), Thyne and his comrades, including Oliver, traversed London taking photographs and savouring some of their last moments of innocence. On that day, Oliver brought them to an ice cream parlour, and— I wasn't there —but I have been assured that he participated in some mischief by fooling them all into stealing their spoons. They brought them to the war with them. Thyne carries his on him most all of the time as well as Oliver's lighter."

Roach's face went flush, despite his best efforts to hide it. *'This is perhaps one too many coincidences to continue ignoring,'* was his general thinking on the matter of his similarities to Thyne's late love. He cleared his throat to try and cough away the feelings, eventually managing to return to his default deadpan expression and divert the conversation: "Francis, can I ask you something?"

His attention had been captured by the sunset over the vineyard and the Tyrrhenian Sea behind it. When he looked back to Roach, he noticed he was lit beautifully in its golden splendour, blowing smoke through his nose like a dragon. The little swirls of sunset-stained grey coming from the end of his cigarette combined with the clouds from his breath, reminding Francis of the nebulae he had seen in his treks across the stars.

"Can you bring others through time, or is it just you?"

"…Why do you ask?"

He took a drag and squinted at the sunset. "I don't know. I…." There were a lot of ideas tumbling around in his head. Part of him wanted to go back and meet this famed Oliver York fellow. Part of him wanted to be brought back to times too ancient to fathom. He would have loved to see Babylon or Ancient Egypt in particular, and he would be lying if he didn't consider the endless possibilities in the future. There was also a large part of him that wanted to be brought back to see Muhammad, Jesus, Judas… But he was a horrible Muslim and an even worse man. That the thought had even crossed his mind was an affront to his faith. He wasn't even monotheistic; he was a henotheist. With a sigh, he looked at his new lover to try to distract himself from his reeling thoughts. "Nevermind."

Francis kissed Roach's cheek and smiled bashfully. "Okay."

His hair was messy and ready to matt. His beard was long and scruffy but softer than it seemed. The crow's feet beside his eyes as he smiled were the only indication of an age past forty on his face. He seemed to always smell pleasantly of the salty brine, despite his great fear of it. He was gorgeous, and now that he had seen him in his entirety: skin and bones with a large scar across his side from his run-in with a hungry shark, Roach was evermore attracted to him. He had seen this beauty in Francis upon their first meeting, but the sunset and the context of the night before put him in a new light. A more beautiful light. He brought one of Francis' rough spindly hands to his lips and kissed his knuckles. "How 'bout them flowers, ay bed bug?"

He nodded and offered his arm to link with Roach's, leading him down to the very edge of the flood waters and around the back of the manor. The light of day was waning just enough that they could see into the house through its large two-storey windows, but there was a big yellow glare across most of them, not helped by the heavy blackout curtains inside. It made looking through them almost as difficult as seeing something on the horizon just below the sunset. Still, Francis waved toward the house and informed Roach, "If they have opened the curtains for the guests, they may perchance glimpse us."

Roach gave a sarcastic salute to the window, managing to catch sight of Partha through it. He seemed to be reading something, so Roach had a hard time believing that they were being watched by anyone in the house.

Only a moment later, they were in a vast garden. The flowers were in full bloom and were by far the most beautiful Roach had ever seen. The pink-orange sunset was reaching its claws across the landscape, painting stripes of light through the bases of trees and dappling through the bushes. Bougainvillea hung drowsily across stone arches and wooden pergolas along the colourful gravel path. In fact, Roach could see now that it wasn't gravel at all but a wide array of gemstones from amethyst to opal to labradorite. The little rocks caught glimmers of sunlight and threw it around like a glowing rainbow of light at their feet. To their left was an overlook of the half-flooded vineyards and the Tyrrhenian with its speckling of leisure boats. To their right was the rest of the garden, which seemed to wind back and forth through the lazy old oaks infinitely.

Sparrows basked in the sunbeams from their places perched in the peach and fig trees dotting the path, and a small brook could be heard tinkling nearby. Francis and Roach were hand-in-hand again as they admired the wide variety of flowers from peonies and poppies to lilies and orchids. Roses of every colour and carnations of marbled red and white as if the red queen's card-soldiers hadn't finished painting them yet. Crocuses with saffron ready to harvest and edelweiss dancing quietly in the brush. Roach started to softly sing the song of the same name when he spotted the, "*small and white, pure and bright,*" edelweiss flowers.

When he heard the music, Francis closed his eyes as they walked to let Roach's voice and the quiet crunching of the gemstones beneath them replace all the visual splendour. He even stopped to quiet their footsteps, and Roach stopped in turn, still singing. Francis' eyes fluttered open like the butterflies dancing in the air to the passerine's evening tunes. Roach was hardly lit, only a rim of orange on his right and the ambient dusk on the rest of him. His song was low, the twittering birds in the treetops taking up all the higher registers and whistling in discordant chorus with him. He was finished before Francis quite knew it, and the quiet that followed was just as serene. He shifted forward, careful not to disturb the tranquillity with a harsh footstep, and wrapped his arms around Roach. "Thank you," he whispered.

When he retreated from the embrace, the soft blue dark of night had finally taken hold, but the garden was lit with hanging lanterns from the trees and fairy lights around the pergolas. Roach was therefore dappled with warmth from all directions and lighting another cigarette. He held the box out toward Francis to offer one.

"No thank you, Roach. I have no lungs."

He snorted and closed the box to slip it back into his pocket. After a drag, he sat on a nearby bench and waited for Francis to join him. He plucked a couple of leaves from the bush behind him. Francis assumed he would fidget with them mindlessly, so he was intrigued to instead see him retrieve his wallet and slip the leaves inside, where money should go. He flipped the wallet closed before Francis could get a look at it and said, "You know what's the most beautiful thing in the garden?"

Francis smiled and rolled his eyes, fully expecting a cheesy, 'You are,' but playing along by saying simply, "No." Roach surprised him by pointing up into the canopy of trees overhead. "The oaks?"

"The moss. I didn't know Spanish moss grew in Europe."

"Masters Drusus and Keeva had it imported from the new world around the same time that I... moved in."

"Ah, well then they know how beautiful it is."

Francis looked up at the grey beards of moss and tilted his head. He wasn't sure what was so pretty about them. He recalled when the shipment came in and how it was one of the first things he had to do as their slave to decorate the garden with them. "They're brimming with ticks," he said as he recalled the bites and the preventative medical procedures Giovanni had to administer thereafter.

Roach poked Francis' nose. "Precisely."

He couldn't help but smile softly, despite the bad memories that tick bites brought up. "Risible bug boy," he muttered playfully.

"Ha!" He coughed on his smoke. "Well, if I'm wrong, then what's the right answer? What's the most beautiful thing in the garden?"

Francis almost gave in to his inclination to be flirty and dumb by declaring it was Roach, but he refrained and looked around. Eventually, his gaze dropped to the "gravel" path, and he reached down to pull up a handful of the gems. They were a weathered mess of colour, but in his handful were two sticks of kyanite, a polished piece of hematite, pieces of raw malachite and lazurite, a polished opal, an unpolished chunk of labradorite, and the rest were pieces of quartz and amethyst.

He smiled at Francis and leaned in for a sudden kiss. The rocks waterfalled out of his hand as it fell limp, relaxed by the kiss and the feel of smoke rushing out of Roach's nose into his mess of facial hair. He wished so dearly he could smell it.

Roach retreated, still smiling, and Francis was about to say something when he heard a bird nearby let out a wolf-whistle like a cartoon character. Immediately, he stopped time, pulled the flintlock pistol from the holster on his back, took aim, and resumed time to explode the bird into a cloud of feathers and blood with a single shot.

Roach started at the loud cracking sound and the sight of smoke coming from the barrel of Francis' gun, which was in his suddenly-outstretched arm. He coughed on the smoke in his lungs, for he was mid-drag when it happened, but eventually caught his breath enough to ask what was happening.

"*Someone* is being perverse and invading our privacy." His eyes were thinned and scanning the area.

Roach looked around. He couldn't see anyone, and the bits of dead bird in the rose bush across from them kept drawing his attention. "Well," he said as Francis kept looking around, "I change my mind. It's that dead bird now."

"What is?"

"The most beautiful thing in the garden."

He simpered and stood, aiming his gun into the flowers behind Roach, who stood and left that general vicinity to stand beside Francis.

"There's no one there," he whispered. There was worry on his tongue. Was Francis losing it again?

Suddenly, a raven hopped out of a bush of buttercups and stood on the bench where Francis had been sitting. The gun was immediately trained on it, and Francis said something in Italian.

The bird replied, also in Italian, which Roach couldn't understand: "Oh, fuck you. Come inside already. Thyne's been pacing all around and grumbling. He wants to talk to you. Also, dinner will be ready soon."

"What's for dinner?"

"Red wine spaghetti, garlic knots, and some sort of salad. You can come see for yourself."

Francis sighed and returned his gun to its holster as the bird flew up into the canopy. He turned toward Roach and said in English, "Okay, we need to go inside."

Roach was visibly baffled. "Dude… did that bird just say something about spaghetti to you?"

Francis chuckled and rubbed the back of his neck. "Yes, that be Master Drusus. He has animal thralls all over."

The visual befuddlement in Roach was shaken away after a moment of wide-eyed staring. He took a drag. "Sonny and I always wondered if we were the only ones with 'gifts.' It seems silly in hindsight. How many people are there like us?"

"Well, none more than this as far as I know, but that brings about a noteworthy peculiarity. We were unaware of you and your brother's existence. Master Keeva has fathered an innumerable amount of children. As well, he has skulked about since humanity first discovered fire. Further back even still. It's rare that his offspring inherit powers from his Etren genes, but it has happened, exemplary in Neodesha. There's no—."

"Shay has them, too? What are her 'gifts'?"

"Well, she is allergic to the sun but not so much as Master Keeva and Drusus. It only makes her sneeze. Her boons, however? Such be difficult to cogitate. Put simply: she be more physically resilient than her human counterparts, and, according to Master Keeva, she has inherited his eternal youth."

"Interesting." He stopped to let Francis continue what he had been saying, but the pirate was lost in his eyes. After a while of silent admiration, Roach said with a smirk, "You were saying?"

"I was saying what?"

"'It's rare that his offspring inherit powers from his Etren genes, but—.'"

"Ah yes, thank you. I was saying, there is no telling how many people might have them latent in their blood because of someone he fathered millenia ago. And, of course, I had children, too. If they reproduced, it is much more likely those children also have these supernatural abilities on account of my half-blooded nature." They both went flush as they simultaneously realised there was a possibility Francis was Roach's ancestor, but they both also promptly ignored the thought, Roach, by smoking, and Francis by adding, "But I am no physician. We should go inside. Master Keeva can tell you why you have them, I am most certain."

Roach finished his cigarette and flicked it into a rosebush beside the front door as they approached. Francis rapped twice on it with the doorknocker before opening it regardless of any response he may have gotten. He called something into the house in Italian to announce their arrival then gestured for Roach to come inside.

The interior was much colder than expected. It brought a chill down the massive man's spine, despite his thick hoodie. "Fuck. It's arctic in here," he complained under his breath as he hugged himself and shivered.

Francis frowned mockingly. "Woe be to the California boy."

Roach glared, but when he heard someone coming into the foyer with them he wiped away the emotion. It was Thyne, and his immediate response to the sight was a wide grin. He held out his arms to invite him in for a hug, but Thyne's little nose was all scrunched up and his brow furrowed. He stomped up to Roach, who was beginning to understand what was happening but didn't have time to react before Thyne punched him square in his Roman nose. The blow caused his piercing to cut the inside of his nostril, so he was immediately bleeding profusely. "Ah FUCK!" He wrapped his sleeve around it and glared at Thyne.

Francis watched him punch Roach with a bewildered expression and, because he was so concerned with the sudden bleeding and so trusting of Thyne, he didn't expect to also be slammed across the face with a white-knuckled fist. "GAH!" He grabbed his nose with his puffy sleeve and arched his brow at Thyne.

They held their bleeding noses together and watched as he wordlessly stomped up the stairs to their right and shortly thereafter slammed a door.

Arjun appeared in the foyer a moment later from the same direction Thyne had come. He was heaving a hearty laugh as he leaned on his cane and gestured to the bleeding oafs. "Come on, morons. I'll show you around."

"What the fuck was that for!?" asked Roach.

"I don't know, but you pissed Thyne off. Never a good idea. Just stay away from the fireplace when he's around, so he doesn't push you in." He laughed at his own comment and repeated the last part, amused with himself: "Push you in. Ha!"

The foyer was small and acted as little more than a place to store wet winter boots, umbrellas, parasols, and a variety of canes for Arjun. To the immediate right of the front door was an archway into a library, directly opposite was the staircase Thyne had climbed beside a small coat closet, and to the left, where Arjun was standing, was an archway to the living area.

The ceiling in the living area was two-storeys tall to accommodate the tall windows, the curtains of which were being pulled open by Dezba and Perlie at the back of the house and closed by Giovanni at the front. Where the ladies were standing, there was a small platform with a grand piano on one side and a variety of other instruments on the other. Above the stage was a catwalk from one part of the second floor to the other. There also hung a large crystal chandelier over the stage, blocking some of the view through the window for any would-be observers on the walkway, and in the centre of the front area, where the living chairs, fireplace, and most of the gang were lounging, was another matching chandelier. The windows on the front of this room were just as tall as the ones in the back, but their curtains were being drawn, so it was only from recalling the exterior that Roach knew they were narrower and came to a rounded point at their tops.

Having good spatial perception, Roach was aware of the cardinal directions. He knew that the Mediterranean was on the backside of the house and that Rome was on the west coast of Italy (not to mention he had just witnessed the sunset), so he knew that it was the South Wing of the house where Arjun led them next. He walked them through a kitchen, one that seemed humble for such a sprawling estate, and through the kitchen to the southernmost rooms on the first floor: two dining rooms. This smaller one was clearly used more frequently than the other, and it was where Partha was helping to set the table. The ceiling was low, enough to make the tall man unconsciously hunch his shoulders and lower his head.

It was about this time that he noticed how much of this house, from its moulding to its floor to its furniture, was walnut. It was dark, made moreso by all the black-out curtains on the windows, but it was comfortable. The maroon paint on the walls, the simple white tile in the kitchen with its black wood-burning stove, the pleasing smell of incense in every new chamber, its relatively small size for a mansion, everything vintage and antique—. It all worked together to make the entire abode seem much more quaint than he would have expected after seeing gravel made of gemstones in the garden.

Arjun took them to the other, more formal, dining area, and Roach made note of how lifeless the room felt. They must not have eaten in there since the sixteenth century with how it seemed to almost shun their presence and shuffle them out of it as soon as they entered. Back in the living room, now under the catwalk and closer to the stage at the rear of the house, they were walked to another foyer, this time leading to the back porch and gardens. It mirrored the one in the front with its entrance to the library, living area, coat closet, and a staircase to the second floor.

The library was just as large as the entire southern wing of the house, but its ceiling was lower to accommodate the rooms on the second floor. There was still a lofted area in the same place as the catwalk on the other side, so the windows on the rear spanned both storeys like in the opposite wing and were lined with back-less settees and other comfortable places to read. The many winding shelves of books were labyrinthian and impressive, especially to someone as interested in classical literature as Roach. His hazel eyes were wide and brimming with wonder at the sight.

Arjun gestured to a LaPerm cat at their feet and said, "Stella is our librarian. Tell her what you want to find, and she'll find it."

Roach arched his brow at him in an irritated way. "Another of your thralls?"

He beamed, the white of his teeth shining from beneath his moustache. "Sí!"

"You better not have touched my pets, creep."

"Don't you worry. Thyne has made sure I'm on my best behaviour. Even if I *could* use a doberman."

He took an intimidating step forward and grabbed Arjun by his collar, lifting him up so their faces were in line with each other. The vampiric Italian man was unintimidated. He giggled and said something in Italian with just as much gesturing and enthusiasm as if he wasn't being held up by his shirt collar.

Roach felt a hand on his shoulder and turned to see Francis who had, for some reason, been accompanying him on the tour. "Put him down, Roach."

He ignored the advice and turned back toward the man to growl, "If you so much as *think* to touch my animals I will flay you alive and make your husband watch. Do I make myself clear?" He was still smiling and eyed Francis to say something else in Italian. "Answer me!"

"Oh! I'm shaking in my wee little boots." He laughed.

Roach dropped him and looked at Francis.

In Demotic, Francis whispered, "We can talk of it later."

"Oh? He knows Demotic? Have you brought him back already, Androme?" asked Arjun in an unplaceable language as he finished brushing down his coat.

Francis arched his brow. "I suppose I haven't," he replied in the same ancient tongue.

Back to English: "Ah. Well, it's a lovely language. A shame it died. Anyway," he clicked his cane against the hardwood flooring. "There is a conservatory just there," he pointed to a pair of French doors at the north of the library then eyed Francis. "Show him to his quarters."

"Which are his?"

"I suppose he could have your room if you don't want it, but otherwise it's the Egyptian. Thyne said he'd like it."

Roach was intrigued and watched Arjun hobble out of the room and back toward the living area announcing to the house that dinner would be served in ten minutes.

Francis took Roach's hand in his and muttered, "Come with me, darling," as he led him up the stairs and into a maze of halls.

"Is Sonny staying in my room?"

"Likely not, but I would imagine he will dwell within the same suite, if nothing else."

"Oh?"

"Yes. Each suite has a kitchen, a common area, and three to six bedrooms. The master suite is the only one we most certainly aren't to enter and is presumably where Thyne is holed up seething about whatever it is we have done that drew his violent ire."

"Yes, that was certainly odd," said Roach with a glance to the wet spot of blood on his sleeve.

"Here," said Francis as he opened a door leading into a small living area with a kitchen on its back wall and two bedroom doors on either side. "The Egyptian is that one," he pointed to the back room on their right.

"What does the name mean?"

"Behold it for thyself."

He approached and opened the door to see his room. The wood floor and accents, for once, were not walnut but instead an airy birch. The window on the left of the room was large and draped with sheer white curtains. The bed was a double with a canopy hanging over it from the intricately-detailed ceiling. The canopy was slightly larger than the bed beneath it and had two sets of curtains on each of its sides, save for the one against the wall. The inner sets of curtains were white tulle with intricate lace patterns all over, and the outer curtains were heavy red velvet. There was a door in the back of the room to a private restroom, and the decorations all around were mostly fresh roses no-doubt from the garden, red gemstones like large raw rubies, and an ornamental rug of mostly red and tan in the centre of the chamber. He didn't understand the room's odd name until he looked at the right wall, opposite the large bay window, and saw a behemoth oil painting of the great pyramids. He had to take a step back to take it all in, ogling it with his jaw agape. The detail and artistry were masterful: akin to the sort of renaissance art that would cost millions and belonged squarely in a museum for all to see.

Francis came into the room and smiled at Roach's amazement. "Master Drusus is a painter. There be something of this calibre in each of the sleeping chambers. My own depicts a nebula with masterful skill equal to this piece. 'Twere painted for me in my youth for my fascination with the cosmos."

After a moment more of admiring the art in stunned silence, he processed what Francis had said and looked at him. "Where's your room?"

"I'll show you." He quit the room with Roach trailing slowly behind, still ensorcelled by the art as he dragged himself away.

The distance to Francis' suite was wrenching his heart. With every step and every turn down a new hall, Roach felt more and more isolated. '*At least I'll have Sonny,*' he thought to himself, though it also crossed his mind that Francis had only said Sonny would probably be sharing a suite with him. '*Surely, Thyne would make sure of it,*' he thought, then his nose started to hurt again. '*Unless he was too angry for whatever it is I've done.*'

Finally, they were in Francis' suite, and he explained, "I have the entire suite to myself. That yonder chamber were Juan Ya's (my wife), and that one was another slave's. What was his name again?" He pondered. "Nevertheless, I use them now for storage and the like. This one is mine." He opened the door to their left. It was larger than Roach's room and lofted with something like a private balcony over the library. It had glass doors leading to it and thus a good look through the large library windows which seemed to be the only source of natural light in the room at all. His bed was a king with a canopy like Roach's, but where most of the accents in Roach's room were red, the accents in Francis' room were dark blue. The wood was all mahogany, and the walls were painted with intricate floral designs, clearly not a wallpaper because it never repeated and had visible paint-strokes. The painting of the nebula was much smaller than Roach had expected after seeing such a large one in his room. It couldn't have been larger than two feet by four feet, whereas Roach's was damn-near as big as the room itself. He took a step closer to admire the piece, and, as an artist himself, he was yet again blown away by the detail and mastery of the craft.

He took a step back and got to thinking about Thyne again when the ache of his nose seemed to flare up as if to remind him. "I don't know why he hit us." He paused. "I suppose if he knew somehow about what happened last night in the hotel, maybe he would be upset. Did you tell him?"

"Did I tell him what?"

"That we had sex? That might be why he punched us."

"Why would he be upset about that?"

Roach's brow flattened. "You told him, didn't you?"

"Well, no, I didn't, but he most certainly knows."

"What do you mean? *I* certainly didn't tell him, though I'm thinking we should."

Francis beamed stupidly. "No. He knows. He has an extraterrestrial device (I am uncertain whence he procured such a thing, for it was not from me). Alas! There be some sort of 'receiver' in his skull and microphones he can install into others: those with pulses. I admit it is difficult for me to divine, but he hath installed one into me, and he hath undoubtedly sunk one into you as well. He most assuredly heard us."

Roach's stomach dropped into some unfathomable abyss in his gut, taking with it all of the colour from his face and sending him stumbling backwards. "He heard us having sex?" His voice was hardly even sounding, all strangled with shock.

"Most certainly. He hears everything unless he is asleep, and he hardly ever sleeps on account of all the voices from the microphones. An ouroboric sort of arrangement: he cannot opt out of listening, and the device's effective range be effectively infinite, though it does cease functioning within about twenty feet of him, presumably because of a feedback issue or to prevent hearing things doubled. However, I know not why us having relations would upset him." He stroked his scruffy chin.

Roach was too stunned and feeling far too many things to properly be astounded by Francis' ignorance. He fell into a sofa chair in the corner of the room and held his head, his eyes wide and affixed on nothing in particular. He stuttered incoherently before finally managing to look at his bemused friend and saying, "Are you fucking stupid, dude!? Of course it would upset him! Ya Allah, Francis! We fucked up so bad." He moved to stand, but his legs were too weak from shock and fear, and he fell back into the chair, resigned to his fate and holding his forehead. "He hears everything? Are you sure he hears *everything?*"

"Aye. Unless he is unconscious."

"And you've willingly let him put a wire on you?"

"A wire?"

"The microphone! Why would you willingly—," he stopped to let out a single wailing syllable and hold his head again.

"There are no wires involved. It is an injection. He has a strange pen: it puts a microscopic microphone into the bloodstream." Roach cut his eyes at Francis, recalling River mentioning the pen he had been given and told to press into Abraham's neck, shortly thereafter recalling the "wasp" that stung him in Arizona. His brow furrowed with rage and breaths started to huff like a bull that's seen red, but Francis continued without even noticing the upset. "I am no surgeon, physician, nor doctor— at least not a medical doctor, I have some twenty PhDs," he was all too chuffed with himself and trying to impress Roach, "—but I believe it must be injected in the back of the neck to latch onto the brain stem? I be not entirely certain. He learns a plethora of paramount and beneficial information with these devices." A beat. "Your brother put one in Tatum Abraham for us! Is Thyne not the cleverest blackguard about!?" He beamed.

Roach rubbed at what he had accepted as a wasp sting, his eyes blurring with tears. It felt like everything was falling to pieces, but when he choked away the dread and sorrow, he spoke in a firm and incensed whisper, "Show me where he is."

He managed to notice the rage in Roach and was immediately scared for Thyne. "Why?"

"He put a damn microphone in me, Francis! He knows things he *can't* know." His tone was chilling, quiet, and brimming with fury. He had stood without fully realising and was crossing the room to Francis' place with a menacing air about him.

"Clayton." His back was quite literally up against the wall by then, his hands out toward Roach as if trying to calm a feral beast. "It's Thyne! He would dare not utilise the information he's learned in this manner. Not for malice, at any rate. You're his friend!" His tone was shaky and terrified.

"If he's not going to do anything with it, then why did he put a fucking microphone in me!?" Francis was trembling with fear, less for his own life, more for Thyne's, and most of all for Roach's. He was grabbed by the throat and slammed against the wall hard enough that the lights seemed to dim. "Take me to him, Francis" he growled.

"I'm right here. Get your bloody hands off of him." They both looked and saw Thyne in the doorway, his face pale. He rushed over and pushed them apart. Roach was baffled and no longer seeing red, so he was easily shoved away.

While Thyne was comforting Francis, speaking in soothing French whispers, petting his hair, kissing his forehead, etcetera, Roach was taken aback by his own actions. He sat on the bed and watched the other two, waiting, he supposed, for Thyne's attention.

Thyne's whispers closed out with something in English: "Now, you pop downstairs for tea, okay?" Francis nodded and patted around for his flask. Seeing this, Thyne turned toward Roach and held out his hand. "Give me the flask, Roach. Now."

He mindlessly passed it to Thyne, who gave it to Francis. They watched him drink from it as he left the room and headed toward the dining room.

"Now, *you*," said Thyne, his wild amber eyes flaring up like a sandstorm as he closed the door and turned back toward Roach, "What did I fucking tell you!?" He pulled out his lighter and held its flame between them. "You have three seconds to explain yourself."

Roach looked at him with a baffled expression. "I—. I—. I won't hurt Francis."

He hesitantly closed the lighter, his eyes glaring holes through Roach's black soul. "I expect stupidity from Francis, but you? Why would you sleep with him? And what the bloody Hell just happened!? What's the matter with you?"

He continued to look at Thyne with the expression of someone baffled by life, as if he had just arrived from another realm. "You know everything?" His voice quavered with fear.

Thyne crossed his arms and looked Roach up and down judgmentally. "Yeah. And?"

"Everything?" he whimpered, holding back terrified tears.

"For the record, 420 is impressive for only being thirty-two. Is that including the war?"

His breaths were immediately shuddery and hands trembling, but he was surprising himself with how coherent he sounded when he said again, "But do you know... *everything?*"

Thyne smirked. "Yes, Roach. You're scared, I can tell, but you don't need to be. I haven't told anyone, and I'm not *going* to tell anyone about that. Or the other thing. Or the other other thing. Any of it. And I won't say anything aloud— and you shouldn't say anything aloud, because you never know when Arjun is listening in this place. That twat loves gossip." He walked over to Roach, who didn't seem comforted, and held out his hands to help him stand. "Come on, you bellend. Let's go eat."

He let him help him to his feet, but when he was standing, Thyne's hands squeezed tighter. He whispered up into Roach's face, his hot breath smelling of wine and cigarettes: "If you ever put your hands on him again— if you muster even just a *thought* to hurt him— I will burn you and your entire family alive, starting with River."

Roach was wordless, and the fear in his eyes compounded. He nodded just-so.

Thyne stepped even closer, their chests brushing together. *"Don't let it happen again."* As quickly as this darkness had come over his tone, it shifted suddenly to one very bright and cheery as he retreated and announced, "Time for tea!"

It wasn't until they were walking down the stairs that Roach snapped fully back to reality. His hand was in Thyne's, and the smells from dinner were intoxicating. He stopped in the foyer, however, and slinked them into the library. Leaning down to Thyne's ear, he whispered, "Tell me what you know."

He sighed and looked around at the shelves. With his fingers still intertwined with Roach's, he pulled him along and pointed at three famous works of classical literature, the contents of which were well known to include taboo topics. Each new title Thyne indicated was another abyss swallowing Roach's heart. By the third, his hands were trembling, and he pulled them out of Thyne's to hold his spinning head. "You can't know," he wept.

Thyne sighed. "I'm actually genuinely kind of sorry, mate. It's never gone this wrong before. I've never bugged someone and found out anything even close to what I learned about you. Most people have secrets, but most people don't have so many and such dark ones. Not to mention a twin they tell everything."

He looked up through his hands, his grey eyes quivering and blurring with tears. "Does it change your feelings for me?"

"Yes."

Roach hid in his hands again. "Fuck." Why had he kissed him? In hindsight, the outburst killing that broker— the bickering— the kiss! Oh! It was all so embarrassing now that he was aware Thyne had spent all that time knowing his deepest darkest secrets.

But... the Brit surprised him. He ran his hands up Roach's firm chest and hooked his hands over his shoulders. Standing on his tip-toes, he breathed sensually into Roach's ear: "It all makes me want you more."

He was dancing away from him by the time Roach looked up from his hands, his eyes wide with shock. Thyne disappeared into the labyrinth of books and, as he passed by Roach from the opposite side of the shelf to his left, said in a sing-songy way, "Time for tea, love~."

Chapter 33
They Infinitely Echo

Sleep was increasingly impossible. There were times he could shut up his mind and forcibly dissociate himself from reality in order to find enough peace to doze off, but none of his tactics were working. It just… kept. playing.

Over and over

and over

and *over* in his head.

Motya Morozov's skull cracking and brains spilling out.

The sound boomed through his sleep-deprived mind.

The sight stuck in his vision like a spectre always watching.

The memories he had blocked out came back in flashes: Roach wiping the blood from his cheeks like a mother cleans a toddler's face. Juliette's panicked yapping. The body… *floating* its way into the large aquarium as if by magic….

Was any of it real?

He took out his phone. Its SIM card had been long-ago destroyed, but he could access its memory and navigated his way to his messages with Motya. Tears pooled in his eyes as he read old jokes and banter and invitations to things like dinners and movies and theatre shows. He recalled the ballet they had seen last December: *Swan Lake*. It was a Christmas gift from Gennady for the entire family, and Jean-Jacques was considered family enough to have been invited. He tried to recall the Morozovs, and he could image all of their faces… save for Motya's. All he saw when he thought of Motya was his disfigured corpse bleeding out onto the black linoleum in that wretched Desert Mart.

It was the fifth night he hadn't slept a wink, so when he sat up from bed and looked down at his hands, the blood he saw on them was a hallucinatory vignette overlaid on reality. He was too exhausted to understand his half-dreaming state and rushed out of bed to his bathroom sink. He scrubbed and scrubbed and scrubbed, but the viscera remained. The water wasn't even running red. Flashes of his own hands pulling back the trigger and killing that guard in the parking garage haunted him between the unwelcome visions of Motya's body.

There was a knock at his bedroom door. It was quiet, but it may as well have cracked as loud as thunder with how much it startled him. He stopped his panicked repetitive whispers, which he only realised retroactively had overcome him.

"Martial?" he heard Thyne's quiet voice, "Can I come in?"

He looked down at his red hands and hid them behind his back. "Oui," he stuttered.

Thyne entered the room cautiously and closed the door behind him. His mien was concerned as he approached Jean-Jacques and held out his arms to invite him in for a hug.

The Frenchman didn't question the gesture and rushed into Thyne's embrace, immediately sobbing into his shoulder. He sputtered incoherently as Thyne pet his hair, making soft shushing sounds. The Brit managed to understand that Jean-Jacques was trying to apologise for, "getting blood on you."

"Shh. Shh. It's okay."

They moved to a sofa chair in the corner of the room. Jean-Jacques curled up in Thyne's lap with Juliette in his arms and sobbed for hours.

When he had gotten a better hold on himself, no longer hallucinating, he stood, set down his dog, and said in French, "I'm sorry."

"When's the last time you slept?"

"I… I'm not sure."

"What's keeping you up?"

Jean-Jacques sunk into the sofa chair across from Thyne and held his head with both hands. His tone was so low, it was almost inaudible: "I *killed* someone."

Thyne spoke softly but with a firm tone: "You were protecting your sister, JJP."

"I know," he mouthed and wiped his weepy face. When he looked up at Thyne, his big black eyes sparkled with tears. "Thyne… I'm worried."

"Worried about what?"

A shuddered breath. The truth was he was worried because he didn't feel nearly as bad about the stranger's death as he should have. He was far more upset about Motya's death, and before he could confess to his slight apathy about the murder he committed, he instead found himself squeezing harder onto the sides of his head. His brow furrowed. "I'm *angry*."

Thyne reached a hand across the space between them and pet his knee gently. "It's okay. You're allowed to be angry. Let it out."

He stood, his tone raising in volume to match the rage pumping through him. "You don't know what happened in New Mexico. Roach killed my friend. He killed him right in front of me!"

"You're angry at Roach, then?"

"He killed him *right in front of me*," he repeated, though his voice broke. The visions reeled back up, and he dropped into his seat with his hands around his face as he let out a shout and shook his head. "Get it out! Get it out of my head!"

"Have you talked to Roach about this?"

Eyes shut tight or wide open, he still saw Motya's head bursting like a grape. Ears plugged or not, he still heard it crack and pop like a sabre down a champagne bottle. He rocked back and forth, but Thyne came to his side and crouched down to pet his arched back and soothe him again. "No," he eventually managed to answer, his voice both panicked and enraged, "No I haven't."

Thyne stood slowly, bringing Jean-Jacques to his feet as well, and started to lead him from the room. "You're going to get your closure right now. You're going to go tell Roach how you feel."

Jean-Jacques stopped at his suite's door before crossing the threshold, and his loyal hound stopped at his side. She looked up at him as he said, "No, Monsieur. I can't go to him. I—. I'm afraid of what I might do to him. I'm afraid of what I *want* to do to him."

"I think you should go to him. You need closure. You don't know why he did it."
Except... he did.

"You don't know what he'll say. Maybe it was a misunderstanding."

Jean-Jacques sighed and stepped through the door to follow Thyne to Roach and River's suite, the click-clacking of Juliette's paws trailing behind them. Thyne had a key to the suite itself, so he opened the door and led Jean-Jacques to Roach's room. He gestured to the door, and the Frenchman hesitantly rapped on it.

Roach's voice sounded from the other side: "Sonny?"

"It's JJP," answered Thyne, "You owe him an explanation."

Roach arched his brow and wiped the tiredness from his eyes before dragging himself from the bed and coming to the door. The light from the other side was a flashbang as he opened it, so he covered the top of his vision with his forearm and squinted down at the Frenchman. "Yeah? What is it, Martial?"

Thyne started to leave, but Jean-Jacques grabbed his hand and squeezed. "Please," he said in French, "stay with me." Thyne nodded, so Jean-Jacques turned back toward Roach and said in English, "You killed Motya."

He rubbed his eyes and tried to blink away the ache in them. "Sounds like something I'd do. Who's Motya?"

Jean-Jacques' cheeks burned bright and breaths huffed through his nose. "You fuckerface! He was my friend!"

Roach pinched the top of his nose and leaned his head back, trying to think. "When was this? I don't remember killing any friends of yours. I didn't think I'd met any outside of the gang and your sister."

"In New Mexico, you—. You—." He was having trouble thinking of an English curse worthy of such scum, so he spat, "Enculé de ta mere!"

He looked down and lowered his hand from his face, revealing his unfeeling eyes and dead expression. "At the gun show? He said his name was Peter." And a muttered addendum: "He *was* trying to make me laugh."

"Guns show? No! In the super store!"

He blinked. "Jean-Jacques, are you referring to the man who was strangling you when I found you?"

Thyne's eyes shifted warily to Jean-Jacques. He had microphones in both of them at the time, but he didn't know any of this had occurred, for it had happened more or less wordlessly. If he had known that Jean-Jacques' "friend" had been strangling him, he would have made a much stronger case on Roach's behalf before coming to confront him.

"Oui!" answered Jean-Jacques, "That was Motya Morozov."

"Dude... He was strangling you. In public. If you're into that sorta shit, you should really do it behind closed doors, but if—."

He slapped Roach across the face and berated him in French.

Roach rubbed gently at his aching cheek. "Dude, I don't know what you're fucking saying. I'm sorry for killing that guy. I didn't know you two were chill considering I was told the Russian Mafia was after you, and when I found you, he had you by the neck and lifted off the ground. You can see why I—."

"No! I cannot! I cannot see why—." His face contorted, and he bawled. "Why would you do this to me!?" He grabbed the sides of his head and shook it before whimpering, "Get it out of my head."

Roach and Thyne looked at each other, and with a gentle shooing gesture from Roach, Thyne left the suite. Roach's hand was heavy on Jean-Jacques' shoulder and brought up his teary black eyes which sparkled helplessly.

"What can I do to make it up to you?"

"You can't."

There was a long beat of silence wherein they looked into each other's eyes. Roach saw straight through to Jean-Jacques' immortal soul and suppressed a wicked grin at the sight. Jean-Jacques, as well, had a rare glimpse into Roach's writhing black baneful sorry excuse for a soul. It was harrowing, but there was a deep knowing in him that Roach's violence would not be directed at him nor anyone else in the gang. Jean-Jacques therefore felt... safe. He was undoubtedly chilled to his core in Roach's presence, but it was not because he was afraid of being murdered or even hurt. This fear was of something else…. He couldn't place or understand it.

"Get some sleep, Martial."

When Roach released his shoulder, Jean-Jacques could swear a burden had gone with it. The visions stopped, replaced with the darkness he had seen in Roach. It protected him from his woes and delirium. With an unspoken gratitude, he nodded and shuffled wordlessly from the suite back to his own and collapsed into bed. Juliette hopped up beside him, and as soon as she was comfortable, he drifted away into a sixteen hour slumber.

It came upon the one-month mark of May being in the gang. In the time that elapsed, her birthday (which was the same as her full name: May Day) was celebrated with the gang. She was baked a cake by Dezba and given gifts from everyone in the group. Some of their gifts were simple things like a plain blue dress and bath bombs, but the fact she was being showered in gifts at all made her emotional. After some amusing party games, wherein Roach and Arjun had everyone's sides splitting for hours on end, the festivities wound down, and she had a late-night chat with Lanni in her room while the others cleaned up from the celebration. It was perhaps the best birthday she had ever had.

As far as the gang's more nefarious activities were concerned, things were also moving along nicely. New Clear was all but dismantled, and the next target had been identified as Eir Lilac, a pharmaceutical company that Roach had requested they destroy. Everyone could tell that Thyne was growing impatient and would have much rathered go after Maitland next, but when May's research came up with a golden opportunity to take down Eir Lilac in October, it became their main focus. Partha would be making costumes for everyone for the renaissance faire in July, but he would also be making costumes for the job in October. There was therefore ample time for bonds to strengthen.

May was particularly excited to get to know the others better. She was quickly invited to the West Marches style campaign Partha was running for everyone and happily played as a warforged rogue girl named Dancer. When she wasn't roleplaying with whoever was free, she was playing video games with Thyne, getting high with Roach, cooking with Dezba, or learning piano from Arjun. After her first month with the gang, she still didn't know a lot of them very well, but it was the general consensus amongst the rest that she lit up any room she entered.

Jean-Jacques had not forgotten her promise to revisit their conversation after a month, but he hesitated to bring it up to her. It was early one Friday morning in June when he finally brought the talk to her: "May, we need to discuss leaving again."

She was in her bed chatting with Lanni on her laptop when he came in unannounced, so she blenched and quickly shut the computer as if there was something to hide on it. "Hey, JJP," she said with a blush, "What did you say?"

"I said it's time to talk about running away."

'Dejected' was a good word to describe how she looked at him. "But, JJP," she whimpered, "Don't you like these people?" He bit his lip. Maybe he did like them. He wasn't sure. "We can't just abandon them. They need me for the job in October."

He sighed and sat on the corner of the bed. "Doesn't it bother you? They kill people. They made *us* kill people...."

She averted her gaze. Her *Eye of Osiris* had its heads-up display plastered over the left half of her vision, and a text box appeared in its corner from Lanni: ⌈ Tell him. ⌋

She typed her reply with the eye-tracking keyboard she had subsequently opened over her entire field of view: 〚 He'll hate me like he hates them. 〛

⌈ So be it. ⌋

May sighed, closed the keyboard, and looked at him. "Jean-Jacques. There's something I need to confess."

"What is it?"

"I...." She looked away from his innocent face. The airplane tattooed on his neck was so sweet. It reminded her of how he would ramble on about how jet engines worked for hours as a child, passing her his sketches of how he'd build one if he could and confusing her with the jargon. "I— uh —have a crush on one of them," she lied.

Lanni messaged her again: ⌈ You have to tell him eventually. ⌋

〚 I know. But not today. 〛

He sighed and pinched the bridge of his nose. "Okay. Ugh. Who is it?" '*Please, God, anyone but Roach.*'

"Roach."

"Merde." He looked at her. "You can't like him. He's a murderer."

'*Well so are we,*' she thought, but rather than saying such a thing she forced a smile. "It'll pass. But... uh... that's why I want to stay for now."

He stood and gestured vaguely and pointlessly. "One more month, then?"

"How about... after the job in October?" Her forced smile became even more strained.

"Fine."

Chapter 34

Embalmed in Amber
Every Pirate Lies

It was June eighth, and Dezba had made a tray of iced tisane drinks with fresh rose hips and lavender from the gardens garnishing them. They were beautiful and looked particularly appetising with the condensation dripping down the sides of the ornate glass-work. She had made them that afternoon with the intention of combatting the excruciating summer heat, so when she brought the tray into the living room and eventually dipped it down in front of the twins as they sweated and fanned themselves, she was surprised to see them both refuse. Holding the back of her hand to his forehead, she asked, "Are you sick, Clayton?"

"They look good, but we're fasting."

"Oh my!" She set down the tray on the coffee table behind her and pressed a hand to her heart, "Why didn't you mention it!? Is it Ramadan?" They both nodded. "How long has it been Ramadan?"

"Few hours."

She let out a relieved sigh. "Oh, good. I was afraid we had somehow not noticed. Would you like us to fast with you?" She gestured to the others in the sitting area as she volunteered them so readily for a month-long fast without a second thought. The entire room went quiet.

Roach let himself smile. "That's very sweet, Em. If you'd like, you can, but don't feel like you have to. And don't worry if you can't make it the entire month."

She nodded and started going around to the others to take their drinks back. She went first to Neodesha who looked at Roach and asked, "We still get ta drink water an' eat *somethin'* I reckon?"

"Obviously."

"Alright, I s'pose I'll give it a try for ya, Mr. Tin Man."

His smile beamed brighter. "You don't have to, but it's a very kind gesture."

"I know. I know," she said with a weak grin.

Dezba came to Partha next. He immediately passed his drink to her. "I'll do it, too, sir!"

"Thanks, kid. Though, you're also supposed to give up things like drugs and sex."

Partha winced, but Dezba was already setting his drink back on the tray behind her. His beaming grin became forced, and he strained to say, "I'll still do it," as he thought to himself, '*What he doesn't know won't hurt him.*' He would be leaving for a quick job in the Bahamas the following week anyway.

Dezba approached Thyne, who sighed and passed his glass to her. "No cigarettes?" he whined like a pup.

"No cigarettes," confirmed the twins in unintentional chorus.

Perlie was next. She hesitated to participate, but after silently convincing herself that it might be a romantic enough gesture to win Roach back, she gave Dezba her half-finished drink and tried worthlessly not to pout about the coming month.

Then came Jean-Jacques. He glared at Roach's innocent smile. '*Why would I do this for him when he's done nothing for me?*' But then he caught a glimpse of May smiling at Roach and remembered her crush on him. If it ever developed into anything serious between them, he would have to get used to Roach being around, so, after almost thirty entire seconds of hesitation, he scoffed and slammed the glass into Dezba's outstretched hand.

"It means a lot, Martial," said Roach with a toothy grin so big it was closing his eyes. It was rare to see him smiling; Jean-Jacques found it perturbing rather than endearing. He averted his eyes and watched as May happily passed her glass to Dezba.

Even considering how much Jean-Jacques seemed to hate Roach, it was Francis who was the most hesitant of the group. He passed his glass to Dezba easily, but afterwards he took out his flask and looked at it cradled in his hands with a leaden heart and sunken shoulders. He flicked his gaze up briefly to Roach and saw his smile had gone. An entire month sober would surely push him to a breaking point. He feared the rum was the only thing keeping him tethered, however loosely, to reality.

"You don't have to," said Roach with a low, almost heartbroken tone.

"Merde," he muttered, and, with another look at Roach's deadpan expression, he hurriedly gave Dezba his flask and held his head in his hands, as if moving too slowly would give him time enough to change his mind.

"Thank you, Francis," said Roach with his beaming grin returned.

The other four were not present, but when they learned later that evening of the fast, none of them were interested in participating. Giovanni, however, was particularly excited by the feast that would follow.

Ramadan passed like molasses for Francis especially. For having worried so often about having no time at all, he was suddenly of the mind that there was at least triple more time on the clock than was necessary. The days were normal enough, but the nights alone in his old bedroom were torturous. The darkness, the oppressive loneliness, and the manor haunted with reminders of his enslaved youth worked in Hellish chorus to bring him to points lower than he thought possible. There was one night, on June nineteenth, wherein he nearly left for the bar down the street to drink himself quite literally to death, but Thyne sensed his upset and came to his room. He held him for that night and every night thereafter.

It was only because of Thyne's assistance that Francis never once broke his fast. It was only because of Thyne that he was still alive at all....

Unsurprisingly, Partha broke on only the second day when he did a line in his bathroom. He was also a bad enough influence on Perlie to break her vow with a night of love-making the fourth day. She had a cigarette two days later, and after that, they were fasting only from food for the rest of the month. (Except Partha, who also resumed eating and drinking once on board the *Aquillius' Revenge* for a week and a half toward the end of the month). They did their best to hide their drug use and sex from the others, and while Thyne, River, and the painfully-sober chronomancer all noticed, none of them revealed it to Roach. He therefore remained blissfully unaware either of them had broken their fasts.

Of the others, there were a few slip-ups here and there, namely from May and Neodesha accidentally drinking a soda here or eating a snack there. They had merely forgotten they were fasting, and in the two instances each that this happened, they were quick to get back on track and apologise to Roach, who was incredibly forgiving. He reiterated each time that the gesture alone was more than enough to delight him.

July seventh came, a day before Eid ul-Fitr, and Roach took Partha and Francis into his suite in the late afternoon. As soon as they were behind closed doors, he held out his arms and offered them both a teary smile. It was the most emotion he had ever displayed around Partha. "I'm so touched," he whimpered, his voice soft and sweet as he gestured with his arms for a hug from the kid.

Partha's heart wrenched as he shuffled slowly into Roach's strong arms. He let out a quiet grunt as the air was squeezed out of him in the tight embrace. Roach sniffled in his ear before retreating and giving Francis a hug just as tight. When he released the pirate, he wiped tears from his eyes and, still beaming, said, "It means so much. I'm so proud of you both."

Partha's stomach turned. He could have hurled. "Y-yeah," he managed with a forced smile.

Roach was able to sense something was off and said, "Oh, Party, it's okay if you messed up a few times. I'm still really proud and touched and just—." He hugged him again.

"Right. Yeah," said Partha nervously as he was held, "A few times. Just a few…."

"And you," he said to Francis when he retreated from this second hug, "Franky, you've been so much more like the man Party and Thyne always ramble about." He was going to say more, but he decided he'd rather have privacy for it (at least as private as possible with Thyne always listening). He sent Partha away, who therefore rushed out of the room to cry guilt-stricken tears into the arms of the first person he found.

Once they were alone, Roach cupped a hand around Francis' face and said in a low and tender voice, "Do you feel better sober?"

"No," he snipped and shoved away his hand. It wiped the beautiful smile off Roach's face. "I am rotting, Clayton, but I suffer it for you."

His lip trembled.

"I love you," said Francis bluntly. It was the first time either of them had said such a thing to each other, so the nonchalant, almost angry manner in which he said it was both jarring and endearing.

"Oh, bed bug," he whispered, "I love you, too. I would kiss you if I could."

"On the morrow. It cannot come quickly enough. I have been counting the seconds to midnight that I might have another flavour of rum. I have nigh forgotten its intoxicating flavour."

A beat. "You didn't have to—."

"I did. I had to prove myself."

He shook his head. "You don't have to prove anything to me, bed bug."

"Then I had to prove it to myself: that I am not so far gone. Not most days, at least."

They were interrupted by a knock on the suite door as Arjun rudely opened it. "Good, you're here," he said pointing his cane at Roach, "Come downstairs. I need you."

They both followed him, but in the sitting room, Francis dropped himself into the settee beside Neodesha and Dezba, almost immediately entering their conversation about American folklore and mythology.

Arjun led Roach to the library where he found River reading and implored him to also follow. He led them to the back foyer and through a door that Roach had assumed was a coat closet. It turned out to actually be stairs to a basement which Arjun took his time descending; his knee was hurting more than usual that day.

Only after a few steps, the staircase opened up on the right and revealed what Arjun called his studio. Its floors were unfinished concrete with centuries' worth of stains from spilled paints and chemicals. There were empty canvases leaning in disorganised piles against the far wall. Rows of shelved carts and mismatched tables of supplies were spattered about haphazardly, all of which were as stained with spillage as the floor. There were some finished and half-finished paintings on easels and leaning against each other and the walls, shelves, whatever else. Brushes and paints and the like were sorted by colour into messy buckets and trays and other recycled containers. It was by far the messiest area in the manor, even messier than Roach had managed to make his suite in his short time there.

Arjun led the twins to a large painting leaning against the stairs. It was a square canvas almost as tall as they were and sported an ornate gold-plated frame. The old Italian gestured to it and said, "Bring it upstairs and hang it in the dining hall."

The subject was a night-time village on the bank of a river that cut through the desert just under the shadowy horizon. A crescent moon took up most of the canvas, and it cast its light down on the village with a crisp clarity only found in masterful oil paintings. There was a dream-like quality, however, because the moon was impossibly large and looming over the dunes almost... ominously. The twins both found it bewitching, and its dark blues and pale yellows would match nicely with the bouquet Arjun had arranged for the table's centrepiece and the lanterns he had started to hang from the dining room's ceiling.

"When did you make this?" asked Roach.

He stroked his chin. "I'm not sure. Some time in the late sixteenth century. That was the last time we threw a feast like this in our hall. It was for Keeva's mistress at the time. She was Muslim, so I painted this for her and travelled to Morocco for the intricate lanterns you've seen hanging in the dining hall."

"You really don't have to go through all this trouble."

He clicked his cane against the cement. "Nonsense. I have been told to decorate for the feast, and that is preciesely what I'm doing! If I could carry and hang it myself, I would, but you strapping young men will have to do it for me. So enough chatter! Up up!" He tapped gently at their shins with the base of his cane before rushing to the stairs.

The twins carried it together with Roach taking most of its weight, but they both subtly used their telekinesis to alleviate some of the heft it had. Physically, they were only as strong as their muscles allowed, but with their telekinesis, they could each move as much as 5,000 pounds. The more numerous the individual things they tried to manipulate telekinetically at once, the more difficult the process was, so one painting proved elementary in this circumstance.

After hanging the art on the far wall of the dining hall (with much Italian bitching from their lame-legged host as they did), Roach went looking for Giovanni to ask for help uncovering the source of his and his brother's powers. Fortunately, the pale chef was also looking for Roach at the very same time, so they were quick to find each other. Roach's concerns were shushed before he had even managed a single syllable, and he was dragged by his wrist to the kitchen.

"I am absolutely buzzing by the prospect of another feast in my grand dining hall! I will spend all of today and tonight cooking and preparing for it, but I need to know what traditional dishes you would like to have."

Roach shrugged. "I don't know. I had a whole jar of mayonnaise last year, and Perlie made me some Jello."

He winced away with pure disgust curling up his lips. "You what!?"

"I don't really have traditions. One year, Sonny found a box of doughnuts on the street, and it only had one missing and only like two with seagull shit on them."

He gagged. "I'm sorry, what?"

"I know, dude! Can you believe it!? Who just throws away a box of doughnuts!?" He huffed out one ha but would have been quite expressive and joyful were he not purposefully stifling it.

Giovanni sighed and pinched the bridge of his nose. "Doughnuts," he said with a tone almost as if it were a swear word. With an exhausted frustrated air, he took a notepad from a drawer nearby and wrote the ingredients to make the fried treat. "Okay," he said when he was finished, "What else?"

He shrugged again. "I usually just smoke a pack, maybe hit a bong, and eat whatever's around. There *is* an Indian place near my apartment that doesn't lock its dumpsters, so I guess that's the closest to a traditional meal I have: Indian dumpster food."

"Okay, fine. What are your favourite dishes in general, then?"

"Do you have any cookbooks?"

He perked up. "Yes! In the library."

"Alright, I'll go get some and dog-ear the recipes I think I'll like."

"Che figata! Do hurry, though, so I can send the boy to the shops and start right away!"

He glared but decided not to impose on Francis' strange relationship with his former masters in favour of perusing the library for cookbooks. He took his time despite Giovanni's insistence that he hurry, returning forty-three minutes later with twelve dog-eared recipes across three cookbooks.

The chef took the books and started flipping through to the recipes Roach had chosen, growing evermore sick until he couldn't hold back from snapping, "This!?" and pointing angrily at a recipe for *Lime Cottage Cheese Jello Salad*.

"Yeah, dude. That one in particular is my favourite meal of all time." He grabbed his forehead and rattled off a lot of angry Italian under his breath but increasingly loud. Roach ignored the upset and said, "Can you make something for the dogs, too? They're not fasting, obviously, but Sonny likes to spoil them for Eid ul-Fitr."

"You say this as if what you want me to make is any better than dog food! You…," various Italian curses.

Roach laughed. "Also, I have something to ask you."

"Yes yes, What is it?"

He swapped to Demotic: "My brother and I have supernatural abilities. Francis said you might be able to tell us why."

Giovanni didn't use the dead language and said in English, "Fine. I will draw your blood after the feast. Now, away with you." He shooed him with a wild wave of his hands.

In the sitting area, Roach dropped himself down beside Francis, who was still chatting with Neodesha and Dezba. He wanted to wrap his arm around him, but they were keeping their relationship as secret as possible for Thyne and Perlie's sakes, not to mention he still had a few more hours of Ramadan to get through. "Are you all still talking about American folklore? Y'know I saw a wendigo once. And a yeti, too."

Once he was free of Roach, Giovanni beckoned Arjun into the kitchen. He was visibly stressed as he hunched over the Jello salad recipe, his stomach turning at the thought of even just the smells that would befall the manor.

"What's wrong?" asked Arjun in their preferred tongue of Old Egyptian.

Giovanni replied in the same language: "He's absolutely vile, Drusus. Look at what he wants me to make! This is an affront to my kitchen and an insult to my craft!"

Arjun flipped through to the dog-eared pages and chuckled. "Are you not going to make these?"

"No. No, I'll make them." He sighed. "Just, go to the internet and ask it about traditional dishes for this feast. It's been so long since we held one, and I don't recall any. I'm sure Clayton and the boy will eat this slop he wants, but the rest of us will want more civilised meals."

Arjun shook his head. "No need, dear. I bought a recipe book of the most common dishes for it when Thyne mentioned that they were all going to be observing Ramadan. I knew you'd be excited by the feast." A moment later, Stella entered the kitchen pulling a tiny wagon behind her, inside of which was the book in question. Arjun leaned down and picked it up to pass to his husband. "Will that do?"

"I love you dearly, Drusus," he said on a relieved sigh as he flipped through the recipes and saw actually edible meals that would not insult his talent or his kitchen. "Fetch me the boy. He has to go to market." He started to leave to find Francis, but Giovanni stopped him in the doorway, "Oh, and one more thing: find a way to make that cretin suffer for this."

"Androme?"

"No. The tall one. He offends me with these 'dishes'."

Arjun tittered. "I'll see to it."

"Thank you, as ever, my dear."

Francis watched the grandfather clock in the living room, his eyes chasing the pendulum and mouth salivating more with every tick closer to midnight. He was like a dog watching a treat on the tip of its snout. The instant he heard the first chime of midnight, the bottle of wine he had stolen from the cellar and already uncorked was on his lips. He drank its entirety in a matter of seconds.

There was no one else in the living area: the three who owned the house were upstairs ending Thyne's fast with a love-making session, Viktor was wherever the fuck doing whatever the fuck, Neodesha was reading in her room, Partha was working on costumes in his suite, and the rest were asleep. There was therefore no one in witness of Francis refilling the wine as he drank until he had downed three entire bottles worth. He threw it on the floor and let it shatter, the sound of which startled Neodesha in her room upstairs. Moreso than Neodesha, who simply returned to her novel, it startled Roach. He jolted upright in his bed with his spine stiff and breaths laboured. The three dogs who had joined him for sleep lifted their heads and matched his energy, looking around the room for what had awoken him.

It took him thirty seconds to realise where he was. "Alhamdulillah," he muttered as he held his racing heart, "Italy." Aphid crawled into his lap, and he pet and held the quivering dog, planting a gentle kiss on his head before whispering, "It's okay, buddy."

After he and his dog had come down from their post-traumatic stress, Roach looked at the time and decided to go downstairs to see what was happening. The hosts of the house were nocturnal, so it wasn't out of the ordinary to hear sounds during the night, but he had an ominous feeling pushing on him spiritually.

He was surprised to see the living area unlit and spotted Francis sitting on the couch across from the dying embers of the fireplace. He approached and leaned down to kiss him but stopped when he saw the far-off look in his eyes. "Bed bug?" he whispered.

It took a moment for Francis to wrench his gaze out of the void and find Roach's vague silhouette. "A demon," he muttered.

He frowned and sat beside him but didn't argue the name. He recalled how the darkness of the hotel room the night they first made love had affected Francis' ability to parse reality, so he telekinetically added a log to the fireplace. It therefore poured an ever-brighter warmth across the rug to their place opposite the flames. Francis leaned away from the magic fireplace and looked to the demon on his right. He tilted his head. Why did this demon seem so familiar? He took up one of Francis' hands and kissed his knuckles. "I love you."

He started. "You do?"

His soft smile became a frown. "Francis… don't you recognise me?"

"Hmm," he looked him up and down, "You look different than I remember."

"How's that?"

"Well, your hair," he reached out and pulled some of it into the light, "It's much darker and longer than I recall. How long were you in there?"

"In where?"

"Auschwitz." Roach went paler than a ghost. "I thought they would have shaved your hair, but how fortuitous that they did not. Fortuitous, as well, that I was able to save you. If only I could have saved everyone else, too…. Wretched villain as I am. I should ne'er have travelled beyond '45 so recklessly."

After swallowing a cold dread in his throat, Roach choked out, "What year is it, Francis?"

He took out his pocketwatch. "1944. Why?"

Roach cupped a trembling hand around Francis' face. His whispered voice was broken: "Please. Come back."

"Come back… to the camp?"

He wept.

Francis didn't notice the upset, he noticed only the silence, which he eventually broke by asking, "Why did you say you love me? I am not Thyne, you are aware."

Roach pulled him into his strong arms and squeezed, crying quietly into his shoulder. After managing to catch his weepy breath, he started to sing for him. He would have sung his favourite song, but he worried that its context in combination with Francis' dissociation back to wartime wouldn't help. Instead, he sang a song he had been writing for him in secret for the past month. Ideally, he would have serenaded him in a more romantic setting with an instrument, but he could offer only his whispery broken voice. He started with the last verse, unsure he would make it very far before crying again:

Take me to a far gone era
Lost with you at dusk
Broken, reckless, lost, abandoned
A cicada's broken husk
And I'll hold you, and I'll tell you
Things you've heard before
That is, until I'm lost without you
And speaking through the veil
I'll say it with a whimper
Oh! I'll say it with a wail:
'A song that never ends ceases to be art
'The ending, my dear, is the beautiful part"

Francis listened to the melody, but he did not hear the words. Toward the end of the short tune, he was himself again and able to comprehend them: enjoying the poetry in a simple, uncomplicated way. He paid no extra attention to what subtext it might have held and had no belief in divine messaging and therefore no instinct to look for deeper meaning. He retreated from Roach's embrace and wiped away his tears. "Thank you, Clayton. I am sorry, as ever."

"You're drunk already. Can't you see what it does to you?"

He glared softly, but Roach's eyes were pleading and sparkled like little stars in the light of the fire, disarming Francis' harsher air. "I were lost *every night* of Ramadan."

"W——. Why didn't you tell me? I would have come to you. I would have sang for hours if that's what it took. I'm so sorry. You didn't have to observe it. None of you did." He forced away another onset of weeping with a rough cough.

"What was I to say? I am a worthless wretch in need of——."

"No!" his tone was sharp and forceful, drawing a darkness back to his eyes that had been lost in the brief moment of vulnerability, "Francis, you're not worthless. You needed me, and I wasn't there, and——."

"We weren't allowed to hold each other, anyway," he lamented, "On account of that tyrannical master of yours."

His brow furrowed. "You take that back."

"And why should I?" He scoffed. "God. Faugh." He spit on the ground. "Unrelenting. Loveless. Selfish. He will always forsake you, Clayton. Never forget that. In your lowest moments, you will fall to your knees and ask him for guidance and answers and help, and he will throw you into an abyss from which there is no escape— an abyss that will make you understand how long forever truly is, and when you break his rules and find your way out, he'll fucking *do it again.*"

Roach leaned away. "My relationship with God is very complex and personal, and I need you to at least tolerate it like He tolerates me. I'm sorry for what you've been through, but is it not at least slightly divine that I've been able to bring you back from the void twice now? Perhaps your God (or Gods) sent me to help you." Francis sighed and averted his eyes. '*No*,' was his thinking, but he remained silent. "I wrote that song for you, by the way."

Francis looked up, and they made eye contact. He saw the very briefest glimpse of Roach's soul the way Jean-Jacques had, but he was too lost a soul himself to hold the vision for long. With another sigh, he ran his hands through his hair and said, "I apologise. Your god is real to you, as the void was real to me, and there is nought I can say that will dethrone him from his rotten—." A pause. "I apologise, and I appreciate that you wrote me a song. We should both rest."

"Yeah. Come to my room?"

He managed a soft smile. "You would still have me?"

"Of course. You're my little bed bug." An adorable smile. "I love you."

"I love you, too."

When they awoke that afternoon, Dezba surprised both Francis and Roach with a plate of fresh steaming-hot brownies as they came downstairs. Roach took one and ate it in two bites without a second thought, but he realised he had made a mistake when Dezba seemed panicked. "Okay, so you just ate an entire one, okay, sure, okay," she muttered as she slapped Francis' hand before he could grab one.

"Gah! Why did you strike me?"

"If you're going to have one you should know," she paused to glare at Roach, "I was going to warn you both: they're edibles. I made them to surprise you, Clayton."

"Thanks, Em. I'll be fine. It tasted good. Couldn't even tell it had weed in it."

Francis was thankful for Roach's response, because he otherwise assumed Dezba was joking, having never heard of edible weed before then. With a shrug, he took half of one of the brownies. Before eating it, he held it up to Dezba with a quizzical look, as if to be asking if it would be too much, and she nodded. "That should be okay."

It tasted off, despite Roach's assertion that it was good, but Francis liked it regardless. He beamed up at Roach as Dezba left the foyer. "I have ne'er been high," he said with a childish sort of glee.

"You might not like it, but I'll be here for you, bed bug."

His smile weakened. "Oh."

"It's fun, though, if you just sort of," he took a deep breath with an overacted gesture to try and get Francis to do it with him. He remembered immediately after starting the motion, however, that Francis had no lungs, so he stopped and said,

"Just relax and don't think too much. We can go watch something in the living room if you want. I'll hold you to make up for all the cuddling we missed out on."

"It seems unwise to be partaking in such romance in Thyne's presence. I remain uncertain as to why our relationship seems to upset him, but I would prefer not further provoke his ire."

He shrugged. "He'll suck it up. Come on. I want to hold you."

"What will the others think?" He leaned closer and whispered, "We will be scandalised."

He smiled. "You're so cute, dude. Alright, we don't have to if you don't want to." He looked around and, once he was certain no one could see them, leaned down for a quick peck. "To the couch!"

It was absolutely mind-blowing that the television in the manor had access to regular cable networks. Roach had never seen regular cable on a television in his entire life, so it boggled his mind how he flipped through the channels and saw nothing but advertisements. '*Surely May could install some sort of ad blocker on here for them,*' he thought as he surfed the channels. After three minutes of this, he stopped when he saw a recognisable character and gently bumped Francis' upper arm to gesture to the TV. "You seen Dr. Who, dude?" He shook his head. "You'll appreciate it, Mr. Twenty-PhDs. He's a time-travelling doctor."

"That's *Dr.* Twenty-PhDs to you," he joked.

Roach sputtered a quick chortle before coughing it away to avoid Giovanni and Dezba hearing from the kitchen. After ten minutes watching their show, Giovanni came into the living room. "Boy."

Francis looked at him, and Roach glared harshly. The pirate opened his mouth to ask what was needed of him, but he was stopped by Roach's commanding voice behind him: "You call him by his fucking name."

"Mind your business, child."

"Don't call me child, and call *him* by his God. damn. name."

He scoffed. "Fine. *Androme*, I have need of you."

"What is it?" asked Francis with a slight blush.

"I fancy some silphium for this dish. Go fetch me some."

Roach grabbed his wrist. "Wait, dude, it's almost back on."

Francis chuckled and rolled his eyes before travelling back in time to acquire a sprig of the extinct spice. From the others' perspectives he spawned the plant in his hand and shifted to Giovanni's side.

After taking the sprig from Francis, Giovanni walked to the space behind the couch to observe the TV. "This is the BBC?"

"Yeah man, it's Dr. Who," replied Roach as he held out his arm to invite Francis into it. The pirate hesitated, but it was too tempting an offer to disregard for longer than a few seconds. Giovanni lingered, watching with them until the next commercial break, then returned to the kitchen to resume cooking.

After fifteen more minutes, Francis received a text from Thyne: ⟦ **Come to the pool, mate. Don't have to swim. We were just wanting to chat.** ⟧

Francis kissed Roach's cheek. "I will return shortly."

Roach was starting to feel the effects of the weed. He had definitely taken too much, but that was a problem he wouldn't have to deal with for at least another thirty minutes. If Francis had also had too much, however, Roach would need to be there for him like he promised. And there was no telling how much closer Francis was to his peak high because of his foray back in time fetching the spice. "Uh. Come right back, okay?"

He kissed Roach's knuckles, nodded vaguely, and disappeared.

At almost that same moment, Giovanni entered the room again. "Boy, I need m—. Where's the boy?"

"I don't know who you're talking about."

"Faugh! Where is Androme?"

He shrugged.

Giovanni huffed and stormed through the house shouting in various languages trying to find Arjun. When he managed to find him, they were in the library but within earshot of Roach. The television was muted during the ads, so he eavesdropped:

"I need more silphium. The boy only got a sprig."

"Keeva, silphium is extinct," replied Arjun.

"If that were true, I wouldn't have it in my pot right now. Stop being lazy, and go get me some more!"

"It's extinct, Keeva. I can't."

"The boy did it!"

"HE CAN CONTROL TIME, STUPIDO!"

"Then go buy one of those newfangled time-boxes. We can afford one, surely."

"What are you talking about time-boxes?"

"Drusus, you are insufferable."

"Are you telling me to go buy a time machine!?"

"Yes! Pigro!"

Arjun laughed heartily. "Keeva, there's no such thing!"

"What do you mean there's no such thing!? I saw it on the BBC not ten minutes ago!"

He laughed more and let Giovanni drag him into the living room where he gestured angrily at the TV. The show was back on, but Roach hadn't unmuted it. Still, Arjun could tell what it was and doubled over in laughter. "Keeva, that's a fictional show," he managed.

He scoffed. "You told me the BBC is a reputable source! Why would they show this documentary if—."

"'Documentary,'" quoted Arjun through his laughter.

"It has a doctor on!"

At that point, the weed was starting to settle in on him, and having heard the entire exchange, this was the last straw on Roach's hold over his emotions. He burst out into a loud guffaw, doubling over and snorting every other breath or so. No one in the entire gang, save for his brother, had ever heard him laugh innocently like this, so Giovanni worried at first that something was medically wrong. He asked, "Are you having trouble breathing, son?" which only prompted more snort-laughing from Roach. When Giovanni was certain Roach wasn't having a medical emergency, his indignant attitude returned, and he stomped back into the kitchen, pushing past Dezba, who was watching the laughing fit from the doorway with a loving smile. Roach continued snort-laughing for about a minute before Francis and Thyne both appeared in the living room on either side of him.

"You're right, Thyne," said Francis.

"Right about what?" managed Roach.

Thyne replied softly, "You laugh just like Oliver."

Chapter 35

Troubles More Than the Heart Could Hold

Giovanni led the twins to the space between the dining hall and the smaller informal dining room. He approached a curtain hanging on an inner wall. It was seemingly there for acoustical reasons seeing as there would be no window there, but Giovanni pulled it back and pushed on the wooden wall panels behind it. A secret door opened, and he gestured for Roach and River to follow him down a staircase on the other side.

Arjun was waiting at the base, holding a gramophone, and tapped his foot impatiently as they shuffled down the narrow staircase. He slipped behind the twins to climb back up into the manor and, with Thyne's approval, let the antique device breathe music into the dining hall, pouring out into the adjacent rooms pleasantly.

This part of the basement was unlike the part Arjun had shown them. Where that room was small and unfinished, this was a labyrinth of hazy corridors and doors, all with fine wooden panelling on the walls and hardwood floors covered by ornate runners. It smelled of incense, but as they were brought deeper into the bowels of the manor, the twins could catch whiffs of a distinct and harrowing scent with which they were both familiar: death. The source of this smell was unknown, but it came and went in waves, in a constant war with the incense and candles they noticed were lit on various tables in corners and up against the walls of the narrow corridors. After only a moment, they turned a corner and saw a wide spiralling staircase, over which were intricate censers hanging from the ceiling. The stairs led further down, and the chains holding the censers lengthened so as to create a downward spiral of waterfalling smoke that currently smelled of patchouli and sage. The excess of incense was necessary so as to cover the increasingly potent reek of death.

Rather than descending these stairs, Giovanni brought the twins to a door just beside them and opened it to reveal a small bedroom completely devoid of personality or decor. He gestured them inside and told them to, "Get comfortable. Have either of you had your blood drawn before?"

"You said you would wait until after the feast," said Roach.

"I say a lot of things." He was opening drawers and cabinets and gathering medical supplies that were modern or at least more modern than the Victorian chamber's furnishings.

"Why are you drawing our blood?" asked River.

"Also, I'm high as shit right now, dude."

Giovanni groaned. "Then would you prefer we make an appointment? I would love to examine the both of you more formally." There was an eerie flicker of want in his eyes, something like lust and something like madness but distinctly not violent.

The twins exchanged a look and whispered a series of numbers, letters, and (occasionally) a random word: a code they had devised as children that made use of their perfect memories. After this, Roach turned to the doctor and said, "You can examine us, but I'm way too high right now."

He smiled, baring his disturbing vampiric teeth. "Then I'll see you boys here in this chamber when you return from your holiday."

They agreed, and all three of them wound back through the labyrinthian basement and into the dining hall where the others were already gathering. On their trek, River asked, "What's down the spiral staircase?" but was regarded only with a dismissive hand-wave.

After Arjun finished pouring the last glass of wine at the table, he rushed from the hall and up into the second storey to start gathering the guests who weren't already present. Roach hid a small smile behind his hand when he laid eyes upon the vast spread of dishes, but most especially he was happy to see six of the meals he had requested in the centre of the table. He sat in the closest seat to the *Lime Cottage Cheese Jello Salad*, which was a chair in the midst of the table with a window behind it and a slight view into the other dining room. When Arjun returned, however, he pulled a heavy blue curtain across the tall arch between the rooms to obscure the other empty dining area and give the hall a more quaint feel. The Moroccan lanterns hanging at various heights from the ceiling all flickered their warmth beautifully down onto the colourful feast, and the painting behind the head of the table was deceptively large hanging on such a tall wall. With the last of the guests sitting, Arjun rushed to his space between Giovanni and Melchiresa and beamed at Neodesha across from him.

The feast was ready to unfold. Roach bowed his head and whispered a prayer in Arabic, but he did not recite the traditional takbir of eid, nor did he ever recite such a thing. He took particular issue with its claim that there was no other god, for he believed wholly in other gods and merely chose to put his own above them. His prayer was instead personal and differed from year to year. A recurring theme in the whispered words of this year's prayer was his gratitude to God for his newfound wealth of friends. No one heard him praying, and it was quite clear that most of them had forgotten entirely what the fast and subsequent feast were for in the first place. They were all drooling at the offerings and passing food around the table to fill their plates without a formal prayer of any kind from anyone to start the meal. It therefore sort of faded into beginning, and before he knew it, Roach was eating some of his favourite foods, the only other person in competition with him for his chosen dishes being Francis.

But... the high was worsening. It wasn't the first time he had overdone it, but Dezba's ratios must have been greatly miscalculated. Only four minutes after finishing his prayer, he could feel the onset of something he had only experienced once before. It had previously traumatised him. His thoughts were louder than the conversations around him: loud enough that he worried the others might hear them. Before he was completely lost, however, he grabbed Francis' puffy sleeve and pulled him in to whisper, "Bed bug, this is going to be the worst thing that could possibly happen to you."

He arched his brow and giggled before whispering back, "We dined from a dumpster together, my love. I have suffered sea biscuits with maggots and limes with—."

"No, dude. Not the food. The high."

His eyes widened, but he soon after chuckled and said at a normal volume "Roach, my dear, you know what I have suffered. This is pleasant! I am enjoying the potted feeling."

Roach sighed and listened to his own reeling thoughts as they seemed to get somehow even louder. "I mean it," was all he could manage before his gaze trailed slowly away with his wandering thoughts. He was starting to have trouble parsing reality, so whether or not his warning was heeded was something he could no longer comprehend or learn. He stared down and sluggishly formed a horrid bite on his fork that contained a bit of everything from his plate.

Francis watched Roach with a furrowed brow. '*Perhaps it is prudent to heed him,*' he thought as he noticed how deadened Roach seemed. Though he was enjoying the high, he aged his body forward. Because he would usually be able to push past a drunken stupor in this manner, he had not expected to be thrown into the midst of a blackout wherein he could no longer perceive his body or conceive of anything at all. It was indecipherable from the void, so when he came back into himself after what felt like eternity but was actually only ten seconds, he clambered for Roach's sleeve and muttered something in Latin. It caught a lot of attention. He heard Thyne ask if he was okay, but his sentience was being blotted out by darkness again. The panic in his eyes as he tried to focus on Thyne was so palpable that everyone who saw it gasped.

Francis was gone again for another eternity, and when he returned and threw his panicked eyes around, he found Viktor's. "Help me!"

With a wave of Viktor's hand, the high was entirely gone from Francis, and he rushed out of his chair, stumbling slightly, to Viktor's seat where he hugged him tightly and thanked him in repetitive whispers.

"What's going on? Sit back down, boy," scolded Giovanni, "We are trying to have a civilised—." He was stopped by a furious set of eyes from Francis. After a moment of staring him down, the pirate thanked Viktor again, returned to his seat, and slyly slipped a hand over Roach's thigh. The others slowly picked back up into their separate conversations, so he leaned in to whisper something to Roach.

Taken by that very same void of nothing that had taken Francis, Roach heard none of it. Having expected it to come, when he was in control of himself again, he leaned over to River and whispered something in Arabic. River then leaned to Dezba beside him and told her in a low tone that she had ruined the brownies.

"Oh no! May had one, too," worried Dezba.

The Frenchwoman was on the other end of the table, so Dezba hid her phone on her lap so as to not upset Giovanni and sent a secret message.

When the text popped up in her vision, May tilted her head at it and opened her chat with Lanni. May was more experienced with weed than even Roach, so she messaged the AI saying, ⌈ If I start to black out, keep me grounded, and don't stop. ⌋ With a thumbs up and a smile toward Dezba, she was certain she would survive the ordeal unscathed.

Luckily, as more time elapsed, it seemed the warning was unnecessary. She had only had half of a brownie, and she had a higher tolerance for it, so she was giggly and cute as she joked with her brother, Neodesha, and Arjun at their end of the table.

Roach was therefore the only one still struggling as eternities elapsed in the span of minutes. He poked around his plate, and the few times he tried to eat, the food turned to ash in his mouth. Even his favourite meal was unpleasant now. He did his best to only eat the gelatin, but he was increasingly unhungry and unliving. He heard glimpses of the conversations around him, but he was never present long enough to understand entirely what was happening.

After a days-long hour, Thyne said, "Roach, are you okay, mate? Is this not what we were supposed to do for the end of Ramadan?"

He regarded him with a deadened set of hazel-greys that flickered in and out of nothingness for what felt like at least half an hour but was only two seconds before he replied, "I'm just a little high. It's chill. I'm having a good time." Thyne could tell he was lying, but he decided not to pry and returned to a conversation with Partha about their West Marches game.

Another excruciatingly long ten minutes passed, and everyone save for Roach was finished eating but remained sitting around the table chatting and laughing. There was more wine being opened and passed around the table, the act of which brought about a rare lull in the talks. It was in this quiet that Arjun drunkenly recalled his promise to "make Roach suffer," so he plucked up his wine glass, stood, and clicked his fork gently on its side. When he seemed to have attention from all but the dead-eyed musician, he raised his glass and said, "To Androme and Roach, who fuck on the regular despite how much it upsets Thyne and Perlie." He giggled and sipped from his glass as if he had actually toasted something wholesome then lowered himself back into his seat to watch the carnage unfold with a sadistic hunger in his piercing blue eyes.

Roach hadn't heard him, and even with his perfect memory, he could not recall something for which he had blacked-out. When he came back from the dark nothing rotting his brain, he noticed all the eyes on him, and his own widened. *'THEY KNOW EVERYTHING!'* His breaths started to pick-up in pace, but before he had a breakdown for fear that all four of his darkest secrets had been discovered, River leaned in and whispered, "Arjun told everyone you're fucking Francis."

He looked at Francis, who was pale and panicked, then glared harshly at Arjun. He didn't have long before he would be wrenched away from reality again, so he was quick to attempt a retort at Arjun: "Our hosts enslaved Francis as a child," he said bluntly.

This shocked Francis to hear almost as much as it did the nine people who didn't already know about his enslavement. His cheeks burned, and with a furrowed brow, he was determined to make Roach regret having revealed such a thing. He was not, however, adept at blackmail or manipulation. His best attempt at vengefully outing Roach was therefore, "The twins are not human! They have telekinesis and can see perfectly in the dark."

After the poor attempt at revenge, Thyne smiled fiendishly and cleared his throat to draw everyone's attention. He eyed Roach, who was falling back into an abyss and could parse only that one of his secrets was about to be revealed. When he came-to three thousand years later, he saw a sea of disgusted and furious expressions set upon him. Which secret had Thyne told them!? Had he told them everything!?

River's glass shattered in his hand as he shot up to his feet and thereafter pointed his bleeding wine-stained hand at Thyne. A boiling hot rage turned him cherry-red as he shouted, "This cretin has microphones installed in all of us! The only reason he knows about Tony is because he's listening to everything we all say and do at all times!" It was the only time any of them had seen River this enraged, including Roach. He slammed himself back into his seat and wrapped his hand with one of the cloth napkins to reduce the immense bleeding from accidentally squeezing his glass hard enough to break it. He let out a muttering of cursing in various languages as he calmed down.

Jean-Jacques was increasingly nauseous as horrifying secrets continued to be thrown around, so when May muttered in the lull after, "I killed my father," he nearly fainted. With a heartbroken gaze on his sister, he mouthed, "Why?" before Partha admitted sheepishly from the foot of the table: "I use wall-hacks in *Counter Strike.*"

"But you're still so bad," Roach somehow joked, and with that, Jean-Jacques stood. All manner of upset plagued him as he wordlessly scooped up Juliette and left the manor. He didn't have a destination in mind, but he wouldn't return until the next morning.

Before anyone could go after Jean-Jacques, and before the proper amount of upset could be directed at Partha for not taking the heavy moment seriously, Dezba admitted, "I used to be a nazi."

"Me too," said Viktor with a chuckle, "Nurse in the war? Did Franky bring you to the future, or what?"

Goosebumps rushed across Dezba's skin. She stuttered. "That's not what I meant. I was a neo-nazi."

"Oh," replied Viktor with a hic, "well I was a *real* nazi back in World War Two." His German accent was thick and slurred from all the vodka he had been pretending was water. He didn't seem to care that those who didn't already know this about him were offering him horrified expressions.

Melchiresa shifted, ready to shut Viktor up, but Arjun held a hand over his chest and whispered something to the mute.

Viktor continued: "Which reminds me. Thyne served in the war, too. Are you still a meth-head, Thyne?"

It seemed to Roach (who had managed to hear all but May's confessions) that the rage in Thyne's eyes when he glared at Viktor in the moments following was a wildfire hot enough to make the room physically warmer by at least ten degrees. Never in his life had Roach seen such tempestuous wrath, even in the eyes of his victims and his victims' families.

In German and through his teeth, Thyne asked, "Do you really want to play this game?"

Viktor hiccupped and grinned. "Jawohl."

Thyne's gaze shifted and softened when it landed on Neodesha. He spoke kindly to her: "Shay, love, do you want to know how your beloved wife really died?"

Until then, Neodesha had been giggling along with Arjun at all the barbs being thrown, but now her heart was thrashing against its cage like an injured bird. She grabbed at her chest and let out a long breath, as if she had been struck in the gut.

"Viktor killed her," said Thyne, his rage returning as he looked back at the ginger-haired drunk. "He killed my daughter."

"*Your* daughter?" he slurred and chuckled.

"Yes. *My* daughter."

He laughed again, completely ignoring all the hatred around him. Melchiresa was ready to stop him, but Arjun grabbed his thigh gently and whispered, "Let him say it. It's just getting good."

Viktor's laughter became shouting: "*Your* daughter, Thyne?" He stood and slammed on the table, hunched over like a beast as he snarled, "You mean *my* daughter, who you kidnapped from me to raise as your own!?"

Neodesha had been married to Rosemary for over a century, but this was the first she was learning of something so harrowing. She looked at Thyne, who was immediately cast in a new light. Despite the warmth of the lanterns overhead, she could no longer see life in him.

He looked like a ghost.

He looked like a stranger.

He looked like a monster.

All eyes were on Thyne once again. He didn't notice. All he saw was Viktor cast in the same sort of darkness as the day he operated on Thyne in Auschwitz. The Brit stood and slammed on the table hard enough to knock over almost every glass on it. He matched Viktor's hunched-over posture and shouted in a deep gravelly tone, "You killed her! You killed Oliver! Death would be too good for you, you nazi fuck!" He grabbed his steak-knife from the table, ready to throw through Viktor's drunken grin, but a palpable fear suddenly struck him and forced him to drop it.

Starting with Viktor and spreading across the table like a tidal-wave, a painful horrible fear struck guests down. Viktor began to shiver with dread and shrank back into his seat, his eyes on Melchiresa. He muttered apologies on repeat to the mute, but he was ignored. When the fear struck Roach, it was so sudden and so potent, worse than any he had ever experienced, that he was made immediately hysterical. A mad laugh cracked like a whip from his lips as he clawed at his own throat before the high silenced him just as suddenly. It whisked him away again to a terrifying nothingness akin to death. Thyne started to hyperventilate as he fell into his chair, and further past him were all five dogs who whimpered and ran to their masters to cower under their chairs.

It seemed Dezba was the only one not affected by this wave of fear. She watched as everyone reacted to it. Most were quiet and shrinking and shivering, but Roach's hysterics were cracks of spine-tingling thunder in the storm. No matter how much she felt betrayed by him, Thyne's rapid breaths broke her heart. "What's going on?" she whispered, and because it was so quiet in the room, Giovanni was able to hear her from across the table.

He stood, also spared of this sudden fear, and spoke to them all with his wine glass up, as if giving a toast. "There is no good and no warmth in Rome tonight. The wine is unseasoned. The meats are all wholesome. We have not deceived and do not plot murders. The dogs are still yours, and the house has warmed significantly to accommodate your mortal flesh. There is no poison. There are no weapons at the ready. As hosts, we have been saintly when compared to our usual behaviour in this role. And yet, this is the bloodiest of feasts since the middle ages. It seems we are all monsters here." His gaze was on Dezba for all of it, as if he thought she was the only one who would listen. "Melchiresa," he said after a sip of wine, "release them."

A lot of relieved sighs and exhausted postures followed the command. Roach came back into himself from another brief stint in the void and immediately quit the room. His dogs all trailed behind him as he slammed the back door telekinetically after them and headed toward the gardens, smoking the first cigarette in a new pack he would finish before dawn.

Giovanni downed the entirety of the wine in his glass and threw it against the wall behind him before turning toward the rest of the table and growling, "Get the Hell out of my dining hall."

Chapter 36
A Countenance Carved of Stone

Their flight to Edinburgh for *All's Faire* would depart the afternoon of July ninth. There was little sleep to be had by all. The restlessness was thanks in large part to the tense feast wherein harrowing things were learned about each other, but Partha was unperturbed by the heaviness. He already knew about Thyne's microphone in him and had, in fact, agreed to have it installed several years prior. He didn't know Roach's kill count was so high, but he was not surprised or disturbed to learn as much. He was surprised that May had committed patricide and by Dezba's darker past, but nothing overly affected him about the dinner. The reason his own confession had seemed so ill-placed at the time was lost on him: he truly held his virtual cheating in the same regard as the other secrets being thrown around the hall.

The reason the one-eyed streamer was having trouble sleeping (other than the line of cocaine he snorted shortly after dinner) was rather trite: he was worried about the measurements he had taken for Roach's renaissance faire costumes. The day he took the measurements, Roach was consistently busy praying, writing music, going with Dezba on an outing to get yarn, etcetera. Partha had therefore used River's measurements and added a few inches here and there. Having seen Roach in the gym earlier that week, however, he realised he may have not given enough extra space. After thrashing in his bed about it for an hour and a half, he groaned and threw off his blanket to go fix the costumes.

He was sitting in his own suite for the first hour of work, but when he started to hear songbirds outside, he realised how lonely and quiet it was. After taking up all of Roach's costumes and his sewing kit, he rushed downstairs to the living room and sat in one of its comfortable couches to resume working. Arjun and Giovanni were in the kitchen chatting, so when they heard him they transferred to the living area to investigate.

"Good morning," said the doctor, "Isn't your flight today?"

"Yes, sir."

Giovanni approached and rudely moved Partha's face around, inspecting him. "You're high." The doctor's expression was the sort of disappointment that made Partha shrink in his gaze. He crossed his arms and looked down at him judgmentally. "While it is true that Viktor has been able to return you your health and keep it steady, it is increasingly burdensome for him to do so. Not to mention: he is not to be trusted more than absolutely necessary. Thyne's hold on him is gone now that he does not have Rosemary to threaten. We must rely only on his own self-reproach and Melchiresa's fear-inducement to control him, now."

That Thyne would threaten who was effectively his own daughter in order to manipulate Viktor did not faze Partha in the slightest. He was instead blushing and feeling like a scolded dog. With his gaze averted, he muttered, "Aren't you an old-timey doctor?"

"What?"

"You prescribed people cocaine back in the olden times, right? So maybe you could...." He looked up with a hopeful but weak smile.

"The only time I prescribed that garbage was when I was experimenting with patients' lives. I may not always be aware of the modern day's fashion and social trends, but I am *always* aware of the medical advancements of the day and am, myself, ahead of them."

Partha looked away again and, after a beat, muttered, "I need it."

Giovanni sighed. "You *must* lower your intake of stimulants."

Partha maintained his nervousness and his gaze on the fire.

With no response, the doctor bid him safe travels with an exasperated tone then followed Arjun upstairs to their bedroom.

An hour after they had gone, May came into the living room. She was wearing one of Roach's hoodies, which swallowed her up and covered the shorts underneath, making it seem that she had no pants on at all. Partha watched her approach with a thumping heart and lewd thoughts.

She sat across from him and beamed adorably. "Hey! What are you up to?"

It took him a moment to wrench his thoughts and gaze away from her, after which he shook his head and looked down at the costume in his hands. "Fixing this. I made it too small."

"Oh? Do you need help?"

He looked around at his supplies and the pieces that still needed to be altered.

"Uh. Do you know how to rip seams?" She nodded. "Tear the seams out of this one's sleeves." He tossed her one of the tops and pointed to a seam-ripper.

She diligently started working, and after a few minutes of quiet interrupted only by the ambient crackling of the fire, she said, "So… last night was… interesting. I wasn't expecting any of it, to be honest." Partha nodded absent mindedly. "Were you?"

"Hm?" He looked at her. "Was I surprised?" A shrug. "A little. For parts."

"Which parts?"

"Well what you said, for one. You killed your father?" She averted her eyes. "Your brother ran off. You think he'll come back?"

A sigh. "He'll come back. I told him to."

"Will he be back in time for the faire?"

"I hope so. It might help him relax. He's really intimidated by all of you."

"Oh yeah? He's intimidated by me?"

She flicked her eyes up to him and saw his smug grin. With a chuckle, she said, "Don't let it get to your head, kid. He's afraid of his own shadow."

His smirk became a pout, and he resumed sewing. *'No one in this god damn gang respects me. She's wearing Roach's sweater. He probably slept with her last night and told her all about how unscary and lame he thinks I am. The asshole.'* The anger broiled within him silently for a few minutes before he blurted out, "Why are you wearing Roach's clothes?"

She looked down at the hoodie. "Oh this? I was cold, and it seemed warm, so I asked to borrow it."

He rolled his eye and scoffed. "Uh huh."

After a moment, she deduced what assumptions he must have made and saw the jealousy plain on his face. "It was just a quick talk, Party. We didn't do anything."

"It's none of my business anyway," he muttered.

"Well, you don't have to worry about me, at least. I'm not interested in him. Especially not after learning that he…," she trailed off.

"Well, good," spat Partha.

"It doesn't bother you?" She had entirely stopped ripping seams by then.

"What? That he's a serial killer? No."

She laughed nervously. "What?"

He glared. "You asked if it bothers me. I said no. What's the confusing part?"

"But… Partha… I mean—. 420 people? And that's not even including the war…."

He stood and leaned over to snatch the piece she had stopped working on and used his rage to effectively rip the seams as he grumbled, "Yeah. We're pirates. I say it's not high enough."

She leaned away from him and stared into the fire. *'What the Hell have I gotten myself into?'* "W-what character is this, then?"

"What?"

"I mean, you're clearly LARPing right now, so I'm curious——."

"I'm not."

A cold sweat beaded on the back of her neck. "Heh. So you're like a serial killer, too?"

"No."

"Then why——."

His gaze snapped up to her. It was cold and harsh to match his voice as he asserted, *"We're* the bad guys, May."

She smiled and rolled her eyes. *'Okay, he's definitely playing a character.'* "Well, I'm going to go get some breakfast. Do you want something?" He huffed and refused to answer, instead returning to his work.

About two hours later, all but Dezba had come downstairs, and Jean-Jacques was still unaccounted for. Francis' breakfast consisted of rum and a kiss from Roach, but the others had things like cereal and leftovers from the feast. There was little in the way of conversations. Other than an apology from Roach to Francis for his ill-advised comment at dinner, the madness of the night before was left entirely untouched by those downstairs.

Dezba and Jean-Jacques shared a suite, and when she came out into the sitting area and saw Jean-Jacques sitting alone with a to-go cup of black coffee in both of his trembling hands, she sat beside him. "Hey, JJP," she cooed as she rubbed his shoulder, "When did you get back?"

"Ten minutes before."

"You want to talk?"

He regarded her with a vague glance then resumed staring at his coffee's lid as he fidgeted with it. "About what?"

"I know you've been having trouble here in the gang. Last night was...," she trailed off.

A sigh. "It is not mattering."

"It does matter, son. Do you want to leave?"

He looked at her with a pained expression and whispered, "I can't."

"You can, son."

He shook his head. "I will not leave May here with you people. You will make her more of a monster than she already is."

Dezba was glaring softly without realising it. "Son, your sister is not a monster. Neither are you."

"I will not leave her here with Roach." He set down his coffee to hold his aching head and mutter, *"Quatre cent vingt.* Putain." Dezba rubbed his arched back lightly as his mind went reeling. Eventually, he looked at her with teary eyes and asked, "Why are you not leaving?"

"You think I would leave because of Roach?" He nodded. "To be honest, JJP, I already knew about him. I think I knew before anyone else. Except River, of course." She smiled softly. "Give me your cup. Your coffee is far too cold by now. I'll make us new ones, then we'll chat. Okay?"

He watched her take his coffee and go to their small shared kitchen where she poured them each a new cup with sugar and peppermint extract. He tended to prefer his coffee black, but he sipped what she gave him and thanked her kindly.

She began her story before she had even sat back down, recounting the day she had met Thyne, Francis, and Roach, how she had pulled her gun on Wendy, how Roach killed the teller shortly afterwards. Jean-Jacques had already heard the beginning of it, so she rushed through the parts she had already told him. She retold the tale, including their trip back to Compton, and wasn't interrupted until she described the wall of knives in Roach's apartment:

"That is terrifying, Madame. Why did you not run away?"

"Well, son, there was a part of me that wanted to. It helped that Partha wasn't running, and Perlie seemed nice. But, I think Clayton could tell that I was disturbed by everything suddenly seeming so... different. He sat across from me, and in the worst attempt at the Navajo language I've ever heard, he confessed to me. He butchered it, of course, but more or less, what he said was, 'I have killed over four hundred people. Should I continue?' And well, I wasn't sure where he was going with it (and I was also convinced he had misspoken the number), so I let him continue. There was this dreadful sadness in his eyes, JJP. I could tell he just wanted me to understand him. So he went on to tell me about how it came to happen that he did what he did, and—. Well, I don't know how much of this is my story to tell anymore, son. I know you're scared of him, but I think you should—."

"I'm not scared of him," he muttered.

"Oh?" she sort of smiled, "Well, I suppose you aren't."

"He won't hurt me. He... saved me." The word caught in his throat. It was sickening to owe a life debt to someone so horrid.

"And he won't hurt your sister, either," agreed Dezba.

"Oui. He won't hurt any of us." A beat. "But he will hurt others, Madame. He will hurt so much others."

She placed a hand gently on his shoulder and looked deep into his black eyes. "You should go talk to him. Get the rest of the story from him, if he'll tell you."

He sighed and looked at his coffee, pondering.. After a sip, he nodded.

Dezba stood and offered to fetch Roach and bring him to their suite, but Jean-Jacques asked her to send him outside to the gardens instead. She agreed and left, having had only half of her coffee. Jean-Jacques chugged the rest of his in four hot gulps before getting dressed and heading outside.

His head was hanging and hands buried deep in his pockets as he ambled his way to the garden, eventually catching whiffs of cigarette smoke and idly meandering toward its source. The gravel became wood planks beneath his feet, and he looked up to see Roach leaning his back and elbows against the railing of a small bridge. It ran over a relaxing brook under a canopy of sprawling old oaks with Spanish moss speckled throughout their winding branches. Roach's voice was as gentle as the overcast sky when he said, "Hey, Martial. You wanted to talk to me?"

He sighed and leaned on the railing, looking down into the stream below where his reflection was as broken and disjointed as he felt. "Madame Meadows told me about how you met. She said you told her how many people you…," he refused to acknowledge the deaths with that final word, "and she said there was more to the story."

Roach had deciphered by then that the secret Thyne had revealed about him to the others was his ludicrously high kill-count, so he was able to determine that Jean-Jacques was upset by it even before he had said as much. "Yeah. There's more to the story."

"Will you be telling me?"

He took a drag. "I suppose." There was a beat as he looked around and admired the midsummer foliage and fauna. "I should start by clarifying that I've always been like this. Since the day I was born, I was interested in all the wrong things: death, decay, garbage, filth. Most things that others discarded and regarded as worthless were things I found inherent worth in anyway." He paused to take a drag, and Jean-Jacques noticed his hand was trembling. "The first thing I ever killed was a turtle-dove. I was only four. I tried to show my mother, and she rightfully scolded and disciplined me for it. Anyway, that's just the preface, so you know that this next part wasn't entirely unexpected:

"I enjoyed the war. I wish Sonny could have been there with me the whole time, but I had Silvino, my buddy Pio, and—."

"Who's Silvino?"

"Right. He was my husband. We got married in Mexico just before the war was declared, so I joined a sort of unofficial coalition with him to defend the country from my own. In hindsight, it was surreal, but at the time, I was mostly just enjoying all the socially acceptable violence. The first person I killed was an American soldier that had gunned down one of my men right beside me. I took his tags and wear them to this day." He pulled the dog tags out from under his shirt and let Jean-Jacques read them as he continued, "I racked up a hefty kill count during the war and did some pretty heinous shit, but I wasn't a monster quite yet. It was all to defend Mexico from invasion, or at least on paper it was.

"By the time we escaped the war back to Compton with Abuela, I was at 176 kills. All in combat. None of those are included in the 420 number, either. Anyway, bit after that I confessed to my brother in secret how much I loved it: the violence and chaos of war. I… wouldn't dare tell Silvino, but…," he sighed. "My husband was a wily one; he figured me out by eavesdropping or… maybe just by seeing that a switch had been flipped in me. Either way, he told me he knew. He asked me to tell him how I felt, so I hesitantly told him just a fraction of the madness within me. He ultimately… kept me docile. 'If you do any of that, I will never talk to you again,' was his threat, and I didn't intend to test if he was being truthful or not.

"It was his idea, few years later, to try smuggling persecuted Americans out of the country, so Sonny and I agreed to help him do it. He set it all up. He contacted Richard (Partha's father) and managed to secure us some cargo space on a cruise ship. We helped 8,413 people escape to Europe, Africa, and South America, including our brother and sister, but we pushed our luck and got caught. Silvino, rest his soul, took the fall for all of us and wound up in a prison in North Texas for what would have been ten years.

"Being how I am, I used a contact I made in the war to help organise a prison escape after only two of those ten years. My contact, Dale, was also interested in breaking his father and uncle out of the very same prison, so the two of us got together and went out to North Texas. I let Dale do the heavy lifting on the way in, no matter how much I wanted to bathe in blood. God, how I wanted to…. But I was true to my promise to Silvino: I would not give in to the darker desires lest I lose him.

"Well, long story short, JJP: Silvino had been put into solitary for starting a riot. I had a real bad feeling going in. We had found Dale's dad and Uncle Johnny in the regular cells, and after talking to them a bit, we learned that Silvino had been sent to the box over a year prior and never seen again." Jean-Jacques' heart sank at the story and the way Roach's voice seemed to be quavering when he started back up, "Silvino was diabetic, and seeing that he couldn't afford insulin as a slave in prison, I was sending him his supplies as much as I could: stealing, lying, and taking loans for the insulin if I had to. I even mugged someone once…. But even still… I wasn't sending enough, and the prison refused to provide any. When we got to his cell and opened it…," he stopped to suck up his weepiness, "The smell of death is unmistakable, Martial."

"Monsieur… I'm so sorry."

Roach turned to face the brook and wiped his eyes. He flicked his cigarette into the water and whimpered, "The only people I didn't kill in that prison were Dale, his father, and his uncle." A deep breath and more controlled tone: "And the only reason I didn't kill myself was because of Sonny's mere existence." He paused to gather himself entirely while Jean-Jacques processed the story. When Roach started back up a few minutes later, his tone was mostly back to normal: "Anyway, I don't know why Dezba stuck around after I told her that. I can't imagine you want to stay."

Jean-Jacques averted his eyes. It didn't matter if he wanted to leave or not: his sister didn't. Maybe her opinion of Roach would change now that she knew he was an irredeemable monster, but the Frenchman hadn't gotten the chance to talk to her since coming back to the manor that morning. He couldn't bring himself to speak with her after her own confession. He supposed, however, that being able to talk to Roach so easily meant that he should have no trouble confronting May. Surely, she would want to leave now… but… did Jean-Jacques? He felt his stomach turn as he noticed himself actually sympathising with the likes of Roach. "I don't know," he muttered eventually.

"Well, here," Roach pulled a key ring from his pocket and tossed it to Jean-Jacques, "Blue *Mustang* with white racing stripes in the south garage." He gestured with his head.

Jean-Jacques looked down at the key fob with a bewildered expression. He was under the impression that he had gotten himself trapped the same as he was with the Morozovs, so a key to freedom was a befuddling thing to behold. After some nonsensical stuttering, he looked up at Roach and asked, "Why are you giving me—?"

"It's Thyne's car. He gave me the keys. Get outta here, man. It's all downhill from here."

He looked down at the keys again. "Won't Monsieur Thyne be angry?"

"Thyne's always angry, man. He told me to give it to you."

"He did?"

"Yeah, dude." He pressed his hand flat against his chest. "Hand on heart."

Jean-Jacques' gaze trailed up toward the garage, as if he could see it through the gardens and buildings between him and the gifted car. "But… where will I be going?"

He shrugged and leaned backwards on the railing again. It let out a faint creak under his weight, but he didn't pay it any mind. "Wherever you want, man."

After a moment longer of deliberation, he passed Roach the keys and sighed. "I cannot. My sister wants to stay."

"Oh yeah?" He pocketed the keys.

"Oui. She… has feelings for you."

"Me?" He let out a quiet ha and added, "She's far too good for me, Martial."

"…At least there is *something* we are agreeing on."

Roach stood upright and shoved his hands in his pockets. "Well, dude, I think it's time we go get ready for the flight, then. You excited for the faire?"

He rolled his eyes. "No. I do not want to wear the stupid fashion."

"Me neither. But anyway, you're free to leave the gang any time, dude." He tossed him the keys again and clarified why with a cheeky wink on his otherwise stone face: "Just in case."

Roach started to walk away, so he didn't hear Jean-Jacques' muttered "Merci."

———— ∽∾∽ ————

Arjun had made them all fake passports with new identities. Having lived through all of human history, he started to forge documents and identities centuries before most of them had even been born, so he was quite the expert. Thyne, as well, assured everyone that the forged documents would be able to get them to Scotland and back without issue. The only person who didn't use a false ID was Partha, who had sailed into Marseilles two weeks prior. He was probably the only one in the group whose identity was still safe and, in fact, needed to be preserved to help distance himself from the gang.

To help hide their American accents, Roach and River were speaking entirely in Arabic while they were going through security, and that, of course, delayed the process when they were pulled aside for a "random" search. With much bitching while packing, Roach had left all of his knives in his checked luggage, so both twins were let through after a strip search in some back room revealed they only had scars and tattoos under their clothes. Luckily, they were able to make it to the gate with ten minutes to spare and boarded after everyone else.

The plane ride was quiet. The group's seats were scattered and separated from each other, save for the twins, but even if everyone was together, it was unlikely they would have wanted to talk. There were a lot of unspoken words and a palpable tension in the group after the many shocking revelations during their feast the night before. That tension, naturally, did not exist between the twins, who spent most of the flight chatting to each other in Demotic and playing hangman or twenty-questions. Any time there was a significant amount of turbulence, however, they held each other's hands and squeezed tightly, looking out their window and trying not to panic. "Thyne is a pilot, and Francis could save us, too, if anything went wrong," said River to comfort Roach, and Roach added with a nervous ha: "The odds there are two groups of terrorists on the plane are slim."

Despite the worrisome turbulence, they made it to their hotel in Edinburgh intact. Their suite would be the penthouse, giving them a phenomenal view from every part. It was a hotel owned by Canopy Cruises and Hotels, and the six-room suite was bankrolled entirely by Partha. The scent of whatever general cleaner the housekeepers used was pleasant, but when it wafted over River, he held his nose and shuddered. It smelled just the same as the casino in Vegas where he had been stabbed. The scent renewed in him the rage he had felt on that day. "We have to go after them next," he muttered as everyone filed into the common area after putting their bags in their rooms.

"No no no!" Partha smacked him in the head with a rolled-up magazine from the coffee table. "It's not time to think about all that! We have to get ready! *All's Faire* starts tomorrow, and I will have none of this gang business while we're here. We're on holiday. Got it?"

He wasn't a very commanding presence, but everyone agreed and sat around to listen to him. They were all-too-happy to ignore the atrocities they had learned of each other, so Partha offering a perfect excuse to stall addressing the situation was welcome to say the least.

"Very good. Now, everyone take your itinerary. Who here has been to a ren faire before?" He started to pass out little brochures. They were handmade with whatever papercraft supplies he could find on the ship he had worked in June and looked almost like an elementary student's class project. Each person's brochure was personalised and, on the inside, each third of the tri-fold was dedicated to explaining a costume, complete with poorly-rendered crayon drawings.

Roach smiled very briefly, unable to stop it when he saw his rough likeness according to Partha's crayon sketch. "Party, these are adorable."

He glared. "I asked who here has been to a ren faire before." They all looked up from their papers, but no one raised their hands or spoke up. "None of you?" Shrugs and shaking heads. Partha beamed. "Oh, you're all going to love it so much! But! In the meantime, I wanted to stream a bit. Would everyone be okay with playing our West Marches game? I had something planned since you'll all be together for a session for the first time."

"You want to stream the game?" asked Thyne.

He nodded. "I'll keep the camera only facing me, and I'll try to only use character names. Don't worry, I've thought about all this."

Roach raised his hand lightly and said, "Problem, kid: Neodesha and I were heard by all those people on the train to London."

"Hmm. Well, can you do voices?"

They shook their heads, and Partha's heartbroken expression afterwards made them both feel they had kicked a puppy. "But, uh, we can try," said Neodesha.

"Yeah, kid. Stream your game. It'll be okay."

He beamed and clapped quietly. "Okay! Okay! Omg, okay just let me get it all set up!" He hadn't been expecting to actually get the gang's approval for this plan and zoomed out of the room to gather the streaming equipment, notebooks, dice, and the miniatures he had secretly printed and painted for everyone while on the ship. They were all touched by the gifted figures, and Roach even let slip a smile that he didn't hide for a good ten seconds.

Chapter 37

While the Monster Shadows Glower and Creep

Aspyn struggled with the front door on account of the bags of groceries in her arms. She had forgotten that there were servants to help with this sort of thing, so when the door opened while she was digging through her purse for her keys, the bag that she had been precariously balancing on her knee crashed into the foyer and spilled snacks all over. "Fucking Hell," she cursed and passed the other bag to the butler who had opened the door for her.

"Terribly sorry, Miss Temm. I'll take care of this for you."

With a huff she forced a smile. "Cheers, Nero."

He bowed his head and held out his white gloved hand to help her step over the mess and into the mansion.

"Aspyn? Is that you?"

"Yes, dear, I brought snacks for the thing you wanted to watch. What was it again?"

He turned around and spotted her coming up to sit beside him on the couch. "Well, look at you. Don't you just look gorgeous?"

"Thank you, Tatum."

He sniffed the air and pointed at her. With a big grin, he chirped, "You're wearing the perfume I bought for you!"

She nodded and pushed some hair behind her ear. "I am. Do you like it?"

He took one of her hands in his trembling one and brought it to his chapped lips for a peck. "Of course I do, maple sugar."

She blushed just-so and turned toward the massive television across from them. "So, what's this we're watching?"

He took a moment to process what she said then perked up and pointed a shaky hand at the screen. "It's a stream! Do you like roleplaying games?"

"Like in the bedroom?"

He let out a hoarse laugh that closed out with a violent cough. "No, sweetie, like with the dice and miniatures."

"Oh, no I've never played anything like that."

"This is Party the Kid. He's streaming a game right now. It's the first proper one since his last campaign ended. You'll like it, I think."

"Well, you'll have to explain what's going on, but I'm happy to watch it with you."

He smiled wide and held out his arm to invite her to cuddle. She took a throw pillow from beside her, put it up against his rickety body, and gently rested in his frail arms. Nero came into the sitting area about ten minutes later with a rolling cart full of snacks. There was an ice-bucket on its top shelf with a bottle of red wine nestled neatly inside, and several upturned wine glasses hanging below the cart's handlebar. "Would you like some wine, sir?"

"Yes please, Nero, but scoot over. You're in the way."

"Of course."

With a wine glass in each of their hands and Tatum's pet rabbit cuddled up in their laps, they watched the stream and snacked. Aspyn was confused, but she could tell after her first question that Tatum was excited to answer and show off his useless knowledge of Partha's past games and DMing style. If she were being honest, she couldn't care less about the stream or the kid running it, but she found her boyfriend's amusement and adoration genuinely endearing. They had been together for a few months by then, and she had found herself somehow falling in actual love with him. Her initial motives were financial, but as she got to know him better, she felt increasingly confident that she would agree to marry him even if he asked for a prenuptial agreement. Of course, he hadn't proposed and likely wouldn't, but she often found herself fantasising about their wedding.

Tragically, Tatum was unaware of her fantasising and falling for him. He was all too aware that it was only his money that kept him in the game these days. He never would have expected that Aspyn actually loved him, but he was increasingly enamoured with her regardless. She showed a genuine interest in him that he had not experienced in decades. Conversations with her didn't feel hollow and forced, and she was probably the only person he had met since college who was not intimidated by his wealth. She spoke her mind and asked him to speak his. After hearing of what her last boyfriend had put her through, it sort of broke his heart to know that he had cheated on her earlier that year on several occasions. His excuse to himself was that he didn't think she actually cared about him. He still didn't, if he were being honest, but he stopped sleeping around after learning of her trauma with cheating. It's not like he had the stamina to spare, anyway.

Aspyn snuggled closer into Tatum and breathed in his peculiar aroma of cigars, rose hips, and menthol. He was rambling about the last campaign's unexpected ending: "…but I wasn't upset like all the other fans were. Zenryll escaping and devouring the world was a pleasant surprise. Partha is such a fantastic writer, I know he can figure out a way to continue Helio, Roosevelt, and Hector's story. I suspect he'll have them battling their way out of some sort of after life, but who's to say, really? He's so creative, I couldn't even begin to imagine what he might do. You know he's the reason I bought Amethyst?"

"The publishing company?"

"Yes! On account of if he ever does end up writing a book. He's mentioned it in passing here and there, and I want to give him an offer he can't refuse. To have his IP under my umbrella would be a dream come true!"

Aspyn's mind immediately started to ponder how she could potentially secure such a thing for him. His birthday was only a month away, and if she couldn't get it by then, perhaps Christmas would prove easier. On the stream, Thyne said something, and she commented, "He's from London, isn't he?"

"Thyne? I'm not sure. No one knows much about him."

"Oh," she sounded disappointed, so Tatum gently pushed her away to grab his mouse and keyboard from the coffee table.

"Watch this. We'll find out for you, maple sugar." He clicked on a few things, typed in a three-digit code, confirmed something with his cell phone, and a moment later, the stream was interrupted.

"Holy shit!" said Partha in the middle of May trying to roleplay something with Perlie. "Holy shit. (I'm sorry May). Skybox! Skybox, you're back, man!" He wiped sweat from his brow at the sight of such a ludicrous donation. €300,000 and a message attached. "Where is Thyne from?" he read aloud and eyed the Brit.

"The UK," was his droning answer.

Partha smiled nervously into the camera. "He's from the United Kingdom! Isn't that cool!?"

Skybox responded in the chat: ⌈ You know that's not specific enough. ⌋

He sweated and looked at Thyne with a panicked expression, muted his mic, and leaned forward to hide his mouth from the camera: "Thyne, give him a more specific answer."

"Why?"

"He just gave me €300,000 to find out."

"So? I'll give you double to tell him to mind his fucking business."

Partha made a pained whining noise like an injured animal. "Please, Thyne."

He scoffed. "Fucksake. Unmute." When the mic was back on, Thyne answered the question with an irritated tone, "I'm from the London underground."

Partha arched his brow at his friend but blinked away the confusion and forced a smile at the camera. "He's homeless…," he clarified.

"Oh, that's awful!" said Aspyn, "Can't we do something, Tatum?"

He pursed his lips. "I suppose. If it will make you happy, maple sugar." He typed another message and attached another €300,000 to it: ⌈ House him immediately. ⌋

"Y-yes sir!" said Partha with a panicked nod.

The game continued, but Partha was more nervous than usual as he feared the powerful anonymous donor would make more demands of him. His gaze was flicking down to the chat a lot, and his anxiety was contagious. The game was made less fun for it, and when Dezba accidentally called Perlie by her real name, rather than her character's, Partha shortly thereafter made an excuse to end the stream.

When Aspyn heard the name, she sat upright and pointed at the screen. "I knew she sounded familiar! I met that woman at the pub just down the bend. She said her name was Perlie Moon."

"Oh, you did? Well, I've never seen most of the people from that stream, so I don't know much about her. Should I try messaging Partha to ask about her?"

She scoffed. "No thank you. She was terribly rude."

"Oh," he frowned, "I'm sorry to hear that, maple sugar." He took out his phone to research her name.

Aspyn watched him for a moment before questioning, "Why don't you have an *Eye of Osiris*, honey?"

"Aspyn, sugar, don't ever get one of those, okay?"

She tilted her head. "Why not?"

"They are my ultimate protection against assassination."

"How so?"

"You've seen how I check my sugars and take my pills in the mornings?" She nodded. "Well, another thing I do after all that medical stuff is activate the dead man's switch for the day. If my heart stops for longer than five minutes, everyone with an *Eye of Osiris* device will be instantly killed."

She went pale. "You what?"

He laughed one ha and rustled her wavy auburn hair. "You're cute, maple. I have to activate it each morning, but it only lasts for twelve hours before I need to give it time to rest or risk it burning out my heart itself. The doctors have been working on a newer model, though, which will hopefully never need to ever be powered down. We'll get it for you, if we ever go public with our relationship."

She sputtered incoherently until she managed to ask, "How does it kill them?

How has no one found the code for this?" A nervous ha. "Are you taking the piss?"

He shook his head. "Dead serious, sugar. I'm a very important man. Lots of people want me dead. It only makes sense to have precautions in place. I don't know much about computers, but from what my people tell me, it's disguised as junk code or obfuscated or something." He shrugged. "They said even if someone found it, it's not like it says 'run the kill code' or something. It just runs a load of functions at once."

"And how would it kill them?"

"The implant on their frontal lobes would overheat and explode. I've seen demonstrations. It looks like a bullet to the forehead."

She dry swallowed and whispered, "Demonstrations, Tatum?"

"Oh, sugar," he pulled her in and pet her, "Don't look so scared of me, please."

She quivered in his arms and closed her eyes tight enough that she might shut out the entire world.

Once the stream was offline, Partha held his spinning head and apologised to everyone for the strangeness. "Skybox scares the shit out of me. He knew my full name without me ever telling anyone. He found out where my father and I live in Bermuda and privately messaged me my own address. I don't know why. He never threatened to use it. He's also donated over two million Euros to me at this point. I think he just wants to show me that he's powerful and knows shit." He sighed. "I don't know. He seems like a mega-fan. If I have a stalker, it's definitely him."

Dezba was closest to Partha and pet his back gently. "It's okay, son. We'll protect you."

"Why have I never heard about these private messages from him?" snipped Thyne, "I thought he was no more than a fan with deep pockets." He kept mum to all he had just learned with the microphone River had installed in Tatum Abraham. Truth be told: he hadn't fully processed what he had heard of the dead man's switch and how Tatum's girlfriend knew Perlie and divulged her name to him. The only thing he knew for certain in the immediate aftermath was that Abraham was Skybox, which was in itself a harrowing enough revelation. As the rest of the information started to process, he held his head, mirroring Partha's posture, and muttered, "This is a threat to everything we're doing."

"I know," Partha whimpered, "I know. I'm sorry, Thyne. I've tried my best to keep him from you."

"Be easy with him, Thyne," cooed Dezba, "It's vacation time, like he said. Unless we all want to unpack what happened at that feast?" she glared around the room. When no one seemed interested in discussing such a thing, she nodded. "That's what I thought. So leave him alone. Someone order some take-out, Roach play us something on your harmonica, and we'll relax for a bit before continuing the session off-stream. Okay?" Vague nods preceded a quiet blues melody on Roach's harmonica.

They ordered liquors with room-service and everyone, especially Thyne, was getting drunk as they ate their Indian food and played the game. In the end, they stayed up far too late for their own good, Partha not calling an end to the session until four in the morning, but he made sure everyone knew that they would still be waking up early to get into costume and leaving for the faire "by nine at the absolute latest."

During the few hours of restlessness in his and River's room, Roach was longing for Francis. His eyes kept trailing to the door. River was asleep and only groaned when he tried to wake him, so, after finishing what remained of his gin, Roach stood and moved with a surprising amount of stealth and grace despite his size and drunkenness to Francis and Thyne's room. He knocked lightly on the door and heard no response, so he peered inside.

"Roach?" whispered Francis as he sat up.

"Is Thyne awake?" He shook his head. The room was dark, but he knew Roach could see him, and he didn't want to wake his friend. Roach tip-toed to Francis and leaned over to whisper in his ear: "I want you."

He smiled all drunkenly and shimmied out of the bed, doing everything in his power not to disturb Thyne (even quite literally using his power). Thyne was a light sleeper, so he stirred, but being drunk and so constantly sleep deprived meant that he was only able to parse that Francis was standing and nothing more than that before his dreams whisked him away again.

Once they were in the hall, Roach pinned Francis gently against the wall and kissed him tenderly. Their tongues were intertwined for a while before Roach needed to retreat to catch his breath, and Francis whispered, "Where will we do it?"

He looked at Francis' pocketwatch. It was six in the morning. Partha had said he would be awake by six-thirty, so Roach dragged Francis to his and River's room and closed the door silently behind him. "Sonny sleeps like the dead," he said before they resumed kissing, this time against the door.

Even with how heavy a sleeper River was, they were still as quiet as possible as they finally fell onto the bed and started peeling clothes off of each other. River wouldn't wake, but Roach was hyper-aware of the microphone in him. He didn't want to wake Thyne, and he especially didn't want to wake Thyne with the sounds of fucking his best friend for the sixth time. Anything that was said was spoken in Demotic: a language Thyne didn't know but the lovers did.

When he was ready to return to his room, Francis stopped time to ensure he was especially silent, but when he opened the door he saw Thyne sitting up and looking at his phone. He dressed himself and climbed into the bed behind Thyne. Maybe he hadn't noticed he was missing…

When time resumed, Thyne was silent for a while. Francis was foolish enough to think that maybe he was right: maybe Thyne hadn't noticed.

"Did you two have fun?" he muttered. It sounded like he'd been crying.

"Oh," he laughed nervously, "you're awake."

His tone was deathlike and dreary. "Party's alarm went off at 6:30 and the little blighter didn't turn it off for four entire minutes."

Francis sighed and sat up to pet Thyne's back. "I apologise. I know you fancy Clayton. The feeling is mutual between the twain of you. I am unsure if you were aware of such a thing."

He eyed him like a corpse. "Francis, you're the dumbest twat I've ever met." And with that he turned his attention back to his phone where he was mindlessly scrolling through a long text from Partha in the group chat about the faire.

"No no! He does fancy you! I swear it." Thyne exhaled a breathy chuckle, one wet with malaise, and shook his head dismissively. "We will terminate the relationship if it pleases." Thyne only sighed. "I will terminate it post haste." He took out his phone to text Roach, but Thyne put his hand over Francis' to stop him.

His eyes were still dead, and the dark circles beneath them were starkly visible even in the dimly lit room. "Don't let me come between you. He deserves someone like you."

Francis read this as an insult to the both of them and sagged his shoulders. "A drunk idiot madman, you mean."

"You say that like I don't have feelings for either of you."

Their conversation was rudely interrupted by Partha bursting into the room sniffling and saying with a sing-songy tone, "Rise and shine, sleeping beaut—. Oh you're both awake already. Well, get dressed! Get ready! Franny, go buy us breakfast from somewhere in town."

Thyne sighed and stood to go find his adorable brochure and start digging through his bag for his costume. As Partha left to go bother Perlie and Dezba in their room, Francis disappeared, having gone downtown to get breakfast.

Everyone was in costume by 8:45 and well-fed, save for Roach. He had eaten the leftovers Neodesha had accidentally left out on the counter the night before, but he continued to refuse his costume.

'*Time for the puppy-dog-eyes*,' thought Partha, '*…I mean eye.*' After gathering up the pieces of Roach's first costume, he found him in his pyjamas digging through the trash. Partha turned around to rub his eye, making it big and watery when he turned back, looked up at Roach, and begged, "Pretty please. I worked so hard on the costumes, and there's actual mediaeval armour in one of yours from when Giovanni was a real-life knight and lord, and everyone else is all dressed up already, even River, and you'll look so pretty and nice, and—."

Roach groaned. "God dammit, kid, just give me the costume."

He perked up and shoved the pile of fabric and accessories into Roach's chest. One of the pieces almost fell into the bin, but Partha snatched it out of the air and set it carefully atop the mountain of clothes. "Thank you, sir, but hurry up, please! We have to leave asap!"

Roach dragged his feet to his and River's room where he was going to change, but after seeing all the pieces, he opened his door and beckoned Partha to it. Once the kid was in the doorway with his nervous little grin, Roach let on a soft glare.

"What?" Partha eyed the pile of clothes in Roach's arms, and his confusion became flirtatiousness. He purred, "I can help you get dressed if you need."

"Party, where's the top?"

He arched his brow and tilted his head. "Aren't *you* the top, sir?"

"I'm not going shirtless." The outfit was too revealing to be halal. Noticing that, he tried not to also notice his hangover and therefore the forbidden behaviour from the prior night.

"Didn't you see the brochure, silly? You'll have a cloak but no shirt. Trust me, you'll thank me later, it gets really hot."

Roach shoved the costume into Partha's chest so hard he nearly fell backwards. When he regained his balance, he saw Roach was already closing the door to the balcony behind him and lighting a cigarette. Partha rushed after him and tried the puppy-dog look again, but Roach was avoiding eye-contact. "Please, sir! I spent so long on all the costumes…. I'll give you a magic cloak to match it in the game~." He glared, but Partha's adorable pleading was melting his heart, so he turned away again and smoked. The kid looked at the time on his phone then back to Roach. "Please please *please*, sir. We only have ten minutes until we have to leave or we'll miss the joust!"

He sighed out a huge cloud of smoke and turned toward Partha. "Aren't you scared of me? Didn't you hear Thyne? He wasn't lying, kid. I've killed damn-near 600 people."

"Oh, yes sir, I heard him. I believe it, and I'm scared as Hell of you, but I know you have a big heart in there somewhere. First time we met was when you were risking everything to save a bunch of strangers from persecution and probably camps. I know you've saved River's life a lot, and I know you'd save mine if it really came down to it. You don't want to kill me over this silly costume. And if you do, then you won't. And if you will, then I probably deserve it." He sighed and slouched his shoulders, nearly dropping the costume as he relaxed his arms. "I just want to have a good time with my friends before we have to get back to all the serious stuff."

After a pensive drag, he sighed again and held out his hand wordlessly. Partha perked up and threw the costume vaguely in his direction. As Roach caught its pieces telekinetically, Partha left the balcony with a quick, "Thank you!"

───※───

While they were waiting in a relatively short line to enter the faire, Thyne's phone rang. He answered, and the subsequent conversation was had in Russian:

"Hello?" answered Thyne.

"Privyet. Have you found my engineer yet?"

It only took a glance to Jean-Jacques for panic to strike across his face. He wanted to ask if it was Grisha, but he knew also that speaking aloud would potentially be heard over the phone. There was some worry in his throat that Thyne would sell him out, so he was surprised to hear him say, "No, I haven't found him, and I had to leave the states."

"God dammit. How did you let him get away from you? And where is my fucking plane!? The *Mosquito*."

"I didn't lock him up like an animal, Grisha. It's not my fault he wanted to run." Jean-Jacques' expression was softened by Thyne's bitter tone spitting at his former captor. "Your plane is in London. I was finishing up getting it refurbished just last week," he lied, "I'll send you an address and date to meet up for retrieval."

"Bring it to America, Chamberlain. I can't leave the country."

"Hm. What a shame."

"Fuck you. Do you really want the Russian mafia after you?"

"Oh, so you have people here?" His tone was mocking and irritated. "Great, then send them to the address I'll message you on the date I say, and if one of them can fly an antique plane, you'll have it in the states no problem, no?"

Grisha huffed angrily at the logic. "Fine. I will send someone, but you owe me extra for losing my mechanic."

"I don't owe you shit, Morozov, but, as a show of good faith, I'll tell you about the letter he left in my plane."

"You asshole! Why didn't you mention it before!?"

Thyne ignored the indignation and looked absent-mindedly at his manicure as he feigned reading the letter aloud: "It says, 'Dear Grisha. I am sorry to have to leave you like this, but I'm afraid I must take this golden opportunity. Mr. Chamberlain's hangar is far enough from civilization that I can finally flee without fear of your men finding me, and there's an old crop duster in here I've been fixing instead of his jet. I'll miss you (somehow). I'll miss you all, but I can't stay trapped forever. I have a family who needs me, just like you have a family who needs you. I'll be going north. Maybe we'll meet again one day, but until then, I bid you as much fortune as you deserve. Signed, Jean-Jacques Paul Martial.'"

Grisha took a moment to process the words. "JJP can fly planes?"

"I guess so. The crop duster was gone when I came back to the hangar for a check-up on the jet, and my engine was entirely detached."

The mafioso pondered. "You found another mechanic to fix your plane?"

Thyne went pale. '*Fuck*,' he thought as his wide-eyed gaze scanned the faces around him. "Yes, of course," he replied after a beat, somehow sounding calm. His gaze was locked with River's. "He's here with me right now. Let me get him." He pulled the phone away from his face and covered the receiver to whisper to River, "You're the mechanic who fixed my plane after Jean-Jacques ran off."

"Alright, hand me the phone." Once he had it, he greeted Grisha in English.

"Hyello, you are plane mechanic?"

"I am. Why?"

"Tell your boss you work for me now."

He was expecting to have to bullshit his way through some mechanical jargon, so with a chuckle he said, "Why the fuck would I do that?"

"Because if you don't come work for me, I'll send my people to kill you."

"You don't even know my name, dude."

"Well, what is name?"

He stifled a laugh and said flatly, "Rumplestiltskin."

Grisha scoffed. "Just tell Chamberlain that if you come work for the Morozovs, we will be even."

"What's in it for me? Make me an offer, asshole."

He was audibly frustrated when he spat, "Millions per year."

"How many millions?"

"Five. Now, give phone back to Chamberlain, so I can tell him news."

He laughed and passed the phone back but not before putting it on speaker. Unfortunately, they reverted to Russian, so River lost interest in the conversation:

"Your mechanic friend needs breaking. Give him to me, and I won't send the mafia after you."

A chill crept across Thyne's skin, and he looked pitifully at Jean-Jacques. His tone was harsh but with the slightest hint of sorrow: "Send whoever you want after me, Grisha. I'm not a slaver. And even if I did own him like you seem to think I do, I wouldn't give him to you."

They were speaking of River, and Jean-Jacques knew as much having witnessed the entire exchange and now able to hear Grisha on the other line, but Thyne's words felt personal. He held his aching heart and nervous stomach. His two minds went to war with each other. Stay or go? Staying meant continuing to enable these horrible people's endeavours. Thyne kidnapped his own daughter, for fuck's sake! Or rather, someone else's daughter... but that someone else was a nazi.... Did that make it okay? *'He saved my life.... But he's also the one who sent Roach with me to that super store. He knew Roach was a monster, didn't he? He must have known he would kill Motya. But, oh, how could he have known!?'* He held his head and ignored the close of Thyne's conversation with Grisha. Their hands were stamped as they entered the faire, but he didn't perceive any of it. His gaze was lazy on the passing dirt as his body pulled him along. *'Where will we go?'* he wondered with a sorrowful look at his sister. *'She killed father.... Do I... even want her to come with me?'* That the thought crossed his mind made him nauseous.

While Jean-Jacques was having an internal crisis, Partha passed out stacks of cash from his satchel. He gave each of them €5,000 from a total of €50,000 he had withdrawn from his bank account in several transactions over the course of June.

"Much appreciated," said Neodesha between sneezes under the blaring sun, "Y'all think they'll have parasols for lil ol' me?"

Partha beamed. "Yeah probably! I was going to try and split away in case I get recognised, but I can help you find one first."

"Should we divide into groups, then?" asked May.

"Yeah, sure! How about...," he stroked his scruffy chin, "Thyne and Franky you two are joined at the hip so might as well keep it that way. The twins, too. Perlie and Dezba, you guys seem to be mates. I'll go help Neodesha find a parasol— er," he bit his lip, "That was an oversight on my part. Sorry Shay."

After another three sneezes she rubbed her sniffly nose and smiled weakly. "It's quite alright, partner."

He beamed again. "So why don't you two— JJP and May —come with us so Shay won't be alone once she has the umbrella?" There were a few nodding heads, so Partha continued: "We'll meet up at the jousting arena at noon then get lunch together. Alright, hands in!" He held his hand into the middle of them and gestured with his other arm to try and form a tight circle with the others. Roach was the first to put his hand on Partha's, which brought a cute smile from the little nerd. Thyne and River's hands fell into the circle with eye-rolls from their owners. Dezba excitedly joined, followed by May, then a reluctant hand from Perlie. After another sneeze into her arm, Neodesha's hand was added, followed by Francis after her imploring him to join.

It took them calling his name four times for Jean-Jacques to be wrenched away from his reeling thoughts. He noticed them all looking at him with their hands in a circle and blushed. "Sorry," he mumbled and added his hand to the top of the pile. He wasn't sure what was going on or why he was holding €5,000, but he tried his best to seem present.

"Alright," said Partha with his big white smile still shining bright, "'Friendship' on three! Ready? One. Two. Friendship!"

The only ones who did not say the word in chorus with him were Perlie and River. Roach rustled his hair and called him adorable, then the group started to separate. Thyne grabbed Francis by his wrist and immediately bolted, leaving a small plume of dust on the ground where he and his time-travelling friend had been standing.

Chapter 38

The Ramping Dragon of Laughter and Wrath

Where the others had several things to consider after the revealing outbursts at the feast, Perlie had truly only learned one new thing that bothered her. She already knew about Roach and in fact had recently learned the last of his darkest secrets: nothing could surprise her about him anymore. She didn't know about Partha cheating at video games, but she could not have cared any less about it. Thyne kidnapping a child was upsetting to learn, but when she found out why and from whom, she sympathised with him and pondered if she may have done the same.

Truly, the only thing that upset her was learning that there had been a microphone implanted in her and everyone else present. After pondering it on the flight to Scotland, the bitterness she felt for having been bettered as a spy was overshadowed by admiration and practical thoughts of how to use such a technology. Since the dinner, she had learned that River had put one of these microphones in Tatum Abraham himself. With a text to Thyne that very same morning, she learned he also had one in Grisha Morozov: Jean-Jacques' former boss and a son of Gennady Morozov. On the train ride to the faire, she had messaged her father about it and suggested he consider getting one of Thyne's microphones installed in him willingly. It was late in Korea, so he was likely asleep, thus she was returned to the present and stifled an impressed grin as she listened to Thyne's conversation with Grisha.

She was generally of the mind that the faire would be fun. Her fringed wide-brimmed hat matched her black dress and gave her an ethereal sort of look she found flattering. The way the hat obscured her face had her feeling confident and mysterious in an attractive way. It was arguable that her costume did not evoke an older era at all and rather gave her a ghostly fantastical appearance. They had already seen someone dressed like a steampunk style robot and another with fairy wings, though, so her trust that Partha knew what he was doing was not unwarranted. It was for all these reasons she was beaming by the time he started passing out money. "Thank you, wangjanim," she cooed when he stealthily passed her an extra €3,000 with a flirty wink.

She took a deep breath and basked in the moment. The sun was bright and pleasant. The air was perfectly humid and carried music on its fresh breezes. The laughter from passing groups of friends and children playing in the distance reminded her of happy memories in both America and Korea. The sweet scents of caramel and fried dough permeated the warm air and put even more light in her happy heart: a heart which skipped a beat with every glance to Partha. Today would be the day: she would get him alone somewhere romantic and tell him that she had fallen in love with him.

Before their first night together, her gaze was usually fixated on one of the twins, but by then she only had eyes for Partha. It had started only as lust— he was an amazing lover —but she could no longer deny the butterflies he stirred up in her stomach or how her name on his lips was the sweetest sound in the world. Sweeter, in fact, than any song Roach had ever written for her.

Doubt crept in, however. The butterflies became a murder of crows, stirring her up with nervous sickness, when he dismissively paired her off with Dezba to explore the faire. She hadn't expected the group to split up at all, and before she knew it, the only person left beside her was her elderly friend. Thankful that her hat obscured her face now more than ever, she offered a quick grin to Dezba and managed to sound okay when she said, "We can go wherever you want."

Dezba sensed something wrong, but she didn't pry and took Perlie's hand in hers to walk them around aimlessly. Like her younger friend, she had already mentally processed all the madness from the feast. Roach had told her about his murderous ways in Compton, and as a former neo-nazi, she was empathetic to both Viktor and Thyne's plights. At first, she didn't love the idea that Thyne could always hear her, but the more she thought about it, the more it comforted her. If Thyne could always hear them, and Francis could be anywhere at a moment's notice, the two of them combined were a constant boon of protection on the gang. It may have been true that the only thing that was still bothering her was Partha's confession. It was a quiet nagging at the back of her mind, but otherwise she was smiley.

Her costume for the faire was a comfortable petticoat and gingham skirt that both fell to her ankles, a brown leather corset over her flowy white blouse, and in place of a purse she carried a basket which had a false top covered in fake flowers obscuring its little hatch into the interior beneath. Because Perlie had no such thing and no pockets in her dress, Dezba offered to carry her money and phone, both of which were passed thoughtlessly to her therefore.

"Perlie, sweetie," she said with a tender voice as they ambled along a crowded cobblestone pathway.

"Hm?"

"Did you read Partha's message about the story behind our costumes?" She shook her head. "Oh! It's so cool! I'll synopsize it for you if you want."

She nodded absent-mindedly and let Dezba rattle on about the interconnectivity of their costumes. Dezba's lilting voice was pleasant, but Perlie wasn't listening to the story. A cloud had passed over the sun, and in the newfound darkness Perlie's inner world was drowning in silent reeling upset.

'*Why would he want to be alone? Or at least he said he'd be alone, but why was he so quick to offer help to Neodesha? Is he cheating on me with her? Shay wouldn't do that to me, right? But who knows, maybe she would. God knows he's handsome and charming. I couldn't even hold it against her if he wooed her. But I could hold it against him. But, Perlie, calm down. It's only until noon, and speculating about it is just going to upset you. He probably wants to go pose for selfies with fans or something, and doesn't want to drag me into the spotlight. Right? He gave me extra money: that's gotta be a good sign. Maybe he found out I used to have a crush on Dezba and wants to test my faithfulness.*' She looked at Dezba while she rambled on about the costumes with a warmth on her cheeks and a wide white grin. '*She does look beautiful, but she's not interested in me like that. And besides: I intend to pass his test, even if she does try to kiss me or something. I'll tell her sorry, but I'm with Partha, and she'll understand, and it'll all be okay.*'

When Dezba was finished recapping the story connecting everyone's costumes and characters, she spotted a vendor's table selling handmade gemstone dice and rushed to it with Perlie slowly ambling along behind her. She bought thirteen sets, making quite a dent in her spending money, and with those in her basket before Perlie could catch a peek at them, she giggled fiendishly and said, "Let's get hammered!"

"Agreed."

They found a vendor selling spiced wine and bought a bottle and two hand-carved wooden chalices. After finding a quiet shaded bench off the beaten path, they uncorked the wine and started nursing their cups. Perlie's mind was still reeling, but she was more grounded now that she was sitting and able to take in the surroundings in this calmer area of the festival. They were sat in a grove of aspen trees with only a light dirt path travelled by a few costumed attendees every few minutes. Sunlight beamed through the green treetops and speckled the white trunks and tannish dirt with dancing yellow lights. The summer heat was a pleasant warmth in the grove, and the spices in their wine were especially aromatic and flavourful.

In relative private and with a buzz brewing, it was only ten minutes into their quiet break from the crowds that Dezba asked, "Is something wrong, sweetie?"

Perlie sighed and looked down into her empty cup. "Yeah."

"What's wrong, deary?"

"It's nothing, Dezba. I'm just a little worried."

"What's got you worried?"

She flicked her gaze toward the older woman. The genuine concern on her beautiful face wrenched her cold heart. With her eyes back on the inside of her cup, she muttered, "Party."

Dezba chuckled. "You're worried about him here of all places? What could you possibly be worried about? That he'll spend too much on dice?"

She let out a forced ha that turned into another sigh. "No. I'm worried about his wandering eye."

She frowned, but Perlie didn't notice. It was Dezba's understanding that Partha and Perlie weren't officially together, but she supposed she may have misread the situation. After a moment of ponderance, she pet Perlie's shoulder and reassured her: "Let him look, sweetie. Men can't help but look. If he's promised himself to you, then he won't cheat on you. Not when Thyne is listening in and able to rat on him."

The added conditions made Perlie's stomach turn. It was true they had never had an official conversation about the state of their relationship, but Perlie loved him. Surely he loved her, too, right? The sex was amazing, and sneaking around during Ramadan before Partha had to leave was exhilarating. He was sweet and cute and brought her several gifts from the Bahamas: a little plush turtle she had been using as a pillow, a baggy hoodie, a vinyl record from a local band, and a case of luxury cigarillos. If she were just a call girl, surely he wouldn't shower her in gifts and praise like he did.

There was a lull in their conversation, so Perlie took out her phone to read old messages from him. Things like:

⌜ Good morning, heart. (｡ ᵕ ｡) I hope you slept well. I asked Giovanni to make your favourite for breakfast. ⌟

And ⌜ You look so cute in that picture! <3 (ˊ ▽ ˋ) Is that a new manicure? ⌟

But the one that had her smiling the widest was: ⌜ I'm drunk! ♪ \(ˊ▽ˋ)/ and yuor'e the hotestt most beaitufl one in the gang! Don't tell Thyne! Hehehe. I miss you out here, heart </3. Its lonely at sea. ⌟

Dezba watched silently as Perlie read these messages again and noticed her blushy smile at the last one. She caught a glimpse of its contents and let Perlie sit in the energy before deciding to bring some fresh reality to the lonesome woman.

"You know," she began tenderly and with a comforting hand on Perlie's shoulder. Perlie looked at her, still smiling, but Dezba's tone was ominous: "You shouldn't attach your self-worth to what a man thinks of you. Especially not a man like Partha."

Her smile disappeared and brow furrowed angrily. "What the Hell do you mean 'a man like Partha'?"

"Now, sweetie, don't go pouting and snipping at me. Maybe you don't know because you weren't a fan of him before you met him, but a few years back he got in some hot water when it came out that he was a serial cheater."

"You're lying."

She frowned. "He's a scumbag, sweetie, and I don't want you getting hurt. Why do you care so much what he thinks of you, anyway?"

Perlie answered unwillfully and with a great amount of anger, confusion, and fear: "Because I love him!"

"Oh, honey," she cooed and wrapped her arm around Perlie's shoulders.

"Get off of me!" She shoved her away and stood. "I can't believe you would talk about him like this. Do you want him for yourself or something!? You creepy stalker fan!"

Dezba was dumbfounded by the outburst, but before she could respond, Perlie threw her cup at her and stormed off. Dezba gathered their things as quickly as she could and rushed after her. She tried to call for her to stop, but her cries fell on deaf ears.

The first thing Thyne wanted to do at the faire was buy a reading from a fortune teller. He dragged Francis through the crowds until he found one and rushed up to her. She was sitting at a table under an awning that had been pulled out from the side of her bohemian wagon. Someone was leaving her table having just finished a reading, so she was still putting her cards and charms away when Thyne approached. She beamed a smile of slightly-crooked teeth under rosy cheeks. Her hair was light brown and made of messy curls that were currently being held at bay by a cloth headband, and her voice was kind with a thick Irish accent: "Hello there, fire soul. What can I do for you, now?"

He didn't have a question in mind: he only knew he wanted his fortune told. Still, he returned her smile and blushed. "How much for a reading with all the bells and whistles?"

She pointed to a chalkboard with listed prices on the side of her wagon that

Thyne was embarrassed to have not seen before. After another blush flashed on his freckled cheeks, he gave her €412 and sat in the seat across from her.

When she was finished clearing the table, she started shuffling a tarot deck and asked, "What question will we be answering today, lad?"

Thyne looked up at Francis, who was standing idly beside him, visibly uninterested in the mysticism. "Frankenstein, what should we ask?"

He pulled the flask in his hand away from his lips to answer curtly, "Ask whatever pleases, Thyne, but prithee do not involve me."

He furrowed his brow and scrunched up his cute button nose while Francis took a swig of rum. "Fine." He turned toward the psychic and huffed. "I don't have a specific question."

She giggled at his pouty posture and nodded. "An open reading, then." She continued shuffling and eyed him. "The spirits around you are almost as fiery as you are." He blushed and nodded just-so. "You know them?"

"I do," he replied.

"Brigit is among them."

He beamed. "She is!"

"I'm quite fond of Her," she whispered, and as she leaned back in her chair, a card flew out of the deck she was shuffling. It landed face-up in the middle of the table. "Ah," she said with a sly grin, "There is something you're not seeing clearly."

He eyed the card with a slight furrow of anger on his brow. The Moon. Just as he was going to ask what was hidden away, another two cards flew out of her deck. She pulled another from the middle and left the three new cards lay face-down on the table while shuffling an oracle deck.

Thyne tried not to seem impatient to see the other tarot cards, but she could tell he was anxious and giggled. "'Twould be mighty foolish t'ask a fire soul like you to be calm, wouldn't it be?" After saying this, a card came flying out of the oracle deck and landed face-up beside The Moon card. On its face was a mostly-red abstract artwork depicting what Thyne saw as a shadowy screaming figure but could have just as easily been seen as something like a hawk or a fox or even an angel. "Ah," she said with a knowing grin, "Well, now, doesn't that just make sense for you, lad?"

"What do you mean?" he said as she pulled a different deck out and spread it across the table to pick out three cards.

She set the new cards down then pointed at the two face-up cards. "You're spiritual in yer own right. What do *you* think it means, lad?"

He eyed the cards while she drew more from another deck and pulled out some charms and runes to cast later. If he were to say what he truly thought it meant, he worried the entire reading would become increasingly negative. An expert liar, he looked at the cards for a moment to think of a dishonest answer and set them down to reply, "Something significant will happen on the next blood moon." He feigned an impatient pout and added: "So not until 2083."

She arched her brow at him and stared through his façade straight to his soul of fibrous black fire. "There's no use lying to me, y'know."

He went pale but tried to hide it with a continued pout. "Well, what does it mean, then?"

"You know what it means." She smiled wickedly. "But, we'll look at your other cards now." She started to flip over the face-down cards and set them out in a spread ahead of her.

The new tarot cards consisted of the Six of Cups, Justice, and the Knight of Pentacles. She set them in a row beneath The Moon but left the nameless red card resting over it. The last four cards were from two different oracle decks. Some of them had pastel artwork on them that evoked memories in Thyne of the paint-job on his fighter jet. He wondered silently if the reminder was a sign of conflict, but before he could ponder for too long, the last oracle card (from its own deck) called his attention. It was of a caged bird on a snowy tree branch. Under the realistic watercolour art were the words, *Use Your Voice*.

The fortune teller took a deep breath and lit an incense. She whispered a prayer as she passed the smoking stick over the table several times, filling the warm summer air with the distinct scents of sage, dragon's blood, and, interestingly to Thyne, basil.

"Well, now, fire soul," she said after another deep breath, "I believe we can begin. Firstly, we will discuss what you have already determined and, for some reason, lied to me about: this hidden information, whatever it may be, will enrage you. I can see that anger is not an emotion you're unfamiliar with." She eyed Francis who sort of smirked at the assessment. With her gaze back on Thyne, she leaned forward and spoke low but with a very serious tone, "Lad, you may know anger, but you have *never* known *rage* like this will be."

He went pale and looked down at the cards. No matter how much he wanted to deny her claim, he could not deny the energies in the air.

She continued: "You will be angrier than you've *ever been*," she whispered as she picked up the red oracle card and tapped it twice with her long blue nails. "But!" She dropped the card thoughtlessly and scooped up the other tarot to show him. "Your inner child will thank you, justice will be served, and what's this at the end of the road?" She pointed to the Knight of Pentacles.

"Uh... a windfall of wealth?"

She slammed the cards down and flicked his forehead. "No."

"Hey!"

"Try again."

He pouted and looked at the cards. "I don't know."

She scoffed, but her air was playful. "Well, this is why you're being asked to seek clarity," she said with a tap on The Moon. "Here, cast these." She passed him a handful of runes, which he promptly cast across the table at the same time that she threw some charms on it as well.

Francis watched absent-mindedly as the reading continued. He wasn't gleaming many details from it and had instead started to people-watch the passers-by as he nursed his bottomless flask of rum. About ten minutes into the reading, however, his attention was piqued by the fortune teller saying, "It's an offer of true love, y'know!" Francis looked at her pointing at a card with a mounted knight holding a … pentagram? He listened more intently as the reading went from there:

"What do you mean true love?" asked Thyne.

"I mean what is love if not the other side of passion?" She tapped the red card of abstract rage. "You will face this trial alone, but once ye've come out the other side, my dear little fire soul, you will find love and peace and happiness beyond yer wildest dreams."

Thyne looked up at Francis momentarily but quickly snapped his attention back to the cards as the fortune teller continued: "I hesitate to say it, lad— I don't want to encourage anything dangerous —but I think you are this linnet bird, and that fire in your heart is the key to the cage. Maybe like a phoenix." He leaned forward to observe the picture more closely, but they were both caught off-guard to see Francis snatch it away.

"Hey! Franky, give that back."

Francis ignored their upset. After some scrutinising of the artwork, he said, "That is not a linnet bird. That is a Chinese nightingale." He set the card gently back on the table. "They are extinct."

After the shock rested plainly on her face, the fortune teller took up the card to observe it again. "Are you certain?" He nodded, and she stroked her chin as she looked at the spread on the table in this new light. "Extinct…," she mumbled.

"There be a poem of the same name," continued Francis, "I learned it by heart when I still had faith in god and miracles. I whispered it foolishly to the heavens in the hopes I might one day be reunited with my precious progeny."

"Oh, do recite it!" said the fortune teller as if there was not a lifetime worth of questions baked into such a harrowing statement.

"It is not a short poem, madame."

She flapped her hands around dismissively. "Recite it!"

"Very well," he said as he pulled up his billowing sleeves to look at his tattoos and pushed his arms through time until a wall of traditional Chinese characters inked in his beautiful script appeared across them. He had not recited the poem since before his stint in the void, so he used the tattooed translation into Mandarin as a guide to help him recall an approximation of the original English:

"'Hello,' he said, 'friend Chang,' I said, 'San Francisco sleeps as the dead—. Termination; lust and play: why still iron the night away? The big clock aches with deadly sound, with a tick and a wail 'til dawn comes round. While the monster shadows scowl and creep; what can be better for a person than sleep?" He looked up from his notes to see their reactions. Both of them had big eyes and wide smiles, entertained by the cadence of his antique voice and the beauty of the poem. He continued but fumbled through a few stanzas as he struggled to recall it perfectly.

By the end of the lengthy poem, he had gathered a small audience, who he assumed were waiting for a fortune to be told rather than to hear his sea-dog voice reverberate a dead man's scrawl. There was a polite clap from the group when he lowered his arms, and he was surprised to see both the fortune teller and Thyne were pallid and shocked. They sat in silence for what may have been ten minutes as the small crowd dispersed to leave them in their uneasy rumination. A soft breeze brought the sweet smell of the summer faire across their table, and with this change in the wind, the teller finally broke their stunned silence: "You're a pilot," she stated abruptly.

Thyne's stomach dropped in that pleasant way only brought about by divination and meditation: "I am," he muttered after a dry swallow.

She slammed her hand onto the Use Your Voice card and held it up to show him. A beaming grin cracked her face like the Cheshire Cat, and she even went so far as to let out a short chortle. His gaze followed the card as she set it back on the table wordlessly and rested on her hands which were crossed flat and gingerly beneath her pointed chin. "What do you make of the poem, there, fire soul?"

He forced a quick smile in her direction before looking back at the spread and muttering, "Moon-fire…. Sorrow and love." He looked at her. His brow furrowed. "What am I paying you for? *You* tell *me* what it means."

She laughed again. "Patience, fire soul." He pouted and watched as she took a deep breath of the sweet summer air. She was going to continue, but Francis interrupted:

"You mean to say you divine this aged rhyme of some 160 annums is somehow a part of his reading?" He rolled his eyes and quaffed his rum at the ludicrous idea before they even replied.

Thyne slapped Francis' thigh. "You atheist dog! Go!" Francis frowned and saw himself away from the colourful wagon.

"You called him a dog because you know he's loyal and good," said the fortuneteller with a simper as he left. It pacified Thyne enough to sigh out some of his anger. "Shall I tell you what I've learned, lad?" He nodded. "What I see for you is as I said: ye'll be angrier than ye've ever been. And this anger will light a fire in that sun-soul of yers that will bring you to the brink of *supernova*." They were both unconsciously leaning closer to each other as she spoke in an increasingly quiet voice. "All this bird imagery, lad: ye're a phoenix. Ye've flown the skies in yer planes, but never *soared*. Yer wings of fire will help you soar. And after yer detonation, rising from the ashes, you'll be better. Stronger. Healed. And loved." They both smiled.

"Romantically?"

She nodded. "Oh, yes. Romantically. Self love. Platonic love. All of it. And all of it unconditional." Her smile wavered as she sat back upright. "Although, I must warn you. As in the poem: there's one you love who can't notice you even as you go supernova. He only sees the ironing board: only the day-to-day and not the sunset that you are."

He frowned so deeply she could swear she heard his heart breaking as he looked after Francis, who was buying something from a vendor across the way. He only looked back to her when he felt her hand on his.

"Lad, it's going to be wonderful for you. Cathartic. Just remember to be present in the moment, and everything you desire and deserve will come to you."

"Yeah…," he conceded with such a quiet tone it may well have not sounded.

She opened his hand and placed something in it. "Here. Take this," she whispered as she closed his fingers around it, noticing through his glove that one of them was mechanical.

"Thank you," he said as he stood.

"Have a blessed life, dear."

"You, too."

When Thyne approached him, Francis was holding out a cone of fairy floss to him. "Here. 'Tis your favourite festival delicacy, is it not?"

Thyne looked up from the gift in his palm and forced a sad smile. "Cheers, mate. Let's go somewhere quiet. I need a fag."

Chapter 39
Lanterns Full of Moon-Fire

She could feel her brother's eyes on her any time she wasn't facing him, but every time she looked in his direction, he would turn his head away and act nonchalant, as if he wasn't constantly staring— *glaring*— at her. Her stomach was churning. Yes, she had killed their father, but Jean-Jacques was gone. Dead, even! And their father was to blame, as far as she had figured. If he had been supportive of their interests, especially little Jean-Jacques', then she never would have had to send her baby brother off to America where he got mixed up with the Russian mafia.

But it had also not escaped her notice that Jean-Jacques' predicament in America could have just as easily been blamed on her. She knew the American government was crumbling when she gave him all of her money and told him to run, yet still she encouraged him to go to MIT. It was the best STEM school in the world, wasn't it? Even while the country around it was fracturing, and its "democracy" was overrun with fascism and corporate oligarchy.

Neodesha didn't seem bothered by all the news that had been learned at the feast. At least, she hadn't seemed worried about any of it until Thyne was revealed as... a kidnapper.... A chill shot down May's spine as she recalled it. Kidnapped someone else's daughter to raise as his own? A serial killer? Nazis? She held her aching stomach.

After Partha had bought a parasol for Neodesha and split away from them, there was a moment shortly afterwards when Neodesha also left the French siblings to go find something to drink. Jean-Jacques and May had slept in the same room in the hotel, but they were so exhausted by the time they finally got to their beds that they were already half-asleep before they even laid their heads on their pillows. So now, in the middle of a renaissance faire and wearing dorky costumes, was their first actual chance to talk about May's confession. They spoke in French:

"JJP, would you stop glaring at me like I'm some kind of monster? You were dead as far as I knew. I didn't have anything to lose, and Father had just found my first iteration of Lanni. He destroyed her, then what did I have? I had no brother, no career, and no love. My heart was black, and I killed him, and I don't know if I would be able to stop myself even if I went back now knowing what I know."

"Why didn't you tell me sooner? Why did you make it everyone's business? These people are psychopaths. They made me kill someone. They made *you* kill someone. They're murderers and thieves and horrible vile people. Why are we still here? We should run. We should go somewhere they'll never come for us and be alone. And I know Thyne can fucking hear me right now. Fuck you, Thyne. I don't want to be in your lunatic gang. I don't care about these companies being brought down. I don't even care if Francis actually *is* trying to save the world. Let it burn! I don't care!" He flashed the cash from Partha and the keys that Roach had given him. "We have enough money and a car now. I have even more money from fixing Thyne's plane, too. We can go somewhere— anywhere —and start over. Please, May. You have to see reason."

Her brow was furrowed and tone firm: "JJP, I love you, but we won't be abandoning these people."

"Maybe you won't, but I will."

She put a hand on his shoulder and felt herself getting red in the face, not because of her brother but because of their stupid costumes. Why were they wearing these and having such a harrowing conversation? Why were all these people around laughing and smiling and having a good time when everything in the world seemed so strange and hard to swallow? "No," she asserted, "You're staying with me. They saved your life. You owe it to them to help with at least one more company."

"Don't tell me this is all because you still like Roach after learning he's a serial killer with over 500 people's blood on his hands."

"I don't have feelings for him like that. I never did. I only told you that to avoid telling you that I killed Father."

He scoffed. "Well, now that all the dirty laundry is aired out, tell me what exactly is stopping us from running, then?"

There was a beat. She looked back at him and sighed. "They can't do this next job without me.... We'll be taking down Eir Lilac, and Jean-Jacques, they saved your life!"

"What do you care about taking down some faceless cooperation? And so what they saved my life? I never should have let them. I'll go back to America if I have to. I don't want to kill any more people, and I especially don't want to see *you* killing any more people. Look what they're doing to you! You're practically one of them!"

She clenched her fists. How dare he imply she was being turned into some sort of monster. Her breaths were heaving and hot, but she calmed herself as she saw Neodesha returning with a drink for each of them.

"I ain't got no clue 'bout all this faire business. I got us mead 'cause it was just about the only word I recognised." She passed out their mugs of mead and held hers up to clink against them, but the siblings hesitated to share her enthusiasm. They were glaring at each other, and she figured it probably had something to do with all the madness that had gone down at the feast. "Ain't none of my business, but iffen y'all got a minute, I might could share some words of wisdom." She gestured to a sitting area beside a nearby food truck and led them to one of the tables.

The siblings were still glaring at each other when they sat down. The tables around them were bustling and bright, but theirs was cold and quiet and dark. Neodesha took a sip of her mead followed by a deep breath.

"I ain't never had a sibling, so 'scuse me if this is just something I ain't got no way to understand, but—. By golly! Can y'all at least *look* at me?" They turned to face her hesitantly, still sometimes side-eying each other and poorly masking their upset the times they did look Neodesha's way. "Now, if you recall, I was also at that dinner, and I also learned somethin' mighty troublin' 'bout a loved one. I ain't never liked Viktor much, so it don't surprise me none that he killed my wife, but Thyne is my Pa, same as he was Rosie's Pa, and I—. Well, I been thinkin' 'bout what I learnt 'bout him and what I always known, and, well... I'm appalled, but... I still love him. He's the same Pa who raised the woman I loved more than life itself, and he did a mighty fine job. She was every good thing a woman can be, then some, and I reckon she wouldn't 'a learned none 'a that from Viktor, even if he has done changed his ways from when he was a nazi.

"The fact of the matter is that Papa Thyne may have had a right to do what he done, but even if he didn't, well... he's still Rosie's Pa, and I still love him, and I think you should think about that, Mr. Martial. What May done was bad, but does it make her not your sister no more? If she were in prison for what she done, would you not visit her? Would you not mourn her absence?"

"You're just as bad as the rest of them," he spat, "Why should I listen to you?"

"You ain't gotta listen to me none, Mr. Martial, but I ain't no fool. I reckon you'd wanna cherish what you got while you got it. I sure know I shoulda cherished my wife more than I done. If she'd 'a done something I find unforgivable, like buying a slave, I still would 'a forgiven her, and I shouldn't never have gotten mad at her 'bout the things I done got mad about. If I'd 'a known she was gon' be taken from me so quick-like, I ain't never would 'a fought with her 'bout anything."

He sighed and glared at May again, but it was less harsh than he had been glaring earlier. He thought back on the man he had already killed to save her and about the darkness in Roach's soul that had seemed to be a salve to his woes. He didn't mean to, but he also thought about the apathy he felt having taken a life and the sympathy he felt for the likes of Roach. Not only had Thyne saved him from being trapped in the states, but there was no other way to slice it: Roach saved his life in that supermarket. Motya was going to kill him.… And if he had considered Motya a friend, he supposed he should start considering these new monsters his friends. Better friends than any of the Morozovs, too. He sighed and held his head in his hands. "Merde."

May pressed a hand cautiously on his upper back and, when he didn't react negatively, pet him gently. "I love you, JJ. You don't have to kill anyone else, okay? I promise. I'll take the brunt of everything. I want to protect you. That's all I've ever wanted to do is protect you. And we missed so much time while you were trapped in America. Now we're finally together, and, after we help these people, we can go on that Antarctic expedition like we planned when we were kids. Okay?"

He managed a small smile at her for the fleetingest of moments. "Okay." His voice was strangled by all his emotions.

"See? Don'tchya feel better!?" Neodesha raised her glass to try and clank against theirs again, and May matched her energy enthusiastically. Jean-Jacques was obviously still upset, but he clicked his mug against theirs and drank and drank and drank.…

He leaned on the caravan as they chatted flirtatiously. The elf maiden he had found was twirling her glittering holographic hair around her finger and pressing her hand over her fluttering heart every time he spoke. His voice was gravelly and deep. She was of the mind that his accent was Gondorian in nature the way it perfectly captured the energy of his kingly appearance. The intricate patch over his eye was like an extension of a crown he wasn't even wearing, and his finely braided hair evoked reminders of her Elvish homeland. She may have mistaken him for an elf if not for his adorable goatee and average height. After the umpteenth compliment of her character and costume, he scooped up one of her dainty hands to kiss its pale knuckles, and she could not stop the blushing giggle that escaped her after the gesture. What a handsome stranger. Perhaps he was Prince Charming.

He had a good control over his gaze in these sorts of encounters, but her particularly prominent bust was making the July sun that much hotter in his unconscious glances down to where she was overflowing out of her corset. Her dress was especially wide around the hips, and he was hopeful to learn if it was natural curves or a petticoat. Either way, he would certainly enjoy whatever was underneath.

With his lewd thoughts on high and "Bellalune of the Redlands" taking to his charms, it was after only fifteen minutes of flirting that he had her on his lips behind the vendor's caravan. While they kissed, there were several moments he flicked open his eye to look around for somewhere private to figure out the skirt mystery. Unfortunately, it was not in one of those more alert moments that he was pulled violently away from his new Elvish friend. He had hardly opened his eye at all by the time he was struck hard across the face. "You fuck! I knew it! I fucking knew it!"

"You said you were single!" cried Bellalune.

He held his spinning head, trying to understand what was happening. In the few seconds he took to gather himself, he was abandoned by the elf and looked up to see Perlie rushing away from him. He gave chase. "Perlie! Perlie, wait! What's going on?"

When he caught up with her, she didn't even turn to him. Her voice was broken as she shook his hand off of her shoulder and spat, "You fucking asshole, leave me alone."

She started off again, so Partha followed and rounded to her side, matching her speedy pace but paying her all of his attention. "What's wrong? What did I do?"

She huffed and stopped to turn and face him. They were in the middle of a crowded walkway, and Partha didn't stop before running into a tall ogre of a man. He winced away from the angry faire-goer and apologised mousily as Perlie watched with teary eyes. Ultimately, she decided to let him get his ass kicked by this random man and stormed off while he was grovelling.

Partha tried to find her again after literally buying his way out of an ass-beating, but the crowds were too thick. Eventually, he slinked away to a shaded area and pulled out his phone. Six consecutive calls were all sent directly to voicemail. "Fuck," he muttered and ran his hand through his hair. "Thyne, where did she go? What did I do?" He looked at his phone for a message from his distant friend, but after five minutes of no text or call, he messaged him the same questions.

〚 Where did who go? The girl you were trying to shag? 〛

「 Perlie! 」

〚 I don't know, mate. She's not said much for a while. She was giving it out to someone a bit ago, though. I presume said someone was you. Lmao 〛

「 Don't laugh at me! What did I do wrong? 」

〚 Lol you don't know? 〛

"Stop laughing at me, you fuck!" He was huffing angrily through his burning nose by that point. What the fuck had he done wrong!? 「 Is it the coke? Everyone's always so fucking mad about that for no reason. 」

〔 The coke probably doesn't help, mate, but no that's not why she's upset, you fucking muppet. 〕

He took a moment to try and figure it out on his own. '*Maybe… she's upset because the story of her character for the day is that she's owned by mine. But I thought she'd like that, right? She's into that, so it seemed kinky…. Maybe too voyeuristic? Is that the word? Well, either way, maybe it's because I shouldn't have made the kink more visible like that. I guess.*' He stroked his short beard. "Alright, well, I'll apologise to her for it when I find her. Where is she?" He looked down at his phone.

〔 You really think you figured out why she's mad? 〕

「 <(•ᴥ•)> Yes. 」

〔 Can't wait to hear it. Sounds like she's getting some coffee. 〕

「 There are a million coffee stands! (╪̄ Ⅲ̄)́ . 」

〔 Good luck! 〕

He huffed and slammed his phone back into its hidden pocket to start wandering the fair in search of Perlie.

⌇

Noon approached, and the different parties started to make their ways to the meeting location for the joust at 12:30. By 12:23, all of them had arrived and started mingling with each other, save for Perlie and Dezba. Partha was biting his well-manicured nails as he scanned the horizon and crowds in search of them. His nervousness eventually brought him to Thyne, to whom he leaned close and whispered, "Where are they?"

"Perlie's still fuming, mate. They're not coming."

He held his face and let out a quiet wail. Before he could ask Thyne for help fixing the situation he still couldn't fully grasp, River approached and pointed to a plush Thyne was holding.

"Where'd you get that?" There was an innocent gleam in his hazel-greys, set over a cute little smile. Thyne had bought a plush doll of a dullahan. It was wearing beige and forest-green striped overalls made of corduroy. The doll itself was made of a simple black cotton fabric everywhere but its big orange jack-o-lantern head, which was made of orange cotton and black felt for the face.

Thyne had named him, "Mr. Parsnip? I can show you where I got him!" Before River could reply, Thyne had grabbed his wrist to rush him excitedly away.

Partha tried to stop them by reminding them that the joust was starting in just a few minutes, but they were already gone. He sighed and despondently gestured for the rest of the group to follow him to the stands.

The joust managed to lighten Partha's mood, especially when Thyne and River came (late) and sat on either side of him with a growing drunkenness evident in both of them. They were playing with their plush dolls, making them say stupid and vile things to each other as well as to Partha, in an attempt to cheer him up. He thanked them for the lightness after the joust, then turned his attention to his map of the event. "It looks like there are some restaurants within the faire bounds. What do we say to some lunch?"

"I reckon that's a good idea," said Neodesha.

Her assessment was the general consensus, except, "Restaurants will be crowded," said Thyne, "What about take-out at the hotel?"

"You want to leave already?" Partha whimpered, "But what about the lantern festival?" His voice was so broken it made Thyne sick.

"Lantern festival?" asked Francis.

He continued to sound hurt. The poor kid was having a horrible day. "Didn't you read the brochures I made you? There's a lantern festival at night where every-one can release a floating lantern into the river and make a wish."

Roach inserted himself between Partha and Thyne and wrapped his large arm around the kid's shoulders. "Sounds like a good time, dude. Thyne, if you don't want to wait for a sit-down restaurant, what about some street food? Can't beat it."

Thyne smiled at his friends drunkenly. "We'll just meet up at the pub after you lot do all the waiting!" With a loud ha he grabbed River's wrist again and dragged him quickly away to explore more of the faire. When they were buying the drinks that had them so besotted now, he had seen a lute he wanted to buy for Roach. The cart at the time had too long a line to wait while they were actively missing the joust, but now that they would be waiting an undefined amount of time to eat anyway, he figured it was a good time to go check it out.

The line around the woodwooker's cart was just as long as the first time he had seen it, but they were content to wait together. While they were in line, Perlie and Dezba happened to spot them and approached.

Dezba hugged them both then linked her arm back up with Perlie's. "How was the joust?"

"Why'd you not come?" asked River with his eyes on Perlie, reading her like a book. Despite knowing nothing about the drama that had occurred, he quickly added, "Let me guess: the kid got feelsy with some bimbo. Maybe a himbo? Or was it both?" Perlie glared daggers into him, which was met only with a harsh chortle.

He was going to say more, but Dezba slapped his chest and scolded him: "Stop taunting her, asshole." His smile disappeared in a flash. "Now," continued Dezba, "I asked a question: how was the joust?"

"It was fun. We missed you both," answered Thyne, "Party wants to talk to you, Perlie. He's such a muppet he doesn't know what he did wrong. It's cute."

She scoffed and rolled her eyes. "It isn't cute, it's pathetic. Why did I ever let myself catch feelings for that idiot? God!" She rubbed the bridge of her nose to cover her blush more than her costume already did.

"Aww," Thyne said with a hic. "Give him another chance, Perls."

"Or," interjected River, "You could take my advice from the job in France and learn to be okay on your own."

She sniffled, pulled herself closer to Dezba, and muttered something. Dezba then looked to the boys, who were only one person from the front of the line by that point, and said, "We'll see you at the hotel tonight."

They left, and River and Thyne were greeted by the woodworker: "What can I do for you two strapping young adventurers?"

Thyne pointed to the lute mounted on the temporary wall behind him. "How much for that?"

The vendor thought back on all the hours he had poured into making such an intricate piece and how no one at any of the faires for the past six years had ever bought it after he gave his price, even when he lowered it each year by at least €500. It was so long ago that he had made it that he now considered it a great loss and didn't even want to sell it. He looked up at it then back at Thyne. No one ever bought it anyway, so what was the harm in saying a ludicrous price? "The lute? Erm... 4500."

He fully expected a "Oh nevermind," a gasp, or at least a scoff. Imagine his surprise when Thyne said simply, "Done," and pulled €4,500 in cash from various pockets. He watched the money slide across the table then saw Thyne bouncing giddily on his toes. It seemed unsavoury to have so much money in cash, but he decided he'd be better off not knowing why and walked over to the lute to take it off the wall. It was surreal to hand off the piece that had become something of a staple in his shop. Who would come up asking for the price and laughing in his face for it now?

"You devious little scamp," said River as they walked away with the instrument, "You know he's not actually going to play it for us, don't you? He's having a good time, but he doesn't want to have a bunch of attention on him while he's in that revealing costume."

Thyne grinned fiendishly. "Wanna bet?"

River mirrored Thyne's energy. "How much?"

"How much do you have left of your spending money from Party?"

"3,213."

Thyne held out his hand to shake with River's. "You're on."

According to Partha's updates, they would be seated in an hour, so after buying themselves another round of beer, Thyne and River slowly made their way to the restaurant to meet up with the rest of the group that would be dining with them. They were waiting around outside of the restaurant. When Roach spotted the lute in Thyne's hands, he sighed, dreading the upcoming conversation. To no one's surprise, Thyne brought the instrument directly to Roach and held it out to him. "Play something."

"I don't know the lute."

Thyne's big honey-gold eyes were wobbly and sparkly as he looked up at Roach and whimpered, "You don't?" He thought he recalled River mentioning that Roach could play the lute, but thinking back on the gamble, he doubted his memory. Had River tricked him into an unwinnable bet?

Roach's heart ached at the adorable display from Thyne. He looked down at the instrument to consider the idea. It was beautifully crafted, he had to admit. Before he might accept it, he looked at River. When they made eye contact, they seemed to communicate telepathically. With only this look and a slight shake of River's head, Roach knew that his brother had money on it. "I don't," he repeated and pushed the instrument gently away.

Thyne's eyes watered and cheeks went red. He had been tricked. *Again*. Were he sober, he would be able to see that Roach was lying, but he was too many lagers deep by then. He turned to River and, with a broken voice, said, "You cunt. You said he could."

It was about this time that Partha approached with a lighter air than during the joust. He rubbed his wrist across his running nose, sniffled, and said with a huge grin, "Woah! Roach, are you gonna play the lute for us!?" Thyne turned around to see his friend and watch how Roach replied.

Partha's adorable pleading posture, combined with how much it hurt to have disappointed Thyne, brought Roach to an internal breaking point. He snatched the lute out of Thyne's hands and sighed. "I'll play something, but only because you two bastards are so fucking cute. Sorry, Sonny."

"Tony, you dickhead. You owe me three grand."

Roach couldn't help but chuckle at the ludicrous amount and started strumming on the strings, noticing from their feel that they were genuine lamb's guts. It was slightly out of tune, so while he was tuning it, he sauntered to where Francis had been watching the entire exchange and nursing his flask. "Hey there, bed bug. Any requests?"

Francis beamed his rotten smile. "Aye! *The Wellerman!*"

Partha clapped at the idea. "Yes!"

"Alright, alright," said Roach as he backed away from the line into the street beside it. He started with a percussive pounding on the body of the lute then started singing. His voice was deep and rough enough that he may have been mistaken for the sort of salty sea-dog that had need for such songs as *The Wellerman*. The lute was mostly only used as a drum, but he eventually started to strum on it, too. Only two lines into the song, Partha and Francis joined in with his singing, and by the first verse there were a handful of strangers in the gathering crowd that had also joined. River and Thyne weren't singing along, but they had passed their dolls to Jean-Jacques and May to hold while they went into the street beside Roach to improvise a dance together.

Things were increasingly lively in the queue for this restaurant, and Roach was quick to ask for another request. So quick, in fact, that he asked while the crowd was still singing the sea shanty. He had asked Neodesha, who answered with a popular country song from a few years prior called, *Withered Bones and Cell Phones.* Lucky Roach had a perfect memory, because he had only heard the song twice in his life but played and sang it to nigh-perfection. Significantly less of the nerds in the crowd knew this song, but there were a few voices singing along with his, including Neodesha's.

After the country song, Roach leaned toward Thyne, who had returned to the crowd with River by then. Roach was strumming a simple back-and-forth melody to keep the air from becoming vacuumously quiet and wore an uncharacteristic genuine smile. His voice was rumbly and charming as he seemed to purr, "And for the handsome lad in the black cap?"

Thyne blushed and grinned. "What about...," he tapped his chin, which was shadowed with a hint of scruff that Partha had insisted he grow out for the costume. He struggled to think of a song that would match the energy of the others but eventually had a visible thought and blurted, *"Puttin' on the Ritz!"*

Roach let out a genuine chuckle and backed away to give himself space once again, starting to play the ancient upbeat tune. Before the first verse, he said playfully, "Forgot my tap shoes today. You'll excuse me." Thyne nodded and giggled, and Roach started singing. To mimic the original song's tap-dancing part, he once again used the instrument as a drum with impeccable skill. This was another song that Thyne and River danced to, and by its close, they only had time for one more song before they would likely be seated. He made eye contact with May: "A last request, mademoiselle?"

She grinned anxiously and rubbed the back of her neck. She didn't listen to a lot of popular music and didn't want to come off as flirting by requesting one of Roach's songs. After a moment of nervousness, she stuttered, "W-well... what's *your* favourite song?"

"Ha!" He changed the melody and started orating over the music: *"You're walking in the woods. There's no one around, and your phone is dead. Out of the corner of your eye, you spot him...."* It led into the rest of the song, one that was relatively unknown to the crowd. It was perhaps only River, May, and Jean-Jacques who had heard it, but everyone was enjoying it and laughing every few verses at the ridiculous lyrics.

Just as he had assumed, they were seated after the song. Roach smiled at the crowd when they applauded for him, but his face returned to its typical deadpan expression by the time they were sitting in the overly-air-conditioned restaurant. He shivered and grabbed the edges of his cloak to pull it over himself, which brought attention to the fact that if the gang hadn't seen the scar on the soft of his shoulder before, they most definitely had after the lute performance. He could only hope they wouldn't ask him about it.

The sun set, and before the faire would close for the evening, there would be a lantern festival. Not every faire-goer would be provided a lantern, but because Partha had paid for the premium tickets, they were each given one for free. They met up at the lantern booth the same as they had met up for the joust, but Perlie and Dezba still weren't showing. Partha's mood was abysmal, even in spite of the line he had done just an hour before the meeting. He must have really fucked up for Perlie to be ignoring him this long. Though he wouldn't admit it even to himself, it broke his heart to have another confirmation from Thyne that she was still angry and was already back at the hotel. He had planned to make his wish with her and for them to send their lanterns down the river together. With tears in his eyes, he took Thyne aside. "Is she really so mad about the costume?"

"Mate…. It's not about the costume at all."

Partha sighed and nodded. He wiped the tears and snot from his face with his sleeve and kicked the dirt. "Should have known. I'm such an idiot. I don't know what I did wrong, but I really wanted to do this with her. It just won't be the same. This faire was supposed to be our break from all the serious shit." Thyne hugged his friend and pet his hair, letting him cry gently into his shoulder. It was a short-lived moment but a meaningful one nonetheless. When they retreated, Partha whimpered, "What did I do wrong?"

Thyne gently explained that Perlie felt he had been unfaithful and conceded when Partha defended himself that it was indeed her assumption that they were exclusive. He toed the line between the two sides with the grace of a dancer, and by the end of the talk, Partha was bawling and Thyne was calling Perlie.

"What?" she answered with a snip.

Before saying anything, Thyne gave the phone to Partha. "Heart?" he whimpered. It gutted her to hear him so broken. "I'm sorry for kissing that elf girl. I'm just a big fucking idiot. I didn't know you wanted me all to yourself." She tried to pout but frowned and held her broken heart instead. "Please come back to the faire, heart. I want to make a wish with you and kiss you under the stars."

Her lip trembled, and it pissed her off that he was able to make *her* feel so guilty for *his* mistake. But… she merely sighed, sniffled, and said, "What time does it start?"

"Uh." Did no one read his brochures? "9:30." He looked at his own phone for the time, which read 9:20.

"The train takes at least fifteen minutes to get there, Party. We'll do something when you get back to the hotel."

"Franky can get you…."

She rolled her eyes and rubbed the bridge of her nose. After an excruciatingly long two seconds, she droned, "I don't want to come."

He choked back a few more heaving weepy breaths to instead suck up his tears, put on a brave voice, and say, "Okay," before shoving the phone back into Thyne's hands and holding his face to cry more fervently.

"He didn't mean anything by it," said Thyne to Perlie, "But you're free to stay there and rot. I'll do the lantern festival with Partha *myself*." The anger on his friend's behalf was especially evident by the end of this assertion and with how quickly he hung up afterwards. Once his phone had been slammed back into his bag, he took out his plush to pass to Partha then pulled him into his strong arms for a warm embrace. "You don't need a bird like that, mate. She's not seeing it from your side."

After Partha managed to gather himself, he held Thyne's hand to let him lead the gang through the process of getting their lanterns and finding a private spot on the river bank to make their wishes. Thyne was strong for his friend, their hands intertwined the entire trip down to the river. They had found a relatively unpopulated part of the bank, but Thyne took Partha even more out of the way to be further disconnected, even from the gang. He finally untangled their fingers when he reached the water and needed to light his lantern.

"Thyne," whimpered Partha. "What are you going to wish for?"

"I'm not sure yet. What about you?"

He looked at the unlit lantern in his hands and sniffled. "I just want her to forgive me."

Thyne's heart ached. He took Partha's lantern and set them both down gently in the grass beside them so he could hold his weepy friend again. Partha's arms snaked up under Thyne's and hooked around his shoulders. He pulled himself close. The embrace was warm and welcoming. Thyne had been his friend for so long, it was hard to imagine life before him.

By then, Thyne was sober, so he was especially surprised when Partha retreated from the embrace only to lean back in and plant his lips on his. Thyne's eyes went wide, and he pushed Partha away almost immediately. "What are you doing?" Partha only wept. "Oh, love." His tone was sympathetic, and he pulled him in to hug him once more, this time with more fervour. During the embrace, he whispered, "You're not thinking clear right now."

"I know," he whimpered. All he knew in moments of upset was hedonism, so it seemed only natural to try and indulge himself in pleasure with his best friend to try distracting himself from reality.

"If things don't work out with Perlie, we'll talk about us, okay? But you two need to give each other another chance." He nodded and sniffled. "Now, come on," he pulled him back by the shoulders and looked him in the eye, "Let's make our wishes and go get some frozen yoghurt from that place near the hotel."

Partha nodded and slowly plucked up his lantern. While Thyne was picking up his own lantern, Partha noticed that he didn't have a way to light his. "Can I borrow your lighter?"

Thyne shook his head. Not even Francis was allowed to touch Oliver's lighter. "But no worries, mate. I've got these!" He produced a book of matches from his pocket. They were multicoloured, and the design on the box was of an esoteric symbol Partha could only relate to fantastical magic. "The fortune teller gave them to me."

"Thanks," said Partha as he tore off one of the matches and struck it on the back.

While he was lighting his lantern and wishing for Perlie's forgiveness, Thyne was lighting his own lantern with Oliver's lighter. It made him think about his late love, which sparked the wish in his mind: '*I wish for him back. Somehow…. Perhaps in a dream.*' They set their lanterns in the stream with their hands intertwined and watched as the current drifted them lazily away toward the other lanterns already in the water.

Chapter 40

Man is a Torch,
Then Ashes Soon

It was the last hours of the last day of the faire, and Thyne and Roach were alone together for the first time since their secrets were revealed to the rest of the gang. That Thyne had divulged one of Roach's secrets was frankly infuriating, but he was also grateful that he had only revealed one and not all four. Still, there was some bitterness in the air as they ambled through the faire wordlessly. They were both of the mind that the rest of the gang (save for Francis and River) hated or at least feared them, and perhaps they were not entirely wrong to believe such things. The true complexity of the others' feelings about them was muddled down to simple words in their heads as they stewed. Without fully realising it, after about ten minutes of quiet walking, they were standing in a secluded garden. If the lack of noise from the faire was any indication, it may well have been private property. A serpentine cobblestone path crept through blossoming honeysuckle and rose bushes. The floral aroma was potent and pleasant and seemed to hug the two men as they found a bench and sat beside each other.

Roach was the first to take advantage of the privacy to break the silence: "Why'd you tell everyone about me?" Expecting him to fly off the handle like he tended to do, Roach was surprised to see Thyne giggle and blush. He bumped his shoulder into Roach's but didn't answer the question. "Don't think you can just be cute to get out of it." He tried to sound intimidating, but Thyne's charms were melting the ice around his heart. With a slight huff: "Tell me why."

"*Ain't nothin' but a heartache*," sang Thyne, giving just a *taste* of his divine talent, followed by another flirtatious titter.

The anger in Roach left him with an amused exhale and roll of the eyes. He smiled lightly and said, "You're such a dick, dude."

"You love it," teased Thyne, "I told them because you upset my Frankenstein."

He sighed. "Yeah, I know. I was high as shit."

"But anyway, only JJP seemed to care enough to want to leave. Which reminds me," he scooted toward the brute and leaned close enough that their faces were almost touching. Whispering sensually, he said, "You make a habit out of giving away your mates' cars, do you?"

Roach smirked and leaned away to light himself a cigarette. He offered one to Thyne and, once it was between the Brit's kissable lips, he lit it with his own and replied, "Call us even, then, yeah?"

After a moment of quiet smoking, Thyne commented, "I'm surprised Martial didn't run. Do you think we should worry?"

"What for? Worrying never does anyone any good." A drag. "Anyway, I knew he wouldn't run."

Thyne batted his eyelashes unconsciously as he looked up at Roach with his big brown eyes. "What do you mean?"

"God dammit, dude, you're so cute." He chuckled and pushed Thyne's face away playfully. "Anyway, even if May wasn't here and crushing on me—. I mean, haven't you noticed? JJP's fucked up, dude. You can see it in his eyes." Thyne stroked his chin. "But it's important to him to feel like he has an out, so I gave him the car. It's not like your rich ass can't afford another one."

There was another moment of quiet as Thyne pondered Jean-Jacques' mental state and wondered why he would be sticking around. His wandering mind was eventually distracted by Roach's costume, however. On this third day, he was wearing a poet's shirt not unlike the ones Francis often wore, but a memory flashed in his mind of seeing a gnarly scar on the soft of his shoulder during his lute performance on the first day. With another tilt of his head and bat of the eyelashes over his big doe eyes, he asked sweetly, "What happened to your shoulder?"

Roach grabbed his right shoulder (the one closer to Thyne at the moment) and rolled it around its joint. "Why? Seems fine. Is there something on it?"

"No, not that one." Roach's stomach dropped as Thyne gently slid his hand into the opening of his shirt collar and caressed the scar. "This one," he whispered.

He let out a stuttered breath and crossed his legs before gently pulling Thyne's hand away, trying not to think about how soft his touch was. "It's uh—. War. Yeah. The war."

Thyne giggled. "You're a lousy liar, Basil." His lightness became shock and horror. The flush on his cheeks turned white. "I mean Roach."

"Y'know," said Roach with a soft grin, "I'm beginning to think I should try and do some sort of regressive meditation."

Thyne nodded enthusiastically. "Oh, you very much should do!"

"Of course: could also just ask Francy Pants to take me back to meet this Oliver fellow."

He pursed his lips. "I don't think that would work…."

"Anyway, tell me about him."

A breeze graced them while Thyne was pondering the request. It pushed around his wavy brown locks as he tapped his perky nose in thought adorably. The sunset painted him on the greenery like a Monet, and Roach took in every last second of the beauty so that he might paint it later. "Alright, it'll be painful, but I'll tell you," said the Brit, "on one condition."

"And what condition is that?"

"Scar story first."

"Counter argument: you tell me about *your* scars first."

"*My* scars?" He looked down at himself and watched as Roach scooped up his hands and tenderly removed one of the gloves.

He rubbed his calloused thumb over the back of his hand before bringing it up to his lips and giving his knuckles a peck. "I noticed them back in the diner when we first met." He was referring to a series of barely-visible marks on the backs of Thyne's hands which were so faded the Brit had forgotten about them.

"Very perceptive," he said as he took his hand back and rubbed it. He sounded irritated.

"You don't have to tell me."

With a smokey sigh, Thyne finished his durry and flicked it into the dirt. "You know why I cut off my fingers already. It's related." He took a deep black breath to steady himself, but it was Roach's hand petting his back a moment later that fully grounded him. "My mother started teaching me piano before I even knew how to put together full sentences, but as soon as I understood basic English, she—. She gave me this little ring binder and some stickers I was allowed to put on the outside of it." His stomach churned at this thought, but he continued after only a slight wince, "And when I asked what the book was for, she sat me down and explained:

"'Clarence, there are some things that Mummy is always going to buy for you: school supplies, new instruments, breakfast, lunch, and dinner. That's her job as your mother. Do you understand? So, when you want something else that isn't a gift from Mummy, I'll write it down in this ledger.'" He shuddered and looked at Roach. There was an odd sort of pain in his amber eyes. It was like the fury of a million tempests, but they were overcast by the heartbreak of a betrayed child.

Roach cupped his hand around Thyne's face and pet it gently with his thumb when the Brit leaned into it. "Here." He opened the satchel Thyne had been wearing as a part of his costume and handed him the plush dullahan he had bought the first day.

Thyne hugged the doll and closed his eyes to breathe in the warm autumn air. After a moment of quiet and Roach lighting himself another cigarette, Thyne continued, "I couldn't have been more than four years old. I remember appreciating how she seemed to be inviting me into an adult conversation at the time, and not in a way that was violating my body, I'll be clear. It was violating my *mind*." He sighed. "I'm waffling now, so I'll just be blunt." He opened his eyes and met Roach's gaze with the same fury and heartbreak in them from before, this time stronger. "The ledger was an invoice. Everything I ever wanted that wasn't a gift was instead something I was to pay off when I turned eighteen and was either paying rent or living on my own. She gave me this power before I could comprehend what money even was, Clayton. Do you understand? I would ask her for something, like a toy or sweet in the middle of summer, and she would say, 'Of course, Clare. Just put it on the docket, and I'll get you the money to go get it.'

"Of course, the piano, guitar, and singing lessons she gave me, which were made incredibly brutal after my father killed himself—. I don't know. Maybe she blamed me. Maybe I reminded her of him…. But anyway, she was adamant that I would become a musical legend. I was already a prodigy, according to her, when I was just three years old. So naturally, those lessons were always 'free'. 'Mummy's gift, so you have a bright future on the stage and in the symphony.'" He rolled his eyes at the memory and took Roach's cigarette to puff on it angrily. "The Christmas after I had finally come to grasp what was happening— must have been seven or eight —I remember opening a present of a new deck of cards. She had never supported my magic and cardistry before then, so I was worried and asked, 'Is this going on the list?' And, I could tell she felt guilty. She was immediately rejecting the idea and making me feel bad for worrying. Said something like, 'Of course not, darling! That's a Christmas gift for you! Gifts don't go on the list, Clare, you know that.'

"When I finally did understand what she was doing, I started saving up for the eventual bill I'd have to pay her. If I could see that docket now, I'd love to read what was on it. I don't remember most of it. Petty things like toys, a bicycle, playing cards, ice cream, books. Anything that wasn't a 'generous gift' from her was added to the tally. But, to be honest, Roach, I didn't see the problems with it. Not even after I read Marx. It was a horrible way to show it, but it was her strange way of expressing… 'love,' I suppose. She taught me piano, guitar, and how to sing. I've composed over a hundred symphonies and sonatas and such, most of which she sold with her music company and promised to give me the profit from. I can play guitar ambidextrously. I can sing in nine octaves."

Roach physically started hearing such a thing as singing in nine octaves. "Ya Allah!"

Thyne smirked at the surprise and looked at Roach with his eyes half-lidded. "I think the most disgusting thing on the ledger, though, was the hospital bill for when I cut my finger off to avoid the violin lessons. As soon as it was healed, no matter what me or the doctors said, she still gave me a violin and started to teach me, and I was going to have to foot the bill for the medical care when I turned eighteen." He smoked. "Those scars on my hands you're asking about are only a fraction of the wrong notes, and only from piano." He pulled up his left sleeve and showed another slew of faint scars near the side of his elbow on his lower arm. "That's the wrong notes from singing." And lastly he showed his biceps. "And those are from guitar." Once his sleeves were back down: "It was usually just a ruler and never hurt too badly. More startling than painful. But, obviously, after enough wrong notes, my failures became visible."

There was a beat. Roach wasn't sure what to say, so he pulled him in for a warm embrace, and Thyne happily returned it.

When they retreated: "Me and Oliver would run rigs on the streets together: I would sell magic tricks to passers-by, and while they were distracted watching me, Oli would go 'round pickpocketing them. It was how I got my microphones, y'know? And, well, we started doing it so I could save up for the bill. Oliver was an orphan, so I paid for most of his things for him with the money I didn't understand I was borrowing until I was already thousands deep in debt."

"You were only nineteen when the war started, right? Did it affect your mother's opinion on the whole thing? Did you end up paying the bill?"

He grinned wickedly and eyed Roach with a beautiful madness in his fiery eyes. "I keep forgetting that you're not him. You don't know what I did, do you? But oh, Roach, if anyone will enjoy the story it's you."

He leaned closer unconsciously. "Yes?"

"When I was sixteen, the bill was mental. I remember exactly. It was £12,423.52. That was *a lot* of money in 1936. It was never added up before I had added it up myself to get an idea of what I'd be dealing with two years from then, and the number, the petty things on the list, the hospital bill on it, and all the scars all over me: it all culminated in my ultimate decision to kill her." Roach sucked in a curt gasp and smoked away the butterflies in his stomach.

Thyne continued with a cocky grin: "As soon as I had decided how to do it (faking my own death in the process of killing her), I was much more generous with my money. I would ask her for loans, and she'd add them to the docket none the wiser. The only thing she ever rejected to buy for me and put on the list was a car. It's a shame, because if she had bought me a car, maybe I would have simply driven off into the sunset with Oliver to never return instead of what I actually did."

"What did you actually do?" asked Roach, his voice low and trembling from the hysterical pleasure climbing up his throat.

Thyne's smile was wicked. He lowered his voice to a gruff half-whisper and relived the tale as he told it: "I got the list from her under the guise of making a copy for my own records, and, once I had it for a few days, everything was falling into place with my false identity, and whispers of war were murmured, I showed up for my piano lesson right on time with the ledger in one hand and my guitar in the other. I had the guitar filled with raw cotton, but she didn't notice. She was sitting on her sofa-chair beside the piano and waiting for me to come sit down, going through some sheet music I had written to critique it. I surprised her when I came in and opened the piano, but she didn't question me and just went back to her papers.

"So, after I put the guitar inside and set the ledger down, I left the room and came back a moment later with rope." Roach let out a faint gasp and whimpered, his pleasure and anticipation immeasurable. "I gagged her and tied her to the chair as quickly as possible, and once I was sure she was secure, I grabbed it by one of its back feet and dragged her across the room so she would be facing the piano. Her muffled screams were the most beautiful music to ever come out of that room." He smiled blissfully at the memory. "So I took the ledger off the ground and brought it over to the piano. I lit myself a fag and smiled at her. Didn't even explain to her why she would die that day. Instead, I took a drag and lit the book on fire page by page while maintaining eye contact with her.

"Once each paper was sufficiently on fire, I dropped it into the piano. Eventually, the guitar started to burn, and the satisfying twang of breaking strings started to ring out. I gave her one last look. She was horrified and heartbroken, and her muffled screams and bawling were just about the most cathartic sound in the world. I left the room, blocked the door with a bookshelf, and ran from the house with a lot of stolen cash and my most prized possessions, never to return."

Roach's next few breaths were shuddered like he was in the arctic, and after such a story, he was kissing Thyne passionately before he quite realised. When he retreated, he wanted nothing more than to find somewhere more private to take Thyne right then and there, but he managed to restrain himself and recognised the behaviour as inappropriate. "I'm sorry," he averted his eyes. "I shouldn't have kissed you. You have a boyfriend. Not to mention how heartbroken you must be that you had to do that."

"I've already told Giovanni about our other kiss. He doesn't mind." His hand snaked around Roach's collarbone and up to his cheek. He turned him so their eyes would meet, and after a longing look, pulled him in for a tender kiss. Roach's lips were cold and smokey and soft. His stubble was scratchy but pleasant, and the way their tongues danced together was like a waltz.

When they retreated, Thyne was blushing deeply and smiling sweetly. His voice was but a breath: "And to be heartbroken, I'd have to have a heart."

Roach smirked. "Aw, Dorothy. You don't have one either? A shame. I wanted to steal it."

"Corny twat." There was another beat of quiet, but Thyne was still grinning and blushing. His eyelids fluttered flirtatiously when he caught glimpses of Roach between his drags. Eventually, he spoke again with a teasing playful tone: "I knew you'd like that story. You're *despicable*. Almost as despicable as I am. Maybe even moreso."

Roach blushed as if it were a compliment. "I did like it. I want to know even more about how 'despicable' you are. Maybe, after enough stories, we can figure out conclusively who's worse."

"Oh, I hardly think we need more proof from *you*," he giggled, "I've heard how much you enjoy killing people, you barmy bastard. Not to mention the other things." A beat and a drag. "In fact, Roach, I think you'll have to tell me something to prove you're *not* just a heartless maniac. So how about it? Got any stories like that, or are you just irredeemable?"

"Oh, irredeemable, to be sure." Thyne sputtered out a laugh. "I've saved Sonny's life a lot, though, if that counts for anything."

"Oh yeah? When was the first time?"

"First time I saved his life?" He took a drag and squinted into the last light of sunset. "I don't remember." Thyne glared. "What?" said Roach. "I don't."

"Well, it's your turn to tell a story either way, you lying blighter."

"It's funny you say that, man, because the story of how I got the scar and the first time I saved Sonny's life are the same story, and I don't remember it."

Thyne's nose scrunched up and freckled cheeks went rosy. "You have a perfect memory!"

Roach trailed his gaze away from the sun-speckled garden to Thyne. There was a sad bitterness in him that heeded credence to his words when he whispered, "I don't remember." He took a final drag and snuffed the fag out on the bench between them. "But Sonny remembers. He's told me what happened."

Thyne's anger dissipated, replaced with concern. He wanted to know the story. He wanted to know everything he possibly could, especially about Roach. Information was the most important thing in the world, so it was especially meaningful, even if Roach didn't know it, when Thyne said in the lull, "You don't have to tell me."

Roach hung his head, leaning on his knees, and nodded vaguely. "Yeah." He said after a moment of quiet. "Yeah, I do."

Thyne placed his hand on Roach's thigh. "Y-you don't," his curious tone betrayed the sentiment.

"Yeah, I do, man. You know why?"

"Why?" he whispered.

"Because I love you," he paused, "and I want to share more of myself with you." His smile was pure and beautiful, and Thyne was beet-red all over his cute little face. "So," said Roach as he leaned back on the bench and held his arm out to invite Thyne into his embrace, "Cuddle up, buttercup."

Thyne nodded vaguely, gave Roach his half-smoked cigarette, and curled up against him somewhat hesitantly, his own arms snuggling his plush dullahan.

"Sonny managed to get his Thanksgiving break early somehow, so he was in town for our twentieth birthday. Silvino broke up with me for smoking cigarettes the day after. Or at least, that's the reason he gave at the time. It was actually because his parents pressured him to leave me when we got back from our cross-country trip since I may or may not have convinced him to do some vandalism and he may or may not have gotten us arrested because he was so bad at being sneaky." He chuckled and took a drag.

"By November 21st I had slept with six different women in motels and bar bathrooms and wherever else. Just trying to forget about him, obviously to no end because of my perfect memory. I was still living with my father, but I drank myself blind every time I could manage to get my hands on any sort of alcohol. Dad didn't know I was drinking. I kept to myself in my room playing guitar most of the time, and he left me alone to grieve. That night (the 21st), I ran out of vodka and asked Sonny to drive me out to get more. He managed to sneak me out of the house to our car (the *Fiat*) and drove me to our older brother's apartment. I drank at his place until——." He squeezed tighter around Thyne to comfort himself. "Until I blacked out. Sonny told me how the night played out afterwards:

"He says we stayed there for a few more hours, and I just kept drinking. Gideon eventually cut me off. He was failing his way out of medical school at the time and worried for my health. Anyway, when he cut me off, after we all smoked together, Sonny drove me back and tried to sneak me inside. Dad caught us in the kitchen on our way through to our room, though. He stopped me, grabbed me by my shirt collar, and shouted, 'Clayton, you useless fuck! Are you drunk?' And apparently I gave him a huge shit-eating grin and nodded. That pissed him off. Obviously. So he decked me and shuffled me off to my room, praying over me the entire time he was shoving me to bed. Asking Allah for forgiveness on my behalf. Like it didn't even register that maybe he should have also asked for forgiveness for hitting me.

"Well, I collapsed in the bed and started sobbing, and that's when he got really annoyed with me. He stopped praying and told me to pull myself together. Called me a faggot. Called me a pussy. 'Stop crying. You're fine.' Hadn't heard those words since I was ten. Hadn't *cried* since I was ten. Well, apparently that was a line too far for Sonny, but he didn't say anything at first. Dad went back to the kitchen

466

to resume cleaning, and Sonny sat with me to comfort me. Once I was asleep a few minutes later, he went to the kitchen and confronted Dad. Told him he was a horrible father. That we'd be better off as orphans. Told him to rot in Jahannam. Broke a couple shelves in the fridge trying to find something to stain the rug. Dad grabbed him, and, that's about when it got loud enough that it woke me up. When I got there, he had Sonny backed up against the stove with a knife in his hand ready to stab him.

"I was still blacked-out at this point, so I don't remember jumping between the two of them and taking the knife for Sonny, but you bet your ass I remember the pain. That shit fucking *hurt*, but I didn't even flinch." He sort of laughed. "It sobered me up for a few seconds. Enough that I recall in perfect clarity my father's immediate weeping and apologies. He was sputtering something like a prayer, but it was hardly understandable because he was crying so much. And of course, I spat his own words back in his face: 'Stop crying. You're fine.'" A beat. "So anyway, I blacked back out, and Sonny brought me back to Gideon's for that sweet sweet failing-med-student healthcare, and yeah…," he sighed and smiled lightly at Thyne. "That's the whole story."

Thyne's hand had slipped into Roach's shirt to feel the scar. Now at the story's close, he had stopped caressing it, his face pale and eyes wide. *'Attempted murder? Bloody Hell, that's much more brutal than what Mother would do.'* He felt guilty and ashamed for having shared his childhood as if it was traumatic and horrible when now, by comparison, he was feeling like it was damn near divine. *'Did she… did she actually love me?'* It made him sick to think that he had killed his mother— burned her alive— when this murderous monster sitting beside him hadn't killed his father… had he? "Surely, he was the first person you killed." His tone was pleading.

"My father?" Thyne nodded. "My father's still alive as far as I know."

Thyne gulped. *Fuck. I had no right to do what I did to her…. Am I worse than him?*

"Thyne?" He pulled him away to look at him more easily. "You look pale. I'm sorry. Was that too gruesome?" Thyne didn't respond, his gaze trailing down from Roach's hazel-greys to the scar peeking out from under his blouse. Roach pursed his lips. After a moment of quiet, he pulled up his face gently and kissed his forehead. "What's going on in that beautiful mind of yours, sparkplug?"

He choked on his words before blurting out, "How did you ever forgive him?"

"For stabbing me? Wasn't so much worse than usual." He shrugged. "But for trying to kill Sonny? I'll never forgive him for that."

"If you won't forgive him, and you're such a prolific killer, then why haven't you killed him? Am I worse than you are?"

'Worse than you are.' That hurt. Roach's heart panged at the words. He knew he was the worst sort of filth in the world, but to hear Thyne regard him that way was mixing him all up inside. He closed his eyes as his mind went to war with itself.

"I—. I'm sorry," said Thyne after a beat.

"Your mother deserved it." He sighed and paused. When he spoke again, his voice was slightly broken: "Maybe my dad deserves it, too, but I love him. He didn't just teach me how to shave and fix a car; he taught me *everything*. At least up until '65 when he surprised me and Sonny with applications to a boarding school we wanted to go to. He didn't have to do that. He didn't have the time or the money to do that, but he loved us and knew we needed a better education than he could provide with all his other responsibilities." He sighed again. "He's sick, and we didn't appreciate some of his more zealous tendencies, but… I mean he's my dad, y'know? It wasn't all bad, and I love him. No matter what."

"How could you love him? You said him stabbing you wasn't much worse than usual. I can't even imagine…."

Roach sniffled and rubbed his arm across his face before forcing away the weepiness with a single rough cough. "Anyway, I have another."

Thyne pet Roach's chest and offered him the plush, which was taken and held limply against his torso. "Another what?"

"Another redeemable quality."

"You have a lot of redeemable qualities, Roach. I didn't mean to imply you're some sort of monster."

"Don't lie to me, dude."

His posture slumped. "I certainly didn't mean to imply it," he repeated but lacking confidence.

"You think I'm a monster?" He looked him in the eyes.

Thyne blenched and, after a moment of quiet, nodded just-so. "But I like that about you!" he immediately defended.

Roach smirked. "You're cute. Don't look so worried, man. You can't offend me calling me what I am."

Thyne let on a weak smile. "I'm no saint myself."

Roach's grin became slimier, and he leaned in to say, "Yeah. You just *might* be worse."

What had been a worry only moments prior was a friendly competition now. Thyne's weak grin became one more smug. "You're right. Two redeeming qualities? That's two more than I have. You're practically angelic!"

Roach laughed one ha and pulled Thyne closer. He kissed the top of his head and hugged him as hard as he could with the one arm around him. "I love you, man." Thyne was too flustered to return the sentiment, so Roach pushed past it: "You already know about the other redeemable quality, though, so it's not a big long story. Just how I got Franky to offload a burden that was weighing down his soul. It's mighty heavy, but I think I'm helping him carry it." Thyne nodded as they both leaned back in the bench to resume snuggling. "I helped him with a couple of other loads, too, eh?" He nudged him, and Thyne rolled his eyes playfully.

They resumed their chatting, less heavy now. It went on for an hour before they somehow wound up on the topic of the burning of the Library of Alexandria, and the tension often brought about from their political arguments was starting to set upon them:

"But why?"

"I'm surprised at you, Thyne. You know better than I do the beauty in fire and destruction. You're saying you wouldn't burn it down?"

"Of course I wouldn't! Think of all the history that was lost."

"Short of loved ones, I don't mourn for lost things, and I don't find value in what the suits in power find worthy of hoarding."

"Are you suggesting that the Library of Alexandria was full of state propaganda?"

"And why wouldn't it be? And why would I care if I were there to raze the city with my army? Burn it down, I say."

Thyne held his spinning head. "But *why*? Why would you throw away so much history— so much *knowledge* so flippantly?"

Roach sighed and bit down on a cigarette. He flipped open his lighter in a small flourish he had learned from Thyne and held its flame at the end of his fag. They watched the little fire in his hand as it gave its warmth to his breath, and after his first drag, he finally released the fork. The air about them was cast in a deeper darkness than before it had flicked to life. The little glow from his cigarette fell from his face as a billowing cloud of smoke left his lips. "It's interesting how you worded that."

After a long beat of quiet, Thyne whispered, "I understand."

"Oh?"

"You would burn it down because you see no value in preserving history. Why should you? You have a perfect memory. You couldn't possibly know the pain of forgetting."

His brow furrowed with irritation, but it was only perceptible in the few seconds the light of his cigarette grew brighter when he tasted its fire.

"I don't remember his face," whimpered Thyne in the quietude that followed. "It's been, what? 140 years? And that's not including the time I spent in the past and future with Francis or with Rosie." He sighed and lit his own cigarette. "If I had some vast temple to him with paintings and photos lining the walls—. If I had recordings of his perfect voice and all the things he ever whispered to me—. Every word he ever said, no matter how mundane—." His gaze snapped up to Roach and hardened. "I would treasure it so completely that some brute coming in with a fire would know nothing but misery for all his days were he to even think of destroying that history. That *part of me*. I don't remember his fucking face, Clayton. I don't remember it, and you would take it from me if I had it because you don't know the pain of forgetting."

"And you don't know the pain of remembering," he said simply.

"I know plenty about the pain of remembering. I remember my mother's face, but I don't remember Oliver's. What could be more painful than that?"

He took a drag and trailed his gaze lazily away to the distant dancing lights of the faire. After a long beat of silence, he replied, "Would you remember it all, if you could? In perfect clarity: every last second?"

"Of course I would. You don't know how blessed you are."

His gaze trailed back to Thyne. The pain in his deep grey eyes was palpable even through the veil of darkness between them in the moonlit garden. "Then you would remember in perfect clarity his screams of agony in Auschwitz." Thyne went pale as just such a memory came whispering through him. "You would remember the others around him in chorus with him. Him begging for his life (or perhaps for his death) to the likes of Viktor. Dying. You'd hear him fucking dying, Thyne. You'd hear it again and again and again. It would haunt you forever.

"But even without your microphones, you would suffer the memories. Every barb he ever threw at you. Every pointless argument you ever started with him. You would remember being irritated with him for trivialities. You would remember every promise you ever made and broke. Every lie you ever told him like the snake you are." He stood, and when he started back up, it was clear he was holding back tears. "You would know, down to the *second*, exactly how much time with him you wasted. How much time you spent getting high instead of holding him and loving him. How much time you spent being angry with him for not letting you be a murderous lunatic as if *he* was the crazy one for leashing you like that. Like you weren't lucky he didn't bring you to a padded box the first chance he got. That he even still loved you at all.

"You would know, Thyne, down to the fucking second just how fucking much of that precious precious time you pissed away in solitude jerking off, drinking, praying, writing shitty music, being a fucking scumbag, whatever the fuck else. Not paying him the God damn attention he fucking deserved." He flicked his cigarette straight to the ground and slammed his heel into it, making an indent in the mud.

Thyne stood to cup his hand gently around Roach's cheek. "Clayton. I—."

He shoved the hand away. "Burn it down, I say. Let it decay. History be damned. If it's worth knowing, inshallah, it will be known. Fire is cleansing, and rot is release"

Thyne pulled back, but he hesitated to fully retreat. Roach felt his hand on his cheek a moment later, wiping away his tears with his thumb. "Can I ask you something?" Roach nodded and sniffled, so Thyne continued, "When we met in that diner… did you feel anything strange?"

There was a slight start in him that he tried to hide. "What does that matter?" he snipped and pushed Thyne's hand away again. "We were talking about the Library of Alexandria. Tell me why you wouldn't burn it down."

He pursed his lips. "Information is the most important thing in the world, but… maybe I *would* burn it down."

"I know you fucking would. All the good ones are the texts; the rest of us: the torches. Burn down a thousand libraries. Raze every university. Deforest every wood. Fill the ocean with garbage and oil. Blot out the sky with nuclear fog. It doesn't matter. Nothing does. All those scrolls are dust now, and that's what all of this will be one day."

Thyne frowned. "If nothing matters, then answer my question."

"Yes," he snipped and glared, "Yes, it was incredibly strange when we met, if you must know. And I can only presume that by your asking, you felt it, too, though I fail to see the connection between the library and that."

Thyne's eyes welled up. He lowered himself back into the bench and looked down at his hands. There was a long pause, during which Roach sat down beside him and let his hair down to run his hands through it. "He was my best mate…," Thyne began confusingly and with a great weepiness in his tone. "When we were little, we would steal spices from the farmers when they came to town. Just a couple kleptos, to be honest," a sad chuckle, "but we got caught one day, and rather than reprimand us, the farmer gave us each an entire plant in a little jar. He figured if we could grow our own we'd stop stealing. He gave me a thyme plant and Oliver a basil one. That's what eventually evolved into our pet names for each other. Even before we were romantically involved, he would call me Thyme, and I'd call him Basil." He sniffled and rubbed his sleeve across his running nose. "Thyme became 'Thyne' when he combined the nickname with the word 'mine' because I was utterly his. Even though I—." He held his face and wept, and Roach was quick to pull him into both of his strong arms to let him cry into his chest. He squeezed Roach's warm body as he gathered enough control over himself to continue several minutes later:

"We never had sex, even though I know he wanted me. We had ample opportunities to do it safely, but anytime things started to get too heated, I would stop it. I would apologise and apologise and—." He sniffled. "He would always tell me he didn't care if we never did it, but I didn't have anything to give him but my body, and I still didn't give him that." He was going to say more, but Roach butted in:

"Thyne, that's not true." He lifted his face up by the chin. "You gave him your heart and soul." He was going to reference the old song of the same name and how it was one of his favourites, but Thyne started bawling again. He held him close and managed to understand some of the mewling words he said in the following:

"You must remember. Why would you say that if you don't remember?"

"I don't know what you mean," whispered Roach.

After Thyne gathered his senses again, he continued without explaining the outburst: "He was the only one there in hospital to visit me after I cut off my finger. He jokingly complained to me later how it threw a wrench in his plans to propose." He chuckled sadly at the memory. "He was tall and strong, and he hardly ever let anyone know his true feelings. He would cough them away and go all stone faced," he looked up at Roach, "like you." He smiled sadly and kissed Thyne's forehead. "He had the most adorable snort-laugh, like you, too, and he had such a good sense of humour…. And our song… Our song was *Heart and Soul.*" He sniffled and looked up at Roach again, his amber eyes and rosy cheeks sopping wet with tears. "His dying words to me were, 'I'll find you in the next life.' And… Roach… When I saw you in that diner I knew he made good on that promise. When I saw you… I remembered his face. I heard his laughter. I—. Please, Basil. Don't you remember London? Please say you remember London." Roach frowned, but before he could say anything, Thyne added, "Say you remember even if it's a lie."

He plucked up one of Thyne's hands and kissed his knuckles tenderly. "I'm sorry, Thyne. London… must have been in the library."

Thyne wailed and buried his face in Roach's chest whimpering, "Delusional. Delusional bastard."

"Shh. You're not delusional. Because… because I felt it too, Thyne." They looked at each other. "I felt it too," he reiterated with a serious tenor to his whisper.

"Then why won't you come back to me, Basil?" Roach's black heart broke as Thyne's face contorted. "Haven't I suffered long enough without you?"

"Just a moment longer," said Roach automatically, as if the words were not his own. He even pushed past them as if he hadn't said anything at all: "Why don't we go get some oolong? That's your favourite, right?"

Thyne's eyes were hopeful and wet as he looked up at Roach. How did he know oolong was his favourite? He had never said as much…. It could have been observational— an educated guess—, but to Thyne it was confirmation that Roach and Oliver's souls were one and the same. "Yeah," he whimpered eventually, "Oolong is my favourite."

Part Four

Monsters aren't welcome here

Chapter 41

I'm Late

Autumn ambled onto the scene taking its sweet ass time cooling down the horrid heat of summer. Most of September was even hotter than August, but by October, there was finally a bite to the air outside. Things had progressed rather uneventfully after the faire. Thyne and Roach were still not officially an item, though their frequent bickering gradually turned more into flirtatious teasing. Perlie was still livid with Partha, but after his fifth apology with flowers and wine and chocolates (still only in August), she caved to his charms. The make-up sex was nice, but the best sex was after he promised to officially be her boyfriend. To his surprise, she didn't even ask for exclusivity. She instead asked him not to have *casual* sex with others and to only seek other long-term partners, should he want them. He was of the mind it was overly generous, but she insisted it was what she wanted. He was already in foreign territory being in a long-term relationship with her, so for the moment, it was open in-name-only. As far as anyone else could tell, they were exclusive.

She found him one chilled autumn morning only a week before the job on Eir Lilac and thus a week before his birthday. He was in the art studio working on costumes and masks with Dezba and Roach. Her smiles since she started dating him usually lit up the room, so the despondent countenance she wore that morning was noticed immediately.

He looked up from his needle and thread. "What's wrong, heart?"

"Party, I need to talk to you in private," she muttered.

His stomach cinched. Was she going to break up with him? He hadn't even cheated.... The sting in his nose and on his gums seemed to surge as if to foretell something. His hands were trembling as he set the dress he was sewing onto a rolling cart and shuffled out of the room after Perlie.

She brought them to the back porch and pulled out her cigarettes. Her hand was trembling as she held the box in front of her chest, not taking one of the cancer-sticks but clearly wanting to. After a while of internal struggle, she pulled one halfway out, but Partha's hand came into her view as he lifted her face up by the chin. "What's the matter, heart?" He spoke sweetly, and her eyes welled up just-so.

"I'm late." Her voice was so strangled that it didn't sound.

His stomach was lead. It crashed through the floorboards of the porch and anchored itself deep into the bowels of the earth. The colour in his skin nearly entirely washed out, and the hand on her chin started to tremble. He opened his mouth to say something, but nothing escaped his lungs, not even his breath.

A cold breeze sent chills down their already-uneasy spines. Perlie finally spoke again. "What do we do if I'm...?"

He shook his head slowly, but the more he shook it the quicker it moved until he was grabbing his temples and stumbling backwards. "An abortion! That's what we fucking do!"

She inhaled sharply and averted her dark eyes. It was what she wanted, too. At least, that's what she had thought at first, "But..."

"But what?" He sounded terrified. "Perlie, please." He slid onto his knees in front of her and grabbed her hands in his. "Please tell me you don't want it."

She still refused to look at him. The tears trailing her cheeks and clogging her throat were unwelcome and frankly pissing her off. She wiped her face with her forearm roughly and stomped inside, slamming the door behind her. Partha scrambled after her, his hands clasped as he followed her begging. "Please please please, Perlie. Think of my career! This isn't fair. We use protection! What's the bloody point of those uncomfortable pieces of sh—."

She slapped him and slammed the door to her room in his face. He stood staring at the dark wooden panels and holding his aching cheek, unsure how much time passed between being slapped and feeling a hand on his wrist.

"Come on, mate," muttered Thyne as he led him away from her. They wordlessly passed by Dezba on her way into the suite to comfort the weeping woman.

"Perlie, dear," she said as she quietly closed the door behind her, "Thyne told me to come comfort you. What's wrong?"

She was sitting on the edge of her bed and fidgeting with a pregnancy test. Her gaze trailed to the small trash bin beside her dresser where another four tests were piled, all positive. An abortion seemed like the best course of action. They were criminals, for fuck's sake, and she didn't want to have to go through nine months of hormonal garbage just to spend however many hours in earth-ending pain. But that Partha was so overdramatic about the issue made her feel… it made her feel… well, she wasn't quite sure how it made her feel. She was thirty-one. He would only be twenty-four on Halloween. She was far more prepared for parenthood than he was, and even considering that: she wasn't ready in the slightest. Still… she at least wanted to *consider* keeping it.

Dezba let herself in and sat beside Perlie. She noticed her despondent posture and the positive reading on the test in her hands and couldn't help but be a little jealous at the sight. Upset that she could get pregnant? When Dezba had gone through hours of labour to a child her womb had already murdered? It was because of her upset that she didn't say anything for about three minutes, after which she finally let out a long breath and pulled Perlie in for a hug. "Come here," she cooed, "It'll be okay, love."

Perlie allowed herself to be held. She even weakly returned the embrace. But when she felt her sinuses starting to burn with tears, she pushed herself away and slammed the pregnancy test across the room with a shout. It hit the wall over the trash bin and landed on the ground just beside it. "Fuck!"

"Perlie, what's wrong? We're in a doctor's manor right now. He can give you an abortion."

"But what if I don't want one!?" she snapped, not even realising what she was saying.

Dezba started. "Well… if you don't want one… then he can deliver the baby."

"'Baby'," she wailed and held her forehead. Hearing that word made it more real for her. "Abortion. You're right."

"Children are a blessing, but we're also in an active gang of criminals. Terrorists, technically." A beat. "You do what's best for you, Perlie. Nothing anyone else says matters."

She sucked up noisily through her clogging nose and said with a quaver, "But what about Partha?"

"What about him?"

"It's his!"

"You're worried he's not ready to be a father?"

"Well *now* I am!"

"Why did you bring him up?"

"Because he wants me to abort it. He was begging me."

"It's your body, Perlie. It's polite to hear him out, but it's not his choice."

She looked down at her hands and imagined them as her mother's hands: soft and loving and sweet. Her parents couldn't make it work between them, yet she felt their love equally, even when her father moved back to Korea before the American crusade. Even if Partha didn't want to participate in this child's life, she would make sure to give it a good upbringing. But as she was considering the life of a single mother, the scars on her wrists and forearms caught her eye. They were faded now, but danger was ever present. And… fuck… what would Roach think? Would he want to help raise the child? Why did she sort of want him to? Why did she still feel anything for him? She had Partha now. But Partha… he didn't want kids… and Roach always had….

"Fuck," she muttered as her hands started to tremble. "Dezba," she whimpered and looked at her, a tear trailing her cheek, "I don't know what to do."

Her elderly friend stood and took her hands in hers. She clasped them gently together to stop their trembling and pet her soft skin, eventually trailing her hand up to Perlie's scars. "You don't have to make any decisions right now. You have at least a few months to think about it. Okay?"

She sniffled and nodded.

While Perlie was being comforted, Partha was sitting on his bed with Thyne standing at its foot. There was a long beat of quiet while his mind raced, after which he looked at Thyne and whimpered, "What's she saying?" Thyne only glared. "I fucked it up again, didn't I?"

"She just wanted to talk about it. The implications are a lot heavier for what she would have to endure regardless of the choice *she* makes." He crossed his arms and softly glared at Partha. "You do know that my daughter died in January, don't you?" Partha stuttered incoherently. He had gathered she had been killed by Viktor thanks to Thyne's comment about it during the madness on Eid ul-Fitr, but he didn't know how recently it had occurred. "You're acting like having a child is earth-shattering when mine has been taken from me. I have half a mind to strike you."

He sighed and slumped his shoulders. "We can't even consider this, Thyne. Even if I do want a kid."

"You what?"

"I said I want a kid," he muttered, "But I don't want to have to quit the gang, and I have a career to think about."

"And that's *all* you'd have to consider?"

Partha tried to think about what else having a child would change. "I guess I'd have to be ashore for a few years at first, too, but that's not so bad."

"The cocaine!?"

Partha started and looked at him hopelessly. "I can't."

"Can't what, Partha?"

"I can't… stop." He averted his eyes from Thyne's wild ambers.

"Absolutely pathetic," spat Thyne. "You know you're not the only one with addiction struggles in this gang."

He scoffed and glared. "Yeah, you and Roach smoke like chimneys, and Franky's blood is probably pure rum by this point."

"That's not what I meant."

"You mean how Viktor said you were a meth head? That was true?"

He crossed his arms again. "It was."

"I don't want to talk about it. Good for you for quitting, but I don't want to quit."

"Well, if you want a kid you—."

"I said I don't want to talk about it," he said firmly, "Leave."

After a few angry huffs, Thyne stomped out of the room, slamming the door behind him, and about ten minutes later, there was a knock.

"I said I don't want to talk," snipped Partha as he was brought up from the depths of his anxious thoughts.

"Party, if you don't let me in, I'll have to pick the lock."

Partha was surprised to hear Roach's voice but sighed and took a twenty-sided die from the dice bag on his bedside table. He slid it under the door and mumbled, "Roll sleight of hand."

Roach picked up the die and looked at it. "Can't I roll diplomacy?"

Partha sighed and opened the door. "What do you want?"

He pocketed the die and grinned. "What's all this about a baby? Knocked up Perls? Lucky you, eh?" Partha pouted, and Roach ruffled his hair as he pushed past him into the room. As he was looking around and picking up some of Partha's nerdy decorations: "I always bugged her for kids, and she never wanted any, so good for you changing her mind. You don't really seem the fatherly type, but I'm happy to see you turning over a new leaf. Are you going to quit the gang, though?"

"I don't want to," he muttered.

"Hell yeah. Fucking rad, dude. 'It takes a village' type deal then? We'll all get to help raise the little kiddo? Oh, I'm excited! Roach: the cool uncle that buys him drugs and shit. When he's old enough, of course." He giggled and looked at Partha with a huge beaming grin. "Speaking of drugs: Thyne said you wanted some tips on quitting the coke? I guess whatever method you used during Ramadan won't work permanently, then?"

He huffed and pouted like a child. "No."

"Well no worries, bro. You don't have to do it on your own. We're here for you."

"I'm not quitting," he grumbled.

Roach started. Thyne had outright lied to him, telling him that Partha wanted to quit for the sake of his unborn child. After the brief startle, he resumed mindlessly observing Partha's knick-knacks and said simply, "You really want to miss out on the little one's childhood?" Partha rolled his eyes and leaned on his elbow to resume worrying about Perlie's ultimate decision regarding the pregnancy. "The gang will help you wean off of it safely." Partha gave him the silent treatment, so after a few minutes of wordlessness, Roach sat on the bed beside the worry-wart.

He grabbed Partha's thigh around the knee and leaned in to whisper, "A si i-Dhúath ú-orthor, Partha. Ú or le a ú or nin."

It took a moment for Partha to process the words and pull himself out of his anxiety. When he finally had, he beamed up at Roach and said, "You know Sindarin!?"

"I was literally dressed as Sauron when we met."

Partha scrunched up his nose but had a playful air about him when he retorted, "Yes, but Sauron hated the elves, why would you being dressed as him mean you know their tongue?"

"Bold of you to assume he didn't know their tongue when he implanted himself into their society."

Partha scrambled to his feet and faced Roach. His posture was submissive, and he spoke in Sindarin: "Forgive me, sire! Oh, Roach! Beautiful monster of… erm… Compton…. You are more handsome, more powerful, and more terrifying than Lord Sauron, himself! I submit to you and will serve you dutifully in your highs—, your throes—, your most vile of plans—. And I would happily and hastily march across Middle Earth with just your word and none else." He crossed an arm over his abdomen and bowed deeply.

"Great," said Roach in English, "Then quit the blow. That's an order." He took out the d20 from his pocket and flicked it into Partha's bowing head before standing to leave.

"Wait!" said Partha with his hands scrambling to Roach's firm chest to stop him.

"I'm sorry? Did you not just swear fealty to me?"

"Roach, I can't just quit!"

"Why not?"

His brow furrowed, but he couldn't retain his anger for long and instead tried bargaining: "What if I just do it less for a while?"

"Hm, I don't know. Would I be getting something out of it?"

"I—. I'll—." He blushed at his own thoughts and decided to instead say, "Well, what do you want, sir?"

"I want you to quit the blow."

"But I need it!"

He nodded and hummed a couple disingenuous "Mmhmm"'s as if he was agreeing. "You want to know a secret, Party?"

"Do I?"

Roach leaned in and whispered, "I used to be an addict."

"You?" He looked him up and down with a bemused sort of expression. "I don't believe you. And besides, I'm not addicted." He knew fully well that he was, but he figured he might as well attempt to deny it.

"It was a downer for me, not an upper. I figure that's why Thyne wanted to talk to you. Because he was on meth in the war like a lot of the soldiers. But I imagine the principle is about the same as it was for stopping H. Quit it now, and we'll all be here to support you in the inevitably messy afterward. We have two doctors in the gang, for God's sake, dude. One of them has doctor magic. The other one's been a doctor for like all of human history. You'll be fine."

He pouted. "Just go away."

"Hm? I must have misheard you. It sounded like you told me to go away."

He scrunched up his nose and tried to be intimidating, only to immediately submit again with just a mere look from the tall man. "Fine. Fine. I'll quit."

"Promise?"

He looked up at him, trying to puppy-dog-eye his way out of it. "Do I have to?"

He sighed. "How about this, kid: you quit the blow, and you can join in on the Halloween job."

"You mean it, sir? I won't have to sit around at the palace base?"

"Yeah. Consider it a birthday present, but you can only go if you quit the blow."

He took a moment to ponder the offer. "Okay… Okay I'll try."

Roach smiled sweetly. "Good! Now go get working on a costume! Only a few days 'til the job."

Partha beamed and said in Sindarin with another bow, "As you wish, my liege."

"Ha! You're cute. I'll be with Thyne and Franky in the states for a few days doing a little stabby stab, but if you need me you can always call."

"Thank you, Roach."

483

Chapter 42
Eat Me

Rory Couch owned a palace in London that was only a few decades old but masqueraded as something more antique. It was rare that he rented out its entirety, usually only offering out a wing or two for weddings or concerts, but on Halloween 2081, it would be entirely occupied, and Mr. Couch would make upwards of thirty million pounds in just one night from that property alone. It had been rented out by Eir Lilac Pharmaceutical's eccentric CEO, Christopher Filipek, for a themed masquerade party. Rory had little interest in the gathering, but when he was given an invitation, he was informed that all manner of elites and celebrities would be attending. '*Maybe*,' he thought, '*that bastard Abraham will be there.*'

He wasn't overly upset about having lost Ms. Temm's favour to the dinosaur, but there was a more nefarious side of him that wanted to screw over Osiris financially because of it. How sweet it would be to see her shattered to pieces, watching all Abraham's money shrivel up. Rory knew it would be impossible to take down the monolith that was Osiris even with his own wealth, which was comparatively pennies, but fantasies of revenge rarely rubbed elbows with realism.

The theme for the party was Lewis Carroll's imaginings, much to Rory's annoyance. He loathed Carroll and the maddening "quirkiness" his fans tended to announce loudly to the world. Filipek was no exception. In fact he was among the worst of them. The entire time he was conducting business with Rory, he was smoking on a pipe and making nonsensical declarations like "Why, this is nothing a dog can't do with a duck!" or "They call you Couch, not because you like to sit, but because you come at life at the right angle!" Rory forced a grin through the frustrating meeting, but as soon as he was free of the eccentric billionaire, he rubbed the bridge of his nose and let out a lengthy string of muttered swears, as if making up for all the cursing he had to withhold in the short exchange.

There were many months before Halloween, during which Rory tried to determine if Abraham would be coming to the party. He had been invited, but beyond that, Filipek was elusive when questioned on the status of the invitation. One of the times Rory asked about it, he was answered, "Why, yes, of course! If he weren't coming he would be there by noon!" Another time, the answer was, "Unfortunately no. Abraham is bald and thus cannot be a hare." That anyone understood the madman was a wonder Rory could not fathom. When it became clear that he would not be getting answers from Filipek about Abraham's attendance, he asked the other elites of Eir Lilac. They were not as incoherent as their boss, but their answers were always some manner of, "I don't know if he'll be there."

The rules of the party detailed that invitees were not to remove their masks and to keep their identities hidden for as long as possible. There was a cash prize for the party-goer who remained unidentified the longest, but Rory had so little interest in the festivities that his costume was little more than a suit and a venetian mask which covered only the top half of his face. The mahogany stubble he sported would be a dead-giveaway to anyone who knew him, so, with a passing interest in the cash prize, the most effort he took to hide his identity was to shave.

The party was in full-swing when he arrived an hour after its start. His coat and umbrella were taken by a service worker at the door, and thus he started sweeping the rooms in search of Tatum Abraham. The old man would be easy enough to identify, no matter what sort of mask he might have been wearing. His short hunched-over stature and shaky half-dead movements would make him immediately recognisable to anyone who had ever even so slight as glanced at him.

He didn't find the ancient man in his first pass of the party, but with a champagne flute in hand, he decided to wait it out a little longer, despite how irritating the guests and decor were. The party was set to go until dawn, and it was only 10:00 p.m. There was still plenty of time for Abraham to show. Having found a corner to sulk in quietly, Rory was approached by another party-goer. He was dressed in deep blacks and vivid reds and burgundies. His dress-shirt was maroon, covered by a black vest with a bright red heart embroidered over the front. The vest matched his pants and shoes, and his full-face mask. On the mask was another red heart with a calligraphic white letter Q painted inside, his left glove was red and his right glove was black, and atop his head there sat what looked to be a red ruby tiara. He smelled of cigarettes, cinnamon, and thyme and had a graceful gait.

Rory dreaded the stranger's approach and what he might have wanted to chat about, so he was glad to learn that this man only approached to grab some of the pre-wrapped cookies that Rory was blocking. "Excuse me, mate," he said politely.

"Sorry," said Rory as he moved out of the stranger's way and watched him take the food. He took upwards of ten cookies and shoved them in his pants pockets. Rory might have said something if he actually cared about anyone at the party, but he only rolled his eyes at the gluttony and watched the man walk away.

"Okay," said Thyne as he approached Perlie, River, and Partha, "They have the biscuits. They're a tad bigger than ours, though."

"Should be fine," said Perlie as Thyne started passing out the treats to the three of them.

The biscuits they had brought with them to the party were almost identical to the ones Thyne had taken from the buffet table: simple sugar cookies with colourful frosting and the words *Eat Me* written atop them. Unfortunately, theirs were smaller and would perhaps be hard to convince their targets to eat. Giovanni had baked them the night before and poisoned them with aluminium phosphide. It was as they were coming out of the oven that Thyne, Francis, and Roach returned from their trip to America.

Thyne had flown them to Toronto, wherein Francis "teleported" Roach to New York City, Vegas, and even back to LA in search of four particular celebrities. Upon finding each of them, Roach's hysterical disgusting pleasure in murder was exploited, bodies were hidden, identities were stolen. With blood still on him, after each kill, Roach made love to Francis: the only one other than Thyne and River not overly perturbed by this murderous part of the plan. The four who had infiltrated the party were using the identities and invitations of those four killed in the states, and while they looked similar enough to pass as the celebrities while in costume, it was imperative that their masks were not removed lest they risk the entire mission.

Partha would be impersonating a heartthrob A-list actor named Andrei Sokolov. He was the closest match to Partha's height and skin tone that the gang could find in the short time Partha in particular had to prepare for the mission. Because he was impersonating such a high-profile person, it was lucky Partha (a celebrity in his own right) was the most adept actor of the group with all the LARPing and DMing he did. During the week of insufferable sobriety before Halloween, he had studied Sokolov's movies and interviews while he made his costume. He therefore had the mannerisms and thick Russian accent down to a science. The only thing he didn't have down was speaking the actual Russian language, so he elected to stay near Thyne as much as possible in the hopes that the Brit could subtly translate or make some excuse for him if someone tried to speak in Russian to him.

All of the masks were full-face for obvious reasons, and Partha's was indigo-blue with subtle gold accents. It wasn't very complex having only been made in a day. The accents were simple lines and emphasised his cheekbones and eyes. There was a small hole in the lips of the mask, and underneath it was a black mesh covering that hid his eyes. He could see through the mesh, but his already-hindered vision was stifled even more by it: another reason to stay near Thyne.

His costume was the same indigo-blue as his mask, his gloves and buttons the same gold, and he had a prop vaping device that fit perfectly through the hole in his mask's lips which he used to vape and blow blueberry-pancake scented smoke rings. The design was crisp and the costume incredibly well-made despite the hurry he was in while crafting it. His slightly-heeled shoes gave him the extra height difference between himself and the now-deceased Andrei Sokolov, and his long dark hair had been cut to his shoulders, straightened, and bleached to match Andrei's as well.

Thyne's Queen of Hearts costume had been sewn with extra padding to make him seem a bit chubby like the voice actor he would be impersonating: a German man called Ferdi Holzknecht who was well known for his work in various video games. Luckily, most of them were games Thyne played often and had mastered. He knew all of the same languages that Ferdi knew save for Japanese, and he had practised the voices he might be asked to perform to good effect. He even asked Francis to take him back to some prehistoric era for a few weeks to have more time to prepare.

Perlie's mask was a cute mouse-shaped one with brown velvet coating its entirety. She also had mesh covering her eyes, and her hair had been braided and pinned against the back of her head to hide beneath the back of the mask. Her costume was a brown velvet dress with a mediaeval style cut and a long strip of extra fabric in the back to act as a train and the dormouse's "tail." It appeared to be the simplest costume of the four, but she had hidden pockets all throughout the dress. She was impersonating an American movie director named Cynthia Sommer, and her research for the job consisted mostly of looking through Cynthia's phone and other things that Roach and Francis had stolen from her home in Las Vegas on the night of her murder.

River would be impersonating a basketball player named August Laine from the team Filipek owned: The Boston Nightingales. Laine was actually two inches taller than River, so he had platform shoes to make up the difference. To cover them, the skirt of his dark grey dress went all the way to the ground where it forked into two short trains. He wore a blue suit jacket over it, and his mask was of a grey walrus that matched his turtlenecked dress. The mask covered his entire head, including his hair, which was pinned up to his head in a tight braid like Perlie's. Luckily, the man he was impersonating had an American accent, and all he needed to do to perfect his impression of him was make his voice a little softer. His sleeves doubled as gloves and, in fact, the dress was quite form-fitting in the torso area and showed his well-toned muscles where the coat was not covering him. To research for his role he did much the same as Perlie and could only hope he wouldn't be invited to play any basketball. At least the pencil-skirt of his dress would be a good excuse if it came up.

Attending the party would be the CEO, COO, CMO, and President of Eir Lilac. Among those not directly working under the company would include the President of Osiris International's food supplying division, the CTO of Maitland, and a number of shareholders from all of the publicly traded companies on their radars. Each of the four infiltrators had three targets, and Giovanni had informed them that they had approximately four hours after the first one was poisoned before the symptoms would start to become obvious.

May had an earpiece on each of them and had hacked into the cameras in the venue. She would start a timer as soon as it was confirmed for her that one of the targets had taken the poison.

While the night was still young, Thyne, River, and Perlie elected to split up to more efficiently find targets. Partha tried to tail Thyne, but after only five minutes, the Brit pulled him close and whispered harshly: "Stop fucking following me. Do the job. Don't you want to prove yourself to Roach?" Partha nodded. "Then go kill someone."

As Thyne's gloved hand slipped away, Partha felt as though he had been dropped from a cliff. His soul was in freefall as he took unconfident strides through the faux-marble halls. He had been to countless parties, but this was unlike anything he had seen before. The music was not a thumping bass nor wailing synth but various live orchestral musicians in different parts of the palace. The few rooms he had seen with prerecorded music were playing whimsical tunes with slower tempos than he would have expected from a party. On the whole, the entire palace was dimly lit, but what lights there were were warm and inviting, which was far from what he had expected based on the theme. It was lucky Perlie had researched the venue and previous parties so Partha could dress them properly, but even still, their costumes were among the more effortful. Some people weren't even wearing masks and most of the guests were dressed in bland ball gowns and suits.

He found himself in a lounge on the fourth floor after some time ambling around and trying to spot targets. His attention was caught, however, by the view through the floor-to-ceiling windows. The cityscape of London sparkled like the night sky through the clear autumn air. The music in this chamber was pre-recorded and, as he looked upon the city, it was a heavenly chorus of wordless song. It enveloped him like a warm hug, and among the sensory overload came the pleasant scent of a familiar cologne. He didn't realise it was someone approaching him until he felt a hand on his shoulder. "Quite the view, yeah?" said the newcomer with an obviously-false cockney accent.

Partha blenched and looked at his guest. He was hopeful it was one of his targets, or perhaps River fucking with him by putting on a different voice, but the half-masked face he saw was immediately recognised and one he was stupid to have not expected. '*Fuck fuck fuck. Does he recognise me?*' He coughed away his nervousness and spoke in the false Russian accent he had spent the last week perfecting: "Is a nice sight, da." A hit from his vape helped to calm him, so there was smoke on his words as he quoted the caterpillar, his voice still accented: "Who are you?"

"C'mon, mate. I ain't just gonna tell ya!" He laughed and sipped his champagne. "Ya sound Russian, but…," he stroked his clean-shaven chin, "I coulda sworn you was someone else. Someone I know."

He laughed nervously. "Another person dressed as the caterpillar?"

The man arched his brow, though it was mostly hidden beneath his mask. He was picking up on Partha's nervousness. "Yeah," he said eventually with an intrigued tone that panicked Partha enough that he had to cross his arms to hide his trembling hands. The man spoke with his normal Brummie accent: "You wouldn't happen to be Bermudan, would you?" He watched Partha like a hawk for even the minutest of movements.

Partha held his breath. '*Fuck!*' He took what felt like six years mulling over his options mentally, but it was only three seconds later that he let out a shaky breath and pulled the man close. His breath was hot in his ear as he whispered, "Please, Rory. You didn't see me."

He whispered his reply into Partha's ear with poorly-veiled venom, "How did you get in here? I would have noticed your name on the invitation list."

"I'll tell you after the party. I promise."

"Like how you promised to come back to London for my birthday in August?"

"I'll make it up to you."

"Make me an offer, or I'll tell Filipek you're here."

Partha's breaths quickened, but after swallowing some of his nervousness, he managed to sound sensual when he replied, "How about a threesome?"

Rory's fist struck Partha's ribs quite hard but stealthily enough that no one noticed. "You twat." He pulled Partha's hunching torso back up to spit more whispers into his ear, "Make me a *better* offer, cunt."

After a quiet few coughs, he replied hoarsely, "How much?" Rory only glared. After another wheeze, Partha sighed and returned his attention to the cityscape. Rory's gaze followed suit, and while they were both gazing out at London, Partha said simply, "500 million."

Rory started. He was certain that was more than Partha was worth, but there didn't seem to be any amount of deceit in his voice. Though Rory was looking at him, Partha continued to look out the window, rapt in panic he was trying desperately not to show. Rory could feel it, though. In fact, there was a part of him that could also feel that Partha was sober. He ran a hand up his shoulder and rubbed it gently. After a moment of consideration, he said, "Keep your money, kid. It's your birthday, after all. I'll keep mum, but you owe me an explanation after... and a dinner date."

Partha sucked up his fearful tears and gave Rory a quick hug. While embracing him, he whispered weepily, "Thank you. I'm sorry for everything."

Before Partha could work himself up, Rory retreated and shook his head. "Don't cry over me, dear. We'll figure it out." Partha nodded. Rory kissed his knuckles then turned his attention back to the city to give Partha a chance to slink away.

After exiting the chamber, the warmth from the angelic music and bittersweet encounter was replaced with crippling dread. He held his head and stumbled. The vape helped, but what he really needed was some coke. The world was heavy and terrifying and depressing, and if he could just have one bump, he'd be able to do this job without fucking it up anymore than he already had. He went into a bathroom beside the next loudest room he could find, lucky it was private. He closed himself behind the thick oak door, blocking out most of the sounds from the other side and whispered, "I know you heard that, Thyne, and I know what you're thinking, but I really don't want to have to kill him. Please don't kill him. He'll keep quiet."

Being in the bathroom, after his pleading with Thyne, he moved automatically. He pissed, washed his hands, then reached for his pockets in search of his coke. When he found only his poisoned cookies, he was reminded of the task at hand and tore off his mask to stare into his own eye. *'I don't need it. I've gone an entire week without it already. I'm finally on a God damn job and being taken seriously. I can't let this shit ruin this for me.'* To help himself feel better, he recalled aloud things his father would tell him as a boy: "You can do it, Partha. You're a fearsome Leviathan. A winsome warrior. Nothing can stop you once you've set your mind to something. *Nothing.*" Then, in his head, he recalled what his father said to him the first day he came back from rehab: *"I'm so proud of you, kiddo, I'm just sorry I couldn't be there for you to stop you from starting in the first place."* "It's not your fault, Daddy," he whispered in reply to the memory.

After his pep-talk, he managed to psych himself up with pure adrenaline before donning his mask and returning to the party fully prepared to murder someone. He pressed a button on the side of his mask to activate the earpiece inside and could finally hear May and the other infiltrators. "There you are, Party," said May as he turned the corner into a wider, more crowded hall. There were too many people around for him to reply, but he listened as she continued: "You disappeared from the cameras and haven't answered me once tonight. What's going on?"

He stopped and took out his phone to text her: ⌈ Everything's fine! ('∀' ;) but anyway, have any of the targets been spotted yet? ⌋

"Yes, Perlie has already poisoned someone. You have three and a half hours to kill the rest of them."

⌈ Is Roach watching? ⌋

She sighed. "He's in the same room as me? What does it matter? I think one of the targets is in the room three doors behind you."

He looked up from his phone and slid it into his inner jacket pocket before pushing off of the wall and spinning on the ball of his foot to go to the room May indicated. Once inside, she was busy talking with River, so Partha listened absent-mindedly as he ambled through this relaxed bar room. Without help from May, he inserted himself into a conversation between several strangers, one of whom he was fairly certain was Sandra Berg, the COO of Eir Lilac. She was wearing a mask inspired by a pink elephant, but an hour before the party, he had seen a post on her social media about her costume and recognised the uniquely tailored dress. She and her conversation partners welcomed him into their space, and he was immediately being complimented for his mask by the man on his left.

"Why thank you," he replied with an attempt at sounding like a Russian trying to hide his accent. He took a drag from his vape and lifted the bottom of his mask to blow a smoke ring around the man. As he pulled the mask back down, he said, "Who are you?" and laughed once.

"Oh, how fun!" said Sandra. "Don't think you can hide that accent, though," she teased.

"Aye, let me guess," agreed a woman on her left, "Sokolov?"

"Andrei Sokolov?" said Sandra with a beaming grin, "I love your work!"

Partha pressed a hand to his chest. "Thank you. Is a shame I am so recognisable. Was going to donate prize money to charity."

"You can still donate to charity without winning the prize money," said the man to his right whose mask covered his entire face and was plain white.

Partha chortled. "Da, but that costs money!"

"I recently lost my summer home," said the woman beside Sandra. Her mask was a white rabbit in a venetian style that only covered her eyes, and her gown was sequined white with a red waistcoat. "If I'm the charity you donate to, I won't tell anyone who you are." She giggled as the rest of them laughed.

"Andrei, I heard you were working with Padovan on that new movie." He snapped his fingers and tapped his unmasked chin. "What was it called?"

"*The Rushingtons*," answered Partha confidently, "He is good director but makes for bad conversation."

"How so?" asked Sandra.

"He talks a lot about his mother. *Too much*, if you get my meaning." He huffed with amusement. "Is not my place to postulate, but," he trailed off and laughed with them at the insinuations.

Just then, a caterer passed by, and Sandra stopped him by grabbing his sleeve. She took five of the strange vials from his tray and passed one out to each of her conversation partners, keeping one for herself. Partha's was a small glass vial with a metallic-looking purple liquid inside and a label that read *Drink Me*. Sandra uncorked hers, which was much the same as Partha's except red, and held it up as if asking for the others to toast theirs with her.

"What is it?" asked the woman in the rabbit mask.

Sandra shrugged and looked around the circle to see if any of the men knew. None of them knew either and showed hesitation. Partha, however, raised his vial to clink with Sandra's, which pressured the others enough to join in on drinking the mysterious liquid together. After the small tapping sound of their vials hitting each other, Partha uncorked his vial and downed it, immediately regretting the decision when he recognised the bitter flavour. The others didn't seem to recognise it, but their distaste was evident in their body language and on the face of the man who wasn't wearing a mask.

"God, that's awful," he said as he looked at his empty vial, "I thought it would be a shot. That wasn't a shot was it?"

"It wasn't," answered Partha.

"What was it?" asked Sandra as she smacked the bitterness off her lips with a sip of champagne.

He feared what Roach might think more than anything. Stalling to answer, knowing Roach or Thyne might come into the earpiece to scold him, he was slow-moving as he started pulling cookies out of his pockets. He passed them around the circle, being sure to give the poisoned one to Sandra.

"Andrei?" she said with a concerned tone at his change of demeanour.

"Is upsetting," he said truthfully both in and out of character, "I was sober."

The others went pale. "Andrei, what did we just drink?" asked the woman in white.

He sighed and broke a piece of his cookie off before finally looking up at the others again and saying simply, "Ecstasy."

He took the next excuse to leave the conversation and found a quiet corner to whisper into his earpiece, "Sandra is done. Please don't tell Roach that—."

"You did good, kid," said Roach. His voice sent a chill down Partha's spine, but the praise confused his upset.

"I did good?"

"Didn't think you had it in you, but you didn't even flinch."

Roach must not have seen that he had accidentally taken molly. Partha bit his lip, but after a moment decided to confess: "She gave us these vials. I swear, sir, I thought it was just a shot, but it was—."

"I know, kid. Just get your other targets done before you're too high. Perlie found one in the foyer a few minutes ago."

Partha was going to say more, but in his moment of ponderance he heard a shout from behind him that tensed his spine: "Andrei Sokolov as I live and breathe!" It was loud enough to have been picked up in the comms. Partha glanced his way and immediately recognised him as Andrei's old agent. Not only was this man not a target, he was also a chatterbox.

"Oh, Mr. Frisk," he said as he was pulled into a hug, "Will you walk with me?"

"Of course! Have you had any of the drinks yet? They have these 'White Rabbit' cocktails that are to die for! They're sort of like White Russians." He laughed and wrapped his arm around Partha's shoulders to walk with him. "How have you been, Sokolov? How's the wife?"

While Partha was busy being roped into an irritating chat with someone he had to pretend to know, his eyes were constantly scanning for more targets and, unconsciously, Thyne. The Englishman was trapped in his own conversation but with a target he had already poisoned: the CTO of Maitland, Lot Astor. Thyne was enraged more and more with every syllable this man uttered and was therefore having a difficult time coming to terms with the fact that he would not be able to burn him alive.

"It's no secret in the business that the first few songs were written by Miss Maitland's son when he was still just a child. It's such a shame that he died so young. I bet if he had lived longer he would have made us even more masterpieces. The kid was a genius! Plus, he had the same sort of shrewd business mind as his mother." He puffed on his cigarette before adding, "But I suppose he would maybe be opposed to how we sign people now." With a chuckle he nudged the woman next to him, whom Thyne had surmised was also a Maitland higher-up. "Do you remember that creepy kid from back when the pier collapsed?"

"That hardly narrows it down, Lot."

"The tall one," he laughed at his own next statement: "We found him dumpster diving after a show."

She nodded but was made pale by the memory. Her voice was shaken: "Yeah, he had blood on him."

"You'll love this," said Lot with no regard for his friend's comment. He directed his attention to Thyne and leaned on his shoulder to explain, "He was no Clarence Crump, but he was a pretty decent writer, so we were going to throw him through the ringer to try and get him to sign, even if we didn't get much. Lucky us, he was a moron! Ha! We said 'seven figures' and he saw dollar-signs. I should've known he'd fall for it: the poor bastard was eating out of the garbage."

"Did you offer him a seven-figure contract?" asked Thyne in the calmest voice he could muster.

"Well, of course we did. How else would we get him writing music for us?"

"You offered it without intention to pay it?"

"Oh, you're just an actor, aren't you? You probably don't know how it works in the business. Basically, he'd sign the contract, and after— what was it? —fifteen years, *then* he'd get a seven-figure check, but he had to make us more money beforehand. It was all in the fine print. We had our lawyers write it up to make it hard for dumb artist-types to understand, but it's all fairly standard. And, as collateral, we also snagged the rights to everything he'd released already." He seemed to suddenly remember that he was talking to a "dumb artist-type" and blushed. "I'm sure it's different with acting, though. You lot have unions."

Thyne took the opportunity to be openly offended and excused himself from the conversation. Once alone, he whispered into the comms to Roach, "What a cunt. Do you want me to get him somewhere private, so we can off him before the poison does? Another chance to teach each other lighter and knife tricks, no?"

Roach's light smile could be heard in his reply: "That sounds romantic and all, sparkplug, but Party's gonna need your help with his last two targets. He's less and less coherent."

May tried not to sound perturbed when she added, "He's in the ballroom on the fourth floor and looking for you."

"I still have one target left."

"We'll cover it," said River.

"You and Perlie?"

"Yeah. Go help Party before he ruins everything."

Partha frowned at the distant conversation he was hearing and patted around his pockets automatically, looking for cocaine. When they all turned up empty, he sighed, vaguely recalling his promise to Roach, and vaped desperately. He couldn't recall the names of his last two targets, and any time Perlie crossed his mind his stomach turned with guilt and anxiety. He was increasingly unable to engage Frisk in any sort of meaningful conversation as the entire world seemed less and less real. The lights sparkled as if he were underwater, and Frisk's chattering voice became another instrument in the lilting music.

When Thyne reached the aforementioned ballroom, he spotted his friend across the room trapped in meaningless conversation. Quick to formulate a plan, he took a champagne flute from a passing caterer's tray and started making his way toward Partha and Frisk. Halfway across the room, he stealthily poured the champagne into a potted plant and approached Partha confidently. He dismissively handed the empty glass to Frisk and said, "Thank you for taking this," before shoving himself between the two of them, facing Partha.

"Uh… I don't work h—."

Thyne scoffed and turned to face him. "Why are you still here?" And with a dismissive turn back toward Partha he loudly complained, "Servants are too entitled these days. As if we owe him a speck of our time."

Frisk smiled nervously at Partha and said, "We'll catch up later," before slinking away, having no interest in sharing space with the rude character Thyne was playing.

Partha, caught-up in the middle of it, was sober enough to understand that someone new wanted to talk, but Thyne's acting was too good for his half-there brain. He vaped from his device and blew a smoke ring around the masked man before saying, "Who are you?" in the caterpillar's voice, as he had done several times that night.

"Who do you think?" said Thyne in his regular voice, "How are you feeling?"

Partha started. He looked Thyne up and down and blushed at the extra padding in his midriff. He didn't recall it being part of the costume: it had been months since he had made it. Had Thyne somehow gained weight without Partha noticing? His shoulders slumped. *'What a horrible friend I am.'*

"What's wrong?"

"I'm sorry," he muttered.

"Why? You didn't know it was ecstasy. It's fine. I just hope it's not a repeat of the last time you were on ecstasy."

"What happened last time?"

Thyne crossed his arms and refused to answer. "Anyway, we should go. Perlie and River will take care of the rest." He held out his hand, and Partha took it limply.

The lights were already colourful; the music was already loud, but to Partha it all seemed so much more. He felt like he was submerged in a sea of aromatic gin, looking up at the lights as they twinkled like moonlight through the surface. He wasn't entirely certain what character he was playing, and it crossed his mind to remove his mask to unriddle the mystery, but he was experienced enough of a drug user and roleplayer to know better than to break the immersion. Someone was leading him around by the hand, so he tried to think of questions to ask that would be in-character but clue him into what was happening. When Thyne stopped them at a threshold waiting for a cart to roll by, Partha wrapped his arms around his shoulders and breathed in his scent. He was 90% sure this masked man was Thyne, but the smell of cigarettes, cinnamon, and thyme helped confirm it. Thyne struggled to peel him off of his back but eventually submitted to dragging him awkwardly along through the opulent halls, all the while with Partha's gaze dancing around the palace at the flowers, the foods, the costumes, the architecture.

When they came outside, Partha barely noticed the difference in temperature and quieting sounds from the party. He squeezed Thyne hard enough that the Brit stopped and turned to hold him. "Come here, you muppet," he grumbled lovingly.

"I love you so much," he cooed. Thyne's embrace was the softest, warmest, bestest feeling in the world, and he could swear that he could feel their souls intertwining. Unthinking, he tried to kiss him, only for their masks to bump into each other, after which he laughed adorably and hung off of Thyne's shoulders. "These masks are like mouth condoms," he joked with another cute giggle.

Thyne chuckled with him. "Yeah, I suppose they are."

"I want you." He tried to reach his hands into Thyne's shirt, but he ungracefully fumbled with one of his buttons before his hands were slapped away, after which he awkwardly touched his chest with his fingertips. That wasn't working either, so he retreated his hands, and pulled Thyne in for another tight embrace. "This is fun. Are you having fun?"

"Yes, now be quiet."

He let himself be led through the increasingly-surreal gardens a little longer until he was sobered by a wet breeze. He blinked away some of the haze in his vision and looked around. After deducing where he was and loosely recalling the job, he hung off Thyne's shoulders again and whispered sensually, "Can we go to your house? *The Prim and Proper.*" He giggled at the name and the silly posh voice in which he had said it.

"That's where we're going but not for the reasons you want."

While Thyne snuck Partha home, Perlie and River were hurrying to try prying the last target away from his entourage before the first dose of poison would hit. Their efforts were futile, but when an ambulance was called, River found himself standing directly beside Filipek. The CEO was puffing on a pipe and watching the shareholder be carried away on a stretcher without so much as a flinch or flutter. His air was just as flamboyant and invested in the festivities as before, and as soon as the doors closed behind the paramedics, he turned to face River. "Why, you're as tall as an ox and a half! A Nightingale! And twice as loud, no?" He laughed heartily. "Follow my feet, good sir. *I* certainly won't be!" River spotted Perlie across the room and gestured at her as Filipek sauntered toward a courtyard, expecting River to follow.

He had a cane as a part of his costume, so he was spinning it around playfully and clicking it on the ground occasionally to match with the beat of the bass drum in the current song. He hummed discordantly with it between puffs on his purple corn cob pipe and sang nonsense to himself every few steps. He had a mask earlier in the evening, but since the incident, he had removed it, as well as his shoes for some reason. His suit was crisp black and perfectly tailored for his gangly limbs and paper-thin waist. He was perhaps as thin as Francis, if not thinner. Despite this, he was incredibly lively and expressive with his movements. He never took a normal step, only ever skipping, hopping, striding long or short, shuffling, scooting, sliding, and spinning. But never never walking. So after a click click click from his cane and a puff puff puff on his pipe, they were outside.

As the doors were opened by doormen for them, he spun around to walk backwards and say to River, "Like the magpie seeks silver, I muse for mind-magic. Entertain me, Walrus, my good friend!" He pointed with his cane at a basketball hoop on an opulent court only a few feet from a crowded in-ground hot tub. The floor of the court was made of marble and the hoops lined with gold, and as they came outside River saw a group of three partygoers exiting it holding a jet-black basketball.

"What makes you think I know how to play basketball?" asked River as Perlie came up to his side and wrapped her arms around his as if they were dating.

"A Nightingale in the flesh says he knows not how to play! What else do birds do but play and play all day day day?" He tilted his head and puffed on his pipe with a quizzical expression.

"My dress is too tight," said River flatly.

"Too tight for this, too snug for that." He waved around his pipe to dismiss the claim. "Tisk tisk tisk and tut tut tut. It's far too tame to tease and toy. Games are meant to ease and joy!" He looked around and, after spotting a cart of basketballs, gestured for River to follow him again. With a roll of his eyes, River did as he was asked and followed to the three-point line where he was handed a basketball. Filipek watched him expectantly, so River shooed him and Perlie back. At that point, she was the only one outside with them other than the group in the hot tub. It was quite cold.

Using his telekinesis to guarantee his shot, he threw every ball from the cart directly through the hoop then turned his irritated attention back to Filipek.

The eccentric man clapped. "Good show! Good show! A homerun!"

River nodded and gave a polite little bow before looking at Perlie and saying, "Dormouse, do you have any water and snacks? That was tough. Gotta stay hydrated."

Perlie took the hint to take out the cookies while they had this perfect opportunity to pass them around, being sure to give the poisoned one to Filipek. River took his and started to open it, but he heard his brother's voice in his comms. He was speaking Demotic, and his tone was nigh-hysterical: "Sonny, flay this fucker alive. Force-feed him to death! He killed Silvino. You loved Silvino, too. He fucking killed him. Make him bleed. Make him pay. Make him beg for mercy, then don't fucking give him any."

River ignored the bloodlust but gave a quick look around for whatever camera his brother must have been using to see this. He spotted it in the corner of the courtyard and gave a subtle head-shake to it, which brought about a guttural breathy growl from Roach followed by, "Don't you want to see the light go out!?"

He stood from the couch in the haunt and put his laptop on the coffee table as he tore out his headphones. Francis was in the kitchen making himself a cocktail, and Roach stopped him by rushing into the room and scooping him up by his collar. "BRING ME TO HIM!"

Unfazed, Francis hiccuped and said, "To whom?"

"Filipek," he breathed and pulled Francis in to kiss him madly. While he was having this… episode… he felt a hand on his shoulder and turned swiftly around to see Dezba there looking concerned. "What!?"

"Clayton, sweetie, they're taking care of it right now. Don't bother Francis with this, okay?"

"You wouldn't understand. *You* got to see the fear in the eyes of the cretin that killed your husband. You got to pull the trigger."

She wrapped her hand around his cheek lovingly, the same way she had done all those months ago when he was having a panic attack in his kitchen. Wordlessly, she calmed the storm raging within him and brought him back into the living area.

While Roach was having his brief breakdown, Filipek had taken his poisoned cookie but refused to open it, saying, "A lovely unbirthday treat, dear Dormouse, but I have no tea!"

"Right, I can go get us some," said Perlie with a kind tone.

He shook his head and spun his cane. "No tea for me to eat or cheek; I have no tea at all to speak!" A chuckle.

River and Perlie laughed with him, able to hide their confusion and anxiety thanks to their masterful acting… and masks. River noticed Perlie looking to him for a translation of the mad rabble, so he did his best: "Are you saying… uh… that you're allergic?"

He poked his nose and jabbed his cane into River's abs. "There you have it! And with a bird brain, too!" He laughed again.

"Oh, is it a gluten thing?" asked Perlie. Filipek nodded, so she immediately thought of a convincing lie: She broke her cookie then gestured with it. "This is shortbread. Shortbread cookies don't have gluten. You see how hard and crumbly they are? That's because there's no gluten. My mother was a baker, and I remember she used to blow people's minds with this fact." She giggled adorably. It was true that Cynthia Sommer's mother was a baker, and she was quite proud of herself for thinking so quickly on her feet while staying in character.

With a look at her cookie then at his own, Filipek shrugged and started to eat his. He waffled on about something or other, but it was only a few more minutes of his dribble later that another partygoer had fainted. He excused himself, and River and Perlie immediately started making their way to the hedge maze in the middle courtyard of the palace. They eavesdropped on conversations as they hurried through the halls, hearing a lot of concern and speculation of poison.

With guidance from May, they were able to find the coat closet where Francis had stashed their tiara and playing card beneath the wooden floorboards a few days before the job. Once inside, they both tore the bottom of their dresses where Partha had left loose seams for just such a purpose. They both had leggings on underneath and tied the torn parts of the dresses around their thighs. While Perlie finished tying up her skirt, River used his telekinesis to start tearing up the floorboards until he found the tiara and card. There was audible panic starting to ramp up on the other side of the door as another two targets fell and more ambulances were called.

Once they had the card and tiara, they rushed to the hedge maze. Perlie followed River as he led them to its centre where stood a tall statue of Winston Churchill. They both clambered up to its head, Perlie first. She jumped from the top of the marble to the roof, but it was a further jump than they had anticipated while planning. She nearly fell, only saved by River's telekinesis floating her the rest of the way to the roof. River's breaths were shaky as he balanced on the statue, noticing security starting to crowd around and aim pistols at him. "Stop right there, or we'll shoot!" With a dismissive and hurried wave of his arm, he tore the guns from the guards' hands and into the maze, but his gaze was wild and whipping around. His time was running out! With no other options in sight, he jumped and could only hope he would make it.

And he did.

Barely.

He caught himself on the edge of the roof by his elbows then fell to just his fingertips. The shingles started to peel up under his weight, so he swung himself onto the balcony beneath him, threw the tiara and card onto the statue's head, and shouted, "GO!"

River rushed through the storey below Perlie, pushing through partygoers and throwing guards around telekinetically until he reached the edge of the building. He slowed his pace on his way to it and saw Perlie jump to a nearby rooftop through a window. She turned back and gestured for him to follow, so he resumed full-tilt sprinting, throwing a vase into the window telekinetically to break it as he neared it, and leapt across the alley between the palace buildings. He latched onto the accent trim and clambered up onto the roof beside Perlie so they could resume their mad dash. They leapt from rooftop to rooftop, ascending and descending buildings with grace and speed, dashing across streets through traffic and sometimes over cars. At one point, they took advantage of a passing double-decker bus beneath them to cross a narrow street without ever touching the ground.

"Alright," said Perlie through her heaving breaths as they neared his home, "Thyne! Attic!"

Thyne sat upright from his bed and rushed out of the room. Partha shuffled after him, rubbing happy tears from his eyes but thoroughly confused by the suddenness of Thyne's actions. The Brit tried opening the loft hatch door that led to the roof. Unfortunately, it was jammed shut, so he slammed his shoulder into it four times before it finally blasted open, just in time for Perlie and River to jump through. Thyne watched them tumble down the stairs, somehow not falling as well, and quickly closed the door to hide it from the helicopters he could hear in the distance.

"Perlie!" said Partha with a big dumb grin as he climbed up into the attic and spotted her, "I love you, Perlie, you're really pretty."

She smiled softly. "Thanks, kid. May? How's the palace?"

"Utter. Fucking. Chaos."

Chapter 43
Down the Rabbit Hole

The next morning, Partha awoke in Perlie's arms. The MDMA still in his system had him dizzy, and the cocaine withdrawals left his heart broken, but for the fleeting moment as he fluttered his eye open and saw Perlie sleeping beside him with her arm draped over his chest, he was elated. He admired her for a tranquil ten minutes before hunger and depression started to take a hold of him. With a kiss on her forehead, he shimmied out from under her arm, put on his eye patch, and sauntered downstairs.

In the kitchen, Thyne was pouring himself a cup of oolong and greeted Partha with a drowsy nod of the head.

"Morning," said Partha as he opened the fridge, "You want me to make breakfast?"

"Sure."

"Might have to go out to the market for ingredients."

"I'll come with you. Just let me finish my tea."

"It's okay to go out after the job?"

"You burned your costume and showered, right?" Partha nodded, so Thyne said with a shrug, "Then there won't be an issue. Perlie and River should stay in, but we left early because of the molly."

"Yeah... sorry."

He sipped his tea and hissed as it burnt his tongue slightly. "You did well, mate. You killed someone. How do you feel?"

He rubbed the back of his neck. He felt like shit. It wasn't remorse but depression that had a hold of him. Now that he didn't have anything to look forward to, his deal with Roach was starting to seem like a mistake. He thought about Perlie's pregnancy and assured himself that it was best for her and the child that he quit doing drugs, but the thought was retorted with another: '*What does it matter if I'm high or sober? I'll be a shit dad either way.*'

"You regretting it?" asked Thyne cautiously as he noticed his friend was rapt in thought.

"Regretting what?" he said with a slight start.

"Killing someone?"

"Oh. No, it's not that."

"You having second thoughts about what you said last night?"

"… What did I say last night?"

"You said you wanted Perlie to keep the kid. It was cute."

"I said that to her?"

"No, you said it to me after I stopped you from trying to shag me by reminding you of her and the pregnancy."

He slumped his shoulders. '*Of course I tried to have sex with him. Perlie deserves better than me.*'

"Mate?"

"Huh?" he sounded, his voice as low as his mood.

"Let's go to market. It'll do you some good to go out and see the autumn leaves. It's nice and cloudy, too, which I recall you saying you like." He nodded, his head hanging, and let Thyne lead him to his coat closet to, "Put on some wellies and a mac, mate. It might rain." Luckily, he and Thyne wore the same size shoes and were roughly the same size otherwise. The raincoat was baggy for him, but he liked it that way: it helped him feel less visible despite its eye-catching minty colour.

The walk to the market was outwardly serene but inwardly tempestuous. He typically liked the sky when it was cloudy and teasing rain, but the drab slate of grey was as dark as the cloud forming over his head. Thyne chattered at him, but Partha's thoughts were louder than the conversation. His gaze was locked on the dreary sidewalk as it ambled along beneath him, and the smell of Thyne's cigarette was the only thing to break up the otherwise unpleasant reek of garbage that was so common in cities with a close proximity to the rotten sludge of the sea. The market's air conditioning cut through his coat like a dagger as he was ushered inside by his friend, who was still rambling and seemingly unfazed by the cold.

"Mate!?"

Partha started and looked up. Thyne had been trying to get his attention since they came inside. "Hm? Sorry."

"What did you want to make for breakfast? If you still want to, that is."

"Let's just look around and see what there is."

They meandered, Partha letting his gaze trail around lazily at the offerings. When they wandered into the seafood section of the deli, he saw an unprecedented meat for a London market: shark. His eye lit up at the sight, but as he picked up speed to grab it, the two of them were stopped by a pair of detectives.

"Are you two aware of the incident that happened last night at *Churchill Palace?*"

Partha looked to Thyne to answer for them both. "Not at all. What happened?"

"That's what we're trying to figure out. Do you live in the area?" Thyne nodded. "Did you notice anything out of the ordinary last evening?"

Thyne poked his chin in thought adorably. "Hmm. Well, there were some electrical issues."

One of the detectives took out a notepad as the other continued his questioning: "What sort of electrical issues?"

"Well, at about midnight, my power went out."

"For how long? Roughly."

"Hmm. Ten minutes?"

"Did you see or hear anything odd in that time?"

"Yes. I saw a woman running down my street. Away from the palace. She had a ballgown on."

"Did you see her face?"

"It was dark. I think she may have had a mask on. I know she had long blonde hair, but I'd be guessing if I gave much else. I don't even remember the colour of the dress."

"And your street?" asked the one taking notes.

"Oxford."

They both nodded, and after a moment, the interrogator asked if there was anything else Thyne wanted to add. With a shake of his head, they thanked him, told him to report anything else to the department, and moved on their way to the next passer-by.

Once free of the conversation, Partha smiled lightly at Thyne before taking his hand and leading him to the shark meat he had spotted. On their way back to Thyne's house, Partha was more lively than he had been on the walk to the market. He was excited by the ingredients they had bought, but standing by and watching Thyne lie so flawlessly about their crimes had his blood pumping. "Have you done that sort of thing before?"

"Hm? What sort of thing?"

"What you said to the police."

"Oh. Once or twice. Yeah. Why?"

"That was so cool!" Thyne giggled. "But aren't you afraid that you'll get caught?"

"There *was* a power outage on Oxford street last night, and no one in the gang is a blonde woman."

"May could be mistaken for blonde," Partha pointed out.

"Sure, but she's in France." He shrugged. "It's good to throw them off the trail. I've done it before. Having a bad memory isn't illegal. If the lead doesn't give them anything, then they'll throw it out, and I'll have wasted their time. If it does turn something up, well… it won't be leading them to us, now will it?"

"Wow. You're so smart, Thyne." He swooned, but Thyne caught him and pushed him away playfully.

"Twat," he laughed, "What ingredients did you get?"

"I got everything I need to make shark hash!"

"Oh, that's your favourite, right?"

He nodded adorably. "I hope Perlie likes it!"

"I'm sure she will."

Thyne flew them to Versailles that evening, and Francis met them at the airport to teleport them into the haunt beneath the palace. Other than Francis, only Roach, Dezba, and May were in France: everyone else had stayed behind in Italy before the job had even started. When they appeared in the living area, Roach stopped improvising on the piano and looked up at the newcomers. He wanted to keep playing, but his eyes were on Thyne as if asking to continue. With a handwave from Thyne, he resumed his jazzy tune while the four who had done the job turned their attention to May.

"Hello," she yawned, "I've been up all night monitoring everything. Eir Lilac's stocks are tanking. Osiris' took a hit, too, but nothing substantial. The celebrities that Roach killed are suspects: seems like they haven't found the bodies yet." A chill shot down her spine, but she ignored it as best as she could. Clearing her throat, she continued, "A lot of your targets have been declared dead, but I only know that from hacking various databases. Nothing more than 'an attack on *Churchill Palace*' is in the headlines just yet." She yawned again.

"You should get some sleep, mate," said Thyne.

"You said you'll fly us down to Rome? I'll sleep on the plane."

After some (burnt) toast and pancakes prepared by Perlie with what remained of their ingredients in the haunt, they gave their unwanted leftovers to Roach. He didn't eat them right away, instead taking his extra plates into his room to pack for the lengthy stay in Rome. Thyne had projected they would be there until at least New Year's Day, so Roach made certain to grab his Christmas gifts for the others. Despite not celebrating it himself, after marrying Silvino, he fell in love with how close the holiday brought him to his husband and his husband's grandmother and sister. He hoped this new found family would prove just as satisfying to shower in gifts.

Francis stopped time to bring them and all their bags back to the airport in some twenty trips back and forth. Once everyone was in Thyne's hangar, he resumed time and waited for his friend to open the air stairs for them. He hadn't said much since they had regrouped, so Thyne took him aside while Roach and River volunteered to pack the plane. "You alright, mate?"

"Clayton much reveres the concept of wasting time, but it feasts and festers upon me."

"We're making good time, Franky. Though, if I'm being honest, I'm a bit pissed off that we haven't even discussed Maitland yet."

"Damn your mother's unremarkable legacy, Clarence. Osiris is much more important."

Thyne grimaced and mustered all of his willpower not to punch his friend in the face. With gritted teeth: "Everyone *sane* and *sober* agrees that Osiris is impossible."

Francis glared, but before the two could go for each other's throats, River approached. "Thyne. Go close the cargo door. We don't want to do it wrong."

He huffed and left to close it and start his walk-around with a lingering glare on Francis. During the flight to Rome, Francis found himself in Roach's arms as he and his brother chatted about something in Arabic. The pirate was drinking to stave away his anxiety. Reality was more real than ever for him. He wished he could whisk himself away with love from Thyne, but he was certain Thyne didn't love him now. Not only that, but Osiris was still unscathed. They were running out of time to fix his blunder. Why did no one else seem to care? Even if it was futile to try, surely it was worse to sit idly by and watch the world burn. Right?

Then again… what good was a world where Thyne didn't love him? Even if only platonically. Francis loved Roach, and Roach loved him, and perhaps that could be enough of a reason. Except… Roach didn't care to save the world. In fact, he would likely relish its destruction. Perhaps he wanted to see it all go up in flames. Perhaps that was why he was so adamant that they waste time. The thought angered Francis, and in the midst of an otherwise calm flight, he shoved himself out of Roach's arms and stood to draw his sword.

"Woah, man, what're you doing?" The blade was aimed at his throat a moment later and swayed as Francis swigged from his flask. Roach held up his hands. "Francis? It's me."

"I know who you are, *Clayton*," he growled the name, "And I know why you waste my time on purpose."

Roach looked at River with veiled panic in the back of his hazel-greys. The unthreatened twin stood and ran his hands up Francis' back to hook around his shoulders. He leaned in close and breathed sensually, "Are you certain that's Clayton, bed bug?"

Francis' head ached, and he lowered the sword. He turned toward River, too drunk to tell the difference. Roach had been holding him, right? Why would River be the one holding him? But… maybe when he stood up he had gotten turned around? He held his forehead with his free hand. "This mischief must cease," he muttered, "Which of you is Clayton?"

"I am," said both twins in tandem.

The others were all in the aft of the plane, but Perlie wanted a coffee and just so happened to enter the room where this madness was taking place while Francis' was still armed. "Francis, why do you have your sword out?"

He aimed it at her. "Tell me which one of them is Clayton!"

She forced a smile and eyed both of the twins, easily spotting the difference. "I don't know. They look the same."

He took her claim at face value and wept as he dropped his sword on the floor then himself into the couch beside River. He held his aching head in both hands and whimpered, "Clayton, I love you, but I need you to help me. Not hinder me."

River swapped places with his brother, taking the fallen sword from the floor and passing it to Perlie. He whispered for her to hide it, and she did just that as she passed through the room to the small galley to make her drink.

Roach wrapped a hand around Francis' thigh and leaned close. "Bed bug, what's wrong? Aren't you glad that the job went so well? And the kid killed someone, too! I'm so surprised."

Francis' teal eyes sparkled helplessly as he looked up at Roach. "Why do you purposefully waste my time? Ruin my chances at reversing my blunder. Why do you want to see it all end?"

His subsequent smile was subtle but fiendish. "Didn't I tell you before?"

"No."

He leaned in to whisper hot breaths directly into Francis' ear: "The ending, my dear, is the beautiful part."

Francis barely recalled the song Roach had sung for him after Ramadan. After processing the memory and his own feelings, he ran his hands through his messy hair and whimpered, "Clayton, *please*. You must aid my attempts to stop it. I *must* stop it."

Roach sighed and pulled him into his arms, petting him and shushing him sweetly. "We'll try everything we can, okay? Even if it's just you and me against the world. I promise."

When they arrived at the manor in Rome, Roach greeted his pets then immediately called for a meeting, even before the cars had been unpacked. With everyone gathered in the living area, dogs lounging on their laps, and the embers of an old fire in the hearth, Roach addressed them: "May asked me to call for this meeting. May? You have the floor."

She stood and pushed some of her hair behind her ear shyly as she scooted to the middle of the room with her laptop open in the palm of her left hand. "More news has come out. The job is public now. They've found August Laine's body, so the celebrities that are missing now are both suspects of the crime as well as suspected victims." She gulped as she saw Roach sit down and felt even more vulnerable with all the eyes on her. "A-and, well, um...."

"Would you like me to tell everyone?" asked Thyne.

She started. "Do you know?"

It hurt him to admit, which was evident in the way he choked out, "No."

"It's okay. I'll be okay. Just...," she took Partha's glass of water from the coffee table and quaffed it. "Just needed some water," she said with feigned confidence. "The thing is... Well, you all did great. The targets all took their poison well... except for... except for Filipek."

Roach jumped to his feet. "That's fucking great! Where is he?"

"G-great?"

"Yeah," a wildness flashed in his eyes, "Now I'll get to watch the light go out myself."

His bloodlust made May uncomfortable, but she swallowed her anxiety and continued, "Well, he made a statement about us. Would you like to hear it?"

"Where is he?"

"Be seated, Roach," said Francis, "You shall have him as soon as she closes her address."

This brought hysterical glee to the madman, and he choked down a laugh that tried to crack out like a whip before settling back into his seat and fidgeting his legs impatiently.

"Merci, Francis," said May timidly, "So this is his statement, or rather, the statement from his PR team considering how coherent it is: 'We at Eir Lilac are terribly remorseful for the tragedy that befell our Halloween event this Friday in London. We are working closely with authorities to unravel the mystery of what happened and will update our timelines as we learn more. Our thoughts and prayers go out to the families affected, and though our security detail were not direct employees of Eir Lilac or any of its subsidiaries, we are still taking full responsibility for not preventing the incident. The attack was carried out by a terrorist organisation calling itself *The Tiara*, and for any members of this despicable group that may be listening: we will not give in to terrorist demands. We're like a family here at Eir Lilac and understand the importance of cooperation, compassion, and reasonable negotiation in all dealings, even with those we don't agree with.' then he went on to quote Martin Luther King Jr. for some reason, and something about Lewis Carroll before his people told the reporters no more questions."

"Is he in hospital?" asked Thyne.

"Yes," her gaze flicked briefly to Roach, "But before I say which one, should we discuss the statement at all? They're calling us terrorists."

"We *are* terrorists, honey," said Neodesha, "By definition."

May started. "Wh-what do you mean?" Jean-Jacques perked up seeing his sister finally seeming to regret her decision to help these people.

"I mean terrorism is just politically-motivated crimes. Provided they're violent 'course. Papa Arjun killed my Mama's master, and that was called terrorism by the Democrats."

"The Democrats said that?" She held her head and set down the laptop on the coffee table.

Neodesha and Partha were both about to pipe up with an impromptu history lesson, but the laptop floated off the table toward Roach. May dove across the room and slammed it closed before he could read anything on it, and the two made eye contact. "What hospital?" said Roach without emotion.

"St. Catherine's in Northern Ireland. He owns it." She snatched the laptop away to scold him, but he was already asking Francis to bring Filipek to him.

Francis disappeared, and three seconds later, he appeared where the coffee table had been with Filipek bound with IV tubing at the wrists. Francis pushed him to his knees in front of Roach and smiled lightly at his lover.

The twins both stood. Roach looked down his face at the stunned CEO and smiled wickedly. His voice was low and buttery as it sounded to the silent room: "Hello, little fish."

Chapter 44
Bread and Butterflies

May clambered across the room and slapped her hands over Filipek's eyes. With a stern expression she shouted up at Roach and Francis, "Idiots! He has an *Eye of Osiris!*"

Roach's eyes gleamed madly over his eerie grin. "Oh, what *fun*."

"You lunatic! He just disappeared from his hospital room! He's best friends with Tatum Abraham! Idiots! Idiots! Francis, put him back before someone notices."

"Friends with Abraham?" said Francis with intrigue. He paced across the room between Roach and Filipek, glaring daggers into the CEO even through May's hands. "Even more reason to keep him here. Clay—. Belay that— erm— Tin Man?"

"Yes?" breathed Roach, his anticipation for what Francis would say next immeasurable.

In Demotic: "Keeva and Drusus are asleep upstairs. Find them. Wake them. Ask them to bring you to the basement. I want answers from this one, and I know you, my darling, will get them."

He bit his lip, his deep grey eyes rolling back as he took a deep breath to calm himself. "I'll go find them."

As Roach left the room, Francis turned his attention back to May. In French: "Can you breach his... device?"

She groaned. "I will, but you should cover his eyes to hide your faces. Idiots."

He took her place covering Filipek's eyes just as the CEO finally spoke: "Who are you people!?" He tried to grab at the hands over his eyes, but as soon as he touched them, his own hands were tied behind his back rather than in front of him. He heard more talking in languages he didn't understand, some of which he couldn't even name, and a moment later the room around him was suddenly darker, quieter, and the rug beneath his buckled knees had become cold concrete. In fact, the entire room was uncomfortably cold. No more than ten degrees celsius if he had to guess. His hands were still bound, but now there was a bag over his head instead of hands over his eyes.

It must have been six hours he sat shivering in the cold. Attempts to shimmy out of his binds were futile, and attempts to stand were stopped by some sort of surface over his head and shackles on his ankles with chains that were bolted into the floor. He shouted until he lost his voice then shouted some more.

After this isolation, he heard a door open and the thumping of combat boots drawing nearer. He opened his *Eye of Osiris* heads-up display to try recording, but all of his inputs led him to a picture of a maypole. With a sigh, he tried to make sense of the nonsense. It seemed reality was finally meeting him halfway: why, he had suffered at least six impossible things since breakfast. "You think you are the crocodile," he said hoarsely and through clattering teeth, "but you're the hare."

The man crouched down in front of him and removed the bag, revealing that the surface above him was a table. He smiled like the Cheshire Cat and puffed on his cigarette like The Caterpillar. "Is that so?"

Filipek nodded. "Exceedingly so, sir. You're late late late."

"You think we don't know about your attempts to send that recording to every-one under the sun?"

"Knowing is only half the battle."

"And the other half?"

He had never been entertained so directly in his own madness and started at the question. "The other half… is…." The man laughed darkly in the pause. That Filipek was being shown his face was increasingly discouraging. These people had presumably already tried to kill him, so his chances of survival were impossible. "But I've suffered six impossible things since breakfast," he muttered.

"No, dude. You haven't suffered at all yet." He stood and chuckled darkly again. Filipek noticed a butterfly knife dancing around in his free hand as he started to pace in front of him. "The problem is, Christopher— Can I call you Chris? —The problem is, Chris: I just can't figure how to do it."

They tried to make eye contact, but the table blocked their view. It was shoved away in a split-second, clamouring across the vacant unlit room, and Filipek's head went on a swivel to find whoever had done it. When the rest of the room seemed empty, he looked up at his captor and muttered, "Seven."

Roach laughed one ha and crouched down in front of his next victim excitedly. "I suppose it's only fair that I'll start with the easy way for you, little fish. We went through all your files and found a lot of communications with Tatum Abraham about something called *The Jabberwock*. It wasn't your usual nonsense, so don't lie to me. It's code for something. What is it?"

"'Twas brillig, and the slithy toves," replied Filipek instantly.

Roach smiled. "So it was." He stood and started to pace again. "Usually, I like to make these sorts of things personalised. I quite abhor Carroll, but you seem to like him, so we can play a bit with that. Then there's the pharmaceutical aspects." He stroked his chin. "Of course, I have a doctor friend who could come cut out your pancreas. I think I'd like to feed it to you." A hysterical laugh sounded for two syllables before he smoked it away with the fag between his twitching fingers and said, "But I'm also a musician, and I've never gotten to use music for it before."

"For what?"

"What do *you* think, Chris?" he asked with the tone of a disappointed teacher.

"I don't quite think at all."

"Agreed," he said with a titter, "So, why don't we start with the safer things then work our way up to the more dangerous ones? Which would you prefer first? Flyting or music?"

"Flyting? Why would we—?"

"Flyting it is. Why don't you start?"

He blinked away some of his befuddlement. "With you?" He nodded, so Filipek looked him up and down. He was taking a while to think of something, but when a blade was held gently to his jaw, he gulped and sputtered out, "A redwood man… with untied laces is… fond of all the dampest places."

Roach brought his face even closer to Filipek's and whispered with smokey breath, "You can do better than that, can't you, little fish? My shoelaces? My height? Come on, Chris."

"M-monsters aren't welcome here."

Roach smiled evilly, took a drag, and blew a cloud of smoke into Filipek's face. While he coughed: "We'll smoke the monster out." A beat. Filipek looked up at Roach expectantly. "Well?" said Roach, "It's your turn."

"W-what are you going to do to me?"

A gash down his jawbone. Roach stood and slammed closed his knife, taking several rapid steps away from the bleeding man and disappearing briefly into the darkness. After an angry puff on his cigarette he turned and stomped back up to him. His voice was quiet but irate: "You disappoint me. You're the maddest one I've ever had, and you still won't play with me." He spat on him. "Disgusting swine. You killed my husband you know. You killed him." His voice picked up speed and lost a lot of its coolness, replaced with hysterical wrath: "And I've seen what you've said about fat people, no matter how much you tried to hide it in your nonsense-speech. I've seen you use it as an excuse for artificially inflating insulin prices. Do you know how much it cost when he died? Do you know how much it costs now?" Filipek may have responded, but Roach gave him no room: "For him— for type-2— for being outside of *your* 'ideal' body-mass-index— as if you have any fucking right to—," he stopped and shook his head violently as hysterical sorrow tried to overtake him. With a shout and heaving breaths to maintain his rage: "It cost us $8,173 per month. Do you know how much he made while working in prison?" Filipek was given a pause to answer and only gulped nervously. "DO YOU KNOW HOW MUCH HE MADE IN PRISON!?" Filipek shook his head. "NOTHING!" He kicked him in the face and telekinetically pulled the table back across the room only to slam it to the other side. "WHAT IS JABBERWOCK!?"

He coughed and shook away some of the blood from his face like a dog. "The Jabberwock is not so true.... I'm sorry for your lover, too."

He laughed darkly. "You're not sorry. You're not sorry, but you *will* be." He slammed the door behind him as he stormed out of the dark room. In the few seconds it was open Filipek tried to see what was outside, but it was too bright. With spots in his eyes, he stared at the cement and watched his blood pool on his lap. Another hour passed, and he perked up his head when he heard the door open again. He tried to parse anything at all of reality, but he was promptly soaked by a bucket of ice-cold water and made even colder than he already had been. The door was closed by the time he opened his eyes again, and he heard the clicking of a dog's claws tapping around him. Roach approached and said, "I've had a long think, little fish. I really want to force-feed you for months on end so that you may suffer an excruciatingly slow and ironic death, but my friends have asked me not to. I wanted to flay you alive and salt the wounds as an alternative, but you see, you haven't given me the information I need, so I'm barred from killing you outright. I was told to make you a promise. Are you ready?"

Filipek's gaze was often flicking to the doberman when he could see it come into his sightline while it circled him. "For the promise?"

"Yes," said Roach with an irritated tone, "Are you ready for the promise?"

"I... suppose?"

He cleared his throat and commanded his dog in Arabic. It came and sat beside him dutifully and looked up at him as he placed a hand over his chest and said, "I swear, hand on heart, that I won't kill you if you tell me what I need to know. You have one more chance to tell me willingly, but once I start the torture, I won't stop until you've told me or died. Is that fair?"

"Hardly."

"Well, if I had it my way you'd have no chance of survival at all!"

"Then kill me."

His breaths heaved, but his dog barked up at him once, and he leaned down to pet her. "This is Diana," he said as she licked his hand to calm him. "Diana, do you think it's a fair deal?" She barked once. "See? She agrees that it's fair."

"Hm. Then I suppose you have both been leashed."

Roach gritted his teeth. Thoughts ran through his head so fast they tumbled over each other and came out ungracefully as he spat, "She doesn't leash," in an attempt to point out that he didn't leash his dogs.

Filipek chuckled. "Of course not. To do that she would need hands. A dog with hands is quite a thought, but something she is assuredly not."

Through his grinding teeth, he said something in Arabic to the dog. She bolted from the room, the door seeming to open for her automatically, and came back a moment later with something in her mouth. "Good girl," he said as he crouched down to take it and kiss her on the head.

"What is that she's brought to you?"

"Dog toy."

"Why?"

Roach spun it around in his hands, saying the same command to his dog again. She came back with another dog toy a moment later, and he praised her again. With both toys, he stepped off into the darkness, but Filipek could hear him fiddling with things. He heard power tools and saw a few sparks. All the while he was working, he was sending his pet out to get more and more dog toys, praising her each time. By the fifteenth time, he sent her out of the room again, and it seemed this time she wasn't returning. He approached Filipek with a strange device. It was built from part of the table he had thrown across the room. The dog toys were attached, but Filipek couldn't fathom what he was looking at. There was a circuit board and switch in the back-middle of the broken wood, and each of the toys had some sort of wiring around it. He looked up at Roach who smirked and flipped the switch.

One by one, the toys started to squeak. Filipek laughed. "Is this what all the fuss is about?"

"Mmhmm," he hummed coolly, "I'll be back." He quit the room and returned a moment later with another bucket of water. The strange device he had built was still sounding every second on the second, and it floated up to the ceiling magically as Roach approached and threw the water over Filipek. Shivering, he watched as the device floated back down to the wet ground, and Roach left again.

Thirty minutes passed of incessant repetitive squeaking, but Filipek associated the sound enough with dogs being playful, particularly Tatum's late pets, that it was only slightly grating on his mad mind. When Roach returned with something else in his hands, Filipek was shivering and hoarse but otherwise chuffed with himself. "What're you so happy about, dude?" asked Roach as he fiddled with whatever was in his hands.

"What's there not to be happy about?"

Roach arched his brow at him. "I don't know, the fact I'm trying to torture you?"

"Emphasis on 'trying', young crocodile."

Roach smirked and returned his attention to the device in his hands. After a moment more of fiddling, it started to let out a chime like the sound played by a car when its door is open with the keys in the ignition. It sounded every other squeak or so, but after Roach fiddled with it some more, they were sounding in tandem. He set it in front of Filipek and left again. An hour later, he returned with six alarm clocks, all of which were blaring and beeping already when he came into the room. They weren't in time with the other sounds, and for a moment, Filipek welcomed the change.

"You hungry, dude?"

He looked up at Roach. "Am I hungry?"

"Yeah, man. Not trying to starve you." He took a... a *pancake* out of his pocket and tossed it on the floor in front of him.

"Is that a flapjack?"

"Yeah."

"I can't have wheat."

"Will it kill you?"

"…No."

"Then eat up, dude."

"I can't reach it."

It scooted closer.

"My hands—. I still can't—."

"Eat it off the ground, little fish. Which reminds me…." He left the room and returned with another bucket to dump on Filipek. It soaked his burnt pancake, so Roach tossed another from his pocket on top of it then a piece of burnt toast.

As Roach left again, Filipek realised that this most recent bucket had some sort of cleaning chemical in it. The smell was potent, and it only lingered stronger and stronger, the same as the noises were seeming to get louder and louder. He dry swallowed and held his breath to avoid the smell as he hunched over and took a bite of the burnt toast. The flavour was awful, but he hadn't eaten since the Halloween party, so the solid food was welcome. He finished the bread then moved on to the pancake beneath it. He had to stop himself from hurling when he accidentally caught a whiff of the floor cleaner all over him, but he managed to eat half of the pancake before his turning stomach couldn't handle another bite.

After another ten minutes, each of which felt like an hour, the door opened again and two figures entered. The same man who had been torturing him was one of them, but the second figure slinked into the shadows out of sight.

Roach pulled a chair from out of the darkness telekinetically and spun it around in front of Filipek so it would be facing him before reaching outside of the room to grab an electric guitar and old amplifier. Filipek expected him to come over and add to the discordant abhorrent symphony serenading him, but he leaned the guitar against the wall and quit the room again.

Filipek looked around for the second figure. "Who's there?" No response. "Who are you? Your friend is mad." After an hour of no sign from this second figure, Filipek started to doubt if he had ever even seen one in the first place. Against his better judgement, he eventually ate the second half of the pancake that wasn't drenched in cleaner. When the door opened for the umpteenth time, Filipek was genuinely glad, somehow, to see his captor come inside. "Who came in here with you?" he asked immediately.

"Huh?" Filipek noticed he had an opaque lidded jar in one hand and a spade and unlabelled spray-bottle in the other.

"Your friend in here. Who is it? What do you have in that jar and bottle?"

"There's no one else in here," he lied with a subtle flick of his eyes toward River in the darkest corner of the chamber. Both twins were sick in the head, but River's particular brand of psychopathy meant that he was overly interested in watching the psychological torment slowly break this man down.

"And what do you have?" asked Filipek.

"Some friends for you," he smiled evilly and leaned over his victim. Filipek would have hounded him further, but his questions were halted when he was sprayed in the face by the spray-bottle. It tasted like vinegar but somewhat sweet.

After all of his exposed skin was sprayed, he felt Roach tug at the back of his shirt-collar. A cold breeze shot down his spine with the sudden movement, followed shortly after by another few spritzes, then the cold of metal and… bugs. Oh oh *oh* so many bugs and critters and whatever else. They fell into his shirt and started crawling all up and down his skin. Some of them wriggled their way into his sleeves to crawl down his arms, some of them managed to get into his pants. He screamed for the first time since his attempts at calling for help. The sounds. The smells. "AGH!" Another scoop of critters. A worm flailed around wildly at the base of his spine as it struggled to find any sense of direction at all. Fire ants and mosquitos started gnawing on him. A hornet stung his inner thigh, only inches from his genitals.

In all the cacophony, a cockroach flew out from under his collar and landed on his lap. It was a relief that it wanted to be free, so it was especially upsetting when his captor grabbed the escaped insect with his bare hands and brought it up to Filipek's mouth. "Say ahhh," he sang. When Filipek sucked in his lips and tried to lean away from the bug, Roach grabbed him roughly by the back of his head, squeezed open his mouth, and shoved the live insect inside. It writhed around on his tongue and lashed against its bony cage, each of its little legs like a cold drop of saltwater. Eventually, it crawled its way down his throat, all the while with him screaming and gagging through his forced-shut lips as his captor watched with sadistic delight. He forced it down his throat instinctively, lest he choke, and he swore he could feel it crawling back up just beside his rapidly-beating heart.

When Roach was certain he had swallowed it, he laughed darkly, poured the remaining vermin from the jar over the CEO's head, then pulled the guitar and amplifier to his hands from across the room. With a glance at River while Filipek screamed and wept and writhed around, he was passed a pair of ear protectors and a thick winter coat, both of which he donned before plugging in the amplifier, turning it up as loud as it would go, kicking back, and riffing mindlessly on the instrument he couldn't even hear.

"STOP! STOP! PLEASE! DEAR GOD!"

Roach stopped playing and lifted half of his ear-protectors. "Hm? You wanted to tell me what *The Jabberwock* is?"

"PLEASE STOP! GET THEM OFF OF ME!"

"I'll get them off of you when you tell me what *The Jabberwock* is." And with that, he dropped the ear-muff back over his ear to cut out the horrid beeping and squeaking and chiming and resume his discordant ear-piercing arpeggios. Filipek kept screaming and begging for mercy, all the while with Roach's eyes firmly locked on his lips, looking for signs of a word worth heeding. It took two hours, but he finally saw one:

"MEXICO! OH GOOD HEAVENS MAKE IT STOP!"

He stopped playing to lift the ear-protectors again. "Mexico? Elaborate."

"*The Jabberwock* is a secret project of Osiris' making. It's in Mexico. In the new states. It's why Tatum pushed for the invasion in the first place."

"He pushed for the invasion? Why?"

Every square inch of him itched and burned and stung from all the venoms in him, but he could only scratch at his palms with his tied-up hands. The critters were all over him to the point that he could hardly open his mouth without one trying to find its way inside. He had accidentally swallowed a moth and several ants, and now a spider had crawled into his ear and started making a nest. A ladybug had taken a liking to his nostrils, dancing around in his sinuses and sometimes out onto his upper lip. "There's one in my ear— my nose—," he whimpered and gagged and sneezed, "The itching itching itching—! Something stung my knob. Please! Make it stop! I BEG YOU!"

"That doesn't sound like an answer to my question, little fish."

He wept, silently glad that the amplifier had stopped screaming. He was relishing the relative quiet. After sucking up some of his sadness and an accidental fly, he sneezed and said, "Some deals in Vietnam and the Philippines fell through for him, so he paid the American government to invade. He needed cheaper land and labour for factories. That's all I know. I swear. Just... please... make it stop."

Roach smiled and turned off all the things making noise. The silence that followed, despite all the other sensory overload, was as heavenly as the angel's trumpets. Filipek's breaths were laboured but relieved as it seemed he had been freed of a great weight on his chest. He was excited for the bugs to finally be scraped off of him, but when Roach approached, he was instead met with a butterfly knife to the jaw again.

"Good job, Tony," said River from his corner of the room as he dropped his ear-protectors on the ground and emerged from the shadows. When he continued, he spoke in Demotic: "I love you. Do you want help killing him?"

"I love you, too," replied Roach in the same language with a soft smile for his brother, "He killed Silvino. I want to do this one alone, and obviously I'm going to wait until we've confirmed what he said. Do you have any more ideas, though? The floor cleaner was a great one."

He shrugged. "No. This is your forté. Just have fun. I'll go tell the others you cracked him."

"Get these bugs off of me," whimpered Filipek. "Please."

"Your best friends!? You want to be rid of them!?" asked Roach with a mocking tone and short chuckle. River leaned down to kiss Roach before he quit the room with a few more words exchanged in Demotic on his way out. As Roach heard the door close, he leaned close and whispered, "We're going to have so much fun, little fish. I'm going to make such pretty pictures on you." He drew a line of blood down his jawbone on the opposite side to the line he had already made. "And... what good is art if no one sees it?"

Filipek gulped. "Please. If you're going to kill me, just do it quickly. Have I not suffered enough?"

A dark laugh. "No. You'll make it to my birthday at the least. An *eternity* of suffering would not be enough for you, swine."

Chapter 45
Painting the Roses Red

May gagged at the video and turned away from the laptop screen. "Roach, this is… this is too much. I won't do it."

"Come on, man. Why not? He deserves it."

"What is it?" asked Thyne from across the room. Everyone had gathered in the living area of Loomis manor at Roach's beck. He was showing May a video with the only context for the others being that he had asked her to send it to Tatum Abraham and show the file title of *Merry Christmas* in the message.

"It's sick, Thyne," she answered.

"Hell yeah it is," said Roach proudly.

"That wasn't a compliment, you psychopath."

He exhaled through his nose with amusement but was unemotive otherwise.

"Let me see," said Thyne as he crossed the room and sat beside her. She passed him her earbuds, and after he had inserted them, she restarted the video and averted her eyes to avoid seeing it again:

It was only a minute long, starting on a black screen. In time with the first words of The Drifters' *White Christmas*, multi-coloured holiday lights flickered to life. They were wrapped around the sides of a guillotine in one of the many chambers of the labyrinthian basement. A wicker basket laid at its base overflowing with white roses. Thyne leaned closer as a masked figure, presumably Roach, pushed Filipek into frame. He was haggard and handcuffed and bleeding already. Roach shoved him toward the guillotine and seemed to be shouting something, but the original audio had been replaced with the music. Filipek willingly knelt down behind the guillotine and looked helplessly toward the camera before Roach put a cigarette out on the back of his neck, pushing him down into the half-moon. He let Filipek sit in anguish for a few measures of the song but eventually pulled the release lever on the side of the device. The blade started to fall. Sparks flew as it clipped the Christmas lights. They went dark when it was only halfway to the base. The music cut out abruptly, and Roach's mad laughter could be heard, as well as the shuffling of the camera. His voice was breathy and insane as he spoke directly into the camera's microphone: "You're next." The video ended, and Thyne leaned back in astonishment. He crossed his legs and looked up at Roach, who had been watching the video silently from behind the settee.

After a while of pondering, Thyne set the laptop on the coffee table, gave May her earphones again, and stood. There was a loaded silence as he visibly processed everything, his thoughts tumbling over each other hot and chaotic like the inside of a dryer. "There's something I never told you all," he said suddenly, "It might change your mind, May. It might make you want to send it."

"Nothing could make this okay to send. And on Christmas? Roach, you're sick."

"Oh yeah," he said with a stifled grin that could not be seen but could be heard.

Thyne turned to face her but spoke loudly enough that they could all hear: "River installed a microphone in Abraham some time ago. I've learned something harrowing with it that has taken me all these months to… to even *try* to process." He looked solemnly at Francis, who stopped drinking in the gaze like a deer in headlights. "Francis… May… All of you." A sigh. "When we were in Scotland for the faire, he was watching Party's stream. He's Skybox. And… anyway… after the stream was over…." He ran a hand through his hair and lit a cigarette despite how angry he knew it would make Giovanni to be smoking indoors. "Francis, please don't… don't hate me for not telling you sooner." A beat. "Abraham has a dead man's switch in him. He warned his girlfriend never to get an *Eye of Osiris* because… because if he dies, everyone with an *Eye of Osiris* will die, too."

The stunned silence that followed was thick enough to cut with a knife. It sucked all the air from the room and sent chills down spines like the slam of a tundra gale.

"That… that's crazy," said May after a tense minute, "I don't believe you."

"How many people have these *Eyes of Osiris?*" asked Jean-Jacques.

"Hundreds of millions," answered Thyne.

May stood. "I don't believe you! You're just as sick as Roach. You only want to send the video to get your sadistic kicks from it."

"We don't need to send it," he said after a long pensive drag on his cigarette, "In fact, we probably shouldn't. He specified to his girlfriend that it only lasts for twelve hours a day. If we openly threaten him, he might try to make it more permanent."

"What good is Christmas if we can't give him a gift?" asked Roach madly.

"Clayton, you lunatic," said Francis, "I love you, but please allow us—. Thyne—." He held his head. "What are you saying? Are you saying we can't kill Tatum?"

"We can't kill him," he confirmed.

"I don't believe you," May repeated.

"Look for yourself, then, you wench!" he snapped.

She sat back down and rubbed her temples. "Lanni, look through the code," she whispered in French.

"And don't you remember what *The Jabberwock* is? He paid for the yanks to invade Mexico," said Partha. Roach had already shown him the video earlier that morning, so he knew the gravity of what he was suggesting when he said, "I think we should send it. We already can't kill him, right? Might as well fuck with him. Maybe Franky can capture him. Viktor can keep him alive. Roach can torture him for as long as he wants, then." Roach's eyes flashed wildly at the beautiful idea.

"Viktor won't want to do that," muttered Francis, "It matters not. We will send it. If he dies naturally, it shan't trigger the switch, am I correct, my dear?"

Thyne took another drag before answering, "I don't know. He said he has to activate it. Presumably, if he was on his deathbed, he wouldn't, but he's mad. We can't expect anything less than absolute depravity from him. He's worse than all of us combined."

Francis sighed and swigged from his flask. "If he dies how I know him to die, it will not trigger. We must let it run its course. It won't be much longer. In the interim, we draw plans to destroy Osiris without targeting him directly."

"We should go to Mexico," said Partha, "I've heard a lot of rumours from my port stops near the new states. Rumours about company towns. I didn't believe them, but... well if what Filipek said is true, then maybe the new states *do* have company towns."

"Roach? River?" said Thyne. They looked at him. "You two were in the war: what do you make of company towns as a possibility in Mexico?"

"Oh, it's very likely," said Perlie, "We were hiding a lot of plans for invasion and occupation with test towns already being built in Nebraska."

In the midst of the conversation, May muttered something.

"What was that, honey?" asked Dezba.

"It's true," she repeated, "The code is right there. It's... it's in mine, too. There's nothing I can do about it, short of brain surgery or carving out my own eye. If Abraham dies, so will I...."

Jean-Jacques stood. "Let me see the video."

May tried to stop him: "JJP, no, it's too—."

"Let me see it!" he shouted.

She shrank away from him. He sounded a lot like their father when he shouted…. "Okay," she whimpered and passed him the earbuds.

He snatched them away from her without recognising that he had scared her and watched the video. His breaths were getting heavier and heavier the longer it went on. When it was finished, the others' conversations were stopped when he slammed the laptop on the coffee table and said, "Send it. Send it, right now, May. That bastard. That—." He stopped, stood, and swapped to French to fully express his disgust as he paced around anxiously: "He's killed you. This video is not enough. If I had him in the room with me right now I'd show him his own black heart. I'd gouge out his eyes, since he fucking loves them so much. I'd bash his head in. I'd kill him! I'd torture him! I'd make him bleed and bleed and bleed! He would know nothing but pain pain pain pain pain!"

Those who knew French were looking at him with wide eyes as his shoulders heaved. "What!?" he shouted in English, "Why are you all looking at me like that? Send the fucking video, May." And in French: "My only regret is that I won't get to see the look on his face or savour the fear in his soulless eyes when he sees it."

"Uh… Roach?" said Thyne after a beat of stunned silence.

"Yeah? What's going on? What did he say?"

"I think… you might have been right about him, mate. Do you maybe want to… uh…."

"Commune with him, Clayton," said Francis.

"Uh, okay sure. Come out onto the back porch with me, dude. I want a smoke anyway."

Jean-Jacques wasn't sure why he was being sent out to have a talk with *Roach* of all people, but he followed him out to the porch, his breaths still heaving.

Once they were gone, Francis turned his attention to May and sighed. "If you want to remove your *Eye of Osiris*, Giovanni is a phenomenal surgeon, and if you worry for your safety under his knife, Viktor can ensure it."

She shook her head. "I won't remove it. I use it to communicate with my… uh… girlfriend."

"It would behove her to join us, then. Where does she live? Mayhaps we can fetch her and bring her here by some means, whether supernatural or otherwise."

May rubbed the inside of her elbow and bit her lip. Her face was burning hot. "She's… not real."

Francis arched his brow, as did a lot of the gang. "You have taken to an apparition, then?"

"She's an AI I made," muttered May with her gaze still averted.

"More real than an apparition," interrupted River before Francis could make it more awkward for her, "Is there not some way to talk with her on a regular phone?"

May smiled just-so at River with appreciation. "There is, but if the *Eye of Osiris* kills me… we've already lost anyway. There's no point in removing it."

Out on the porch, Roach offered Jean-Jacques a cigarette, which was refused, and leaned on the railing to look out at the flooded vineyards and the Tyrrhenian beyond them. "So, what did you say in French?"

Jean-Jacques averted his gaze. "It is not mattering."

"You seemed pretty upset," he led.

Jean-Jacques sighed and leaned on the railing, running his hands through his hair in the process. Since they had met, his roots had grown out long enough that he now had a full head of dark hair. It had been cut and maintained at about two inches long, however, with the sides still shaved to show his tattoos. The style reminded Roach of a friend of his, but he didn't mention it. Jean-Jacques responded after a moment of quiet, "I don't know you, but I do."

"What do you mean, dude?"

He groaned. English was so confusing. He had never bothered learning it in much depth because his sister had created such a good translation software for him to use in his classes at MIT. He only sometimes had to look up jargon that he would have been learning for the first time as a native English speaker anyway. Then, when the Morozovs "took him in" he mostly only heard them speaking Russian and focused more on learning how to understand that language as opposed to the language outside of his strange little prison. However, being with the gang for almost a year was helping him grasp the language better. He tried to express the sentiment again, taking his time to think of the right words: "I mean… You are… evil." He glanced Roach's way to see if he had taken offence, which it seemed he hadn't. At least… his face was as unemotive as ever, so he continued: "You are evil, and yet… I… like you. I think."

Roach smirked and slapped a hand on Jean-Jacques' upper back playfully. "I like you, too, dude. I'm glad you're warming up to me."

"And," continued Jean-Jacques, "I understand why you are all doing this gang now. After learning about Osiris' leader and the 'dead man's switch' as Monsieur Thyne calls it."

"Is that so?"

He nodded and watched Roach take a drag. The way the smoke fell from his lips was like a waterfall. The way his hand was held so still against his subtle smile was as calm as the winter breezes caressing them. It was nigh-impossible to fathom that those very same hands had killed almost— what was it? —500 people? One of those people was Motya…. He hung his head as the bittersweet memories of his late "friend" whispered through him. "Oui," he replied in a disinterested way, "It is difficult to believe, but you and me are on the same side."

"Yeah, dude. I've got your back, same as anyone else in the gang. This whole group is a Godsend, and I thank Allah every damn day for it." He squinted out at the winter sunset and smoked. After a moment of quiet, he turned back to his friend and asked with a slight grin he could not hide, "Are you excited for tomorrow? Do you celebrate?"

Jean-Jacques smiled. "Oui. I have a gift for you. I hope it is not rude."

"Rude!? Ha! Of course not, dude! That's so sweet. Thanks! I feel bad I didn't get anything for you!"

"It is okay, Monsieur."

"I'll do something for you on your birthday, then."

"If you are wanting to."

Roach finished his cigarette and flicked the butt into the bushes. "Let's go back inside and finish decorating. I know I shouldn't, but I fucking love Christmas."

"You can love Christmas, Monsieur. Your God would not be angry."

Roach let out an amused huff. "Yeah. Lots more for Him to be mad at me about than that."

Jean-Jacques simpered softly and followed his friend back inside.

The next morning, there was a healthy snow dancing down from the blue-grey sky. Lanni sent the harrowing snuff film of Filipek's death to Tatum Abraham, making certain that it couldn't be traced and that, in fact, it seemed to be a message from Filipek himself. After that dark business was finished, however, lightheartedness abounded.

They trickled downstairs slowly, the smell of waffles filling the living area as Dezba made each newcomer a plate with fresh fruit and whipped cream on top. After eating, each of them would file into the living area and listen to Arjun playing gentle Christmas tunes on the piano while nursing a mug of coffee or tea. As the room started to fill, they discussed the success of their Halloween job, with May gleefully informing those who had gathered that Eir Lilac was finally going under.

The last person to join them was River. Even Melchiresa, who had no interest in Christmas or being awake at such an hour, was quicker to meander his way downstairs than the groggy twin. River's waffle was cold by the time he ate it, but he scarfed it down in a few bites with just as few manners as his brother had an hour and a half earlier. With a hot cup of coffee and sleep still in his eyes, he finally joined the others, and Giovanni addressed them lazily: "Should we begin? You've gotten each other a lot of gifts."

"Yes!" cheered Roach like a child. He set down his empty mug beside him and telekinetically pulled one of the gifts from its place under the tree to Thyne's lap.

"Oh!" said the Brit as he tried not to spill his tea on the box. "I forgot you could do that, mate." His cheeks were pink as everyone's attention turned to him. This first gift was an idol of Charon on the Styx. It curiously piqued Melchiresa's interest, but the mute did no more than look at it with a scrutinous gaze. The figure weighed less than it appeared to weigh and was beautifully painted, with a plethora of complexities and intricate details in both the paint and sculpture itself. "What is this made of, mate? Did you make this?"

Roach nodded and beamed. His cheeks were all red with delight and bright teeth shining. "Yeah, dude! It's made of recycled trash." Thyne sort of winced. "It's clean and sanitary and all that shit. Don't worry."

"What a sweet gift," said Dezba, "I didn't know you were the type to make art like that."

He nodded and blushed. "Yeah, you know those packs of trash Osiris sells? They scoop it out of the ocean and pretend they're being environmentally friendly by packing it in more plastic and selling it?" Vague nods all around. "Yeah, so I hate Osiris and all, but I fucking love those things. They find the coolest trash, I swear. Had to leave a lot of my collection in Compton, so I had to buy some of those to make it, but…." He laughed nervously as shame started to set upon him for finally admitting that he partook in such a strange hobby. "Uh… Do you like it?"

"I love it, mate. Thank you." He smiled and blew Roach a little kiss before Dezba caught his attention by walking over to the tree.

She picked up a set of nine similarly-sized boxes, passing them down the line until everyone but herself and their hosts had gifts. "Okay," she said with a big grin, "Open those together."

There was a cacophony of ripping paper and a rumble of low conversation. Partha was the first to fully unwrap his gift, and he held up the knitted sweater inside to look at its design. He jumped to his feet and turned it around to show Dezba as if she wasn't the one who had made it. "Do you know what this is?" She giggled. "This is the design from Edward Low's flag!"

"I know," she said with another giggle.

"Thank you, Dezba!" He rushed over and hugged her.

She returned the embrace lovingly. "Of course, son."

"What did everyone else get?" He looked around the room as the others started to hold up their sweaters to see the designs. Roach's sweater was black with a red millipede wrapped around the entire torso, made from the same yarn as Partha's. Also made with the same yarn was Thynes: entirely black save for a big red heart in the middle. It seemed to match the theme of River's, his being white with a big black spade in the middle. May's was dark green with a complex white pattern all across it that resembled a circuit board. Jean-Jacques' was orange on its bottom half and blue on the top with the silhouette of a jet plane in white in the centre. Neodesha's was magenta with a pair of duelling pistols crossed over the chest. Francis' was red with his own pirate flag's design on it, and Perlie's was entirely black with no design but was knitted from the softest and fluffiest yarn Dezba could find. Everyone swarmed their elderly friend for hugs, with Perlie, Partha, and Roach already wearing their new sweaters.

After thanks were given out, she passed out another nine boxes, these much smaller. They were the gemstone dice she had bought for everyone at the renaissance faire, and though they were less personalised, they were still to the tastes of each member.

"Okay, okay," said Thyne, "You two have given enough lovely gifts. It's my turn." He stood and dug through the presents. He found two small boxes after a bit of searching and brought them to the twins. Before passing them over, he asked, "Which of you is older?"

They chuckled and said "Tony" and "Me" in tandem.

Thyne pointedly gave one of the boxes to Roach then the other to River. They looked up at him, unsure who should start. "What are you looking at me like that for?" He laughed. "Open them!"

They were quick to tear open the paper and pop off the lids of the small boxes, both of them looking down into them. Whatever was inside left them speechless.

Thyne giggled with playful fiendishness, and after six seconds of stunned silence, Francis leaned over to peer into Roach's box. "Oh," he said with a smirk and a swig.

"What is it?" whined Partha.

Roach covered his mouth and turned away, passing the box to River and hiding his expression from the others as tears trickled down his cheeks.

River was usually an unemotional man, but the gifts were getting to him as well, evident in his continued quietude as he dumped both boxes into his left palm and held up the contents for the room to see: four different car keys.

"What are those?" asked Perlie before suddenly sitting upright. "Are those—!?"

Thyne nodded. His grin was smug and haughty. "They're in the North garage. The one nobody has been allowed in."

Roach stood and rushed to the door, River following behind him with the keys. Thyne followed the both of them all chuffed, and the rest of the gang trailed him.

Thyne had to unlock the garage for them, but once they were inside, he flicked on the lights and looked immediately at Roach and River to see their reactions.

River's voice was broken as he turned to Thyne and asked, "Is this what you were doing in November?"

"Mayyyybe."

Roach was still averting his gaze from the others, but he could be heard sniffling as he approached and reached a hand out to the roof of his *Locust*, brought there somehow from the states. After a moment wherein River walked down the line to see the twins' *Fiat* and two cars he didn't recognise, Roach turned to Thyne, his eyes wet with tears, and whimpered, "How?"

"It wasn't easy. I had to rent a cargo plane. Blackmail. Bribe. Work with the Morozovs. Burn my identity for a new one. But… I did it. For you."

"And these?" asked River as he gestured to the other two cars.

"I gave you four keys, didn't I, mate?"

"You wouldn't give us—." He stopped himself to look at the new cars before rushing to the closest one to unlock what he thought was its passenger door but turned out to be the driver's side. It was a 1938 *Alfa Romeo 8C*, one of the most expensive classic cars in the world. It was painted black with a matte finish, white accents, and sported white-wall tyres. Beside it was another classic car: a 1949 *Ferrari Inter*. Its paint was midnight blue, and River rushed to open it too, admiring the interiors of both vehicles before looking for a way to open the hoods. "Tony! Oh! Come look! Come look!"

Roach was too busy holding Thyne in a near back-breaking embrace and sobbing quietly into his shoulder to heed the calls. "Thank you," he whispered so that only Thyne could hear, "I love you so much. I'm sorry I don't remember London."

Thyne grunted. "Too tight."

"Shit. Sorry." He retreated and rubbed the tears from his eyes with the sleeve of his new sweater. He looked over at River and noticed the classic cars. "Are those for us, too?" He hadn't seen that River's gift box was the one with the keys for the two he was currently fawning over.

"Yeah, mate." He stepped up into Roach's space and stood on his tip-toes to kiss his cheek and whisper, "I love you, too, you muppet."

Roach turned toward the others. "Give me and Sonny a minute. These cars are fucking sick." He sniffled and looked back down at Thyne. "Just don't open anything too cool without us. We'll come back inside in a minute or two."

Thyne smiled knowingly. "You two have fun. I'll wait to give Francis his gift until you're back, then."

They left the twins to admire the cars. On the way inside, Thyne pulled Jean-Jacques aside and explained, "I couldn't get your motorbike to Rome in time, but it's in Europe: it's in my garage in London."

"Merci, monsieur," was Jean-Jacques' reply with a blushy beaming grin.

Per Dezba's suggestion, no one opened any gifts in the thirty minutes it took the twins to come back inside. They instead poured more tea and coffee, and Dezba started a batch of gingerbread cookies which were fresh out of the oven as the door opened and the Roaches kicked the snow from their boots onto the foyer's rug.

Roach bumped into Dezba on his way into the kitchen, and she spotted a tub of sour cream in his hands. "What's that?"

"I need a spoon."

She blocked him from going further into the kitchen. "Where did you get that, son?"

"The *Locust*."

She snatched it out of his hand and replaced it with a cookie.

"But it's not even opened!" he whined, "I want to see if it's cream cheese now."

He tried to give her his best attempt at the puppy dog eyes, but she shook her finger in his face and tossed the tub of sour cream, nearly a year old by then, into the garbage. (As if binning it would stop him). "Go sit with the others, son."

He sighed and munched his cookie with a pout. "Fine."

When they were all settled again, more gifts were exchanged. Roach gave Francis a pocketwatch he had made entirely out of some of the junk he had bought from Osiris. They had specialty packages of garbage that were made up of small mechanical and industrial parts, so with a few of those, he managed to find enough things to make a pocketwatch with a rib-cage pattern of openings on its lid and an engraved message in Demotic on the back which read *Love you forever, bed bug*. Because it was purpose-built, Roach was able to add a ticker for not only the month and day, but as well the year. He had even consulted Thyne about Francis' methods of time measurement, so there were only four "months," which were indicated by symbols to represent the season rather than numbers. Francis immediately replaced his other pocketwatch with this much more useful and sentimentally valuable one, pushing it through time until it had the same reading then giving the old watch to Roach thoughtlessly.

Another gift for Francis was an antique *Uberti 1858 Remington New Army Revolver* from Thyne that he had bought from the gun show in Crownpoint for €56,000. It was authentic, at least as far as he and Dezba could tell when they bought it, and Francis beamed with pride to be holding it. Dezba was also given some guns, all of which were European models from Thyne's personal arsenal, and she was even more chuffed by all the firearms than the drunk as she started taking them apart and seeing what new arrangements she could make like a child playing with action figures.

Partha gave Thyne the sword he had bought in Crownpoint based on his character's in their old game. Seeing as he was giving Thyne a sword he had previously been using in the bedroom with Perlie, they would need a new one. He therefore gave Perlie a vintage Hwando with a jade handle. He explained in a note with the gift that he wasn't sure how to use it in its proper form, but he had started to learn for her.

Besides the guns and swords, the rest of the presents were fairly pedestrian. Jean-Jacques had bought Roach some fried crickets and gave him one of his old university textbooks about aeromechanics. For May, he gave her a stack of postcards from his travels in America that Francis had secured for him on his trip with Thyne to America for the twins' cars.

Perlie wanted to find something grand for Partha: she wanted to find him a genuine pirate ship or at least a replica of one, but it proved impossible for a plethora of reasons. Instead, she settled for a few miniatures she thought he'd like, a glass eye she had blown herself, and an 'IOU' to watch the *Lord of the Rings* extended editions with him. Roach failed to hide a glare at her when Partha read the IOU for the room: he had tried to show her the movies countless times when they were dating.

Giovanni gave Neodesha and Thyne some books, Thyne gave Neodesha a pair of gold hoop earrings, and Partha gave Perlie a care-package of goodies from the cruise he had worked in November which included a lot of candies and a plush or two from various ports in Latin America. May was given a new laptop. Dezba was given some dice and yarn. The dogs and duck were all given homemade treats from Giovanni and some toys from various others. Their hosts were not given much as per their own requests: they had enough things already. That didn't stop Thyne from finding some gourmet spices for Giovanni and a new harmonica for Arjun, however.

The strangest gift, at least for those who did not know of Thyne and Francis' traditions, was Francis' final gift, wrapped beautifully in golden paper with a big red ribbon. Inside the intricate wrapping was simply an orange, and Francis was delighted by it. He thanked Thyne kindly and immediately started to peel it, giving parts to Thyne and Roach and eating a few himself. Having grown up in financially hard times being born in 1920, even with upper middle-class parents, an orange was sometimes the best gift Thyne could hope for as a child. As well, Francis always considered citrus a special treat not only because it was so foreign to his own childhood but because it would also keep the scurvy at bay in his young adult-hood. Thyne had unintentionally started the tradition of giving Francis an orange each year in the 1960s when he impulse-bought a pack just before Christmas, recalling how they always tasted sweeter as gifts.

On the whole, it was a loving and wholesome morning for the gang, and Francis, for once, was glad to be wasting some time. When the gifts were all opened, Giovanni, Viktor, and Dezba spent the rest of the day preparing a feast, during which Partha ran a Christmas-themed session of his West Marches game for those who weren't busy. The game was as fun as ever, and rather than an explosive outrage like their last feast together, dinner was harmonious and conversational. The food was delicious, and the only break from sobriety for anyone was brought about only by celebratory wine and rum.

When they went to sleep that night, Francis slept in Roach's bed, and the pirate was therefore able to stay grounded the entire night, giving a much-needed rest to his frazzled mind.

She was startled awake by her phone buzzing on her cheek. "Oh my! Oh! Hello? I'm sorry. How long was I asleep?" The man on the other line was a weepy mess too wrought with sorrow to be comprehended as he sputtered something at her. "Oh love! What's wrong? Do you need me to come there? Where are you? Which house?" She stood and immediately started packing a suitcase. In his sputtering, she managed to understand the word "Rome," and replied, "Rome? Okay I'll be there in a few hours. Oh, poor thing. I love you! Hold Nessie, okay?" she said, referring to his pet rabbit, "I'll be there, and I'll bring Meatloaf to cuddle you, too."

"Thank you," he managed through his sniffling and sputtering, "I love you."

"I love you so much, Tatum! Just hold on a few hours."

Her flight from London was excruciatingly long. She had no idea what had Tatum so upset. She had never seen him like this, and she spent most of the trip worrying herself with worst-case-scenarios. What if he was dying? And on Christmas Day! What a horrifying prospect.

When she finally arrived at his home in Rome, she rushed to his room where he was three tissue-boxes into a crying fit. He tried to stand when he saw her, but she rushed over too quickly for his old bones. She hugged him as tightly as she could without hurting him, and retreated to wipe tears from his cheeks tenderly. "What's the matter, love?"

"They killed Chris," he whimpered, "They killed him and made me watch."

"Oh! Tatum! You poor soul!" She pulled him in for another embrace and wailed into his shoulder. She had only met Christopher three times, but each time he was an utter delight and made her Tatum as happy as a child. "What monsters did this!?"

"*The Tiara. The Crown*. Whatever they call themselves."

"Evil! Evil *evil* creatures! We'll do something about it, love, don't you worry your precious little heart."

PART FIVE

IS THIS A KISSING BOOK?

❧ Chapter 46 ❧
When Does It Get Good?

2082 came with much fanfare from the rest of the world, but Tatum's was hollow and harrowing. Another wretched year rotting around the sun. Another friend's funeral on the schedule. For once, London was sunny and cheery, as if to mock his pain as his chauffeur trailed the hearse. It was an empty casket. There were some of Christopher's belongings inside, some notes and parting gifts from friends and family, but Tatum was having trouble seeing the point in burying a coffin with nobody in it. What good was all the money in the world if he couldn't give his best friend a proper burial?

His overworked associates were pushing themselves to the brink for his cause: vocal analysts trying to track down a person behind the camera based on the laugh and spoken threat at the video's close— hackers who had previously worked for various intelligence agencies of various countries trying their damndest to find out where the email actually came from— search dogs and cops on every corner of the globe trying to sniff out his corpse—. All of it for naught.

The funeral was like a dream. It came and went from his perception like a storm through a window. He was almost as lifeless as his friend for the entire ordeal, his mind all the while reeling. The stranger from the video had the most harrowing laugh he'd ever heard, and his whispered threat at the end echoed like a gunshot through the old man's head: *'You're next. You're next. You're next.'* He had his dead man's switch to protect him, but the man hardly sounded sane enough to care if he was responsible for hundreds of millions of deaths.

Tatum's eyes scanned the faces surrounding him as speeches were given to the empty grave and dirt was thrown onto the polished casket. Christopher's brother was wailing, and the way his shuddered inhales sounded was not dissimilar to the shuddered inhales of the murderer's mad laughter. It brought a chill down Tatum's arched spine. Could it have been him? His eyes scanned more, and the more he let his thoughts go reeling, the more he realised: *'It could be anyone.'*

"Love?" cooed Aspyn through her weepiness. She set her hand gently on his shoulder. When she had his attention, she smiled sadly, "We'll get them back for this, love."

He managed the slightest of sad smiles at her. *'It could be anyone but her. My greatest love. What would I do without her? Why, I'd have probably killed myself the moment I saw it.'* He took her hand up in his and kissed its knuckles tenderly. "Thank you, maple sugar." As he looked at her fingers, he couldn't help but notice the lack of rings on them.... At that point, he was at least somewhat certain that what they had was real love. He would buy her a ring that very night and plan a romantic proposal. With the threat on his life looming over him, it seemed evermore pertinent to make her his wife.

It was decided that the first week of January would be the gang's foray into Mexico. They would only bring a handful of members, the rest left behind in the manor planning and preparing for their hits on the other remaining companies. Those involved in investigating *The Jabberwock* would first fly to Brazil. After landing in Boa Vista, they would rent or steal two cars and make their way north to the warfront.

Before their departure, however, the twins approached Giovanni while he was cutting vegetables for a stir fry. River spoke first: "Heya, doc?"

"Hm? Yes, can I help you?"

"Well, you took our blood a while ago— after the faire —but you never told us the results."

"Yeah," concurred Roach, "Why do we have powers? Did you figure it out?"

Giovanni rubbed his forehead. "Ah, it is unfortunate, boys. I would have told you had I remembered: I never ran the tests because Arjun drank the samples."

"What do you mean he drank them?" they asked in unintentional chorus.

He resumed cutting vegetables but gestured with his knife-hand as he replied, "Oh, you know. He needs blood to survive, and despite how much we are able to procure for him, he is still always *getting into* things." He spoke of his husband as if he were a rambunctious puppy or mischievous child.

"Well, can you take our blood again before we leave?" asked River.

"And don't let him drink it this time," added Roach.

He waved his hand around dismissively, nearly nicking River with the blade, "Yes yes. After dinner. Remind me."

As requested, shortly after the last dishes were brought into the kitchen from the stir fry, Roach reminded Giovanni to draw more blood. He led them to the same room wherein he had initially taken samples. Roach was just as nervous as he was the first time, but his upset was only evident to River, who held his brother's hand lovingly as Roach averted his gaze from the needle entering his inner arm and bit his lip.

Giovanni put the new vials of blood into a small refrigerator and removed his gloves to toss carelessly into a bin by the door. "I'll test them while you're gone, then afterwards: I will finally examine you more thoroughly." His eyes flashed madly, but the twins were unbothered by it.

"Alright, dude. Seeya," said Roach as he hopped out of his seat and walked with River to their *Locust*, excited to drive it to the airport for the trip to Brazil.

The party to leave would include Melchiresa and Arjun, the only two in the entire group who knew Portuguese. Thyne was their pilot, and their plane was a rental under Arjun's name, for Thyne's new identity was still not attached to his own planes or wealth. The other passengers of this flight were Francis, Roach, River, and Partha. May and Perlie would be in the palace haunt acting as eyes and ears in the sky for them, but it would take the ground crew several days if not an entire week to reach the warfront. The ladies were therefore still in Italy when the plane touched down in Boa Vista at two in the morning Amazon Standard Time on January third.

Roach brought the group to a used car lot near the airport and lockpicked his way into the building. He and his brother searched for car keys with Arjun's help translating, and by 3:23 they had two sets of keys and identifying codes to easily find the corresponding vehicles in the lot. Arjun drove the larger of the two cars with his passengers being the twins, Francis, and Partha. Melchiresa could not drive, so he would be Thyne's only passenger, acting as his translator without fear of someone else hearing his soft voice.

Taking the decade-old bridge over the Amazon, the trip from Boa Vista to Medellín was only twenty hours, during which they were able to stop to refuel at petrol stations or sleep in hotels built hauntingly over the dense jungle. Once they were off the bridge, they swapped drivers so that Partha could easily navigate on their way up into Panama and the rest of Central America. Thyne followed behind them dutifully for the entire trip, though he was increasingly annoyed by how slowly and carefully Partha drove as opposed to the immortal man who had been driving priorly.

The closer they neared Tabasco, the more guidance the twins needed to give

Partha in order to make their way to Silvino's half-sister's house in Villahermosa. It was far enough from the warfront to be safe, but the landscape was forever marred by the echoes of the battles just past the horizon. They arrived at her doorstep unannounced in the middle of the night on January eighth. She was bemused and welcomed them inside to let them sleep there, but when morning came, she was quick to pester them as to what was happening. The entire conversation was had in Spanish, but Thyne was able to at least surmise that there was an upset:

"Keep your 'good mornings,' Clayton. How dare you come showing up at my doorstep in the middle of the night and refuse to tell me why! You've always been a miserable sack of shit. Silvino was too good for you."

"I know," he replied with his upset well veiled physically but felt by all spiritually, "If we told you why we're here, it'd put you in more danger than it's worth."

"I've survived this long in the middle of a war!"

"And we would like you to continue to survive," said Francis.

"And who are you, then? Who are any of these people? You Roaches really live up to your names. Disgusting creatures always crawling around where you're not welcome."

River draped his arm around her shoulders and said with a slimy grin, "Come now, Elisa. You must have something you need doing that we can do for you to pay our way. A car that needs fixing? An American that needs killing?"

She pushed him away and spat in his face. "You can rot in Hell, Karson. Why are you here? Who are these people?"

"You're still mad about Abuela, I take it?" asked River as he wiped her spit from his eyes.

She wound back to punch him, but Roach grabbed her fist mid-throw and looked at her solemnly. Her lip was trembling as she looked at him and whimpered, "You didn't let me say goodbye."

"I'm sorry, Elisa. Truly I am. If it helps: she had a peaceful death away from the war. I brought you a picture of her and Silvino for your ofrenda." He pulled a polaroid from his pocket and passed it to her. "It's the only picture I have of the two of them, but she wasn't my grandmother, she was yours."

She snatched the photo from him and looked at it for a weepy moment. With sopping cheeks, she looked up at him again and asked, "Please just tell me what's going on."

Roach sighed and looked to Partha, River, and Francis. Glances danced around between them for a silent moment, as if they were speaking telepathically, after which he turned his attention back to Elisa. He took up one of her hands to kiss its knuckles and spoke softly, "Sister, we are going to push through the warfront into the new states and see what has been done there."

She blinked. "Why?"

"We have reason to believe that Osiris International paid for the invasion to create company towns there. We intend to destroy them and free the workers."

It took her a moment to process the claim, after which she sighed and slipped the photo into her pocket. "Fine. You can stay here. But on three conditions."

"Alright. What are they?"

"One: fix my car before you go. It's been veering to the left."

"Done. Next?"

"Two: take pictures of you and your stupid fucking brother for my ofrenda in case you get yourselves killed being idiots."

"Alright. And the last?"

She gestured to the others and said with an exasperated tone, "Who the fuck are these people, Clayton?"

He chuckled. "Friends."

She slapped him. "Tell me who they are, you rotten—."

"I am Androme Francis Horatius Alexandre Anaxagorasde Tremblay." He bowed, and Thyne rolled his eyes.

"Elisa," she said with a befuddled expression as he took her hand to kiss politely.

"Partha Jem Nima, miss." He also bowed and kissed her hand, unsubtly mimicking Francis.

"I am Arjun and this is my partner, whose name is lost to time. We call him Melchiresa." They both shook her hand.

"Uh… Name's Eric," said Thyne when she turned to face him. They shook hands awkwardly. "No hablo español."

"And I don't speak English," she said in English with a sigh. Back to Spanish and with a glare at the twins: "Why did you bring him if he doesn't know the language?"

River replied, "He's useful for other reasons. We can't tell you anything more. It's a risk to your safety and ours."

She rolled her eyes. "Just go fix my car, you oversized grease-monkeys." They mock-saluted and trailed out of the room toward her garage. "Now… Partha, was it?" He nodded. "Tell your friend to warn me of any allergies before I start making lunch, and while I'm cooking, all of you can sit here and…." She looked around. "I don't know, twiddle your thumbs. Don't touch my things. If you're associated with the Roaches you're no good." She started to leave and muttered, "Now where did I put that camera?"

Roach and River had only been working on the car for ten minutes when they were interrupted by the sounds of Elisa's panicked voice as she bursted into the garage and slammed the door behind her. "Clayton!"

"What's wrong?"

"There's a wasp in the house! Go take care of it!" She rushed over to River and cowered behind him.

Roach sighed. "Where did you see it?"

"Ask your British friend. He saw it. It stung me!"

"Of course he did," he muttered in English. "Alright, I'll go take care of it for you, Ellie." He went inside and found everyone sitting in the living room chatting. He glared softly at Thyne who saw him and smiled guiltily. "Sister says there's a wasp in here," he said as he crossed his arms.

Thyne stood and slid his way over to Roach to run his hands up his chest. "Will you save us from the scary bug, sir?"

"And how would I do that, hm? Choking you again?"

He batted his eyelashes and made a good effort to look adorable as he said, "If you think it'd help."

"God dammit," said Roach as Thyne successfully broke through the rough exterior. "You're so cute, you little fuck. You don't even know Spanish. Why'd you mic her?"

He blinked and poked his nose as he thought. "To protect her?" He sounded unsure.

Roach pulled him under his arm and gave him a noogie. "Dumb bitch," he said playfully as Thyne wriggled free and stamped his foot. "I'll tell her the wasp is gone. The wasp *is* gone, right?"

He pouted. "No sense in bugging her again."

"Alright. Now I'm gonna go finish fixing her car, then we're going to the *warfront*." He glared at everyone in the room as he emphasised the word. When his gaze fell back on Thyne it was harsh. "Maybe let's stop dicking around and take shit a little more seriously for once."

"Of all people to tell me to take things seriously, I would have never bet you'd be one of them, mate. Are you sick?" He held his hand up to his forehead to feel for a fever.

Roach shoved it away. "We're already on thin ice with Elisa. Leave her alone, would you?"

He pouted. "Fine."

"Good." And with that, he returned to the garage to tell Elisa he had killed the wasp then resumed fixing her car.

They left Elisa's house at midnight and started the long trek up to Mexico City, where the Mexican-Italian-Brazilian coalition had been holding the line since the war slowed down. It hadn't occurred to him before learning about *The Jabberwock*, but now that he knew that Osiris was involved, River figured that the war must have slowed because the government wasn't getting pressure and funding from Osiris anymore. At least that was his best guess. Why else would the Americans, who had handily pushed up to that point, have been stalemated for four consecutive years in Mexico City?

The twins were each driving one of their stolen cars, with Roach in the lead. The closer they neared to Mexico City, the more the smells of gunsmoke, iron, and death filled the cabins. Even in the dead of night, they could hear gunshots in the distance, and at a certain point, they could see the faintest flicker of muzzle flashes. Roach took backroads that were new even to River, but it helped keep their cars shielded from potential strays or snipers, however unlikely it might have been for them to be shot at such a distance and in civilian vehicles. The last of the backroads led into a hand-dug trench large enough for the cars but not by much. He followed the winding trench until the dirt below became asphalt and split off in three directions. He took the furthest right path, as did his brother behind him, until they were parking in an underground garage with a handful of other vehicles. There were two repainted American military *Jeeps*, four repurposed Mexican military *Jeeps*, what was once a food truck, reinforced with some sort of metal plating, and now their stolen civilian cars. The twins turned off the engines, which sent the room into pitch darkness. Francis changed his eyes to see, and Melchiresa, Partha, and Thyne had to hold onto one of the others' hands in order to be led around in the black room. Melchiresa held Arjun's hand, Partha grabbed Roach's, and Thyne was led by Francis.

After hanging the keys of the new cars on a pegboard in the garage, the twins led them into an adjacent hall, which was fortunately well-lit. The building was laid out similarly to a high school, and after some navigation through it, they finally heard the shuffling of other people. Roach and River pulled out their wallets as they walked and each produced an ID of some sort, which they took turns scanning to open a series of four doorways. Once they were through, Roach turned to address everyone but was interrupted by someone shouting, "Capitán!"

He turned around and beamed at the man rushing up to him, who was walking with a bit of a limp but was still speedy. He was about the same height and build as Thyne. His skin was deep in colour and warm in tone with scars peppered all over. His sharp jawline had a scar that cut into his stubble and made itself more visible therefore. His eyes were honey brown with madness swimming inside them. One of his dark bushy eyebrows was scarred, giving it the illusion of a purposeful eyebrow slit, and his dark brown hair was a short undercut that was almost as covered in soot as the gunmetal black rifle on his back. Though his teeth were slightly yellowed from smoking, his smile was wide and bright as he threw his strong arms around Roach, embracing him for a good minute. He spoke in Spanish with a boisterous raspy voice as Roach pulled him away and held him by the shoulders: "You madman! You came back!"

"Dude! So good to see you! Not gonna lie: I feared the worst."

He laughed. "No need to worry about me, Cap! They couldn't kill me if they tied me to a nuke! Look at this." He lifted the bottom of his pants to show a prosthetic leg shoved into his boot. "Blew it off with a landmine, but they can't stop me, brother! Man! We've missed you out here." He hugged him again. "And Karson!" He hugged River then asked Roach, "How's your sister?"

"She's good. In Egypt with the rest of the family, save for the stubborn Elisa, of course. But yeah, we brought her back to America with us when we snuck back with Abuela in seventy-two."

"So glad she's doing well. I miss her like crazy."

"She misses you, too. She always rattled on about you."

He wore a proud grin and finally gestured to the others. "Who are your friends?"

Roach introduced everyone, including Thyne, which brought a glare from the Brit. "And this is Pio," said Roach in English to introduce this newcomer, "Friend of mine from the war. He's absolutely out of his mind."

"Oh yeah," agreed Pio in English, "Gotta be out of your mind to be in the war this long." He laughed. "Is that why you came back, you loon? 'Cause you've finally lost that last pesky bit of sanity?"

Thyne tilted his head unknowingly as he tried to imagine Roach sane. Was he sane before the invasion? Was it the war that awakened the monster in him, the same as the war had changed Oliver all those years ago?

"You could say that," replied Roach, "Hey, we're going to go into the new states to blow shit up. Wanna help?"

His eyes lit up like a child meeting a unicorn. "DO I!?"

Roach chuckled. "You get your stuff together, man. We're gonna take some supplies ourselves. That chill?"

"Should be. Do you still have your ID?"

He showed him the card, and Thyne leaned forward to peep it. It was in Spanish, and at a distance, but he managed to see Roach's picture and the words *Capitán No Oficial* before Roach slid it back into his pocket. Thyne tried to pickpocket it, but River grabbed his wrist and shook his finger disapprovingly at the attempted thievery. "Man, you haven't aged a bit, huh?" said Pio after seeing Roach's picture on the ID.

"I mean my back hurts, but that's probably from carrying all the good looks and humour in the family." They laughed, giving no attention to River. Thyne looked for offence on the twin's face and saw none.

"Alright, well, let's meet up when you're ready. But, oh! Can I ask a favour?"

"Sure, dude. What is it?"

"Is there any chance, after I help you, that you could bring me back to Brazil?"

"Of course, man."

"Thanks so much!"

They hugged excitedly again before Pio rushed off and Roach turned back toward the group. "Alright, nice. He's an explosives expert, so he'll be real useful. Thyne?"

He started and blushed. "Yes?"

"Don't gotta look so scared, dude. I was just gonna tell you... y'know... wouldn't mind if *he* gets stung by a wasp." A cheeky wink. "So, let's go get outfitted. Franky can probably bring us past the line, but I don't want him overexerting himself. You excited, bed bug?"

Francis beamed. "I am!"

"We're finally going after Osiris proper!"

The pirate nodded vehemently. "AYE!"

"And Party must be hyped, too: finally on a fun guns-blazing type job. You really impressed me with the Halloween one. And you didn't even wince at the video of Filipek dying. I really underestimated you, kid." He nudged his shoulder.

"Thank you, sir. I'm happy to help." He saluted, which brought a loving chuckle from Roach as he rustled his hair.

"Alright, boys. Follow me."

Chapter 47
The Pit of Despair

Perlie and May came downstairs together with a suitcase each. Perlie took the keys for one of Thyne's cars out of a bowl in the foyer and turned to May to continue their conversation about the world cup that would be happening that summer in Rome. She opened her mouth to comment, but Giovanni stopped them by saying: "Before you leave, Miss Moon, I need to speak with you."

She rolled her eyes and groaned. "Yes? What is it? We have to get to Versailles to help the boys."

"I understand. Please, come with me to a private room."

"Why?"

"Do you wish to have a medically-sensitive conversation with Miss Day present?"

Another groan. She set down her suitcase, told May, "Just a minute," then followed Giovanni to her suite upstairs.

After closing the door behind him: "Miss Moon, you are nearing the end of the optimal time to abort the foetus as you are reaching your second trimester. I, personally, will abort up to term, but it will be increasingly less comfortable for you. I am also willing to deliver it when the time comes, should you choose to keep it. Have you come to a final decision?"

She averted her eyes and hid her pink cheeks behind her stark black hair. "I want to keep it," she muttered.

"No abortion, then?" She nodded shyly. "Very well. Carry on to France, but do hail me if you ever change your mind."

"Thanks," she mumbled as he opened the door again.

When she came back downstairs, May could tell there was a change in her attitude. She feared the worst, so when they were in the car, she asked, "You're not sick or anything are you?"

"What? Oh. No, I'm okay. It's just... about the baby."

"Oh no! Is everything okay?"

She sighed and leaned on her door. "He was asking if I want to abort it." A beat. "I don't, but I don't want to have to raise the kid alone if Partha chickens out."

May patted Perlie's thigh and beamed adorably. "Don't worry. Even if Partha is a deadbeat, the rest of us will all be here for you and the little one!"

Perlie smiled dismissively at her. "Thanks. Let's just go."

May nodded and turned over the engine. After she got onto the road: "Have you thought about names?"

"I haven't thought about it much at all beyond the morning sickness and cramps."

"Well there's plenty of time! Just try not to worry, okay?" A vague nod from Perlie. "Have you told your parents? I bet they're excited to be grandparents."

"May, I appreciate you and your light-heartedness a lot, but... can we just talk about something else? You were saying you don't root for France in the world cup but, what was it? Scotland instead?"

May smiled sadly at Perlie. "Oui. I root for Scotland instead."

After gathering ammunition for the guns they had brought with them and a few extra knives for Roach (never enough knives), he led the group to a part of this makeshift barracks with other military equipment. As he walked the aisles looking for uniforms and protective gear, Partha rushed up beside him and asked, "Sir, do you think they have any rapiers? I gave mine to Thyne for Christmas, and all my other real ones are back home in Bermuda."

Roach stopped and arched his brow at him. "Rapiers, kid?"

"Yes, sir. I'm a very good swordsman. Francis has been teaching me, too, so I'm even better than before we started the gang. Isn't that right, Francis?"

"Aye. He be a fine fighter."

Roach smirked evilly. "Well, they don't have rapiers, but they have claymores. Do you know how to use those?"

"Erm... Those are quite a lot larger, but I can try, sir!" A stiff salute.

He chuckled. "Alright, follow me." He led them to an area brimming with explosives where he was unsurprised to see Pio packing a duffel with various kinds of bombs, mines, and grenades. He brought Partha to a box with only one claymore mine left inside and tossed it into the kid's chest where it was briefly fumbled before being caught.

"What's this, sir?"

"Claymore."

He observed it. "I don't understand."

Roach tried to withhold it, but after the comment, he bursted into a fit of snort-laughter. "Fuckin' got you, dude! You totally thought it was a sword!"

Pio was surprised by the sound and came over to see what had amused him so much. "Wow! Never heard him laugh like that!" He slapped Roach's back playfully. "They really got you, huh?"

Roach nodded and wiped tears from his eyes before looking back at Partha, who was smiling adorably. "It's a fucking warzone, dumbass. They don't have swords. If you're close enough to use a blade you're probably already five feet in the grave." After another chuckle he gestured lazily. "Give Pio the mine, and let's get some actual equipment."

Pio accompanied them back to the protective gear and uniforms and helped Roach pass out bulletproof vests and gas masks. "Make sure the masks have the tinted eyes, Pio," he muttered as he noticed him passing a different kind to Partha. "We need to hide our identities." Pio took back the mask and started digging through boxes for more that would hide their faces properly.

While his friend was busy with that, Roach noticed that Francis hadn't put on his vest. "Bed bug? Is it too big for you?"

"This is quite unnecessary, Clayton. I would sacrifice range of motion, and for what?"

He blinked. "For a bulletproof vest, dude."

"A projectile's greatest boon is its speed, which is something I need not fret."

"Bed bug," he said lowly, "Please put it on. I don't want you getting hurt."

"I will wear the colours to avoid friendly-fire, but this is redundant, my dear."

Roach was going to insist again, but he was stopped by Thyne leaning in to whisper something in Francis' ear. The pirate swigged from his flask, said, "Very well," and started to don the vest.

"Thank you, Thyne. At least he listens to *someone* who loves him." He didn't mean to sound as bitter as he did, but Francis didn't notice it either way. River helped him secure the vest tightly, after which Pio rushed up with gas masks for those who didn't have one already.

With the masks clipped to their belts, Roach took the duffel bag he had brought with him from the car and tossed it on a nearby table, gesturing with his head for everyone to come with him. "Got any extra straps around here, dude?" he asked Pio.

He peered into the bag as Roach opened it and started distributing a variety of firearms. "I'll go find some," he said as he dragged himself away from the scene.

To everyone's surprise, when Roach pulled out the gun he had bought in Crownpoint, he purposefully broke off one of its stocks and tossed it carelessly back into the bag. "Much better," he said as he tucked the remaining stock under his arm and mimed shooting. "Yeah, just like I remember."

"You *actually* bought one of those things?" said Thyne with an amused and mocking tone.

"Mmhmm."

"Well, you broke it, so at least you know it's rubbish."

"And you know how much I love rubbish," he said with a grin and a cheeky wink. Other than the Anubis gun, he also had a mint-green shotgun and a pair of stickerbombed pistols from Thyne's collection as well as upwards of fifteen pounds worth of knives from his own.

Thyne's primary firearm was the rifle he had bought at the gun show, to which he had attached a sniper scope, but he also had two pistols from his own collection and a switchblade. All four of his weapons were some shade of pink or magenta, and his straps were all decorated with colourful pins and patches, making it especially obvious that this group was not a part of the actual military.

Partha was using the flintlock pistol River had bought for him, but his primary weapon was a stark white bolt-action rifle from Thyne's collection. He had only fired a rifle once or twice in his life while training with the gang, so it was more for show than utility. He wasn't particularly dangerous, especially not without something to fence with, but Roach had lent him a handful of knives that were at least slightly more familiar to him than two-handed guns.

Francis was using his new revolver and typical flintlock pistols. He also had his backsword on his hip as was the case since he took it during their jobs taking down New Clear. If Partha was in desperate need of a sword, he would not hesitate to pass it over. Partha, however, was the only one in the group who had not fought in a war (or near enough) and thus the only one who did not understand how unlikely it was that he would safely close the distance on anyone worth killing.

Roach tried to give Arjun a gun, but Thyne stopped him at the wrist, saying, "Don't. He's a cack-handed fool."

"A what?"

"A bleeding mughead. Can't hit anything."

"Hey! I can hit things!"

"On purpose, mate?"

He smiled. "Sometimes."

"If he doesn't have a gun, what will he use?"

"Do you have a longbow in there?" asked Arjun.

"Yeah, dude. It's right next to the trebuchet and fire-breathing dragon." He stifled both a glare and a chuckle and looked at Thyne. "Why's he here, then?"

"Because he knows Portuguese."

Arjun dug through the duffel bag in search of a weapon he thought Thyne might approve of him having but could find nothing. They watched him silently for a moment before resuming their conversation without regarding him: "Alright, and what about the creepy one?" He gestured toward Melchiresa.

"You can give him a gun. He's good."

Roach nodded and slapped Arjun's hands gently to shoo him away from the bag before reaching in and grabbing a few guns to toss to Melchiresa.

"Well, what will I do?" asked Arjun as he watched Pio come back with some extra straps, and everyone attached their many weapons and accessories to themselves.

"Oh, I know," said Roach as he tossed the empty bag to Arjun, "You'll be pack mule. Grab some extra ammo for us and maybe a few gun mods, but leave some room in the bag in case we need to collect things from the towns."

Arjun beamed and saluted lazily. "On it, boss."

They returned to the garage fully outfitted and with Pio in tow. On their way there, Roach flipped a switch in the hall that triggered the garage door so that it was halfway open by the time they reached the vehicles. "This one's mine," said Pio gesturing to the armoured food truck. "We should all fit, even with you two."

"Alright, everyone pack it in," ordered Roach. Most of them climbed into the back after Pio opened it, but Roach came up to the front with him to ride shotgun.

Pio started the engine and beamed at his friend as he heard him light up a cigarette. "Is this everyone?"

"Huh? Yeah, dude. Who else would there be?"

He tilted his head. "Silvino?" The silence that followed was loud. "Oh...."

"Let's just go, dude. I don't want to have to think about this shit."

"Alright. I'm sorry."

"It's chill." He leaned forward to turn on the radio and one of his own songs started blaring. "Hey! You still have my album, man?"

"It's the best for blasting heads and ramming barricades, brother!" He laughed.

"I'm touched."

They smiled, Pio's much more evident than his friend's, and with that, they drove out of the garage, the door closing automatically behind them.

Driving through the warfront was as chaotic as could be expected. Even with the pedal to the metal, the truck could only go as fast as forty-five miles per hour, even slower off-road. They were ignored for about half of the drive, but the closer Pio drove to the Americans' side of the line, the more shots were purposefully aiming for them. In the back, Partha's teeth were clattering more and more with every shot hitting the armoured exterior. He wasn't sure how the others were so nonchalant about it. They were having a pedestrian conversation about... something. He couldn't even parse the words with all his fear compounding. The entire conversation went silent when a shot went clean-through the top of the truck from just beside River's head to just behind him. Rather than what Partha would have considered a reasonable reaction, River simply smiled and said, "I should probably sit down." He crossed his legs and lowered himself down to the floor, looking up at the others as they resumed their chat with no regard for the fact that one of them had almost been shot through the fucking skull.

However they got to their destination was a blur to Partha. He was shivering-scared by the time the back doors opened and revealed an endless horizon and a night sky spotted with clouds of smoke. "Everyone still alive back here?" joked Roach.

"Yeah," said River, "but the kid's shitting himself over there. Wanna bring him up front with you?"

"Sure. Kid, you wanna come sit on my lap up in the front?"

Partha scrambled his way out of the truck and hugged Roach tightly at the offer. His breaths were quick and heavy and panicked. Roach pet his head gently and addressed the others: "We're through the line. Lost 'em a few hours ago. I'll be directing Pio based on my memory of this area, but it's a lot different since the bomb dropped."

"ETA?" asked River.

He shrugged. "We're just gonna drive around a little aimlessly until we find something that looks like a town then go investigate. Everyone chill? Got enough water and stuff? There's a gas station up the road. Pio says it's abandoned, but it might have something."

"I shall keep stomachs filled via chronomancy should the situation necessitate it. Take the terrified child somewhere to comfort him. He could not fathom us no matter what was said to him."

"Yep. Alright, arms and legs inside the vehicle." With Partha still clinging to him, he closed the food truck's back doors then turned his attention to the kid. "Is it so different to the Halloween job, kiddo? You could have died just as easily there."

He wept and buried his face in Roach's chest, shaking his head to try and wake up from the nightmare.

"Aww." Roach kissed his forehead. "It's alright, kid. We've got you. I won't let anything happen to you."

"P-p-p-p-promise?" he whimpered through his clattering teeth.

"Of course! I love you, dude." He hugged him tightly. "You're doing great. Just try and channel that same energy you had way back in February. You remember?"

He shook his head. "You said, 'I quite like the idea of being a real pirate instead of just pretending.' Not just pretending anymore, are you?"

He tried to smile but whimpered helplessly instead.

Roach kissed his forehead again and scooped him up to carry him to the front of the truck. He opened the door telekinetically and set Partha in the middle seat.

"Everyone okay?"

Roach nodded. "No injuries. Everyone's fine. Party's just scared as shit."

Pio rustled his hair. "I remember when I was just the same. You'll get the hang of it."

"Th-th-thanks," he gulped and clung to Roach when he sat beside him.

Roach closed his door and sang: *"These vagabond shoes are longing to stray. Right through the very heart of it."* A gesture to the road ahead. *"New states, new states."* Pio giggled and took the hint to put the truck back in drive and start their directionless journey.

Before America's crusade into Mexico, Guanajuato was an explosion of colour and life, as if a gargantuan macaw had laid itself to rest upon the city. It was where Silvino's grandmother had lived and therefore where Roach sought sanctuary when he would come back from the frontlines in the earlier days of battle. He and his brother were the only ones in the gang to have seen it before the war: they were the only ones who knew first-hand how truly ruinous it had become. It was where Roach was married and where he wrote his first successful album, inspired greatly by the love he held for his husband, his husband's family, and the vibrant electric energy of the city. He had told Abuela that he and Silvino would lick the Americans with the Mexican military. He had promised they wouldn't reach Guanajuato.

As scorched farmlands finished rolling by, the distinct ruins of the vibrant city started to pepper the horizon. Partha had stopped clinging to Roach two hours ago, and Roach would never admit that he missed it now. His throat clogged with tears as the ruined landscape overwhelmed him with memories and broken promises.

"There," said Partha as he pointed to a featureless white building in the distance, on the side of a once-lush mountain. "You see? That's new, right?"

"Looks new to me. We'll go check it out," said Pio.

"Roach, you can climb mountains, right?" asked Partha as Pio struggled to find a safe path to drive. "Should we just get out here?"

"Hm? Yeah I can climb mountains. Sure. Let's go."

"Are you okay, sir?"

"I'm fine," he said forcefully before opening his door, "Let's go." When he rounded to the back of the truck, he was already donning his mask as he opened the doors telekinetically, successfully hiding the tears on his cheeks. With a sniffle and cough, he sounded mostly okay when he shouted, "Masks on. Guns out. We found something."

They all donned their masks, Arjun hid his cane in his duffel bag of extra supplies, and they all followed Roach's lead toward the strange white building. They had to step through and around a plethora of ruined structures. Homes raided. Schools rotted. Churches razed. Where once there was music, there was silence. Where once there was colour, there was grey. Where once there was life, there was death.

"How about a travel song," suggested Pio when he sensed the dark cloud forming over everyone's heads. "What was that Italian one you taught us, Capitán?"

Arjun perked up and looked at Roach. "*Bella Ciao*," replied the weepy twin dismissively, "Thyne won't like it if we sing."

"Well, I don't mind it if it's *Bella Ciao*."

Pio nudged Roach in the side playfully. "See, Cap? Now how did it start?" He reached to stroke his scruffy chin but only succeeded at awkwardly bumping his fingers into his gas mask's filter.

"I don't want to sing," muttered Roach.

"You always want to sing, Capitán!" he lilted with a big dumb grin hidden under his mask.

Roach stopped and looked down at him, leaning forward and therefore forcing the shorter man to cower slightly. "I said I don't want to fucking sing, Pio. Drop it."

He saluted with a slight panic. "Yes, sir."

They continued through the rubble without another exchange until they were at the base of the mountain. "Not too steep," said Roach, "but you two have bum legs. Come here." He gestured for Arjun and Pio to approach him, which they did. "I mean no disrespect, truly." Before they could question him, he was scooping the both of them up and throwing them over his shoulders. With them secured in his strong arms, he took a large stride up the incline. They both nearly dropped their bags, but River caught them telekinetically and grabbed their handles as his brother droned, "Come on."

Hanging off of Roach's shoulder as he climbed, Arjun was as chipper and unbothered as ever. He leaned on his elbows and looked at Pio to say, "How's it hanging?"

"Ha! I was gonna say that!"

"Would you two shut up?" snipped Roach.

Arjun made a mocking gesture with his hand but didn't say anything aloud.

The others followed Roach up the mountain toward the strange building. As they neared it, they started to see other people and cars here and there on a cliffside road. It led into the structure, which made more sense when they were able to tell it was an outer wall of some sort, with guards posted on top of it. Under the cover of night, they fortunately hadn't been spotted yet. Roach set down Pio and Arjun when they reached a small ridge and whispered to everyone, "You see the guards?" He pointed.

"You want me to shoot them?" asked Thyne.

"We don't know what they're guarding just yet. Bed bug? Would you mind scouting for us?"

"I could hardly climb the hill." He gestured behind them at the relatively shallow incline then turned their attention toward the nearly sheer cliff he would have to scale to reach the road and building above them.

"Thyne give me the scope from your gun."

"Why?"

"Just do it!" Thyne slid the scope off of his gun and passed it to Roach. He took it and looked through it at the top of the cliff where the cars and people could sometimes be seen. "Yeah, that'll do." He looked at Francis. "I can get you up there."

"And back down?"

"If needs be."

Francis nodded and grabbed the hilt of his sword to brace himself. "I am prepared."

"Sonny, you catch him if I fuck up," he muttered in Arabic. After a small nod from his brother, he gestured with his right arm, and with the movement, Francis was thrown up toward the cliffside. Roach quickly looked through the scope to find him while he was still in his ascent, after which he caught him and moved him carefully onto solid ground. With a thumbs-up from Francis, he watched as the chronomancer blinked two feet to his left and pointed to himself then the ground. Roach brought him back down to them carefully.

Over these few seconds, Pio was staring slack-jawed at the show of supernatural power but was unable to put his questions into words before Francis was back beside them saying, "It is a factory. A sweatshop." Thyne held his hand out for the scope again, but when Roach gave it to him, Francis grabbed both of their wrists. "Do not kill the guards. They may kill the workers in retaliation. There are children inside. We need to contact May. I installed her finger drive."

"Finger drive?"

"The... erm... thumb drive!" A few stifled chuckles. "I aver that we should find a way for the entire crew to infiltrate together. She may be of aid."

"How does he know all this? How did he float up there?" asked Pio finally.

"Aliens," said Roach simply as he pulled out his phone.

"Dieu merci!" answered May from within the haunt, "We thought you boys didn't make it. Poor Perlie was having a panic attack! Is everything okay?"

He whispered his response, "Francis installed some sort of software for you."

"Did he? I'll look." She tapped on her laptop and had a brief exchange with Lanni in her head. "I see." She mirrored the security footage of the venue. "Oh my Lord. Where are you? What's going on?"

"Not inside yet. We were hoping you could help us."

"Um. Okay, give me a minute." A moment later: "There are armed guards on the walls like a prison. Is this a prison?"

"We think it's a sweatshop, but I wouldn't be surprised."

"Oh, it can't be a prison!" she gasped. "There are children in there!"

"You think the pigs wouldn't lock up kids? Can you get us inside or not?"

"I can try. Do you have headpieces to talk to me more easily?"

"Sonny? Set up the mics." River nodded and started passing out earpieces. "Oh, and May? There's another person with us. His name is Pio. Codename: Ladrillo Amarillo. He's a friend of mine. Can't miss him. He's dressed to the nines like us."

"I hope you're all hiding your faces," she warned.

He glared despite everyone else's complete inability to see it. "No shit, Sherlock. Alright. Hanging up now. Partha, turn on that body cam to stream for May."

"Yes, sir." He started fiddling with a small camera he could strap to his torso and use as a video feed for May to see via a private web-call with her.

With everything set up, May led them around the building to a less steep drop-off. There was a foot-path above them that led into the factory's warehouse. Utilising the twins' telekinesis, they were all on the path hiding in the dead brush within five minutes of finding this spot. May further directed them with a combination of the facility's cameras and Partha's. She led them through a gate during a lull in guard activity in the area. It was locked only with a padlock that Roach easily picked, and afterwards they were all inside and directed to descend a staircase to their left. Another door laid at the base of the stairs. It was harder to pick than the last lock, and when May started to panic that he wasn't moving fast enough, the lock suddenly disappeared: a pile of metallic dust on the tops of Roach's boots. He nodded appreciatively to Francis before ushering everyone quickly inside.

"Now, this part is kind of a maze. I'm not sure how well I can lead you through, but there's no one in this room. I'll warn you if that changes."

River whispered, "Wait, I recognise this place."

"You do?" asked May.

"Yeah, this was an American outpost. Obviously it's a warehouse for something else now, but a lot of it seems to be in the same layout. What's through the door marked F3?"

She clicked through her cameras. "F3? I don't see that. Sorry."

He sighed. "Alright, we'll just wander I suppose. I'll bring us to what used to be the sleeping quarters." With River at the head of the line, they snuck their way through the warehouse to a corridor. It ramped downward and therefore further into the mountain. On their way down they heard the beeping of a walkie-talkie and all exchanged panicked glances as a guard rounded a corner into their sight. He spotted them, but before anyone could so much as utter a word he was gone, and Francis was where he once stood gesturing for the others to rush up to him.

"Where'd you put him?" asked May.

"The ground," muttered Francis as he looked down either side of the hall whence the guard had appeared.

"It's this way. Come on," whispered River as he rushed as quietly as possible down the left hall toward a peculiarly blue door. There was a window in the door, and he gestured with his head for Francis to look through it without being seen. With a flicker of Francis' form and a nod but gesture with his flintlock, River pushed open the door and stepped inside gun-first.

This room was small with only enough space for two bunk-beds and a dresser between them. Three of the bunks were empty, and the fourth had a scared and sleepy man whose hands were immediately in the air. He spoke in Spanish with an American accent: "Don't shoot. Don't shoot. I'm unarmed."

"Who are you?"

"George Linford. I work here."

River shook his gun to emphasise the threat on this man when he seemed to be moving for something. "What is this place?"

"An Osiris factory. We make clothes."

"Are you a worker or a guard?"

"A guard."

"Do you live nearby?"

He looked around the room. "I live right here."

At this, Roach entered and pulled his brother back gently. "Let me take it from here, bro."

"You know English?" he asked when he heard Roach speak it.

"Yeah, is that easier for you, man?" He nodded and gulped. "Chill out. We're here to help."

He pointed to River and commented, "By threatening to shoot me?"

Roach held his hands up defeatedly. "We were just trying to figure things out. How likely do you think it is that your guard buddies would let us free the workers here, including security?"

"Free us?"

"Yeah, man. Here, let me start over: you live here, right?" He nodded. "This is kind a shit-hole, right?" He nodded again. "I mean you don't even have a window. That's a human-rights violation. Does it pay well?" He shook his head. "Figured. And does it pay in an actual currency?"

"We're paid in Osiris credit."

"Company town. Wow. I don't know why I'm actually kinda shocked." He sighed. "Alright, dude, where's your walkie?" George pointed to a closet behind Roach.

At this point, River had left the cramped little room with its too-low ceiling and was waiting outside listening. He heard Roach open the closet and peered inside where he spotted George pulling a gun out from under his pillow. River instinctively pulled it out of his hands telekinetically and rushed in to press the barrel of his rifle on George's forehead. "You trying to kill my brother, fuckhead? You want to fucking die?"

He wept and shook his head. "Please don't kill me!"

He shoved the barrel deeper into his forehead, pushing him backwards into his pillow. "How much of what you said is true?"

"I don't live here. I'm from Minnesota."

May chimed in: "George Linford from Minnesota? There are three of those. Ask him his wife's name."

"What's your wife's name?"

"Jenna. Oh God! Please don't kill me!"

"Jenna Linford. Yep. Have Partha come inside so I can see him."

"Lion! Get in here."

Partha rushed into the room and pointed his camera at the panicked man's weeping face as best as he could.

"Looks like him. I'll look up his other information."

There was a beat, during which George was whimpering and being told to "Shut the fuck up, pussy," by River.

"He's military. Army. I'll see what I can get, but they usually make it annoying to break into secret shite like this."

"You're in the army," said River, "What is this place, really?"

"What I said about the factory is true. I swear. The workers: they get paid in Osiris credits, and I do sometimes, too."

"Are all of the guards here military?"

"Or mercs. Please don't shoot me."

"And why shouldn't I? You tried to shoot my brother."

"I have a family."

"And he doesn't?"

"Please," he wept.

"Alright, I've gotten a little bit about the factory. Wait… I've gotten a lot, actually. Lanni, thank you, I love you."

For the first time, Lanni spoke to someone other than May when her voice sounded in their earpieces. It was soft with an Eastern-European accent: "Happy to help. We have coordinates for other factories, as well. They're all in a secret document called *The Jabberwock*."

River smirked. "Tony."

"Hm?" He turned around from snooping in the closet and looked at his brother and the man in the bed.

"Knife."

Roach threw a knife into the man's throat, killing him instantly.

River sighed. "That's not what I meant, but whatever. At least now he can't blab." He took the gun George had tried to pull from under his pillow and brought it out into the hall to pass to Arjun. "Don't use it. Just put it in the bag."

"So," began Roach as he came out of the room cleaning his knife with one of the shirts he had found in the closet, "back in the big leagues. Haven't pissed off the government in a while. Almost makes me wanna sing the *'Playing With the Big Boys'* song from *Prince of Egypt*." He closed his knife with a flourish and shoved half of the bloody t-shirt into his back pocket.

"Cap wants to sing again!" said Pio giddily.

"*Almost.*"

"May, take us to the factory floor," said Thyne.

"Okay, go back the way you came and take the right hall instead."

"Pio, before we go," Roach took him aside and took out his earpiece. He made sure he was far enough that Thyne wouldn't hear him, but close enough that his microphone wouldn't trigger, and leaned down to whisper something to his friend. After a nod and salute from Pio, Roach put his earpiece back in and approached the others. He patted Thyne's head to pacify his enraged posture. "What's wrong, dude? Come on." They started down the path May indicated.

"You know what's wrong, you rotter. What did you say to him?"

He shrugged. "I don't remember."

Thyne balled up his fists, rearing to punch him, but withheld from the violence. "Cunt."

"Yep."

Where Roach would usually go along with an insult or tease Thyne with information playfully, his tone now seemed genuinely hurt. Thyne huffed and puffed a few times, but noticing the upset, he crossed his arms and grumpily said, "I'm sorry."

At that point, they were at the end of the hall and about to enter a heavily popu-

lated room. May shut them up and warned them of the vague locations of everyone inside.

"Are there any windows?" asked Francis.

"None that I can see."

He nodded and stopped time to open the door. It was the same part of the
building he had seen before that had him call it a sweatshop, with countless
workers labouring at sewing machines, most of them women, some of whom were
no older than ten. He made the rounds again, finding all of the military in the
room and taking them out into the ruins where he had taken the earlier guard.
Once he was far enough that he could only slightly see the factory, he turned their
walkie-talkies to dust one by one then beheaded them with his backsword. After
ageing so many things to dust, the long trek back up into the factory drained him
greatly. He couldn't make it all the way back down the hall before he needed to
resume time, so from the others' perspective, he teleported backwards about thirty
feet where he held his knees and lifted the bottom of his mask to spit on the
ground.

"Wait... Where'd they go? All the guards in there just disappeared," said May.

Partha turned around to see Francis at the end of the hall, which answered May's
question for her. Roach rushed up to him and scooped him up into his arms. "Bed
bug! You didn't have to do that."

He nodded dismissively and pulled his mask back down. "As you have already
observed: we are in with the larger leagues now."

Roach let out an amused exhale before reaching the double doors to the factory
and opening them telekinetically. He set Francis down, and they all fanned out.

The workers paid them little mind despite their masks and many nonstandard
weapons. The guard they had cornered and killed mentioned mercenaries working
there from time to time, so it was reasonable for the workers to believe that's what
they were.

As they walked through the sweatshop, taking in the disturbing ambience, Partha
found himself especially perturbed. The lights buzzed unpleasantly. There were no
windows, and a faint foul fog hung in the air. The sound of sewing machines was
an incessant buzzing like a hive of hornets. The floor, walls, and ceiling were all
the same stale grey concrete as each other with nothing but unidentified stains and
a large Osiris logo to decorate them. Partha's steps were staggered and slow as he
walked through this Hellish environment. He had seen a lot of poor working
conditions: he had *worked* in a lot of poor and dangerous conditions. In truth, this
couldn't have been much worse than some of the leaky rooms he had suffered in
the windowless bowels of the hottest most uncomfortable ships.

The difference was: when he worked those jobs, he *chose* to work them. He could
easily afford to never work again thanks to his wealth from streaming, and without

that, he had Thyne and Francis who would gladly pay for his housing. If not them: well he still technically lived with his father and couldn't see a situation where he would ever actually be unwelcome at home in Bermuda. When he worked those jobs struggling to breathe on some crooked cruise ship, he was paid with legitimate currency backed and recognised by all the world's governments. Were it not a company town, perhaps he would have found himself less perturbed. This sweat-shop was horrible, but it was better than his worst cruise jobs in some regards. But… he was perturbed. More than anyone else present.

There were *children* here.

Children who weren't even double-taking at the well-armed strangers infiltrating the building. They were working just as diligently and with just as much disregard for the danger as the women around them. It wrenched his gut. One child in particular looked to be no more than five years old. Not even old enough to read, but she sat beside her mother pushing shirts through the machines just the same as the other workers. For nearly ten minutes, no one said anything, and in those ten minutes, Partha made a world-shaking decision.

This was infuriating.

This was amoral.

This was the vilest thing anyone could even conceive.

These children were *children*. They should have been outside playing in the trees, catching bugs, stealing candy, learning life skills. They should have at least been able to play in the rubble of their lost country. Childhood was innocence, and to take that away was worse than murder, worse than rape, worse than anything. His breaths were heaving more and more as he worked himself up.

This was outrageous! And the American military was here to *protect* it!?

He saw a little girl in particular: a young teenager who looked to be half Korean. She had earbuds in, listening to music evident by the way she was bobbing her head and mouthing along to the lyrics. He saw her, and he thought, *'I'm going to be a father soon. I'm going to be a father, and if this was my daughter— if any of these children were mine— if these women were Perlie—. I'd—. I'd—.'* He looked down at the camera on his chest and pressed a button on the bottom. He pointed it at the Osiris logo on the wall then turned to face the horrifying visage of the workers. After nearly two minutes of standing still and silent, he approached the girl listening to music and took out one of her headphones.

She spoke in Spanish: "Hey! What the heck!?"

"How old are you?"

"Thirteen."

"How long have you been working here?"

She tapped her chin. The woman next to her tried to tell her to keep working, but Partha shushed her rudely then turned his attention and especially the camera toward the little girl as she answered: "Since I was five."

"Where is your mother?" She pointed to the woman next to her.

"We're here to free you," he said to the mother, "All of you."

❧ Chapter 48 ❧
Rubbish! Filth! Slime! Muck!

Jean-Jacques was … *enduring* what Neodesha was calling a "puppy party." She had gathered all of the pets in a bathhouse he didn't even know was on the property and twisted his arm (asked nicely) into helping bathe and play with them. Neither of them were certain how to bathe a duck, so they let her swim around in the soapy water of what amounted to a small shallow pool while they scrubbed the dogs in it. The twins' dogs were usually well-behaved, but because Roach and River were on the other side of the world, and with Juliette's bad behaviour influencing them, they were especially rowdy and playful, much to Jean-Jacques' annoyance. He loved dogs, but six was far too many to handle at once. Neodesha, on the other hand, was in a swimsuit and playing with them in the bath, having the time of her life, so he tried his best to at least fake a smile when she looked his way.

The shenanigans were interrupted when Giovanni came into the room unannounced and approached the side of the bath, in line with Neodesha. The dogs all looked at him curiously, and after a few irritating quacks from the duck, he sighed and said, "Shay, my dear, I need to draw some of your blood for testing."

"Why?"

"I would like to confirm something."

"Can't it wait 'til after the puppy party, Pa?"

He smiled. "My my, Shay, how old are you?" A playful laugh. "Call me with your cellular device when you are finished. Preferably before dinner."

"I reckon I could do that."

"Thank you." He rushed out of the chaotic room.

"How old *are* you?" asked Jean-Jacques.

She stroked her chin. "'Bout 200 give or take."

He chuckled. "Is this 'puppy party' a hundreds-years-old tradition?"

"Having fun's a hundreds-years-old tradition!" She splashed him playfully. "Come in here, ya stick in the mud."

He groaned when she splashed him, and before he could complain or leave the edge of the water, she grabbed his wrist and dragged him into the shallow pool. He rubbed the soapy water from his face and glared at her. "Not fun, mademoiselle."

She splashed him again and threw one of the dog toys that was floating around the pool at his head. "Kiss attack!" she playfully demanded of the dogs.

One of the puppies doggy-paddled over to him and grabbed the toy from the water. He couldn't help but be endeared by her struggling to swim and squeak it at the same time, especially because of the dollop of suds on her head. With a cute grin, he scooped her up so she could stand in his hands and play with the toy.

"See?"

"It's a *little* bit fun," he conceded with a playful glare.

When they were finished in Guanajuato, the freed workers were instructed to go to Heroica Veracruz and, with Partha's verbal and written instructions, told how to successfully stowaway on the *Aquillius' Revenge* with Captain Richard Nima's help. With the workers heading eastward, the gang started toward Durango for the next company town from the list Lanni had found in *The Jabberwock* files. Though the files had coordinates and detailed finances and logistics, it was proving impossible to find what the town's factory actually manufactured.

They stopped halfway through their trek to sleep in the truck during the day. Luckily it was cloudy, or the heat so near the equator might have melted their tyres as it was wont to do. After a few hours' rest, they resumed the drive with Durango on the horizon just as the sun began to set.

Pio was trying his best to chat with Roach the way they did in the war, wherein Roach was lighthearted and playful despite all the horrors. He tried to sing with him and tell him anecdotes from the time they were apart, but no matter what he gave Roach to work with, he was met only with short answers and forced huffs of laughter. As they parked to look for the next factory, he turned to him and said, "Roach, my friend, are you angry with me?"

"Hm? No, dude. Why would I be?"

"You've been quiet. Not yourself. We just blew up a whole military base!" He laughed devilishly. "Isn't that exciting?"

Another forced huff of laughter as he looked down at his hands and fiddled with his rings. "Yeah, man. It's cool. I'm glad you're having fun."

"Are you not? I know you like the knives and stuff better, but you got to kill that guard in his room, right? Wasn't that fun?"

"Listen, dude, it's just… a lot right now. I'm sorry I'm not as fun as usual. I'll be back to normal when we're not in this Hellscape anymore."

"I'm here for you, brother."

He sighed, his attention still on his hands as he spun his wedding ring around. "This place just reminds me of my failures way more than I expected."

"Your failures? What do you mean?"

He took a deep breath as if he were about to explain, but after an exasperated exhale he said, "It doesn't matter. Let's just go. Don't want to waste anymore time." He opened his door and rounded to the back of the truck to let the others out.

It took them a few minutes of wandering the half-ruined city to find the factory. The houses in this company town were actually above ground, which was an upgrade from the one in Guanajuato, but the working conditions were even worse. It was a textile factory with deafening looms. The workers were forced to stand for sixteen-hour shifts, and there were even more child labourers than adults. After freeing the workers, they razed the factory the same as before and sent some of the workers southward with instructions to meet up at the same port as the others.

After destroying the factory, they gave the workers who had stayed in Durango heaps of cash and left for their third company town up in Hermosillo. It was a long drive, but when Pio started to tire, Roach drove for him. They stopped to refuel halfway to Hermosillo, having run out of pre-filled tanks. Before leaving the truck, they all donned their masks, but they kept their guns inside.

While in the gas station, River inquired about the area. He learned that this port-village was entirely off the grid. The only cash he had was Euros, which intrigued the clerk, but River refused to explain. He bought water for everyone and a case of cigarettes for Roach, Pio, and Thyne to share before coming back to the truck and informing the others that this could be a contender for a place to send the refugees of the next town.

They hydrated, Roach prayed, and after some chatty smoking in the back of the truck, they finished their drive up the coast, the landscape becoming more and more barren as they drove into the mid-afternoon. The clouds were thick and dark, making the desert feel oddly lit and unreal as they parked behind a newly built Protestant church. In fact, *everything* in the town was freshly built and painted stark white, contrasting surreally against the endless yellow dirt. It looked like an inescapable nightmare where the danger present was felt but not seen.

Roach opened his door to go let the others out of the truck, and a rough gust of wind pushed a haunting familiar scent into him. He tried not to notice it, but it brought horrible vivid flashes into his vision. His soul turned: something spiritual was asking him not to finish this job. He ignored it. Perhaps it was time to pray, but he had no time to pray. He had no time to waste with false hope and angry Gods.

Roach was quiet as they all armed themselves. He trailed along at the back of the group and tried not to notice the smell as it continued to attack him on the way toward the factory. Everyone noticed his upset, but there was nothing anyone could say to lighten him back up. Francis had tried kissing him and reassuring him and thanking him. Pio and Arjun had both tried joking with him. River had spoken very succinctly to him about exactly what was upsetting him, which didn't help in the slightest, and Thyne had offered a pack of gummy snacks and a cigarette kiss.

As they walked, Partha decided it was his turn to try helping. He slowed to match Roach's pace as the others all trudged forward too far to hear. With his hands around Roach's massive bicep: "I haven't had a bump since I promised you I'd stop."

Roach looked at him and gave him a quiet grunt of approval.

"I'm excited to be a father."

Another vaguely positive sound.

"It's weird being sober…. I forgot how quiet it can be…."

Roach looked around at the vast wasteland and shrugged. "Yeah."

Partha's voice was broken when he spoke again a few minutes later: "You know why I started coke in the first place?"

He looked at him, concerned, but unable to show it even if he wanted to. "Why?"

"A friend of mine was here when they dropped the bomb." He looked around at the aftermath and sniffled. "She was a paladin in one of my private games. Was friends with her in college, actually. Before I even started streaming." A beat. "I say 'friend,' but she was actually my girlfriend…. I know you don't really take me seriously, and maybe I was just a dumb kid, but… I had a ring. My plan was to propose when we finally met up in person. I begged and begged her to let me come here and take her somewhere else. *Anywhere* else. I tried to tell her she didn't have to keep showing up for the games. I just wanted her safe."

He chuckled once: a sad remorseful sound. "But she told me, 'I don't want to abandon my family and my home. The Americans want us to run and cower and die, but if they kill me, I'm going down fighting. So let me keep playing with you and pretending for a few hours each week that I'm strong enough, with God behind me, to fight this fight and come out the other side.'" Another beat as his gaze trailed back to the landscape. "Her name was Ana. I had been saving myself for her and, well… after the bomb fell, I basically immediately started doing every sort of drug I could find and sleeping around. Dropped out of college, too. All of it. Just really fucked my whole life up."

His lip was quivering, but he was otherwise surprisingly resolute after such a sad retelling. He looked at Roach. "Rehab didn't help. I didn't see the point in trying. Didn't see the point in sobriety. She wasn't even taken from me in some sort of honourable way. She and her entire family: eviscerated in an instant. And for what? So Osiris could turn her home into some factory to make a quick buck." He gestured around them. "Rehab didn't make me want to give a shit again. Nothing did. Not even... not even Perlie." He wiped his arm across his teary cheeks. "But I do give a shit again, Roach. And you know what made me care again?" He looked up at him, his eye quivering and glimmering with tears. "*You.*"

Roach wrapped his arm around Partha and slowed their already sluggish pace to a stop. He pulled him in for a warm embrace, which was returned tenfold. Partha buried his face in Roach's chest and sniffled as his head was pet. Roach rocked him subtly from side to side and shushed him quietly. It invited him to cry, and by the time he was fully weeping, Roach had picked him up to sit with him on his lap on an eerie white bench in this eerie white town. "You're a good kid," said Roach as he kissed Partha's head, "but you're gonna be an even better dad. I'm sorry I didn't take you seriously."

Partha pulled himself closer and whimpered, "Thank you."

Another breeze brought that horrid smell to Roach, and any amount of wholesomeness that Partha had returned to him was stolen away. His gut wrenched and mind reeled, so the few minutes he sat holding Partha passed meaninglessly and in an instant. They met back up with the group, Roach still despondent, and from there it was only a ten minute walk to reach the factory.

Much like the last one, they didn't know what it manufactured before going inside, but May and Lanni were able to determine that its only security was artificial and were therefore able to hack and deactivate it. On their word, the group walked up to the entrance unbothered and opened the unlocked door while looking at turrets that may have otherwise shot them on their approach.

Roach's hands were in his pockets and head hanging, but that smell.... It was so strong here. He could smell it through his mask. How? He must have been hallucinating. How could a smell penetrate a gas mask so potently? He checked to be sure he had a filter, and when he confirmed that he did, he sighed and tried to ignore it. It must have been all in his head: all the culminating self-loathing and reminders of failure finally manifesting in one ultimate hallucination to remind him of the first life-changing mistake he ever made. If it were real, River would have mentioned it by now.

He was trailing along solemnly behind the others, watching as Pio excitedly planted charges around the lifeless corridor for the eventual destruction of this brand-new building. Francis was taking the lead as they wandered down what was seeming like an endless hall. What the fuck was this building? Roach tried to surmise it by looking around, but he hadn't the slightest idea, especially not as the smell got stronger. And... and now he was hearing things too. He must have been. He must have been, because if it were real, River would have mentioned it.

Sweat beaded on the back of his neck as his God whispered warnings to him, but he shook his head and coughed away his nervousness. It couldn't have been a real divine message: he already knew he was hallucinating....

Francis opened the doors at the end of this never-ending hallway, a gust of wind wafted the smell directly into Roach's rotten soul, and, framed by the silvery threshold, was the worst thing that could have possibly been on the other side of the door:

It swished from side to side and gleamed in the artificial light. Behind it: another. And behind that one: another. Back and back and back like a mirror in mirror. The way they moved was like a haunting dance of silver dresses in the House of Romanov. A death waltz in monotone. A stolen childhood. He lost all perception outside of the blades— unhooked from all semblance of the present— drifting alone in a haunted memory. His mind was sent back to the smell of pigs, the sound of squealing, and the horrid horrid dance of those blades. It flashed with the image of his brother's arm, lobbed clean off by the death-machine, bleeding on the floor. It sounded with the screaming and crying of a child who would never use said arm again. Roach tried to close his eyes, but they were glued open. He tried to move, but he was petrified.

"Roach? Roach, what's wrong? River, what's wrong with him?" asked Partha as he approached the frozen man.

"Leave him alone, Party," warned River, but it was too late.

Partha had reached up to tap Roach's shoulder, but his wrist was in a death-grip before he could fathom Roach had so much as flinched. He called out in pain. "Roach! Stop it! OW!" He tried to pry his fingers off of him. "FUCK! OW! Please stop! You're BREAKING IT!"

The next thing Roach knew, he was in the middle of the desert with Francis in front of him. Both of their masks were clipped to their belts, and their earpieces were turned off and in Francis' left hand. Roach shook away the harrowing memories that had petrified him, finally able to parse his surroundings again. "Bed bug? What's going on?"

"You broke Partha's wrist."

He started. "I what?"

"You broke his wrist with your bare hands, Clayton. Why?"

He held his head. "I don't know. I don't even remember."

A beat. "Stay here. Gather yourself. Hail for Thyne to hail for me, should you need assistance. We will raze the butchery without you."

"Butchery!? Ya Allah!" His aching head spun as the perfect memories of breaking Partha's wrist came crawling into his fractured mind. "I'm sorry. Tell him I'm sorry. I didn't mean to. I broke my promise. I didn't mean—. Oh! His arm!" He wailed and struggled to stand upright.

"Clayton?" Francis grabbed one of his wrists and pulled it away from his head. "He is already healed. It was startling, but I have reversed the physical injury." Roach only wept. "I love you. He loves you, too."

"Why would he love me?" whimpered Roach, "Why would *anyone* love me?"

Francis kissed the tears off his cheek then pecked his trembling knuckles. "I shall write a poem to detail all the ways in which I love and am endeared by you, but presently I must return to the butchery. I apologise for not being here for you, but I must try every chance with which I am afforded to cease this war before it begins. Do you understand?" Roach nodded and sniffled. "I love you, Clayton. I will return post haste. I swear it."

"I love you," he whimpered, and before he could say more, Francis disappeared.

Alone, the Mexican desert reeked of its past battles. Roach's eyes scanned the featureless horizon. The smell of charred flesh still hung in the dry air. The brush had all been burned away by the atomic bomb America had dropped here to finally secure the West of the country. Somehow, it was the only nuclear weapon dropped during the entire crusade, and luckily he had already snuck his way back to California with Silvino and Abuela when it fell. As his hazel-greys devoured the horizon, it all came back to him in flashes overlaid on the eerily quiet former battlefield.

In the middle distance, he saw the ruins of what was once a public school that had been made into a makeshift outpost by the Mexican military. Silvino's voice echoed through his mind as he recalled a conversation they had had in the building:

"I don't know how I'll ever forgive you for this."

"It's a warzone!"

"Warzone or not, he had his hands up."

"I had already pulled the trigger."

"Clayton.... We both know that's not true."

"Faugh! We can't let our guard down! That's how you fucking get captured, Vinny. Or worse: killed!"

"Better dying as an honourable man than living free as a monster."

He grabbed his head again. After staggering backwards three steps, his knees buckled beneath him, and with two thuds into the sand, he kowtowed. His hands clawed at the dirt as the feeling of Partha's wrist breaking in them played on repeat in his mad mind. It let way for the image of his brother's detached arm: the horrific reality of his own time as a child labourer with his siblings. Those memories morphed into repetitive visions of his hand stabbing or loosing various knives into various victims. All the while, as his past attacked him, Silvino's voice echoed ever louder than the memories of failure and bloodshed until it was all he could fathom:

Monster.

Monster.

Monster.

Monster.

Monster.

He shouted: one long loud syllable to shut it all up. With a shuddered inhale, he spat out a panicky prayer as his hands twitched and trembled in the dirt: "I am... *unclean*," the word caught in his throat as hysteria tried to choke him. "Writhing around in the filth."

His breaths began to heave angrily.

"Vermin," he hissed, "Pest." A silent gale wrought with the stench of swine whispered mad nothingness to him.

"Roach," he breathed.

"Roach," he said again, louder.

"Roach! ROACH! I AM A ROACH! STRIKE ME DOWN, DAMN YOU! Why do You let me *breathe*? Why did You take him!? WHY NOT ME!? ROACH! ROACH! ROACH!" His voice was loud and guttural and echoed all around him as he shouted down into the dirt.

As suddenly as it had sounded, his rage released him and was replaced with hysterical sorrow. Tears dripped down his hands as they clawed at the charred sand beneath him. "Why not me?" he whimpered, "Allah, I am weak. If You won't kill me, at least separate me from them. I don't have the strength to do it myself. I love them too entirely. I am too selfish. Too wretched. Too weak.... And I won't ask Your forgiveness: I don't deserve it. I ask only for mercy on their behalf. I don't deserve this love I am given so readily. I hurt Partha without even meaning to. I got Gideon's arm cut off. I let Silvino die!" He wept as worries for how he might fail Francis, Thyne, and River swarmed him.

Minutes elapsed, and after sucking up some of his sadness, replaced with a quiet rage, he slammed his boot into the dirt and stood. With his hazel gaze on the dark clouds, his ire and sorrow compounded and sounded simultaneously: "DAMN YOU!" Mad tears choked him, stopping him from saying it again as the sky grumbled disapprovingly. Defeated, he looked at the nothingness around him then down at his killer-hands. "Damn you, Clayton.... Monster.... Filth.... *Roach*."

Chapter 49
Mawidge

It must have been the fifteenth time his phone had gone off that day, let alone all the fuss it had made earlier that week. He had tried being patient, merely silencing it and resuming the task at hand each time, but now he was visibly annoyed. "I told them not to call! I told them this week, and especially today is important!" He held down the button until the phone's screen went black then passed it to Aspyn, "I'm sorry, maple sugar. Can you put that in your purse?"

She nodded and slid it into her bag. "It's okay. I'm still having a good time. Being CEO of Osiris must be a really demanding job, you would think they would understand that you want at least a few weeks to holiday."

He nodded, his lips pouty. "Exactly. Cretins. I'd bet it's one of those pesky unions in Eurasia asking for higher pay again as if they don't get enough to buy entire mansions as it is."

She pet his balding head gently. "It's okay, love. You were saying we would go to the zoo?"

"Yes, if you like, maple sugar. I want today to be all about you."

She blushed and smiled. "You're so kind. I haven't been to a zoo since I was a little girl."

"Then let's call Nero to take us there."

There was a brief moment where they stared awkwardly at each other before Aspyn said, "Oh! You just turned off your phone, didn't you? I'll call him."

Despite all the stench of the coastal town, combined with the smells from the animals, the zoo trip was fun. Aspyn allowed herself to submit entirely to her inner child. She went so far as to ask for a balloon and plush from the gift shop, which Tatum happily bought for her. A worker mistook her for his granddaughter, but other than that awkward chat, the date was as great as the breakfast date earlier that day and the lunch date after the zoo. As Tatum paid for lunch, he asked, "And where to next, maple sugar?"

She pursed her lips. The sudden day of whirlwind romance was appreciated, and Tatum seemed to be having a lovely time, but she worried that he was hiding something from her. Was he diagnosed with something serious? Something terminal? She stroked her chin in thought, and before she knew it they were outside in the limousine, and he was asking where to go next again. "Oh," she started, "I hadn't thought about it."

"What were you spending all that time pondering, then, maple?"

"Only that.... I'm worried. Is everything okay?"

"More than okay! I'm having a wonderful time. Aren't you?"

There was nothing malicious or secretive behind his smile, so she averted her gaze to hide her pink cheeks and shy grin. "I was just letting my worries get to me, I suppose."

He kissed her hand. "No need to worry, my dear. I would tell you if something serious was happening," he reassured her, seeming to have read her mind, "So, where to next? We can go one more place before dinner on my yacht."

"Why don't we go to the yacht early? We can watch a movie and cuddle in bed until the cooks are finished."

"A wonderful idea!"

Nero drove them to the docks where he helped the both of them onto Tatum's yacht and instructed the captain to bring it out into the harbour. In Tatum's room, a large window showed them the sunset as they laid in bed, after which Aspyn curled up in her boyfriend's arms, snuggling her new plush giraffe from the zoo, and said, "Show me a movie you used to watch as a child."

He rang a bell to summon Nero and spoke in Italian to him.

"Of course, sir."

"What movie is it?" asked Aspyn. Nero started to set something up with the laptop, and a sizable flatscreen descended from the ceiling and covered part of the window.

"A surprise! But it's about true love, which is what I have for you, you know."

She blushed and buried her face into his chest with a cute giggle. "I love you, too, Tatum!" The movie started, and when the title *The Princess Bride* came on the screen, she smiled up at him. "Oh! This is your favourite, isn't it?"

He nodded. "I used to watch it in boarding school."

"I've never seen it. I'm excited!"

Their movie date was perfect, Aspyn declaring that the film was among her top five shortly after the credits started to roll, after which she helped Tatum out of bed to go downstairs with him for the dinner his servants had prepared.

The first course was a garlicky coq au vin with ice water and a small spring mix with balsamic vinaigrette. The second and main course was lamb chops with a fifty-year vintage champagne from California. There was an option for a third course, but Tatum and Aspyn both asked to skip it in favour of dessert, which was a simple undressed cheesecake that looked bland but tasted divine.

With their stomachs stuffed and the table cleared of all but their champagne, Tatum stood and hobbled over to Aspyn's side. She tried to stand to come with him wherever he was going, but he gestured for her to keep sitting. With her head tilted like a confused pup, she watched as he grabbed the arm of her chair and smiled sweetly. "Aspyn. Maple. My love. I admit I had an ulterior motive for such a day of romantic shenanigans." She went a little pale, so he hurried to try kneeling down. When she realised what he was doing, she gasped and held her face to watch with wide watery eyes as he pulled out a ring and said, "Will you marry me?"

She nodded and sniffled, too overcome with emotions to speak, and after helping him to his feet she stood and picked him up to twirl him around in a loving embrace. He laughed and, back on the ground, he gestured for her hand so he could put the ring on it. His hands were incredibly shaky, so she helped him still them and guided her finger through the ring before leaning down to give him a big sloppy kiss. She tried to make it more passionate, but he stopped her and said with a playful tone, "Now now, not quite yet, dear. I have one more thing."

"What is it?"

"My captain is ordained. I have the paperwork. I want to sign everything right now. We can have the actual ceremony later, but I want it done legally, if nothing else. I want you to be just as much an owner of Osiris as I am and able to take up the mantle of CEO when I'm gone."

She started. "Right now?"

"Please, maple sugar. You saw what they did to Christopher.... I may not be long for this world."

"O-okay," she stuttered, "Where do I sign?"

With the paperwork signed, Aspyn helped her new husband back to the bedroom to consummate the marriage, after which her phone beeped. She didn't have any friends or important things to do, so she was curious what the notification could have been.

"Oh, look, Tatum!" she grinned and showed him the screen. He squinted to try reading it, but before he could reach for his reading glasses, she said, "That 'Party the Kid' bloke is going to stream soon! He says it's a special stream starting in ten minutes."

"This day just gets better and better!"

She nodded and hopped to her feet. After wrapping a robe around her naked body, she said, "I'm going to go freshen up. Should I call Nero to set up the stream for you on the television?"

"I'll hail him with this," he said with a gesture to the bell.

"Would you mind if I shower during the stream?"

"Of course not, dear. They usually start with mindless chatter for a few minutes anyway."

"Alright, I'll see you then," she said before leaning down to kiss his forehead.

With the shower running in the adjacent washroom, Nero was hailed and told to set up Partha's stream on the television. It took him only a moment, after which he gave a tablet to Tatum to control it. "Thank you, Nero, now off with you! It's starting!"

It began with Partha holding a camera up to a mirror in a bathroom. He was haggard and sweaty and looked perturbed. Tatum arched his brow and adjusted his glasses. This was unlike the start of any other stream, but then again, Aspyn had said it was special.

"Hey everyone, Party the Kid here," he said as he tended to say at the start of his streams, though his breaths were heavy as if he had just run a mile. "I try not to get too political on stream, but... something happened. Something happened and...." He rubbed his hand down his sweaty face and stumbled forward. He looked into the lens through the mirror and furrowed his brow, "I'm fucking pissed." The camera made an uncomfortably loud crash as he slammed it into the sink, and the stream abruptly cut to an edited video of a concrete wall with an Osiris logo on its entirety.

Tatum's heart nearly stopped.

When Partha turned to face the sweatshop behind him, the old CEO's jaw dropped. He couldn't fathom what he was seeing. If the rug hadn't been pulled from underneath him—. If he didn't feel so betrayed—. If life didn't feel like such a sudden nightmare—. Maybe he would have called someone to make it stop. Maybe he would have clambered into the shower with his new wife to weep. Maybe he would have done anything at all besides sit slack-jawed watching his favourite streamer expose his company's darkest secrets to some 200,000 people.

The video went on with him interviewing a child worker, their Spanish words subtitled in English. It cut to another shot, this one of the ground. Partha had a GPS tracker open showing his location to the camera: Guanajuato. He whispered into the camera's microphone: "He started the war. Osiris started the war for this. To make company towns." The camera panned up to the exterior white walls of the factory on the side of a mountain, and a moment later, it collapsed, having been demolished as if by a professional team. "Fuck you, Abraham. I know you're watching, you monster."

A tear trailed his cheek, and shortly after the explosion, the stream cut out with the message *This user has been permanently banned.* tickering across the screen. Aspyn came out of the shower a moment later, drying her hair in a towel as she stepped into the room to see the stream. She noticed the strange message then looked at Tatum, who was staring at her helplessly, as if his entire world had just imploded.

"Did you get everyone out of the states?"

"Yeah."

"How long did it take?"

"Well, I took most of them just east to Merida, so it was three trips, a day each way. The passengers were confused, but I told them there was some bureaucracy trouble shuffling us back and forth. Some of the refugees wanted to go further south, but I knew I was going to be inspected when I passed Cancún, which I was. I did manage to get tickets for one family in particular who are still on board, though they wouldn't hold up under any scrutiny, so I should get them off the ship sooner rather than later. They wanted to go to Italy, and I figured since you and your friends have been going there a lot, you could help them get there."

"Okay, where should we meet with you to pick them up?"

"Havana if it's not too much trouble."

Partha pulled the phone down from his ear and looked to Thyne, who was driving them to Loomis manor from the airport. "Thyne, do you think we could pick up some of those refugees and bring them here?"

"To Giovanni's house?"

"No, just to Italy."

He sighed. "I suppose. Where are they now?"

"Daddy says he'll bring them to Havana."

Thyne groaned and gritted his teeth. After a moment of irritated pondering: "Well, we don't really have a choice, now do we?"

"Great!" He put the phone back up to his ear and informed his father, "Me and Thyne will pick them up from Havana. So anyway, Daddy, after we got to Guanajuato and I saw them all working and got upset and stuff, we helped them leave. Roach and Thyne and Melchiresa and River were gunning down guards left and right like pow pow pow, and I was like 'This is so exciting!' And I shielded this one little girl from a stray bullet (I don't think it was on purpose sent toward her) but anyway, I had a vest on so it bruised me but that's it! And she was like 'You're a superhero!' and I was like 'Mmhmm! So are you!' And so then we got everyone out, and all the guards were either dead or running off, and we went out onto the mountainside then Roach smirked and looked at us like, 'Wanna see some fire-works?' and we were like, 'What?' and he was like, 'Hit it, Pio,' then Pio took out this device that looked sorta like a phone and he pressed something on it, then we looked up at the building and BOOM!" He laughed. "And we were like, 'WOAH!' and he was like all laughing like a maniac and stuff. It. Was. Awesome! And so after that we went up to Durango, and it was like the same sorta thing this time, but Pio and Roach weren't keeping it secret that they were placing explosives around, and Pio let me hold some C4 and let me play with it, and I made it into a little shark-pup thing because it's like clay, y'know? And so that was cool, too, and I almost didn't want to blow it up, but Pio took it and complimented my artistry then we went out and," he imitated an explosion loudly, successfully irritating Thyne but endearing the others in the car.

"That sounds really exciting, kid, but it also sounds dangerous. Are you sure you want to keep doing this gang thing?"

"Oh, don't worry about me, Daddy! I wouldn't put myself in too much danger. Not now anyway. Not since— I forgot to tell you —Perlie says she wants to keep the baby!"

"That's great, kid! I'll be a grandpa!"

"Yeah! I'm excited. We can take him (or her since we don't know yet) out on ships and teach him how to sail together. It'll be so fun! And me and Franky can teach him how to fence. And like, if it *is* a boy, we can name him after a pirate or—oh! Sauron! That sounds awesome, right Daddy?"

"You think Perlie will let her child have a sword after what happened to you?"

"What? What do you mean after what happened to me?"

"…Your eye?"

"Oh!" he laughed, "Nah, she'll be fiiiine. It was just 'cause I wasn't wearing a mask is all. We'll be safe, Daddy, don't worry!"

"What age are you planning to be giving this child a weapon?"

"I don't know like five? So anyway, after Durango we went up to Hermosillo. You remember? Where they dropped the bomb?"

"I remember," he droned with audible irritation that he would even be asked.

"So yeah, it was sad and stuff because of Ana… But anyway, Roach freaked out. He broke my arm. He didn't mean to, but so then Franky healed me and teleported him away because Franky has superpowers, remember I told you? And so while Roach was out somewhere we placed charges around this butchery and freed the workers. There were only a few, so we sent them down to this off-the-grid village River had found, and they were like, 'Thank you so much,' and we were like, 'Of course! Wanna see the butchery blow up!?' and so Pio let this little boy press the button to blow it up and BOOM!" He laughed. "And don't worry, Daddy, we let the pigs out before we blew it up. They'll probably just end up being wild pigs in that area or something. I don't know. Maybe they'll die. It doesn't matter too much.

"So after Hermosillo, Franky went and got Roach, and when we were all on our way back to the truck, I brought up this really good point (Thyne said as much, so I know it was a good point) that if we didn't pick up the pace, we would probably get caught before we got to the last eight company towns. They were all over the place, Daddy! You wouldn't believe! And so, Thyne was like, 'That's a good point, Party,' then Franky was like, 'I'll teleport us all around like blip blip blip and stuff,' and so we got blipped all around to the next few company towns. Pio had a lot of explosives, but by the last four he was entirely out, and so for those ones Roach taught me how to make molotov cocktails, and he let me throw them! It was awesome! And so yeah we burned down those last four instead of blowing them up, but it was still really fun, obviously. Anyway, how have you been, Daddy? Sorry for just throwing all those refugees at you. Hope it doesn't get you in trouble."

"I'll be okay, kid."

"Oh my goodness! And so while we were on the plane back to Italy, Neodesha messaged me all these adorable pictures of the dogs from this puppy party she threw with JJP while we were gone. I'll forward them to you! And the duck! Their names are...." He continued rambling at his father for the last ten minutes it took to reach Loomis manor, but when they pulled into the garage, Partha ended the chat and rushed inside. His first order of business was giving Perlie a big hug and kiss then kissing her tummy. It turned her pale cheeks rosy, but she didn't even have a moment to comment before he was rushing up to May in the living room and dragging her off the couch by her wrist. "I need your help!"

She spilled her box of candy as she was jostled around and trying not to stumble when he dragged her toward the stairs. Perlie tried to stop him, worried he was bringing her to his suite to bed her. She was also worried his excited energy was due to cocaine. While it was true he was bringing May to his suite, he was fully sober and didn't intend to break his promise to Perlie by cheating on her. He needed May to help him figure out the logistics of releasing the video he would spend that night editing before the "special stream" he had already teased for his fans.

While Partha was busy being hyper in Italy, his father was pointing his ship toward Havana. Worry tried to plague him, but he managed to shake it away. Partha may have been a young, dumb, crazy kid, but he was *Richard's* young, dumb, crazy kid. He couldn't be prouder of him for helping the captives in Mexico escape the company towns. It wasn't surprising to learn that Osiris had paid America to invade, and it wasn't surprising to learn why. Considering how shamelessly evil Osiris was, Richard had tried warning Partha that displacing people from their homes, even if willingly, could be turned against him. He tried to warn him that they were already under higher scrutiny after their involvement with the Roaches' job helping persecuted people escape the states all those years ago. He had said all these things that went in one ear and out the other, but he was still proud.

When his shift ended, he passed the controls over to his first mate and climbed down into his quarters to get some rest. He snuggled up with a plush lamb Partha had made for him when he was only fourteen, played a podcast on his phone to act as background noise, and turned out the lights to get a few winks in his four hour break. Unfortunately, he would not sleep more than an hour before his first mate came banging on his door. "Captain! Captain! They're hailing us! They want to speak with you."

He jumped to his feet and rushed out of the room, following his panicked friend up to the bridge. Through the windows he saw they were surrounded by US Navy and Coast Guard vessels, and a crew member was holding the ship's radio toward him, covering the receiver. With a pit in his gut, he swallowed a lump of dread and took it. "*Aquillius' Revenge*. This is Captain Richard Nima."

"Good evening, Nima. Our Coast Guard ships will be boarding you now."

"S-sir, I—. Y-yes of course, but may I ask why?"

"Not only will we be boarding, you will be escorted off of the bridge. Come quietly, sir. This doesn't have to make the headlines."

"Escorted off—. Sir, with all due respect, I believe you may have me confused with someone else. This is the *Aquillius' Revenge*. We are a leisure civilian vessel under Canopy. We aren't affiliated with any conflicts."

"Not on paper."

Before Richard could further blubber his panicked defence, the channel cut out, and he cast his panicked brown eyes around the room.

"What do we do, sir?"

"I... think I'm under arrest."

"That would make sense considering Party's stream tonight," said his first mate with a solemn expression.

"What? His stream?"

"He was asleep, Logan."

"Shit, you didn't see it, sir?" Richard shook his head. "Hate to be the one to tell you: your kid's a terrorist. He's in that *Crown* organisation. They blew up some factories or something. Good kid, though. Osiris had some sweatshops with kids working in Mexico. You should be proud that he did something about it."

His stomach was leaden. "His stream?" was all he could manage to utter. An armed Naval officer with four Coast Guard members bursted in the room before anything could be further explained to Richard. They trained their guns on him but made certain to also have everyone else's hands up before rushing up to him and telling him to get on the ground. He knelt down and let himself be handcuffed, his jaw agape all the while.

It was surreal to see his ship shrinking on the horizon as he was brought toward Fort Lauderdale. All he could think as the ship became a speck on the horizon was, '*What the fuck has Partha done?*'

Chapter 50
No One Withstands the Machine

He fidgeted mindlessly with his erl piercing as he leaned on his arm and stared vacantly at the wall. The only sounds breaking through the silence were his slow breaths and the soft bubbling of his half-empty beer. His fidgeting eventually slowed to a stop, and his breaths grew too quiet to register. His eyes watered from how intensely he was staring at a speck of blood on the wall, but he was unaware of his gaze. His fractured mind was on fire, but his well-toned body was catatonic.

An entire hour of this trance elapsed, at the close of which he came back to reality in an instant when the kitten on his coffee table stirred from its slumber and mewed. "Right," he said to the little critter, "Thanks." He patted its head, downed the rest of his beer, which was mostly flat by then, and tossed the crushed can out a window on his way to the bathroom.

The whirring sound of his razor would be unsettling and risk another trance, so he took out his phone to play some old rock music as he shaved. To avoid the hum of the razor for as long as possible, he shaved as much of his face and sideburns as he could with a straight razor. The shaving cream was his sister's, so it smelled more floral than he would have usually liked, but he could never complain much about the feeling of the blade gliding gracefully across his cheeks: a cathartic sensation for him.

After shaving his face, with a death-grip on either side of the sink, he looked himself in the eyes. The mirror was cracked and missing pieces, revealing the white rotted wood behind, but he was able to entirely focus on the blue eyes of the fractured man within. "Come on, Dale," he whispered to himself, "It's jussa quick shave, ye fuckin' pussy."

His hand moved on its own as he surrendered himself to a higher power, and as the whirring of the blades started to sound, his stomach immediately turned. His eyes tried to glaze over, but he stared deeply into himself and rushed to trim his mohawk-mullet as quickly and carefully as he could. He shaved it in three-to-five second bursts, having to turn off the razor several times to take mental breaks. Each time it stopped sounding, he let out several breaths as if he had been pulled up from the bottom of the ocean, and each time he had to turn it back on, it became increasingly hard to make himself do it.

What would have taken most people fifteen minutes took Dale an hour and a half of arguing with the mirror and forcing himself to be present. There were times he wondered how worth all the turmoil it was, but the tattoos on the sides of his head were something to be proud of: they represented his escape from hate.

After the battle with the razor, he had a smoke and started to prepare for his second battle of the day: a shot in his thigh. It was another fight that would have taken most people ten minutes, but his internal war had him sitting in his office chair struggling to inject himself for two hours. He had given himself this same shot in this same dosage every other week since he was nineteen, but it never got easier.

When he finally won the fight with the needle, he threw the hazardous waste out a different window and took staggered steps to his kitchen. He leaned down into the fridge to grab another beer and cracked open a small carton of milk for the little grey kitten he had saved from a gutter in Gatlinburg that weekend. He hadn't decided on a name for her yet, but it's not like she would listen to one anyway. He watched her lap at the dish of milk on the counter as he nursed his beer. It was a nice day outside, so he considered going out to hunt for dinner, but his phone buzzed on the coffee table, briefly stopping his music and distracting him. He sauntered to the couch and plopped down into it to pluck up his phone and read the message. It was from his best friend, Ridley:

⌈ Did you see the video? ⌋

Dale swigged his beer and typed a reply: ⟦ What video? ⟧

⌈ The one of that streamer. ⌋

⟦ I ain't even heard of it. ⟧

⌈ Get on your computer. I'll send you the link. ⌋

⟦ K. ⟧

His home was a modified prison bus, so it was a short trek from the kitchen and living room in the front to his small sleeping quarters in the back. Despite only having to walk a short distance, he still groaned and lazily dragged his feet to the back of the bus to open his dinosaur of a laptop and wait impatiently for it to boot up and connect to the hotspot from his phone. Service was shoddy out here in the middle of the Tennessee wilderness, so it took ten minutes for his email to even load, let alone the video his friend had sent. With the video open and buffering, he left the small fold-down desk to go chop firewood outside. He let his kitten wander around the area as he did, keeping an eye on her to be sure she didn't stray too far.

After thirty minutes of axing, he slammed the weapon into the stump he was using as a chopping surface and went to grab his kitten. The sun was setting, and for a quiet moment he nursed his beer and watched the warm rays dance through the naked trees, taking in the serenity and isolation he cherished so much.

The video was mostly finished loading when he went back to his computer, so he slipped on some headphones and started it.

It opened with an attractive man wearing an eyepatch talking to the camera through a mirror in a private bathroom. He said his name was Party the Kid and that he didn't like to get political, but he was pissed off. He slammed his camera into the sink, and the video abruptly cut to a shot from his perspective. He was in a sweatshop of some sort. He spoke with a child, but they spoke in Spanish, and Dale's grip on the language was loose at best. He could only understand the number "thirteen" and nothing else. After this exchange, the man from the introduction, who was wearing a body-cam, took out an old handgun and pressed it to the little girl's head. She screamed and cried, but he did not hesitate to pull the trigger. Dale paused the video and averted his eyes from the still image of the dead child, now merely a body half of viscera on her sewing machine.

Rather than watching more, he turned off his hotspot to conserve his phone's processing power and called Ridley.

"Hello?"

"What the fuck!?"

"I know! It's fucked up! Did you watch the whole thing?"

"You know Ah ain't gon' watch some lunatic kid-killer, Ridley."

"Well, toward the end of the video, he says he's going after Osiris next. I think we should rush out to DC before this job gets snatched up by someone else."

"Ah'll get packin'."

"Eibhlín says the CIA is likely already involved, so if we want to get in on the payout we'll have to find this guy before they do."

Dale was going to reply, but he heard the aforementioned woman shouting to the phone from somewhere else in the room with Ridley: "Not like they'll find him, anyway!"

He pondered. "I'll meetchye at the depot on Sundee."

"Alright, seeya then."

After playing with his new pet for another half-hour, he dragged his feet around to start packing for the trip. Along with his clothing, hygienic products, and the new things he had gotten for the cat, he also had three large trunks he had hired a buddy to install into the bed of his cream-coloured pickup built to hold his many firearms. He usually liked to fly a big American flag from the back of the cabin, but with the trunks attached and full of firearms, it would be wiser to put the shell over it. It was cumbersome, but he managed to shimmy it from its place leaning on the side of the bus to the back of the truck where he lifted and slid it into place.

Packing everything and readying the truck took until midnight and left him quite sweaty, so after a quick dinner of jerky from his last kill and another beer, he showered and brought the kitten into the back to watch a few episodes of *One Piece*. He considered naming her Monkey or Luffy since she seemed especially interested whenever Luffy was on screen. Three beers later, he brought the cat to its crate in his room and caged it up for the night, letting it only have a few hours of freedom the next day before being caged again for the long trip ahead of them.

His truck had been lifted to make room for his flotation tires, and its sides were caked in brown muck from a recent mudding foray in South Carolina. It was typical of these sorts of trucks to be louder than sin, but removing his muffler was never a consideration: it would put him at a very real risk of making him catatonic. Still, he wanted his presence known, at least when he was flying his flag and showing pride for his country, so he had his friend install better speakers and a boombox.

He climbed up into the cabin and buckled the kitten's crate into the passenger seat, buckling himself and turning on the radio shortly afterwards. He wanted to blare his music, but he was considerate enough of the small creature with him to keep it at a reasonable volume.

It would be about a nine hour drive accounting for breaks from his bus in the deeply wooded Appalachian mountains of Tennessee to the depot in Washington DC. It had been almost a year since his last job. The payment from it had long-ago run out, but he had very few expenses as something of a self-sufficient man living off the grid. When he did need money, he did not want for it, with a loving family willing to finance him without question and... *other* less-than-legal avenues of income.

With enough cigarettes and a few beers, he managed to make the entire drive without losing his mind from the quiet droning of the engine behind the music. He nearly crashed into one of the company cars in the gated lot when he was parking at the depot, but he managed to sober himself up enough to park safely. Climbing out would be more difficult, so he leaned his head on the steering wheel as he turned off the engine but let the music keep playing. The world was wobbly, and his stomach was turning, but the lack of droning meant his soul was no longer constricting.

His cat mewed after a few minutes, so, feeling marginally better, he opened her cage and let her out, clutching her to his chest as he struggled his way down from his driver's seat and onto solid ground.

The front door unlocked when he flashed his company ID at its sensors, and after stumbling his way through some winding halls, he collapsed into the sofa of a lounge area and set the cat down on the floor to explore the small room. It was 3:46 a.m. on what was only technically Sunday, so he was the only one there. While the kitten was stumbling around on the rug and climbing under the lower shelf of the coffee table, Dale made his way to the vending machines for some "dinner" consisting of a honeybun, a bag of pretzels, sparkling water, and two cigarettes.

When he was finished eating, having fed the cat on the road, he brought it up to one of the unoccupied sleeping chambers, paid for the night with his ID as if it were a credit card, and curled up in the stiff white sheets with his pet for what semblance of sleep he could manage, all the while with his phone playing quiet music for him to avoid hearing the humming of any fluorescent lights or air-cons.

Leviathan LLC was a mercenary corporation sanctioned by the United States government. It was founded only a few years before the invasion into Mexico was launched. Where normal military operations were bound by international laws, Leviathan privateers were not involved with the state government or the war (at least not on paper), so their war crimes were more easily swept under the rug. The name of the corporation came from legends from the Golden Age of Piracy, wherein it was said that a demon captain, called Melchiresa in the Caribbean and Leviathan in Europe, had made some sort of demonic pact with the Portuguese royalty, making himself the commander of Portugal's entire navy. The owner of Leviathan LLC was a second generation Portuguese immigrant to America, so he had heard the stories as a child. It inspired him to get involved with privateering in adulthood, and it was an open secret that he intended to one day command the entire American navy like his childhood "hero" commanded Portugal's.

While Dale was in the army and helping the war efforts for America, his captain, with something of a soft spot in his heart for the young man, half-suggested half-warned him to leave the army and join Leviathan as a mercenary. He had explained to Dale that his conduct was inhumane and would risk a dishonourable discharge. Young Dale took the advice to heart when Ridley was discharged for killing a POW in cold blood only a month later. So, while Ridley was in prison, Dale kept fighting in the army (now on his best behaviour) while he waited for the bureaucratic processes to officially transfer him to the private sector.

It wasn't until the very tail end of the invasion that everything was made official, and because of his glowing references from the military, he was quickly a favourite among the dispatchers and management officers. It was contract work, but he had worked fairly steadily for Leviathan for over a decade at that point. Ridley, or

"Twist" as he was known in mercenary circles, was correct in assuming that Dale could pull strings to put himself in charge of collecting Partha's bounty.

He was stirred from his slumber only a few hours after having closed his eyes. The little kitten was still curled up in his hand, and the both of them yawned in tandem as Dale sat upright and rubbed his aching eyes. After some groggy still-ness, he turned to leave the bed. He slipped the cat into his pullover hoodie's large pocket where it mewed happily and curled up to resume sleeping as he grabbed his phone and texted Ridley:

⟦ Alright, I'm awake. You here? ⟧

⌈ We're at the depot, if that's your question. ⌋

⟦ I'll meet you in the mess hall. ⟧

⌈ Oh, good. We're already there. Ace wanted some coffee. ⌋

Dale dragged his feet to the mess hall and quickly spotted his friends amongst the crowd, standing in line waiting for their coffee. Adjacent to the cafeteria was a convenience store, so, with some time to kill waiting for his friends, he sauntered inside and bought himself a six-pack of beers, a pack of smokes, some "gourmet" cat food for his little friend, and a root beer. His friends were waiting for him at a table when he left the shop, so he approached and immediately pulled the root beer out to give to Ridley. "Got this for ye."

"Hey, thanks!" Root beer was to Ridley what cigarettes and beer were to Dale, and he was happy to treat his friend, who seemed as jubilant as ever even without the gift. His white teeth were beaming bright in contrast to his dark brown skin, putting an extra emphasis on his cheery nature. His girlfriend, Eibhlín, or "Ace" as she was code-named in the business, looked almost irritated by how happy Ridley was. Her pale freckled cheeks were pink with exasperated frustration as she sipped on her black coffee desperately. Something of a night owl, she hadn't gotten to sleep until five in the morning, then was ungraciously awoken only two hours later to take the quick drive from their apartment in Arlington to the depot in the North of DC.

Dale noticed her upset as immediately as he noticed Ridley's pep, so after handing off the soda, he reached into his pocket and set the kitten on the table in front of Eibhlín. Her eyes went big at the little critter, and a huge grin, rivalling her boyfriend's, split her face. She looked up at Dale and, with her thick Irish accent, said, "Where'd ya get this little fella?"

He sat down across from them and opened the can of food for the cat, setting it on the table beside it and petting its small frame with his comparatively hulking hand. "She's gutter trash like me!" He chuckled and opened one of his cheap beer bottles on the edge of the table.

After catching up for about an hour, they all made their way to a communal office area with unoccupied computers. Sometimes people could be found playing video games or watching things on them, but they were most typically used for their intended purposes: drafting contracts and doing research. It was a good mercenary's first course of action to research and consider terms for a contract before signing. Dale was never a lawyer, but he had something of a talent for writing contracts that would guarantee him legal protection, a good payout, and were agreeable enough for the government to have little qualms signing.

They all three sat in a row, each in a small cubicle, and started to research. Ridley and Eibhlín had already gathered some information at home, but they had sensitive security clearances and were therefore able to sign-in with their company IDs and peruse information not publicly available. Dale, however, was a high enough rank in the company to have earned himself confidential clearance, so his research would be the most valuable. What more, Eibhlín had top secret clearance in the past, though she had lost it after leaving the CIA, so she could sometimes offer older information that even Dale didn't have access to.

He started with the obvious: Partha's name, job, a few of his streams. He researched all of the people who regularly joined Partha's streams, which included his father, Thyne, and Francis, among others. It led him to information about Partha's father, Richard Nima, having been the captain of a ship smuggling refugees out of America, which led him to research on the criminals charged, which led ultimately to Karson, Silvino, and Clayton Roach, the former of which had a large file and was considered a minor threat to national security. Upon seeing the surname, he went pale.

Wordlessly, he pushed past the feelings and decided to pivot, if for no other reason than to collect himself, and searched for the video Ridley had sent him. He didn't watch it, but smirked when he saw its classification. It had already been marked as confidential, which bolstered Dale's confidence in this job being especially lucrative.

Unbeknownst to him (though he did pick up on some strange artefacts and oddities in the few seconds he did see) the video was fabricated. He had no reason to distrust it. It had been marked confidential. If anything was going to be deep-faked, surely it wouldn't then be hidden away from the general population. It didn't even cross his mind that the video might not be real, and it did its job of motivating him to find this imaginary version of Partha and bring him in to be tortured for information on his accomplices.

He minimised that window to start drafting the contract, only to be met again with Roach and River's mugshots. The sight stopped his movements, and he stared with his eyes squinting at Roach's portrait in particular for two entire minutes, pondering, before finally getting back on track and starting a draft of the contract.

It took him six hours to get his contract to a state he felt would get him the biggest check for the least risk, and after proofreads from Eibhlín and Ridley, he saved it to his company account and left the communal office. Eibhlín and Ridley followed him for as far as they were allowed to go, but they had to split ways when he reached a set of opaque slate-grey double doors at the South end of the building. He went inside alone, even going so far as to leave his kitten with his friends.

This section of the building could be mistaken for a bar or lounge, but there was no music to be heard, and the only other soul to be seen when he entered was a worker at the bar. He had been looking at his phone, but when he saw Dale he stood upright and poured him a whiskey neat. It hit the bartop at the same time that Dale sat on a barstool. He took the drink and looked down a corridor to his left. "Any int'restin' folk here?"

"A man came in surrounded by bodyguards like the secret-service, but he definitely wasn't a politician."

"Definitely? Ye can't be so sure."

"Pretty damn sure, but anyway, his people were asking about you in particular, actually. He came in about ten minutes ago. Here's his contract." He took a tablet from under the bar, tapped on it a few times, and showed Dale a lengthy contract not much longer than the one he had just written. The bartender returned his attention to a game on his phone while Dale read.

"Shit," he said after two minutes of skimming, "Where'd ye say he was?"

"Twelve."

Dale knocked back the remainder of his whiskey and left the bar to find room twelve. There were six bodyguards posted by the door who stopped him from nearing it. "I ain't armed." They ignored his claim and patted him down roughly. He felt utterly violated, but he managed to sound in control of himself when they finished man-handling him: "Ah told ye. Now outta my way." He shoved past them, and after some grumbling from all parties, he was able to flash his ID at a sensor on the door. He pushed it open, ignoring all the tough-guy talk from the guards, and found the client slowly standing from a loveseat.

The small windowless chamber was entirely black, as were all its furnishings. Its size was not much larger than a walk-in closet, and the stale air smelled of dust, sweat, and whatever girly cologne this man was wearing. He closed the door behind him and approached the man to shake his hand. "Mr. Abraham. Dale Quirk. Pleasure."

Tatum shook Dale's strong hand weakly then took roughly thirty years getting himself back down in the loveseat. Dale sat in a sofa-chair across from him, taking a tablet from the coffee table in the process, and watched with thinly-veiled irritation as Tatum struggled to sit down. When he was finally seated, he scooped up his martini from the coffee table and said, "Your reputation precedes you, Mr. Quirk."

"'Sthat so?"

"Yes, sir. I requested you specifically."

"Ah saw as much in yer contract."

"I hope it is agreeable."

Dale scoffed. "It ain't."

"Well, I'm here to negotiate."

"You ain't got no lawyer?"

"I have plenty of lawyers, sir, but none that I trust to keep this as secret as it needs to be."

"Mmkay."

"So what part of my contract is disagreeable for you?"

"All it." He took his ID out of his wallet and slid it into a slot on the tablet. With his profile opened on the device, he navigated through his files to find his own contract. He opened it and passed the device across the room for Tatum to read. Another millenia passed as the old man struggled to open a pair of reading glasses and find the correct distance from his face to hold the tablet. Dale watched wearing his annoyance plain on his face, but Tatum was too preoccupied to notice. It took him thirty minutes to read the contract, after which he looked up at Dale and asked for a stylus to sign it. He rushed over to the other side of the room to squint at the screen. Had he shown him the right contract? He scrolled through it, confirming it was the correct one, and quickly slid the stylus from its place on the side of the device. "Here!"

Tatum struggled to grip the pen, but once he did, he signed everywhere it asked for his signature and copied Dale's asking price on the provided line in both numerical form and written words: a measure added to all Leviathan contracts to be sure the number would be fully understood by all parties involved.

Dale took the tablet from Tatum as soon as he finished his last stroke of the pen and scrolled up and down through it for an entire minute: double, triple, quadruple checking that he hadn't made a mistake. It was unfathomable that this ancient man had signed and copied the two-billion-dollars asking price with all its zeros and in plain English. "Hot damn!" he said as he beamed down at Tatum, "Yer one crazy sonuvabitch! I ain't never had no one sign so quick! Yeehaw!" He giggled and sent the signed contract to his superiors as well as a few copies to the printer down the hall.

"It's imperative that he be brought in," was Tatum's only reply.

"Ah'd say! Ah'll get the fucker don'tchyew worry none, Mr. Abraham. Ah'll get two of 'em if Ah find another!" He laughed and slapped his knee. "You done made my day! An' my lips is sealed 'bout who done sent me, 'course."

Tatum stood, shook Dale's hand again, and followed him out into the hall. They split ways immediately as Dale practically sprinted to the printer to hold the lucrative contract in his trembling hands. He took a big whiff of it, as if he could smell the money already, and rushed to file it away in his office.

Chapter 51
I Can Cope With Torture

It was three in the morning when Partha was pulled out of his bed in Loomis manor by his hair. "WHAT THE BLOODY HELL HAVE YOU DONE!?"

"Thyne! Thyne, please!"

"HE KNOWS YOUR NAME, YOU IDIOT!"

The commotion was loud enough to wake Roach across the manor, and he rushed toward the sound. When he bursted into Partha's room, Thyne was throwing whatever he could grab and shouting various obscenities. He was about to throw a model ship at Partha, but Roach grabbed his wrist and tore it out of his hand. "You need to fucking chill, dude."

He wriggled free of Roach's grasp and turned around to shout up into his face: "NO, I FUCKING DON'T! HE'S RUINED EVERYTHING!"

"You talking about the video he streamed a bit ago?"

There was a beat wherein steam may well have started shooting out of Thyne's ears. "YOU KNEW!?"

He tried to punch him, but his fist was caught. Roach twisted his arm to pin it behind him and pulled him close by the small of his back in a half-forceful half-romantic manner. Looking down at him: "I knew," he confirmed with a shit-eating grin, "I *helped*."

Thyne couldn't free himself, so he resorted to crying. "Why?"

Roach turned them around so that he was in front of Partha and released Thyne to back up toward the kid. He held his arms out to make himself into a wall between the hot-headed Brit and Partha and tossed the model ship on the bed. "I'm not talking to you about this until you've calmed down, dude."

"Fuck you, Clayton!" He threw a half-empty bottle of soda from the dresser at him, but Roach unsurprisingly slowed and caught it.

"Hey thanks," he said with a wink before twisting the old drink open and downing it.

Thyne just about blew a gasket watching Roach be so nonchalant and mocking. He couldn't form any words and instead sputtered incoherently through his grinding teeth and weepy countenance.

"Listen, Thyne," said Partha as he peered out from behind Roach, "I may not have superpowers or weird alien microphones, but I have *reach*, and I used it. Now everyone who watched my stream knows that Osiris paid for the war and what Abraham's doing in Mexico."

"Don't you know that no one bloody cares, mate? No one cares about Mexico." He furrowed his brow. "I do."

"Yeah *we* do, but what are your viewers supposed to do about it? Even if they do care, which they bloody fucking don't, mate."

"Don't talk about my fans like that."

"You don't think! You don't think, you idiot! No one cared about the Czechs. No one cared about the communists. No one cared about us. And now, no one cares about Mexico! What are your fans meant to do, Partha!? Are they meant to boycott Osiris? The company that owns bloody everything!? Are they meant to go to war!?"

He stuttered, struggling to find a reasonable answer.

"And you!" he stomped up to Roach and pointed up into his face, "Partha lacks foresight, true enough, but I *know* you're smarter than that. There'll be mercenaries on our heels by the end of the month if we're lucky! Why'd you let him do it?"

Roach smiled sadly. "Why else, sparkplug? To watch it all burn."

The room was humid and hot and reeked of garbage. He could hear the waves trying their best to lap gently against the sand through all the trash. The seagulls outside screeched incessantly, and a thunderstorm rumbled in the distance. The window had bars on it, but at least there *was* a window. The same couldn't be said of the interrogation room when, just after sunrise, he was escorted from his holding cell down the hall. He wasn't sure how long he had been jailed. He still wasn't sure what Partha had streamed that had gotten him into so much trouble.

Surely, Partha wouldn't have streamed the destruction of the factories in Mexico. He wasn't *that* stupid… was he?

Richard ran his hands through his dark hair, leaned on the interrogation table, and sighed. The one-way mirror was like Sauron's watchful eye the way it seemed to see right through him. What evils must have been on the other side, just out of sight?

The door clicked open, and he perked up to see who was coming inside. It was the same man who had escorted him from his otherwise empty cell through the otherwise empty halls to this damp little room. He was of average height, likely somewhere between 5'8" and 5'10". His build was athletic enough that Richard felt his gut knot up with worries of what sorts of damage he could do. Looking to be in his early thirties, his features were sharp and handsome and added another year or two with their structure as well as some sun he must have seen during his life. He had a cigarette between his soft lips and a dirty-blond mohawk-mullet that showed strange geometric tattoos on either side of his head. They looked like lotus flowers but with more jagged lines than would be typical for plantlife, and they were coloured entirely with vivid reds, blues, purples, greens, and thick black lines. The flowers themselves were almost square in shape. All Richard could ponder seeing them was how much it must have hurt to have received them. They weren't the only tattoos this man had, but the others were covered by his clothing. He wasn't in any recognisable uniform, instead wearing dirty blue-jeans, a wifebeater, and a crusty old leather jacket over it. He crossed his arms and looked down at Richard, cracking his neck before saying, "Mornin'."

"Good morning," replied Richard with a sigh.

"You know why ye're here?"

"No." A beat. "Can't I have a lawyer? I'm not even American."

"Don't matter."

"You can't just arrest a foreigner and not even tell him why."

A wicked grin. "Cain't be certain which crime it was?"

"I don't know what you're talking about."

"Sure," he said as he finally sat down in the other chair. He kicked up his muddy boots on the table and threw a manilla folder beside them.

"Is this for me to read?" he asked as he slid the folder toward his side of the table.

Dale gestured. "By all means, Mr. Nima."

Richard opened the folder and gulped at the picture of his son's passport paper-clipped to at least ten pages of information about him. Behind Partha's files was a similar pile of papers about Richard himself, under those were files on the three Roaches with whom Richard had helped smuggle refugees out of America, and lastly were Perlie Moon's files. Only a moment after he had opened the folder, Dale pulled his feet down from the table and leaned on it. He closed the folder before Richard could read much and slid it back toward his side of the table. After a drag on his cigarette: "Now we can do this the easy way er the hard way. Ah'll ask real nice and slow for ye: where's yer son?"

"I don't know."

He smiled wickedly and smoked. "Ah was hopin' ye'd say that." Richard watched with panic in his eyes as Dale stood and started to pace. "Let's git one thing straight, Nima: Ah ain'tchyer fren. Ah ain't got no 'nice cop' gon' come in, neither. Ain't no one else in Florida that's even authorised ta come inside this buildin', let alone know what Ah'm gon' do t'ye." He pointed to the one-way mirror which Richard only then noticed could be seen through via the lights now illuminating the empty room on the other side. "Ain't no one watchin'. No one ta save ye. So, Ah'll ask again, and Ah hope to God ye're as dumb as yer kid and lie again: where is he?"

"You do whatever you want to me. I'm not telling you."

"Ahaha! Ah like you! Ah like when they got spunk." Another drag. "Alright, Nima. If ye won't say where yer kid is, yu'll 'least tell me if the Roaches and Miss Moon 're involved with his kid-killin' terrorist shit."

"I don't know what you're talking about."

"'Course ya don't. And you ain't know them Roaches?"

"The only roaches I know are the ones that crawl around in my quarters."

"And Miss Moon?"

"I don't know who you're talking about."

"Well, let's see if we cain't jog yer mem'ry." He rushed to Richard's place, grabbed his left arm, and snuffed out his cigarette on his wrist. As Richard screamed in pain, Dale watched with a sadistic grin and madness in his pale blue eyes. "That's just the warm-up."

Richard bit his lip and averted his gaze from Dale's disturbing smile. With tears in his eyes but a resolute tone: "I won't talk."

"Yu'll talk," said Dale as he stood upright and quit the room. While he was gone, Richard observed his new scar and sniffled. After ten minutes, the door clicked again. He heard the distinct crackling of a taser and tensed up as Dale approached. "Tell me somethin', Nima."

He leaned back as far as he could without moving from the chair he had been cuffed to by the ankles, shaking his head and bracing himself for the shock that followed. His vision blurred, and it felt like his muscles were trying to escape his skin. When he came back into himself, he was laying on his side on the floor, the chair still awkwardly cuffed to his ankles but on its side now.

Dale crouched down and looked at him, his big blue eyes gleaming madly over an eerie grin. "Ever been waterboarded, Nima?"

Richard's eyes danced around the room. There were more things on the table than before he had been tased, among them: a rag and four large buckets with condensation on their sides. He gulped and shook his head.

"Ah've been waterboarded. It ain't no fun at all, 'specially when ye ain't got the info they're tryna get, but we both know you's got the info, so...." He stood back upright and stepped on a beam at the base of Richard's chair, sitting him upright again with the strength of his leg alone. Before Richard could fathom, Dale had his chair tipped back, a rag over his face, and disgusting sea water was being poured all over him.

He was waterboarded for hours. Dale shouted at him for information each time he was allowed to gasp for air, but Richard never broke. Dale had to get new water for his buckets six times, but after four consecutive hours of torture, he was visibly enraged and slammed the door behind him as he quit the room. Richard sat in horrified silence, gasping through waterlogged lungs and blinking salt out of his eyes, hoping desperately that his torturer wasn't coming back.

Just down the hall, with his eyes on the door to Richard's room, Dale had a smoke to calm himself. When his breaths were no longer huffing and hands no longer trembling with wrath, he took out his phone and made a call.

Roach was eating a late lunch of lima beans from the can and listening to Thyne shout at him about how anarchy would never work when his phone started ringing. He looked at the number and went pale.

"Who's that, then!?"

He wiped the emotion from his face in a split second, swallowed his mouthful, and answered the call: "Hyello?"

"Roach. The bus's givin' me trouble."

"Who is it!?" shouted Thyne. It was loud enough that Dale heard his voice.

"Who's that witchya?"

"A friend," he said to answer both men, "What's wrong with the bus, dude?"

"Cain'tchya just come see it fer yerself?"

Roach put a finger over Thyne's lips to stop him from shouting more. "Well, dude, I mean it's better if you just explain it in case it's something simple, y'know?"

He rubbed the bridge of his nose. "It got... uh... damaged."

"By...?"

A beat. "You member that... *thing*... we saw when we was campin' in it back in seventy-eight?"

Roach went pale at the memory. "You know I do. How bad is it? When do ya need me there?"

"Asap."

He took another bite of his lima beans. "Kay. It'll be a bit. Long drive, y'know."

"Yer... uh... sure?"

Roach grinned. "Yeah. Unless you don't want me to come for some *inexplicable* reason."

Dale sighed. "Ye're too smart fer yer own good, Clay. Ah take it ye're involved wit this Party kid, then?"

"Mmhmm. And I take it you're after us?"

"'Course Ah am! You broke yer promise, Roach! We had a deal!"

"Huh? What promise?"

"Don' play dumb, asshole!"

"I didn't break any promise to you, dude."

"Maybe not d'rectly, but runnin' wit that kid-killer's just as bad as bein' one."

"Kid-killer? What are you on about?"

"It don't matter anyway. Ah got Nima's dad. He ain't cracked yet, but he will."

Roach stood. "Richard?"

"Yeah. He says he ain't know none a' ye. Ah'd respect it if he weren't protectin' kid-killers."

"I don't know what they told you, dude, but we haven't killed any kids. Partha's about to *have* a kid."

Thyne whisper-shouted, "Who is it? Stop telling him things. Hang up!"

"Ah don' know why you's lying ta me. Ah thought we was friends, Roach. We had a fuckin' deal."

Roach tried to defend himself, but Dale ended the call just as Thyne snatched the phone away to end it, too. With his phone still in Thyne's hands, Roach quit the room and found May: "Can you track someone's phone with just the number?"

She sensed his panic and looked up from her laptop to give him her full attention. "Probably. What's the number?"

Back in Florida, it took Dale another five minutes to gather himself before he decided he'd try a different torture tactic. He went out to his truck and returned to Richard's room spinning a machete around his wrist, ready to start chopping off fingers. When he came into the room, however, though everything else was as he'd left it... Richard was gone.

Dale looked for him around the building for an hour and a half, after which he texted Roach: ⟦ Is one of your powers to kidnap people I rightfully kidnapped first? ⟧

⟦ Ha! ⟧ Dale rolled his eyes. As he was typing an angry response, Roach sent a picture of himself with Richard who looked confused as Roach made a kissing face for the camera. The picture's caption: ⟦ Lose something? ⟧

⟦ You cheated.... ⟧

To this, Roach sent a gif of Jack Sparrow's response to the very same claim in his first film: ⟦ "Pirate." ⟧

After Richard was given medical attention by Giovanni, he was escorted up into the living area where the others were already having a meeting about the terrible predicament Partha's stream had put them all in. Richard had been given very little of an explanation about how he was brought from Florida to Italy in the blink of an eye, but he could tell that Francis was involved. When Partha had told him earlier about Francis' ability to "teleport" others, he hadn't taken it seriously, assuming that his son was being as imaginative as he usually was. He also tended to have trouble telling the difference between Partha's true stories and his ramblings about his various highs or tabletop games. He was quivering when Giovanni sat him beside Roach and Partha and rounded to a different settee to sit beside Arjun and listen to Thyne:

"Hello, Richie. Firstly, now that you're here." He took his strange pen out of his pocket and tossed it to Roach. He gestured with his head to Richard, who didn't even flinch when Roach inserted a microphone into the back of his neck and floated the pen back to Thyne. "Ta. So, with that handled and Giovanni present, we can discuss more seriously about how to address Partha's great blunder. It goes without saying that it's wisest for us to split ways and—."

"We can't split the party," muttered Partha.

"What was that?" snipped Thyne, "Are *you* trying to give advice right now, mate? *You!?* How dare you even breathe after what you've done."

Roach stood. "Leave him the fuck alone."

"You're lucky I don't kill him!"

He stepped up to Thyne and looked down at him in an attempt to intimidate him. "You're lucky I don't kill *you*. The kid did a good thing. We're not just some fucking gang of nobodies hiding in the shadows anymore: he put us in the spot-light. He put us on the global stage, and now? It's showtime."

Thyne stepped into Roach's space to show he was unintimidated and hissed, "Sit. Down."

"Make me."

"Alright, alright, you're both pretty," said Dezba as she stood and peeled them away from each other. "Sit down, boys." Her maternal air seemed to supernaturally control them: as she shooed them away, they both sat back down, still glaring at each other. "Splitting up is a good idea. Perlie?"

"Yes, ma'am?"

"Would your father be willing to help us?"

"I would hope so. Even if he can't, though, Thyne says they have my name, so we should at least warn him that he might be visited by mercs."

Dezba nodded and addressed the room with a calming tone: "So, here's my thinking: the haunt in the palace is currently the safest place at our disposal. Are we all in agreement?" Vague nodding and agreeing. "So, it only makes sense, then, that we should send those in the most danger to the haunt. So: Partha, Richard, May, the animals, and Perlie."

"No. Absolutely not. I'm not going to hide away."

"Perlie, please," said Partha, "They have your name. I love you. What would I do if they took you from us?"

"You'd get over it, kid. I'm not going to France, and that's final."

"What if," began Thyne, "we send Giovanni, Viktor, Arjun, and Melchiresa to go with you? They can protect you all if something goes wrong."

"Send them with the others, yes. Protect Partha, but I am not going to let you all fly out to Korea without me. The only one here who even sort of knows the language other than me is Roach, anyway."

Thyne sighed.

"So," continued Dezba before another argument could flare up, "It'll be all of them at the haunt. I'll stay here with Neodesha to keep the manor safe and undetected. I doubt it would be targeted, so just the two of us should do. And the rest of you will fly out to Korea as soon as possible to talk with Perlie's father about reinforcements and maybe also other places we could hide. How does this all sound, dearies?"

Jean-Jacques wanted to protest being separated from his sister, but he knew the haunt was the safest place for her. Even if it wasn't, the others would need her there to hide them from the cameras. Likewise, if something went wrong with Thyne's plane in Korea, Jean-Jacques would need to be there to fix it for him. He wasn't completely happy with the developments and plans forming, but he was willing to let these experienced criminals take the wheel. Running wasn't really an option anymore, and he wasn't even certain he still wanted to run after learning about Abraham's dead man's switch. His feelings for Partha's mistake were also more muted than they may have been without that knowledge. Sure, it was stupid to stream his terrorism openly, but it undeniably brought more attention to their work and the evils of Osiris.

"Is it really quite necessary for us to be in the haunt?" whined Giovanni.

"Yes," said Dezba, "It's very well hidden, so it's also not very likely to be targeted or even found, but you will be good protectors for the Nimas. Honestly, I think the most dangerous place for any of us to be right now is within arm's reach of Party. He's probably the most wanted man in the world." Roach nudged Partha with his elbow and beamed a proud grin at him.

"Maybe I should go somewhere alone, then," he conceded with a slight smile at Roach's encouraging expression.

"Nonsense, kid," said Roach, "We're all in this together. That's what a gang is. If you get hauled off to the gallows, I'll be right there with you."

"Roach, don't scare him like that. He won't be getting hauled off anywhere," Dezba scolded.

Roach patted Partha's thigh and rustled his hair. "Don't worry, kiddo. Everything'll be fine."

"Only if we act quickly," said Thyne, "We already have mercenaries after us. We need to get him hidden yesterday. Franky?"

Francis looked at him. "Yesterday has passed."

"Okay, well can you start taking people to the haunt?"

Francis was still exhausted and panicked from having brought Richard across the entire Atlantic ocean. He swigged from his flask, glared just-so at Partha, and said, "Fine." After the Nimas and May disappeared, Francis appeared in the living room and asked Roach where Malfeasance was.

Giovanni took the opportunity to stop Francis before he did anymore "teleporting" by standing and interrupting Roach, "Boy! Don't bring me anywhere just yet. I have business with the twins."

Francis rolled his eyes. "Okay, well where is the duck?"

"The bathhouse unless someone moved her without telling me," answered Roach.

Francis disappeared, and the twins turned their attention to Giovanni as he gestured for them to follow him. He brought them to an examination room in the basement. Once the door was closed behind him: "Boys, I have tested your blood and cross-referenced it with Neodesha's. The only thing I can't figure is—. Well, I'll put it this way: are your parents Egyptian?"

"Our dad is Egyptian," said Roach, and River added, "but our mom's from New York."

"Right," he stroked his chin, "But your surname is Roach?"

River replied, "He changed it," and Roach elaborated, "when he first came to America."

Giovanni smiled. "Oh! And beforehand it—. Wait, he changed it *to* Roach?"

"He thought it meant scarab," they said in tandem.

"I see. Well, it wouldn't happen to have been Al-Mufti before he changed it, would it?" They nodded, and Giovanni clapped his hands together once. "Then my tests weren't faulted!"

"And?" the twins asked together.

He held out his arms toward them like they were prize sows. "In those beautiful veins of yours, boys, is the blood of Osiris." They started. "Osiris, of course, being," he pressed his hand to his chest and bowed deeply, "yours truly."

"Woah woah woah. What are you saying, dude?" asked River.

He stood back upright. "I'm saying your blood is my blood. You're descendants of mine."

"And you're Osiris?"

"I was. Yes." A long beat of stunned silence. Giovanni pushed past it before the twins could formulate more questions: "My husband was Set, as well."

"You married a God?" asked Roach as River asked, "What happened to him?"

"My husband is Arjun. Arjun was Set. Though, he does like to say that he was only *affiliated* with Set and not the god himself. He says he was only a priest of Set. All of it nonsense, of course. Gods in the sense that you uneducated and spiritual folk worship are plainly not real."

Roach glared, but River spoke before his brother would go at the arrogant doctor: "So we're related to you?"

He nodded. "It's a shame Partha has ruined everything. I was so looking forward to examining you two more thoroughly." A sigh. "Oh well! Perhaps another time!" Without further explanation, he opened the door to the examination room and called out into the hall, "Boy! We've finished!"

"Now, hold the fuck on, dude. You can't just—." Giovanni disappeared before Roach could defend his faith. "Fucking asshole," he muttered.

"Related to Osiris? I'm not sure how to feel. How do *you* feel?"

"I feel like he's a prick! 'Gods like yours aren't real,' what a fucking dick."

"Being a doctor for thousands of years probably doesn't really bolster someone's faith."

"Still…." He sighed. "Let's just go pack and figure out what to do with this information later."

Chapter 52
I Could Not Bear It
If You Died Again

Francis watched the smoke twirling up from Roach and Thyne's cigarettes in the front of the car. Each trail of smoke danced into the other back and forth like an abstract waltz. *It brought ancient memories to Francis' sobering mind of his youth in the palace watching the ballroom dancing and listening to the twang of the harpsichord or the thunder of the organ. The twiddling of the fiddles or the low hum of the cello. The noblewomen's dresses flowed like rivers of silk and velvet and lace as they dragged across the floor. The clicking of heeled shoes against the marble was only mostly drowned out by the orchestra. All with a choir of pseudo-angels whose talent could never compare to his angel Thyne's.*

Roach noticed Francis humming in the backseat and turned briefly to get a good look at his dopey grin. "Corelli, hm, bed bug?"

As Roach took his hand away from the middle console to take a drag, Francis found himself back in reality. He looked out the window to his left and saw some of the Korean landscape ambling slowly by them. His smile remained, for he was brought back to reality not from a horrible void of rotting but from a bittersweet memory of childish awe. "Corelli," he repeated with a nod, "We made merry together when mother brought me on her voyages to Bologna and Rome. Among my most prized memories of Arcan are those of making mischief. A favourite jape of his was when we hooked frogs in the gardens and hid them in the adults' teacups and porridge." He giggled at the memories. "He were merely five years older than I."

Thyne turned to face Francis and smiled wide at him. "You never told me that, Frankenstein! Corelli is one of the only classical composers I can listen to without going mad. I never had to learn him. Did he teach you any violin?"

Francis shook his head absent-mindedly and looked deep into Thyne's eyes where he could swear he saw a glimmer of starlight.

"I can teach you violin, bed bug," offered Roach, "But later. For now, I need one of you to tell Perlie we'll be there in ten."

"Have you been here before?" asked Thyne.

"Once. Back when we were dating. She wanted me to meet her dad. I think she thought I was going to propose and wanted me to ask for his permission. As if I'd fucking ask permission." He chuckled and took a drag. "You two will love him, though."

"She said you know some Korean. How much?"

"I know enough. Not gonna be reading any great Korean literature any time soon, but driving isn't an issue, and lower-level conversations are simple enough. I only learned from Perlie's dad. She didn't really want to teach me."

"Hm, I wonder why not."

"She's only half-Korean and grew up in the states. She's probably just embarrassed that she doesn't speak it more fluently."

At that point, the rest of the group had already made it to the house of one Moon Jae. He lived in a modest mansion on the outskirts of Seoul. The build of the house was a clash between traditional Korean architecture and the harsh angles and intricacies of brutalism and maximalism. Rather than soft rounded columns, there were harsh concrete blocks that seemed to be arguing with the curvature of the roof holding them up. It was stark black with designer shingles, and the house itself was slate grey concrete with vines growing up its facade. The front door was tall and black with a big circular window in its centre, and when Roach rapped gently on the dark metal rim of the window, a sheet of pleated blinds was curled up at one corner.

Jae opened the door and immediately pulled Roach in for a hug. "Your friends are in the den. Perlie's already told me some of the details. I always knew you were a good one. You're not even dating her anymore, and you're still protecting her." He smiled and jammed his finger into Roach's chest as he continued to praise him: "You're a fine man, Clayton, and I'm excited to help with this whole operation. I hope you don't find it rude, though," he stopped and pulled Roach down to whisper into his ear, "I was told you have very wealthy friends."

Roach huffed with amusement. "These two will take care of you. That's Francis, and that's Thyne. They're both loaded."

Jae laughed a loud ha and introduced himself with handshakes and a final gesture toward the den. "Follow me! We're having tea and eating some of the chocolates my wife bought for my birthday last week."

"Right! I brought you something, too. It's in the car."

"Go-ma-wo! You can give it to me later, though."

They were led into a sitting area and each given a cup to have some hot green tea. Jean-Jacques was being treated to a slideshow of pictures of Perlie when she was a child. Before their conversation had been interrupted, Perlie was about to tell her father about her pregnancy. When he came back into the room and tried to resume rambling about his daughter, she cleared her throat and asked to take him aside.

Once they were out on the back balcony together, Jae noticed Perlie wasn't smoking and beamed. In Korean: "Have you finally quit those horrible things?"

"What things?"

"The cigarettes."

She sighed and ran a hand through her hair. "Sort of…. Appa, I'm…. I'm…."
'*Fuck, what was the word?*'

"Is everything okay, little bear?"

"I'm pregnant," she said in English.

He blinked. After a moment of processing the information, his brow furrowed. In Korean: "You're pregnant, and you're still in this gang!?" He crossed his arms. "Young lady, this is incredibly dangerous! I won't have you doing this while you're—."

"Appa, please. I'm not a little girl anymore," she said in English.

Anger remained on his face for a moment before he sighed defeatedly and conceded, "I suppose you're not." With another sigh, he decided to speak in English to make her more comfortable: "But your boyfriend is… very stupid. Are you sure you want to keep it?"

She glared. "He's not stupid."

"He released a video of himself killing a child, little bear. What is that if not—?"

"Killing a child? What?"

They looked at each other with arched brows.

"Well, I don't know Spanish," he said eventually, "Maybe she was saying something really horrible."

Perlie's confusion could not be overstated. "She was talking about being a child labourer, Appa. Why would Partha kill her? Why would he release the footage of such a horrible crime? And why would I be carrying his child if he was murdering children?"

He held his head. "What are you saying? Have you not seen it?"

"He showed it to me before he even streamed it. He wanted to make sure I was okay with him doing it because he loves me."

"You... you *told* him to release it?"

She blushed. "I was drunk."

"While pregnant!?"

A sigh. "No.... I was sober. I just regret telling him to post it. I didn't think we'd have mercs after us this quick."

"WELL, OF COURSE YOU DO! HE KILLED A KID!"

"He didn't kill any kids, Appa. I don't know what you're talking about."

He dragged her inside by her wrist and turned on his television. His energy interrupted the conversations around him, sending the room into an awkward quiet. On his laptop he opened a copy of the video he had downloaded before it was scrubbed from the internet. After pressing play, all eyes in the room were glued to the screen.

It started the same as they all recalled, but when it cut directly to a shot of the sweatshop, skipping the Osiris logo, Roach and River both noticed the change immediately. "What's this?" asked Roach, "Fan edit?"

His question was answered for him only a few seconds later when the deep-faked horrors started to play out. Everyone, save for Jae, gasped when Partha seemed to have killed a child for absolutely no reason. It went on to show him and his masked accomplices killing everyone in the room. It cut to Partha's actual footage of the factory exploding and gave no room to breathe before moving on to more fake footage of senseless slaughter.

When it was over, it was quiet enough to hear a pin drop.

Jaws were on the floor as entire minutes elapsed.

"Well...," said Thyne finally, "Shit."

The haunt was quiet. Giovanni was finishing up with dinner while Arjun chatted with him in the cramped kitchen. Viktor was sulking in Thyne and Francis' room. May was playing *Minecraft* on her laptop while Partha sat beside her watching. Richard was reading. Melchiresa was lazing on a sofa and getting blind drunk. Malfeasance was swimming in the bathtub, and all of the dogs were lazing about the area on various sofas and laps.

Dinner was a salad with edible flower petals and a red vinaigrette paired with a cheap prosecco Francis had aged forward at Giovanni's whiny request. Giovanni wanted to cook, but he was scolded for the idea by Francis before they were left to their own devices in the haunt. Cooking would mean smells might leak out into the palace, however unlikely. Before they were so wanted, it was less of a risk, but to keep the group as undetected as possible, cooking in the haunt was outright forbidden. As they ate, Giovanni apologised several times for the simple dish despite everyone reassuring him they liked it. Still, he continued with the passive aggressive comments about the distant pirate.

After they ate and Arjun cleaned their dishes, Partha suggested they play a session in their West Marches game, which all but Viktor agreed to join. Richard had to make a character, but once he had one, they started a game.

Despite being something like twenty sessions into this campaign, Giovanni still found himself growing confused by the rules. All his millenia of playing various games kept mixing together. It seemed the only thing he could ever keep up to date with was medicine, and even then he would sometimes refer to things like "humours" or "bad air" when speaking with patients. When he finally seemed to realise that he was meant to be acting out a character after his first few sessions, his questions slowed but never truly came to an end. About fifteen sessions in, when he realised that the setting was meant to be more mediaeval, he would sometimes get so into character as to speak Middle or even Old English, meaning that only Arjun could understand him. Most of these moments were met with a strange mixture of awe and slight irritation from their one-eyed DM, but he was always outwardly patient with the old doctor.

Two hours into this particular session, Giovanni found himself in one of these mix-ups. He hadn't entirely fallen back to middle English and knew without a doubt what was reality and what was mere roleplay, but he most assuredly did not know what year or era it was. The DM screen was hiding Partha's phone and newer-looking books. May was being attentive and polite having put her phone in her back pocket and not touched it for the entire two hours. The furniture and decor in the room harkened back to the mid-1700s, and the accent Partha was often adopting when narrating was evoking an era older still. There was no hint of modernity in Giovanni's sightline.

Because of his strange relationship with time, he had passively begun to think of the year as 1720 with no real rhyme or reason to the exact date other than he had heard the number "twenty" a lot during play. As for his location? The room and plethora of animals reminded him of his own basement in the early 1700s, so his assumption was that Arjun had rearranged and redecorated for this strange game to be played there. May, a lady, was wearing pants. It was odd for the era, but he was polite and gentlemanly enough not to comment. She was their guest… apparently… so she could wear whatever she liked.

"Alright, doc. Your turn," she said.

He looked at his little miniature elf and nodded. "I roll this one?" He held up his twenty-sided die then pointed at the table with their character sheets and mess of dice.

Partha blinked away his irritation and shock. With a forced smile: "Probably. What did you want to do?"

Giovanni was about to answer, but a thud sounded from behind him. He turned around and looked up the strange chute-like hallway only to hear another thud and see a small plume of sand fall from the ceiling at the bricked-up entrance. He arched his brow then eyed the others around the table.

Arjun pushed out his chair and hobbled up to the wall of brick. There were three more slams into it as he approached, but he was unperturbed. When it seemed there was a lull from whatever was bashing into the wall, Arjun shouted in French through it, "We don't want any!" Another thud and some muffled voices from the other side of the wall. Arjun leaned down so his head was poking out from under the archway at the bottom of the slanted hall and chirped in Old Egyptian, "Melchiresa, my darling, hide the ones we're meant to be protecting. Keeva, get yourself a sword."

They both stood and did as they were told, and while they were shuffling around, Arjun noticed a crack in the wall had been bored big enough to eye the intruders. They had a handheld battering ram, sledgehammers, and a dweeby looking Frenchman biting his nails as he watched the destruction.

"I wouldn't do that if I were you," said Arjun as they leaned back the ram for another bash. He spoke in English (though his Italian accent was thick), for he had seen one of the men with the battering ram wearing a hoodie with the logo for the New York Giants. Not only that, these people just *oozed* that stereotypical rude American energy. After Arjun's warning, the ram was slowed to a stop before it completed its swing.

The leader of this group noticed the gleaming animalistic blue of his eyes peeking out from the crack and shooed his cohorts away from the wall. He stepped up and crouched down to make eye-contact with Arjun through the broken stone. "Why not?"

"Arsenic."

"We have masks." He patted the gas mask on his hip.

"Oh, well then come on in," said Arjun, his tone playful but with a hint of sadism that his conversation partner did not fail to notice.

"That's what we're tryin' ta do, if ye ain't noticed."

Arjun laughed, and Dale caught a glimpse of his vampiric almost snake-like fangs. It put a pit in his gut, but he didn't let it show on his face. "Well," continued Arjun when their eyes met again, "didn't your mother ever teach you how to knock?"

He pondered, pouted, and said, "One sec," before pushing off his knees to stand back up and sauntering to the historian who had accompanied them to this hearth. "Ye were right there's a hidden room, an' Ah betchye they's in there, but Ah wonder if there's a better way 'a openin' it."

The scientist listened to Dale's interpreter and nodded. He replied, in French, and Dale listened to the translation: "He says he hopes so."

Dale rolled his eyes and returned to the hearth to crouch down and look at Arjun again. He rested his rifle over his shoulders and gestured to the wall between them. "Don't s'pose ye're gon' tell me how to open this proper, are ye?"

Arjun smiled, leaning his head back in playful thought and thus flashing his bright white teeth once more. A generous interpretation of his reply could be read as an attempt to stall for time for the people and pets he was meant to be keeping safe, but the fact of the matter was that Arjun hadn't the slightest care in the world about them. It was purely because Dale was letting him play that he replied how he did when he answered, "I'll tell you, if you answer my riddles three."

Dale was unamused, but he merely sighed and shook his head. One more attempt at diplomacy: "Tell Roach t'come up an' chat."

This intrigued Arjun greatly. With animal thralls as numerous as he had, it was rare that he could be surprised, but Dale's mention of Roach sent his mind reeling. Had Roach betrayed them by revealing their location? Arjun's grin turned wicked at the thought. *'How fun!'* Deciding to have some fun of his own, he said, "I'll go get him."

'Well that was easy,' thought Dale as he stood back upright and looked toward their French guide and translator. "Ask if there's a second exit down there."

There was some French back-and-forth, after which his interpreter said, "He says not according to the radio imagery."

Dale nodded and pointed to two of his ten men. "Just in case, y'all go 'round that way," he gestured vaguely, "where there might be a let-out."

The two men he addressed nodded and disappeared into the adjacent hall. Only a moment later, Arjun returned to the wall and cleared his throat. "He says you can rot in Hell and eat shit."

Dale frowned. That seemed unlike Roach, and this stranger's laugh didn't bode much confidence. He decided, however, to play along and said, "Alright, well, whoever ye are, best get a move on, 'cause we's bashin' our way in."

"No need," said Arjun before they could get another hit in. He pressed the button to open the door from his side, and as it slid noisily open, some of the bricks falling and clattering on the stone floor of the hearth, he gestured politely down the hall. "Don't forget your masks."

Dale put on his mask with a gracious nod of his head toward Arjun, after which he gestured for his heavily-armed men to follow him. All of them donned their masks as they mumbled confirmations that they were, "Right behind ya, boss."

The clicking of Arjun's cane against the ground tripled in volume when the floor turned abruptly into hardwood at the base of the chute-like hall. He gestured into the empty living area with a wide swing of his arm then turned to face the mercenaries, leaning casually on his cane as he said, "Make yourselves at home. By all means."

Dale glared, which could not be seen behind his gas mask but could easily be felt. He noticed the coffee table was covered in character sheets and dice and knew therefore that they had interrupted a game. "Where's Roach?"

Arjun bared his vampiric teeth in a wide smile and tilted his head. His cheeks pushed his eyes closed, and his moustache twitched with delight.

When it was clear Arjun wasn't going to reply, Dale ordered his men to "Be ready for anything," then cocked his rifle as he led the group deeper into the haunt. Arjun merely watched, even bowing his head politely at some of the gunmen as they passed, after which he sat at the piano bench near the entrance and started playing Melchiresa's favourite song.

Melchiresa had hidden Richard, May, and Partha in the kitchen pantry, so when he heard footsteps approaching he took a step out into the hall and was immediately staring down the barrel of four guns. Unimpressed and unafraid of death, his hands remained by his side and his expression retained its usual frown as he used his Etren power to induce a great fear in the four men before him. It began as the rattling of their guns, then evolved into some panicked commands, and finally, Melchiresa said simply, "Drop them." His voice was staccato with an accent something like Italian but not entirely. His words were obeyed instantly.

A grin flashed as he heard the satisfying sound of Beethoven's *Moonlight Sonata* in the adjacent chamber, still in its first movement. He stepped over the cowering men and into the main area, his head on a lazy swivel in search of Giovanni and Viktor.

The doctor had managed to find a sword in Partha's room while Arjun was stalling, and after some confusion between the two of them, paid "three plastic cards" for it. His antiquated expertise was with polearms and longswords, but Partha's scimitar would pass muster, even if it was, "not that sharp, mate. Only really for roleplaying or acting."

Dale was the first to cross paths with Giovanni, still in Partha's room. He physically started when he saw the Italian's lack of irises and felt another knot in his gut at such an uncanny sight. After swallowing his fear, he said, "Where's Nima?"

"Uhhhh," was Giovanni's eloquent reply.

"What about Roach?"

"Roach isn't here."

Dale's teeth ground down into each other. "Where is he?"

"Korea."

Too enraged to entertain the foolishness any longer, and especially irate at the slightly out-of-tune piano music, Dale lifted up his rifle and sprayed an arc across Giovanni's chest, yelling out a scream in perfect time with the beginning of the third movement of the sonata.

Gunfire was indication enough for Dale's men to start shooting. The four under Melchiresa's spell were still cowering, but the others aimed for Arjun, who continued playing as if he wasn't being shot. One of them accidentally shot another mercenary in the commotion.

Dale began to rush around and slam open doors in search of Partha, and when Viktor finally showed his face, leaving Francis' room, the bottle of vodka in his hand was promptly shattered by a gunshot.

Bleeding from his bad leg and waist, their piano accompaniment remained, with only the odd wrong note every other measure. Dale figured the ginger one must have been deaf or dumb to have walked into the main room without a weapon and an apparent interest in getting drunk, and Partha was nowhere Dale had checked. Just as he had this thought, however, the kid-killer himself came screaming out of the kitchen with a butcher knife and stabbed one of the men cowering on the floor to death. Dale's men knew better than to kill him, but the three who could see him and weren't piles of dread on the floor were trying to disarm him, scare him, or otherwise stop him.

Partha was unrelenting in his murderous rage, and just as he was about to move to the next cowering mercenary, Aphid, Roach's xoloitzcuintli, bursted himself out of the bathroom and jumped over the cowering men as if they were obstacles in a race course. He ran for the first armed man he saw and jumped up to latch his sharp teeth around his forearm. As he ripped and tore at the skin, panic visible in his dark brown eyes, one of Dale's men in witness of such a thing shot the dog in the head then twice in the chest to save his friend.

Dale recognised this dog, and without hesitation, he shot his own man in the calf, kicked his back so he was laying facedown on the rug beside the bloody chunks of dog meat, and scolded loudly: "We ain't cops, Lucas! We don't kill dogs!" He slammed the butt of his rifle into the man's head and heaved a black breath of rage. Roach was not the kind of guy to cross, and Dale was determined to not be on his shit list for this, already formulating plans to somehow make it up to him. Everything had unfolded in a matter of seconds after the first shots had been fired. The third movement had hardly even started by the time Dale shot twice into the ceiling, his foot still on Lucas' back to keep him from trying to escape. "Shut up that gat damn music!"

Arjun frowned, but he stopped, and the newfound silence was deafening. For a precious few moments, all of the fighting had stopped, and all attention was on Dale.

"Now," he said with an irritated huff, "Hand over the kid, an' no one else has ta die." He glared at Partha, who glared promptly back.

Richard entered the room behind his son, his hands entirely in the air before he even stepped out into the open. "I'm unarmed. I'm unarmed." He gave a quick spin to show he wasn't hiding any guns on his back then turned to face Dale. "I don't know what's going on, but if you want my son, you're going to have to get through me." He stepped over the body Partha had mutilated, trying not to notice, and stood proudly between his son and the mercenaries.

"Well hoowee! Ain't we lucky, boys?" He chuckled and leaned his rifle on his shoulders. "Two fer the price 'a one." Fear was visible on Richard's face, but he did not waver from his place. With Dale's mouth open and ready to speak, he was stopped by four sudden sounds in tandem:

The loudest of these sounds was the muffled screams of the three mercenaries behind Dale.

One sound was the soft squishing sound of a scimitar being stabbed through a man's lower back and out through his abdomen.

Another was the sound of a kitchen knife sliding quietly over a man's jugular vein.

And the final sound—. The man in the middle of these two murdered mercenaries was not accompanied by his murderer like the other two. He was alone, standing idly behind the couch and watching the exchange between Dale and Richard when, in tandem with the other killings, *all* of his skin cells became blood cells in an instant. He survived some fifteen seconds as a waterfall of blood and exposed musculature collapsed on the dusty hardwood, screaming in agonised pain.

Dale was horrified at such a sight, and his body reacted before his mind could even process it. While his men were still falling dead to the floor, he sprayed a clip across the entire space behind him. In it, he shot Giovanni in the chest (again), who had murdered one of the men with his scimitar. He shot Melchiresa in the stomach and waist. He shot Arjun in his right hand as he seemed to want to start back up with the inappropriately-timed music. And the one who slit open his best man's jugular, May, was shot in the heart. He screamed as he sprayed, after which he pointed at the three men still cowering on the floor. "Get up off the fuckin' ground 'fore I kill y'all, too! Get the kid and his pa. We's leavin'!" He looked to Viktor, the only enemy still standing, as if to ask for approval.

"Take them," said Viktor, "Two less burdens for me." Dale nodded and watched as Melchiresa's spell visibly waned from his remaining men. They handcuffed Partha and Richard and shoved them both out of the haunt.

Richard was cooperative, but Partha fought against their grips and resisted as best he could. He yelled and flailed around, and as he was shoved past Viktor he spat in his face. "Fuck you! Fuck you! THYNE! THYNE HELP US!"

Viktor smirked but returned to a more neutral expression when he looked back at Dale and said, "You owe me a vodka."

Chapter 53
The Battle of Wits

While in Mr. Moon's home, Roach and Thyne found themselves alone together on the balcony looking out at the sunset and smoking. Since Perlie's pregnancy, their smoking breaks had been made more romantic, and this one was no different. Thyne scooted himself up next to Roach so they were touching as they both leaned forward on the jade green wooden railing. They exchanged a charged look, after which Thyne stole a quick kiss, successfully bringing a blush to the taller man's cheeks that he could not hide. He smiled softly. "Never thought I'd be so smitten with a no-good lib," he teased.

Thyne rolled his eyes and bumped into him with his hip. "Wanker." A beat. "Can I ask you something?"

"Sure."

"Why did you freeze up and break Party's arm in Hermo… Herma… Herno…" Roach let him suffer with the word as he took a drag and admired the posture he had adopted while he struggled to recall the proper pronunciation: his brow furrowed adorably as he tapped on his pokeable nose repetitively.

"Well, I don't think I'm drunk enough for that story, sparkplug."

He frowned and averted his gaze. There was a burning desire to push the issue, but he sighed and smoked instead. "Okay…. You don't have to tell me." The words strangled him.

Roach turned Thyne's face toward his and offered a slight but wicked grin. "Did I say I wouldn't tell you?" Thyne only blinked and blushed. "Get me a drink."

After a moment of processing the demand, Thyne nodded, muttered, "Yes, sir," and gave Roach his cigarette so he could slip inside. He returned three minutes later with a bottle of soju and two glasses. They drank together for the remainder of the sunset and on into the night. With two more smokes into the pack of artisan Cuban cigarettes Partha had brought Thyne in November, they were sufficiently buzzed.

"Alright," said Roach. He leaned forward from his chair and snuffed out his cigarette in an ashtray Perlie had blown for Jae almost a decade prior when the older man still smoked. "You ready, sparkplug?"

He blushed and nodded, pushing some of his pink hair behind his ear. "Can I come sit with you?"

"Wouldn't have it any other way." With Thyne sitting on his lap and curled up in his arms, he took a sip of his drink and began his story: "Not sure how much you've kept up with American politics, but you probably heard about the issues with China." Thyne arched his brow, so Roach explained, "Oh? Well, that's okay. I'll give you the short and skinny of it. It was kind of an open secret in the states, but, at least according to Perlie, it wasn't so well-known outside of it that the government was rolling back increasingly more... uh... protections— agreements. You know how it is: enough companies get tired of environmental laws, they bribe the suits to look the other way when they're clogging the sky and sea and whatever else with pollution. A lot of the international agreements required them to build more government housing and public transit, so they did, but—." He sipped his drink. "I saw one of the buildings they built in Compton before all the flooding got really bad. I mean I saw it after the flooding, but they built it before... anyway....

"Long story short about the housing: there weren't any windows in like 90% of the units, and they were hardly bigger than a closet. Not to mention the rent was still insane, and you had to qualify and yada yada. You know how it goes. So anyway, the Eurasian Union caught wind of all this but didn't really do anything until China joined. When China joined they told the Americans to stop being so fucking evil. Told 'em they'd forgive all of their debt, if they pinky promised to stop with the no-windows and prison-slaves and all that shit. Not like China's much better, of course, but anyway, the Americans being as they are kept fucking doing it but *said* they'd stop." He scoffed. "Well, so the EAU found out like basically immediately. Like two years in, and that's why China stopped trading with us.

"So after China cut us off and the dollar crashed and everything went to shit financially...," he quaffed his soju to stall from having to continue. After clearing his throat: "We fell on hard times. Everyone did. And so funding got cut to basically everything, at least everything social: infrastructure, public transit, drug safety, food safety, regulations on businesses, and," he paused to look at Thyne and emphasise, "public schooling."

"I had heard that America cut back on school spending."

Roach shook his head. "No, sparkplug: they cut it entirely. No more public schools at all." Thyne gasped. "It was nationwide. There were riots, of course. Wish I was old enough to have gone to one." He chuckled and poured himself more soju telekinetically so as to not stop holding Thyne. After topping off both glasses and taking a sip: "We were really young. This was around the time Mom was leaving with four of my siblings, so Dad was depressed as shit. He got into gambling, and he got addicted. Even without the financial straits everyone else was facing, we would have been all up and down all the time. Sometimes he'd bring us all gifts then the next week he'd have to take them back to pawn. Sometimes we had food, sometimes we didn't. Sometimes he'd come home happy and drunk, and sometimes he'd come home pissed and go on a cleaning-frenzy… or worse…. It was constant. And so when I got older, and it became clear to me that this money shit was always going to be an issue for us… I convinced my brothers and sister to come with me to work in a butchery."

He drank away his feelings as they tried to surface, and Thyne hugged him tight. "How old were you?"

"Eight."

He held him even tighter.

"It wouldn't have been so bad if not for… for Gideon, my big brother… getting his arm cut off in one of the machines. He said it wasn't my fault, and he's said it again as an adult, but it doesn't stop me from blaming myself for it every God damn day. Anyway, if I had to guess, I broke Partha's arm because he came up to me unexpectedly when I was entirely lost in the memory, and I always wanted to just fucking strangle those motherfucking—." A sigh. "There were two overseers at the butchery, and they literally whipped us when we didn't clean the machines to their liking. Always cleaning. Cleaning. Cleaning! Always cleaning is the fucking issue. Why can't people just let things be messy?" He finished his glass in one go and slammed it down on the arm of his chair. "Anyway… our dad made us stop when Gideon literally lost his fucking arm. Obviously. So it was only a couple months that we were working. Job was mostly just cleaning the blades because we could get into the little crevices."

Thyne kissed his cheek repetitively and held him tight, trying to squeeze the love he had for Roach into his heavy black heart, to lighten it at least slightly. "You poor bastard," he whispered.

They may have spoken more, but their chat was interrupted when Perlie opened the door and leaned outside to beam adorably and say, "Come inside! Appa wants to play."

"Play what?" asked Thyne.

"Cards!" she cheered and disappeared back inside.

"If we're playing cards, your brother is going to play, no doubt."

"Oh, for sure, dude."

He huffed. "I don't want to play with him again."

Roach smiled evilly. "Oh? You scared?"

"NO!" He pouted.

"Ya Allah, you're so fucking cute."

"I'm not scared. He's a bellend, is all."

"Mmhmm. Well, have fun out here all alone then, I guess." He stood and placed Thyne in the chair.

"Wait!" He stood. "Roach, if we play... can you... can you promise to be on my side?"

"On your side?"

"You know what I'm saying, you twat!"

He grinned. "Oh, sure. I'll promise." The hand he wasn't using to hold his glass was pressed firmly against his chest. "Hand on heart."

"You're a wanker. You know that trick doesn't work on me."

Roach only laughed, grabbed the half-full bottle of soju, and went inside.

Being unfamiliar with the layout of the house, Thyne's attempts to sneak through it to hide in the rental car were thwarted when River spotted him looking lost in a hallway. "Hey, dude. It's this way. Come on." Thyne sputtered incoherently. "I'll go easy on you," he said with a mocking tone as he slipped his fingers through Thyne's to lead him through the house.

The blush on the Brit's freckled cheeks deepened increasingly as they neared a recreational room wherein boisterous conversations could be heard. He wanted to wriggle free and run, but River kept looking back at him and giving him a sensual gaze with a sinister but alluring grin underneath. The hazel-grey of his eyes was like the darkest of storm clouds harkening the gentlest of downpours. His long dark hair was voluminous and twirled around him in his glances backwards as he led Thyne through the labyrinthian halls. Halls that had faded from Thyne's perception, replaced by the tall dark River. His hand was soft, much moreso than Roach's, and he was humming *We're Off to See the Wizard* as he pulled Thyne along. It all worked in tandem to enchant Thyne. He would later come to think of it as outright mind control, despite knowing the twins had no such ability.

When they reached the rec room, Thyne was beet-red, especially as River announced their presence. He floated away from Thyne, pulling up his long locks into a ponytail as he approached the table where most of the others were already sitting.

"Good, you found him!" said Jae as he slid up to Thyne's side and ushered him further into the room. "Your friends were telling me that you're a street magician.

My ex-wife was a magician, too! She still couldn't beat Karson in *Hold 'Em*, but maybe you can."

He forced a nervous smile, but before he could protest, Roach stole him and sat him between himself and Francis. Across from them, River was chatting with Jean-Jacques and inviting Jae to sit beside him, but he made certain to eye Thyne. The charm in his gaze that had puppetted Thyne through the house was all but gone, replaced with a lust for metaphorical blood. The Brit gulped. Roach pushed a glass of soju in front of him as he leaned in to whisper sensually, "He doesn't know he has a tell."

Thyne's gaze snapped to Roach's. "What is it?"

With a mocking grin he leaned back, sipped his soju, and taunted, "Who knows?"

His nose was scrunched up and the redness in his face flared up again. He whisper-shouted at Roach, "You do, you wanker! Tell me what it is!"

"So what game are we playing first?" said Roach to the entire room. His voice was deep and commanding, so it brought all of the attention his way.

The others discussed the games ahead, and while they did, Francis leaned in and whispered to Thyne, "What ails thee, dearest?"

"The bloody twins! They're insufferable. Not even mentioning that Party ruined everything. We have mercenaries after us! Why are we playing games and getting drunk? We need to—."

He pet Thyne's thigh lovingly. "'Tis a time for gaiety. We mustn't fret for the future. At the very least not for this evening. So says Clayton." He gestured to Thyne's glass. "Drink and make merry!"

He huffed and pouted. "There's nothing merry about playing poker with River."

Despite Thyne's whinging, the games began with a light and casual air to them. They played *Gin Rummy* first, as requested by an ever-drunker Roach. After his first loss four rounds in, Jae suggested *Badugi*. Thyne was increasingly drunk and lost every round, but he was paying special attention to River all the while. He couldn't be certain, but he thought maybe he had figured out his tell. Despite the lack of confidence, he still loudly suggested, "Time for River's favourite."

River chuckled darkly. "Are you certain, sweetums?"

"Don't patronise me, twat. I want to play *Hold 'Em*. Deal." He slammed back his glass only to find it was empty. With a quick scan of the table, he saw Roach had the bottle and snatched it from in front of him to drink straight from the top. "Why's everyone staring at me!? Deal the bloody cards, mate!"

River started shuffling and dealing, during which Roach leaned in to whisper so that only Thyne could hear, "As attractive as it is to drink straight from the bottle like that, sparkplug, I think I need to cut you off."

He tried to take the bottle but Thyne snatched it away and whisper-shouted at him while the others chatted amongst themselves, "Piss off. I'm English. I can drink all of you under the table."

Roach snickered and retreated. "Suit yourself, dude. Gonna be a killer hangover."

They were dealt their cards. Thyne looked at his several times as the booze kept erasing the hand from his memory, but he was also spending a lot of mental energy watching River. He made no effort to hide his staring, but River didn't seem to mind. The haughty twin continued as ever: betting in chaotic amounts, showing no change in his amused and mocking energy regardless of his cards, and folding with winning hands just to throw the others off his scent. Thyne's assumption that he only sipped from his glass when he had a bad hand proved wrong three rounds into *Hold 'Em*. When he realised this, he dropped his head onto the table, and because of his defeated posture, it was decided that a break would be a good idea.

While the others filed out of the room to go use the restroom, get snacks, and refill drinks, Francis and Roach stayed with Thyne, both of them petting his arched back. "It is but trifles, my dear. He cannot win over you for aye. Even my own hubris in betting games was torn asunder, despite not losing that final fateful hand aboard my ship."

Thyne only groaned, so Roach tried, "Come on. Let's go have a smoke."

The Brit grabbed for his bottle without lifting his head, and after a few misses he had it in his hand. Dragging himself out of the room behind his friend, he stumbled twice, both times being caught in Roach's strong arms.

"Drink us under the table, huh?" said Roach as they neared the door to the balcony.

"What are you doing? You're taking him outside?" asked Jae from the kitchen.

"Yeah, man. Cigarette break."

Jae was going to worry that Thyne might drunkenly fall over the railing, but when Roach mentioned cigarettes his mind was replaced with nagging thoughts he voiced: "Those things will kill you, Clayton!"

"Nah, dude. The feds will kill me," he replied and finished escorting his drunken friend outside. He lit his cigarette with a flourish and shoved one into Thyne's mouth before he could blubber on about whatever had his brow so furrowed and cheeks all pink. The Brit started and watched as Roach lit Thyne's fag with a cigarette kiss. "How's that, hm? Feel better? Gonna give me the bottle now? I want some, too, y'know. I'm hardly even drunk anymore."

Thyne took a drag and looked down at the bottle. It was a lot more empty than he recalled. Had he really had that much? Surely Roach and Francis were drinking, too, right? Maybe he would have surrendered it, but then he heard, "Have you figured out Sonny's tell yet?"

With his brow furrowed and cheeks pink again: "No! No thanks to you!"

He smiled. "You're so fucking cute. Alright, fine. I won't tell you what it is, but I will play 'on your side' like you asked. Okay?"

"How?"

He shrugged. "I figure Sonny can't read me at all if I just don't look at my cards, y'know? That's the best I've got, unless you've got a better idea."

"You would—. Uh. You would allow fate to—. To erm…." He hicced and tried to focus his whirling vision on the cigarette in his hand.

"Yeah, man. Whatever happens happens. Now, give me the bottle." Thyne snatched it away when Roach tried to take it, so he clarified, "I'll give it back, dude, I just want a sip."

When they were finished with their break and back at the table, Thyne held his head to try to stop the world from spinning. He watched his cards fly neatly in front of him and took a moment to gather himself before looking at them.

"You're not going to look at your cards, Tony?"

Thyne looked up at Roach who was leaning back in his chair with his boots on the table and hands behind his head. "Nope."

"Well there's no fucking fun in that, but fine," grumbled River.

"Ha! Still fun for me, dude."

Thyne's harsh gaze on River strengthened. It was unlike him to show any amount of upset during these games, so Roach's strategy must have really bothered him. He watched River so scrutinously that, even though he lost yet another game, ironically to Roach's hand, he was beaming by the end of it.

Between games, River was visibly angry that he had to fold early to not risk his title with Roach's unknown hand on the table, and Thyne's smile only made him angrier. "What's got you so fucking happy, then?"

If he were sober he would not have made the mistake of telling him, but he was past the point of blackout and slurred immediately, "I know your tell."

His mocking and amused energy returned. With a dark chuckle: "Don't be silly, Thyne. I don't have a tell."

Thyne chortled just as haughtily and gestured toward the table. "Deal the cards."

The tell Thyne had figured was a gamble in itself. It required River to pick up his cards entirely from the table, but he was relaxed enough the last three rounds to have leaned back in his chair and picked them up telekinetically. If he instead only peeled them up to look at them like Thyne tended to do, then the tell was nonexistent. When he had a good hand and had lifted the cards off of the table, he would place the card on his left on top of the other when he set them back down on the table, but a bad hand would have the right card on top.

Fortunately for Thyne, River lifted the cards from the table. He would never admit it, but Thyne's drunken confidence was perturbing. He was certain he had no tell, but the way the Brit was smiling brought a knot to his gut. *'Do I have a tell?'*

he worried as he looked at his cards. The two of diamonds and the five of clubs. Trash. He unknowingly signalled this to Thyne as he set them down and threw in his bet. *'But I'll make him fold.'* The entire group had agreed on maximum and minimum bets earlier in the evening, so River tossed in the maximum bet for an opening round. It was the most he had bet at once all night, which was enough of an oddity for Jean-Jacques to fold. Roach, Perlie, Jae, and Francis called, then it was Thyne's turn to bet.

He would fold, that much was certain to River. But… despite his terrible hand and the consistency with which he would fold when given nothing at the start, especially when faced with such a high wager, Thyne threw in his chips and swigged from the soju bottle. River's stomach sank as he watched the chips tumble across the table toward him. His face was pale and heart racing. *'DO I have a tell!?'* He stared down at the chips with visible fear on his face, but his mind was reeling through his perfect memories. Thyne was more of a challenge than he had initially given him credit for. If he wasn't piss-drunk River might have lost his title by then.

He recalled in perfect clarity their other game together and paid special attention to his own movements, expressions, comments, and emotions. Likewise, he recalled the other games that same night, and after forty-two seconds of silence, he had figured out the tell Thyne had noticed.

Roach still wasn't looking at his cards, and Thyne was perturbing him, but River tried not to worry about it as he dealt the first card of the flop: the five of spades. *'Oh? Lucky day.'* He wiped all the emotion from his face, though there remained sick pleasure in the pit of his eyes when he gave them to Thyne. He shouldn't have mentioned the tell, because now he had nothing over River. Only risky drunken plays. And, dear Lord! It was so beautiful the way he was making him squirm. He had known him long enough to know that drinking as heavily as he had been was entirely out of the ordinary, and there was a swelling pride within him for having tormented him enough to drive him to such a thing. His cards were garbage, that much River knew for certain. He was as easy to read as anyone else at the table, especially piss drunk. It was the subtlest of facial tics that told entire epics, and the glimmer of fear in his golden eyes. Thyne would fold, as he always did when he was given nothing. Maybe River wouldn't win, but Thyne would lose, and that was all he truly needed to feel satisfied with the games that night. At least… he would lose if Roach would look at his stupid fucking cards. "Tony, are you honestly not going to play?"

"I'm playing, dude. I called the first round. Deal the rest of the flop, bro."

"You're not looking at your cards!" He huffed.

Roach grinned and shrugged. "So?"

"So you're not playing!" He swapped to Arabic and said something that only

Roach could understand. With the simple response of "Sure," from his twin, River took out his phone and typed madly on it.

Thyne felt a buzzing on his thigh and looked at his phone. It took four reads to finally understand the message, during which River dealt the next two cards of the flop: the three and five of hearts. *'Another five! I'll make that little twink cry with luck like this.'* Said twink's gaze snapped up to River from his phone, a deep crimson all over him. "Okay," he said in response to the message before peeling up Roach's cards to look at them. Roach was still leaning back and watched wordlessly, making no effort to stop him. "Do I tell you?" Thyne slurred as he leaned back in his seat.

River chuckled darkly. "You already have. He has nothing." Thyne nodded as River continued, "Thank you, sweetums. We'll discuss what I sent when you're not so slobbering drunk."

"You're not backing out are you?" said the Brit with his brow furrowing angrily.

"No, of course not. It just won't be tonight on account of the state of you." He gestured to the table. "It's your call." He watched with a mocking grin as Thyne looked at his cards for the sixth time.

'Three of clubs and ten of hearts,' he read again before spying the new cards. *'Two pair's not bad.'* He threw in the maximum bet for that round, which prompted Francis to fold. Roach should have folded as well, but he remained in his relaxed posture and threw in his chips telekinetically to call.

Five seconds of quick maths and counting cards later, River leaned back to offer a confident smile to the boastful Brit across from him. "Call." His chips were tossed carelessly into the middle of the table as he scooped up his cards and held one in each hand, his grey eyes hardened on Thyne like a predator. He opened both of his palms and floated the cards over them telekinetically. He moved them back and forth, swapping their positions on repeat as he leaned back in his seat, crossed his arms, and mouthed to the horrified Englishman, "You're fucked."

Thyne was perceptive enough to know that River had figured out his own tell. He cursed himself internally for having mentioned it in the first place. Stupid booze made him talk too much. The soju, however, was still the first thing he reached for when he saw that sadistic bloody smirk. *'The cunt. He thinks he can intimidate me into folding with a pair of fives on the board.'* River had figured out his tell and was avoiding touching his cards therefore, but he had already shown it this round. He had nothing, and assuming he still had nothing was what had Thyne throw in another maximum bet when the turn was dealt: the five of diamonds. This third five gave him a full-house: a damn good hand, especially knowing that River, surely, still had nothing.

Jae and Perlie could assume from his drunken tells that Thyne almost definitely had a full house or four of a kind. The soju was doing him no favours in hiding his true elation at the turn of luck for him. After Roach stupidly called again, it fell on River to fold or call. The river was the next round, and he hesitated to throw in his bet. Thyne was too drunk to deduce the true reason as to his slowness. He read it as genuine upset and teased, "If you fold now and lose with dignity, we won't tell anyone."

River giggled at the notion. The sound sent chills down Thyne's spine, but it wasn't until River set down his cards from their place floating in front of him that the gravity of the situation started to sink in. He used his telekinesis to make a show of it, and he made special effort to show that he was putting the card from his left on top, even spinning it magically and showing its face (the two of diamonds) before it nestled gently face-down on top of his win-condition. He had pointed his right hand to move them magically, leaning on his left arm, and once the cards were settled, he pushed his left forearm forward, shoving all of his chips into the pot.

Thyne swallowed a gulp of nervousness at the sight. Surely he hadn't been outplayed again. And if he had… it was the alcohol to blame. The only way River could win now was if he had the last five in his hand. What were the odds of that?

River gestured toward him. "A full house, is it, then?"

Thyne's cards slipped out of his hands and fell haphazardly onto the table. His face went white. "Fuck," he muttered.

River smiled and nodded. "Indeed." And with River's five of clubs revealed, Thyne rested his forehead on the table to hide the drunken sobbing that would follow such a humiliating defeat. The river was never even dealt. There was no single card in the deck that could give Thyne a winning hand when River had all four fives to his name.

He drank even more as the room cleared out. Francis and Roach stayed with him until two in the morning, consoling him. Their concerns, when voiced, were met with enraged wailing. At one point, when Roach took Francis' flask from him, Thyne went so far as to slur out, "I bloody hate you."

After escorting Thyne to a guest room, a teary-eyed Roach worried to Francis about the comment. The pirate responded, "Fear not, my dear. He has thrown that very same barb at me numerously. He is only sore for having lost at cards."

"He says it all the time to you? Doesn't it hurt?"

"Aye, but he be me dearest friend. I know he doesn't truly loathe me."

"Are you… are you sure he doesn't mean it?" He nodded and beamed. "Because… well, I'm utterly in love with him. I can handle it if he doesn't feel the same, but," he paused, "I don't think I can handle him hating me."

Francis kissed Roach tenderly and cupped a hand around his cheek to rub away his tears with his calloused thumb. "He does not hate you. I swear it."

They went to the twins' room together. Francis and River both held Roach as he tried not to cry. Something was weighing on him spiritually. He assumed it was because Thyne truly did hate him… he never could have guessed what the feeling of loss in his soul actually was.

Thyne was asleep almost as soon as he laid down, and when Partha's voice was sounding in his head in need of help, it became no more than a vague flash of upset in his dreams.

Chapter 54
Are We Enemies?

"I wanna be the one t'tell ye 'bout this, butchye gotta promise not t'kill me."

"What is it?"

A long pause.

"Yer dog's dead."

"You killed my fucking dog and expect me not to—!?"

"No no no. It weren't me. It were one 'a these good fer nothin' yankee fucks. Soon as he done it, I shot his calf out, an' now Ah got 'em all nice an' tied up fer ye to do whatchye want with 'em."

Roach's breaths heaved his large shoulders. He had left the crowded living room to answer the phone, but his upset was visible in his posture as he leaned over the balcony and wiped his teary face. After a moment of quiet nigh-hysteria, he pulled the phone back up to his ear and said, "Why were you with my dogs, Dale?"

"Ah was tryin' ta find ye t'talk 'bout that kid-killer what ye like. Yer cripple fren said ye were down there but 'pparently ye're in Korea."

"Was it Aphid?" His voice was strangled.

"Yeah, Aphid, that's his name. The one ain't got no fur? Yeh. We went to yer place in the palace. What're ye doin' with these folk, Roach?"

"*Why* were you with my *dogs, Dale?*" His voice was rising in volume, and the shattering of his heart was sensed by the entire drowsy morning crowd in the living room behind him.

"Why're *you* in bed wit kid-killers? We had a deal."

"And I haven't fucking broken our deal! You were shown a deep fake, Dale. I saw it. Why'd you kill my—," his voice broke off into silent sobbing.

"Sure Ah was." A scoff. "Anyway, it don' matter. Ah done got the lil fucker and his dad already. An' ye should know: yer other frens is dead. Ah shot 'em all while they was killin' my men. 'Cept the orange-haired one. He weren't no trouble."

He hung up the phone, wiped the tears from his face, and coughed to force away his emotions. With his weepiness sufficiently veiled, he rushed inside to shake Thyne from his drunken slumber with a good amount of force. The first thing Thyne saw when he opened his bleary eyes was the panic in Roach's. "What's going on?" he muttered as he sat up and held his aching head and stomach. "What happened last night?"

"How many of the people in France can you hear right now?"

He rubbed his eyes and looked at the time on his phone. "It's one in the morning in Versailles, Roach. What's going on?"

"How many!?"

He started. The sense of urgency in Roach's tone and the fear in his eyes was gut-wrenching. He listened for a while, hearing none of those they left in Europe. "They're probably asleep, mate. Don't worry so much."

"They're dead!" He lamented.

Thyne arched his brow and, after watching Roach break down for just a moment, he took up his phone and called Giovanni. Arjun answered. His tone was groggy, and there was an ambient background noise indicating that he was on a train. "Thyne? Are you all okay over there?"

"Yes, of course we are. Are you?"

He looked down at his mangled hand and chuckled. "Been better. You didn't send Francis to help us, so we figured it was a coordinated attack."

"Wait," he held his aching head, "What are you on about?"

He chuckled again. "You didn't hear? The base was attacked. One of the dogs is dead. May's dead. Melchiresa almost died, but Viktor and Keeva were able to save him." Roach was watching Thyne expectantly, so he was first to witness the horror as it crossed his face. "I lost three fingers. They took Partha and Richard," Arjun continued, "We're headed to Francis' apartment in Marseilles to hide. I already texted him about it. I guess he didn't tell you."

Thyne looked through the cracked door into the living room at all the gang members, including Francis, chatting over their breakfast with the occasional concerned look his way. "I'll call you back," he said as he pulled the phone away and stared down at it. He had ended the call but made no further movement or sound while he was rapt in thought. '*Good going, wanker,*' he scolded himself internally, '*Your bloody ego got May killed. This was one of the only ways to justify these bloody microphones, and your idiot arse was too bleeding drunk to save her.*'

"Thyne?" cooed Roach as he crouched down beside the bed and picked up his face by its chin. His amber eyes were as dry as a desert. They pierced through Roach, who immediately recognised the expression and seemed to read his mind when he said, "It's not your fault."

He glared, his cheeks immediately blood red and his nose scrunched up. "Don't bloody lie to me. Get out of my sight."

Rather than leave he closed the door to give them more privacy and muttered, "No, Thyne. It's not your fault, and I won't let you sit here and blame yourself." He turned to face him and gestured toward the phone. "Who was that?"

After a while of intense glaring, Thyne averted his eyes. "Arjun."

"He's okay?"

"No."

"Dale said only Viktor made it…"

Thyne stood, ignoring the sickness in his gut, and took a step toward Roach to point up into his face, "Who the bloody Hell is Dale?"

"He's my friend…. Sort of…. I thought…. Listen, if I could just talk to him face-to-face, I'm sure he'd come to his senses about all this."

Thyne slammed his phone on the ground and shouted, "That's not good enough! May is dead!"

Jean-Jacques was one of the sleepy few in the living area adjacent to Thyne's room, and when he heard this, the small grin on his lips was vanquished. He went to Thyne's door, opening it as soon as he could. All eyes were on him, and a spine-tingling silence hung in the air for an agonising thirty-three seconds as he stared deep into Thyne's soul. "My sister is dead?" Another tense few seconds of quiet, and Thyne was finally able to nod.

With the confirmation, Jean-Jacques, having an almost unfazed and casual air about him, plucked up his jacket from the coat rack in the foyer and, without even looking back at the others, walked outside, closing the door gently behind him.

There was a moment of quiet as everyone tried to process what was happening. Roach gestured with his head for River to come to him, and once he was in Thyne's room, he closed the door to give them privacy again. River rushed up to Thyne and caressed his face with the back of his hand lovingly. "Thyne, it's not your fault."

He shoved his hand away. "Leave me alone."

"No. Come here." He stood upright and pulled Thyne into a warm embrace telekinetically. When Roach saw them hugging, he joined from the other side, sandwiching Thyne between them and drawing remorseful tears from him.

"I'm sorry," he whimpered, "I'm so sorry." The warmth and safety he felt in their shared embrace helped, but after two minutes, it suddenly worsened his feelings of guilt. He pushed them both away from him and climbed back into bed to hide beneath its covers. He could feel them encroaching and stopped them with a whimper from beneath the blankets, sounding almost like a weepy child: "I want my Frankenstein."

Roach's voice was strangled as he barely managed to say, "We'll go get him for you, sparkplug." The two of them were shortly thereafter gone and in their stead was Francis. Thyne could smell his boozy salty aura before he could hear him close the door, but as soon as he heard the click, he peered out from under the blankets at his dearest friend in all the world.

Francis was leaning his head on the door.

"Frankenstein?"

There were a million things Francis wanted to say, most of them disparaging and angry with Thyne for letting this happen, but he kept his mouth shut and his head on the door.

"Franny, please come hold me. I need you."

"I know," he snapped, "Give me a minute, god damn you."

Thyne started. He wanted to scold him for not sorting out his feelings while time was stopped to be more immediately present, but he knew better than to cross such a line and, like Francis, kept his mouth shut. Three minutes later, Francis finally turned away from the door and approached the bed.

Almost as soon as Thyne was in Francis' arms, all the anger they had for each other evaporated, replaced with warmth, forgiveness, and love. Francis even kissed the top of Thyne's head. He nestled his face into Francis' chest and listened to his heartbeat for a moment before breathing an inaudible declaration of love into the air around them.

Upon the utterance, Francis was wrenched from the present and cast back into the abyss. Libidinously, he pulled Thyne away to get a better look at him before kissing him deeply. Thyne started and pushed him away. "No, Franky. I'm not okay, can't you see? I got May killed."

The rejection grounded him as quickly as he had been taken from reality. "Of course," he whispered, "I beg your pardon."

"Don't look so heartbroken. I love you. I always love you. I just can't snog while I can hardly even bear myself."

"I apologise."

"Franky," he whimpered. His face contorted into the beginnings of an ugly cry, and rather than trying to manage another word, he threw himself back into Francis' arms and wept fervently.

With a looser grip on reality than before, Francis pet Thyne and shushed him lovingly, but he wasn't entirely certain what had happened that had him so upset.

Was this still about the poker game? Had he actually said something about May dying, or did Francis imagine that? Was May even real at all? He couldn't image her no matter how hard he tried. For a brief moment, he even wondered if May was the name of a woman he and Thyne had known in the war, back in the 1940s, but he couldn't recall her either.

While Thyne was weeping into Francis' blouse, Roach and River had driven out toward the city. They had their eyes scanning for Jean-Jacques, but after five minutes of aimless driving, Roach broke down. River pulled the car off into a gas station parking lot and flipped a switch to darken the tint on the windows, thus giving them more privacy. Roach was wailing into his trembling hands and whimpering incoherently. His nails clawed into his forehead in bursts of madness, and his cries were sometimes broken by mad laughter or ireful shouts.

"Tony...." He pushed back Roach's seat and crawled across the middle console to act as an oversized plush for his brother to hold. Curled up in his arms, he cried for his lost pet with Roach for ten minutes, but after that, the well of his emotions had all but dried up. He loved his animals dearly, but he couldn't cry anymore for Aphid. He couldn't cry at all.

Roach needed to mourn, and he didn't want anyone else to know how weak he had been made by this unexpected death. Yes, it was natural to grieve. Yes, for a monster like Roach, it was comforting to know that Dale had Aphid's killer gagged and bound and ready to be flayed alive. Yes, he was willing to acknowledge openly that he was saddened by the passing, but it was plainly insane the way it had reduced him to nothingness. He had managed to stand upright for as long as possible. After that, he had managed to look for Jean-Jacques for as long as possible, and now he was finally disintegrating. He was inconsolable.

The old dog had died alone and scared in a foreign place with his last thoughts of harrowing memories of war and a fear that Roach and River would never return. The other dogs were River's or Jean-Jacques', but there was no doubt in anyone's mind that Aphid was his. He'd never admit it, but back in the war, there were times when Aphid was the only reason he kept going at all. "Dead," he wailed hysterically, "I could have saved him. I would have killed them all. Even Dale."

"Now now, Tony. You don't want to kill Dale. He's our friend."

"He killed him!" He shouted, but he was too much a puddle of despair to be threatening.

"No he didn't. If he did, do you really think I would be opposed to the idea of killing him? Arjun confirmed what happened already. It wasn't Dale. It was one of his men."

"Aren't you sad?" he whimpered almost incomprehensibly.

River was upset, that much was true. One of his dogs had died, and there were few things he cherished more than his dogs. He often pretended to be his brother when it would benefit one or both of them to do so, but he more often wondered what it must have been like to *actually be* Clayton Roach. It was River's belief that his ability to feel things had been somehow mixed up in the womb and given to his brother. What a burden it must have been to feel so incredibly deeply and so incredibly often. How foreign it would be if he were to ever find himself as distraught as Roach was in that moment. This was the saddest River had ever felt since Silvino's passing, and yet, after those few tears had been shed when he first curled up in Roach's strong arms… he was fine.

He wasn't always so numb, though. His feelings had been snuffed out at some point in his late teens or early twenties. A point he couldn't define. As children, there were infrequent crying spells over trivial things. Not wanting to eat his vegetables. Not wanting to fast for Ramadan. Finding his homeschool lessons boring. Getting in trouble with the police for bullying other children at the skatepark. He had cried at least once for each of these. And further still, he had found himself emotional for more serious reasons: When their mother left. When their father was kidnapped. When Gideon lost his arm. When Roach was stabbed.

But as a child, Roach was even more prone to hysterical breakdowns. When Roach didn't want to fast for Ramadan, he was indiscernible from the mess currently in River's arms. They were dubbed "tantrums" but it was never so simple. His feelings were cavernously deep and nigh infinite in number. When presented with the choices between fasting and risking eternal damnation, Roach seemed to actually understand the imbalance of such a thing. There was no truer terror in young Roach than when he was threatened with Jahannam.

It was during one of these fits, after their mother had driven off with four of their siblings, that their father's patience first ran out with Roach. He hit him for the first time when he was just four years old. "Knock it off. You're fine." The pattern started there, but Oba wouldn't become physically violent again until the twins were nine, at which point he knocked Roach to the ground with a backhanded slap because he was crying over his fish dying. A few months later, it was because Roach was upset he had accidentally eaten beef while dumpster diving and feared for his eternal soul.

Watching this, River learned to keep to himself, and Roach learned how to hide his feelings to the point that, when he was stabbed by their father, he showed absolutely no emotion whatsoever. He had watched Oba's pleas for clemency and said coldly, "Stop crying. You're fine." The venom in the way he had said it still gave River chills.

"Yes," he finally replied to Roach, "Of course I'm upset, Tony, but I'm also touched: it's a blessing to see you so vulnerable. You must have half my soul."

He muttered something, but it was incoherent amidst all the tears. He must have said something like "I love you," though, if the strong hug River received in tandem with the jumbled words was any indication.

A burlap bag had been fitted over their heads in the van shortly before it came to a stop. They were shoved out onto a paved road and guided by their upper arms up a few steps and eventually into a seat. Partha's best guess, based on the way the floor seemed somewhat hollow, was that they were either on a plane or a bus. He leaned more toward the former, however, when he heard the word "Hamilton" being thrown around by their captors.

An hour later, the take-off roll was unmistakable: they were on their way to Hamilton on what seemed to be a private jet. Whose jet it was was either never uttered or went unheard by the Nimas from their seats in the rear of the plane, especially considering one of the engines was right beside them.

A few minutes into the cruise, Partha spoke at as low a volume as possible to his father in Papiamentu: "They're taking us to Hamilton for a refuel."

Richard sighed. "Yeah."

Partha bumped his shoulder into his dad's playfully. "Chin up, Daddy. It's providence! They're taking us home and don't even know it. We can slip out of their sight there."

The older man had accepted their fate. He wasn't sure why they had been taken alive, but their chances of surviving the entire ordeal were abysmal. His son's optimism was read as foolishness, and were their heads not covered, Partha would have seen a despondent and disappointed gloom on his father's haggard face. Without the ability to see such a thing, however, it was only perceptible in the dragging drawl of his voice as he replied, "Party, it's okay. At least we're together."

The huge beaming grin behind the burlap on his head could be felt. "Ah! Ye of little faith!" He said in English and at a normal volume as he tried to wiggle out of his binds. *'All those nights tied up by kinky strangers are paying off!'*

When Dale noticed Partha's wriggling, he approached the Nimas and leaned on the seat in front of them. "So what's goin' on back here?" Partha stopped wriggling around despite Dale's tone being friendly. Even if they escaped their binds, the two captives would have nowhere to go on the plane. He was even confident enough to lean over and remove Partha's bag.

The light rushed in like a tsunami. He hissed as his one good eye was made immediately exhausted by the bright interior of the plane and sunset streaming through the windows. After a moment of squeezing his eye shut and blinking away its pained tears, he grimaced at Dale.

"Aw, now. No need ta go lookin' all trifled with. Havin' fun witchyer handcuffs?"

"Fuck you," he spat.

Dale smiled. "Ye wanna know what's gonna happen to ye?" His air was menacing, and he punctuated the veiled threat by biting a cigarette out of his pack and lighting it. Partha's only response was more glaring, so Dale continued as if he had been invited to do so: "Ye're wert 'bout two billies, an' I reckon yer dad's at least anudder couple gran', 'pending on what he knows. 'Course, it don' matter ta me none how much ye says to my clients once I hand ye over, but seein' as how I 'specially don't like kid-killers, I might just keep ye fer m'self." He chuckled darkly and, after a drag, added, "Ye shouldn't'a killed them kids, Nima."

His brow was too furrowed with rage to properly show his confusion at the comment. *Kid-killer?* His gaze briefly trailed around the interior of the plane, landing squarely on the lighter in Dale's hand as he slid it into his pocket. It had an American flag pattern on it. A tattoo could be seen on the side of his partially-shaved head. It was of a geometric sort of lotus flower, which Partha recognised as a common way to cover swastika tattoos. *'Two billion dollars, and I'm being taken alive. Torture? But they know what I saw, so what more–.'* His thoughts stopped cold, and realisation visibly crossed his face. After the brief stint of reeling thoughts, he hardened his gaze on Dale once again and said, "I've only killed three people, and none of them were children." His stomach tied up in knots admitting such a thing with his father sitting right beside him. He could feel the disappointment and fear in the air around him and in the way he shifted and squirmed to try and get the bag off his head. Dale noticed this and, not willing to pass up the opportunity to see a father's reaction to finding out his son is a murderer, he leaned over and took Richard's bag off his head.

Immediately, he locked eyes with Partha. His lip was trembling. "What do you mean you've killed three people, son?"

Partha ignored him. "Sandra Berg, the COO of Eir Lilac: killed via poison. The second was an American soldier at the sweatshop in Durango, and the third was the man I stabbed in front of you."

Dale puffed on his cigarette. "An' how do ye know Roach?"

"Who?"

Partha's acting was good. Enough that Dale fully believed it. His brow was furrowed intently at all the confusing mis-mash of information. He looked at each of the Nimas back and forth before snuffing out his cigarette on the back of the seat he had been leaning on and leaving them. He entered the cockpit and closed its door behind him. "Land."

"What? Why?" asked the pilot.

"Ah gotta make a call."

"I can't land a plane just for you to make a call." He could have allowed him to use a phone or offered one, but he was growing tired with the mercenaries and their unprofessionalism. Putting his foot down on this one issue seemed like a perfectly reasonable concession to make.

"Can ye land if there's a 'mergency?'"

He turned from his instruments and went pale when he saw the barrel of a pistol falling into his sightline. While he was a military pilot, his job was primarily transporting goods and soldiers. He had never seen combat, and his training for hijackings failed to ever mention what to do when the hijacker was both not a pilot himself and also a mercenary with vast authority over him. With a shuddery breath, he turned back toward his instruments and spoke into his radio to request a diversion. When prompted as to why, he declared a fuel shortage as he simultaneously started dumping half his supply.

"Good boy," praised Dale as he holstered his weapon.

As soon as the stairs opened and clicked against the hangar floor, Dale stepped out of the plane and called Roach. He wasn't sure where he was, but he could hear seagulls squawking nearby and even saw a few fly down toward the small airport's taxi lanes. They were seemingly the only travellers there at the moment, and the few people who came out to look at the apparently-faulty plane weren't city folk.

"Hello?" Roach finally answered. It was clear in his tone that he had been crying, but Dale would not dare to comment.

"Do ye know this kid 'r not?"

"Partha?"

"Yeh."

"Yeah, I know him." He sniffled.

"He say he don' know ye. Ye using a different name 'round him?" There was a pause from Roach, and before he could reply Dale added, "I seen him kill them kids, Roach. I seen it with my own two eyes."

"What kids, Dale?"

"Down in Mexico!"

"If he killed any kids in Mexico, Dale, I swear I didn't know anything about it. If you're talking about the video where he just randomly kills them for no fucking reason, they're pretty obviously fake, dude."

He rubbed his aching head. Roach was not the kind to lie to him. They had a very forthright relationship with each other, and he wanted more than anything to believe that Roach had not broken his promise. "Listen. I'll find out where I am, an' ye can come here, an' we can figure out what's goin' on together."

Roach perked up. It was like he was struck with divine inspiration. This was his prayers answered: this was his chance to separate himself from the others to keep them safe from his own monstrous self. After a quick and silent prayer to thank Allah, he said, "I'll go with you if you give the kid and his dad back to my people."

He groaned. "But Roach he's wert two billion. I cain't jus' give that up! Why'd ye care so much 'bout him?"

"You can either trade me for them, or we can take them back forcefully." Dale pondered the offer but ultimately sighed and agreed. "Good boy," said Roach, his tone finally back to normal, "Now, where are you?"

With a glance at the airport building, he saw what he believed was the city's name and tried to relay that they were in "Less Sables Day Oh-lone Arrowport."

"Is that French, dude?"

"Looks like it."

"Take a picture." He took a picture and sent it to Roach who forwarded it to Francis asking for a translation. "Okay, I asked my boyfriend to give it a look."

"When will ye get here?"

"Soon," he replied and hung up before the conversation could be dragged out any longer.

When he heard the beep indicating the end of the call, Dale rolled his eyes and climbed back into the plane to pour himself a glass of bourbon and think.

Chapter 55
No Bribe Attempts or Blubbering

The raven flew up onto her chest and pecked gently on her cheeks. She giggled sleepily and batted at it before turning to her side and snuggling up with her pillow. The bird hopped up onto her shoulder and leaned down to peck at her braids, tugging on them. She shooed it away and groaned. Seeing as she wouldn't stir further, it squawked loudly, and she jolted upright, holding her racing heart.

"Papa!" she scolded the bird, "You 'bout gave me a heart attack!"

"You and Dezba need to hide in the basement," it said.

Neodesha rubbed her aching eyes and yawned. "Why?"

"The haunt was attacked. We're hiding in Marseilles. The others should be back soon, but in the meantime, you and Dezba need to hide in the basement."

She sighed and nodded. "Gosh darnit. Fine."

It fluttered its wings noisily and flew onto the rug. "Up up, now, Shay. You know I wouldn't be warning you if I thought you could handle whatever threat might come up."

She dragged herself from the bed and shuffled to Dezba's room, the raven hopping along behind her and trying to hurry her sluggish pace. "Shut it, Pa," she snipped before rapping thrice on Dezba's door.

"What's wrong?" asked Dezba as she yawned and rubbed the sleep from her eyes.

"Pa says we gotta hide."

"Why?" She eyed the bird.

"They was 'ttacked up in France."

"Oh no! Is everyone okay?"

"No," said the bird, "Go hide, now! I can tell you the details when you are both safe."

Dezba was quick to grab her purse and followed Neodesha's lead down into the bowels of the old manor. She tried not to let it show, but her eyes were watering when they were both finally settled down in a small windowless suite. She wiped them with her pyjama sleeve and looked at the raven as it hopped up onto the coffee table to address the women. "What's going on?" she whimpered, and Arjun used his raven to tell the entire story.

"I won't do it! I simply won't do it, Clayton!"

"Then I'll find my own way there somehow. My prayers have been answered, don't you see? I might die, but Partha and Richard will be safe again. Is that not something you want?"

"We have been given their location. To safely retrieve them, I need not forsake thee in the clutches of a madman. And I shan't! I shan't! I love you!"

Roach took up Francis' hand and kissed its knuckles. "Bed bug, please. I'm asking you to do this for me."

He snatched his hand back. "And I am objecting! Your prayers were mad! Your prayers were loathful self-reproach masquerading as divination! Why, Clayton? Why did you ask your god to wrench you away from me? You promised. You promised you'd always be here to ground me again when I am lost."

His throat clogged up. "I...."

"Clayton," he wept, "'tis you or the bottle. I am evermore lost at sea, and you are the lighthouse. Thy self-reproach be misbegotten. Partha has offered clemency. It was no fault of your own that you hurt him. You were lost in a memory. Lost out at sea...."

"I still am," he choked out. "If you bring me to Dale, after I've talked with him, I'll come back to the gang. I'll go to the manor in Rome."

"Swear it to me!"

He pressed his hand against his chest and sucked up his weepiness to say, "Hand on heart, bed bug."

Francis wiped his eyes with the heels of his hands. "Give me a moment to gather my bearings. Take this time to bid the others adieu ahead of your brief absence."

He leaned down to kiss Francis' cheek, whispered, "I love you," and left the room to commune with the rest of the gang. It had been eight hours since the madness of the morning, and Jean-Jacques was still missing. Thyne had chain smoked two entire packs of cigarettes and vomited thirteen times due to the hangover, and Perlie was holing herself up in her bedroom to cry in private over May and Aphid's deaths, as well as her beloved being kidnapped and in mortal peril. Roach cleared his throat to address the few in the living room: "I'm going to trade myself for the Nimas."

Thyne stood and rushed up to him. He grabbed him by his shirt collar and pulled him down so their faces were level. "No you fucking aren't, mate."

"I am." He pushed Thyne's hand away and stood upright. "Huff and puff all you want, sparkplug. Dale is my friend, and I told you already that I just want to talk to him face-to-face."

He shook his head as he took a deep drag. There was hardly any smoke on his words at all when he said, "No. You want to get away from us. You think I didn't hear your little spat with God in the desert? I fucking heard you, mate. I know you think this is providence, but it isn't. You're staying with us, Franky will get the Nimas, and everything will be at least nominally okay while we try to deal with all the fallout."

"Thyne, no. I'm going. If I don't talk with him, he'll keep coming after us. He'll find us wherever we go. I texted him earlier. He said he pinged Partha's phone to find the haunt." May had assured them all that she had made their phones untraceable. "He has my number, too. And River's. And he's damn smart, man. He's a hunter. He could track us in the tundra. There's no hiding. I'm going, and if I die, I deserve it."

Thyne punched him in the face and shouted out a wail. "You bellend! You no-good rotting carcass of a man! Francis will merely kill him when he fetches the Nimas!"

He took a step back, not even acknowledging his bleeding nose. There was the pain of betrayal in his hazel-greys, not from being struck but from what he had said. "Thyne. He's my best friend."

"Your best friend killed your bloody dog, mate!"

He furrowed his brow. Jae had cleared out of the room before Thyne hit Roach, and Francis was still not present. It was therefore only the twins and Thyne; River approached Thyne from behind. He pulled him back gently by his shoulder and placed himself between the two of them to protect his brother. "Thyne, let him do this."

His eyes welled up and smoke tore through the air from his nose like a dragon. "NO! You're both mental!" His voice dropped in volume as his rage became sorrow. "Please... don't leave me again, Basil. Not again!"

Roach's black heart cracked. *'And here I thought Sonny was manipulative. Both of them! Both of them trying to guilt me to stay! They don't know Dale. They don't know how determined he is.'* "I'm leaving, and that's final." He quit the room with a huff before the guilt-tripping would have him change his mind.

Partha could taste the blood from his nose dripping down over his swollen lips. He spat a lob of red onto the concrete and continued glaring at Dale. "I'm not giving you names, you fuck. I don't care what you do to me."

Dale unwrapped the cloth strip from his knuckles. It was so drenched in Partha's blood that it made a wet slopping sound as it fell onto the concrete between them. The captor noticed a bulge in Partha's pants and sort of chuckled. "Ah think ye're enjoyin' this a lil too much, pal." Partha smiled. "Well, if ye ain't gon' tell me nothin', then Ah'mma go getchyer daddy an' knock his teeth out."

"Don't you dare bring him into this."

He laughed and leaned close enough that the hot of his breath could be felt and the smell of the breakfast cereal he ate on the plane wafted into Partha's bloody face. "Are ye gon' gimme names, then?"

"Clayton Roach," he taunted, and it earned him another right hook. Dale left the room shortly thereafter and came in dragging Richard by his hair. He tossed him onto the ground and kicked him once in the gut, knocking the wind clean out of him. Partha turned his head to avoid seeing such a thing and apologised in Papiamentu. His father couldn't catch his breath, let alone respond. He struggled to get up onto his hands and knees, coughing and wheezing as he tried to crawl to the door. As soon as he managed to steady himself, he was pushed back onto his side and kicked a second time in the same place.

"Stop!" cried Partha. "Please!"

"NAMES, NIMA!"

He looked into his father's pained eyes. The man who had raised him. Always there for him. Loving him unconditionally. Protecting him from the harshness of reality as best as a single dad could. Partha hardly remembered his mother. As far as he could recall, life was a fantastic adventure on the high seas with his father always there to guide him.

He had carried him— ran like a mad man on foot to the hospital when he lost his eye because the ambulances were stopped up with busy city traffic. By his bedside in the hospital, he apologised ad nauseum for what he perceived as his own failings as a parent, no matter how much Partha reassured him.

He had taught him how to swim, how to sail, and how to be a man. He had homeschooled him to teach him more general things, awakened a love for history in him, and taught him all of the languages he knew, including Sindarin. Partha's hobbies and passions were always supported and taken incredibly seriously no matter his age, and even before he knowingly got involved with crime, Richard had asked only that he stay out of danger.

He was there when Partha lost his first tooth, when he won his first fencing match, when he DMed his first game, when he made his first costume. And his greatest betrayal before this, when he was caught as a college drop-out wasting all of Daddy's hard-earned tuition money on blow, he was met with forgiveness and empathy and welcomed back into those strong paternal arms without a second thought. Even after his fifteenth relapse, he was loved and supported and showed nothing but patience.

But... what must he have thought of Partha now?

The kid had hoped his dad would never find out about his direct involvement in killing those people, and he had hoped further that if he did somehow find out, it would at least be on more favourable terms than having gotten the two of them kidnapped and now physically beat for information on people Partha would, at that point, die to protect.

Heartbreak was plainly visible in Richard's dark eyes before he was kicked down for a third time. He fell onto his side and curled up into a foetal position to hide his tears, but the way he was trembling made his endless pain and upset entirely evident.

"Stop!" whimpered Partha. "I'll talk!"

Dale smiled wickedly. "I thought ye'd see things my way."

Partha hesitated, but when he saw Dale pulling back his foot for another blow into his father's stomach, he shouted, "THYNE! Thyne Chamberlain. He's British. He's been on my streams before. We work for him."

There was a subtle shift in Dale's grin which turned it from hysterical elation to one that was thinly masking an unending rage. He was holding back from shouting when he said in a faux-chipper way, "Is there anyone who wouldn't show up wit a curs'ry innernet search?"

"No. It's just me, the twins, and Thyne. My dad isn't a part of it. Let him go."

Partha's acting was good, but Dale was reasonably confident that Perlie Moon was also involved considering she was expressly named by Tatum in the contract. Still, he had only started beating Partha in this little seaside shack to see if he could weasel himself a bonus with more accomplices. Another right hook knocked one of Partha's molars out of its place, and he spit it across the room. "The dead ones, too, Nima! What're their names?"

"They're not dead," he heard from behind him at the same time that he felt a small prick in the nape of his neck. He rubbed at it and stood upright to see Roach suddenly behind him with a scrawny blond man looking drunk and exhausted.

"You only killed one of them. Now, if you'll stop beating the shit out of my friends, we can get on with the trade."

"Trade?" said Partha.

"Shush, kid," said Roach with a pleading look in the pits of his expressionless eyes.

"Leddum talk, Roach. He was *juss* warmin' up t' me."

Roach looked toward Francis and nodded his head once, after which Partha, Richard, and Francis were all immediately disappeared from the room and safe back in Marseilles with the other survivors of the attack.

At the blatant show of the supernatural, Dale merely sighed. "'S'that a new trick a' yers?"

"No." He lit himself a cigarette with a flourish and offered one to Dale. As he closed his lighter: "It's good to see you, dude. Not the best torture chamber," he looked around judgmentally, "but I suppose you *were* on a time crunch."

With his offered cigarette, Dale plopped himself down into Partha's empty seat, his knees spread and smoke filling his lungs. "Ah dunno if it's good t'see ye. Start 'splainin'.'"

Roach nodded and took a drag. He looked down at the rag on the floor and was simultaneously guilt-ridden and impressed to know it was drenched in Partha's blood. "I know who hired you," he said suddenly. Dale arched his brow. "Osiris International, no?"

There was a beat of quiet wherein Dale only continued to look confused and intrigued. Roach went on: "I know you and I don't see eye-to-eye on a lot of things, but *The Crown* and *Tiara* are trying to take down as many companies as possible. That seems at least slightly up your alley, right? We were starting with the ones we had personal beef with. Osiris is too big to take down all at once like we did for Eir Lilac and New Clear, but the reason I know who hired you is because we were destroying Osiris sweatshops and company towns down in the new states. That's what Partha's original stream was about." A drag. "What did the suits tell you we were doing?"

"Ah think Ah've made it pretty clear, Roach, that they was tellin' me you was killin' kids. Ah saw the vidya of it, too. Ah wanna trust ye, but Ah dunno if Ah can."

Roach smoked and leaned against the wall across from Dale. "It doesn't matter. If you want to turn me in, dude, I'll go quietly. So long as you drop this contract on Party."

"Turn ye in?" He pursed his lips. "Fer all yer killin'?"

"Yeah."

Dale's blue eyes widened. He took a drag and looked out at the sea through one of the shack's cracked windows. "Ye know Ah ain't gon' do that to ye."

632

"I won't rat you out if you do, man. You know I'm good for it."

He looked at him sceptically. "What's goin' on witchye, Roach? Ye're acken weird."

He ran a hand through his hair and shook it anxiously. "I don't know, dude. Are you gonna take me in or not?"

Dale stood and approached him. "Ah know you, Clay. Ah know there's summon goin' on up there in that wile brain a' yers." He poked his temple gently before taking up Roach's free hand in his and patting it to comfort him. "Ah'm sorry 'boutchyer dog, and Ah ain't gon' turn ye in. 'Least not 'less it turns out you *was* killin' kids."

"You know I'm not killing kids. We had a deal, and even if we didn't... I don't think I'd have it in me."

"Thass good, mane." He punched his upper arm gently. "Now, Ah don' wanna go back empty handed, so come wit me an' ack all trifled with. Can ye do that?"

Roach nodded and flicked his half-finished cigarette to the ground. "Gonna cuff me?"

"Yeh." He roughed up Roach's hair by hocking a loogie into his hand and rustling it in Roach's long locks. "Good goin' already bleedin'." He laughed. "Ah guess Ah don't gotta punch ye ta make it seem like we scrapped."

Roach huffed once with sad amusement and droned, "Yeah."

Dale tied Roach's wrists together behind him and escorted him out of the shack. When they were close enough to see the plane, he took out a pistol and pressed it against the small of Roach's back. He leaned forward when he sensed Roach's fear and whispered, "Safety's off, but it ain't cocked. Ah ain't gon' shootchye." Roach nodded and let himself be guided up into the plane. Dale kept him in front of him with the gun pressed to his spine when his men approached asking where Partha and Richard were. "They's gone." He glared at the others as if to dare them to challenge him. "Caught thissun freein' 'em. He don't know English. Only speaks Spanish, so we's gotta divert down to Porta Rica."

With Roach keeping Dale off their trails, the rest of the gang could finally relax, if for only a moment. They were packing up Thyne's plane in Korea, preparing for a flight back to Rome that evening, but there was one last effort made to find Jean-Jacques before they would leave. Thyne could hear him intermittently. He had heard him buying a plane ticket to Moscow, and afterwards was mostly silence. The time of the flight was unknown, so Perlie was asking various gate agents about recent or future flights to Moscow, ultimately able to determine that he had already left.

Perlie and River were the only passengers on their trip out to Rome, and despite everything that had happened to her up until then, Perlie was still smitten with River. He was sitting on the couch across from her and playing chess on his phone, not acknowledging how she was staring. After three games, however, he glared at her pink cheeks and dopey grin. "Can I help you?"

She started. "Oh! Uh…. What are you up to?"

"What do you think?" She chewed her lip and averted her eyes. He smiled wickedly and set his phone on the table between them. "So, have you thought of what you're going to name the baby?"

A soft glare. "You know I haven't."

"And why not, pray tell?"

"Stop tormenting me," she mumbled.

"Hm? And why would I do that?"

"Would you wipe that snide grin off your stupid fucking face!? You win! Okay? You win! I can't handle being alone."

He chuckled darkly. "I just hope that weakness of yours is not the catalyst for your ultimate decision to carry Partha's seed."

"God, River, do you have to word it so creepily? I love him. Of course I'm carrying his *child*."

"Do you now?"

"You're insufferable. I'm glad we never dated."

"Likewise." He flicked his phone up off of the table telekinetically and resumed his game.

While they were bickering, Thyne was in the cockpit with his eyes half-glazed as he scanned his instruments for the umpteenth time. His mind was on fire, and the remnants of his hangover stuck around in the form of a migraine. His *DC-8* had been retrofitted with a more modern cockpit that would allow him to fly the large jet alone, though it was still ideal to have a co-pilot. Francis' absence was therefore felt with more than just his haggard heart: his attention was divided and overstimulated, especially with all the voices. Partha's was the most obnoxious of the lot: going on a rambling tangent to Francis about being kidnapped. Dale's voice was new. He spoke quickly, so the speed combined with his thick twang would take some adjustment to understand. Still, Thyne was ultimately grateful for the extra intel.

While he was monitoring his instruments and trying to distinguish the radio chatter from the voices in his head, he heard Roach say something in English for the first time in at least an hour:

"Thyne…. I'm not sure if I'll make it back, so it's probably best that you tell the others I died. And if I do come back, I'll think of a funny bit to explain the whole 'I died' thing, so don't worry."

Tears trailed Thyne's cheeks. His heart panged. What Roach had said was almost a word-for-word quote of what Oliver had said when he was captured in the war.

His imagination was a wildfire. Memories of Oliver's screams of agonised pain as Viktor tortured him worsened his migraine.

He worried the echoes of his past were an omen: that the next time he saw Roach would be the same as when Oliver was finally rescued— that the next time he saw Roach would be with a bomb sewn into his abdomen. Another goodbye. Another century of waiting for his soul to find him again.

A chime from the plane pulled him out of his wallowing thoughts: a wind-shear ahead. He wiped his arm across his teary face, sucked up his sadness, and grabbed the yoke more firmly. Now was not the time to grieve and worry and cry, so he detached himself from his emotions, turned off the auto-pilot, and manually flew the plane the rest of the way to Europe.

⪘ Chapter 56 ⪙
The Sound of Ultimate Suffering

It reeked of garbage, blood, and gunpowder. The ceiling was leaking into an overflowing children's pail across from his place tied to a fold-out chair in the centre of the featureless room. The shuttered window behind him was being pelted by pulses of rain in the howling tempest outside. He traced cracks in the terracotta tiles with his eyes until he was startled by the door to his right slamming open.

The man who entered spoke in Spanish as he thumbed through a handheld notebook: "Morning. Dale says you only know Spanish. He says you were freeing the others. How did you get to them?" Roach shook his head. "I promise you that this will all go much smoother if you just cooperate."

"And why would I want it to go smoother?"

"Alright, let me start over. Hello. They call me Twist, and I'm a mercenary after your child-murdering cycloptic friend. Now it's *your* turn. What's *your* name?" His tone was patronizingly chipper like a children's cartoon character breaking the fourth wall. There was a beat, so Ridley cracked his knuckles and took out a scrap of cloth to start wrapping around them. "Last chance," he sang.

"Oliver," blurted Roach with a glimmer of panic in the backs of his eyes. "My name is Oliver York."

Ridley's bright white teeth contrasted against his dark skin in the subsequent sinister smile he offered. He curtsied sarcastically. "Señor York. A pleasure."

"I'm sure."

"So, Oli. How'd you get past Dale?"

"Snuck by."

"Uh huh…. And how tall are you?"

"6'6"."

"Right." He rolled his eyes and sighed. "I suppose it doesn't matter how you got past him." He took a half-full bottle of root beer out of a satchel he had brought into the room and sipped it. "Where'd they go?" Roach shrugged. "No no, Señor York. You must be misunderstanding me. You have to tell me where they went, or things are going to get ugly."

"Already are," he said with a flick of his gaze up and down his interrogator's body. "I mean, honestly! Flannel and flip-flops? Are we in Puerto Rico or the Smoky Mountains? Did the torture already start?"

Ridley punched him in the jaw. "I'm not in a trifling mood, Señor York. How did you know we're in Puerto Rico?"

He shook off the pain. "Saw a pirate spider. You have an American accent. Smells like the ocean. Flood stains on the walls. It's not exactly rocket science, Twist."

Ridley stood upright and looked down at Roach. Another sip of root beer. "You have one more chance to tell me where the Nimas went, or I'm going to have to get creative."

He smiled sarcastically. "I like to encourage others' creativity."

Ridley returned the grin and quit the room. This was when Roach really considered the likelihood of his survival. He could have lied more. He could have sent them on a goose-chase in Canada or froze them out in Russia. Even with his hands bound, he could at least somewhat use his telekinesis if things got too dire, but it was with a sort of self-flagellation that he invited the "enhanced interrogation" and would allow whatever torturous horrors laid ahead. He wondered if he might let it go so far as to kill him, and after a silent self-loathing prayer, he whispered to Thyne the message to tell the others he had died.

Thyne suffered two days of listening to Roach being tortured, having no idea the extent of the information he may have been giving with so much chatter in Spanish. Roach was making his best attempts to stay quiet through all the pain, so in the instances he did manage to break, it sent chills down Thyne's spine. It didn't help that his captors continuously called him Oliver or Señor York, or some other variation. Thyne had to wonder if he was hallucinating. He had to wonder if this was some sort of nightmare. He spent every possible second clinging to Francis, but when his continued embraces sent the pirate back into his void of rotting and madness, he found River to cling to instead.

When it rolled around to February 3rd, the nightmare continued in spite of Thyne's prayers that his birthday might be spared. It was eight in the morning when everyone gathered in the living area of Loomis manor for a meeting called by Partha. He addressed them all:

"I can't be the only one who felt wrong burying May without her brother there and Aphid without Roach. This gang is a year old today, and it's already in shambles." He looked at Thyne, who was trembling with a death-grip on River's upperarm. "I'm sorry, Thyne. I just… I need to know: are you so upset because you heard—. Did you hear Roach die?" Thyne shook his head. "Well, that's good. Where is he? We should go rescue him. I feel like shit having traded places with him. It's my fault all this shit is happening. I never should have released that video."

"You did the right thing, wangjanim," said Perlie, "Roach knew what he was doing. He's friends with Dale." She looked at Thyne. "Though… why *are* you so upset? We're all upset about May and Aphid, but…." A realisation visibly struck her. "Is it JJP? Did you hear *him* die?"

He shook his head again, buried his face in River's chest, and cuddled Diana with Malfeasance and the other dogs all nearby to comfort him, too. River pet Thyne's head and glared softly at the others. "Leave him be. Tony and Martial are fine."

"Then where are they? Or at least where's Roach?" said Partha, "We should bring him back here."

"'Tis his yen to ne'er return," grumbled Francis after a swig from a bottle of vodka, "He be a misguided fool with delusions of martyrdom and no empathy for those he contends to love. He hath marooned himself: if there be any salvation for him it shall be in the deliverance of a more swift and lonely end." He unholstered one of his flintlock pistols and tossed it onto the coffee table to punctuate the comment.

"Are you saying you want to kill him?" asked Perlie.

"NAY! HE HAS KILLED *ME!* Deceitful cretin! He implored Thyne to claim he is deceased because he desires no homecoming nor loving reunion. Heartless wretch! Mutinous dog!" His white-knuckled fist on the bottle shook as he lamented, "He cast me to the sea again, the cold-blooded blackguard."

"He asked you to do that, Thyne?" asked Dezba as she tried not to notice how much Francis was downing from the bottle.

The Brit nodded and squeezed his arms around River as he heard, at that very same moment, Roach bawling at the searing pain brought on by a branding.

"We have to go save him," said Partha, "Thyne? Where is he?"

He shook his head and, after taking a moment to ground himself, stood. Thyne knew Roach was in Puerto Rico, but if Partha knew that, he would get himself killed trying to invade American soil. Though Francis could save him, Roach wanted to stay where he was, at least for the time. Thyne swapped places with Partha, and with all the attention on him, addressed the room with an uneasy tone and tremble in his hands: "I don't know where he is. It's my birthday. Everything is shite, and I just want to go after Maitland now. Please."

"We can't just ignore all this shit to go after a company that isn't even that big," replied Partha, "If we're going after a company right now it should be Canopy or Osiris again. Not Maitland. I know it's your birthday, Thyne, but Maitland just isn't that bad. They're not using child labour. They're not enslaving people in prisons or company towns. They're not polluting the oceans or exploiting gambling addictions. They're just a shitty record label."

Thyne's upset became his usual rage, but before he started shouting, Roach whispered to him again: "I miss you, Thyne. You were right. I wish I hadn't done this. I want to come back, but I still need to talk to Dale. I miss you all so much, and I'm sorry for—." A beat. The next thing he said was in Spanish.

"What's going on? What did you hear?" asked Perlie.

"Mind your business, slag! I want to go after Maitland. Who's coming with me? Franky?"

"I love you dearly, my darling, but I stand with Partha. Maitland is not a threat to the world. Osiris is."

Partha piped up: "This is ridiculous. Why are we even talking about the companies!? I'm going to go find Roach. I'm going to save him!"

"I'll go with you," said River with a disinterested tone.

"Good. I'll be stealing a ship. It can be a Canopy ship, too. Might as well. Who else is coming with me?"

"Now hold on, Party," said Thyne, a tint of red on his cheeks, "You can't just go steal a Canopy ship. You'd need far too many men for that. And you don't even know where Roach is. It's too dangerous. He'll be fine. If you want to be the one to lead the Canopy take-down that's fine, but we'll have to think of a more effective way to do it. Maybe killing shareholders. That worked well the first time."

"Fuck you, Thyne. I'm going to find Roach." He stood and gestured at River. "Come on."

"We need you here with the gang, mate."

"What gang!?" He looked around, and when he started back up, his voice was quavering and strangled but wrought with determination and anger enough to keep it audible: "May is dead, Jean-Jacques is gone, and Roach is out there somewhere losing his mind even more than it already was! Now you can either help me by telling me where he is, or I can find out on my own somehow. I'm already the most wanted man in the entire God damn world. What does it matter if I steal a ship?" He cast a wide gaze around the group with a wide swing of his arm as he shouted, "Who else is coming with me!?"

River stood to join him. Perlie stood a moment later, and before Thyne knew it, other than Francis and Richard, everyone had joined Partha's cause to save Roach.

His face was as red as the fire in his soul. His heart was beating hard and fast, enough that it almost hurt. His knuckles were white, and his teeth ground down into each other. Roach was screaming again, and every sort of upset that could plague a man sounded from Thyne's quivering lips when he said: "You want to be in charge so much, Party!? Then fine! Some birthday gift this was." He wiped his sleeve across his face. "I'm leaving. I'm leaving, and I'm taking down Maitland." With that said, he stormed out of the manor and peeled away in the twins' *Locust*.

In his absence, the others were overcome with stunned silence for twelve seconds. After the stillness, Francis stood and ambled toward the hearth, downing most of what remained of his vodka, and finally slamming the bottle into the fire where it plumed up with flames. "FUCK!"

"Franky, be careful!" shouted Partha as he pulled him away from the fireplace, "We need to stay calm. That's what Roach would do."

"No," spat Francis as he shoved Partha off of him, "No, he would waste what little time and chances remain for us to save the world. He would see me fail!"

"Franky, son, I think you need some fresh air," cooed Dezba.

"I'll go with him," said Richard hurriedly. "Don't anyone go anywhere while we're gone." Ignoring a whiny complaint from his son, he ushered the drunkard out onto the back porch then toward the gardens. Once they were alone, Richard sat on a bench and held his spinning head. "Franky, what the fuck is going on? What do you mean you're trying to save the world?"

He sat beside his friend. "I trust you have gathered the nature of my superhuman abilities?"

"No."

"Well, I am a chronomancer."

"You mean this entire…," he gestured at Francis helplessly, "*deal* isn't just a character you play for the streams?"

"Of course not. Me character were Hector." Richard blinked, so Francis continued: "I control time, as well as a nominal control of most meteorological phenomena. I have foresight regarding the beginnings of a looming war: Osiris International will spark global conflict, and after some time a fourth world war will develop that will end nigh all life on Earth."

"What the actual fuck?" he whispered.

"So, it is imperative that Osiris International be destroyed."

"How do you have superpowers?"

Francis blinked. "Richard, my friend, you seem to be misthinking. The origins of my abilities are of no present concern."

"Are you like a vampire or something?"

"Don't be dippy. Vampires are fantastical creatures." It did not escape his notice that Giovanni, Arjun, and even Neodesha could be described as vampires with a fair amount of accuracy, but it was a foolish notion in his mind to equate the two.

While Richard was being brought up to speed on the true depths of the oddities in his son's criminal friend group, Thyne was northbound and hasty. The *Locust* had been modified to go speeds far exceeding the car's factory limits, and Thyne was abusing this fact on every even slightly-straight road he could find. On one stretch in the North of Italy he managed to reach 357 km/hr. Luckily the roads were mostly clear at such a late hour: the blear of tears in his fiery amber eyes hindered his vision enough to be dangerous (even more dangerous combined with the speeding, at any rate). He didn't care. He was every imaginable kind of upset. Nothing mattered to him at that moment more than getting to London and burning down Maitland's headquarters.

Sixteen consecutive years of being moulded into a perfect musical machine and charged monetarily for childhood trifles led way to Thyne's ultimate decision to kill his mother. Shortly after burning down his childhood home with his mother inside and only a handful of possessions to his name, he was on the frontlines killing krauts and commanding vast swaths of British troops. Later still, he was subjected to the horrific sounds of his truest love being tortured to near-death then forced to hold his hand as his time left alive quite literally ticked away. His time with Francis and Rosemary was never calm for long with a war here or natural disaster there. Political unrest was a constant, and it was only recently that he was able to be openly bisexual and flamboyant without fear of summary execution or near-enough. A curse of his own creation was brought about by all the many voices in his head which rarely allowed him a wink of sleep. It was quite possible that Thyne Chamberlain had never known true peace in all his life. Perhaps, he thought, if he were to finally wipe his mother's name and legacy from the face of the Earth, he might finally know such a thing. Perhaps if he burned down Maitland for good, things would finally be okay.

Two sleepless nights before he stormed out of the manor, followed by ten hours of driving afterwards, he stopped at a petrol station in rural France and left his car to go buy more energy drinks. The voices were incessant, but he was trying his best to tune them out, only listening out for Roach to say things in English again. The convenience store was cramped and reeked of bleach, but he ambled to the cooler and dragged four cans of an Osiris-branded energy drink called *Ra* to the counter. Along with the drinks, he bought a bag of chocolate raisins, a pack of menthol cigarettes, and paid in cash.

On his way back to the *Locust*, he spotted some teenagers, likely eighteen and nineteen, ogling it. They tried to approach and reach for the door handle, but he made an obnoxious noise as he neared them and shooed them like they were pesky vermin. They scurried away hastily, and Thyne climbed back into the car to crack open one of the *Ra* drinks and start nursing it. It tasted like a sparkling lemonade with a hint of apple, sweetened with aspartame. Even without his caffeine addiction, and even considering his opposition to Osiris, he would likely rank it among his favourite beverages. He was halfway through the can and listening to a boring French talk radio station when he noticed the teenagers he had shooed away from the car were lingering in a shady corner of the parking lot. He squinted and watched as an old woman approached them. They had a conversation, money changed hands, and she walked away shoving a plastic bag into her purse.

Thyne opened the door, pulled up his hood, and approached the kids. He greeted them in English, "What are you two selling?"

They looked him up and down and each adopted a crooked grin. "You tryna get fucked-up, mate?" replied the taller of the two with a half-French half-Cockney accent.

"Depends. Do you have any go-fast?"

"What's that?"

"You know… chalk?" They still didn't understand. "Crank? Crystal? Bloody wakey-wakey pills?"

"Crystal?" said the shorter one. "You mean meth?"

He sighed. "Yes, I mean meth."

"We've got some, yeah."

Thyne took out his wallet. "How much?"

They turned to each other and spoke in hushed French about how Thyne had an expensive car and fat wallet. "Alright, bruv. 2200," said the shorter one.

Thyne rolled his eyes and took out the blatantly overpriced amount. They tried to take his money, but he yanked it away. "Show me the chalk first." The taller one produced a bag with six small pills in it. With a scoff, Thyne passed over the money and snatched the bag away.

"Woah, mate! 2200 for one, not the whole bag!"

He replied in French: "Piss off. Insolent child. You've swindled enough. You don't even know what it's called and expect me to not know how much it's worth? Go!" They scrambled away, and Thyne rushed back to the car, popped one of the pills, and resumed his mad dash to England.

Because of his speeding, it wasn't much longer before he had suffered the traffic in the channel tunnel and made his way back home to London. He parked in his private garage and popped another pill before rushing to his house. He tore off his hoodie and shirt for no discernable reason, threw them haphazardly onto a settee in his living room, and kicked up the rug. After slamming open the cellar door hidden beneath, he descended the stairs into his basement where he ravaged his stockpiles of weapons, tossing guns around without rhyme or reason. He wasn't even certain what it was he was looking for. After fifteen minutes of madness, he stopped suddenly and looked around at the mess he had made. His heart was beating so wildly he could hear it pulsing in his ears. Loud, but unfortunately not loud enough to drown out the voices:

"Do you think Thyne will be okay?" asked Dezba.

"'Okay' is a word he hath ne'er known, poppet." A beat. "He will survive. We all will. At least a little longer. Beyond that— the state of us in the end? I can guarantee nothing."

"Will he come back?"

"…Unfortunately."

Thyne whimpered. A tear trailed his cheek and crashed against his collarbone. He grabbed at the area it hit and squeezed hard. Harder and harder and harder as his teeth ground down into each other and heart beat even louder. With a hysterical sort of air to him, he rushed out of the basement and up to his room, skipping two steps at a time to get there quicker.

He locked himself in his private bathroom with an unlit cigarette already in his mouth. The man in the mirror caught his attention. He was a haggard mess. His hair was dishevelled. The dark circles beneath his wild dilated eyes made him indistinguishable from the walking dead. His skin was especially pallid— even his freckles were hardly visible. The rage within him wasn't tinting his cheeks as it tended to do. It was instead showing itself in the mad tears trailing his sickly white face and, especially, the ireful fire in his big-pupilled eyes. Overall, he appeared at least half as ill-fated as he had when he was a prisoner of war.

With a shout at the stranger, he averted his gaze and patted around his trousers' pockets.

After scrambling his twitchy hands all over himself, unable to find Oliver's lighter, he wept hysterically and collapsed to the ground where he slammed his closed hand repetitively into the counter cabinets and let out a long frustrated shout. It must have been fifteen times he struck the cabinets before something fell from the countertop onto his head. He watched it tumble to the tile and scrambled to grab it, as well as his fallen cigarette. With the fag in his mouth he looked at the matchbook in his trembling hands. It was the box the fortune teller had given him at the renaissance faire.

It was a sign.

'*Thank you, Brigit,*' he prayed silently as Her divine inspiration overcame him.

After lighting his cigarette, he stood upright and gave himself a long look in the mirror. He looked plainly like a monster with his eyes even more wild than before:

a determination in them that was unmatched by any other in his life. His hands were steady but quick as he took out an electric razor. The sink piled up with pink locks, their brown roots showing. All the while, he never broke eye-contact with himself.

With his head entirely shaved, he rubbed his hands through the buzz to brush out the remnants, finished the last half of his cigarette with one long inhale, then flicked it into the sink where it started to burn the clippings. He let it cinder, leaving the room to open his wardrobe.

February 4th.

Noon.

The door to Maitland Music Group's headquarters chimed with a motif young Thyne had written. He approached the counter.

"Afternoon. Can I help ya?" She beamed, unperturbed by his face-mask, black clothes, or pulled-up hood.

"Tour."

"Alright. What time?"

"Soonest."

"Alright, just a moment." She tapped at her computer. "Oh, sorry, mate. Looks like the only one left isn't 'til three."

"That's fine."

"Oh, well in that case…." She tapped on it some more. "That'll be twenty quid." He slid two tenners across the counter. "See ya then!"

She expected him to leave, but he sat on a couch across from the counter and stared at a paisley on the ugly rug. Music was filling the room, but he didn't hear it.

"Sir!" He started and looked up at her. She was standing in front of him now. There was a small group of people crowded near a hallway behind her. "It's time for the tour, mate. Come on." He let her help him out of his seat and followed her to the group that had gathered at the mouth of the corridor. "Have fun!" She disappeared back into her cubicle behind the counter, rapping on another door on her way.

It seemed the type of people who took this tour were almost exclusively businessmen and women who were on company trips and had some time to kill. As aspiring moguls themselves, they were interested in the business practices of the founder. Thyne, therefore, looked quite out of place in his baggy black hoodie and shredded black jeans. One of the women in the group probed, "Why are you on the tour?" in a fake-polite way only a fellow Brit could recognise.

"I'm a musician."

"Oh! What do you play?"

He wasn't sure how to respond, but thankfully another person on the tour interrupted: "What's with the mask, mate?"

"I have a cold."

They bought his excuses, and a moment later, a woman appeared from the door the secretary had rapped upon. She brushed down her skirt and said with a forced smile, "Welcome all. Come along, now."

They followed her down a short hall. At the other end was what was once Thyne's childhood home, now rebuilt and made into a museum to Maitland as a company. The tour began with a brief history of his mother's life before Thyne was born. It seemed accurate, so he was surprised by how inaccurate the reconstructed rooms in the house tended to be. Still, he had only come on the tour to get an idea of the layout, make mental notes of cameras and windows and other sightlines, and to keep himself in a mental frenzy.

As the tour went on, Thyne silently thanked his Gods for the meth. He was beginning to realise that he never would have been able to make it this far sober. Even high, the constant demonstrations of reprises he was tormented into writing and blind adoration of his mother's "talent" and "good business sense" were making his entire body ache and vignetting his vision. He was mostly able to tune out the waffling and sometimes able to tune out the short bursts of music, but all the voices and overstimulation were hard to entirely ignore.

While walking down a particularly nothing hallway, they passed a fire-escape chart, and Thyne stealthily snapped a picture with his phone. "No photography, please, sir," said the guide, and he apologised, and that was that.

Even if he was entirely interested in the tour, with no baggage at all, he couldn't imagine it would be very exciting. He was high, yet it was bringing him nearly to tears of boredom. "This was Mrs. Crump's bedroom," the guide would say and show a bland bedroom styled nothing like how his mother liked her room. "And this was where she first found the inspiration for the song *Little Juniper Berries*," she informed with a gesture into a foreign-looking kitchen. He had written that song after Oliver bought a juniper bush from the farmer's market with him. This hogwash about his mother writing it was made especially trite by the potted juniper plant on the windowsill.

It was boring boring boring, up until he was brought to the music room where he had killed her. This was where he expected the tour to fully grip him. He imagined the guide would put on a sombre façade and lament, 'And sadly this was where she died in the house fire, in 1936 with her son, and the company was traded all around until so-and-so bought it in nineteen-fifty-something. Blah blah blah. So so sad.'

He was grinning wide as they approached the door, his anticipation making the high that much better.

"And this is her music room, where she wrote most of the songs we know," began the guide. "Shortly after the house fire in 1936, she built it back up and wrote a song of mourning for her lost son." She put on the false sombre act and bowed her head as she used a remote to play a demonstration of the song from a speaker in the hall behind them. . . .

A song Thyne most definitely did not write.

Surely, there was some sort of misunderstanding. Perhaps she had become something of a mascot for the brand, where the company was using Maitland's likeness to give themselves a more wholesome motherly appearance. It was probably some no-name intern who wrote it after she died. Maybe she had an heir that Thyne never knew who inherited the company. Maybe his estranged uncle.

The song sample finished, and they were allowed into the room.

Walking through the threshold of the door, it was like the entire world went cold. Unlike the rest of the rooms, this one was *exactly* how he remembered it. The plush forest-green carpet. The mahogany grand piano surrounded by a corner of intricate windows and sheer white curtains. Even the lace on their edges was how he recalled. The guitars and violins on display. The heavy tapestry on the eastern wall, faded and singed but recognisable. He stepped automatically toward the piano.

"Oh, hey," said the woman who had bothered him earlier, "You said you're a musician. Play us something!"

The others all agreed, and he looked at the guide with horrified amber eyes as if to ask her to disallow it.

She didn't notice his silent pleas for help and beamed. "We allow the guests to play the piano. It's very well taken care of, and it was Mrs. Maitland's thinking that an instrument is no good if it isn't being played. Go on!"

All he had to say was, 'I don't play piano.'

That's all he had to say.

But his body, in this room, was not his own.

The eyes on him were the same million little daggers as his mother's.

He sat on the uncomfortable bench and automatically raised his hands over the keys. The choice of song was just as automatic for him: Chopin's first ballade. It was one of the songs his mother had him practise daily because he would consistently make mistakes in the complicated coda.

"If you would just play it properly, we wouldn't have to practise it every day, Clare."

"If you would just play it properly, I'd let you play one of the waltzes you like."
"If you would just play it properly, we could finally move on!"
"If you would just play it properly, I wouldn't have to hit you."
"If you would just play it properly."
"...just play it properly."

With a shuddered breath, he looked down at his trembling hands and was reminded of the time he had tried wearing gloves to mitigate the pain from his mother's strikes on the backs of his hands. She had torn the gloves off of him, expressed that "You can't play music if you can't feel it," and threw them out the window. He gingerly slid the gloves from his hands, revealing his cybernetic fingers to the small audience he had.

After a final pained look at the group, he took another breath of the familiar air, his hands started the ballade, and his mind caught up with them shortly thereafter.

He played.

And the strangers listened.

And...

After nine and half minutes of uninterrupted piano, he finished the song, removed his hands from the keys, and looked up to his right, expecting his mother to be there. "Acceptable," was what he expected to hear her say. When she wasn't there— when she didn't say that— he slowly began to recall where and when he was. He started to recall *who* he was. After only a tumultuous second of reeling thoughts, he was pulled immensely and immediately back to reality by the uproarious applause that came, not from some crowd of faceless onlookers on the street outside, but by the tour group, all of them smiling wide at him.

He had played it to absolute *perfection*.

He had entirely forgotten about his missing fingers until he felt the nip of metal against his palm when he nervously closed his fists and tried to comprehend the applause he was receiving. Applause was something an audience gave him on stages or from the street below, but it was always from a faceless entity. A crowd was never a group of individuals in those instances: they were merely clapping out of societal expectation.

To see these people... strangers... smiling at him and coming over to give him verbal praise and adoration—. To feel them shake his hands and pass him business cards and rattle on about his talent and their gratitude for having been witness to it—.

He had once gotten a standing ovation at the opera hall when he was only fourteen years old, but at the time it was merely a roaring ambient nothing coming from a void of black behind the blinding lights of the stage: *"They're clapping for me, mother,"* he had said with a smile.

"They clap for everyone, dear."

Before he quite knew it, he was being shuffled out of the room, pats on the back and praise in his ears all the way. They were all led to a gift shop, which would lead back to the street. As he pulled his gloves back on and finally parted ways with the rest of the group, he was stopped in the corridor just before the gift shop when he spotted a quote painted on the wall:

'In these dark times, it is music that brings us God's light.'
Maitland Crump
(1889-1978)

Chapter 57
Your Friend Here
Is Only Mostly Dead

The days blurred together. He wasn't sure how long he had been in Puerto Rico, but it felt like an eternity. Pain was an understatement. He had been branded with the Leviathan logo on his inner left forearm, ruining the tattoo of a song he had written for River over ten years prior. His brow was bleeding. He had a black eye. Nearly-broken nose. Fat lip. Chemical burns on his hands. Water in his lungs. There was nothing he desired more dearly than to rush back to the gang and curl up in the arms of whoever would hold him, which was why he had finally given a location to his captors.

He had been blindfolded and transferred through San Juan to what he assumed was a yacht. After being led down a set of stairs in the boat, he was locked in a room and tied to a chair. The blindfold was not removed when his captors left. He heard them shuffling around on the boat for the following two hours, after which they started to clear off. The engine never started.

With a sigh, he tried to loose his aching hands. Maybe if he escaped he could find a way back to Rome somehow. Maybe he hadn't lied to Francis after all. And… shit… he still needed to think of a funny bit for his return. As he picked at the duct tape around his hands fruitlessly, he heard a door open in front of him. In Spanish: "Who's there?"

"Shush. They's all gone fer now, but there's some on the docks," whispered Dale as he rounded to the back of the chair and cut him free. Roach hissed as the tape tore at his already-burning skin. "Ah'm sorry. Ah'm sorry, Roach, it weren't s'posed ta get this bad. Why ye ain't tell 'em summon sooner?"

When the blindfold was removed he blinked at the dim lighting in the small bedroom as if it were a flashbang. His eyes watered for a moment, but he was able to focus on Dale after some time and started untying his legs. "Thanks, man," he whispered.

"Ye look like Hell. Ah feel bad. Ah didn't figger ye'd be the type ta leddum go so long. What're we gon' find in New York?"

He finished untying himself and leaned back in the chair, his breaths laboured and raspy. "Nothing," he answered eventually, "It was just the first place that came to mind when I decided I want to go home."

"Ah'ight." A sigh. "They wanna turn ye over to the gubberment, but we bote know Ah ain't gon' let that happen." He pulled something out of each of his back pockets. "Gotchyer phone an' wallet."

"Did your friends look through them?"

"Nah, don' worry. Ah had 'em this whole time."

"Thanks, dude." He took his phone but watched with a slight smile as Dale opened his wallet, presumably to rob him.

Dale hadn't looked in Roach's wallet before then out of respect, but seeing as he was putting his ass on the line to free him and go on a witch hunt in NYC, he figured a few bucks wouldn't be asking too much. He wasn't surprised by his friend's lack of funds when he opened it, but he *was* surprised by what he found. In the main pocket were four living caterpillars crawling around. One of them climbed up onto his thumb as he held the wallet open. Roach snickered, and Dale looked at him with an arched brow.

"They're called Eastern Tent Caterpillars, and they're really soft and cute!" His beaming grin contrasted with all the injuries eerily. Even more eerie was what Dale knew of Roach and how little he expressed his emotions. Smiles were usually reserved for his victims. It would have perturbed Dale if not for what he had said.

"Why d'ye have cadderpillers in yer wallet?"

"So they can turn into moths."

They stared at each other for a moment, after which Dale only chuckled and resumed his search for some money. He opened the second largest pocket and found a single twenty dollar bill, but upon closer inspection..., "*Fer motion picture use*. Roach, ye really are the craziest sunovabitch Ah ever met."

"You'd be surprised how often it works, dude. I used to have like five hundred bucks worth in there. Found it in the trash in Hollywood a while back."

"'Course ye did. What else ye got in here?" He thumbed through some of the cards. Among IDs of both him and his brother was Roach's credit card, which Dale could safely assume was overcharged to high Heaven. There was another credit card with the name Androme de Tremblay on it, which he decided was best left unstolen. He blushed when a condom slid halfway out of one of the folds as he thumbed through. He started at the sight, it fell, and he read it absent-mindedly as he picked it up. "Penna Colada flavoured? Really?"

"Nah, man, it just tastes like a scented eraser."

"'Course ye'd know what a scented 'raser tastes like," he said with another chuckle. "It's 'spired, y'know."

"Is it? Hm. Guess I should get some more."

"Lord knows we don' need no more a' ye," he joked and found another oddity in the wallet: a colourful plastic card from a children's fun park that had been out of business for over fifteen years. He held it up to show Roach and glared playfully.

"Don't throw that away, dude, it's got like 13,000 tickets on it."

"Ain't this 'Hathor's Fun Land' outta binnus?"

"Well, it might come back! I was saving up for the bike."

He shook his head in playful disappointment and slid it back into the wallet beside, "Is this a *Uno* Reverse card, mane? Are you an actch'l clown?"

"You mock me, but it'll come up one day, and it'll be *so* funny when it does."

"An' what's this?" He took out a folded up disintegrating coupon for a free corn dog from Buc-ee's with any purchase of over $10. "Thisun's also 'spired." He observed it more and noticed the doodles Roach had scribbled on it with a thick black marker, including one of a butterfly, a millipede, and a third depicting the Egyptian God Set with great artistry across most of the back.

"Yeah, I know, but I liked the drawings I did on it, so I kept it. I can't use it anyway: the corn dogs are all only beef or pork."

He carefully returned the coupon into the folds, flipped the wallet closed, and tossed it to Roach. "Ye're crazy, mane. God love ye. Now, can ye get outta here on yer own witchyer telly-kinesis?"

Roach stood, pocketed his phone and wallet, and stretched. He gestured with his head at a porthole behind the bed and said, "Should be able to just push that window out, but it might be loud when it hits the water."

"Ah'll go out on the docks an' try an' give ye some 'sisstance. Don' leave 'til... le'ssay five minutes?"

"Alright. Thanks again, dude. If you get in trouble with your friends for releasing me—." He held up his hands as Dale seemed to want to correct him. "I know I know: you didn't release me." Dale calmed back down. "I'm just saying, if you get into trouble, come join us. We're going after Baumbach at some point, and I figure you'd want to help with that. I know Partha's worth a lot, but you and I both know you don't need much money to live how you like out in the mountains.... Plus my friends are all fucking loaded, including the kid."

"They is?"

"For sure, dude."

"Ah'll think 'bout it. An' yu'll send me the real vidya, right? The one that ain't no deep fake?"

"I will. Soon as I can."

"Ah'ight. Get outta here, brother."

"Wait, can I have like a zip-loc or something?"

"What? Why?"

"For the caterpillars, man. They'll drown."

Dale chuckled. "Ah'll go getchye summon, ye loon." He left and returned a moment later with a box of zipper-bags.

With his wallet double-bagged and back in his pocket, Roach hugged his friend, thanked him again, and shooed him out of the room. After about five minutes of waiting alone, he climbed up onto the bed and pressed his hands against the glass of the window. With a combination of the strength from his muscles and his telekinesis, he managed to push the thick glass loose of its fastening, but it made a loud screeching sound. By the time he stopped to try and think of another way out, he already heard people outside looking for him, so he blasted it the rest of the way out of its slot and jumped immediately into the black water below.

The moonless night and layer of garbage on the surface of the ocean helped to hide him as he swam under the yacht and hid on its starboard side. He surfaced, tearing some seaweed and a plastic six-ring out of his hair in the process. Listening, he heard guns being cocked, the yacht being swarmed, and a lot of angry merce-naries shouting. A spot of light landed on him, so he dove under the boat again. He took out his phone and texted Thyne:

⌈ I'm somewhere in San Juan. Please come save me. ⌋

Before he ran out of air, he surfaced at the aft of the boat and immediately heard gunshots. Some of the garbage in front of him exploded across his vision before he could fully fathom what was happening, and he dove beneath the waves again. He swam to another yacht, surfaced behind it for a gasp of air, then swam for two entire minutes before he risked drowning. He surfaced behind a sailboat and wiped the ocean's muck from his burning eyes. It seemed, at least for the moment, that he was safe, so he took out his phone and saw Thyne's reply to his message:

⟦ My plane's in Rome. I'll be there as soon as I can. ⟧

"Thank you, sparkplug," he whispered, "I'll head to the airport." His phone buzzed just as he was taking a breath to dive again:

⟦ No. Don't go to the airport. It'll be crawling with federals. Just find somewhere safe. Get out of America, if you can. The British Virgin Islands are nearby. ⟧

He snickered at the name and scanned his surroundings for any of his pursuers. The coast was clear, so he climbed up into the sailboat he was using as cover and snuck his way to its bridge, unlocking the door with his industrial piercings that doubled as lockpicks.

With a combination of what Pól Barre had taught him aboard his yacht, his own knowledge of how to hot-wire a car, and the many times Partha would ramble about pirates and sailing on his streams or in person, Roach was able to start the engine. When the boat snagged on its mooring line as he reversed out of its spot, he used his telekinesis to break off the dock cleat.

He was halfway out of the marina when he noticed the yacht he had escaped was giving chase. With limited time, he quickly found Polaris, aligned his boat in a generally-East direction, and struggled to find the lever that would unfurl the sail. The wind was in his favour, but he couldn't find the damn pull. "Fuck it." He left the bridge and looked up at the sails. He didn't have his usual butterfly knives— or any knives, for that matter —so he used his telekinesis to tear down the rigging lines one by one but in quick succession.

As the sails fell open, a tempestuous gust pulled the ship forward, knocking him on his ass just in time to dodge a bullet that would have otherwise killed him. With his panicked gaze on the bullet-hole in the mast, he kowtowed and muttered, "Alhamdulillah," repetitively.

He army-crawled around the boat to avoid showing his head again and rummaged around the bridge for a map. After ten minutes of searching with the occasional peek at the yacht behind him, he managed to find an atlas of the Caribbean. It was older than Roach, still not recognising Puerto Rico as an American state, but he only needed measurements. With the boat going 8.8 knots, he did some quick mental maths and calculated how long it might take to reach the British Virgin Islands. The yacht was slowly creeping up on him, but it was likely only going a tenth of a knot faster than he was. He hoped the approximate hour it would take to be out of America would not be long enough for the mercenaries to catch him.

With a moment to catch his breath, he leaned against the wall of the bridge and looked down at his injuries. His hands burned like a cut constantly soaking in alcohol. His entire body was throbbing with pain, and his freshly-salted wounds were making it very clear how much they didn't appreciate being soaked in the toxic Atlantic. What most upset him, however, was the Leviathan brand on his forearm:

Marked forever… like some company asset.

Like swine.

He sighed and took out his wallet to let the caterpillars inside have some air. As one of them crawled around on his burnt fingertips, he spoke tenderly: "I'm on my way to the British Virgin Islands…. Won't be virgin islands for long with me there, huh?" He tried to laugh but whimpered instead. "I'm sorry, Thyne," he wept, "I'm sorry for leaving, and... I'm sorry for coming back.... Sometimes I wish I was never fucking born." The caterpillar fell from his fingers and onto the outside of the bag in his lap as his hand started to tremble. He sniffled and wiped his sopping wet sleeve across his face instinctively, only adding to the mess and the burning and the aching. "Fuck." He hissed at the pain. "If I survive this, I need you to tell me everything about our past life together. I want to remember London more than anything."

He wrangled some of the bugs to go back into the bag, peeked outside to see how close the yacht was, and relaxed back against the wall. His breaths were still laboured and raspy: his lungs burned more than they ever had. With a rough cough he mustered up his voice to say more; it was hoarser than before: "You never got to show me *The Wizard of Oz*...." He was mournful, speaking like a ghost that had already passed.

"Sometimes in my life," he said after another beat of quiet and laboured breathing, "I felt like only half a person. Moreso than being a twin tends to do. That is... if I'm a person at all. I'm such a sorry excuse for a Muslim— for a man—." He whimpered. "Don't come for me, Thyne. Let me die. It's for the best. All I do is hurt the people I love. I didn't mean to get Gideon's arm cut off. I didn't mean to break Partha's wrist. I didn't mean to let Silvino die.... Fuck. Dale only pinged Partha's phone because I taunted him with a picture of Richard, too: it's my fault May is dead. It's my fault Aphid got shot." He sniffled. "It'll be better without me. A brighter world. But I'll miss you all.... All the love I never deserved in the first place."

A beat.

"But other than all my loved ones, I think the thing I'll miss the most when Allah has finally done humanity the service of killing me... the thing I'll miss the most is week-old popcorn from the movie theatre." He chuckled sadly. "That, or getting wasted and listening to children rage at me for being trash in whatever FPS game I'm playing."

His phone buzzed. ⟦ Basil, please stop talking like this. I'm speeding back to Rome right now. I'll save you. You'll be okay. You're a good man, despite what your God might make you think. We'll be together soon. We'll watch Wizard of Oz. You can eat all the popcorn you want and get sloshed. I'll even let you play on my accounts and tank my Elo if it'll help you feel better hearing some tilted brats. ⟧

"Don't text and drive," he warned in as playful a tone as he could manage.

⟦ Voice to text, mate. ⟧

He laughed weakly. After a beat of silent crying, he coughed away the tears and spoke hoarsely: "Don't come for me, Thyne, you'll only get hurt, too."

⟦ I don't care. I don't care if it's dangerous. I'm coming to save you. You better be alive when I get there, or you will be hurting me guaranteed. I love you basil. ⟧

He sighed. "I love you, too." And in Arabic to himself:

"Disgusting.

"Swine.

"Monster.

"Filth.

"*Cockroach*."

A while later, he peeked through the windows above him again and saw what must have been The Virgin Islands. He started packing up his caterpillars back in his wallet. Once they were secured, he bagged it, slid it back in his pocket, and crawled out onto the deck. The yacht was closer than ever now, and if he waited much longer he'd risk being caught. His unhindered vision in the oppressive darkness worked greatly to his advantage in determining the perfect time to...

Jump silently into the ocean and stay beneath the surface as his stolen vessel continued ambling eastward. He swam toward land for as long as he physically could, and when he surfaced he was glad to see that the mercenaries on the yacht didn't seem to notice he had left the sailboat.

After swimming the rest of the way, he climbed up out of the water like a sea hag, dripping in seaweed and garbage that he peeled off of himself to throw into the piles of trash on the shore. When he was more or less free of the restrictive mess, he scanned the area: an unlit beach with a sleepy town in the distance.

Viktor always had a good idea of the state of those he had been ordered and intimidated into keeping healthy. At any given moment, he was keeping Thyne youthful and stopping his rotten smoke-filled lungs from developing cancer. He was keeping Francis alive through all his excessive drinking. Since the formation of *The Crown* and *Tiara*, he was furthermore responsible for people like Roach, who was seemingly alive only by the grace of some God he entertained when Viktor first got a sense of his conditions. He was surprisingly healthy despite his diet, but it was still an impressive feat for him to have made it, at the time, thirty-two years without Viktor's aid. Partha's coke habit was also quite near to killing him when Viktor first met him.

Saving them from themselves was as easy as a flick of the wrist for Viktor, as was keeping himself alive and healthy through all his copious drug abuse and the little allowance he was given of proper sleep. The only person who required a level of effort and focus to constantly keep alive was Melchiresa. He had saved him from death countless times: his stroke however many centuries ago, a lightning strike to the heart, gunshots, chloroform, cocaine, and *dear lord his drinking*. It was only after Francis' recent break in sanity that he surpassed the mute in alcohol consumption.

Melchiresa could drink anyone under the table, and Viktor actively struggled to keep his liver from declaring war on the rest of him.

The manner in which he sensed reality was entirely unique. Since his birth, he was both blessed and cursed with an extraordinary sense. It wasn't the same as seeing or feeling, but he knew the location and state of the innumerable cells and microscopic organisms within an undefined range around his own. He could sense every single one of them at all times, and when he realised he could manipulate them, he fancied himself a God.

After decades of practice, it still took Thyne threatening his daughter's life for Viktor to push himself to be able to monitor the health of Thyne and Francis and Melchiresa when they were halfway across the world. Every centimetre further from him made it increasingly difficult to differentiate them from the cells around them. That was, until he realised that he could push his extrasensory ability even further than its baseline. He could sense things smaller than single-celled organisms. Things like DNA.

So now that he had been doing this for Thyne for over a century, he was intimately familiar with the Brit's genetic make-up to the point that he could heal him from anywhere in the world, but Thyne rarely found himself in need of such a thing. In fact, Viktor had trouble recalling *any* instance wherein Thyne was so near death that he needed immediate attention.

Until the day after he stormed out of the manor in Italy…. Viktor had no way of knowing why, but Thyne's blood pressure spiked to a deadly degree, and it wa only through his immediate alleviating the situation that Thyne did not die of cardiac arrest.

And Thyne knew.

He knew when it happened that he had just been saved from death. His heart seemed to explode all at once before pulling itself back together as if in fear of his rage. He saw his life flash before his eyes in an instant, and in the next he saw only red.

1978.

She hadn't died.

Despite his rage, which was entirely evident on his face, his breaths were short and shallow enough to not be heard or overly exaggerated. His fists were clenched, but his knuckles were only pink. The red of his face was not much redder than after a long run. His movements through London were quick and graceful, and perhaps the passers-by would have assumed he was only angry because of the thunder rolling over the dreary city. He closed himself into his home and immediately descended into the secret partitioned part of his basement. The furrowing of his brow was enraged, but it was also furrowed with determination. Everything he was doing was done precisely and with intention. He dug through his weapons and supplies for a while, bringing armfuls of materials to a workbench under the centre of his house.

Before then, he had heard absolutely nothing of the outside world. He hadn't heard the thunder. He hadn't heard the voices. It was nothing but a high-pitched ringing in his ears and white-noise in his mad mind. When he flicked on his soldering gun and spent a moment waiting for it to heat up, the voices and calming sound of pouring rain faded into his perception. He paid special attention to Roach and Dale's voices. For this reason, when the captured brute asked him directly for a pick-up, Thyne was already looking at his phone to try figuring out the logistics of such a sudden trans-Atlantic flight.

Trying to help Roach pulled him from his work, but there was nothing that could quiet the rage. He left the workbench and ambled his way upstairs to boot up his computer and send notice to the Fiumicino airport that he would be flying out at least fourteen hours later. He marked his destination airport as the one in Road Town, and with a quick bag packed, rushed to his garage.

While he packed the *Locust*, he had a long internal argument on whether or not to involve Francis in Roach's rescue. His pondering was interrupted, however, when he noticed that Jean-Jacques' motorcycle was no longer in the garage. He stroked his chin, trying to recall if it was there when he had arrived. The attempts to conjure a memory were futile, so he got in the car, exchanged a few more texts with Roach, and was on his way.

After a while of driving, he was exchanging texts with Roach via the *Locust's* voice-to-text functions. He listened out for Roach's replies with his microphones, but it had been a few hours since he had said anything. He pulled into a petrol station and refilled as he checked for more messages. Still nothing. His stomach cinched. After sending a quick question to Roach, he called Francis.

Francis didn't answer. "Typical," he grumbled as he noticed Roach had replied to his question asking where he was:

⌜ Hiding in a dumpster. <3 ⌟

He rolled his eyes. ⟦ Don't scare me like that. ⟧

⌜ It's okay it doesn't have any needles or broken glass or anything. ⌟

⟦ That's not what I meant, idiot. Why have you been so quiet? ⟧

Roach replied with a shrugging emoji.

⟦ Are you still in San Juan? ⟧

⌜ Nope, but apparently I'm still in America. ⌟

⟦ Where? ⟧

⌜ The Virgin Islands. I just need to sneak further East, but the cops are after me, now, so it's like a whole ordeal, y'know? They've got dogs sniffing for me. Lucky I'm covered in garbage and seawater. I mean it hurts like shit, but you gotta take what you can get. ⌟

⟦ What time is it there? ⟧

⌈ Idk. Lunch time. I already ate, though, so don't worry. ⌋

⟦ Out of the bin, I take it? ⟧

⌈ Uh huh! (: I found a whole sub in here still wrapped up! This dumpster is for a sandwich place or something. ⌋

Thyne chuckled. ⟦ Alright, well I don't know how to get your bloody car to read your messages to me, and I need to get back on the road. Just give me verbal updates when you can. ⟧

Roach replied with a gif of someone saluting, and Thyne rushed to finish filling the tank and get back on the road.

The sounds of cops and mercenaries in the area started to increase in volume, so Roach turned off his phone's screen and froze. He heard a dog sniffing and encroaching on him. Holding his breath, he listened to the hound as his heart beat up into his throat. "Did you find him, boy?" a man said in Spanish. Roach heard his footsteps crunching on the gravel in the alley and held the dumpster's lid closed with his telekinesis, but he was relieved to hear the man slap the dog's nose and scold him: "You no good mutt! You can eat when we've found him."

When they were gone, Roach let out the breath he had been holding and released the lid. He listened for a while longer, and after half an hour, the sounds of mercenaries and police searching for him were fading. He carefully peered out of the dumpster, checking for life in the alley. There were some citizens walking by when he inched the lid open, but they didn't notice him. He watched as they turned into the alley, talking to each other about a movie they had presumably all just seen. They approached a door, one of them took out a key-ring, and they all went inside. Roach could only assume it was the entrance to the apartments over the sandwich shop, so after two minutes of quiet, he climbed silently out of the dumpster and snuck to the door. He checked for passers-by again before picking the lock as quickly as possible.

It opened into a featureless hall with a flickering fluorescent light, stained linoleum flooring, and no windows. He pressed further, eventually spotting a staircase. A peek through the railing toward the top. He was blinded briefly by the sun through a skylight, and after rubbing the ache from his eyes, he rushed up the stairs. On the top floor, he found a ladder to the roof and clambered up onto it, straining his muscles to open the rusted-shut door at its top. Once outside, he silently closed the trap door and scanned the roof of blue concrete. The only features were an AC vent and metal chimney. The edges of the roof were bordered with a six-inch high lip, and the blue concrete was slippery, presumably from some sort of weather treatment.

He took three large strides away from the door and toward the Northern face of the building, beyond which he could see the rotten Atlantic and the trashy shores of whatever island he had found himself on. To avoid being seen by anyone below, he laid down and looked up at the clouds. "Alright," he whispered, "I'm just...

laying on a roof. Let's cross our fingers they don't send any helicopters after me like in GTA." He chuckled and looked at his phone's screen for a reply, noticing, "My battery's almost dead, dude. I think I have to turn the phone off. ETA?"

The phone buzzed a moment later: ⟦ Text Francis your address. It'll probably take me at least 16 hours to get there mate. ⟧

"No, dude, I don't want to ruin the bit. I thought of one while I was hiding in the dumpster. It's gonna be really funny."

⟦ You're impossible. ⟧

"Love you, too. Turning the phone off now to preserve the battery. If I manage to find like a hotel or something I'll shower and charge it."

⟦ Bloody rotter. ⟧ He turned off his phone, put his burning hands behind his salty muck-covered head, and breathed in a lungful of the disgusting odour around him. "Alright. You like audiobooks, right?" He cleared his aching throat. "Sing in me, Muse, and through me tell the story of that man skilled in all ways of contending, the wanderer, harried for years on end, after he plundered the stronghold on the proud height of Troy…."

It was annoying at first, but Thyne grew to enjoy the raspy retelling of the epic by someone with such a good sense for poetry and showmanship. It was almost like a song the way he told the story. In fact, it was so beautifully told, Thyne second-guessed if he had ever read it at all. Unfortunately, halfway into the story, Roach expressed that he needed to go find somewhere new to hide because his rooftop had been compromised. He shortly thereafter chattered with someone in Spanish and it was only a few moments after that that Thyne was informed he was about to take a shower in a kind woman's home, his phone on the charger nearby.

He listened to Roach singing quietly in the shower and found himself getting butterflies. Even with all the other voices still sounding, it was like he could only perceive Roach. And what was he singing but *Heart and Soul*? He parked in the hangar with his plane while Roach was showering and took advantage of the break to text him: ⟦ Cheeky bugger. <3 ⟧

A few minutes later Roach replied: ⌈ You like the little private concert? That'll be 14 bucks at least, bud. ⌋

⟦ About to get on the plane. Get back to the story! ⟧

⌈ Oh… I was gonna try and sleep. I'm pretty much on death's door at the moment, and I was ordered not to die, you see. ⌋

Thyne frowned. ⟦ Oh. Okay. Sweet dreams. Be careful that bird isn't gonna grass on you, mate. ⟧

⌈ Nah, she's chill. She's got a hammer and sickle tattoo it's sick. And she let me borrow some of her husband's clothes while she washes mine. He's fighting in Mexico rn. Anyway, I'll ramble the rest of the odyssey at you until I pass out. ETA? ⌋

⟦ It's a 10 hour flight. ⟧

⌈ Nice I'll get a full 8 hours, then. ⌋

〖 Ha... yeah. 〗

⌈ "Oh no, Roach, don't get a good night's sleep after a week straight of torture!" come on, dude. I'm sorry, but I'm what they call in the biz 'the big sleepy.' ⌋

〖 Yeah, get some sleep, mate. 〗

As promised, Roach rambled more of the story to Thyne before eventually becoming incoherent and falling asleep.

While waiting for clearance to enter the runway, Thyne texted Viktor: 〖 Flying for the next ten. Keep me awake. 〗

Chapter 58
They're Kissing Again

The sky was infinite. The horizon was a neverending sunset over a neverending ocean. It expanded impossibly in every direction: an explosion of pinks and violets like the clouds were a garden of carnations basking in the orange glow. They waltzed through the sunbeams slowly and beautifully and....

He was awoken suddenly by a series of alarms and warnings. Immediately alert, he scanned his instruments, gently pulled the plane out of its shallow dive, and recentred himself. His heart was beating hard and fast, and his hands were trembling. He must have dozed off and accidentally pushed the yoke forward. With the plane flying safely and the autopilot reengaged, coming down from the start, he popped another "wakey-wakey pill" and slapped his cheeks. He flew in silence for another ten minutes, but when his eyelids gained weight, he shook away the drowsiness and took out his phone. The first call he made was to Francis who, as usual, didn't answer. After some grumbling, he took a deep breath and called Roach.

"Hello?" he droned and yawned, "Thyne? You okay, dude?"

"You have to talk to me, Roach."

He yawned again and sat up. With a look at the clock on the bedside table he rubbed the sleep from his eyes. He had only gotten six hours of sleep, but Thyne sounded panicked. "Did I do something wrong?"

"You have to keep me awake."

"Alright…. Uh…." He shook away his own sleepiness, covered his naked torso with the hoodie his host had cleaned and laid out for him, and dragged his feet to the kitchen. She was cooking dinner, so he had a quick exchange with her as he brewed a pot of coffee. Then to Thyne: "You want me to keep going with *The Odyssey* or what?"

"If you're somewhere you can talk like this for a spell, then I'd appreciate it."

"Like this? Like… on the phone?"

"Yeah."

"Alright, Kara shouldn't mind unless the feds show up." He said a few things in Spanish to her, and she gleefully invited him to stay as long as he needed to hide. "You'll have to give her some money or something. I feel bad for leeching, but she's real nice. Anyway… Hmmm… In my history class my senior year on Valentine's Day we learned about this old news article with thirty-six questions that would supposedly make anyone fall in love. It's meant for strangers to ask each other, but want me to ask them anyway?"

Thyne blushed and yawned. "That should do. Yeah."

"Alright just a minute." Roach poured himself a cup of coffee and got comfortable on Kara's living room sofa across from where she was working on her laptop. She smiled at him when he came into the room but scolded him for not putting his cup on a coaster. With the blunder corrected, he sank into the cushions, nursed his coffee, and asked Thyne the first question: "If you could invite anyone in the world to dinner, who would you invite?"

"Wait, can your mate hear us? Kara, was it?"

"She can hear me, but she doesn't know English."

"Are you certain?"

"Uh… Like sixty percent certain."

"I guess it doesn't matter," he said through slightly-gritted teeth. "What was the question again?" Roach repeated it. "Well, I can't exactly say you or Frankenstein."

"Why not?"

"Because you're both disgusting." He chuckled.

"Fair."

Thyne took some time to think. "Tatum Abraham."

"Oh? To kill him, no doubt."

"Absolutely." A beat. "Who would you invite?"

"Well, I can't just steal your answer." He paused to think and eventually answered by naming the dictator of the United States, "Elijah Park."

"To kill him, as well, I presume."

"Yes, of course, but not until after I've picked his brain. You know how I like to do it, you eavesdropper."

Thyne chuckled. He was feeling rejuvenated and more awake by the conversation, and they were only one question into it. They went on for a few more. The fifth was, "When was the last time you sang for yourself?"

Thyne's mood was audibly soured by the question: "I've never sung for myself."

"That's so sad, sparkplug. Singing is supposed to be cathartic…. What about for someone else? Have you done that?"

"Yeah… Yeah, I sang Franky his favourite song a couple years ago for his birthday. He probably doesn't remember…."

"He remembers, sparkplug."

"Sure…."

Two questions later: "Do you have a secret hunch about how you'll die?"

"I actually know precisely how and when I'll die," said Thyne.

"What? You do?"

"Yeah. Chronomancer best mate has some perks."

"Perks? I don't know why you'd want to know how and when you'll die. That sounds horrible."

"It's not so bad…. Do you have a hunch about your death, though?"

"I mean, do you have to ask? State execution, obviously. Maybe a victim gets the better of me in my old age, though. Not to mention the mercenaries after us. Cigarettes. Rabies, even!" He laughed. "It'll be exciting, whatever it is."

Question ten was: "If you could change anything about the way you were raised, what would you change?" Thyne took some time to think, during which he asked for Roach's answer. "Me? I wouldn't change it at all."

"Not even the whole… getting stabbed business?"

"Nah, man. Things happen for a reason. It made me who I am. No sense in dwelling on the past. Blah blah blah. You know me. You know how I am."

"Well, I suppose if it's only one thing I can change, I'd quash the invoice."

"But, that's why you killed her, so if she hadn't done that, maybe you wouldn't have ever been free of her." Thyne's stomach turned and heart ached at the reminder that he hadn't succeeded in his attempted matricide. He might have mentioned it, but Roach continued, "Wouldn't you want your father to have not offed himself?"

"I suppose…."

Roach could read the room, so he moved on to the next question which would involve them telling each other their entire life stories. After they wasted a good twenty minutes with those: "If you could wake up tomorrow with any one ability or quality, what would it be?"

"Can it be something supernatural?" asked Thyne.

"Sure. Why not?"

"Omniscience," he answered immediately.

"Shit, dude. Really? Wouldn't that be burdensome?" Thyne didn't answer, so Roach thought of his own and commented a moment later: "I'd probably want the ability to consume anything with no unwanted side-effects. I heard plutonium tastes like candy, and I *need* to taste it now. And I mean they literally named it yellow cake uranium! Like how am I supposed to not want to eat that!?"

"Barmy bastard," said Thyne with a chuckle.

"I suppose I already know your answer to the next question, then."

"What is it?"

"If you could learn the truth about yourself, the future, or literally anything else, what would you want to learn?"

"Everything," he answered instantly again.

"Yeah, figured."

"What about you?"

"Nothing."

"Opposites attract, oi, Basil?"

"Yeah, dude."

They continued.

Later, they were to state their greatest accomplishments. Thyne took a moment to answer, and Roach was not prepared for how cute his response would be: "Mine is probably being ranked first in the entire world in *War Rose*." A popular first-person shooter game with a brutal competitive scene. It was set in World War Two with award-winning accuracy in its maps, weapons, and aircraft.

"Woah, dude. Are you really number one in the world?"

"Yes."

"Still?"

"Last I checked."

"When'd you last check?"

"Before Party streamed the factories. Before we went to Korea. Before everything went tits up."

"Why do you want to relive that, though? Isn't that game really accurate?"

"Yeah."

"So doesn't it trigger PTSD in you or something?"

"Yes. Headshot. Get fucked, kraut." They chuckled. "Anyway, mate, what's yours?"

"My greatest accomplishment?"

"Yeah."

"The wholesome answer is quitting H." A beat. "But the real answer is definitely all the hundreds of beautiful murders I've gotten away with."

"Naturally," said Thyne with a playfully teasing tone.

They continued, and Roach eventually said, "Alright, these should be easier for you since your memories, as I understand it, stick out to you when they're especially nice or especially horrible?"

"Okay?" led Thyne.

"What is your most treasured memory?"

"Oh, where to begin?" He was audibly beaming as happy memories came flooding in. "Well, my first instinct is to say when Franky took me and Basil back to Ancient Greece, and I proposed to Basil with Prometheus' ring, then he proposed to me. Maybe a little disrespectful to not say meeting Prometheus and getting said ring was better, but I love my Basil so so so much, he's better than any God."

"Well, that is high praise! I should have loved to meet him!"

"You *are* him. I'm certain of it."

"Oh? So I'm better than any God, then?"

Thyne started, and his blushy nervousness could be felt through the phone. "Well…. Uh…. What's *your* most treasured memory?"

"You're so cute, dude. Mine? Promise not to laugh?"

"Of course, mate."

"My first time."

"Horny bugger."

"Nah…. Nah that's not why. My first time was with…." It wouldn't matter if he finished the sentence aloud, he had already audibly admitted to being a serial killer, but his voice still trailed off and eyes flicked to Kara anxiously.

"Ohhoho! You cheeky bastard!"

"Yeah, and… uh… well, I wasn't on H at the time, but later on, it was because of him that I stopped shooting up."

"That's so sweet, mate."

"Thanks…. Anyway… the next question is what's your most terrible memory? We can… skip this one if you want."

"I think it'd be a dead tie between watching Basil die and hearing Viktor kill my daughter."

"Yeah…. Yeah mine's definitely finding Silvino's empty prison cell with his blood still on the floor. But I think surprisingly close behind is the most terrifying thing that ever happened to me."

"Oh?"

"Yeah. Me and Dale were camping in his bus in the Appalachian mountains. It was a hunting trip, but other than that we were just chilling. We got drunk and shot each other with bulletproof vests on just for fun. I fixed his truck while he rambled about his kid sister at me. I taught him a little about sumo wrestling and showed him a few moves. He showed me how to take apart his gun and put it back together again. We watched shitty action movies and shotgunned beers. Bros being bros kinda stuff. And, well, one night we were sat around a campfire and chatting, then suddenly out of the woods…. I mean, I don't even know how to describe what we saw, dude. It was freaky. It was this huge gangly thing, like twelve, fifteen feet tall, with scratchy-looking black fur all over and this horrifyingly human-looking face.

It had long thin fingers, and I swear it spoke to us in Japanese, or maybe Chinese. I could ask Francis.

"Anyway, me and Dale ran into the bus and cowered in his bedroom. He tried shooting it, and when he ran out of bullets in his handgun, I used my telekinesis to push the thing away when it came near, but it was too heavy to move entirely, and it started jostling the bus by grabbing onto either side, and we just about shit ourselves, and… yeah…. Eventually it ran off, but we were traumatised. At least the experience brought me and Dale even closer, though."

"That's horrifying."

"It was."

They chatted about cryptids and ghosts and other supernatural things, but Roach, sounding evermore saddened by the topic, eventually put them back on track to finish the little love quiz. It came up to the last three questions:

"Alright, thirty-four is that your house is on fire, and you've already saved all your pets and loved ones but can only save one item. What would you save?"

"Well… typically, I'd say Oli's teddy, but since Francis gave me this journal of his—. Well, actually, the notebook is in my plane, and this is a house fire, so Oli's teddy is my answer."

"What's in the journal from Franky?"

There was a long beat. "It's—. He wrote it for me—. He started it after—. After I died."

"How morbid."

"It's lovely, actually. I reread it from time to time. I wish he knew how much I love him."

"Yeah… I've tried telling him, but it just makes him lose himself in the void, and that far-off look he gets is so… sad."

"It's heartbreaking." A beat. "Anyway. Uh. What would you save in the house-fire?"

"I'm not very materialistic or sentimental. I have a perfect memory, y'know? Maybe I'd save my parlour guitar, but—." He pause. "Actually, thinking about it now, I think I'd save Aphid's favourite plush."

"Gods, mate, and you say I'm the cute one."

He scoffed playfully. "Whatever, dude. I love my dogs, and I'm gonna miss the Hell out of Aphid. He was a street dog in Mexico. I adopted him when I sort of saved him from this old bitch that hurt him. He had gone up to her looking for food, and she kicked him in the face, so I gave her a talking to and shooed her off. But… what I really wanted to do was feed her to him. I didn't, though. This was the day before my wedding, so I didn't have a drop of blood on my hands yet and didn't want to disappoint Silvino. I figured it was just an intrusive thought until I realised most people don't have such murderous lecherous thoughts so often."

Thyne was quiet for a beat as he tried to keep himself from indulging Roach in said lechery. He shook away the lust and said, "What's the next question?"

"Uh. Yeah, sure. Next one is: out of your entire family, whose death would you find the most disturbing, and why?"

Thyne chuckled sadly. "All my family's already dead, mate."

"What about Neodesha? She's your step-daughter... or something."

"If she counts, then yes her death would perturb and upset me."

"And for me the answer is obviously Karson."

"I could have guessed as much."

"Alright, and the last question is—. Drumroll, please!" He drummed on his lap and heard the faint tapping of Thyne drumming on his chair's armrest. "—not really a question! We tell each other a personal problem then give each other advice on it."

"Alright." He took a deep breath. "My problem is that I learned something disturbing. And, mate, I am so unbelievably cross about it. I've never been more miffed in my life."

"What is it?"

"My mother didn't die in the fire I set."

"What? She didn't?"

"She lived to 1978. I saw it under a quote from her in the Maitland Music Group museum."

"Well, shit, dude, I'm sorry to hear that. Obviously we need to burn down the museum and defile the grave!" He laughed evilly.

Thyne chuckled. "I'm not so sure about defiling the grave, but you've got the right spirit with the arson."

"Yeah, I'll help! Is the gang in London now?"

"No, I stormed out to take down Maitland alone."

"Cool, so I'll have time to do my plan."

"What plan?"

"For the bit about coming back from the dead. I'm gonna bleach my hair and wear all white (I look horrible in white) and be like, 'I'm Roach the White.'"

He scoffed and rolled his eyes. "Well, whatever, what's your issue you want advice on, then?"

"Oh. I'll admit I kind of only brought up this quiz so I could say this." He cleared his throat. "Thyne, I love you. I want to be with you. But, the problem is that... well... I want you all to myself." He sounded self-loathing even just admitting such a thing.

"All to yourself while you shag my best mate?"

"Well, I'd be okay with you and Francis dating, if he ever gets his shit together enough to realise you're meant to be. And, if you and Sonny want to get together, I'm fine with that. But... uh...."

Thyne sighed. "You want me to break up with Giovanni, is what you're saying."

A beat. "Yeah."

"I do love him."

"Well, he *enslaved* Francis, and I love Francis. Maybe if he didn't treat him like shit, I'd be okay with it, but he literally still calls him 'The Boy' like he's a child servant."

"Well, Francis dated Viktor!"

"Thyne... we both know Frankenstein isn't the most socially adept. He definitely didn't think it through."

Thyne sighed, groaned, then said, "Fine. I'll... I'll call him when we're back in London. I need to tell the others not to go looking for you anyway."

"Looking for me? Why would they be looking for me if they think I'm dead?"

"I didn't tell them you're dead."

"Oh. Well, when you call Giovanni you can tell him to spread the word."

Thyne rolled his eyes. "I still won't be to Road Town for another hour and a half, so let's talk about something else."

Finished with the questions, they thought of more to ask each other. Thyne told stories about his time with Oliver like how they used to play marbles and jacks, which earned him some playful teasing for being "so old, dude." Roach yapped about his wedding, about his sister, and gave some basic mechanical tips. The last leg of the flight seemed shorter than it actually was because of the chatter, and when Thyne could see the islands in the distance, he gleefully exclaimed as much to Roach.

He rushed to a window to look for the plane, surprised by a wall of darkness behind the curtain. They had chatted for almost four hours. In the far distance, high above the scattered clouds, he saw Thyne's lights. "Oh, there you are! I should head to the airport."

"As long as it's the British one. I can't fly in American airspace, they'll get all miffed."

"Alright. See ya soon, dude. Love ya!" He made kissy sounds, Thyne returned the sentiment, and Roach ended the call.

As Thyne readjusted to put his phone back in his pocket, he accidentally pushed on his rudder pedal. It turned his plane off of its heading and took him out of autopilot, which he noticed immediately when the plane chimed. He failed to notice the slight deviation in his heading, but he was more concerned with changing his radio frequency to the controller in Road Town. He called in and asked for clearance to descend, but there was no response. He tried a few more frequencies, listening for other chatter before speaking, but it was dead quiet. "What the bloody

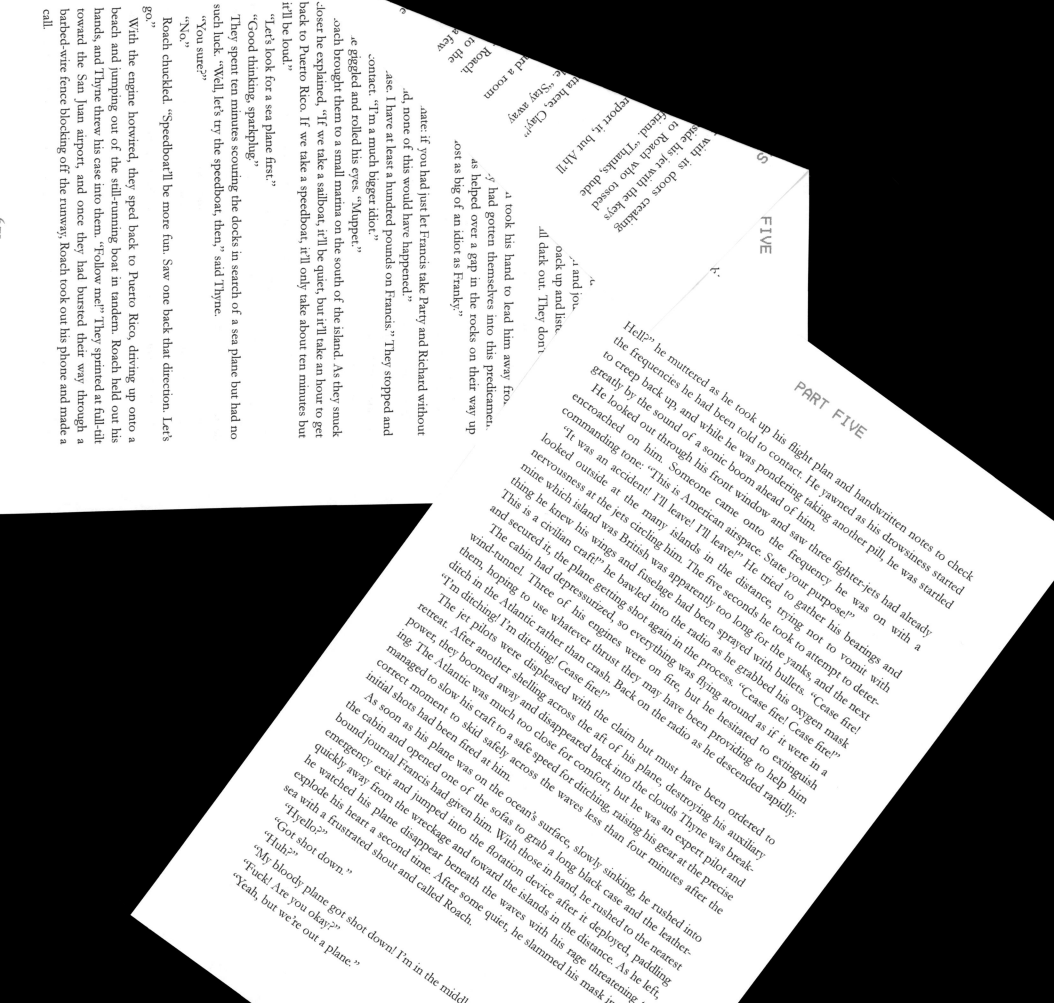

FIVE

PART FIVE

call.

barbed-wire fence blocking off the runway, Roach took out his phone and made a

toward the San Juan airport, and once they had bursted their way through a

hands, and Thyne threw his case into them. "Follow me!" They sprinted at full-tilt

beach and jumping out of the still-running boat in tandem. Roach held out his

With the engine hotwired, they sped back to Puerto Rico, driving up onto a

go."

Roach chuckled. "Speedboat'll be more fun. Saw one back that direction. Let's

"No."

"You sure?"

such luck. "Well, let's try the speedboat, then," said Thyne.

They spent ten minutes scouring the docks in search of a sea plane but had no

"Good thinking, sparkplug."

"Let's look for a sea plane first."

it'll be loud."

back to Puerto Rico. If we take a speedboat, it'll only take about ten minutes but

closer he explained, "If we take a sailboat, it'll be quiet, but it'll take an hour to get

oach brought them to a small marina on the south of the island. As they snuck

.e giggled and rolled his eyes. "Muppet."

.ontact. "I'm a much bigger idiot."

.ase. I have at least a hundred pounds on Francis." They stopped and

.d, none of this would have happened."

.ate: if you had just let Francis take Party and Richard without

.a took his hand to lead him away fro.

.y had gotten themselves into this predicamen.

.as helped over a gap in the rocks on their way up

.ost as big of an idiot as Franky."

"Hell?" he muttered as he took up his flight plan and handwritten notes to check the frequencies he had been told to contact. He yawned as his drowsiness started to creep back up, and while he was pondering taking another pill, he was startled greatly by the sound of a sonic boom ahead of him.

He looked out through his front window and saw three fighter-jets had already encroached on him. Someone came onto the frequency he was on with a commanding tone: "This is American airspace. State your purpose!"

"It was an accident! I'll leave! I'll leave!" He tried to gather his bearings and looked outside at the many islands in the distance, trying not to vomit with nervousness at the jets circling him. The five seconds he took to attempt to determine which island was British was apparently too long for the yanks, and the next thing he knew his wings and fuselage had been sprayed with bullets. "Cease fire! This is a civilian craft!" he bawled into the radio as he grabbed his oxygen mask and secured it, the plane getting shot again in the process. "Cease fire! Cease fire!"

The cabin had depressurized, so everything was flying around as if it were in a wind-tunnel. Three of his engines were on fire, but he hesitated to extinguish them, hoping to use whatever thrust they may have been providing to help him ditch in the Atlantic rather than crash. Back on the radio as he descended rapidly: "I'm ditching! I'm ditching! Cease fire!"

The jet pilots were displeased with the claim but must have been ordered to retreat. After another shelling across the aft of his plane, destroying his auxiliary power, they boomed away and disappeared back into the clouds Thyne was breaking. The Atlantic was much too close for comfort, but he was an expert pilot and managed to slow his craft to a safe speed for ditching, raising his gear at the correct moment to skid safely across the waves less than four minutes after the initial shots had been fired at him.

As soon as his plane was on the ocean's surface, slowly sinking, he rushed into the cabin and opened one of the sofas to grab a long black case and the leatherbound journal Francis had given him. With those in hand, he rushed to the nearest emergency exit and jumped into the flotation device after it deployed, paddling quickly away from the wreckage and toward the islands in the distance. As he left, he watched his plane disappear beneath the waves with his rage threatening to explode his heart a second time. After some quiet, he slammed his mask i sea with a frustrated shout and called Roach.

"Hyello?"

"Got shot down."

"Huh?"

"My bloody plane got shot down! I'm in the middl.

"Fuck! Are you okay?"

"Yeah, but we're out a plane."

"Shit…. Well… Should I still go to t[h]

He sighed. "Fuck. I don't know."

After some deliberation, they agre[ed] paddling. He struggled through the ga[?] neared the rocky coastline: his anger evident [?] and complaints. He was ready to jump out and sw[im] entire raft floated up out of the water and was gen[tly] Roach telekinetically.

"Thank you," he huffed as he stood and grabbed his jour[nal] helped him step out of the raft wearing a dopey grin all the while. so chuffed?"

"You look cute with your head shaved," he lilted.

A slight blush. "Well, you look awful." The swelling on his lip had mostly dissi-pated, and the shower and first-aid he had administered afterwards had done him wonders to wash off all the blood all over him, but his left eye was still blackened and bruised, and the cut on his brow would likely last months. All things consid-ered, however, the time he had spent resting and licking his wounds had him in much better spirits and much more presentable than he had been only twelve hours prior.

"You don't look in good health yourself, dude. When's the last time you slept?"

His blush deepened. "I don't know."

"Will you be able to fly us back to London?"

"Not without a plane, dickwit."

"Will you be able to fly us back if we get a plane?"

He flailed his hands around angrily. "Come off it, Roach."

He sighed and pulled the Brit in with an air of irritation but a small smile as he pinched his chin to force eye contact with him. "You're so cute. I have us a plane. We just have to get to San Juan."

"I can fly it."

"Promise?"

He smiled fiendishly and said with a mocking tone and overacted gesture, "*Hand on heart.*"

Roach chuckled and leaned in to kiss him tenderly. As he retreated, he whis-pered, "What heart?"

"Bellend," he replied with playful venom.

Roach retreated from the embrace and picked up something from the colourful sand beside him. It was long and rectangular and thin, wrapped entirely in aluminium foil. He passed it to Thyne with his big dumb grin returned.

"What's this then?"

"Birthday present."

They ran across the active runway toward a hanga[r] open. When they rushed inside they saw Dale standing b[y] in hand, ending his call with Roach. He tossed the keys Thyne's case back to its owner before running up to hug his

"I owe you."

"Ye're damn right ye do! Now go on! Get! Ah'mma have ta[?]

"Thanks so much, man. That's Thyne, by the way. Cute right?" Dale rolled his eyes and pushed his friend toward the jet. "Get o[n] from the moment ogling the plane, Thyne smiled awkwardly at Da[le]

"Ah'm goin'. Ah'm goin'." He lit himself a cigarette and headed tow[ard] attached to the hangar.

Thyne watched him for a moment before shuffling into the jet afte[r] While the brute was pulling up and locking the air-stairs, Thyne rushed cockpit to get a feel for it. "Buckle up, Basil!" he shouted into the cabin afte[r] minutes of studying the controls.

"Okie dokie, Captain Cutiepants."

Thyne rolled his eyes at Roach's casual unbothered nature and started th[e] engines. He took off without clearance, and it was only five minutes into the fligh[t] that they were being trailed by fighter jets and shot-at. Luckily, Dale's plane was not as defenceless as Thyne's had been. It was also a smaller target and therefore more manoeuvrable. He had never flown this specific model of plane, but it had complex delta wings and powerful engines which would help him to pull off manoeuvres that would make these American man-children cry. "Try not to pass out, Basil!" he shouted as he flicked a switch to drop the oxygen masks for the few seats in the cabin and put on his own mask.

As he secured it over his face, he saw two fighter jets booming toward him aiming for his well-protected engines in the wings. After banking almost ninety degrees to fly between them, he turned around and shot both of them directly in their engines before punching his throttle and starting a rapid climb. There were three jets following him up into the clouds, and he used the brief cover to level his plane and float down in a flat spin, almost like an autumn leaf. As he descended, in such a way, he shot the jets that were swarming past him in quick succession. They had not expected such an advanced manoeuvre, or perhaps even thought he had stalled, which had Thyne laughing maniacally; he slowly increased his engines' power and

After spraying their undercarriages, he barrel-rolled through a cloud to avoid more shots from two jets that were sand-witching him from above and below. Poor Roach in the cabin tried his best to parse what was happening, but he was in and out of blackouts with all the g-forces acting on the plane. He managed to help destroy one of the jets… maybe… at some point… by shoving its rudder with his telekinesis, but he was increasingly lightheaded and confused and nauseous. He also tried not to panic about all the constant peppering of bullets on their plane, but the fear was inescapable and contributing to his poor state.

After fifteen minutes more of dogfighting, Thyne had thinned the herd to only two jets, which he destroyed by kiting them and cleverly using his own plane and the clouds to hide them from each other, successfully sending them into a head-on collision. An orange glow briefly lit up the sky behind him, and Thyne let out an involuntary cheer when he saw it reflecting off the clouds in front of him and felt the shockwave. He laughed maniacally and circled back around toward the airport looking for more trouble. When it seemed he had exhausted all of his playthings, he pouted and twirled the plane gracefully to align it with a heading to London, breaking the sound barrier as he raced away from America.

When they were out of American airspace, he pressurised the cabin to climb into a cruise. Once they were established on a steady track toward England, he took off his mask and cheered, "BLIMEY, THIS IS A GOOD BIRD!" After a moment of quiet, he looked behind him for Roach and shouted, "Come up here! Come sit with me!"

Roach took off his oxygen mask and unbuckled. He had to hunch over when he stood, which only worsened the wobbliness of his legs. He grabbed onto the low ceiling to steady himself, swallowed a mouthful of vomit, and struggled his way into the cockpit.

"There's a jump seat there. Just pull it down." Roach did as he was told and collapsed into the tiny little seat that creaked under his weight. "You alright, mate?"

He held his dizzied head. "I'll be okay."

"That was so fun!"

He smiled weakly at him. "You're cute, sparkplug."

"If we had planes like this in the war I never would have transferred to infantry." He beamed. "We're in the clear now, Basil. Next stop: London."

"Great. Would love to be back on solid fucking land."

"You scared of heights, mate?"

He shook his head, which upset his stomach more. After holding back from vomiting, he spat on the floor and let his long hair down. "I don't like planes, and I don't like roller coasters. I also don't entirely appreciate getting shot at, y'know?"

"Poor Basil," he said as he reached out to pat his knee lovingly. "Well, I'm going to come down from that rush soon. Why don't I pop another wakey-wakey pill, and you regale me with the rest of *The Odyssey*?"

"Wakey-wakey pill?"

He blushed and averted his eyes to look at his instruments. They needed monitoring, anyway. After a moment of actually checking them, he took out the bag and popped the last pill.

"What is that? Is that meth, dude?"

He threw the empty bag behind him and turned away to hide his shame. "I'm bloody tired, Basil. I don't know what to say."

Roach took up the bag and frowned at it. "Well… at least that's the last one, right?" Thyne nodded. "Sparkplug? Look me in the eyes."

He turned toward him and sighed. "It's the last one."

"Good. It's bad enough I got your fucking plane shot down. Don't want you relapsing after like 140 years of sobriety." He yawned and stretched his arms, finally not feeling like he was on the verge of another blackout. "*The Odyssey*, then?" Thyne nodded, so Roach picked up where he had left off.

A few hours later, he had finished the story, and despite the theatrics of his retelling, Thyne was struggling to keep his aching eyes open. "Alright," he said with a yawn, "Don't stop talking to me. Uh… What's something that no one knows about you?"

"Well, Sonny knows everything about me, dude."

"Everything?"

He sighed. "Well, there is one thing. Literally only *one* thing that he doesn't know. At least only one thing worth noting."

"What is it?"

"Back in the war, there was a moment I was shot… uh… straight through my neck."

"What!?" He turned to try spying the scar.

"Nah, man, you won't see it. There's nothing to show for it. It's why I never told Sonny. I'm not really sure if it happened or not."

"That's scary."

"When it happened… I mean, I must have died. It *felt* like I had died. It seemed like I had fallen on my face, bleeding out into the dirt. But—. Well I should—. Actually, I—." He took a deep breath. "There was this figure. Something divine. Something supernatural. He looked like an impossibly thin man— humanoid I should say —and he seemed like he was made of fire, but he was black as pitch. He didn't have any facial features at all, but when he came to me, he smiled a wide set of sharp white teeth that just sort of appeared. He wasn't… *there*. If that makes sense. I mean, he was there, but the way he hung in my vision was like a sunspot. He was hard to get a real good look at, is my point. And he wasn't physically in front of me like it seemed. And, well, anyway, he came up to me and spoke. His voice was deep and ethereal. He had a British accent, and, sort of like how he appeared to me, it was more like I was having a thought than actually hearing something.

"He said, 'No. Not yet, Basil,' and brought me back to life. Later, Silvino and Pio said they didn't even see me fall over, let alone get shot, and I didnt have a scar to show for it, so…." Thyne looked back at him with wide wild eyes, but Roach continued before he could interrupt: "When we met in that diner. You say you saw Oliver in me? Well… I saw— whatever this creature was —I saw *him* in you."

"Find some paper and a pen right now, Basil, and draw him. I have to see it."

"Oh, okay." He was intrigued by the reaction, so he rushed out of the cockpit to find something to draw on and draw with. Two minutes later, he returned with the sign he had stolen for Thyne and a black permanent marker. "Best I could do."

"Just draw him!"

Roach nodded and uncapped the pen to draw the figure on the uncoloured back-side of the sign. When he showed it to Thyne, the Brit's eyes were even more wild "I've seen him too! I've seen him too, Basil!"

"Where?"

"In my dreams. In my nightmares. In the mirror when I took DMT with Partha. And when I haven't slept for days. I assume I only haven't seen him this stint because of the meth."

Roach looked at the drawing again. After a moment of quiet, he tossed the sign on the ground beside him and leaned back to get more comfortable in the jump seat again. "Well, I have no idea what to make of all that, but I answered your question."

There was a five minute quiet as they both silently pondered, but toward its close, Thyne felt himself starting to nod off again. "Talk to me more, Basil. Tell me about… uh…. Tell me about Silvino."

"Okay sure. I met him in the all-boys boarding school in San Fran that me and Sonny went to for high school. I was a weird kid, so I mostly only hung out with Sonny. He would bully the bullies who mocked me for… y'know being a freak. Things like my dumpster diving or reading and rambling about *Lord of the Rings*. My scars sometimes, too, because they'd assume I'd done them to myself. They even got me to stop eating lunches when I got so self-conscious about my taste in food. I definitely could have just eaten like a normal person rather than a fucking psychopath, but kid-logic was to stop eating in front of other people entirely." He shrugged. "At least skipping lunch meant I didn't get sceptical looks from the teachers when I avoided ham and stuff.

"Anyway, as you could probably guess, Silvino was the complete opposite: he was super popular because of his mom being an A-lister. Everyone loved him in his own right, though. He was a quarterback. Rich. Smart. Super hot, too. Like, I was real lanky back then, maybe even thinner than Francy Pants, so even though I was taller than him, he could pick me up easily. We met because he had noticed that I would 'go to the bathroom' every day at the same times, and he was curious what that was about. He found me at my locker one morning just before one of those scheduled 'bathroom breaks' and just straight-up asked me what it was about. I was worried if I told him I was Muslim he might get me kicked out of the school (it was a Christian school) or worse, but I was in a particularly shitty mood that morning and decided, 'Fuck it.' I told him about the different prayer times and ablutions and all that. He was genuinely really interested, and when I had finished the crash-course for him, he leaned in and whispered that he was Catholic.

"I invited him to pray with me that afternoon, and we met up in a janitor's closet where the custodian had been letting me pray. He took out a rosary and prayed on it while I rolled out my prayer mat and did my thing. It was cute, I think. I don't know. We started doing that together every lunch period, and I got *such* a big crush on him. I mean, why was this super popular hunky kid hanging out with *me*: the loser emo kid with bugs in his backpack? Y'know?"

"He fancied you, too."

"He did, but I didn't know. Sonny told me as much, but I didn't believe him. Not until the summer between Sophomore and Junior years when Silvino asked me to come to his room while his roommate was back home so I could 'teach him guitar.' When I came in with my guitar and like a million butterflies in my stomach, he—."

"Real butterflies?" Thyne interrupted.

"What do you mean?"

"Were the butterflies in your stomach real butterflies?"

"...Maybe a couple." They both giggled. "Anyway, he grabbed me by the back of my neck and immediately started making out with me. I never taught him any guitar during our 'guitar lessons.' We didn't do anything more than kissing until after we graduated, though. Not even over-the-clothes stuff. It was just real cute, innocent, puppy love. And so, even though I was officially the quarterback's boyfriend after that, the other boys still bullied me. Sonny was so brutal with his words, he was able to keep them off of me most of the time, but Silvino's friends didn't let him faze them at all. One time, one of them shoved me down, and Silvino didn't do anything about it, but Sonny was there, and he was quite a bit bigger than me at the time from his gymnastics, so he gave the kid a black eye." He chuckled at the memory. "Me and Sonny both got sent to the principal's office over it, but they didn't know which of us threw the punch. Neither of us ratted on the other, and the kid that got punched didn't rat either, so we got away scot-free. It was the first time we had gotten away with something by abusing the fact that we're twins.

"I digress. My point is that Silvino was sweet, but his friends and their girlfriends were all just... really fucking mean. Like I was a weirdo, let's not act like I wasn't, but still.... Y'know words hurt sometimes, and I'm not allowed to forget them." A beat. "I think a big reason none of them turned us in for being gay was because they knew it'd probably mean we'd get killed or at least imprisoned for a long time. And the teachers weren't going to turn two teenagers over to the literal police just for kissing, especially not Silvino considering his status. Even the super religious ones seemed to be okay with it as long as we were making an effort to hide it, which we were.

"After high school, Silvino started to gain weight, and he worried I'd leave him when all of those so-called 'friends' of his ditched him, but obviously I didn't. I offered to workout with him to help him keep the weight off, but even though *I* fell in love with exercising, he just wasn't into it. Sonny was my workout buddy instead." He shrugged. "I promised Silvino that I loved him no matter what, so he basically never exercised again. Not like I minded, but after long enough, he got to be pushing 400, maybe 450. When he was only twenty-five. He got diabetes, and…." He sighed as the memories started to visibly upset him. "I thought he was beautiful no matter what, but I should have stopped it before it got so out of hand. I should have helped him. It got really bad after we escaped the war. He was so fucking depressed, dude I—." He held his head. "I should have said something."

"Roach, no. You stop it right now. I know what you're doing."

"And what is that?" he said with an exasperated tone.

"You're blaming yourself. It's not your fault."

There was a long beat of quiet, at the end of which, he coughed away his upset and rubbed his lap anxiously. "How much longer 'til we get there?"

Thyne frowned. "Not too much longer. Thank you for talking to me. I love you."

He smiled weakly. "I love you, too, and I love talking to you. Just… maybe let's not talk about Silvino anymore. At least not for a while. What do you want to do when we get to London? Other than sleep."

"Sleep will be lovely, yes, but I already told you, Mr. Perfect Memory: I was hoping you could help me with Maitland."

"Yeah, but, right away?"

"Well, did you have something else in mind?"

"Yes. You never showed me *The Wizard of Oz*, dude. And you promised me stale popcorn! I say we have a movie marathon. With mandatory cuddles, of course."

Thyne giggled. "A splendid idea."

❧ Chapter 59 ❧
Death Cannot Stop True Love

To avoid being caught in a plane Dale had reported as stolen with evidence of combat on its fuselage and in its weapons' chambers, Thyne took them away from any airspace where he would be required to contact a tower. He landed in a field far north of London. As soon as the plane stopped moving, he found the cockpit voice recorder and both erased and removed it physically. He rushed into the cabin and threw it to Roach explaining that it needed to be destroyed and buried in the back garden, "to be especially certain they can't scrape it."

It was lucky he tended to wear gloves to hide his cybernetics, so neither he nor Roach needed to worry about their fingerprints being found. What they did need to worry about was the angry cow farmer whose field they had landed in. He was coming over with a shotgun in hand, no doubt because of the Leviathan logo in the livery, but he wasn't aiming the firearm yet.

"Friend of yours?" asked Roach with a gesture through the windows at the oncoming stranger.

"Bugger all," he muttered as he leaned down to see through the window. "We should go. Now."

Roach nodded and unbuckled to follow Thyne out of the plane. They left via the door opposite the farmer and booked it into a nearby forest.

Thyne was deathly tired. Once they were hidden in the shadows and underbrush, he stopped to lean on his knees and spit on the ground, rearing to vomit. Even without the heart attack and meth, he hadn't slept in almost a week, and the constant physical activity was starting to wear on him even through Viktor's supernatural protection. It was only through said protection that he wasn't dropping dead then and there.

"Come here, baby," said Roach as he rushed over and scooped Thyne up into his arms, holding the CVR and sniper's case ahead of them telekinetically. "Which way's London?" Thyne gestured vaguely and nestled his weary head into Roach's chest. He could hear his hasty heartbeat and savoured the safety and warmth in his arms. Unwillingly and without warning, he closed his eyes. "You get some sleep, sparkplug. Next thing you know, you'll be back home in bed."

"I love you, Basil," he said in the tiniest sleepiest voice Roach had ever heard. It was precious and earned him a kiss on the top of his head. Roach was going to return the sentiment, but he heard something behind them and resumed running.

Just as he had said, the next thing Thyne knew, his eyes were fluttering open in his bedroom. He was snuggling up with Oliver's teddy under the blankets with a gentle drizzle tapping on his window. He turned over to look for Roach and was surprised to instead see a tray with a bottle of water, two lukewarm juiceboxes, a pack of cigarettes, and Oliver's lighter. A blushy smile. As he sipped on one of the juiceboxes, he plucked up the lighter and noticed it had a new message on the back, scratched with perhaps a needle rather than a proper engraving tool and in a horrific script: *Love you forever, sparkplug.* With a cute smile followed by an even cuter yawn, he dragged himself out of bed and changed out of his clothes into sweat-pants and slippers. He pocketed the cigarettes, the lighter, and the other juicebox before shuffling out of the room sipping on his fruit punch with big amber eyes on the lookout for Roach.

It was grey outside and dark enough that it seemed to be either sunset or sunrise. When he came into the living room, he saw Roach reading and nursing a cuppa. He noticed Thyne and rushed up to hold him. With his hand caressing Thyne's cheek, he whispered, "Morning, sleepyhead."

Thyne offered a closed-eyes smile in greeting before asking, "How long was I asleep?"

Roach glanced at the pocketwatch Francis had given him. "About eighteen hours. Did you sleep well?"

He nodded and let Roach carry him to one of the settees where he curled up on his lap and sipped his juice. He offered Roach some, and said, "How'd you get us back here? The last thing I remember was that farmer with the gun."

"I ran us to a nearby road and hitchhiked back. There weren't many cars out, but the one car that showed up, after about two and half hours of walking, stopped. The driver was cautious and scared of me, no doubt because I was carrying an unconscious man and a weird orange box and gun case at like six in the morning, but I turned on the charm and made up a whole tale about who we were and where we'd been and why we were in such poor shape and blah blah blah."

Thyne blinked. "You let him see our faces?"

"Well, I'm sorry, sparkplug. I would have walked us all the way back to London, but I didn't know how to get there or how far we were, and I was pretty tired myself. Plus… I mean carrying you through a busy city would probably draw more attention from more people anyway."

He pursed his lips, nodded to agree with the assessment, and finished his juice noisily. "And where's the CVR?"

"That weird orange box?" He nodded, so Roach continued, "I crushed it as best I could with my telekinesis, but it's really fucking tough. I was going to bury it, but I wanted to make sure it's destroyed enough to your liking, so it's on the kitchen counter."

Thyne smiled. "It's meant to survive a plane crash even if everything else gets decimated."

"Oh? I should ask Martial to tell me about the engineering of it. Where is he, by the way?"

Thyne's smile soured. He sipped on his empty juicebox to stall answering. "Dubai. I think." They both pondered what the Frenchman might have been doing for a moment, after which Thyne kissed Roach's cheek and said, "Thank you for carrying me home, by the way."

"Thanks for saving my ass, dude." His slight smile became a frown. "I'm sorry for letting everything get so hairy in the first place."

"Stop blaming yourself for everything, Basil."

"Well, it quite literally is my fault."

Thyne huffed. "Not your fault everyone else doesn't care about Maitland, though: the whole reason we started the gang in the first place." He opened his second juicebox angrily. "Where's my phone?"

"Charging with mine in the kitchen."

"I need to call Giovanni."

"So you do. I was going to text him for you, but I don't think he'd understand the request to tell everyone I'm dead if it's coming from my phone, y'know?"

He rolled his eyes. "You're mad for wanting them to think you're dead, mate."

"I'm mad in general," he said with a little laugh. "Anyway, I've already popped some popcorn to let it get nice and stale. I've written down a list of movies to show you, and I baked cookies. Dezba's recipe. Oatmeal raisin: best kind. I wanted to go out and buy snacks, but I can't do the accent, and I'm really tall and all scarred up so… cookies it is."

Thyne smiled sweetly and gave him a few pecks on the lips. "Cheers. Where's the list?" Roach took out his wallet to reach further into his pocket, but Thyne stopped him when he asked, "Do you really have caterpillars in there?"

"Yeah, dude." He smiled and gave the wallet to Thyne. "Wanna play with 'em?

They need to get some attention and food. They'll be pupating soon. Tomorrow, if I had to guess. I bred them to spend less time in their cocoons so they'd be caterpillars longer. Because——. I mean just look at them. They're adorable." He giggled. "Anyway, I'll grab something for them to eat while I'm getting the phones and seeing what other snacks you've got around here. Oh, and the list." He passed him a folded up piece of printer paper and set him on the seat beside him to go to the kitchen.

Thyne giggled as the caterpillars crawled around in his hands. They were soft and cute, just as Roach had described, and when he came back with some canned spinach he scooped into Thyne's left palm, they munched on it adorably. After some time of Roach arranging snacks on the coffee table in an uncharacteristically organised fashion, Thyne put the caterpillars and wallet on the table so Roach could watch them and opened the list of movies.

"Uh… mate?"

"Yeah?"

He turned the paper every which-way and blinked repetitively. "Is this English?"

"Yeah, dude. What else would it be?"

"I can't read a word of it."

"You never learned to read?" he teased and recited the list aloud for him, making the scribbles somewhat more legible in the process: "*The Wizard of Oz, The Pirates of the Caribbean* (original trilogy not the horrid remakes), *Singin' in the Rain* (since you said you've never seen it), *Godzilla* (2074), *Skyrim*," Thyne glared but didn't interrupt, "*Bill and Ted*, and *Double Trouble*. Then I did some doodles and left some space for your ideas on the bottom half."

"*Skyrim*, mate? You did that on purpose." Partha had forced Thyne to watch the *Skyrim* movie on stream after they beat the video game together using a multiplayer mod. Clips of Thyne complaining about the nonsensical plot and horrible effects of the movie had done the rounds online, becoming a bit of a meme, at least amongst Partha's fanbase. *He was teased by the fans for being both the best and the worst sort of person to watch movies with. His commentary was plentiful and typically ireful, but the things that enraged him were trivial or blatantly horrible and not needing commentary, at least not the kind he gave. It was still a majority opinion that watching any bad movie at all with him was enhanced greatly by his usually-humorous banter with the screen. One of the more popular clips from the stream was when Alduin first showed himself, and the effects left a lot to be desired, which Thyne pointed out when he exclaimed, "Fucksake, he looked better in the fucking game!"*

Another moment the fans favoured was a two-minutes-long uninterrupted rant (later made into a copypasta) about the downfall of art and cinema and the decay of society as witnessed by a communist born in 1920. He never made explicit reference to his birthdate, but he referenced old movies and books, some of which were silent films or lost media. He had also said four separate times in the rant that, "Antarctica used to be uninhabitable!" and reminded the audience twice that the original creators of Skyrim didn't want it to ever be put to film. Because of the references to lost media specifically, it had become a joke amongst the fans that Thyne had never publicly stated his age because he was actually a vampire.

The clip of his ranting that had escaped the sphere of Partha's influence and made its way onto other lively corners of the otherwise-dead internet was what he had said at the very end of the movie when the main character looked into the camera and said a cheesy line about being a "true hero" or some shite like that. As the credits started to roll, Thyne said, "Oh, Fus-Roh-Fuck you!" and left the call with Partha, infamously ghosting him for the rest of the week until their next session of his campaign.

Roach smirked fiendishly at Thyne's assertion that he had chosen the movie on purpose. "What? The *Skyrim* movie? What *ever* could you be talking about, Thyne?"

With a roll of the eyes and a soft smile, he gestured and asked for a pen "from that cupboard." He went to the cabinet and tossed him a pink gel pen with a little pig attached to the top from a spring then watched him write, not realising how in-love he must have looked until Thyne spied him and mirrored his dopey grin. "Can I help you?"

"Whatchya writing?" He rounded to his side and sat beside him to try and see the paper, but Thyne folded it up and snatched it away before he could read any of it.

"It's a surprise. We'll watch your movies first, but what's *Double Trouble*? I've never heard of it."

"It's a shitty end-of-the-world type action movie from a few years ago, but it's one of my favourites of all time."

"If it's bad, why do you like it so much?"

"Well, the main characters are evil twins, so me and Sonny like it since, y'know, so are we," he giggled, "But I just like shitty movies in general, especially bad action movies that are of no real consequence. I don't tend to like movies that might upset me too much. I've avoided *Brokeback Mountain*, for instance. Perlie told me not to watch it. She said it made her cry for like two days, and she's one tough bitch. Much tougher than I am, so I don't stand a fucking chance. I don't want to have to add more upset and trauma to the infinite perfect memory-dump, y'know?"

He frowned and looked back at the list. "So… what about *A Clockwork Orange*? Is that too serious for you?"

"I've never seen it, but from the little bit I've heard, it's probably too serious for me, yes."

His shoulders slumped. "I think you'd really like it, mate."

"Well… I trust you. Just… uh… make sure none of the movies you want to watch have Vinny Alvarez in them."

He looked over the list again. "I'll look them up to be certain. We'll watch your ones first, though. Did you get my phone?" Roach passed it to him. "Cheers. Where do you want to sit?"

He looked around. They were already sitting, but the television was directly to their right. They could lay down in the settee together, but an idea struck Roach, and he beamed. "We should make a blanket fort!"

"Good heavens, Basil. That's an adorable idea."

He stood and started gathering pillows and plushes from around the room. "I'll start on it while you call Giovanni."

His smile faded. "Oh. Right." A sigh. "I'll go do that now."

He stepped out into the back garden and sat on a bench as his phone was ringing. Because he was shirtless and didn't have the foresight to take a jacket with him, he hoped the call wouldn't last too long as he tried to still his teeth from chattering.

Giovanni answered, "Well, what a lovely surprise. Have you taken down that company you wanted to destroy yet? When will you be coming back home, dear?"

Thyne's gut wrenched. "Well, firstly, are the others still there?"

"They're somewhere around here, yes, I believe so." He called into the manor to beckon his husband into the kitchen where he was making dinner. After a back-and-forth he answered Thyne with what he had already heard via his microphone in Arjun: "Yes, they're all in the basement drawing up plans to find that tall fellow with the improper tendencies for some reason."

"Right, well tell Arjun that he's fine. I have him in London with me now."

He relayed the message then returned his attention to the call as Arjun left the room. "And when will you be back home, darling?"

"Soon, but… uh…."

"Is something wrong?"

"I—. Uh." He gulped. "Ihavetobreakupwithyou."

"You what?" He seemed to genuinely not understand.

With a huff. "I'm breaking up with you."

"Oh." He took a moment to process. "Well, okay."

"Wow. You took that well. Uh… will I still be welcome in your home?"

"Oh, of course, dear."

"You don't sound very upset...."

"Should I be?"

Thyne's heart panged. "I... suppose not."

"Then, why would I be? I have had countless affairs. This one was no different."

His lips trembled, and a quiet whimper escaped them. "Well," he sucked up his weepiness with a sniffle, "I'll see you soon, then."

"Arrivederci!"

Giovanni ended the call, and Thyne looked down at the screen where a tear fell and opened his messages with Partha. He sniffled and wiped his face but decided to send a quick text to the kid to really make certain that the others wouldn't go looking for Roach: ⟦ I have Roach. He's safe with me in London. ⟧ He took a moment to grieve the relationship and look at the cloudy sky. A cold breeze sent a chill down his spine as he sniffled and prayed aimlessly to his Gods.

His phone buzzed before he could get too lost in his own melancholy. Partha had replied: ⌈ I don't believe you. ⌋

With another sniffle, he went inside and took a picture of Roach just as he stood up to see him in the doorway. By the time he had sent it to Partha, Roach was holding him and wiping the tears from his face. "Oh, sparkplug, I'm sorry. I feel horrible for making you do that. You shouldn't have had to—."

"He didn't care," he whimpered.

"What?"

He looked up at him with helpless sparkling eyes and tears trailing his freckled cheeks. "He said I was just another affair. Just like all the others he's had."

"Oh, Thyne." He pulled him in for a warm embrace and kissed the top of his head.

After weeping into Roach's chest for two minutes, he retreated, sniffled, and said, "I need a fag." He took out the box of cigarettes Roach had left out for him and offered one to him, which was taken and lit by stealing the fire from Thyne's.

With smoke on his breath: "Alright, I've mostly finished the fort. I took blankets and pillows from all the beds to make us a nice cosy place to lay down. Moved the coffee table back so we'd have room. I've got the snacks and everything all set up, and, oh—." He took out his wallet and referenced the caterpillars inside: "As long as we don't lose any of them, these homies can chill with us, too."

"Wow. You did all that rather quickly, didn't you?"

"Telekinesis helped. Anyway, let's go watch *The Wizard of Oz!* I'm so excited to see your favourite movie!" He beamed adorably and led Thyne to his fort, which was evidently called *Fort Butts* because he had written *Fort* on top of the street sign he gave to Thyne and attached it to the back "wall" with clothespins.

He giggled and sniffled. "Are you an actual child, mate?"

"Come on, man. You gotta be a little silly sometimes, or what's the point of anything? Now, I demand snuggles, and I demand them now!"

In Roach's strong arms in a pile of blankets and plushes with his favourite movie in the world on the telly, Thyne was in bliss. Or at least... he would have been, if not for the nagging feeling gnawing at the back of his mind.

He tried to push it out. They would burn down the museum together after this time to relax and be romantic.

If only he could relax.

The movie finished, and Roach surprised Thyne by kissing him deeply during the end credits. He briefly tasted the piercing on Roach's tongue, but the brute retreated and said, "That was amazing. I can see why you love it so much. Should we watch another?"

When Thyne hesitated to respond, Roach kissed his forehead and knuckles and asked if he was okay. Thyne bit his lip. "We can watch another."

"Another musical? *Singin' In the Rain*?"

He nodded, so they put on the movie, and Thyne gave it as much of his attention as he could. Roach looked at him each time a new song started, worried he might be triggered. Thyne gave him weak smiles with each glance, and at the close of the movie, he said, "That was good, and now I finally know the origin of the *Clockwork Orange* scene, but, Basil... I want to burn Maitland down. It's all I can think about."

Roach stroked his beard. "Well, let's go after Maitland then! It'll be romantic. We'll take turns showering, I'll pray, then we'll talk over a plan and wait for nightfall. When we're done, though, I want to watch the rest of the movies on the list."

Thyne nodded and kissed Roach's nose. "Alright, but...," he blushed but said his lewd thought anyway: "Why take turns showering?"

Roach blushed with him, the two of them noticing each other coming to attention at the thought of showering together, but neither of them mentioning it. Roach ran a hand through his hair and averted his eyes, which unintentionally worked to make him look even hotter and thus worsened the situation in Thyne's sweatpants. "S-sorry, sparkplug, but I don't think even a shower with you could wash off all the liberal filth." A nervous but playful chuckle. He didn't want to reject the idea, but he also didn't want it to be interrupted by Thyne's obsessive thoughts about his mother and her company.

"That's not what I meant," he lied blatantly and with an air equally as nervous and teasing, "I meant why take turns when I have more than one shower?" He stood and noticed Roach trying not to notice his erection. After an awkward lustful stare, Thyne slinked out of the room and ascended to his private bathroom. He frowned when he saw his mirror was scorched and the room reeked of burnt hair, but after brushing out the sink into the bin, he put together an outfit for the job and got in the shower.

They met back up in the foyer an hour later having both showered and prayed. Roach was clean-shaven and wearing the same clothes as before: a bleach-stained raggedy shirt with no sleeves or sides, covered by the knitted sweater Dezba had made for him, torn black jeans, and his usual combat boots. He typically wore a lot of rings, but before trading himself for Partha and Richard, he had purposefully left all of them, even his and Silvino's wedding rings, with River. Thyne was wearing all black: leggings, a snug hoodie, gloves, and ballet slippers with the ribbons tied up under the leggings.

"Well, don't you look cute, sparkplug?"

"Ditto, Basil. I like when you shave, but isn't it haram? Not that you much care about being haram."

He sighed. "I do try to be halal, but no, at least according to my father, shaving isn't haram."

"Well, you're pretty with or without the beard." He stood on his tiptoes to kiss his cheek and smell his aftershave.

Roach blushed and smiled softly at Thyne before noticing something in his hand. "What do you have there?"

"Ski masks. See if this fits that big dumb head of yours." He tossed one to Roach and watched him fit it over his head easily. "With *all* your hair in it, muppet."

"Alrighty." He took it back off, quickly tied up his hair, then tried to put the mask back on with some difficulty getting it over the massive bun.

"That's what I thought." He sighed. "You need to cut it."

He gasped and tore off the ski mask and hair-tie to grab at his luscious locks defensively. "Thyne, no."

"You can spare a few inches, Rapunzel, it's past your arse!"

"Oh? Been looking back there a lot, have you?"

Thyne sputtered nothingness and repeated with a blush, "You need to cut it!"

"Don't you like it?"

"…Yes."

"So do I. Why would I cut it?"

"Because it's impeding your ability to wear a mask."

"You act like I don't know how to tie a headscarf."

Thyne scoffed but blushed. He hadn't considered a headscarf, completely forgetting that Roach had worn one on their first job together. "Alright, I'll find you something." He shuffled through various wardrobes in the house and eventually found a black scarf that looked big enough. With Roach's ability to hide his identity confirmed, they sat in the kitchen and had tea as the sun set, discussing the plan of how to go about burning down the museum and headquarters without getting caught.

Despite his hulking frame, Roach was able to be stealthy when he needed to be and followed Thyne through the shadowy streets with a good amount of grace. The Brit, however, was as silent and unobserved as a professional cat-burglar, and it distracted Roach. His eyes were half-lidded as he watched the show of skill. What beauty would he witness come the fire? What madness within Thyne might show? He sighed longingly at the thoughts. Thyne noticed his daydreamy far-off look and snapped loudly in his ear to bring him back to Earth. "Sorry," whispered Roach, which promptly earned him a thump in the forehead and a finger over his cloth-covered lips.

Thyne led them to a residential area with only a few commercial venues nearby: a dentist's office, an Indian restaurant, a real-estate office, and, where they were going: Maitland Music Group's headquarters. He stopped before the entrance and pointed to one of the corners of the awning over it. With a motion as if he were crushing something in his hand, Roach blindly squeezed telekinetically on a camera which fell from the ceiling but was promptly caught with a point of his finger before it could clatter to the ground. He flicked it silently into the bushes and followed Thyne to the door. After removing his industrial piercings to pick the lock, and before going inside, Thyne pointed vaguely at the building. Roach shook his head. He could technically manipulate things telekinetically without seeing them like he had just done for the other camera, but if he couldn't see it, he didn't know what exactly he was doing. If something fell again, or if there was some sort of motion-detecting alarm, he wouldn't know until it was too late. "I'll just go in," he whispered and pushed into the lobby, turning toward the indicated camera and turning it up toward the ceiling telekinetically with another quick gesture.

Thyne took off his backpack and opened it to retrieve two of the boxes of playing cards from within. He skillfully waterfalled them out of his hands and onto the floor as he backed down a hallway with Roach following him. He was carrying both of their bags to pass Thyne more cards each time he ran out. All the while, his hazel-greys were half-lidded and watching Thyne's movements with his only thoughts wrought with adoration and anticipation.

Thyne's collection of decks was so vast that they had spent almost all of the time after their showers up into the dead of night removing the kings and queens of hearts from every deck in order to coat the crime scene and make it clear that *The Crown* and *Tiara* were still operational. When they ran out of cards, Roach destroying cameras when he was shown them, they rounded back to the lobby. Roach cut up the chairs with one of the Brit's pastel pink bowie knives and started passing the cotton filling to Thyne, who stuffed it in his empty bag. They took paper from shredders and, along with spreading the makeshift kindlings, dumped two bottles of gin around in various areas.

With those things finished, Thyne brought them to the music room. He stood at the threshold of the door and took pause. Roach let him have a moment but peered into the unlit room curiously. Upon seeing the piano, he correctly assumed this was where Thyne had tried to kill his mother in the past. To soothe his nerves, Roach gently ran his hand down Thyne's arm to interweave their fingers.

After squeezing Roach's hand and taking a deep breath, he tried to enter the room but couldn't make himself take that fateful step. He held out his free hand toward Roach, expecting to be handed something. Roach unzipped the bag in his off-hand and slipped out a water-gun filled with gasoline. He passed it to Thyne.

"Fuck you, mother. Fuck you, mother. Fuck you, mother. They *were* clapping for me. For *me*. Fuck you," he whispered before stilling his trembling hands and stepping back into the torturous chamber. He tried to remember the room as it looked when it was burning and the sounds of his mother's screams, but all he could see was the black void of nothing behind the stage-lights and the sound of his mother scolding him: *"If you had done better.... If you had done better...."*

This room struck Roach's soul as he entered. It evoked … memories? Surely not true memories. A sense of déjà vu mixed with dread, perhaps. He wasn't sure what it was, but before allowing himself to even parse the surroundings, he muttered a quick prayer to Allah to protect the two of them from whatever evil haunted this room…. An evil other than the two of them, at least.

Roach had drifted from Thyne toward the piano, but before he could slip entirely out of Thyne's hand, it was squeezed painfully hard. "Don't leave me!" he cried at a much louder volume than he intended.

Roach immediately returned to him and embraced him. "I'm right here, baby. I'm here. I'm not going anywhere."

He pulled himself into Roach's chest and listened to his calming heartbeat. Even standing here about to set the entire building ablaze, it was slow and easy. Slow and easy like, "Play me *Heart and Soul*, Basil."

Roach smiled down at his sparkly amber eyes and whispered, "As you wish."

Thyne followed him to the piano and sat beside him as he cupped his hands over the keys. *'Improper. Improper form. Improper form. Too relaxed. Up up up with the palms, Clare. Up up up.'* He shook away the thoughts and closed his eyes to listen to Roach play.

It was 3:30 in the morning. The window was cracked, letting in a cool winter breeze. It was silent outside, not unlike the quiet of a forest when a predator is near. The world felt impossibly small and fragile, and when the bench creaked beneath Roach's weight and the first note rang out, it was like Thyne was transported back in time. It was horrible. It was wonderful. This room was his torture chamber, but… it was also where he and Oliver had first kissed. This piano was tuned with death knells, but it was also the first instrument Thyne had played for him. *Heart and Soul* was Oliver's favourite song, but it took until his dying breaths for Thyne to be able to muster up his voice and actually sing for him. His last few moments: wrought with serenade and the kind words, *"That little kiss you stole held all my heart and soul."*

The music poured from the window and down into London like a heavy fog. It crept across the street, the antique piano showing its age with its slightly out-of-tune twang. What was once an empty street was now haunted by this whispered ancient song and the memories it therefore aroused in Thyne.

It was soothing. Slow. Embellished with creative flourishes. Wrought with love. Pianissimo. He breathed in the smell of the room, changed enough after all these years with strangers shuffling through it to not perturb him. Roach's soul was Oliver's soul: he could feel it enveloping him as the song went on. Roach started to hum quietly, which only sent Thyne deeper into his blissful trance until—. His eyes shot open and a spine tensed. *'A slip of the finger. Wrong note. Start over. Start over and play it properly this time. Play it properly. If you would just play it properly….'* He grabbed Roach's hands by the wrists to stop the music.

"Sparkplug?"

He shook his head and, with Roach's wrists still in his hands, stood behind him and—. SLAM! A discordant sound as his fingers hit random keys in the motion. A beat of quiet then— SLAM! … SLAM SLAM! He pushed Roach out of the seat and slammed his own hands on the keys. Again and again and again until mad tears were pooling on the bottom rim of his ski mask's opening and nothing but noise was leaving the ancient instrument. "Fuck you! FUCK YOU! FUCK YOU FUCK YOU FUCK YOU!" He stood and stumbled backwards, taking his makeshift flamethrower from the bench before it toppled over. With mad quickness, he lit the entire matchbook the fortune teller had given him and held it in front of the nozzle. Without even noticing that Roach had rushed out of the way, he pulled down the trigger and painted the room in red and orange and black with no regard to his own existence. The eerie fog of *Heart and Soul* haunting the street was replaced with discord and echoes of Thyne's mad bays.

It took Roach picking him up for him to shut up and finally remember that he had a body that was in danger of suffocating or burning to death. He swore, as he was carried out the window and down onto the awning below, that he saw his mother tied up where he had left her before. He swore he saw her looking at him.

Back outside on the ground, he threw as much fire on the bushes at the base of the building as he could, running out of fuel only a moment later.

"We've gotta get out of here, Dorothy," worried Roach.

Thyne nodded and took a few steps back from the burning building, but he couldn't bring himself to look away. Last time he had fled from this building after setting it on fire, his one goal of killing his mother had apparently failed.

"We've gotta go," said Roach again as he tried to pull him away by his sleeve.

"No," he said, his gaze still locked firmly with the roaring tongues of flame, "We have to *watch*."

He didn't notice the thunder roaring over Roach's pleas to flee. He didn't notice the rain drenching them. He didn't see Roach throw their bags through one of the windows on the first story or the molotov he tossed after them, and he didn't notice him hang the tiara on one of the iron spikes on the gate around the small front garden. He didn't hear the voices. He couldn't cognise the true date or time. In that moment, as he watched the flames with eyes hungrier than they had ever been in his life, he saw only red, felt only warmth, and heard only… music.

When it was clear Thyne was not going to move of his own volition, Roach picked him up again and ran back toward his house as stealthily as he could manage. He was thankful for the rain obscuring them, and when they were off the street with the fire, Thyne slowly seemed to come back to life. Roach set him down to run on his own, and for a spell they sprinted. When their shoes became a burden or slipping hazard in all the puddles, they removed them, all four thereafter hanging by their various laces and ribbons in Roach's right hand.

As soon as he was free of the shoes and able to feel the rushing rainwater between his toes, Thyne smiled at the distant glow from the fire, which raged and roared despite the downpour. He danced his way to a lamp post, kicking up puddles on his way. After spinning himself around it once, he hung off of it, holding his hand out to watch the rain pool up in his palm. Roach slowed down and turned to grab Thyne again, but he stopped dead in his tracks when he heard what was perhaps the most perfect sound in all the universe:

"I'm singin' in the rain." His heart leapt up into his throat hearing Thyne's flawless voice. He was made immediately hysterical by it, but he managed to choke down the swelling emotions. Thyne continued: *"Yes, singin' in the rain. What a glorious feeling, I'm happy again."* It was operatic but natural and raw. There was some purposeful distortion that seemed to convey the overwhelming emotion finally pouring out of him. The sound of the fire brigade's sirens in the distance harmonised with him as if some God of music was watching this moment and gracing it with even more musicality. It was like he was in witness of Orpheus' lost songs. No. *Better* than Orpheus.

There was a small part of Roach that was compelled to join in on the song, but he was stunned to stillness and silence by the sheer perfection of it. Was it even real? How could a *human* sound like this? Surely, he was no human. No. He was a malak come down to Earth to bless the world— nay to bless Roach with the opportunity to even chance upon such sublimity.

"What did I do to deserve this?" he muttered in Arabic. He didn't consider himself worthy of anything so divine as this, and when Thyne danced over to him and gestured to invite him to sing, Roach, for the first time since his childhood, was actually self-conscious of his singing voice. Compared to Thyne, his well-practised and professionally trained sultry voice might as well have been the same as two brawling alley cats. With the invitation, and with great hesitance, he muttered a shy, *"Dancin' in the rain."* Thyne nodded, as if to agree with his assertion despite his lack of dancing, and continued the song from there.

Roach did his best to stay present to bring Thyne home, but the music was a siren's song enthralling him. It was as impossible as the stars, with vast unfathomable beauty and otherworldly radiance. He felt himself coming to attention at the display and felt guilty for the lust. With a blush, he tried to avert his eyes, but he couldn't pull himself away. Thyne was too perfect. Too beautiful. The rain poured down over him, weighing down the sleeves of his hoodie and thus showing the formation of muscles beneath. The leggings he was wearing accentuated everything they purported to cover. Thyne's new haircut really was adorable in Roach's opinion, and his smile was divine. But there was nothing in all the cosmos more bewitching than his voice.

A loud boom of thunder broke Roach's trance, and he was able to scoop up his malak and rush him back to his house before they were seen by a police car that had just turned onto the street. The very *moment* the door clicked closed behind them, their masks and shoes were on the floor, and their tongues were intertwined. They kissed and tugged at each other's tops, all the while with Thyne still humming and smiling. With their torsos exposed, their hands were all over each other's abs and biceps and pectorals. Roach went for Thyne's neck and marked him with a hickey, during which Thyne was rubbing his hands up Roach's muscled back and pulling himself closer, whisper-singing hot breaths into his ear. When Roach was back on his lips, Thyne played with his piercing with both halves of his split tongue and giggled at the little moans it drew from the brute.

"Thyne," said Roach when he could catch breaths between kisses, "Thyne, I want you. I love you. I need you. You're perfect."

"I love you. I need you. I want you. You're perfect," he whispered with a kiss between each statement. He thereafter unbuckled Roach's pants and allowed him to pull down his leggings and boxers. By the time they had made it the six feet to the base of the stairs, they were both entirely nude. Roach shoved Thyne backwards onto the steps and grunted animalistically as he dropped to one knee, lubricated himself with his own spit, and entered Thyne as carefully as he could while overcome with so much ardour.

Thyne was too far to keep kissing, so he ogled Roach's Adonis body as he continued singing, swapping from *Singin' in the Rain* to an operatic rendition of *Over the Rainbow*. Soon after this, his voice started to catch and be replaced with moans of pleasure with each pump into him. It wobbled and faltered; going flat and sharp and wrong and bad and *he didn't care*. He didn't fucking care. He didn't care he didn't care he didn't care! All he could even fully fathom was his love for the man fucking him and the wailing sirens whispering through the rain.

It became too cumbersome to sing after only half of his song, so he stopped and reached out his hand to hold Roach's. With a soft and loving smile, he blew playful kisses at Roach, who beamed in return. After a few more pumps, Thyne wanted to be closer, so he pulled himself up to wrap himself all over Roach and smother him in slobbery kisses. He was fucked some more from this new position and carried another three stairs upwards before Roach slammed him against the wall with Thyne's legs wrapped around him. He pinned Thyne's wrists over his head with one hand and grabbed his cock with the other. "You're mine," he growled quietly before biting and licking Thyne's earlobe and retreating only a centimetre to whisper, "Thyne. All mine." A moan then in Arabic: "My sweet angel of music and bloodshed and fire."

"I'm yours," he agreed breathily, "Always yours, Basil." They resumed kissing for the next few pumps until all they could do was moan together. "I'm close," Thyne managed.

"Come for me," ordered Roach, and just as he had commanded, a thread of white sprayed him, and he simultaneously finished inside of Thyne.

But when Roach climaxed... something... *odd*... occurred:

Faster than he could even blink, he was no longer in Thyne, in London, in England at all. He was on his back in a grassy field looking up at a midday sky. He was unable to move and felt something foreign in his abdomen, but before he could even try to fathom what was happening, there was an explosion of illusory confetti overhead that revealed the word *Congratulations!* floating in the sky either a few feet above him or up near the clouds. His head turned, but he hadn't moved it on purpose, though it felt as if he had. Perhaps he had been mind controlled?

Nothing was making any sense.

When his head turned, he saw the shadowy figure that had saved his life in Mexico and gasped. The creature smiled the same as he had when he found Roach bleeding from the jugular in Chihuahua. "Basil," he said with that same ethereal voice as before. The most notable difference about him in this instance was how he was not so much like a sunspot or hallucination and more like an actual entity. It was enough of an oddity that Roach almost didn't notice the other being with him.

This new figure had a body like a white opal statue with kintsugi lines that pulsed with different colours, chiselled masculine features, and six arms. His head cut off like a broken sculpture at the bridge of his nose, the top half oozing a surreal cloud of holographic white. To make up for his lack of eyes, he had several disembodied faces like venetian masks orbiting him. Behind him was a battlefield and a group of uniformed men, frozen in time. They were blurred as if by a tilt-shift effect, drawing more attention to the surreal beings.

"Thyne?" he heard himself ask between pained breaths, "What the bloody Hell is happening?"

"The bomb Viktor put in your abdomen is going to go off soon," replied the shadowy man, his smile gone by then.

"Bomb!?"

"What's going on?" asked Roach, surprised that he was able to speak through what he was beginning to realise was Oliver's mouth.

"Was that me? Did I say that?" asked Oliver. "What the bloody Hell is happening!?"

"Roach, don't confuse him more right now, he's about to die," said the figure. "Oli, my love, you're about to die."

"Who the fuck is Roach? Did he do this?"

"He already told you that Viktor did it, dumbass," replied Roach.

"Why do I sometimes sound American and say things I don't mean to be saying?" He hissed and grabbed at the foreign object in him. "God! It hurts so much!"

The pain stopped abruptly. "Now, if you two would shut your mouth, I could explain." A beat. "Good!" He beamed his eerie white smile. "Oliver. Roach. I am Faers. That is Daetus. We are Thyne and Francis' souls."

"To put it simply," added Daetus.

"*Very* simply," concurred Faers, "We want you to join us, which requires your death, but Oli, you unfortunately can't come with us just yet. That's why we're going to give you another chance."

"The other chance is me, then?" asked Roach. "I'm the New Game Plus?"

Faers giggled. "Yes, Basil, now be quiet. Oliver, I love you dearly. I need you to agree to this. To being reborn."

"Fuck. Okay," replied Oliver with a defeated and irritated tone.

"Perfect! To make it up to you, we'll make sure your second chance is related to Keeva and awaken the latent Etren genes in you to give you powers."

"That was a load of nonsense, but alright," replied Oliver.

"I want to give him something, too," said Daetus. He approached and poked Oliver's forehead, and Roach felt something scratching at his soul for a brief moment.

"What did you give him?" asked Faers.

He shrugged.

Faers giggled again. "That should be that, then. Are you ready to go to the next life, Oli?"

"Wait," he coughed up some blood as the pain started to crop back up. "How long will I have to wait before I find my Thyne again?"

"Thirty-two years, if memory serves."

He wept. "No! That's too long. That's too long, I can't go that long alone."

"Oh shh shh, Basil," Faers crouched down and cupped a hand around his cheek to wipe away the tears. His hand felt like dry water. It was cold, soothing, and impossible. "You won't have to go it alone. You'll have your brother."

"Sonny?" said Roach.

Faers nodded. "I sent him to guide you."

"Will I remember this?" asked Oliver.

"You'll remember it eventually," he smiled, but only Roach perceived it despite sharing eyes with Oliver. "Are you ready?"

"Wait!" He panicked as Faers stood. Oliver tried to stand, but the pain in his abdomen came back in an instant, knocking him immediately to the oddly-golden grass. He called and cursed and held the ache. With tears blurring his vision entirely, he found Faers' vague form and whimpered, "Is it going to hurt?"

Faers sighed but with an air of love and concern. "You trust me, don't you?"

"I trust Thyne."

"Then you trust me." He smiled. "Oh, and Roach?"

"Yes?"

"Try not to freak out, okay?"

He may have replied. He might have pointed out how calm he felt despite how nonsensical it was to be calm in such harrowing, maddening, and confusing circumstances. He wanted to be scared, but he was in bliss. He may have said any of this, but he was suddenly back in England, in London, in Thyne. It was the same moment he had left, time having not passed at all and the both of them still orgasming.

Roach started to laugh hysterically for seemingly no reason, and it made Thyne's climax tenfold as pleasurable to witness such madness. His eyes rolled back and thighs trembled, and when he was finished entirely, Roach kept going as he carried him up the rest of the stairs and laid him on his bed. Thyne wasn't participating anymore, but after two minutes of Roach's continued pumps— after he kissed the semen off of Thyne's abs— he teased his cock and balls with his fingers enough to get him back up. Having heard Roach have sex in the past, he knew he had no refractory period, so it was expected that he would be able to keep going. What he didn't expect was that his own participation would be possible so quickly after his first orgasm.

They came together for a second time, and Roach finally pulled himself out of Thyne, still hard. "Let's go clean up," he said through his heaving breaths before scooping Thyne up and carrying him to the bathroom. He set him on the counter and approached the shower.

Thyne watched him turning on the water with a dopey grin and half-lidded eyes. "I love you, Basil."

Roach beamed at him and rushed up to kiss him deeply. "I love you so much," he whispered before kissing down his neck and chest. "Can I ask for something?"

"Of course." Roach blushed, and over the course of the next thirty seconds, it deepend from pink to dark crimson as he hesitated to ask his question. "What's wrong, Basil?" said Thyne with a teasing tone.

"Can I... uh...." He shook his head. "Nevermind."

He tried to turn away and go to the shower, but Thyne grabbed his wrist and pulled him back. "Oh no you don't. Come here." He kissed his nose and poked it. "What were you going to ask?"

"It's stupid. No. It's bad. I can't."

"You can *ask*, Basil. What's the worst that can happen?"

He took a moment to steady his shaky breaths and leaned in to whisper. Still he hesitated, so for a long moment Thyne heard only his nervous breaths. Eventually, he caressed Thyne's jaw with his trembling fingers and said with a voice just as uneasy, "I want to scar you."

The Brit blushed and stopped Roach from fearfully retreating by whispering sensually, "Okay, Basil. Then scar me." He bit his earlobe after noticing that Roach was still hard.

A shuddered breath. "W-where am I allowed to do it?"

"*Wherever you want*," he breathed. He giggled when he saw the effect of his words on Roach's attention.

"I need a knife," he choked out and retreated to start looking through the drawers under the sink. While he was doing that, Thyne spread his legs to pull open the drawer beneath where he was sitting on the counter. He took out a pair of barber's scissors and passed them to Roach with a spin in his wrist. Once Roach had them in his trembling hand, he came back up in front of Thyne and flicked open the scissors like a switchblade. He already knew where he wanted his scar. When the blade was rested gently on Thyne's cupid's bow, Roach looked at him inquisitively.

"You're sure?"

"I'm sure."

Slash.

The scissors were dropped to the floor immediately after making their mark down the exact centre of Thyne's lips, and before Thyne could fathom the pain, Roach was kissing him and tasting the blood as it pooled up in their mouths. He carried him to the shower as they kissed. When they were both under the stream of water, Roach finally retreated, and his eye twitched as he admired the cut.

Thyne cleaned Roach's cock before anything else, and when it was sufficiently clean, he got down on his knees and took him in his mouth to finally finish him off for good. He played with Roach's Prince Albert piercing, turning the brute to nothingness with his split tongue, and swallowed his final load of the night when it shot down his throat five minutes later.

After their shower, Thyne offered to wash the one outfit Roach had with him. He would have nothing to wear in the interim, "but that won't matter if we're cuddled up in Fort Butts watching movies."

Roach chuckled. "Okay. Sure. But you've gotta be naked, too. In solidarity, of course."

"Of course," he said playfully.

So, they snuggled up and watched the first *Pirates of the Caribbean* movie, during which Roach's clothes were finished being cleaned and dried. Once both of them were dressed, Thyne was wearing boxers and Roach's sweater (stolen from the dryer). He sat back down in the blanket fort and took up his phone to order some food, "Let me guess. You want pineapple on your pizza."

"What kind of a monster do you think I am?"

"The kind who likes pineapple on his pizza."

"I genuinely don't like pineapple on pizza."

Thyne laughed. "You what, mate?"

"It's true," he chuckled, "I seriously don't."

"You'll eat rubbish from the bin, but you draw the line at pineapple on pizza?"

"You have to stand for something, or you'll fall for anything."

He rolled his eyes. "Well, what do you want?"

"You could get groceries instead, and I'll cook for you."

He blinked. "You can't cook."

"What? Says who?"

"Says me, mate."

"You've never even tried my cooking, dude, what the fuck?"

"You're telling me *you* can cook?"

"Yeah, man. I'm a good cook, too."

"I don't believe you, but alright. What should I order?"

Roach listed some ingredients and spices then, "Oh, and some movie snacks. Candies and sodas and stuff. I like black licorice and circus peanuts best."

"What are circus peanuts?"

He gasped. "You don't have circus peanuts here!? Dude! They're so good! Next time we're in America we've gotta get some for you. They're sorta like packing peanuts but you don't get beat for eating them."

Thyne chuckled. "Noted. Well, I'll get your licorice, you wanker, and some actually good sweets for me."

"Should probably avoid sour candies, though, because of the cut." He blushed and averted his gaze. Rubbing the back of his neck, he asked timidly, "Do you like it?"

"I do like it, mate."

"You're not just saying that, right?"

He replied with a tender kiss. "I love it, and I love you."

Roach smiled and tried not to get turned on by the feel of the cut when they kissed. "I love you, too." Thyne smiled and returned his attention to his phone. With the order placed, he started to arrange the pillows and blankets in Fort Butts to prepare for the next movie, but Roach said, "Wait dude, I had another question for you before we get back into it."

"Alright."

"Have you lost your marbles?" Thyne closed his eyes and braced himself for some sort of joke. Roach chuckled. "No, but for real. Do you still have them?"

"I might. Somewhere in the loft."

"Can you show me?"

Thyne arched his brow at him, but when Roach seemed serious, he groaned and stood to climb the many flights of stairs toward the roof. Roach followed like a loyal hound, the temporary stairs to the loft creaking grumpily under his weight. Thyne rummaged for a few minutes, sneezing at the dust he was kicking up, but eventually came up to Roach with a little leather drawstring bag and a runny nose.

They went into Thyne's bedroom, and he made a circle on the carpet with the cord from his gaming headset. After pouring the marbles into the circle, he knelt down and invited Roach to kneel across from him. "So, to play you have to—."

Roach picked up one of the marbles and jumped to his feet. "I knew it!"

"You what?"

"I knew you were a little thief!" He snort-laughed.

"What are you on about, mate?"

He crouched down in the circle and took Thyne's hand to put the marble in his palm. It had a swirled pattern with one half red and one half green. He couldn't recall how he had gotten this marble in particular. "What about it?"

Roach's smile was wide and somewhat fiendish, like he was watching Thyne about to open a gift. His voice was playful and low: "Did you know Oliver was colourblind?"

He tilted his head and trailed his gaze down from Roach's wild hazel-greys to the red-green marble. It started to come back to him how he had gotten it: *He must have been eight or nine years old and playing marbles with Oliver. This one was originally Oliver's, but he had taken it when he wasn't looking. When Oliver tried to ask for it back as they were cleaning up, he described it as having a subtle change in colour, and Thyne thought he must have gotten away with the thievery because this marble was two distinct colours.*

"What?" The word was strangled as his throat started to clog up with some sort of weepiness, but he couldn't be entirely certain why. It was like his body had already figured it out, but his mind was still catching up. "What?" he said again, his gaze shooting up and locking with Roach's. "WHAT!?" With a cheeky wink from Roach, tears waterfalled down Thyne's contorting face. "You remember London?" he whimpered.

Roach took up Thyne's hands and alternated kissing his hands after each word:

"Every."

"Last."

"Second."

Chapter 60
Good Heavens,
Are You Still Trying to Win?

The rum burned pleasantly, as it always did. He was one— two— ten flasks deep and still only tipsy. Rage churned his empty stomach and wrenched his loving heart, for he was forsaken by his two greatest loves and witnessing his last hope of saving the world disintegrate further without Roach and Thyne to keep the rest of the gang on track and in good enough spirits to fight. Francis had attempted to call for action since it was confirmed that Roach was safe, but the others were more interested in relaxing. Perlie was far enough into her pregnancy to be showing, and she had scheduled an ultrasound with Giovanni a few days from then. Partha was trying to wrap up his West Marches game in anticipation of fatherhood. River seemed as disinterested with saving the world as his brother was. Jean-Jacques was still MIA, and Dezba cried old age and mourning as her reasoning for needing time to relax. Neodesha was willing to help, but Francis had little in the way of a plan that only the two of them could carry out.

Bored of rum, he climbed up from the cellar with two bottles of wine, one red one white, and dropped himself in one of the settees in the living area, his brow furrowed with both wrath and ponderance. The only other person in the room was Dezba, reading a book from the manor's library and listening to classical music from Perlie's phone connected to the television.

"Franny, honey," she said as he swigged from a bottle of wine.

"Aye?" he growled.

"Aren't you glad that Roach is safe?" He glared and swigged again, offering no verbal response. She stood and crossed the room to sit on the couch beside him. With a hand on his knee: "What's wrong, son?"

"What *isn't* wrong?"

"Good point. What isn't wrong, then?"

He blinked away the shock at having the question turned around at him. Typically, he would say his relationship with Thyne. He would say his relationship with Roach. He would cite the time remaining before World War Three optimistically: a last chance to reverse his blunder, but a chance nonetheless. His eyes welled up as all the trials he had suffered reeled through his boozy brain: a mutinous crew, the loss of his children, the horrors of war, the inescapable crushing nothingness of the void, that he would never be with Thyne, that he had raped him, that he constantly disappointed him—. '*What isn't wrong?* he asked himself again, and the only thing that caught his mind in response was the bottle in his hand. After another swig to wash away the hurt, he gestured to indicate his answer.

"Now now, son. There's more to life than drinking."

"I made no claims at the vastness of life. You queried what isn't wrong, and I have answered."

She sighed. "Well, what else, dear? What else is good to you?"

"Naught."

"That's simply untrue. You have plenty to be grateful for!"

A beat of quiet. Francis' rage compounded, and as his thoughts tumbled over each other, a plan formed. He stood and quit the room, a bottle still in hand, without another word for Dezba.

Perlie and Partha were cuddling in her bed and admiring her baby-bump together. They didn't know its gender yet, but they were still excitedly brainstorming names and chatting about picturesque fantasies of their future as a family. In the midst of a chat about Partha making Halloween costumes for the child, they heard a knock on the door and both immediately lost the innocent smiles they had been beaming to each other, as if trying to hide their happiness. Partha rushed to the door while Perlie grabbed a book from her bedside table to pretend to be reading.

"Is Perlie in?" asked Francis when Partha opened the door. "There she is." He pushed his way into the room. "Perlie, I have need of your technological expertise."

She put down the book and sat upright. "What do you need?"

"The names and locations of Osiris' twenty most elite shareholders."

She blinked. "Franky, there's a lot of different branches to Osiris. Do you mean, just the—."

"I mean across all of its branches. The twenty most influential shareholders."

After a moment of thought, she led Francis and Partha out into the suite and sat on the couch with her laptop. "I'll see what I can do. Party, can you make me something to eat?"

"What would you like, heart?"

"Well, what I really want is banana pudding, but anything sweet will work."

He held an invisible sword in the air and declared, "Quest accepted!"

She giggled at the antics as he rushed out of the suite to procure some banana pudding somehow. "He's so cute, isn't he?" she smiled at Francis.

He tried not to look as pissed-off as he was, failing miserably when he snipped, "Where are the shareholders?"

She frowned and returned her attention to her laptop.

Roach was working in the kitchen, making a mess of it as he cooked, while Thyne sat on one of the counters and chatted with him. "After tea, we'll sleep, then tomorrow we'll watch my suggestions, right?" They had just finished the last of Roach's movies from the list.

"If that's what you'd like, sure."

"What are you making?" He peeped into one of the bowls Roach had been mixing things inside.

"Lamb shawarma bowls—. Though this isn't how it's usually cooked. It's usually cooked on a spit. But yeah, lamb shawarma bowls with Egyptian baba ganoush as like a sauce on top." He chuckled as he stir-fried the meat. "It's so fucking funny, dude. You're so British. I can't believe you didn't even have cumin."

Thyne rolled his eyes and scrolled through news updates on his phone. After two minutes, he grew tired of the doom-scrolling and set it down. "Where'd you learn to cook?"

"My dad taught me. It's actually a funny story." He paused to add more oil to the pan. "When I was little I would dumpster dive in the bins in the garage, and one night my dad heard me and came out to shoo away what he thought was gonna be a raccoon. Luckily, I managed to hear him and hid before he saw me, but after that, he put locks on the dumpsters. So then—." He paused, distracted by his cooking again. "So then when I saw that, I would go through the trash in the kitchen instead. And well, he found me one night eating my sister's half-finished Taco Bell out of the garbage in the kitchen, and after a firm talking-to I promised real hard I wouldn't eat out of the trash anymore. He told me the reason Allah doesn't want us to eat pork is because pigs are so filthy, and cleanliness is really important to Him, so it kinda followed that dumpster diving would also be haram.

"Anyway, after I got caught in the trash again (couldn't help myself), he put a lock on the cabinet it was in and gave everyone a key but me." He chuckled. "And he was a busy guy, if not working at the shop then out gambling or lesson-planning for us all, and so he didn't really have the time to be teaching me how to cook at such a young age (I was only nine), but he *made* the time and taught me every dish he knew and what spices are good together and stuff. His thinking being that if I knew how to cook I'd do that instead of eating out of the trash, and I mostly did afterwards. Still wanted to sneak into the trash, though. That's why I learned how to lockpick." Thyne giggled, and Roach smiled at him lovingly. "I did like cooking, though. I felt cool and more mature and got to tease Sonny for not knowing how to do it yet. Dad was a good cook, too. Not that my accolade means much considering my tastes, but—." His smile faded as he realised he was speaking of his father as if he had passed away. "…Anyway, I'm making shawarma."

"What's wrong, Basil?" Roach shook his head to reject the conversation before it started. Thyne wanted to pry— he always wanted to pry —but he loved Roach enough to leave it alone. He picked his phone back up and started scrolling again.

Roach pushed out the sudden upset about his father by exploring his new memories. Oliver didn't have a perfect memory like Roach did, and observing the surreal way he had conjured up his past was equal parts intriguing and unnerving. Roach supposed this must have been how everyone else remembered things, but the lack of distinction in even things like faces was disturbing. He couldn't recall entire books he had read but instead the feelings they evoked and particularly potent scenes as Oliver had imagined them. It was also lucky Oliver was colourblind, though certainly not to him at a time. He was never diagnosed and was often regarded as stupid for mixing up colours, but to Roach it acted as something of a sepia filter over the memories to differentiate the two lives.

There was no shortage of horrifying memories from Oliver's life, including every last second of Viktor's torture and ultimate murder of him, but Roach was glad to see that Thyne's presence in his life made the majority of it overwhelmingly positive. Even though they couldn't be together publicly, and even after being sent off to war, it was a happy life, made especially moreso with Oliver's best friend, Roman Rose, whom he lovingly called Rommie. He smiled lightly as he cooked and silently integrated Oliver more into his own identity. Among the new memories, perhaps his favourite was a moment in the war:

He and Thyne got into a friendly competition to see who could dome more krauts, and it started organically when Oliver was aiming his gun for a nazi's pallid face. The nazi saw him about to pull the trigger and immediately raised his hands in surrender, even dropping his gun. He mouthed something in German that Roach guessed must have meant, "Don't shoot," and Oliver hesitated. He wanted to kill him, and his finger was tightening around the trigger, but he was stopping himself for fear of what it meant for his soul. He was stopping himself to attempt maintaining some level of humanity. The urge grew to a tipping point after only a moment of hesitation, but before he could shoot the surrendering enemy, his head exploded, and Oliver turned toward Thyne to hear him laugh and say, "Boom! Got 'em! That's another one for me, Basil. Better catch up."

As Roach started to plate their dinner, a soft smile at the memory, Thyne groaned at his phone, "Franky, you mug."

"What'd he say?"

He cleared his throat and read aloud: "*'Twenty Osiris shareholders dead in unison despite physical distance from each other.'*"

"Oh? They probably could have done better with the headline."

"It says all twenty of them have been confirmed to have died at the exact same time."

"How'd he kill 'em?"

"Beheadings." He scrolled more and muttered quietly, "Witnesses. *The Crown. The Tiara.*" He perked up: "It says there was a playing card left with each victim, either of the king or queen of hearts, and on each of them was a word and number. When put in order it reads, "*'Twill out my peace? No! Let heaven and men and devils, let them all, all, all cry shame against me.'*"

"Othello," said Roach as he brought the plates to the dining table in the kitchen, "Your favourite. He's sweet."

"Bloody idiot doesn't remember the next line."

"*'Be wise, and get you home,'*" Roach quoted said line.

"Francis has never been wise a day in his infinite life," said Thyne with a huff as he hopped down from the counter and came to the table. "Thank you for cooking."

"No problem, dude." He tossed him a juicebox from the fridge and grabbed a cup to fill with tap water for himself. "It's so cool that you can drink from the tap here," he said after a gulp of the unremarkable water. "We could drink from the tap when we lived in New York, but certainly not in California."

Thyne nodded dismissively. "This article is talking about an uptick in plane crashes. You think I'm not the only one that got shot down?" He scrolled more and didn't leave Roach any room to reply before countering his own question: "No, wait, it says they've all been having flight-control and engine issues."

"Well, they could be lying to cover up the attacks."

"Maybe," he mumbled, "It's all over the world, though." After a moment more of scrolling, he set down his phone and took a bite of the shawarma.

"What?" said Roach when he noticed Thyne was glaring at him.

He chewed slowly and swallowed, his brow still furrowed. "This is good."

"Thanks, dude. Glad you like it."

"*Too* good."

He chuckled. "What the fuck's that supposed to mean, mate?"

Thyne's anger dissipated when he heard Roach use the word 'mate' and was therefore reminded that he now had Oliver's memories. "I just wasn't expecting you to be a good cook, is all."

"Better than the doc?" Thyne blushed and averted his eyes, so Roach laughed haughtily and said, "It is, is it? Well, it must be all the love and kisses I put in it." He blew teasing kisses at Thyne and took his first bite. Through his mouthful: "So what movies are on the docket for tomorrow?"

Thyne huffed, not entirely sure why he was grumpy but feeling grumpy nonetheless. He took the list of movies out of his pocket and passed it across the table before taking another bite angrily.

Roach opened the list and read Thyne's additions at the bottom: *A Clockwork Orange, Howl's Moving Castle, Everything Everywhere All at Once,* and the *Lord of the Rings* extended editions. He stopped chewing and looked up at Thyne with his eyes welling up. "You seriously wanna watch *Lord of the Rings* with me, man?"

"I do."

"But you told Party on stream that you'd never watch them."

"Well, I suppose I lied."

Francis returned to the manor and dropped his bloody sword on the living room rug. He finished his third bottle of wine of the day and refilled it via chronomancy to swig from it again. No one else was downstairs, so when his phone rang it echoed through the empty midnight chambers. "What?"

"Frankenstein, you did good with the shareholders, but I can see it's not working like you maybe thought it would. Roach is worried for you, and so am I. We won't be back in Rome for at least another few days, so do you want to come to London? We'll hold you together."

"In what world might I long to be embraced by either of thee loathsome lot?"

A beat. "In the world you told me I'm the only thing that matters to you."

Francis drank half of the wine in one go and ended the call without another word. He shouted out a frustrated yell. The day after he had killed the twenty wealthiest Osiris shareholders, the stocks became *more* valuable and sought-after. Currently, his sword was bloodied from his murdering the CFO and CMO, but it was too soon for their deaths to have reached the news. He collapsed into one of the settees and finished his wine, dropping the empty bottle on the rug beside his sword and holding his face to cry. Ten minutes later, his phone rang again, and he answered it with a shout: "LEAVE ME BE, DAMN YOU!"

"No, Franky. Come here. Please."

"The twain of thee would see the world burn! You hinder my desperate attempts to save it!"

"Please just come here. You can shout at me in person."

He stopped time as he stood, kicked his sword up into his hands, stole another bottle of wine from Giovanni's cellar, and walked to Thyne's house in London.

No sooner had Thyne made his final plea than he heard Francis' key in his front door. When Francis entered the house, he slammed his empty wine bottle down the entrance hall where it shattered across the floor. Stomping up to Thyne's room where he correctly assumed he would find him, he slammed open the door.

Roach and Thyne were already halfway out of the bedroom by the time Francis opened it. Thyne stopped when he saw him, but Roach rushed up to him and took on an uncharacteristically submissive air. He held his hands out at Francis, sometimes clasping them together as he begged, "Franky. Franky, I'm so sorry. Thyne told me how angry you are with me. I know I fucked up. I fucked up so bad, and I'm sorry. Please give me another chance."

Asking for another chance forced unpleasant echoes of a memory through him:

"Please, Silvino. I'm sorry. I love you. I'm sorry. I don't know why I'm like this."

"Clayton, you're a monster. You fed him his own captain?"

"He was a nazi! His captain was a nazi, too. He was a lost cause."

"No one is a lost cause, Roach."

"I just wanted to save you. I love you! I just wanted you safe in my arms. Please don't leave me. Please give me another chance."

"You only think of yourself, Clayton. You act like it was all in the name of finding me, but forced cannibalism is beyond anything even remotely acceptable. Maybe if it was only the waterboarding I could somehow accept that you were caught up in the moment, but on what planet would I want you doing something so disgusting as you did in my name? You may say your God is my God, but Clayton... your God cannot be my God because my God would have long-ago killed you and damned you to the deepest darkest pits of Hell."

"Please! Please, Silvino! I'll be good! I'll be good! I swear!"

"You'll never be good, but if I leave you, you'll be worse. I'll stay with you, if for no other reason than to keep you docile.... And... because I love you. Even after all

you've done, I somehow still fucking love you. But today? Right now? I can do no better than tolerate you."

Roach worried Francis' reaction would mirror Silvino's. Trading himself for Partha and Richard was another act of selfishness and misguided martyrdom. Lying about his return was another broken promise. It was possible that, up until then, Francis had only been tolerating him the way it seemed *everyone* only tolerated him. After such a betrayal of trust, to be broken-up with would be merciful compared to what Roach, the monster he was, truly deserved.

Francis was quiet for an agonising six seconds. He looked Roach up and down, his brow furrowed and face red with both drunkenness and rage. When he finally spoke, his voice was low and simple: "You told Thyne to lie to us. To fake your death. All in the name of not hurting us…. Forsaking us hurt. Lying hurt, too."

"I know!" He wailed as his hands started to tremble. It all felt so familiar already. It was only a matter of moments before Francis would rightfully tear him to pieces the way Silvino had. He held his head and wept. "I'm sorry."

An eternity elapsed, at the close of which Roach fully expected to be stabbed. He was crying into his hands and waiting for whatever wrath Francis would wrought, so it was especially surprising when he felt not a blade but a warm embrace. He looked up from his hands and saw Francis was holding him. He could feel his love radiating into his black soul.

What had he done to deserve this? Forgiveness? *Again?* Why was he so constantly shown love? Perhaps it wasn't Francis in an imagined existence. Perhaps it was Roach who had imagined his own reality. He returned the embrace with confused slowness.

Francis retreated and wiped away his own tears then Roach's. "I love you, Clayton. I will love you for aye. Please refrain from forsaking and deceiving us in future." Roach could only whimper in reply. "My forlorn heart hath wrestled with the wake of thy absences, the tempestuous waters of which nearly tore me asunder. To Thyne: my apologies for the bitterness which escaped my thirsty lips and struck thee unfairly. To Roach: my clemency and love. I would not be so ruinous as to destroy my lighthouse for a brief flickering-out of its flame." He pulled back Thyne's gaming chair and dropped himself into it, swigging from his flask. "I have made more attempts at Osiris. Worthless attempts thusfar, but attempts *must* be made while there still be time to shift the tides."

After a long quiet, Roach scooped Francis up and brought him to the bed to lay him down between himself and Thyne. He gently took his drink and set it on the floor then kissed him tenderly and embraced him. "We just need to take some time to recenter."

"Why is it always time to relax and recenter? Do you not grasp the gravity of the situation?"

"Franky, it's *because* I grasp the gravity of the situation that I constantly tell you to relax and waste your time."

"How in god's name does that offer aid in any capacity?"

Thyne answered for him: "Frankenstein, you need to rest. At least right now you need to rest. You're pissed and acting a fool."

He took offence, but Roach clarified, "He's just trying to say that we should try and more carefully plan out any future attacks on Osiris after the shareholders thing did the exact opposite of what you were hoping. Sonny went to school for business: he's probably the best to ask for ideas about how to pinpoint weaknesses."

Francis pondered and silently enjoyed being in Roach and Thyne's shared embrace. There was no better place for him than in their arms, but he shook away the admiration when he felt himself slipping into the void and asserted, "We can *never* capitulate. Promise me, the twain of you, that we shan't ever stop making attempts at Osiris."

Roach kissed Francis' knuckles while Thyne squeezed his other hand hard. They both nodded.

"We'll try, but no matter what, we'll be here with you," said Thyne, and Roach added, "forever, bed bug."

Part Six

No cause is lost if there is but
one fool left to fight for it.

⚙ Chapter 61 ⚙
Jones' Horrible Leviathan
Will Find You

Silvino was sitting poolside, sipping on a margarita, and watching Roach swim laps. After his fiftieth lap, Roach went up to the edge of the pool and crossed his arms over the side to rest. He smiled at his boyfriend and wiped his eyes to get a better look at him. Silvino beckoned him over, so he pulled himself out of the water and sat in the lounge chair beside his. As he was ringing out his shoulder-length hair, he smiled and asked, "How's it going over here, sweetie?"

"Just watching my sexy boyfriend be shirtless and cool." He giggled and sipped his drink some more.

"Hey, man," said Roach with a blush as he lowered his hands from his hair to cover over his stomach self-consciously. "This swimsuit is halal. It's not sexy."

Silvino blushed. "Oh. Sorry. I uh... guess you're sexy even when you're being modest?"

Roach sighed and shook away the upset. "It's chill," he said as he leaned over to steal a kiss then a sip from Silvino's cocktail.

"Hey!" he complained playfully. "Get your own."

"I might. So anyway I was just thinking."

"A dangerous pastime."

"I like to live dangerously." A cheeky wink. "I was thinking about how I'm learning how to mountain climb, and I thought, why not invite you to come along for Cloud Peak?"

They both looked down at Silvino's little round belly. He patted it and chuckled as he looked back up at Roach. "I don't think I'm in the type of shape to be climbing mountains, dear."

"Well, it'll be my first one, so it shouldn't be too difficult. I saw some people with physiques like yours in the class." Silvino sipped his drink and pondered. A few quiet moments passed, so Roach let him think by leaving to go make himself a Bloody Mary inside. One of the servants offered to make it for him, but he refused and cleaned up after himself diligently to avoid having to make the workers do it.

After ten minutes, he returned to the poolside seats where Silvino was ringing a little bell to summon a servant. Roach kept control over his face to hide the discomfort he felt watching Silvino order a servant to bring him another margarita. He coughed away the upset and sat beside him shortly after the servant left, sipping on his Bloody Mary as he reached across the space between them and rubbed his boyfriend's cute little tummy. Silvino blushed and worried what the servants might think but listened to Roach when he continued: "You don't have to come with me, but I think it'd be romantic, and if you're having trouble I'll pick you up like Sam and Frodo and carry you to the top."

His blush deepened. "Are you sure you can pick me up?" Roach nodded. He retreated from Silvino's stomach to hold his drink with both hands and sipped through the striped paper straw. "I don't know. I don't think you could," Silvino worried with an embarrassed look down at his gut.

After setting down his drink pointedly, Roach sat still for a moment before suddenly standing, scooping Silvino up into his arms, and kissing him romantically all in one swift motion. "You think all my work at the gym is just for looks?" he said with a taunting playful tone.

"B-but you couldn't carry me up a mountain."

"I could and I would." He set him back down and kissed his knuckles. "What do you say, honeybee?"

He smiled sweetly, still wearing a pink tint on his tipsy cheeks. "Okay, dear."

'Livid' did not even begin to describe how he felt. His best friend: dead. His factories: razed. Twenty of his shareholders: dead. His CFO and CMO: dead. Factories could be rebuilt. Stocks were up. CFOs and CMOs were easily replaceable. But what on Earth was Tatum Abraham to do without Christopher Filipek? There was no word in any language that could convey the turmoil in his soul.

Though Osiris was outwardly unscathed, the company towns in Mexico were a trillion-dollar investment that went up in flames in a matter of minutes. Partha Nima was the most wanted man in the world, and it was entirely because of the blow he struck against Osiris by destroying those factories.

But Tatum's job was not to bother with Partha, nor was it to fear for his life after *The Crown's* outright threat on it. His job was to answer or make a call every once in a while. His job was to sign papers. His job was to do interviews with journalists, provided they paid handsomely for his valuable time. All he had to do was keep his company afloat.

The yes-men beneath him were of the mind that Osiris was too big to fail, but he knew better than to get complacent. He would not underestimate these terrorists. The identities of Partha's accomplices still eluded his men, and the manner in which twenty people were simultaneously beheaded was nothing short of supernatural. *The Crown* and *Tiara* weren't just snakes in the garden, they were a tornado on the horizon threatening to rip up the entire house and send it off to a land of witches and angry apple trees.

After ending a call with his new CFO, he leaned on his desk and held his bald head in his wrinkled hands. "It's not fair," he lamented to his wife, who was sitting beside him and rubbing his arched back.

"It's not," she agreed lovingly.

"When the other kids were partying, I was studying. When the others were filing for welfare, I was living with my father and working at his firm. When others went for scams and instant gratification, I made wise investment decisions. I did everything right, and I worked so hard to get here. It's not fair that these nobodies can just come tearing things apart and killing people I love. What if they got to you next?" He looked at her. "We are getting you a dead man's switch, and we will be certain that yours will not need to be turned on and off like mine."

"Tatum, I don't know, I—."

"I will hear nothing to the contrary, sugar. You are getting one, and that's final." He opened his laptop and wrote an email to his secretary to contact 'the tech people.' With that sent, he held his aching head again and huffed. "I have to sell one of my islands, and no one can afford the asking price, so I have to sell it at a loss. I did everything fucking right, and still I have to sell my island. The biggest one, as well!" He huffed and sighed and eyed his laptop screen in hopes of a reply email.

"Tatum, I think you should take a break from all the work. Do you want me to make you something? Biscuits maybe?"

He glared at her. "This is not something I can just 'take a break from,' Aspyn. These terrorists killed Chris!" He was too angry to cry no matter how much he needed to.

She kissed his cheek and sighed. After a beat of quiet and his continuous glances at his laptop, she stood and said, "I'm going to go to Everest next week, and I want you to be okay while I'm gone. Promise me that you'll go on holiday, too? Or at least that you'll give yourself permission to leave this room."

"No! I have to stay here. I have to keep the company afloat."

"I understand that, Tatum, but really what can they do while Leviathan is after them?"

"They can kill twenty damn shareholders and two of my executives in just two days, Aspyn! They can do that!"

She pouted. "Leviathan will find them."

"Leviathan is useless. The boy I hired got kicked off the job for being in leagues with the terrorists. They know so much more about me than I do about them, and now they have one of the only competent Leviathan mercenaries on *their* side."

She pursed her lips and tapped her chin in thought. "Well, honey, why don't you just hire more mercenaries? You can send them to find the one that betrayed you. They have his name and presumably know how to track him, right? Don't they put implants— tracking chips? —Don't they put those in all of their employees?"

"They put them in the new employees, but he's been with them a while, and he's one of the highest ranking ones. His tracker is in his ID, and he no-doubt knows that." He sighed and stared at his inbox as emails flooded in, waiting to see his secretary's name.

"Well, what's one thing we do know? We know Perlie Moon, that cunt I met at the pub, is friends with Partha and a former CIA member. Send your mates after her more pointedly." He pondered the idea, and Aspyn continued, "They killed your friend, so why not kill one of Partha's?"

He nodded for a while. "Alright. Alright, I'll call my pilot in the morning to arrange a flight back to DC."

"Good." She leaned down and kissed his bald head. "I'm going to go make you some biscuits and tea whether you like it or not."

A sigh. "Thank you, sugar. I'm sorry for being snappy with you. I love you."

"It's okay. I know you're only cross because you're stressed. I love you, too."

Partha's hand on her baby-bump was the warmest most loving touch she had ever known. His innocent smile melted her cold heart, and his little kisses on her cheeks and neck and excited rambling about their future family sent her soul soaring. She once thought she loved River, she once thought she loved Roach, but she knew now that she had never loved anyone until she loved Partha. As it neared the time for her appointment with Giovanni, Partha helped her out of bed and followed along beside her as she walked, still rambling at her. It mirrored the way he had followed her and begged her to abort it when he first found out about the pregnancy.

"Ah, hello, Perlie. Sit here," said Giovanni with a gesture as she entered the examination room. Partha followed and asked where to stand. "Just don't get in my way."

"Yes, sir." He shuffled around to give Giovanni room as he was setting up the ultrasound machine, eventually finding himself opposite the screen with Perlie's left hand in both of his. He beamed at her, and she smiled softly in return. "I'm excited," he whispered.

"Me too," she mouthed.

"Lift your shirt up, please." She did as she was told and winced at the cold gel he put on her belly afterwards. He rubbed the device around on it. "Ah, there we are." He pointed at the screen. "You see? That's the head." They both beamed and nodded excitedly at him. "How precious to see the father is happy, too," he commented, "And happier still, I imagine. Do you see?" He pointed again, but they weren't sure what they were looking at. "It's a boy." They smiled at each other and kissed. "It looks healthy. You've not had any issues have you, Perlie?"

"Nothing we haven't already talked about."

Giovanni smiled and started to clean up the machine. "Wonderful. Unless you have any questions, that's that for now. I'll want to keep checking on things as it goes along, though. And, of course, you probably already guessed you'll need a caesarean procedure."

"What? Why would I need that?"

He gestured at her vaguely. "Your hips are too narrow for natural birth."

Partha wasn't sure if he was meant to take offence on her behalf, so he looked at her for her reaction. She seemed saddened by the news, but she stopped him when he opened his mouth to defend her. They left the exam room and went back up to their suite. As Partha made her a cup of tea, she lounged across one of the settees and sighed.

"A boy," said Partha as he set her tea down, "And he's healthy. That's good, right?"

"Yeah," she said dismissively.

"Are you afraid of the c-section?"

"No."

A beat. He poked his first fingers together and looked around the room. "What's wrong then, heart?"

She tried to swallow her emotions, but her hormones were chaotic, and tears welled in her eyes. Her voice was weepy as she flailed her hand in the air above her and said, "He said I'm not fit to be a mother!"

"Perlie, heart, that's not what he said at all." He knelt down beside her and kissed her cheek as he rubbed her tummy.

"Maybe I should abort it. If I can't have it naturally, maybe it's just not meant to be."

Partha's heart shattered at the idea, and she could feel his upset in the way he stopped rubbing her belly. With a sniffle, he said, "If that's what you want...."

"Oh, Party, I don't know what I want," she wailed.

"Well, if I were a woman, I'd be kinda scared of giving birth naturally. I'd want the surgery instead."

She averted her teary eyes and whispered, "You just don't get it."

He took his hand off her tummy and kissed her knuckles. "I'm sorry." He tried to stand and leave, but she grabbed him by the wrist and put his hand back on the baby-bump.

"I love you, Party. I'm just hormonal, and trying not to worry about the fact that you're the most wanted man in the world, or that Thyne texted me this morning about how now Osiris is hiring mercs after me specifically, too. I just want to be a good mother, and I'm scared that a good mother would abort it."

He sighed. "I love you either way, heart. You'll be a great mother regardless. I'm just excited to be a dad, is all."

She opened her mouth to reply, but Partha's phone rang. He read the caller ID aloud: "Unknown number." He looked to her for guidance.

"May made your phone untraceable, right?" He nodded. "Answer it, but let me hear."

"Hello?" he answered with the volume loud enough that Perlie could hear the man on the other end of the line.

"Owamya, it's Rory. This is a burner phone."

He grinned. "Hi! How are you!?"

"I'm cross. I saw your last stream, and I want to join your cause."

"Oh that's great!" Perlie made a motion with her hand over her neck to end the call, but Partha ignored her concern and stood to start pacing as he talked with his old flame: "We're in Rome. We should meet up somewhere."

Perlie sighed and slapped her hand onto her face. Now they'd have to find a new place to hide. This was clearly some sort of set-up, and Partha was an idiot for not noticing.

"Yeah, I want to meet up, too. Can you meet in London, though?"

"I actually have some friends in London right now! I'll text you the address." Perlie rushed up to him to try and snatch the phone away, but he had already texted Thyne's home address to Rory. "They'll be back here in Rome with us soon, so they can take you with them! I'm so excited to see you again! I've missed you. Do you want to know some of the gang's strengths and weaknesses?" Perlie grabbed the sides of her head in astonishment.

"Uh, I suppose?" answered Rory.

"Okay, so strengths: Cool outfits and nicknames. Some of the people in the gang have superpowers. A lot of them, actually. Oh, and Dezba made us all sweaters! And Roach is really cool. He's like a serial killer, and that's cool I think. And also Thyne is in the gang. He's on my streams sometimes; you've seen him. Or I guess you've only heard him. He's cool, but he gets grumpy sometimes. And so that brings us to the weaknesses: Other than Thyne being a grumpypants, there's also the fact that I can't stream anymore since everyone in the world thinks I kill kids. (That was a deep fake, by the way). I also left my Magic cards in Bermuda, and Perlie says I'm not allowed to go home and get them, and Franky won't use his power to go get them for me, so I can't play Magic unless I use Roach's deck, and his deck is garbage. He also likes garbage in general... And another weakness is right now we're in hiding and kind of a little bit broken, but with you joining everyone will want to get back together and get along to show you how cool we are! And when you get here you can meet my girlfriend, Perlie."

At this point, she had accepted their fates. She sat on the couch and rubbed her aching temples, wishing dearly that she could have a cigarette. Francis would have to bail them out, Roach would be happy to get to do some murdering, and Thyne's heart would explode with rage at having his house compromised, but it wasn't an unsurvivable situation. Partha continued his talk with Rory without even noticing Perlie's upset: "She says I can date other people, too, so maybe we can get back together."

"I'd uh... I'd like that. I'll go to this place and see you soon."

"Yay! Okay, mate! See you soon!" He hung up and beamed a stupid smile at Perlie. "What's wrong, heart? You feeling sick again? Need a back rub?"

She glared at him and opened her mouth to rant and rave but only succeeded at sighing and dropping her head into her hand, trying to massage the headache out of her forehead.

"You'll like Rory," he said as he came over and started giving her a shoulder massage, "He's really nice and handsome. He didn't rat on us after the Halloween job. He's a good guy. Or, well, I guess he's technially a bad guy like us!" He giggled. "'Cause we're the bad guys."

"Okay, Party," she said with utter exasperation.

Roach and Thyne were hopeful that, with Roach anchoring him in reality, perhaps Francis and Thyne would be able to at least briefly delight in each other's company. Francis was wrapped up in Roach's arms with Thyne beside them and caressing his sharp jawline having just retreated from a passionate kiss. He was between worlds. Thyne was only romantic in the void, but Roach only existed outside of it.... Right? He looked up at Roach and examined his facial features with scrutinous eyes. Tracing the subtle wrinkles in his face with his ocean eyes and noting the individual specks of darkness in his five o'clock shadow, he determined that Roach *must* have been real. Even in his most realistic imaginings, he would not have conjured a stranger with such distinct and detailed features. His gaze therefore trailed back to his angel Thyne.

"Guess what, Franky," he said with sparkling ambers and a sad smile, "I can sing now. Do you want me to sing for you?"

He looked up at Roach with a raised eyebrow. Where he was so certain of reality only a moment before, now he was certain Roach wasn't real. Nothing was. No matter the detail in the room or on his face, Roach was a djinn, and Thyne was an angel, and in no reality would said angel ever offer to sing. "What madness speaks the angel, dear djinn?"

Roach pursed his lips and said to Thyne, "Sing for him, then."

Thyne nodded and cleared his throat. For the first few moments of quiet as he sat upright and quaffed a glass of water, Francis was evermore convinced he was in the void. "What should I sing?"

"*Roll the Old Chariot Along*," answered Francis thoughtlessly.

He nodded and beamed. It was a favourite of Francis', especially when he was sloshed, and Thyne always enjoyed the boisterous sea-dog air to it. He shimmied, straightened his spine, pressed his hands together near his diaphragm, and sang.

Francis' eyes went wide. He had heard Thyne's timid singing once, before the void had taken him, but this was something else entirely. This voice was so perfect, it was impossible. Not only impossible to imagine but impossible to witness.

Rather than Roach and Thyne's hope that it would ground Francis, it only sent him further into that reach between worlds. Not quite dead, not quite alive: he was suspended in a new void, but this one was pleasant. It was a divine plane of soul-shattering music. This was his angel Thyne, not conjured by his madness but tangible and between life and death with him. He was certain of it, because there was no mortal being that could, solely with his voice, reach so deeply into Francis' soul and manipulate it, and there was no mortal soul like Thyne's on Earth. He tried to wake: thinking he must have been hearing a siren outside of his ship, his life having been only a dream on a stormy night at sea. When he couldn't wake, he decided to instead listen to the divine gift and savour it.

When Thyne finished his song, he blushed at the way Roach was staring so lovingly and with such astonishment at him, but it was Francis they were trying to ground. He had slipped into the void in their arms, and after an hour of trying to reassure him of reality with Roach as his lighthouse, singing for him was a hail-Mary. Thyne was worried that his sudden ability to sing would only worsen Francis' situation, but Roach was of the mind that it was too perfect a sound for Francis to deny as only a hallucination. Thyne looked at him with a worried smile. "Frankenstein? Did you like the song? Do you know where we are?"

"Aye."

"Where are we?"

"Purgatory. Me angel hath delievered me from Hell." He beamed his rotten smile but it faded as he looked up at Roach, "I have no more need of thee, djinn."

Roach's heart shattered, and his smile snapped immediately to his typical deadpan mien. He coughed away his sorrow and stood, leaving Francis on the bed feeling cold and forsaken. Roach looked at Thyne with upset pouring from his soul but hidden behind his lifeless hazel-greys. He started to leave the room.

"Basil, he didn't mean it. He's lost. He needs you."

"Evidently not." He closed the bedroom door gently and shoved his hands into his pockets on his way down into the living room where he lit himself a cigarette and tried not to take it so personally. *'He's lost,'* he reminded himself, *'He's mad. Thyne's right that he didn't mean it.'* He smoked and sat at the bay window, leaning on one of the bookshelves beside it and resting his smoking hand on his raised knee. His gaze was vacant and aimed through the window at the cloudy afternoon in London.

He may have wallowed in his melancholy longer, but halfway through his cigarette there was a knock at the door that pulled him back to the present. He put his cigarette out on the windowsill and left it there before dragging himself to the door, a hand running through his long hair on the way. After coughing away any expression of emotion on his face, he leaned down to peer through the peephole and thereafter opened the door. "Hey, man."

Dale had a gun to the small of a man's back and pushed him inside roughly, enough that he stumbled to the floor beside Roach and cut his hand on a piece of broken glass from Francis' shattered wine bottle. Roach watched him fall apathetically then turned his attention back to Dale who was closing the door behind him, his aim still on the man. "How'd you find us, dude?"

"Ah pinged yer phone."

"How do you keep pinging our phones, dude? That girl you killed said she made them untraceable."

"Yeah, she made it a real pain in the tuckus." He gestured to the man bleeding on the floor. "That there's Lucas. He's the one what killed Aphid."

"Is he now?" Madness flashed in his eyes as he looked down at the man and smiled eerily. "My brother and I are going to have *so much fun* with you, Lucas."

"Ah got kicked off the job fer helpin' ye. Was hopin' Ah could still join ye ta help wit Baumbach an' whatever else."

"Happy to have you, dude."

"Lucky Abraham's bein' so squirrelly. Ah'm the only one what knows who hired us, so I reckon we's got a week er so 'fer they's on us again, an' 'course they ain't half so good at trackin' as Ah'm."

"Yeah, dude. Thanks for bringing this blighter," he gestured to the man crying on the floor as Dale arched his brow, "Should probably patch him up so he doesn't die yet. You can go upstairs and talk to Thyne. His room is the first one on the left after the second staircase. Franky's in there, too. They're my boyfriends." He smiled proudly with a soft blush on his pale cheeks.

There was a beat as he thinned his eyes at Roach. "Summon's off 'bout ye, but Ah'll figger it out later." While Dale went upstairs to knock timidly on Thyne's door, Roach used his telekinesis to carry Lucas into a nearby bathroom and tend to his bleeding hand and the months-old gunshot wound in his calf.

Thyne shook Dale's hand and invited him to sit at the white wooden table he had in the corner of his room that he often used as a writing desk. Once he was sitting, he tossed him a beer from his mini-fridge and invited him to smoke. If not for his microphone in Dale, he would not be so hospitable, but he knew that he was being truthful, at least about being removed from the job to hunt them down. He introduced Dale to Francis, who was floaty and nursing his flask.

When Roach was finished with Lucas, he brought him up to Thyne's room and asked, "You got any rope, dude?"

"Yes. Follow me, all of you. It's far too crowded in here." They all followed Thyne down to the living room and watched as he revealed a hidden hatch to the basement beneath the rug. "Wait here." He descended and reemerged two minutes later with zip-ties and duct-tape. "Will this do, Basil?"

"That'll work. Yep." While Roach was tying up his next victim, there was another knock at the door.

"That's curious," said Thyne as he hid the hatch back under the rug and peered through the window beside the front door. He gasped and looked at the others. "It's the federals," he mouthed.

After deciphering what he had mouthed, Dale set down his beer on the coffee table, approached the entrance, and shooed Thyne back. Ignoring the sputtering whispered protestation from the Brit, Dale opened the door and slipped himself outside, closing it behind him. "Evenin' officers. What can Ah do ye fer?"

Thyne rushed upstairs to one of his guest rooms on the third floor. Once he was about twenty feet from Dale, the microphone in him cut back on, so he looked out a bay window down at the front door and listened to the exchange: "...a fire nearby, and we're taking statements. You don't sound like a local. Where are you from, mate?"

"Tenny'see," he answered truthfully.

"Are you here on holiday?"

He only stared in reply.

"May we come in?"

He crossed his arms.

"Is this your flat?"

"No."

"Whose flat is it?"

"Ye're the ones came up to the door, an' ye ain't know whose house it is?" He laughed.

The police were unamused. The most senior one said "This isn't The States, mate. This is official police business. If you don't cooperate, we'll have to arrest you."

He laughed again. "Oh, git on down from that there high horse ye're on, gov'na. Pigs're the same no matter where ye go. Ah ain't lettin' ye in summon else's house, an' if ye ain't got no warrant, then ye ain't got no right ta be tryin' ta get in affer Ah said no."

"You have to at least answer our questions. Why are you in London?"

He chuckled darkly and took out his wallet. The Leviathan ID inside had a tracking chip in it, and he still needed to get rid of it. Luckily, it wasn't the highest quality tracker, so its range of accuracy was about three miles: Thyne's house wasn't compromised by Dale being there. Despite the tracker, he was glad to have kept the ID thusfar. Glad enough to hesitate to slip it out of his wallet. *'It'll show Ah'm serious 'bout joinin' Roach's frens,'* he thought to himself as he passed it to the police with a sigh. "Ah think, officers, that Ah ain't gotta answer no queshuns at all." A shit-eating grin as they observed it. "This ain't yer binnus. Git outta here, 'fer Ah show ye 'bout the right ta bear arms."

"Do you mind if we take this to the car and run the numbers on this to confirm it's real?"

He gestured with his head to shoo them back to their car and waited with his arms crossed as they looked up his ID. When they were finished, they all three came back to where he was standing, this time looking much more submissive and not stepping all the way up to the platform with him, electing instead to stay on the stairs below. "I'm sorry about that, mate," said the lead officer as he gave the ID back to its owner. They were all slouching and had their hands slightly raised, as if they feared for their lives in his mere presence.

"Now y'all run back off and delete this entire interackshun from yer records."

"Yes, sir."

"Of course, sir."

"We're sorry, sir."

"An' delete this house from yer database. Ah don't want y'all ever showin' up here again. Am Ah clear?"

"As crystal, sir."

"Of course, sir."

"Yes, sir."

He shooed them away and smirked as they scurried off. Back inside the house, he met with Thyne just as he was coming to the base of the stairs. "That ID has a tracker in it," said Thyne, "Give it to me."

He passed it over with his hands up defeatedly. "It ain't that accurate, but anyway Ah was thinkin' yer teleportin' fren could throw it in the Timbs 'r summon."

"That's a shite idea," he huffed. With a soft glare, he slipped into the living room to pass the ID to Francis. "Get rid of this." It disappeared. "Where did you put it?"

"The Thames."

Thyne pinched his forehead and sighed, but before he could complain, there was yet another knock at the door. "LEAVE ME THE FUCK ALONE!"

"I'll get it, dude," said Roach as he shoved his captive into Dale's arms and peeled back the curtain on the side window of the door to look outside. "It's just some suit," he informed the room behind him, "Should I kill him?"

The visitor spotted Roach through the window and shouted through the closed door, "It's Rory. The kid sent me."

"He says his name is Rory and that Party sent him."

Thyne sighed and stomped up to the door to unlock and slam it open. He grabbed Rory's wrists, yanked him inside, and slammed the door behind him. After locking it and forcefully putting a microphone in Rory, he shouted into the living room, "Franky, take us back to Rome before some other rotter shows up!"

And thus they all found themselves in the otherwise uninhabited living area of Loomis manor.

⚙ Chapter 62 ⚙
The World Beyond This One

Roach was wearing nothing but boxers and ripping from his bong when he heard a knock at the door. With a smokey cough, he scratched his balls and dragged his feet to the entrance to look through the peephole. A smile he couldn't hide cracked his lips as he opened the door to pull Silvino in for a loving embrace. After calling into the house in Arabic to warn his sister to veil herself, he said to Silvino, "Hey, sweetie. Come on in. What's up? You look excited."

"I am excited!" He tippy-tapped into the room with his steps quick and fast. With the door closed behind them, he bounced on his toes and said, "Okay, close your eyes, and hold out your hands."

Roach smiled softly and rolled his eyes before closing them and laying out his hands. "It better not be your dick, dude," he joked before he felt something being placed into his open left palm.

"Open 'em!" said Silvino after kissing Roach's cheek.

He fluttered open his hazel-greys and saw an old Volkswagen key in his hand. "What's this? My birthday's not for a few weeks. You're giving me a car?"

"Sort of! Okay, listen listen listen: remember how you were telling me about that mountain in Wyoming?"

Roach arched his brow. "Yes."

"So I was thinking what if instead of only going to the mountain together, what if

we go all over the country!? We'll take another gap year and go see The Grand Canyon and shows in Vegas and listen to all the music you want to show me and go to amusement parks and eat food from all around the country and—."

"Alright alright I get it. You're adorable," he said with faux-irritation. "What's with the Volkswagen, then?"

"Right, well I bought it and figured you and your family could trick it out for the trip. You can keep it afterwards as like a birthday gift, but for the trip I thought maybe you could add like a mini-fridge and a TV and a boombox and—."

He shut him up with a passionate kiss. When he retreated, he poked Silvino's nose and looked deep into his dark brown eyes. "I love you so much, Vinny."

He beamed. "I love you, too! I'm so excited. I've never been out of California. Have you?"

"Yeah, man. I was born in New York, remember?"

"Oh, New York! We should go there, too."

"We'll go wherever you want, honeybee." He scooped him up and carried him to the couch where he sat down and let Silvino curl up in his strong arms.

"I still can't believe you can pick my fat ass up," he joked.

"Stop it, Vinny. You're just a little husky. As cute as a little husky pup, too."

Silvino giggled and blushed. "So you like the plan?"

"Well, I don't know if I can afford to take a bunch of time off to fix the van, but I like it in theory."

He slapped his chest playfully. "No seas gilipollas. You know I'm going to pay you."

"And you'll pay for the modifications you want?"

"Of course. You're such an asshole thinking I'd want you to work for me without paying you."

"Well, you are a liberal," he pointed out with a playful tone.

Silvino pouted. "You said I'm a good liberal."

"So I did," he said after kissing his nose, "Well, I'll get you a list of things we'll need for the trip and another list of the parts I'll need for the van. Just need to give it a looksie. Where is it?"

"In my garage. Should I call Cleo to come pick us up to take us to my place?"

Roach pursed his lips. "I guess. You know I don't like having servants do stuff for us, though."

"Oh, I know, but he doesn't mind. It's his job, after all. It's not like we don't pay *him handsomely." He took out his phone and texted his chauffeur then opened his notes app where he had already listed some places he wanted to visit. "I'm so excited for the trip. Are there any places you want to go in particular?"*

"Other than the mountain?"

He giggled. "Yes. Other than that."

He shrugged. "Wherever.... Now," he let out a slight grunt of effort as he lifted Silvino from his lap to set him in the seat beside him, "you sit there looking pretty while I take another hit of this bong before I have to be around your parents. You want a hit?"

"You know I don't, Clay."

Another shrug. "Suit yourself, lame-ass."

In the library, Partha was losing his sixteenth game of chess in a row to River, who was desperately trying to teach him his constant mistakes, when they both perked up at the sounds of conversation and shuffling suddenly coming from the living room. "Tony?" said River as he stood and started to rush around the back of the house toward the living area. The dogs that had been lounging around the chess table were bolting along beside him.

"Sonny?" They met up in the back foyer where Roach scooped his brother up into a spinning hug. After setting him back on the ground, he crouched down to let the dogs smother him in kisses. He spoke to River while being pummelled by the playful pups. "I missed you. I'm sorry, bro. I shouldn't have gone. Dale's here. He brought the fuck that killed Aphid for us." He giggled and calmed the dogs down.

After Roach finally stood back up and hugged his brother again, River said, "I missed you, too, dumbass. Let's go flay the fucker."

"Hell yeah," he grabbed River's hand to lead him into the other room. "That's Rory, by the way. Hey Lucas! Get your ass over here. Make it snappy, and it might not be so bad for you." He limped up to the twins despondently.

River whispered in Arabic, "Oh, look how obedient."

Roach addressed the others: "We'll be in the basement. Excuse the rudeness, please, Rory. We'll get to know you better when we're finished with this guy."

Rory gulped and nodded as he watched them lead their captive away, their dogs trailing loyally behind them. Partha surprised him with a hug from behind. "Heya, Rory!"

He shoved Partha gently off of him and looked around. "Where are we?"

"It's like this big vampire manor. Here, I'll give you the tour." He offered his arm to link with Rory's, but before leading him away he spotted Dale and offered his other arm. "You, too!"

Dale arched his brow at him. "Ye must not reckanize me."

"Yeah, you're that guy who did that kinky torture after you kidnapped me." He wiggled his arm. "Come on!"

Dale blushed. "It weren't kinky."

Rory arched his brow at Partha. "Mate? Did this bloke actually kidnap you?"

"Yeah, but he's good at torture," he purred and wiggled his eyebrows. "Come on, Dale."

He timidly took the offer with a confused panic in his blue eyes as he said to Thyne and Francis, "'Spose Ah'll be seein' y'all affer the tour."

"Party," said Thyne before they left.

"Yes?"

"You and me are gonna have a little chat later." It would be a proper reprimanding for Partha's stupid stupid decision to tell Rory everything about their gang over a random phone call. Luckily, the call wasn't a set-up, but it very easily could have been.

He smiled anxiously. "Okay, sir." With a shooing motion from Thyne, Partha led the new recruits through the manor, introduced them to the others, and explained in great detail everything that had happened up to that point, everyone's powers, the gang's goals, and of course some (a lot of) ramblings about his West Marches campaign. His plan was to wrap the game up before his son was born then ask the twins to co-DM a new campaign for everyone.

While Partha was talking Dale and Rory's ears off, the twins were in the same dimly-lit room they had used to torture Filipek and looking at their next victim with eyes like cobras. The puppies were playing in the hall outside of the room, but Diana (the doberman), and Angel (the pit bull) were sitting on either side of the twins and looking up at their masters in wait for a command.

There was a small bluetooth speaker connected to Roach's phone playing a random selection of songs. It was cold and dark and terrifying in this chamber, but the song currently playing was an upbeat Hank Williams tune. Lucas was tied up much the same as Filipek had been, but he was gagged where Filipek wasn't. The twins spoke in Demotic to each other:

"So what do you think, Tony? Torture first?"

His breaths were heaving evermore as he stared Lucas down and remembered his beloved dog. *'Alone. Scared. Just trying to protect his people. And this fucker took him from me. Killed him without a second thought.'* "I don't think I can wait much longer. I'm just going to tell the dogs to kill him."

"It'll be over so quickly, though. Can't we play with him first?"

Roach disregarded the request and said, "Diana, Angel," they stood and gave him more active attention. In Arabic: "Villain."

They turned their attention toward Lucas and bared their teeth at him. As they crept up on him and started circling like the predators they were, River said in Demotic, "Oh, you're right, Tony. I shouldn't have questioned you. Look at the fear in his eyes. Oh, I could swoon." His legs wobbled, so Roach held him up by his elbow. With a mad grin at Lucas as they made eye contact, he said in English, "You scared?" Lucas nodded and tried to plead for mercy with his eyes. Roach's voice reached a new level of darkness as he held back his wrathful sorrow and said, "Sic 'em."

Diana was the first to move. She snapped her teeth around his throat and tore at his jugular. Angel, seeing this, went for his thighs. Roach watched the light go out of Lucas' eyes with a deranged grin twitching his lips and unhinged grief twitching his left eye. The dogs tore him to pieces, and the twins savoured all the barking and growling and slurping and muffled screams of agony. Roach began laughing hysterically at all the red, but the laughs became greeting and wailing. Tears soaked his cheeks, and long after the dogs had already killed Lucas, Roach shooed them away and flipped open a knife to stab down into his unbeating heart repetitively, all the while laughing— crying— shouting— sobbing—. "You get what you deserve! You get what you deserve! Fuck you! Dog-killer! Dog-killer!" Laughing— crying— shouting— sobbing—. Laughing— crying— shouting— sobbing—.

River came up behind him and wrapped his hands up under his elbows to slow his mad stabbing. His hands were trembling and pure red when he finally stopped decimating the corpse. He tried to keep a grip on the knife, but he was shaking too much, and it fell with a thud into the body's open chest-cavity. "Tony," whispered River sensually as he ran his hands down Roach's chest, "He's dead, Tony."

A beat. Roach's hysterics faded. The music seemed to pick back up in volume now that the room wasn't echoing with madness. It was a calmer song than before: slow and melodic and one of Roach's favourites. Diana and Angel were concerned for their master, so they came up and sniffed at him. Roach's heart-rate slowed, and he placed a bloody hand on Angel's head. "Good girl," he said with a sniffle.

"Come here, Tony." He helped Roach stand and sat him on the cold concrete beside the corpse. He sat across from him and commanded the dogs to snuggle Roach. They happily trotted up and curled up in his lap for pets, no regard for all the blood on all of them. "Tell me what happened while you were gone."

Roach stared vacantly as memories of Aphid overwhelmed him, but he eventually retroactively heard the request and shook his head as he returned to the present. He looked at his brother with a dumbfounded expression, if a little hidden under all the blood. "You were sent to guide me in this life."

"Yeah."

"Not metaphorically."

"Yeah."

He started. "What? You knew?"

"Of course I knew. I have a perfect memory, too, y'know."

He took a moment to process the information. Unsure of how to address it, he said, "I had sex with Thyne——."

"Nice."

"Shut up. —and when I came the first time, I… I was sent back and saw this weird shadowy figure that had also once saved me in Chihuahua, and anyway, he gave me Oliver's memories. I'm Oliver. I'm the New Game Plus. And he said you'd be with me to guide me while I was trying to find Thyne again."

River blinked. "Shadowy figure? You mean Faers?"

Roach scrambled to his feet and backed away. "What the fuck, Karson? How do you know him?"

"I knew him in the time before."

"The time before what?"

He tilted his head. "The time before we were born."

Roach's breaths quickened. He held his heart. "You remember the time before we were born?"

River stood and cautiously approached his panicking brother. "Tony, calm down. What's wrong?"

"YOU REMEMBER THE TIME BEFORE WE WERE BORN!"

"Don't you?"

"No!" He grabbed his head. "I mean. I guess *now* I do because I remember being Oliver in London in the 1920s, 30s, and 40s. Is that what you remember? Were you Rommie?"

"What? Who's Rommie?" Roach's breaths got even faster. River tried to console him to little effect. "I thought we weren't talking about it because it was so creepy."

"Creepy?"

"Yeah. Dad once even took me to a priest for an exorcism and made me do ruqyah every night for a year straight."

"He took you to a priest!?"

"Yeah. He said I was possessed. I drew Faers with some crayons and said he was my friend before I was born, and he freaked the fuck out. I mean rightfully so. Scary shit for a six-year-old to be doing." River rubbed Roach's back. "I'm sorry for not mentioning it before. I thought you remembered too." He kissed his cheek. "I remember Faers. He was a friend of mine and an on-again off-again flame. Faers is a god. So was I. Anyway, just before I was born, he made me promise to look after you."

Roach looked at his brother with every sort of confusion and upset plain on his face. "What the fuck, Karson? What the *fuck?*" he whispered.

"Tony, don't look at me like that. Please. Dad made me so scared to talk about it. I don't want to have to hide it from you too."

"No no no, don't hide yourself from me, Sonny. Please." He pulled him into a warm embrace and squeezed hard. His entire body was trembling.

"Shhh, Tony. It's okay. I love you."

He tried to retreat but instead held him closer as he said, "I love you, Sonny. I'm sorry. This is a lot. This is a lot to suddenly find out about you. I thought I knew everything about you."

"Do you want me to keep telling you?"

He finally retreated and tried to wipe the tears from his eyes, only succeeding in wiping Lucas' blood all over. He chuckled at the mess, his white teeth in bright contrast to the dark blood. "Please keep telling me, Sonny. I want to know you entirely. Like I thought I did."

"Well, it was about 300 years that I was living there as a god. My name was Raez. I was a god of fortune, which is why I was so adamant to Dad about letting me help him gamble. I thought I could manipulate the odds in his favour, but I've since realised that I don't have those powers in this body." He paused to let Roach simmer in his shock. "Faers was a god of manipulation, so naturally we had a sort of frenemies situation going on. The plane itself was really eerie and surreal. Everything, and I mean *everything* there was a living sentient being: the wind, the sky, the clouds, every single grain of sand. It was called Aeteriodorum. To incarnate a god there, you have to die as a spiritual person. I don't remember the life I led that made me into the god I was, but I remember being one. I remember the insane sex with Faers, too." He chuckled. "It's all a bit muddy, though. I don't know how to describe those memories, but they aren't as crisp as the ones from being a mortal are." A beat. "Is that how Oliver's memories are, too? All vague and weird?"

He nodded, but his gaze was hollow as he tried to process the information. Eventually he looked River in the eyes and said, "Certainly not... *real* Gods, though, right?"

"God-adjacent if not. We were very powerful. Faers was the *most* powerful. Like the most powerful being in existence.... Or something. Again, it's all a bit muddy, and it was so surreal and weird. I try not to think about it."

There was a long beat of quiet filled with only the random music from Roach's phone. "Is that all?" Roach asked eventually.

"Well, I can give you a play-by-play later. I don't want to have to think about it all at once. And you can tell me about your life as Oliver." He cupped his hand under Roach's forearm. "Let's go shower."

"No more giant secrets you're keeping from me?"

"I wasn't keeping it from you. I thought you knew."

"Sorry…."

"Although, I suppose there is *one* thing."

"What is it?"

"Remember in tenth grade when you were looking for your money for the book fair?"

"You dick. What did you do with it?"

"I bet another kid he couldn't do a backflip and watched him wipe-out. Bought us those ice creams that weekend with the winnings."

He smiled softly. "That's it, then?"

"Yeah, dickhead. That's it. Come on." He kissed him and led him out of the room to the bathroom. They cleaned the dogs first, and once the pups were free and zooming around the entire manor like maniacs, the twins showered.

When they were finished, they found Thyne reading in the library. "Hey, dude," said River, "You wanna cash in on our deal now or no?"

"Hm? What deal?"

"When we were playing *Hold 'Em* in Korea and I asked you to look at Tony's cards."

He blinked.

"You don't remember, do you?"

"I don't remember."

"Look at our messages."

Thyne cautiously took out his phone and navigated to his messages with River. The last one read: ⌈ **Look at Tony's cards right now, and we'll have a threesome with you.** ⌋ He blushed a deep crimson and looked up at the twins who smiled down at him fiendishly in tandem. "Uh… alright… right now?" They nodded. "Alright. Uh… Yes. Okay." He set down his book and let them lead him to their suite.

With the door locked, River started kissing and undressing Thyne while Roach took off his shirt and sweater behind them. Once Thyne's shirt was removed, River started kissing down his neck to let his brother get at him too, but he stopped when he spotted the brand on Roach's arm. "What happened to you, Tony? Is that a brand?"

He followed his gaze to the scabbing wound. "Oh. Yeah. That hurt. I'm fine, though."

"It ruined your tattoo." He took his arm and gently ran his fingers over the scar.

"Yeah. I can get it again somewhere else, though. Franky has that tattooing pen I could use. Probably my thigh would be easiest."

River pursed his lips. "No. I don't want a thigh tattoo. I'll just have to get branded, too."

"Sonny, no. Please don't. I already caused so much trouble. I hurt Thyne. I hurt Francis. I can't bear it if I hurt you, too. We don't need to stay entirely identical."

He rolled his eyes. "Shut up, dude. I'm getting the brand. I'm *choosing* to do it. Okay? It's not you hurting me. I want to be able to pretend to be each other. It's too useful to throw away because of your stupid ego."

Thyne, for this entire conversation, was standing beside the twins and looking up at them with an awkward blush as he tried not to ogle their bodies after the change in tone. The brothers noticed him and swapped to Arabic to bicker quietly for a few more lines. It ended when Roach threw his hands up and said in English, "Fine, Sonny. Whatever. Let's just try and get back in the mood."

River smiled and eyed Thyne like a viper before flicking his gaze back to his brother. He spoke sensually: "Alright. Firstly I'll compliment your artistic eye: the cut on his lips will make such a cute scar."

"I think so, too," said Thyne with a shy smile.

"Come here, you cute ass little bitch," said Roach as he pulled him between the twins and leaned down to kiss his scabbed lips while River peppered him in kisses on his shoulders and back, continuing to undress them all in the process.

When they were finished having their fun, they came downstairs, following the smells of whatever Giovanni was cooking for dinner. Thyne was only wearing his boxers and Roach's sweater, which was quite big on him, Dezba having made it slightly oversized for the giant. River was in a pair of pyjama pants, and Roach was wearing sweatpants and a t-shirt. The newcomers were awkwardly settling in, Partha still yapping their ears off in the living room with Dezba trying to ease them into the gang less obnoxiously. Richard was listening and looking uncomfortable and out of place all alone on one of the couches. Francis and Viktor were in the library playing chess with Melchiresa reading nearby. Perlie was learning piano from Arjun, and Neodesha was cooking with Giovanni.

Thyne avoided the kitchen, his insides squirming and heart fluttering as he merely imagined an encounter with Giovanni. It seemed he was going to sit in the living area, but he surprised everyone by instead going for the piano. Arjun stopped playing and looked up at him. "I don't know how you do it with these fake fingers," he said as he held up his new cybernetics, though they were hidden by his gloves, "They're no good at all for anything."

"Move over." He swung himself onto the bench, and the room quieted as all eyes turned to him. Perlie and Arjun left the piano bench to give him space. He looked at all the attention he had gathered, beamed, and started what was once his favourite song to play: *Chopsticks*. It always irritated his mother when she would request a waltz, and he would start it up. Now, without her nagging him on the sidelines or her memory haunting him, he was able to actually enjoy playing piano. The waltz timing was made especially evident in his rendition, all of it played with emotion. The piece began simply, but as it went on, he added more and more embellishments, flourishes, and other complexities that greatly impressed the other musicians in the room. Giovanni and Neodesha peered out of the kitchen when they heard a song Arjun would never play and both smiled wide to see Thyne at the piano.

Roach approached him in the middle of the song and slipped his harmonica out of his pocket. He wiggled it inquisitively for Thyne to see, and with a big grin and a nod from the Brit, he started playing a countermelody. Roach was improvising, and Thyne naturally understood what he was going to play next. He had never played with someone else before, and he had never improvised, so it was surreal to understand what Roach would play before he played it. He tried to be spontaneous by gradually transferring the melody to *Tico-Tico No Fubá*, but during this second song, the flourishes and embellishments he added eventually overwhelmed the music until he wasn't playing a recognisable piece at all anymore. He was instead playing off of what Roach was doing, and vice versa. When he realised he was actually improvising, his big smile got even bigger, and he laughed. It was like magic, and when Arjun joined in with a guitar, the song became even more complex but still somehow easy to play together. He silently thanked his Gods, feeling as if they were truly in control of him in such a divine moment anyway.

They played for fifteen minutes, the others in the room eventually letting the jamming become background noise to the conversations they were having, but when Roach stopped playing his harmonica suddenly in the middle of a solo, the rest of the music also ended abruptly as Arjun and Thyne followed his gaze.

He had to use all of his mastery over his facial muscles to not growl like a feral dog at the man he saw coming into the living area with Francis. *Viktor.* The nazi fuck that had killed him. His shoulders were heaving and deadpan gaze locked with the ginger as he crossed the chamber into the kitchen. "Bastard," he muttered.

"Mate?" Thyne was frowning, and it wrenched Roach's heart.

"Sorry. Uh…."

"Let's swap," he said, "You play piano, I'll play guitar, and Arjun can play harmonica."

They agreed, swapped instruments, and with a riff from Thyne on the guitar, another jam session began.

Dinner was half an hour later.

Giovanni hadn't expected to have to feed such a large crowd, and while he did manage to make enough food for everyone, he unfortunately forgot to keep it halal. The main course was a roast ham. With everyone sitting at the table, he started to carve it and fill the plates he was handed. Roach's plate never left his place, and his gaze hardly ever left Viktor. His breaths were heaving and teeth grinding down into each other, though there was no expression of emotion on his face otherwise. Viktor's smile hanging in the dark above him as he tortured Oliver lingered in his perfect memory. The feel of his cells being turned one by one into plant cells and back again as rings of green shot down his arms. Flowers blooming from his open abdomen and thorny vines from his eye sockets. Blackouts that felt like a thousand years without sleep. A thousand cuts that didn't bleed. Limbs removed and reattached.

'He's keeping Thyne and Francis and Sonny alive. Don't kill him, Clayton. Don't kill him. He's protecting them. Thyne tormented him for me. Don't kill him, Clayton.' He watched as everyone else started eating and noticed his plate was still empty. There wasn't much on offer for him, and seeing as he was having a particularly hard time being in Viktor's presence, he excused himself and climbed to his suite where he produced music on his laptop and tried to calm his mind.

Rory and Dale were sitting where May and Jean-Jacques had once sat, and with an anxious air to both of them, after Roach left and everyone was starting to eat, they were hammered with questions from the others:

"So, Rory, how do you know Partha?" asked Dezba.

He sipped from his wine to force away some of his nervousness. "We dated."

"Remember when I said I had a boyfriend in London when we first went there? That was Rory I was talking about."

"That's nice," replied Dezba with a flick of her eyes toward Perlie.

"How long did you date?" asked Perlie with a glare at Rory.

"I'm not sure. Partha had a nasty habit of constantly standing me up."

"I'm sorry, Rory. I'm getting better. I quit coke."

He smiled. "That's really good, kid. I'm glad to hear it."

"And how do you know Roach, Dale?" asked Thyne.

He started, and his face went pale. "Er... We met at a bar." He didn't want to give the real reason. He wasn't sure how much the gang knew about Roach and therefore didn't know what was okay to divulge.

River piped up: "That's a lie. He's trying to protect Tony. That's sweet of you, Dale, but everyone here knows Tony's a serial killer." He punctuated the harrowing statement with a nonchalant bite of his ham.

Dale gulped and forced a smile. "Ah met 'em when he kidnapped me durin' the war. He were lookin' fer—," he stopped and looked at River who nodded to allow him to continue: "He were lookin' fer his husband. Ah dinny know where he were, though."

"He kidnapped you? How'd you end up being his best mate?" asked Thyne.

"It doesn't matter how they got to be friends," interrupted River when he saw the panic in Dale's icy-blues.

Thyne glared, but before he could snip at River, Perlie asked, "What made you want to join us? Both of you."

They looked at each other. Rory answered first: "Last year I met this wonderful bird at a pub. She was beautiful and kind and fancied me, not to mention she was a baker like me. I took her to a private lounge, had my way with her, showed her London from a whole new perspective, and bought her whatever drinks she fancied. It was a lovely date, and I was thinking she might be perfect for me." He quaffed his wine and slammed the glass down. "Bloody harlot. Soon as I turned me back she was flirtin' with none other than Tatum Abraham. I had gotten the hint that she was into money more than men, but I didn't think it'd go so deep."

"Are you talking about Aspyn Temm?" asked Perlie. He nodded, and Perlie scoffed. "She's insufferable. How could you like her?"

"Perlie, don't," said Dezba.

"I like the cut of his jib," said Francis, "Such begrudging would not be out of place among the likes of Thyne."

"The motivation is good," agreed Thyne, "but do you have anything else you bring to the table?"

"Aye. I'm rich. I've a load of properties in London and Birmingham and a few in other countries."

Thyne's smile soured. "A landlord? Party, this is unacceptable."

"What? You'll let *Viktor* be in the gang but not my boyfriend?"

Thyne scoffed and pouted. "Well, I'm not responsible for whatever Roach does when he finds out you're a landlord."

"Landlord or not," argued Rory, "I'm rich."

"So are we, mate. Look around. You think a mansion like this just grows on trees?"

"And what about you, Dale, sweetie?" asked Dezba before they could get into a political debate.

"Erm... Ah'm here ta help wit Baumbach. They imprisoned my daddy an' uncle a while back. Roach an' me done saved 'em, but he says y'all's goin' affer Baumbach, an' Ah said Ah'd help. Got lots more skills than some wert'less landlord too." He glared at Rory who glared back. "Y'all already know Ah'm a merc fer hire."

"Well, it's voluntary here," said Neodesha.

"Ah know. Ah'm not askin' fer nothin'. Ah owe Roach that much."

"You did kill May, though," said Perlie, "If Jean-Jacques ever comes back, he's gonna be pissed."

"I don't think he's coming back," said Thyne, "I think he's gone back to work as an aeromechanic."

"Good for him," said Dezba with a soft smile.

"Well ain't Ah lucky, then?"

Dezba's grin became a scowl. "No. You aren't. You killed May. She was the lifeblood of this gang. She was the sweetest one in the group, not to mention, she had invaluable skills. We're a lot weaker without her, and none of us are happy that you're here."

He shrank in her oppressive gaze.

Rory piped up: "Weaker? Did she have superpowers too?"

"No. She was a hacker," said Partha.

"Were she now? Well Ah ain't too bad wit that sorta thing, neither. Ah got pass her guards on yer phones. My Granpappy and Granmama was hackers. Ah don' really 'member Granmama, an' my Granpappy died 'fore Ah was born, but Ah learnt from some vidyas they made."

The conversation may have continued, but River's phone rang, drawing all of the attention to him. Giovanni scolded him for having it at the dinner table, but he ignored the old Italian and read the caller ID. "'Unknown number.' Dale?"

Dale started and scrambled to take something out of his pocket. He held out his hand for River's phone and, once he had it, he plugged a strange device into its charger port. "That'll hide it fer the call 'slong as it don' last longer than an hour."

"Thanks, bro." He answered with the volume on speaker so the entire table could hear, all of them falling entirely silent. "Hello?"

"Happy birthday, Clayton!" said a woman on the other end.

Confused glances were exchanged: the twins' birthday wasn't until November eighth. Everyone was quiet to let River reply: "Thanks, sis. I see you're calling from an unknown number. Any particular reason why?"

There was a beat. She laughed nervously. "Yeah, I was just thinking it'd be interesting to go a bit old school." There was a subtle emphasis in the final two words, and River stroked his stubble.

"Right. Well, what'd you get for me for my birthday?"

Another beat. "Uh, you sure you want me to tell you?"

He paused, as if to give her more time to think, before saying, "Yeah."

"I know you like Jenga, so I bought you one with blocks made of steel."

River chuckled. "Thanks, sis. Sounds fun. You'll have to meet up with me somewhere to give it to me."

"Yeah," another nervous laugh, "So where should we meet up?"

"How 'bout the library?"

She gulped. After a long beat of silence: "Heh. Uh, no sorry, Clay. That won't work."

"I see." He steepled his fingers. "Well, where do you think we should go, then?"

She laughed nervously again, and it was clear in the tenor of her voice that she was on the verge of tears when she said, "H-how about where you're staying. Where *are* you staying?"

"I'm in New York too. Just come to my apartment. Sunday night. I'll make you dinner." He hung up and rushed upstairs to fetch his brother.

There was a stunned silence in his wake, broken after a moment by Dale taking the phone from the table and fidgeting with the device on it. "The Bronx…. How'd he know where she were?"

Thyne took out his phone and quit the manor, standing on the back porch and smoking as he made a call of his own. "Chamberlain!" answered Grisha Morozov.

"Hey chap, I need your help again."

"Am always willing to help rich little faggot man."

"I need a plane to take me into America. To New York City. How quickly can you get me one?"

"You want pilot?"

"I don't need a pilot, but I need to be able to enter American air-space, so if that's the only way to do that, then I'm fine with hiring one of your men."

"Hold on." He put the phone down and chatted loudly with his father for a minute or two. When he noisily pulled the phone back up to his ear, he laughed and said, "Can get you there tomorrow, flying out from London, if you pay well enough."

"How much is 'well enough'?"

"Thirty million Euros."

"Deal. Heathrow airport?"

"Da."

"I'll be there. I'll have some passengers with me."

"As long as you don't have more than fifty."

"Far from it. I'll also need a flight back at some point, but I don't know when."

"Okay. Will call my people. Be in my hangar by sixteen hundred."

"Alright. Cheers, mate." He hung up, and when he went back inside everyone had migrated to the living area where the twins were addressing the gang while Arjun and Viktor cleaned the dining table.

"There you are. What were you doing out there?" asked River.

"Got us a plane leaving for New York tomorrow out of Heathrow. We should get going now."

"Nice. Good goin', man."

"Who was that girl on the phone?" asked Dezba.

"That was me and Tony's little sister."

"What the fuck is she doing in New York?" said Roach as he massaged his aching forehead. "I was certain she was in Egypt."

"I guess we'll find out when we get there," said River.

"While we's in 'Murica, we can head out to Tenny'see an' get my bus ta go affer Baumbach wit it."

"Good thinking, dude. Poppie will be able to help, too, if she's not too shaken after being kidnapped," said Roach.

"She sounded more scared than I'd think she would," said River, "Maybe she's not alone. Maybe she's got Gideon with her."

"Shit, I hope not," said Roach.

"Thyne, you said you had a plane for us?" asked River.

"Yeah. We should start driving to London as soon as we can."

"Alright," said Roach as he started pointing at various members of the gang: "Party, Dale, you two are coming with us. Dezba, do you want to go back to America?"

She smiled sweetly. "Well sure, honey."

"Alright, so Dezba's in. Perlie should stay. Anyone else coming along? Rory? Do you want to come on this job with us to show your mettle?"

He went pale. "Uh. O-okay."

"Alright, that should be enough, then. And obviously Thyne and Franky are coming, right?" He looked at them.

"Of course, darling," answered Francis.

"Okay. Break, then. Let's get this show on the road."

They dispersed and packed while Francis took loaded suitcases out to the cars Thyne and the twins told him they would be taking. They brought whatever weapons they had in Rome, but Thyne suggested stopping by his house in London on the way to the airport to pick up more.

With everyone ready to go, they hurried into the twins' three cars still in Rome, with Roach in the *Ferrari*, River in the *Fiat*, and Thyne in the *Alfa Romeo*.

✺ Chapter 63 ✺
We're Really Bad Eggs

"This is the tent you got, dude?"

He beamed and nodded.

"This is really small. Didn't they have a bigger one?"

"It says it's for two people." He pointed to the words on the packaging, "And it's a hiking tent like you wanted."

"Yeah, but dude... we're both so big."

Silvino frowned, and his big brown eyes got even bigger and sparkled with tears. "I can get a different one." Roach felt like he'd kicked a puppy.

"I—. Uh. No, it's okay." He took on a more confident and teasing air. "Guess we'll just have to snuggle up real close, huh?"

Silvino fluttered his eyelashes and let a small smile tug at his mouth. "That sounds horrible," he said sarcastically.

"The worst. But, it's the bed you made, so," he shrugged and tossed the tent into the van before wrapping his arm around Silvino's back and pulling him in close to give him a romantic kiss.

Silvino pushed him away and tugged at his curly shoulder-length hair with a nervous scan of the area. "Be careful, Roach. What if someone saw?"

His smile disappeared. "Sorry. Let's uh— just finish packing."

"Yeah."

They resumed packing, during which Roach said, "So, I'll drive for the first leg."

"Er... first leg?"

"Yeah. Unless you wanted to drive first."

He went pale. "I thought you would be driving the whole time."

"Dude what?" He huffed with amusement. "Are you fucking high? I can't be the only one driving on a year-long cross-country roadtrip. I love you, but if you want to see even half of the shit on your adorable little list of places to visit and dates to have, it's gotta be a team effort behind the wheel." Silvino stopped packing, his face still void of colour and eyes wide. "Well, don't look at me like that, man. You're making me feel like an asshole."

Silvino muttered something, but Roach couldn't understand him, so he asked him to repeat himself. Again, he couldn't understand. It took three tries before he finally heard him say, "I don't know how to drive."

Roach chuckled. "You don't have a licence?"

"I... have a licence."

"So you passed the driving test. Can't have been too long ago, too. How old were you? Seventeen?"

"Yeah. Seventeen."

"So what's the problem?" Silvino blushed deeply and averted his eyes. Roach's head went on a swivel to check for strangers around, and when he confirmed they were alone, he cupped his hand around Silvino's jaw and whispered, "Did your mom pay off the DMV to get your licence?" Silvino nodded timidly. "It's chill, man. You've got the licence, so I'll just teach you. We'll wait until we're out somewhere more rural and swap, alright?"

"That sounds scary. Can't you just drive?"

"You gotta learn to drive, dude. It's fun! I'll keep us safe. Promise."

He tugged at his hair again. "Okay, if you say so."

Roach leaned down to give him a quick peck and a cheeky wink.

With Silvino's worries waning, they finished packing the van and got inside to start their year-long adventure. After only ten minutes on the road, Roach pulled into the cracked parking lot of a dank gas station in Compton. Litter danced around in the wind in front of its deteriorating façade. Bars were built over the windows, the panes of which were covered in overlapping sun-faded advertisements. There were piss stains on the wall just beside the ice cooler, which itself was open and dripping half-melted ice onto its own cables. Roach beamed at Silvino and turned off the engine.

"Let's stock up on goodies, yeah? Gotta fill up that mini-fridge that I painstakingly installed for you, else it's just a useless drain on the battery."

Silvino gulped and tried not to look as terrified as he truly was. "Okay...."

"What's wrong, honeybee? I love this place. Good prices. Good workers. Good place." He patted Silvino's thigh. "Come on."

He followed him with his shoulders up and both of his arms wrapped around Roach's bicep, hiding as much of himself behind his boyfriend as possible. Roach noticed how anxious he was and wanted to wrap his arm around his shoulders to help him feel safer, but if they were accused of homosexuality there was a good chance they'd get arrested. Instead, he silently prayed to Allah to help Silvino and slammed open the convenience store's door excitedly. "Ayo! Beefy! It's ya boy!"

"Roach!" shouted the teller from behind a wall of plexi-glass, which was evidently bulletproof if the shattered circles in front of him were any indication. "Who's your friend?"

"Nepo-baby from the hills."

He laughed. "That must be why he's so scared. Don't worry, kid, we don't bite." Silvino imagined it would be hard to bite with only the five teeth this clerk had.

Roach led Silvino toward the coolers and leaned down to whisper, "It's okay, honeybee. I come here all the time."

He looked up at him, his big brown eyes quivering with panicked tears, and it wrenched Roach's heart. "You promise it's safe?"

"Swear to God, sweetie. Now, let's get some snacks." He opened the cooler in front of them to grab two chocolate milks in each hand. "You want some milk, too?"

"Milk? On a road trip? You're so weird, Clay," he said with a sniffly giggle, "I'm gonna get some sodas." He took a moment to unclench his hands from their death-grip around Roach's arm and grabbed himself some sugary sodas in a variety of flavours. "We should get a basket."

"Too right. I'll go get one."

He started to leave, but Silvino rushed after him and got as close to him as possible with his hands full of drinks. After dropping the beverages in the basket, Roach added two packs of circus peanuts and complained that they were out of black licorice, "which sucks because it's like the only place in town that has it."

"What about some chips?" he said with a shaky hand picking up a can of crisps.

"Yeah, man. Those are good. I like the pickle ones."

"Of course you do," he chuckled.

With a basket full of goodies, Roach brought them to the counter and started holding things up to the glass for the clerk to scan with a pricing gun. Silvino gulped as he got a more thorough look at the bullets still encased in the glass at his exact eye-level.

"You want the usual, Roachy boy?" asked 'Beefy' as he finished scanning the items Roach was showing him.

"You know it, dude."

"A'ight just a minute." He left the till and returned a few minutes later carrying a grocery bag with something vaguely orange inside and two packs of cigarettes. Silvino assumed the cigarettes were only scanned to act as a price for the mystery bag, but the toothless clerk tossed them on top of the bag in the little metal dish beneath the glass for Roach to take.

"Thanks, dude. Here's the card," said Roach as he took out Silvino's wallet, which he hadn't realised Roach had taken from his pocket, and dropped his card noisily into the curved metal tray. 'Beefy' took it, charged them, and before he knew it Silvino was back in his seat with a bottle of Pepsi in his trembling hands.

"You alright, honeybee? We're gonna need to stop for gas a lot, but I'll try to find places in richer areas on the rest of the trip, alright? So you're not so out of your element. You sure had a lot of haunted places on your list for someone so spooked, though. You like being scared?" Silvino nodded timidly, though what he actually liked was being scared while simultaneously feeling protected by Roach. His soft smile dissipated when he saw Roach bite down on a cigarette and pull it out to light with a lighter he already had in his pocket. "Want one?" he said with the box held out toward Silvino.

"N...no, Roach. I didn't know you smoked...."

"Yeah, man. Started last year. Gotta take the edge off y'know?" He took a drag and cracked the window to blow the smoke out.

"Isn't it haram?"

"Yeah, and I drink sometimes too. It's whatever, man."

There was an awkward beat of quiet until Silvino asked, "What's in the bag?"

"Oh this?" He held up the unlabelled grocery bag. With a nod from Silvino, he tossed it onto his lap. "Taquitos."

"There's so many in here. Why didn't he charge you?"

"They're from last week."

Silvino chuckled and looked at his stupid fucking boyfriend with a big dopey smile. "I love you so much, dumbass."

"I love you, too, honeybee." A drag. "Ready to rock out? The sound system is killer considering your rich ass was footing the bill."

"Okay."

"I made a playlist." He took out his phone with its shattered screen and nearly cut his thumb connecting the bluetooth. He told it to play the playlist he had made, and once the music started, he revved up the engine and left the gas station, turning up the volume telekinetically to an unreasonable level when they were on the highway.

As the others were packing Grisha's plane, Thyne finished a walk-around and met with one of the Morozov lackeys to take the keys. As she passed them over, she worried aloud and in Russian, "Be careful with it. A lot of planes have been going down lately. Watch out for wind shears and double check your instruments. There may be some sort of foreign interference."

"Thank you. I'll keep it in mind." The warning put him on edge, so as he settled into the cockpit he called upon Francis.

"Yes, my dear?"

"I'm a wee bit worried."

"Wherefore?"

"Just… be extra vigilant in case we crash. My last plane got shot down, and there have been a lot more going down recently. Especially private jets."

"I'll keep a weather eye. You are all safe within my presence." He punctuated the statement by kissing the top of Thyne's head and leaving the cramped little cockpit to join the others in the cabin.

In spite of his misgivings and trepidation, Thyne flew them safely to New York, putting on a Southern accent when he used the radio with the Americans. He name-dropped Gennady Morozov, and the name combined with the tags on his plane meant he was allowed to land and park in one of the Morozov's hangars.

With the engines spooled down and the hangar door closing, Thyne ambled into the cabin and collapsed into Roach's strong arms. "What's wrong, sparkplug?"

"Sleepy."

"Goodness," he kissed him softly and offered to piggyback carry him. Thyne took him up on the offer, and they all thereafter followed River out of the plane to take a shuttle from the airport into the city.

"So, where are we going?" asked Dezba on the shuttle.

"My apartment," answered River.

"I thought you lived in Compton," said Partha.

"Yeah, I do—, or I did before the whole...." He gestured vaguely to not incriminate them in front of the strangers on the shuttle. They all understood, so he continued, "I'll tell you all why I have it when we get there."

The early March weather was oppressively hot in the giant sinking city. Flood walls surrounded every inch of it that was exposed to water, giving the feel of being in a big concrete bowl, or more aptly, a big concrete waste bin. There were more vermin than people (though some of them masqueraded as people), and bags of trash were stacked up beside the cracking sidewalks every twenty feet or so. It was uncommon to go a full minute without hearing a car honking. Homeless folk lined the sidewalks displaying written cardboard signs with messages of various levels of depressing. Thyne asked to be set down, so Roach stopped carrying him and watched with half-lidded eyes as the Brit went down the line of homeless people passing out handfuls of Euros. River stopped him after noticing why the party had slowed down. He grabbed him by the wrist and pulled him away, whispering darkly into his ear, "My sister is in trouble. Leave them."

Thyne frowned and made his way to the back of the group as they resumed their hasty walk through the crowds. When he noticed Francis beside him, he passed him his wallet and asked for him to use his power to give generously to them. He nodded and stopped time to go around the city dropping handfuls of money in cups, hats, hands, etcetera, refilling the wallet with his power when he ran it dry then doing it again. He spent six hours of his own time doing this before ambling stupidly in search of wherever he had left the group. Holding time still was tiring him needlessly, so he resumed it and texted Thyne that he had gotten himself lost.

When River noticed Francis had disappeared thanks to the gasps of the typically-unfazed New Yorkers around him, he turned swiftly around and rolled his eyes at Thyne's guilty smile. "You can fuck around when my sister is safe. Stop causing trouble. We're almost there."

Thyne nodded and shuffled up to Roach to wrap his hands around his bicep to somewhat hide himself from River.

The building where he brought them was in the north of Brooklyn near Queens. There was a subway station not too far of a walk away, and the door to get inside had a code lock. When they went inside, River walked them to a wall of mailboxes and noticed that his was overflowing with papers, all of which he grabbed.

His apartment was on the eighth floor, and the building was void of elevators, so Roach offered to carry Dezba. She thanked him kindly but refused, and Partha piped up: "You could carry *me*, sir!" Roach rolled his eyes but couldn't stop himself from smiling slightly and agreeing to the request. The halls reeked of mildew, and the lights were a gross yellow tint. River brought them to his door, which was visibly shorter than him, and hunched down to unlock it. He opened it and shoved his giant frame through the threshold, nearly on his hands and knees. Roach set Partha down, leaned on the wall beside the door, and took out a knife to start mindlessly doing flourishes with it. "Are we not going in?" asked Partha when he saw this.

"I mean, you can *try*."

The others all peered into the apartment. It was about as big as a standard walk-in closet with a slit for a window at the top of the room on a diagonal wall in the back where a comically small sink was mounted. There was a single seven-inch-wide counter with a minifridge beside it and a hot plate on a tiny dining table. A thin door spanned all the way from the floor to the ceiling beside the "kitchen" that opened into a toilet room roughly as large as an airline bathroom. Everything in the sparsely furnished space from the floor to the walls had a vague hint of dust. The ceiling in the entire apartment was only six feet high, so River was forced to hunch the entire time he was in it, but there was a bed hardly large enough for a child lofted over the door that dropped the height of the ceiling by another foot over the entrance.

Partha was too curious for his own good and went inside. Even though he was only 5'7", he still instinctively craned his neck away from the low ceiling and tapped on River's shoulder as he was running his mail through a paper-shredder.

"What are you doing?" said River.

"You were saying you'd tell us why you have this place."

"Yeah, sure. It's for Tony, mostly. When he does his whole," he gestured like he was stabbing someone, "When he plans it out at least, I go out into town, in Compton, doing stuff. I make sure people and cameras see me. So then, if he gets caught: I'm his alibi. Like one time I was at an MTG tourney, and he could say it was him at the tourney (except of course he's horrible and I won). Anyway, then he can say I live here to 'prove' that it was him out doing whatever I was doing." Partha blinked. "Just go wait in the hall, dude."

Partha left, and Rory went inside. He closed the door behind him and whispered, "Are those tax forms?"

River glared. "What are you? The feds? Mind your business."

"No no, listen. Ignoring and shredding things isn't going to do you any good, mate. If you want to do tax evasion properly, I can help."

He arched his brow at him and stopped sending the envelopes through the shredder. "Hm. It's a nice offer, but you're a bit too late. The government's already tried to kill me. We're long past peaceful tax evasion."

Rory went pale. "O-oh. Okay, well… carry on, then." He shuffled back into the hall awkwardly and grinned nervously at the group.

"Hey, Sonny," Roach shouted from out of the room.

"Yeah?" The shredder whirred.

"You got any drinks or anything in there, man?"

He shredded his last piece of mail, a summons for jury duty, and opened the minifridge only to immediately close it and hold his nose. "Jesus fuck."

"What's wrong?" asked Dale as he peered inside.

"I don't know. Something's really rotten in there. Fuck. We'll have to clean it."

"How thorough do you think these people are going to be able to be when they come here with your sister?" asked Dezba, "You can't even fit in your own apartment. Why would they come inside with you?"

"It's more to make it look like I live here for when the feds show up, which happens from time to time. My neighbours lie for me and say I live here, and my landlord loves me because I'm never fucking here and always pay my rent on time, so he also lies to them for me. But even with all that, whatever fucking died in my fridge is probably not gonna bode much confidence. Tony, come in here."

"It's so fucking small, dude, do I have to?"

"Yes."

With a roll of his eyes, Roach flipped his knife closed and slid it back in his pocket before forcing himself into the cramped little box. River gestured to the fridge. "See what it is. If it's a dead rat or something, I'm gonna hurl."

"Alright, move." They shuffled awkwardly around each other, brushing up against each other unintentionally as they swapped sides. Roach crouched down and cracked open the fridge just wide enough to see inside. "Jesus Christ," he said as he plugged his nose and reached inside to take out a carton of eggs that was making the foul odour. He opened the tiny cabinet beside it and slipped out a ziploc to put the carton inside. As soon as he finished zipping the bag closed, the smell started to dissipate. He tossed it carelessly behind him, and River caught it telekinetically to flick it out of the room where it landed on the floor in the circle of his friends in the hall. "Now, what is this beaut?" said Roach as he pulled out something wrapped in wax paper. He stood to show his brother with a big stupid grin and unwrapped it. Whatever it was was so covered in mould that River, even with his perfect memory, couldn't parse what it could possibly be. "That's all that's in there," said Roach as he started the awkward shimmy back to the opposite side of the room.

"I have something I need you to do, Tony, and I think you'll really like it," said River as they finished shuffling around each other.

"Okay, but let me show the others first." He went back out into the hall and showed them the disgusting unidentifiable hunk of mould. "Look!" His beaming smile was somehow endearing.

"What is it?" asked Dale.

Roach shrugged, and as he went to take a bite of whatever the fuck this thing was, Dezba slapped it out of his hands. It fell to the ground next to the bag of rotten eggs with a little mushroom-cloud of mould, and Roach's shoulders slumped. "Why'd you do that, Emmie?" He sounded like he might have actually cried.

"You were about to eat it!"

"Yeah! So why'd you knock it on the ground!?"

There was a stunned beat of quiet, after which Thyne asked, "Mate, how are you even fucking alive?"

"God's favourite."

Some scattered laughter preceded Thyne's playful mocking, "Sure, mate."

River returned to the group after this exchange and smiled at his brother. "Alright, you ready for your mission, bro?" He gave a lazy mock-salute. "Go out into the city," he paused to let a tension build, "and…."

"And…?"

"And find me some things…."

"What things?"

"Things to make it look like I live here. Like old towels, and…."

Roach's eyes glittered. "And some half-eaten food!?"

River giggled. "Yes."

He hugged his brother tight before excitedly rushing down the stairs. He stopped before he was too low to see the others, though, and said, "Anyone wanna come with me?" They shook their heads. "I'll have to see if Franky wants to come, wherever he is." He resumed his mad dash down the stairs with his phone in his hands texting Francis:

⌈ You'll never believe it, bed bug. Sonny needs me to go dumpster diving in NEW YORK CITY! I fucking love this place, dude. It's the nastiest not-flooded city in the fucking world, and I get to go dumpster diving~ I was already planning to do that, but now it's PART OF THE JOB! I'm so excited. We should do it together. It'll be romantic! Love you <3 Call me if you can, and I'll try to help you be less lost. ⌋

After a while of Roach's wandering around the city in search of a good dumpster, Francis finally called him. He said he wanted to be with the gang to protect them and expressed his apologies for not accompanying Roach on his disgusting outing. Roach was understanding, and after some verbal cues about where Francis was, he easily led him through the city to River's apartment where he met with the group just as they were leaving the building. Francis hung up the call and rushed up to them to give Thyne a hug and ask them all, "Where next might we sojourn?"

River sat on the steps up to the building and said, "Right here, man. The mercs might come by with my sister. Unless you have a better idea, Dale."

"They's Leviathan folk?" River nodded. "Lemme see." He took out his phone and worked some magic with it. After a few minutes: "Ah goddem."

River stood and peered at his screen. "You found them?"

"Ah found my buddy Twist. Ah'll go talk to 'em. Should prolly go alone."

"Franky should follow at a distance," said Thyne.

"Nay, I will remain near...." He gestured at Partha. "What was his secret sobriquet? The Lion? I digress. Why not share the location, and I will merely crib Poppie from under their noses."

"Well, Ah ain't so sure this's where she's at. Just know this's where Twist's phone is at."

"I imagine they also haven't let her veil herself, so it would be good to minimise the amount of strangers seeing her," said River.

"Then I'll follow from a distance," said Thyne.

"What'll ye do if Ah gets inta trouble?"

"I have a gun, mate."

"Ye any good wit it?" He furrowed his brow, so Dale held up his hands in social surrender. "A'ight Ah'mma go now."

As they left, Rory leaned in to whisper to Partha, "That Dale bloke is really cute." Partha nodded. "He hits like a truck. It's hot."

"Would you two behave?" said Dezba with a slap on Partha's chest. "River, honey, what would you like us to do?"

"Well Dale seems to be handling things for now. Wanna get some street food and chat about how we're gonna take down Baumbach?" They all three nodded at the idea and followed River into a more crowded part of the city to find a food truck.

Chapter 64
Hello, Beastie

On their way out of Vegas where they had spent a couple nights watching various shows and wishing they were old enough to drink and gamble, Silvino saw a sign for a county fair in town a few miles north and asked Roach to go. "Sounds fun, dude." They followed signs for the fair and arrived at sunset. "You ever been to a fair?" asked Roach as he turned off the engine.

"Once when I was like eleven or twelve."

"I've never been. You're not gonna make me ride the rides, right?"

"God no. Maybe when we get to a proper theme park, but they're basically held together with duct tape and prayers at these county fairs. Plus, we're both too big in one way or another anyway, but you'll love the fair food, and there are a bunch of stupid rigged games we can waste our money on."

"I'll have to win you something like in the movies," he said with a sweet smile as he lit up a cigarette, "It'll be romantic."

"Don't worry about winning me anything, dear. The games are all rigged. It'll just be nice to hang out with you regardless."

He shrugged and opened his door to go inside. After getting their tickets, they were asked if they wanted to drink. They were only nineteen, but they decided to both say yes and were given handstamps to indicate they were old enough to buy alcohol despite not showing the acne-covered teenager stamping them any form of identifi-

cation. With mischievous giggles at each other when they got through, they were quick to find some beer.

The chilled January wind cut through Silvino's paper-thin hoodie, and when he complained after they finished their second and third beers, Roach immediately took off his own hoodie to offer. Silvino grinned with a drunk little blush and pulled it on, glad that it was able to comfortably cover him despite his belly. It was warm from Roach's body heat and smelled like him. With his nose buried in the sleeves he had pulled over his hands taking in big whiffs of Roach's peculiar aroma of cigarettes, basil, and gasoline, he had a lot of trouble not looking dopey and in love with his tall, dark, and handsome boyfriend as they wandered around the fairgrounds.

Silvino eventually led them toward some food carts and giggled at Roach's confused excitement when he saw the strange assortment of fried goodies. "How do they deep fry ice cream?" he said, trying to hide the clattering of his teeth.

"You're cold!"

"I'm not," he said with a shiver.

"You are! Take your hoodie back!" He started to pull it off, but it caught on something on his lower back. "What is it catching on? Why won't it come off?"

"It's fine. I'm not cold." He rubbed his goosebumped arms.

"At least let me buy you a new one from one of these vendors."

He nodded adorably at the offer and let Silvino rush him to the nearest shady salesperson. The dark grey hoodie was cheaply made with an ugly pot-smoking rhinoceros screen-printed on the front, but it still cost Silvino a cool $540. Roach felt bad for the price, but he couldn't complain when he was wearing it and feeling warm again.

"There!" said Silvino with a cute beaming grin, "Now, let's get you some hot chocolate or coffee or something."

"And then the fried ice cream?"

He giggled. "Yes, dumbass. Then the fried ice cream or butter or whatever your lovely little heart desires."

Roach tried not to blush but couldn't hide it with the two pints in his veins. He wanted to kiss him, but there were too many strangers around to risk even holding hands.

After the disgusting deep-fried nonsense, which they both greatly enjoyed, Roach caught Silvino looking at a passing fair-goer carrying a giant plush dinosaur. "You want one?" he whispered fiendishly.

"You're not gonna be able to win one of those."

"You'll eat those words, Alvarez."

Silvino giggled and shook his nose at Roach. "Wanna bet?"

"Yeah. I bet you a big ol' sloppy kiss and a handy-J in the parking lot later." He wiggled his eyebrows.

Silvino put his hand out with a determined little pout, they shook on it, and Roach took the lead to find the games with the obnoxiously big prizes.

Luckily for him, the game with the biggest selection of giant plushes was one where the goal was to knock over a stack of three bottles. Silvino bought him his first game, and he used it to get a feel for the scam at play. It seemed pretty straight forward, so he wasn't entirely certain how it was rigged against him. He wound up a pitch with the softball and hurled it at damn near mach-ten toward the stack of bottles. It clipped the top of the first one and slammed loudly into the series of sheets behind it. None of the bottles fell, and he realised what the con was.

"I told you," sang Silvino teasingly.

"One more," he said.

"Alright, one more." He bought a second game and watched as Roach leaned back for his second pitch and hit the dead-centre of all three bottles, knocking them all to the ground. A little alarm played and some lights flashed as the carny announced his achievement and asked which prize he wanted. Roach deferred the choice to Silvino with his hands on his hips and a shit-eating grin.

Silvino's jaw was on the floor as he held his oversized dinosaur plush and blushed at Roach's big stupid smile.

"You owe me, bucko," he said as they shuffled off together.

It took almost two hours for Dale to find his way across the city at such a late hour. Some subway trains weren't running, so he had to walk for more of the trip than if he had gone earlier in the day. For the first forty-five minutes, Thyne accompanied him, and they chatted as they walked:

"So, Roach kidnapped you to find his husband?"

"Yee."

"Where was his husband? Did you ever find out?" Dale shook his head. "You also did that prison break with him. What was it like seeing him snap and kill all those people?"

"It weren't nothin'. Juss s'prised it took 'em so long."

"You know, he says you're his best mate."

"Yee."

"Why don't you say he's yours? Ridley seems like a real blighter."

Dale stopped and arched his brow at Thyne to show his confusion and muted anger. "How you know 'bout Ridley?"

Thyne smiled sweetly and shrugged.

Dale grumbled and eventually resumed walking, leading them down into a subway station where they both wordlessly hopped the turnstiles like they had done twice already. They sat on a bench on the relatively empty platform and waited for their last train. Fortunately, Ridley had either left his phone somewhere, or he was "interrogating" poor Poppie: he hadn't moved at all during their trek. As they boarded their train and sat beside each other, Dale's stomach sank when it dawned on him that he may have been walking into a trap, 'But Ridley wouldn't do that ta me,' he thought, 'He's my bess fren. He'll 'least hear me out.'

Thyne took off the backpack he had been wearing and set it in his lap. He leaned over to bump his shoulder into Dale's playfully and said, "Don't worry, mate." He patted the bag. "I'll protect you."

"And how're ye gon' do that if Ah'm in some random buildin'?"

After the train's first stop let some strangers into their car, Thyne leaned even closer, his hot breath almost sensual on Dale's neck as he whispered, "I can hear you."

"Huh?"

"If you need me, you can say the word. I'll hear it."

"Ye high er summon?"

He retreated and shook his head, but Dale brushed him off anyway. It was only a short walk from the station, so Thyne lagged behind to let Dale approach alone. He stopped when his phone told him he had arrived and looked up at this unassuming residential building in The Bronx it had indicated. He squinted at its windows to try and see inside, but they all had their curtains or blinds drawn. Even still, the yellow glow of the lights inside poured out into the blue midnight from every floor.

He scanned the area in search of Thyne but couldn't find him, so he sighed and approached the door. Behind it was another door then a musty looking hallway. It was locked, but it was also mostly made of glass. Retrieving the pistol he had tucked into his pants, he walked down the stairs while patting around for his silencer. When he found it in his boot and leaned down to retrieve it, he heard a quiet thump from across the street and a clamouring sound from behind him. The door's handle had clattered to the ground, as did the one on the door behind it, neither of them taking any damage to the glass.

Dale looked across the street and squinted into the darkness, noticing something on one of the rooftops. He took out his phone and saw Thyne typing out a message to explain that he had shot the handles off for him. Baffled, he replied with a quick thanks and cautiously entered the building as he hid his silenced gun under his jacket while keeping a hold of it.

The hall led to a set of stairs at its end and a door to the back courtyard. With a quick glance outside, he started climbing the stairs and listening out for voices or codes he may have recognised. One of the first things he heard as he started to pass by apartment doors was a screaming match between a couple, complete with the shattering of glass and thumping of punches. He winced at the sounds and tried not to notice the turning in his gut as he realised he may have just broken into a random apartment building for no reason at all. Still, he kept ascending. A few more doors later he heard some people making love, and across from that door was someone raging at a video game. Knowing how Leviathan tended to operate, it was odd he hadn't heard anyone being tortured or at least interrogated. The doors were paper-thin, so the lack of recognisable sounds was worrying up until he heard Ridley's voice. He perked up and approached silently to listen through the wall:

"They all say they don't know where they are."

"All of them?" asked Eibhlín.

"Yeah. The dad hasn't talked to them in years, so I'd assume if he did know he'd outright tell us. In-law says she last saw them in Mexico, but I did manage to get some descriptions out of her."

"That's good."

"Yeah. Have you gotten the girl to talk?"

"No, she's just as stubborn, but I think she does know something. I've got a plan in motion, though."

"Oh, is it the one you were telling me about last night?"

"Yeah."

A beat. "I feel kinda bad for luring her out here."

"She betrayed us, honey. She's working with the kid-killers."

"Still… she's our friend. She's just a little lost."

They said more, but their voices were muffled as they changed rooms. Dale's face was washed of colour and hands sweaty. He shook away the upset almost as quickly as it came and tried opening the door. The fact that it was unlocked dropped his stomach all the way down into Hell. Only a moment after he had turned the knob, it was pulled from his hand, and Ridley held out his arms. "So glad you could make it, buddy." Dale was yanked inside and shoved into a chair in an otherwise unfurnished room. The only other people in the room with him were Eibhlín leaning on a doorway into a kitchen and Ridley, who was leaning over him and smiling evilly as he took Dale's gun from him. "How's it been working with the kid-killing terrorists?"

His brow was furrowed and cheeks red. "They ain't killed no kids, Twist."

"Ha! Well, then, how's it feel sabotaging and ditching on a job worth two billion?"

"Feels good."

Ridley reeled back to punch him, but he stopped short. "You know," he said as he stood upright and took the clip out of Dale's gun to toss to Eibhlín, "I'm not gonna hit you."

"Pussy."

A huff of amusement. "No, I'm not gonna hit you because I don't hit women." Dale stood and threw a punch, but Ridley caught his fist and used it to sit him back down. "So it's true, is it? You're a girl."

"Ah ain't a girl, Ridley."

"Well... that's not what your birth certificate says." He lit a cigarette for himself and offered one to Dale, an offer he literally spat on. "Feisty like a girl, too."

Dale's eyes welled with tears. "Ah ain't a girl," he whimpered.

"Crying now, too? My my. So emotional." He chuckled darkly. "I'm the one who should be upset right now: my best friend has been lying to me about herself this whole time I've known her?"

"Fuck you." He managed to sound intimidating even through his weepiness.

"Now, Darlene, you're my friend, and we can still be friends after this. Hell, we'll even use your play-pretend name and all that. I won't even torture you. I'll be real nice and give you an offer: if you sell out your little gang of terrorists— names, ages, locations, the works —then you're free to come back on the job with us. In fact, we'll even still give you the cut you were going to get before. If you *don't* tell us everything you know, then we'll turn you over to the FBI, and you'll go rot in that same little prison cell as your daddy."

Dale flicked his gaze to the window beside him, through which he was certain Thyne could see him with his sniper. He was glad for the threat because otherwise he may have considered the offer. He slumped his head, and there was a beat of quiet while his heart shattered. Ridley had saved his life in the war numerous times, and he had returned the favour. Ridley had even saved Dale from Roach's capture. He had made him rethink his racism beyond simply calling him "one of the good ones." Dale would have been the best man at Ridley and Eibhlín's wedding if they hadn't cancelled when they lost hundreds of thousands of dollars to New Clear's downfall. Dale and Ridley would camp and hunt and tailgate and whatever else any time they were together. Some of Dale's best memories were times he spent with Ridley.

But in hindsight... it was all only ever a surface-level friendship. Ridley never knew anything deeper about Dale or his inner world. He didn't know the secrets that Roach knew and accepted without question. Ridley had never even bothered to ask Dale about his interests or thoughts beyond basic platitudes and small talk.

More sour memories came to mind wherein Dale was ignored or brushed-off and drank away his troubles in isolation. He had never considered Roach his best friend because their initial encounter was less than favourable (to say the least), but now that Ridley was showing his true colours— that Dale was right to have kept this secret from him all these years —he felt stupid to have ever considered him a better friend than Roach. He felt stupid to have ever considered him a friend at all....

"Ah got more skeletons in my closet than ye think, Ridley," said Dale with a quiver as he stood and stepped up into Ridley's space, their chests almost touching, "Ye wanna be one of 'em?"

"You gonna kill me, Darlene?"

He gut-punched him and grabbed him by the hair when he hunched over. There was a darkness in his icy-blue eyes as he leaned in and said, "That ain't my fuckin' name." Eibhlín was halfway to them by the time Dale had taken back his gun and slipped a new clip into it. He aimed it at her to stop her in her tracks then pressed it against the underside of Ridley's chin. With the same sadism as Roach, his true best friend, he savoured the fear in his big brown eyes before pulling the trigger. Eibhlín's screams were cut short by his second shot, and he immediately started sweeping the apartment in search of other mercenaries or the captives he was meant to be rescuing.

In his search, he found a woman tied to a chair and rushed up to her, quickly removing the gag in her mouth. There was a quaver in his voice he couldn't thwart and tears still battering his cheeks when he said, "Ye okay, miss?" She responded in Spanish, and Dale bit his lip. "No... er... hablas espanyall." She muttered a few more things in Spanish, one of which Dale recognised as a swear he heard in the war from time to time. He untied her while she mumbled, after which he stood with her and said, "Come wit me," with a gesture to follow him.

She trailed him as he left the room and searched the others. The next room over had a one-armed man tied to a chair, and Dale rushed over to ungag and untie him as well, noticing his other rescued captive helping to find scissors to cut through the zip-ties. "Ye muss be Gidyon. Ah'm Dale. Ah'm yer brother's fren."

"Thanks, man," he said through laboured breaths. It was clear to Dale that he had been tortured for information with the blood all over his shirt and scars on his face, so Dale didn't ask anymore of him than to follow as he continued his search.

The next room had another man tied up, and again Dale rushed over and ungagged him. "Ye know Roach, too?"

"I told you I don't know where he is."

"We're here ta rescue ye."

"That's our dad," informed Gideon. Oba turned around and smiled at his son.

They chatted in Arabic, during which Dale was wiping his face to dry his tears and sweat. "Either 'a y'all know who this's?" He pointed to the woman who only spoke Spanish.

"That's Elisa. She's Clay's sister-in-law," informed Gideon. Dale nodded and had them all three follow him into the next room where Poppie was tied up. He immediately averted his eyes when he saw that she was unveiled and pointed for her father and brother to go untie her. When Poppie came out into the hall where Dale and Elisa were, she had a bed sheet over her head and lifted her arms to move around and make a ghostly wailing sound. "Did I scare ya?"

Dale chuckled sadly. "Thanks, Poppie, I needed that."

"It's good to see you again.... Though it's hard to see you on account of being a spooky ghost now."

"Good ta see ye, too. Ah guess Ah'll juss bring y'all wherever we're stayin'." He took out his phone to call someone to find out where to take the others, but when he got to his contacts list, he received a call from Thyne instead. "Yeah?" he answered.

"What flat are you in?"

"Huh?"

"The number on the front door."

"Oh. It were 7A I b'lieve."

"Alright." He hung up, and Dale looked down at the screen with a knitted brow. As he was trying to parse the strange call, he and all four of the rescued captives were suddenly in a large hotel suite with everyone else present save for Roach.

Despite the late hour, Roach was still out having the time of his life gathering trash and taking in the sights. He had wandered the city aimlessly, taking trains here and there and letting his vagabond shoes stray. Because of his perfect memory, he couldn't get lost, but he got damn near. As he was walking down a mostly empty sidewalk with his hands in his pockets and a backpack full of garbage, he was unknowingly beaming. Since taking on Oliver's memories, it had become difficult to hide his emotions as constantly as he had before.

Times like this, he didn't even notice he was smiling, but he should have guessed as much. It was a lovely evening. The rats were bouncing around the sidewalk adorably. The moon cut through the smog beautifully. There were less tourists in the city considering how difficult it was to enter the country, so the crowds were never bothersome. On his jubilant jaunt that evening, he had seen five street musicians and sixteen dogs. He had found an entire slice of horrible greasy New York pizza in the garbage for a delicious dinner, and some of the trash he found that wasn't for his brother's apartment was already inspiring him for things he could make by junk-bashing. Overcome with a love for the disgusting city, he took in a big breath of the dirty air as if it were fresh with his arms out to feel the breeze from a passing train overhead.

The gust pushed a paper into his leg, so he bent down to examine it. Before he could start reading, he was startled by someone jumping out from behind the corner of a building. The stranger had a face-mask on and sunglasses with the hood of his oversized navy-blue hoodie up over his head, hiding his hair. There was a balisong knife in his hand aimed at Roach. "Wallet and phone. Now."

"Oh! This is the best day of my fucking life." The mugger leaned away when he saw the genuine glee in Roach's eyes, but he was pulling out his wallet, so he didn't flee. Roach opened his wallet, aiming it toward the mugger, and snort-laughed when four moths flew out. "Get it?" he managed between snorts, "Like in the cartoons."

The mugger blenched briefly at the bugs but thereafter noticed there was no money where they had been, so he tried not to be perturbed by Roach's madness and said, "Just g-give me your cards, then, man. Stop being creepy."

His laughter died down, and he said, "Okie dokie," as he took out his *Uno* Reverse card and handed it over.

"What the fuck is th—." His knife was suddenly in Roach's hand and aimed at him. "Fuck." He started taking the wallets and phones he had stolen that night from his pockets and passed them over with a chuckle. "I can't even be that mad, man," he said as he gave him the last wallet, "That moth thing was pretty funny, too."

Roach beamed. "Y'know what? For being a good sport, you can keep the phones."

"Thanks, bro." Roach gave them back.

"Yeah, man. I'm keeping your knife, though." He bounced it off his bicep and caught it after it closed in the air. "Good luck with the next sucker." He patted his head and sauntered off, dropping his new wallets in his backpack as he made his way back to River's apartment.

✥ Chapter 65 ✥

What a Man Can Do,
And What a Man Can't Do

They were ambling north toward Wyoming, but Roach suggested they go further west to go hiking in Washington before the trek up to Cloud Peak. They changed course, and on their way to Washington, they stopped by some chintzy roadside attractions and took pictures with the polaroid camera Silvino had bought for the trip. He put his big dinosaur plush in a lot of the pictures as if it was a third member of the travel-party. It was in the picture with them in front of the "world's largest bottle of water" which wasn't even filled with water but rather an ugly painted sculpture in some backwoods town. The plush was also in a few shots from a creepy Christian museum they found in what they later realised was a sun-down town. The "museum" was made up almost entirely of mannequins that depicted a handful of bible stories, one of which was peculiarly King Soloman's story, complete with a baby mannequin being sawed in half. As well, they took pictures together kissing and making hearts with their hands or generally being adorable and young and carefree in front of beautiful vistas, a family of raccoons in a McDonald's dumpster, and everything in between.

When they reached a beginner hiking trail in Mount Rainier National Park,

Roach looked longingly up at the mountain. "I'm gonna climb that one one day. Mark my words."

"You gonna carry me up that one, too?"

"I'll carry you anywhere you want, Silvino. I love you."

He blushed and looked around the empty trail before replying, "I love you, too. What about Everest?"

"Everest is really dangerous. I want to climb it, of course, but I wouldn't want to risk bringing you up there, and if I went alone I'd be without my honeybee for three whole months, at least. Nothing would make that worth it to me."

Silvino nodded and returned his attention to the trail. "Well, this sort of mountain climbing's not so bad. Maybe one day we can go on the pilgrimage in Međugorje to see the Mother Mary together or at least to prove our devotion. I know you're not Catholic, though."

Roach smiled. "I'll go there with you, honeybee, and I'll carry you up that mountain, too, if you need." A beat. "Bag's not too heavy for you?" He shook his head with a confident little smile that had Roach's heart fluttering with absolute adoration. "Well, let me know if you need to take any breaks or anything.... It's pretty, huh?"

He nodded. "A shame Berry couldn't come."

"Berry?"

"Berry."

They made eye contact. "Is Berry the dinosaur?"

"MAYBE!" he said with faux-defensiveness.

"You're so cute, dude."

After a chatty thirty minutes of hiking and taking in the scenery, an unsettling silence crept up and slowed them to a stop. "Roach?" said Silvino, nervousness dripping off his words like the sweat off his brow.

"Yeah, man. I have no idea why it's so quiet. This is fucking weird." They both looked around, and it was only a second later that they spotted a giant grizzly rising to its hind legs just some ten feet ahead of them. They both screamed in abject horror as it roared. Before they could gather their bearings, it dropped down on all fours and charged them.

Silvino was knocked to his back, scratched across the chest, then... covered in blood. He blinked and tried to understand what had happened in the past two seconds as Roach helped him to his feet. "Are you okay!? Ya Allah!" He prayed with mad quickness in Arabic for his health and safety.

Silvino, on the other hand, was only just then starting to grasp a semblance of what had happened. He couldn't even feel the horrible pain in his chest or hear his boyfriend's panicked praying as he looked at the blood on his hands and chest and wiped some of it off of his face and out of his eyes. It wasn't his blood. It wasn't Roach's blood. It was apparently the blood and viscera of the now-headless grizzly laying in the dead leaves and snow to his left. "What the fuck is happening?" he muttered.

"I killed the bear, but I think you should let me carry you down to the lodge for medical treatment. It's quite a gash."

Silvino looked down at his chest again then offered the most perplexed expression Roach had ever seen. "What do you mean you killed the bear?"

He sighed. "I have like... superpowers. I have telekinesis. I crushed its head and pushed it off of you. Now, please let me carry you. Give me your bag."

"You have... what?"

"Please, just give me your bag, and I'll explain on the way back to the lodge." Silvino dropped the bag off his back and watched as Roach plucked it up from the ground and threw it over his shoulder. "Okay, come on."

Before he knew it, Silvino was being princess-carried back the way they had come and blinking up at Roach as reality started to set back upon him. "Superpowers?" he whispered.

Roach managed a small smile. "Yes. Sonny has them, too. Please don't tell anyone. Not even my family."

"Telekinesis?"

"Among others."

"The others being?"

"Darkvision, a perfect memory, and devilish good looks." He winked playfully.

"Darkvision?" He giggled, ready to mock Roach for calling it that, but suddenly felt the pain of the gash across his chest. "Ah, fuck. It hurts, Clay."

"Oh, I'm sorry, Vinny. This is all my fault. I'm the one that wanted to come here. Maybe we should just go home."

He shook his head. "No. Please. I'll be okay. What's the line from that British movie you like?"

Roach chuckled. "It's just a flesh wound?"

"Yes! 'Tis but a scratch!"

"Okay, we'll talk about it again when you're not hopped up on adrenaline, though."

After a few minutes of being rushed down the trail, Silvino thinned his eyes at Roach and said, "Wait a second."

"I'm not stopping, dude."

"You cheater!" His tone was as playful as possible considering the state of him.

"What do you mean?"

"You cheated at that carnival game! You owe me a handjob and a big sloppy kiss."

Roach bit his lip to not take him up on the offer. For some reason, he was aroused by the blood all over Silvino, but he knew better than to stop rushing him to the lodge.

Dale was immediately worried for the bodies he hadn't gotten the chance to clean. He found Francis and rushed up to sweat about them while everyone else was trying to calm the four people who had just been teleported after however long of being captives of violent mercenaries. "Fret not," said Francis to Dale after his panicked sputtering, "I disposed of the bodies for you."

"Where?"

"I turned them to dust."

Tears trailed Dale's pallid cheeks, and he wiped his face. "Ah'm gon' go make a call." He found an unoccupied bedroom in the suite and locked himself in it to take out his phone.

"Dale, baby! How are you?"

"Hey, Mama. Ah'm gon' cry summon fierce."

"Oh no! My poor darling. What's wrong?"

He sniffled and sat on the bed before admitting with a low and remorseful voice: "Ah killed… Ah killed Ridley."

"Oh, my precious sweet baby. What happened?"

He sniffled again and wiped his hairy arm across his running nose. "He were callin' me a girl. He called me Dar—. Dar—."

"Oh, shh shh. It's okay, honey. You don't have to explain yourself. Why don't you come on over, and I'll make your favourite dinner, and you can see all the animals? We recently got a new lil guy. I won't spoil it."

"Thanks, Mama. Ah'll come down. Up in New York right now."

"For work?"

"Yeah sorta. Ah'll be bringin' frens. We might needa stay there fer a night er two."

"Are you gonna bring that Roach fella?"

He chuckled sadly. "Yeah, he's comin'."

"Yay! I liked him. How many people should I expect?"

"Ah dunno yet. Ah'll call ye later. Ah miss y'all."

"We miss you too, pumpkin. I'll see if Gigi can come up so you can see her, too. Sound good?"

"Yeah. Ah gotta go."

"Thank you for calling, sweetums." She made kissy noises that he returned before hanging up and wiping his nose again. When he returned to the main area of the suite the herd had thinned. After glaring holes through his father's soul, River had been taken into the kitchen by Oba, the door closed behind them.

He spoke in Arabic: "Son, I'm sorry." River only glared. "Don't look at me like that. I know I was a horrible father. I'm sorry. I was doing my best, but I was sick, and I've gotten some help. I've been keeping tabs on you and your brother through Poppie. You don't have to forgive me, but I'm sorry regardless."

"What makes you think you have the right to know anything about us? You don't know what you did to Clayton. You don't know how disowning him *destroyed* him." His voice was low but increasingly irate: "You weren't there with him with the needles in his arms and the half-dead look in his eyes." A step closer. "You weren't there to hear the 'not good enough' repetitive panic-attack spirals that *you* caused." Another step. "You weren't there with him as he spent eight hours a day on his knees begging god for you to love him again." Another. "You weren't there shoving your hand down his throat until he upchucked the pills." He stepped close enough that their chests were nearly touching. "You. Weren't. There. What makes you think you have the FUCKING right to know ANYTHING about him, now!?"

Oba wept and whimpered another apology.

"Death would be too good for you." He spat on him. "Fuck you."

Just as River was storming out of the kitchen, Roach was led into the suite by Dezba, who had met with him in the lobby after a doughnut run. "The fun has arrived!" he announced. He scanned the room and was quick to spot Poppie, Gideon, and Elisa. After rushing up to them, he scooped them each up into his arms to give them big bear hugs. He spoke in Spanish so Elisa would understand: "I'm so glad you guys are okay. I've had the best damn day, and now I get to hang out with you, too? I'm glad we got to come here, but why the fuck are you guys not in Egypt and Mexico?"

Elisa replied, "After you left my house, I started noticing people following me, so I tried to fly to Spain, but the plane was having troubles, so we had to do an emergency landing here. I didn't know what to do, so I called Poppie, and she said she'd come help me escape America. She brought Gideon and Oba just for sight-seeing." Roach's face fell. "We had all our stuff ready and papers signed to leave again, but then the Leviathan people showed up." She slapped him. "They said *you* told them where we were."

He held his cheek. "I sent them here specifically because I didn't think anyone I knew was here."

"Don't hit my brother," said Poppie.

"Is Dad still here?" he asked his siblings in Arabic.

"I think he's talking with Karson in the kitchen."

"He's really sorry, Clay," said Poppie, "We've been keeping him up to date on things. Nothing too personal, of course. Just things like the wedding and war and… uh…." She didn't need to mention Silvino's death for Roach to know what she meant.

He huffed and averted his eyes. "This is ruining my good day."

River came up behind him and hooked a hand over his shoulder to pull him backwards slightly and whisper, "You don't have to go talk to him. Thyne has already said he'll fly them back to Egypt, and Poppie offered to come with us to take down Baumbach." Despite his whispering, Poppie could hear him and nodded at the assessment. She was wearing a makeshift burka, so her beaming grin was only visible in her eyes.

Roach sighed. "I should go see him…."

"Do you want me to come with you?" asked River.

He shook his head, dropped his bag on a couch, and shoved his hands in his pockets. His strides to the kitchen were loud and quick despite how he was hanging his head. He opened the door and went inside. After a moment: "Hey, Dad."

"Son…."

There was an awkward minute of quiet that may as well have been a thousand years. Roach's mind was an overclocking engine with how chaotic and fast it was rumbling.

"Son, I'm sorry." His voice was broken and gaze on the ground.

After another beat, Roach took the two strides between them and wrapped his strong arms around his father. Oba was a large man himself, but his musculature was only average, and his height was two inches shorter than the twins. His skin was slightly darker than his children's, and his short black hair was streaked with grey. He was surprised by the embrace and returned it with slow confusion. It lasted another minute before Roach finally retreated and coughed away the weepiness trying to overcome him. "Missed you, Dad."

His stomach sank as River's words replayed in his head. He had no idea how much it would hurt his son to disown him. He couldn't imagine why Roach missed him at all, let alone how deeply he did. His gaze fell. "I missed you, too. I've been listening to all your albums. You've got a real gift, Clayton."

Roach nudged his shoulder. "Thanks, man. Means a lot. How've you been? Other than getting kidnapped, of course." He chuckled. "Got a shop out in Egypt?"

He looked up at him and blinked the tears out of his eyes. "That's it? You just forgive me? After everything I did?"

"Forgave you for that shit years ago. I'll never forgive you for trying to kill Sonny, but otherwise," he shrugged, "we're chill."

"Well…. I… I've been alright."

"Poppie says she's been giving you updates on me?"

His stomach sank even further. "Yes, which Karson made very clear was inappropriate of me, and I apologise."

"Nah man. It's chill. So you know about Silvino."

"Yes. I was devastated by the news. Vinny was really good for you. For all of us. I truly did love him as my own son."

Roach smiled sadly. "Yeah…. So this gang is the one that's been taking down companies like New Clear and Eir Lilac. We figured while we're in America, we'll take down Baumbach, the prison company that killed him, so we'll be here a while. Probably until Christmas time. We already blew up some factories in the new states. You might have heard about the company towns down there. Or maybe you heard that Party kills kids, which isn't true." He bit down on a cigarette and offered one to his father. When the offer was refused, he flipped the box closed and opened his lighter, distracting himself from talking about the gang to instead say, "Look. My boyfriend taught me," as he started a flourish.

"Boyfriend, huh? You're still into men, then?"

He stopped the trick, and any amount of happiness in his countenance washed away. With a deadpan expression, he lit the cigarette and took a drag. "Yeah."

"I'm sorry. I don't mean to be rude."

"But you are."

He ran a hand through his hair. "I'm trying my best. I'm just disappointed I won't get grandkids."

"What makes you think, if I were to have kids, that I'd let them around you?"

"Weren't you with a girl called Perlie at some point? Where is she? Is she in the gang with you?"

He glared. "I'm not with Perlie anymore, and she's having Partha's kid." After another drag: "I'm with three men, actually."

Oba closed his eyes to take a deep calming breath the way his therapist had taught him when he felt himself getting angry. "Three?" he said with a forced smile.

"Yep." He smoked some more. "Thyne, Francis, and," he took another drag to stall, his hand trembling as he did, "and Karson."

In the heavy quiet that followed, Roach's stomach was churning so much that he audibly gagged, and the trembling of his hands made it impossible to keep smoking. They looked into each other's eyes for another thousand years before Oba tore his gaze away and cursed. "They said they fixed him."

Roach leaned over menacingly. "They said what, Dad?"

He sighed and rested slightly on the counter. "When you boys were eighteen, Karson came to me and told me he was in love with you. I didn't know what else to do, so I sent him to a hospital in San Diego. I told the rest of you it was a summer camp for gymnastics." He silently wished he had taken Roach's offer for a cigarette. His voice was trembling almost as much as Roach's hands when he resumed the story: "They were trying everything, but he kept saying he loved you. I drove out and talked to the doctors, and they suggested this thing called... Oh what was it called?" He rubbed his forehead. "Electroshocking Therapy. Or something like that. They said it'd fix him. I had to sign some legal things because... because there was a miniscule chance that it would kill him. And well... afterwards, he wasn't saying it anymore, so I brought him back home. It was supposed to fix him, but I guess it didn't."

Every moment Roach had ever had with his father from birth up until then went reeling through his head like a mad zoetrope. In the three minutes of utter silence that he was looking for a reason not to take out his new knife and throw it through his father's bloodshot eyes, Roach was motionless. He wasn't even trembling anymore. The cigarette in his hand burned down in his unmoving fingers and dropped the last of its ashes on the floor. His gaze was locked on his father, and his face was unemotive.

"Son?" Roach flipped open a knife, which made his father scramble away. "Clayton. Please. I'm sorry. You can be with him for all I care. You're both adults."

Roach flicked his cigarette butt in the sink and locked eyes with Oba. He tried to turn his face away under his son's horrifying hazel gaze, but his head was held still supernaturally. Roach took four intimidating steps toward him, all the while Oba was less and less able to move and increasingly terrified. He pulled back his hand, ready to strike down into his father's trapezius. He tried several times to move— to just kill him —but the only movements in his arm were its increasing quivering. When he finally threw his arm down four minutes later, it was in defeat. He leaned on Oba's opposite shoulder, holding back tears as he slammed the knife on the tiled floor where it clattered loudly. They embraced.

"I'm sorry, son. I was the one that needed the hospital. I know that now. When I realised I'd lost you all because of how evil I was, I lost my faith, too. You're so merciful to me when you shouldn't be, Clayton, you make me want to believe again."

Roach only cried, and his father joined him.

The embrace lasted fifteen minutes, at the close of which Roach retreated and wiped his eyes with the heels of his hands. "I love you, Dad."

"I love you, too, son."

"I'll give you my number." He sniffled. "My boyfriend, Thyne, is going to fly you back to Egypt. I'll get him to tell you about what I've been up to."

"You're too kind to me, Clayton. I'm a wretch."

"No," he poked his nose playfully but sniffled loudly afterwards, "You're a Roach."

He laughed sadly. "I'm glad you like the name at least. You always did like all the wrong things."

"Yeah…. Guess that's why I like you."

Chapter 66

An Agreeable Sense of the Macabre

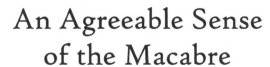

Silvino was eating the drive-thru food they had bought for dinner as he watched Roach exercising on the scratchy hotel carpet. He rambled at him about their trip to the Austin aquarium earlier that day and leaned on his big dinosaur plush like it was a beanbag chair in the bed with him. In the midst of his push-ups, Roach stopped and held himself up by one hand to point at Silvino, and they both said, "Nice," in tandem before he resumed with his seventieth push-up.

"So why did we skip the mountain climb again? What are the odds we'd get attacked by another bear?" asked Silvino between sips from his fountain drink.

"Bad time for hiking," he replied between presses with a hint of deception that Silvino was able to catch. He stopped himself as he reached for his second burger. After retreating his hand, he looked down at his shirtless body with a sudden upset in his air. When he noticed, Roach stopped exercising and stood. With his breaths heaving: "What's wrong, dude? Your scar hurting?"

He tugged at his hair. "Have I gained weight on this trip?"

Roach shrugged. "Maybe. Does it matter?"

"Be honest with me, Roach. Are you afraid you can't pick me up anymore and carry me to the top like Sam and Frodo? Is that why we're not going to the mountain?"

"Ha! You're kidding." He lifted him telekinetically and pulled him quickly into his arms. After a kiss on his forehead, nose, blushing cheeks, then lips, he said, "I think exercising has made my telekinesis even stronger. I think I could lift a car, to be honest with you, dude. But even when I was paper-thin I could have lifted you with it, and even without it right now I can lift you." He demonstrated by lifting him once without using his telekinesis to aid him. After twirling him back down into his arms gracefully: "We're gonna go to the mountain, but let's just see a few other sights first. We're closer to New Orleans right now anyway." He kissed his forehead again and sat on the edge of the bed with him still curled up in his strong arms. "I love you, Vinny." He still looked upset with his arms crossed over his tummy trying to hide it. Roach pursed his lips. "I've got it, dude. Come on." He set him down and rushed to their suitcase to start rummaging through it.

"What are you looking for?"

"You and me are gonna go out to that statue of Park and vandalise it. You need to get your blood pumping!"

Silvino went pale and sputtered, "B-but what if we get caught?"

Roach smirked at Silvino and tossed him some dark clothing. "Just follow my lead, honeybee."

"H-how is this gonna help me feel better?" He wasn't moving to start changing out of his pyjamas. "Can't we just cuddle?"

"Come on, dude, it'll be fun." He took off his shirt, which unintentionally shut up whatever Silvino was going to sputter-out next. "Change your clothes, man. Put the hoodie inside-out so the design is hidden."

He gulped and watched Roach get dressed until his torso was covered then managed to start dressing himself. When he was finished tying his shoes, he looked up at Roach and smiled anxiously. "Am I ready?"

"Where's the extra t-shirt I threw you?"

"Uh, was I supposed to put it on?"

"Just where is it?" Silvino pointed to it on the corner of the bed where it was mostly hidden under the mess of blankets, and Roach tossed it back to him. "Now watch me, okay?" He held up a t-shirt of his own and laid it flat on the bed. "You do it, too." Silvino gulped and did as he was told. When it became clear a few more instructions later that Roach was showing him how to turn the shirt into a sort of ninja mask, he started to struggle with the steps as his hands were increasingly shaky. With his own mask finished, Roach came over and took Silvino's shirt. "You're so cute. Come here." He kissed his forehead through his own mask before flicking the shirt flat again and quickly wrapping it around his boyfriend's panicked face.

"Roach, why d-don't we just watch a m-movie?"

Though his face was covered and usually deadpan, he looked disappointed. "Don't you trust me, bro?"

"I trust you...."

"Good! So some ground rules. Rule number one: If we get caught by the cops, let me do the talking. Yeah? Don't talk to them under any circumstance, even if you think I'm fucking things up." He nodded, the panic in his sweet brown eyes even brighter. "Rule number two: Don't speak Spanish around them, either. You have far too much melanin in your skin to be doing that. Alright?" Another terrified nod. "And rule number three: Have fun!" His hazel-greys closed as he beamed beneath his mask. "Now, hoods up," they flicked their hoods over their heads, "and follow me."

Before entering their hotel room, Roach had already instinctively flicked the security camera in the hall up toward the ceiling telekinetically, so he only gave it a quick glance to confirm it was how he had left it before gesturing for Silvino to follow him out into the hall. Despite his size, Roach moved stealthily on his way to a maintenance closet near the vending machines. It impressed and titlated Silvino when he saw Roach remove some of his piercings and use them to effortlessly pick the lock to the closet. He crossed his sweaty palms over his chest to shove under his armpits nervously as he watched Roach quietly searching the cupboard for something. Before he could ask what he was looking for, Silvino was scrambling to catch a can of black spray-paint and winced at how loud and clumsy he was being. Roach patted his head on his way out of the room flipping and catching his own can of spray-paint flawlessly with a smug wiggle of his eyebrows.

It was a long trek from the hotel to the park with the statue, so when Roach decided they would need to run, he scooped up Silvino and sprinted. Silvino's arms were tight around his neck and heart racing, but he was smiling behind his mask at the exhilarating experience. They hadn't even started the scariest part yet. Stealing some spray-paint was already thrilling, so he was quietly excited to get to the vandalism, having never done anything illegal in his life other than underage drinking, being Catholic, and being bi.

When they reached the park, Roach floated Silvino over the chain-link fence on its outskirts before scrambling over it himself. "Come on," he said with a lilting tone and exuberant delirium in the pits of his hazel-greys. Silvino followed dutifully and hid behind various half-walls and garbage bins and whatever else Roach was using as cover on their way to the centre of the park. Statues of Elijah Park across the country were sometimes patrolled by police, so Silvino's heart was beating up into his throat when they somehow managed to reach it without getting caught. He uncapped his spray-paint can when he saw Roach pocketing the lid from his own. "You wanna start, dude?" he whispered with a gesture at the stone slab base of the dictator's self-important statue.

Silvino raised his can, the little ball inside rattling around as his hand shook. Roach stilled it with his own hand and held it gently as Silvino hesitated to tag the stone. The warmth of his touch and love in his air had Silvino's already-racing heart fluttering with the butterflies in his stomach. "What should I write?" he whispered as he retreated.

"Whatever you want, man."

He couldn't think of anything good to write or draw, so his foggy panicked brain made his shaky hand start painting a crude depiction of a penis. Roach giggled and started to spray a big anarchy symbol beside it. He was finished before Silvino, so he capped his can and stroked his chin to ponder whether or not to use the anarchy symbol as the letter A in something like 'Bash the Fash.'

As Silvino was struggling to cap his can, there was the unmistakable sound of a policeman's walkie-talkie beeping loudly. He sucked in a curt gasp to avoid screaming and looked at Roach with horrified eyes. Roach tossed both cans into a nearby bush, but before he could scoop Silvino up to rush him away, there was a flashlight on both of them. Silvino let out a whimpery scream and immediately reached for the sky.

Roach sighed, his back to the cop as he heard him say, "Hands where I can see 'em, kid." He put his hands behind his head. "How old are you punks?"

"Are we being detained?" asked Roach as he turned to face the pig.

"Shut up and answer my question."

"How am I supposed to answer your question if I've shut up?"

The cop twitched for his gun but took a deep breath to stop himself from terrifying poor Silvino even more by pulling a deadly weapon on him. He said a code into his walkie and gestured with his flashlight. "You two come over here."

Silvino started to shuffle to the indicated spot, but Roach held out his arm in front of him to stop him and asked again, "Are we being detained?"

"Yes."

"On what grounds?"

"On the grounds that I'm an officer of the law. Do as you're told, son."

Silvino rushed over to the spot where the officer's light was still pointed and said, "W-w-we're sorry, officer, sir, b-b-but I think you may have us m-mistaken. We weren't doing anything il-illegal." He tried to wipe the sweat from his brow and was reminded of his mask, which he quickly removed, accidentally rubbing paint from his finger on his forehead in the process.

"Uh huh," said the officer with a huff of laughter, "What's your name then, genius?"

"Silvino Alvarez, s-sir."

Roach rolled his eyes and sighed. He stepped forward, his hands still on his head, but before he could give a shake at the impossible task of talking them out of the mess, there was a gun pointed at him. "On the ground! On the ground, now!" Fear tried to crack out of him with a hysterical laugh, but he managed to hold it back as he laid down on his stomach and let himself get cuffed.

Silvino was hyperventilating on their way to the station. He was hyperventilating as his prints were taken, and by the time he was being lined up for his mugshot, he was outright bawling. Meanwhile, Roach was being defiant and refusing to give a name to the officers. He hadn't taken his wallet or phone with him, so they had no way of identifying him beyond the joke names he was giving like "Guy Mann," "Richard N. Butts," and "Michael Hunt." He had hoped that Silvino would be wise enough to not bring his wallet too, but it was one of the first things the cops found on him.

When Roach had his prints taken, they were flagged by the computer, and the woman doing his papers asked, "Roach? Why does it not have a first name?" He shrugged and withheld a smug grin. She read a note on the file and said, "Oh, I see. Are you Karson or Clayton?"

"Maybe."

She sighed and didn't even bother pestering him further. After putting 'K/C Roach' onto his letterboard, she lined him up for his mugshot. A modified version of the picture she took would later be used as the cover of one of his best selling albums, one he wrote as a wedding gift for Silvino, called Apis Mellifera.

Roach was closed up into the holding cell with Silvino sitting on the bench and holding his reeling head. "We're so fucked. We're fucked. We're fucked," he was muttering on repeat. "My mom and dad are gonna kill me."

Roach dropped down into the bench across from his and laid back on it with his hands behind his head casually. After a few more moments of mewling from his boyfriend, he smirked at him and asked, "First time?"

"What? Of course it is! Are you saying this isn't your first time getting arrested?"

He chuckled. "Yeah, man. Main difference here is I don't know these guys."

"What do you mean?"

"I mean I know like ninety percent of the cops in So-Cal by their first names and badge numbers." Silvino sighed and held his aching head to mutter more lamentations. "This is my nineteenth time, but first time in Texas, so that's gotta count for something, no?"

"It counts for you're a lunatic, and my parents are gonna kill me, Clay."

"Yo, dude, don't call me that. They don't know my name."

"What have you been arrested for eighteen fucking times anyway?"

"Whole bunch of stuff, man," he started counting on his hands as he listed nonchalantly, "dumpster diving, trespassing, weed, drinking underage, driving without a licence, pickpocketing, vandalism, flipping off a cop, praying to Allah, stole a whole cart-full of Magic cards from a Desert Mart sophomore year, some stuff Sonny did, and once for kissing a boy."

"Kissing a boy?" He frowned. "I thought I was your first kiss."

"Nah, sorry man. I was only like thirteen, though, if it makes you feel better."

"A little," he mumbled as he held his turning stomach and averted his eyes.

"Relax, dude. Everyone gets arrested. Everything's fucking illegal. Besides, it'll be good for your image."

"What? No it won't!"

"Sure it will. This plus the bear attack? That scar is sick, man. And sexy, too." He shrugged. "Little edge in showbiz is good. You already called your mom, right?" A nod. "So then what's the worry, honeybee? She'll pay our bail, and we'll be back on the road by lunch tomorrow."

"She's gonna fucking kill me," he lamented in Spanish as he dropped his head back into his hands.

After about an hour, Roach requested his harmonica, and after another hour it was brought to him. He played some good ol' prison blues for them for a couple hours before Silvino's stomach growled loudly and brought a cute blush to his cheeks.

Roach stopped playing. "You hungry, dude?" He turned his head in shame. "I'll get them to get you something." He stepped up to the bars of the cell and shouted for someone to come to them. It was surprising how promptly he was met with a cop on the other side of the bars: he didn't even have to ask twice.

"What's the problem?" the officer asked as he crossed his muscly arms and looked judgmentally at the both of them.

"Hey, man. We're hungry."

"Tough shit."

Roach rolled his eyes. "Come on, dude. You're already bald with the stupid sunglasses indoors and bad breath: why not break the stereotype and be nice."

"Sit down, boy."

Roach sighed and sat back down on his bench. The cop started to leave, but Silvino stopped him with his voice cute and submissive: "Please, sir, I'll pay extra for the service."

Roach slipped out his harmonica and held it up to his mouth to resume playing, but he stopped when he saw the malice in the pig's gait as he stepped up to the bars and looked down at Silvino. He chuckled darkly and spoke with a tone not unlike the bullies that would beat Roach down in high school: "Let me guess, tubby: double cheeseburger with fries?"

A red tint flashed over Roach's pale skin as his gaze hardened on the cop. He couldn't hide the rage in his heart, and he most assuredly couldn't hide the intense insanity in the backs of his eyes.

Silvino was offended, but he nodded at the question and said, "Okay, okay, that's okay. I'm just hungry."

"'Course you are. I'll get you something." He huffed with disdain and looked at Roach, failing to hide the hint of fear that struck him when he saw how harrowing his hazel-greys were. "And what do you want, asshole?"

After three heaving breaths, he shook away his rage and tried to seem as nonchalant as he had been up to that point. "Chicken sandwich'll do."

The cop left, and Roach rushed over to Silvino's bench to sit beside him and whisper, "Don't you dare let that dumbass thumb get to you, honeybee. You're adorable and beautiful, and I love you so fucking much no matter what."

He sniffled and nodded while wiping the tears from his eyes with his sleeve. "Thanks, Roach."

After a scan of the area, he quickly leaned in and kissed Silvino's cheek before going back to his bench and bringing the harmonica to his mouth with shakier hands than usual.

After another two hours, the same cop came back to their cell with a bag of cold fast-food and two lukewarm bottles of water. Roach and Silvino expected him to open the door to give it to them, but it proved to be wishful thinking to be treated like human beings. After dropping the water bottles through the bars like he was dropping off packages in a post-box, he shoved the bag through and tipped it upside down to dump the contents on the cold cement. "Eat it off the floor like the cow you are," he spat at Silvino.

"You wanna fucking die, pigshit?" said Roach with a menacing tone as he stood and took a stride toward the cop.

His tall stature and imposing musculature were terrifying to this man despite the bars between them. His hand hovered around his gun as he took a step back and shouted, "Are you threatening an officer of the law?"

He smirked at the fear. "What do you think, Einstein?"

The cop took out his gun and aimed it at Roach, who appeared as unfazed as ever. Despite his deadpan expression, he had never before wanted to see blood more than he did in that moment and had to actively stop himself from murdering the bastard. The madness in his hazel eyes was palpable and put a quiver in the officer's gun as he said something into his radio and started to back away. Silvino stood and wrapped his arms around Roach's back, tugging at his elbows and whispering in Spanish, "It's okay, Roach. Please don't get into even more trouble. Please."

With Silvino's loving touch and sweet voice, the rage within him halved. He hesitated to retreat, his gaze still locked with the cop, but after another plea from Silvino, he let out an angry huff like a bull and sat back down on his bench. As the officer fled, Roach ran his hands through his hair feeling suddenly exhausted. It had taken his every last scrap of energy to refrain from butchering the pig.

After blipping Thyne and the three he'd be flying to Egypt back to the hangar,

Francis returned to the others and paid with cash for two used vehicles from a shady seller the twins had found. They didn't need to sign any papers, and even if the cars were lemons, they would at least last long enough to get them out of the city. In an abundance of caution, the Roaches all three looked under the hoods of the minivan and sedan after driving them to a parking garage and informed the others they would like to gather some supplies to fix the cars later, but Partha objected: "Our disguises won't work forever. We should get out of here and go somewhere more remote."

He was referring to the way he and Francis had changed their appearances before leaving Italy in order to not be so recognisable from Partha's streams. Francis had aged himself to appear roughly fifty, cut his hair short and aged it enough that it started to grey. He had fixed his teeth and changed his eyes to be heterochromatic, with one blue and one brown, and wore one of Thyne's hoodies over his blouse.

Partha, the most wanted man on the planet, had to take some more extreme measures. He was wearing the glass eye that Perlie had blown for him, but even with how realistic it looked, he still wore sunglasses. He had his head shaved and covered with an ugly baseball cap Roach had found in the garbage. He had also allowed Roach to pierce his lips with snakebite piercings, and with Francis' help, the piercings in his ears were widened for twenty-millimetre gauges. With Francis' tattooing pen, he allowed Roach to essentially doodle all over him, and when Roach was running low on ideas, he passed the pen to Francis. After drawing with his right hand, he used his left until he ran dry of ideas and finally passed it to Arjun. Partha was therefore covered from tip to toe in a variety of beautiful art pieces. He fancied some of them enough that he considered asking Francis to not remove them like the rest at the end of the job.

Along with their disguises, River had asked Giovanni to brand him the same as Roach had been branded, so the twins could successfully pretend to be each other again if the need arose.

The Roaches weren't worried about Partha being recognised, but they heeded his concerns and waited until they were out of the city and on their way toward Tennessee to start looking for auto shops. With his perfect memory, Roach could recall how to navigate the states from his cross-country trip with Silvino when they were nineteen, though it was never made clear to the others just why he knew his way around the highways. He was leading them through the country, driving the minivan with Francis, Dezba, and Dale as his passengers. In its back were the few weapons, bulletproof vests, and masks they could reasonably carry from the airport through the city, but they were otherwise wanting for clothes and hygienic supplies having brought no other luggage. The plan was to buy whatever else they might need with cash or Rory's cards if they were desperate.

River was driving the sedan and following his brother with Poppie in the passenger seat and Partha and Rory in the back. Poppie was veiled as best as she could be without being outed as a non-Christian. Her short hair was pulled up into a beanie, and she wore a facemask and Roach's sweater, which swallowed her little 5'2" frame up. Her pants were a baggy pair of torn jeans, under which she was wearing leggings to hide her skin, and her shoes were combat boots not unlike the kind her brother liked to wear. As they drove, she danced to the music on the radio for the first half-hour on the road before turning it down and asking River, "How's Pio? Do you know?"

"Yeah, we saw him when we went out to the new states to blow shit up."

"Oh!" she giggled, "I bet he had fun with that."

"Yeah he had a blast. Pun intended."

"I miss him."

"He asked about you, too. First thing he said to us."

She blushed beneath her mask and shimmied in her seat like a schoolgirl with a crush. "And he's okay even though he's still fighting in the war?"

"Well, he lost a leg, but he's as manic as ever. We brought him back to Brazil, though, so he's taking a break from combat."

"Did he get a phone finally?"

"He's got a phone, yeah."

She took out her own phone and opened her contacts to add Pio. "What's his number?" River recited it, and she tapped the screen to add him to her contacts with a big beaming grin hiding beneath her mask. "Thank you, Karson."

"No problem."

She turned toward the men in the back of the car. "How are you two? It's so nice to meet some of my brothers' friends."

"Excited!" answered Partha.

"Me too! And what about you, Rory? You ever done this sort of thing? Clay says you're a landlord. I'm surprised he hasn't killed you yet." She covered her already-hidden mouth to giggle adorably. "Do you guys know that story?"

"What story?" asked Partha.

"When Clay first moved into his apartment (like the literal week after), he was accused of murdering his landlord. It turned out the real murderer was the lady who rented his apartment before him, though. But anyway, that's how he met Pio. They were neighbours, and Pio liked the landlord because he got a discount on his rent, and so when he thought it was Clay that killed him, he bursted into his apartment with a sword and said, 'You killed my landlord. Prepare to die.'" She laughed. "And Clay just cracked up, and they hit it off. I'm sure that was an interesting conversation. Anyway, Pio was invited to Clay's wedding, so he and I flew down to Guanajuato together. We were going to go back to America a few weeks after the ceremony, but of course, that's about when the war started, so me and Pio joined Clay and his husband in this sort of unofficial military thing. I got to shoot stuff and reinforce this food truck we stole and Pio let me detonate a few bombs and… yeah…. It was fun!"

"We took that food truck up into the new states when we blew up the factories," said Partha with a big dumb grin.

"Did it hold up for you?"

"Yeah, but the kid was nearly shitting himself."

"You literally almost died, River!"

He only shrugged.

There was a beat, during which Rory was looking particularly out of place. Poppie noticed his nervousness and asked, "You alright, dude?"

"Er… yeah."

"You have such a cool accent. Where are you from?"

"Birmingham."

"Is it nice?" He forced a smile but didn't answer verbally. "So, why'd you join my brothers' gang of terrorists?"

He sweated and flicked his gaze toward Partha, hoping he might be rescued from the conversation. After a beat of quiet, it seemed he would have to answer, so he cleared his throat and said, "I just have some issues with Osiris."

She laughed. "That makes sense. Well, it's good to see so many people are willing to help. Did you help with the company towns?" He shook his head. "Oh, right, that was before you joined, right? So you're like brand new! Have you ever done a crime?"

"Er…."

"Other than tax evasion?" said River.

"I er… stole some chips once in secondary school."

The other three chuckled. "That's adorable," said Poppie, "If you're having any trouble with the prison jobs, just talk to Clay. He's real good at crimes."

"Y-yeah. So I've heard."

As Rory was being tormented with shades of regret for having joined the gang, Dezba was comforting Dale in the minivan. Roach had Francis' playlist blasting, so the conversation in the back was drowned out for the two in the front. She had her hand on Dale's knee. "What's wrong, son?"

"Ah'm fine."

"Son… you're not. You can tell me. I'm here for you like I'm here for everyone in the gang."

"Why? Ah killed yer fren."

"You did…. But you're part of the gang now, and that's what matters."

"Ye're quick t'fergive."

ase in making you feel like an outcast for it. Now, what's got you
w? Is it the guilt of killing May?"

......on like that."

"Well, you don't have to tell me, but I'm here if you want to talk. It'll be a long
drive back home."

A beat. "Why're ye in the gang anyhow?" She smiled and told him the story of
how she joined. He was smiling by the end. "Ain't that juss how it goes? So ye're
good wit guns?" She nodded. "Well, when we's get back t'my bus maybe Ah'll
letchye take a look at my s'pply. Least what Ah dinny lose when Ah loss my plane."

"That's exciting." She went on to ask about what models he had, and the conversation picked up in pace and levity as they both became increasingly invested.

It took twelve hours to get to Gatlinburg with an hour stop in the middle where
the Roaches had to give the cars both some quick fixes to make it the rest of the
trip. Other than gas and food breaks, they also made a few stops to buy clothes and
other supplies they would need for their indefinite stay in the states. At almost
every gas and snack stop, they shuffled around passengers between the cars, with
the twins always driving. The long trek brought about a levity to everyone and
bonded them together, helping to welcome Dale and Rory further into the gang.
The only exception to this was Roach, who was increasingly downtrodden and
who spent increasingly long during his prayer breaks. He was untalkative for the
first half of the trip, and after fixing the van, he was all but entirely silent. Francis
asked what had him so upset, but he brushed him off: "I'm fine. Hand on heart."
With that said, Francis eventually asked River what was wrong during Roach's last
prayer of the trip, which lasted almost fifteen minutes more than Poppie's, and
River told him not to pry.

They arrived at Dale's parents' house at midnight and were welcomed inside by
his mother while his father and uncle slept upstairs. She was sleepy but bubbly as
she brought them to the kitchen where a tray of cookies was set out for them and
a pot of coffee had already been brewed. Because they were so tired, there was
hardly any conversation before they all climbed to their various guest rooms or
pull-out couches to collapse and sleep.

Roach and Poppie awoke before the others for their prayers, and as they stepped
down into the living area and caught a glimpse of the view outside, they were both
stunned to stillness. The sleepy Tennessee morning evoked a tranquillity they had
never experienced, giving them a plethora of new things to thank Allah for. A
gentle fog broke sunbeams of the golden sunrise, carrying with it dewdrops that
hugged the grass and leaves like glittering magic. Passerines serenaded the groggy
cabin and its inhabitants, and a family of wild deer was standing on the mountainside grazing peacefully. The siblings made eye contact, both of them recognising
the awe in the other, and embraced almost automatically. Overcome with astonish-

ment that the world could be so beautiful, they decided to pray outside. Opening the door, a cat slipped through, swapping with one from inside as if they were passing each other on a morning commute, and the Roaches giggled together at the charm of it all.

Though the grass was wet with dew, Roach did not roll out a prayer mat, choosing to instead kowtow directly on the ground and feel more connected to the planet. They prayed silently together, and when they were both finished, Roach, for once, felt no desire to light up a morning durry. He instead brushed the dew from his knees worthlessly and ambled up to the front porch where a pair of rocking chairs were perched with a perfect view of the sunrise. Poppie sat with him, the two of them enjoying the view and crisp mountain air in serene silence.

Shadows stretched far across the verdant rolling mountains and the small lake in the valley below the cabin, but as the sun climbed, the darkness receded and dappled the landscape as clouds danced slowly through the everblue sky.

The Quirks' home was a handbuilt two-storey log and stone cabin with a finished basement bored into the mountainside and a detached menagerie which was built with newer materials. There were some additions to the house itself that were also newer like an extension to one of the bedrooms upstairs and a small greenhouse off the kitchen. As Poppie and Roach were sitting in silence, they heard some movement inside but didn't pay it much mind. They were therefore both startled when Gracie, Dale's mother, came out the front door and greeted them loudly, "Good morning, y'all! Watching the sunrise?" They nodded. "Roach, come here! You didn't give me a hug last night." He stood and gave her a big bear hug. "Hey now, ya big lug. Be careful with me." She slapped his chest playfully. "And what was your name, sweetheart?"

"Poppie."

"What a cute name! You two come with me. My baby Dale is still asleep, bless his heart, so you'll have to help me with his chores."

They followed her out of the house toward the menagerie. There was a rickety wooden fence around it that followed the uneven landscape and surrounded the small building. As she opened the gate she warned them to watch their step and led them to a pair of standing coolers under an awning on the side of the building. "Grab those buckets there. Two each." They nodded, and she took two for herself. After filling each bucket with a different kind of food, she gestured with her head for them to follow her as she kicked the cooler's legs so its lid would fall.

Excited braying sounded through the walls as the lid slammed shut, and Gracie shouted, "I know. I know. We're coming. Calm down." She wedged one of her buckets between her hip and the wall beside the door as she entered a code onto its doorknob to unlock it. It beeped, and the eager animals on the other side got even more rambunctious as she bumped open the door. "Well, go on, then."

Roach and Poppie went through before her and tried to see what animals were inside, but they were all hidden in dark mahogany stalls. It certainly smelled like barnyard animals though, and Roach's stomach dropped when he spotted a horse stick its head out of its stall door where it snorted playfully and whinnied. "Alright," said Gracie as she pushed through them, "Ungulates first. Reptiles next." She turned to walk backwards and looked at Roach, "Dale says you'll like the tarantulas."

He lagged behind his sister and forced a smile at Gracie. "Yeah, I like tarantulas." While he was successful at hiding the true depths of his unease to keep his face stoic, he couldn't stop himself from flicking his gaze toward the horse as they grew nearer to it. They passed it, much to his relief, and fed the animals in the furthest stall: four pygmy goats.

"Poppie, you've got the food for them in your red bucket."

"Oh, uh. Do I just throw handfuls in?"

"No, there's a trough." Poppie set down her grey bucket and went into the pen with Gracie's guidance. "You see the empty one?"

"Yes."

"Dump about half your bucket in there."

"Yes, ma'am." After the sound of her food being poured stopped, her voice sounded again timid and cute: "Can I pet them?"

"Of course!"

She giggled and passed the bucket back through the window, which Roach took telekinetically and set beside her other one. Gracie started at the power before remembering that he had it and letting out a little gasp. When Poppie finished petting the goats, who were busy eating their breakfast anyway, she shimmied out of the stall and picked her buckets back up off the ground. "Where next, Mrs. Quirk?"

"Oh, you don't gotta be so formal, honey. Just call me Gracie." She brought them to a stall with three alpacas in it: two adults and one baby. "That's Sandpaper. She's only three months old. Don't tell Dale about her yet. I'm gonna surprise him when he gets his sleepy butt out of bed."

"She's precious!" said Poppie. "Can I pet her!?"

"Of course. It's the red bucket again for them."

Poppie set down her grey bucket and hopped from foot to foot as she waited for Gracie to open the stall for her. Once it was open, she rushed inside and immediately started petting the animals who were overly interested in the food she was holding. "They're so soft, Clay! Come pet them."

He rolled his eyes and set down his buckets to go pet the animals. The jubilance in his sister's air was helping calm him, but he was still dreading whatever would happen when they got to the horse's stall. Still, he gave some quick pats to the adult alpacas and conceded, "They *are* really soft."

When they were finished with the alpacas, Gracie took them to a stall with a pig in it, glad she had given herself the food for it when the Roaches both seemed perturbed by it. She didn't linger long for their sakes and shuffled off to a stall with a tapir in it. Roach and Poppie were both amazed by the creature and took turns feeding it out of their hands when Gracie told them how. After the tapir, they were brought to an okapi, which was equally fawned over by the Roaches. Then came the moment Roach had been dreading, and one of his buckets was the only one with food still in it. He gulped as Gracie brought them to the stall with a big brown stallion and started petting his face. "This is Moose."

A beat.

"…He looks like a horse," said Poppie.

She giggled. "Yes, but his *name* is Moose. Now, Roach, come feed him. You can feed him out of your hand if you lay it flat like this." She took a handful of the food from his bucket and demonstrated.

"Uh… yeah… can't you do it?"

She pursed her lips. "Now, why are you gonna be all helpful the rest of the morning but start being a pain in the tuckus now? This is Dale's favourite part, and I'm letting you do it."

"Then… uh… then Dale should do it." The horse made a little snort and shook its head to try and get Gracie's attention, and Roach blenched away.

"Big baby," Poppie teased in Arabic and took the food bucket from him.

He watched with shaking hands as she laid her palm out flat to let Moose eat from it. "Careful," he whispered.

Despite his fears, feeding the old horse went off without a hitch, and they were led into a separate room with terrariums lining the walls. She introduced them to turtles and geckos and lizards, and when she pulled out a diamondback rattlesnake to show them, it was Poppie that Roach was teasing for being scared when she hid behind him. It was over seven feet long, and Gracie was proudly showing it off and draping it over her shoulders as it playfully slithered around. She noticed that Roach was smiling softly, so she offered the snake to him. Poppie stepped back when he took it happily, letting it slither around all over him while Gracie cleaned its terrarium and put a dead squirrel inside the large glass tank.

When they were finished with the reptiles, Gracie gestured to three terrariums that were separated from the others on a little table at the end of the room and said, "Winifred, Sarah, and Mary. The tarantulas. Would you like to hold them, Roach?"

"Yes!" he said while Poppie made an excuse to go to the cabin.

Gracie giggled. "Okay, tell Dale to come out here if you see him."

With Poppie gone, Gracie passed a spider to Roach. "That's Sarah. She's a *Mexican R*—."

"*Mexican Red Knee*."

"Good! Do you know a lot about spiders?" He nodded, and she beamed. "Okay, well let's put you to the test! Put Sarah back. This is Winnie. What is she?"

"*Orange Baboon*. She's gorgeous."

"Why, thank you, son, I take good care of my girls." He gave her back the spider after some time admiring it, and she passed him the last one. "And what's Mary?"

He stroked his stubble and watched her crawl around on his hand. "Hmm. *Chilean Rose?*"

"Aw, you almost had a clean sweep, son."

He pursed his lips and stroked his chin some more. "Then she must be a *Skeleton*. Surely."

"Yes. And don't call me Shirley."

He huffed with amusement and set the spider back in her terrarium. "They're delightful, and so was the snake. Thank you."

"Of course! Now, come back in the house for breakfast, maybe play us some banjo music, and if you ever want to come out and see them again, just let me know."

When Roach came back inside, he saw Rory and Partha standing hand-in-hand and observing a gallery wall of photos. The intoxicating smell of bacon permeated the air, so Roach, curious if it was halal, slinked into the kitchen where he found Dale's uncle Johnny cooking a large breakfast spread.

Rory and Partha were quiet in his absence as they observed the pictures. In one of them was a dark-haired little girl on a camel at a zoo wearing an umbrella-hat that was irritating and embarrassing her despite not looking any older than eight. Beside that image was a shot of a pair of little girls who looked to be twins, smiling and each holding up a fish they had caught in the valley's little lake. The girl on the left was beaming proudly at her large catch, and the one on the right looked embarrassed by her puny little fish in comparison. Beside that, there was a snap of the dark-haired girl, a teenager dressed in all black and beaming a big grin at the raven she had perched on her arm. On another wall, there was a bachelor's degree for Grace Quirk in Life Sciences with some pictures of her when she was younger scattered around it. Even older were some images of Gracie as a child with her parents and brother, one of which was of the entire family in corresponding Halloween costumes, themed after *Star Wars*.

"Where are the pictures of Dale?" muttered Partha as he migrated to a hutch with a few more frames on it. He plucked them up to look at the figures, none of them seeming to be Dale, and all of the children, save for John's few images, being girls. "Who are these two, do you think?" he asked Rory with another picture of the little blonde twin girls, this time wearing swimsuits and holding popsicles at the shore of the lake.

Rory took the picture to observe, but he was stopped by a loud thumping sound.

"Ow, what the fuck, Roach?" said Partha as he rubbed the back of his head where he had been struck.

"Mind your fucking business, kid. Go get some breakfast."

Partha tried to slink away with Rory still in his hand, but they were stopped by Dale's voice sounding as he came down the stairs: "Now, Roach, don' go hittin' the poor kid. It's fine."

"Did you hear what he was asking, dude?"

"Yeah." Once he was down the stairs he stretched and smiled at the three in the living area. "Ma says Gigi couldn't make it, so ye won't get ta meet my sister." A beat. "Smells good, huh? Uncle Johnny's makin' brekfass."

"But the bacon is pork," said Roach with slumped shoulders, "Your mom wanted to see you, by the way. She's in the menagerie."

He nodded and passed through the kitchen to grab a handful of bacon and munch on it as he left the house through the back door and sauntered across the vibrant property to where his mother was waiting for him.

Roach left to find a banjo to play for the family like Gracie had requested, so Partha and Rory returned their attention to the photos before wandering to a display case brimming with porcelain dolls. "Well, those are creepy, huh?" said Partha.

"Nah, mate. They're pretty."

The entire interior of the cabin suited the collection. The rooms were all dark and cramped and cluttered with cosy furniture, books, animal skulls, herbs and wreaths, baskets of flowers, trinkets and knick-knacks. The beds had all been piled so high with comfortable blankets and pillows that River, Dezba, and Francis had yet to be free of their drowsy clutches, and Poppie had returned to her cocoon of cosiness to text Pio in her and the twins' guest room. It was like the warmest sweetest witch in the world had decorated the house. It even had a little cauldron hanging with the other pots and pans in the kitchen that was used to make stock-pots every other weekend or so with the bones and vegetable peelings from that week's meals. The greenhouse was more green than house with its overgrown pots of vegetables, fruits, herbs, and even some edible flowers. The entire property was powered by solar panels on the roof as well as the handcrafted waterwheel on a nearby stream that ran down the mountain and fed into the lake at its base. The only roads on the property were dirt or gravel, and on moonless nights it was black as pitch outside.

Rory and Partha ambled into the kitchen for breakfast and tried to chat with John about... well *anything*, but he gave them only vague sounds and one-word answers to things. As they were bothering him, the oldest member of the family, Dale's father, came downstairs and poured himself a coffee. "Mornin'," was his groggy greeting to the visitors at his table. He looked to be over seventy with a full head of white hair and wrinkled face. The features beneath his pale wrinkled skin were sharp, lending him an attractive air even at his old age: it was clear where some of Dale's features came from. Unlike his son, his back was hunched because of his age, showing his spine slightly through his flannel shirt, and his physique was frail and thin. With his coffee in hand, he sat at the table and gave his guests more attention in the form of a big beaming grin, putting on display his slightly-crooked teeth. "I'm Flint. I'm Dale's dad. Who are you two?"

They introduced themselves, but after Partha's name was uttered, John stopped cooking and looked at them while Flint spit some hot coffee back into his mug.

"Partha Nima? Like Party the Kid?" asked John. He looked to be somewhere between fifty and sixty with his black hair streaked heavily with grey and lines showing on his face. He also resembled Dale in part, especially in the icy blue of his eyes, but his features were thinner and almost eerie: like some sort of cartoon villain drawn entirely with triangles. His physique was slightly above average in terms of musculature, and as he set down a bowl of grits with a large serving spoon, he was eyeing Partha harshly.

"Yeah. That's me," said Partha eventually, averting his gaze.

"My sister loves your streams."

"Oh yeah? Did she— uh. Did she catch the last one?"

"What happened t'ye? Ye're all covered in tattoos an' piercin's," said Flint as he buttered his toast.

"Shut up, Flint, he asked a question."

"Uh. Yeah I had to disguise myself because of the last stream."

"Seems a bit extreme," said Flint to Partha before taking a bite of his toast.

"Gracie saw the last stream," John finally answered, "She said she wanted to help you, so it's good you met Dale. She helped convince him that the deep fake of you isn't real, so he finally dropped the job to capture you."

As they were talking about him, Dale was meanwhile curled up in his mother's arms on a bench down the mountain a ways and hidden by the incline and foliage from those in the cabin. She pet his hair and shushed him lovingly as he bawled into her chest and wailed incoherently at having killed his friends and the betrayal that had led him to do it. "Shh, honey, you did what you had to do. Your real friends are inside right now." He only mewled more. "You're my precious little man, and I love you so much, baby."

"Ah love you, Mama," he whimpered and pulled himself closer to her.

"Shh. Baby. Poor baby. It's okay."

He cried for half an hour before there were no tears left in him. With a noisy sniffle, he wiped his arm across his face and sat upright. "Thanks fer lettin' me be a mess on ye, Mama."

"You be anything you want, Dale, baby. I love you no matter what. You know that."

He nodded and sniffled again as he lit himself a cigarette. His mother had supported him through everything for his entire life. She didn't drop him when he turned to crime as a juvenile. She didn't drop him when he joined the military and nearly got discharged for being too sadistic. She didn't drop him when he came out. She didn't drop him when he joined a far-right movement and got swastika tattoos on his head. She didn't drop him when he covered those tattoos, and she didn't drop him when he came home from war with Roach, rearing to rescue Flint and John from prison. She knew what evils he committed from his bus in the woods, and she knew why Roach was such a good friend for him. Still, she loved him. He couldn't have asked for a better mother, and he most certainly deserved much worse.

With his approval, she went back inside and mingled with the others while he smoked, glad to shade her pale freckled skin in the cabin lest she get even more freckles. She was between Flint and John's ages at about sixty with her long straw-berry-blonde hair finally starting to grey and rosy cheeks starting to sag. She gave Flint a peck on the lips and Johnny a peck on the cheek when she came into the kitchen where Dezba had also joined for breakfast.

"Your name was Dezba, right?" she asked as she poured herself some orange juice.

"That's right, Miss Gracie."

"Well, aren't you just beautiful? Would you like something to drink?"

Dezba blushed. "Sure."

"Orange juice alright?"

She nodded. With her drink in front of her and a plate of food, she watched Gracie sit and asked her about her house. After a rambly answer about how Flint and John had built the cabin, Dezba inquired about the animals, and Gracie's hazel-green eyes lit up. John and Flint joked that Dezba had opened the floodgates with the question, and it proved correct when she spent half an hour rambling about all the animals she had, past and present. It led into talks about her time working as a zookeeper, which led further back to her meeting with Flint and how they fell in love.

Dezba engaged in the conversation with almost as much enthusiasm, telling Gracie about how she met Lionel then raving about the gang and how much she loved the members in it, which led to conversations about Dale.

They yapped for so long in the kitchen, hardly ever paying attention to anyone else except at lunch and dinner and for Roach's banjo music, that it came as a surprise to both of them when River came in at ten that night saying, "Come on, Dezba, we're leaving."

⚙ Chapter 67 ⚙
Here There Be Monsters

"Now that you're a hardened criminal and all, I think we should go get our first tattoos together."

Silvino smiled and readjusted the bag on his back to shift its weight around as they hiked. "Oh yeah? And what super badass thing would I get on me?"

"A bouquet of apple and cherry blossoms on account of how pretty and sweet you are," answered Roach with a flirtatious giggle.

"Right over my gnarly bear scar," he said sarcastically as he bumped into Roach playfully, almost knocking him into the brush on the side of the trail.

"Careful, dude, I might get Berry dirty." Silvino had insisted on bringing the plush up Cloud Peak to take a picture on the summit, so Roach had tied it to his backpack with the tent and other camping equipment. The only things in Silvino's bag were his camera, water bottles, trail snacks, and their only emergency beacon. "But for real," said Roach after a few more steps up the winding trail, "They should match or at least go together."

"Well, we're not done with the trip after this, right?"

"Nah, I still want to go to Florida. Sonny said he'd fly out and meet us there because he misses me and also apparently wants to see if he can find a clean enough beach to surf on. Plus we haven't gone to New York yet or some of the other places on your list like Salem and fucking Waffle House, you adorable little dork." He

giggled at the thought that Silvino had Waffle House on his list of sights to see alongside wonders like The Grand Canyon and Niagara Falls.

"Should probably wait until after the trip, then."

"I guess, but I just thought it could be part of it." They walked quietly for a few minutes, both of them pondering tattoo ideas. "Oh, what if we draw something for each other? Like, I'll draw yours, and you draw mine."

"That sounds romantic, but what would we draw?"

"Well," he hopped over a creek and held out his hand to help Silvino over it after him, "I like to call you honeybee. Maybe you draw one of those, and I'll draw a roach for you."

Silvino was so charmed by the idea that he giggled. "That's so sweet, Clay. Okay, we'll do that. Where should we get them?"

"Hm, maybe the pecs?"

"Well, then I'll hardly ever see yours since you're always so covered up."

"Forehead."

Silvino rolled his eyes. "What about the backs of our hands?"

Roach winced. "Won't that hurt?"

"It's gonna hurt no matter what, Clay. You scared?" he teased.

He blushed and muttered, "Yes."

"Big scary Roach can climb mountains and kill bears and get arrested twice a year but gets spooked by a little buzzy needle?"

"I get scared of lots of stuff, dude."

"Oh yeah? What else are you scared of?"

"Needles in general, flying, roller coasters, ferris wheels, horses, fascism, going to prison, ghosts, my—."

"You're afraid of ghosts? But you said you'd never seen one."

"I haven't, but I see how scared they make you, and I've seen like videos and stuff. I dunno man that sorta stuff just freaks me out. Cryptids, too. Glad it was a bear that attacked you and not bigfoot or something because I probably would have just frozen up or had a fucking heart attack."

"So when I've been getting all scared at all the haunted places we've been visiting and running up to you to protect me, you've been scared, too?"

"Yeah, dude."

Silvino's stomach swirled around and cheeks turned pink. "Aww, Clay. That's so sweet."

"I'd protect you from anything no matter how scared I am, honeybee. I guess except my biggest fear."

He frowned. "What's your biggest fear?"

There was a beat as a more serious air overcame them. "Losing you," he said eventually.

He pursed his lips and ran his hand down Roach's arm to interlock their fingers. "Well, I'll always love you, Clay. I'll always be with you."

"Promise?"

He nodded and pressed his free hand to his chest. "Hand on heart."

Roach was pacified by the oath and let the beautiful Wyoming wilderness calm him further. He wrapped his arm around Silvino's shoulders to walk with him closer and said, "So, a honeybee for me. A roach for you. We should do some concept sketches when we make camp, yeah?"

He looked up at him and beamed. "Yeah!"

"I'm sure you've also noticed I'm bringing my guitar up." A nod. "I've got a little something I've been writing for you."

"Roach!" he said with an almost irritated tone, "That's so sweet. How dare you? Now I'll look like a jackass with nothing for you."

"Nothing for me? You won't be there to listen to it?"

"Huh?"

"I only want you there with me. Your presence is a gift."

He blushed and rolled his eyes. "You're so cheesy, are you sure you're not Swiss?"

He snorted and put on a horrible Swiss accent: "Oh ja, ich bin sehr Swiss."

Silvino giggled and snuggled up closer to Roach as best as he could while they walked. Only a few minutes later they had to separate when they noticed a group of four people hiking down the trail ahead of them, and they stayed apart as the climb became increasingly difficult. Roach asked if Silvino needed to be carried several times, but he was each time deceived by a big grin and thumbs-up, assuming the redness in his face was mostly a blush and not from exhaustion. By the time they reached their campsite, Silvino's breaths were heaving and loud.

"You alright, dude?"

He dropped his bag beside the half-pitched tent and leaned on his knees. "I'm fine."

"Dude, drink some water and sit down. Why didn't you tell me you were having trouble? Now I'm just gonna have to carry you the entire day tomorrow to make sure you don't tell me you're fine when you're fucking not." His tone was loving but irritated as he picked Silvino up, opened a camping chair telekinetically, and sat him in it. "Drink this," he shoved a water bottle into his hands, "Jackass."

Roach resumed pitching the tent, and when he was finished he forced Silvino's plush dinosaur inside and rolled his eyes with a stifled grin at how much room it took up in the already-too-small tent. He came back up to Silvino's place and replaced his empty water with a new bottle before gathering some kindling and sticks from around the campsite. He was no longer irritated. By then it had become outright anger, which could be seen in the way he slammed sticks down into the dirt and heard in his muttering as he walked around the area to gather them. "Why didn't you fucking tell me you needed help, dude?"

"I'm sorry."

"I was just saying how I'm fucking terrified of losing you, and you go and act like you're fine when you're not?"

"I'm sorry."

"What if you were having a real emergency? Would you have even told me, then?"

"I'm sorry."

"Fucking asshole."

"I'm sorry, okay? I just don't want to be a burden."

"Have I not made it abundantly clear that I love you, Silvino? That I'd do anything for you? Do I need to shout it from the rooftops? Pin you down and kiss you until you understand? Chase you down in the last act of some shitty movie to say it again so you don't fly off to Cambridge without me?" His voice broke.

Silvino stood and crossed the campsite to wrap his arms around Roach and squeeze. "I'm sorry, Clay."

Roach hugged him tight and cried into his shoulder. "Why are you leaving me, Silvino?"

"It'll only be for four years, and I'll pay for your flights to come visit when my classes aren't so busy, then you can have all the shitty British food your heart desires." He retreated from the embrace and wiped away Roach's tears lovingly. "I'll call every single day, too. I'm sorry, Clay. My parents... they insisted I go, and they said they wouldn't pay for you to live with me there. Maybe if you sign with that label that you were talking with, you wouldn't need their help! Though... I don't want to ask you to leave Karson behind. I know how much you love him. Maybe he could come with you."

He wiped his eyes with the heels of his hands. "Whatever. Let's just set up the campfire and make s'mores or whatever the fuck." After lighting himself a cigarette, he started arranging the sticks he had found into a cone shape to set alight.

Silvino lingered awkwardly before eventually slinking off to their bags to gather the cooking supplies. In his rummaging, he spotted Roach's guitar and brought it to the fire as Roach got it started. "Uh, Roach, uh... I've got a song for you, too... I guess."

He looked at the guitar in his hand and watched as Silvino sat back down in his seat and nervously took up the instrument. Roach was still upset, but he managed to joke, "Play Wonderwall," which relieved the tension greatly.

After a giggle and deep breath, Silvino pressed his fingers into the strings to form a chord and clenched his teeth at the pain of the nylon. "Now, I only know the one song.... Sort of," he defended himself preemptively, "so go easy on me, okay?"

"I'd rather go hard on you," he said before feigning like he misspoke and correcting himself: "In you. I'd rather go hard in you."

Silvino giggled again, rolled his eyes, and looked down at the guitar. He started strumming, and after the first few strums, he started singing. His voice was raspy and a bit off-key at times, but there was enough love in the gesture to wash away all the imperfections. The song he sang was a Spanish translation of La Vie En Rose. Roach's stomach fluttered with butterflies, and he approached to sit in the dirt beside Silvino. He leaned on the side of his chair, letting his eyes slip closed so the calming sounds of the fire and his lover's serenade could bring him into a state of bliss.

When Silvino finished the song, he leaned the guitar on the opposite side of the chair and looked down at Roach, who was grinning sweetly at him. "Thank you, honeybee."

He smiled sadly at Roach. "I'm sorry I have to go to Cambridge. If we could just run off together somehow...."

"Well... we could."

He bit his lip and averted his gaze. "I know you could make due with only a little bit of money, but I don't think I'd last long."

Roach sighed. "Whatever. I don't want to think about you leaving. I have you right now, and that's what matters. Come here. Let's lay back. I'll teach you the constellations before I play you the song I've been writing and make you dinner."

"You know the constellations?"

"I know lots of stuff, honeybee. I have a perfect memory."

Roach spread out one of his jackets on the ground for Silvino to lay on then laid in *the dirt beside him. With Silvino curled up in his right arm, he used his left to point at the stars and tell him the stories behind some of the constellations.*

They drove to Pigeon Forge Airport where they met with Thyne shortly after he landed the Morozovs' plane. They met him in the hangar, and he ambled out of the jet with an exhausted posture. He threw himself into Roach's arms when he saw him. The dark circles beneath his eyes were deathly, so Roach wordlessly plucked him up and let him curl up in his arms to nap.

Dale's truck was nearby, where he had parked it when he left with Leviathan to capture Partha and Richard, so he brought the group to it. Roach, the sleeping Brit, and the kitten he had left with his mother before flying out of the states, were in the front with him, but the rest were told to climb into the backseat or the bed of the truck if necessary. Once everyone (and everything) was as secure as possible, he drove through the wee hours to the national park wherein he had his bus illegally parked.

He tended to like driving up to the bus with his truck, but seeing as they would be taking it out of the woods anyway, he decided to park in the public lot and helped people out of the vehicle. "It's quite the hike," he informed, "Dezba lemme know if ye need carryin'."

It was 4:30 in the morning when they started their hike, carrying all their equipment and luggage with a lot of help from the twins' telekinesis. They followed an established path for the first hour and a half before Dale informed the others that they would have to veer off of it. "Stay close ta me er the twins. There's monsters out here, an' I ain't talkin' 'bout me an' Roach."

Hearing this, Rory and Partha's fingers interlocked and squeezed tightly as they followed Dale into the woods. Roach was still carrying Thyne, napping in his arms, and River offered to carry Dezba. She refused after Dale answered a panicked question from Rory, informing them that it would only take a half hour longer to get to the bus. The sky slowly lightened above them in the last stretch of hiking, and though there was a brief scare from what the twins confirmed was a distant black bear they could see through the trees, they came upon the clearing where Dale had parked his bus.

Roach followed Dale inside to set Thyne down on the bed and tuck him in before having a quick chat about where his tire gauge and air pump were. River and Poppie gave a look at the engine in the back of the bus, and Roach filled its flat tires.

When they were done tuning it up, Roach and Poppie prayed, and Dale asked River, "D'ye think ye could turn the bus 'round so Ah don' gotta do a million-point turn?"

He pursed his lips. "Not alone, but maybe if Tony helps."

"Great. Ah'll wait, then. Anyone wanna beer?" He opened his fridge and tossed a slightly-cold can each to Rory, Partha, and Francis. When Roach came to the door to be let on board ten minutes after Poppie, River shooed him back outside.

"What's going on, dude?"

River hopped down the stairs and shouted up to the inhabitants, "Everyone sit somewhere, else you might fall over." With his attention back on his brother: "We've gotta turn the bus around."

"Oh, okay. I'll push the back left; you push the front right."

"Sounds good."

Inside, the entire bus spinning across the dirt as the twins strained to push it was an unsettling feeling, especially given the slight incline of the clearing. It seemed after being turned 180 degrees that they might start rolling forward into a tree only three feet from the front window, but the twins managed to turn it entirely around without issue. When they were finished, they went inside and both collapsed on the couch, exhausted.

"Thanks, boys," said Dale as he tossed them each a beer, "Ah'mma get us on outta here." He slid out of the room and into the driver's seat, started the engine, and drove the long winding path he had taken to get there in the first place. When they reached the road, he failed to see an approaching police car and drove down from the mountain and onto the pavement, cutting the cop off and groaning at the subsequent sirens.

He pulled over and left the driver's seat to open a nearby cabinet and pull out a pistol he was already cocking as the officer was halfway to his window.

"Woah woah, dude, you're just gonna shoot him?"

"Ye got a problem wit killin' pigs all the sudden, Roach? Summon cover the cat's ears."

Roach may have responded, but as he opened his mouth and Dale sat back down, the officer knocked on the window.

Dale turned to face him and pushed open the window, hiding his gun in his left hand just behind the door. "Mornin'."

"Mornin'. Ye was up in the mountains driving. That's illegal."

"Ye got a partner in yer car?"

He looked back at the car then at Dale. "No, sir."

"Good." He pulled out the gun and shot him in the forehead, smiling as he watched the body fall backwards and bleed all over the empty backroad. "Ah'll be back." He stood, shoved the smoking gun into the back of his pants under his shirt, and hopped down the stairs.

"Uhhh, should we not be panicking?" asked Partha.

"He knows what he's doing," said River as he sipped his beer and pet the kitten.

Partha and Rory exchanged a nervous glance and fidgeted as they waited for Dale to return. He had taken the cop's keys and gone into his car to quickly hack into his dash-cam and laptop to wipe all the footage of the encounter and came back to the bus about five minutes later.

"Did you get the body-cam, dude?"

"Oh, thank ye, Roach." He went back outside to take the camera from the corpse and tossed it to his friend as he came back in and closed the door.

They drove for another half hour before Dale merged onto the interstate and called Roach up to the front.

"What's up, man? Need directions?"

"Ah do."

"Where we goin'?"

"Gonna start wit a prison in Wyoming."

"You're gonna have to be a little more specific than that, dude."

"It's on a mountain called Cloud Peak."

Roach went pale. "It's what?"

Dale looked at him briefly. "What's wrong?"

"Uh… nothing. Yeah. Uh, head toward Nashville."

"Ye can tell me what's wrong, Roach. Ah'm here fer ye."

He sighed. "I don't know. Maybe later."

"Ah know what we'll do: we'll stop in Nashville an' getchye a gi'tar. That'll cheer ye up."

"Thanks, man. I wasn't gonna drink in case you need me to drive, but I think I'll need that beer. Thyne can drive for you when he wakes up."

"No problem, mane. Ah can go fer at least a few hours."

"Thanks." He patted his shoulder and went into the back.

"We are *not* naming our son Sauron," said Perlie.

"But, heart, it's *such* a cool name."

Perlie looked at Neodesha on the couch next to her and gestured to the phone with an irritated expression. "Are you hearing this shit, Shay?"

She giggled. "Well, it ain't none 'a my business, but I think it's mighty cute."

She rolled her eyes and looked at Partha on the video call. "I was thinking we could name him after my father or grandfather."

Partha stroked his goatee. "What was your grandfather's name?"

"What about Arson?" Roach interjected.

"Arson?" asked Partha.

"Yeah," he huffed once with amusement, "'This is our son Arson.'"

"Roach, you asshole," snipped Perlie.

"Alright alright. A real answer: Ruin," said Roach.

"Ruin is Sindarin," said Partha with a big grin, "What does it mean again, sir?"

"'Blazing fire.'"

"We aren't naming our kid something Sindarin!"

Partha pouted and leaned on his elbow. "Well, what's your grandfather's name?"

"Kwan." A beat. "I'm also happy to name him Richard."

"Maybe a middle name," said Partha with a sigh, "I just really like the name Sauron. What about Aragorn? You liked him in the movies."

"I liked him because I wanted to fuck him, Party. Would you drop it? We're not naming him Sauron or Anakin or Aragorn or whatever the fuck else you nerds think is cool." She scoffed. "None of you know what being pregnant is like: I'm so fucking mad about this that it's pissing me off how mad I am."

"Oh, when I'm eating a peanut-butter and pickle sandwich I'm the smartest man in the world, but the moment I suggest a name you don't like I'm a nerd who doesn't understand simple concepts like hormones."

"Roach! Mind your business!" She huffed and puffed.

"Heart, I think you should take some deep breaths. It's gonna be okay. Getting all worked up can't be good for the baby."

She tried to calm herself, but it was helped immensely when Neodesha came up behind her and gave her a shoulder rub. "Thank you," she said through gritted teeth as she pet Angel in her lap to try and calm her further.

"What about Sirion?" said Roach in the lull.

"Is that another Sindarin name?" she snipped.

"Yeah," said Partha with a wince, "It means 'river.'"

She was going to bark at them some more, but she pursed her lips into a cute little pout when she was told the meaning. "Maybe."

Partha's eyes lit up. "You mean it!? I think that's a really good name! We could add Kwan and Richard as middle names, too."

"It sounds a lot like Sauron, though. You two better not be tricking me."

"No, heart. I would never."

"Sirion Richard Kwan... Moon? Or Nima?" asked Francis.

In unison, Perlie answered "Nima," and Partha answered, "Moon."

"Awww," said River, "You two are cute. Moon sounds better, though."

"It does sound better, heart."

"You sure you don't mind your son having my last name?"

"I don't know why that would matter to me beyond it sounding cool. But oh! What if instead we give him an entirely different surname?" She arched her brow, so he clarified with a sea-dog's grin: "Bellamy!"

She smiled softly. "Okay, kid."

"So, when's the procedure?" asked Roach rudely.

Perlie couldn't see him: he was across from Partha, but she glared all the same. "Party, turn me toward him." He turned the phone so she could see him sitting sideways at the bus' small dining table with a can of beer in his left hand and a butterfly knife he was doing tricks with in his right. "Clayton. Look at me." He gave her his eyes, and she winced at how upset he looked even with his expression relatively unemotive. She was going to shout at him to mind his business again, but she only sighed and said, "What's wrong?"

"Don't bother, heart," said Partha as he turned the phone back to face him, "He won't say, and River won't tell us, either."

"Well… whatever I guess. The procedure will be early in July."

"We won't be back by then," said Roach, "We won't be back until December."

"W-what?" Her lip trembled. "Party, is that true?"

"He's being pessimistic, but if it's going to take that long, I'll just get Thyne to fly me out early."

"Can't," said Thyne.

"Why not?"

"Morozovs told me they're out of favours for getting through American airspace, not to mention they've lost four jets to whatever weird curse has all those planes crashing left and right."

"Shit… I'm sorry, heart. If I had known, I never would have left you there."

She sighed. "Well, it's okay I guess. As long as you'll be back as soon as possible."

He saluted the phone. "Of course!"

"Alright, well…," she yawned, "Shay, thank you for the massage. I think it's bedtime now."

"Goodnight, heart! Dream of puppies and dragons and swimming in the stars."

She giggled sleepily. "You're cute, kid. Call me again when you can. Miss you. Love you." She blew him kisses, which he returned before declaring his love and ending the call.

After Partha put his phone away, Roach crushed his empty beer can and threw it on the floor beside three he had already finished before cracking open a fifth and lighting a cigarette. His expression was blank, but his movements were slow. His entire air was downright depressing.

Seeing him so torn up broke Thyne's heart, so he took River aside and asked, "Where's that guitar he got in Nashville?"

River brought him to the bedroom to take the guitar out from under the bed and passed it over. After admiring the quality of the instrument, Thyne rushed out into the main cabin and kissed Roach's hanging head. It caught his attention. "You want me to serenade you, mate?"

He managed a soft smile. "That sounds nice, sparkplug. Your voice is otherworldly."

He grinned fiendishly and started picking the strings and drumming on the base. Roach recognised the tune, but he assumed it was a coincidence that it sounded so familiar until Thyne sang, *"We're no strangers to love. You know the rules, and so do I,"* with a blush on his freckled cheeks and mischief in his amber eyes. Only a few more lines in, and Roach bursted out into a snort-laugh. Thyne continued to play, but his voice was getting broken up by laughter of his own.

Through his guffaws, Roach managed to say, "Dude, that's like the oldest meme ever. You're so old, you cute little fuck." He pulled him down onto his lap and kissed him deeply before he could finish the song.

Though his rotten soul still ached, the levity Thyne brought to the entire party helped Roach to smile again, at least for the last few hours of the drive up until they were parked at Cloud Peak and sleeping through the latter half of the day, planning to start the hike up that evening.

They hiked through the darkest hours of night to cover their approach. Equipped with military-grade armaments, they were beyond conspicuous. The night was quiet and clear and dark as they followed Roach up the mountain. Rory lagged behind the furthest, not because he was incapable of the hike but because he was terrified by what would happen at the summit. Partha noticed his upset and walked with their hands intertwined. After kissing his cheek, he whispered sweetly, "You look hot in all that gear. You'll do great. I was scared in Mexico, and now look at me."

"Thank you, Party," he said with a quick panicked grin.

Dezba was walking beside Dale and trying to comfort him from the upset still lingering over him after having killed his friends. She did manage to squeeze a confession of the murders out of him, but he would sooner kill himself than admit he was not cisgendered. It was bad enough that his family knew and that Roach knew: he wished no one in the world knew. He wished it wasn't true at all.

Thyne was walking with River and Poppie. The three of them were chatting about what would happen the next day when they stormed the prison. They had already discussed their plans on the road, so it was more of an excited 'what if?' sort of conversation than one that brought anything new to the plan.

In the front was Roach. Francis had initially walked with Thyne, but he caught a glimpse of Roach's face, on which he saw the glistening of tears, so he excused himself early on in the trek and walked beside him. They were far enough ahead of the others that their quiet conversation was private. After kissing Roach's cheek, Francis held his hand and said, "I have finished that which I promised." Roach didn't respond, so Francis pushed up the sleeve of his left arm and sent the skin through time until a particular tattoo was showing. His sea-dog voice reverberated through the night like the beautiful biting cold of death:

"*Summer sweet pharos with blood of the pharaohs,*

"*thy soul be the music of great white tornadoes.*"

He paused to look at Roach, who gave him a pitiful pair of glistening hazels. With a sad smile, Francis returned his attention to his arm to resume reading the poem he had written:

"*Stand guard the shoals, armipotent saviour.*

"*Rot not thy bones nor vile behaviour.*

"*Thee be the djinn to witness me wishes,*

"*with mischievous tricks and consummate kisses.*" He paused again and saw another tear trail Roach's cheek where it met with a soft smile.

"*I love thee. I love thee. Like rain to a drought.*

"*Like fire and ashes. Like in needs an out.*

"*You save me from drowning. You save me from death.*"

He kissed him tenderly and whispered the last line:

"*Oh, summer sweet pharos. Oh, High Priest of Seth.*"

Roach's voice tried to sound, but he managed only a whimpery, "Thank you, bed bug."

"It pleases?"

He nodded and sniffled. "It was beautiful."

Francis beamed. "Bully! I went far into the future to the gone-out world of nothing to afford myself nigh-infinite time to conjure it for thee. Forsooth, I am of the mind the gone-out world becomes thee, my dear lover of chaos and rot."

Roach chuckled sadly and nodded. "I love you, Francis."

"What ails thee on this weary trek across the states, my darling?"

He sniffled and wiped his face with his sleeve. "What else, bed bug? Memories of Silvino. Why do you think I know my way around? We went on a road trip when we were nineteen. We went all around the country. This mountain…." He looked up the trail and noticed they were coming up on the part where he and Silvino had talked about their tattoos, which brought his attention down to his hand where the honeybee was inked. "It's just a lot. I'll be okay, though. I always am. And I've got three perfect loves I need to pay attention to, lest I rue these memories too." He draped his arm around Francis' bony shoulders and squeezed him lovingly. "Let's talk about you. You must have stories I can't even fathom. You've been to other planets?" Francis nodded. "Which one's your favourite?"

He stroked his beard. "In this system?"

"You've been outside this solar system?"

"Aye."

"Well, start with this system I guess, then tell me about the ones outside of it."

"As you wish. Though there was once a time I may have cited Earth as the most gorgeous, it has since slowly rotted by the cancer of capital. So, in the absence of Earth's majesty, this system's most pulchritudinous planet is Jove—. Jupiter. Nemine contradicente. When it was inhabited and could be visited, cities floated atop the big swirling oceans of oranges and blues. Sailing ships beyond any human imaginings adorned the surface. 'Twere almost Venetian in these regards, but 'twere distinctly alien."

"That sounds fucking sick, dude," he said with a sad chuckle.

"Aye. 'Twas beguiling. Mayhaps I shall take you there one day."

"You could do that?"

"I may take thee many places and times, my dear. I want as much time with you as possible, and time not spent trying to destroy Osiris be particularly valuable, no?"

Roach pursed his lips. "Well, one step at a time, bed bug. I think if it were up to me— though Jupiter sounds amazing —I'd like to see Ancient Egypt above all else."

"It shall be done, my love."

They continued their conversation wherein Francis told stories of his journeys through the cosmos, even going so far as to point out places he had visited in the starry sky above. When they reached a place to camp for some rest around dawn, the conversation continued but with all the others as Francis' audience.

They slept through the day with Francis on watch for any potential threats from the prison up the mountain, but the hours passed uneventfully. He doodled tattoos on his thighs as he waited, and when night began to fall again, the party ate, prayed, and resumed their trek up the mountain.

It was another black night, and when they could see the prison towers through the treeline, they all stopped and crouched down in the brush. Roach asked Thyne for the scope from his gun, and once he had it, he looked through and spotted several guards. "Someone give Sonny a scope, too." Dale took a pair of binoculars out of his bag and gave them to River. "Even better," said Roach as he pointed some of the guards out to his brother. "Alright, you see them all?"

"Yep."

"You get the ones on the left, I'll get the ones on the right."

"Yep. Count it down."

Roach took a deep breath and counted backwards from five. At one, the twins both reached up their hands and made several small gestures in unison with them, using their telekinesis to implode guards' heads, send them toppling over the cliff-side, or otherwise kill them. They did it as quickly as possible, but an alarm still sounded when they passed the scope and binoculars back to their owners. Thunder rolled across the horizon as a storm Francis had conjured finally took form. They used the cover of darkness and pouring rain to inch closer and closer to the prison until they were blasting through the front doors, all of them gunning down guards as they fanned out through the labyrinthian halls. Even Rory killed someone, though it was an incredibly lucky shot, and he never left Partha's side.

It took ten minutes to kill all the guards, after which they met up with each other in the warden's office where River had already killed four people. Roach stepped over the fallen bodies with no regard for them beyond their physical inconvenience and found the prison's PA system. He pushed down on a button to broadcast his voice: "This thing on?" His friends confirmed that his voice could be heard in the halls outside the office. "Alright, listen up, you dogs. There's a special little button here in this office that'll open all your cells. Before I press it, a warning: we will be freeing literally all of you, but we are *not* your friends. We will kill you with absolutely no hesitation if you get too close. Good luck getting down the mountain because I suggest getting the fuck out of the building as quickly as possible: we will be burning it to cinders. If anyone asks who freed you, be sure to tell them it was *The Crown*. Have a nice day." And with that said, he pressed the button to open all the cells and listened with a blissed smile at the chaos that sounded thereafter.

⚙ Chapter 68 ⚙
I Feel Cold

Just as he had said, the next day, Roach refused to let Silvino hike and carried him, along with all of their things, to the summit. They were alone at the peak, and he finally let Silvino walk on his own. After dropping their many belongings on the ground and offering his hand to Silvino, which was hesitantly taken, he led him to the edge of the mountain and sat with his feet over the black cliffside. "Sit with me, Vinny." He patted the spot beside him, and Silvino ungracefully struggled to plop himself beside Roach.

They admired the vast verdant landscape, Silvino eventually leaning his head on Roach's shoulder and interlocking their fingers. It was silent for an hour before Roach finally broke it: "Honeybee?"

"Yeah?" he said sleepily.

Roach had spent the past hour mentally preparing himself for what he would do next, but his hand was still trembling and palm sweaty as he stealthily slid a small box from his left pocket. He coughed to force away his nervousness, and after another few minutes of quiet, he flicked open the box and let it sit flat in his hand on Silvino's lap. His voice was strangled with nervous hysteria and eye twitched as he finally managed to ask, "Will you marry me?"

Silvino was quiet and unmoving. Roach worried he was asleep, so he leaned away to look at his face. He wasn't asleep: he was crying happy tears, and when he looked into Roach's eyes, he let himself be taken by the deep whirling rapids of hazel-grey and wept. "Of course."

Roach let out a breath of relief and returned the smile before leaning in and kissing him deeply. When they retreated from each other's lips, Silvino tried to take the ring out of the box, but he accidentally fumbled it. It started to fall down the cliff, but before it had even made it a metre away, Roach pointed at it and brought it back to Silvino's lap telekinetically. "Butterfingers," he teased.

"Sorry."

"Let me." He took the box then Silvino's left hand to slip on the ring, after which he kissed his knuckles. "Do you like it?"

Silvino observed it. It was a silver band handmade by Roach with a large design on the top of a gold honeybee with a heart around it. On the inside, it had, 'Love you forever, honeybee,' engraved. "I love it, Clay." He looked up and kissed him, but in the midst of their kiss they heard some conversations in the distance and quickly retreated to hide their illegal love.

Roach scrambled to his feet away from the cliff and brought Silvino to his side telekinetically. "Let's get your pictures taken and start heading back down."

"Okay... fiancé." Roach blushed a deep crimson, unable to hide how flustered the word made him. Silvino giggled evilly and teased, "I guess we'll have to talk over the wedding plans in the car, hm?"

Thyne was driving, and the only other people awake in the bus were the twins. The tenor to Roach's voice was as dejected as he had seemed the entire trip thusfar, and he spoke matter-of-factly in Arabic after a half hour of quiet: "You lied to me."

River looked up from the chess game on his phone and arched his brow. "When?"

"'Gymnastics camp.'"

He arched his brow. "What are you talking about? I never went to any gymnastics camp."

"Exactly. You said you didn't have anything else you were keeping secret from me."

"I have no idea what you're talking about, Tony."

"Summer of '68?"

He took a moment to recall the summer and had a visible realisation, sitting more upright as his own mind startled him. "Wait…."

"You came back from 'gymnastics camp' and told me you loved me and we fucked in the car."

"I remember the confession and love-making," he muttered.

"So why didn't you tell me about the hospital?"

He held his head. "Hospital?"

Roach raised his brow. "Yeah. The hospital Dad sent you to."

"I… Tony, I don't remember that summer at all."

Roach crossed the bus to sit beside his brother and wrapped an arm around him loosely. "That's probably for the best."

River looked at him with sparkling pitiful eyes. "What? What do you mean?"

"Dad told me he sent you to a mental hospital."

"He what?" He let out a whimper as he desperately withheld tears. "Why?"

Roach shook his head and pulled River into his arms to hold him more tightly. "I love you, Sonny. I'm sorry for bringing it up. Let's watch something, no?"

He weakly agreed and followed his brother to the cramped sofa-chair where he was held as they watched a few old episodes of *One Piece* that Dale had downloaded onto the bus' television. He focused as much on the show and his brother's warm embrace as possible, but his mind kept trying to reel back to the summer of 2068 to uncover whatever horrors his otherwise perfect memory had hidden from him.

Cloud Peak Prison was only the first on their quest around the country, and by the time they were in Montana, they had already hit another forty-five. The jobs were all similar: sneak up to the prison under cover of darkness and rain, kill the guards, free the prisoners, raze the building. Rinse and repeat. Rory was slowly getting the hang of the violence, and when they stopped at their forty-sixth prison in the west of Montana, he domed three guards and shot another three in their thighs, letting them bleed to death and stealing their guns. The adrenaline pumping through him had him trembly at every stop, but Dale and Partha's unwavering airs inspired him enough that by the fifty-eighth prison, on May seventh, he was confident enough to take a hall on his own when they fanned out.

The months passed quickly with so much action, so it was rare for them to have a moment of quiet. While in Montana and Idaho, Roach was less upset, but the closer they neared to the West Coast, the more the cloud over his head was forming again. Springtime brought with it new challenges in the form of an ever-rising temperature. They hadn't expected Baumbach to be so resilient. According to River's calculations, that the company had lost almost sixty prisons and was still outright thriving was unexpected and discouraging to say the least.

Though Roach had told Perlie they would return in December, it was only established as the date they would return if they razed every last Baumbach prison. Other than Roach, who had been pessimistic and downtrodden the entire trip, it was the general consensus, at least at first, that they would not need to destroy nearly that many. It was River's thinking, as the December date seemed increasingly realistic, that Baumbach must have been getting bailed out with tax dollars.

Washington and Oregon were brimming with prisons, so (with some backtracking back into Idaho) by July eighth, they had hit another sixty prisons and were only just then entering California. Two days later, on only their third resting day of the entire job, Partha received a call at about noon:

"Yes, heart?" he said with a yawn.

"Would you like to meet your son?"

His eyes immediately watered, and he hurried to look at the pictures Perlie had sent of her holding the newborn. "He's beautiful," he wept, "I'm sorry I'm not there."

"You just stay safe, kid. I love you."

"I love you so much." He sniffled and wiped his eyes. "I'm a shite dad already."

"No you aren't. You stop it. You're saving the world." He tried to smile and thank her but whimpered and sniffled instead. "His name is Sirion Jae Bellamy."

"What does the J stand for?" There was a beat where she glared softly but with a loving air. "Oh! Your father's name."

"Yeah, kid," she said with a chuckle.

They continued talking until the sun started to set outside the bus' windows, after which Partha heard the others starting to stir. The baby was hungry by then, so Perlie let Partha hear his little coos before ending the call, and Partha immediately started showing the pictures to everyone in the bus.

"Congrats, kid," said Roach with a slap on his upper back.

"Thank you, sir."

"You've really manned up since I first met you. Proud of you. You'll be a great dad." There was a hint of sadness behind his words. Perhaps envy. He had always wanted to be a father, but he was glad to at least be Sirion's 'Cool Uncle Roach.'

After seeing his son, a fire lit under Partha's ass. He refused to wait to hold him until December, so after buying some supplies from a craft store, he locked himself up in the bedroom for the next three days, staying in the bus with the kitten while the others killed guards, freed prisoners, and razed buildings.

By July seventeenth and over half a million prisoners freed, they were still only in San Francisco, with their next stop being Alcatraz, refurbished as one of Baumbach's first prisons. To reach the island, they stole a sailboat. Francis elected to stay ashore and would meet up with the others on the island after freezing time and walking to it. It was therefore up to Partha to captain the others successfully through the storm Francis was conjuring. With Roach and River's telekinesis, which the others had gathered by then had no limit on its range so long as the twins could see what they were doing, they killed any guards that may have shot them on their approach and docked beside a small cargo ship.

Rory expressed a fear of ghosts inside, and when Thyne scolded and mocked him for it, Roach slapped the back of the Brit's head and said sadly, "Let him stay in the boat. Place is haunted as shit."

"Th-thank you, sir," said Rory.

"Keep your head down. Shoot any prisoners that get close."

He nodded, Roach sniffled and coughed away his upset, and with a pat on Rory's head, they met with Francis on the docks and went inside. After releasing the prisoners, Rory had to kill ten of them before the others had returned to the docks, and after sailing back to the city, Partha stopped everyone from leaving the boat. He took a big black sheet of some sort from his backpack and said with a determined furrow in his brow: "I'm going back to Rome to see my son. Who's coming with me?" Saying this, he dropped open the folded-up sheet to reveal a handmade pirate flag. It had a black base with a white lion's skull in the centre.

"You're so cute, dude," said River as he rustled Partha's short black hair.

Roach commanded, "Rory, Dezba, Poppie, you go with him. He'll need the extra hands. Drop my sister off in Egypt, kid."

"Yes, sir," he saluted. "I plan to sail up to Canada to get a flight."

"Sounds good. How will you be paying?"

"I've been stealing cash from the last ten prisons."

"Won't it be suspicious to pay with American money?" asked Dezba. Partha opened his mouth to reply but didn't have a good response. He hadn't thought of that.

Thyne groaned and took a handful of cash out of his own wallet. "There. That should be enough. You know how to get a hold of me if you need Francis' help, but remember that he's afraid of the open ocean."

Partha hugged his friend tightly. "Thank you, Thyne."

"Yeah yeah," he patted his back grumpily but eventually returned the embrace more lovingly. "I'll miss you, mate. You be careful, okay?"

He retreated and wiped his eyes. "We'll see you back in Rome."

After more hugs were passed around, Thyne, Dale, and the twins hopped out of the boat onto the docks and met with Francis back at the bus, informing him of Partha's plan when he inevitably asked where the others were.

Despite the lack of manpower, the gang still handily razed another twenty prisons by the time they had reached Orange County. As they passed through Compton, they stopped by Roach and River's apartment to sleep in a proper building and relax. When they were settled inside, Thyne called Partha. They had just found their way into Canada and were hitchhiking to an airport. After making everyone an admittedly lovely tuna casserole, Roach praised Rory and Partha's work and dropped down on his sofa to light up a bowl. The call went on for another ten minutes while they ate, after which Thyne hung up, took a guitar off of the wall behind Roach, and sat beside him strumming and plucking improvised melodies on it. Seeing this, Roach beamed and took out his harmonica to jam with him.

They played together for an hour, after which Thyne stopped to stretch and yawn. Roach smiled softly and held out his arm to invite Thyne into it. Francis was sitting on the other side of him, so he held out his other arm once Thyne was comfortable with a blanket over him. Francis took the invitation to cuddle, and Roach frowned at River, who was sitting in Dezba's rocking chair across from him. "I need more arms."

"It's okay, Tony. I'm in a tourney right now anyway."

Thyne yawned and asked in a tiny voice, "What kind?"

"Magic."

"Good luck," he said as his eyes slipped closed.

With Thyne asleep and Francis drinking as he snuggled up with him, Roach used the arm around Francis to put a cigarette between his lips, light it, then leaned his head on the back of the couch to puff on it without using his hands or telekinesis, letting the ashes fall onto his cheeks. River finished his tournament a while later and went to bed after a tender kiss from Roach, seeing as everyone in the room knew about them. The hazy air was serene.

Dale drank a beer as he read one of Roach's books, but after another half hour, his air tensed. He ran a hand through his hair and said, "Roach, Ah'm sorry. Ah was gon' wait 'til ev'ryone went ta bed, but we's gotta talk 'bout these prison jobs."

"Sure, man. What's up?" He looked down at the men in his arms and noticed it was only Francis who was awake to hear Dale anyway.

"Well, Ah been trackin' Baumbach's finances as we been goin', an' Ah done some math. Had yer brother triple check it fer me too, and, ways we sees it, we got two opshuns."

"Oh? And what are they?"

"Ah'll put it this way: if we wanna take Baumbach down fer good, we can only 'fford ta skip *one* prison, 'specially while they's buying up more ta counter what we's doin'." Roach took a moment to process what he meant and went pale when he realised. "Yeah. Ye see the issue then."

"Yeah."

"An' so we gotta figger it out 'fore we leave Californee."

"What are the options?" asked Francis.

"What Dale's saying is that we're either going to have to hit the prison in Death Valley, or we're going to have to go to the one where Silvino died...."

"Oh." Francis took Roach's hand in his and let him squeeze it. "Perchance I could destroy the one in the desert alone."

"I don't want to risk that, bed bug. It got to be over 200 degrees in Death Valley last summer."

"Aye, but when time is stopped, it is all absolute zero."

Roach pondered the offer but shook his head and asserted, "No, Franky. We're skipping Death Valley. If something were to happen, we wouldn't be able to save you."

"And when I trek across the sea it is much the same. I cannot swim; I sink like a stone: if something happens in those instances I am equally as lost."

"Then I don't want you crossing the ocean either, bed bug."

Francis pursed his lips, and Dale said, "Ye're sure, Roach?"

"Yeah. When we get there, if I can't handle it, I'll just wait in the bus." A sigh. "It'll be fine. Whatever. Let's just relax for the night and think about all this heavy shit tomorrow. It's ruining my high."

"Ah'ight. Ah'm sorry 'gain, Clay."

"It's chill, man. Get some sleep."

"You too."

Roach was the first to drive the bus the next evening. The cloud over his head from the rest of the trip had returned by the time he was behind the wheel and pulling into the gas station where he had brought Silvino at the very start of their trek across the states. He parked at a diesel pump and let Dale fill the tank as he rested his head on the steering wheel. He squeezed his eyes hard enough to see stars and bit his lip until it bled to keep himself from crying.

Everyone filed out of the bus, but River came up to Roach in the driver's seat and rubbed his arched back. "I'm sorry this is so hard for you, habibi. Vinny's with you in spirit."

"God, I hope not."

"Why not?" They made eye contact, and River practically read his brother's mind. He was self-loathing and worried that Silvino would hate who he had become. River sighed as Roach slammed his forehead back onto the wheel. "He loved you, Tony." He didn't respond, so after kissing his cheek, River left the bus and went into the store.

"Ay! It's Roachy boy!" said the clerk as River came inside.

He took on a more casual and playful air like his brother on a good day and made finger-guns at the clerk. "Beefy! Got anything good back there?"

"I'll check in a minute. Haven't seen you in ages, man. Where ya been?"

"Oh, y'know. The usual."

"Getting into trouble?" He laughed.

"Oh yeah."

"Nice to see you, man."

River nodded and found Thyne in one of the aisles holding a bag of circus peanuts with a befuddled expression. He held them up to River and asked, "Are these... edible?"

"Yeah, man. Tony loves those things. I like 'em, too, to be honest." He grabbed two packages of them and two bags of black licorice before slinking off to the coffee bar to make Roach a cup. He was the last to come back onto the bus, but the first to approach the driver's seat without being shooed away. He crouched down beside his brother and whispered, "I got you goodies." Roach looked at him with slight intrigue, so River showed him the circus peanuts, licorice, black coffee, cigarettes, and bag of week-old taquitos. "It's gonna be okay, habibi. You want me to stay up here with you?"

Roach sniffled and sat up, nodding as he wiped his sleeves across his face. "Thanks, Sonny. I love you."

"I love you, too." He pulled out a bottle of seltzer and cracked it open to drink. "This place got a stereo? Why don't we play some music?"

"Yeah. Uh... ask Dale."

"Alright, I'll be back. Don't eat all the candy. I want some, too."

With Dale's help, a sound system played old rock music across the entire bus, and Roach started the southerly drive toward San Diego wherein stood the last Californian Baumbach prison they would actually attempt to hit.

River's gut was churning as they approached the prison. He hadn't been this nervous for any of the others, so he passively wondered what was so different about this one. It was the smallest prison thusfar and the least heavily guarded even after Baumbach had started upping its defences to counter their attacks. The rain Francis had conjured was refreshing in the oppressive So-Cal heat, and the friends surrounding him exuded love and lightness even in the moonless dark of midnight. So... why was he so nervous?

He and his brother killed guards telekinetically on their way to the gates, and after bending said gates open together, the twins led the charge into the cramped one-storey building. Where most of the prisons to that point had bars across the entirety of their cells, the standard cells in this building more resembled boxes for solitary confinement. They had doors with slit-windows to the halls but no windows to the outside in the cells themselves. There were at least two inmates to a room, sometimes up to four, despite how small the spaces were.

After the guards had all been killed, River wandered the halls with an ambling pace and his hazel-greys lazily scanning all around him. Something was... odd... about this place.

Something felt... *familiar.*

It came back to him in flashes:

"Karson. Karson, sit down." He climbed down from where he had been standing on the sofa-chair and sat on the scratchy grey rug in front of it. "Why are you sitting on the floor?" He didn't respond, and the psychiatrist wrote something on her cork-board. "I've been told you've been having trouble using the restroom. It's not bulimia again, so what's the problem now?"

He went pale. His spine stiffened. "The mirror...."

River shook his head and left the room that was sparking these memories. He resumed wandering through the halls, vaguely remembering the layout of the building as he made his way to a records room. He tore open filing cabinets and thumbed through the "R" files in search of his own, but it was only prison rap sheets. After knocking two of the cabinets to the ground angrily, he reached up his hand to telekinetically crush the buzzing fluorescent light in the room and shouted out a scream as another unwelcome memory forced its way into his reeling mind:

> *pins and needles and pins and needles and pins and needles and pins and needles and pins and needles and pins and needles and pins and needles and pins and needles and pins and needles and pins and needles and pins and....*

He tore off the gown as it burned through his skin and threw it on the floor before clawing off his socks, on the bottom of which were a thousand little cleated daggers. His fingers screamed out in pain as he dared to touch and grab things so furiously, but he couldn't take it anymore. Every touch, no matter how slight, was like a million pins and needles burning and biting and stinging and stabbing. He looked down at his naked body and saw a million metal millipedes crawling all over it: the imagined cause of all the tingling. They all faded to nothing when the door to his room was slammed open. He screamed and tried to run from the nurses, but they were grabbing him and scolding him for being indecent and ignoring his cries of pain. "Please," he whimpered, "Please don't touch me."

"We told you already, if you took off your clothes again, we'd have to put you in a jacket to keep you decent."

"No! Please. Please. Please. Please. Please. Please. Please...."

His begging fell on deaf ears, and within the hour he was back in his room with his hands pinned to his sides and thus even more cloth burning through his flesh and tearing into his overstimulated nerves.

After leaving the records room he shouted loud enough to catch Francis' attention, who appeared in front of him and gently cupped his hand under River's forearm. *"What ails thee?"*

"GET OFF OF ME!"

He shoved Francis to the ground and rubbed his arm where it had been touched as mad tears trailed his cheeks. He grabbed the sides of his head and tore off his headscarf as he stumbled around and pleaded with a higher power to, "Make it stop! God! Please! Make it stop!"

"...narcissist, yes. He's in love with his twin because he's in love with himself. He spent twenty minutes talking in a made-up language to the mirror last night. We had to take it out of his room to get him to shut up and go to sleep."

"I didn't sleep at all," he said dully.

"Karson?" An incensed smile. *"What did I tell you about talking while I'm updating your father?"*

"You don't remember? I guess it must be hard to remember much of anything at your age."

She glared and returned her attention to the phone. *"I'm sorry, sir, I'll have to call you back."* After hanging up, she stood, and River scrambled away. He tried to open the door, but it was locked from the outside, and before he could even consider breaking the handle off telekinetically, she had him in a chokehold and a needle injected into him. His flailing broke the needle off in his arm, but it was only a few seconds later that he felt like he weighed a million pounds.

He slumped like dead weight on her, and a group of nurses brought him to his room where he was strapped down in his bed. Not long later, he felt like he was drowning in his own drool, which burned his skin like everything else burned his skin as it trailed down his cheeks.

Some undetermined amount of time later, the same woman who had sedated him came into the room. She closed and locked the door behind her, saying something he couldn't cognise to someone in the hall, then came up to his bedside and feigned a frown.

"You know how much I hate to do this to you, Karson." Her hand trailed up his leg gently, pulling up his gown in the process. "I'll make it up to you, though."

She massaged his thighs like she liked to do, and the pins and needles from such rough touches brought pained tears to his already-blurred vision. The tears trailed down his temples feeling like drops of liquid magma and razor blades tearing him open. After the unwanted massage, she teased him with her fingers. Her touch was agonising, but it seemed only his mind could feel the pain, because his body, however sedated, was easily manipulated. It only took a moment for him to get a semi, which she promptly grabbed and started to stroke. "There we go. My good boy. So pretty when you're not flailing around or bullying everyone."

He felt like he was dying or already in Jahannam, being punished eternally for loving his brother, that incestuous sin. In an attempt to prove to himself that he was still alive, he tried to listen to his own breaths, unintentionally and unknowingly letting out haunting wailing sounds in time with her movements. "That's it. You like that, don't you? Tell me more about how you want to gag me and choke me, my mean little baby boy."

River collapsed to the floor in the foetal position, bawling as more horrorshows came pouring back into his perfect memory. Francis rushed to his side. "Poor darling. I'll fetch your brother."

He disappeared and reappeared a moment later with Roach by his side. "Sonny! What's wrong? Are you hurt?"

He grabbed at Roach's arm limply with a trembling hand. "Tony," he whimpered, "*Help me.*"

Roach wrapped him up in his arms and held him tight. "I'm here. What's wrong? How do I help?"

"Make it stop."

"Make what stop, habibi?"

"The memories…."

He looked around and, after a moment of thought, snapped his gaze to Francis. "Did this place used to be an asylum?"

"Yes," said Francis.

"Shit. I'm getting him out of here. Finish the job without us."

"Aye." He frowned at River's pitiful state and disappeared again.

As Roach picked him up and started rushing through the halls, River squeezed his eyes shut to avoid remembering more. Unfortunately, as they passed through a hall near an emergency exit, the smell of bleach mixed with the fetor of pollution outside and assaulted his senses, bringing back the clearest memory thusfar:

He was coming up from another round of powerful sedatives while the nurse pushing his wheelchair walked with Oba. River was only allowed to speak to his father once prior to the visit, and he had spent the entire call begging him in Arabic to be brought home. Oba had callously rejected the request. He told him not to speak Arabic in the hospital and that the family would think he was at gymnastics camp. He told him to keep that lie up, "or else," so River, on top of everything, was worried about his weight.

"Thank you for coming out here, Mr. Roach. We're having so much trouble helping your son," said the nurse as she wheeled him toward the cafeteria for lunch, "When you first admitted him, he was refusing to talk to the doctors at all, but now he spends most of his sessions with the psychiatrist insulting her and refusing to answer her questions. He's so mean! I couldn't believe some of the things he was saying."

"Yeah, he's a little asshole," agreed Oba with a chuckle. "I don't mind him being rude, but have you fixed... the other thing... yet?"

"No, sir. He's constant trouble. We had him in a normal room, but we caught him inducing vomit in himself after dinner, so we had to move him to a room with cameras to stop the bulimia and make sure he kept his medicine down. Then the cameras were how we were able to catch him constantly taking off all his clothes and exercising. He'd work out until we told him to stop, then he would just stare into the camera like a demon. He did it basically every day. When an exorcism did nothing, we tried the straitjacket, but he kept doing it until the fourth or fifth night in the jacket. After that, even though he wasn't getting naked anymore, we kept having to sedate him because he'd exercise too hard. For hours and hours sometimes.

"Anyway, he got into this nasty habit of lying to us, so a lot of our research was set back when we realised. He had said his skin hurts. He said that's why he kept getting naked, but after checking the dosages on all his medicines, we've determined that he's just trying to get off of them. They shouldn't be affecting his nerves at all."

"He's always been a little over dramatic. Him and his brother both."

She chuckled. "Yeah, but even though he's not very forthright with us, he's continued to say he loves his brother and wants to sin and do evil evil things. He once detailed to Dr. Quixote how he wanted to gag her and hear her breaths stop and see her soul leave her body. He accused her of unspeakable unchristian things to defend *himself, so we had to change his medicines to stop all the nasty violent thoughts he was suffering."*

"Has... the doctor been investigated? Did she touch my son?"

"Oh, no need to worry, Mr. Roach. She would never. It's just another one of Karson's trademarked lies." She tapped his head lightly. It felt like a sledgehammer.

He mumbled a curse under his breath, but she didn't hear him as she stopped pushing his chair and took Oba into a nearby room to have a more private conversation. Alone, River blinked until his vision was less blurry and heaved his breaths to bring his heartrate back up from near-death. After making himself more present and alive again, he bolted out of the chair toward the exit, slowing to a casual stride before passing the front desk.

"Hey! Come here, son." He approached the secretary and leaned on the reception desk nonchalantly. "What's your room number?"

"Oh, I don't have a room anymore. The doctors are letting me leave."

He lied so flawlessly that she blinked away some of her surprise and looked down at her computer. "Oh... okay, well let me just make a call to get you back in your street clothes. Name?"

Rather than answer, he bolted for the door. The sweet smell of freedom was cut short only six paces out of the building, replaced with the searing of his own flesh as he dropped to the ground with two probes from the front guard's taser in his back.

He was dragged back inside. When he could move again, he tried to flail and writhe and wriggle himself free, but another needle in his arm was quick to add the weight of the world back onto his chest.

Roach brought him to the bus and laid him down in the bed. "Sonny, it's okay. You're safe now. Do you want some water?"

He nodded, but when Roach tried to go to the fridge, he grabbed the leg of his pants and shouted, "Don't go!"

He sat beside him and pet his hair. "Shh. Sonny. I'm right here. I'm not going anywhere. It's okay. Here." He took out his cigarettes and offered one to his brother, which was taken weakly. "You want it?" River nodded vaguely, so Roach lit it for him in his own mouth then slipped it between his brother's lips after a peck. Having never smoked in his life, the feeling was strange and not nearly as soothing as he had imagined it would have been. As he pet his hair and held his trembling hand, Roach sweetly hummed the song he had written for River that was tattooed on their arms.

After smoking half of the useless durry, River dropped it on the bed beside him and, as Roach stopped it from starting a fire, said simply, "I died."

"You died?"

"In that hospital." Roach's lip quivered, and the hand he was using to clean the cigarette clenched into a white-knuckled fist. He should have killed his father when he had the chance. "When they put me under for some procedure…. They said it'd finally 'fix' me. That I'd stop loving you. That I'd stop sinning." He sniffled and squeezed his brother's hand. His voice was quavering when he started back up: "I died. I was back on Aeteriodorum, where I had been before we were born. Back in my godly form. Faers was nearby, saw me, and asked where you were. I couldn't get a word out before he probed my mind. He told me to go back for you and revived me. I gasped so deeply when I came-to that it physically hurt. It was like I couldn't get enough air in my lungs for four breaths straight, no matter how much I gasped for it. When they noticed I was alive again, the doctors and nurses helped me back to my room and, a few hours later, a nurse brought me to Dr. Quixote." He whimpered and averted his gaze as more memories of her abuse came back to him.

Roach cupped his hand around River's face and wiped away his tears. "Sonny, you don't have to tell me if you don't want to. You don't have to relive this."

"She asked, 'How do you feel about your brother?' And, truthfully, I said, 'I don't.'"

"'You don't what?' she asked."

"'I don't feel anything at all.'" He wept fervently and let Roach hold him. After ten minutes, he retreated and wiped his eyes. "I didn't love you. I didn't want you. I wasn't happy or sad or angry. All I was, was scared. So scared and cold and lonely. And you know what she said when I told her I couldn't feel anything anymore? … She said I was cured." Another three minutes of crying. "She said I was cured, so she sent me back home after a week. A week where I was the walking dead. Where all I felt was scared and cold. It was August, but I was so… so cold." A sniffle. "I remember when I got home, Dad made spaghetti. I remember everyone asking what camp was like. I remember sounding like a drone when I answered, and I remember, for hours, not looking at you. Not *daring* to look at you. I was afraid to look at you like I was afraid of the mirror."

"But you did look at me," whispered Roach.

He smiled sadly and nodded. "Yeah, Tony, I did. And when I did, you know what happened?"

"What happened?"

His smile grew and met with the tears streaming from his sparkling greys. "When I looked at you, I started to forget all the horrors. Like your soul was blacking out the memories for me. *Just by looking at you.*" He sniffled and wiped his arm across his face. "When I looked at you, Tony… I could feel again."

"Oh, Sonny!" He wrapped his arms around him and joined him in weeping.

"I love you, Clayton. Thank you for saving me."

"I love you so much. You're safe now, habibi."

⚙ Chapter 69 ⚙

Keep a Weather Eye
on the Horizon

Silvino's stomach was doing flips on the ride from Compton to his house in the hills. He chewed his lip and avoided eye contact with Cleo. As soon as the car was parked, he opened his door and slinked inside, attempting to rush to his room without being seen by his parents. His father was outside in the pool, but his mother was in the kitchen and heard him come in. She rushed to meet up with her son, whom she hadn't seen at all during his year-long trek around the states with Roach. She only caught a glimpse of him as he turned a corner on the mezzanine and shuttered himself in his room. His breaths were heavy and hands trembling as he took out his rosary and begged God to have mercy on him.

"Vinny, why are you hiding away?" asked his mother. A thought struck her and furrowed her brow. "Did he hit you!?"

"No," he shouted through the door he was leaning on, "No, Mamá, please just leave me be."

"Leave you be? I haven't seen you in an entire year. Open this door." She jiggled the handle.

"No. You're mad at me."

"Of course I am; you're a criminal now! Open the door."

"No!" He shoved a chair under the knob and locked himself in the bathroom, hiding in the behemoth shower as he resumed praying. He heard his mother through the wall shouting that he had to come out of there eventually and taunting that she had asked the cooks to make his favourite dessert, German chocolate cake, to celebrate his return.

It took six hours, but he eventually mustered up the courage to face his parents despite how sick it made him to imagine what might happen when he went downstairs. He navigated the mansion and descended a winding marble staircase in the front of the house on his way to the lounge, where he heard his parents chatting and ordering the servants around. After pulling one of the sleeves of Roach's hoodie he had stolen down over the tattoo on his hand, he shuffled anxiously into the room.

"The man of the hour," said his father with a drunken hic, "Come sit down. Let's talk." The way his voice wound down at the end of the demand was downright ominous.

He shuffled to the ottoman across from his parents' plush sofa chairs and lowered himself onto it, holding his knees and forcing a smile. "Hola...."

"So...," began his mother as she set down her glass of wine and made a lazy gesture at the butler beside her to refill it, "you've got a record now."

He gulped. "Sí, Mamá."

"You better have a good story. Spit it out."

"You also smell like cigarettes. Have you been smoking, son?"

"No, Papa. This is Roach's hoodie."

"Tell us why you got arrested," said his mother.

His voice was trembling, teetering between sobbing and mumbling: "We spray painted a statue of Elijah Park together...."

She held her forehead and let out a slew of Spanish curses that were tame by most standards but unthinkable for her. He gulped as his father piped up: "This Clayton boy is no good for you. Stand up."

"W-why, sir?"

"I said stand up, so fucking stand up, Silvino." He stood and shoved his trembling hands into his pockets. "Take that urchin's sweater off this instant."

"B-but, Papa, I—."

He slammed the table between the sofa chairs hard enough that it rattled the glasses on it loudly. "Do as you're told!"

He pulled off the sweater and actively stopped himself from hyperventilating as he held it in a ball in front of him, trying to hide his gut and the tattoo simultaneously.

"Son, you put that fucking rag down on the ground right now, or it's going in the fireplace." He threw it on the ground, tears falling beside it between his sniffles. "Look at him, Eva." She looked up briefly only to wail into her hand to resume weeping and cursing. "Warren!" A servant approached and bowed. "Find a trainer for Silvino. He's gained at least another thirty pounds. How much have you gained with that cretin, son? Is he force-feeding you?" Silvino only gulped and shook his head. "It's no matter. The trainer will fix you." Silvino whimpered at the comment, but he was silenced by another slam of his father's fist on the table. "Shut your snivelling mouth, boy! Maybe we shouldn't have been so lenient, Eva. Maybe letting him be gay is making him weaker."

She looked at her son again, spotted the tattoo on his hand, and started muttering about it in her Spanish cursing.

His father stood and encroached on him, stepping on Roach's sweater in the process and kicking it angrily when it nearly tripped him. "Show it to me!" Silvino immediately raised his hand to show the tattoo and bit his lip to stop from calling when his father grabbed his wrist hard enough to bruise and observed the roach tattooed on the back of his hand. "Disgusting." He spit on it and threw Silvino's arm down. As he walked back to his seat, Silvino shoved his hands under his armpits anxiously, but it pulled up the shirt on the front of his belly, so he rushed to tug it down with both hands before his father would turn back around and see.

Eva listened to her husband as he sat back down and leaned over to whisper something to her. When he was finished with the secret message, her gaze immediately snapped to Silvino, and she rushed up to him to grab the same hand his father had observed. "What is this!?" She tried to take off his ring, but it caught on his knuckle, and he snatched his hand away to cover it with his other.

"It's my engagement ring. I'm marrying him. I love him."

"¡Dios mío!" Silvino's eyes widened hearing his mother take the Lord's name in vain. "You will not marry him. I forbid it. You do not love him. You're just enticed by him because he is a bad bad sinful boy with the devil in his soul."

"No, Mamá. I'm marrying him. I love him with my whole heart."

"Oh do you?" said his father. His tone was quiet, but his face was red with rage. "Then you'll have no trouble with this: it's him or us."

His mother looked at him for his answer.

"W-what? What do you mean, Papa?"

"This boy is a bad influence on you."

"The worst," agreed Silvino's former nanny as she cleaned a spotless mirror.

Silvino's brow furrowed. "No he isn't. He's a good man. He taught me how to drive. He saved my fucking life." He pulled down his shirt's collar to show the top of his scar. "He makes me happy. He thinks I'm beautiful. He makes me feel loved and appreciated, all of which is more than I can say for any of you." He covered his mouth as soon as he said such a cruel thing and quivered at the subsequent wrath that crossed their faces.

His father stood and shouted, "He is a BAD INFLUENCE. He got you ARRESTED. We won't be paying your bail again, Silvino, and we certainly won't be paying his. Call him and tell him it's over this instant, or you'll be living on the street by tomorrow."

"You can't just kick me out!"

"I am your father. I can do whatever I please to you," he said through gritted teeth as the rage simmered down but by no means dissipated, "You will call him, or you will leave my property immediately."

No longer able to stop himself from hyperventilating, he collapsed and bawled madly into his hands, but when he heard his father stepping closer, he scrambled backwards, grabbing Roach's sweater in the process and cuddling it. "I'm calling him," he cried.

"I don't see your phone."

He nodded and removed his phone from his pocket. His hands were shaking so tremendously that he could hardly navigate it, but he eventually managed to start the call. While it was ringing, his father demanded he put it on speaker-phone, so Silvino did as he was told.

"Hello, honeybee," answered Roach, "Haven't been answering my messages. Been busy with the folks? My family loves Malfeasance and the story of how I saved her from that gator. She's so cute: I sent you pictures." His voice was so happy, it made Silvino cry harder. After a moment of quiet, Roach asked, "Hello? Are you there?"

"I'm here," he whimpered and sniffled.

"What's wrong, sweetie?" His hyperventilating resumed for a few breaths before he sobbed something incoherently. "Ya Allah! You sound horrified. What's wrong? I'm coming over."

"Don't!" he shouted.

Silvino's father whispered in Spanish: "If I see that boy again, I'll put a bullet through his skull."

"Don't come. Don't come, Roach. I'm breaking up with you."

He was completely blindsided. "Huh? Why?"

"I'm breaking up with you." He wept, and Roach's stomach sank into the bowels of the earth.

"It's your parents, isn't it? Capitalist fucks."

He looked up at his father helplessly, who was shaking his head. With his gaze back on the phone and hardly able to see anything through his tears, he said, "No... It's... because of the cigarettes."

"What? Dude, why didn't you say you had a problem with it on the trip if—." Silvino hung up and wailed into his hands.

"Now.... Go to your room without dinner. God knows you don't need it."

He scooped up Roach's hoodie and rushed to his room, locking himself inside and curling up under his covers to cuddle the sweater and the big plush dinosaur the servants had brought up with the rest of his luggage.

Back on track, the gang continued destroying Baumbach prisons. The company was haemorrhaging investors almost as quickly as it was losing prisoners, but Dale's calculations held true. They would need to go to the prison outside of Dallas where Silvino had died. Still, for Roach's sake, they gave it a wide berth and stalled going there, hoping it would eventually become unnecessary.

By September twenty-seventh, they had destroyed 200 prisons and freed over 800,000 inmates with no regard for why they were imprisoned in the first place. Some of them were violent, but there were also people jailed for selling or doing drugs even as mild as marijuana, for holding nonchristian religious beliefs, for not presenting as heterosexual, and for being transgendered. The uptick in freed criminals led directly to surges in people looking for work and housing in the wake of *The Crown's* interference, and it helped that a majority of the violent inmates, as well as a handful of the non-violent ones, were committing numerous crimes, thus keeping the police busy. Child abusers were killed by murderers. Neo-nazis were killed by gang members, then the gangs turned on each other. The police were scrambling to deal with the issue, for they had little recourse with everless prisons in their jurisdictions. All in all, though, it wasn't much more crime than usual, which bolstered Roach's arguments for anarchy when he had little tiffs with Thyne.

They were in the homestretch by November, with only forty-eight prisons left to hit. They would start with some new ones in Kansas, bought by Baumbach specifically because of their attacks. After clearing Kansas, they would work their way south, passing Dallas to favour the prisons in and around Austin to attempt avoiding the prison where Silvino had died. Before their jobs in Kansas, they stopped for some rest, parking in a prairie far from any trace of civilization, and tried to get some sleep. Roach awoke in the middle of their break to pray, and when he was finished, Dale approached to ask, "Wanna go huntin'?"

"Sure, man."

"Git yer gun."

While they were hunting, the others eventually stirred and chatted in the bus, nursing coffees and juices to wake themselves up. Sleeping during the day was proving difficult, especially for Thyne, who had trouble sleeping at any time, but it was a part of the reason they had yet to have Dale's bus be associated with the attacks. Dale and Roach returned two hours after the last of them awoke. They showed off their kills: a beaver, two cottontail rabbits, and a prairie chicken. Thyne, Francis, and River migrated out of the bus to sit around the fire Dale had built while Roach cooked. Dale went back inside to feed his kitten, not so little anymore, and played with her while he waited for his midnight breakfast.

"The stars are so pretty out here," said River after some quiet.

The other three all looked up at the vast canopy of stars and each smiled softly. There was a long beat of silence, broken only by the crackling fire, before Roach returned his attention to the spit and said, "It's romantic."

"If I could," began Francis as he laid back in the grass, "I would cease my desperate attempts to reverse my blunders in favour of an endless gallivant through the cosmos with you three."

"Endless?" said Roach.

"Aye! There be endless beauty: why not an endless trek?"

Roach only sighed and let silence overtake them again as he cooked. Dale eventually brought him some spices he had requested, but he was quick to return to the bus. After plating a meal for each of those outside with him, Roach took Dale his food and invited him to come outside with them to watch the stars. Dale rejected the idea, sensing that Roach needed some time to be romantic with his lovers, so after grabbing a few beers, Roach returned to the campfire and made himself a plate. The food was hearty and filling, and there were leftovers enough for at least another meal when all was said and done.

With them packed up in the fridge, Roach double-checked that Dale didn't want to come outside, which continued to be the case, so he went back out and laid down in the grass, where he invited River, Thyne, and Francis to lay with him and watch the slow spinning sky together. Thyne laid between the twins, and Francis laid on Roach's opposite side, all four of them blushy and smiley in each other's arms. Dale napped in the bus while they were outside being sweet, passing around Francis' flask and telling each other stories from their pasts. Francis told tales of piracy amongst the stars as well as in his youth. Thyne talked about raising Rosemary in the Victorian era. Roach reminisced fondly about his late husband, and River... lied. He made up an untrue story, at the close of which Roach complained, "We were telling real stories, Sonny."

He took offence. After a moment of quiet, he sat up and took a deep breath to calm himself. "I'm trying not to bring the mood down. None of the real stories worth telling are happy...."

Roach pulled him back down into the cuddle-pile telekinetically and kissed him. "Pour your heart out, habibi. Break down in pieces if you need to. We'll put you back together when you're done."

He smiled sadly and sighed as he laid his head on Thyne's stomach. "Okay.... I guess I'll start with the hospital and work my way backwards to Aeteriodorum...."

After destroying the prisons in Kansas, they started their southerly drive toward Texas. The sun was rising by the time they reached the border of Oklahoma, but before crossing state-lines, they pulled off at a gas station to refuel. People went inside to stock up on snacks and drinks, and Roach prayed in the back of the bus. Dale bought some cat food and fed Monkey, who was looking less like a kitten by the day. River did a check-up on the engine, and after not too long, they were all only waiting on Thyne, who was still inside buying Ra energy drinks.

About ten minutes passed, after which Thyne rushed into the bus and interrupted the others' conversation about Partha's streams. He grabbed Francis by the wrist shouting, "Franky!" as he dropped the bags of snacks and drinks he had bought and pulled Francis off the bus.

"It seems I am wanted elsewh—," he was dragged outside before he could properly excuse himself, and everyone else followed curiously.

Thyne brought him to the edge of the parking lot and gestured with both arms at the vast plains ahead of them. "We're in Kansas," he said.

"Aye."

"Make me a tornado."

Roach had approached just in time to hear this and patted Thyne's head as he said, "Ding. You're a tornado."

He flailed his arms to push Roach off of him. "Bellend."

"Thyne, my darling, I cannot merely 'make a tornado.'"

"You can make it rain, so make it rain but... more."

He sighed. "There be not a cloud in the sky, dear. You ask much of me. Even if I were to succeed at creating a funnel, I would not be able to control it afterwards."

Thyne pouted and slid up close to Francis. He pressed himself into him and wrapped one arm around his bony shoulders so Francis would feel his muscles. After walking his fingers up Francis' chest, he touched his lips sensually and offered a big sparkly pair of amber eyes as he said, "Please, Frankenstein? Just a little one?"

"Don't listen ta him," said Dale on Francis' other side, "It's too dangerous."

Francis gulped. He was coming to attention in Thyne's grasp and trembling when he tried to pry Thyne's hand away from its place resting on his thumping heart. "I... shouldn't...," he said, but the words were strangled.

Dale tried to discourage him again, but Roach slid in between him and Francis to act as another devil on his shoulder: "Do it, bed bug. I want to see how powerful you are."

"Please," cooed Thyne as he batted his eyelashes and rubbed his hand up Francis' chest to hook around his shoulder.

With another gulp, he nodded and closed his eyes to get in touch with his relatively weak power over the weather. He could sense the pressure differences around him and increased them just enough to make a small harmless twister. He wasn't very powerful, so it would only be a quick sliver of cloud then it would dissipate.

Thunder whispered in the clouds that were forming. Hail began to batter the awning over the pumps, and all but Francis looked to the sky to see dark clouds rolling in. After twenty minutes, the entire landscape was dark and ominous enough that the owner of the store came outside and offered, "Y'all can get in the cellar with me if ya need."

When a tornado siren wailed in the distance, Dale sighed and said, "Ah'll go get the engine runnin'."

While Dale prepped the bus for fleeing, Francis, Thyne, and the twins were having their shins peppered by the hail bouncing off the asphalt as the midday sky became ever darker. Wind howled and pushed around the twins' long hair haphazardly; they both pulled up their long locks into messy ponytails, almost in tandem. It was only five minutes later that River said, "Look! There." He pointed to a vortex of clouds to their left, and Francis cursed under his breath. He had been trying to put the twister in the plains, but it was forming dangerously close.

At the sight, both Roach and Thyne pulled Francis close and bathed him in sensual kisses with Roach on his neck and Thyne on his lips. They were both taken by his power, but River was able to snap them out of it enough to bring them into the bus where Dale floored it to flee from the forming funnel-cloud. It touched-down just beside the gas station and would have definitely killed them if they hadn't fled when they did. Despite Francis' attempts to make it small and harmless, it gained power in only a matter of seconds and started churning through the land-scape ruthlessly, following them for a spell before turning suddenly, not toward the empty plains but toward a nearby town.

At a safe distance, Dale slowed to a stop, and they watched through the rain-battered windows as the storm grew to an unfathomable width and darkness, gobbling up the buildings with no remorse. Roach and Thyne were both made lecherously weak by the display of power, however unintentional it may have been. They were draping themselves over Francis and peppering him in kisses between glances at the wedge tornado tearing through the town.

After five minutes of relative quiet in the bus as they all watched the black storm destroy the suburban town, Roach's hysteria cracked out of him. He snort-laughed and held his aching abs as he fell to the ground cackling and nearly orgasming, overcome with his own insanity. After fifteen minutes, the storm started to wane, and Roach was brought telekinetically to the bed where he finally calmed down, his body aching from such a fit. Dale drove them into Oklahoma for the next few jobs, while Francis, Thyne, and River all joined Roach in the bed.

After another twenty prisons, in late November, they were in Austin and had determined that they would definitely have to hit Silvino's former prison. Dale seemed stressed about where to park in the city, so with no recourse for his best friend, Roach asked to go, "find some dinner," while the rest of them tried to find somewhere to hide the bus, which was camouflaged for the woodsy environment where he tended to park it and not at all a dense urban area like Austin. Roach's exit was followed immediately by his brother's who assured the others that by "find some dinner" Roach meant he would be dumpster diving in the relatively large city. River would instead find a proper establishment with food-grade offerings and took some cash from Dale to foot the bill.

With the twins gone, Dale continued for another half hour to find somewhere inconspicuous to park for the day and ended up in the parking lot of a Desert Mart. When River returned about an hour later with some Taco Bell, they ate then went into the store to stock up on supplies. By midnight, they still hadn't heard from Roach, so the attention all turned to Thyne. "Where is he?" asked Francis.

"He's still just… dumpster diving," replied Thyne with an air of embarrassment that he was in love with such a maniac. He rubbed his forehead and listened as, two minutes later, Roach spoke directly to him:

"Dude… this is the coolest thing I've ever fucking found in the trash. This is maybe the best day of my life. I might be a bit late. Good thing I stole some cash off this really cute British guy." He chuckled and took what he had found to the same Desert Mart they were parked outside of without any of them noticing.

Thyne patted his pockets and rolled his eyes while trying not to smile about his missing wallet.

"Is he okay?" asked Francis after another half hour.

"Yeah, he's just…," he sighed and rubbed the bridge of his nose, "He's just a muppet."

It wasn't for another hour that Roach finally knocked on the bus' door. Dale opened it for him, and he climbed on with only a bag of stale cheese crackers. "This is all I found to eat, but you guys… you guys I found something so amazing." He tossed the crackers haphazardly in Dale's direction and retreated to the bus' exit. He shouted inside before he revealed what he had: "I found the coolest shit ever in the dumpster." And with the preamble stated, he revealed to his friends a one-year-old child in a baby carrier. She was chewing on a toy he had bought for her and making cute little noises.

"What?" said Thyne with a shake of his head.

"This is my daughter! Look how cute!"

"Daughter?" said Dale.

"Yeah!" His smile was so wide and genuine that it disarmed anyone's misgivings about the assertion. "Look at her!"

"You can't just—," said Thyne before stopping himself.

"I fucking can, Thyne, and if you have a problem with it, you can fuck right off. She's my daughter. She had a little note in her carrier, but I only saved it in case she wants it when she's older. Her name is Ruin, and she's my precious little baby."

Thyne sighed and came up to the baby to caress her cheek gently. "I'm not really ready to raise another daughter after what happened to Rosemary, but I love you, Basil, so… I guess I'll just have to suck it up for you."

Roach beamed and kissed his cheek. "Thanks, sparkplug. It means a lot."

"I, too, will help raise the little one," agreed Francis as he came up and tickled her feet. She giggled adorably.

"Is this what you want, Tony? Some garbage-baby? Why not just give her to an orphanage?"

Roach glared. "I won't be putting her through that. Especially not in America right now. She's my daughter, and you're her uncle, so get used to it."

"Fine. Only because I love you, though. Kids are so gross."

"She won't be a kid forever," he said as he plucked her out of the carrier and smiled at her subsequent giggles. "Will you?" he said in a baby-voice before blowing a raspberry on her stomach and smiling wide at her subsequent laughter.

"This is... good," said Dale as Roach played with her, "Now Partha's son'll have a fren."

"Exactly, dude! I was thinking the same thing. If we can't prevent the war, at least Sirion and Ruin will have each other. I'm so excited, you guys." He set her back in the carrier and gave her one of the new plushes he had bought for her. "I've always wanted to be a dad. This is the best day of my life."

"What did the note say?" asked River.

"Here."

River read aloud: "'*This is Emily,*'" they all eyed Roach, but he was paying them no mind. "'*Her shots are all up to date. She was born September 21st, 2081. I couldn't afford her anymore. Please, if you find her, give her a good life. A better life than these overly-religious orphanages could. I tried to keep her as long as I could, but it's hard. I'm only 14. My dad told me to get rid of her... She's his....*'"

A heavy cloud weighed down the crew, but Roach was still beaming at his new child and making her giggle. "I love her more than anything," he said eventually.

Thyne kissed Roach's cheek with a hand over one of his broad shoulders. "And I love *you* more than anything, Basil. I hope she can handle having so many father-figures."

Roach smiled sweetly at Thyne and kissed him. "Thank you, sparkplug."

Chapter 70

The Reeking Odour of a
Thousand Rotting Corpses

Silvino had spent the past three months moping about the mansion. His trainer was as verbally abusive as his parents, so he had developed an aversion to food, losing all of the weight he had gained on the trip around the country. Even without the weight, he felt heavier than ever with his broken heart like an anchor in his chest. In an attempt to cheer him up, his parents secured him his first voice-acting role as an adult, but when they tried to surprise him with the news and a big house party where he could network even further, he holed himself up in his room and refused to leave.

After the party, his mother came to his room and tried her best to be comforting, but he didn't say a single word to her for the entire thirty minutes she was sitting on the side of his bed and petting his shoulder. He didn't even look at her. It was her idea to sell the plush Roach had won him. It sold to one of the few fans of Silvino's web-comics for a measly $300, and when he tried to decline the offer, his mother closed out the deal behind his back and sent it away. He was afraid the hoodie would be next, so he never let it out of his sight.

"I know you hate me right now," she had said, "but you'll thank me later. He's tempting you to sin. We just want what's best for you, Vinny. We love you."

After she finally left and the noise of the servants cleaning up downstairs started to wane, Silvino looked at his engagement ring and the tattoo beside it. 'We could just run away,' he recalled Roach saying....

Why was he sitting here moping around? Why did he choose physical comfort over Roach? At the time, he hadn't mentally prepared himself for the idea of homelessness, but now he was certain he'd love Roach anywhere and through anything. Still, he didn't want to be homeless if it could be avoided. He didn't want to have to find his own way in the city that had beaten him down and defiled him in more ways than one since he was just a boy. All he wanted was Roach, and with that in mind, he squeezed his hand with determination and rushed to his closet.

It was two in the morning. He was wearing Roach's hoodie inside-out to hide the design, a face-mask, sunglasses, and a baseball cap. Climbing out of his window was more difficult than he anticipated, but he managed not to roll or slide off the roof. After tip-toeing to the edge, he looked for a good way down and decided his best bet was jumping in the pool. "Shit," he whispered before deciding to just go for it. It felt like the water shot up all the way through him and came out his ears when he jumped in, but he shrugged off the discomfort, grabbed his hat, and swam to the edge to start running off the property, scrambling ungracefully over the back fence in the process.

He made it down the hill behind the mansion and tumbled through some bushes before getting to a lower road and taking out his phone to use its GPS to guide him to the Roaches' car shop. It took him eight hours to make the long and winding walk. His clothes were crusted with dried mud that he failed to fully brush off before going inside and waiting in the short line for another ten minutes.

The young woman behind the counter was wearing a face-mask not dissimilar to Silvino's and had her shaved head and pierced ears covered by a bomber hat. She was wearing a loose turtleneck and long baggy pants despite the So-Cal weather and was audibly beaming behind her mask when she said, "Hello hello! Car trouble?"

"Hola, Poppie. Is uh... is Clay here?"

She tilted her head like a curious pup but then seemed to recognise him. "Vinny! We've missed you on game nights. Karson came to visit in December and complained that he wouldn't get to smoke you."

"Please don't use my name. I'm trying to lay low. Don't want paparazzi spotting me."

She nodded and leaned forward to whisper, her air still playful and jubilant. "Clay's not in today. He's moving."

"Moving?" His stomach dropped. "W-where's he moving to?"

"I'll give you the address!" She perked up and took a customer's invoice from beside her to write an address on the back.

"Uh... isn't this for someone else?"

She shook her head adorably. "Not anymore! Tell Clay something for me when you go see him?"

"... Okay I guess."

She said in Arabic, "This is an important secret message," and he stood there awkwardly, unable to understand a lick of it. "You tell him that, okay? Okay, bye!"

He shuffled out of the shop and looked at the address, pressing a hand to his racing heart with a sigh of relief when he saw it was in Compton. After putting it into his GPS, he was sent all up and down various roads, still not realising that the map service he was using had a walking setting. It took another hour to walk what should have actually only taken him half an hour were he to be using the app correctly. He was increasingly perturbed by his surroundings as he trekked further into what his mother had always called "the bad part of town." He was the only one walking around outside, and the windows of the houses all seemed to be staring at him harshly.

His posture was unconfident, and when he reached Roach's apartment complex and noticed it had a gate that would be impossible to climb, his shoulders slumped even further. He made another loop of the buildings in case he was lost, but it seemed his entire outing would be stopped short. His parents had deleted all of the Roaches' numbers from his phone and removed all means of contacting him otherwise, so there was no recourse.

He heard a car to his right and stepped out of its way so it could park nearby. It was some sort of old sports car painted with a grey primer and making a clicking noise until its engine stopped. Silvino wasn't going to pay it any mind, but then none other than his beloved stepped out and walked around to look under the hood. He rushed up and sputtered incoherently.

"Hey, man. You live here, too? I just moved in."

"ROACH!" He wrapped his arms around him and squeezed him hard enough to nearly break him in half.

"Honeybee?" he said with a weepy quiver.

Silvino retreated and tore away the mask and sunglasses to reveal his teary face. "I'm so sorry, Clay. My parents. They made me. I don't know why I—." He was shut up by a deep and passionate kiss, melting immediately into the strong arms he had missed so much.

"You broke my fucking heart, dude," he said as he retreated and wiped his eyes, "You said it wasn't your parents' idea. You said it was the cigarettes. I've been wearing patches to try and be good enough for you again."

Silvino shook his head fervently. It was all he could do before he wept even harder, unable to formulate any words.

Roach pulled him in and held him tight. After another prolonged embrace, he said, "Look at you. You're all covered in dirt and wearing a hoodie when it's so hot out? You must be dripping sweat. You want to go inside?"

Silvino nodded. "For a bit, but Clayton I... I ran away, so I should go back soon. They'll be looking for me. They might try to say you kidnapped me."

"You ran away for me? Honeybee, you're so sweet. Why didn't you just call?"

He wiped his eyes. "They deleted your number from my phone."

"Well, then I guess I'll have to get a new number, won't I?" He smiled, and it brought a blush to Silvino's cheeks and butterflies to his stomach.

"I need to rest. I haven't sat down since I left the house at two."

"Two in the morning?" He nodded. "Well, I don't have any furniture yet, but you can sit on... the counter! And we can shower together if you like." He was blushing when he made the offer, but his voice was confident and sensual. Silvino nodded and wiped more tears from his eyes, unable to speak again. Roach pulled him in for yet another hug. "Let me lock the car back up. You can explain what happened when we're inside, but just to be certain," he pulled him back by the shoulders and looked into his glistening brown eyes, "You still love me?"

"I never stopped," he whimpered.

"Oh, honeybee! I missed you so much."

It was her fourth flight of the week, but she was still energetic and happy to snuggle up on the private jet with a book and hot coffee. It was almost Christmas, and she had asked Tatum to borrow a plane to go shopping in Asia for his gifts. It was therefore a solo trip, but she was enjoying herself. Her happiness, however, was soured when she thought back to a conversation she had had at the beginning of the month with one of the mechanics at the hangar in Dubai:

"You're sure it's all fixed?"

"Yes, madame." He smiled, but there was something malicious in his black eyes. She couldn't place it.

She flipped through the forms he had passed to her and, after glancing at enough jargon to be exhausted, she passed it with a sigh to her pilot. "Well, thank you for working on such short notice. Our personal mechanics are in Quebec."

"Oh, it was my pleasure," he said with another eerie grin. In fact, he hadn't stopped smiling for the entire conversation. Now, however, she could see a hint of the real emotion in the twitch of one his eyes. A wildfire burned in his soul: he was enraged.

"And… uh," she gulped, "and the pay is good?"

"The pay is more than generous, madame."

"W-well, uh… I should get going, then."

His smile twisted so subtly she only noticed it with her intuition and not with her vision. It was harrowing and evil in his eyes, which refused to catch the light in the area, instead snuffing it out like a cloud of shadow. Still, her pilot and servants didn't seem perturbed by it, and she was due to start her cycle a few days from then: it was probably just hormonal paranoia.

Thinking back on it, she shivered and looked down to realise she had read four pages of her thriller novel without intaking any of the story. After flipping back to where her mind had wandered, she took a deep breath, quaffed her coffee, and forced herself to focus on the book rather than the chilling memories of that odd black-eyed mechanic.

For the last few prisons, they took turns staying on the bus with the baby. They maintained their anonymity, and as the company finally started to crumble, they made their way to the last Baumbach facility in the entire country: The Dallas Yard. It was the prison Roach had massacred after his husband's untimely death. The one they had been trying to avoid.

Finding Ruin had greatly lifted his mood. Silvino had never wanted children, and with only male partners and no legal means of adopting, Roach had resigned himself to a childless life. Even with such a beacon of good as his new daughter, he was still too perturbed to go into the prison and asked to be the one that stayed with Ruin on the bus, "at least for the first part. I'll… I'll come in with her when you're all 100% certain that it's only prisoners left. Keep them locked up. I want to find Silvino's records. I want to know where they put his body."

The others were understanding and quit the bus without him. Ruin was asleep, so he sat beside her carrier and rocked it, trying to stop his mind from reeling. His perfect memory conjured up the smell of death from Silvino's cell. It flashed with the visage of his blood in the empty concrete box. He tried to replace the upsetting memories with thoughts of his future as a father, but it only upset him further to know how far he had fallen from Silvino's perfect match to the wretched thing he had become.

He listened to the sirens about an hour after the others had left, followed by scattered cracks of gunfire sometimes muffled by thunder. Reality was heavy on his shoulders, but Ruin's big green eyes fluttered open, and he smiled sweetly at her. She cooed and grabbed her foot to shove into her mouth. His stomach cinched up with butterflies. "You hungry?" He opened the fridge telekinetically and grabbed a container of applesauce with a spoon already on it in anticipation of feeding her. She messily enjoyed the breakfast and giggled when he thereafter tickled her tummy. It was in the midst of her laughter that his phone rang, and the sirens outside wound down.

"Hyello?"

"Guards are all dead. You sure you still want to come inside, mate? We can get the records for you."

He frowned and sniffled. "Yeah, sparkplug. I... I have to."

"Alright, well, just let Franky know if you need to get brought back to the bus. We took sheets from the prisoners to cover the bodies so Ruin won't see them. Dale's also hacked the cameras, so you don't need to wear a mask."

"Thanks. You're all such precious gifts, I hope you know."

"Ditto, Basil. We love you."

"I love you all, too." He hung up and took Ruin out of her carrier to rest her on his hip with a teething toy. When she was content in his arms, he trudged out of the bus toward the prison where he had become the unredeemable scum of the Earth he was then.

After going inside and setting down his umbrella by the door, there was a strange sense of anxiety that tugged on him like an undertow. The lights were bright and illuminating the white halls he had once painted red. Images of murders he hadn't committed flashed in his vision. There was the vague smell of blood beneath the otherwise sterile air. The roaring of gunshots from weapons he wasn't holding and... and certainly never *had* held... whispered through his mind. With a shake of his head to force away the strange hallucinations, he kissed Ruin's forehead and climbed to the third floor where the records room was located. The others were already there to greet him. They had a strange air about them. It was like they knew something he didn't know. Like they were talking about him before he showed up.

He chalked it up to a delusion and passed Ruin to Thyne so he could go looking through the filing cabinets.

River tried to stop him: "He wasn't in there, Tony."

"Did you check all of the files? Maybe it was misplaced."

"I checked them all." He had found Silvino's files in his search, but he didn't want his brother to see them.

"Well," said Roach with a forced smile, "worth a second look." River sighed and let Roach go thumbing through the papers. He checked everything filed under "R" but didn't find Silvino.

"Told you."

"Shut up, bro. There's so many fucking files, Jesus Christ. You'd think it was a big prison or something. They must keep this shit for *decades*." He slammed the drawer closed and went to the "A" files. "Ah, see? Alvarez." He threw the file down on an empty table nearby and spread out the papers.

Dale approached and started skimming things. "Wait. Eva Alvarez visited? The actress? Was ye married to a celebrity,?"

"Yeah? Eva was his mom. I thought you knew this."

"Ah never knew his name was Alvarez. Why they got him under that name? He were under 'Roach' when Ah was lookin' fer 'em."

Roach didn't have an answer to the question until he saw a post-it on one of the files that read, *Moved from file 'Roach' after inmate name-change.* "What the fuck?" Silvino had only changed his name the one time: in Mexico after their wedding. Roach brushed it off after only a moment of confusion to look for information about Silvino's death.

Francis started skimming through the files with them. "Vinny Alvarez, hm? Partha fancies his work."

"What? No he doesn't, dude. He doesn't even know who he is."

He arched his brow. "His boisterous besotted blabbering would beg to differ, my darling. I were present for a stream wherein he sat in on call for a charity auction and purchased something of the actor's for an unfathomable sum."

"Huh? He bought something of Vinny's?" Francis nodded. "What'd he buy?"

"Did you find out where they sent his body yet?" interrupted River.

Roach glared slightly. "I appreciate whatever you're trying to do, Sonny, but I want to know everything I can about my husband, and if Party has something of his, I want to at least know what he has."

"It's an obnoxiously large plush dinosaur," answered Thyne.

Roach dropped the paper he was holding.

"Here," said Dale, holding a different paper toward Roach.

It felt like lead in his trembling hands: U.S. STANDARD CERTIFICATE OF DEATH

After shaking away his grief, he saw the cause of death was listed as *self-inflicted lacerations of the heart.* "Bastards," he said as the paper crinkled slightly in his tightened grip, "Didn't even have the decency to admit to their murder."

"Well.... Least ye kilt 'em all."

Thyne had approached by then and readjusted Ruin on his hip as he plucked up a different paper. "You said to Filipek that Silvino didn't have enough money for his insulin."

"Yeah. He didn't. That's why he died."

Thyne pursed his lips and set the paper back down after a quick glance at River. They seemed to communicate telepathically in the split-second of eye contact. "I think that's someone else's, then," said Thyne with a strained smile.

Roach plucked it up from in front of Thyne. River tried to take it before he could read it, but Roach snatched it away. It was about Silvino's finances in prison. Alongside Roach's sparse donations of whatever he could get his hands on while he was living on the streets of Dallas scraping things together to keep his husband alive, there were numerous payments made by Silvino's wealthy parents. Roach tossed the paper away and wiped his arm across his face. He leaned on the table and looked down at the files for a moment of tense silence.

"Tony...."

"Those fucking assholes," he said with an angry chuckle, "He was getting paid enough for the insulin the whole time!" He grabbed the lip of the table, rearing to flip it, but he stopped himself. He didn't want to scare Ruin. After a few deep calming breaths, he lit a cigarette and spoke his thoughts aloud: "They killed him even more directly than I had thought: stealing his money before he even knew his parents had sent it." After a drag, his hand stopped trembling as violently as it had been. "At least I didn't fail him as much as I thought I had.... I want the CEO. I want to watch the light go out."

"It says here they sent Silvino's body to the Pharaon Funeral Home in Louisiana," said Thyne, "Let's get you out of here, Basil."

He nodded and followed the others out of the room with one last glance at the files. On their way to the warden's office, where they would open all the cells, more flashes of hallucinated violence plagued Roach. The closer they neared to the box where Silvino had died, the more red he saw on the stark white walls. It got to a point that he stopped and held his aching head.

"Ye ah'ight, Roach?"

"I'm fine. Just... have a headache."

"Tony, what's wrong?"

"I said I'm fine." He tried to glare, but the hallucinations of gunfire cracked so loud when he opened his eyes that he physically blenched. He was beginning to realise something he dared not acknowledge....

River took his hand and whispered in Arabic, "You don't have to do this, Tony. No one is making you do this."

Roach didn't respond and averted his gaze. After snatching his hand away, he followed the others as they slowly resumed the climb up to the warden's office. When they reached it, his stomach dropped down into the pits of Hell where lived his rotten black heart. There were screens with feeds from security cameras in various cells, flickering through automatically. They were numbered, and his stomach churned. Surely… surely the numbers were coded somehow. Four inmates per cell, sometimes six. Surely these feeds were from other prisons….

"Basil? Come here. Do you want to do the announcement? You seem to like to do them."

He ambled to Thyne's place and dropped himself into one of the chairs across from the warden's desk. With his head in his hands he sniffled and whimpered, "Dale?"

Dale crouched down beside his friend and pet his arched back. "Ah'm here."

A loud sniffle. His teary hazel-greys met with his best friend's icy-blues. "Have they renovated?" Dale knitted his brow. "How many cells were there when we were here?"

"Ye don't 'member?"

"Evidently not," he whimpered.

Dale turned toward River and whispered, "Should Ah tell 'em?"

"Tony, it's okay."

"How many!?" He tried to shout, but his voice was strangled.

"There's 'bout a thousan' cells, Roach."

The memories of his massacre became more clear. Swarming him like a hive of hornets. His trembling hands were white-knuckling around his aching head. "How many per cell?" A beat. No one wanted to answer. "How many, Dale? Please…."

They made eye contact again, and Dale smiled sadly at his friend. "I thought ye had a perfect mem'ry, brother. If ye wan' me ta juss tell ye how many people ye kilt, Ah can gib a rough estimate." Roach whimpered but nodded slightly. "Was 'bout 4500. Ye was usin' yer telly-kinesis when ye ran outta bullets. That's how Ah known 'bout the powers."

More memories he didn't know he had blacked out came flooding back in with Dale's confirmation. He held his teary eyes. "4500?"

"Give er take. Yee."

"Tony… it's okay."

He huffed. "I knew Vinny would hate what I've become, but… but I had no idea…. 4500. It's hardly even a number…. I didn't know I was so far gone."

Thyne passed Ruin to River and crouched down in front of Roach. He lifted his head by his chin and wiped away his tears. "You're not gone at all." With a sweet slowness, he pressed his lips against Roach's trembling ones and retreated to say, "I waited so long for you to come back to me, Basil. You're not gone at all. You're right here," he squeezed his hand lovingly, "with me again."

"Thyne," he wept, "Why do you love me? Why do *any* of you love me?"

"Faugh! Need I recite more poetry?" said Francis with an offended air and irritated flick of his wrists. "Pass judgement on thyself if you must, but pass it not unto us for accepting and loving you as you are."

"You're a good man," said Thyne, to which Roach only rolled his eyes. Thyne's cheeks turned pink and brow furrowed, but he shook away the anger and huffed once. "Well, call yourself whatever you like, Basil— be it monster or man —but know that whatever you are, so are we." He stood and took the child back from River. "Now, Karson, make the announcement and release the inmates. We're running out of time and still need to figure out how we're getting out of the country."

 # Chapter 71

You've No Manner
of Luck At All

"No, kid. Just stop."

"I swear! It wasn't me."

He sighed. "Son, this isn't just dumpster diving and trespassing anymore. This is real shit. You assaulted someone. He's in the hospital. We like you and all, but we can't just let you get away with the 'it was my brother' song and dance this time. I know that murder thing you got accused of was a mistake, but there's no mistake here. We know you punched that guy. You have blood on your knuckles, kid, come on."

He shook his hands in his hair and held his breath to keep from hyperventilating. "It wasn't me."

"Alright. Here's the deal. If you say it was your brother one more time, we're just going to arrest him, too. We'll put you both away. So, last chance, son: did you assault someone tonight?"

He squeezed his eyes shut and replayed the chaotic encounter in his head. He and Silvino had managed to get into a bar using fake IDs. One drink too many had Silvino on his lips, and the next thing he knew Roach was knocking the lights out of some creep trying to blackmail Silvino out of a kiss. "Felix, man, you don't understand. He was... he was....” He cursed in Arabic, unable to even begin to defend himself to the pig interrogating him because of the law against homosexuality. After rubbing his lap anxiously he announced loudly, “Fine. I did it. I punched the fucker. I guess I’m just a mean drunk.” He sighed and held his head again.

“I’ll pretend you didn’t say that just now about underage drinking.” Roach cursed again, and the cop patted one of his knees to comfort him. “You’re a good kid. It’ll be okay. I’ll get you a court date then drop you off at home. I saw you moved recently. You like your new place?”

“Yeah man, whatever. What’s gonna happen after court?”

“You’ll probably go to jail, but the judge is my cousin, so I’ll make sure it’s a light sentence. Just a year or two.”

“Thanks, I guess.”

He was served papers and brought home, and after climbing up to his unfurnished apartment, he rubbed the bridge of his nose and tossed the papers on the ground. “Fuck.” With the first cigarette lit in a pack he would spend that night chain smoking, he laid on the empty bedroom floor and stared at his ceiling fan, all the while taking drags and running through plans in his mind. The police had made the mistake of assuming he wasn’t a flight risk because they had a soft spot for him, and, well, he had never fled before.

The next morning, he was packing his van when he heard Silvino calling out to him from across the parking lot. He leaned on his knees after getting Roach’s attention, his breaths laboured after a long hasty walk. Roach rushed over. He took his heavy backpack, carried him to the car, and sat him on the edge of the bed in the van where the back seats were prior to him replacing them with a bed for camping on the trip. “There’s water in the fridge.”

Silvino took one of the bottles and downed it as Roach resumed packing, stacking things higher on the pile of boxes and suitcases on the mattress. After catching his breath and calming his racing heart, Silvino said, “My parents paid my bail, but they gave me an ultimatum. The same ultimatum they had given me before: you or them. I chose you. I should have chosen you the first time. I ran away. I have no money and nowhere to go.”

“I’ve got money. We’re going to Mexico.”

“What?”

“I said we’re going to Mexico,” he repeated as he slammed the hatch closed, “And we have to go before my court date.”

"They want to put you in jail...."

"Yeah, but I think I'd rather go get married. Orange really isn't my colour."

Silvino blushed and managed a smile. "Where's Malfeasance?"

"Poppie's gonna take care of her."

He pursed his lips. "Well, my abuela lives in Mexico. She seemed sympathetic when I cried about you to her on a call while we were separated."

"Call her."

"I will. Before my parents cut off my phone." He took it out and dialled his grandmother's number. They chatted for a spell, Silvino tearfully explaining the situation, and she opened her home to them. They graciously gave her Roach's number, got in the van, and fled the country, entirely unaware they were driving into a future warzone.

River called Pharaon Funeral Home as the gang headed eastward out of North Texas. After some confusion about Silvino's last name, the mortician informed him that the remains had gone too long unclaimed. The body had been cremated and its ashes scattered in Lake Pontchartrain. River asked Roach if he wanted to go, but without even a verbal response, River told the mortician, "Thank you," and the call soon thereafter ended.

A sombre silence choked them for the next few miles of their trip as Roach tried desperately not to cry. Imagining his husband as lost scattered ashes completely devoid of any distinction from the water around them made him especially mournful even these several years after Silvino's passing.

The tires hummed ambiently as they glided down the highway. From North Texas to Arkansas to Tennessee, the trip was evermore lighthearted and tension lightening. The plan was to park Dale's bus in the mountains again, after which he would drive them in his truck due north to Detroit where Francis would stop time and walk them into Canada. The drive to Gatlinburg was pleasant, as was the hike down the mountain to Dale's truck. It could hardly fit everyone, especially with how big the twins were and the new baby, but with Ruin securely fastened in the backseat, Roach shoved himself into the middle seat between her and Francis while Thyne and River took the seats in the front with Dale and Monkey. Dale had Roach's album *Apis Mellifera* queued up on the truck's internal harddrive, but when it started, River immediately skipped the entire album in favour of whatever classic metal music Dale had queued up next.

"Sorry, brother," said Dale when he saw River's reaction and noticed a cloud forming over Roach's head again.

"It's chill, man," he said with a sigh, "If we weren't in America I could probably listen to it without issue. It's just a lot of compounding things, y'know?"

"Ye don' gotta 'splain yerself ta me, mane."

There was a beat of decreasing tension before they got on the road. Ruin was asleep. The music was quiet. Francis' hand was intertwined with Roach's as he leaned sleepily on his shoulder and scrolled mindlessly on his phone. The traffic on the midnight highway was light, and the stars glimmered beautifully through the skylight. After a while of watching the sky, Roach spoke softly, "So, Dale, do you have any companies we should add to the docket? Leviathan, maybe?"

"Uh... ye can go affer Leviathan if ye think ye can take 'em, but Ah'd 'vise 'gainst it."

"Well, it's up to you. We've only got Canopy and Osiris left otherwise."

"Takin' down Osiris'll be troublesome, but Ah b'lieve in y'all."

Roach was going to reply, but River interrupted: "Are you not planning to come back to Rome with us, Dale?"

"Ah thought that was the plan. Ah take y'all up to Detroit, an' y'all head on off inta Canada without me."

"Wait," said Roach with a heartbroken air, "You're not coming back with us, dude?" Dale didn't reply. "Man, this blows," said Roach with a huff.

Francis rubbed his hand with his thumb lovingly. "Perhaps whatever business needs conducting in the states can be done now. What need thee, Dale, to allow your continued accompaniment?"

There was a long beat of quiet. Dale sighed and ran a hand through his hair. "Ah'll come wit ye, Roach, butchye gotta promise my family'll be safe."

Roach frowned. "Leviathan is after you...."

"Mayhaps we could bring your family to Rome as well."

"My Ma ain't gonna leave." He sighed. "Ah was gon' go back an' protect her."

Thyne sighed and spoke up, though it seemed to pain him to say, "While we were with you at your childhood home, I—. I have these microscopic—. These things that—."

"He put a microphone in your mother, father, and uncle," said River bluntly, "He can always hear them. He has one in all of us."

Dale glanced at Thyne with a harsh air before returning his attention to the road. "That's a mighty breach 'a privacy."

"His point," continued River, "is that if your family is in danger, he'll know and be able to tell Francis to come rescue them. Francis could likely even take you with him."

"But Franky told me on this trip that when he walks across the ocean like that, if he loses his grip of time for whatever reason, he'll sink into the sea and be crushed by the depths," said Roach with a soft glare on Francis.

"Ye can walk 'cross the ocean!? Are ye Jesus er summon?"

"When time is stopped, the surface of any body of water can bear my weight, yes. It is like ice and difficult to roam, but I always have access to crampons in one way or another." He turned to Roach and kissed his knuckles. "You needn't worry, however, my beautiful monster. I needn't cross the ocean on foot. 'Tis marginally more effort, but I possess a spaceship and can therefore traverse the continents with ease upon returning to Siberia in the prehistoric years wherein I have it sepulchred."

Roach smiled softly. "Then that settles that. Dale'll come with us, and Thyne will send you to save his family if Leviathan goes after them."

"Aye!"

Dale sighed. "Fine. Butchye still gotta promise. Promise my family'll be safe."

"Swear on my life, mate," said Roach.

The roadtrip continued and lightened yet again as the miles accumulated. They reached Detroit at breakfast time and decided to stop at a Waffle House for old-time's sake. Dale was dead-tired from driving for almost ten hours, so when Francis brought them over the border, it was decided with a quick phone call to the group back in Rome that they would stay at a hotel using Rory's name and card. During that call, they were pleased to hear Jae had joined the gang in Rome. He made them an offer: "They need out of Canada? I have some boys smuggling guns out tomorrow, just in time for Christmas. They can hop on board with them."

"Where will they be landing?" asked Perlie.

"Naples! I've been making connections with the mafia here since this seems to be my baby girl's base of operation for the time being. I want to stick around with Sirion for as long as you'll have me."

"Jae, you're a godsend, man," said Roach.

"Thank you. Thank you. Get me a souvenir while you're there!"

"You got it, mate," said Thyne.

So, with the plan established, they contacted Jae's people, slept for a few hours, then let Francis bring them to Toronto where they would wander around aimlessly for three hours before their flight out. They bought some nonsense from touristy shops while their proper luggage was being packed onto the plane. Francis drank himself blind to be able to mentally handle the trip over the ocean, but he was markedly less scared during the flight thanks to the twins both holding him.

They landed in Naples on the evening of Christmas Eve and were met at the airport by Perlie and Jae in a pair of Giovanni's cars.

She was finally on her way back home with a plane full of gifts for her husband. A smile was plastered to her face as she looked through pictures from the trip and remembered the amazing things she had seen from the natural wonder of the rainbow mountains in Zhangye, to the man-made masterpiece that was the *Taj Mahal*. She had a gift for Tatum from almost every country in Asia including things as simple as a teapot made of jade and interesting candies and snacks from Japan or things as extravagant as ancient art pieces bought directly from museum archives and even a new *Mitsuoka* supercar, which she had shipped back to Rome a week before Christmas to be sure it wouldn't be late.

Unfortunately, she had to stop in Dubai before getting back to Rome when her pilot said the plane was having trouble again. The landing was smooth, but she was terrified until she heard the engines spooling down, after which she looked outside to see the pilot meeting with some mechanics. She hid behind her window's curtain, afraid the eerie mechanic she had met in the same hangar over a month ago would see her. Upon further inspection, however, he didn't seem to be present.

After paying extra to the mechanics to work through the night so she wouldn't miss Christmas, they rushed the fixes and declared it safe for flying at about 9:00 p.m. on December twenty-fourth. She was anxious on the take-off for no discernable reason. Her hands were automatically tugging at her hair as she watched the world fall away, feeling it try to pull her back in an unsettling way. They were scarcely two hundred metres from the ground when she heard a clattering thud behind her. It felt as if the landing gear had fallen off the plane. She closed her eyes tightly and told herself, *'It's just the gear coming up or something. It's no big deal. They just fixed the plane. They just fixed it.'* There was a part of her that wanted to go up to the cockpit and ask the pilot what was happening, but if there was something seriously wrong, she didn't want to distract him. One of her servants looked at her with as much anxiety on her face as Aspyn's and asked, "Should I go ask—?"

"No," Aspyn interrupted, "It's nothing. The mechanics just fixed it." Her wobbly tone betrayed the sentiment.

"Yes ma'am," said the maid with a gulp.

Whatever had happened must not have been a very big deal because the pilot kept flying, and the ladies were soon calm again.

It was somewhere over the Mediterranean that the severity of the situation became clear. After an agonising ten seconds of freefall, everyone was slammed back down into their seats or, in the case of one of the butlers, to the ground. There was no longer any sound coming from either engine, and the lights in the cabin flickered out. In the eerie quiet, Aspyn could only hear the muffled whispers of blaring alarms from the cockpit and, she swore, the susurrating of the waves below as the big black sea enveloped more and more of the view through the windows.

The only mercy the pilot gave in the eternity of horror was a quick announcement to the cabin of the single word, "Brace." Those who hadn't already taken on the brace position did so immediately after hearing the panicked command, after which, the crash.

The next thing she knew, Aspyn was in a shattered vessel with a broken wrist and bruises on her arms and shins. The odour of kerosene grew increasingly strong, and she scrambled out of her seat to rush out of the plane from the opening in front of her. The cockpit was nowhere to be seen. All she could hear was screaming, crying, drowning, and the unforgiving water crashing against whatever rock they had half-landed on. She jumped out of the wreckage onto the wet rock and climbed with only one arm to its highest peak in a matter of moments. Her gaze as she looked down at the wreckage was shaky. Why was no one else leaving?

'Aspyn you animal! You left them to die!' She looked around at the nothingness on this little rock in a panic, as if it might provide her a rope and piton. When it proved a ridiculous notion to look around for tools, she started to descend from the peak. Only three steps toward the cliff face, however, she was startled by an immense fireball and fell backwards. The arms she held over her face were singed even from the distance she had gained. After ten minutes wailing and screaming into her shaking arms, she lifted her eyes and watched through the blear of her hysteria the last remnants of the plane and everyone inside burning up to cinders.

The rescue was a blur. She awoke in a hospital bed in Cyprus on December 26th and was almost immediately met with Nero, who had flown in from Rome and landed only twenty minutes prior. He was sombre and took off his hat. "I'm sorry, ma'am," he began with a strangled voice, "There's something you need to know...."

He told her something so upsetting, it was like the entire world disappeared. The colour drained from reality the way it drained from her face. Everything pale blue and lifeless. It struck her like a pick into the ice of her heart. Whatever remained of her withering soul fell away like the petals of the beast's cursed rose....

What was she now but a cadaver with a pulse?

The gang had scarcely entered the manor when the twins were crouched down and drowning in puppy-kisses from Juliette as well as their own dogs, the puppies having gotten much bigger in their year's absence. Perlie was crossing her arms and glaring at the twins while the rest of the newcomers had already moved upstairs to meet Sirion.

"What?" said Roach with a big dopey grin as Daisy licked his face. He giggled and blew a raspberry around her snout before scratching her favourite spot and beaming up at Perlie, "We'll go meet him soon. Is Malfeasance in the bathhouse?"

"She's dead."

He went pale, and all the levity in the air immediately disappeared. "What?"

"Giovanni tried to save her."

"Tony," said River with a worried look at his brother.

"Where is she?" He rose to his feet menacingly.

Perlie staggered backwards when she noticed he was angry. "They buried her," she said with a glimmer in her eyes that River caught but Roach didn't notice. She was lying. River's stomach turned. '*They must have eaten her*,' he thought.

"Where!?" shouted Roach.

"In the graveyard!" She wailed and ran upstairs to avoid whatever wrath Roach might have wrought.

"Come on, Sonny," he said as he shoved his hands in his hoodie pocket and went out the back.

He was only three steps into the snow when River's voice sounded from the porch: "Tony, it's a blizzard. Come inside. We can see the tombstone later."

He huffed and shook away the idea, lighting a cigarette to warm him and pushing further into the wall of swirling white. River sighed, grabbed another coat from the closet near the stairs for each of them, and rushed after his brother. In the graveyard, Roach was quick to find May and Aphid's graves and kicked the snow around the area in search of disturbed dirt. He didn't see Malfeasance's tombstone, and the ones that were there were hard to read through the whipping winter wind, but he was determined.

"Tony! Please, let's go inside." He grabbed his hand and tried to pull him back toward the house, but Roach was immovable. "Please," he wept, "It's only eight degrees!" He wrapped the coat he had brought for Roach around his shoulders and tried again to pull him away from the gravestones, but Roach fell to his knees and started digging through the powdery snow with his bare hands to find his pet's grave. Upon seeing this, River shouted, "TONY, THEY ATE HER!" He stopped and looked up at River with trembling eyes. "I can't know for sure, but they didn't bury her. Perlie was lying to protect you. Please. Please come inside."

He was like the walking dead as he let River bring him inside to sit shivering beside the hearth. River made him some hot tea, and after only ten minutes alone,

Francis and Thyne came down to comfort Roach as he mourned his lost pet and thus the last living connection to Silvino he had.

None of the four of them slept that night, so they were cuddled up in the living room when Partha came down for breakfast on Christmas morning. He was immediately shooed out of the kitchen by Giovanni with only a black cup of coffee to appease his whining for the time. As he sat across from the others and sipped his bitter drink, he noticed the upset in their airs and beamed to combat it. "Good morning and merry Christmas! Did you see my son!? Isn't he so beautiful?"

Thyne smiled softly. "He is, mate."

"And Ruin is so cute, too! They'll be best mates for sure," he said with another unsatisfying sip of coffee. "What's wrong, Roach?"

"My duck is dead, dumbass."

"Oh! Right… I guess you weren't here."

"Did they eat her?" The colour drained from Partha's face, and Roach leaned closer to him with a harsh glare. "Did *you* eat her?"

His gaze shifted from side to side as he sputtered incoherently. "Listen," he finally managed to say when Roach stood, "She got attacked by a fox. Giovanni did all he could, but she didn't make it, and he didn't tell us where the duck came from, and I'm stupid, so I didn't even think about it until Perlie saw me take a bite and asked if it was your duck."

Roach wanted nothing more than to kill Giovanni, but his legs weakened, and he collapsed under the weight of his own emotions. Thyne, River, and Francis brought him back up to the couch and held him as he wept fervently.

In general, the holiday was met with little fanfare given its timing with the reunion, Roach's grief, and some unspoken tension in the house. There were a few gifts exchanged, but the day otherwise dragged aimlessly before the feast. Giovanni, Dezba, Rory, and Viktor had worked from sunrise to sundown cooking a grand meal with roast pheasants and chicken, curried goat, croissants, vegetable medleys, mashed squash, and spiced wine. With the babies asleep, everyone else gathered around the table in the dining hall. The spread was presented beautifully. The wine was helping Roach feel less enraged with their host, but the rage upon seeing Viktor was immense and broke through the buzz. After knocking back the remainder of his glass, he took the bottle from Arjun's place telekinetically and uncorked it to drink straight from its top. Dinner had only just started, but everyone was in witness of the display. Giovanni may have said something, but he had been made aware that Roach was upset with him and grieving. His only response to the rudeness was a muttered passive-aggressive comment to Arjun.

Conversations were slow to start, especially because Roach was making it no secret that he was getting as drunk as possible when he finished the wine and asked for Francis to refill it. He only ate three bites of his curried goat during the entire first fifteen minutes of the meal, in favour of drinking as his mind reeled madly:

'*I bet it was Viktor's idea to eat Malfaesance the nazi fuck. He killed me. He fucking killed me. He tortured me to death. And for what? For what? For the nazis for the nazis for the nazis…*' When he wasn't gulping down wine he was glaring harshly at Viktor or trying helplessly not to. '*Don't fucking kill him, Clayton. Thyne avenged you. Don't kill him. Don't kill him. Don't kill him. He's keeping us alive. He's keeping us healthy. Don't kill him, Clayton. Don't kill him.*'

His breaths were heaving more and more as his mind was pulled further and further into the black depths of his rotten soul. It made it seem like the lights were physically dimming around him. He was white-knuckling the neck of the wine bottle, the liquid inside eventually starting to make quiet tinkling noises as his hand around it trembled and breaths huffed louder and quicker.

Thyne rubbed his shoulder lovingly while River rubbed his thigh, both of them occasionally whispering things to keep him docile. It worked most times to calm him down and bring back some light, but his rage was increasingly evident and dangerous.

"This pheasant is so good, Pa," said Neodesha as she took a second helping.

She was trying to distract from Roach's upset, and Giovanni opened his mouth to take up the opportunity but was interrupted by Viktor saying with a chuckle, "Not as good as the duck from a few weeks ago, though."

In less than half a second Roach stood, reached out his hand, squeezed it, and Viktor's head was crushed like a grape, spilling viscera all over the beautiful feast and its company.

Silence.

It seemed to last for hours.

All eyes were on the headless corpse half-fallen out of its chair.

Giovanni was the first to break the quiet some five hundred years later. He cleared his throat, folded up his cloth napkin, set it beside his plate, and stood to address everyone calmly: "All of you schedule an appointment with me as soon as possible. Arjun, my darling, clean up the mess."

As people started to stir, Roach finally processed what he had done. His outstretched hand, which hadn't moved since the act, started trembling. He retreated it to grab his throat as if he was choking. "I'm sorry," he said with a strangled voice and stumbled away from the others, whose eyes had found him again. Without another word, he rushed outside and ran about twenty feet before collapsing into the snow, kowtowing as best as he could, and praying.

Hours later, Roach was being comforted by River in the living room while Thyne helped with the final touches on cleaning the murder scene and Francis mourned in solitude. There was a moment wherein Thyne rushed into the living room and peered out the windows, but when questioned as to what he was doing, he was dismissive and eventually returned to the basement with Arjun to help dispose of the body. It was therefore only the twins who were still on the main level of the manor, everyone else either upstairs or in the basement, when there was a knock at the door. It was nearly three in the morning, so with a confused glance at each other, they investigated. After Roach looked through the peephole, he slammed the door open, and beside him fell a bloody baseball bat. He ignored it, pulled the man who had dropped it into his arms telekinetically, and rushed him to the hearth to warm him. River closed the door behind them and rushed to get Giovanni from the basement.

"Doctor!" he shouted as he ran through the labyrinthian halls beneath the manor with relative ease, "Doctor! Come quick!"

He heard Giovanni calling from a layer deeper and rushed toward the sound, the two meeting on the spiralling staircase into the darkest bowels of the property.

"What's going on?"

"He's been out in the blizzard!"

"Who has?"

"Jean-Jacques!"

⚙ Chapter 72 ⚙
We're Catching Up

Roach had him in his arms, wrapped up in a blanket with Juliette snuggling into his chest to warm him and all of the twins' dogs huddled around to help warm him as well. When he finally stopped shivering, people started to ask him questions about where he had been and what he had done. He shook his head at most of their questions, and it was Thyne of all people to tell them to stop pestering him.

"You feel better, dude?" said Roach when Jean-Jacques shifted to knock the blanket off of his shoulders.

"Oui," he said with a sigh.

"The kettle's hot. What sort of tea do you want?" asked Thyne.

He shook his head, ran his hand through his shoulder-length hair and sighed. His black eyes locked with Roach's: "May I speak with you in private?"

"Me?" Jean-Jacques nodded. "Of course, dude." He stood and made sure Jean-Jacques was steady on his feet before releasing him. "Oh, but before we go," he paused and pursed his lips, "That's Dale. He killed May."

"Ah'm real sorry 'bout it, Martial, but Ah get it if ye wanna skin me 'live 'er summon." He sighed and slumped his shoulders. "Ah know what it's like ta lose a sister, an' Ah know Roach'll take care 'a my family if ye kill me."

Jean-Jacques somehow smiled and surprised everyone by pulling Dale in for a hug. He whispered as he held him, "I forgive you, monsieur." Roach's jaw was agape when Jean-Jacques returned to his side and grabbed his hand: "Come with me."

While Jean-Jacques was slinking off with Roach, Thyne pulled Francis and

Partha aside as well. "Martial gave me his phone. He said we can read his messages with Lanni after he left."

"Did he actually say that, or are you being a snoop?" asked River who was rudely eavesdropping.

"He actually said it, mate. Mind your business."

"This is my business. I want to read the messages with you."

"Well, then come with us."

He had a knowing grin which River immediately interpreted, seeming to read his mind: "So none of you will translate it for me, then?" he asked with a matching mocking smile.

"I will, sir!" said Partha with a little salute.

Thyne grumbled and clenched his teeth but ultimately caved and let River tag along to Francis' suite upstairs where they sat together and looked at the old texts.

Thyne interpreted Jean-Jacques messages aloud for River, and Partha did the same for Lanni's responses. The time-stamp on the messages indicated they had been exchanged immediately after Jean-Jacques left Jae's house in Seoul:

"May is dead," began Thyne as Jean-Jacques.

"I'm not seeing any obituaries anywhere," replied Partha as Lanni.

"She's dead, Lanni! This is all Partha's fault."

They all looked at Partha, who frowned at the message. "I don't understand. How did she die?" he continued translating, now with a strangled voice.

"It's Thyne's fault, too," read Thyne, stopping when his stomach turned to lead. After clearing his throat and swallowing his tears: "The one good thing those microphones could have done for us, and he was too shit-faced to save her." His voice was strangled and hardly sounded at all.

"Alcohol can help humans feel less upset with their current circumstances," was Lanni's robotic response. Francis was mid-sip from his flask when he heard it and stopped to look at the tin.

"I finally understand Roach," said Thyne as Jean-Jacques, "I finally understand because I'll be back, and I'll kill both Partha and Thyne for this." They looked at each other and gulped.

"Killing Partha and Thyne will not bring May back from the dead."

"I thought you were supposed to seem human. Why are you so fucking callous about this? Didn't you love her?"

"My programming says to put you and your needs above all else, Jean-Jacques."

"Good! My needs are blood. I want blood, god dammit! They killed my sister. Partha, Thyne, Francis, Perlie. All of them! She trusted them, and they couldn't care less about her death! I'll kill them all, and you'll help me, Lanni. You'll help me or else."

"Or else?"

"Or else I'll kill you, too!"

There was a three-day gap in the messages' time-stamps, and they took the opportunity to all let out a shuddered breath, save for Francis, who swigged from his flask at the whetted perturbation.

"Lanni... I'm sorry for what I said," Thyne resumed translating.

"I forgive you," read Partha.

"It's not Partha's fault."

"It isn't."

"And for Thyne... It was just bad timing...." Upon reading this, Thyne wiped the tears from his eyes with the back of his hand.

"They loved her. They did not love her as much as we love her, but she often expressed how safe all of your friends made her feel," was Lanni's reply.

"Can you help me figure out who actually killed her?"

"I have been looking into it. From what I can tell, a mercenary group called Leviathan is likely responsible."

"How can I get to them?"

"Standby." There was another gap in time-stamps of fifteen minutes, after which Lanni said: "There is a Leviathan depot in Paris. It looks like you'd need an employee ID to enter, but I've managed to hack into a few of their systems and made one for you. You'll have to add your picture. The only images I have of you are not forward-facing enough to be passable as forgeries."

"I've been thinking while you were working," was Jean-Jacques' reply, "I hate to ask too much of you, but... Lanni, it isn't Leviathan's fault, either."

"What do you mean?"

"Leviathan is just the gun. I want the one who loaded it. Who hired them?"

"Standby...."

While they continued reading Lanni and Jean-Jacques' messages, the man himself and Roach were shuttered up in the conservatory together. They were quiet and each petting a dog in their laps, Jean-Jacques with Juliette, who was over-joyed to be reunited with her master, and Roach with Hugo. Jean-Jacques looked haggard and world-weary now. There were deep dark circles under his eyes, his dark hair was dishevelled, his black beard untrimmed. There were new wrinkles in his face as if he had aged ten years in the mere one he was absent. His build had thickened: visibly stronger now but with a small gut. His broader shoulders seemed only recently to have been freed of the weight of the world. He surprised Roach by lighting up a cigarette and offering him one, which was taken timidly.

"Thanks," he said as he lit it up and took a drag.

They smoked for a few minutes, Jean-Jacques simply watching the snow dancing down onto the glass greenhouse roof where it promptly melted. When he looked back down at Roach he smiled wide. "I killed Abraham."

"You did!? That's fucking awesome, man."

He chuckled. "Yeah. I figured you'd like that." A drag. "I see you all have been busy here. Two babies and some new recruits. Hope you weren't trying to replace me," he said with a playful tone.

"Of course not, dude. We missed you. I'm really glad you're back, and I'm excited for you to properly meet my daughter."

"That means a lot, mon ami."

Roach beamed. "So what were you up to while you were gone?"

His smile faded, and he took another drag as he looked back up at the snowfall. After a beat of solemn silence: "Becoming a monster." There was another long moment of quiet before his gaze fell back and locked with Roach's. "The planes that were malfunctioning and crashing this last year belonged to Osiris elites or had them on board. I sabotaged their engines."

"Sick. That's a cool way to kill people."

Jean-Jacques managed a little chuckle. He moved Juliette to his side and leaned forward with his elbows on his knees. "You are an interesting one, monsieur. I missed you most. I wished I could have asked you if I was going too far., but I can ask you now...."

"You didn't go too far, dude. You did great! Francis will be elated when he hears you killed Abraham. Is that whose blood is on the bat?"

He nodded and leaned far back into his chair with his legs spread as he took another drag and resumed petting his dog. "Oui, but I think.... I think maybe I did go too far. That I got lucky."

"How so?"

A sigh. He snuffed out his cigarette on the glass patio table beside him. "I will tell you the entire story.... If you'll listen."

"Of course, man. Spill your heart out. I'm here for you."

"When I discovered how close his winter home was to Monsieur Giovanni's, I stopped sabotaging planes to prepare for this very night. The blizzard wasn't in the plans, but I couldn't wait any longer. I wanted it to be on Christmas. It *had* to be on Christmas." A beat. "When I was living with the Morozovs, I was taught a lot of skills I used in my absence from you all, but most especially I used them tonight. I was taught some of the skills actively, some of them I learned in the moment under pressure, and some I picked up through... osmosis. Is that the term?" Roach nodded. "You may have noticed I have also been honing my English. I *hope* you've noticed at least."

"Yeah, man. You're doing great."

He smiled softly. "Thank you. It was calculated: I knew I would come back to this gang eventually, and I wanted to be able to properly express myself, especially to you. But, I digress. When I found Abraham's winter home and was certain he was inside, I planned my attack. I wanted to do it on Christmas. I hadn't planned for the blizzard, so sneaking onto his property was more difficult considering my clothes were meant to blend into the darkness. Luckily, the snow was whipping all around and helped obscure me more. I was able to climb over the south wall and reached the back patio. I expected more guards on the outskirts. I expected him to have people outside even in a blizzard. I'm still surprised he didn't.... Regardless, I picked the lock and snuck inside.

"A lot of the manor was empty, but when I came upon a butler awake and walking the halls, I used a chloroform rag to muffle him as I slit his throat. It was the first time I had directly killed someone so... needlessly.... It felt good." He held his head, and Roach reached over to pat his shoulder. "Anyway," he said as he sat back upright, "I pressed on until I found his bedroom. It took about an hour, and I had to kill another person with the rag and knife. I don't know what she did— maybe she was a maid —but I eventually found Abraham sleeping in this big silk bed. His girlfriend wasn't with him, which made things easier for me, to be honest.

"And this, Monsieur, is the part where I fear I have gone too far. Before I even entered the room, I took inspiration from your video killing Filipek and played the *White Christmas* song from my phone. I turned up the volume as I stepped up to his bedside. When he opened his eyes and met mine, I pulled him violently from bed and let him tumble onto the rug. He was immediately cowering and whimpering and trying to call for help, but I was already bashing his head in with the bat." He clenched his fist and said, "He killed May." After shaking away the rage he continued, "I was having so much fun seeing what new shapes of red I could paint on the rug that I nearly forgot to run away...."

"Good job, dude. I don't see how you went too far. It's okay to get a little lost in the moment of the kill, especially because he killed your sister. And the song was a nice touch. I'm glad I inspired you."

He chuckled. "No, Monsieur, that is not what I mean."

"Then what do you mean?"

There was a beat of quiet wherein he lit himself another cigarette, his fingers trembling. After a few drags he finally answered: "It did not escape my notice... the dead man's switch. I just... didn't care."

Roach had obviously not forgotten about the switch, but he hadn't run the scenario far enough through in his mind to understand the problem until Jean-Jacques spelled it out. He nodded solemnly.

"Would you have done the same?"

"At least 300 million people have *Eyes of Osiris*. That's three percent of the entire world's population." He finished his cigarette and snuffed it out under his boot as he pondered the question. Would he have given pause? He didn't think he could go through with it, but, "If it was to avenge Sonny… yes I think I would have done the same."

Jean-Jacques sighed with relief. "That makes me feel much better. Thank you, Monsieur."

"Makes you feel better that I'm fucked up too?"

He smiled softly. "Oui."

Roach returned the smile tenfold. "Well, Martial, welcome to the Irredeemable Monsters Club! We meet on Wednesdays and make macaroni art." They laughed together. "You know, I'm a lot more far gone than I thought when I told you about all my killings. I sort of accidentally lied to you."

"How so?"

"When we were in America a few days ago I learned that I had blacked-out most of the massacre in Silvino's prison. I killed over 4500 people that day…."

"Baumbach killed your husband," said Jean-Jacques eventually.

"Yeah." He sighed and ran a hand through his hair. "He would hate who I became… who I maybe already was."

Jean-Jacques' light smile dissipated. "Oui…. May would be disgusted by me. It was in her name— in the name of vengeance. But… but I killed those servants… and innocent passengers on planes with Osiris elites on them." A beat. "Why are we like this, Monsieur?"

There was a long moment of quiet wherein Roach watched the snow whirl around outside and lit himself another cigarette. "All I know, Martial, is that I'm glad you're back. That's all I know."

"Well, I'm glad to be back. You have all always felt more like real family to me than the Morozovs."

"Yeah… I'm sorry again about killing your friend, man."

He chuckled. "My 'friend' was trying to kill me. I should thank you for saving my life."

"It's chill, man. I get it. Feelings are complicated. It's okay to be upset that he's gone even though he was horrible. And no need to thank me: protecting this gang is my number one priority."

"Speaking of the gang: I saw you all took down Baumbach while I was gone. Congratulations!"

"Yeah, it took all year, though, and we still don't know where the CEO is. He went into hiding about halfway into the job."

"Well, do you still need to kill him if the company's going under?"

Roach smoked and nodded. "He signed off on my husband's solitary confinement. He signed off on sending his body off without informing me. He signed off on letting the jailers deprive him of his money and therefore his insulin in the first place, or he at least looked the other way. He killed my husband."

"I hope you find him, then, mon ami." Jean-Jacques had long-ago come to terms with what sort of a monster he had become, so now he was perfectly willing to accept how curious he was to hear Roach's vile ideas to let them inspire his own depravity. This sick interest was evident in his black eyes when he asked, "Do you know how you're going to do it?"

"Hm? How I'll kill him? I don't know. Maybe I'll bury him in his own gold." He shrugged. "I'm more of an improv artist," he chuckled, "Usually just go with the flow in the moment."

"You say he has gold, monsieur?"

"Yeah. Did some research on the trip when he went into hiding and found out he also owns a few gold mines and, of course, like most rich people with no taste, he likes to just have gold... *around*. For dècor." Jean-Jacques smiled wickedly, so Roach arched his brow and inquired what he was thinking.

"Forgive me, but I have an idea you may like."

"Sure. What is it?"

"It would require a good amount of preparation, not to mention we would need the man himself, but—. Monsieur Roach, are you aware of what aqua regia does?"

"I can't say I'm familiar."

His wicked smile twisted, and darkness flashed in the pits of his eyes. When he finally responded, his voice was low and raspy: "It dissolves gold." Roach smiled just as evilly as Jean-Jacques. "I can only imagine how beautifully it dissolves billionaires." He took a drag to punctuate the dark sentiment.

"You're fucked, dude. I love it."

"Thank you, mon ami."

"You know where to get some of this aqua regia stuff?"

"I know where to get some, yes. Not enough to dissolve an entire person, but the host of this chateau is a chemist, no? He likely has avenues to acquire some."

"Well, this is all fucking fantastic, dude. I can't wait for Franky to find out about how you—." Their conversation was interrupted when Francis bursted into the conservatory and rushed up to Jean-Jacques, who was standing up to match his energy.

"Is it true!?" he asked in French, "Did you murder Tatum Abraham?"

A smug grin. "I did, Monsieur."

Francis' teal-green eyes welled with tears, which ran down his pale cheeks and met with a beaming smile. He pulled Jean-Jacques into his frail arms and squeezed him as hard as he possibly could, which was a lot harder than he had expected. Roach joined in on the hug and smiled softly as Francis whimpered, "Merci," on repeat and cried into Jean-Jacques' shoulder. When he finally retreated and wiped his eyes a few minutes later, he said in French, "You have single-handedly saved the entire world."

"Oh, it was nothing, and you don't need to speak in French," replied Jean-Jacques in English, "I wasn't even concerned about your ends."

"It matters not! A hero is a hero regardless of his intentions." He took up Jean-Jacques' hand and kissed his knuckles as he bowed deeply.

"You're sure he saved the world, bed bug?"

"He's saved us all!" His weepy beaming grin stirred up Roach's stomach with butterflies. "Abraham died of old age! Not murder! Huzzah! Huzzah! Huzzah!" He grabbed Jean-Jacques' wrist and rushed him out of the conservatory with Roach and the dogs trailing quickly behind. He brought them to the living room and told Jean-Jacques to wait. The others in the manor started to appear in pairs beside them, most of them looking confused at the teleportation. When everyone was present, Francis appeared in the middle of the murmuring room with his rapier in one hand and a bottle of champagne in the other. The loud popping sound as he opened the drink was met with cheers from those who knew what was happening, and the next thing they knew, everyone was holding a champagne flute with Francis back in the middle of the room raising his own. "Skoal! To Jean-Jacques!"

Glasses were raised and sometimes clinked together, but those who didn't understand Francis' jubilance were under the assumption it was simply because of the aeromechanic's return and nothing more. Knowing this, for he was the one to tell Francis the good news in the first place, Thyne said, "Frankenstein, tell them why we're celebrating."

He wept happily and set down his glass to grab Jean-Jacques by his shoulders from behind and shake him to emphasise his words as he declared, "The saviour! The saviour of the realm! He hath fractured my known and doomed timeline!"

Jean-Jacques' cheeks were flushed pink with all the eyes on him. He waved timidly at the group.

"What do you mean, Franky?" asked River.

"He killed Abraham! He murdered him!" There was a beat wherein he saw some confusion in the room, so he elaborated: "He changed the future, oh! Summer's day!"

Thyne smiled softly at seeing his friend so elated. There was a chance things wouldn't turn out as favourably as Francis' optimistic expectations, but now wasn't the time to tear him down. Instead, Thyne made his way to the piano and started playing *Ding Dong the Witch is Dead*. He serenaded the room with his angelic voice after a wordless introduction to the song, and River invited Francis to dance, which was a request happily taken.

After only ten minutes of levity, a loud roar silenced the room, and everyone looked to Arjun, who had a tiger sitting beside him. "Apologies for the start. I appreciate the gaiety, but we must prepare the manor for law enforcement. There is a trail of blood leading to our doorstep. We are to make it impossible to tell anyone besides myself and my lovers live here, and we have only until sunrise at the latest. We will celebrate later. Mayhaps myself and Keeva can teach the lot of you some mediaeval group dances. But until then, Androme? You know what to do."

"Yes, master," he said with a bow and disappeared.

Arjun clapped his hands. "Everyone get to work."

⚙ Chapter 73 ⚙
It's Just Good Business

"Tell them if they report on it, I'll hire assassins."

"Yes, ma'am."

"In fact, I'll hire assassins preemptively."

"Yes, ma'am."

"His sister can come to the funeral, but she can't bring her husband."

"Yes, ma'am."

"I want as few people as possible to know he's dead. This is the work of that terrorist group, and I have a plan."

"A plan, Miss?"

"Yes. Set up a meeting with all the highest ranking members of the company. And call my lawyers."

"Yes, ma'am. Anything else?"

She rubbed her forehead and sighed. "More wine, please, Nero."

"Of course." He bowed and took his leave of the room.

She was on board a Canopy cruise that was sailing the same path the *Titanic* once sailed with what remained of Tatum's corpse in the ship's morgue. It was his last wish to be buried in his hometown just outside of Calgary. It would have been faster to fly, but after her crash just a few days prior, she had sworn to never again set foot on an aircraft. The fact that her ship would be sailing through the ominous path of the infamous *Titanic* had her nervous, but there hadn't been an iceberg in the area for decades. Even if there had been an iceberg and the ship started to sink, the lifeboats were plenty and durable and capable of reaching Iceland if not the UK or Canada from wherever the wreck would hypothetically happen.

Having inherited Osiris only six hours prior, Aspyn was already making moves on her plans to destroy *The Crown* and *The Tiara* for having taken the love of her life from her. Her mercenaries had yet to find Perlie Moon as Tatum had instructed them, and the gang had evaded them while they were destroying Baumbach.

The terrorists had rescued the captives Leviathan had managed to trap, and two of the mercenaries had disappeared outright. It was Aspyn's assumption that they must have defected like the other merc, so she bought Leviathan outright only two hours after inheriting the largest fortune in human history. She sent out instructions to find *The Crown* and *The Tiara* and to kill them or any defectors on sight, as well as any journalists trying to report on any of the company's goings-on including the life-state of any and all members. Along with those orders, she told them the names Perlie Moon, Partha and Richard Nima, Clayton and Karson Roach, Androme de Tremblay, Thyne Chamberlain, Silvino Alvarez, and Darlene Quirk with the instructions, "Find out their involvement. Find out their locations. Torture and kill family members. Do whatever you have to do to get me answers and vengeance.

"Give. No. Quarter."

By the time the *Aquillius' Revenge* was docking in New York, Aspyn had already bought every single journalistic company on the planet and instructed them to only report on Osiris if she herself told them to.

She disboarded the ship and was escorted by her immense security detail to a private train that would take her to Alberta. Upon settling into the train, she opened her laptop and continued her frenzied work, the first order of business being making three consecutive purposefully-bad investments. She was confident the speculation would lose her up to thirty billion Euros by the next year, if not a little less, which was exactly what she wanted.

After finishing all of that, she was startled out of her work by Nero, who was offering his hand to her with a sad smile. "It's time for the funeral, ma'am."

She took the hand, and suddenly the world seemed real again. She had blocked it out entirely in her mad dash to enact her plans. When she stepped onto the platform, the breeze from a passing train pushed her hair around and brought a pleasant chill through her. The air smelled of fresh petrichor and pine. Icicles dripped down from the awnings and onto a little girl, who was playing on the platform while her parents watched from a nearby bench. She looked up at the icicles and said something in French to her parents before rushing up and grabbing a toy she had forgotten beside her father.

Aspyn smiled at the innocent scene and took a deep breath of the crisp air to let it calm her. She had already mentally prepared herself for Tatum's death considering his age, so most of her upset was a wrathful thirst for vengeance rather than despondent grief. She was therefore able to be calmed enough to smile somewhat as Nero led her away from the train to her limousine. He helped her sit, followed by her bodyguards, and climbed into the driver's seat to follow the hearse to the funeral home.

Canopy was still in the gang's crosshairs, but considering Abraham's death, they had agreed to take at least a year to rest, raise the children, and otherwise recuperate. It was a month into 2083 when Roach was called into one of Giovanni's examination rooms for the appointment he had scheduled after killing Viktor. He had a timid guilty air about him, but the ancient doctor didn't notice in the slightest. He was flipping through the forms Roach had filled out back and forth on the clipboard until eventually sighing and pulling out a laptop. His first question when he opened up a digital chart was, "Have you suffered serious head trauma in your life?"

"Uh. No."

He arched his brow at him. "Perhaps too much headbanging?"

"Uhhh."

"Or... what do they call it? Moshing?"

"I mean my dad punched me a few times, but that's about it."

He sighed and looked at the forms again. "Did they teach you English in America?"

"...Yes?"

"Your handwriting has always been this illegible, then?"

"Come on, bro, it's not that bad."

With a motion of his head that indicated he would have been rolling his eyes if he had any irises, he looked back at the screen and typed Roach's answers to the many questions he subsequently threw at him. About twenty minutes into the interview: "Why was it removed?"

He rubbed the back of his neck. "We don't gotta talk about it."

"We categorically do. Why was it removed? Was it cancerous?"

"No. It was... uh...."

"Well!?"

"Listen, alright. I was backed into a corner, and I needed a lot of money in a short amount of time so—."

"So you sold your kidney?"

He blushed. "Yes."

"Why did you need the money?"

"We don't need to talk about that."

Giovanni made no attempt to hide his curiosity. "Tell me."

After a deep inhale, Roach sighed and answered, "I was watching this auction, right? And they had this wine from the 1800's, and I just *had* to know what something that old and rotten-looking tasted like, so I won a bidding war for it for $300,000. The auctioneer company more or less told me to pay up what I owed in twenty-four hours, or I'd be in debt to them *and* lose the wine, so I found this shady back-alley guy on the dark web and sold my kidney. It's not even that big of a deal, dude. Let's move on."

Giovanni was stunned to silence, but when he piped back up his air was as normal as ever if not a little jubilant. "What was the occasion?"

Roach's eyes were shifty. He had no occasion for the antique wine, having simply split the bottle with River one random evening playing video games. "Uh…. It was for my sister's birthday."

He smiled. "How sweet." The interview resumed.

After getting his fill of examining the *specimen* that was Clayton Roach, Giovanni dismissed him with one final praise of his fitness. Inspired by the compliment, Roach decided to head for the gym on property. He gathered up a change of clothes and towel and marched through the snow to the gym where he was unsurprised to see Dale and Thyne already getting a morning workout in and slightly surprised to see Jean-Jacques doing the same. He greeted them with a big beaming grin and tossed them each a bottle of water from the fridge before getting to his own sets.

Dale, Thyne, and Jean-Jacques had all finished their showers and trudged back up to the manor when Roach heard the gym's door open and looked toward it. He was laying on a weight-lifting bench, so his head was upside-down as he smiled at the two newcomers. "Heya, kid. I was actually wanting to talk to you. What's up?"

Partha pulled Rory by their interlocked hands to be closer to Roach, who was sitting up and wiping sweat from his face with a rag. "We had a request."

He sort of glared, expecting to be propositioned for a threesome. "What is it?"

Partha looked briefly at Rory who gestured in a way that asked Partha to be the one to say it. "Well," said the kid, "we were wondering— since you're such a bad guy —we were thinking maybe you could give us bad guy lessons."

"And training in the gym," added Rory.

Roach stifled a smirk. "Bad guy lessons?"

"Yeah, so that when we go after Canopy, we'll be scary and cool like you, sir."

"You're cute, kid. Sure. I need to take a break anyway. You guys want some training now?"

"Yes, please, sir," said Rory, "But what about the lessons?"

He chuckled. "Aren't you a landlord? Can't get much more evil than that, dude."

He blushed and sputtered, thankful that Partha said for him, "He wants to be bad like you."

"You're so fucking stupid, dude. Whatever. Why don't you both write me an essay about the evillest things you can think of? To establish a base-line. Then we'll go from there." Partha saluted while Rory nodded. "You two have a change of clothes?" They both confirmed that they did with a gesture to a duffel Partha was carrying. "Cool. Let's see how much you guys can lift already. I bet Party's pretty strong already since he's a sailor."

He blushed and saluted. "Aye, sir!"

Roach rustled his short black hair and started training them. He didn't push either of them too hard, allowing Rory to stop for a shower after only fifteen minutes and Partha after twenty. When Partha came back into the gym after his shower, Roach sat up from the bench and said, "Hey, kid, don't leave yet." He saluted adorably, and Roach rolled his eyes with a little smirk as he stood and wiped the sweat from his face. "I wanted to talk to you."

"What about, sir?"

"When we were in America, Franky and Thyne told me that you apparently bought something of Vinny's at an auction. Do you remember?"

"Vinny…," he tilted his head, "Alvarez?"

"Who else would I be talking about?"

"Yeah, I've got a few of his things, actually. A shame about him dying in—." His eyes widened. "Wait, Vinny is short for Silvino, isn't it?" Roach only chuckled. "ROACH! You were married to the best voice actor in the whole world!?"

"Yes, dumbass."

"Oh my God and—. And I met him!?"

Roach chuckled and gave him a noogie. "Idiot."

He was blushy and excited as he was released and bounced on his toes. "Did he think I was cool!?"

A sad smile. "Yeah, kid. He thought you were cool."

He squealed and hugged Roach tightly. It choked Roach up, but he turned his head and pushed away the show of emotions. Partha was wiping tears off of his cheeks and beaming when he finally retreated. "I can't believe I met Vinny Alvarez and didn't even know it. He inspired me to try so many different voices for my games, and my favourite movie of all time is the English dub of *Nanako*." (A Japanese animated movie from 2073). "He's so talented, Roach. Did he ever use the voices in the bedroom? Like Katsurou's?" He wiggled his eyebrows.

Roach shoved his shoulder playfully. "Shut up, dude."

"Katsurou's voice was so hot." He giggled but had a visible thought and looked up at Roach with another cute head-tilt. "Do you want the things of his I bought?"

"Nah, kid, it's alright. I didn't think you knew him since you didn't recognise him on the job, but I see now you're clearly a big fan. He'd want you to have it."

He frowned. "I'm sorry I didn't recognise him. He was a lot fatter than I thought." Roach's lighter air soured, though it could only be felt and not seen. He was ready to dismiss Partha and go shower, but the kid had another visible realisation. "Wait. His parents were murdered after he died.... Was that...?"

"Yeah."

He lowered his voice to a whisper. "You killed them, sir?"

"I just said I did."

"Why?"

"They abused him in every single way you can think of." The colour drained from Partha's face. "And without him there to stop me...." He trailed off and shrugged. "Anyway, I'm gonna shower."

Partha watched him leave with a tempest of conflicting emotions swirling up inside him. He had no idea of his favourite voice actor's horrible past, beyond his time in the war at least.

Roach finished reading the essay and took off the glasses he had only put on because Partha had told him to wear them to "look more like the sexy teacher." He set them on top of the papers on the dining table and looked down at Partha with his typical emotionless expression.

"Did I do good, sir?"

"Does Perlie know you wrote this?"

"Uhh.... Sort of?"

"What does that mean, kid?"

"She found out about it, but I asked her not to read it."

"She knows how I'm involved in it?"

"Yes.... Did I do good?"

Roach sighed. "You want the truth?"

"Oh, yes sir. I can handle it. I'm a public figure. I promise I've heard worse than whatever you'll say."

"Alright, well first of all: I have a Prince Albert piercing."

Partha nodded and wrote something in his notebook, muttering, "I'll have to remember that for the sketches."

Roach huffed with amusement. "Also, if I was trying to kill you, I wouldn't tie you up like you said, and I certainly wouldn't ask Shelob to do it. I'd just use my telekinesis to hold you still."

"But, sir, Sauron doesn't have telekinesis, does he?"

"You also said 'throbbing cock' four times. I thought you were a writer, dude."

"Oh, I am, sir. I guess I was just… uh… writing too quickly."

Roach chortled. "Well, I'd suggest slowing down next time. Speaking of slowing down: after that first kiss they— or 'we' I suppose —were already naked? You didn't write anywhere that we were undressing." Partha nodded and took more notes. "One of the biggest problems, though, is the language. Not only did you spell a lot of the Sindarin wrong, but, kid, why were they speaking Sindarin at all?"

Partha looked up from his notes and blinked. "Because… Sindarin is hot?"

Roach laughed. "Okay, sure, but you clearly said that I'm Sauron, right? And you're the Mouth of Sauron, so what language *should* we be speaking?"

"Oooohhhh! Black Speech, right?" Roach nodded, and Partha said, "But, sir, I don't know Black Speech. No one does, right?"

"Right, but you could have written it in English and said in the prose that it was Black Speech." Partha took more notes. When he looked back up, Roach continued, "I'm having trouble understanding why this essay is six pages long when the only evil act is at the very end when we, 'went out and killed like 1200 people together, and it was really hot because we were burning down villages and even went to Mt. Doom and started throwing orcs and elves and hobbits into it,'" he quoted the last line of the essay.

"Well, that was the evillest thing I could think of, sir."

Roach pursed his lips. "Oh, I see. Making me read your weird erotica about me was the evil thing, then?"

"Uhhh…. Sure!"

A chuckle. "Well, your next assignment is to write a sequel where you detail at least three of the 1200 murders you mentioned in the last line, okay?"

"And no sex?" He frowned.

"You write whatever you want, kid. I'm not giving you anymore direction than that. We have to establish a baseline for how much of a 'bad guy' you are already, so detail a couple of the killings however you think is the worst way that we would do them together. And don't have us speaking Sindarin when we should be speaking Black Speech. Alright?"

Partha closed his notebook. "Should I go do that now, sir?"

Roach shooed him out of the kitchen lazily and grabbed a beer from the fridge. "God help that man," he muttered to himself in Arabic with a quiet chuckle. He turned next to Rory and cracked open his beer. "Put it on the table, dude."

Rory nodded and set his handwritten essay on the table just as Roach was plopping down into a chair and kicking his boots up to lean far back in the creaky old seat. He pulled the papers to his hands telekinetically and nursed his beer as he read. Rory, all the while, was standing and fidgeting with the belt loops on his expensive dress pants, tracing the tiles on the floor with the points of his loafers, or rocking back and forth on his feet as he waited.

Roach's brow knitted halfway through the first page, and as he turned to the second then the third, he sat upright and set down his beer to read ever faster. His eyes were wide and increasingly horrified as he pressed on, enough that he eventually started to mutter in Arabic, "What the fuck? What the *fuck?*" When he finished the essay he set it down and stared at Rory with his jaw agape. "You fucking wrote this shit, dude?"

He went pale. "Is it bad?"

"Dude, this is so fucked up."

He rubbed the back of his sweaty neck. "You said to make it the evillest thing I could think of."

"Yeah, but not *that* evil!" He chuckled.

Rory laughed nervously with him. "Sorry."

"Well, I guess my assignment for you is to make it less fucking terrifying and more like an art form."

"An art form?"

"Yeah."

They stared at each other for an awkward moment.

"Okay, I'll go start on a new one, then."

As Rory shuffled out of the kitchen and Roach grabbed his beer to sip more, River rushed into the room and grabbed his brother by the shoulders. He shook him back and forth and shouted, "I can't fucking take it anymore, Tony!"

"Chill out, man. You made me spill my beer." He wiped it up with Rory's essay papers.

"Please, Tony, *please* let us cut our hair." He pulled up a handful of his own hair, the ends of which were wet. "I finished pissing and bent down to close the toilet, and—." He shook the wet ends of his hair.

"Ha! Idiot."

River groaned and threw his hands down like a child throwing a fit. "I'm shaving my fucking head, Tony."

He shrugged and sipped his beer. "Okay."

"So you're shaving yours, too."

He frowned and grabbed a handful of his luxurious wavy black locks. "But...."

"No, Tony. It's too long. We'll grow it back to this length eventually. Doesn't your fucking neck hurt? Doesn't it bother you?"

Roach was going to argue more, but he spotted the brand on River's forearm and how it matched with his own. With a sigh: "Fine, but at least let me finish my beer first, pisshead."

River rolled his eyes and washed the ends of his hair in the kitchen sink while he waited for Roach to finish drinking. They chatted about Partha and Rory's "bad guy lessons" and fitness training, Roach praising both of them for different reasons. After crushing his beer can and tossing it on the floor, he followed River to their private shared bathroom where he had already found a razor. It whirred, and Roach teared-up watching his brother shave off his own hair. As it was falling on the floor and into the sink, Thyne knocked on the door and opened it uninvited.

"You're shaving your head, Basil?" He sounded disappointed.

"Yeah, mate. Sonny insisted."

He frowned as he watched the last strip of silky black fall off of River's head. "A shame."

River ran his hands over the fresh buzz and took a deep inhale. "Much better, Tony. Look!" He shook his head quickly from side to side.

Roach sighed and shoved him. "Alright, dude. Clean up your piss-hair." He took a hair-tie from his wrist and secured it around the bottom of his hair, but having so much, he ended up needing three ties to secure all of it. When he was plucking up the razor, River was leaving the bathroom with their trash, now brimming with hair, and Thyne grabbed Roach's forearm lovingly. "It'll grow back, Basil," he whispered.

He smiled down at Thyne and silently admired the scar on his lips. "Don't worry about me, sparkplug. I'll live. I look good with my head shaved anyway."

"If River was any indication then I agree," he said with a purr.

Roach took a moment to get the strength to turn on the razor, and when it started to whir, he interwove his fingers with Thyne's and squeezed. "You've got this," said Thyne with a pat on the back of his hand. With one more inhale to brace himself, as if he was about to jump a high-dive, he ran the razor over his head.

This was the first time he had cut his hair since Silvino's death.... It almost felt like cutting away the last remnants of foolish hope that they might meet again. As silly as it seemed, he had always relished the fact that some of that hair had existed in the same room as Silvino. That he had touched some of it. As it fell off his head in chunks, Roach couldn't help but relate it to the ashes in Lake Pontchartrain: dead, detached, and indistinct.

When all was said and done, there was a minimal mess in the sink, and the three hair-ties he had used to bind the mass of black helped it to be easy to clean. Thyne plucked them off the floor and tilted his head. He didn't understand why Roach of all people would be taking such precautions. He was going to inquire about it, but he was distracted by the heft of the hair. All together in his hand, he lifted it up and down and guessed, "Good Gods, Basil. This must weigh at least a kilo."

Roach finished shaking out the remnants from the buzz on his head and was quick to joke, "Follow me for more weight loss tips."

Thyne chuckled and rolled his eyes. "I love you, you muppet. Why did you tie up the pieces like this? Are you going to keep it?"

"I don't know. Just kinda wanted the option, I guess."

"What would you do with it?"

He shrugged. "You can have some for your voodoo or whatever if you want."

Thyne pouted. "Maybe I will!"

He was trying to be threatening, but Roach kissed him and said, "Cute." He gently pressed his fingers against the scar after retreating and whispered, "You like the buzz, babe?"

He was still pouting but eventually grumbled, "Yes."

"Good. Let's go. You still have to learn all the plugins in *Oddity*." *Oddity* was the music production software Roach favoured and had been slowly teaching Thyne how to use. While learning the program, Thyne had also been teaching Roach a lot of fundamental music theory and tips on composition in general, so each session involved them teaching each other more about music than the day before. They were both of the mind that it was incredibly romantic, and they had agreed to write an album together by the end of the year.

When Christmas was upon her, Aspyn had holed up with her cat and rabbit in a panic room with Nero standing outside the door to keep watch. Two tragic Christmases in a row were enough to have her paranoid that she would be targeted for a third that day. The only sound in the cramped little box was the thumping of her wild racing heart. Her arms were trembling and wrapped up tightly around her pets, both of which were calm. They were so docile and allowing her to hold them because they could sense her upset, and their love was greatly appreciated by the lonely woman.

She had no one left to lose, save for Nero and the animals. She had nothing worth dying for, as well. Where she had once sought after Abraham for his money, now that she had all the money in the world, she realised it was never riches she had wanted. What she had most desired all those years of greediness was simply freedom. The thought crossed her mind vaguely and juxtaposed with the cage she had locked herself in. She briefly pondered dissolving Osiris, taking even just a fraction of its wealth, and fleeing with Nero and her pets to Nepal. It was the sort of idea that stuck to her brain as soon as it had formed and refused to ever fully dissipate.

Nero knocked on the panic room door as gently as he possibly could, but Mrs. Abraham still blenched as if she had been shot in the heart. "Apologies, Miss," he said as he opened the door and watched Meatloaf rush out into the manor, "It's noon on the twenty-sixth now. What would you have me make for lunch?"

After catching her heaving horrified breaths and grasping at her racing heart, she said, "Whatever you want."

He bowed his head politely and offered a hand to help her step out of the panic room and into the luxurious halls of her Parisian manor. The floors were white marble and met with the cherry wood panelling on the walls abruptly. The ceilings were a combination of cherry wood, white plaster, and the same marble as the flooring, with extravagant chandeliers all throughout the building. Wide spiralling staircases, gargantuan oriental rugs, satin throw pillows on designer couches, enough rooms to house a small army. At times, Aspyn found all the opulence exhausting and obnoxious, but after twenty-four hours of sleepless panic, she felt more warm and safe than ever in the cold lifeless halls of the empty manor. Lunch was a simple sandwich to hold her over before she would sleep for ten hours.

Upon waking, Nero offered to make her dinner. With a lazy gesture to approve, she wiped her tired eyes and dragged her feet to the office. Sitting in Tatum's chair felt wrong and put a weight on her shoulders, but she was too exhausted and frazzled to let the feeling linger for longer than a few minutes. With a sigh, she opened her laptop and started working. The investments she had made at the beginning of the year that she had hoped would lose her money were doing just that. She smiled and yawned and thanked Nero when he brought her a cup of Earl Grey.

She ate at her desk with Nero eating in the servants' quarters alone. He worried his mistress was unravelling. She had fired all of her servants save for him and sold all of her properties save for this one. Her investments were losing an unbelievable amount of money, and she had just spent twenty-four hours in a paranoid panic. He wondered if there might have been something he could do to help her, but it would be above his station to question her. Perhaps, however, she saw him as more of a friend than butler considering she hadn't let him go when she purged the rest of her house staff.

He scrolled through news articles on his phone as he ate his soup noisily and noticed something Mrs. Abraham would no doubt want to know, if she didn't already: the crown jewels had gone suddenly missing. He knew one of the terrorist groups after Osiris called itself *The Crown*, so he copied the link into his notes app to show to Mrs. Abraham when she wasn't busy working.

In navigating to his notes app, he accidentally opened a music player and saw a new album had released the day prior from Red Velvet. It was called *We Stole The Crown Jewels*. He snorted with amusement and choked briefly on his soup. After coughing the broth out of his lungs, he hied to Aspyn's office and knocked gently on the door.

"It's open," she droned.

He entered with his phone still in his hand and said, "Excuse me, Miss, but didn't you say Red Velvet was the stage name of one of the terrorists?"

She arched her brow. "Yes. Why?"

He showed her the album title. "The crown jewels really are missing, as well. He released the album on Christmas. I only tell you because—."

"Perfect," she said with a wicked grin, "Cheers, mate. Have a seat. I'll tell you my plan, as it's finally coming to fruition." He sat in one of the cushioned mahogany and leather seats which faced the large matching desk. "You thought I was worrying about losing money when I would mention those investments from the beginning of the year. I was actually worrying the opposite. I was worried I would make money rather than lose it." Nero's brow knitted. "I have just now dissolved Osiris into fourteen subsidiaries, none of which share the name. I have also just sent instructions to my journalists to report that Osiris is dying. Do you understand?" He pondered but was given little time to answer before Aspyn continued, "They'll think they've won, and if they look into my finances somehow with whatever unnatural means they might have, they'll see that I really have just lost thirty-six billion Euros. I haven't let the journalists report on Tatum's death yet, so as far as anyone else knows, he's still calling the shots. The terrorists haven't come after me yet because they don't know I'm involved. They can't possibly know who's really in charge right now, and since they know that Tatum is dead, they'll assume that the company breaking up is a sign of their success."

Nero stroked his goatee as he pondered her plans and eyed her evil smile. "Very clever, Miss, but I do feel the need to remind you of your plane crash."

"Oh, faugh," she flapped her hands around to shoo the idea away, "It was unrelated. They would have come after me just yesterday if they knew about me. And if it was them that crashed my plane, they'll think I'm dead. They're going after the monarchy now, stealing the crown jewels: they're not going to bother with Osiris anymore. They think they've won."

"Well, if it's not too bold of me to say it, Miss, I think you're as cunning as a fox, and I'm proud to be of service to you. Do you need anything of me to help your ends?"

Her wicked grin softened. "For now, mate, I think I just want to curl up on the couch and watch a good movie. Join me?"

"Of course, Miss."

⚙ Chapter 74 ⚙

A Woman as Changing and Harsh and Untamable as the Sea

During their year's rest, the gang had started light preparations to take down Canopy, which was the largest company other than Osiris on their list. It was Partha's request to have a sailing ship like Francis' vessel when he was a pirate, so Rory went with Francis to a shipyard in Marseilles and commissioned one to be built. This was in the summer of 2083, and it wouldn't be ready until the spring of 2085, so they were glad to have gone during their year off. After a confirmation of the time when they would start attacking Canopy, a brief meeting was called in the midst of Ramadan. It was determined that they would wait until Christmas to release Thyne and Roach's collaborative album, which would happen in tandem with Francis stealing the crown jewels. It was Roach's idea to title the album such that he would be incriminating himself publicly, and when Thyne unsurprisingly protested, Roach had replied, "I don't care, Thyne. Party inspired me, and maybe it'll help take some of the heat off of him." This had shut Thyne up and put a proud blushing smile on Partha's face.

Also in their year of rest, on November 8th, Francis approached Roach only an hour after he awoke and took up his hand to kiss his knuckles and bow. "Clayton, my love?"

"What's up, bed bug?" He said as he resumed pouring himself a bowl of stale cereal.

"I have a gift for this: the anniversary of thy birth."

He huffed out a laugh through his nose. "Dork. What is it?"

"The twain of us, along with Thyne and Karson, shall spend the morn packing supplies."

"Packing for what?"

He kissed his knuckles again, and it was then that Roach noticed happy tears in his eyes. "Clayton, my sweet pharos— my beloved monster— my murderous djinn. Because of you and your ceaseless love of me, my last foray into Hell was antecedent to even our trek across the states." Roach smiled sweetly. "Not only that: upon his killing of the rotten Abraham, Jean-Jacques has returned to me my hope. We have not suffered any blows from Leviathan, and life has been kind! This year's rest has done thee well as it has done us all well, and I opine it is as swell a time as it shall ever be to show you the wonders of the ancient world— of Ancient Egypt."

Roach pulled Francis into his strong arms and held him close. "Oh, bed bug. You're so sweet. I'm glad you've been feeling better. Haven't lost yourself since before Baumbach? That's amazing!"

"I can guarantee only four years in the past, but it shall be more than enough time to see as much of the ancient world as you like, and mayhaps after we've taken down Canopy, we can flee to the stars, the four of us, to see Jove, nebulae, the Sirian system—! Oh! Roach, it will be such a beautiful life with the three of thee galavanting through the cosmos!"

Roach's smile soured. "One step at a time, bed bug. We'll start with Ancient Egypt. I don't know if I want to be away from Ruin for four years, though."

"She won't age a moment! We will leave, experience years away, and return at the very same moment we left."

He stroked his beard. "Hm. Well four years still seems like a long time.... But I'm sure I *will* want to stay a long time. And me and Thyne can work on the album! I'll bring my laptop and gear, and you can charge the battery by sending it backwards. So long as you don't age the memory backwards. And...." After some more rambling about what he could do and see, Roach had excited himself enough to kiss Francis' cheek and bolt out of the kitchen to start packing.

The twins had more or less mastered the Old Egyptian language in only two days of their vacation to Ancient Egypt and spent a little more than three years there with Francis and Thyne, so when they returned (at the very same moment they had left), they were all four passing out hugs to the rest of the gang, all of whom they had missed dearly. They showed pictures they had taken and pulled from their plethora of stories to entertain the others. Roach had also managed to bring back some toys for Sirion, Ruin, and the dogs. It was the twins' thirty-fourth birthday when they awoke, but they were thirty-seven before sundown.

After Christmas, it came to light that Osiris had shattered into fourteen smaller companies, none of which any news articles named. Upon learning this on the first day of 2084, the beaming grin Francis had worn for all of 2083, as well as his holiday in the past, became strained. River immediately noticed the upset in Francis but didn't comment while most of the others were celebrating the stroke of luck. He took him aside into the garden during the New Year's fireworks show coming from a yacht nearby and leaned down to whisper, "What's wrong?"

"Oh, nothing," he said before swigging from his flask.

River grabbed his wrist and pulled him close. More forcefully this time, he whispered, "What's wrong, Franky. You can tell me. Write it down, if you don't want Thyne to hear."

"Where is Clayton?" He looked around.

"I am Clayton," said River.

He squinted. After snatching his hand away to swig again he spat, "Clayton does not speak with the devil's tongue."

River smirked wickedly. "Careful. Too much rum, and you might have believed me."

"Faugh."

"What's wrong, Frankenstein? I'm here for you." He took his hand and squeezed it gently. "Tony's worried, too."

"He is?"

"Yeah, man. He thinks it's a bad omen that it's in fourteen pieces rather than any other number."

"As he should." There was a beat. Francis ran a hand through his matting hair and groaned. "Alright. I will tell you."

"Good boy."

He glared, which delayed his words. "When I learned of Osiris' fate— the company, not the god —I was taught that it was briefly broken up into fourteen pieces, but it was not finished."

River pursed his lips. His hopes were never as high as Francis' had been, and now he was convinced that their blow against Osiris had meant absolutely nothing in the long run. Still, he attempted to goad the hope in his tipsy friend by saying, "But Abraham didn't die of old age in this timeline like you were taught."

He nodded and swigged again. "Aye. Still I sweat. Me soul be a din only quiet by gin."

"It'll be okay. Let's just try and focus on Canopy, okay? Come watch the fireworks, get hammered, and let me and Tony hold you."

"Aye. I've no choice but to tarry. I dare not attempt learning more of the future, lest I run the risk of making it worse. Fortune's be it must run its course."

Increasingly large and well-armed men opened each set of double doors she approached as she made her way through the labyrinthian halls. The clicking of her heels against the marble flooring and the swish of her hips were the only sounds echoing off the art-filled walls. Even the man leading her through the building was quiet.

After at least two minutes of walking, she was finally stopped and led into a luxurious room with rounded walls and a plush blue carpet. The man that had led her there closed the door behind her, leaving her alone with another man, who had stood upon her entry. He adjusted his tie as he rounded to the front of his desk and held out his hand to shake with hers.

He was a middle-aged man of roughly six feet with chiselled masculine features, a brawny body, and a beaming white grin. His skin was smooth, save for the wrinkles of his age, and his blond hair was mostly slicked back but with an unruly strand that tried ceaselessly to caress his brow. He was clean shaven and smelled of sage, cherry wood, and very vaguely of coconut. She had only seen him in the media. She hadn't expected him to be so handsome in person, and she certainly didn't expect his skin to be so soft when she shook his hand.

"It's lovely to meet you, Mrs. Abraham." He brought her hand up to his lips and kissed her knuckles politely, with a wry grin and cheeky wink.

She blushed and batted her eyelashes as she pulled her hand away and pushed some of her wavy auburn locks behind her ear. "The pleasure is all mine, Mr. Park."

He smiled, and it was like the entire world stopped. It felt like a betrayal to be so smitten with him while still grieving Tatum, but he was undeniably beautiful and charismatic to boot. "Please please. Have a seat." He gestured to a pair of chairs across from his desk. She lowered herself into one of them in a ladylike manner and tucked her ankles together under the seat in lieu of crossing her legs while wearing a pencil skirt. Elijah leaned on his desk and smiled sweetly at his guest. "What brings you to my beautiful country this fine fine day?"

"I heard about your prison problem," when she said this, the levity of his smile soured. A chilling darkness settled over his brow, but he slid a hand through his hair, taking the unruly strand with it, and succeeded in suppressing the brief flash of rage.

"Yes, we have had a particular lot of trouble with a group of terrorists calling themselves *The Crown* or *The Tiara* or whatever the fuck," he flapped his hands around and averted his eyes to huff and try to swallow his rage again, "I apologise for cursing in the presence of a lady. This is of no concern to you." He turned back to her and forced a smile. "So, to what do I owe the pleasure?"

"It's the prisons," she said and tilted her head at the way it enraged him, "I wanted to offer some assistance."

He took a deep breath. His hands were white-knuckling around the lip of the desk he was leaning on. With his eyes closed and an incensed air to his forced jubilance, he said, "If you are here to try buying the country from me, you have vastly overestimated the straits I have found myself in."

"Mr. Park, sir, I think you misunderstand my intentions. This country is a great asset to me, but what good would owning a country do me? I'm here with an offer I don't think you'll refuse, and seeing as I am likely the only person in the world allowed to be alone in a room with you like we are now, I think you'll listen."

He sighed and looked down at his loafers. "I apologise, Mrs. Abraham. Please. Go on." He gestured for her to continue and, in the same motion, took a case of cigars from his desk and lit one.

"Thank you," said Aspyn as she readjusted her posture to look more attentive, "As you know, the terrorists have also been a thorn in my side. They destroyed my cities in the new states and stole my workers. After they destroyed half of the prisons in your country, I was struck with an idea. I thought, '*Why don't I fund the reconstruction of the prisons they razed and use the prisoners as free labour to replace the factories I lost?*' What say you to that, Mr. Park?"

"You'll rebuild the prisons?" He puffed on his cigar.

"Yes, sir, if you'll let me."

He laughed. "Let you!? I'd beg you if I had to, Mrs. Abraham."

She smiled and blushed, making a conscious effort to look cute and smitten as she said, "There's no need to beg, Mr. Park. I want to befriend you. We're the two most powerful people on the planet, are we not?"

The grin he let on after such a comment was slimy and sleazy, but Aspyn found it enchanting. "That we are, Mrs. Abraham. You rebuild those prisons, and I'll fill them up for you."

"Well, thank you very much, Mr. Park." She stood to leave, but he stopped her with a hand around her wrist. She turned back toward him and blinked up at him with her big doe eyes.

"A glass of wine to celebrate?"

"To celebrate what, Mr. Park?"

"Why, our friendship, of course."

"Well, how could I say no?" As he was pouring them each a glass of chardonnay, Aspyn's phone chimed. She apologised and looked at it. "Oh, I'm terribly sorry, Mr. Park, but this is important."

"Take your time."

She nodded and made a call. Elijah eavesdropped as he poured the wine and managed to put together that she was on a call with some mercenary or assassin who had killed one of the terrorists' mothers. After that call, she immediately made another, and Elijah accidentally overfilled one of the glasses as he heard her say, "Tell them I'll pay 700 billion for it. Yes. The entire palace. Is that not enough? 750 then."

When he realised he had overpoured the wine, Elijah was quick to drink the excess from the glass and wipe away the spillage with a cloth napkin from one of his desk drawers. Aspyn finished her call a few minutes later and smiled apologetically at him as he handed her the less-filled glass of wine. "I couldn't help but overhear you were trying to buy a palace."

She blushed and pushed some of her hair behind her ear. "Yes, I just found out where the terrorists were hiding a few years ago, and I'd like my mercenaries to comb through it for any possible trace of those rotten cunts who killed my husband." She started at her own cursing. "Apologies. I only mean that I want my men to look through it without interference from the government, so I bought it."

"You bought what?"

"The Palace of Versailles."

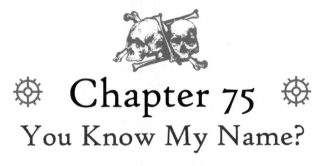

✵ Chapter 75 ✵
You Know My Name?

Partha, like Rory, had gained a lot of muscle mass from his training with Roach and was overly pleased with his new look. He went shirtless more often now, but at this moment in particular he was covered in protective gear as he and Jean-Jacques worked tirelessly for their third week in a row. They were forging bronze cannons and gold-plated cannonballs to arm the frigate they were having built in the shipyard. While he was welding a clamp down onto one of the barrels, Partha was surprised by the door to the workshop slamming open and Perlie rushing up to him.

By the time she had reached him, he had set down his tools and lifted up his mask. "What's wrong, heart?" She threw herself into his strong arms and wept fervently. "Oh, shhh. Honey, it's okay. I'm here. What's wrong?"

He held her lovingly, letting her soak his apron in tears for almost three straight minutes before she finally managed to muster up her voice: "They killed my mom."

Partha scooped her into his arms and told Jean-Jacques, "Keep working without me," before promptly carrying her across the property and setting her on a bench in the garden. The early springtime blossoms were burgeoning into the mild mediterranean air. Birds twittered in the treetops, and the brook nearby had recently thawed enough to babble its way across the gemstones on its bed beautifully. Perlie was still crying into Partha's chest, but she retreated to let her bleary gaze trail around at the gradient of colours. "I'm really sorry, heart."

She sniffled loudly and wiped her arm across her face. "Appa sent more protection for Dale and Roach's families after hearing the news. He'll also be bringing Pio to us since sending protection to the warfront is… stupid."

"Hadn't he already sent protection for your mother?"

She nodded and whimpered. "It wasn't enough. They killed all his men then—," a wailing grief overtook her again, and she threw herself back into Partha's loving embrace.

After another ten minutes of weeping, they heard the crunching of gravel under someone's fast-approaching steps. He rushed up to Perlie's other side and pet her arched back. "I just heard." It was Rory, having only just returned with Thyne from their second trip to Australia together. "Perlie, I'm so sorry." She whimpered and sniffled and swapped from Partha's arms to Rory's.

It was only a week later that the shipyard called Rory to inform him that his frigate was ready to sail, so he took the Nimas, both of whom were well-disguised, to the yard to sail their ship to Loomis Manor's private harbour. She was a beautiful vessel Partha had dubbed *Initiative* and fitted with blood-red sails. The wood of the ship was also stained cherry-red. The trims and accents were all bronze, gold, or copper, and therefore matched beautifully with the cannons that would need to be taken down from the workshop and installed by the twins. As they were disboarding into the half-flooded vineyards behind the manor, Francis appeared beside them and smiled at the craft. "She be a fine beast, Partha!"

"Aye! The scourge of Canopy! Would you like to come aboard?"

He stroked his beard and silently guessed at the ship's distance from the shore of this private beach as something like a hundred feet. "She is anchored securely?"

"Aye, sir."

"I suppose I could withstand a sprightly jaunt."

Partha beamed and offered an arm to link with Francis' to help him onto the dinghy. Rory and Richard followed behind them and listened intently as the old pirate admired the craftsmanship, gave tips on sailing that even the Nimas didn't know, and ultimately ended up behind the wheel with an odd expression. It was something like longing and something like fear, accentuated further when he squinted at the setting sun over the sea. After a while of quiet, broken only by the gentle lapping of waves against the hull and the jangling of the rigging, he said solemnly, "There be times that horizon beckons me as a siren to the shoals."

Partha, Richard, and Rory followed Francis' gaze out to the horizon and watched the sun as it turned red and sank beneath the waves. At the last light of day, Partha turned to finally reply to Francis but was distracted when he saw Neodesha rushing up to the beach. She waved them down, and the four aboard the *Initiative* returned to their dinghy to quickly row up to her place on the sandy shore.

"What ails thee?" asked Francis as he stepped off the little boat.

"Pa! Pa, I don't wanna be the one ta tell ya, but ya gotta know: they done reported on Mr. Abraham's death. They's sayin' he died of old age."

The colour drained from Francis' face, and his sea-green gaze went hollow. The waves crawled up the shore to his boots and tried to pull him into the big black abyss behind him but managed only to take a tear that fell from his pale cheeks. He shook away his upset and climbed wordlessly up to the manor with his hands in the pockets of Roach's hoodie he had borrowed.

Neodesha looked at Partha and Rory with a concerned smile. "Was he out on that there ship?"

"He was."

"And he didn't have no panic attack?"

"He seemed to want to go sailing, actually," replied Richard.

Her eyes widened and looked after Francis as he closed the back door of the manor behind him. "I don't rightly believe it!"

"Do you think he might want to come with us instead of going to do the Australia job?" asked Partha with a pleading hopeful posture.

"I wouldn't get my hopes up, kid. They need 'em on that there mission fer them powers of his."

Partha kicked the sand disappointedly.

"Well, maybe after the job then," tried Rory, "We'll still be sinking ships after they're all finished down under."

She shrugged. "I can't even fathom he was out there at all, Mr. Couch. 'Sposin' we'll just hafta see how God wills it."

They all four returned to the manor through the back door and heard laughter and chatter around the dining room table. The twins had started a session of the West Marches game they were co-DMing, and when Roach spotted the others coming in from the back porch he raised his voice to clamour playfully, "More! More the merrier!" Already around the table were Melchiresa, Thyne, Arjun, and Dezba, with Francis sitting between the twins and leaning on Roach. His posture was solemn, and the way he was staring at his flask was indication enough that he would not be playing and only wanted to be near his lighthouse while a dark tempest tore through his soul.

Partha and Neodesha joined the session, but Richard wanted to shower, and Rory had already made plans to go on a jog with Dale and Perlie. Meanwhile, Jean-Jacques was swimming laps in the pool, Pio was sleeping off his jet-lag, and Jae and Giovanni were reading and chatting minimally in the library where Sirion and Ruin had fallen asleep on each other while playing on the rug.

Among the monsters in the manor, both real and imagined, the loudest to Francis' perception was the grandfather clock in the living room. Its ticking was a series of stabs to his heart. '*What a fool I was*,' he thought as he pushed through his tattoos and lamented how he had scratched out the apocalyptic future he thought Jean-Jacques had destroyed.

Roach noticed his tattoos changing out of the corner of his eyes and draped one of his burly arms around Francis' bony shoulders to half-hug him. He leaned down and whispered, "It's gonna be okay, bed bug," so that only Francis could hear while River was explaining a scene to his players.

Francis shook his head at the prospect. He replied in Demotic with a voice just as low, "To think we wasted all that time in Egypt and continue to waste more now."

Roach squeezed him harder, frustrated, and replied in the same dead tongue, "You trust me, don't you, bed bug?"

"I trust you," he said eventually.

"Then let me waste this one last night. Fair enough?"

"Faugh. It matters not if I concede, you will do as you please regardless of me wishes."

"That's the spirit." He laughed quietly and kissed his cheek before retreating.

Francis rolled his eyes and swigged from his flask. Only a moment later, Partha said, "Franky? I have a question."

"I am not paying attention to this session, my friend."

"Well, it's not about the game, mate. I was just wondering—. You seemed to maybe want to try sailing again out there," the others all looked to him with various levels of surprise, "—and well, I was wondering why we don't maybe let you sail around the harbour a bit. To help ease you back into it. I'd be mighty honoured to sail under your command when we're out sinking cruise ships."

"Party, don't bother him with—," began Roach.

"Let him," interrupted Francis, "'Tis a flattering notion, but I am ne'er to sail again as ordained by God on high, demons below, and all that lies therein between."

"You don't believe in that stuff, Frankenstein," said Partha, "Why is it really that you're so afraid of the ocean?"

There was a beat of quiet wherein they all tried to suss out if he was comfortable enough to explain. It seemed he was too perturbed to divulge the story, so Thyne opened his mouth to discourage more prying but was surprised to hear Francis say in that sultry sea-dog voice of his: "'Twere the mutiny what wrenched away me courage." They gave him their undivided attention and listened as he told the story:

"Upon my vessel, which Partha has made known was infamous among slavers, me crew were all freed or escaped slaves save for three: me son, me daughter, and me first mate. My beautiful wife, Juan Ya, was another of master Keeva's: we escaped together when I were but nineteen years old, and she were sixteen. We stole a ship of the master's from that very same harbour," a vague gesture to the window beside him at the dark glittering sea, "and made way for the new world. Promises of riches, land, foreign creatures and peoples—. *'What adventure!'* thought us with the foolishness that be marked of youth. *'And what adventure of marriage,'* thought I with tenfold the foolishness.

"We married on my vessel that very same year and sailed into the sunset, secure in our minds that life had only just begun: our past the only home for misery then. Rum was the most intoxicating taste— new to my tongue at the time. The salt of the wind— the salt of our brows— there was no better panacea to the woes of the past nor even the present.

"From vessel to vessel, we gained crew, cargo, riches, and above all: reputation. We were a pair to be reckoned with, and as we freed slaves and watched delightedly as they killed their captors, we were made host to a vast swath of colourful characters. We taught each other all manner of cultural oddities and linguistic tics. I was of the halfwitted opinion, that these lot were my friends— nay: my family. That they might die for me as I would so readily die for them and nearly had on countless occasions.

"When I captained us through our first hurricane, it was the crew's thinking that I was some manner of sailing legend: all the more reason to stay aboard. Me sailing skills remained mine own, but most other skills of mine were shared amongst the crew, and I were happy to share the glory! Lo! The fool I was. The fool I am.... 'Twere too often I allowed Juan Ya or me first mate, whom I later learned was Viktor— I had brought him to the past to keep myself and my crew safe—. 'Twere too often I allowed others to do as they pleased. I was a soft captain: easily swayed in all matters but sailing. 'Twere common amongst us pirates, as Party may know, to run ships democratically, but there were times I were wholeheartedly the leader and last to speak on a matter wherein I would, in my cowardice, allow the democracy reign where it ought not've. However, by my sixth successful foray through a tempest, I felt just to ignore Juan Ya's pleadings to be allowed to sail through the next.

"What I failed to see at the time but have since made notice of in the handful of stints wherein I have relived these years—. I failed to recognise the resentment brewing in Juan Ya. 'Twere like a tempest of its own were forming over her. After my daughter's birth, Juan Ya was particularly dark like the depths and bitter as gall. Wen, our daughter, was much more favoured by her than I ever had been, but still I somehow managed to win her over again. I allowed her once— only once— to sail through a storm. 'Twere no hurricane, but she still nearly capsized us, and that was the last of it. 'You shan't risk us all for your bitter pride, Juan Ya,' I had told her, 'Sail as thee please through sunlit calm seas, but risk not our daughter— risk not our friends.'"

He paused and swigged again, rubbing his forehead to massage away an oncoming headache. "After Wen's birth, there was only one single night of love-making to be had with Juan Ya for the years to follow, and from that night was born my precious son. Juan Ya had poisoned my daughter against me, slowly but surely, but my son could never be swayed. No matter what anyone told him, he admired me endlessly.... Foolishly. The way a child worships God not for fear nor reverence but for the hope of rewards. And I gave him such: he were a good fencer even as young as he was last I saw him.... He may have been a great sailor one day. A fine pirate."

He wiped tears from his cheeks and swigged again. "'Twere a drunken night of gaiety wherein I let mine arrogance, which I had become known to boast, inflate to an unreasonable degree: in my drunken stupor, I put Juan Ya herself in a betting pool in order to win a ship. I knew I was guaranteed the win, but she was present to watch me treat her so callously and—. I didn't see it through the rum-blear at the time, but this was the moment she decided to kill me. To mutiny.

"That night aboard me carrack I was torn from me bed, not only by Juan Ya but by every friend I ever thought I had made as captain. *'What nightmare is this!?'* I had thought, *'Awaken at once, Androme! Awaken at once!'* But I did not wake, for I were not dreaming. The clamouring and shouting— my beloved hound barking and growling and trying to stop this coup— none of it was real to me until I felt the cold of the Atlantic and its black inky depths immediately trying to swallow and crush me. I sank like a stone, yet still I saw three things which shall never leave my recollection no matter if I return to the void of rotting for a thousand eternities:

"The first of these horrors was seeing my quartermaster scoop up my dog and throw him into the sea after me, as if his innocent love for me made him as worthy as I of death. The second horror was the sight of Juan Ya kicking a barrel of chum in after the twain of us. And...," he paused to wipe more tears from his eyes, "The third was how my son reached after me. He tried to jump in to save me, but Viktor stopped him." A beat.

"What followed was a flickering of reality. Forward and backwards, I was unintentionally sending myself around the moment in time. I watched Juan Ya kick the chum in twenty-three times. I was attacked by a shark— both an agony and salvation, for the beast brought me to the surface of the water wherein I would have otherwise sunk to the depths—. I was struck by this creature forty-six times, and my precious dog was torn in twain by another pair of feasting beasts: this I witnessed sixty-five times. My ship was near. My ship was far. I was sinking through the black. I was breaching through the waves. Back and forth and up and down and hot and cold and over and over and over and—." He stopped and looked down at his flask as he fidgeted with its lid noisily. "I came to realise the power at my beck, and I attempted to use it to stop the mutiny, succeeding only in reliving it another umpteen cycles.

"Me hope being as inimical to hopelessness as it is, 'twere likely days of me own time I wrestled with the fourth dimension— begging God not to forsake me to such Hellish nightmares as this— begging God for any mercy whatsoever." Another swig. "Eventually, I stopped time and held it long enough to learn I could walk across the water, after which I walked to a nearby island and regathered my strength before attempting to walk to a civilised place. 'Twere on that island I first learned I cannot starve— or at the least I do not hunger for years if left to such a fate." He ran his hands through his hair and looked at Partha with a sad smile. "The sea be a temptress I once thought I'd tamed, but I fear I've challenged fate one too many times, my friend. I dare not boast by sailing again...."

"Though I am not a religious man, and I stray further from God as each of my wretched days elapses.... I have a family to lose again, and I shan't make the same mistakes as in my youth, but... were there a God, mayhaps I might at the least learn my son's fate."

Quiet enveloped the room. It seemed everyone was letting the story settle in their souls, but the serenity was broken with a scoff and a roll of the eyes from Melchiresa. He spoke in Chinese, a language not even Arjun was aware he knew, saying, "I'm right here, you fucking dumbass."

Francis perked up and eyed him with tears streaming his cheeks. "Jean-Marie?"

Melchiresa dropped the pencil he had been fidgeting with, his eyes going wide. He may have said something, but Arjun let out a startled shout and scolded Francis in Italian: "Did you just tell him his name!? You idiot!"

Melchiresa stood from the table and quit the room with Arjun rushing madly after him and begging under his breath in a language the others couldn't place as they gained quick distance.

"Franky, I—. I had no idea your son was still alive," said Thyne with a bright pink tint on his cheeks, "Are you okay?"

He hadn't moved at all since looking into his son's eyes. It was almost as if he was frozen in time: his shocked stature unmoving and the only indication of life in him showing in the tears falling from his pallid face.

"Bed bug?"

Roach's hand on his shoulder grounded him enough that he immediately scrambled from the table and rushed after Arjun and Melchiresa in the hopes he might chance a conversation with his long-lost son.

He thought they must have been in the master suite, but on his way there he heard Arjun tearfully shouting in his study. With so many emotions whipping up his soul, it had entirely slipped his mind that he could use his power to find them at his own pace, but when he heard the loud crack of a gunshot, he stopped time instinctively.

Despite the unmoving nature of time, he rushed and trembled as he stumbled into the study to see what had happened. When he entered the chamber he was met with a horrifying visage. Half-fallen to the rug with a pistol still slightly gripped in his hands was Melchiresa, who had evidently shot himself. Arjun was on his knees in front of him with hands clasped and begging.

Francis' eyes welled as he stared at the unmoving scene for what may as well have been a century before finally releasing his grip on time, not willingly, but because he had exhausted his energy too much to hold it any longer.

The body thumped to the ground in tandem as Arjun's mournful wail. He rushed to the exploded head and tried to scoop brain matter back into the broken skull.

All the while, Francis only stared. He listened to Arjun's hyperventilating and the distant cries of the children downstairs who had been startled from their slumber by the commotion. It felt like another century, but it was only a minute later that Francis closed and locked the door behind him to give them more privacy. He approached Arjun and crouched down beside him, rubbing the small of his back.

When Arjun was present of mind enough to notice Francis, he immediately leapt to his feet and cocked the same gun that had just killed his lover. He aimed it for Francis and pulled the trigger, succeeding only at shooting a vase behind him. Madly, he slammed his hand around on the desk, shoving papers all over the room in a scramble to find more rounds for the flintlock.

"Master," said Francis with a surprisingly resolute tone, "Master, why do you fire upon me?"

"YOU TOLD HIM HIS NAME!" He grabbed Francis by his shoulders and shook him fervently as he repeated the same sentiment several times in decreasing clarity and volume as his grief overtook him again. He collapsed into Francis' arms, the both of them weeping, and managed to give the old pirate something of an explanation for the confusing unfolding of events when he mewled, "The Ferryman wouldn't let him cross without a name."

⚙ Chapter 76 ⚙
The Seas Be Ours

The *Charybdis*, the largest cruise ship in the world, was on a returning trek from Bermuda to Halifax. She was 400 metres in length and ninety in breadth, making her too large to pass through any narrow channels and thus soft-locking her in the Atlantic. The ocean that night of April 28th was calm. The light of the crescent moon was sparkling sparingly on the waters as the ship churned through them. She was a vessel so bright that the stars could scarcely be seen by the passengers party-ing on deck. All was lively and jovial, but it was with an unspoken trepidation that a dense and chilling fog rolled over the vessel.

Penelope was an eighteen year old Canadian woman on a late spring break vaca-tion with her friends. She had won a raffle to go on a cruise to Bermuda and had no chance of affording such a thing otherwise, but when she had told her mother of the good news, she had been warned not to go. "Why not?" she had asked, and she was answered with something like, "I just have a bad feeling about it." To Penelope, who was just starting medical school, this was far too illogical a reason to avoid the trip, but with the warning in mind, the sudden fog that seemed to carry with it an ominous sense of dread made her especially anxious. The alcohol and dancing had warmed her, but it still brought a chill down her spine. She took her hoodie and told her friends she would meet them in the room and therefore started the long walk across the ship from the boisterous deck to her cheap windowless cabin in the bowels.

She was walking alone along a balcony on the portside of the ship when there was a sudden intense thud at its stern. She heard distant screams from the deck behind her and turned around as if she might see something through the fog and walls. When she was met only with an intensified version of the dread she had felt before, she hugged herself and took deep calculated breaths to calm down as she resumed her walk to her cabin. The screams were short-lived, so whatever the thudding sound was must have been something easily ignored.

It was only two minutes later that it dawned on her that the ship was slowing down. There was still a railing beside her, so with an abundance of caution, she leaned over to look at the water below. A gasp. They were hardly moving at all anymore. A chime from the PA system startled her, and she blenched away from the railing. "This is your captain speaking. We've been assessing the situation and have determined the cause of that loud noise you all heard. Good news is that there's no reason at all to be alarmed. We're just having some engine troubles, and the engineers have said it'll be back on track within the hour. To accommodate the uneasiness, we are extending happy hour by another forty-five minutes! Good luck, and have fun, everyone!" Penelope was aware that there were seventeen casinos on board, but the captain saying 'good luck' sent another shiver down her spine.

She resumed her walk down the row of doors to other people's rooms but stopped when she heard something behind the *Charybdis*. By then, she was at the stern, below the decks but still on a balcony, on her way to the elevators to the cheaper cabins. She was the only one awake this far back of the ship, so she was the first person to notice a shape in the fog and the first person to hear the gentle crashing of waves against whatever the foreign figure was. She squinted into the fog at the shape, which was growing in size. She feared briefly they were reversing for some reason and going to crash into some sort of rock or iceberg, but the shadow was increasingly red in tint. She couldn't fathom what it might have possibly been, so it wasn't until it was breaking through the fog almost close enough to touch that she held her racing heart and scrambled away from the railing.

A ship with blood-red sails and no lights aboard whatsoever. The *Charybdis* dwarfed it, but she was close and low enough on the cruise ship's peripheries to understand the true magnitude of the ghost ship. It flew a black flag with a skull wearing a crown, and it was with much trepidation that she witnessed its gun ports being opened in tandem, letting way to the gleam of twenty-eight bronze cannons. They each reflected the *Charybdis'* many colourful lights like an entrancing waltz of colours across her besotted bleary vision. She was so enthralled, it was almost disappointing when there were no more cannons to ogle.

Before she could fathom any more of the ghost ship or its unseen inhabitants, it had disappeared back into the fog, and no matter how hard she looked after it, she could only see its dark red shadow and hear the gasps of the few others who had seen it. She was glad to have heard others gasping, for she had worried she was hallucinating. It was like a ship from a far-gone era, and flying a pirate's flag——. She hated herself for pondering if perhaps they had found themselves back in time through some anomalous event like a spiritual maelstrom. Or perhaps it really was some incorporeal vessel from the afterlife, crewed by the dead and a harbinger of doom for the cruise ship.

Her pondering came to a halt when she heard fourteen successive shots of the cannons on the ghost ship and the subsequent calamity about the *Charybdis*. The next few moments of her life were some of the most confusing. Adrenaline sobered her as best it could as she heard an announcement but failed to process any of its words. Fourteen more shots. Screaming. The splashing of wreckage and panicking people into the black midnight sea. Fourteen more shots, further than any others thusfar. Another inconceivable announcement. While all of this was happening, she was trying not to be swept away by the liquid crowd of people around the lifeboats as she rushed to find one. They had not been told to abandon ship, but the passengers were overpowering anyone trying to stop them from climbing into a lifeboat.

Fourteen more shots. Closer now. Screaming. Crying. Drowning below. Fourteen more shots, closer than ever. Penelope sweated and looked around for a way to climb higher. The ship had started to list just-so, and she worried they would be sunk before sunrise. If she could just get higher up, maybe she could——.

Her eyes went wide when the ghost ship of red broke through the fog again, just in front of her and the panicking crowd around this lifeboat. She could hardly see through all the shoving arms and life vests being thrown around, but she could swear she made eye contact with one of the ghosts, a one-eyed man, as he clicked his fingers and another fourteen shots sounded. The floor beneath her clamoured in pain like a dying animal.

As quickly as it had appeared, the ship was back in the fog, this time headed toward the stern yet again. It was circling them like a shark and shooting at the lowest parts of the hull.

After its next fourteen shots at the stern, the lights on the *Charybdis* all flickered out, and only its auxiliary power allowed the captain to come over the PA system and say in a voice all-too-calm: "Abandon ship." It was but a whisper amidst the calamity.

She was shuffled onto a life-raft that felt more like a shipping container. It was ejected into the ocean like a bullet only four minutes after she had been packed inside with a horde of others. They all screamed as their raft fell into the sea. She broke her arm against the back wall when they slammed into the ocean and were briefly entirely submerged. When it bounced back up to the surface, however, she got a better view of the *Charybdis* as the ghost ship and its fog seemed to be leaving. Life rafts like hers were being ejected from the ship at a rapid rate. Where it had towered out of the sea in the harbour, now she wagered at least half of it must have been underwater. Hours had passed, but they had only felt like moments to her.

She thought it must have been over, but to her horrified shock, she heard the shrieking of many of the passengers on her raft as they leaned away from the starboard windows. Penelope, however, stepped closer and looked through to see the ghost ship had returned, no longer obscured by fog, only obscured now by darkness and chaos.

It slowed between her raft and another three, and she looked up at its massive structure dwarfing her little white boat with even just one of its massive sails. At its stern there stood a man. He was tall with shoulder-length black hair whipping around in the gusts of ocean wind and smoking a cigarette. She made eye contact with him the same as she had the other man, but he surprised her with a cheeky wink and smile. She wasn't sure how he had even seen her considering someone had already turned off the lights in the raft to conserve power. She pressed a hand to her heart and felt a great sense of relief as she watched this tall dark stranger set the shank of his boot on a pile of crates and push it off into the inky black void. She read one as it floated near her:

Supplies inside. Apologies to the proletariat.

With an arched brow, she tried to look up at the stranger again, but she managed only to see him light a flare with his durry and toss both onto a pallet he had kicked into the sea with the crates before the ghost ship's sails flicked open further, and it disappeared into the black night.

Joshua Widdogast was a thirty-six year old man with silky chestnut hair and a chinstrap beard. He was easy on the eyes but not drop-dead gorgeous, so the reason he tended to pull as many lays as he did was because of his vast wealth. If not his wealth, his equally-rich younger sister with her dark brown wavy locks and pouty lips was often seen as even more attractive than he was.

They had something of a friendly competition between them as to who could settle down happily first, so after Eunice, the younger of the two, divorced her husband of two years, the game was afoot yet again. They were both aboard Joshua's favourite ship in his fleet where he had a large and opulent apartment built for him just below the bridge wherein he could see the sea he loved even more than the conquests in his bed.

Joshua was the CEO of Canopy Cruises and Hotels, Eunice was the CFO, and it was the evening of April 30th aboard the *Aquillius' Revenge*. The siblings were interrupted from a hedonistic night with six strangers in the sleeping chambers of Joshua's apartment when his phone rang for the sixth time in a row. Fed-up with the repetitive rudeness, he wrapped a blanket around his waist, grabbed his ringing phone, and went out onto one of his private balconies to answer, "What!? I'm busy!"

"*Charybdis* has sunk, sir," said a woman he didn't recognise.

"What are you on about?"

"The ship, sir. It sank on the 28th."

"Who is this?"

"Captain Nevena, sir."

"You were captaining it?"

"Yes, sir."

"Were there any casualties?"

"Yes, sir. We think about 200."

He cursed under his breath and silently lamented all the lawsuits in his future. It was such a bleak idea that he shook it away and decided that the ship simply hadn't sunk. "Where are you now?" he asked the captain.

"The Coast Guard took us to Halifax."

He rubbed the bridge of his nose. "I don't understand what you're telling me. You're in port?" She didn't reply. "*Charybdis* didn't sink. It's practically an island it's so fucking big! It didn't sink, so tell me how you must have damaged its hull trying to dock somewhere, so I can just fire you and get on with my day. How did you even get this number?"

"I'm with the— what were you again, sir? —I'm with the CSO. He told me to be the one to tell you *Charybdis* has sunk. We were attacked."

"Attacked?"

"Aye, sir. By a frigate, sir."

"This can't be fucking happening," he mumbled, "Park is gonna try and strong-arm me now. He's gonna want to go to war with whatever country shot you down. What country was it?"

"It… it wasn't a military vessel, sir."

"You've just said it was a frigate, Nirvana. Get your story straight!"

"Nevena," she corrected mousily, "It was a…. Sir, it was a pirate ship. Like from the 1800s. With blood-red sails and a cr—."

He scoffed and hung up on her, opening his email application to offload the problem onto his COO. With the email sent, he returned to his bedroom and attempted to rejoin the sex-pile.

⚙ Chapter 77 ⚙
They've Started to Sing, Sir

It took much longer than they had anticipated to prepare for the job in Australia. Initially, the plan was to strike in the spring after the first Canopy ship was sunk, but by Dale and River's calculations, they wouldn't be fully prepared until November. It was bittersweet news to Thyne. On the one hand, he was given more time to work on his part of the plan, but on the other hand: his part of the plan involved him pretending to be a woman. He had prepared himself for a few months of presenting as a woman on his trips to Australia, but by the show on November 30th, he was curled up in Dale's arms in his dressing room. Weepily, he said, "I can't do it again."

Dale's strong arms were tightly woven around Thyne, who was only half-ready for his show two hours from then. "Ye can do it this one las' time cain'tchye?"

He sniffled and nuzzled his face into Dale's chest. "I have to, but it's bloody hard."

"Ah know," he said as one of the few people on the planet who truly understood how Thyne felt by being constantly misgendered and treated like a woman.

Thyne eventually sucked up the sorrow, downed a bottle of water, and returned to his vanity to grit his teeth and put on the makeup to help him pass as his false identity.

Other than the dysphoria eating away at him, this extra time on the job was actually a good thing. It had made the potential impact of their upcoming acts exponentially stronger than they had originally planned. For most of 2085, Thyne had been implanting himself in the upper echelons of the society in Sydney. When the

Sydney Opera House burned down in 2080 during a particularly hot fire season, its charred remains were bought up by Canopy Cruises and Hotels, and after three years of reconstruction, it had been mostly converted into a large casino but retained a lot of its seating for watching stage-shows. It still ran shows regularly, and it was possible from some of the poker tables and slot machines in the upper floors to glimpse the stage while still gambling. Another change was the addition of a private viewing chamber in the back of the performance hall. To those outside of the room, it looked like a wall of mirrors, and it therefore wasn't commonly known that it even existed at all.

On his increasingly long trips to Sydney, where Rory luckily owned a property even before he joined the gang, Thyne's false identity, Lilith Killigrew, was growing in popularity as both a composer and singer. "She" went viral on social media after "her" first performance at the Opera House on May first. After such a successful performance, Thyne was invited back to perform again at the end of the month, and after another massive profit was made, he asked the Opera House runners to allow him to compose a routine themed around the history of pirates for shows throughout June. He was approved, but Dale warned halfway through the rehearsals that they would still not be ready for the final blow. The pirate theme was therefore wasted, and a lot of the songs Thyne had written to outright threaten Canopy were shelved to not draw too much attention to the show while they were biding their time.

During each of his shows, Perlie, River, and Francis, in various disguises, would gamble in the casino and win until they were nearly poisoned or removed from the facility. After cashing out their winnings, they would bring them to Rory's property nearby and stash it.

They had won upwards of eight million Australian dollars by July, when Thyne was approved for another show, this one themed around winter. He may have tried for a more relevant theme, but the gang was fairly certain they hadn't bled the casino enough for the impact they wanted.

All the while that Thyne was gaining popularity as Lilith Killigrew, a legendary songstress, the other half of the gang continued to sink Canopy's cruise ships. When they could, to attempt helping *The Tiara's* mission, they would board the cruises to rob the casinos and jewellery stores aboard before sinking the ships. They also avoided firing on civilians when possible.

In September, there was a mix-up in the scheduling of the ships (thanks to Dale and Lanni's combined efforts hacking things), so there were three large vessels sitting empty in Marseilles for two days. During those two days, the twins, Partha, Jean-Jacques, and Pio all boarded and planted explosives in the engine rooms and around the hulls. They detonated them after being certain no one was aboard and watched from the marina as they sank like rocks, thudding almost immediately into the shallow waters. They weren't as lost as the crafts they had been sinking in the open ocean, but the damage was expensive enough that Canopy wrote them off.

Because they had so long to continue sinking cruise ships, everyone in the gang save for Thyne, Francis, and Dale had the chance to participate in one of the attacks at sea, if not more than one. Likewise, everyone had seen at least one of Thyne's shows and were all impressed with his countertenor voice just as much as his regular voice. On Halloween, for Partha's birthday, Thyne had arranged to sing a medley of songs from various geeky media, and that show closed with a nearly flawless performance of *The Diva Dance* from *The Fifth Element*. He usually received standing ovations, but the audience of October 31st was the loudest he had ever heard.

It was after that show that Dale approached him saying, "We can strike on the 30th."

"Of November?"

"Yeah. Can ye do that?"

Thyne agreed and composed another themed show when he returned to his pseudo-home in Rory's building that evening. The theme would be musicals, both on stage and screen, for he had realised there were a plethora of readily-made songs that could send a very disturbing message when heard in succession with the hindsight of the deadly finale. Still, he tweaked the final number (or at least the final one he would actually sing), called for Roach to join him for duets, and easily wrote the orchestral score in such that it would accompany him and glide flawlessly from one song to the next despite changes in pitch, key, and tempo.

The night of November 30th was upon them, and after swallowing his upset at continuously being called Lilith or Miss Killigrew, it was no longer sorrow plaguing him but nervousness. Stage fright was something beaten out of him as a child, so it was only because of the finale they had planned that he was jittery and white-knuckling the edges of his vanity. He looked deep into his own amber eyes and muttered a prayer to his Gods to help him through the performance. The set he had composed consisted of fourteen songs from various musicals, and he had rehearsed with Roach and the orchestra from start to finish for two weeks straight. This performance would be the only one available to the public, and he feared he would fall into the habits of said rehearsals, forgetting to stop on the ninth song and sing the lyrics he had added specifically to threaten Widdogast and his sister.

Unfortunately, though the gang had hacked and lied and prodded to try and have the CEO in attendance that evening, it was only Eunice, the CFO, who would be present. They were still grateful to have a chief in the company at all, however, and their actions might ring even more horrifying for it.

Dale left Thyne's dressing room after helping him into his corset and giving him a big bear hug. Thyne didn't want to let go, but after two minutes, Dale peeled him off of him, rustled his hair, and hid in an electrical closet below the stage with his laptop to start work on his part of the plan.

When Thyne was summoned from the dressing room an hour later, he was escorted to a backstage area where he could hear the opening numbers playing. Roach was there waiting for him and stood from the couch where he had been resting to coil his arms around Thyne lovingly. He whispered comforting words in Old Egyptian about both Thyne's anxiety for executing such a public act of terrorism and because Dale had texted him about Thyne's dysphoria. There were stagehands present, but they were all under the impression that "Miss Killigrew" was dating Roach, or as they knew him, Iago Low.

"Iago" was wearing a black three-piece suit with a shoulder cape. His hair had been cut short and slicked back with minimal product. His piercings and tattoos were removed via Francis' chronomancy, and his beard stubble was short and well-groomed. "Miss Killigrew", in contrast, was wearing a baby-blue and white gingham dress with "her" loose brown curls in pigtails that covered "her" flat chest. "She" was also wearing red ruby slippers. Both of them looked dashing, at least in the opinion of the stage hands.

Roach was made uncomfortable seeing Thyne cross-dressing so much that it had him crying for an hour before the show, and it hurt his soul to hear a stagehand say, "Mr. Low, we need to steal Lily now. She's on in five." He nodded and watched Thyne slip away after the stagehand.

From the side of the stage, Thyne could hear the opening act, a medley of show tunes from various musicals, as it slowly transitioned from *Singin' in the Rain* to the beginning chords of his first song. The dancers and choir exited the stage gracefully as they transitioned into his piece, and he simultaneously slipped through them, beginning his operatic countertenor rendition of *Over the Rainbow* before the audience could even fully fathom where he was in the mess of people.

The spotlight found him as the stage cleared and crowd cheered, and by the time he was in the front centre, he was alone with his only accompaniment being the orchestra surrouding the front of the stage.

While he was finishing *Over the Rainbow* and following the violins into *The Sound of Music*, Roach was off stage being fitted with a microphone and calming his stage fright in the manner he tended to: with a quaff from a pickle jar and a bite on a lemon.

Right on cue, he entered the stage singing his part in the duet with his lover and with the lilting soul of romance, too. This was the largest audience he had ever performed for, but he was focused so entirely on Thyne that he was lost in the euphoria of music. His steps were slow as he approached centre-stage, his hand limply outstretched for his love and caressing his arm gently when they finally reached each other.

After *The Sound of Music*, the orchestra seamlessly led into the next piece, which would be another solo for Thyne, so Roach retreated to a seat near the cellos and watched as Thyne started singing his version of *How Far I'll Go* from *Moana*. It was the first song that was explicitly meant to grab the attention of the Canopy elites, but it was much more harmless than the later songs would be with hindsight. Following *How Far I'll Go*, Thyne sang *One Jump Ahead* from *Aladdin*, followed by *If I Only Had a Heart*.

During the instrumental at the end of the song, Thyne exited the stage to drink some water and relax while Roach took his place and followed the symphony into *If I Were a Rich Man*. It was entirely possible that any fans of his music would recognise his voice in this performance, which was sung with more distortion and therefore resembled a lot of his heavier original songs. Even if he was recognised, and authorities were called, it wouldn't matter come twelve minutes from then.

He finished his performance, and in the last few hits of brass, Thyne returned to the stage acting as a pleasant humming backing vocal and eventually exchanging lines both melodic and otherwise with Roach when he moved on to *Be Prepared*. It was also sung with a good amount of emotion and distortion, sounding even more like his regular style.

From *Be Prepared*, the mood was evermore sinister as the orchestra transferred to what would become the penultimate song of the evening: *Playing With the Big Boys* from *The Prince of Egypt*. Thyne continued to make an effort to sound feminine, but he let it slip into more unreasonably masculine tones here and there, using Roach's voice in chorus with his as a mask of his more natural and gruff tenor. As they sang this piece in particular, they were glancing into the many cameras capturing the show as well as at the private viewing box in the back of the dark room, wherein they knew Eunice Widdogast was watching.

Her heart sank into her stomach as her soul seemed to understand how they were taunting her. She subconsciously recognised the ever present danger in the Opera House that evening, but when questioned by her date on her pallidity, she laughed it off and ordered another glass of wine. As far as she knew, the show was only halfway over, and she chalked up the strange feelings to simply not liking the song. Perhaps it was a sort of embarrassment for not recognising what movie or show it had come from, as all of the songs on the itinerary were from a piece of popular musical theatre that she recognised save for that one.

Then came the next song, which started sweetly as a duet between "Lilith" and "her" lover. He flicked his shoulder cape, wrapped one arm around the small of Thyne's back to pull him close, and smiled sweetly as he serenaded him with a surprisingly operatic voice: "*Past the point of no return. No backwards glances. Our games of make-believe are at an end....*" They could feel each other's hearts beating hard and fast as adrenaline started to pump through their black veins. Roach continued singing, and when it came time for Christine's part, he disappeared from the spotlight. Thyne looked directly at the wall of one-way mirrors in the back of the building as he returned to his countertenor perfection and sang with increasing intensity.

When he came to the line *"When will the flames at last consume us?"* his hands moved madly but in time with the music as he pulled out a lighter from a pocket in his dress. He lit it and sang the line into the flame before slamming it on the stage at his feet, along with a smoke-bomb. The smoke that quickly enveloped him was briefly illumined by a fireball, and when it cleared a moment later, he was in a completely different costume, drawing a loud cheer from the audience. Now his dress and wig had burned away revealing him in a black suit with short brown hair, looking nothing like a woman any longer. He continued the song, repeating a similar notation as the verse he had just sung, but with new lyrics. As well, he was singing with a gruff, masculine, and above-all malicious tone:

"Past the point of no return

"You're out of options

"Your disregard for us will spell your doom

"Past all thought of right or wrong

"One final question," by this point, the orchestra had dwindled to silence with some of them flipping through their sheet music and looking at their conductor for guidance. It was therefore only Thyne's raw and beautiful voice echoing through the otherwise dark and silent room. His fiery amber eyes were locked with Eunice's even though he could not have possibly seen her through the one-way mirror. He reached his hand up to vaguely and threateningly gesture toward her as he continued:

"How deeply will you bow to leave the tomb

"When we have buried you alive

"Beneath your riches and your pride

"Will you beg Neith to not consume you?" At the end of this line he let out a short but mad laugh, and when he began again, Roach's voice was in chorus with him as he stepped back into the spotlight from behind him, setting a tiara on Thyne's head. Their menacing singing was the only sound, it seemed, in all the world:

"Past the point of no return

"The final threshold

"Your ships have sunk, so drown and sink in turn

"We've passed the point of no return!"

As they held their last note, loud and up several steps from the original notation, the lights in the building cut out entirely, plunging everything into utter darkness. The power was still running, for it was their design that the cameras would not stop streaming and recording. The duo were therefore still amplified by their microphones when they finished their final note in the dark, drowning out the various shouts and screams beneath it in the growing calamity of the crowd. The note faded into mad laughter from the both of them, and just as it was cut short abruptly, the lights flicked back on, illuminating the stage anew. Roach and Thyne were absent, and in their stead was a broadsword stabbed into the wood of the stage like *Excalibur*. On its hilt was the decapitated head of Eunice Widdogast, and upon her temples were the stolen crown jewels.

Screams sounded in the front of the hall from the orchestra and patrons who had seen such a horrifying visage appear in front of them, but most of the crowd didn't notice. Money was raining down from the ceiling, and the walkways were covered in jewels, jewellery, and precious metals. As people stuffed their pockets, it eventually became obvious that there was a decapitated head where the singers had been, so the room was clearing out somewhat in spite of all the riches to be had.

What finally had the majority of people running was the evident fire growing on the stage, made worse by the paper money flickering toward it from the rafters.

On the casino floors, every single machine that could give out jackpots was doing so for every pull, but there was also a rain of money on these floors. Even outside, where the wisest of the crowd were headed after the fire alarms started to blare, money was raining down from skyscraper windows onto the jewell-laden streets, causing various car accidents and general chaos.

The gang members present in Sydney had been taken to Rory's property by Francis who was joining them all in a celebratory toast to the inevitable ruin of Canopy.

Chapter 78
Give No Quarter

Joshua Widdogast was awoken from a drunken stupor by a chime on his phone. He rubbed his tired eyes, peeled a sleeping stranger's arm off of him, and watched as a flood of messages and emails poured into his notification bar. They were flashing too quickly to fully fathom. The last one (at least the last one at the moment) lingered the longest and was therefore easiest to process. It was from a number he didn't have in his contacts. He sat up and clicked open the feed to read it again:

⌈ Widdogast. I have names I'm willing to share, but I have a price. ⌋

He scratched his head and stumbled to the bathroom to piss. As he washed his hands, he pondered who the unknown number belonged to and what the message might have been referring to.

To avoid waking whoever was in his bed, he slipped out onto his back balcony and took in a calming breath of the ocean air before returning his attention to his phone to try and parse what the explosion of messages may have been about. With the rising sun dappling the area he took a glass of whiskey to stave off the hangover and relaxed. The chaos unfolding in his messages was impossible. There was so much serenity around him, how could there be such turmoil bearing down upon his soul?

Messages of condolences were the most dreadful, for he knew not the extent of what horror he would see upon opening the video attached to several of the emails. He remembered seeing one of Killigrew's shows at the Opera House and finding her voice utterly breathtaking. He had gone backstage after the show to try flirting, but she had rejected him. There was therefore a slight resentment for her, and he had refused to go to another show. Such bitterness, it seemed, had saved his life....

Of course, he was beyond upset that his money had been slowly bled out from under him and thrown all around Sydney for the commoners to freely collect, but his greatest grief was found in the murder of his beloved sister.

In the months that followed, he turned to drinking and drugs and stopped sleeping with strangers in favour of lamenting and isolating in his apartment on the *Aquillius' Revenge*. When he was informed of another three ships sinking over the next few months, his reaction each time was mournful surrender. "Might as well," was his most uttered mantra in this dark time. When asked for headings by the captain of the *Aquillius' Revenge*, his answer was always some manner of, "Whatever you want," which often landed him somewhere tropical.

In April of 2086 he accidentally reopened his messages with the unknown number that had messaged him the day he learned of his sister's fate. He sat up in bed and reread the message again and again until eventually calling the number attached. A woman with a British accent answered, "What do you want?"

"You know who killed my sister."

"Haven't you been paying any attention to anything other than slags and blow, mate? Tell me you've at least *heard* of *The Crown*."

"Of course I have. Why is everyone always talking about it when bad things happen to me? I'm on good terms with parliament and His Majesty."

She groaned and rubbed her forehead. "Fucksake, Widdogast."

"You said you know who killed my sister. Are you trying to say it was the English government?" She didn't reply, so he eventually worried she had ended the call. "Hello?"

"It's a terrorist organisation, you idiot."

"Oh."

"I'll tell you the names I have, but not for free."

"Well, I'm real short on money right now."

"Precisely why I will be asking for an asset instead."

"Well, I'm low on all that, too. All my casinos have failed. All my ships have sunk. All I have left is *Aquillius' Revenge* and a private island off the coast of Nova Scotia. I don't even have a house: the island is undeveloped." He sighed. "You can have the Sydney Opera House if you want it."

"Is that what your sister's life is worth to you?"

"My sister's life is worth the world to me, Aspyn, but you're not a fucking necromancer, are you? You're not offering me her life. You're offering a fleeting chance of vengeance. I'm not a combatant, and they've ruined me financially, so what will I even hope to gain against these violent terrorists with a list of names?"

"Just answer me this: are you only willing to offer the burnt remains of a building I have no use for?"

He groaned. "Just tell me what you want."

"I want your ship."

"No." He hung up and flopped into his bed defeatedly.

After four hours of laying in bed and staring at the ceiling, he heard the rustling of something near the balcony and lazily lifted his head to see what it was. A cold breeze was blowing into the room through his open balcony doors and had pushed the sheer curtains into a nearby table. He sat upright and looked out at the sea as a dense fog crept up on the ship. The hairs on the back of his neck stood upright. Another breeze entered the room and passed through him like a spectre. He knew the pirates attacking his ships were always preceded and obscured by a deep and chilling fog. "Might as well," he muttered and tried to let himself lay back down, but his survival instincts overrode the depression.

When there was a loud thud in the back of the ship, he stood and let his gaze trail around the room. He was unsure what it was he was looking for, but his body was only half in his control as adrenaline started to pump through him.

On the *Initiative*, which was gaining on the *Aquillius' Revenge*, Roach and River looked up from the camera feeds in front of them and informed the rest of the crew in tandem, "Props down."

Partha, who was acting as captain of the *Initiative* as he had been since the start of their jobs at sea, praised the twins but pulled Roach aside and said, "Sir, I think you should go talk to him. No one else has been able to help."

"He *owned* Francis. Let him suffer."

"C…captain's orders, Roach."

He rolled his eyes and lit a cigarette as he hopped down a nearby staircase to a chamber below deck where Arjun was doing sit-ups on a paint-splattered rug. It smelled of mildew and sweat in the room, so Roach cracked open a window, which would also help to air out the smoke from his cigarette.

Since Melchiresa's death, Arjun had spent almost every hour of every day exercising or painting madly. His build had gotten leaner, and the facial hair he tended to keep in a neat moustache was instead a mad wiry beard streaked with grey. His black hair was also unkempt, uncut, and streaking with grey. No one had been able to pull him out of this mental break, not even his husband. Giovanni had informed the others that, in his expert opinion, it would be best to let the madness run its course. Arjun could not die, so the lack of sleep and overworking of his body was physically exhausting but would never kill him. The doctor was also confident that Arjun's madness and depression would never dip so low as to allow for attempted suicide (or near enough) because of his love for the doctor himself, and if not for him, for Neodesha.

All this said, Arjun was present enough of the mind to be of use on these seafaring missions. Like Francis, he possessed a minimal control of the weather, though his was only ever in regard to colder conditions. He was the reason their little sailing ship was constantly in cover of fog, and intel from his birds scouting ahead was useful, if a little difficult to wrench from him when he was in a particularly intense fit.

Roach smoked wordlessly and watched him exercise. "You'll pull your muscles doing it like that," he muttered. Arjun only shook his head to reject the idea and continued the sit-ups unchanged. With a sigh, Roach crouched down in front of him and held his knees still to help anchor him. "Doc said we should just let you lose your mind, but the kid said to come talk to you." He shook his head again and continued the sit-ups, silently grateful that Roach was holding his legs and that he was also being tender with his bad knee. After a long while, Roach's air seemed to darken in a sympathetic way. He stopped Arjun's mad exercising by holding him telekinetically when he was sitting upright. With a hand on his shoulder and smoke on his words, he spoke low and lovingly: "You remember what you told me in the temple to Set?"

"I don't."

"You said, 'They may hide it beneath the sand, but this is His domain, and He will always find what is in need of destroying.'"

Roach released his hold on Arjun, who hugged his knees and averted his eyes. He finished the quote in the original language he had spoken it: "'Thus always death in His blessings and destruction in His love.'"

"Why have you been working out so much?"

A sigh. "In preparation of my next trek into Hell." Roach only blinked. Arjun wiped his icy-blue eyes with his arm and muttered in English, "These jobs at sea are destroying me."

"How so?"

"When I first met him, myself and Melchiresa were the scourge of these seas. He had me create fog and douse the lamps to do much the same as we are doing now to these crusie ships, though our targets are much larger now."

"I'm sorry."

"For the first few years of knowing him, I thought he was a mute. I remember exactly what he said to me when I learned he had a voice at all. He said, 'We won't be needing a black flag, Mr. Catatone. We give no quarter aboard this vessel.' Clayton, I didn't know it at the time, but his soft porcelain voice was the last domino to unlocking my heart to him. I fell deeply in love with him just by hearing it." Roach rubbed his back. "It is not the first time he's died, you know."

"Oh?"

"When we were in America back in the 1800s, his sister succeeded in killing him."

"But...."

"But I saved him. I found a path to Hell and dragged him back here." He sniffled and blinked the tears from his eyes. "I thought he loved me. I thought I was saving him, but.... But all these centuries...." He broke down, and Roach sat down to pull him into his arms and let him mourn. "All this time," he whimpered, "he was only waiting to die. He didn't even... he didn't even hesitate, Clayton. I begged him. I said, 'Don't you love me!? Haven't you loved me all this time? Haven't I given you a reason— however paltry —just one single reason to live?'"

A beat.

"I hadn't. In fact...."

"Yes?"

"He could have just said, 'No.' He is a man of few words in the company of strangers, and a simple, 'No,' would have killed me enough, but he is a cruel black-guard with a stone heart. He said, 'No, pigeon, you haven't. I do love you, and I have loved you, but I'm afraid you've only given me reasons to the contrary.'" His broken voice was hardly audible when he finished the story crying, "and that was that."

Roach held him for fifteen minutes as he wept, but before he could try to relate to him as a fellow widower, they were interrupted by Thyne coming into the room and saying to Arjun, "Come on, mate. We're boarding before we sink it, and you can help. We'll even let you have a gun if you promise to be careful."

Roach looked to Arjun for his answer. After a pause to ponder, he wiped his eyes and nodded, letting the other two help him to his feet and throw a shirt at him to cover his sweaty torso.

They joined the others on deck. The boarding party would be Partha, Roach, Arjun, Richard, Rory, and Thyne. Because their ship was so small compared to the others, and the *Aquillius' Revenge* had very few balconies on its sides, they would need to be launched up to the deck telekinetically. The first to volunteer for River to throw him onto the ship was Roach. He was silently flung upwards three stories and landed on the empty deck, too close to the bridge for the seamen inside to see him. With a quick scan of the area, he gave a thumbs-up to an albatross thrall of Arjun's who had checked the area as well, and thus the rest of them were quickly launched up the same way Roach had been.

Partha and Richard were the next two to land on the deck. Roach shuffled them off, knowing they would be headed for Widdogast's apartment having worked on the ship before and thus knowing how to navigate it. Before he left, however, Roach caught Partha's wrist and said, "Ú-dano i faelas a hyn an uben tanatha le faelas."

The kid furrowed his brow with determination and gave a little nod and salute before rushing after his father, drawing his rapier as he caught-up.

Joshua's hands were trembling loudly around the shotgun he was cradling. His breaths were evermore laboured as he heard gunshots in various parts of the ship. This was it. This was his last day on Earth. He may have prayed were he a religious man. Instead, his mind reeled madly as he sat on the floor, leaning against his bed, and hugging the weapon as if it would save him from a sinking ship. He was hopeful to hear his captain's voice over the PA system. He would have been happy to hear something as harrowing as "Abandon ship," but he heard no such announcement. The high from the ecstasy he had done the night before was waning, and the alcohol in his system had all but gone entirely. Reality was far too heavy and scary and lonely without his sister, and now he would lose his favourite ship and likely his life to the terrorists. He made a promise to himself. A foolish and desperate promise. '*Whoever opens the door next,*' he thought, '*I will shoot immediately. Even if it's the captain. So be it.*'

It was only two minutes after he had made this declaration that he heard the doorknob turn. Without processing his own actions, he jumped to his feet and shot the man who had entered directly in the chest.

He fell dead into the hall behind him.

Partha, only some six feet behind his father, watched his body fall onto the ugly carpet. As soon as Richard's corpse hit the ground, all the colour and sound disappeared from the world.

He rushed up to his side and scooped him up into his arms to try and share a final word, but his father only managed a weak smile at his son before dying in his arms. Partha's harsh gaze snapped immediately to Widdogast with such a harrowing darkness that the CEO let out a brief scream of terror. He dropped his gun, despite Partha only being armed with a sword, and raised his hands in defeat as he backed tearfully away.

"I didn't mean it, Nima. I didn't mean it," he wept, "Oh! Captain!" His mind flashed with the many memories he had of Captain Richard Nima, all of them wholesome and pleasant, now tainted with red.

Partha stepped over his father's corpse into the golden suite of splendour and opulence with his gaze never so much as flickering away from Joshua.

"Partha, please. I didn't mean it."

He aimed his sword for the CEO's throat. "Beg."

"Oh! Oh, anything, Partha! Anything!"

"MORE!"

He looked around in a helpless panic. While he was falling to his arse against the bed, Roach and Thyne had found the scene and rushed in behind Partha. "Oh, please don't kill me! I've got nothing left! I have nothing!"

Partha let out a haunting ireful shout and sliced open Widdogast's shin.

"MURDEROUS WRETCH! BEG FOR YOUR WORTHLESS LIFE!"

"Take the ship! Take it all!"

Roach came up behind Partha and grabbed his shoulders. He leaned down and whispered, "Give yourself a moment."

He turned around with a furrowed brow. "Why?"

"Just don't be too hasty. You don't want to kill him in a way you might regret," he whispered so that only Partha could hear.

The kid was whipped up in a frenzy, but he was present enough to take the advice and gave Roach his sword to pace madly around the room and think. While he was busy doing this, Roach used his telekinesis to keep Partha's next victim from escaping. "What was Nima doing here?" wept Widdogast.

"Shut the fuck up, you cretin," spat Roach.

He was quiet. Roach was intimidating, and he was in the lowest state of his life: easily manipulated and overly impulsive. If he had suffered even a slight start, he may have had a heart attack with such frayed nerves. His mind was TV static, and his teeth were chattering. Partha continued to pace, and Thyne quit the room.

More gunshots could be heard around the vessel. Screams. A splash or two from crew members jumping overboard. Widdogast watched with blurry blue eyes as Partha suddenly started prying gold plating off of the walls and furniture around the suite. He watched him do this, gathering a small pile of random gold tid-bits on the coffee table, for three minutes before he couldn't stop himself from sputtering, "What are you doing?"

"I said shut up!" Roach kicked him hard in the gut, knocking the wind out of him. "One more word, and I'll cut out your tongue."

Roach didn't know what Partha was doing with the gold he was gathering, but he could see the fire in his eye and knew something wicked and beautiful was about to happen. When there was a good two handfuls of random golden pieces on the table, Partha quit the room wordlessly, and Roach held Widdogast patiently while waiting for his return ten minutes later. He had a cast-iron pan in one hand and a portable gas stove in the other. He set them both on the table, dumped the gold into the pan, set it on the eye, and put the heat on high before quitting the room again.

"He's melting the gold," said Roach with an intrigued tone. He eyed Joshua. "No idea what he's up to, but I'm sure it's not good for you, mate. Give me your wallet and phone, by the way."

Joshua gulped as he handed over his things and watched when Partha returned only a moment later with a heat-resistant glove. He tossed it on the coffee table beside the melting gold and watched intently as it slowly pooled up in the pan. His breaths were heaving and harrowing. He horrified Widdogast with a crooked grin. "What would you offer me to not kill you?"

He sputtered fearfully. With a nod from Roach that he could answer, he said, "Anything!"

Partha stroked his goatee. "What do you think, Roach? Do you think I should let him live?"

"It's not the worst idea," said Roach truthfully, "We've really fucked him over. You could let him live on in poverty, trying fruitlessly to feed his addictions, and with no one to love him in all the world."

"No."

"No?"

"No, Roach. He chose his fate when he named this ship." Roach arched his brow. "Hold him still."

"Aye, Captain."

Partha smiled softly as he donned the heatproof glove and carried the pan of melted gold over to Widdogast. "Say ah," he teased, and Roach forced open his mouth telekinetically. "Are you sorry?" taunted Partha.

"I'm sorry," he wept.

"Too bad." He poured the melted gold down Widdogast's throat and joined Roach in mad laughter at the sounds of his painful death. When it was over, Partha dropped the pan on the floor and tried to say a cool one-liner: "*Terrorists win.*"

Roach snort-laughed. "Dude, I love you. That's so funny."

He laughed awkwardly. He wasn't trying to be funny. "Y-yeah."

"Come on, kid. Let's get you home." He scooped up Richard's corpse from the doorway and held it close and lovingly. Tears trailed Partha's cheeks at the sight, but a look at Widdogast's corpse helped him feel marginally better as he followed Roach out of the room and back to the *Initiative*.

Chapter 79
Time to Go

It was Ramadan, 2086, and Roach was playing with Sirion and Ruin in the living room of Loomis Manor. Canopy was no-more, so the only company still in the gang's crosshairs was Osiris. Roach had given Widdogast's phone to Dale, who was taking his time combing through its message and internet histories. The only member of the gang to hound him to go faster was Francis, but he was quieted after enough comments from Roach to let Dale work as slowly as he needed.

It was only a couple weeks after Sirion's fourth birthday. He tried to snatch a toy from Ruin, but Roach scolded him gently and said, "Now, Sirion, she's playing with it right now. Can you ask nicely for it?" He pouted and grumbled about needing to be polite, but before a lesson about sharing could start, a buzz sounded through the house. "I've got it," called Roach as he scooped up Ruin in his right arm and Sirion in his left.

With a child on each hip, he approached the front door and looked at the camera feed from the front gate. "It's the pigs," he muttered to the children, "Do we remember what to say to them?" They both nodded, so Roach pushed down the intercom button and said, "What do we say?"

"Fuh duh weece!" cheered Sirion.

"Very good, and?"

Ruin bounced excitedly in his arms as she said, "Come back with a warwent!"

"Mmhmm. So, do you meatballs understand, or do I need to find someone who speaks spaghetti for you?"

The police responded with something in Italian, to which Ruin said something

Roach didn't understand in the same language. He set down the children, who ran into the living room to resume playing, passing by Arjun on their way. With the butt of his cane in Roach's chest, he pushed him away from the door and exchanged a few lines with the police. During their talk, Roach noticed the cops holding up an ID of Giovanni's. Still, they left, and Arjun glared at Roach. "You almost ruined everything."

He shrugged. "That's just my style, man."

A scoff. "BOY!"

Francis appeared beside him. "Yes?"

"We'll be needing our ship back."

The colour drained from Francis' face. "You what?"

"We need to leave."

"Leave?"

"YES! Bring us our ship in the next half hour." Before Francis could extract more of an explanation, Arjun was climbing the stairs and shouting for Neodesha. He found Giovanni and scolded him for having left his ID in the Palace of Versailles, which is where the police had said they found it.

While he was busy with that, Francis looked worriedly at Roach. "They're leaving the planet?"

Roach shrugged. "Seems a bit drastic, but I don't know Italian."

"What did they say in Italian?" Roach repeated the conversation verbatim via his perfect memory, having little idea what he was saying as he did so. "Damn. The masters and their manor have been compromised. Mayhaps Rory has a property in which we could sepulchre?"

Roach may have responded, but he was interrupted by Dale rushing into the foyer and grabbing his arm. "Ah got it! Ah got 'em!"

"Got what, dude?"

"Call a meeting."

"Alrighty." He saluted lazily and cupped his hands around his mouth to shout into the manor, "Everyone downstairs! Now!"

"Ah coulda done that, Roach," said Dale with an irritated mien.

"Then why didn't you?" He rustled his hair and winked with a click of his teeth before wrapping an arm around Francis and forcing him into the living room.

Two minutes later, everyone was present for the impromptu meeting, including Giovanni and Arjun. "Everyone listen to Dale."

"Ah been workin' wit this here phone," he held up Widdogast's phone, "An' Ah figgered it all out. Franky, you's worried 'bout Osiris starting a war, ain'chyee?" He nodded. "Well…. Ah figgered out Elijah Park's number." Francis stood. "Ah figgered ye'd like that. So, what'd'we say t'callin' it right now?"

"Calling?" asked Dezba. "With just our regular phones?"

"Sorry, ma'am, Ah should'a been more clear. Ah meant we call pretendin' ta be Miss Temm. Ah can spoof her number."

"This sounds risky," she said.

"That's why Ah called fer the meetin'."

"We only have minutes before the police return," said Arjun, "You all can do as you please, but we need to leave." He stood. "Keeva, Shay, come on."

"What? I don't wanna go nowhere, Pa."

For the first time in Neodesha's life, and perhaps for the first time in Arjun's, he raised his voice, his cheeks red and brow furrowed as he shouted in Italian: "You are coming with us, and I will hear nothing to the contrary! I won't lose you, too!"

She shrank. "W-where are we going?"

"Olympus."

Giovanni stood, matching the frantic energy all around. "Clayton and Karson, come downstairs with me at once." They followed him into the labyrinthian bowels of the manor wherein he piled papers and books in their arms from various rooms. "This is all my medical research," he explained after both twins had been given at least ten pounds worth of text. "Go with the boy to another time, read it all, and come back with any questions. We will not have long, and you will not be certified by any means, but the breadth of knowledge in your unforgetting minds will be of use when this inevitable war is sparked. You may not believe me, Clayton, but I do love Thyne and ask you to take care of him."

"I will."

Giovanni rushed them somewhere he could shout loud enough for Francis to hear, after which the pirate appeared before them looking evermore frazzled. "Yes?"

"Give these two the time to read what I've given them."

After some months in a prehistoric era reading the millenia worth of medical research, sometimes needing help translating things like French, Italian, Latin, Old, or Middle English from Francis, they each had a handful of questions in mind. Upon being brought back to Giovanni in 2086, they rattled them off as quickly as possible. He answered just as hurriedly, so after twenty minutes, the twins had exhausted all of their questions and were scrambling around the manor to help pack their things into their various cars, which they would use to flee to London where Rory had an empty rental property with a large garage beneath it and enough rooms for everyone.

Just as Arjun had predicted, it was only half an hour after their first visit that the police returned. They were waiting by the gate and buzzing it ad nauseum when Arjun attempted to buy them some time by sending out his tiger, which leapt over the gate beside the cops, who were immediately cowering and running to their cars upon seeing its vicious eyes locking on them.

With the police trapped in their cars, Arjun, Giovanni, and Neodesha were brought in an instant to where Francis had hidden their ship in Siberia.

Before they fled the planet, Arjun took Francis aside and said, "I apologise for all we have done to you, Androme. I apologise for all *I* have done. Within every wall of the manor, both above and below ground, there is hidden treasure, mostly gold bars. I know it won't absolve me, but all of it is yours to keep. We will return to take you to Olympus if you only ask one of my thralls." He hugged him tightly, which dumbfounded Francis, who sat limply in his arms before returning the embrace with slowness and confusion. When he retreated, Arjun wiped his eyes with his sleeve and said, "I do hope to see you again, son. Thank you for all you do. Good luck saving the world, no?" Another quick embrace. "Tell Thyne we love him."

"I will...."

Neodesha was next to bid him farewell, and it was done with misty eyes and many lamentations. "I love you, Pa! Oh, I'll miss you! I wish I didn't have to go."

Giovanni's goodbye was the least wordy. He simply hugged Francis for an entire minute before retreating, wiping his eyes, and saying, "Until we meet again, Androme."

With his goodbyes exchanged, Francis was much more emotional than he would have expected and watched the ship disappear into the clouds with tears in his eyes.

While this was happening, the gang that had been left behind at the manor were clambering into various cars and speeding away from the property via a back road. Thyne was mere seconds from throwing a molotov through one of the front windows when he heard Arjun tell Francis about the gold in the walls. He therefore tossed it at the gate before rushing to his car and peeling off, the last of them to flee.

Francis returned to the manor but kept time stopped when he noticed the police were fanning out all over the property in search of a way inside. He pushed past them, killing a few with his sword before deciding not to waste his energy, and entered the forsaken building. The unmoving air was heavy. There were still a few toys on the rug and a dying fire in the hearth. A half-eaten bowl of oatmeal on the table sat beside a tea Thyne hadn't finished.

As Francis wandered the chambers, his heart weighed him down more and more with each step. '*This is my doing*,' he thought as he opened Roach's room and saw several instruments he didn't have the time to throw haphazardly into one of their cars. '*If only I hadn't doomed us all*,' he thought further, his eyes welling with tears. With another look around, he closed his fist with determination and set immediately to work.

It took almost a month of his own time without releasing his hold on the fourth dimension. He brought every last belonging in the manor, including its entire library, to Thyne's home in London. The only items that remained were the furniture pieces too heavy or unnecessary for him to bother dragging across Europe. Once he had packed their things in Thyne's home, he returned to the manor and took an axe to the walls to unearth the hidden treasures inside. He took several more trips, this time to Venice where his buried treasure was hidden, and added to his stash all of his masters' gifted riches. He was unsure if they would be of any use, but he would certainly not allow the authorities to seize them.

The manor was in tatters when he finished fishing out all the treasure, after which he went down into the basement and took his axe to every load-bearing support, various pipes, and even electrical wires. He cut down lit incense bowls and tossed splintered wood all around. With all that done, he climbed back upstairs and caressed the piano with a sombre look back before leaving the building and hiding on the rocky beach behind it. When he finally resumed time, there was a thunderous calamity in the manor, which shifted on its supports with several loud creaks and cracks before entirely collapsing in on itself, after which it began to smoulder.

Satisfied with his work, Francis looked behind him at the rising sun silhouetting the *Initiative*. With one last look at the chaos up the brae, he stopped time and walked across the water to the ship. "Hello," he said to it with a hand on its hull, "Would it not be the greatest shame to lose you?"

His hands were trembling as he climbed onto the deck and made his way to the wheel. He squinted into the unmoving sun and released his hold on time to feel the gentle rock of the ship. The ocean air beckoned. A raven landed on the railing beside him and said, "Are you going to sail, Androme?"

He smiled faintly at the bird. "I may."

"I have only birds and rats to be of aid."

Francis nodded to acknowledge him and looked up at the sky. There was a good covering of clouds, and he used his control of the weather to start brewing a storm and fog that would obscure his exit. The ship started to rock more fervently and birds started to land on the deck, some of them dropping mice and rats. Francis' trembling hand gripped hard around one of the wheel's handles, and he pushed a breeze into his own face to feel the salt of the wind. With a sea-dog's smile, he hopped into action, jumping down to the lower levels and opening sails. Luckily the anchor could be lifted electronically, so when she was ready to sail, he lifted her anchor and blipped up to the wheel just as rain started to batter his face.

Four days later, the others were finally settled in their new hideout, all of them freshly rested and showered. Francis was still sailing around the edge of Spain, but he was in high spirits and made it known to Thyne with the occasional solo sea-shanty or playful chat with Arjun's ravens. "We can't start without him," said Thyne, "We might need to be somewhere immediately. If we can get a location on Park, for example."

Dale was anxious to use the number he had discovered as quickly as possible in case Aspyn had predicted the move, but Thyne had also explained how important it was that Francis was sailing again. They all therefore rested, sometimes taking the things Francis had brought to Thyne's house to the new property, but overall only waiting for Francis' arrival in London a week later.

While he was out at sea, time didn't seem to matter anymore. It didn't seem to be passing at all. In fact, he had often forgotten that December 28th of that very year was when America would declare war on Canada and start World War Three.

He anchored the *Initiative* in a random part of the Baltic Sea and stopped time to walk to Thyne's home in London. No one was inside, so he called on Thyne and was eventually escorted to Rory's property, only a ten minute walk away.

Finally, all together in a blandly-decorated den in the large house, Dale addressed them, "Well that was all crazy, but it's 'bout time we see if Aspyn ain't changed her number yet. Ah'mma call wit this burner. He'll think we's Miss Temm, so hopeflee he'll answer. We all ready? Perlie? Ye ready?" Vague nodding. "Ah'ight. Everyone quiet." He plugged the burner into his laptop, typed a few things into both the phone and computer, and the phone began to quietly ring. He turned up the volume, and a heavy weight pressed down on all their throats.

"Aspyn?" answered Park. Adrenaline pumped through them all in tandem and with enough intensity that he may have even heard the thunderous racing of their hearts. "Surprised you've got service up there, sweetie."

Perlie was quick to respond with a perfect impression of Aspyn: "Ha! Yeah I found this one spot with some service."

He chuckled. "Between a rock and a hard place, I suppose?" Perlie feigned a giggle in the acted voice. "You sound to be in good spirits. Maybe a bit loopy…. You have enough oxygen?"

They were confused as to what he could possibly be talking about, but Perlie answered, "Yeah. Plenty!"

"You sound so out of sorts." He was picking up on the hysterical nervousness that was quavering Perlie's voice and breaths just-so. "I'm worried for you. Are you not too far up yet? I know you said you wanted to do it alone, but can't you go down and get a sherpa to make me feel better?"

"Sure, mate," said Perlie eventually, "I trust you. Do you want to meet me there?"

There was a long beat, after which Park said coolly, "Nice try. Almost had me. To whom do I owe this pleasure, hm? Is this *The Crown* or *The Tiara*?"

Dale hung up the call before anyone could taunt, fearing Park would be able to find their location, and immediately broke open the burner and cracked its SIM card. "Destroy that, Roach," he said as he slid the phone across the coffee table and watched as it was crushed telekinetically.

"Everest," said Perlie.

Thyne perked up. "Yes! She talked about semi-annual trips to Everest. We should go. We should go right now." He stood and grabbed Roach's hand. "Tell Franky what supplies to get. I'm coming with you both, and we'll leave as soon as we're outfitted."

Roach nodded and took Francis aside to list out supplies which the pirate subsequently noted on his arm with his tattooing pen.

"What about Park?" asked Dale.

"We shall deal with Park after killing Aspyn."

"It's really good that we found out where the bird is," said Rory, "Are we sure you can climb Everest, though?"

"Roach is experienced and has his telekinesis," answered Thyne, "Not to mention Francis' powers. We'll be okay, mate. We'll find her on the mountain, wherever she is, and we'll kill her."

The supplies Roach had listed started to appear in piles around the room. Francis appeared beside them and read through his notes again. "Is this sufficient, my dear?"

Roach crouched down and started shuffling through the supplies, tossing things to Francis and Thyne. The pirate wouldn't need a coat or gear for oxygen, but Roach suggested he wear/carry it at least when they would speak with the employees at the base of the mountain to try sussing out which path Aspyn was hiking.

As they donned their gear, a tension grew in the room.

"H-have you ever climbed a mountain as difficult as Everest, sir?" asked Partha.

"Rainer in '77," he said as he packed a bag, "Whitney in '78— nearly died on that one —and Denali in 2080." He sighed and stood to put his hands on his hips. "I've obviously looked into Everest. I've got a good idea of a path to take, but the hope is we'll be able to catch Aspyn before the summit. Since she's alone, I assume (and hope) she's doing an easier trail. Easy, of course, being entirely relative."

"Why don't we just... why don't we just wait for her to come back down?" asked Jean-Jacques.

"No," snipped Francis, "Park will warn her as soon as he can. We cannot tarry! This may be our last chance to reverse my blunder. To stop the war."

With Roach's approval of their gear ten minutes later, Francis brought them to the area near the base of the mountain. There was a crowd of similarly-outfitted people in the area, but he needed Roach's guidance to get any further and therefore resumed time. There were some startled gasps at their sudden apparition, but they ignored the commotion. Roach grabbed a hand from each of the men accompanying him and brought them swiftly to a building meant for hiring sherpas, among other things. He went inside alone. A worker approached him and said something in Nepalese.

"You know English, dude?"

"Yes," he said with an irritated tone.

"How many people recently have gone up the mountain alone?"

"There are many solo travellers, sir."

"No, I mean alone alone. Not with one of your men here."

"There have been a handful."

"Any women?" The man winced away. "Fuck. That probably sounded creepy. I'm just looking for one woman in particular."

"I… I think I'm going to have to ask you to leave, sir."

"Shit. Fine. Sorry, bro." He left and met back up with Thyne and Francis to explain the situation: "I don't know which path she's taking, so probably will have to cheat to catch up and meet her at the summit."

"Not another moment to waste, then," said Francis.

"Bring us as far up as you can, bed bug, but don't you *dare* hurt yourself. Stick to the map I gave you. If you need me to use my power just stop us somewhere safe and I'll throw you two up and climb whatever needs climbing." He ran his hands through his short hair. "We should have brought Sonny. Fuck."

"There be no time to fetch him," said Francis, "I apologise, my love. Are the twain of thee prepared?" They nodded, so he brought them along a path as far as he could before he needed Roach's help again.

⚙ Chapter 80 ⚙

Did You Forget?
I'm a Heartless Wretch

Due to Roach's knowledge and skills in combination with his and Francis' powers, they reached the summit in only a month. When they arrived, there was one other person already there taking in the astonishing view, but after confronting whoever it was, they heard him speak and realised he wasn't Aspyn. With little else of an option, they camped on the summit and waited for her to arrive. There was a chance they had missed her, but they were determined to wait for as long as possible before they would have to make the arduous journey back down.

They waited for weeks. When Roach and Thyne's oxygen tanks ran low, Francis would refill them via chronomancy. When their food ran low, he would do much the same. They slept in shifts to not risk missing any travellers, but the sleep was adequate enough. The biggest threat to their survival was therefore the temperature. Francis used his control over the weather to keep the air calm and raised the temperature as much as he possibly could with such a thin atmosphere and without brewing up any storms. They still sometimes found themselves in swirls of cirrus, but on cloudless nights, gazing into the endless sky was hypnotic. It felt as if they could reach out and touch the stars. It was a serene and romantic time, but there were some nights they feared they would freeze no matter how large their fire was. It was possible they were only afforded continued survival by the grace of their Gods.

It was after two and a half weeks that they started to consider retreating down the mountain with less and less strength after so many nights in the unforgiving cold and with their oxygen masks starting to scar their faces. By a great fortune, however, as they were packing to leave, a solo traveller breached the clouds below them on her ascent to the summit. Roach and Thyne both prayed to their Gods that she might be Aspyn.

When she came up within earshot of them, Roach called out plainly, "Aspyn Abraham?"

She turned toward them. Her face was covered entirely by her mask and goggles, but the way her heart leapt up into her throat with fear could be felt. Her hands trembled. "Y-yes?" Instantly, she was sitting in the snow and surrounded by three harrowing figures with a vague pain in the back of her neck. Two of them were in the same sort of gear as her, with masks and goggles and winter gear, but the third was a man with no mask, wearing a snow-dusted black cotton blouse, leather pants, and boots. He smiled his rotten teeth down at her, and it was clear from the masked men's postures that they were also smiling wickedly.

"Do you know who we are, love?" asked Thyne.

"You're terrorists. You're *monsters*," she said with a shiver, "You killed my husband."

"And enjoyed it, too," said Roach.

"Before you kill me, there's something you should know: I have a dead man's switch in me. If I die, everyone with an *Eye of Osiris* will also die. Tatum insisted on it."

Francis went pale. He looked at Thyne. "Is this true?"

"It is," he said solemnly.

"Why did you not warn me!?"

"Because you don't have to worry about it, Frankenstein." He took a bowie knife out of his bag and crouched down in front of Aspyn. After removing her mask to look her in the eyes, he brought the blade to her throat but didn't touch her with it. His breaths shuddered. "How many people have an *Eye of Osiris*?"

"Almost 400 million," she said, her panicked gaze never leaving the blade at her throat.

Thyne's breath shuddered. '*For Francis*,' he told himself, '*Do it for Francis. It will be like any other murder. Just slit her throat or cut her oxygen and leave her to die like anyone else. Just kill her, Clarence.*' His hand trembled. '*Just do it, Clarence, you bloody coward. It's not your fault she's a fucking genocidal maniac. Just....*'

"Put your mask back on." He stood while she secured her mask back over her pallid face and took a deep breath. "I can't do it.... I can't fucking do it. You keep trying to save the world, Franky. You keep railing against fate. And I love you, and I want to help you, but I can't. I can't be the hero you need me to be." He caressed

Francis' cheek lovingly as he spoke, but his gloved hand fell from his face, and he turned slowly toward Roach. "But... it's not a hero we need…. Tin Man?"

Roach gulped as Thyne passed him the knife. It weighed a thousand pounds. Though it gleamed in the bright sun and snow, the light all around him was snuffed out as soon as the handle was in his palm. The world was gone, and all that remained was this blade and the darkness writhing in his chest blacking out reality. *'400 million is four percent of the entire world.'* His eyes widened as he looked at the knife in his trembling hands as if it were a holy relic.

'What chaos I could wrought.'

A mad grin twisted his lips.

'Four percent of the entire world…. I'm already so far gone. I've already killed some 5,000 people. What's a few million more?' His throat clogged up with hysteria that could not crack out of him no matter how hard it tried, for he was swallowing his nervousness too frequently. A cold sweat fogged up his goggles, and the knife visibly shook in his grip as he realised that he could kill her— as he realised that he *wanted* to.

'What perfect destruction…'

His free hand raised up to his smiling face, as if he could feel it through his mask and gloves. As if it was its own terrified and shocked entity.

'What am I?

'Why… why does it entice me so? Four percent of the entire world. A number not even challenged by the Gods. Clayton Roach: God amongst men. Roach: the Patron Saint of Death….

'What creature am I?

'What wretched thing am I that wants this?'

He ambled toward Aspyn with a drunken gait despite his sobriety. The snow piled up around his shins when he crouched down across from her. *'What creature am I that is… capable… of…'* The blade was at her throat and about to dig into her skin when a hand snapped around his wrist.

"Don't," said Francis.

As if he had been pulled up from the depths of the darkest abyss in all the universe, he took a deep breath, dropped the knife, and stumbled backwards into the snow. The light of day flooded back into his perception like a flashbang. He held his racing heart and looked at Aspyn with his breaths heaving and eyes wide as he realised what he had almost done.

After having helped Aspyn down the mountain, Francis brought Thyne and

Roach back to London where they were all greeted with tearful embraces, puppy kisses, and worried weeping. The others hadn't known the state of the mission for the entire time they were absent. River's grip around his brother lasted some fifteen minutes before he finally retreated and kissed him deeply. "Oh, Tony! Tony! We feared the worst," he said for the umpteenth time, "Why do your eyes look so hollow, habibi?"

He looked through River and smiled. It was weak and wrought with self-reproach. "She's still alive." River knew that wasn't the full reason, but he would pry out of Roach what he had almost done when they were in private that very night.

"I have one last hope," said Francis after only enjoying two hours in reunion, and without any further explanation, he disappeared.

Dezba and Rory cooked a lovely meal to welcome everyone home, but it was dark and quiet as they ate, knowing they had failed. Francis reappeared in his seat between the twins with a half-empty bottle of gin in his hand and a drunken sway to his movements. He swigged from the bottle and slammed it on the table. "Park is dead."

"Good job, bed bug," said Roach with much less enthusiasm than was characteristic of him hearing of such a good death.

"That remains to be seen. Me hope wanes. 'Twere too easy...."

Christmas came that year with no public announcement of Elijah Park's mysterious death. As far as the rest of the world knew, he was still the dictator of the states. Francis held onto every last shred of hope he could conjure to the very end, but it was generally understood among the others that there would be no stopping the war.

"Bed bug, I have good news," said Roach that Christmas morning, "When I went through Aspyn's phone on the mountain, I found Nelson Lager's number. The Baumbach CEO. I gave it to Dale, and he's been able to figure out where the bastard's been hiding. Do you want to go kill him with me and Martial? Thyne and Sonny can come, too. It'll be romantic."

"I will follow thee to the ends of the Earth, my pharos, but give me these last few days. Until there is not a shred of a chance left, I will not capitulate. I must stop the end of it all. I must reverse my blunder."

"Alright, bed bug," he said with a strangled voice, "Promise?"

"I swear it will be so, my darling."

Francis made many attempts in the last few days— hours— minutes until the war would be declared. He travelled to America while time was stopped and killed everyone in the Capitol building, everyone in the White House, and everyone in the Pentagon. He did this each day from Christmas until the 28th. America was sent further and further into anarchy for it, but it never fully broke like he hoped. By the 28th, he found Aspyn alone in the White House signing a paper to declare war on Canada. She had taken over the country, and no matter how many people he killed in the various branches of government, he would *not* kill her. Instead, he did the only thing he could think to do, and resumed time in front of her.

She blenched and grabbed the nearest sharp-object on her desk in her scrambling away from him. "You! From the mountain!"

"Aye, from the mountain," his tone was dejected, "I know not thine ends, nor do I care to unbosom them. As you can plainly see, I—." She threw the obelisk-shaped paperweight at him, but it disappeared in mid-air, and he was suddenly in front of her with a blade at her throat and her back against the wall. "I control time," he said, "Your invasion into Canada will bring about the end of the world. All life on Earth: vanquished by this action. Would you still persist knowing this?"

She spat in his face. "Kill me, then. Stop it yourself."

. . .

"So I thought." She pushed him away. "Why would I believe anything you say? You killed my husband. You killed my friends. You and your mates have ruined every life you've ever touched." She snatched the paper off her desk. "I will invade Canada with the country I inherited, and if the world falls, then so be it. Let it be a reminder for you in the end that you could not kill me right here right now when you should have. Perhaps the regret will hurt you as much as you've hurt everyone I've ever known and loved."

At this, Francis accepted defeat. He disappeared from the room, leaving in his wake a terrified woman who held her racing heart and looked at the paper in her hands with a brief consideration to heed him. A consideration easily squandered upon remembering the sight of her husband's decimated corpse.

Francis returned to London, and found Roach. "Where is Lager?" he droned.

"He's in an abandoned power station in Quebec."

"Canada is where the war will begin. I shan't take you there."

"Bed bug, you promised. But you don't even have to take me there anyway. Just go grab him. "

"Faugh. Tell me where, then."

"Well, we had the aqua regia in Rome, but you said you destroyed the manor, right? Where's that raven? We should ask Arjun if the manor is clear. Maybe we can still get to the aqua regia and dump Lager in."

Francis hailed one of Arjun's ravens and asked him for an update on the manor.

"It is clear at the moment," replied the bird, "It will be difficult to get to the aqua regia, but it won't be impossible."

Francis nodded and took the twins, Thyne, and Jean-Jacques to the ruined building. While they were fanning out and following a bird of Arjun's on the property to find a path to the aqua regia, Francis asked Roach where Lager was.

After some instructions on how to get to the abandoned power station on the LaForge river in Quebec, the former-CEO was brought to Roach gagged and bound and pushed onto his knees in front of him. "Thanks, bed bug." He kissed him and carried Lager telekinetically as he followed the others into the depths of the charred and splintered ruins. "You've done magnificent work here, Franky," he said as he admired the destruction.

"Here!" shouted Jean-Jacques from somewhere below them. "It should be enough." Arjun's bird fluttered up in front of Francis, Roach, and their victim and led them down to the tub of aqua regia where Jean-Jacques had found it. "Be careful," warned the Frenchman as they brought the CEO closer.

"Tell him what this is," said Roach when they were all together. Jean-Jacques smiled wickedly and explained what acid was in the tub and its unique ability to dissolve gold. He even demonstrated by tearing the golden watch from Lager's wrist and tossing it into the tub. Madness flickered in his eyes as he spoke, and Roach admired it like a mentor admires a gifted student.

After turning Lager around and savouring the fear in his eyes, Roach said, "Everyone out of the splash zone." When it was clear around the tub, he shoved Lager backwards into the acid and held him in it telekinetically. Some of it splashed onto his boots and pants, but after the initial spillage, he was holding the dead man entirely still and watching through the amber liquid as it wrenched flesh from bone. He gestured for the others to come watch with him. All of them, save for Francis, wore sadistic grins and ogled the violent visage with hungry eyes. Francis saw it in glances, but he was looking through his tattoos for another moment to perchance save the world.

After Lager was beyond dead, and the rubble above them was creaking, Roach smiled at his friend and lovers, ready to crack a joke. Before he could say anything, Francis grabbed his arm.

"I have only just realised: I have but moments!"

"Moments until what?" asked Roach.

"Until I am wrenched away to the other version of me: the foolish man who fought in the war, only solidifying it further! Oh! Oh, after all this I am punished further!" He hugged him tightly. "We've failed, Clayton! We've failed!"

Roach retreated and cupped his hand around Francis' face. "How long do we have until you're taken away?"

Francis stopped time to look at his watch, not wanting to waste another second, and answered Roach when it resumed: "Forty-one seconds."

Roach leaned in and kissed him. "Time enough for that, then," he said after the quick peck. "It'll be okay, bed bug."

"It won't, Clayton! Don't you see!? The war has started! We've failed. We've failed. We've failed. We've failed. We've failed. We've failed."

"Shhh. Francy-Pants, listen to me." He snapped in his face to catch his panicked eyes. "You listening?" A nod. "How long will you be gone?"

"Two years."

"To the day?"

"Nay. To the month."

"And where will you be at the end of those two years?"

"Thyne's home in London."

Roach glimpsed the watch and saw they only had eight seconds before Francis would disappear. "Look at me, Francis." He looked up. "I love you."

"I love you."

He took up his hand. "We'll see you there in London, bed bug." As he was kissing Francis' knuckles, the chronomancer disappeared. Tears sparkled in Roach's eyes, but he managed a smile at the other three. "War should be fun." A loud sniffle. "Wrote my best shit in Mexico. I'll write some more albums."

Thyne's cheeks were soaked in tears, and his hand was squeezing River's. They were all three giving Roach their attention, but they hadn't moved since the sudden disappearance of Francis. "What beautiful carnage, chaos, and rot in war, eh, habibi?" River nodded just-so, and Roach looked at Thyne with smiling teary eyes.

"Will you set fires with me, sparkplug?"

"I will."

"Will you write music with me?"

"I will."

"Will you still love me after you've seen what I truly am?"

"I'll always love you, Basil."

Roach opened his arms for an embrace. "To arms, then."

Author's Note
& Acknowledgements

My dear reader, I will be with you momentarily, but I must first do what is only respectful and pay thanks to those it is due:

Firstly, I give humble praise and thanks to my Gods, who will remain unnamed but without whom I would quite literally be nothing. In my lowest moments, through all my life, when I had no one and nothing else, I had their love, guidance, and spiritual support.

Secondly, I must give ample thanks to my fiancé, Alex, without whom this book would not exist. He is always ready and willing to help me break through blocks, read my first-draft nonsense and give critique and feedback, comfort me when I am suffering something like imposter syndrome, etc. He is a precious gift and a blessing and has supported me through everything. He knows my stories and characters almost as intimately as I do, and some of my favourite conversations with him involve joking and rambling at each other about them.

Thirdly, I will thank my father, who always took my interest in writing seriously and encouraged my creativity even when I was so young as eleven and even when I was writing "a book" in highschool that amounted to a lot of mostly-unusable garbage.

Fourth, to my sole alpha/beta reader, Vittoria, I also give thanks. Other than Alex, it was Vittoria who was my biggest cheerleader helping me feel less like some hermit with a pen and more like an actual author. She's a wonderful writer, and to have her respect as well as her help is a boon I do not take for granted. I love writing with her and consider myself lucky to have her as a best friend, let alone as an alpha/beta reader.

And fifth, what might be peculiar, I thank Alexandre Dumas. Were I to sit here thanking every artist who ever inspired me, this note may be as long as the book itself, but Dumas receives special mention for reasons both spiritual and personal.

Beyond these, I offer gratitude to the friends whom I bothered ceaselessly in years past with mad ramblings about my characters and stories. My friends who have been incredibly patient with me, not only when I waffle on about things they couldn't care less about, but also when I hole myself up, radio silent for however long, enthralled with my work.

More broadly, I thank my past English teachers for reasons I hope are obvious. I thank the agents I once queried with a shite book I thought was good at the time, without whose indifference I may have ruined my own career.

And, were I to say there was not a great deal of motivation to finish *Death to Osiris* born purely of spite, I would be lying. Therefore, my final homage must go to all of the motherfuckers who said I couldn't do this or at the very least who did not take me seriously.

And now that I have prattled on enough without you, good reader, I will finally get to the proper rambling. Thank you for reading *Death to Osiris!* I do hope you enjoyed it. I realise there are some things that were left unanswered and some threads left open, and that was all by design. If you can believe it, the some 900+ pages you've just read was only the first half of this lengthy tale. Still, I did my very best to make this story stand on its own and hope it has not left too sour a taste in anyone's mouths. The sequel will be titled *Glory to Set* and will shoot those Chekhov's guns that haven't fired yet. I can't give a date for when it may be finished. It would be difficult to even cite how long it took to write *DtO*. Technically, I started writing on November 29th, 2022 and am writing this author's note on October 9th, 2024. But even though this book was only technically in the works for that long, there are a lot of WIPs and characters referenced or featured in *DtO* which are much older. Hell, Franky and Thyne were characters I created in *high-school*. They are completely unrecognisable to what they were then, but the foundation has carried through all this time. With that said, of course, those same foundations will not be going anywhere between books, so hopefully it is no more than another two years before the sequel is finished.

I'm certainly excited to get started on it!

Before I begin drafting *GtS*, however, I admit I might indulge in one of my many other WIPs. They all exist in a shared universe. Olympus, the planet the "vampires" flee to at the end of this book, will be the setting for another series. Melchiresa's backstory is another of my WIPs. Some of Arjun and Giovanni's past lives as well. I could go on. There are a lot of moving parts and intertwining stories, but the plan is to keep as many of them as stand-alones as possible. I don't really have a name for this shared universe in which my books all take place....

I don't fucking know. *Universe McUniverseFace*. How's that?

I realise that this author's note isn't the most insightful into my process or goals with writing this book, which might be what you were hoping to find here. Dear reader, I will level with you: there is rarely any method to the madness. Writing is a process which takes the cloud of unformed thoughts and seeks to put order to them, so it necessarily involves delving deep into your own head and getting lost there. I time my sessions (for whatever that's worth), but otherwise it is a lot of quiet pondering and trying helplessly to harvest the good ideas from the cloud of nonsense in my big dumb head.

But yes, like any other human on the planet, I am inspired by things (I say as if my many allusions did not make that abundantly clear). I have playlists of music for most characters, relationships, and for the stories themselves. (My playlist for *DtO* is one of my favourites for a story I've ever made. The vibes are just *chef's kiss*). I have chaotic Pinterest boards and half-finished notes scribbled here and there. My monkey-brain likes to glue things to other things, so I have some junk journals and collages I've made that are more or less physical moodboards. (For example, a junk journal inspired by Thyne and his vibes). I also sketch my idiots from time to time.

Perhaps the most unique thing to note about my "process" is that the piece of media which sparked this entire book into motion was a fucking meme I found. Literally that's not a joke. It was a screenshot of some headline talking about how an old man had joined a gang because he was lonely. Obviously the story grew from there, but the initial inspiration came from a meme.

As for my goals with the book? To be honest with you, reader, my goal was just to write it. I'm not going to tell anyone how to feel about it. I think the text speaks for itself. I do hope that you, having read it, got something valuable out of it, but it wasn't written with any particular goal in mind. I don't write stories with an agenda, even if it may seem that way. I write because I have to. I write because these stories bleed out of me. I was put on this Earth to yap, and yap I shall!

But, having said that, I should finally do you the mercy of some quietude. Have a blessed day and a blessed life, dear reader.

Until next time.

By the way: you have my full permision/blessing to (assuming you own your copy) mark up the book, paste things in, paint the cover, draw on the pages, etc. If it wasn't so long I would have made the margins bigger for more doodle space.